Praise for Janet Dailey and her bestsellers

Masquerade

"In MASQUERADE, Janet Dailey's latest romantic suspense novel . . . the reader never doubts that Remy Jardin will be strong enough to resolve everything for her —and our—satisfaction."

—*The New York Times Book Review*

"Dailey deftly crochets together past and present as she unravels the mystery. There's something for every escape reader in this bestseller—history, suspense and romance."

—*The Wichita Eagle*

"MASQUERADE has all the old Dailey charm and skill."

—*The Rockdale Citizen*

Rivals

"A Sure-Fire Winner"   —*Publishers Weekly*

Heiress

"The complexity of [the sisters'] relationship fascinates . . . . She moves her story ahead so purposefully and dramatically . . . . readers will be glad they've gone along for the ride."

—*The Chicago Sun Times*

THREE COMPLETE NOVELS

JANET DAILEY

THREE COMPLETE NOVELS

JANET DAILEY

MASQUERADE
RIVALS
HEIRESS

WINGS BOOKS

New York • Avenel, New Jersey

This 1994 edition is published by Wings Books,
distributed by Random House Value Publishing, Inc.,
40 Engelhard Avenue, Avenel, New Jersey 07001,
by arrangement with Little, Brown and Company.

Random House
New York • Toronto • London • Sydney • Auckland

Text design by Kathryn W. Plosica

Printed and bound in the United States of America

Library of Congress Cataloging-in-Publication Data
Dailey, Janet.
   [Selections]
   Three complete novels / Janet Dailey.
      p.   cm.
   Contents: Masquerade — Rivals — Heiress.
   ISBN 0-517-11822-X
   I. Title.
 PS3554.A29A6   1994
 813'.54—dc20   94-17966
                         CIP

8 7 6 5 4 3 2 1

CONTENTS

Masquerade

1 ～

SHE SIPPED AT the wine in her glass and watched with marked indifference the lewd gyrations of a short, fat man garbed in the costume of Bacchus, a wreath of grape leaves encircling his bald head and a toga stretched tautly around his protruding stomach. His partner wore a simple black cocktail dress, a collection of ribbons and bows in her hair, and festive makeup that included glittering pink eye shadow and blue stripes on her cheeks. Near them, a woman in a high, powdered wig, a fake mole, and a gown from the court of Louis XVI danced with a man in a red tuxedo with devil's horns on his head.

Turning from the sight, she let her gaze wander over the hotel's renowned rooftop garden, ablaze with light from colored lanterns strung all around, tiny fairy lights wound through the potted plants and trees, and votive candles on all the tables. Tonight it was the site of a private masked party—one of those intimate little affairs with two hundred or so guests, many in costume but some, like herself, choosing only a mask. Hers happened to be an elaborately feathered, hand-held one in amber satin that matched the dress and fur-lined stole she wore. It was lowered now, revealing the sculpted lines of her face, its expression untouched by the band's driving rock music, the laughter, the voices that filled the night air, a babble of French and Italian with a smattering of German, Dutch, Swiss, and English rising here and there—voices of people caught up in the party madness that gripped Nice, the undisputed queen city of France's Côte d'Azur, the party madness of Carnival that encouraged its revelers to celebrate all that was flesh, to don masks and shed inhibitions, to conceal and reveal.

Reveal. She finally looked at him, feeling the anger rise in her throat—along with the hurt and bitterness of disillusionment. He stood some thirty feet from her, his face partially hidden by the black satin mask he wore, fashioned to resemble a pirate's eye patch. A pirate—criminal of the high seas. My God, how appropriate, she thought. Looting, plundering, destroying in the name of —there was only one word for it—greed.

She took a quick sip of the wine, but it couldn't wash away the disgust, the revulsion she felt. Her fingers tightened on the glass's slender stem. What was she doing at this party? Why was she going through the motions of pretending everything was all right when it wasn't—when nothing would ever be all right again?

A waiter said something to him, and he lifted his head sharply, then nodded once and moved off, coming directly toward her. She took a quick step closer to the roof's edge, with its spectacular views of the gardens below and the Mediterranean beyond. She didn't want to hear any more of his explanations, his justifications.

But he wasn't walking toward her. He was heading for the entrance to the rooftop terrace to her left, a firmness in his stride that spoke of purpose. Curious, she turned and stiffened in alarm at the sight of the dark-haired man in a business suit waiting for him. What was he doing here? He belonged a half a world away. She watched as the two men met and immediately moved off to a quiet corner, away from the throng of party guests.

Why was he here? What was this all about? She had to find out. She cast a cautious glance around, then slipped closer.

"—realizes what went on that night. She's put two and two together and figured out what we did and how we did it."

" 'We'? You told her I was involved?" he demanded, anger and accusation in his tone.

"I didn't have to. I told you she figured it out. That's why I called. I felt I should warn you. So far, I haven't been able to make her listen to reason."

They were talking about her. She almost stepped out from behind the concealing fronds of the palmetto plant and confronted them both with her knowledge. She wanted them to know they weren't going to get away with this. But his next words stopped her cold.

"If she can't be made to see reason, you've got to shut her up. She can't be allowed to tell what she knows. There's no place for sentiment in this. She's proved that. And you'll never have a better opportunity than now. Kidnappings, accidents happen all the time in Europe. Back home, she'll be just another statistic."

She felt her mouth and lips suddenly go dry with fear. He wouldn't agree to that . . . would he? He wouldn't hurt her. He couldn't. Not him. But his face was in profile, shadowed by the mask that covered his right eye, making his expression unreadable.

There came a sigh, heavy with defeat. "I don't see any other choice."

No! She backed up a step, moving her head from side to side in mute denial, not wanting to believe what she'd heard.

"Are you going to arrange it, or do you want me—" The wineglass slipped from her fingers and crashed to the terrace floor. Both men turned and stared directly at her. There was a split second when she couldn't move, paralyzed by the accusing look in their eyes. Then she turned and ran. "Stop her! She'll destroy everything."

She looked back and saw his familiar face, half concealed by the mask, coming after her. She brushed past a slim young man in a Degas ballerina costume and pushed through the doors to the bank of elevators, conscious of the shock, the disbelief that blurred everything but the panicked need to escape.

He reached the elevators to the rooftop terrace just as the doors to one of them slid shut. He punched impatiently at the button to summon another, gripped by his own kind of fear, the fear that came with guilt and desperation.

He couldn't let her get away, or all would be lost. Why couldn't she see that? Why was she doing this? Why was she making him do this?

At the lobby, he emerged from the elevator in time to see her dart through the hotel entrance and into the street. He hurried after her. A cab pulled away as he stopped outside. He lifted a hand to call another, then saw her cutting across the street toward the Espace Masséna. If he lost her in that mob of revelers in the square—he couldn't let that happen.

But it did. The crowd swallowed her.

Where was she? The black mask cut off his peripheral vision to the right, forcing him to turn his head to scan the boisterous throng on that side of the Espace Masséna. There was a loud splash behind him, accompanied by a woman's shriek of laughter. His back was to the square's fountain, with its spectacular pillars of water shooting some forty feet into the air. He swung around, his glance briefly resting on some madcap brunette frolicking in the fountain's pool. The instant he identified the woman as a stranger, he looked away, resuming his search and unconsciously clenching his hands into tight, trembling fists.

Ignoring the tangle of confetti at his feet, he took two quick steps toward the boulevard. In one direction, only a short stroll away, was the Promenade des Anglais with its glittering casinos and palatial hotels, bastions of privacy and exclusivity for the wealthy and celebrated. In another lay the narrow, cobbled streets of Nice's Old Town section with its mélange of galleries, outdoor cafés, and *boîtes de nuit*. Beyond that were the Baie des Anges and the Mediterranean.

He hesitated, then stopped. Three-story-tall cartoon figures, garishly outlined in a blaze of colored lights, mocked him from the distinctive roccoco red buildings that flanked the square. He swung abruptly to his left, only to be met by the taunting grin of the giant papier-mâché King Carnival enthroned on the square.

For an instant, he glared at the figure, then swept his glance over the milling crowd again. How could she have disappeared so quickly? He scanned the throng, seeking the amber shimmer of her satin gown, the streaks of gold in her sun-lightened brown hair, and the gleam of the topaz brooch she wore at her throat. Again he saw no sign of her, and he felt the knot tighten in his stomach.

Someone jostled him from behind. Instinctively he turned, protectively lifting a hand to cover the slim wallet tucked inside the inner breast pocket of his black tuxedo jacket, well aware that Mardi Gras celebrations always attracted a sizable contingent of pickpockets as well as sun-and-fun-loving tourists. This time his caution was unnecessary as a fair-haired German raised a wine bottle to him in an apologetic salute and then reeled away, his arm hooked around his svelte companion.

He absently brushed at the wet splatter of wine on his sleeve and turned back. At that instant he saw her, near the sidewalk of the tree-lined boulevard, looking warily about, poised for flight. But she hadn't seen him yet.

He came up behind her and caught hold of her arm, his fingers curling into the satin of her stole. "You're coming with me—now."

She pulled back, her head coming up, her gaze clashing with his, her temper willfully set against his, stubbornly resisting him. "So you can have me kidnapped? Murdered?"

For an instant everything inside him went still. "It doesn't have to be that way. If you'd just listen to reason. Nobody got hurt in this. No one."

"What about the company? This could destroy it." She threw him another angry and challenging look, only this time it was colored by hurt and accusation. "But you don't care, do you?"

"I had no choice."

"Didn't you?"

His grip tightened on her arm, checking the pivoting turn she made away from him and steering her into the concealing shadows beneath a tree. "You've got to understand—"

"I'll never understand!" she flared, then her voice grew all tight and choked. "How could you do this? Who are you? I don't even know you anymore."

The revulsion, the distrust she showed for him broke the thin thread of his control. Seizing her high on both arms, he began to shake her, mindless of his roughness. "Don't you realize what's at stake? How can you betray me like this? If you truly love—"

"Stop. Stop it!" As her hands came up to push at him and end the violent shaking, the rodlike wand that held her satin mask struck against his upper lip, sending a needle-sharp spasm of pain through his face.

Stunned by the blow, he instinctively released her to explore the injury with his fingers and tongue. He tasted blood and realized that she'd hit him. She'd hit *him*. A sudden rage welled up in him and he lashed out, backhanding her across the face.

The force of the blow sent her reeling backward against the tree. The momentary gratification he felt vanished when he heard the cracking thud of her head striking the trunk a second before she crumpled to the ground.

"My God, no." He took a step toward her, automatically reaching out to her with his hands. "I didn't mean to, I swear—"

But she didn't move.

"Hey?!" someone shouted, the voice American in its accent. "What's going on there?"

He shot a quick glance over his shoulder, regret, fear, and guilt warring for control. He hesitated for a split second, then took off across the boulevard.

Two T-shirt-and-denim-clad twenty-year-olds ran to the pool of amber satin lying in the shadows by the street. The one with dark-rimmed glasses knelt down to check her pulse while the blond sporting a California tan started after the fleeing man.

"Let him go, Brad," his buddy called him back. "You'll never catch him anyway, and this girl's unconscious."

"Is she hurt bad?"

"I don't know, but we'd better get an ambulance."

"And the police," his friend added.

BLACKNESS. SWIRLING, EDDYING, trying to pull her deeper—away from that distant light. She fought against it, straining toward that light, obeying some inner voice that said she must reach it. But it hurt. It hurt so much.

One last time she kicked for it. Suddenly it was there—glaring on her eyelids. She'd made it.

She struggled to open her eyes, fighting the lids' heaviness. The light—she didn't understand why it was so bright. Something was wrong. Dazed and disoriented, she looked about her in confusion, not recognizing the stark walls or the drab curtains at the windows.

A man loomed beside her, his features blurring for an instant and then coming into focus. "Where—" Her lips were too stiff, too dry; she couldn't get the words out. She moistened them and tried again. "Where am I?"

"*Américaine*," someone said softly, very softly, giving the word the French pronunciation.

Groggily she tried to locate the source of that voice and finally saw the balding man standing at the foot of the bed, dressed in a comfortable tweed coat and a turtleneck sweater. He looked like a kindly old professor.

"You are in an hospital, mam'selle," the first man replied.

"A hospital." She frowned at that, certain there was somewhere else she was supposed to be. "I have to go." Something told her it was important. "I have to leave." But the instant she tried to lift her head, pain knifed through her and the blackness rushed back, threatening to swirl her away again. Somehow she managed to hang on, clinging to the sound of the man's voice even though she couldn't actually hear the words; they came from too far away. Finally the black pain receded to the edges.

"—lie quietly." The voice was clearer now. "Do not try to move."

She opened her eyes again, focusing on his regular features, etched with tired lines. "Who are you?" She searched without finding anything familiar about this plain-looking, brown-haired, brown-eyed man.

"I am Dr. Jules St. Clair." A faint smile edged the corners of his mouth. "And what is your name, mam'selle?"

"My name. My name is—" She frowned, not understanding why she couldn't think of it. But when she tried, there was only a confusing blankness—and a throbbing pressure in her head that wouldn't go away. "I—I can't remember it." She saw the doctor's somewhat startled look, followed by the quick narrowing of his eyes. She felt a rising sense of panic and fought it back. "What's happened to me? This pain. I—I can't seem to think."

"You have suffered a head injury, mam'selle—a concussion. I will have the nurse give you something for the pain so you can rest."

"But my name—what is it?" Even as she made the weak demand, she was conscious of the welcome promise of his words. She was tired, so very tired of fighting to hold the pain at bay, tired of struggling to penetrate this thick, bewildering mist in her mind.

"Later, mam'selle. There will be time for all your questions later," he said.

Without the strength to argue with him, she closed her eyes. Distantly she heard the doctor murmur instructions to someone else in the room. She sensed that he was no longer standing beside her, but she didn't bother to open her eyes again to see where he'd gone. She drifted instead.

At the foot of the hospital bed, Dr. St. Clair picked up her chart and began making notations on it. Inspector Claude Armand watched him in silence for several seconds, then asked, "Is it possible she cannot truly recall her name?"

"Yes," the doctor replied, without looking up from the notes he was making. "Patients with head injuries such as hers are frequently confused and disoriented when they first regain consciousness. Some memory loss is not uncommon. In the majority of cases, it is a temporary condition."

"How temporary?"

"That is difficult to say, Inspector. A few hours, a few days, a few weeks." His shoulders lifted at the impreciseness of his answer as he finished the last of his notes and retracted the tip of his ball-point pen with a sharp click. "Your question leads me to assume that no one has come forward to identify her."

"No one."

"Personally, Inspector Armand"—he paused to hand the chart to a waiting nurse—"I find nothing unusual in our mystery lady's inability to remember her name. But she was admitted—what?—nearly thirty hours ago. How could someone forget to remember such a beautiful woman? To me, that is strange."

"*Oui.*" But it wasn't the *how* that puzzled Inspector Armand as he left the hospital room. No, it wasn't the *how* so much as the *why*.

3

SUNLIGHT STREAMED THROUGH the hospital window, setting agleam the shiny satin fabric the young nurse held up for her inspection. "It is beautiful, *non?*" declared the short, stout woman, whose olive skin and dark hair revealed her Mediterranean origins.

She ran her hand over the gown's skirt, which lay draped across her lap. "It is very beautiful," she agreed, then sighed, fighting back a bitter discouragement to admit, "but I don't remember ever seeing it before, let alone wearing it."

The nurse glanced at the balding man by the window, dressed in a corduroy jacket of charcoal gray with a pearl-gray turtleneck under it. A pair of glasses framed with gold wire sat on the bridge of his nose. With a downward tilt of his head, he peered over the top of them and signaled to the nurse, with a slight flick of his hand, to take the gown and its matching stole away.

Only the jewelry remained—the antique brooch and the diamond-studded topaz earrings. She didn't recognize them either. She pressed her fingers to her temples and tried to lightly massage away the pressure. Earlier, a nurse had given her something that had reduced the throbbing pain to a dull ache—an ache that kept her on edge. But she wanted nothing stronger—not now, when she needed to think.

"Is that all I had when I was brought in to the hospital?" Each time she looked at the man by the window, she had to remind herself that he was an inspector. He didn't look like one. If she had guessed his occupation, she would have said he was a headmaster or a schoolteacher—someone of authority who could be stern and benevolent by turns.

"*Oui*, you had nothing else." He removed his glasses and returned them to the breast pocket of his jacket. "No identification, no passport, no hotel key, no purse."

"Could my purse have been stolen? What happened? The nurses couldn't tell me. Do you know?"

"You were seen by two young men—Americans—struggling or arguing with a man at the Espace Masséna. They think he may have struck you—which would account for the bruise by your mouth. When they saw you fall to the ground, one of them shouted, and the man ran off. Bits of tree bark were found when the laceration to the back of your head was cleaned here in the hospital, and later, traces of blood and strands of hair the same color as yours were found at the site. From that we assume that when you fell, you struck your head on the tree, resulting in your injuries."

Those she knew about. The doctor had enumerated them for her when she'd seen him earlier—the bruise near her mouth, the laceration to her head, which had required twelve stitches to close, the hairline fracture to her skull, the concussion, and—a rare total loss of memory. Total in the sense that all details of her personal life had been lost, but not her store of knowledge.

"I know where the Espace Masséna is—and the flower market on Cours Saleya. And Nice is in France; the capital is Paris—" She broke off the spate of facts. "Why was I at the Espace Masséna?"

"I assume to participate in the Carnival festivities."

"Carnival. It comes from the Old Italian word *carnelevare*—which loosely translates as a 'farewell to the flesh,'" she murmured, remembering that and so much more. "It's pagan in origin, isn't it?—a spring rite of the Greeks to celebrate the miracle of propagation, an annual event that the Romans subsequently corrupted with lewdness and the followers of Christianity eventually absorbed into their religion, making it an acceptable feasting time before the Lenten season. The custom of masking came from the French—along with the name Mardi Gras."

The inspector smiled faintly. "Nothing is ever what it seems, is it, mam'selle?"

"What about me?" she asked, suddenly intense. "What do I seem like to you?" As he hesitated in answering, she suddenly realized she had no idea what she looked like. She was trapped in the body of a person she knew absolutely nothing about. "Is there a mirror somewhere so I can see myself?"

After taking a moment to consider her request, he nodded. "I will find one for you." He left the room and returned within minutes with a small hand mirror.

A tension threaded her nerves as she took it from him, then slowly raised it to look at the reflection her face made. Her eye was first caught by the swathe of gauze around her head and the purpling near her mouth, which swelled part of her lip. She touched a lock of her shoulder-length hair, the tawny color of cognac, then noticed the paleness of her face. She wondered whether it was caused by the absence of makeup, the harshness of the light, or the drabness of the hospital gown.

Not that it mattered, she decided, and instead directed her attention to the strong refinement in her features—the good cheekbones, smooth jawline, and solid angle to her forehead and chin. Her eyebrows were a sandy shade of brown, thick at the inner corners and arching naturally in a graceful sweep. Amber flecks shimmered in her hazel eyes, and her dark-brown lashes were long and thick, tipped with gold at the ends. Her lips were well shaped, with a full curve to the lower one and a bowing arch to the upper. With the slightest lift of their corners, attractive dimples appeared in her cheeks. Except for a faintly troubled darkness in her eyes, the image in the mirror looked dauntless and proud, a hint of daring about it that seemed to eagerly seek challenge.

Was that her? In frustration she lowered the mirror. It was no use. She didn't remember that face. She didn't remember anything.

"Who am I?" she said with impatience. "Where do I live? What do I do? Don't I have family, friends? I've been in this hospital for almost two days. Why hasn't anyone missed me? Could I have come to Nice alone? The gown—" She remembered the designer label it had carried. "It was by St. Laurent. Does that mean I'm wealthy?"

"It is possible," the inspector conceded. "Though it is also possible the gown and the jewelry were gifts from a generous lover. The Côte d'Azur attracts many with income in rarefied brackets. And they, in turn, attract beautiful women to the area."

"And you think I'm one of those women."

"Perhaps." He shrugged noncommittally. "However, most—even today—are poor Bardot imitations, with tumbling blond hair, voluptuous curves, and pink, pouting lips. Few have the appearance of class you possess."

"I think that's a compliment. Thank you," she murmured with a trace of dryness.

"It was." His mouth curved with the same droll amusement she had shown. "In any case, beautiful women may arrive in Nice alone, but they seldom remain alone very long."

"Then you think I knew the man I was seen struggling with?"

"The two of you could have been engaged in a lovers' quarrel. Or—he wished to make your acquaintance, and you rejected his advances."

"But why would I go to the Espace Masséna at night, during Carnival, without an escort, and without a purse?" she argued. "Or was the man a thief who stole my purse? That could have been the cause of the struggle—and it would explain why he ran."

"But why would he take your purse and not your jewelry?"

"I don't know." She sighed wearily, confused and frustrated by the constant blankness, the absence of any answers to the questions. "There has to be some way to find out who I am. Somewhere there has to be a room with my clothes in it, my makeup, my jewelry."

"Inquiries are being made at all the hotels and pensions in the city," he told her. "But you must remember, during Carnival people frequently stay out all night. Therefore, the absence of a guest from his or her room for one night normally would not be worthy of notice. Two nights in a row, that is another thing. If we are fortunate, I may know something tomorrow."

"I hope so. I *have* to find out who I am."

He arched an eyebrow at her curiously. "You say that with unusual urgency, mam'selle."

"I know." She heard the troubled note in her voice and tried to explain. "I have this feeling, Inspector—this vague yet very compelling feeling—that I'm supposed to be somewhere. It's important. It's more than important. It's as if something terrible will happen if I'm not there."

"Where?" It was asked quietly, almost indifferently, as if to gently jar loose a fragment of her memory.

But it didn't work. "I don't know." This time her voice was choked with the frustration and strain of trying to recall. But the more she struggled to remember, the harder her head pounded. Suddenly she didn't have the strength to fight them both. She sagged back against the hospital pillows and shut her eyes tight, hating the blankness.

"I have overtired you with my questions. I am sorry," the inspector said, his voice gentle with regret. "You rest. I will come back tomorrow."

Then he was gone and she was alone again—alone with the emptiness of her memory, an emptiness she seemed powerless to fill. With a turn of her head, she gazed out the window at the brilliant blue sky that had given the Côte d'Azur its name. If only there was something she could do, somewhere she could go—but where did a person go to find her memory?

FROM THE HOSPITAL CORRIDOR came the murmur of typically hushed voices, the rustle of stiff polyester uniforms, and the whisper of white-stockinged legs brushing together in a striding walk. But no one approached her door, and no bouquets of flowers relieved the starkness of her room or sent their sweet fragrance into it to cover the sharp antiseptic smells.

Agitated, restless, and tired of staring at the walls that echoed the blankness of her mind, she threw back the covers and sat up, swinging her legs over the side of the bed. A wave of dizziness hit her. She gripped the edge of the mattress and waited for the room to stop spinning, then slowly lowered her feet to the floor and stood up. Immediately she felt a coolness against her skin where the hospital gown gaped in back. But she had no robe to cover her—no clothes at all other than the evening gown. Turning, she pulled the blanket off the bed and draped it around her shoulders Indian-style.

She was halfway to the door before she realized she was obeying that faint inner voice that said she had to leave, that she was needed somewhere. But where? Why? And why the urgency? Was she in some kind of danger? The man she'd been struggling with—had he deliberately tried to hurt her, or had he been trying to make her go somewhere with him? But where? And what was the danger? From whom? And where were they now?

Driven by the endless questions, she crossed to the window with its post-card view of Nice, the city of fun and flowers, of sun, sea, and sex, a city that sizzled softly by day and crackled with action by night.

In the distance the sunlight sparkled on the deep blue Mediterranean waters of the Baie des Anges, ringed by private beaches, crowded now with wall-to-wall sunburned flesh and languid egos. Closer were the red-roofed ocher buildings and Italianate churches of the town's old section, with its narrow streets opening to form little squares.

She hugged the blanket more tightly around her and searched the scene with her eyes, a scene so reminiscent of paintings by Matisse and Cézanne. Here the dreaded mistral that roared down the Rhône Valley twisting and turning trees was but a breeze to stir the fronds of the palm trees along the Promenade des Anglais, and the architecture was distinctly Mediterranean in character rather than French, a reminder that less than a century and a half ago Nice belonged to Italy.

Was it somewhere in Nice that she was supposed to be? Was that what had brought her here? But how could she be sure she didn't live here? The inspector claimed that she spoke English with an American accent, but she was fluent in French. The designer gown, the jewelry—it was possible she was a wealthy American living abroad, perhaps in Nice itself. After all, she knew the names of its streets, the location of a marvelous little tea shop on the Rue St. François-de-Paule, and . . . but a frequent visitor to the city might know such things too.

If she wasn't supposed to be here, though, then where?

Her head started to pound again. She turned from the window, absently massaging her temple.

Inspector Armand stood inside the doorway, his relaxed stance conveying the impression that he'd been observing her for some time. She lifted her head sharply at the sight of him, her glance quickly taking in the shiny bald top of his head, the dark-gray hair shading to white at the temples, the pleasing plumpness of his features, and the keenness of his blue eyes. She hadn't heard him come in. He had slipped in quietly—like a principal slipping in to the back of a classroom to silently observe.

"I see you are up and about today," he said, his sharp-eyed gaze continuing its assessing sweep of her. "That is good."

She took a quick step toward him, then stopped, every muscle in her body strained taut. "Have you found out who I am?"

"Regrettably, *non*. Our check of the hotels has turned up nothing. The whereabouts of all their guests have been accounted for, and no belongings have been left in any rooms, other than the normal one or two items that a departing guest might forget to pack."

She had tried to brace herself for this answer, but it was still frustrating to hear it. "And I suppose no one answering my description has been reported missing."

"*Non*."

She sighed. "What now, Inspector?"

"Now, we widen our search to include apartments, homes, villas, yachts. . . ."

"It will take time to check all those out." She looked down at her hands and the tight lacing of her fingers on the blanket, the tension, the turmoil, knotting them as it knotted her.

"Unfortunately, a considerable amount of time."

"I don't know if I can wait that long to find out who I am." She forced her hands to loosen their grip on the edge of the blanket. "There must be some other—quicker—way."

"When you saw Dr. St. Clair this morning, was he able to tell you anything?"

There was a wry pull at one corner of her mouth. "If you mean other than his opinion that the laceration to my head is healing nicely, no. But he's arranged for a specialist to see me this afternoon. A psychiatrist or psychologist, I don't remember which."

"Perhaps he will be more helpful."

"Perhaps." She sighed again. "If only I could remember something—anything."

"Maybe it is more convenient not to remember."

He suddenly had her complete attention. "What do you mean by that?" She saw the close way he was watching, observing every nuance of her reaction to this rather startling remark. "Do you think I'm faking this amnesia? Why? What would I gain by it?"

"I have asked myself that too."

She stared at him, stunned by the implication of his words. "My God, do you think I'm some criminal? Why haven't you run a check on me?"

"It was one of the first things I did—merely as a matter of routine, you understand." His mouth curved in a faint, apologetic smile that took much of the sting out of his suspicion.

"Obviously your 'routine' check didn't turn up anything, or I'd be arrested."

"The results were negative," the inspector admitted.

"You don't still think it's a possibility?"

"In my profession it is never wise to rule out any possibility until the truth is uncovered."

"I suppose it isn't. Right now I just wish I knew something. I am so tired of this endless circle of questions."

"Life is a question, is it not? And we spend our whole life trying to find the answer to it." A smile made his cheeks rounder. "But it is ironic, *non*, that many people wish they could forget their past, while you seek so valiantly to remember yours."

At that moment a small, quick man with bushy hair and beetle brows bustled into her hospital room, a clipboard and manila folder tucked under his arm. "I am Dr. Gervais. Dr. St. Clair asked—" He stopped and blinked at the inspector. "You have a visitor."

"Inspector Claude Armand." He smoothly produced his identification.

"You are here to question the patient?" The doctor blinked at him again, with a certain vagueness in his expression.

"And you are here to examine her." The inspector smiled, but as usual, the smile didn't reach his eyes. "You have no objection to my sitting in, do you?"

The doctor seemed momentarily taken aback by the request, then lifted his shoulders in a brief, indifferent shrug. "You may stay or go, as you wish." With that settled, he turned and introduced himself to her again. "Dr. St. Clair tells me the injury to your head has caused a defect in your memory."

"A defect—that's an understatement, Doctor. I don't remember anything. Not my name, my address, or my family—assuming I have one."

"Hmmm," he said, as if he found her response most interesting, then flicked a hand in her direction. "Please make yourself comfortable, and we will talk about this."

"In other words, lie down on the couch," she murmured dryly.

He gave her a startled look, then glanced around the room. "There is no couch," he said, then the curious frown that had pulled his heavy brows together cleared in a dawning realization. "Ahh, you make a joke. It is good you have retained your sense of humor."

"It is one of the few things I've retained." Avoiding the bed, she crossed to a chair and sat down, conscious of the inspector standing quietly to one side, silently listening, observing.

The doctor sat himself down in the other chair and crossed his legs at the knee, one foot swinging in a nervous rhythm as he arranged the clipboard on his lap and opened the manila folder to leaf through the papers inside. "Shall we begin?" he said.

After thirty minutes, during which he tested her current memory retention, asked numerous general-knowledge questions, and questioned her extensively about her past, specifically her religion, her patience was exhausted.

During a lull, she demanded, "What are we accomplishing with all this, Doctor?"

He gave her a look that seemed to say the answer was obvious. "I am attempting to determine the extent of your memory impairment. Amnesia has many causes and takes many forms—senility, alcoholism, electroconvulsive therapy, acute encephalitis, brain trauma. . . . In severe cases, amnesia symptoms primarily stem from damage to such brain structures as the mammillary bodies, circumscribed parts of the thalamus, and—"

She broke in, shaking her head in confusion. "You are being too technical, Doctor."

"My apologies." There was a quick bob of his bushy head. "My initial findings tell me that you have what we call traumatic amnesia, as a result of the concussion you suffered. This is a common aftereffect of a severe head injury."

"But when will my memory return?"

"That is impossible to say. It could be today, tomorrow, next week, next month." He leaned back in the chair and pulled thoughtfully at a thick eyebrow. "It will probably return gradually, with pieces of your past coming back to you—perhaps in chronological order, from the most recent, or perhaps haphazardly, like pieces of a jigsaw puzzle that finally fit together."

"But it isn't permanent?"

"There have been cases where the patient has never recovered his memory, but they are rare." He hesitated, then added, "However, it is altogether possible that you may never remember the events that immediately preceded your injury."

"In other words, I might not remember the identity or description of the man I was seen struggling with," she concluded.

"Correct."

"You haven't said anything about treatment." And that omission bothered her. "What about drugs or hypnosis?"

"Hypnosis is frequently helpful in cases of hysterical amnesia—where there is no physical cause, no damage to the brain."

She stared at him. "Are you saying that all I can do is sit and wait for my memory to come back—if it does?"

"Essentially, yes."

"I don't accept that. There has to be something I can do." She rose to her feet and crossed stiffly to the window. "There has to be."

"You cannot force your memory to return, mademoiselle. The more you grasp for it, the more elusive it becomes. It is better to relax your mind and allow your memory to return naturally."

"It's bitter prescription you offer me, Doctor," she murmured, unable to keep the note of frustration out of her voice.

"But it is the best one." He spent another few minutes briefly lecturing her about time and healing, then left.

She stood at the window, fighting tears and railing at her helplessness. Then a faint stir of movement intruded to forcibly remind her of the inspector's presence in the room. She threw him a quick glance then tilted her head a little higher, fixing her gaze on the colorful sails of the pleasure craft in the bay.

"The good doctor wasn't very helpful, was he?" she said.

"No, although it was apparent from your conversation with him that your knowledge of medicine and anatomy is limited. I think it would be safe to assume that you are not associated with the medical profession."

"But I must do something—have some interest." Made restless again by this blankness, she turned from the window.

"The dress you were wearing is an expensive one. Perhaps you are wealthy and do not have to work at anything."

"Maybe. But I can't imagine myself being idle—or flitting from one fashionable resort to another, occupying my time solely with parties and charity events. A life like that would be too aimless."

"What do you think you might do, then?"

She searched her mind for an answer, then sighed. "I . . . don't . . . know."

"Tell me what you know about the law—the first things that come to your mind."

"Free association, you mean?" She looked over at him, her curiosity piqued by the thought.

"Something like that, yes."

"The law." She closed her eyes and tried to relax, letting her thoughts flow spontaneously. "Corporations, felony, fraud, writs, subpoenas, habeas corpus. . . ." She felt herself trying to grope for words, and shook her head. "That's the extent of it. Let's try something else."

"Banking."

"Numbered Swiss accounts, deposits, rates of exchange, interest, loans, mortgages, checking accounts, savings."

Again the well of terms quickly dried up. It was the same with advertising, petroleum, interior design, motion pictures, computers, and the travel industry.

Refusing to give up, she insisted, "Let's try another."

The inspector hesitated, then said, "You are fluent in both French and English. Perhaps you are an interpreter. When I begin to speak again, simultaneously translate what I say into English."

"All right." She focused her gaze on his mouth and waited, a tension heightening all her senses despite her attempts to relax.

He began talking at a rate that was neither fast nor slow. "I was born in the Maritime Alps and grew up in Levens, a peaceful village at the entrance to the Vésubie Valley. . . ."

She was able to follow along for the first half dozen or so words, then she began to stumble, the words tangling as she struggled to listen to what he was saying while translating what he'd already said. The harder she tried, the more jumbled everything became.

"Stop—please." Laughing at her mangled translation of his words, she lifted her hands in mock surrender. "I can't do it. I can't split my concentration that way."

"It is difficult, *non*?"

"Yes," she replied emphatically, then her amusement at the abortive attempt faded as discouragement set in. "What else is there, Inspector?"

"It is always possible, mam'selle, that you haven't been trained for anything."

"Except to be beautiful and decorative, you mean."

"You say that with a touch of disdain."

"I suppose I do." But she wasn't interested in her reaction to that. "This feeling I have that I'm supposed to be somewhere—if it's true, then why hasn't my absence been noticed? Why hasn't someone missed me?"

"Perhaps when we find out who you are, we will learn those answers as well."

"But when will that be?" she demanded, all her frustration and anxiety surfacing as she turned from him and paced to the window, her arms folded tightly in front of her, her fingers curling into the blanket. "How long will I have to wait?"

After a short silence, the inspector spoke. "I have arranged for a photographer to come and take your picture today. The newspaper has agreed to print it in tomorrow's edition. Perhaps someone will recognize your photo and come forward."

"Perhaps."

When he took his leave of her, she responded automatically but didn't turn from the window, her attention riveted on the brilliant blue sky outside. Like the endless swirl of questions in her mind, it seemed to go on forever.

"WE'VE LOCATED HER," the man said into the telephone, studying the grainy newspaper photograph before him, transposed onto thin facsimile paper. It showed a young woman, bandages circling the top of her head and a bruise standing out sharply against the paleness of her skin. There was no hint of desperation in the eyes that stared back at him. Instead, they looked insistent, determined, demanding.

"Where?" came the sharp, quick response from the man on the other end of the line.

"At a hospital in Nice."

"A hospital?"

"Yes. I've just received a copy of an article that's appearing in the morning edition of their paper, accompanied by a photo of her." Once more he scanned the article in the French-language newspaper. Mostly it was a collection of pertinent facts, and little else, listing her height at five feet four and a half inches, her weight at one hundred and thirteen pounds, her hair dark blond, her eyes hazel, and her age estimated to be in the mid-to-late-twenties range. All of these details he already knew about her—with one enlightening addition. "My French is a little rusty, but it appears she has amnesia."

"Amnesia. My God, does that mean she can't remember anything?"

"Apparently." He couldn't keep the note of satisfaction out of his voice. "The article refers to her as the 'Demoiselle de Mystère.'"

"This is great news."

"I know."

"You've got to get to her—quickly."

"My thought exactly."

"I mean it. We can't afford for her to remember and start talking. I'm counting on you to keep her quiet. And if you can't, I will. I'm in way too deep to let her destroy me. I'm sorry, but that's the way it is."

"Don't worry." There was a sharp click, and the line went dead.

She looked at the grainy black-and-white photograph, finding it strange that she felt so detached. On second thought, she decided that it wasn't so strange, considering she didn't recognize that woman at all.

Too bad the photographer hadn't waited another twelve hours to take her picture. Dr. St. Clair had removed the turban of gauze from around her head early this morning, leaving only a small, square bandage to protect the deep cut, and her shoulder-length hair covered even that.

And the doctor had also hinted that she would soon be well enough to be released. Which raised a whole new set of problems. Where would she go? How would she live when she had no clothes, no money, and no name—other than the melodramatic one the newspaper had given her, "Demoiselle de Mystère." She suspected it could have been worse. They could just as easily have dubbed her "Mademoiselle X" or something equally trite.

Checking a sigh, she folded the newspaper shut and laid it back down on the table in the small waiting room. As she rose from the chair and pulled the blanket-robe higher around her shoulders, she wondered if anyone would see the photograph and recognize her. It wouldn't be wise to count on that, though. No, she needed to start planning what she was going to do once she was released from the hospital.

As she passed the nurses' station and turned down the corridor to her room, she decided to ask Inspector Armand to recommend a jeweler who would give her a good price for the antique brooch and topaz earrings she'd been wearing. Once she had money, then what? Should she stay in Nice and look for work— Heaven knew what kind? Or should she leave? And go where?

Distracted by the sound of a raised voice, she looked up from her absent contemplation of the floor. There was a man standing in the corridor directly ahead of her, not far from the door to her room. He was upset about something, judging from the anxious attempt by one of the nurses to placate him. Curious to learn what the fuss was all about, she took another look at the stranger.

Dressed in a sport coat in an elongated herringbone design, a beige brown tie of woven silk, and mocha trousers, he stood easily over six feet tall. His heavy-boned features were lean and angular, with none of the carved sleekness about them that might have persuaded her to consider him handsome. It was a hard face, an unforgiving face that gave the impression that cynicism lurked just below the surface. Yet there was something compelling about his looks—something ruthlessly masculine—that she couldn't deny.

"I don't care whether you make a habit of losing patients or not," he said to the nurse, plainly unplacated. "But I suggest you find this one—now!"

"*Oui, m'sieur.*"

He turned on his heel, then stopped abruptly when he saw her walking toward them. Suddenly his eyes seemed more black than gray, with glass-sharp splinters of interest in them.

"Remy." His deep voice rumbled the name.

Who was he talking to? Was there someone behind her? She glanced back, but there was no one in the corridor. When she squared around, the man was there before her, his hands seizing her by the arms and pulling her to him, a harshness in their grip that spoke of feelings he had tried to control and couldn't. And she realized he was referring to her. She was Remy.

Too stunned by the discovery to resist, she let him gather her to him. The fine woolen texture of his sport coat against her cheek, the musky sandalwood fragrance of a man's cologne that clung to it, the faint tremors within him— those and a dozen other impressions registered on her at once. But most of all she was struck by the overwhelming feeling that it was right for her to be in his arms. It was where she belonged.

Savoring the feeling, she leaned into him and let the hands that glided with such familiar ease over her back press her even closer to him. She was conscious of her pulse quickening in pleasure when he rubbed his mouth against the side of her hair.

"I was about to turn this hospital upside down looking for you, Remy."

Remy. It was the second time he'd called her that. Was that her name? She tried to remember, but she couldn't penetrate that wall of blankness to make it familiar.

She sensed his withdrawal an instant before his hands pushed her an arm's length away from him. She caught the glimmer of anger in his hardening expression, an anger that suggested he regretted the action that had swept her into his arms. Yet the light in his eyes remained dark and bright as his gaze traveled over her face in a quick inspection.

"The photo I saw showed your head in bandages." Reaching up, he traced one side of her forehead, which had earlier been swathed in gauze, his touch incredibly light and gentle.

She should know him, but she didn't. "Who are you?"

He stiffened as if she'd struck him, then pulled his hand back to his side, his mouth curving in a humorless smile. "Obviously someone you'd rather forget."

"That isn't what I meant."

"This is Monsieur Cole Buchanan," the nurse volunteered, handing her a business card. "Your family owns an international shipping company. It is exciting, *non?*"

Before she had a chance to look at the card, footsteps approached. "It seems I have arrived late with the news," came Inspector Armand's familiar voice.

"News," she repeated blankly, still trying to make sense out of all of this.

"*Oui.* I came to tell you that your brother would be arriving shortly to take you home."

Struggling to hide her shock at his announcement, she quickly looked down at the card in her hand. Cole Buchanan's name appeared in bold type in the center of it, with the title of President listed directly below his name. This man couldn't be her brother. She inwardly recoiled from the thought, aware that her reaction to him when he'd held her in his arms a moment ago had been anything but sisterly. She remembered the way her body had arched in a sexual response—the gliding caress of his hands on her back—and the momentary desire she'd felt to turn her head and find the male lips rubbing so sensually over her hair.

She forced herself to look at the company name and logo that headed the card—the Crescent Line. She stared at the name, waiting for it to spark some memory, no matter how vague. But nothing came. Instead, she felt uneasy. Why?

"Is something wrong?" The deep-voiced question came from Cole Buchanan.

"No." Why was she so quick with her denial? Something *was* wrong, but what? And why didn't it feel right to ask him about it? He was her brother. "It's just that—I don't remember anything about the company or about shipping."

"You've never been involved in the actual operation of the company."

Was that criticism she detected in his statement? But a glance found nothing in his expression to suggest that. If anything, he seemed sharply alert, watchful—his look almost guarded.

"You don't remember anything, do you?" He made the observation somewhat thoughtfully.

"She suffers from amnesia—" Inspector Armand began.

"I know," Cole interrupted, a trace of aloofness in the glance he gave him. "I was informed of her condition, but I hadn't realized it was total."

"You said my name is Remy." She focused on that, compelled by a need to challenge and confront. "Who am I? What am I? Where do I live?"

"In New Orleans . . . Louisiana," he added, as if she might not remember that fact either. "You still live at the family home in the Garden district."

Images flashed in her mind, images that came and went too quickly for her to grasp and hold and discover what they meant, images of ancient moss-draped oaks, graceful wisteria arches, and scrolling iron lace railings. Were they her memories, or merely a knowledge of the place? She couldn't tell.

"Do you remember something?" the inspector asked.

"I'm not sure," she admitted, then looked at him and realized, "You two haven't been introduced. This is Inspector Claude Armand. He—"

Cole Buchanan broke in firmly and extended a hand in formal greeting. "A pleasure, Inspector. I know the family would want me to pass along their thanks for the efforts you've made in Remy's behalf." He sounded warm, sincere, and polite—but aloof. She was struck by that. Inspector Armand was a stranger to him, and she had the impression that he wanted to keep it that way. He wasn't interested in making friends, in allowing people to get close to him—just as he'd pushed her an arm's length away. Why? She was his sister. She remembered his initial embrace of her, the depth of feeling he'd shown—and subsequently regretted. Why? Distracted by these thoughts, she missed the inspector's response and discovered that Cole was speaking again. ". . . arrange for her release, we need to leave. I'm sure you can understand, Inspector, the family is very anxious to get Remy safely back to New Orleans."

New Orleans. This time she picked up on the words, a certainty rushing through her. "That's where I'm supposed to be. That's where I'm needed. New Orleans." She laughed softly in a release of tension and turned to the inspector. "At last we have that riddle solved. And so simply, too."

"What riddle?" Cole asked.

"I've had this feeling—ever since I came to, here in the hospital—that there was some *place* I was supposed to be. It was important, I knew that, but—" She stopped. "Why is it important?"

"I don't have any idea," he replied, without even the slightest hesitation. "How long will it take you to get dressed and be ready to leave?"

"Forgive me, M'sieu Buchanan," the inspector inserted smoothly, politely. "But there are a number of questions I must ask you first."

"Questions—why?" She found it impossible to tell what the inspector was thinking—or suspecting.

"We may have learned who you are, but we have yet to determine the identity of the man you were with," he reminded her.

"And you think—" she began, then turned to look at Cole Buchanan, "—he might be that man."

"I wasn't. As a matter of fact, I wasn't even in Nice at the time."

"And what time was that, m'sieu?" the inspector asked, then extended a hand, palm up. "May I see your papers?"

"Of course." With barely disguised impatience, he reached inside his sport coat and took out his passport, then handed it to the inspector. "You will find they are all in order, Inspector Armand, and they will prove that I am exactly who I claim to be." Then he glanced at her. "This won't take long, Remy. In the meantime, why don't you get ready?"

"I have nothing to wear—no street clothes," she said, aware of the inspector glancing through his passport with more than casual interest.

"I anticipated that and picked up a couple of outfits for you on my way here."

"*Oui.* We left the boxes in your room," the nurse added.

The inspector nodded his acquiescence. "I would prefer to speak privately with M'sieu Buchanan. It is my job to ask questions, *non?*"

"Following the routine again, are you, Inspector?" she said, remembering the check he'd run on her to see if she had a criminal record.

"But of course." He smiled.

"In that case I will leave it in your capable hands to determine whether I should go with him or not." She said it lightly, but with an underthread of seriousness running through her voice. She didn't remember him, and she only had his word that he was her brother. Still, there was New Orleans. She had to get there. No matter what other doubts she had, that certainty remained strong.

As she entered her hospital room and closed the door, she saw the inspector return Cole Buchanan's passport, observing, "You travel a great deal."

"On business, yes." The rest of his reply was muffled by the door.

The boxes were there, exactly as the nurse had said, containing two outfits complete from the skin out—lacy lingerie, sheer stockings, shoes, and a chocolate-brown pantsuit with a blouse of cream-gold silk as well as an oversized turtleneck sweater of cranberry silk knit with a matching full skirt of silk broadcloth.

Mindful of the long flight potentially ahead of her, she chose the pantsuit. It fit perfectly, as if it had been made for her, yet it was brand-new. She wasn't sure why she felt so surprised by that. Cole Buchanan was her brother, so naturally he would know her size and taste in clothes.

Fully dressed, she sat on the edge of the bed and listened to the voices in the corridor, the inspector's calm and low-pitched voice making its inquiries, and Cole Buchanan's deep-voiced replies, always short, sometimes impatient, sometimes angry. Finally there was a knock at her door.

"Come in."

Cole Buchanan stepped into the room, his glance sweeping over her with unflattering indifference. "You're ready, I see. I'll settle your bill with the hospital and be back to get you—" He paused and glanced somewhat cynically over his shoulder. "With the inspector's permission, of course."

"Of course." Inspector Armand walked into the room and stayed when he left. "You will soon be leaving us for New Orleans—for home."

From that she concluded that he was satisfied with the answers Cole Buchanan had given him. "Was he able to tell you anything about that night?"

"Regrettably, *non.* The case remains open." He walked over to her and took her hand. "If you should remember—*when* you remember," he corrected himself, "you contact me."

"Of course. And thank you, Inspector, for everything."

He shrugged. "It is my job."

* * *

Twenty minutes later Remy emerged from the hospital into the brilliant Mediterranean sunlight. Automatically she slowed her steps and breathed in the tangy freshness of the air, ridding her lungs of the strong medicinal smells they'd known for days.

She turned to say something to Cole and nearly collided with him, unaware that he'd been following so close behind her. His hand came up to steady her as his glance came down, lingering for only a fraction of a second on her lips—but that was all it took to spark the thought of being kissed by him and to shatter the comfortable, companionable feeling she'd had toward him since they'd left her room. She was stunned that such a thought could cross her mind, even fleetingly. He was her brother. She should never have let the inspector's questioning of him reinforce her initial reaction to him as a man.

"Sorry," she said quickly, conscious of the faint heat in her cheeks and the rare embarrassment she felt.

"It's all right. The car's over there." With a gesture of his hand, he pointed her toward a shiny gray Citroen parked in the visitors' area.

She moved briskly toward it, this time sharply aware of his footsteps directly behind her. When they reached it, he stepped ahead of her in one stride and set down the suitcase he'd provided for her clothes, then unlocked the passenger door for her. Eluding his assistance, she slipped quickly onto the seat and waited while he closed the door. In the rearview mirror, she watched him open the trunk to stow her suitcase inside. But he didn't immediately close the trunk again. When he did, she noticed that he'd removed his sport jacket. As he slid behind the wheel of the car, he reached back and laid it on the rear seat.

Instinctively she knew that despite the ease with which he wore the expensive sport coat, he was more comfortable in shirt sleeves. He hadn't always worn a suit and tie; he had learned to wear them, and to wear them well. Yet, strangely, she couldn't imagine anything but the finest cloth against her own skin. Why was that?

"Ready?" He directed the full brunt of his sharp, strong features, lean almost to the point of gauntness, at her.

She nodded and looked away, silently wishing he hadn't removed his jacket. She didn't want to notice that the muscles beneath his shirt were the hard, ropy kind that came from work, rather than the bulging perfection that came from workouts. He had the polished look and confident air of a highly successful executive. So why did she think he'd fought his way to the top? Why did she have the feeling that despite the streak of gentleness she'd detected when he'd so lightly run his fingers along her forehead—that despite that, he could be cruel in a tight place? How did she know with such certainty that he could play the quiet game—as now—or the quick one?

And why was she so physically aware of him as a man? She shouldn't be, but the close confines of the small European car seemed to make it impossible for her to be otherwise. With each breath she inhaled the masculine fragrance of his cologne, and the sight of his tanned hands on the wheel filled her side vision, reminding her of the feel of them spread across her back. . . . Abruptly she broke off the thought, damning the sudden uneven beat of her pulse.

"How old are you?" She directed her gaze to the front.

"Thirty-five," he replied, a thread of puzzlement in his deep voice.

"How old am I?"

"Twenty-seven."

Which meant he was literally her big brother. Was it a case of hero worship? Had she always idolized him? Surely it wasn't unheard of for a sister to recognize that her big brother was sexually attractive. After all, she was a woman, and since she had no memory of their sibling relationship, wasn't it logical that she would react to him strictly *as* a woman? It was the only rationale for her behavior that made sense.

"You said you saw the photograph in the newspaper," she remembered. "Were you here looking for me?"

"No, I arrived in Marseilles yesterday on business. The company has an overseas office there," he inserted in explanation. "Frazier called me this morning about it."

She frowned. "Who's Frazier?"

"Your father."

"Is that what you call him?"

"Yes." He turned the car onto a main street.

"Do I?" she wondered.

"Occasionally."

"Frazier." She tried out the sound of it, but she couldn't summon any image of him, and stopped trying. "And my mother—what's her name?"

"Sibylle."

Still nothing. She rested her head against the seat back and tried to relax. "At least I know I have a family, even if I can't remember them. There were times when I wondered if I did—when I wondered if anyone was looking for me." She frowned again. "Why did it take so long for you to find me?"

"No one realized you were missing until almost two days ago, when you failed to return home on your scheduled flight. At first they thought you had missed your connection and would be arriving on a later flight. When you still didn't turn up, they contacted me to see if you had changed your plans and were flying back on the corporate plane with me. Of course, you hadn't—and the search for you began at that point." He paused, glancing at her sideways, his mouth twisting in something that passed for a smile. "Right after that, they discovered your clothes and your bags were still in the closet of your stateroom on the yacht. And Frazier realized you hadn't gone off by yourself for a few days, as everyone had assumed."

No wonder none of the hotels had been able to identify her as a guest. She'd been staying on a yacht. "Then originally I came to Nice with my parents."

"You joined them here. They'd been cruising the Mediterranean for a week before that. Then you and most of the family flew over for a couple of days to celebrate their thirty-fifth wedding anniversary."

"Were you here?"

"No. I was in New Orleans, nearly half a world away."

"Working," she guessed, picking up again on that charged intensity about him, the air of a man driven to succeed. "You work all the time, don't you?"

Briefly he met her glance, then gave his full attention to the traffic in front of them. "You've told me that before."

There was no amusement in his voice, which made her think she had criticized him about that in the past. She decided it was a subject better not pursued, but it brought up another question.

"What do I do? You said earlier I wasn't involved in the company. But I can't imagine myself doing nothing."

"You're heavily involved with the Louisiana State Museum. You act as a docent, and you assist in the authentication of certain items donated to it—specifically seventeenth- and eighteenth-century French porcelain, your special field of knowledge."

She suddenly had an image of an antique jardiniere with flowers and cupids painted in reserves on its sides and embellished with gold against a distinctively pink background. She knew instantly that it was a Sèvres piece done in the *rose Pompadour* color. Maybe she wasn't an expert, but she was highly knowledgeable in that field. She knew that in the same inexplicable way she knew other things.

The things he'd told her—her original purpose in coming to Nice, the reason her family had failed to miss her—all of it sounded very logical, very plausible, even believable. Yet . . . something wasn't right. None of it explained this feeling she had that she was urgently needed at home, that there was some kind of trouble.

Sighing, she turned to gaze out the window and looked blindly at the ocher buildings they passed. As the gardened boulevard made a curve, she recognized that they were traveling down the Avenue Félix Faure, approaching the Espace Masséna. Tensing slightly, she straightened in her seat, waiting for that first glimpse of it.

Then, there it was, the towering sprays of its sparkling fountains visible through a break in the row of shade trees and slender cypress, and the grinning face of the giant papier-mâché King of Carnival peering down from his alfresco throne. She scanned the stand of trees by the sidewalk, wondering which one she'd struck her head against. At the same time, she couldn't help thinking how beautifully serene the square looked with only a scattering of people strolling its landscaped walks.

Belatedly she noticed that Cole had stopped the car at a pedestrian crosswalk. A woman walked in front of them, pushing a baby stroller. Smoothly he shifted the car into drive, and they rolled forward again. A moment later she was surprised when he failed to turn at the next intersection and continued straight ahead onto the Avenue de Verdun instead.

"If you had turned back there, we could have taken a better route to the airport and avoided all this traffic."

"I know," he said, slowing the car to make the turn onto the palm-lined Promenade des Anglais.

"Then why are we going this way?" She frowned. "I thought you said at the hospital we were flying directly to New Orleans."

"We are—as soon as I eliminate the problem with your passport."

"*What* problem with my passport?"

"You don't have one . . . yet. Hopefully it will be waiting for us when we arrive at the hotel."

6

MINUTES LATER HE pulled up in front of the entrance to the Hotel Negresco. A plume-hatted doorman in a scarlet-lined blue cloak and high, shiny boots stepped forward and opened the passenger door for her. Taking his gloved hand, Remy let him assist her out of the car, then turned and waited, watching as Cole slipped back into his sport jacket, its rich herringbone wool skillfully concealing the strong build of his upper body. Idly she studied the solid, angular bones of his face, covered by skin that was deeply tanned and without a wrinkle.

With an odd certainty she knew that nepotism had nothing to do with his position as president of the family shipping business. It was his competence, his aggressiveness, his ability to lead and command that had gained him the office. Suddenly, without any effort at all, she could picture him on the wharves in his shirt sleeves, moving among the longshoremen, as tough and strong as they were. And just as easily she could see him in command of a board meeting, respected—however grudgingly—for his canny business skills. *Grudgingly*—why had she thought that?

But she didn't have an opportunity to analyze that very definite impression as she found herself now standing face-to-face with him, the rock gray of his gaze boring into her as if searching for something. For an instant the air seemed to crackle around them, charged by a tension that flashed between them. She held herself still, wondering what he was thinking. What did he want?

The whole sensation vanished as if it had never been when he said, "Shall we go in?"

"Of course." She swung sharply about and crossed to the hotel's entrance, conscious of his long-reaching stride easily keeping pace with hers.

Once they were inside, her glance swept the hotel's magnificent interior. The Hotel Negresco was typical of the many palatial hotels scattered along the Côte d'Azur, but it had a style and gloss that was all its own. It was officially listed as a historic monument, though Remy suspected that it could more accurately be called a monument to excessive consumption. Used as a hospital during World War II, it had been restored with an ostentatious hand. To the undiscerning eye, the glass-domed and marble-floored Salon Royal might resemble a gaudy if stunning piece of costume jewelry, but the one-ton chandelier was nothing less than Baccarat crystal, and the tapestry on the wall was a genuine Gobelin.

Cole's hand moved to the small of her back, the sensation of it blocking out everything else as he guided her to the registration desk. She was acutely conscious of the sudden longings that ran through her—a desire for intimacy, to touch and be touched. Why? Had it been that long since she'd been with a man?

"Am I married?" she wondered suddenly.

"No." If he found her question unexpected, he gave no sign of it.

"Divorced?"

"No."

"Have I ever been close?"

"To which? Marriage or divorce?" he asked, showing her the first glimpse of his humor.

"Wouldn't it have to be marriage?" she challenged, a faint smile dimpling her own cheeks. "I understand it comes before divorce."

"I guess it does," he agreed, then seemed to withdraw from her, a remoteness shuttering his expression. "You were engaged once."

"What happened?"

"He drowned in a boating accident on Lake Pontchartrain."

She immediately felt a sharp twinge of sadness. "What was his name?"

"Nick Austin."

Did the name mean anything to her? She couldn't tell. All she had was a vague feeling of something—someone—from long, long ago. Then the curtness of Cole's answer registered, and she looked up, encountering his glance, oddly cool and remote. "You didn't like him."

"I didn't know him."

Again he spoke curtly, as if he resented any mention of her late fiancé. Why? Surely he couldn't have been jealous, could he? Jealous that some other man had come first with her? Then another thought occurred to her.

"Cole, are you married?"

He shot her a quick look before answering, then abruptly dropped his glance. "No."

She was stunned by the relief she felt at his answer—and by the swift rise of possessiveness she'd felt just before it. She didn't follow him when he crossed to the desk and spoke to one of the clerks. She was too busy trying to come to terms with the discovery that the possessive feeling had been jealousy.

Then he was walking back to her. "He hasn't arrived with your passport, so I've arranged for a suite. I didn't think you'd want to wait around the lobby until he comes."

She stiffened at the hint of sarcasm in his remark, and its implication that she would regard waiting in the lobby as something beneath her. She started to challenge him on it, but the arrival of a bellman deterred her—for the time being.

In silence she went up in the elevator, down the hall, and into the suite of rooms. There she crossed to the window of the richly furnished sitting room and waited while the bellman went through the ritual of showing Cole all the suite's amenities. Finally she heard the click of the door latch signal his departure, and she swung from the spectacular view of the bay's deep-blue waters.

Without looking at her, Cole locked the door behind the bellman, then loosened the knot of his tie and unfastened the top button of his shirt as he started across the room toward the telephone, which rested on an ebony secretaire. "I'm going to order up some coffee. Do you want anything?"

"Yes, I'd like to know what you meant by that remark you made downstairs. Or was that some brotherly gibe?"

"Brotherly?" he stopped, an eyebrow lifting sharply. "I'm not your brother, Remy."

Her mouth gaped open. She couldn't help it. "But . . . at the hospital . . . I thought. . . ." She stopped, trying to remember exactly what had been said—and by whom.

"I am not your brother, Remy," he repeated, his mouth slanting in a hard and cynically amused line.

"Then who are you?"

"Exactly who I claim to be—the president of the Crescent Line, Cole Buchanan."

"Inspector Armand said my brother was coming to take me home," she remembered. "If you aren't my brother, then where is he?"

"Gabe should be arriving at the hotel anytime now—with your passport."

"Then who am I? What's my name? Remy what?" she demanded, confused and angry—and making no attempt to conceal it.

"Remy Jardin."

Remembering how guilty she'd felt over her attraction to him, she walked over to confront him, her temper showing. "You bastard!" She lashed out, striking at his face, but in a lightning-fast move he caught her wrist and stopped it short of its target. When she brought her other hand up, it was caught too, and held in the vice of his fingers. "Why didn't you tell me at the hospital you weren't my brother?" she demanded, straining to pull free of his hold but not deigning to struggle openly against it.

"I never said I was. If you assumed that, that's your problem. Not mine."

"You let me think it," she accused.

"I have no control over what you think or what conclusions you reach. If I did, then—" But he cut off the rest of that sentence. "I had no idea you thought I was your brother, Remy. If I had, I probably wouldn't have told you differently. Do you know why? Because amnesia or not, you have an incredibly strong sense of family. You might not have left the hospital with a stranger."

"The end justifies the means, is that it?"

His head came up sharply at that remark. "Believe what you like, Remy. You always do."

Looking at him, she became conscious of the harsh grip of his hands on her wrists and remembered the pressure of them when he'd pulled her into his arms, the way they had moved over her with accustomed ease, and the natural way he had spoken her name. More than that, she remembered the way she'd reacted to him. "Are we lovers?"

Slow to make her change of mood, he lowered her hands and absently rubbed at the insides of her wrists, where his fingers had dug in. "Yes."

"I should have guessed," she said, then wondered, "Why didn't you tell me?"

"You didn't remember. I thought it might be better that way."

"Why?" she asked, then immediately guessed, "Have we been arguing?"

"You could say that." His reply had the ring of an understatement.

"About what?" Was this the trouble she'd sensed? The reason for that feeling of urgency?

"Does it matter, considering you don't remember?" He let go of her hands and crossed to the window, massaging the back of his neck in a gesture that revealed strain and tension.

"Do I love you, Cole?"

He released a short, explosive sigh. "How the hell am I supposed to answer that, Remy?" She said nothing, letting her silence prod him. "You've told me you do," he said finally.

She walked over to him. "Cole." She waited for him to look at her. "Do you love me?"

His gaze locked with hers for an eternity of seconds. Then his arm hooked itself around her waist and pulled her to him as he lowered his mouth onto hers in a deep and loving kiss that had a hint of roughness to it. She remembered the familiar rightness of being in his arms, but she hadn't guessed at the powerful range of feelings it could evoke.

He dragged his mouth from her lips and rubbed it across her cheek. "You turn me inside out. You have from the first day we met," he murmured against her skin, his hot, moist breath fanning out to offer its own stimulating caress.

"When was that?" She closed her eyes, reveling in the feel of his mouth moving along her temple, into her hair, and behind an ear.

"Roughly a year ago—at a party Frazier gave at Antoine's after I came on board as the company's new CEO."

He still remembered vividly the first time he'd seen her. At that moment she'd been for him the only living thing in the room, her face softly lighted and softly shadowed, her shoulders straight and graceful, her presence creating its beauty and its imperative call. Frazier had introduced them, and he'd taken her hand, the fragrance of her nearness arousing all his male interest in a reaction that was both quick and reluctant. The glimmer of gold in her eyes had seemed to sparkle just for him, but he hadn't been fool enough to believe it . . . then.

"And you fell for me right off, I suppose." She raked her fingers through his hair, flexing them almost like a cat as her parted lips grazed along his jawline.

"Are you kidding? I swore I wouldn't get within ten feet of you." It was a vow that common sense told him he should have kept.

"What happened?"

"About six months ago I got within ten feet of you, and all hell broke loose." He meant that literally. Trouble had erupted almost from the moment they'd gotten together—and grown steadily in the interim. But it was moments like this, when he held her warm and cushioning body close to him and tasted the fiery flavor of her kiss, that he could almost convince himself he didn't give a damn.

"Now *that* is the first thing you've said that I believe," she murmured, seeking and finding his lips.

For her this was like the first time, because she couldn't remember the other. That he had been her lover she did not doubt. Her body knew him, and her heart knew him, even if her mind couldn't recall him. This was the man she loved.

Yet the sensations of being loved by him were all brand-new. She couldn't get enough of the feel of his hands on her back—kneading and caressing in their foray down her spine to her hips—or the taste of his tongue in her mouth, thrusting and mating with her own. His chestnut-dark hair was thick and full beneath her fingers, smooth but a little on the coarse side, slightly rough, like the rest of him.

Wanting more, she strained to get closer to him, her back arching, her hips pressing, her body aching to be absorbed by him. Frustrated, she bit at his lip, inadvertently drawing blood. She heard him stifle a faint sound of pain and rained the spot with light kisses of apology as she brought her hands down, encountering the muscular wall of his chest, rising and falling with the heaviness of his breathing. She tried to run her hands over his chest to the wide points of his shoulders, but his jacket got in the way and his shirt barred contact with the flesh beneath it.

Impatiently she tugged at the loosened knot of his tie. But Cole's hand took her place, yanking it the rest of the way loose and stripping the tie away. When she pushed at his coat, he shrugged out of it. While their lips continued to consume each other with desperate greedy kisses, she set to work on his shirt buttons. But the third one defied her efforts, a thread of the buttonhole catching it and refusing to let it go. Gripping both edges of his shirt front, she pulled them apart, and the rest of the buttons snapped off one after the other. Her hands moved freely onto his bared chest, all hard, bronzed flesh over sinewy muscle, smooth and hot to the touch, like satin over sun-baked steel. But it wasn't enough to feel it; she wanted to taste it, too. She pulled away from his kiss and brought her lips down to the pulsing vein in his neck. She felt the faint tremor that shuddered through him.

"Someday, Remy—" His low voice vibrated against her hair, husky with disturbance, as his fingers curled around the collar of her jacket. "Someday you're going to pay for all the shirts you've ruined."

Openmouthed, she ran the tip of her tongue over the ridge of his shoulder, licking the hot saltiness of his skin, then lifted her head, tilting her face to him. "Make me pay, Cole," she whispered the dare, her eyes gleaming as she gazed into the darkening smoke of his. "Make me pay now."

Accepting her bold challenge, he pulled the front of her jacket apart and dragged it off her shoulders, momentarily forcing her arms to her sides before she could slip free of the sleeves. With the same impatience she had shown toward him, he ripped her blouse open, sending buttons flying into the air. Not content with that, he pushed the blouse off her, dragging the thin straps of her lace teddy with it and exposing the golden cream of her shoulders. Her blouse had barely touched the floor when his fingers took hold of the front of her teddy, indifferent to the expensive lace, and pulled it down, his large hands immediately cupping and covering her small but highly sensitive breasts.

She gasped softly at the sudden swirl of raw pleasure that swept her up, but his mouth came down to smother the sound and steal the rest of her breath. She wrapped her arms tightly around his neck and forced him closer, parting her lips to invite the mating plunge of his tongue. As his hands slipped to the sides of her waist, she arched against him, flattening her breasts against the muscled wall of his chest, needing to feel the heat that came from flesh against flesh.

She wanted him. She wanted all of him, with a fierceness that staggered her completely. What kind of passion was this that erupted so violently? The desire for him had been there all along, thrumming just below the surface. Now it had burst wide open, making her feel incredibly strong and incredibly weak at the same time.

His hands tightened on her waist and effortlessly lifted her, the iron band of his arm circling below her hips to hold her tightly against him, her feet dangling inches from the floor. He carried her that way, with their mouths locked in a kiss, to one of the suite's bedrooms. Remy didn't know which one and didn't care as she kicked her shoes off along the way.

In the room he stopped short of the bed and let her body slide slowly down his chest until her feet touched the floor. Immediately his hands were at the waistband of her slacks, seeking its fastener. Catching his urgency, she hurriedly began to finish undressing him.

Within minutes their clothes were a puddle on the bedroom floor and she lay naked beside his nude male body. At last she had time to explore at her leisure. Levering herself up on one elbow, she rolled her lips off his mouth, briefly grazing them across his square chin, then turned her head to admire that expanse of bare chest and shoulders.

There was a power and a discipline inherent in his muscled form that pulled at her and challenged her to touch him. She pressed her mouth onto the solid curve of his shoulder, then let her lips follow its ridge to the strong column of his neck before wandering down to tactilely explore the hollow at the base of his throat, conscious all the while of the caressing play of his hands over her back and ribs, stroking, teasing, stimulating, and encouraging her. Moving lower, she rubbed her mouth over the square flatness of his breast, then paused to lick at the excitingly small nub of his nipple. She heard the rumble of approval come from deep inside his chest, and she smiled. She slid her hand lower, across the flatness of his stomach, its muscles tensing at her touch, and into the silken curl of hairs at the very bottom of it. When her fingers curved around him, he groaned a muffled curse.

An instant later his fingers tunneled into her hair at the sides and grabbed a handful. She gasped a protest as he hauled her up and twisted her onto her back, letting go of her hair and catching her arms, spreading them above her head and pinning her wrists to the bed, his weight holding her down.

"No," he said against her lips, catching the lower one and lightly nipping at it with his teeth. "I've been away from you too long, Remy. And I'll be damned if this is going to be over before it's begun."

He again caught her bottom lip between his teeth and tightly nipped at it. She groaned at the action that both teased and aroused. Then she felt satisfying pressure of his mouth on hers once more as he kissed her long and deep, drawing from her feelings she hadn't known existed. She was going soft inside and she knew it as he kissed his way over every inch of her face, then paused to sensually chew at an earlobe. When he nibbled his way down her neck, delicious shivers tingled over her.

His arms continued to pin hers to the bed, but she lay there a willing captive, trapped by the urgent need to absorb this myriad of sensations. When his tongue licked at a taut nipple, a curling started deep in the pit of her stomach. She moaned at the ache it produced and finally realized that he was doing to her all the things she had done to him. And it was wonderful. Wonderful.

She arched her back, pushing her breast at him and trying to make him take more of it. When he did, a raw sound of satisfaction came from her throat. Cole stole a glance at her, watching her head roll from side to side, her eyes closed and her lips apart. At last he could stand it no more. He had to touch her. He released one of her wrists and slid his hand down her arm and onto her body.

She was deceptively small and delicate, everything perfectly proportioned, from the narrowness of her rib cage and hips to the petite roundness of her breasts. But he knew the strength and power packaged in her delectable form. Not so much a physical strength as the mental one that came from a strong and indomitable will, a will that gave her boldness and the supreme confidence to be exactly what and who she was. And the power in her—she had the power to make him hunger, to make him ache, to make him vulnerable.

Yet none of that mattered to him as he played with her breasts—with his hands, his mouth, and his tongue. He listened to her sighs, her whimpers, and her moans, expressions of the sexuality that lived within her.

As he ran his hand up her leg to cup the soft swell of her bottom, she shuddered. "How could I have forgotten the way this feels?" she whispered achingly. "How could I, Cole?"

He didn't have an answer for that, but he drew himself up and murmured against a corner of her lips, "Does it matter? Does it matter *now?*"

"No," she groaned, and she turned to his mouth, carelessly commanding, "Love me, Cole."

He kissed her and she was all motion beneath him, her hands, her lips, her body exhorting and demanding satisfaction. He knew she didn't understand the urgency that pushed at both of them. She didn't realize this might be their last time together. But he did.

At this moment and in this place, she belonged to him and he was hers. That was the only certainty. It wasn't enough, but it was all he had, and he seized it.

She sighed his name against his neck, then raked her teeth across his shoulder. "Don't make me wait anymore, Cole. Take me now."

He couldn't resist her—not then and not now. He felt her shudder as he shifted onto her and spread her legs apart. Her breath caught on his name when he entered her. She was hot; she was tight; she was moist. Robbed of all thought by her, he could only feel as she wrapped her legs around him, her hips driving him even as he sought to drive her. The pressure built like the approach of a summer storm, all light, wind, and heat. Then the fury of it was upon them, and release came in a torrent that buffeted both of them and left them wrapped tight in each other's arms.

NESTLED IN THE CROOK of his arm, Remy snuggled closer and rubbed her cheek against his chest. She wondered at this dichotomous reaction of hers that had her feeling both supremely content and oddly energized.

She tilted her head back to look at Cole, then couldn't resist reaching up to trace the sharp outline of his jaw with her fingertips. "Is it always like that with us?"

"Not always." There was a sexy laziness to the smile he gave her. "Sometimes it's even better."

Mockingly skeptical, she retorted, "That is impossible."

He caught her hand and pressed her fingers to his lips, a faintly mischievous glint in his gray eyes. "You're probably right."

His response surprised a laugh from her, the admission so contrary to the typically male boast of sexual prowess that she'd expected to hear. "You amaze me."

His look turned faintly serious. "Try not to forget that." There was a brief silence in which neither of them stirred, and then Cole said, "We'd better get up, Remy."

She made a soft protesting sound. "Not yet. I'm too comfortable."

His arm tightened slightly around her, offering a silent agreement that they would remain as they were awhile longer. She closed her eyes and breathed in the musky scent of their passion, still lingering ever so faintly in the air. She wished she could hold on to this moment, never have to stir, never have to remember. She frowned at the latter thought. Why wouldn't she want to remember?

She tensed, something flashing in her mind. It had to do with Cole. She was sure of it, in that same strange way she had been sure they were lovers without being able to actually remember any part of their affair.

She lay there mentally straining to recall what it was that she should remember about him, trying to make that indistinct impression of trouble become a memory. She couldn't. It had slipped away from her.

Sighing in frustration, she was swept by a surging restlessness, her previous contentment gone. "I think we'd better—" As she started to rise, his hand slid limply off her hip. She turned and discovered he was sound asleep.

Smiling, she laid a hand on his shoulder to awaken him, but the sight of his harshly masculine features composed in the peace and innocence of sleep stopped her. Deciding it couldn't hurt anything to let him sleep a little longer, she withdrew her hand and slipped quietly from the bed.

She crossed silently to the bedroom's private bath and closed the door behind her. She showered quickly, then donned the terry robe the hotel had thoughtfully provided and slicked the wetness of her hair away from her face with her hands. Cautiously she opened the door to the bedroom and peeked around it. Cole was lying in exactly the same place and position.

She walked noiselessly over to the mound of clothes on the floor and began picking them up, remembering the haste with which they'd been stripped away. Separating the garments, she laid them out in neat His and Hers piles, then went into the sitting room to find the rest of them.

When she saw the phone on the secretaire, she hesitated and glanced toward the bedroom. On impulse she picked up the phone and dialed room service, ordering the coffee Cole had wanted when they arrived. She felt pleased with herself, knowing that when he awakened, she'd be able to serve him coffee in bed. She liked the idea of pampering him a little.

In no hurry, she gathered the clothes from the sitting-room floor and carried them into the bedroom. She laid Cole's on his stack, then took her own into the other bedroom, where the bellman had left her luggage. She opened the largest case and began sifting through her clothes, trying to decide what to wear.

The ringing of the bell to the suite's outer door interrupted her. She turned with a faint start, not expecting room service to be so prompt. Running silently on bare feet, she hurried to the door before the waiter could ring the bell again and waken Cole. She unlocked it with one hand and opened it with the other, automatically swinging it wide.

A man in a navy-blue suit stood outside, a stone-gray raincoat draped over one arm and a slim black leather briefcase clutched in the opposite hand. The tense, worried look on his face vanished, and relief sailed through his expression.

"Remy. It *is* you. Thank God." Issuing the fervent declaration, he stepped into the room and hastily set his briefcase on the floor, tossing his coat on top of it and never once taking his eyes off her.

As she stared at him, another image of that same face sprang into her mind —an image frozen in a hearty laugh, his brown eyes crinkling at the corners, a wayward lock of tobacco-brown hair falling onto his forehead.

"Gabe." She recognized her brother, and flashes of childhood memories started coming back to her—memories of Gabe pushing her in an old rope swing, racing his horse against hers along the levee, and teasing her unmercifully about her first date. Gabe, always laughing, always reckless, always carefree. No glint of mischief danced in the brown eyes of the much more mature version of her brother that stood before her now, but the ready grin was there, this time ringed with gladness and relief. When he opened his arms to her, Remy went straight to them, letting him catch her up close and hugging him back.

"I can't believe this," she said, remembering him as he briefly rocked her from side to side, then set her away from him as if needing to look at her again.

"I would have been here sooner, but—Cole had taken the corporate jet to Marseilles, and I had to catch a commercial flight. Then there was a delay for mechanical trouble, and—" He stopped and sighed heavily, happily. "You don't know how good it is to see you, Remy. Don't ever pull a disappearing act like that one again. I thought we were going to have to turn the world upside down to find you."

"It isn't something I want to go through again either."

"When I saw the photo, I knew it had to be you," he said, then chided, "You do realize that had to be the worst picture ever taken of you. I mean, the bandages around your head, the bruises . . . what happened?"

"I don't know—correct that, I don't remember."

"Then this business about the amnesia—it's true?" His expression turned serious, almost grim. Suddenly he wasn't the same—he wasn't the young, smiling Gabe she'd known. "You don't remember anything?"

"No. Just you. As a matter of fact, you're the first thing I have remembered." She paused and took hold of his hands, conscious of the strong bond she felt with him, then lifted her glance to study this new, older face of her brother. "You've changed from the Gabe I remember, though. You're not the teasing, laughing, full-of-the-devil teenage brother anymore. You've grown up and become a responsible adult." Smiling, she reached up and gave the lapel of his navy suit coat a flick. "You've even gone conservative on me."

"But it's what every well-dressed lawyer is wearing these days," he replied with a glimmer of a smile.

"You're a lawyer?"

"It was the next best thing to becoming an actor."

She laughed at that. "You always were a ham," she said, then suddenly remembered, "Your field of practice is maritime law."

"With the family in the shipping business, what else could I choose?" He paused, again sobering slightly. "We've all been so worried about you, Remy, I —Dad had almost convinced himself you'd been kidnapped or murdered or— something equally horrible."

"I wish I could remember him. . . ." She frowned at the absence of any image, any feeling, any impression evoked by the mention of her father. "Maybe when I see him," she said, trying to shrug it off. "Too bad he didn't come with you."

"He wanted to, but he couldn't."

"Why?" Seized again by that feeling of trouble, she became tense. "Has something happened to him? Is he sick?"

"No, it . . . it just wouldn't have been wise right now, that's all. Besides"— he smiled quickly, as if to cover that slight hesitation, and hugged an arm around her shoulders—"you've got your brother the lawyer here, and I'll be much more useful than Dad if we encounter any difficulties with customs or immigration. By the way, where's Cole?"

"Slee—"

"Right here." Cole stood in the doorway to the bedroom, calmly tucking the tails of a crisp new shirt inside the waistband of his mocha trousers. "I see you made it, Gabe."

"Yes, finally." Despite the easy smile her brother gave Cole, she sensed a change in his attitude, a faint, barely perceptible withdrawal. Why? Didn't he like Cole? Or had he merely been surprised to find Cole standing there?

"By the way, thanks for picking up Remy from the hospital," Gabe added.

To Remy it sounded more like an afterthought, one dictated by good manners rather than sincere gratitude. And that impression reinforced her initial feeling that her brother didn't think all that highly of Cole. Yet she couldn't detect any hostility from Gabe, only a wariness.

Cole shot him a look that Remy could only describe as sardonic as he buttoned the cuffs of his shirt. "Thanks aren't necessary, Gabe." Without a break, he said, "If you two will excuse me, I'll get my jacket and see about rounding up our flight crew so we can head back to New Orleans."

The instant Cole left the suite, Remy turned curiously to Gabe. "You don't like him, do you?"

He had difficulty meeting her gaze, and briefly raised his hands in an uncertain gesture. "You can't possibly know how damned awkward your amnesia makes things." He stopped, meeting her glance. "You haven't said how much you remember about Cole—if anything. But you two were—pretty thick for a while."

"I know that much." She smiled, mostly at the memory of the extremely satisfying moments she'd just had with Cole.

"You don't know how relieved I was when you finally broke up with him."

"We broke up?" Somehow she hadn't gotten that impression from Cole.

"He didn't tell you that, did he?" he guessed, his very tone making it an accusation.

"I knew we'd been arguing," she replied carefully.

Gabe shook his head in disgust, a grimness about his mouth. "I always knew that man had no scruples, so why am I surprised that he'd take advantage of your amnesia?"

When he looked at her, Remy glanced away, resisting—resenting—the implication of his words. Not twenty minutes ago she'd believed herself in love with Cole. The feelings, the emotions had been real; she didn't question that. But could it be that they were wrongly placed, as Gabe was suggesting? Had Cole deliberately lied to her? Or, at the very least, told only a half truth? But why?

"Why did we break up?"

"You never gave a reason—not to me, anyway. And I never asked. I felt you'd tell me if you wanted to. But I do know that as far as you were concerned it was final. You were through with him."

"Did Cole accept that?"

"No."

Gabe's answer confirmed what she'd already guessed—Cole wanted her back. That was why he'd been so quick to make love to her when she'd shown she was willing—eager. Had he hoped it would be the start of reconciliation between them? Did she want that? How could she know, when she couldn't even remember why she'd broken off their affair? Obviously she hadn't stopped loving him, which meant he must have said or done something that she'd found impossible to forgive. But what? And was it connected to this feeling she had that it was urgent—critical—for her to return to New Orleans?

"To tell you the truth, Remy," Gabe said, "I never approved of your becoming involved with him. Call it the protective instincts of a brother who wants only the best for his sister—and who knows that Cole Buchanan isn't the man for you. I always thought you'd end up regretting it. And believe me, there's no satisfaction in knowing I was right about him all along."

"What do you mean? How were you right about him?"

He turned away, plainly uncomfortable with her questions, and walked to a window, unbuttoning his suit jacket and pushing it open to rest his hands on his hips. "I wish you could remember for yourself. I don't like being the one to say these things, but—I guess someone has to tell you." He stared out the window. "The man simply doesn't have the same values, the same principles as you. He comes from a totally different background, a different environment. True, he was born and raised in New Orleans, the same as we were, but on the other side of the river, in Algiers. You can't get much further removed from the Garden district than that."

Remy nodded absently, remembering the desperately poor and crime-ridden area of Algiers, located directly across the Mississippi River from the French Quarter. The contrast between Algiers, with its dilapidated shotgun houses and scrubby yards, and the Garden district, with its colonnaded antebellum mansions, its lush, green gardens, and its tree-lined streets, was unarguably a stark one.

"And you can't grow up in an area like Algiers," Gabe continued, "without coming away with some of its hardness, its ruthlessness."

Frowning, she recalled her own impression that Cole possessed both traits to some degree, but she didn't consider either one to be something that should be held against him, as Gabe was implying. And this talk about different values and principles held criticism as well.

"You don't trust him, do you?"

He hesitated, then angled his shoulders toward her, briefly meeting her eyes. "No, I don't."

"But he's the president of the company. If that's your opinion of him, then why—"

"Look." Gabe turned from the window and raised his hand in a silencing gesture. "At the time, we thought he was the best man for the job. He had the experience, the qualifications—and a helluva reputation for turning troubled shipping lines around. As far as all the talk we heard that his methods were sometimes less than orthodox—nothing illegal, at least nothing that was ever proved—we chalked it up to disgruntled competitors. After all, every head-hunter we talked to mentioned Cole Buchanan as a solid candidate for the position. A man's name comes up that often, you hire him."

"And now you suspect him of doing something wrong."

He seemed startled by her comment, which was half guess and half supposition—startled and a little worried, as if he'd said more than he'd intended. "We're getting off the track here. We were talking about you, and why I didn't like the idea of your getting mixed up with a man whose name has been linked with some sharp—maybe even shady—dealings. As for the company, maybe it's the lawyer in me, but I don't like the employment contract he got. It ties the board's hands and puts too much power in his. In my opinion Buchanan's grabbing for power, and you were part of the grab."

Had that been it? Logically she could see that it was more than possible. A man who had been raised in the squalor and poverty that marked so much of the violence-ridden Algiers section, and then risen from it to preside over a major shipping line, obviously had to be aggressive and ambitious. After sampling the heady taste of power, he could have decided he wanted more.

"How could I represent power to him?" She lifted her curious, troubled glance to Gabe.

"You own a substantial share in the company, and you sit on the board," he replied, studying her with affectionate patience. "And the family is not without some influence."

Remy suspected that the latter was a gross understatement, but she didn't dwell on it, her thoughts turning instead to the other things Gabe had said. With no memory of her own, she found herself seizing on every scrap of information and trying to make it mean something—specifically, something that would explain this feeling of trouble she had.

"You mentioned that Cole had a reputation for turning companies around. Does that mean the Crescent Line is in trouble financially?"

He gave a light shrug. "The company has lost money the last couple of years—nothing dramatic, certainly nothing to be overly alarmed about. All businesses experience a slump now and then."

"Then that wasn't the reason you hired him." Absently she ran a hand through her hair, which by now was nearly dry, trying to piece things together.

"No. Dad wanted to retire. He'd already put thirty years into the company, and Marc had never been involved in the operations side of the business."

"Marc—who's he?"

"Dad's brother—our uncle." He frowned at her for an instant, then his forehead cleared. "I forgot. You probably can't remember him either."

"No, I can't."

"Marc's a couple of years younger than Dad—brown eyes, dark, curly hair with just a touch of gray sprinkled through it." Gabe paused, as if trying to think how else to tell her about him. "After Grand-père died, he and Dad took over running the company. It's almost too limiting to say that Marc handles the public-relations side. He's the spokesman for the Crescent Line—the labor-relations man, the representative, the company's goodwill ambassador. The man's phenomenal, Remy. He knows even the newest employee by name. He can go down on the docks, take off his jacket and tie, and swap stories with the longshoremen over a beer like he was one of them. That same night he can put on a white tie and tails, mingle with a bunch of visiting dignitaries, and exchange views on global politics with all the ease of a diplomat. Everyone likes him. He's so charming and warm it's impossible not to."

But the only image she had of her uncle was the one Gabe had just drawn for her. She had none of her own. "Sorry." She shook her head in regret. "I still can't remember him."

"What about his son, Lance? He's the same age as me—our birthdays are just a couple months apart. He works for the company too, in the accounting end of it." He watched for some indication that his words were striking a familiar chord—and found none. "Maybe it would help if I told you that you don't like Lance."

"Why?" she asked, surprised by his assertion.

"You seem to think he's too full of himself, a little too contemptuous of women."

"Is he?"

"Probably," he conceded. "But the way they practically fall on their backs if he so much as looks at them, it's not really surprising that he doesn't have much respect for them. I used to be envious of him when we were in high school together. It was the closest I ever came to hating him. If he was around, not a single girl would look my way."

"By that I assume you mean he's handsome."

He laughed softly at that. "Actually the phrase 'handsome as the devil' could have been invented to describe Lance—dark hair, dark eyes, and a sexy, brooding look. He's the bad kind that mothers warn their daughters about and daddies meet at the door with a shotgun—and girls go crazy over."

"He sounds like a bachelor playboy." She was conscious of her teeth coming together in an almost instinctive reaction of disgust and dislike. But was she reacting or remembering? She couldn't tell.

"A bachelor? No. He's been married for three years and has a two-year-old son and another baby on the way. A playboy?" Gabe tipped his hand from side to side in a gesture that indicated that the decision could go either way.

"In other words, he's a married playboy," Remy concluded, a little acidly.

"Let's be realistic," Gabe protested, obviously coming to his cousin's defense. "If you're at a party and you keep being served up a tray of sweet, delectable morsels, are you going to have the willpower to say no every time it's offered? No man is that strong, Remy."

"And Lance is a little weaker than most, isn't he?" she guessed—or was she guessing? She wished she knew, then shook off the question as unanswerable, just as so many others were. "You said he works in the company's accounting department?"

"Yes. So you see, neither Lance nor I was interested or qualified to take over as president. Which meant we had to look outside for someone to replace Dad."

The ringing of the suite's front bell was quickly followed by a heavily accented voice announcing, "Room service."

"That must be the coffee I ordered earlier," Remy said, and automatically went to the door.

The waiter swept into the sitting room with an elaborate tray balanced on his upraised palm. He made a production out of setting the tray down, arranging the china cups and saucers, setting out the cream and sugar, and adjusting the placement of a flower vase, totally indifferent to the heavy silence stretching over the room.

He picked up the stainless coffee server. "Shall I pour, madam?"

"No thank you."

"Very well, madam." But he practically sniffed his disapproval as he presented the bill to her with a slight flourish.

Remy hastily scratched her name across it and passed it back to him. When the waiter left, she locked the door behind him, then turned back to the room.

"Would you like a cup of coffee?" She walked over to the tray and picked up the coffee server.

"Please."

Remy filled both cups with steaming coffee, then reached for the creamer. "Heavy on the cream and light on the sugar, right?"

"Right," he said. "You're starting to remember things."

"I hope so," she said, feigning a nonchalance she didn't feel.

"What happened, Remy? What caused this amnesia? I never really got the story straight. Was there an accident, or what?"

"According to the police inspector, I was seen arguing or . . . struggling with a man." She sipped at her coffee, remembering the bruised and swollen soreness of her lips. "He struck me and I fell backward, hitting my head against a tree trunk. It knocked me out. When I regained consciousness in the hospital, I had a dozen stitches in my scalp, a concussion, and—amnesia. I had no idea who I was, where I lived, or what I did, and I didn't have any identification on me."

"This man who hit you—did they catch him?"

"No. He ran off and disappeared into the crowd. The police couldn't get much of a description of him, and of course I wasn't able to remember any of it. I still don't know if he was somebody I knew, somebody I recently met, or a total stranger." She stopped. "Do you know anything about that night, Gabe? Why was I at the Espace Masséna? What was I doing? Where was I going?"

"We were all at a party that night . . . at a hotel not far from the square," he replied hesitantly, as if uncertain how to answer her questions. "You, me,

Marc and Aunt Christina, Lance and his wife, Julie, Diana and Kathy and their husbands—" He caught her blank look at the last two names and paused to explain, "Diana and Kathy are Marc's daughters, both younger than Lance." A rueful smile tugged at his mouth. "They're our cousins, but—to be truthful— they're both kind of shallow and vain, more concerned with being seen with the 'right' people, wearing clothes by the currently 'in' designers, and sending their children to the 'right' schools than they are with anything else. . . . Anyway, they were there that night too. But the last time I remember seeing you, we were all at the party. Then you were gone. I assumed you'd gone back to the yacht. I wasn't surprised. After all, one Carnival party is pretty much the same as another. And when you weren't on board the next morning, no one thought anything of it. You had planned to leave that day, and we thought you had. I never guessed—none of us did—that something had happened to you. We wouldn't have left if we had."

"I know."

She heard the key turn in the lock and turned with a slightly guilty start as Cole walked in. He stopped, his gray eyes locking on her, but she had difficulty meeting them, no longer certain she could trust him, yet bothered by the feeling that her doubt was somehow a betrayal.

"Were you able to round up the crew?" Gabe asked.

"They're on their way to the airport now to file a flight plan and obtain all the necessary clearances. We should be able to take off as soon as we get there."

"Give me twenty minutes," she said, and she walked quickly from the room.

FROM THE PORTHOLE window of the corporate jet, Remy watched the golden light of a slowly setting sun spread its color over the beaches and buildings of Nice. As the jet climbed over the tinted waters of the bay, the grand hotels along the Promenade des Anglais—those towers of luxurious elegance—diminished in size, the famed Castle Hill landmark, with its sparkling waterfall, visible from almost anywhere in the old section, was reduced to a vague knoll of ground, and the backcloth of verdant hills and distant mountains that ringed the city rose to dominance. Then the plane made its banking turn on its prescribed departure pattern, and Remy leaned back in her seat and tipped her head against the headrest.

They were going home. She was going home—home to New Orleans, to Louisiana. Yet she felt no sense of anticipation, only a kind of vague dread.

"Tired?" Gabe asked from his seat across the narrow aisle, mistaking the barely audible breath she'd released for a weary sigh.

"Not really." Though she wished she was.

The seat-belt light flicked off. Giving in to a surge of restless energy, Remy picked up her purse and got out of her seat. As she turned to walk down the narrow aisle to the lavatory, her glance encountered Cole's. He was in the cushioned chair directly behind hers, the point of his elbow on the armrest and a forefinger curved across his mouth in a thoughtful gesture.

What was in that steel-gray look of his? Remy found it impossible to tell. He had a face that revealed his inner feelings only when he chose. She hesitated an instant longer, then walked back to the lavatory and studied her own reflection in the mirror, wondering if she was that good at concealing her feelings. She doubted it. On the contrary, she suspected that she'd never bothered to learn to control her feelings or her opinions. From reviewing her own recent actions, she recognized that she was invariably blunt, even with those she liked or loved.

She freshened her makeup, touching the wand of brown mascara to the tips of her lashes, adding a few strokes of blush to the high contours of her cheekbones, and applying a fresh coat of peach lipstick to her lips. When she was finished, she ran cold water over her wrists, trying in vain to cool the agitation that pulsed through her. Giving up, she dried her hands on a towel monogrammed with the company's initials, then retrieved her purse from the sink counter.

When she stepped out of the lavatory, Remy immediately noticed Cole standing in the plane's small galley, his tall frame slightly stooped to avoid bumping his head on the curved ceiling. He had a coffeepot in one hand and a cup in the other. At the latching click of the lavatory door, he angled his upper body toward the sound, his gaze centering on her, as impassive as his expression.

"Coffee?" He lifted the pot in an offering gesture. Remy started to accept, then recalled that caffeine frequently contributed to the effects of jet lag. As if reading her mind, Cole said, "It's decaffeinated."

"Then I'll take a cup." She moved into the galley opening and watched his hand tip the pot to pour coffee into a cup. When he passed the filled cup to her, their fingers inadvertently brushed. Her glance locked with his a second time, the memory of the way she'd felt when his hands had loved her suddenly vivid. She remembered clearly the violent harmony of their lovemaking, and the deep emotions she'd felt for him—emotions that she now hesitated to call love.

Something hard flickered over his lean features, thinning the line of his mouth before he abruptly turned away and reached into a cabinet for another cup. Had she revealed her doubt? Remy wondered. Probably. Because she did doubt—both her feelings and him.

"Why didn't you tell me we'd broken up instead of letting me think we'd only been arguing?" She wrapped both hands around the sides of the cup, as if needing the warmth from the hot coffee.

He looked at her, the line of his mouth finishing its cold-smiling curve. "I was sure Gabe wouldn't waste any time telling you that."

"Why didn't you tell me?" she challenged. "Don't you think it was slightly deceitful not to?"

"I suppose now you're regretting what happened." He raised the coffee cup to his mouth.

"Yes, I am." She watched him take a slow sip of the coffee. Instantly she recognized her mistake and lifted her glance from his mouth to his eyes, willing the uneven beat of her pulse to stop. Doubts or not, the attraction was there, strong and swift. "I wish I'd waited until I could remember our love relationship before I resumed a sexual one with you." Remy looked down at the cup and her hands, so tightly wrapped around it. "I wish—" She broke off, stopped by the futility of the phrase.

"Don't we all," Cole murmured dryly.

She looked up, suddenly and intently curious. "What do you wish?"

His gaze made a slow search of her face, a glimmer of longing in his eyes and a trace of anger in his expression that the longing was there. "I wish I'd told Mrs. Franks I was too busy to see you and never allowed you to walk through that door."

It took a second for Remy to realize what he meant by that. "That's when you got within ten feet of me six months ago, isn't it?"

"Yes."

"Will you tell me about it?" She was curious—more than curious—to learn the circumstances that had brought them together. "I need to remember. Who's Mrs. Franks?"

"My secretary." He looked at her, hearing the sharp buzz of the intercom that day and remembering his absently curt response. . . .

"Yes, what is it?" he demanded, without looking up from the operations cost report for the month of July.

"Miss Jardin is here to see you," came the reply over the speaker.

"Who?" He frowned at the intercom, which now had his undivided attention.

A short silence followed, then his secretary's voice spoke again, faintly prompting, faintly embarrassed. "Remy Jardin."

"Frazier's daughter." His frown deepened. "What—never mind." Cole flipped the report shut and leaned back in his chair, his curiosity aroused in spite of his better judgment. "Send her in."

Almost immediately the doorknob turned. Cole automatically stood up when she entered his office, the manners insisted upon by his mother too deeply ingrained to be ignored. As impossible as it seemed, Remy Jardin looked more attractive than he remembered from their one brief meeting several months before. Her hair was a fresh tawny gold in the room's artificial light, its rich color deepening the pale tan of her skin. Good breeding defined all the regular features of her face, a face made graphic by some warm, frank curiosity lying within.

As she crossed the room, the whisper of coral silk shantung drew his eye to the soft summer dress she wore, the cut of the diaphanously thin material designed to flow over her natural curves in a deliberate but subtly body-conscious style. He saw her glance make an inspection of the corner office—the standard old-world executive kind that had required the sacrifice of a small mahogany forest to panel the walls. A smile touched her lips when she noticed her grandfather's portrait hanging in its customary place, and it lingered as she stopped in front of the massive desk, the gold flecks in her hazel eyes glinting with a warmth and a touch of amusement that was oddly appealing.

Wise to the ways of her kind, he waited for the dip of her chin and the provocative glance issued through the sweep of long lashes. It didn't come. Instead she faced him with a somewhat surprising directness.

"I thought you would have had this office redecorated by now," she said. "Everything's exactly the same as when my father sat behind that desk."

"Considering the company's financial situation, I thought the money would be better spent elsewhere," he replied easily, aware that the width of the desk precluded the need for a handshake. "Please have a seat, Miss Jardin." He motioned to the two captain-style chairs with leather seats in front of his desk.

"Thank you."

He waited until she was seated, then sat down in his own chair. "I'm sure you'll understand when I say that this visit of yours, Miss Jardin, is more than a little unexpected. Just what is it you wanted to see me about?"

"I came to take you to lunch, Mr. Buchanan," she announced with all the smoothness and self-assurance of a wealthy young woman too accustomed to having her own way.

He reacted swiftly, instinctively, disguising it all behind a polite smile. "Sorry, I—"

"I've already checked your schedule, Mr. Buchanan," she interrupted. "You don't have any appointments until three o'clock. And this is business."

"What kind of business?" He breathed in the scent of her perfume, a blend of sweet gardenia and sandalwood, as bold and feminine as the rest of her.

"Company business."

"Really? You'll forgive me if I seem surprised, but I understood you took no interest in the business—except to attend board of directors' meetings when they're called and to collect compensation of your attendance at those meetings."

She didn't bat an eye at his implied criticism, but her tone was a degree or two cooler. "You're quite right, Mr. Buchanan. I've never been involved in the actual operations of the company, but I do take an interest in who's running it. Now that you're in charge, I think it's time I found out more about you."

"Wouldn't it have been wiser to do that *before* I came on board, Miss Jardin?"

She smiled, not in the least nonplussed by his question, and he couldn't help noticing the attractive dimples that appeared in her cheeks. "You know the old saying, Mr. Buchanan—'better late than never.' Besides, you piqued my curiosity when you informed my father last week that you weren't interested in being nominated for membership in his krewe. I believe your exact words were 'I don't give a damn if the club is one of the most elite and politically powerful Carnival organizations in the state.'" Her smile widened. "Poor Daddy is still suffering from the aftershock of your refusal." She paused, considering him with undisguised interest. "According to your résumé, you grew up in New Orleans, so you must know there are people who would pay anything merely for the chance to have their names mentioned in the same breath with a nomination."

"I'm not Uptown, Miss Jardin, and I have no desire to mingle with your Uptown crowd." When he said "Uptown," Cole was referring not so much to a place as to an attitude.

"You could make some very important contacts."

"Perhaps. But these 'important contacts' didn't do your father much good, did they? They certainly haven't kept the Crescent Line out of the financial trouble it's in. That's why you brought me on board."

"So it is." She started to say something else, but the strident buzz of the intercom interrupted her.

"Yes?" He heard the tension in his voice. Dammit, why was he letting her get to him?

"I'm sorry to bother you, Mr. Buchanan," his secretary replied, a faintly worried edge to her voice. "There's a delivery man here with a package for you. He said he had instructions to bring it here—"

"Yes, I've been expecting it. Go ahead and accept delivery on it."

"But one side of it has been . . . crushed in a little. Before I accept it, maybe you should open it and see if there's been any damage—"

Cole didn't wait for her to finish as he moved out from behind the desk and started for the door, murmuring a slightly distracted "You'll have to excuse me" to Remy. As he walked into the outer office, his glance skipped over the pencil-thin Mrs. Franks and the brown-uniformed delivery man standing in front of her desk, then zeroed in on the rectangular package propped against the side of the desk. With clenched jaw, Cole surveyed the caved-in front of the cardboard container, then walked over to it and removed his pocket knife from the pocket of his trousers.

He took his time opening the package. If there was any damage, he didn't want to make it worse through careless haste. When he finally lifted the ornate, gilded frame out of the wood-reinforced box, he drew his first easy breath at the sight of the seemingly unscarred print, matted in pale blue.

"Has it been damaged?" Mrs. Franks asked anxiously.

"Except for a couple of nicks in the frame, it doesn't appear to be." But he carried it over to the couch and set it on the seat cushions, crouching down to examine it more closely. He ran his hand lightly over the surface, tactilely searching for any break in the smoothness of it and finding none. Satisfied at last, he withdrew his hand and allowed himself to gaze at the old print for the pure pleasure it gave him.

At almost the same instant he became aware of a stir of movement beside him, the soft rustle of silk whispering against silk as Remy Jardin sank down beside him. She reached out and traced her hand over the picture.

"This is an old sporting print. They were very popular between the mid-eighteenth and nineteenth centuries, before photography became widespread." She threw him a slightly surprised look. "Prints like this—especially in such excellent condition—are fairly uncommon."

"I know." His glance skimmed her blond hair, the color of dark honey, its loose windblown style the kind that invited a man to run his fingers through it.

She turned back to the picture, admiring it with keen, appreciative eyes. "It's a marvelous work—so much detail, so much genteel refinement . . . surrounding two boxers."

"Pugilists," Cole corrected. "The English regarded boxing as a noble art and a gentleman's pursuit, while Americans have tended to think of it as the sport of underclass ruffians. This particular print depicts the international match between the American John C. Heenan and the English champion Tom Sayers. The portraits of the important personages at ringside include, among two hundred others, Prince Albert, Thackeray, and the cartoonist Thomas Nast."

He straightened from his crouched position, catching her elbow and drawing her up with him, ignoring the speculating light in her eyes. But he found it impossible to ignore her. She was attractive, too damned attractive, and his reaction to her was that of any normal, healthy male. Unfortunately he'd thought he'd acquired an immunity against her type.

"Do you want me to put in a claim for damages to the frame, Mr. Buchanan?" his secretary asked.

"No, it's not worth the paperwork. Just sign for the delivery." He picked up the framed print and carried it into his office, aware that Remy Jardin was following him. He leaned the painting against the walnut credenza behind his desk, then turned to glance at her. "Was there something else you wanted, Miss Jardin?"

She smiled faintly. "I invited you to lunch, remember?"

"I remember." But he'd hoped she'd forgotten—or changed her mind.

"Surely you aren't going to refuse to have lunch with one of the directors of the Crescent Line, are you?"

He wanted to. Every instinct warned him to steer well clear of Remy Jardin. He reminded himself that he wasn't twenty years old anymore. He knew who she was and what she was—and her subtle look of class and breeding didn't impress him. He wasn't about to be taken in by her kind again.

"Where are we having this lunch?" he asked, deciding to get it over with and be rid of her.

"Galatoire's." Her smile became more pronounced. "But don't worry, Mr. Buchanan. Directors don't have expense accounts, so you don't have to be concerned about the company ultimately paying for it."

But he had a strange feeling that *he* would pay for it, somehow.

They walked to the restaurant in the French Quarter—although *walked* wasn't really an appropriate word for it. Nobody ever *walked* in New Orleans in the summer. The heat, the humidity, the languor in the air always reduced the pace to a leisurely stroll, a pace that let the sights, the sounds, the atmosphere of the city known as the Big Easy seep in.

When they crossed Canal Street, the dividing line that separated the Central Business District from the narrow streets and tightly packed houses of the Vieux Carré, Cole felt it sweep over him—the iron grillwork on the balconies, the doors leading to hidden courtyards, the clip-clop of a carriage horse, the muffled notes of a trumpet wailing to a Dixieland beat, and the heaviness in the air. He tried not to listen to the low, smoky pitch of her voice and to concentrate instead on her words. He tried, but he couldn't.

In the years when he was away from New Orleans, he'd forgotten the sexual energy that sizzled beneath the city's surface—a sexual energy that was erotic, not the sleazy packaged kind that could be found all up and down Bourbon Street, but rather the subtle, sultry kind found in the diaphanous dress she wore and in the steamy air, thick with the scent of magnolias. Why hadn't he remembered it during the six months he'd been back? Why now—with her? Had he avoided the memory deliberately, or had he really been that busy? He wanted to believe the latter.

By the time they reached Galatoire's, the long line of people that typically stretched out the door and down the block at lunchtime had dwindled to a mere handful. A word to the maître d' and they were immediately ushered to a table in the large, brightly lit room, mirrored on all sides. The restaurant hummed with gossip, the rise and fall of it untouched by the lazy rotation of the ceiling fans overhead.

Addressing the waiter by name, Remy Jardin questioned him on which of the seafood items were truly fresh that day, treating him with an easy familiarity that spoke of a long-standing acquaintance. Cole listened somewhat cynically, aware that in her rarefied circle such relationships were frequently cultivated as a means to avoid ridiculously long waits at such places as Antoine's, where a waiter's name became a secret and very necessary password.

At the conclusion of her consultation with the plump-cheeked Joseph, she chose the oyster en brochette for an appetizer and the lamb chops with béarnaise as her main course. Cole ordered the shrimp rémoulade and the pompano à la meunière.

When the waiter had retreated out of earshot, Remy Jardin murmured, "A word of warning. If there's something you don't want the whole city to know, never talk about it in front of Joseph. As Nattie would say, he has a mouth bigger than the Mississippi."

"Who's Nattie?"

"Our cook—although she's been with us so long, she's practically a member of the family."

"I see." He had an instant image of a stout black woman—the plump-cheeked Jemima type—and withheld comment, realizing that he should have known. Her kind always had some relationship like that that they could point to to show their liberalism.

After a moment's pause, with that direct gaze of hers quietly studying him, she said, "I admit the pompano sounded good. I was tempted to order it myself. Are you a seafood lover?"

"Truthfully, my favorite dish is red beans and rice." If he'd expected to shock her with his less than sophisticated tastes, he was wrong.

She laughed, an audacious gleam lighting her eyes. "Don't tell Joseph, but it's my favorite too." She reached for the glass of crisp, dry rosé wine the waiter had brought her earlier along with Cole's bourbon and branch. "Nattie makes the best red beans I've ever tasted—hearty and creamy, seasoned just spicy enough—and serves it over the fluffiest bed of rice. And the sausage is homemade, stuffed by Nattie herself. You'll have to come to the house for dinner sometime."

"I'm afraid I'm too busy for socializing, Miss Jardin."

"So I've heard. In fact, my brother's convinced that you're a workaholic."

"Perhaps if your father and uncle had paid more attention to business and less to socializing, I wouldn't have to put in the long hours that I do now."

"I asked for that one, didn't I?" She tipped her glass to him in a mock salute, then took a small sip of wine and lowered the glass. "I don't recall seeing anything in your résumé about a family. I assume you have one."

"I do," he replied, deliberately uncommunicative.

"Any brothers or sisters?"

"None."

"What about your parents? Where are they?"

"My father died when I was eight. My mother lives here in New Orleans."

"She does? Do you see her very often, or—are you too busy?" she taunted lightly, a small smile taking much of the sting out of her words.

Maybe that was why he answered her instead of telling her it was none of her business. He wasn't sure. "I usually call or stop by her shop once a week or so—and occasionally I go over to her place for dinner in the evening."

"What kind of shop does she have?"

"A small antique store."

"Really? On Royal?"

He smiled wryly, faintly, at that. "No, on Magazine. Her shop draws the blue-jean-and-sneakers trade, not the hat-and-white-gloves one."

The waiter Joseph returned to the table with their appetizers. When he retreated, Remy speared a bite of oyster with her fork. "What types of antiques does your mother sell?"

"They're not antiques as much as they are collectibles—period toys, lace curtains, bric-a-brac, wicker pieces, things like that."

"What's the name of her shop?"

"The Lemon Tree. Why?"

"Just curious," she said with a graceful lift of her shoulders, an action that briefly drew the thin material of her dress more tightly over her breasts, momentarily delineating their roundness—something he didn't want to notice. Yet as much as he wanted to deny it, a sexual awareness of her existed in him. It had ever since their slow stroll to the restaurant, ever since she'd walked into his office—ever since he'd met her that first time, six months before.

He stabbed a piece of shrimp with the tines of his seafood fork and tried to ignore the thought. "I thought this lunch was to talk about business."

"I never said that," she replied, quickly and smoothly. "I said I wanted to get to know you better." She paused in the act of forking another bite of oyster to her mouth. "By the way, where did you manage to find that print?"

Cole hesitated an instant, then said, "When I was in London last month I had some time between appointments, so I stopped in at Christie's, and there it was."

"Christie's—really? That's where I took my training in eighteenth-century French porcelain." She smiled absently, as if some thought had just occurred to her. "I wonder if Jacques the jackal is still there."

"Who?" Cole frowned.

"This absolutely insufferable man—French, of course—who was an authority on *everything*. Nobody could stand him. But he had this laugh that sounded like a hyena." She paused and arched an eyebrow in his direction, her eyes glinting with amusement. "You wouldn't believe the lengths we used to go to to get him to laugh—especially if there was an important client around."

"I think I can." He nodded, imagining the conspiracies among the trainees to make the man break up with laughter.

"I thought you'd be able to." She showed him an unsettling smile of shared humor, then turned her attention back to her appetizer. "Are you a collector of sporting prints?"

Cole remembered the quiet appreciation in her expression when she'd seen the print. It would have been easy for him to talk to her about his interest—which was precisely why he didn't.

"I doubt that five—six"—he corrected himself —"prints would be considered a collection by your standards."

"Really? And what *are* my standards?" She sounded amused.

"I'm sure you and your friends generally collect original art, not prints. But that's all I can afford."

She picked up her wineglass and raised it to her lips, holding his gaze and murmuring over the rim, "You don't have a very high opinion of me, my family, or my friends, do you?"

He hesitated, then chose to be blunt. "Frankly, no."

"Why?" She studied him thoughtfully, curiously.

Finished with his shrimp rémoulade, he laid his fork aside and coolly met the silent challenge of her gaze. "Look at the pathetic shape the Crescent Line's in now, and you'll find the answer to that. You and your family bled the life out of it, paying stock dividends to yourselves when the company couldn't afford it, when that money needed to be reinvested. You were solely concerned with yourselves and maintaining your style of living. You didn't give a damn about what might be best for the company—until it appeared that the company might go broke."

"Guilty as charged, I'm afraid," she confessed. "Although in our defense I would have to say that initially none of us realized the situation was quite so serious."

"It was—and is. Perhaps if you had studied the balance sheets and asked some questions at the directors' meetings instead of rubber-stamping whatever your father or uncle put in front of you, you would have found out."

"You're right, of course," she admitted again, untroubled by his criticism of her. "Although I felt that since I knew nothing about the business, they were better qualified than I to make decisions."

"As one of the owners, Miss Jardin, you should have made it your business to know instead of donating all your time to the museum, playing at being a docent and dabbling in acquisitions."

The dimples appeared in her cheeks again. "That sounds remarkably like a suggestion that I should be working in and for the company. Obviously you didn't intend for me to take you literally, since I can't imagine you being an advocate of nepotism."

The waiter came back to the table to remove the dishes with the remains of their appetizers and serve them their main course, his presence eliminating the need for Cole to respond to her remark and creating a lull in the conversation.

"I am curious about something else," she said when Joseph left. "Considering the company's financial problems and your opinion of us, why did you take the job?"

"Simple. You—the company—met my terms."

"Yes." She paused reflectively. "And your terms were: full and complete authority over all facets of the company; any decision you made was final; no approval required from the board of directors. If you succeed financially in turning the company around within three years, you are to receive ten-percent ownership in the company, plus some very favorable stock options."

"Then you did read my contract."

"Honestly? I read it for the first time the other day after Father told me what you said he could do with the nomination to his krewe."

"You admit that?" He was surprised by her candor.

"The truth hurts, but—yes, I do. Of course, I console myself with the knowledge that despite past mistakes, we at least had the good sense to bring you on board."

"First interest, now flattery, Miss Jardin?" he mocked.

"I don't suppose I could persuade you to call me Remy."

"What would be the point?"

"Why not say . . . in the interest of establishing friendlier relations between owners and management."

"I repeat, what would be the point?"

She laid her knife and fork down and rested her elbows on the table, folding her hands together and thoughtfully propping up the point of her chin on top of them. "You resent who I am, my background, don't you? You do realize there's nothing I can do about it. And I'm certainly not going to apologize or feel guilty because I happened to be born into the Jardin family. I had no control over it. Or—is that my problem?" She raised her chin long enough to flick a finger in the direction of his hand.

"Is what your problem?" Cole frowned.

"You prefer brunettes with short hair." She reached over, plucked a dark hair from the sleeve of his suit jacket, and held it up as evidence.

"Sherlock Holmes you're not, Miss Jardin." He took it from her and let it drop to the floor. "That happens to be cat hair."

"You own a cat?" She picked up her knife and fork and cut another bite of lamb chop.

"You've obviously had little experience with cats or you'd know that nobody ever *owns* one. You may occasionally share the same living quarters, but that's about all."

"And this cat you *occasionally* share your quarters with, what kind is it?"

"The alley variety. Its pedigree is the street."

"Does your cat have a name?"

He hesitated. "Tom."

"You're kidding." She stared at him incredulously, then burst into a laugh.

In spite of himself, he laughed with her. "Not very original, I admit, but the name suits him."

"I wouldn't do that very often if I were you."

"What?" Suddenly he found himself captivated by her gaze, unsettled and disturbed by the warmly interested glow in her eyes.

"Laugh," she said simply. "It makes you seem human."

He caught himself wanting to respond to her as a man, and immediately steeled himself against that impulse. "I'll remember that," he said, wiping the smile from his face.

"Other than occasionally sharing your digs with Tom, collecting sporting prints, and dining with your mother now and then, what else do you do? Are you interested in sports? Football? Soccer? Tennis?"

"I don't have time."

"You must do something to stay in such great shape," she said, running her gaze over the width of his shoulders and chest. "And somehow I can't imagine you working out in a gym with weights."

"Actually I do try to make it to the gym a couple-three times a week to spar a few rounds."

"You mean—you box?" She seemed uncertain that she had understood him correctly.

"Yes." Dammit, why was he telling her this? Had it been deliberate, to remind him how he'd met . . . ? But Remy Jardin's reaction was different. There was no look of fascination for what many regarded as a violent sport, nothing that even remotely resembled an attraction to blood and gore.

"An art collector who boxes. What perfect therapy it must be," she marveled. "Personally, I can't think of a better way to get rid of frustration and repressed anger than to unleash it on a punching bag. How long have you been doing it?"

"I started boxing when I was a kid. My mother figured I'd be getting into fights anyway, so she decided it would be better if I did it in a ring under supervision, instead of with a gang in the streets."

"Obviously it worked."

"For the most part."

"I'm almost afraid to ask what kind of music you like?"

"A little jazz, a lot of blues." Too late, he caught himself and wondered why in hell he was answering these questions of hers. He knew better. She wasn't his kind. Nothing would come of it.

"Then you must like Lou Rawls. Have you seen his show at the Blue Room? From what I've heard it's drawing rave reviews."

"The tickets are sold out."

"Really." She gave him a knowing smile and a bold glance. "It so happens I have two tickets for tonight's show. Gabe was supposed to go with me, but he has a heavy date tonight—with a weighty legal brief, he claims. I can't think of a single reason why I shouldn't take you instead."

"I suppose next you'll try to convince me this invitation is all in aid of friendlier relations between ownership and management," Cole replied cynically. He signaled for the waiter to take away his plate, then ordered coffee.

"Are you suggesting that that's wrong?" The coffee arrived, the matchless New Orleans–style coffee, a blend of dark roasted coffee beans and chicory, brewed strong and black, with the option always provided to dilute it with hot milk.

Cole drank his straight, and he noticed that Remy Jardin did too. "I'm suggesting . . . that you find yourself another escort—one suitable for a Newcomb girl."

She looked at him in surprise. "How did you know I went to Newcomb College?"

"Considering it's a tradition in the Uptown set, it was an educated guess. No doubt your mother went there, and your mother's mother—right on down the line."

"Where did you go to college?"

"I can assure you it wasn't Tulane," he replied, trying not to think about the scholarship he'd almost gotten to that university, a scholarship that was ultimately given to someone else whose family had the "right" background and a depleted bank account. "Your brother went there, didn't he? And obtained the mandatory law degree to go with the rest of his impeccable family credentials."

She propped an elbow on the table and rested her chin on the heel of her hand. "Your logic escapes me completely. What does all this have to do with refusing to go see Lou Rawls with me?"

"Some relationships between certain people are deadends from the start. This is one of them, Miss Jardin. And I don't see any reason to start something that will never go anywhere."

"How can you be sure of that?"

"It's simple, Miss Jardin. People—like water—seek their own level." It was a truth he'd learned the hard way, on more than one occasion.

She arched an eyebrow at that. "And you accept that?"

"It isn't a question of accepting it. It's reality."

"If women had that attitude, we'd still be in the kitchen."

"Somehow I doubt you have ever seen the inside of a kitchen—except maybe to complain to the cook."

"I think you'd be surprised at how well I know my way around a kitchen, but that's not the point." She shrugged idly, her eyes never leaving him. "You disappoint me, Mr. Buchanan. I thought you were more of a gambler."

"I don't play longshots, if that's what you mean."

She laughed, and the throaty sound of it worked on his senses. "I've been called many things, but never a longshot." She reached into her lap for her purse. He heard the snapping click of the clasp opening. She took something out of it, then presented it to him in a flourish, with a twist of her wrist. "Here's a sure thing, Mr. Buchanan. *One* ticket to this evening's show . . . and look." She wiggled it. "No strings attached."

He took it from her, then hesitated warily. "What's the catch, Miss Jardin? What's behind this?"

"No catch. And if it was prompted by anything, then it's probably something Nattie once told me."

"What's that?"

"A little sugar never hurt a lemon."

He smiled in spite of himself and slipped the ticket inside the breast pocket of his suit coat.

A half-dozen times that afternoon, back in his office, he took it out and looked at it. Each time, the sight of it gave him pause. And a hundred times he debated with himself whether or not he should go.

In the end, he showered and changed at his apartment, then went to the Fairmont Hotel, which, like most New Orleans natives, he continued to think of as the Roosevelt. He was shown to a table for two in the hotel's supper club, the Blue Room. The emptiness of the chair opposite him stared accusingly back. One word from him at lunch, and Remy Jardin would have been sitting there. He wondered if he could stand to stare at it all night. Finally he decided he couldn't, and he started to get up.

That was when she walked in, dramatically feminine in a high-necked two-piece dress of silk jacquard, inset with embroidered lace at the throat and with another wide swathe accenting the hem. Her hair was piled on top of her head in a crown of soft curls, a style that was both sophisticated and sexy.

"Sorry I'm late. I hope I haven't kept you waiting long," she said, as if he'd been expecting her to come all along. Had he?

"Remy." It was out. He'd said her name.

"Yes, Cole," she replied softly.

"Nothing." Ripping his gaze from her, he moved briskly to pull out the other chair at the table.

"Nothing," she mocked playfully, following after him to take her seat. Her dress was a pale shade of ivory, but the effect of it was anything but virginal, as Cole discovered when he saw the back of it. It plunged all the way down, giving him a glimpse of the tantalizing hollow at the base of her spine. "Your longshot comes in, and all you can say is 'nothing.'"

"I see you changed for the occasion." He took his own seat, rigid, tense, every instinct telling him to walk out now.

"You like my dress?"

"*That* isn't a dress. It's a weapon."

"Mmmm, a lethal one, I hope." She smiled, deliberately provocative.

"Just why have you set your sights on me?" He leaned back in his chair, trying to put more distance between them and negate the effect she was having on him. But he heard the whisper of silk over silk as she crossed her legs under the table.

"Frankly?" Unexpectedly, her expression turned serious, her look soberly contemplative. "Initially—as I told you before—I came to see you out of sheer curiosity. I wanted to meet the man who wanted no part of one of the most elite krewes in New Orleans. When I did, you were—at least at first—almost exactly what I expected. Then I saw the way you looked at that print. You weren't calculating its worth, as I've seen *many* collectors do, or even imagining how much it would impress others, as some do. No, it was the print itself that appealed to you—the style, the technique, the use of colors, the feelings it evoked. I suppose I recognized that look because so often that's the way I feel when I come across a Sevres figurine I've never seen before." Pausing, she continued to look at him, seeing him, studying him. Then she seemed to realize how serious she'd become, and she quickly smiled, picking up the water glass in front of her, a faintly mocking gleam in her eyes. "Something tells me you aren't as hard, as cold, or as cynical as you may seem—not a man who's sensitive enough to understand cats."

Cole leaned forward, uncomfortable with the things she was saying. "Is the analysis over, or should I see if the management can provide us with a couch?"

"Now there's an intriguing thought."

"What? Analyzing me?"

"No—having you all to myself on a couch for an hour."

He didn't remember much of the show. He was more conscious of the play of light and shadow across her face with the changing of the stage lighting, and of the absence of any rings on her fingers when she clapped enthusiastically at the conclusion of each song. Her vitality, her zest—her passion—that was what he recalled when the show was over.

In the lobby of the lavishly decorated turn-of-the-century hotel, Cole guided her through the milling throng of show-goers, slow to disperse. "I wonder how lucky I'll be getting a taxi," Remy remarked.

"You didn't drive your car tonight?" He'd taken it for granted that she had.

"No. I had Gabe drop me off on his way back to the office to tussle with his weighty legal brief," she replied, then sent him a challenging sidelong glance. "You wouldn't happen to be going my way, would you?"

Another imaginary handkerchief had been dropped. Cole had the feeling he'd been following a trail of them all day. Each time he picked one up and returned it to her, he discovered that he'd gone a little further than he'd planned. The hell of it was that he *wanted* to be led like this.

"I could arrange to go that way," he heard himself say.

"I know you *could*, but will you?"

He answered that a few minutes later when he helped her into his car. During the short ride to the Jardin family home in the Garden district, the fragrance of her drifted through the car, accompanied by the whisper of silk that came with her slightest movement. The intermittent glow from the street lamps along St. Charles Avenue, their light broken by the heavy branches of the old oaks on either side of the esplanade, kept her constantly in his side, vision, occasionally highlighting a refined cheekbone or shadowing the delicate cut of her jaw. He had the feeling that from now on the ghost of her would always ride with him.

Following her directions, he turned off St. Charles onto a side street, then turned again and parked the car in front of one of the many old mansions that graced the district. He got out and walked around to open her door. His mother was old-fashioned in many ways, and she'd raised him to always walk a girl to her door, not to let her out at the curb and drive off. It was too deeply ingrained in him to be ignored, even though he knew it would be a mistake to walk Remy to her front door.

Beyond the delicate lacework of the iron fence and the dark shadows of the lush foliage, the white Doric columns of the mansion's pillared front gleamed wanly in the moonlight. He lightly kept a hand on her elbow as they walked up the banquette to the yard's black iron gate. She pushed it open. The hinges were too well oiled to creak—like the family that owned the property, Cole reminded himself.

The lights inside the main foyer spilled softly through the leaded glass windows that flanked the big oak door, forming pools on the hard cypress flooring of the front gallery. When they reached the door, with its gleaming brass knocker, she turned to him and held out a key. He stared at it, aware that if he reached for it, he was picking up another lace hankie.

He willed his expression to remain bland as he took the key from her outstretched hand and inserted it in the lock, silently cursing his mother for the first time in his life. He gave the key a quick turn, telling himself all the while that this was not a date. He didn't have to kiss her good-night. He didn't have to kiss her at all. Hearing the slide of the bolt, he turned the doorknob and pushed the door inward. As he swung back to give her back the key, she held out her hand, palm up. He hesitated, then dropped the key in the center of it.

Her fingers immediately closed around it, the polished sheen of her nails flashing in the foyer light. "I enjoyed the show—and your company tonight, Cole." The golden gleam in her eyes challenged him, dared him. "Thanks for the ride."

"You're welcome," he replied automatically.

"Good-night," she said, then—to his surprise—she stepped past him into the foyer and made a graceful turn to shut the door on him. When it was half closed, she paused and said, as if only then remembering, "By the way, I met your mother this afternoon. I liked her."

Stunned, he shot out a hand, blocking the door from swinging the rest of the way shut. As he shoved it back open, she calmly turned and advanced into the foyer. He charged after her.

"You saw my mother? Where?"

"I went by her shop on Magazine after I left you at Galatoire's," she said without so much as a backward glance, and she gave her evening bag a toss onto a side table, then crossed to a set of French doors that led onto an expansive courtyard.

"Why did you go there?" He demanded to know the reason, pushed by a half-formed annoyance that rippled through him at this invasion of his private life.

She looked over her shoulder, her dimpled smile faintly mocking. "Can't you guess?" she said, and she pulled both doors open wide, then walked through them into the night-darkened courtyard.

"I don't want to guess, Remy. I want an answer." He followed her outside and immediately felt the liquid heat of the summer night wash over him.

"Very well." She stopped on a wisteria-covered walkway flanked by white columns, and turned, leaning her shoulders against one of them. "I wanted to meet the woman who gave birth to a man like you."

Facing her, he couldn't hold on to his anger. He still felt heat, but now it was part of the voluptuous ease of the night. "Why? What difference could it make?"

"Because I gambled that you'd come when I gave you that ticket this afternoon. I hoped that by seeing your mother I might get some sense of whether or not you'd show up." She paused for a fraction of a second. "When I gave you that ticket, I never once said I wasn't going. You had to know, in the back of your mind, that there was a good chance I'd be there. So . . . if you came tonight, I knew it had to mean you were interested in me, despite what you said."

"And if I hadn't come?"

There was a tiny lift of her shoulders in a shrug. "Then I would have had to accept that you meant exactly what you said. Not that it matters. You came."

"Yes—I did." And he was regretting it, too—especially now, alone with her, with this sultriness in the air.

"I know what I want, Cole. And I want to know you better." She tilted her head to one side. "Am I too aggressive for you? In a man, I know that's a trait to be admired. But some men find it off-putting in a woman. Do you?"

"No." There was a tightening in his chest—in his whole body. He couldn't get his legs to move, not backward or forward. "What exactly do you want from me? Have you become bored with your proper world and decided to find someone *improper* to liven things up for you?"

"Could you liven things up, Cole?" In a single, fluidly graceful move, she straightened up from the column, and he discovered how close to each other they were standing. She lifted her face to him. "Can you liven me up?"

She was waiting for his kiss, and he knew it. Just as he knew he was going to kiss even before he framed her upturned face in his hands, his thumbs stroking the slender curve of her throat and feeling the heavy thud of her pulse. She looked small and delicate to him, like a porcelain figurine in a glass cabinet at his mother's shop—so very fragile, despite the directness of her eyes. Slowly he lowered his mouth onto her lips. They were soft and incredibly warm. He rubbed his mouth over them, holding himself in tight restraint. But it wasn't easy—it wasn't easy when what he really wanted was to plunder their softness, taste their heat, and make them part with his name. A second later that desire became action.

Suddenly his hands weren't steady—nothing about him was steady. He pulled back, shaken by how completely she had broken through his will. When she swayed toward him, he slid his hands onto her silk-clad shoulders, keeping her at a safe distance.

There was a radiance to her face that he didn't remember seeing before as she lifted her hand and traced the shape of his mouth with her fingertips. "Do you always kiss like that?"

"Not always." His voice sounded too husky, too thick, revealing too much of the way she disturbed him.

She released a breath of soundless laughter. "I don't think there can be any doubt: you do liven me up—in every way."

Watching him, listening to him tell of that night, Remy felt the strong pull of attraction. She could easily visualize her persistence and his resistance. "What did you say to that?" she asked when he paused in his telling.

"I didn't say anything. As I recall, we didn't need words."

The air seemed to hum between them, vibrating with a sexual tension, as it must have that night. "Did we make love?" Remy wondered.

"No. It was too soon—too sudden for both of us."

"I suppose it was." She noticed the guarded way he was studying her, the hint of wariness in his gray eyes, a wariness that suggested that he'd been hurt before. She thought back over his description of their first meeting and the remarks he'd made about the so-called Uptown crowd. "Cole, what happened to make you so distrust someone with my background—my family?"

A grim, almost bitter smile twisted his mouth. "Which time, Remy?" He turned back to the galley counter. "More coffee?"

"I—" Suddenly the plane started to shudder and buck violently, throwing Remy sideways against the counter and knocking the cup from her hand.

In the next second she was grabbed roughly by the waist and hauled against the opposite bulkhead wall, pinned there by the heavy crush of Cole's body. She found herself engulfed in the feel of him, the smell of him. The wild buffeting of the plane continued for several more interminable minutes before it settled into a mild shaking.

As Cole drew back, his hands continued to grip the hold he'd found. "Are you all right?"

"Yes." She had room enough to nod, though, like him, she wasn't sure it was over. Unsteady, shaken, she was conscious of a throbbing pain in her hip. No doubt she'd bruised it when she was thrown against the counter. But she was growing more conscious of the pressure of his hips as they held her against the wall, the hard, unmistakably male outline of him making itself felt.

"It looks like we encountered some turbulence."

Looking at him, Remy knew that the outside turbulence had moved within. "We certainly did," she said. And it increased further as the gray of his eyes darkened on her.

"Remy, are you all right back there?" Gabe called, his voice followed by the sound of his footsteps coming up the aisle to the galley.

His approach chased away the moment of awareness between them, and Cole pushed away from her, his hands moving to lightly grip her shoulders before falling away entirely.

"I'm fine," she repeated the assurance she'd earlier given Cole. But by then Gabe was already in the galley opening, his gaze immediately fastening on her in concern. Feeling the need to say more, she added, smiling, "A little shaken, but unharmed. I came to get a cup of coffee. Which now happens to be all over the floor," she noticed. "Hand me some towels or something, Cole. We'd better get it wiped up before one of us slips on it." The plane shuddered again, and Remy immediately grabbed hold of the edge of the partition to steady herself.

"I'll clean it up," Cole said. "Go back to your seat and buckle up. Get some sleep if you can. It's going to be a long flight."

She went back to her seat, not to sleep but to mull over some of the things Cole had told her. It was obvious that she'd been the pursuer. And it was equally obvious that he hadn't found it easy to trust her because of previous encounters with "her kind." He seemed so strong, so hard, that *vulnerable* certainly wasn't a word she would have used to describe him—until now. What *had* happened to make him so leery of her? Had he told her? And did it matter? Without trust, no relationship could survive. Was that what had ultimately caused her to break it off with him? Had she become tired of constantly being forced to prove to him that she cared—tired of defending her family's actions?

And that brought up another thing: according to Cole, the company was in serious financial shape. In fact, he'd blatantly accused her family of draining it of funds. Earlier Gabe had admitted that the company had been losing money, yet he'd been very definite that it was nothing serious. Which was the truth? And what could either of them gain by lying?

9

SOMEWHERE OVER THE ATLANTIC, Remy managed to doze off. When the plane began its descent to the New Orleans airport, Cole touched her shoulder. "We'll be landing in about ten minutes," he said. "Check your seat belt. There's rain and fog in the area, so it might get a little bumpy."

Groggily she acknowledged his advice and tried to wipe the sleep from her face as Cole passed the same message on to Gabe, then sat down in his own seat and buckled up.

With the dimness of the cabin lights, there was little glare on the plane's windows. Turning, Remy gazed out the window at the stars glittering before the rising moon. Below, a blanket of dark clouds hid the city. She felt oddly uneasy, unable to summon any excitement at the prospect of being reunited with her family—of returning home.

After a fairly smooth descent, the plane broke through the clouds roughly four hundred feet up. All looked black beneath them. Belatedly she remembered that the airport was located on the edge of the swamp and Lake Pontchartrain. From out of the black, the runway approach lights gleamed, twin trails of light pointing the way through the darkness and the wispy fog.

A cool, light rain fell as Remy stepped off the plane at New Orleans' Moisant International Airport. One of the ground crew ushered her to the building, sheltering her from the pattering drops with an umbrella.

After a minor delay as they went through immigration and customs, Remy walked into the terminal building itself, flanked by Gabe and Cole and trailed by a porter with their luggage. Cole tipped his head toward her, his gaze fixed on some point ahead of them as he murmured, sotto voce, "It seems the whole family turned out to welcome you home."

Following the direction of his gaze, Remy located a group of people waiting to greet them. She faltered for a moment. Strangers. They looked like total strangers, all of them. Until that moment she hadn't realized how much she'd hoped that seeing them would spark a memory, if only a long-ago one—as seeing Gabe had done. But there was nothing.

Refusing to give up, Remy focused on them individually instead of viewing them as a whole, starting first with the woman with the anxious look on her face. A soft-brimmed hat, the same teal-blue color as her raincoat, covered short blond hair that had been artfully faded to a flattering shade of platinum. Her gloved hands held a clutch purse that she gripped tightly.

When the woman saw Remy approaching, her anxious look disappeared, replaced by a glowing smile that gave a soft, Renoirish radiance to her delicate features. "Remy, my darling." Her voice caught on a happy sob as she glided forward and embraced Remy, hugging her close for a moment, then drawing back to look at her. "It's so good to have you home. You gave us such a scare, vanishing like that. What are we ever going to do with you?" She ran a gloved hand tenderly over her cheek and smoothed the side of her hair in a soothing, motherly gesture. "How are you? Are you all right? They told us you have amnesia. Gracious!" She blinked in sudden surprise. "Do you remember me? I'm your mother."

"You grow roses." She had a fleeting image of this same woman in a wide straw sun hat, with a basket of freshly cut roses on her arm and a pair of garden shears in her white-gloved hand. That was it. That was all. But it was something, a tiny piece of memory that allowed Remy to truthfully say, "I can remember that."

"Gracious, yes, I grow roses. Prize roses."

"How about me? Do you remember your kindly old father?" asked a low, jesting voice.

Less certainly, Remy turned to the man who was obviously her father, her searching glance taking in the bright twinkle in his brown eyes, the almost total absence of gray in his dark hair, and the tanned, healthy vigor of his face. "I wish I could say I do remember you, but . . . I can't." She saw the flash of stark hurt in his eyes and regretted her candor. Smiling, she reached for his hand. "Right now, it's enough to know I have a father who loves me."

She could tell that her words had pleased him as he gave her hand a squeeze. "What father could not love a daughter like you?" Then his gaze centered on the faint discoloration near her lips, his expression taking on a look of shared pain. "Remy, do you remember anything at all about what happened that night?"

"No. Nothing. And the specialist at the hospital told me the odds were I would never remember the events directly leading up to my injury. That part of my memory will probably be lost forever."

"I . . . I see," he murmured, his glance dropping to her hand.

"Now, Frazier." Her mother slipped a gloved hand under the crook of his arm. "That awful incident isn't something we should be dwelling on."

"Of course not," he agreed, somewhat hesitantly.

"Well, it doesn't matter whether you remember me or not, Remy," another voice broke in, its heartiness a contrast to her father's quietly serious tone. "I insist on having a hug from my favorite niece."

Remy turned to her uncle, a slim version of her more robust father, impeccably groomed in an Italian suit, his handsome features beaming with a smile. "You must be Uncle Marc," she managed to say before she was smoothly drawn into his arms, a dry kiss planted on her left cheek.

Then he stepped back, holding on to both her hands. "Let me have a look at you," he said, giving her the once-over, then winking. "I must say, you look none the worse for your adventure." He paused to sigh in contentment. "Ahh, Remy, you can't know how worried all of us have been about you."

"And you can't know how much I needed to hear that a few days ago, when I felt totally lost and forgotten." She smiled.

"Never forgotten, Remy," he insisted firmly. "Never for one minute."

She laughed. "Do you always know the right thing to say?"

"I try," he said, lifting his shoulders in a shrug of modesty.

"I can't imagine you could have forgotten me, Remy—your dear cousin Lance," a low voice challenged, silken with mockery. "Especially when you consider I'm your least favorite."

Turning, she forced herself to calmly meet the lazy, taunting regard of his dark, nearly black eyes. "In that case, maybe I shouldn't say it's good to see you, Lance."

He stood before her, one hand idly thrust in the side pocket of his pleated trousers, in a pose of negligent ease that smacked of arrogance. His hair was the same near-black shade as his eyes, its thickness skillfully and smoothly combed away from his face. His lips had a woman's fullness to them, yet on him it looked sexy instead of effeminate. And when he smiled—as he was doing now —there was a faintly sarcastic curl to his upper lip. Gabe was right—Lance was "handsome as the devil."

"I don't know why anyone worried about you," he said. "Your memory may be impaired, but your tongue is as sharp as ever."

Before she could show him precisely how sharp it could be, three women converged on her with effusive welcomes, hugging her and kissing the air near her cheek.

"You look marvelous, Remy," declared one of Marc's daughters, a raven-haired Southern beauty with dark, flashing eyes and a beauty queen's empty smile. "When they told me you had amnesia, I thought you'd look, well, haunted, your eyes all shadowed and your face pale and wan. But here you are —the same old Remy."

"We heard they put a dozen stitches in your head," the other chimed in, craning her neck to see where they'd been taken.

"Not a dozen," Remy corrected automatically.

"Well, however many it was, they don't show. Your hair covers it beautifully. Aren't you lucky you don't wear it short? Think how funny you would have looked with a bald spot in the middle of your head."

"She would simply have had to wear a hat to cover it, Diana," the first inserted, which meant she had to be Kathy, the older of the two.

"It's almost a pity you don't," sighed Diana, who was a less striking version of her sister. "According to *W*, hats are *in* this season."

"Is it true, Remy, that you don't remember anything?" Her aunt Christina, a plump, matronly woman who had obviously given up the battle of competing with her daughters' looks, finally squeezed in a question.

"Yes, is it true?" Kathy immediately took up the thread. "You don't remember anything? Not even about the—"

"This isn't the time to besiege Remy with questions," Marc smoothly cut across his eldest daughter's words. "She just stepped off the plane from a long and very exhausting flight. She can tell us her story later—after she has had time to rest."

"And we are all dying to hear it," Kathy put in, then added with a hint of resentment and envy, "Amnesia. Leave it to you, Remy, to come up with something so spectacularly unusual."

"Not by choice, I assure you." Remy smiled, their prattle sounding vaguely familiar to her. No doubt she had been irritated by it in the past, but not tonight—not when she was standing here literally surrounded by family, embraced by a sense of belonging.

As she idly swept her glance over them, she noticed that Cole wasn't there. A slight turn of her head and she found him, standing well apart from them—alone. She was suddenly struck by the feeling that he was an outsider, he didn't belong. Unbidden came a wash of voices through her mind: "not one of us" . . . "methods less than orthodox" . . . "native shrewdness" . . . "not suitable at all" . . . "ruthless, cunning."

Staring at the hard and so very cynical look on his face, Remy realized that much of that was true. Cole Buchanan hadn't been born into that uptight, Uptown New Orleans world of hers, where lineage was everything, where certain standards of conduct were quietly expected, where you were judged by the high school and college you attended and the number of Mardi Gras courts you were invited to participate in. She told herself that none of that mattered, yet . . . she felt trapped by this lack of memory that kept her from knowing whether or not she should believe in him. Part of her wanted to go to him, to include him in this moment, but she was afraid to trust her instincts—perhaps for the first time in her life.

"How much does she remember about—"

Remy recognized Lance's voice, its tone dropped to a conspiratorial level, an instant before Gabe broke in with a quick, quiet "Nothing."

She pivoted toward them. "I remember nothing about what?"

"Gabe," her uncle inserted smoothly as he clamped a hand on her brother's shoulder. "I don't believe any of us have thanked you for flying all the way there and bringing her back."

Remy started to point out that Gabe hadn't been alone, as her uncle Marc had implied, that in fact Cole had been the one to make the initial contact, but when she glanced at Cole, his back was turned to them, and he had a briefcase in one hand and a heavy garment bag slung over his other arm. Something tore at her throat when she saw him walk to the exit without so much as a backward look.

"Hey, Sweet Cheeks." Lance snapped his fingers in front of her face. "Have you lost your hearing as well as your memory?"

"I'm sorry—I wasn't listening." Still confused and troubled by Cole's abrupt departure, Remy forced her attention back to the family, looking from one to the other in a vaguely distracted way. "What did you say?"

"It doesn't matter," her father replied, his look gentle with concern. "Marc was right. That long flight has taken its toll on you. We need to get you home so you can rest." He reached in his pocket and took out a set of keys. "Bring the car around, Gabe, so we can get the luggage loaded."

Remy discovered that she was tired, more tired than she had realized. It had been a long day, a confusing day, with too much happening, too many new faces and new names—including her own. And with the fatigue, the dull pounding in her head had returned. There would be time enough to sort through everything tomorrow—after she'd slept.

10

A SLOWLY RISING SUN burned through the remnants of the dawn fog and gave the air in the Quarter an unusual crystalline quality. But the damp chill remained, and Remy shoved her hands a little deeper into the pockets of her shaped double-breasted blazer of black wool, glad of the sun-gold sweater she wore beneath it and the wool slacks in a black-and-white houndstooth check covering her legs.

She'd awakened at dawn, too restless and edgy to stay in her room until the rest of the house stirred. Her first thought was to wander the house and see if familiar surroundings might arouse some memories, as Dr. Gervais had suggested. She'd roamed the lavender and plum parlor, then gone to the solarium with its cushioned rattan furniture and profusion of potted plants, but an inner tension had made her too impatient to absorb the things around her. And the emptiness of the house and the hollow echo of her footsteps had haunted her.

Finally she'd been driven outside, into the mist-shrouded courtyard, a mist thickened by the steam rising from the heated swimming pool. All the while, the urge to leave—to go—had become stronger and stronger. The compulsion seemed somehow linked to that feeling she had that she was needed somewhere.

At last she'd given in to it and left a note in her room, telling her parents she'd gone for a walk. She'd left the silent, sleeping house and set out, letting the compulsion guide her, hoping it would lead to the recovery of more memories. When the streetcar had come by on St. Charles, she'd climbed aboard and ridden it all the way to Canal, then found herself crossing the street into the French Quarter.

As she wandered down the narrow streets of the Vieux Carré, Remy was conscious of the stillness and quiet of its sleepy abandon. It was too early for the syncopated clop of the carriage horses, too early for the street musicians, the mimes, and the dancers, too early for the artists to hang their canvases on the iron fence around Jackson Square, and too early for last night's Mardi Gras revelers to be up and about. It was as if she had the city all to herself. But no, not quite all to herself, she realized as a man in a T-shirt and shorts lifted aside the curtain of a second-floor window and groggily peered out at the early morning. Then Remy saw a woman's hands slide around his middle and spread across his chest. His mouth curved in a lazy smile as he turned and let the curtain fall. Remy smiled too—a little wistfully, though, made restless again by her own longings, longings intensified by the languor of the street.

Moving on, she let her gaze absorb the old buildings that lined the streets of the Quarter, absently admiring the mellow beauty of their stucco exteriors and the rails of iron lace along their balconies. Yet there was nothing in their facades that hinted at the hidden courtyards within. Was anything ever what it seemed? This was the French Quarter, but the architecture was Spanish.

The soft, melodic notes of a clarinet drifted across the stillness. Remy paused to locate the sound. There on a balcony sat a black man, still wearing his white shirt and black suit from the night before. He had his feet propped up on the cast-iron railing and his chair tipped back on two legs while he played his song to the early-morning sun. There was no wail to it, no lively jazz melody. It was soft and sad and yearning.

And that was New Orleans too, Remy realized. For all the face it showed to the world of wild fun, steaminess, and good times, there was a subtle melancholy behind it. This was the home of jazz, but it was also where the blues had grown up. What was the French phrase? *Les tristes tropiques.*

Remy started walking again, picking up her ambling pace, needing to escape that sweetly pensive clarinet. She no longer wanted the quiet and solitude of the Quarter. There was one place that was never still, no matter the hour, day or night, and Remy headed for it, slipping down the alley between the Cabildo and the St. Louis Cathedral, with its soaring triple spires, and emerging on the cobblestoned street facing Jackson Square, its gates still locked. As she skirted the square and started past the historic Pontalba Apartments, a silver cloud of pigeons erupted in flight, their wings thrashing through the aromas of beignets and freshly brewed Louisiana coffee.

With a cup of the chicory-flavored coffee from the Café du Monde, Remy climbed to the top of the levee and faced the turgid, earth-smelling Mississippi River. The cathedral bells rang the hour and a delivery truck grumbled by on Decatur. Before her curved the crescent-shaped bend of the Mississippi that had long ago given New Orleans the nickname Crescent City.

There was always activity on the river, always something happening, always something moving. Towboats and barges, merchant ships and tankers, pilot boats and paddle wheelers. Traffic on the Mississippi was always two-way, oceangoing vessels gliding slowly along the east bank and off-loading barges hugging the west.

Remy took a sip of her coffee and wrapped both hands around the cup, absorbing the heat through its Styrofoam sides. The smells, the sights, the sounds appealed to her. She saw a tanker riding low in the water, heading downriver, the throb of its engines trailing across the morning to her. From somewhere upriver came the deep-throated blast of a whistle.

As she watched the tanker, suddenly, unexpectedly, something else flashed through her mind, passing so quickly that it took her a full second to realize that the image had been of another tanker wrapped in darkness and fog. It was so fleeting that nothing more than that registered. She stared intently at the tanker moving downriver, willing the image to return, but it didn't.

Impatient, she turned away and began to wander up the levee, drawn by the restlessness of the big river. When she reached the wharf area, Remy kept walking. Then she saw the company insignia, the same one Cole had had on his business card—the letter C joined by an L at its lower curve—painted on the side of a building. She stopped, faintly stunned. Had her subconscious been directing her to the company wharf all along? Why?

She stared intently at the building, a little weathered-looking, a little dirty, like most of the wharves along the riverfront. She tried, but she couldn't make it seem familiar to her. Was it purely an accident that she'd stumbled onto it? Refusing to accept that possibility, she walked around the long building to the dockside.

A sleek merchant vessel was tied alongside, the tall crane on its deck busy off-loading the cargo from its hold. For a moment Remy stood and absorbed the scene before her—the loud whir of the crane, the rumble of forklifts, the shouts of the deckhands and longshoremen, the lingering odor of diesel fumes, the smell of the river, and a thousand other scents she couldn't identify.

A long, low wolf whistle pierced the air, followed by a coarsely flirtatious "Hey, baby, whatcha doin' tonight?"

Out of the corner of her eye Remy saw the brawny, big-smiling dockworker looking her over. As he turned to make some remark to his buddy, another shorter, slighter man walked up, dressed in a white short-sleeved shirt, with a clipboard in one hand and a shirt pocket full of pens and pencils. He said something to the man who had whistled at her. He spoke too low for Remy to hear, but his tone was definitely angry.

Some memory suddenly flickered, distracting her. She frowned, realizing she'd almost remembered something. But what? She focused her attention again on the ship tied up to the dock, something telling her that the memory was connected to it.

She wasn't aware of the man scurrying over to her until he spoke at her side. "I'm sorry about that, Miss Jardin. That crazy Bosco, he got the head of a duck. He didn't mean no harm. He jus' didn't know who you were."

"It's all right, really."

"You be up early this mornin'. Was there something you be wanting, Miss Jardin?"

This time her ear caught the Cajun accent of his voice, but it helped her not at all. "No. I was just walking." She noticed the company insignia emblazoned on the vessel's smokestack. "This ship, what's it called?"

"She's the *Crescent Lady,* jus' come in."

Something flashed in her mind, but once again it came too quickly and passed too quickly for Remy to grasp it. She strained to recall it, oblivious of the man hovering anxiously beside her. It was something important. She was certain of it.

"Excuse me, Miss Jardin, but I got to be gettin' back to work," he said finally. "If you be needin' anything, you jus' tell one of the boys to fetch Henry for you."

"Thanks." Again she responded automatically, without really hearing what he'd said. There were more flashes, coming in rapid succession now. She stood motionless, trying not to think, letting them happen. She didn't see the man walk away. She didn't notice the looks she received or the subdued voices around her, the talk restricted to the job at hand, the rough camaraderie suppressed by her presence.

One minute, two minutes, five—Remy had no idea how long she stood there staring at the ship. Then a hand gripped her arm and roughly pulled her around.

"What the hell are you doing here?" Cole was furious. When Henry had told him she was out on the dock, he hadn't believed him. "Don't you know better than to walk along the waterfront at this hour?"

Whatever else it might be, New Orleans was a major port city. And like any port area, it attracted its share of unsavory elements. Cole knew that; he'd grown up with it. But she hadn't.

"I've been here before." She stared at him, her eyes moving over his face with a strange, faraway look—as if they were seeing him, yet not seeing him. "You brought me"—she paused, her glance drawn to the vessel lying at dockside —"to see the newest ship in the line, the *Crescent Lady.*"

Cole stood perfectly still, saying nothing, recalling that afternoon clearly, vividly—everything from the warmth of the sun on his back to the way a vagrant breeze had played hide-and-seek with the jersey material of her skirt.

"What—no champagne?" Her side glance playfully chided him. "I thought you were bringing me here to christen the newest ship in the fleet. I'm disappointed."

"That ceremony is only observed when a vessel is launched for the first time. The *Lady's* a year old." He walked her to the gangway, his hand riding on the small of her back, conscious as always of the faint sway of her hips and the natural heat that flowed from her body.

"And I suppose there's some silly superstition against christening her a second time," she said, then released a sigh of mock regret. "I've always wanted to break a bottle of champagne over the bow of a ship."

"You'll have to wait until the company can afford to commission a new ship to fulfill that fantasy."

"How can we even afford this one, considering the dire financial shape you claim we're in?"

Cole ignored her taunt. "The loss of the *Dragon* was a blessing in disguise. When the insurance company paid off on the claim, I used some of that money and raised the rest through conventional sources to buy this ship."

She shot him a quick look. "Then this is what you spent the insurance money on."

"Not all of it."

"I remember my father was upset," she said, unconcerned. "He thought there should be some distribution of dividends."

"That money belongs to the company—not to your family."

She laughed. "You love having power over my family's purse strings, don't you?"

The ship's captain was waiting to welcome them aboard, which checked any response Cole might have made to her assertion—not that he would have denied it. A part of him thoroughly enjoyed the power he exercised. And another part would have gladly traded it for some control over this—*thing*— that had erupted between him and Remy almost three months ago. They'd been seeing each other regularly ever since, meeting two, sometimes three times a week, usually at his apartment, occasionally going out to dinner or some local festival or public concert, or taking in a new exhibit at the museum or a gallery. He never went to any social function with her, flatly rejecting any suggestion of hers that he meet her friends.

Lately, though, they'd kept more and more to his apartment. He'd thought it would help. He'd thought he could handle this . . . affair they were having. He'd thought he could use her, the same way she was using him. But how many times during the day did he have to make himself stop thinking about her? How many times had he sat at his desk, staring at reports and visualizing her slender white body lying beside him, the gold flecks—like rays of sunshine trapped in her hazel eyes—glittering with desire just for him?

Yet none of it would last. He knew that—and that knowledge was his shield.

Cole introduced Remy to the ship's captain, Peder Van der Horn, a ruddy-cheeked Scandinavian with yellow-gray hair. After a brief tour of the vessel— limited mainly to the galley, the officers' quarters, and the bridge, due to the constant activity on deck as the ship was loaded with its first cargo for the company—the captain left them on the deck of the bridge for a few minutes, giving Remy an opportunity to observe the high-speed lifting cranes as they transferred the specially designed containers onto the ship to be stowed in the cellular grid of the below-decks compartments.

Alone with her, he became aware of the silence—if it could be called silence, with the noise of the cranes and the shouts of the longshoremen. He moved to stand beside her at the rail, deliberately focusing his gaze on the activity on the weather deck.

"The *Lady*'s operating costs are going to be substantially lower than those of the *Dragon*, the ship she's replacing. Not only does she require a proportionately smaller crew, which cuts our labor costs, but those containers reduce the risk of pilferage, which decreases the insurance rates. And using containers means she can be unloaded and reloaded in a matter of hours, so less time is spent in port, again lowering the cost of the crew—and she can also make more trips, which adds up to more profit for the company," he said, talking to fill the void between them. "As the captain explained when we were on the bridge, the higher-than-average service speeds she's capable—"

"Enough," Remy broke in, holding up her hands in mock surrender, then laughing and shaking her head. "It's no use, Cole. I'll never be able to tell a container ship from a tanker."

"That isn't exactly something to brag about," he chided, faintly amused.

"That's no brag—it's a fact." She turned her back to the rail and leaned her elbows on it, letting the breeze play through her hair. "Now, if you want to talk about porcelain, that's something else."

Her remark served to remind him that she was porcelain and he was ordinary river clay. Neither fact was he likely to forget, even if she pretended to. His glance strayed to the ferry in the distance, plowing its way across the swirling channel waters to the landing on the opposite bank. Cole turned from the rail to watch it.

"The ferry's making its run to Algiers." He nodded his head in its direction, pointing it out to her, then watching as she turned to look, pushing back the strands of tawny hair that blew across her face. "That's where I grew up—in a ramshackle house off Socrates."

Properly it was called Algiers Point, the origin of its name long ago lost. During French and Spanish rule, slave pens had been built there to hold newly arrived blacks from the West Indies and Africa. Although separated from it by the Mississippi, Algiers was a part of the city of New Orleans, called black Algiers by many, and not because of its origins.

"Some say Algiers is where the blues got their start," Remy said, gazing at the jutting point of land. Then she turned her head and fastened her eyes on him with typical directness. "Have you been there lately? There's some marvelous renovation and restoration work going on. In fact, it's becoming a fashionable place to live."

Cole sensed immediately that that was more than just an idle comment; it had some other overtones in it. "Are you suggesting I could become fashionable?"

"I don't know," she returned lightly, a tiny smile teasing at the corners of her mouth. "Do you think you could be a candidate for renovation and restoration?"

"No."

She laughed. "I didn't think so. And truthfully, I can't imagine you being anything other than what you are. 'Take it or leave it'—that's you." She pushed away from the rail and swung to face him in a lithe, graceful move, then slid her hands up the front of his shirt without any interference from his suit jacket, since he'd left it in the backseat of his car, along with his tie. "And I'm so glad I decided to take you."

He stopped her hands before they crept around his neck. "The question is, where do you plan to take me, Remy? Your family doesn't approve of this—affair—we're having."

The faint smile never left her face, but her fingers stopped their caressing play on his shirt as she withdrew from him and stepped back. "Has someone said something to you about us?"

"No." But he wasn't surprised by that, either. "Your father is in an awkward position. I may be good enough to run the family business, but I'm not good enough for his daughter. I can't pass the blood test—the one that checks the amount of 'blue' blood in a man's veins."

"Why do you keep bringing up this nonsense?"

He saw the anger slowly building in her expression, and ignored it. "Because it's true, whether you want to admit it or not."

"Do you want to know what's true, Cole Buchanan?" It flared hotly then, yellow fire flashing in her eyes. "It's true you were raised in Algiers and I come from the Garden district; you were poor while I had plenty; you struggled to survive, but for me, life was yachts on the lake, summer dances, and Carnival balls; you worked your way through college and I attended an expensive one; you've fought to get where you are, and I haven't! And I say, so what? My God, do you think I judge a man's worth by where he's from or what he was?"

She said it now—with the same heat, the same outrage, remembering it clearly, both the words and the emotions. Hearing her, Cole again felt that surge of feeling breaking through his restraint.

That time, those months ago, she had abruptly turned from him. But he hadn't let her stalk away in anger. He'd caught her arm and spun her around, needing to see her face, needing to see she'd meant it. Then he'd kissed her, there on the dock, amidst the whistling approval of the longshoremen, and her anger had turned to a loving passion.

The urge was in him to replay the rest of the scene to its former conclusion —and the desire was there in her eyes too. But he'd believed her then, he'd believed she was different, he'd believed—and he'd paid the price for it, a price that might still go higher. No, too much had changed, too many things had changed. He wasn't a believer anymore—and, more damning than that, neither was she.

Cole watched the light of desire fade from her eyes, and he never moved, never reached out to keep it there. Maybe he ought to. Maybe she'd forgotten. Maybe she never would remember—except he knew her family would see to it that she did.

The morning breeze blew a lock of hair across her cheek. She brushed it back, breaking eye contact with him in the process. "I remember that moment," she said quietly. "That is what happened, isn't it?"

"Yes." He sounded curt, and he knew it. Trying to cover it, he glanced at his watch. "I have to be at the office in ten minutes. You'd better come with me, and I'll arrange for a taxi to take you home."

Remy shook her head. "I can walk."

"Not at this hour, and not in this area." Taking her arm, he steered her away from the dock. She briefly stiffened in resistance, then abandoned it and let him guide her to his car.

As they drove away from the wharf area, Remy sat silently in the car. When she'd left the house this morning, she'd hoped she might remember something. She had. She'd found another piece of her memory—in many ways a beautiful memory. Yet . . . afterward, she'd had the strongest feeling that she'd lost something. Why? Why did she think that? Why did she feel it?

She stole a glance at Cole. Even in profile, his strong-featured face wore that same cold and forbidding expression he'd shown her on the dock. It was as if he hated her—this same man who'd made love to her so fiercely, so desperately, so thoroughly, only a day ago. Why had he changed? What had she done? Or—was it something he'd done?

She felt herself tensing, straining to recall, and immediately tried to make herself relax. Her memory wasn't something she could command to return, as she'd so painfully learned.

Seeking a diversion, Remy fixed her attention on the business district of New Orleans, rising before her with its canyonlike streets running between lofty buildings, an eclectic collection of architecture, with examples of nineteenth-century styles intermingling with the concrete-and-glass towers of the twentieth century. She waited for Cole to turn on Poydras Street and enter the heart of it. Instead he made the jog and turned in to the entrance to the International Trade Mart.

"What are we doing here?" She directed her bewildered frown at Cole when he opened the passenger door and offered a hand to assist her from the car. "I thought you had to be at your office."

"This is where the corporate offices for the Crescent Line are located," he replied, waving a hand in the direction of the thirty-three-story building as she stepped out of the car without his help.

"I don't remember that." Why? she wondered. "Have they been here long?"

"Since early in the sixties, shortly after the building was completed. I understand it was your grandfather's decision to move the company headquarters here." He took her arm and guided her toward the entrance. "A smart move, considering that some twenty-eight foreign consulates and trade offices are located in the Mart, as well as a number of import-export businesses, barge lines, and other shipping companies."

She would have commented on this rare expression of approval for something one of her family had done, but she was still bothered by the discovery that the company offices were in this building. She didn't dispute him, exactly; she just had a vague feeling there was something he wasn't telling her—something she *almost* remembered for herself.

"There's a taxi pulling up now." His hand tightened on her arm.

When he started to steer her toward it, Remy pulled back. "No. I don't want to go home yet. I want to see the offices."

He opened his mouth as if to argue with her, then clamped it shut and swung toward the building.

When they reached the fifteenth floor, she saw the company logo on the door, gold lettering edged in black below it spelling out the name THE CRESCENT LINE. The world map showing the major ports and shipping lanes that dominated one whole wall of the reception area was too typical of a decor associated with shipping. So were the models of racy clipper ships and sleek, modern vessels.

She followed Cole down the wide hall to the executive office area. She responded automatically to his secretary's greeting but didn't pause by her desk when Cole did.

"Have they arrived yet?" Cole asked as Remy wandered restlessly around the outer office, searching for something familiar, trailing a hand over the armrest of the leather sofa, wondering if it was the one Cole had set the framed print on to inspect it for damages, then moving on when it failed to strike any chord in her.

"Not yet, Mr. Buchanan," the painfully slim secretary replied, adding, "I put a stack of letters on your desk that require your signature."

Remy paused in front of the door to his corner office, vaguely aware of

Cole's saying, "Miss Jardin will be leaving shortly. Make sure there's a cab waiting downstairs to take her home."

"I'll see to it right away."

Remy's hand reached for the doorknob as she realized it was imperative that she see inside. She turned the brass knob and gave the door a push, letting it swing open. She hesitated, then walked slowly into the room, the heels of her boots sounding loudly on the hardwood floor until they were muffled by the cushion of the thick Tabriz rug.

The morning light coming through the large windows gave a lustrous glow to the paneling, revealing the mahogany's rich patina—a patina that her mind told her couldn't be achieved over a few decades. A century, perhaps, but not mere decades. The wine leather chesterfield and wing-backed chairs in the small sitting area showed the wear of many hands. And the massive kneehole desk was clearly an antique—Sheraton, she thought.

More bewildered than ever, Remy turned and found Cole watching her from just inside the door. "I don't understand. This office is . . . old."

"Yes. Your grandfather moved the company headquarters but kept his office. It was dismantled in sections—floors, walls, and ceiling," he said, thumbing a hand at the coffered mahogany ceiling above them, "and then reassembled here, with allowances made—grudgingly, I'm told—for the Mart's larger windows."

"Subconsciously I must have been remembering how very old this office was—without remembering it had been moved here." She reached down and gave an antique globe a turn in its Chippendale stand, wondering if she'd played with it when she'd come here to see her father as a child.

"If you've satisfied your curiosity, or whatever it was, I have work to do," he stated, abruptly and briskly crossing the room to his desk.

Remy looked up, well aware that he wanted her to leave and doubting that his reason was solely the press of business. "I do have one other question."

"What is it?" There was a hardness in his expression, as if he was setting himself against her, as he'd done at the docks.

"Why did you leave the airport last night without a word to me or anyone else?"

"I have a question for you: why didn't you come after me?"

"I don't have an answer for that."

"And maybe that, in itself, is an answer."

"Maybe it is." As she moved away from the globe, the light from the window glared on a framed picture, obscuring the subject and drawing her attention to it. In her mind's eye she had a fleeting glimpse of a silver-haired man, stiffly posed in a boxy jacket with wide lapels. "Grand-père." She immediately identified the brief image. "Is that his portrait?"

Without waiting for Cole to confirm it, Remy walked over to see for herself. She stared in surprise at the somewhat dashing figure in oil, dressed in a black frock coat and a silver brocade vest. His hair, far from being silver, was a deep, dark shade of red, cut fairly short, just covering the top of his ears and parted slightly off-center—the only hint of anything even slightly tamed about him. His eyes gleamed with laughter, and a smile lifted the corners of his mustache and creased his deeply tanned cheeks. The whole impression was one of a strong, vigorous man who relished challenge regardless of the odds.

"Who's the man in the portrait? Is this painting one of yours?" The instant the words were out, Remy turned with a start, paling slightly. "I've asked you that before, haven't I?" He nodded that she had, then waited, as if to see what else she remembered. But it was all blank after that. "What did you tell me when I asked?"

"It's a portrait of the company's founder. I found it buried under a hundred years of dust in one of the company's warehouses along the waterfront."

She took another look at the painting. "How strange. He doesn't look like a Jardin at all."

"That's because he isn't a Jardin," Cole stated.

"What? That's impossible. A Jardin has always been the owner of the Crescent Line."

"Not always. Certainly not in the beginning. That man—Brodie Donovan —started the Crescent Line."

"Donovan." Inwardly she wanted to reject everything Cole said, certain that he had to be wrong. But she couldn't remember. Was he right? Was this another piece of information about her family trapped behind that wall of blankness?

"By rights, Remy," Cole went on, "your name should be Donovan, not Jardin."

"What are you talking about?" she demanded, thoroughly confused.

He started to answer, then glanced at the connecting door to the outer office and paused for a fraction of an instant, smiling without warmth. "Maybe you should ask your uncle to explain."

Remy swung toward the door that had been left open. Marc Jardin stood with one foot inside the office, his dark eyes narrowed at the portrait, his mouth compressed in a tight line of displeasure. Then the look was gone, wiped away without a trace, a bland smile in its place.

"This is a surprise, Remy." He walked across the rug to her.

"Uncle Marc. Good morning." She was certain he'd overheard the statements—the assertions—Cole had just made about their family, yet he seemed to be deliberately ignoring them. Why? Did his silence mean they were true? Or was Brodie Donovan a subject he didn't wish to discuss in front of Cole? Some little voice inside her head said, *Family secrets should stay just that.* She obeyed the dictum and followed his lead, explaining instead, "I went for a walk this morning and . . . this is where I ended up."

"What brings you to the office so early, Marc?" Cole inquired with a faintly aloof indifference. "At this hour you're usually huddled with your buddies at the coffee shop of the Hotel Pontchartrain, aren't you?"

"Usually," her uncle admitted. "But with the meeting this morning—"

"There is a meeting scheduled for this morning. But what does that have to do with you?" There was a forbidding coldness in Cole's expression, which seemed to cause the temperature in the room to drop several degrees.

"I felt I should be here," Marc Jardin replied, his smile becoming a little forced around the edges.

"Why?"

A redness began to creep up her uncle's neck. "Why?" He laughed, a little self-consciously. "I am an officer of the company, Cole, as well as a director and major stockholder."

"So you are," Cole agreed. "But I think you've forgotten that *I* do the talking for the company now. And your presence isn't required."

"I see," her uncle murmured, a stiffness—a rigidity—in his expression and his stance.

Realizing there was no way he could make the graceful exit that his pride desired, Remy spoke up quickly. "If you aren't needed here, could I persuade you to give me a ride home, Uncle Marc?"

He turned, a flicker of gratitude showing in his dark eyes. "It would be my pleasure, Remy." He offered her his arm in mock courtliness. Remy took it and walked out of the office at his side.

11 ✒

ENSCONCED IN THE PASSENGER seat of her uncle's gray Mercedes, Remy listened to the soothing sound of his voice as he drove along St. Charles Avenue, en route to her home. As he had from the moment they'd left Cole's office, Marc Jardin talked about his son and daughters and their children, telling her about the recent parades and festivities his grandchildren had attended and recounting amusing incidents concerning their reactions to them. Remy smiled at the appropriate times, but her attention drifted, her glance straying out the window to observe the morning brightness along the avenue—seeing it now without the darkness that had shadowed it the night before and without the swirling fog that had layered it in the early dawn hours of this morning.

Reminders of the current Carnival season were visible all along the popular parade route, brightly colored beads—the "throws" from the floats—winking at her from the branches of the majestic oaks lining the street, and plastic cups—the ever-popular "go-cups" that held revelers' favorite spirits—lying almost hidden beneath the azalea bushes planted the length of the neutral ground, their tightly budded blooms nearing the day when the median strip would burst into its pink glory.

And here and there Remy caught a glimpse of the official Rex flag of the elite Carnival club flying in front of a stately home in the Garden district, safe behind elaborate wrought-iron fences and guarded by towering magnolias. Seeing the insignias, she recalled that by tradition, only former rulers of Mardi Gras—the ex-Rexes and their queens—were allowed the privilege of displaying the purple, green, and gold flags in front of their homes. Purple for justice, green for faith, and gold for power, of course.

But the trappings of Carnival made her wonder all the more why Marc Jardin was deliberately steering their conversation away from any discussion of what had transpired in Cole's office. Why wasn't he telling her who Brodie Donovan was? She remembered the way he'd glared at the portrait, and she was certain he'd overheard Cole assert that this Donovan man had founded the Crescent Line. Yet he'd said nothing about it, and given her no opening to ask him. By the same token, she hadn't forced the issue. Why was she reluctant to question him?

The opportunity to correct her self-imposed silence was lost as her uncle announced, "Here we are," and swung the Mercedes between two narrow wrought-iron columns, the scrolled gates of the mansion's former carriage entrance standing open to admit them. "It must be good to be home again after the ordeal you've been through."

"If you had said that to me two days ago, in Nice, I probably would have agreed with you," Remy replied as he parked the car in front of the old carriage house, which had been converted into a four-car garage. "Now I have a feeling that the ordeal has barely begun."

Saying nothing to that, he let a silence fall between them, a silence that seemed even more pronounced after the stream of banal conversation he'd maintained during the drive here, and it convinced Remy that her statement might be more accurate than she'd realized.

When they walked into the mansion through a side entrance, she was immediately greeted by an array of tantalizing aromas. Her uncle paused and inhaled deeply in exaggerated appreciation. "Smells like that Nattie has been baking up a storm already this morning."

"It's about time you got back here." At the end of the hall stood a tall, spare black woman, wearing a businesslike white apron tied firmly around a black uniform. Her hair was cut close to her head at the sides, then allowed to pouf in a mass of pepper-gray curls on top of her head, a cut that was both stylish and practical and that showed her high cheekbones to their best advantage. Her dark eyes narrowed on Remy. "It seems to me that knock on your head took away more than your memory. It took some good sense along with it—going off for a walk before it gets light."

"You must be Nattie." Remy walked toward the woman, waiting for the sight to spark some memory.

"Considering I'm the only black woman in this house, I don't see how you could mistake me for anyone else."

Remy laughed in surprise. "Are you always this blunt?"

"If I am, I got it from you." The quickness of her retort led Remy to believe this conversation might be typical of past exchanges.

"Where's—" Marc began.

"Mr. Frazier and Miss Sibylle's in the solarium having their morning coffee," Nattie interrupted, anticipating his question.

"I'll let them know you're home," he said to Remy, then set off, striding briskly toward the white-wood-and-glass room.

"They did find the note I left, didn't they?" Remy wondered, belatedly.

"I found it," Nattie replied, "when they had me take a tray of morning coffee up to your room. Right away your momma started worrying that if you'd lost your memory, how were you going to know where you lived to find your way back?"

"I promise you I could have."

"Try convincing her of that," Nattie countered, shaking her head in a gesture of exasperation.

Despite the familiar way the black woman spoke to her, Remy noticed that she hadn't once asked her where she'd gone or why she'd left or what she'd done. She remembered that Cole had said she regarded Nattie as practically one of the family, but obviously not to the extent that she felt she had to account to the woman for her comings and goings—and it was equally obvious that Nattie didn't expect her to.

Suddenly Nattie reached up and curved a pink-palmed hand against Remy's cheek. "I'm glad you're home. I was worried about you," she declared, a little too brusquely, then quickly drew away her hand. "I don't know why I'm standing around here talking to you when I've got work to do. Go tell your momma and papa breakfast will be on the table in twenty minutes. And ask Mr. Marc if he'll be staying."

"I will," Remy promised, but Nattie hadn't waited for a response as she started for the kitchen.

Smiling, Remy turned and moved off in the direction her uncle had taken earlier. Without Nattie's presence to distract her, she found her thoughts immediately swinging back to replay the morning's events—with Cole and with her uncle. As she approached the sun-filled solarium, she heard voices and automatically slowed her steps.

"It never occurred to me that Buchanan would shut you out of the meeting," came her father's voice, its muttering tone underscored with both irritation and worry. "This complicates things."

"That's a mild way of putting it," her uncle replied. "Now we'll have to look for some other way to find out what this so-called proof is that the insurance company claims to have. Until we know that, we can't be sure which will be the best way to proceed."

"Why don't you arrange to meet privately with the representatives from the insurance company—somewhere away from the office?" The suggestion came from Gabe. "Use the meeting as a means to express the family's concern about their allegations."

"However valid that reason is, at this stage, Gabe, I don't think it would be wise," Marc Jardin stated. "It could suggest to them that we think there might be some truth to their charges. We could lose a valuable negotiating edge that way."

"Truthfully," her father inserted, "I'm more concerned that the insurance company may carry out its threat to make this whole business about the *Dragon* public. A scandal like that would be extremely damaging."

"I wouldn't worry about that, Dad. You can bet the insurance company wants to avoid that as much as we do. But Marc's right. Before we can take any action, we have to find out what kind of case they have—if any."

"And Buchanan knows it," her father muttered. "That man is so damned cunning."

Remy used the pulsebeat of silence that followed to cross the last few feet to the solarium's open glass doors.

"Good morning." She felt the layer of tension in the room, a tension not betrayed in the smiles of its occupants—her father seated in a cushioned rattan chair, her mother at the serving cart stirring cream into a coffee cup, Gabe at the many-paned windows leaning a shoulder against the white framework, and her uncle, Marc Jardin, standing in the room's center, as if he'd halted in the act of pacing the room. "I'm supposed to inform you that breakfast will be on the table in twenty minutes—and to ask if you'll be joining us, Uncle Marc."

For an instant Remy was struck by the realization that although she recognized who each of them was, she didn't recognize any of them. They were family, yet they were still strangers—people she didn't remember. That was true even of Gabe and her mother. The childhood memories she'd recalled about her brother didn't tell her any more about the man he'd become than the fleeting image she'd remembered of her mother in the rose garden told her about what kind of woman she was. Unconsciously Remy tilted her chin a little higher and mentally tried to shake off the disturbing thoughts.

"I'm afraid I won't be able to stay for breakfast this morning—as much as I would like to indulge in some of Nattie's delicious blueberry muffins. I need to get back to the office." Marc Jardin set his cup and saucer on the serving cart.

Remy spoke up quickly to forestall his departure. "Before I came in, I overheard you talking—something about some allegations the insurance company is making against the shipping line? What's that all about?" As she glanced at each of them, she caught the quick looks they exchanged. "Is it something I'm not supposed to know about?"

"It doesn't matter if you know, Remy," her uncle declared, his smile gentle in its reproof. "They're simply taking issue with a claim we've made. You know how insurance companies are. You pay their outrageous premiums, and then when you file a major claim on a policy, they go through all the fine print to find a way to avoid paying up. Which is precisely what they're doing in this case."

Remy frowned. "But you made it sound so serious—"

"Aaah, Remy." Her uncle sighed a laugh and curved an arm around her shoulder, giving her an affectionate squeeze. "Business is always *very* serious," he declared in an exaggeratedly sober tone, then looked at her father. "Frazier, do you remember when we decided it was time to change the company logo for the Crescent Line? We agonized and worried over that for more than a month."

"Gracious, yes," Sibylle Jardin inserted as she crossed the room to give Gabe the cup of coffee with cream. "The way they carried on and argued, you would have thought the fate of the world hung on their decision."

"See what I mean?" her uncle said, then gave her shoulder a pat and released her. "I've got to be going." Lending action to his words, he walked to the doorway and paused in the opening to look back. "I'll call you as soon as I know something, Frazier."

"Right."

Remy watched him leave, wondering whether the situation with the insurance company was as forthright as he'd made it sound, or if this was the trouble she had sensed. But how could it be? She took no active part in the operations of the shipping company; both Cole and Gabe had made that very clear. Therefore, she wouldn't be needed—not in the vital sense she felt—even if the shipping line were truly experiencing a crisis. It must be something else.

"Would you like some coffee, Remy?"

Remy turned from the now empty doorway. "Please," she said in acceptance, then observed the way her mother lightly pressed a hand on her husband's shoulder as she passed his chair—and the way he reached up and absently patted it—an exchange that spoke of affection given and returned, of a bond apparently strengthened by thirty-five years of marriage.

It made her wonder if she'd observed such exchanges before—or if she'd taken them for granted.

She watched her mother pour coffee from the silver pot into a china cup, noticing the delicate look to her hands, the medium length of her clear-polished nails, and the half-moons at the base of them. The blue veins standing out along the backs of her hands were the only indication of age, their presence betraying an otherwise youthful appearance.

Lifting her glance, Remy saw that it was the same with her mother's face— the initial impression was one of youth, and only a closer look revealed the faintly crepey quality of the skin around the eyes and mouth. Yet none of it detracted from the quiet elegance, the aura of studied grace about her. Or from the inner strength Remy sensed she had—not the "steel magnolia" kind, but something gentler, warmer. She wondered what her relationship with this woman had been like. Had Sibylle Jardin been a role model for her? Had they been close? Somehow Remy couldn't imagine confiding her deepest secrets to the woman, but—she couldn't imagine quarreling with her, either.

As for her father, her relationship with Frazier Jardin was an even bigger mystery, since she remembered absolutely nothing about him. She glanced his way again, seeking some feature, some characteristic, some mannerism that might spark a memory, no matter how small. But there was nothing, nothing but the sight of his face, drawn in sober, thought-filled lines, the darkness of his eyes all shadowed with concern—or was it fear?

"Your coffee, Remy."

Distracted by the prompting statement, she looked away and took the cup and saucer Sibylle Jardin handed her. When she glanced back at her father, he had tipped his head down, and she was even less certain whether what she had detected in his eyes was fear or merely deep worry.

"Do you mind if we all adjourn to the dining room?" Gabe asked, pushing away from the window frame with a shove of his shoulder. "If we stay in here, I don't think I'll be able to resist the temptation to stretch out on that sofa and catch up on some of the sleep I lost flying halfway around the world and back."

"Tired, are you?" Remy smiled at him in sympathy, seeing the shadows, the puffiness around his eyes.

"Tired?" He raised an eyebrow, questioning her choice of words. "I feel like I need toothpicks to prop my eyelids open."

"Don't do it," she advised in mock seriousness. "It would definitely hurt."

"What's a little pain when you're numb with fatigue anyway?" he countered, walking over to her and draping an arm around her shoulders, leaning his weight on her. "I don't suppose I could persuade you to carry me to the dining room, could I?"

"As heavy as you are, I'd collapse before we made it to the door."

"I was afraid you'd say that." He straightened slightly but kept his arm around her, drawing her along with him as he set off for the dining room, followed by their parents. "Tell me, where did you get the energy to go for a walk so early this morning?"

"Easy. I was already halfway around the world; therefore all I had to do was fly back." It was a nonsensical exchange, yet Remy was conscious of how naturally she slipped into it with him. And that ease suggested a closeness between them that had transcended childhood.

"I wish I'd thought of that. Which shows you how tired I am," he said with a mock grimace of dismay. "So—exactly where did you go on this walk of yours?"

"I caught the streetcar and rode to Canal, then strolled through the Quarter. You'd be surprised how peaceful and quiet it is at that hour," she continued. "After that I stopped by the Café du Monde for coffee, then wandered along the riverfront for a while and suddenly found myself at the company wharf."

"The wharf." Beneath the shock in her father's voice, there was censure. "That area is no place for a decent young woman to be walking alone in."

"That was Cole's reaction when he found me there," Remy admitted as she turned in to the dining room, a study in orchid and soft, cool blues. The long walnut table held place settings for four, the richness of the wood gleaming beneath the light from the bronze doré chandelier overhead, a twin to the one in the main salon. On the marble top of the French Empire serving table sat a tall crystal pitcher full of freshly squeezed orange juice, along with four glasses. Remy slipped free of Gabe's draping arm and crossed to the serving table with its mirrored base—a "petticoat" table. "Actually Cole put it a bit more bluntly— something like, 'What the hell are you doing here?'"

"I wondered how you came to be with Buchanan this morning." Her father sat down at the head of the table.

"That's how." Setting her cup and saucer down on the marble top, she picked up the juice pitcher and filled two glasses, one for herself and one for her waiting brother. "Afterward he insisted that I ride to the office with him and take a taxi home from there." She gave Gabe his glass, then picked up her cup and went over to sit down. "But when we—"

"No, not there, Remy," her mother admonished when she started to pull out a chair. "That's where Gabe always sits."

She let go of the carved chair back as if the wood had become hot to the touch. She was stunned to discover how awkward and uncomfortable she suddenly felt. Another scene from another time sprang into her mind, a scene when she was seven or eight years old, a scene where her mother had informed her that she couldn't sit there—"That is Gabe's place"—a scene where she had childishly stomped her foot and protested, "But he always gets to sit next to Daddy."

Remy stared at the chair she'd almost sat in—the chair next to her father— and murmured, "I didn't remember."

"You can sit there, Remy." Gabe motioned her back to the chair. "I don't mind."

"No, I don't think so." She knew she'd be uncomfortable sitting there now. Instead she pulled out another chair, down the table from his. "I'd rather sit here."

"If you say so." He shrugged and sat down in his customary place.

Her father picked up the conversation as if the interlude over the chairs had never occurred. "It's curious that you weren't able to find a taxi at the Trade Mart. Usually there are several around in the morning."

"There were this morning, too," Remy admitted. "But I wanted to see the company offices."

"Why?" He gave her a startled look, his hand halting in the midst of reaching for the glass of orange juice Sibylle had set in front of him.

Rather than attempt to explain the vague feelings that had prompted her visit to the offices of the family's shipping line, Remy said instead, "Curiosity, mainly. I wanted to see if I would remember it."

"And did you?" Gabe asked.

"As a matter of fact, I remembered the portrait of Grand-père that always hung on that one wall," she replied, just as the connecting door between the dining room and kitchen swung open and Nattie walked through, a tray balanced on her upraised palm. Frazier Jardin set his juice glass down again and leaned back in his chair, a smile lifting his somber features.

"Ahh, breakfast at last," he declared lightly. "It smells wonderful, Nattie."

"Of course it does," she retorted, and put a plate in front of him, laden with the morning's fare of eggs Benedict topped by lemony bright hollandaise sauce and garnished with fresh strawberries, raspberries, pineapple, and colorful kiwi. "Whatever I make always smells good and tastes better. You know that, Mr. Frazier."

"My waistline reminds me when I forget," he replied drolly.

Nattie chuckled and continued on to serve his wife.

"By the way," Remy said as she unfolded her napkin onto her lap, "would someone mind telling me who Brodie Donovan is? Cole claimed he started the Crescent Line. Is that true?"

Her father stiffened instantly, resentment and anger in every line of his face. "In the strictest definition, I suppose he did." He sliced off a portion of his eggs Benedict. "The man was a war profiteer who made a fortune running the blockade during the War Between the States. He smuggled in satins and silks, whiskey and wines, and endless other luxuries, selling them for high dollar at a time when the South was begging for medical supplies and drugs, food for the table, and blankets to keep its people warm. The ships, the company name, may have been his in the beginning, but it was a Jardin who made the Crescent Line a respected shipping company," he concluded forcefully, and Nattie made a scornful, disbelieving sound in her throat. Frazier immediately fired a look at her. "Is something wrong, Nattie?"

"Not with me." She set Remy's plate in front of her, then calmly met his gaze. "Is something wrong with you?"

He glared at her for an instant, then Gabe spoke up. "Wasn't it Balzac who said that all great fortunes have been founded on a crime?"

Frazier Jardin turned his sharp look on Gabe as Nattie returned to the kitchen with her empty tray. "That is not amusing, Gabe."

"Sorry." He immediately lowered his head in a show of contrition, secretly directing a quick, smiling glance at Remy.

"All that's in the past, and better left there—regardless of how Buchanan chooses to look at it," Frazier stated curtly.

"Yes, but—" Remy began, wanting to ask him why Cole had said her surname should be Donovan instead of Jardin.

"It's the present we need to discuss," her father interrupted. "Specifically your amnesia, Remy, and what we need to do about it."

"Do about it," she repeated in startled confusion. "What do you mean?"

"When I learned about your condition, I called Dr. John—"

"Who's Dr. John?" The name meant nothing to her.

"Dr. John Lucius Sebastian has been the physician for the Jardin family for years. He took care of your grand-père in his final years and delivered you into this world," he explained patiently. "Even if you can't remember, I'm sure you can appreciate that he's developed a personal interest in you—a fondness for you—over these many years. Naturally he was disturbed to learn about your amnesia. Your mother and I talked with him at length about what could be done. He recommended a clinic located outside of Houston. Their staff has had considerable experience treating cases such as yours."

"Dr. John said it was very beautiful there," Sibylle Jardin inserted. "It's one of those secluded, sylvan settings, peaceful and quiet. Every . . . *guest* . . . has a private cottage on the grounds, complete with maid service and your own private chef if you wish. It's almost like a resort, really."

"Are you suggesting I should go there?" Remy looked from one to the other, not wanting to believe what she was hearing.

"Dr. John assured us that its facilities and its staff are the best to be found anywhere. He knows we wouldn't want anything less for you." Her father calmly carved off another bite of the rich egg dish. "I thought we could fly you over tomorrow. They have their own landing strip—"

"No." Her quick and angry denunciation of his plans sounded unnecessarily loud even to her own ears.

" 'No'? What do you mean?" He seemed stunned by her objection.

"I mean—I'm not going," she replied in a more controlled but no less firm voice.

"But why?" he protested. "You can get the kind of care and treatment you need there. The whole purpose is for you to regain your memory. Surely you want that as much as we do."

"Of course I do."

"Well, they can help you accomplish that, Remy."

"They can't," she argued. "The kind of amnesia I have can't be treated with drugs or psychiatric therapy or hypnosis. Believe me, I inquired about every possibility while I was in that hospital in Nice, trying desperately to find out who I was. Unfortunately my amnesia is caused by brain trauma—the kind that requires time to heal. The specialist was very definite on that point."

"I'm not prepared to accept that," Frazier said. "I think we should have a second opinion. After all, who was this specialist you saw? What were his credentials? How can you be certain he's kept up with all the latest medical advances?"

"I checked." She stabbed at a bite of Canadian bacon drenched in the congealing hollandaise sauce, feeling inexplicably angry and unsure—but at what? At her parents? Why? Weren't they merely acting out of concern for her? Or were they attempting to control her life? Had they done that in the past? Was that what she was subconsciously reacting to?

"If your amnesia is something that requires time to heal, then surely the clinic would provide an ideal setting," her mother suggested. "There you can rest and relax, have an opportunity to recuperate free of any stress."

"I can do that here, Mother," she insisted, then laid down her fork. "Why are you two so anxious to get rid of me? I haven't even been home twenty-four hours yet."

"We're anxious for you to get your memory back, Remy," her mother declared, a pained look in her expression. "It isn't that we don't want you here. We do. But we're trying to think not of ourselves, but of what's best for you."

"The best place for me is right here." Again she was overwhelmed by the feeling that she *had* to be here; it was vital. Just for an instant she wondered whether, if it wasn't for this feeling, she might have let them persuade her to go to the clinic. "I've started remembering things—Gabe, you, Grand-père's portrait. Dr. Gervais told me that familiar surroundings might revive memories for me. What better place than here, in the house I've lived in practically all of my life?"

"I have to agree with Remy." Gabe spoke up for the first time. "If she's starting to remember things, she should stay here with us. Hopefully we can help her to remember more."

"Perhaps," Frazier conceded, indicating a definite coolness toward the idea. "Personally, I'm still not convinced the clinic isn't the best place for her."

"I—" As Remy started to reassert her position, Gabe laid a silencing hand on her arm.

"Let me argue your case. I'm your brother the lawyer, remember?" He winked and gave her arm a reassuring squeeze. Grateful for his support, Remy smiled back and held her silence as he turned to their father. "What time is your committee meeting this morning, Dad?"

"Ten o'clock. Why?"

"I was thinking you could ride downtown with me. It would give us a chance to talk over Remy's situation."

"We've already talked it over."

"So?" Gabe shrugged. "We'll talk it over again. But let's not argue about it now and ruin a perfectly delicious breakfast."

"All right," Frazier Jardin agreed, albeit grudgingly.

No further mention was made about the clinic for the rest of the meal, yet the issue hung in the air with Damoclean insistence. However well-intentioned her parents might be in wanting her to go there, Remy knew she couldn't—and wouldn't. She couldn't leave New Orleans, not until she remembered why it was so important for her to be here.

12

SOON AFTER NATTIE cleared the breakfast plates, Gabe and Frazier Jardin left the dining room together. A few minutes later Remy heard the sound of a car pulling out of the driveway. She took a sip of her coffee, conscious of the silence that had fallen between her and her mother, and of her own odd reluctance to break it.

"Remy," Sibylle began in a hesitant yet momentous tone, "I don't want you to misunderstand about the clinic."

"I'm not going, Mother, and that's final."

"But we only want you to go because we truly believe it's for your own good." She sighed, regretting her initial abruptness. "Thanks for caring, but—"

"Gracious, Remy," her mother broke in with a soft, breathy laugh. "You don't have to thank us for caring. We're your parents. We love you."

"I know." She wished she could remember feeling a similar closeness to them. She wished she could remember this house—this room.

Automatically she looked around it, seeking something familiar in its furnishings. Her glance fell on the footed Sèvres bowl on the serving table, ornately gilded and adorned with a view of the gardens of Versailles, all on a background of royal blue. Intuitively Remy knew that the piece was from the very early 1800s, the golden age of topographical porcelains. And she knew, too, that the footed bowl had long been a family heirloom.

"Did I ever determine whether that bowl was an individual piece or part of a service?" She sensed that the question was one that she would have been lured to investigate.

"You always believed it was part of a service, but I don't recall whether you were ever able to find another piece sufficiently like it in style and design to prove it," her mother replied. "Two or three years ago, however, you were able to locate the source material for the engraving on the bowl. In fact, you obtained a copy of the original painting. It's somewhere about, I'm sure." She lowered her cup to its nesting place on the china saucer and tipped her head curiously to one side. "Why? Have you remembered something?"

She shook her head. "Only that it's been in the family for years."

Sibylle started to respond to that, then stopped. "I almost forgot. Paula called for you this morning. She'd heard you were back and wanted you to come to a little dinner party she's having tonight. Isn't it amazing how fast news travels in this town?"

"Who's Paula?" Remy tried, but she couldn't make the name seem familiar to her.

"Paula Michels. Well, she was a Michels before she married Daryl Gaylord. The two of you have been the dearest of friends since childhood. Actually there were three of you—you and Paula and Jenny D'Anton."

She shook her head in defeat. "I can't remember either of them."

"I'm sure you will . . . in time."

"Yes," Remy murmured, silently wondering how much time it was going to take. "Am I supposed to call Paula back?"

"It isn't necessary. When she told me about the party, I went ahead and made your excuses. I—I hope you don't mind."

"No, that's fine."

"I thought you'd want to spend tonight here at home with us." Something outside the window caught Sibylle's eye. "The florist's van just drove in. I hope the flowers are better than the ones he sent last week. The daisies drooped terribly, and the petals of the day lilies were turning brown around the edges. Unfortunately I was out of the house when the delivery man came, or I never would have accepted them. It was nearly six when I returned home, and by then it was too late to do anything about it. And the Girards and the D'Antons were due to arrive for dinner in less than two hours. At seven o'clock, there I was, trimming the brown off the lilies and wrapping wire around the drooping stems of the daisies, trying to salvage something so we would have a few fresh bouquets in the house. Worse than that, the roses didn't last three days. I warned Robert that if this week's flowers weren't absolutely exceptional, I was returning them en masse and taking our business elsewhere." She removed the linen napkin from her lap and laid it beside her coffee cup and saucer. "Excuse me while I inspect today's delivery."

"Of course." Remy watched her leave the room. With her own coffee finished, she had no desire to linger at the table by herself. Leaving the dining room, she drifted aimlessly across the wide central hall into the main salon.

For all the subtle grandness and the touches of antiquity in the high-ceilinged room, it had a comfortable, lived-in quality. Magazines cluttered the Louis Napoleon console, and a lap robe of white cashmere lay carelessly draped over the back of a Victorian sofa covered in a vibrant plum brocade and flanked by matching chairs. Next to the tufted easy chair, upholstered in a cream velvet material with a thin purple stripe running through it, stood her mother's petit-point frame, and beside it her tapestry sewing bag.

A walnut whatnot desk sat in the corner by a window. Remy wandered over to it and idly ran her hand over the top, wondering if she'd sat here to do her schoolwork, and stared out the full-length window instead. Briefly she touched the pale orchid sheers, then smiled when she noticed the puddling of the orchid damask draperies on the floor—a typical yet subtle display of wealth in the old plantation days, and a tradition that had once more become fashionable. Turning, she looked again at the room, noting the black marble fireplace and the Oriental rug on the floor, its strong tones repeating the richness of color in the room.

How many hours had she spent in this room? Hundreds, no doubt. Yet nothing in it stirred up memories.

Suppressing a sigh at the continued blankness, Remy crossed to the entrance hall, which was dominated by the graceful curve of the grand mahogany staircase. Her glance strayed upward to the ornate frieze that outlined the ceiling and the elaborate plumed medallion from which the bronze doré chandelier was suspended. The walls were covered with a scenic wallpaper, its blue panorama a replica of a historical design made famous by Dufour. A Brussels carpet stretched the length of the hall's cypress flooring.

Something flickered along the edges of her mind, and she closed her eyes. The image she saw was the same one before her now—except that boughs of shiny green magnolia leaves were wound around the stairs' carved balustrade. She heard the echoes of giggles and saw herself scampering down the steps, trying to reach the bottom ahead of Gabe. Papa Noël had come. Papa Noël. Yes—as a very little girl, she had called Santa Claus by his French name.

From the mists of that memory came another, of the Carnival season of her debutante year, when she'd glided down the steps in her ball gown, a stunning creation in white satin and lace studded with shimmering beadwork and rhinestones—and another time in a different ball gown, adorned with snowy aigrettes and pearls. To her mother's glorious delight, Remy had been named Queen of two balls, an honor so rare as to be almost without precedent—and an indication of the power and prestige attached to the Jardin name.

Frowning, Remy tried to recall what her feelings had been toward it all. Had she enjoyed the whole social whirl of parties, suppers, and balls, or had she participated grudgingly, regarding the entire business of being presented to "society" as outdated in today's liberated world? Neither one—she'd seen it as a duty, and her acceptance of that duty as a recognition of her family . . . just as her failure to be accorded honors would have been a reflection on them.

"Certain things are expected of you because you are a Jardin." She heard the words in her mind, but she couldn't remember who had spoken them. Yet they stayed there, softly ringing, subtly applying a pressure that she felt even now.

Remy opened her eyes, breaking the spell. And the entrance hall became once again merely the entrance hall of a mansion, faintly haunted by long-ago memories. She hesitated a moment longer, then walked across the Brussels carpet, past the base of the staircase, to the double set of doors opening onto the gentlemen's study.

Pausing a few feet inside the room, Remy let the rich loden green of the walls close around her. A pair of freestanding walnut bookcases flanked the fireplace, again made of black Carrara marble artfully streaked with gray. Near the windows stood a library table of dark ebony and tooled black leather. The deep colors, the heavy solidity of the furniture, and the leather-covered sofa and chairs gave the room a definite masculine aura that appealed to her.

She wandered over to an old platform rocker, covered in dark green leather and studded with brass. On the ebony side table next to it was a well-thumbed copy of Virgil's *Aeneid*. She ran her hand lightly over its worn cover, then caught the faint, fragrant aroma of tobacco, and her glance was drawn to the walnut pipe stand next to the book.

Images flashed through her mind like pictures caught by the shutter of a rapidly clicking camera. She tried to focus on the images and hold on to this rush of memory merging with the background. Suddenly she could see her father relaxing in the rocker, not a single strand of his dark, curly hair out of place. His somber features wore a smile of pride and approval as he reached out to take something from her.

The pipe. Unerringly Remy picked up an old briar pipe, its stem half chewed, its charred bowl scraped clean of tobacco ash and char. Beside it sat a sterling-silver tamper with his initials etched on it—the one she'd given him for Christmas when she was twelve years old. Remy looked down at the rocker, remembering, hearing the texture of her father's voice, warm with praise and affection. The love in it filled her—just as it had done all those years ago.

Her mother walked into the study, carrying a Baccarat vase filled with a spray of white tulips, their ivory color accented by lacy green fronds of maidenhair fern and delicate baby's breath. Seeing Remy, she faltered slightly in surprise.

"You startled me. I didn't realize anyone was in here." She went over to the library table and placed the vase on one corner of the tooled leather top. "Aren't these white tulips magnificent? Robert sent them as a gesture of atonement for last week's floral fiasco. I thought they'd look perfect in here, and I know your father will enjoy them."

"I remember him, Mother." She was too caught up in the wonder of the memory to care about the bouquet of rare white tulips. "I remember Dad." No longer was he a stranger to her, a face without significance, a name without personal meaning. "He used to let me fill his pipe with tobacco—and he showed me how to pack it so it would draw properly. He wouldn't let anyone else do it but me—because I was the only one who could do it right." She gazed at the pipe in her hand, conscious of the lump in her throat, a lump that came with the discovery of how much she loved him, how much she adored him.

Before, she hadn't been sure what her feelings for him had been—if they'd been close. Had he cared? Or had Gabe, his son, been the recipient of all his attention? Now she knew. "This is his favorite pipe," she remembered.

"Yes . . . unfortunately. I've been wanting to throw that smelly thing away for years, but Frazier won't hear of it. Why? I'll never know. It isn't as if he doesn't have others," Sibylle declared, waving a hand at the numerous pipes in the walnut rack.

"You don't know how relieved I am," Remy confessed. "It's bothered me that I couldn't remember him."

Sibylle smiled gently in understanding. "It's bothered him too . . . as I'm sure you guessed. He was very worried about you, Remy. And he felt guilty that we'd left Nice assuming you'd gone off on your own for a few days—as you'd planned to do. When we finally realized something was wrong, he kept insisting over and over that we should have known you wouldn't have left the yacht without telling us good-bye."

"He shouldn't have blamed himself for that."

"I know, but he did. And it only added to an already stressful situation. He let it work on him. For that matter, he still is." She fussed with the floral arrangement, adjusting a tulip stem here and moving a frond there. "I'm certain that's why he was so sharp with you at breakfast."

"You mean when I argued with him about going to the clinic," Remy guessed.

Sibylle threw a startled look over her shoulder, then quickly tried to cover it with a hasty, "Yes, that too."

Remy knew immediately that she had guessed wrong. "You were referring to when I asked about Brodie Donovan, weren't you?"

After a brief hesitation, Sibylle admitted, "Actually, I was." She turned back to the flowers. "I do wish you hadn't asked your father about him—although it wasn't really your fault. That Cole Buchanan's responsible for resurrecting that whole thing. He had no right to take your grand-père's portrait down and put that other one in its place. It may be a terrible thing to say, Remy, but I hope you never remember any part of the attachment you once had for him. I was so afraid you were going to do something foolish—" She let the rest of the sentence hang unfinished.

"Like marry him?" Remy suggested, suddenly realizing that Sibylle Jardin would find it impossible to approve of a man with Cole's background.

Her mother turned from the vase of tulips. "Remy, is it so wrong for me to want to see you safely married to a good man?"

Remy had the feeling "acceptable" should have been parenthetically inserted after "good." "Mother, I could never marry *safely*," she protested with a faint laugh.

"Security is not something to be scoffed at. Marriage comes with no assurance of happiness, Remy. For a woman it's always better to love wisely."

"Is that what you did, Mother?" She found herself becoming angry.

"I am devoted to your father, and he to me. We have had thirty-five wonderful years together," she replied in quick defense. "And a great part of that is due to the many things we share in common—the same backgrounds, the same set of friends—"

"The same views on what and who is acceptable," Remy inserted. "Forgive me, but I find this conversation disgusting."

She turned on her heel and started from the room. But before she had taken three steps, her mother was there, catching her arm.

"Remy, I'm sorry. I truly didn't mean to offend you with the things I said," she declared, looking genuinely contrite. "I may have sounded like a snob, but I've seen what happens when two people from vastly different backgrounds marry. I've seen the embarrassment, the gaucherie, the stiltedness at social gatherings, and the valiant attempts to bridge the two levels. Soon it doesn't matter how exciting the marriage may be in the bedroom. In reality, the bedroom makes up only a small portion of a marriage. If it can't survive outside the bedroom, ultimately it won't survive at all. That's why I'm glad you didn't make a disastrous mistake with that Buchanan man. Do you understand?"

Remy nodded, slowly, a little stiffly. "I understand."

"I hope so." She curved her hand along Remy's cheek. "I know you're finished with him, and I'm sorry I brought up his name."

She was finished with him. Everyone was saying that, including Cole. Yet this morning on the dock, when she'd seen that container ship and recalled their previous visit to it, she'd remembered how completely she had loved him and how furious she'd been at his insinuations that his background was somehow a barrier between them. And she'd remembered, too, how his mouth had come down on hers in a claiming kiss. Even now she could feel the sensation of its lingering heat.

Afterward, when he'd lifted his head and she'd seen his dazzling smile, she'd forcefully declared, "I love you, Cole Buchanan. Nothing and no one will ever change that."

But something *had* changed it. And that part of her memory was blank.

"You look tired, Remy. It's to be expected, though, considering you were up and about before the sun," Sibylle chided gently, and she tucked a hand under Remy's arm, guiding her toward the hall. "Why don't you lie down awhile and get some rest?"

"Maybe I will." But Remy wasn't sure it was fatigue she was feeling as she let Sibylle walk her from the study to the entrance hall.

Her mother stopped at the base of the curved staircase. "You do that, and I'll go take care of my flowers. The house will be brimming with them when you come down—the way I wanted it to be when you came home."

Remy watched her move off in the direction of the solarium, then turned and climbed the winding steps to the second-floor hall. The door to her bedroom stood open. As Remy approached it, she heard someone moving around inside, humming an old jazz tune and injecting a lyric here and there. She immediately recognized Nattie's voice and smiled, entering the room as the woman proclaimed in song, " 'I got Elgin movements in my hips with twenty years' guarantee.' "

"Only twenty years?" Remy teased as Nattie reached for the remaining pillow lying at the head of the antique tester bed. "That's a shame."

Nattie shot a startled look at her, then straightened up and moved her hands onto her hips. "Have you come up here to lie down?" she challenged. "Because if you have, there's no sense in me making up this bed."

Remy glanced at the bed, all its covers thrown back and its feather pillows piled on the floor. She couldn't imagine herself doing anything but tossing and turning in it, regardless of what she'd thought when she came up here.

"No, I think I'll shower and change into something else," she replied, and she began unbuttoning her double-breasted jacket of black wool. Nattie leaned across the mattress again to pull the last pillow off the bed. "Do you do all the housework too, Nattie?"

"Me? Clean this big house?" Nattie shook and punched the plumpness back into the pillow, then tossed it on the floor with the others. "There wouldn't be enough time in the day. No, you've got dailies that come in twice a week to do all the cleaning and washing. Me, I make the beds, cook the meals, and keep things tidy."

"I wondered." Shrugging out of her blazer, Remy walked to the closet, crossing the Aubusson rug, patterned in the room's soft greens and golds. She opened the door and walked into the large closet. As she took down a shaped coat hanger, she looked around the closet and frowned. "I thought these old homes didn't have closets."

"That used to be an alcove. Back in your grand-père's day, his daddy boxed it in and made it a closet." Nattie's answer was accompanied by the sound of the top sheet being whipped over the mattress.

Remy fitted the jacket onto the hanger, fastening a button and hanging it on the rack with other tops. "How long have you worked for the family, Nattie?" she asked when she emerged from the closet.

"Come the third of November, it'll be twenty years." She smoothed the top sheet and deftly turned its hem back in a precise crease.

"The third of November. Is it so memorable that you know the exact date?" She walked over to the bed and leaned a shoulder against one of the carved mahogany posts at the foot of it.

"I know because I went to work for your family two days after I lost my restaurant, and that was on All Saints' Day." She said it very matter-of-factly, yet her long fingers hesitated in their edging of the sheet.

"You had a restaurant." Remy wondered if she'd known that.

"For six months I did. It was a fine place, too. I called it Natalie's—'course I gave my name the French pronunciation. I thought it would make a better impression on folks." She paused a moment, her expression taking on a faraway look, and then she laughed, and the laugh had a self-deprecating ring. "Why, when I opened those doors, I thought in no time at all folks would be saying Natalie's in the same breath with Antoine's and Brennan's. Which shows what big ideas I had."

"What happened?"

"I went broke, that's what happened. All that schooling I had in France in haute cuisine, all those years working in the kitchens of those other fine restaurants doing prep work when I knew I was better than those men chefs, all my dreams"—she lifted her shoulders in a shrug that Remy knew couldn't be as indifferent as it appeared—"gone."

"Why?" she protested, experiencing some of the hurt Nattie must have felt.

"It goes back to that same old thing—you put a man in a kitchen and people call him a chef; you put a woman in a kitchen and she's a cook. And when you put a black woman in a kitchen, people expect her to cook soul food. They want to see neck bones, gizzards, oxtails, and dirty rice on the menu, not potage of cauliflower with caviar, roast duck in port sauce, or feuillet of squab. There I was, broke, in debt up to my ears, with a nine-year-old girl to raise. My grandma had worked for your grand-père for nearly forty years. She got me this job here, and here's where I've been ever since."

"I'm sorry, Nattie."

Again she shrugged, pulling the quilted comforter over the sheets. "That's the way it goes sometimes."

Remy shook her head in vague bewilderment. "How can you sound so casual about it? You have to be disappointed, hurt, angry, bitter—something."

"I feel all those things and a few more," Nattie admitted. "I just don't show it like you do. People who are born poor and raised poor don't. It's been bred out of us, probably because there's too many things that can break our hearts. Having crying jags, throwing tantrums, getting all blue and low, that's for wealthy people who can afford it."

Remy immediately thought of Cole, remembering that steel control he had over his feelings—so much control that she'd wondered if he felt anything deeply. Maybe Nattie had just given her the answer to that as well as to his cynicism.

Thinking of Cole reminded her of the things he'd said about Brodie Donovan —and Nattie's reaction to the explanation her father had given. "At the breakfast table, when my father was talking about Brodie Donovan, I had the feeling you didn't believe him."

"I didn't." She took the pillows from the floor and piled them two deep at the head of the bed.

"Why?"

"Because that's not the way it was."

Remy frowned at her. "How do you know?"

Nattie looked at her and smiled sagely. "The folks who come into this house through the front door, they see the big white pillars, the mahogany staircase, and the crystal prisms dangling from the chandelier. But the folks who come in the back door, they know where the dirt is."

Unable to contest such a keen observance, Remy instead asked, "But why would my father tell me something that wasn't true?"

"Probably a case of wishful thinking." She flipped the quilted coverlet over the pillows and tucked the edge behind them. "Sometimes you want a thing to be so, and you wind up pretending it is. A lot of families rewrite their history that way. Look at what happened back when New Orleans was struggling to become a town and the men were wanting women to marry them. The French government sent eighty-eight over here, all of them inmates from La Salpetriere. Correction girls, they called them. Then, seven years later, in seventeen twenty-eight, the government started sending girls picked from middle-class families, who had some housewifely skills. They were known as casket girls because of these little chests filled with their clothes and such that they brought with them. And today you'd be surprised how many fine old Creole families can trace their ancestry to one of them casket girls. But all of them correction girls must have been sterile—not one of them has any descendants. Amazing, isn't it?"

"Very," Remy agreed, smiling, then she became serious once more. "Tell me what you know about Brodie Donovan, Nattie. Who was he? Did he start the Crescent Line? How did the Jardins acquire it from him?"

"Let's see. . . . " Nattie picked up a throw pillow covered in the same pastel yellow-and-green floral print as the coverlet, and paused as if gathering her thoughts. "I don't know how much you can remember about New Orleans' history, or whether that's been lost along with the rest of your memory, but back in the early part of the eighteen-thirties, shortly after the four-mile-long Pontchartrain Railroad between the city and the lake was built, some businessmen from the city's new American section decided to dig a canal through the swamps so the melon schooners and other ships from Mobile could have a shortcut to the Mississippi River. Raising the money for the six-mile-long canal wasn't a problem, but finding the labor to dig it was. They couldn't use slaves, for a couple of reasons. You see, by then it was against the law to bring Negroes from Africa into the country to be used as slaves, which meant they'd have to buy slaves that were already here. Considering that they needed thousands for the job, that was too expensive—especially because they knew a lot of the slaves would likely die from working in the swamp."

"Why would they die?"

"Well, think how miserable the working conditions were back then—the sweltering heat, thigh-deep mud, and swarming insects, not to mention the snakes and gators. And don't forget, yellow fever was the scourge of Louisiana in those days," Nattie reminded her. "It wasn't until after the turn of the century that they discovered that mosquitoes carried the disease. Before that, most people thought yellow fever was caused by 'effluvia' from marshy grounds like swamps.

"Anyway, they decided black slaves were too valuable to work in such a place," she continued. "So the next-best thing was to import laborers from Ireland. It wasn't long before ship after ship started arriving in New Orleans, crowded with Irish workers.

"Brodie Donovan was fifteen when he got here in eighteen thirty-five along with his father and three of his brothers. Like most of the Irish, they went to work digging the canal. Within a year he lost a brother to yellow fever and his father to cholera. In the seven years it took to build the canal, thousands died from cholera and yellow-fever epidemics. For a time there were so many bodies they just tossed them in wheelbarrows and dumped them in graves dug along the banks of the canal." Nattie paused a moment to reflect. "It's kind of ironic when you think about it, but the prevailing attitude back then was, who cared if an Irishman died? There was always another waiting to take his place.

"Brodie Donovan was an old man of twenty by the time that New Basin Canal was finally finished. He and his brothers went to work on the wharves. According to my grandma"—Nattie laid the pillow on the bed, propping it against the headboard—"Brodie Donovan first dreamed of owning his own ship during the voyage from Liverpool to New Orleans. That may be true, but I figure it stayed only a dream until he went to work on the riverfront."

A faint musing smile edged her mouth, and her eyes took on a faraway look. "The riverfront of old New Orleans must have been a sight to see back in those days. 'The master street of the world,' they called it then. Vessels of every size and kind—clipper ships, ocean schooners, river packets, cutters, steamboats, smacks, flatboats—they lined the levee for four and five miles, tied two and three deep sometimes. I think Brodie Donovan saw the steamboats arriving, with every available inch mounded with cotton bales, and he talked with rivermen, heard them tell about all the bales waiting upriver for transport to

New Orleans and beyond. He saw, and he heard, and—he turned his dream into a plan.

"After about a year on the riverfront, he and his brothers left New Orleans and went upriver to Bayou Sara. There they got a contract from a local planter to clear a section of wooded land he owned; their payment was the timber from it. They used that timber to build themselves a flatboat. Then they loaded it with cotton and floated down the Mississippi to New Orleans, where they sold their cargo and the flatboat. They went right back upriver and did it all over again. After just three trips, they bought an old steamboat. Two years later they bought another, then two more each year after that. Finally, in eighteen forty-seven, Brodie got his first oceangoing ship—a schooner. And that was the start of the Crescent Line."

"It sounds like the American dream," Remy declared.

"It was." Nattie nodded in emphasis. "After a couple of voyages with his schooner, he sold off his riverboats and bought more ships, bringing his total to four within a year. A remarkable feat when you consider that less than fifteen years before that he'd been wading in mud digging a canal."

"But how did the Jardin family get the shipping line? And why did Cole tell me my surname should be Donovan, not Jardin?"

"That's because of Adrienne."

"Who's Adrienne?"

"Adrienne Louise Marie Jardin," Nattie replied. "She was one of those dark-haired, dark-eyed Creole beauties people like to write stories about. Both her parents died when she was a baby—victims of a yellow-fever epidemic. Adrienne and her older brother, Dominique, were raised by their grand-père Emil Gaspard Jardin and a maiden aunt they called Tante ZeeZee.

"Now, you gotta understand there've been Jardins in New Orleans almost from the beginning, back in seventeen eighteen. By the time Brodie Donovan met up with the Jardins, they owned a lot—real estate in the city, bank stock, a cotton plantation in Feliciana Parish, and a couple of sugar plantations south of Baton Rouge, just to name some of the larger things."

"In other words, they were wealthy," Remy inserted.

Nattie snorted. "Hmmph, they were one of the wealthiest Creole families in the city."

"You said Brodie Donovan met up with the Jardins. When was this?"

"He met *Adrienne,*" Nattie corrected. "The year was eighteen hundred and fifty-two. . . ."

13 ⌒

LIKE A FOREST of barren timber, the high, proud masts of the ocean steamers and sailing ships lined the levee, towering against the blue sky, the gray canvas of their sails tightly furled. Their decks and gangplanks seethed with activity, stevedores scurrying back and forth, darky roustabouts shuffling, their bodies canted sideways by the weight of the cargo carried on their shoulders, sea captains pacing in impatience, more roustabouts rolling bales of cotton up the staging and into the holds, press gangs forcing more bales into the ships with their powerful cotton screws, and sailors in the garb of a dozen different nations sauntering ashore or staggering back on board. And the noise, the endless, deafening noise, a cacophony of shouts and curses, hooting laughter and challenging brag, "coonjine" songs and work-gang chanteys, clanging bells and deep-throated steam whistles.

And the wind carried it all, a wind heavy with the ultrasweet odor of molasses and pungent with spices, a wind that stirred up floating wisps of cotton from the mountainous piles of bales stacked on the levee, dotting the air with them.

From the vantage of the levee, Brodie Donovan viewed it all—its jostle, its din, its smells, and its energy familiar to him, more familiar than his own home. He raised a hand in a saluting wave to the captain on the deck of the *Crescent Glory*, then turned his back to the scene and adjusted his hold on the small, flat bundle he carried in his left hand.

Directly ahead of him stretched the tightly packed buildings and narrow streets of the city's old French section, still the bastion of aristocratic Creole families. Canal Street—so named for the ditch, actually a kind of moat (but never a canal), that had once run its length, when New Orleans was a walled city—was the unofficial dividing line that separated the old quarter from the brash and bustling American section, now the city's commercial center. The offices for his shipping company, the Crescent Line, were located in the American section, and most days he would have turned and headed up the levee in that direction. But not today. Today he had an errand in the Vieux Carré.

Striding easily, he went down the levee's sloping bank, past the tin-roofed shanties stocked with cheap trinkets for the sailors, past the grog-shops with their many eager customers, and past the oyster stands. The street beyond was clogged with freight wagons, the river commerce turning New Orleans into a city of drays pulled by mules in tandem.

As Brodie picked his way between them to the other side, he recognized some of the drivers and called easy greetings to them, lapsing into a heavy brogue. "Hey, O'Shaughnessy, why would you be holding your head like that? Was it too much to drink you had last night?" "Micheleen, tell your pretty missus I'll be stopping by for some of her scones—when you're not home, of course!" "Is that a black eye you got there, Dolan? Did you forget to duck again?"

And they responded in kind: "Well, if it ain't himself—or should we be calling you Your Honor now?" "Would you look at the vest he's wearing? 'Tis fancy he's getting." "What would you be carrying in that package, Donovan? Lace kerchiefs for to be blowing your nose with, maybe."

There was affection in their gibes, affection and pride for one of their own who'd made good—and hadn't forgotten them. Like Brodie, the Irish draymen were survivors of the bloody ditch, as they called the canal.

He may have been one of them, but he wasn't like them. And the difference lay in more than the fineness of the black frock coat and brocade vest he wore, or the flat-crowned black hat on his head and the gleaming leather of his boots. The difference had been there even when he was dressed as shabbily as they.

True, Brodie felt the same strong loyalty to his own that they did, and had his moments of dark moodiness, though they were rare. He loved a good laugh and his temper could be quick. And like them he was fiercely independent, but that need for independence had directed him on a different path and turned his thinking in other directions.

Sure, he'd slogged through the ditch's muck and mire beside them, smelled the foul stench of the swamp and the rotting corpses along its banks, and fallen into his cot at night bathed in his own sweat. But never once in that swamp had he thought of Ireland's green valleys and sparkling brooks—not like they had. For him, the thought that had kept him going, that had given purpose to the sweat and weariness and death around him, was the dream that someday *his* ships would steam through the canal he'd dug . . . ships like the one he'd sailed on to America. He'd dreamed it, and the riverfront had shown him how he could make it happen. A roundabout way, to be sure—first flatboats, then riverboats, and finally his ships. But he'd learned that there was always a way, even if it wasn't a direct one.

Leaving the bedlam of the riverfront behind, Brodie entered the old quarter, his glance straying to the new triple spires of the St. Louis Cathedral, which replaced the old bell towers, changing the area's skyline—a change made even more pronounced by the recently added mansard roofs of the Cabildo and the Presbytère and the twin three-story, redbrick and wrought-iron structures built in the Renaissance style by the red-haired Baroness Pontalba, housing magnificent apartments in its upper floors. Brodie doubted they would be the last changes the old Place d'Armes would see. There was currently a lot of talk about changing its name to Jackson Square in honor of the hero of the Battle of New Orleans. It would happen. Americans now held the majority of seats on the city council, and they'd see that it did—the Creoles be damned.

Two more strides and his view of the spires was lost, buildings rising up on either side of the narrow street, their facades smoothly stuccoed and painted in mellow shades of peach or blue or pink, all of them dominated by their tall double-storied galleries, supported by iron posts set in the curb and edged by waist-high railings of delicate iron filigree in a dozen different designs. Brodie walked beneath the overhanging galleries, shaded from the sun, which gave a springlike warmth to the morning in place of winter's usual gray damp.

Drays rumbled and rattled over the dirt streets, occasionally sharing the muddy thoroughfare with fancy carriages pulled by high-stepping blooded horses in gleaming harnesses. Directly ahead, a white overseer with a whip supervised the rare cleaning of the street's cypress-lined drainage ditches by a gang of chained and collared slaves—runaways, most likely.

Brodie continued along the brick sidewalk—a banquette, the Creoles called it—past neat little shops and slave pens with heavily barred windows, past corner fruit stands and flower stalls, past travelers ogling the sights of the renowned city, past young, richly dressed sons of aristocratic Creole families, perhaps en route to fencing lessons with some of the many masters who ran schools on Exchange Street, or merely off to share a cup of coffee with friends, and past an ivory-skinned and incredibly beautiful mulattress—a *femme de couleur*, a free woman of color, her status declared by the brightly colored madras kerchief wrapped around her head like a turban, her eyes properly downcast, her satins and jewels closeted in her little house along the ramparts to await the pleasure of her white lover. Brodie touched a hand to the brim of his hat and nodded a *Bonjour* to a young Creole miss and her glaring chaperone, noting the quickly averted glance and smiling to himself at the hastily whispered *"Yanqui."*

To the Creoles of Louisiana, all Americans, regardless of their origin, fell into two categories: the unlettered, uncouth, and hell-roaring river crowd were all *"Kaintucks,"* and the rest—the merchants, the planters, the wealthy, and the scholars—were *"Yanquis."* To the first, the Creoles turned an icy shoulder, but as for the second—well, time, the overwhelming numbers of Yankees, and, most of all, economic circumstances had forced them to develop a tolerance of them. They did business with the Yankees, drank coffee with them, and attended the same social functions, but rarely was a Yankee invited to dine in their home. True, marriages between Yankees and Creoles had taken place, but Brodie had observed that in most cases such marriages were largely to the benefit of the Creole family, the union either bringing with it desired holdings or cementing a liaison of particular interests.

The Americans and the Creoles represented two totally different cultures. After nearly fifty years, they'd learned to coexist—warily at times, occasionally clashing, but always competing, however subtly.

Unlike most of his counterparts in the American section, Brodie had taken the time to learn the Creoles' language, though he often found it to his advantage to pretend he neither spoke nor understood it—at least not as well as he did. And he'd learned to control his impatience and not press for a decision on some business matter, instead allowing the conversation to follow leisurely lines before finally arriving at the subject—if it did at all. As a result, a good share of his business came from the Quarter, and several valuable contacts in Europe as well. Yes, he did a lot of business in the Quarter, but not all of it with aristocrats.

On the corner a blind Negro played his violin, his curly gray hair bared to the sun, his slouch hat turned upside down on the brick banquette in front of him, and a pair of black-lensed spectacles partially concealing the heavy scarring around his eyes. Brodie stopped and dropped a dollar into his hat.

"Merci." The old man bobbed his head the instant he heard the clink of the silver coin against the smaller ones.

"How goes it with you, Cado?" Brodie interrupted, addressing the old free Negro in French.

There was a quick cocking of the old man's head at the sound of his voice. *"Michie Donovan,"* he said in immediate recognition of the voice, addressing him by the Negro's gumbo contraction for *Monsieur* as he continued to saw the bow over the strings, never once missing a note. "Old Cado is fine, suh, especially today with the sun warming my old, tired bones."

"Is there any talk going around?"

"There's a lot of weeping and praying at the Gautier house on Royal. The young Michie Gautier, he took offense at some little thing said by a planter from upriver. They met at dusk under the oaks. Now blood bubbles from the young Michie's wound where the planter's rapier pierced his chest."

"A punctured lung," Brodie murmured, then asked, "Is there nothing else?"

A small grin appeared. "Michie Varnier from the Julian plantation lost fifty thousand last night in a game of brag. I think he'd sell his cotton cheap today."

Brodie allowed a faint smile to curve his mouth. "You play beautiful music, Cado." And he dropped two more dollars into the old man's hat.

"So do you, Michie Donovan. So do you." The old black man chuckled and immediately launched into a few bars of an Irish jig tune as Brodie moved away.

At the curb, Brodie waited for two heavy drays to clatter by, then stepped into the muddy street and hailed the next one. The driver hauled back on the reins and called a whoa to his mules, cussing them out in a fine Gaelic voice as Brodie climbed onto the running board and balanced himself there, tucking the bundle he carried tightly under his arm and taking a pencil and notepaper from inside his coat pocket.

"Would you swing by the Crescent Line office for me, Flannery, and give this message to my brother Sean?" He hastily scratched it on the paper, folded it, and handed it to the drayman, ignoring angry shouts and raised fists from the drivers of other wagons that had been forced to halt as well.

"Sure I'll be doing it for you, but it's a whiskey you'll owe me, Brodie Donovan," the red-headed Flannery declared as Brodie hopped down.

"Get it in Sean's hands in ten minutes and 'tis a bottle I'll buy you—and not tell your wife."

" 'Tis a deal you've got, and I'll be holding you to it." He cracked the whip above the long ears of the mule team and slapped the reins on their rumps, urging them forward with shouts and curses and hollering at the wagons ahead of him to "Make way!"

Dodging the freight wagons that quickly filled Flannery's breach, Brodie crossed to the other side of the street and walked down two doors to the millinery shop of Madame Rideaux, where a small sign in the window promised the latest in styles from Paris. The fulfillment of that promise was wrapped in the bundle under his arm—the most current fashion plates from France, only two weeks old, courtesy of his ship the *Crescent Glory*.

He stepped inside and closed the door behind him, then started toward the rear of the shop, automatically scanning the front area for the henna-haired proprietress who wavered so insecurely between the unctuous smiles of a shopkeeper and the haughty airs of a customer. His eye was first caught by the shimmer of velvet the deep, rich color of garnet. It drew his glance to a young woman clad in a velvet walking dress, her back turned to him as she tried on hats in front of a freestanding counter mirror. Brodie noticed two things simultaneously: the small span of her waist, accented by the wide circle the skirt made, and the jet-black of her hair, in lieu of the typical dark-brown color of most Creole women's tresses. Obviously she had some Spanish blood mixed in somewhere.

In the next stride, Brodie saw her reflection in the mirror and halted abruptly, stopped by a sharp kick of feeling that momentarily stunned him. There was a perfection to her oval features that he could only liken to that of a cameo, her expression serenely composed yet possessing a subtle vibrancy that gave immediate life to her face. He stared, knowing he had to find out who she was but unwilling to move from this spot, for the moment content to gaze at her.

Suppressing a sigh of dissatisfaction, Adrienne Jardin laid the bonnet aside and picked up a dress cap of pearl-colored silk, trimmed with a wreath of velvet leaves, flowers, and ribbons. She slipped it on, first letting the ribbons hang, then tying them in a loose bow. As she turned her head slightly to view her side reflection, she saw another face in the mirror—a man's face. For the briefest of seconds her eyes locked with his in the mirror. A small crease appeared between his dark eyebrows, his glance flicking to the bonnet, as he gave a faint shake of his head in disapproval.

Adrienne immediately broke eye contact with him and fixed her gaze on her own reflection, stiffening in annoyance at the man's boldness, his rudeness. No doubt he was a Yankee. Did he think his opinion of the bonnet mattered to her?

To make matters worse, she discovered she didn't like the bonnet, either. She kept it on a little longer, playing with the ribbons, tucking a dark curl in here and rearranging another there, trying to make it clear, when she finally did take it off and lay it aside, that her decision hadn't been influenced by his reaction to it. All the while, she pretended to take no notice of his reflection in the mirror, acting as if her peripheral vision hadn't observed his wide and slanted brow, the slight break in his otherwise straight nose, his well-formed chin, which neither jutted nor receded, his high, broad cheekbones, and his sharply angled jaws— or the deep mahogany red of his hair beneath his black hat, and the dark brown of his eyes. Honesty forced her to concede that he was handsome—in that rough, raw way Yankees usually were.

As she picked up a white silk bonnet trimmed with satin roses and white lace, Adrienne wondered what he was doing in Madame Simone's shop. She remembered hearing the shop door open, but she had no idea whether he had entered alone or with another. Had he accompanied his wife, perhaps? Or his sister? Or his demimondaine? The last seemed most likely. There was a picaresque quality about him that would prompt him to appear in public with such a woman.

Discreetly Adrienne scanned the interior of the shop, turning her head this way and that as if inspecting all angles of the silk bonnet on her head, while bringing every corner of the room into view. But *non*, there was only Tante ZeeZee at the counter with a patient clerk, engaged in what was, for her, an agonizing decision over which pair of gloves to purchase. As if gloves would help her appearance, Adrienne thought with a sudden twinge of pity for the woman who had raised her. Poor Tante ZeeZee had inherited Grand-père's very prominent nose, a feature that on him looked most noble, but on her . . . Adrienne understood why her aunt had acquired such an inordinate fondness for the jade-green absinthe.

She looked again at her own reflection, discovering that she was back to her original question: what was the Yankee doing in Madame Simone's shop— alone? Had he business with the proprietress? But of what kind? He was too well dressed to be a tradesman, and he hadn't asked after the woman, who had been called to the rear of the shop to handle some minor emergency in the cutting room.

With rising curiosity, Adrienne let her glance stray again to his reflection. Again eye contact was made, and again she saw the faint frown and slight shake of his head, rejecting the latest bonnet. And yet again, Adrienne pretended to take no notice of him. She recognized that it would be a simple matter to move to another mirror, but that would be an admission that she was aware of his attentions, and she didn't want to give him the satisfaction of knowing she was in any way affected by his presence. It was always best to ignore these Yankees.

Yet sheer perversity prompted her to try on a singularly unattractive bonnet with an extra brim, reminiscent of a calash and appropriately called an "ugly."

The mirror showed that it was all of that and more. She allowed the barest trace of a smile to touch her lips as she darted a quick look at the Yankee. His eyes were downcast, as if he were hiding the humor in them, while his mouth twitched with a smile, bringing into play a pair of very attractive creases in his cheeks. Again there was a shake of his head, but this time it seemed to be more an expression of amusement.

Hiding her own smile, Adrienne removed the bonnet and picked up a hat that had appealed to her earlier, of a somewhat sophisticated style, with a black lace demi-veil spilling from the brim, the effect slightly dramatic. She tried it on and liked it immediately. She felt certain that even the Yankee would approve of this choice. But when she stole a glance at his reflection to observe his reaction, he wasn't there!

Startled, Adrienne threw a quick look over her shoulder to the place where he'd been standing, but he'd disappeared. The instant she realized what she was doing, she squared around again to face the mirror, stunned by the strange disappointment she felt. A second later she was doubly stunned to see him standing before her, next to the mirror. She was extremely conscious of the quick, small beats her heart struck—from the shock of finding him there, of course. There could be no other cause.

"The hat is very attractive." He spoke in French, his accent definitely American and his voice deep-pitched. "Unfortunately it hides your eyes. And I'm certain you've been told before that you have very beautiful eyes, black-shining like the sea on a moonless night."

She made no response. Frankly, Brodie would have been surprised if she had. Well-bred Creole misses didn't address strangers, and she was unquestionably well-bred. But it wasn't necessary that she speak to him; she had a very expressive face, and what it didn't tell him, her actions did.

She had regained her composure with remarkable swiftness after initially stiffening in surprise at finding him so near. There'd been no betraying blush of discomfort, no hint of alarm in her eyes. More than that, there'd been no indignant walking away. She'd stayed—out of pique? Out of pride? Out of curiosity? Brodie didn't particularly care what her reason was. She was there, and she was listening—however much she might be coolly pretending not to be.

The hat with the veil was exchanged for a white straw bergère with a wide, soft brim, a wreath of flowers encircling its flat crown and pink satin ribbons dangling at the sides. Instead of turning her into a picture of virginal innocence, the hat made her look even more alluring, yet . . . there was nothing of the coquette about her.

This time Brodie made himself shake his head in rejection. "I admit the brim would protect your face from the sun, but it would also force a man to keep his distance. I wouldn't want you to be wearing it if you were on my arm."

Again his remark was met with silence. She removed the straw hat and replaced it with a bonnet that had plumes of white ostrich feathers sweeping down its sides. Brodie frowned in exaggerated disapproval.

"*That* would be guaranteed to tickle a man's nose and turn any whispered word into a sneeze."

The corners of her mouth deepened with the faintest suggestion of a smile, the only outward indication that his observation had amused her. Brodie didn't need any other.

When she removed the bonnet, she automatically lifted a hand and smoothed any disturbed strands of hair into place, the action drawing his gaze to the black sleekness of her hair, parted in the center and drawn back into a small knot near the back of her neck.

"In all honesty, mam'selle, your hair should never be hidden beneath a hat or bonnet. It is its own adornment, a midnight curtain gleaming with starshine," he declared softly when she reached for another bonnet. "Covering such beauty should be a sin."

Calmly she slipped her own velvet bonnet onto her head, its rich garnet color matching her walking dress. Without once looking at him, she began to secure the trailing ribbons beneath her chin with a small posy of artificial flowers.

Madame Simone emerged from the rear of the shop, took one look at Brodie, and rushed over, her expression running the gamut from horror and fury to panic and outrage. "I regret the delay, Mademoiselle," she blurted. "If this gentleman has been bothering you in my absence—"

"On the contrary, Madame Simone," she spoke at last—in flawless English, her voice round and soft and reserved. She could, Brodie thought, handle men as she pleased. "I believe it is I who have been bothering him." Brodie smiled and resisted the urge to throw back his head and laugh at this very astute and provocative observation. She had indeed been bothering him . . . in the most stimulating way. "If you will excuse me, Madame, I believe my aunt has completed her purchase."

With a graceful turn, she glided away from them. Madame Simone started after her, but Brodie caught her arm. "Introduce me."

"*Nom de Dieu*, you do not realize—" she whispered in frantic protest.

"Introduce me," he repeated in the same low undertone, then held up the bundle he was carrying. "Introduce me, or these drawings will end up in the muddy bottom of the Mississippi instead of in your back room. And for your information, the *Sea Star* was damaged in a storm during her crossing and limped into Havana. She'll be a week being repaired. Which means it will be more than a week before your competitor, the modiste Madame Trussard, receives *her* copies of the latest fashions."

"A week," she breathed in excitement.

"Introduce me."

She straightened, the chance of stealing a week on her competition overcoming any reservations she had about the wisdom of granting his request. Turning, she fixed a smile on her face and walked with him over to the young woman and her chaperone, a woman of indeterminate age whose face bore no family resemblance at all to her charge's.

"Monsieur Donovan, allow me to present Madame Jardin and her niece, Mademoiselle Adrienne Jardin," the proprietress declared, then completed the reverse introductions. "Mesdames, this is M'sieu Brodie Donovan. He is the owner of the shipping company the Crescent Line."

Madame Jardin gave him a baleful look. "You are a *Yanqui*."

"Regrettably, yes. It was a tragic circumstance of birth over which I had no control. I hope you will not hold it against me, Madame, Mademoiselle." He inclined his head to each of them in turn and caught the amused, and approving, smile that curved the lips of Adrienne Jardin—and the dark glow in her eyes that revealed definite interest.

"A pleasure, Monsieur Donovan." She nodded her head, acknowledging the formal introduction.

"Yes, a pleasure, m'sieu," her aunt repeated with little conviction. "Now we must say adieu."

"Not adieu . . . *au revoir*. We will see each other again," Brodie stated, looking straight at Adrienne Jardin when he said it and realizing that his patience would be sorely tested by the careful manners and correct ways of doing things dictated by Creole society. He watched her leave the shop with her aunt, then turned to the proprietress. "Jardin. Where have I heard that name?"

"It is Emil Gaspard Jardin's name, you know. It is whispered that he owns half of the Vieux Carré and a half dozen plantations on the river. Adrienne is his granddaughter," she replied, and held out her hand. "You obtained your introduction—for all the good it will do you. I will take my package now."

Brodie gave it to her. "What makes you think it will do me no good?"

"You heard the old crow of an aunt," she said, tearing at the brown paper around the fashion plates. "You are a *Yanqui*. And Emil Jardin clings to the old attitude toward *Americains*."

"We'll see." He knew there was a way around him. There were always ways.

Leaving Madame Simone to her intense perusal of the drawings, Brodie exited the shop and paused on the banquette to gaze after the departing figure in garnet. The strains of Cado's violin came to him. He turned and crossed the street to the blind fiddler's corner.

"Emil Jardin, Cado—where does he live?"

"You want to know about him?" Startled, the old man missed a note.

"I want to know about his granddaughter Adrienne, everything you can find out. Does she assist in the marketing? If so, when? Is there a regular hour? The theater, the opera, where does she usually sit? What invitations has she accepted? What balls and masquerades will she be attending? I want specific dates and times."

"But such details—"

"The house servants will know them, and house servants can be encouraged to talk." This time he didn't drop coins into Cado's hat. Instead he slipped some folded bills into the pocket of the old man's coat.

14 ~

NATTIE MOVED AWAY from the bed and picked up the satin robe Remy had tossed over the arm of the loveseat earlier that morning. "I'm sure it won't be any surprise to hear that Brodie Donovan got detailed information about Adrienne's daily activities and plans." She carried the robe to the closet and hung it on a padded hanger on the back of the door. "And during those next two weeks, he *arranged* for their paths to cross several times. Twice he was at the pillared arcade of the old French Market when she went there with her aunt to do the day's shopping. He attended Sunday mass at the St. Louis Cathedral, where her family worshiped. When he found out she had a fitting at Madame Trussard's, he waited at a nearby café until she came out, then *chanced* to meet her on the street. And there was the opera too.

"In those days," Nattie explained, "four operas were performed every week at the Théâtre d'Orléans, two *grand* and two *comique*. When he found out which operas she was going to, he got tickets to two of them, seats in the dress circle. My grandma said that between acts he visited her box. 'Course, he didn't get to talk to her every time he *accidentally* saw her."

"But Adrienne must have encouraged his pursuit of her and guessed these weren't chance meetings." Remy curled an arm around the bedpost and sat down at the foot of the mattress, wrinkling the coverlet Nattie had so carefully smoothed.

"Sure she did," Nattie agreed quickly. "There's no doubt she was just as attracted to him. Part of it was probably that he was different from the young Creole men she knew. He dressed well, but he wasn't a dandy, like some of them were; he wasn't a quarrelsome braggart, all obsessed with honor and dueling; and he observed all the proprieties back then without acting like he was bound by them. And his being a Yankee probably added a touch of the forbidden, too. Besides"—Nattie shrugged—"doesn't every young girl at some time in her life dream of meeting a man who can thrill her—a man who's bold and handsome, who will defy anything to have her for his own? Times may change, and people with them, but not in the ways of love or our dreams of it— man or woman."

Remy couldn't argue with that.

"Anyway," Nattie continued, "after those *chance* encounters, Brodie then found out Adrienne was going to a ball at the St. Louis Hotel. That's where nearly all the fashionable balls were held—at least the ones attended by the Creoles. The Americans had their parties at the St. Charles Hotel . . . in the American section of town. This particular *bal de société,* as they called it, was a private-subscription affair. Brodie Donovan probably had to use all his contacts in the Quarter and twist every arm he could just to get his name on the invitation list. And then he had to pay dearly for the privilege of attending the ball. In a way, he was as single-minded in his pursuit of Adrienne Jardin as he'd been in building his shipping company—not minding the time, the effort, the cost, or the risk. . . ."

Tall pillars circled the famed rotunda of the St. Louis Hotel, its beige-tinged-with-pink marble floor gleaming beneath the high dome of its elaborate and ornamental ceiling. Paintings covered the walls, and a long bar of solid marble curved halfway around the room. And the patrons were as finely appointed as the decor—including Brodie Donovan. Wearing the requisite white gloves with his black tailcoat over a white waistcoat, Brodie picked up a brandy from the polished top of the marble bar and idly swirled it in its glass. With a turn of his head, he glanced again in the direction of the room's entrance and ignored the poke of his starched-stiff collar.

The cadence of the music rose as the band played a quadrille. Brodie scanned the file of dancers on the floor, doubting that he had failed to see her arrive, but verifying it all the same. Satisfied that she wasn't among the dancers, he swung his gaze to the ball guests milling about along the outside circle by the towering pillars. White satins, cream taffetas, pastel silks, gowns adorned with flowers, glittering beads, and sequined lace, but none worn by the dark-haired, dark-eyed Adrienne Jardin.

He took a sip of brandy and glanced at a group of guests entering the rotunda. He recognized a planter and his family from upriver and started to turn away, then spotted an elderly woman in a drab stone-colored gown, her headdress of lace and pink ribbons barely able to conceal the spreading thinness of her gray hair. It was Adrienne's sour and rather sad aunt.

A second later the planter and his family veered to the right, and there she stood, her black hair swept high on her head, a blood-red rose at the side, the low-cut corsage of her silk gown baring the rounded points of her pale shoulders. Suddenly every edge of the night was sharp and biting, and every scent was sweet and keen. His restlessness and impatience vanished at the sight of her.

He pushed his brandy glass back onto the bar counter, then stiffened as he saw the man at her side, lean and elegant in his black evening clothes. He had Adrienne's ebony hair and equally dark eyes, and there was a faint similarity in their features, though his were more sharply cut. Dominique Jardin, Adrienne's brother and the only grandson of Emil Jardin. Through him the Jardin legacy would live on.

Brodie breathed a little easier, but not much. According to Cado, Dominique Jardin was not a Creole dandy to be taken lightly. At twenty-five, he was a veteran of more than a dozen duels, his skill with a rapier reportedly rivaled only by that of his fencing master. More than that, he and Adrienne were exceptionally close for a brother and sister. It was said he was proud of her beauty and extremely protective of her reputation.

Thoughtfully Brodie reached for his glass of brandy and took a minute to study this new obstacle. In the past he'd had only Adrienne's chaperoning aunt to be concerned about, and she'd been relatively easy to circumvent. Her reputation for Gallic thrift was renowned in the Quarter; Brodie'd merely had to wait until she was haggling with some merchant, then he could be assured of having Adrienne all to himself. Cado claimed the old spinster used the money she saved to buy absinthe on the sly. The house servants said she was a secret tippler.

Unfortunately Dominique Jardin shared no similar failing. On the contrary, he was said to be as sharp and as quick as the rapier he wielded, a fitting heir to assume the family mantle, a man to be approached directly. Brodie took a last sip of his brandy and pushed away from the marble bar to wander slowly, casually in their direction.

As Adrienne advanced into the domed rotunda on her brother's arm, she acknowledged the waving of hands, the nodding of ornamented heads, her gaze always moving, being careful not to miss a sign of recognition from any dowager, and to maintain a composed smile of interest. The lively strains of a quadrille filled the room, rising above the bright hum of gaily chattering voices and the sweeping rustle of stiff taffetas, satins, and silks, the soft whisper of her ruched gown lost in it, the caged crinoline of her petticoat holding the circular fullness of the skirt away from her and giving her the appearance of gliding over the gleaming marble floor.

Here and there she and Dominique were detained by gloved hands reaching out to stop them. "Adrienne, if only your *mère* were here to see how beautiful you have grown."

And another declared, "Ah, *chère*, but it was only yesterday you went to sleep in our box at the opera."

"Dominique, you remember our daughter Gisette."

"Where is your grand-père? I had hoped to see him this evening."

Dominique explained that a small emergency at one of their plantations upriver had required their grandfather's presence, but that he was not expected to be away long—a day or two, perhaps. Then they moved on, strolling beneath the galleries that circled the domed ceiling.

As the last notes of the quadrille faded, Adrienne watched the dancers leaving the floor, conscious of the fine tension that had her tightly gripping the handle of her closed fan. Again she skimmed the faces of the men garbed in the mandatory black evening dress, ignoring the women with their satiny shoulders and shimmering gowns, not admitting to herself that she was looking for anyone in particular.

Before the dance floor had completely cleared, the band struck up another tune, a waltz this time. Dominique turned to the older woman on his other arm. "Come, Tante ZeeZee. Permit me to have this first dance with you."

She harrumphed in response, her expression scornful of the invitation, but her eyes warmed with affection when she looked at him. "I am too old to be whirled about the floor like a dervish. You have done your duty by asking me; now let us speak of such foolishness no more."

"Now I am hurt that you refuse to dance with me, your favorite nephew," Dominique teased, something only he could get away with.

"Hmmph, you are my *only* nephew," she retorted. "And your feelings will recover quickly from the slight. It is better that I take my seat along the wall with the rest of the ancient tapestry. If you wish to be kind, later you may bring me a glass of absinthe."

Leaving them, she went to join the other matrons along the wall, ensconced on seats provided for those who sat out the dancing. There she would spend her evening, listening to gossip and occasionally inserting an ascerbic comment of her own. Adrienne considered again the loneliness of her aunt's life, relegated to the role of glorified servant, the chatelain of her father's house, dependent on him for her existence—a loneliness assuaged by two things: the jade-green liquor and Dominique.

"You almost coaxed a smile from her," Adrienne observed as she cast one of her own at her handsome brother. "She adores you so."

"Is that bad?" He drew his head back, feigning an affronted look.

"Very. You are adored by so many women now, one more may fill your head with conceit," she replied in jest.

Instead of maintaining the light banter, Dominique turned serious. "But it is not I who am adored by so many women so much as it is the Jardin name and the wealth it portends."

She looked at her brother, his remark reminding her of the many duties and responsibilities that would one day be solely his to bear, burdens he'd been groomed to assume almost from the day of his birth. How old had she been when she'd first recognized that no matter how much her grandfather loved her —and he'd never given her cause to doubt his love for her—she would never occupy the place of importance in his life that her brother, Dominique, held. While she was the delight of her grandfather's life, Dominique was his heir. Through him Emil Jardin would know his immortality. Through him the Jardin name would be carried on. It was the way of things, and she loved her brother too much ever to resent his position.

Studying the clean lines of his profile, she announced, "Any woman who looks at you and sees only that is unworthy of the man you are."

"Praise from my sister?" Dominique raised an eyebrow in mock amazement. "What other surprises will this evening hold, I wonder?"

"Let us hope many." Adrienne turned again to the couples taking the floor and skimmed the host of guests crowding at the edges. Out of the corner of her eye she caught a hint of burnished red, deep and dark like mahogany. He was here. Not thirty feet away. Exchanging pleasantries with Monsieur Rousseau. She let her glance linger on him for an instant, more than a little pleased to discover how magnificent he looked in formal dress, the white silk cravat tied in a small, precise bow at his throat, the black tailcoat splendidly emphasizing the width of his shoulders. Then she looked away, her smile deepening with the sudden rush of exhilaration. "Perhaps there will even be wonderful surprises."

Although she kept her eyes steadfastly averted from him, she knew the instant he moved on—toward her—and yet she maintained the pretense of being unaware of his approach, instead watching in satisfaction as other feminine heads turned to cast curious and admiring glances his way.

She waited until his tall shape had entered her side vision, then allowed her wandering glance to encounter his. But the knowing glint in his brown eyes made her wonder if she'd fooled him at all.

"M'sieu Donovan," she said, acknowledging him first.

"Mademoiselle Jardin." He inclined his head in a show of respect, his gaze holding hers a fraction longer than propriety allowed, reaffirming his interest, and then he moved on to her brother—again showing a surface observance of convention.

"Dominique, allow me to present Monsieur Brodie Donovan." Adrienne quickly and smoothly made the necessary introductions. "My brother, Dominique Jardin."

She heard the coolness of her brother's response and witnessed the testing handshake the two men exchanged. The subtle inquiries Dominique made were what she'd expected, and the proper replies Brodie Donovan gave, she'd anticipated.

In the last two weeks Adrienne had made a few, very discreet inquiries of her own about Brodie Donovan and learned that he had earned the respect of several leading businessmen in the Vieux Carré, all of whom remarked on his courtesy, his patience, and his business acumen, always adding, "If only more *Yanquis* were like this one."

But her few encounters with him had made her aware that while he may have *adapted to* their ways, he hadn't *adopted* them. He was not at all like the young Creole men she knew, never fawning in his attention like the limp-wristed ones, never swaggering with his chest thrown out expecting to be noticed like the strutting cocks of the walk, never leering like the self-styled Lotharios whose looks gave her a crawling sensation wholly unlike the excitement she drew from the quick, amused eyes of Brodie Donovan.

No, there was a directness about Brodie Donovan that he never tried to disguise, as evidenced by the way he looked at her—the way a man looked at a woman he desired and intended ultimately to have.

"With your permission, M'sieu Jardin, I would like to have this dance with your sister," he said, and fixed that look on her.

She felt Dominique's gaze on her and turned to meet it, unaware of the dark glow in her own eyes as she gave a barely perceptible nod to indicate her assent to the request. His expression immediately became thoughtful, probing, with a trace of frown appearing. But he smiled and nodded his consent to Brodie Donovan.

"You have my permission," he said, surrendering her.

When Brodie offered her his arm, Adrienne placed her hand on his sleeve and let him lead her onto the dance floor. As he moved to face her, she was confronted by the wide set of his shoulders and the white expanse of his cambric dress shirt. She felt the strong curl of his gloved fingers on her hand and the warm press of his hand on the curve of her waist, guiding her into the first steps of a waltz, the bulk of her skirt keeping a distance between them. She lifted her gaze higher—to the smoothly hewn line of his jaw and chin, then to his mouth, faintly curved in a warm, lazy line.

"You dance well, M'sieu Donovan." She met his stare, conscious of the pleasant disturbance it created within her.

"For a Yankee, you mean." The corners of his mouth deepened into a smile that brought the carved lines in his cheeks into play.

Adrienne laughed softly at the phrase he'd probably heard a thousand times, which he had now turned onto himself. "You dance well—for anyone," she insisted.

"A compliment from the beautiful Mademoiselle Jardin." He tipped his head to her in silent acknowledgment, amusement glinting in his eyes. "I can think of only one thing that would give me greater pleasure this evening."

"And what is that, m'sieu?" She matched his bantering tone, making the question half serious and half jest.

"A kiss from your lips."

Unconsciously she lowered her glance to his mouth, for an instant imagining. . . . Aloud, she wondered, "How do you have the boldness to speak to me this way?"

"How do you have the boldness to listen?" he countered, his hand tightening its grip on her waist as he whirled her into a series of concentric turns that robbed her of her breath and gave her no chance to respond. When he finally resumed their former pace, it seemed inappropriate to allude to either of his remarks.

The song ended, yet the phrase would not leave her—"A kiss from your lips," "A kiss," "kiss." The words echoed over and over again in her mind each time she met his gaze that evening, each time she danced with him, each time she thought of him.

Again he came to claim her for a waltz, and again she took to the dance floor with him, the pressure of his hands, the length of his gliding steps, the sight of his face before her all now familiar to her.

"Do you realize, m'sieu, this is the twelfth time we have danced together this evening?" she said, aware of the speculating looks currently being directed their way.

"You've been keeping count," he observed, then smiled that slow smile she'd come to expect. "So have I."

"People are beginning to notice."

"Let them. Whatever they're thinking, it's probably true." He slowed their steps and stole a quick glance around. "Are you tired of dancing, Mademoiselle Jardin?"

"Why?" she asked, startled by the unexpected question.

"Come with me," was all he said as he calmly led her off the floor, as if to stop dancing in the middle of a waltz was the most natural thing to do. Unhurried, he guided her through the ring of onlooking guests. Adrienne saw they were heading in the general direction of the exit onto St. Louis Street. She said nothing when his fingers pressed down on her arm to check her steps, as if they were about to linger. He cast another surreptitious glance around them, then drew her toward the exit. He exchanged one conspiratorial look with her, and then they slipped from the domed ballroom and moved quickly down the long arcade of fashionable shops. Her aunt would be shocked that Adrienne had deliberately eluded her chaperoning eye, but she didn't care, not now.

Halfway down the arcade, the music and the susurration of voices became muted. Again the pressure of his hand checked her steps. She swung around to face him, feeling wonderfully wicked, especially when she saw that look in his eyes. They were near a recessed entrance to one of the shops. Adrienne wandered over to peer in its window and then turned, drawing her hands together behind her back and leaning against a corner of the entrance.

"You should not have brought me here," she said.

He rested a hand on the framework above her head. "You shouldn't have come. Why did you?"

Adrienne answered him honestly, directly. "I wanted to be alone with you."

She heard the faint sound of his indrawn breath as his gaze fastened on her lips. She watched his mouth move closer, her eyelids slowly lowering until her lashes closed with the first warm touch of his lips against hers. The initial contact was light and exploring, a brush here, a faint pressure there, her breath slipping out to mingle with his. Then his mouth came the rest of the way onto hers, covering all the surfaces of her lips in a tender yet stirring kiss.

When he lifted his head, regret quivered through her. Slowly she opened her eyes to look at him, stunned to discover that he hadn't taken her into his arms. Their lips had met, but that had been the only contact. There was still space between them. She searched his face, seeking some answer to this heady tension that held her. His eyes did their own searching of her.

"Adrienne," he rumbled her name.

Almost simultaneously his hands moved onto her, pulling her to him as his mouth came crushing down again. Some remote part of her mind noted that she hadn't given him permission to use her given name. But this Yankee wasn't the kind to wait for permission. He took what he wanted—as he was taking this kiss. She gave him all he asked for and more, her hands winding around him, her fingers curling through his hair. Heat flowed through her, but she made no effort to identify its source. There were too many other revelations claiming her attention as his delving kiss unlocked all her closely held hungers and exposed to her, for the first time, the deep and passionate values she held within.

When he broke it off, she looked at him wordlessly, conscious of the unsteady beat of her heart and of an inner trembling that had nothing to do with weakness—rather, it was evidence of the powerful effect of his kiss.

His smile seemed a little unsteady too. "I think it's time I spoke with your grandfather."

"Yes," she said in absolute and full agreement. "He is away. We expect him to return the first of the week." Reaching up, she traced a finger over the curve of his mouth, remembering the sensation of his lips on hers. "You've had your kiss. Your pleasure in the evening should be complete."

"Yes, but now my life isn't." He caught her fingers and pressed them to his lips. "We'd better go back to the ball before I behave like a Yankee and spirit you away from here."

As they retraced their steps to the rotunda, Adrienne unconsciously held her head a little higher, secretly pleased by how womanly she felt. When Brodie suggested a glass of champagne on their return, she agreed, glad of the opportunity to have a few moments to herself to explore these new feelings. But her time alone seemed all too brief as Dominique joined her.

"You look very happy about something," he said.

"I am," she admitted. "M'sieu Donovan is going to ask Grand-père for permission to call on me."

He looked at her in shock. "Adrienne, have you taken leave of your senses? He is a *Yanqui*."

"I know."

"Grand-père will—"

"—will storm and stomp about, call upon all the saints, glower indignantly for a day or two, and then ultimately grant permission," Adrienne concluded confidently.

"How can you sound so sure of that?" Dominique shook his head, harboring his own doubts of the outcome.

"Dominique," she chided with a reproving smile. "When has Grand-père ever denied me anything I have wanted?"

"But you have never wanted to see a *Yanqui*," he reminded her.

15 ✍

THE VERY WALLS OF the house on Royal Street reverberated with the fury emanating from the library on the second floor—which, following the Continental style, was the structure's main story. The chandelier in the room quivered with the force of voices raised in anger. It had begun within seconds after Brodie Donovan was summarily ordered from the premises.

Emil Jardin stood in front of the library table, his silvery head thrown back—not with pride for the young woman who was now before him, but with outrage. His deep-set eyes were not bright with love for this granddaughter who was the delight of his winter years; they were burning black with ire. His hands didn't reach out to stroke her hair or caress her cheek; they flailed the air in indignation. His voice didn't croon to her in affection, each sentence punctuated with *"ma petite"* or *"ma mignonne"*; it lashed out in full Gallic temper.

Adrienne had seen her grandfather angry before, even furious, but never like this, consumed by a rage that purpled his face and made the veins in his neck stand out. She didn't flinch from him. Instead she let her own temper rise to clash with his.

"You could have had the simple courtesy to listen to him!"

"Listen to what? More of his offensive declarations of interest in you? *Non,* never! I would rather God strike me dead than hear him speak your name. *Non!"* he repeated forcefully, gesticulating with his hands. "The doors of this house are forever shut to that *Yanqui* barbarian!"

"You have no right!" she protested, just as loudly.

"I have every right. This is my house."

"It is my house too."

"And you are my granddaughter. You will do as you are told, and I forbid you to speak to this man again!"

"You forbid?! Why?" Adrienne demanded, her hands clenched in fists at her sides. "Because he is a *Yanqui?* This prejudice of yours toward the *Americains* is archaic. They are here. They have been here. Even you do business with them."

"*Oui,* I do business with them. And my grand-père, he did business with Indians. But he would no more have allowed them into his house than I will have that *Yanqui* enter this one!"

"You are not being fair!"

"*Chut!"* He demanded silence from her. "I have made my decision. There will be no more discussion on this, do you hear? Now, go to your room."

"I am not a child to be ordered to my room, Grand-père. I am a woman."

"A woman who has foolishly allowed her head to be turned by a quick-tongued Yankee. That your Tante ZeeZee allowed you to speak to this—this—man is an outrage, and that she failed to inform me is unforgivable. You will see him no more, Adrienne. This is the end of it!"

"*Non*, you are wrong!"

"Do not defy me in this! I will not permit it."

Glaring at him, Adrienne recognized that she was too angry to reason with him, and he was too angry to listen. She turned sharply on her heel and stormed from the room, slamming the door behind her, the loudness of it rebounding down the side hall. She hesitated, feeling the silence of the house, its quiet reminding her of the eerie stillness that preceded a violent storm.

There was a movement at the end of the hall. Turning, Adrienne saw her black maidservant Sulie Mae peering cautiously around the corner. Hastily she caught up her skirts and ran quickly and noiselessly down the hall—in the opposite direction from her room. The young brown-skinned woman stepped out to meet her, glancing anxiously past her toward the library door. Adrienne took her by the arm and drew her into the main salon, out of sight, then whispered urgently. "Sulie Mae, when M'sieu Donovan left, did you see which way he went?"

"*Oui*, Missy." She bobbed her head in quick affirmation. "He turned like he was goin' to Canal."

Adrienne tried to remember how long ago that had been. Five minutes? Certainly not more than ten. "I want you to go after him, Sulie Mae, and bring him back here."

"Here?" She drew back in alarm. "But Michie Jardin, he say—"

"I know what he said," Adrienne cut in sharply. "But you do as I say. Bring him here. I will meet him in the carriageway. Now, go. *Vite*."

Like all the homes in the Vieux Carré, the Jardin house was built flush with the banquette, its galleries of iron lacework extending over it, but it kept its back turned to the street and faced the courtyard within. Two entrances provided access to the house. The first was a formal doorway set between half-columns and crowned by an arched fanlight, up a short flight of steps from the banquette; the second was a carriage entrance, marked by heavy double doors with a smaller opening cut into one side. Behind the doors was a tunnel-like passage paved with flagstones. At the end of it stood a pair of tall, scrolled iron gates that led into the sun-splashed courtyard with its lush greenery and weathered fountain.

In the middle of the darkly shadowed *porte cochère* there was another arched opening, and a wooden staircase that curved up to the main residence on the second floor. At the foot of the steps, within the arching frame, Adrienne waited anxiously, impatiently, hearing the clatter of mule-drawn drays in the street and listening for the creak of the small gate that would signal Sulie Mae's return.

Just as she stole a glance around the corner, the dark-green gate swung inward and Sulie Mae stepped cautiously into the passageway, pulling her shawl more tightly around her shoulders, her head bound in a kerchief, the pointed ends poking into the air like a pair of horns. She saw Adrienne and looked back over her shoulder, motioning for someone to follow her inside. A second later Brodie ducked his tall frame through the gate and stepped to one side, letting Sulie Mae close the gate behind him. He seemed to resist Sulie Mae's attempts to hurry him down the passageway to the opening where Adrienne waited. As he came toward her, she noticed the stiffness—the erectness—of his posture, hinting at tautly controlled anger, but it wasn't until he was closer that she saw the hardness in his expression and the cold look in his eyes. She hesitated, guessing how insulting, how contemptuous her grandfather must have been when he'd ordered Brodie from the house.

He stopped in front of her, the muscles along his cheek and jaw standing out in sharp ridges. "Your Negress said you wanted to see me." His voice was as hard and cold as the rest of him.

"I do." She moved aside to let Sulie Mae scurry past her up the stairs. "You spoke to Grand-père—"

"He has refused permission for me to call on you."

"I know. He has forbidden me to speak to you." She searched his face, looking for some glimmer of the warmth she'd once seen in it. "Do you intend for this to be the end of it? Will you stay away, as he has ordered?"

His gaze bored into her, dark and angry. And Adrienne recognized that hardness as pride.

"No," he said. "Never."

Then his hands were reaching out to drag her to him, and she went eagerly into his arms, tilting her head up to receive the satisfying crush of his mouth. Again she felt shocked alive by his kiss, and more certain than ever that this was how it should be between a man and a woman.

"There's a way," he muttered against her cheek. "There has to be."

"Yes." She drew back, needing to see his face. "My grand-père is a . . . a stubborn man. But he means well. He thinks he is protecting me, and I have yet to make him understand that I have no wish to be protected from you, Brodie."

A corner of his mouth lifted in a near smile. "You make my name a melody."

"Do I?" She laughed softly, breathlessly, exhilarated by the look of desire that had returned to his eyes. Then she heard her aunt's voice coming from the courtyard, and she tensed in alarm. "You must go—before someone sees you." She cast an anxious glance over her shoulder. "I will speak to Grand-père. Not now. In a day or two, when he will be more reasonable," she said as she hurried him toward the small gate.

"Do you know the blind fiddler, Cado?" He stopped at the gate, not yet opening it. "He plays on the corner of Royal and St. Philip."

"The Negro with the violin? I have seen him," she admitted. "But I never knew his name."

"If you need to reach me, leave a message with him, and he'll see that I get it." He opened the gate, then paused halfway through it. "If I don't hear from you, I'll be back."

"A week," she promised. "No more than that."

Thunder rumbled low and ominous as rain fell in slanting torrents, filling the garbage-strewn gutters, turning the dirt street into a quagmire, and inching over the sidewalks. Only those who had to ventured out, and they hugged the buildings, seeking what little protection the overhanging galleries offered from the wind-whipped rain. The rest stayed inside and waited for the deluge to pass.

From the shelter of the covered carriageway, Adrienne watched the street, a full-length cloak of Burberry cloth covering her dress and hooding her face. Few vehicles plowed through the deep mud on Royal Street, and still fewer pedestrians scurried along its banquette. None noticed the small gate held partially ajar, or the woman on the other side, silent, calm, and determined.

A closed carriage approached, pulled by a team of matched bays, their ears flattened against the rain. The driver swung the team close to the banquette and brought the carriage to a halt next to the cypress-lined ditch. The door to the carriage swung open. Adrienne darted from the shelter of the *porte cochère* and climbed inside before the driver could alight to assist her.

With a crack of the whip, the carriage lurched forward. Inside, Adrienne pushed back the hood of her cloak and finally met Brodie's gaze. She briefly wondered why she felt no awkwardness, no anxiety, no guilt—only this calm, smooth certainty. Brodie said nothing, waiting for her to speak first.

"Grand-père remains adamant in his decision. He will not tolerate even the mention of your name."

"That doesn't change the way I feel," he said, leaving unspoken the question of whether she wanted to reconsider her position.

"Nor the way I feel," she assured him, firmly.

A small smile touched his mouth. "In that case we're left with the Yankee thing to do—run away together and elope."

"*Non.*" She had already considered that option and rejected it. "Flight carries with it the inference of wrongdoing, of guilt, of shame. I feel none of those things with you."

"I can't disagree with you. But neither am I going to allow your grandfather to keep us apart. You'd better understand that, Adrienne."

"I do."

In the last six days she'd had a great deal of time alone to think—about them, about herself, about life and what she wanted from it. She'd seen the loneliness of her aunt's spinster existence, the isolation of a single woman, her dependence upon the charity of a relative. And she'd seen the unhappiness of a loveless *mariage de convenance*, the tension, the bitterness, the resentment of young brides as they tried to pretend they didn't know about the concubines their husbands kept in those little cottages on Rampart Street. Ever since she'd been old enough to be aware of these things, she'd been determined to marry for love. She had never doubted that she could. She was a Jardin, and the Jardins had risen above the need to further their power base through marriage.

She had never guessed she would choose a Yankee to love. And she'd never guessed that her grandfather's dislike of them was so deeply ingrained.

Twice this past week she had tried to reason with her grandfather, and both attempts had ended in arguments. She hadn't tried again, recognizing that more quarrels would only harden him. And tears and pleading wouldn't work with her grandfather; he disliked weakness, even in women.

While Dominique sympathized with her plight, he wouldn't side with her against their grandfather and suggested instead that she accept that their grandfather was a better judge than she of what was best for her. As for Tante ZeeZee—she was a woman. Her grandfather would no more listen to her than to Adrienne.

Her acceptance of his demands was out of the question. She would never submit to that.

Open defiance of her grandfather was unthinkable—scandalous.

All of which left only one option: she had to arrange for her grandfather to realize that the best thing would be for her to marry Brodie Donovan.

"We will see each other, Brodie, as often as we can." She twisted sideways in the seat to face him and reached up to trace the high arc of his cheekbone. "For now, we will have to meet like this."

Irritation flickered through his expression. "Why? You can't believe he's going to change his mind."

"In time he will, yes." She smiled confidently.

He looked at her, then slowly shook his head, his mouth reluctantly curving in a smile. "Why am I agreeing to this? What kind of spell have you cast over me?"

"Brodie. Do you think you are the only one who feels this enchantment?" she asked, feeling slightly wiser than he.

"I'd better not be." He drew her hand from his cheek and carried it to his mouth, pressing an evocative kiss in the center of its palm, his eyes never leaving her face. "How long before I have to take you back to your home?"

"Not long," she said regretfully, glancing up at the upholstered ceiling of the carriage, listening to the tattoo of the rain on its roof. "Already the rain is letting up. When it stops, the streets will be crowded." She left it unsaid that that would greatly increase her risk of being seen leaving his carriage.

"You don't know how tempted I am to tell the driver to keep going—how tempted I am to kidnap you and never take you back. I want to spend more than a few minutes with you, Adrienne."

"You will. I have begun to spend my evenings alone in my room, retiring immediately after supper, refusing to attend any of the parties or the opera. Grand-père thinks I am sulking, and I have not attempted to disprove him." She paused for an instant, marveling at her own daring yet never questioning her decision. "At night there is little traffic on the street, few people to notice a carriage going by—or stopping very briefly. We would have time to be together then—perhaps two, even three hours."

Brodie frowned in amazement, hearing her words and seeing the cleverness, the intelligence in her plan—and observing her seemingly unshakable calm. Rebellion against family dictum was so rare as to be almost nonexistent in aristocratic Creole families. That she was even in this carriage with him in the daytime, unchaperoned, showed stunning boldness. But to suggest meeting him at night—alone—for several hours. . . . It humbled him a little to think of it, especially when he considered how strict her upbringing had been. And he wondered if she wasn't putting too much trust in a gentleman's honor—his honor. Didn't she realize that if he were really a gentleman, he'd never see her again?

"Is there a place we can go when we meet? I know of none," she confessed, calmly looking to him.

"I do." He knew the requirements without asking—somewhere private where they wouldn't be seen or recognized. "My home. About three miles from here."

There was one small flicker of hesitation, and then she smiled. "I would like to see your home."

"When?"

"In a day or two. I will send a message to you."

16 ❧

A WAXING MOON, a shimmering crescent in the night sky, joined the dusting of glittering stars to look down on the collection of elaborate homes with expansive front lawns that had sprung up in the partially wooded outskirts of the city, built by prosperous Americans on the former site of the old Livaudais plantation. Stately processions of towering columns, Corinthian and Doric in design, faced the streets, the wide galleries borrowing the lacework ornamentation of iron railings from the Creoles, and the interiors adapting to the subtropical climate of New Orleans with rooms sixteen and eighteen feet high, wide doorways, tall windows, and folding shutters that could be thrown open to admit the flow of air.

Brodie Donovan stood at a parlor window in one of those homes—his home, finished only a few short months before, its grandeur befitting the residence of a successful shipowner. Yet, looking into the mirror-black night, he had only to close his eyes and remember the unbelievable green of his native Ireland, the two-room mud house that had been his home, the meager meals that had been served on its crude table, the patched and worn clothes that had covered his back, the hunger that had been in his belly, and the smell of peat burning in the hearth. He had only to close his eyes and remember the sensation of the swamp's mire tugging at his legs, drying on his clothes and skin—the suffocating heat, the *zzzizzing* buzz of attacking mosquitoes, the trembling and aching of exhausted muscles, and the stench, always the rank, malodorous smell of the miasmal swamp.

It didn't matter that he'd left it all behind; it hadn't left him.

If Adrienne had seen him then, she would have given him a look of cool disdain and drawn her skirts aside to avoid contact with him. In all the times they'd met and talked, he'd never told her about any of it. Oh, he'd told her of Ireland, described the green of its countryside, the rocky promontories of its sea cliffs, the sparkling waters of its springs and lochs, and told her of the grand wakes—the keening and weeping in one room and the toasting and tale-swapping in another. And he'd recounted the story of how he'd started his company and built it, as well as his plans for the future.

There was a truth to all of it, but not the whole truth, not the parts that might change the way she looked at him. Did he think she wouldn't love him if she knew? Did he think he wasn't really good enough for her? Was that why he went along with meeting her in secret—because he didn't feel he had a right to be seen with her in public?

But this was America. There was no rigid separation of the classes here; a man was not forever bound to one station. He could rise—as Brodie had done. Look at his clothes, look at this house—they were as fine as anything Adrienne's family possessed.

The darkened windowpane reflected his scowling look. Brodie turned from it, irritated by the blackness of his mood. But he knew the cause of it: she was late. He glanced at the clock on the black marble mantel. The carriage had left to pick her up more than an hour ago. Had something gone wrong? Why wasn't she here? Had there been trouble? He cursed himself for not going with it and for waiting for her here instead.

He glared at the emptiness of the richly furnished parlor, the many crystal pendants of the Waterford chandelier increasing the spray of candlelight that filled it. Once he'd enjoyed this room, taken pride in its beauty. Now, when he looked at the sofa where they always sat, part of the walnut parlor set he'd bought for the room from Prudent Mallard, he always imagined her there. Sometimes, when he was alone, he'd run his hand over the curved armrest where her hand so lightly rested. And sometimes he swore the rich red velvet held traces of her fragrance.

There was no more contentment in this house for him, no more satisfaction. He remembered how proudly he'd shown it off to her the first time she'd come. Now every room was marked with the memory of her reaction—the sound of soft, indrawn breaths of admiration, the sight of a hand trailing in approval over a mantel, even the occasional carefully worded criticism offered under the guise of a suggestion.

Dammit, where was she? Brodie spun back to the window and searched the darkness beyond for a glimpse of the carriage. Would she come? Would she notice the magnolias the gardener had planted in the front lawn, or the newly laid flagstoned walk in the rear, the beginnings of the courtyard she'd thought would be attractive there?

The bright light pouring from the parlor beckoned to her. Adrienne quietly closed the rear entrance door to the wide hall and let the light guide her to the parlor, then paused just inside to face Brodie with clear-shining eyes as he pivoted from the window toward her.

"Adrienne!" Disbelief flickered across his face. He took a step toward her and then stopped, as if expecting her to disappear. "I didn't hear the carriage."

"When you were not at the door to meet me, I thought you might have given up on me." She quickly unfastened her cloak and swung it off her shoulders. "Grand-père brought guests home to dinner unexpectedly. I had to wait until they had left and Tante ZeeZee had retired to her room."

"You're here. That's all that matters now." A smile came to his mouth.

The sight of it was all Adrienne needed as she crossed the room with no memory of her feet touching the floor. He swept her into his arms and wrapped her tightly around him, covering her lips with a fiercely tender kiss.

Almost before it had begun, he was breaking it off, raking his mouth across her cheek, murmuring a husky and rough "I've missed you."

She closed her eyes, thrilling to the emotion vibrating so thickly through his voice. "And I have missed you, Brodie," she declared, just as thickly.

"It's been hell these last two days—wanting to see you, wanting to hold you, wanting to be with you."

"It has been the same for me." Adrienne rubbed her cheek against his, feeling its smoothness, its chiseled bone structure, its heat.

With an effort, he lifted his head and framed her face in his hands, looking at her with heavy-lidded need, a smolder and a sparkle in his eyes. "I was standing at the window, wondering where you were, wishing you were here with me. And when you came through that door, I thought you were a dream I was having. It's a dream you are, Adrienne—a dream most men carry in their minds but never see."

"I am no dream."

"No," he said, none too certainly, his mouth slanting in a near smile. "But I've been thinking, Adrienne—what is a man? There's stars he wants to reach, but it's the earth that stains him. Man was meant for the earth, but he can look at the stars. When you appeared tonight, it was like I was seeing a star suddenly blaze and fall to fill the sky—to fill my night . . . and my life." He paused and deliberately lapsed into a lilting brogue, trying to lighten the seriousness of his feelings. " 'Tis loving you I am, Adrienne Jardin."

She drew a small, quick breath, conscious of the sudden soaring of her heart, and smiled. "And 'tis loving you I am, Brodie Donovan." She used his phrasing, moved by the simple sincerity of it.

Humor, warm and glinting, mixed with the desire for her in his eyes. "It's bold you are again, mocking me with my own words."

"It is no mockery." Smiling, she ran a caressing hand over the angled line of his jaw. He caught it and pressed the tips of her fingers to his lips. "I love you. You are the man I want for my husband. It is your children I want to have, your home I want to keep, your bed I want to lie in."

For an instant he gripped her fingers so tightly that she thought he would break them. Then he was murmuring her name in a groan as he smothered her lips with a kiss that was warm, hard, and demanding. Adrienne was stirred anew by the flood of sensation washing through her. She had no doubt that this was what she wanted—the heat, the need, the near desperation.

His mouth shifted, pressing rough kisses over her cheek and eye. "I want that too," came the thick words against her skin. "I want you."

She felt the faint tremors that shook him, the struggle for control. But there was no place for control in this moment of giving—this release of feelings too long held back. She knew that, as a woman knows it.

"I want you, Brodie." She drew back to look at him, taking his hand and drawing it inside the lace collar of her jasper silk walking dress, laying it against the bare skin of her breastbone, the heel of his hand resting on the top swell of her breast. "Do you feel the pounding of my heart? Do you feel the trembling within? It is for you."

He was still, so still he could have been made of stone. Only his eyes were alive to her—so very alive to her. "You don't know what you're saying, Adrienne."

A smile touched her mouth, at once warm and amused. "You likened me to a star, but I am not something to be regarded and admired from afar. I am a woman to be loved by a man—by you. The stars are outside, Brodie. We are here."

"Aye," he breathed the word, his hand slipping lower, finding the roundness of her breast beneath her gown's corsage. At his touch, an indistinct murmur of pleasure broke from her. "We are here."

His head bent. His lips brushed hers, then came back to plunder and invade. As she tasted the hardness of his tongue, Adrienne knew that this was what she 'wanted—his hands on her, his mouth on her, his muscled body pressed tightly to her. It was what she had always wanted.

He swept her into his arms and carried her from the parlor, up the curved staircase to the master bedroom on the second floor. The soft glow from a lamp on the bedside table illuminated the full tester bed, with the lace baire rolled up and the bed linen turned down, the massive rosewood armoire along one wall and the pale-blue carpet on the floor. He lowered her feet onto the carpet and continued to kiss her. She felt his fingers at the fastenings of her dress, and then it was swinging loose.

Soon her clothes were in a pile at her feet. Brodie drew back to look at her standing before him, proud, bold . . . beautiful. The back-glow of the lamp-light made the thin material of her chemise appear transparent. His mouth went dry. She looked small and delicate, with a narrow rib cage and a waist so small he could span it with his hands, and slender hips that were yet wide enough to cradle a man. He wondered how a form so fragile could hold so much strength —and how a pair of eyes could look at him with a desire so deep it rivaled his own.

"You are beautiful." His voice was husky as he let his gaze stray to her hair, swept back in its smooth knot. She reached up and pulled the securing pins from it, combing it loose with her fingers and drawing its length forward over one shoulder. "This is the first time I've seen it down," he said, and he ran his hand under the silken length of it, a knuckle grazing the peak of her breast, further sensitizing it. Then the ends of his fingers were along her throat, his thumbs under the point of her chin, tilting it up. "You have such full and giving lips."

He lowered his head and she closed her eyes, anticipating the hard demand of his kiss. She was startled—wondrously so—when he caught her bottom lip between his teeth, the light nibbling sensation arousing a whole new shimmer-ing ache within her. A sigh whispered from her as he brushed his mouth over her parted lips, saying against them, "It's sweet they are too—like wild honey."

He tasted them, his tongue tracing their outline, then stroking their inner softness. She swayed against him, her hands clutching at his middle as the world spun behind her closed eyes at this excitingly evocative kiss that was not really a kiss at all. An instant later she discovered that his fingers were no longer at her throat. Instead, they were at the front of her chemise, undoing its fasten-ings with a deftness that surprised her.

Only a moment later, when she stood naked before him, her chemise joining the rest of her clothes on the floor near her feet, Adrienne felt no self-con-sciousness, no awkwardness. She knew by the soft hiss of his indrawn breath that the sight of her more than pleased him, and the look in his eyes con-firmed it.

Needing no invitation, Adrienne moved against him, the fine texture of his linen shirt brushing against her bare skin as she curved her hands behind his neck and drew his head down, urging his mouth to take its fill of her lips. When he did, her tongue began a slow and silent seduction. His hands glided down her spine, the faintly rough feel of them somehow stimulating to her as they pressed her hips against him, then roamed free over her waist, her ribs, her breasts, in even more stimulating play.

Swept by a desire to touch him as he was touching her, she tugged the hem of his shirt free and ran her hands under it and onto his hard flesh, reveling in the sudden contraction of his stomach muscles. Abruptly he gripped her arms and pushed her back, then pulled off his shirt, baring his torso to her.

His sun-bronzed skin gleamed in the lamplight, lean muscles rippling in his chest, shoulders, and arms as he unfastened the flyfront of his trousers, then hesitated. "Do you want me to turn the lamp down?"

"No." If there was color to her cheeks, it was not from embarrassment as she watched him strip off the rest of his clothes. When he stood before her, she was stirred by the magnificent breadth of his chest and shoulders, the tapered trimness of his hips, and the long columns of his legs. "You are beautiful," she said.

Succumbing to her fascination with the innate power of his body, she spread her hands onto his shoulders, rubbing her palms over their hard, coiled muscles. But the feel of him only whetted her appetite for more as she pressed her mouth to his chest, running her lips and tongue over its lean ridges and the tiny nubs of his male nipples, tasting the warm, salty flavor of him and inhaling the earthy and invigorating scent of his skin.

Before she could protest, he scooped her up into his arms and strung a trail of hungry kisses across her cheek, jaw, and lips as he carried her to the tester bed. He lowered them both onto it. Neither of them needed its relative narrowness to force them to lie close together, facing each other, their lips joined in an intimate kiss, their hands alternately caressing and pressing. There was no sense of urgency, only a desire to pleasure each other to the fullest. It incited a passion stronger and hotter than lust.

Adrienne felt consumed by heat—the furnacelike heat of his body that seemed to envelop her from head to toe, the moist heat of the kisses he burned over her face, lips, and throat, and the curling heat from within that spiraled through her with such a pleasant ache. His hands lifted her higher, with a strength and an ease that she'd come to expect. Then his lips brushed her breast, and she gasped at the fresh explosion of sensation. His hands had fondled her breasts and teased her nipples into erectness, but never his lips, his mouth, his tongue. When he drew a nipple into his mouth, Adrienne shuddered.

Brodie felt her tremble with pleasure—the pleasure he gave her as he tasted, tempted, and teased. He had never known such power or such humbleness as he heard her breath catch on his name. She was small, delicate, and fragile but more than strong enough to hold him—to move him. For all the lust, all the passion, all the desire that coursed through him, he was driven by a need to cherish and protect her. She belonged to him, and he was determined to show her how beautiful it could be for them, no matter the ache that grew hotter and hotter within him. He waited until her hips rubbed against him in eager insistence, until her hands pressed and urged in desperate demand, until the sounds coming from her throat revealed the intensity of her longing. Only then did he ease himself onto her, the caress of his hands subtly positioning her body to receive him.

She had a moment of making the small discovery that he wasn't too heavy for her. Nor did his greater height cause any awkwardness. They fit together naturally, the way God had intended. Then she could think of nothing but his hard body, the damp earthy smell of him, the wild taste of his mouth—and the kiss that swamped her, drawing her into some dark, secret place where there were only the two of them.

"I'll not hurt you, Adrienne." His voice rumbled against her skin. "I'll never hurt you."

But she knew he was wrong. It was inevitable that he would hurt her. Three years ago she had gone to her aunt with stories she'd heard from other girls in the convent about the horrible agony a woman was expected to endure on her wedding night when she was impaled by her husband. Tante ZeeZee had explained that a woman would feel pain when her maiden veil was torn by a man's entry, but she said the discomfort would pass in a little while and not return. Knowing that, Adrienne had no fear.

Yet the pain never came. She could feel him inside her, the slow and lazy, oh so very satisfying stroke of him, but each time she felt the beginnings of discomfort, the pressure was withdrawn. Then it would begin all over again, invading a little deeper.

She didn't understand, and she didn't care, not when it felt so good and the ache inside only became wilder and sweeter. Suddenly she felt a sharp pinch, followed by the incredibly wondrous sensation of him filling her. Her tiny gasp became a shuddering sigh. They were one, rising together in a harmony of rhythm that was its own form of beauty.

"THE MAGNOLIAS." REMY stood at the French doors leading onto the second-floor gallery, staring at the towering trees with green, leathery leaves on the front lawn. She turned to Nattie, faintly stunned by the realization. "Brodie Donovan built this house. I never thought . . . I assumed . . . even though I remember that the Garden district was originally established by wealthy Americans, it never occurred to me this house was built by anyone other than a Jardin. I should have known that the Jardins, being Creole, would have lived in the Vieux Carré."

"This was Donovan's house, all right," Nattie confirmed with a nod of her gray head.

"Then we got not only the shipping line from him but this house as well. How?"

"I'm getting to that." Nattie waved a hand at her, demanding patience. "Anyway, there's no doubt Adrienne knew exactly what she was doing when she went to bed with Brodie. By that I'm not saying that she didn't give herself to him for the same reason any young woman gives herself to the man she believes she loves. But she had other reasons."

Remy frowned. "What other reasons could she have?"

"Don't forget, in those days a woman was compromised merely by being alone with a man for an extended amount of time. And Adrienne always

intended for her grand-père to find out that she'd been secretly meeting Brodie
—at the appropriate time, of course—*and* she wanted her grand-père to know
without a doubt that she'd been irreparably compromised. There was even a
good chance she was going to have his baby. She figured her grand-père not
only would have to accept Brodie Donovan, but he'd also insist that they get
married." She paused briefly. "I think Adrienne had images of the two of them
reigning over both American and Creole society, living a life still cushioned by
the wealth and prestige of the Jardin name."

"Obviously that didn't happen," Remy guessed as she wandered over to an
old rosewood prie-dieu, suddenly wondering who had knelt on its padded
knee-rest to pray. Had it belonged to Adrienne? "Why? What went wrong,
Nattie?"

"She didn't think about what might happen if her brother found out she was
seeing Brodie. Which is exactly what happened," she replied. "By that time
she'd probably been meeting Brodie secretly for almost a month, no oftener
than twice a week. Now, when she came back from seeing him, she never used
the stairs; she always came through the courtyard and entered the house that
way. She figured if she was seen she always had the ready excuse that she hadn't
been able to sleep and had gone outside to take some night air. . . ."

Adrienne moved along the cool, dim passage of the *porte cochère* to the scrolled
iron gates at the end of it. She paused there and listened to the receding clop of
hooves and the muted clatter of the carriage as it departed on Royal Street. She
hesitated a minute longer, letting her ears adjust to the new silence and her eyes
to the uneven darkness of the courtyard beyond the tall wrought-iron gates.
The silvery glow from the moon highlighted the shininess of the magnolia's
green leaves and gleamed on the central fountain's bronze statue, of a woman
balancing a basin on her head, over which water flowed in a melodic whisper.
But there was no sound, no movement other than that. And no light shone from
the *garçonnière*, the narrow wing that extended from the main house and provided private quarters for the unmarried males in the family as well as for the
occasional guest. The Lenten season had arrived, bringing an end to the winter's lively social season, so there were no guests, and the absence of any lights
in the windows assured her that Dominique had retired for the night.

Carefully, Adrienne opened one side of the double gate and slipped through
into the garden patio, closing the gate quietly behind her, then pushing back
the hood of her cloak. Deliberately holding her pace to a wandering stroll, she
moved along the brick walk that circled the fountain and its reflecting pool.
The night air was scented with the fragrance of the shrubs and trees that were
planted in abundance throughout the courtyard—honeysuckle vines entwining
with the ivy to cover the high brick wall in the rear, sweet olive and fig trees
shading the rosebushes, and crepe myrtles, gardenias, and camellias crowding
the edges of the informal parterre.

By the time Adrienne reached the outside steps to the second-floor gallery,
all her tension was gone. It wasn't necessary to feign insouciance as she climbed
the stairs, thinking back on the pleasurable two hours she'd spent with Brodie
and savoring the stimulating memory of their moments of lovemaking, warmed
anew by it.

As expected, her room was dark, but her black maidservant Sulie Mae wasn't hovering at the French doors, waiting to unlock them and admit her, a necessity forced upon them by the nightly check her grandfather made before retiring to insure that all the doors were securely locked. Adrienne tapped twice on the glass. Almost immediately the familiar shape of the round-bosomed Negro woman appeared on the other side of the glassed doors. She fumbled briefly with the lock, then swung the door inward. Adrienne glanced down the length of the deeply shadowed and empty gallery and then stepped into her room, unfastening the front of her cloak, preparing to remove it and hand it to her servant.

A voice came out of the darkness, low and ominous—her brother's voice. "You may go now, Sulie Mae."

As Adrienne stiffened in alarm and swept her eyes over the black shapes in the darkened room to find him, a lamp-wick that had been no more than a faint speck of light was turned up, throwing a bright glow over the room. Dominique stood beside it.

"Michie Dominique, he say I gots to let him in," Sulie Mae murmured, her eyes round and dark with apprehension as she met Adrienne's accusing look. Then she hurried from the room.

Adrienne turned to face her brother, unconsciously tilting her chin a little higher at the sight of his cold and forbidding expression. "Dominique," she began with forced lightness.

"You were with the Yankee—and do not add to your shame with lies of denial."

She was stunned that he knew. How had he found out? Had Sulie Mae betrayed her? Recognizing that the answers were irrelevant, Adrienne dismissed the questions from her mind and admitted, "I was with him, yes. I love him, Dominique."

"And what of Grand-père?" he challenged in a voice that was all ice, his stare raking her. "How could you betray his trust? How could you bring this dishonor to him, to the family?"

"My love for Brodie is no dishonor, but Grand-père has refused to see that," Adrienne asserted. "He left me no choice."

"And you have left me no choice."

As he came toward her, Adrienne instinctively took a step back, intimidated by this man who seemed so unlike the brother she knew. "What do you mean by that?" she demanded, belatedly realizing that he wasn't approaching her—instead, he crossed to the gallery doors, which Sulie Mae had left standing open. "Are you going to tell Grand-père?"

He paused in the doorway. "I would never deliberately say or do anything that I knew would hurt him—as you have done." He stepped onto the gallery and quietly closed the door behind him.

She believed him. He wasn't going to tell Grand-père about her assignations with Brodie Donovan. She felt momentarily weak with relief, aware that it would have ruined all her plans if her grandfather had found out from Dominique—but now she would have to alter those plans. She couldn't count on Dominique's keeping silent for long.

She realized she had to talk to her brother, make him understand the reasons for her actions. Not now, though. Tomorrow, when he was not smarting so from what he considered to be her betrayal.

Not for the first time in her life did Adrienne rail at society's duality of standards, which demanded strict observance of rigid moral codes by women but imposed no such inhibitions on men, leaving them free to drink, gamble, carouse—and install café-au-lait-skinned concubines in little cottages on Rampart Street.

When Adrienne entered the dining room the next morning for breakfast, only her grandfather and her aunt were seated at the table. Dominique's chair was empty. She murmured a greeting to her grandfather and nodded to her aunt, who was always sour-tempered in the morning, quick to speak sharply to the servants at the least clatter of dishes.

"Dominique is late this morning," Adrienne observed, taking her customary seat on her grandfather's left.

"*Non*, he arose early," her grandfather replied as he slathered raspberry sauce over a flaky pastry.

"Then he has left?" Adrienne asked, frustrated that she was being denied the chance to speak to him privately.

"He had his horse saddled more than an hour ago," her grandfather confirmed, then added vaguely, "He made some mention of an appointment."

"Did he say when he would return?"

"Not until evening."

All through breakfast, Adrienne debated her next move. Before she'd left Brodie last night, she had arranged to meet him again tomorrow evening. Now she decided that until she reached some type of understanding with Dominique, it wouldn't be wise to keep the appointment. But to cancel it without a word of explanation—she couldn't do that, either. No, she had to advise Brodie of this new situation, and she could do that only in person. She couldn't run the risk of having a note fall into the wrong hands.

The instant she returned to her room, Adrienne summoned Sulie Mae. "I want you to take a message to the old fiddler Cado. Tell him, 'She will meet him at the market this morning,' " she said, deliberately not mentioning Brodie's name and trusting that the mere fact that she would risk a daytime meeting would lend an urgency and importance to her words.

The black woman drew back, shaking her head vigorously. "No, Missy, I can't do that. If Michie Dominique find out, he have Michie Jardin sell me."

In no mood to be opposed in this, Adrienne retorted, "You must, or *I* will have him sell you."

Two hours later Adrienne lagged behind her aunt, scanning the throng of shoppers and merchants gathered under the pillared arcade. The din was ceaseless, with hens squawking in their crates, merchants shouting out proclamations of their wares, parrots screeching from their cages, customers calling greetings to this person or that, and all of it abrasive to her as she kept watching for Brodie.

Stall after stall of fishermen proudly displayed their morning's catch, grayblue bodies of fish gleaming in the sunlight, hard-shelled oysters piled in mounds, crayfish wiggling and brandishing their claws, dingy gray shrimp spread in layers six or seven inches deep waiting for a spiced boiling pot to turn them a delectable pink, and lazy crabs stirring reluctantly. But none of them tempted Adrienne's aunt as she continued on to the fruit and vegetable section to inspect the prickly pineapples for freshness. While she haggled with the vendor, Adrienne surreptitiously looked for Brodie. But he wasn't here either.

Nor was he among the butchers busy carving cuts of meat to order from fresh carcasses—nor among the huddle of flower merchants or the roughly clad bayou hunters with their assortment of wild fowl, turtles, and alligators. Worried, Adrienne looked around openly. Hadn't he got her message?

The clinking of foils echoed from the fencing room, followed by a well-modulated voice proclaiming, *"Bien.* Let us try it again." Again there was a ring of steel as rapiers met.

With ill-concealed restlessness, Brodie rose from his chair in the academy's austere office and crossed to the window, clasping his hands behind his back, fingers gripping each other tightly. He stood there—for how long, he didn't know—his tension mounting at the sound of clashing blades.

Then it stopped. There was a polite murmur of voices and then he heard footsteps approaching the door. Brodie pivoted from the window as the door opened and the academy's master walked in, a lean-visaged man with a deceptively warm and pleasant look. His fencing mask was tucked under one arm, and his other hand loosely held a tipped foil. Yet there was ever an alertness about him that spoke of well-honed instincts, muscles, and senses trained to react in fractions of seconds.

"Brodie, how good to see you, my friend. I regret that I had to keep you waiting. It was a rare morning lesson, you understand." Each movement was lithe and supple as he laid his fencing mask and glove on the writing table and placed the rapier beside them. "May I offer you coffee, or perhaps a glass of wine?"

"No," Brodie refused abruptly, and came straight to the point of his visit. "I need your advice, Pepe," he said, familiarly addressing the renowned fencing master José Llulla by his more common name. A Spaniard by birth, José "Pepe" Llulla was unlike most of the fifty or so masters with fencing schools strung along the flagstoned Exchange Alley. He did not dress extravagantly, affect the manners of a dandy, or try to enter the ranks of Creole society. More than that, he saved his money and invested it in various businesses—a sawmill, a grocery, a slaughterhouse, a barroom. It was through his many ventures that Brodie had first met this man who had lived the life of a seaman before becoming a *maître d'armes,* considered by many to be the finest swordsman ever to draw a blade in New Orleans.

"You seek my advice? I am flattered, Brodie."

"I have been challenged."

Merely saying the words recalled the coolness of Dominique Jardin's expression when he'd confronted Brodie outside the offices of the Crescent Line an hour earlier—and brought back the flicking brush of the man's glove against his cheek. There'd been no display of anger, no hot words. The challenge had been delivered in the precise, courteous manner dictated by the duello, the dueling code.

"You have been challenged—this is wonderful, *mon ami!"* the *maître d'armes* declared, smiling in delight. "Congratulations."

"Wonderful?" Brodie snapped. "I see nothing 'wonderful' in it."

"But of course it is wonderful," Pepe insisted with an expansive wave of his hand. "You have been accepted at last. A challenge cannot be issued to one who is not an equal. Tell me, who is your opponent?"

"Dominique Jardin."

A black eyebrow arched sharply. "A formidable rival, and a veteran of many duels—all of which he won with his blade. You are fortunate that he challenged you. The choice of weapons becomes yours. I suggest that you choose pistols."

"I'm not going to fight him."

The Spaniard stiffened, his look turning hard and cold. "You must."

"Dammit, I can't, Pepe. That's why I'm here. That's why I needed to see you. You know the proper procedures. There has to be some way this can be avoided, something within the letter of that damnable dueling code."

"If Monsieur Jardin chooses to accept an apology from you for whatever it is you have said or done over which he has taken offense, then there is no need for a duel to take place, and there is no loss of honor for either party. However, the apology must be tendered within the prescribed time. Once you meet on the field of honor, it is too late."

"You can forget the apology," Brodie said with a sigh. "He wouldn't find it acceptable."

"Then you must meet him."

He shook his head. "I can't."

"Then I advise that you get on one of your ships and leave, M'sieu Donovan. To refuse to meet him is tantamount to cowardice. You would be finished here in the Vieux Carré. And I suspect your American associates would lose their respect for you as well."

"I'm not leaving."

"You came here for my advice. I have given it to you. Since you are afraid—"

"I'm not afraid of him, Pepe. If there was no one else involved, I would meet him with shotguns at a handkerchief's length. But that isn't the case."

The Spaniard looked at him with new curiosity. "Someone else is involved? Who?"

"His sister, Adrienne. I intend to marry her, Pepe. Now do you see how impossible this situation is? No matter what choice I make, I lose. If I refuse to meet him, I'll be branded a coward. I'm not sure I could live with it, even knowing that it wasn't true. And I doubt Adrienne could bear the shame of it even if she knew I'd done it for her. As you pointed out, I'd be finished in this town, and if she married me, she'd be finished too. On the other hand, if I accept his challenge, she'll never agree to marry the man who killed her brother."

" 'Killed.' " Pepe Llulla laughed easily, lightly. "You Americans and your notion that every duel must mean the death of one. Honor is satisfied with the mere drawing of blood; a scratch on the cheek or the hand is enough. I myself have been in numerous duels, and regardless of the stories you may have heard to the contrary, the occasions when I have inflicted a fatal wound were few. Most are still walking around, sporting the scars from their encounter with me." He came over to Brodie and clamped a friendly hand on his shoulder, smiling broadly. "Accept Monsieur Jardin's challenge. Meet him on the field of honor. Shoot to wound and pray to Le Bon Seigneur that his bullet does not strike a vital organ. Then allow the beautiful mademoiselle to nurse you back to health, let her be angry with you for dueling, let her fuss at you and love you all the more."

Brodie hesitated, then slowly smiled. "I knew there was a way."

"It is not without risk, *mon ami*," Pepe reminded him.

"But it's a risk worth taking."

"Have you chosen your second?"

"My brother Sean, I guess. I would ask you, Pepe, but I'd rather not draw you into the middle of this."

"Perhaps that is wise," he conceded indifferently. "Have you considered the time, the place, the weapons, the distance?"

Brodie gave him a dry look. "Pepe, I've been spending the last hour trying to figure how to get out of this duel, not how to carry it out."

"May I suggest you arrange to meet him late this afternoon—at four or five o'clock? It is never wise to allow yourself too much time to think about what is to come."

"If you say so." The haste suited him. But his own thought was that he wanted this duel over with before Adrienne could find out about it. It was her nerves he wished to spare, more than his own.

"The oak grove on the Allard plantation is the common choice of sites. Everyone knows it. You may as well meet him *sous les chênes*." The Spanish master began slowly to pace the room, thinking, planning, deciding on details. "As for weapons, I have a fine pair of Navy revolvers. Have you handled one before?"

"Yes." Brodie nodded, remembering his river days. Only a fool traveled the Mississippi on a flatboat unarmed.

"You may have the use of mine, then. I suggest you set the distance at thirty paces." He allowed a brief smile to show. "After all, it is not your desire to kill your opponent, *oui*?"

18

THE AFTERNOON'S WARMTH lingered over the courtyard, ignoring the long shadows of twilight that stretched across it. Adrienne betrayed none of her inner agitation as she wandered along the bricked walk. Pausing, she pretended to admire the perfection of a red rose while mentally she screened out the musical fall of the fountain's water and listened intently to the muted sounds coming from the street beyond the thick walls that enclosed the courtyard.

Where was Dominique? Already lights gleamed inside the house. If he didn't return soon, she would have no opportunity to speak to him privately before it was time to dress for the evening meal. Then what would she do? Postpone it until tomorrow? She doubted her nerves could stand it; already they felt brittle from the strain.

Again she resumed her apparently idle stroll along the parterre. Then came the groan of the tall wooden carriage gates swinging open, and the noise from the street grew louder. Adrienne turned to face the courtyard's scrolled gates, tense, expectant. She heard the clop and clatter of a horse and carriage in the flagstoned *porte cochère* and almost turned away, realizing that it couldn't be Dominique returning; he'd left on horseback, not in the family carriage. But who would be coming to call so late in the day?

A black groom hurried from the stables to hold the horse's head when the open carriage stopped before the flight of stairs. Drawn forward, Adrienne saw a short, slightly pudgy man alight from the carriage. She recognized Victor Dumonte, a contemporary of Dominique's and one of his closest friends. How oddly disheveled he looked, she thought, his cravat all askew, the front of his shirt stained. As he turned back to the carriage, he saw her and froze.

"Victor." She went to greet him and welcome him to the house, manners permitting her no other choice. Leaving the private patio, she passed through its wrought-iron gates and approached the carriage. "It is good to see you. But if you have come to speak with Dominique, he is not here. He left early this morning and has yet to return."

"I know." He took a quick step toward her and stopped again. Adrienne was struck by how unusually pale he looked, with no pink-cheeked glow to his face. He took her hands and she felt the clamminess of his skin, the sensation eliminating any further doubt that he was ill. Even his eyes had a sick look to them. "I—" Victor started to say something more, then stopped and looked back at a second man now stepping down from the carriage.

"Dr. Charron." Adrienne glanced at the gray-goateed man in surprise. His tall beaver hat sat firmly on his head, and a pair of spectacles rode the high break of his nose. He carried a walking cane but not his black medical bag. Adrienne saw it sitting on the carriage seat. "This is unexpected. I—"

The doctor wasted not a breath on a greeting, his expression stern, his manner grim. "Where is your grand-père?"

"He is inside," she began, then frowned in bewilderment when he brushed past her without a word and hurried up the stairs. She turned back to her brother's friend, feeling the first glimmer of apprehension. "What is it? What is wrong, Victor?"

He looked down at her hands, his grip tightening on them. "There was a duel, Adrienne," he said in a low, choked voice.

She stared at the sickly pallor of his face, suddenly remembering how many times Dominique had called on Victor to act as his second—and how frequently Dr. Charron had served as the attending physician. "Dominique?"

When he lifted his head, there were tears in his eyes. "He was shot, Adrienne."

She made a small sound of protest, her eyes racing to the carriage as the driver and the family's Negro groom gently carried her brother's motionless form from it. For an instant she stared at Dominique's face, noticing how very white it looked against the black of his hair—the moment filled with a strange unreality.

She shook it off. "We must get him inside at once. The doctor will need his bag—"

"*Non.*" He checked her attempt to pull away. "Adrienne, he is dead."

"*Non,* it is not true!" She glared at him, furious that he had dared to make such a claim.

"I swear it is."

Ignoring his earnest plea, she twisted free of his hands. "I do not believe you. It cannot be." She moved immediately to her brother's side, his still body cradled in the arms of the liveried black driver and the old groom. She saw no wound of any kind—the front of his linen shirt showed not a trace of blood. But when she laid a hand against his smooth cheek, she was shaken by the coolness of his skin. "It is a mistake. It must be!" She leaned over him, sliding her hand around his middle—and stopping abruptly when she felt something damp and sticky.

A pair of hands gripped the points of her shoulders. She didn't resist them when they pulled her back, away from Dominique. She looked at her own hand, seeing the dull red stickiness on her fingers and palm. It was blood, but it wasn't warm, it wasn't bright—it wasn't . . . life.

From somewhere behind her came a moan of pain that sounded more animal than human. Turning, Adrienne saw her grandfather on the stairs, leaning heavily on the wooden rail. He seemed to become an old man before her eyes, his proud shoulders bowing, his stiff back hunching, his face turning as ashen as his gray hair as he stared at the body of his grandson.

Slowly, as if each step required all the strength he possessed, he came the rest of the way down the stairs and halted in front of the body. With eyes as dead as the man before him, he looked at the doctor.

"Who did this?"

"A *Yanqui.*"

Adrienne stiffened.

"Who?" her grandfather persisted.

"Brodie Donovan."

"*Non,*" she whispered in protest.

Her grandfather lifted his head at the name. "He lives?"

The doctor nodded. "A shoulder wound. Nothing more."

Adrienne tried to be glad, but she was too numb. Over and over again she kept remembering the statement Dominique had made the night before in her room: "And you have left me no choice." She should have known what he meant by that. She should have remembered his inflexible code of honor. But never once had she considered what her brother's reaction might be to her activities. No, her whole attention had been concentrated on placing her grandfather in a position where he would be forced to accept Brodie.

"Dominique." A rasping sob broke from her grandfather as he said the name. Bending, he kissed a colorless cheek and murmured softly, brokenly, "Blood of my blood. My life."

She saw his shoulders shake with sobs more wretched for their silence. The first of her own rose in her throat. *Nom de Dieu,* what had she done?

"I don't understand," Remy said in confusion, pushing herself off the bed to pace the room. "If Brodie intended only to wound him, what went wrong? Was his own aim thrown off when he was shot?"

"No. It was one of those freak things nobody could have expected," Nattie replied. "Brodie's shot struck Dominique in the arm, but the bullet hit a bone and glanced off, entering his body and going right through his heart, killing him instantly."

"Then it was an accident, a horrible accident."

"It was that, all right."

"Surely Adrienne knew."

"Brodie told her."

"Then he saw her again." For some reason, Remy'd had the feeling that Dominique's death had meant the end of their affair.

"Briefly—at the St. Louis Cemetery, when her brother was laid to rest in the family tomb. . . ."

The sky was blue and cloudless, the sun warm and bright, its rays spilling between the leafy branches of the oaks and magnolias to cast their light on the whitewashed stucco of the cemetery's many "mansions" of the dead, built close together in a precise pattern that reminded Brodie of the houses standing shoulder to shoulder along the narrow streets of the Vieux Carré. Here too—in death as in life—many generations slept under the same roof.

Absently he adjusted the black sling that held his left shoulder immobile, his eyes never leaving Adrienne's veiled face. The filmy black net shaded her features but didn't hide them. From this distance they appeared to have been carved out of white marble, so cool and blank did they look, not a tear falling to glisten on her cheek.

Not so her aunt. Her weeping hadn't slackened since they'd arrived at the cemetery. Now that it was time to leave, it grew worse. Brodie watched as both Adrienne and her grandfather helped the grieving spinster to her feet. Emil Jardin himself bore little resemblance to the autocratic patriarch Brodie had faced a little more than a month ago; his eyes were dull and haunted, his firm stride reduced to a shuffling gait.

He stared at the three of them for a moment, huddled together in their black mourning dress yet unable to draw comfort from each other. Then Emil Jardin signaled to Adrienne that her assistance was no longer necessary. She stepped back, letting him lead her aunt away from the mausoleum. She started to follow, then hesitated and looked back, tilting her head to gaze at the family name, JARDIN, carved above the temple's bronze door, ornamented with laurel leaves and seraphim. She was frozen there for a timeless second. With an effort, it seemed, she dragged her glance away and trailed after her grandfather and aunt, staying a few paces behind and letting her grandfather deal with the mourners who had lingered to offer their condolences in person.

It was the chance Brodie'd been waiting for. He'd come hoping he'd be able to speak to her, even though he knew there was nothing he could say that would enable her to forget what he'd done. But he needed to talk to her—he needed to tell her how much he regretted it, he needed to say the words for his own sake.

He glanced at her grandfather's gray and tear-wet face as he passed by, then stepped out from between two temple-shaped tombs to intercept Adrienne when she approached. She faltered for an instant, then stopped.

"I had to come," he said. "I swear it wasn't deliberate on my part." In his mind's eye he saw again the grove of old oak trees dripping with gray moss, that moment when he'd brought the barrel of his revolver to bear on Dominique's long, lean shape thirty yards away, sighting on his arm and squeezing the trigger, that instant of relief he'd felt when he'd seen Dominique's arm jerk even as a bullet slammed into his own shoulder, the force half turning him so he never even saw Dominique crumple to the ground, the glimpse of everyone running to the limp form lying on the spring-green grass, the shock of hearing someone cry out, "He's dead!" and his own disbelieving protests insisting that his shot had been true, that Dominique had been wounded in the arm, without knowing the bullet had ricocheted off a bone and into his heart. "I'm sorry," he finished tightly.

"We each have our cause of deep regret." Just for an instant she let her own intense pain show. "My brother is dead. My family is dead. Everything is dead."

As she walked away, Brodie knew exactly what she meant. He felt dead inside knowing he'd never see her again. The steady beat of his heart was a lie.

"Of course, Adrienne didn't know how wrong she was," Nattie declared from her perch on the arm of the bedroom's overstuffed chair. "Not then."

" 'Wrong?' What do you mean?"

"I mean she was pregnant, but she didn't realize it until a couple weeks after the funeral."

Remy sat down on the loveseat, all the pieces starting to fit together. "And even though she was pregnant with Brodie Donovan's child, her grandfather refused to let her marry the man who had killed her brother. And that child is the reason Cole said our name should be Donovan instead of Jardin."

"That's true, though there's one thing wrong with what you're saying. You see, the question of Adrienne marrying Brodie was never raised—not by old Emil Jardin, and definitely not by Adrienne."

"Why not? I would have thought—"

"You're forgetting the guilt she felt," Nattie broke in. "As far as she was concerned, she was the one who'd killed Dominique. Brodie had merely been the instrument of his death. Considering how much she loved her brother, that alone would've been a heavy load of blame to carry, but she had the added guilt of knowing that the family name had died with Dominique. That's why when she learned she was with child, instead of that knowledge filling her with deep despair, it gave her hope. That's why she wouldn't let her grandfather arrange a marriage for her even though she knew the scandal, the shame, the disgrace she would face by having a child out of wedlock back then."

Remy slowly shook her head. "I can't imagine Emil Jardin agreeing to that—not with his pride, his sense of family honor. However much he may have wanted the family line to continue, he couldn't have tolerated the humiliation of a bastard child continuing it—especially Brodie Donovan's. He did know Brodie was the father, didn't he?"

"He guessed. It wasn't too hard. . . ."

"This bastard you carry comes from the seed of that *Yanqui*, is this not true?" The glitter of loathing was in his eyes, a loathing born of disgust, a match to the pain that rasped his voice. "The same *Yanqui* who killed my Dominique. It is why he challenged him."

"*Non*," Adrienne denied that, her calm like an armor that not even his trembling rage could penetrate as she stood before him in her brother's darkened bedroom, the drapes pulled against a world that continued to go on. The room was exactly as it had been on the afternoon of his death—a change of clothes for dinner neatly laid out on the bed, his shaving things arranged on the bureau, the basin of water kept full and fresh by a servant. The only alteration was the tapers that burned in his memory on the prie-dieu. For it was here that her grandfather came to pray. In the days and weeks since Dominique's death, he had divided his time between this bedroom and the family tomb, isolating himself with his grief and sharing it with no one. And in all this time he'd hardly spoken a word to anyone, sitting in silence at meals, staring at the plate before him, and rarely touching the food on it. "Dominique knew only that I was meeting . . . him in secret." She deliberately avoided referring to Brodie by name, and spoke quickly to make her case. "It matters not who the father is, Grand-père. My child will be born a Jardin and raised a Jardin. He will know no other name, no other past. Through him, our family will live."

"Through a bastard." The words were spoken low, thick with the disgrace inherent in the phrase.

"*Non*, Grand-père." She smiled faintly, serenely. "This life that grows within me is God's will. He has taken Dominique from us, and He has given us this life in return." She moved toward him, lifting her hands, but he drew back stiffly. "No one can take Dominique's place—in your heart or mine. I know that. But God in His wisdom has allowed me to conceive this child."

"To punish you for your sins," he said bitterly.

"*Non*, Grand-père. It is so I may atone for them," Adrienne replied with a certainty of heart. "My son's origins need never be known. Your friends are aware that we have distant relatives in France.\In May, when the fever season approaches, we will sail for France to visit them. After my son is born in November, we can return home . . . to raise the baby of a Jardin cousin, orphaned at birth."

And that would be her punishment, her pain—the knowledge that she would forever have to deny to the world and to her own child that she was his mother. It could be no other way. Just as she would have to live the rest of her life knowing she had killed her brother, as surely as if she'd pulled the trigger herself.

A knock at the door broke the thick silence in the room. In response, her grandfather snapped an impatient "*Entrez.*"

The bedroom door swung open under the push of his black manservant's hand. "Michie Varnier is here," Gros Pierre announced. "I told him you don't want to see no one, but he say he gots to talk to you. He say there's an emergency at the old Clinton plantation."

"See him, Grand-père," Adrienne said, quietly urging him to speak to the man who served as his secretary and assistant, handling the details for the family's many and varied business interests. After Dominique died, her grandfather had ceased to care about any of it and had let the full responsibility fall to Simon Varnier. "You have reason to care about the future. When you think on what I have said, you will see I am right." She held his look an instant longer, then turned and left the room.

"Is you going to see him, Michie Jardin?" the black asked, then added, "He sure was powerful upset."

Emil Jardin gave no sign that he'd heard him, his gaze lost on some distant point. Then he roused himself and nodded absently, "*Oui*, I need to see him."

* * *

"Finding out about the baby gave old Emil Jardin reason to go on, all right," Nattie declared. "But it was never the reason Adrienne thought she'd given him."

"What do you mean?" Remy asked, even as she guessed at the answer.

"I mean he set out to destroy the man who had taken his grandson's life and ruined his granddaughter."

"The Crescent Line." She had a sudden, sinking feeling that she knew how her family had acquired the shipping company.

"You've got it." Nattie pointed a long finger at her in affirmation. " 'Course, it wasn't something he could do overnight. And it wasn't something he could do without placing some money in the right hands—and as successful as Brodie'd become, that meant a considerable amount of money. Her grandfather ended up selling his sugar and cotton plantations to raise it. While he was doing that, he had his man Simon Varnier find out who Brodie was doing business with, both here and abroad, where he was getting his cargo, who was working for him, who he owed, and how much. After a couple months—about the time Adrienne and her Tante ZeeZee left for France—he put his plan in motion."

"And there was nothing Brodie could do to stop him, was there?" Remy mused aloud, recalling the power and influence Emil Jardin had possessed through connections long established.

"At first he didn't even realize what was happening. You've got to remember, he loved Adrienne. He'd taken it hard, losing her that way. For a while he lost interest in everything, including the Crescent Line. When things started to go wrong for him—his captains leaving him to command other ships, his crews going off on shore leave and not coming back, mysterious fires breaking out aboard ships, cargo spoiling on him or getting damaged, the insurance companies hiking the premiums on him—he thought he was having a run of bad luck. Within a year, nobody wanted to sail with him, nobody wanted to ship their goods on his vessels, and nobody wanted to sell to him. And the last was the part that ended up making him suspicious. The others he could understand. People tend to be superstitious; if they thought his ships were jinxed, they'd steer clear of him. But not to sell to him—that didn't make sense. . . ."

An overcast sky spread a premature gloom over the Vieux Carré, the black clouds hanging low and heavy as Brodie made his way along a narrow street. In the far distance, lightning danced, but the clatter of drays and the street noise masked any faint rumble of thunder. Casting a weather eye at the approaching spring storm, Brodie judged it to be another three or four hours away. He welcomed its coming, wanting a release from the charged tension in the air.

As he neared the corner, he found his steps slowing. He rarely came to the Quarter anymore, not since. . . . It still hurt to think of her, to see the places where he'd met her, to remember her smile and the shining black glow of her eyes. A year, and the pain was still as fresh as if it had been yesterday, especially here in the Vieux Carré, where she lived.

He spotted the old blind fiddler at his customary place on the corner. Brodie stopped and almost turned around, not wanting to talk to the black man who had relayed so many messages from her, afraid he wouldn't be able to keep from asking about her. He forced himself to think of the Crescent Line and the trouble it was in—and of his suspicions about its worsening situation, suspicions that it was more than bad luck.

He walked up to the fiddler and dropped a silver dollar in his hat. "How have you been, Cado?"

The old man stiffened at the sound of his voice and stopped playing, something he'd never done before. Startled, Brodie watched as the man bent down and fished around in his hat, then straightened up and held out a silver dollar.

"Your money ain't no good no more, Michie Donovan."

"What the hell are you talking about, Cado?"

Centering on his voice, the black man pushed his hand against Brodie's middle. "Take your money and go. Leave old Cado alone."

For an instant Brodie warred with his anger, torn between ripping the coin from the man's hand and smashing his fist into that cold black face.

"You've turned against me too, have you, Cado?" he muttered, seizing the black man's wrist, taking the silver dollar from his unresisting fingers, and flinging it into the gutter.

When he started to shove past him to cross the street, the old man murmured under his breath, "Four o'clock. The shoemaker's shop on Dumaine."

There was only one shoemaker's shop on Dumaine, a narrow hole-in-the-wall affair. A hand-painted plaque by the door identified the owner as Louis Germaine, F.M.C.—a free man of color. The door was propped open, letting in the heaviness of the storm-laden air. Promptly at four o'clock, Brodie walked into the shop, which was redolent of leather and polish.

An ebony-skinned man in a leather apron sat at a cobbler's bench. When Brodie walked in, he looked up, hesitated, and darted a quick glance at the open doorway, then nodded his head in the direction of a curtained opening in the rear of the shop.

When Brodie approached it, Cado's voice came from behind the thin curtain. "There's some boots on the counter to the right of you. Look 'em over, Michie Donovan, and don't give no sign you can hear old Cado. There's eyes everywhere."

Brodie did as he was told. "What's going on, Cado?"

"You made yourself an enemy," came his low reply. "I knew you'd be coming to old Cado. I been listening and I been hearing. The word's out: a man does business with you and he be finished in this town."

"Who put the word out?" Brodie picked up a boot and pretended to examine it, his fingers digging into the soft leather.

"You mean you ain't got that figured out?"

"I have my suspicions."

"If you're suspicioning old Emil Jardin, you'd be right," Cado said, and Brodie swore under his breath. "Ain't no use in that, Michie Donovan. You got more troubles coming your way. Talk is he bought up the notes on the ships and your house. I figure he's jus' waiting for the right time to say you gotta pay."

Brodie hung his head, knowing Jardin would pick a time when he was certain he couldn't scrape the cash together. "All because that damn bullet had to ricochet," he murmured to himself, realizing that the bullet had taken away more than Dominique Jardin's life, more than Adrienne from his side. Now it was going to cost him the Crescent Line. A part of him didn't care—and hadn't cared since he'd lost Adrienne.

"I'm suspicioning it's more than that, Michie Donovan. He ain't after you jus' cause you killed his grandson in a duel."

Adrienne. The old man was getting back at him for meeting her in secret, Brodie realized, but he said nothing, feeling too sick inside.

Cado began talking again. "When they come back from France last December, they brought a baby with them, a little boy child. Claimed he didn't have no momma and no papa."

"I heard." Brodie nodded indifferently.

"The house Negroes say Missy Adrienne love that boy like he was her own," Cado declared, then paused for several seconds. "The house Negroes, they say that boy got red hair. Real dark red hair . . . about the color of yours."

In the heartbeat it took for the implication of those words to sink in, Brodie reacted, whipping back the curtain and stepping into the back room to grab the blind man by the collar of his gray shirt. "What're you saying? Speak plain. Is the boy my son?"

"Ain't no one can tell you that for certain sure but Missy Adrienne, her aunt, or Old Emil. It's a fact, though, she was feeling poorly before they left. And when they come back, they didn't have none of their servants with them—gave them all their freedom and left 'em in France. That says to me old Emil didn't want them to come back here and do no talking. Then there's that red hair of his. Where would a Jardin get red hair? If you ask old Cado, there can only be one place—and that's from his daddy."

Brodie loosened his hold on the blind man's collar, never having wanted to believe anything so much in his whole life. "His name," he said thickly. "Do you know it?"

"Jean-Luc Étienne Jardin."

"Jean-Luc. Luc." He liked the sound of that.

But was he his son? The question drove Brodie from the shop and up the street. He turned on Royal and didn't stop until he reached the Jardin home. A cool breeze brought the smell of rain to him as he hesitated briefly, then went directly to the pedestrian gate cut into the tall wooden carriage doors. He opened it and stepped through into the tunnel-like passageway of the *porte cochère.* He moved briskly to the stairs and took them two at a time, then paused at the top. The second-floor gallery was empty, the French doors leading onto it from the house standing open to admit the fresh breeze.

The indistinct murmur of voices came from inside, their tone and texture definitely feminine. Brodie paid no attention to them and listened instead for another sound. When he heard the gurgling laughter of a baby, he followed it to a pair of open doors and walked in.

He paused a moment to let his eyes adjust to the deeply shadowed interior, then looked around. It was a bedroom, the set of silver brushes and combs on the rosewood vanity table telling him it was a woman's bedroom. He heard the happy coo of laughter again, coming from a corner of the room. He spotted the tall crib, draped in lacy mosquito netting. There was movement behind it, a waving of arms.

The last few steps to the crib seemed long. Almost hesitantly, Brodie lifted the netting to look at the baby inside, conscious of the quick beating of his heart and the tightness in his throat.

A baby, sitting up by himself, looked back at him with wide, startled eyes.

His hair was dark and thick, with a telltale glint of red showing in it. He scowled at Brodie as if expressing his annoyance at being surprised, then grabbed at the silk hem of a blanket and flailed the air with it.

Brodie hooked the netting over the bar, freeing his hands so he could trail a finger over that smooth cheek. "It's a fine-looking lad you are, Jean-Luc." As he drew his hand away, the little boy grabbed for it, squealing with delight when he caught hold of it. As the child tried to pull himself upright, Brodie could feel the straining of his small muscles, and he smiled. "You're a bit young to be standing, aren't you?"

But he reached under the boy's arms and set him on his bootied feet. Then, having gone that far, he picked him up—a little awkwardly, his hand momentarily tangling with the long linen gown the baby wore before he managed to smooth it over his long, chubby legs.

"Somebody should tell your mother you look like a girl in this thing," Brodie murmured, receiving another scowl in reply. "As hefty as you are, there's no doubt you're a boy."

The scowl faded into a look of fascination as Jean-Luc stared at Brodie's mouth and chin, his hand coming up to investigate, little fingers curling onto his lower lip. Brodie caught at his hand and freed his lip from the boy's fingers, then chucked him under the chin with his own little fist. Jean-Luc gurgled a laugh, breaking into a wide smile. Brodie wanted to laugh too, but the pleasure he felt was too deep, too intense; it choked him instead. Just for an instant, he hugged the boy to him and pressed his lips against his temple, breathing in the baby-cleanness of him.

Suddenly, unexpectedly, he had the sensation of being watched. He looked over his shoulder at the door to the hall. Adrienne stood inside it, dressed in black, just as she'd been the last time he'd seen her, at the cemetery. The color suited her, bringing out the darkness of her hair and eyes and the luminous whiteness of her skin.

For a long moment, words wouldn't come to him. He had the feeling she'd been standing there for some time. He turned slightly, and her gaze went from him to the baby in his arms, then back to his face.

"I wanted to see my son."

She said not a word, her expression remaining serenely composed, yet there was a shiny brightness to her eyes, the shiny brightness of tears—happy tears, proud tears. Her look eliminated any vestige of doubt that the child was his.

A jagged bolt of lightning flashed from the dark clouds, lighting up the late-afternoon sky. It was followed immediately by an explosive crash of thunder that shook the glass panes in the French doors. Jean-Luc whimpered, his lower lip jutting out in an uncertain quiver. With the second clap of thunder his whimper became a full-blown wail, and he stiffened in Brodie's arms and turned, stretching out needing hands to his mother. When Adrienne came over, Brodie reluctantly surrendered him to her, watching those small arms cling to her and listening to the shushing croon of her voice.

The wind and the rain came next, driving across the gallery and sweeping through the open doors. Brodie knew he should leave, but he continued to stand there, gazing at the two of them, a thousand *if-only's* going through his mind, his heart twisting with each of them.

"Adrienne?" Footsteps and the rustle of layers of silk swishing together came from the hall. "Is that Jean-Luc crying? What is wrong?"

Adrienne took a step toward the hall door, calling, "The storm has frightened him, Tante ZeeZee." She looked back at Brodie, her eyes begging him to go.

He hesitated, then reached out and stroked Jean-Luc's silken hair and let his fingers run lightly over her hand as it cupped the back of the boy's head, feeling the softness, the warmth, of her skin. Suddenly he didn't trust himself to stay. He turned abruptly and went out the way he'd come.

When he left the shelter of the *porte cochère*, closing the gate behind him, he paused, oblivious to the sheeting rain. He remembered the sensation of holding the baby in his arms, the little fingers pulling at his lip, the softness of him, the strength of him. A son. He had a son. He walked down the street smiling, tears mingling with the rain that streamed down his face.

19

THE CARRIAGE ROLLED across Canal Street and entered the brash and raw American section of the city. Emil Jardin sat stiffly erect on the tufted leather rear seat, his gaze fixed on some distant point, not deigning to glance around him. Usually his eyes had a flat, dead look to them, coming alive only when Brodie Donovan was mentioned. They were alive now.

His gloved hands adjusted their grip on his silver-handled cane. "This attorney, this—" He lifted a hand to gesture, searching for a name.

"Horace Tate," Emil Jardin's ever-precise, ever-fastidious secretary, Simon Varnier, supplied the name.

"*Oui*, Tate." His hand returned to its resting place atop the cane, which he carried more out of habit than out of necessity. In his youth Emil Jardin had carried a *colchemarde*—a sword cane. Everyone had, back then. Although he was too old and too slow for such a weapon now, he liked the reassuring feel of a cane in his hand. It was his gavel, tapping the floor for attention; his pointer, directing that attention where he wanted it to be; his rod, administering sharp raps of reprimand; and his scepter. He took strength from it. "This Tate, he told you nothing about this information he claims to have on Donovan?"

"He said he had information on the Crescent Line, not Donovan," Simon corrected, with his customary insistence on exactness. "Information he was certain would be of enormous interest to you. He refused to tell me what it was. In fact, he was most adamant that he would speak to no one but you."

"What of this warning he issued?"

"*Warning* is my word. M'sieu Tate *strongly advised* that you make no further move against the Crescent Line until you had spoken with him. He indicated that you may wish to take a different course of action once his information is in your hands."

"What could this mean, I wonder?" Emil Jardin murmured, his gray eyebrows drawing together to form a thick, solid line.

Simon Varnier took him literally and responded with his own speculation. "We know Donovan has been trying to sell three of his ships. Perhaps he has found a buyer for them. Or perhaps he has obtained financing from some unknown source. If he has, then it would not be wise to demand payment at this time for the notes you hold."

"What do you know of this Tate?"

"Very little. He landed in New Orleans on the first of March, barely a month ago. He says he is from St. Louis, but he arrived not by riverboat, but on one of Donovan's ships that had stopped in Boston. I suspect that is how he came to know about Donovan's situation."

"But how did he discover my interest in him?"

"He refused to disclose his source."

"He will disclose it to me before this goes further." He didn't like the idea that someone new to the city had learned so quickly that he was the force behind the move to crush Brodie Donovan—to crush him slowly, to make him suffer, to make him feel the pain, the grief, the humiliation and shame that he, Emil, knew. The man had destroyed lives—his, Dominique's, and Adrienne's. It was only right that he be destroyed, and only fair that a Jardin be the instrument of his destruction.

As the carriage slowed, Emil Jardin lifted his head and took note of his surroundings, looking down the prominent length of his patrician nose at the string of hastily constructed clapboard buildings. On only two other occasions in his life had he found sufficiently strong reason to venture into the *Yanqui* section. Both times he'd sworn that nothing would induce him to repeat the experience of being in the midst of those jostling, crude, loud-talking *Americains*, always hurrying, always demanding, always greedy.

"If this attorney was so anxious to share his information, why could he not have come to the Vieux Carré?" Emil grumbled when the carriage rolled to a stop in front of one of the clapboard buildings splashed with whitewash. "Why was it necessary for us to come to *this* place to meet with him?"

"I explained that," Simon Varnier said patiently. "Horace Tate is a cripple. A childhood injury left him without the use of his right leg. He has great difficulty getting in and out of a carriage, and he could not have walked the distance from his office to yours."

"I cannot think what information this man could have to give us that would be of any value." But he had to find out, and he stepped down from the carriage.

Horace Tate's office was as spare and inelegant as the building's exterior. A collection of worn law books occupied crude shelves of bare, rough wood, and more sat in a trunk waiting to be unpacked. There were scratches and gouges in the oak panels of the large kneehole desk that dominated the room. Emil Jardin walked straight to it, looking neither to the left nor to the right, his gaze fastened on the man behind it—though he seemed hardly a man, with his dusting of freckles and thatch of hay-colored hair. His quick smile had the eagerness and innocence of a boy's. He reminded Emil of a young man who had barely reached his majority, coming to the city fresh from the river bottoms, whose view of the world had been obscured by the back end of a mule pulling a plow—an impression reinforced by the ill-fitting suit and poorly tied cravat he wore.

"Mr. Varnier, it's good to see you again," he greeted them, speaking in English with a thick country drawl. "And you must be Mr. Jardin. Forgive me if I don't get up, but this leg of mine makes it mighty awkward." Emil observed the limp and crooked sprawl of the attorney's right leg under the desk, and the pair of sturdy canes propped against the plaster wall behind his chair. "Have a seat." Horace Tate waved a hand in the direction of the three chairs crowded in a semicircle in front of his desk.

Emil ignored the chairs and the invitation, choosing to stand, certain, now that he'd seen Horace Tate, that their meeting would be an extremely brief one. "Let us not waste time, M'sieu Tate."

"I agree." The voice came from somewhere behind him to his left. Emil turned and stiffened in shock.

Brodie calmly met his thunderstruck look and raked his thumbnail over the lucifer, then held the flame to the tip of his cigar. "Surprised?" he queried between puffs.

Purpling, Emil Jardin swung back to the attorney. "What is the meaning of this? It is an insult. An outrage." He stamped the floor with his cane. "Come, Simon. We are leaving."

He turned and flashed a look at Brodie, as if expecting him to try to stop him. Brodie merely shrugged his indifference. "You can stay or go. It doesn't matter to me. But you might want to take a look at the documents Mr. Tate has for you. They could make for some interesting reading."

Emil glared at Brodie for a long moment, then thrust a hand at his assistant. "Let me see these documents."

Horace Tate silently passed them to Simon Varnier, who gave them to Emil Jardin as Brodie wandered over to the far side of the desk. "Pull out a chair for him, Simon. I think he'll want to sit down."

Emil had barely got past the first paragraph when his hand began to tremble and the color drained from his face. "What is this?" He sank into the chair Simon had pulled out for him.

"Exactly what it says," Brodie replied. "You seem so anxious to destroy the Crescent Line, I thought you might like to know I don't own it anymore."

His fingers curled into the papers, crumpling their edges. "You cannot do this!"

"It's done—all legally signed, sealed, registered, and recorded," Brodie waved the cigar at the papers. "You don't have to let them stop you, though. You can still go through with your plans to ruin the Crescent Line. Of course, it will be interesting to see how you'll go about demanding payment on those notes from your own great-grandson. But I forgot. You refer to Jean-Luc as your ward, don't you? Then as his legal guardian, you should know that he's now the owner of a shipping company and a house. If you'll read further, you'll see I've named Mr. Tate here, Father Malone, and Adrienne as the administrators of his properties until my son turns twenty-one."

"How—" Emil choked off the rest of the question.

"How did I find out Jean-Luc was my son? It was a good job you did of muffling my sources of information, but you failed to silence all of them."

"You cannot prove this."

"I can't prove it, not legally. But he is my son. I know it and you know it." Brodie moved to the corner of the desk, dropping his air of coolness and seeking the confrontation he'd arranged.

Emil Jardin rose from his chair and hurled the documents down on the desk. "I will see you in your grave for this."

"Maybe you will. But my death—whether by your hand or by God's—won't change the one thing that matters: Jean-Luc is my son. He may carry the Jardin name, but he has Donovan blood."

On that note Emil Jardin stalked from the room, his cane pounding the hardwood floor with each stride.

The honking of a car's horn somewhere outside jarred Remy into the present. "Then Brodie gave the Crescent Line to his natural son," she murmured. "Emil Jardin didn't steal it from him."

"It wasn't for lack of trying," Nattie declared as she pushed off the armrest of the stuffed chair.

"And Brodie? What happened to him?"

"He died in August of that same year."

She remembered the threat Emil had made, swearing he'd see him in his grave. "How? Did Adrienne's grand—"

"No one knew for sure—except Brodie and old Emil. They say he died of yellow fever. Old Bronze John, they called it back then. Maybe he did. That summer of eighteen fifty-three saw one of the worst yellow-fever epidemics ever to hit New Orleans. Somewhere around fifteen thousand died from it, although some claim the figure was more than twenty thousand. Upwards of sixteen hundred died the same week in August that Brodie did. There were so many bodies needing to be buried, officials didn't bother with death certificates. Which is why there's none showing the cause of Brodie's death. And by then there weren't enough gravediggers to keep up with all the work. Coffins were stacked up like crates in a warehouse. The situation got so desperate they dug trenches and dumped the bodies in common graves. That's where Brodie ended up—in an unmarked grave. It was a terrible, terrible time."

"And Adrienne?"

"She and her family escaped it. Like always, they left the city the first of May, before the fever season arrived. She knew what was going on here. The whole world knew. People from all over the country sent gifts of food and money," Nattie said, then paused. "Adrienne never married. Wore black the whole of her life—for her brother, folks claimed, but I think she wore it for Brodie too. Every All Saints' Day, she went around and placed flowers on the common graves of the yellow-fever victims—because she didn't know which one Brodie was in. Old Emil couldn't have liked that, but I guess by then she didn't care whether he did or not. Old Bronze John took Father Malone too. And five years later Horace Tate was killed when the boiler on a riverboat exploded. He'd been on his way to visit his family in St. Louis."

"And Adrienne ended up as the sole administrator for her son."

"That's right. And that's how Emil Jardin ended up running the Crescent Line —and the Union blockade during the Civil War. Made a fortune at it, too. Why, it wasn't nothing for one of his ships to net almost a half a million dollars in *one* round trip. And the war went on for four years, with the ships making anywhere from five to ten trips a year. Most Southerners lost everything they had in the war, but old Emil Jardin got rich—or Jean-Luc did, since it was really all his, and old Emil didn't live long enough to enjoy much of it. He died in eighteen-seventy, after Jean-Luc turned eighteen."

"Then the Jardins were the war profiteers," Remy mused absently, and she leaned against the curved back of the loveseat. "I wonder how Cole found that out? I suppose if he went far enough back in the company records he would have found a copy of the document transferring all Brodie's interest in the Crescent Line to Jean-Luc. Maybe there was even some mention of his death in eighteen fifty-three—long before the Civil War started."

But it didn't explain why he had dragged Brodie Donovan's portrait out of storage and hung it in place of her grandfather's. He had to know it would upset her family, especially her father—which meant it had been a deliberate act. Why would Cole want to deliberately antagonize him?

"Are you still going to take that shower and change?" Nattie wanted to know.

"Yes." She nodded, still preoccupied with her thoughts.

"I'll lay you out some clean towels, then."

As Nattie headed for the adjacent bathroom, Remy rolled to her feet, restless again. She crossed to the French doors, unlocked them, and stepped onto the front gallery. Like twin sentinels, the two magnolia trees stood guard over the front lawn, magnolia trees that Adrienne had suggested Brodie plant.

Remy paused for a moment, then walked to the railing, its delicate ironwork a tracery of leaves and flowers. She let her gaze wander over the lawn, the wrought-iron fence that surrounded it, and the quiet street beyond.

Catty-corner across the street, a navy-blue sedan was parked at the curb. Remy noticed the driver sitting behind the wheel, her eye drawn by the incongruity of his dark hair and neatly trimmed salt-and-pepper beard, which looked more salt than pepper from this distance. He appeared to be writing something. She guessed he was a salesman. At that moment, he looked up. Realizing that he'd seen her, Remy turned from the railing and walked back to her room, not wanting her presence to be taken as an invitation for him to come pitch his wares.

As she entered the room, she glanced at the antique tester bed and stopped, suddenly wondering if Adrienne and Jean-Luc had lived in this house after Emil Jardin died. She was certain they must have. How else could it have become the family home? And if it had been haunted with memories for Brodie, how much more haunted it must have been for Adrienne.

A pink-palmed hand waved in front of her face. Startled, Remy blinked and focused her gaze on Nattie's high-cheeked face. "Sorry, I didn't see you."

"I guessed," she said dryly. "The towels are all laid out for you, and your robe's hanging on the back of the door."

"Thanks."

"What's wrong?" Nattie frowned at her in puzzlement. "You looked like you were in some kind of a trance."

"I was thinking about Adrienne, remembering how much she liked the social life back then—and how much she pitied her Tante ZeeZee. Yet she ended up just like her, a spinster—alone. I wonder where she found the strength to do it."

"Honey," Nattie said, offering another one of her sad and sage smiles, "a woman is like a teabag—you never know how strong she is until you get her in hot water."

Remy laughed, yet she had the feeling that somewhere nearby, trouble seethed. Where and of what kind, she couldn't remember. But she needed to be there. Why? To prevent what? To stop whom?

20 ~

THE MUSEUM COMPLEX on Jackson Square wasn't the place. At least her visit to it hadn't given her any indication that it was. Remy stood at one of the desks in the museum's office area, closed to the public, and absently twined the telephone receiver's coiled cord around her forefinger.

Gabe's voice came over the line. "If you're calling to tell me you're too tired to go to the museum this afternoon, I'm not surprised—considering how early you were up this morning."

"Actually, I'm calling from the museum."

"You're there?" She could hear the frown of surprise in his voice. "I thought you were coming to my office at two-thirty so we could go together."

"I was." After spending all morning wandering the house, she'd been on the verge of going crazy from inactivity. Then her brother had called around lunchtime to let her know he'd talked their father out of sending her to that clinic outside of Houston. In passing Remy had mentioned she was thinking about going to the museum later on, and Gabe had immediately insisted on going with her. At the time, she'd agreed. It wasn't until later that she'd known she would prefer to see it alone—with no one to distract her with talk—so she could be open to any impressions, any memories, any sense of trouble. "I was too restless sitting around the house, so I left early and came here to look around on my own."

"Then you've already been through everything."

"Yes." She couldn't keep the dispirited tone from her voice.

"You seem . . . discouraged. Weren't you able to remember anything?"

"Unfortunately, no," she said on a sigh. Nothing had been familiar to her— not any of the layouts, not a single exhibit, not one member of the staff, nothing.

As she idly scanned the bank of television monitors, part of the museum's security system, on the opposite wall, she noticed an older man standing near the traveling exhibit. With his dark hair and distinctively whitish beard, he looked exactly like the man she'd seen in the car in front of her house. Obviously she'd been wrong to assume he was a salesman. He must be a tourist. It was odd, though, that he was wearing a suit and tie. Most of them dressed much more casually, especially in the daytime. And he certainly wasn't very interested in the exhibit. The way he was looking around, Remy had the impression he was searching for someone.

"What are your plans now?" Gabe asked, distracting her attention from the black-and-white monitors. "Are you going to stay there for a while, or head home?"

"I don't think so. I'll—"

"Don't tell me. I think I can guess, " he broke in. "You're going to Canal Place and see if you can buy out Saks and Gucci's this time."

He sounded so certain that Remy frowned. "What makes you say that?"

"Because you always go on a shopping binge when you're depressed."

"I do?"

"You do," he declared, with an undertone of amusement. "I'd offer to carry your purchases for you, but I've got some paperwork I should catch up on. Why don't we meet at La Louisiane for drinks at, say . . . about four-thirty? That'll give you almost three hours to shop."

"All right," she agreed, though she had no desire to go shopping.

There was a hesitation on the other end of the line, as if Gabe sensed her reluctance. "Remy . . . you aren't going to get yourself lost or—wander down to the docks again, are you?"

"No. I promise." She smiled at the phone.

"Good. I'll see you at four-thirty, then."

"At La Louisiane," she confirmed, then hung up the receiver when the line went dead. "Thanks," she said to one of the staffers, who nodded in response.

As Remy started to leave the museum's administrative offices, a young woman in her early twenties came bounding up to her, her dark hair cut in a short, sleek bob with a full fringe of bangs. She stopped abruptly, exclaiming in delight, "Remy! When did you get back?"

"Last night," she replied, silently wondering who this girl was.

"How was the Riviera? I expected you to have a gorgeous tan that would make all of us poor working girls green with envy," she said, scanning Remy from head to toe. "That's a gorgeous outfit. Did you get it in France?"

"It was in my closet." She had no idea where she'd bought it.

"I wish I had your closet," she responded, casting an openly admiring eye over the hunter-green paisley jacket and blouse that Remy had paired with a navy skirt and red belt. "Have you got time for a cup of coffee or something? I've got about an hour before my tour gets here, and I'm dying to hear all about Mardi Gras in Nice. It can't possibly be as crazy as it is here."

"I'd love a cup—" Remy began, then stopped, a wry smile curving her mouth. "This is awkward. I'm sure I know you, but—I can't remember who you are. You see, I . . . . " She hesitated, but there was no way to say it except straight out. "I have amnesia."

The girl gave a jaw-dropped look. "You're kidding."

"I wish I were."

"Oh my God, you're not kidding," she declared. "For heaven's sake, what happened? How? Oh, Remy, you've got to tell me all about it." She reached out to clutch at her hand, then laughed self-consciously. "I forgot. You don't remember me. I'm Tina Gianelli. We both started working here at about the same time."

With that, she caught at Remy's hand again and practically dragged her back to the employee area, sat her down at a table, and demanded again to know all about it. Remy briefly filled her in, keeping to the basic facts and concluding with, "I came to the museum today hoping something would be familiar, but when I wandered through the various exhibits, I felt like a stranger looking at things I'd always known about."

"In a way, you *have* been something of a stranger around here lately," Tina stated, combing her fingers through one side of her hair and giving it a flipping toss. "You're hardly ever here more than two or three times a week, and then only for a couple of hours. It's certainly not like it was in the beginning. Of course, the circumstances were different then."

" 'Different'? In what way?" Remy studied her curiously.

"You came to work here shortly after your fiancé drowned. I think you wanted to lose yourself in something, and the past probably seemed safe—without a lot of constant reminders of him, if you know what I mean," she said, then added quickly, "By that I'm not implying this was nothing more than distraction. You seemed to really enjoy working here. Heavens, when you weren't helping with the tours, you were persuading some family friend to either loan or donate an item to the museum—especially things for the eighteen-fifties house and the Mardi Gras exhibit."

"But you're saying that lately I've lost interest in my work here," Remy guessed.

"It isn't that you've lost interest, exactly. I've just had the feeling there isn't enough challenge here for you." She paused and cast a rueful smile at Remy. "I'm afraid I'm putting this badly, but—it's like you enjoy this as diversion, but it's not satisfying enough to be your life's work. Am I making any sense?"

"Possibly more than I realize," Remy murmured thoughtfully, then lifted her shoulders in a light shrug. "Who knows? This amnesia might turn out to be a good thing and make me take stock of my life and decide what it is I want—and don't want—to do with the rest of it."

"Wouldn't that be something? Truthfully, I've always wondered why you never got involved in your family's shipping business, but I suppose when you live with your family, you don't want to work with them every day, too," she said. Then she suddenly brightened. "I've got an idea—why don't you tag along on this tour with me? It might be just the thing to help you remember."

Remy glanced at the large wall clock. "I'd better not. I'm supposed to meet my brother for drinks at four-thirty—"

"You are! That's nice. Although I'll never understand why it takes some sort of crisis to shake a family up and make them pay attention to each other. I guess we get too caught up in our own lives. I remember when my mother was in that terrible accident last summer and my brother flew home. We sat down and talked—I mean really *talked*—for the first time in years. I learned so much about him that I never knew."

"Hey, Gianelli," a voice called from the doorway, "your tour's here."

"Already," she protested and flashed a look at the clock. "Wouldn't you know, they're early? Look, I've got to go," she said, pushing to her feet. "Give me a call, OK? And don't use amnesia as an excuse. My number's in your address book—under G for Gianelli."

"I'll remember," Remy said, and followed her out of the room.

Outside the sun was bright and warm, the weather atypical of the gray and damp dreariness of a New Orleans February. Yet Remy couldn't bring herself to appreciate it.

At the corner, while she waited for one of the city's many mule-drawn carriages to roll by, she looked back over her shoulder at the museum that had
been another dead end in her search, her glance falling on the entrance just as
the man with the grizzled beard emerged in some haste, stopping to quickly
scan the street. Guessing that someone had failed to meet him as planned,
Remy briefly empathized with his anxiety and frustration. She felt those things
too, only in her case they were colored with discouragement as she crossed to
the other side of the street.

She was beginning to doubt this feeling she'd had that she was desperately
needed somewhere. It didn't appear that she was *needed* anywhere. And she was
beginning to suspect that this inner compulsion was really only a desire to give
meaning to her life. It made sense—a good deal of sense.

Yet there was that man in Nice, the one she'd been struggling with. Why?
Over what? Who was he? The description from the witnesses was so vague that
it could have fit almost anyone—including the bearded man.

Remy sighed and a second later realized how fast she was walking. She
slowed her steps and looked around to get her bearings. She was on St. Ann.
She glanced at the old buildings, noting the smooth plaster covering on them,
chipped here and there to reveal powdery red brick beneath. Cars were parked
along the curb, lining one whole side and turning the narrow thoroughfare into
a one-way street. As she neared a pair of tall wooden gates, the entrance of an
old *porte cochère*, she idly wondered if a courtyard could still be found on the
other side.

Garbage cans and black plastic trash bags were piled in front of one of the
scarred doors. A scruffy long-haired cat rummaged through the contents. He
saw her and crouched low, as if to flee, regarding her with suspicious green
eyes. Except for a patch of white at his throat, he was all black—and big,
weighing at least twenty pounds. The tip of his left ear had been chewed off,
and Remy guessed that his long hair hid even more scars.

She started to smile, then stopped, realizing, "You're Tom, aren't you? You're
Cole's cat."

When she took a step toward him, the cat flattened his ears and showed his
fangs in a silent hiss, then lashed the air with his tail and bounded to the top of
a metal garbage can. Stunned, Remy watched as the black cat hurled himself at
the old wooden carriage gates and clawed his way over the top with an alacrity
a boot-camp trainee would have envied.

Was he really Cole's cat? Cole lived in the Quarter, didn't he? She was almost
certain he'd told her that. And she had a vague memory that his apartment was
located somewhere on St. Ann. She looked again at the old carriage doors the
cat had disappeared behind. Was this the building?

A few feet away, a recessed doorway marked the entrance to it. Remy hesitated momentarily, then walked over to it and pushed it open. A wide cool hall
stretched away from the door. French doors, their glass panes grilled and barred
for security, stood at the opposite end. On her right, a curved staircase led to
the second floor.

When she stepped into the hall, she noticed the row of mailboxes. Pausing,
she stared at the first one, the one marked 1A, the one with the smudged
lettering that read C. BUCHANAN. Remy hesitated again, then crossed to the
side door near the end of the hall.

There was no bell, only a large brass knocker cast in the shape of a roaring lion with a heavy ring suspended from the corners of its mouth. She studied it for a long second, then reached up. Of their own volition, it seemed, her fingers slipped inside the lion's mouth—and touched a key hidden in a hollow at the back of its mouth. As she slipped the key into the lock and gave it a turn, she told herself that she wasn't really trespassing—she only wanted to see if his apartment was familiar to her, if it would spark some memory.

The well-oiled door swung silently inward. She walked in and quietly closed the door behind her. The living room was a masculine mix of heavy, solid furniture and large overstuffed sofas and chairs, rough-textured tweeds, and smooth leathers, all in deep earth tones of brown, tan, and burnt red.

In her encompassing gaze around the room, Remy noticed a framed sporting print hung at eye level on the cinnamon-glazed wall near her. The scene depicted a boxing match held amidst an unspoiled landscape, with a throng of well-dressed spectators crowded around an alfresco ring, turning it into a sea of top hats. In the center of the ring two pugilists in tight-fitting breeches, their hair neatly combed, faced each other in the old-time upright stance. She knew immediately that it was the print that had arrived that day she'd gone to his office to take him to lunch.

She swung around to look at the other framed prints on the living-room walls. There was a foxhunting scene hanging above the heavy-beamed mantel, the scarlet red of the riders' jackets against the gleaming coats of their mounts catching her eye. And near the hallway on her right was a Currier and Ives print of a harness race.

The hallway. It led to the bedroom. Suddenly, in her mind's eye, she could see the golden gleam of brass accents on the lustrous black iron bed, the mixed blue of the striped spread, the clutter of men's things on the dresser—and Cole lying on the bed, cushioned by propping blue pillows, bare to the waist, the coverlet down around his hips.

Abruptly she turned from that image and found herself facing the far door in the living room. What was behind it? She couldn't remember. Curious, Remy walked over and gave the door a push, then swung it open wider to see more of the kitchen, with its heart-of-pine cupboards, beamed ceiling, and gleaming array of copper pots. Tucked in a corner of it was a small dining alcove with windows facing the courtyard without.

More images came to her—vague at first, then sharpening with clarity. Cole standing at the stove stirring something in a copper pot, steam rising from it, a towel wrapped around his waist. Then she was there, moving to his side, offering him some morsel and ordering, "Taste."

Obediently Cole lowered his head and let her feed it to him. "Mmmmm, good," he said, with a faint trace of surprise and a quick licking of his lips to savor every bit of it. Then, still stirring the pot with a long wooden spoon, he arched his arm and let her duck beneath it to fit herself to his side.

"I told you I knew my way around a kitchen," she chided.

"Know something else?" he said, dropping a playful kiss on the tip of her nose. "I think you know your way around the cook too."

Suddenly a noise—a scraping of metal, a click, something—shattered the image. Remy swung away from the kitchen, letting the door shut on it as the front door opened. A pulsebeat later, Cole filled the doorway, his suit jacket slung over his shoulder, his shirt unbuttoned at the throat, his tie draped loose around his neck. He saw her and stopped, still holding the door open, the key still in the lock. A sudden brightness leapt into his gray eyes, erasing the tired, drawn look. Just as quickly, it was shuttered again.

"What are you doing here?" The tightness in his low voice gave it a husky quality.

"Tom was outside. I recognized him." She felt his tension—her tension. "Then I found the key in the lion's mouth."

"I always left it there for you. You used to come here and wait for me to get home from the office." He stopped, a muscle working convulsively in his jaw. "You don't know how many times these last couple of weeks I've wanted to see you waiting for me when I walked through this door."

There was a rawness in his look and his expression, an ache that suddenly made him appear . . . vulnerable as he stood there, holding himself so stiffly, so rigidly.

"What was it like between us, Cole?" Remy took a step toward him, then halted, realizing she needed to keep the room between them. "What did we do? We shared more than the bedroom, didn't we?"

"We did, yes." His reply was clipped, almost as if he didn't trust himself to say more.

"Tell me about us, Cole," she insisted. "I need to know. I need to remember. Did we stay here in the apartment? Did we go out? Where? What did we do?"

Turning from her, he pulled the key out of the lock and pushed the door shut. "Sometimes we stayed here and tried out our culinary skills on each other," he replied with a touch of wryness as he walked over to the leather recliner, tossing his jacket over the back of it and pulling his tie from around his neck to lay it on top. "Other times we went out for the evening and had dinner at some restaurant."

"Which one? Did we have favorites?" Remy asked, pushing for a more specific answer, not at all surprised that the evening's entertainment had consisted of no more than dinner. New Orleans was a great food town. For most natives, dining out was neither a prelude nor an ancillary activity, but an event in itself —something to be not hurried but relished.

"Mr. B's, Cafe Sbisa, L'Eagles—"

"L'Eagles—that was one of your favorites," she remembered, visualizing the interior of the small, classy restaurant with its deep coral walls and European country decor. "You always claimed you liked to go there for the cold crawfish fettuccine they served, but it was really the collection of antique prints that you went there to admire."

Some of the remoteness left his expression, replaced by warmth as he conceded, "It was probably a combination of both."

"Where else did we go for dinner?"

"Every now and then we'd venture uptown and eat at the Garden Room in the Commander's Palace or else at Brigsten's. Or when we got the urge for a good po'boy or a meal of red beans and rice, we usually went to Mother's Restaurant on Poydras. And of course there was always Galatoire's."

"Where we had lunch that first time." Remy smiled.

"Yes," Cole nodded, then continued, "Other than that, some evenings we'd go to a concert. Or if someone one of us wanted to see was playing at the Blue

Room, we'd go there. Other nights we'd wander down to Preservation Hall and listen to them jam." He looked at her, a faint smile slanting the line of his mouth. "After the first time you heard the wail of Kid Sheik's trumpet, you became a die-hard jazz fan."

Preservation Hall—that aging and tattered building with its doors thrown open on most nights to let the unamplified music within spill onto St. Peter and Bourbon streets. Remy could almost hear the gritty notes of the trumpet growling its song in the old club's smoky atmosphere, yet—oddly—it was Cole's face she could see, "feeling" the music, "grooving" to it, letting it speak to him, move him, lift him. As she strained to recall more, it all began to fade.

Frustrated by these near memories that were little more than impressions, Remy pressed on to something else. "What about the weekends? Did we do anything special? Go anywhere?"

His eyes were on her, a reflective quality in their gray depths. "You were always dragging me off to flea markets, hoping to find some treasure among the junk. Or if you saw a notice for an estate auction in one of the outlying parishes, we'd go to it—especially if they listed porcelains among the items."

"Did I ever buy anything?"

"Once. You discovered a Meissen vase, then felt so guilty because you'd paid only fifteen dollars for it that you gave it to a charity to be sold at their benefit auction. Actually"—he paused briefly—"it usually ended up that you did the browsing and I did the buying."

"The statue of the horse," she said suddenly. "I remember—it was that plaster of Paris kind with glitter sprinkled over it, like the ones they used to give away at carnivals for prizes." But there was more, and the memory of it drew her closer to him. "When you were a little boy, your father took you to a carnival and won you a horse like that at one of the booths on the midway. That's why you bought it, isn't it? For sentimental reasons."

"Yes."

Seized by the feeling that she was on the verge of remembering more, she didn't let him continue. "There was something else we often did on the weekends. What was it?"

Cole frowned slightly and shrugged, as if he wasn't sure what she might be referring to. "If the weather was nasty, we'd rent some movies at the video store and watch them here."

Remy took an eager step toward him. "What kind of movies?"

East of Eden—"

"*On the Waterfront*," she remembered as another scene flashed before her.

It had been a damp and drizzly Saturday afternoon in November, the misty rain gathering on the panes of the doors to the courtyard and trickling down the glass. She and Cole had been encamped on the sofa in front of the television, reclining in each other's arms, their feet propped up on the coffee table, which was already crowded with a pair of bottles of Dixie beer and a bowl of popcorn dripping with butter.

When Cole had shifted her out of his arms to get up and change the tape, he'd given her a playful swat on her behind. She had instantly retaliated with a kick in the pants and had then bounded to her feet, assuming a fighting stance, dancing around on the balls of her feet, bobbing and weaving like a boxer and throwing jabs at Cole's arm.

"Whatsa matter, tough guy?" she taunted. "Am I too much for ya?"

She threw two more quick punches that Cole fended off with the flat of his hand, his gray eyes regarding her with open amusement. "That'll be the day, kid. You've got lousy footwork."

"Lousy, eh?" She danced back, sniffled loudly, and brushed her thumb across the end of her nose. "I'll have you know—I coulda been a contender," she declared in her best Brando imitation.

"You could have been a contender, all right—for the role of Funny Girl."

"Oh yeah?" she challenged, and she hunched her shoulders, crouching down and rubbing her thumb over her nose again, "Why do boxers do that? Do they all have runny noses, or what?"

"Wouldn't you if yours kept getting bopped all the time?" His hand snaked out and sharply tapped the tip of her nose. Grinning, he immediately caught the fist she aimed at him. "Come here, you idiot."

When he pulled her into his arms, Remy pretended to resist, protesting, "Foul. Clinches aren't allowed."

"Can you think of a better way to feel out an opponent?"

"I think you mean feel *up*," she said in mock reproof as his hand cupped her bottom. "Or is that called going below the belt?"

"That's *hitting* below the belt."

"Like this?" She punched him low in the stomach.

He grunted, more in surprise than in pain. "Now you've done it."

When he caught her up to him, she smiled in satisfaction, but a second later she was squealing with laughter. "No! No! Don't tickle me! Don't!"

She twisted, turned, pushed, trying to elude the tickling fingers that had her convulsing with laughter, but there was no escape from them, not even when she collapsed on the chocolate-colored shag rug, too weak to stand. They rolled around on the floor until she was laughing so hard she could barely breathe.

"I give up," she cried between shrieking giggles. "Uncle. Uncle!" Mercifully, he stopped, and she drank in air, each breath a sigh as she relaxed against the floor, gradually becoming conscious of the pinning weight of his leg hooked over hers, an arm propping him up alongside her. She saw his grin and accused, "You don't fight fair."

"Who's fighting?" he countered softly. "I think I went down for the count at your hands weeks ago."

She caught her breath at the simple declaration so freely made, and lifted a hand to run her fingers through one side of his thick hair. "Are you as happy as I am, Cole?"

The laughter went out of his gray eyes, a sudden and serious intensity claiming them. "Every time you walk into a room, Remy, every time I see you, you"—he seemed to momentarily hesitate over the words—"you make my heart smile."

"It's that way for me too," she said, his words describing exactly the swell of buoyant, happy feeling inside her each time she saw him. She ran a finger down the side of his cheek to his lips. "Who was she, Cole? The one who hurt you—the one you always think I might be like?" She felt the tensing of his muscles, that move to withdraw from her both physically and mentally, and slipped a hand behind his neck to prevent him from rolling away. "You were in love with her, weren't you?"

"I was nineteen. I was in love with who I thought she was."

She ignored the curtness of his answer, recognizing that he used it to hide an old hurt. "Tell me about her, Cole."

"There's nothing to tell." This time he succeeded in pulling away from her as he rolled over and sat up, his back to her.

"I think there is." She sat up too, but made no attempt to touch him. "How did you meet?"

There was a long pause, and she thought he was again going to refuse to discuss her, but then the words came . . . grudgingly, tersely. "She liked boxing—the blows, the blood, the bodies glistening with sweat. To her it was primitive and exciting. She saw me box. Afterward—she was outside waiting for me. . . . She had so much class—not like anyone I'd ever met—I guess I was blinded by it."

"You started seeing each other," Remy said, quietly prompting him to go on.

"Not all that often. I was going to college, holding down a full-time job to pay for it and boxing on the side to earn some extra money. I didn't have a lot of free time for dating. Mostly she came to see me work out at the gym. Then afterward we'd go somewhere for a beer. Correction—I'd have a beer; she'd have a glass of wine. She didn't seem to care that I didn't have the money to take her out to Antoine's for dinner. It was enough that we were together—at least, that's what I thought."

"But you found out differently, didn't you?" Remy guessed. "How?"

"I made the mistake of going to her house one afternoon to see her—one of those cozy little mansions uptown near Audubon Park," he added with more than a trace of sarcasm, then paused again. "The shock on her face when she saw me standing in the foyer—I'll never forget that . . . or the anger that followed. I remember she said, 'How dare you embarrass me by coming to my house!' I turned every shade of red there is, and walked out." He tipped his head back and gazed at the ceiling. "It's funny, but the thing that hurt the most was knowing I'd told her about my father. I'd never been able to talk to anyone about it before. I . . . " He shook off the rest of it and lowered his head.

"Your father?" She frowned curiously. "He died when you were eight, isn't that what you told me?"

"Yes." Again his answer was clipped.

"How?"

With a turn of his head, he looked at her, something hard and unforgiving in his expression. "In a head-on collision with another car, driven by a very eminent—and very drunk—former state senator from *your* district."

Remy breathed in sharply, realizing that she knew exactly who he meant. The senator had been one of her grandfather's closest friends, a man whose political career had been cut short by an automobile accident that had left him paralyzed. She'd heard the story a dozen times as a child. "But I had always understood—"

"—that my father was the one who'd been drinking?" Cole inserted. "That was a lie. I know. I was there."

"You . . . were in the car?"

"Yes."

She stared at him, remembering the shock, the panic, the terror she'd felt that day on the lake when she'd seen her fiancé, Nick Austin, overturn in his speedboat. She'd waited with her heart in her throat for him to surface and wave that he was all right. He hadn't. And the search had begun, a search that lasted four agonizing hours before his body was recovered. The shock of witnessing the accident, of discovering how tenuous life was, how insecure—she'd had trouble coping with it. It was part of what had driven her back to the family home—the solidness, the security it represented. That was three years ago; she'd been twenty-four. How much harder it must have been to lose someone you loved at the age of eight.

"Cole," she murmured, feeling the fear and pain he had to have experienced.

"He'd taken me to the zoo. My mother was working. She couldn't come with us. We were on our way home. It had started raining. Suddenly there was a glare of headlights right in our eyes. I remember my dad yelled something. Then his arm was across me, pushing me back against the seat. Then there was a lot of noise of glass breaking and metal. . . ." He paused and drank in a trembling breath. "My dad was lying on my lap, and there was blood all over. I knew he needed help, but I couldn't get the door open, so I had to climb out the side window. The police came and I grabbed one of them and took him back to the car to help my dad. Then his partner calls to him—'Jesus Christ, Hudson, get over here quick! You aren't gonna believe who's driving the other car!' The cop grabs my hand and shoves a bloody handkerchief in it and tells me to hold it against my dad's neck to stop the bleeding. I remember hearing the cop say, 'My God, it's the senator,' and the other cop said, 'Yeah, and he's drunker than a sailor.' After that all I can remember is crying and holding that handkerchief on my dad's neck, but I couldn't make the blood stop. It was all over my hands . . . on my arms . . . I was too little. I couldn't do it, and the cops never came back to help me. They were too busy saving the senator."

And Remy knew that along with the senator's life, they'd saved his reputation, placing all the blame on the other driver, the one who wasn't alive to deny it.

She didn't say anything. She simply put her arms around Cole and held him tight.

Reliving the scene in her mind, Remy felt the same pain all over again. She released a long sigh and discovered she was gripping the back of the sofa. As she lifted her head, her gaze happened to fall on the television's blank screen. Instantly she stiffened.

"We watched television another time, but it—it wasn't a movie." Frowning with the effort of recalling it, Remy turned to Cole, then remembered in surprise, "It was you! You were interviewed by one of the local news stations. Why? Wait—" She broke into a smile as it came back to her. "It was because of the annual Christmas party for the company employees. You'd arranged for it to be held on board one of our ships. And you had Christmas lights strung on all the decks all over the ship. The whole thing was so unique that the television station sent its anchorwoman out to cover the story."

Remy turned to stare at the television again, seeing the interview—Cole standing on the deck of the ship, casually dressed in a turtleneck and navy blazer, a breeze playing with the ends of his hair, the camera gentling his hard-edged features and imbuing them instead with a quiet strength and character.

"This is festive and fabulous, Mr. Buchanan," the anchor, a stunningly attractive black woman, had declared. "What gave you the idea of holding your employee Christmas party on board one of your ships?"

Cole flashed her one of his rare smiles. "With as many attractions as our city has to offer, it's easy to lose sight of the fact that the port of New Orleans is second in activity only to that of New York City. And there are years when our export tonnage has surpassed New York's. The company has always been proud of the fact that New Orleans has always been the home port and the headquarters of the Crescent Line, ever since its founding more than one hundred and fifty years ago. Ships and shipping have always been our business. But when you spend most of your time behind a desk in an office, you tend to forget that. Recently I realized how few of our employees—not to mention any of their families—have ever had the reason or the opportunity to set foot on the deck of one of our ships. . . . When it came time to plan our Christmas party this year, I saw this as the perfect chance to correct that situation and remind everyone what the Crescent Line is all about."

"Approximately three months ago, you lost one of your ships. Did that play any part in your decision?"

"It's true one of our tankers sank in the Gulf during a storm—fortunately with no loss of life or any damage to the environment. Which means we have that much more reason to rejoice in this holiday season."

With that statement from him, the reporter concluded the interview, and Remy turned on the sofa to hug Cole in delight. "You handled that question perfectly. But how quick and clever you were to brag about New Orleans' status as a port *and* work in a plug for the company at the same time. And here I always thought Uncle Marc was the expert at dealing with the media," she said, then poked him in the ribs. "But I'm not sure I liked the way you flirted with that reporter."

"I wasn't flirting—merely turning on the charm," he replied, with a faintly smug smile. "In all business, there's a time to play hardball—and a time to play it soft."

"You've never played it soft with me," she retorted in mock complaint.

"I should hope not," he chuckled, the glint in his eyes giving an entirely different meaning to the word *hard*.

She poked him again. "That isn't what I was talking about."

Remy couldn't remember what had happened next, though she could guess. But it didn't matter; the memory had prompted her to wonder about something else. "Did we spend Christmas together?"

"Christmas Eve," Cole replied.

"What did we do?" She crossed to the leather recliner where he stood.

"We drove up to St. James Parish and watched them light the bonfires along the levee—"

"To light the way for Papa Noël," Remy inserted, recalling the tradition, allegedly begun by early settlers in the area, of building giant bonfires along the Mississippi River to help Papa Noël find his way to their new homes. She smiled to herself, remembering the little boy—no more than seven years old—who had scoffed at the whole proceeding.

"Don't you believe in Santa Claus?" Cole had asked.

"No!" the boy had responded emphatically.

Cole had crouched down to the boy's level. "It doesn't matter . . . because Santa Claus still believes in you. He always will."

When Cole had stood up from the boy, she'd marveled aloud, "You still believe in Santa Claus, don't you?"

"Of course," he'd replied with a perfectly straight face. And she'd suspected he really did.

Realizing that Cole was talking, Remy forced herself back into the present.

"—came back to the apartment and exchanged our gifts, then we went to midnight Mass together."

"What did you give me?" She had the feeling it had been something special.

"An antique brooch."

Remy frowned, certain there'd been some sentiment attached to it. "Had it belonged to your mother?"

"My grandmother."

She breathed in sharply and unconsciously pressed a hand to her throat. "It was set with topaz, wasn't it?" Even before Cole nodded affirmatively, she knew it was the brooch she'd been wearing that night in Nice. "Cole, why did we break up? What did we argue over?" It was suddenly imperative that she know.

"The same thing we always argue about—your family and their destructive greed. Now—" He cut off the rest of it, a grimness thinning his mouth. "Look at you. You're already bristling."

It was true. She didn't try to deny the flash of temper his words had sparked. "What do you expect, Cole? They're my family."

"And we're at another impasse," he observed curtly.

"That wasn't your attitude when we were in Nice, at the hotel," she reminded him. "Why? Why have you changed since we came back? This morning at the dock—and later, at your office—it was like you were pushing me away from you. Why?"

He studied her for a silent moment. "Last night . . . at the airport . . . seeing you wrapped again in the bosom of your family, I realized you'll never love me enough to trust me and believe in me over them."

"How can you say that? I love you."

"In your way, yes."

She covered his mouth with her hand, wanting to cut off the things he was saying. "That isn't true. I love you in *every* way."

He dragged her hand from his mouth, his fingers gripping it. "Don't make this any more painful than it is, Remy. You don't know how much I want to believe you."

"But you can," she insisted. "I was wearing the brooch you gave me the night I was hurt. Don't you see? I wouldn't have been wearing it if I was still angry at you, if I didn't want us to be together again."

With a throaty groan, he pulled her to him. As his mouth moved over hers with a pressure that was urgent, his tongue delving, filling, Remy discovered that nothing had changed from the hotel room in Nice—she felt the same immense shock, the same feeling of deep need satisfied.

In the bedroom, Cole undressed her. He wouldn't let her help. This was something he wanted to do himself. He peeled off her clothes, layer by layer, touching, stroking, caressing as he went. She was beautiful, with her high, firm breasts sized perfectly to fit the cup of his hands, and her hips, thighs, and legs with their silky, woman-soft curves, and the warm smoothness of her body beneath his hands. He looked at her—into the gold-flecked glitter of her hazel eyes—and saw the deep, bright glow of love for him.

Reaching out, he pulled down the blue-striped coverlet and the sheet, then lifted her and laid her gently in the middle of the bed. He stepped back and shed his own clothes while she watched with half-closed eyes, resting on her elbows. He had a magnificent body, muscular and flat, but she'd thought that from the first moment she'd seen him. She lay back against the pillows, languid with anticipation as his eyes grew needy and dark and his final nakedness gave away his rising desire—his bold desire.

His knee touched the bed, and the mattress caved in beneath his weight. Leaning over, he pressed a warm kiss against her belly, and she felt the curling sensation of it deep inside. Her arms reached out for him, drawing him to her, his length stretching out alongside hers, as his mouth came down.

He intended to be gentle, to make the kiss sweet and lasting, but he'd been too long without her, he was too hungry, too starved. He tore his mouth from hers and pressed another hard kiss against her jaw, then into her neck, the fragrance of her surrounding him. His mouth found hers again, her lips parting, seeking and eager in accepting the deep strokes of his tongue.

Gripped by the fierce need to touch, to kiss, and to taste, he held her to him with both arms and legs as they tumbled together on the bed, her belly straining against him and the twin peaks of her soft breasts flattened by his chest. The sweet woman smell and the sweet woman taste of her drove him on.

His hands slid into her loose hair. He loved the silken feel of it, the silken length and the scent of flowers that clung to it. He stroked her body, cupped her breasts, and probed the petal-like folds of her until she arched against his clever fingers. He kissed her breasts, his mouth gently suckling, his teeth gently nipping, and she writhed beneath him, her fingers digging into his hair to keep him there. She reached down to touch him, her hand encircling, stroking. He heard his own grunt of raw pleasure. "Love me, Cole," she whispered into his ear.

A cheek muscle flexed as he realized she was killing him slowly, softly. Then he was inside her, thrusting deep, his moans lost in hers. He wanted to make love to her slowly, completely. He wanted her to belong to him again, and this time to make it last. He braced his weight with his hands, the muscles in his arms trembling with the strain of holding back, but she arched her hips against his. It wasn't his restraint she wanted, but all of him.

He plunged into her, then plunged again and again, the tempo rising, the pressure building, the pleasure sharpening until it broke over and through them, disseminating and decimating them in a thousand white-hot shards of sensation.

21 ✐

REMY SLIPPED ON the paisley patterned jacket of silk charmeuse and fastened its one button, then glanced at Cole sprawled over half of the pale-blue bed sheets, for a moment watching the even rise and fall of his bare chest in light sleep. She smiled faintly, still warm inside with the feeling that she had been well and truly loved. She moved to his side of the bed and sat down on the edge of the mattress, then slowly, quietly she leaned forward—with every intention of disturbing his slumber—and nuzzled his ear, lightly breathing into its shell.

"You fell asleep on me again," she accused softly, feeling him stir a second before his hand glided onto her back, the silk of her jacket sliding over the matching blouse at his touch.

His hand stopped. "What is this?" He turned his face into hers, seeking and finding the corner of her mouth. "What are you doing with clothes on? I didn't take them off for you to put them back on, you know."

"I know." She let her lips brush over his mouth, eluding his attempt to claim them in a kiss as his hand resumed its caressing foray, now joined by the other. "But I have to go."

"Oh no you don't," he said in a lazy denial, his encircling arms tightening to keep her with him. "You're going to stay right here with me . . . in my arms . . . in my bed." He punctuated each pause with an evocative nibble on her neck.

"I'd love to." She closed her eyes, strongly tempted to take off her clothes again and crawl back under the covers with him. "But I can't." Sighing her regret, she spread her hands over the hard plane of his chest and used them to level herself partially away from him. "I'm supposed to meet Gabe at four-thirty, and it's going on four o'clock now."

"That's no problem." His hand moved onto her hip, rumpling the navy wool of her skirt. "Call him up and say you can't make it. Tell him something's come up. It would be the truth," he said somewhat wickedly, tipping his head far to one side to pointedly look past her at the very noticeable protrusion of the sheet around his hips.

Remy looked too, and smiled mockingly back at him. "You know what they say—what goes up must come down."

"Ahh, but it's the *come* part of 'come down' I'm interested in," he said.

She pretended to be critical. "Once is never enough for you, is it?"

"Not with you, it seems."

And she understood exactly what he meant. No matter how well their bodies might know each other, it didn't seem that either she or Cole had exhausted the mysteries they discovered each time they made love.

"I really do have to meet Gabe," she said with reluctance.

His gray eyes lost their teasing look and turned needing and dark. "Stay with me, Remy."

"It's my first night back. I need to spend some time with my family."

His hands ceased their wandering and simply held her. "You're running true to form, Remy. Amnesia or not, your family still comes first with you."

"Let's not argue about this." The potential for it was there; she sensed it in the dead quiet of his voice.

"You're right. It would be useless anyway," he said dryly, then forced a smile.

Another kiss and a few more whispered words and she left, retrieving her purse from the living room on her way out.

On the banquette outside his apartment, Remy breathed in the air, scented with the thousands of aromas of the Quarter, everything from the mustiness of the past to the Cajun spices of today. The long slant of the sun's rays cast a mellow light over the old buildings. It was, Remy decided, an absolutely gorgeous day. She started walking.

As she rounded the corner onto Bourbon, a hand hooked her elbow. Reacting instinctively, Remy switched her clutch purse to the other hand and threw her weight into the would-be purse snatcher rather than away from him. Her shoulder connected with something solid, drawing a grunt of surprise and causing him to loosen his hold. She pulled her arm free, and at the same instant caught a glimpse of a heavily grizzled beard in her side vision. The man in the car outside her house—and at the museum!

She swung around to confront him. "Who are you? What do you want? Why are you following me?"

A dozen impressions registered at once: the neatly trimmed beard, heavily streaked with white, that failed to hide the thickness of the man's neck; the top-heavy quality of his build, with massive shoulders and chest tapering to boyishly slim hips; and the keenness of his pale-blue eyes, a keenness that immediately reminded her of Inspector Armand's.

"I'll ask the questions, if you don't mind, Miss Jardin," he said, unsmiling. "You are Remy Jardin, aren't you? I guessed it was you I saw on the balcony this morning."

"I repeat, who are you?"

"Howard Hanks." With two fingers, he produced a business card from his breast pocket and offered it to her. Remy glanced at it, then at the wallet that he flipped open to his identification. He was a licensed investigator—according to the card, working for an insurance company.

Remy looked at the business card again, conscious of the odd churning in the pit of her stomach and of the alarm bells going off in her head, warning her not to tell him anything. It was crazy—she didn't even know what he wanted from her. Whatever it was, why did she feel she needed to conceal information? What information?

She took the card from him, stalling for time until she could decide what to do. "Do you normally accost people on the street, Mr. Hanks?"

"Only those who refuse to accept—or return—my phone calls and claim to be indisposed when I come to their houses." He gestured toward the entrance of a nearby bar, a gold signet ring flashing on his left hand. "May I buy you a drink or a cup of coffee?"

She hesitated. "I have an appointment at four-thirty—"

"This shouldn't take long."

"All right—coffee, then." But it wasn't the quiet insistence in his voice warning her that he wouldn't take no for an answer that convinced her to accept—rather, it was the realization that she had to know what this was about, had to discover the reason for this feeling of danger she had.

Her low heels made a hollow sound on the dirty and old hardwood floor as she walked into the bar ahead of the investigator. The place smelled of beer, bourbon, and old cigarette butts; its atmosphere consisted of its lack of any pretension of class—with its dingy smoke-stained walls, round wooden tables with initials and dates carved into their tops, sturdy but cheap wire-backed chairs, and an old bar that was probably mahogany under its layers of grime.

Remy crossed to the table by the corner window. She sat down in the chair facing Bourbon Street, with her back to the view of Cole's apartment building. The bearded Howard Hanks sat down opposite her, on a seat still warm from his last occupation of it.

He held up two fingers to the bartender. "Coffee."

She laid her purse on the table and lightly clasped her hands together on top of it. "For your information, Mr. Hanks, I was out of the country until yesterday, so I wasn't avoiding your calls—as you implied. I simply wasn't here to accept them. I'm sure you were told that."

Remy was careful not to admit that she hadn't been informed of his calls. She could only guess that in all the anxiety and the relief of having her home, her family had simply failed to mention them. As for this morning, it was possible that she'd been in the shower when he came to the door. Nattie would have known that, and her mother might have heard the water running. But that didn't explain why she hadn't been told that he'd been there to see her.

"There was some mention of your being in France, but everyone was very vague about your exact whereabouts."

She could have told him that they hadn't known, but she was reluctant to say anything about her hospital stay or her amnesia. The bartender arrived with their coffee. Remy moved her purse aside as he set two mugs in front of them.

"Cream or sugar?" Hanks asked, holding up a hand to keep the bartender from walking off.

"Neither, thanks," she directed her answer to the bartender, who immediately returned to his station behind the bar. She wrapped both hands around the thick stoneware mug. "You said you wanted to ask me some questions, Mr. Hanks. What about?"

"The sinking of the *Dragon*."

The *Dragon*. She'd heard that name before. Marc Jardin had mentioned it this morning in the solarium. What had he said? Something about fearing the insurance company might go through with its threat to make this business about the *Dragon* public. Later, when she'd asked him about it, her uncle had dismissed it as a typical hassle with an insurance company over a claim they were attempting to get out of paying. But . . . at the wharf, when she'd remembered the previous time Cole had shown her around the container ship, he'd said that the loss of the *Dragon* had been "a blessing in disguise"—that he'd used the insurance money to buy this ship. Had the insurance company paid the claim, or hadn't it?

"What about the sinking of the *Dragon?*" she asked, and took a sip of the chicory-strong coffee.

"What do you know about it?"

"Why should I know anything about it?"

"You are a stockholder and director of the Crescent Line, aren't you, Miss Jardin?"

"Yes."

"Then tell me what you know."

"About what?"

He shot her a look that was both tolerant and wryly amused. "Spare us both the dumb-blonde act, Miss Jardin. I know you graduated cum laude from New-comb College."

"If you've checked on me to that extent, Mr. Hanks, then you must know that my role as a company director is basically a titular one. I have very little knowledge of the company's operations. I've simply never bothered to involve myself in the family shipping business."

"In other words, you want me to believe you don't know anything about the *Dragon.*" The skepticism in his voice was as thick as river fog.

"I'm aware that we lost a ship, and I'm also aware that the insurance company has been causing trouble over the claim."

"Wouldn't you, if you discovered that someone had fraudulently collected on a cargo that didn't exist, after deliberately sinking its container ship in deep water to conceal that fact?"

Stunned by the charge, she blurted, "That's ridiculous. Why would anybody do that?"

"Why, indeed, would anybody try to collect twice for the same cargo?"

"Collect twice?" She frowned, her mind racing at the implication of his words as she feigned confusion. "I'm afraid you've lost me, Mr. Hanks. Exactly what is it that you're saying?"

"That tanker was empty when it went down, Miss Jardin. At some point, between the time it was loaded here in New Orleans and when it sank in the Gulf, that cargo of crude was off-loaded. Once the tanker ran into the storm and heavy seas being reported in the Gulf of Mexico, it was sunk—probably with the aid of some strategically placed explosive charges."

"But you don't know that for a fact, do you?" The conversation she'd over-heard in the solarium—she remembered that her father, Gabe, and Marc had been talking about finding out what proof the insurance company had, if any.

"Miss Jardin, there are basically only two ways to scuttle a ship—open the sea cocks and flood her, a process that could take as long as twenty-four hours, or blow out her bottom with explosive charges and send her to the sea floor within minutes."

"And you think that's what happened to the *Dragon?*" she managed to chal-lenge him before taking a slow sip of her coffee, wondering if it was true and telling herself it couldn't possibly be. So that was why her family had sounded so worried. These were serious charges.

"I'd bet on it."

Remy shook her head in denial. "I'm sorry, but your theory doesn't make good sense—or good business. Why would we deliberately sink one of our ships simply to collect on a cargo that you claim wasn't on board?"

"The *Dragon* was an old tanker, Miss Jardin. I doubt she could have had more than a few voyages left in her before she would end up in a scrap heap. You probably collected more from the insurance company for the ship than you could have got if you'd tried to sell her . . . not to mention the tax losses the company will get out of it."

"But if she was that old and in such bad shape, then she could easily have broken up in the storm and gone down *with* her cargo of crude oil."

"Then why wasn't there any oil slick?"

"Maybe her tanks—or whatever you call them—weren't ruptured," Remy argued, then lowered her cup to the table, lacing her fingers tightly around it. "In any case, these charges against the Crescent Line are preposterous. My family would never involve itself in such dishonest activities."

"What about Cole Buchanan?" His quiet question hit her like a fist.

"Cole," she repeated dumbly, then tried to laugh off her shock, conscious of the sick feeling in her stomach. "Don't tell me you suspect he's behind this so-called insurance scheme?"

"Why not?"

"Because it's absurd. What would he have to gain?" At the moment Remy was too stunned to think it through for herself. She needed the insurance investigator to provide the answer.

"Money, of course."

"How? Where? Not from the insurance company. The claim money would be paid directly to the Crescent Line . . . unless you're about to suggest that he's stealing funds from the company."

"Not directly. But he could have sold the shipment of crude oil, off-loaded it onto barges waiting downriver—or into a pipeline—and pocketed the money himself. Your company wouldn't be losing anything, since it would be collecting on the shipment from the insurance."

"I don't believe that." Yet she found herself remembering the comment Gabe had made about Cole's name being linked with some shady dealings in the past.

"Why not?"

"Because I don't." She loved Cole. How *could* she believe that about him?—but then she wondered if it wouldn't be closer to the truth to say that she simply didn't *want* to believe it. She went on as if she had no doubts. "If that's what you think, you should confront Cole with your suspicions, not me."

"I have. Naturally, he denies everything."

"Then why are you talking to me? I've already told you I have nothing to do with the comp—"

"But you do have something to do with Cole Buchanan." He smiled. At least Remy thought he did. With that thick, silvery growth of whiskers above and below his mouth, it was difficult to tell. "I think it's safe to say you know Cole Buchanan quite well—certainly well enough to visit his apartment."

"It's no secret that Cole and I have been seeing each other, but I don't see what that has to do with this."

"I thought perhaps he might have said or done something unusual in the past few months—bought you an expensive present or been a little freer with money, maybe received some unusual phone calls . . . anything out of the ordinary."

"Nothing that I can remember." Which was the truth. Of course, she didn't tell him she could remember almost nothing about her past, including these last few months.

"Think about it. Maybe something will come back to you. If it does, my phone number's on the card. Be sure you call me. I wouldn't want to see you get into trouble over this."

"That almost sounds like a threat, Mr. Hanks."

"I'm sure you've heard the term *accessory*." He stood up, took a money clip from his pocket, peeled two one-dollar bills from it, and dropped them on the table. "I appreciate your time, Miss Jardin. Let's stay in touch."

Alone at the table, Remy let in the wash of questions she hadn't dared think about with the investigator looking on. Was it true? Was there an insurance fraud? Was this the trouble she'd sensed? Was Cole a part of it? Had she known that? Was that the reason she'd broken off with him? Had she seen something or heard something, as the bearded Mr. Hanks had suggested? Was that why it seemed so imperative that she be here?

"More coffee, Miss?"

Startled, she glanced at the stained-glass pot in the bartender's hand and quickly shook her head. "No—thank you," she said, breaking free of the questions whirling about in her mind and gathering up her purse.

By the time she reached La Louisiane, the shock of the information had worn off. She swept into the lounge and spotted Gabe at the large mahogany bar, the gleaming centerpiece of the elegantly appointed room. He'd obviously been watching for her. The instant he saw her, he picked up two drinks and gestured to a quiet corner table. She met him there.

"It's about time you got here," he said. "I was starting to worry about you. You realize you're almost fifteen minutes late?"

"I was detained."

"I gathered that."

She opened her purse, took out the investigator's business card, and laid it on the small cocktail table in front of her brother.

"What's this?" Idly he picked it up, then went still. "Where did you get this?" he asked, too casually.

"Mr. Hanks gave it to me personally."

"You've seen him?"

"Yes. He had some questions to ask me"—she closed her purse with a sharp snap —"about insurance and fraud—and the sinking of the *Crescent Dragon*. That was what you and Father and Uncle Marc were talking about this morning, wasn't it?" she said stiffly. "Why didn't you tell me about it then? Why did all of you pretend there was nothing to worry about, when you knew better? When you knew this man—"

"Remy, you've already been through enough this past week. We all agreed there was no need to tell you about this. And we were right. Look at the way you're trembling."

"It's because I'm mad," she said, and tried to cool the angry tremors of her hands by wrapping them around the cold, moisture-laden sides of the iced drink. "You should have told me."

"Maybe we should have, but you don't have any involvement in the company—"

"But I *am* involved with Cole—as Mr. Hanks was so quick to point out."

"What exactly did he say?"

"He all but accused Cole of being the one behind this fraud scheme, and he suggested that I might have seen or heard something suspicious."

"What did you say?"

"What could I say? The little I can remember might as well be nothing." An olive was impaled on a red plastic saber in her glass. Remy seized the miniature sword and began stabbing at the ice cubes.

"Is that what you told him?"

"I said I didn't remember anything unusual happening. I didn't tell him why."

"Is that all?"

"Why all the questions, Gabe?" she demanded. "Am I being cross-examined by you now?"

"Of course not." He smiled at her so gently that she felt churlish for having snapped at him. "I was curious, that's all. I hate seeing you all tense and upset like this. It's what we were trying to avoid."

"Is it true, Gabe?" She turned to him, earnestly, seriously. "Was the *Dragon* deliberately sunk? Is it fraud? Is Cole a part of it?"

"To tell you the truth, Remy, we don't know. Obviously we don't want to believe it, but . . . I can't imagine that the insurance company would throw around accusations without having some proof of wrongdoing, though we haven't been able to find out what it is. And Cole's not talking." He paused for a fraction of a second. "Hanks didn't happen to reveal anything to you, did he?"

"No," she said, and sighed. "Unfortunately, I didn't ask whether he had any proof. . . . The more I think about it, though, most of what he said sounded like conjecture."

He absently rattled the ice cubes in his glass as if considering the possibility, then shrugged. "It could be they're just fishing," he conceded, taking a sip of his drink.

"Fishing? Why?"

"Insurance scams involving old—and supposedly fully loaded—ships on the high seas happen more frequently than any insurance company cares to admit, and they're next to impossible to prove with the evidence 'twenty thousand leagues under the sea,' so to speak. The *Dragon* might fit what they see as a pattern."

She didn't believe that, and she didn't think Gabe did either. He was only trying to play down the situation for her benefit. It wasn't working.

"What if Hanks is right, Gabe? What if I do know something?"

"About all this?" His glance was openly skeptical. "You would have told us, Remy. If not me, then Dad."

Maybe not. She might have kept silent—not necessarily to protect Cole, but to give him a chance to quietly rectify the situation. Maybe she had even threatened that if he didn't, she'd go to her family with what she knew and give them grounds to demand his resignation—or to break the contract and vote him out of office if he refused to resign. Yes, she could think of a dozen reasons why she might initially have kept silent. It might have been why she'd planned to go off by herself for a few days in France—to give herself time to think and decide what was the best thing to do.

"You're worried." He reached over and covered her hand with his, giving it a squeeze. "Don't be."

"Why don't you tell the Mississippi to flow backward?"

"I mean it, Remy. In the first place, there's nothing you can do. And in the second, you need to concentrate your energies on getting better and not get all worked up over this. Let us handle it. OK?"

If he'd patted her on the cheek and told her not to worry her "pretty little head about such things," his message couldn't have been plainer: leave it to the menfolk to handle. Southern chauvinism, in its place, could be nice; it could be sweet. But this was life, her life, and her business—as much as it was theirs. But Gabe would never see it that way. He couldn't.

"You will tell me what's going on, won't you? I'm in the dark about so much now that I don't think I could stand not being kept informed about this."

"The minute we have some hard facts, I promise I'll tell you."

Which meant that he'd only tell her things that would reassure her. If she wanted something more than a watered-down version of the truth, she'd have to find it herself.

THE MINUTE HER MOTHER left the next morning to keep her standing Thursday appointment at the hair salon, Remy headed for the public library, a drab concrete and glass example of fifties architecture located at the intersection of Tulane and Loyola avenues.

She scanned the newspaper article printed on the computer screen. The account on the sinking of the *Crescent Dragon* had been relegated to page 3 of the paper's front section, running only slightly more than half a column in length and obviously not deemed newsworthy enough to rate a follow-up story.

Why should it be? she thought. There'd been no loss of life, no daring rescue at sea, no harrowing days spent in lifeboats by the crew, and no major oil spill, and no one in the crew had been from the New Orleans area—or even from Louisiana. If it hadn't been for the fact that the tanker was owned by a local shipping company and went down in the Gulf of Mexico, Remy doubted the newspaper would have devoted more than a paragraph to the story—if it had covered it at all.

She read the article again. According to the captain—one Titus Edward Bartholomew from Cornwall, England—the combination of the vessel's age and the heavy seas had caused a structural failure in the tanker's hull. At approximately 10:00 P.M. on the night of September 9, the ship had begun taking on water. Twenty minutes later, with the pumps unable to handle the flow and the tanker foundering badly, the captain gave the order to abandon ship. Twelve hours after that, a passing freighter saw the distress flare fired from the lifeboats and picked up the crew. A search of the area by the Coast Guard yielded some debris, but no evidence of oil spillage.

The only thing Remy found in the entire account that was even remotely suspicious was the tanker's failure to issue a distress call, or Mayday—evidently the ship's radio had chosen that moment to quit working. In fact, problems with the equipment had been reported earlier—perhaps conveniently?

What had she hoped to find? She wasn't sure. A clue, maybe—something that would lead her to look somewhere else. If there was one in the article, she didn't see it. Just the same, she asked for a hard copy of the story and waited while a word processor printed it out.

Where did she go from here? Would the company files have more information? They would definitely contain the names and addresses of the rest of the *Dragon*'s crew. But how was she going to get to see them? She'd never taken an active interest in the shipping business before, so she couldn't just walk in, and ask to see the files without drawing attention to herself—and her search. *That* was the last thing she wanted to do—especially after last night.

By the time she'd gotten home the evening before—after somehow, somewhere making a wrong turn and not knowing it until she discovered she was on the River Road and had to double back—Gabe was already there. She'd walked in to hear him and her father locked in another debate over her.

"I'm not even going to guess how that Hanks character managed to track her down. But as far as I'm concerned, this changes things. Remy is going to that clinic. I want her safely away from here—away from all these questions and charges."

"That isn't the way to handle this, Dad," Gabe had protested. "She needs to be here with us, where we can keep an eye on her—not three hundred miles away."

"The clinic is the best place for her. I don't care what you say."

"Dad, she's already said once that she won't go. If you try to make her, she'll fight you—especially now. Is that what you want? To be at odds with her? I don't think so."

"Frazier," her mother had inserted tentatively. "Maybe he's right."

A long and heavy sigh had come from her father. "I don't know. I just don't know."

"Where is Remy?" her mother had asked worriedly.

"I don't know. She left before I did. I walked her to her car—"

At that point Remy had taken her cue and walked in. "Would you believe I was halfway to the airport before I realized where I was? I guess I thought the car knew the way home, so I didn't pay attention."

There'd been no further mention of the clinic or of Howard Hanks—not in front of her, anyway. But what she'd heard was enough. Her family was determined to protect her, to shield her from this "unpleasantness" over the *Dragon*—for her own good, naturally.

Maybe they'd always treated her like this, but this time she couldn't let them. These allegations of fraud had to be the trouble she'd sensed. She knew something, she was certain of it—maybe something that would either clear Cole or convict him. She had to find out what it was. She couldn't sit back and twiddle her thumbs, waiting for her memory to return—if it ever did.

Assuming that the charges of fraud were true, more than one person had to be involved in it. Somewhere there was proof of that. Maybe the company files could provide it.

But once again, the question was, how was she going to get to them? That was her next problem. She paid for the hard copy of the newspaper article and left, arriving home a good twenty minutes before Sibylle returned from the salon.

The newspaper print blurred. Not that it mattered, Remy thought. She'd read the article so many times she practically had it memorized. She lowered the copy to her lap and let her gaze drift restlessly around her bedroom. The blackness of night pressed against the glass of the gallery doors and threw back a fuzzy image of the room. Remy couldn't help noticing how relaxed she looked, lounging on the loveseat clad in a jade satin robe—the proverbial lady of leisure. She knew a closer look would have revealed her tension.

She glanced at the digital clock on her bedside table and sighed. The minutes were ticking away with all the speed of stampeding snails. She considered going through the drawers of the small escritoire again, but she'd already spent the afternoon doing that, and had found little more than bank statements, blank checks, a sheaf of embossed stationery with matching envelopes, an odd letter or two from what she presumed were girlfriends of hers—letters she obviously hadn't gotten around to answering—and an address book filled with names and phone numbers of people she couldn't remember, with two pages devoted to family birthdays and anniversaries. There was a date calendar for the new year, but the notations in it were few, limited to the month of January and containing mostly reminders of dinner engagements, somebody's party, museum meetings or tours, and a dental appointment, and concluding with the time, airline, and number of her flight to Nice.

Cole's name didn't appear anywhere. Remy didn't know whether that meant that she'd already broken up with him by the time the new year started or that she hadn't needed to be reminded of her dates with him.

The drawers had yielded no diaries or journals—not that she had expected any. Even now she had no compulsion to commit her thoughts to paper. And there hadn't been any lists of things-to-do. If the contents of those drawers were a reflection of her life, she obviously led a very carefree existence—no responsibilities, no demands, no obligations.

Had she always let others do things for her? Like Nattie, who cooked the meals, made her bed, tidied her room, and saw that she had clean towels for her bath. And the dailies, who cleaned the house and did the laundry and the ironing. And her mother, who planned the meals, managed the household, arranged the dinner parties, and kept fresh flowers in all the rooms. And her father, uncle, and cousin, who ran the family shipping business that provided her with an income—though it wasn't her only income. According to some papers she'd found in the desk, she had a trust fund of some sort. Set up by her grandfather, she thought.

But what had she ever contributed—except to put in her appearances at the board meetings? Had she always let others provide for her needs, let them have the work and the worry of the shipping line while she breezed through life—until now? But it couldn't have taken until this minute for her to realize what she'd been missing. No, it had to have happened earlier, or she would have never been nagged by this feeling of trouble at the hospital in Nice when she hadn't known anything about herself. Had she been jolted into awareness by the insurance company's charges of fraud and her own now-lost knowledge of it? Or had it started before that? Maybe with Cole's criticism of her ignorance about the company's financial situation?

My God, how horribly and painfully ironic that would be, she thought, and then she heard footsteps and muffled voices in the hall outside her door. Hurriedly she snatched the latest issue of *Harper's Bazaar* off the floor next to the loveseat and sandwiched the copy of the newspaper article between its pages. A second later there was a light rap on her door.

"Come in."

As she'd expected, her parents walked in, her father in white tie and full evening dress, her mother gowned in a soft chiffon cloud of deep rose pink, a silver fox stole around her shoulders. They were off to another gala event, one of literally dozens strung in multiple strands through the Carnival season, which began on the sixth of January—Twelfth Night—and ran all the way to Mardi Gras, gathering momentum all the while.

"We wanted you to know that we're leaving now," Sibylle Jardin declared, casting her a concerned smile. "Are you sure you'll be all right here alone?"

"I am twenty-seven." Remy automatically smiled, then caught herself and remembered not to look too bright, too cheerful—or too anxious for them to leave. "I think that's old enough to stay home alone at night, don't you?"

"Yes, but . . . with you being ill and all—"

"I have a slight headache . . . probably from fatigue. It's nothing more serious than that. I promise."

"Just the same, we'll give you a call later and make sure you're all right," her father said.

"No, don't. You'd be alarmed if I didn't answer, and I wouldn't," she said, thinking fast. "I was planning on disconnecting my extension so I wouldn't be disturbed if the phone rang."

"I suppose that's sensible," he conceded. "You know where we'll be if you need us."

"I do. Has Gabe left already?" She thought she'd heard his car, but she wasn't sure.

"About ten minutes ago."

When her father made a move toward the door, Remy quickly encouraged it. "You two enjoy yourselves tonight, and don't worry about me. I'll be fine."

After a few more flutterings of concern from her mother, they left. Remy waited until she heard the Mercedes pull away and let another ten minutes drag by for good measure, then ran silently across the second-floor hall to the master bedroom. For an instant she stared at the solid brass doorknob, conscious of the hard thumping of her heart and the nervous churning of her stomach, and then she closed her hand around it, gave it a turn, and slipped inside. She felt exactly like a thief sneaking into her parents' bedroom—but she hadn't come to steal, only to borrow.

She flipped on the lights and went directly to the bureau. There, on top of it, in the oval tray that held her father's loose change, an empty money clip, and a pocketknife, was a key ring with some half-dozen keys looped on it. Smiling in triumph, Remy scooped it up. The smooth fall of his trousers—with no jangle of keys when he walked—had earlier encouraged her to believe that he was carrying only his house and car keys, leaving the rest behind. What they all went to, she didn't know, but she was counting on the fact that when he'd resigned as president of the Crescent Line, he hadn't returned his key to the office.

Back in her room, Remy pulled on a pair of navy-blue slacks and a matching raw-silk sweater, grabbed a fawn-colored suede jacket from the closet, and left the house.

Thirty minutes later she was inside the International Trade Mart, standing in front of the entrance to the corporate offices of the Crescent Line. Neither the first nor the second key fit in the lock. Remy flipped past the next two, which bore the Mercedes logo—possibly spare keys to her mother's car. She tried the fifth key. It slipped right in. She gave it a turn, and the lock clicked open.

The office lights were on. For security reasons? Or had someone forgotten to shut them off before leaving? Or—was someone here? Remy stepped partway into the reception room and listened intently for some creak of a chair, a rustle of paper, the faint click of computer keys, a cough—anything. Silence. Not trusting it, she inched the door closed and moved stealthily forward to investigate, in the process discovering how loud the sound of cloth brushing against cloth was, how dry her mouth could be, and how acutely tense her muscles could become.

But there was no one about. She was alone. She drew her first full breath and began her search for information. She glanced at a computer terminal. A touch of the right keys would call up all the information she wanted—assuming she could figure out the access codes. But it was the documentation for the computer entries that she really wanted to see.

She went to the file cabinet. Locked. She started down the row, pulling at drawer handle after drawer handle. Locked, locked, locked—they were all locked. She sagged against the last cabinet in frustration and combed a hand through her hair, trying to think.

The file clerks had to have keys to them. Did they take them home? Drop them in their purses or pockets to get buried in the bottom or sent to the cleaners—or left on the kitchen table? They wouldn't take that risk; they'd leave the keys in their desks. She found a set in the first drawer she looked in, and went to work.

It took Remy fifteen minutes to figure out the filing system, and another twenty-five to gather together all the paperwork relating to the tanker's final voyage. Armed with the names of the crew from the ship's manifest, she shifted to the payroll records, pulling each man's file.

Unwilling to take the time to study all the documents now, Remy turned on the copy machine and glanced through the papers while she waited for it to warm up. All of them appeared to be simple and straightforward—a list of the stores and their associated invoices, a bill for the cargo of crude oil and a copy of a check representing payment in full for the same, charges for fuel and marine services, copies of some kind of licenses or permits, employee rate cards and personal information. Yet something bothered her. She had copied all the documents and was halfway through the crew's records before she realized what it was.

Hurriedly she copied the rest, stuffed the copies into a blank folder to take with her, returned the originals to their proper files, and began going through other employment records to see if maybe—just maybe—she was wrong. She wasn't.

The crew that had sailed aboard the *Crescent Dragon* on her last and final voyage—from the captain to the lowliest seaman—had never worked for the Crescent Line *before* or *since.* Judging from the records, it wasn't uncommon for a seaman or a first mate, or even a captain, to work for the company only one time. But an entire crew? No, that was too coincidental to be anything other than suspicious—very suspicious.

Remy stared at the crew names, many of them Oriental, possibly Korean, and thought how funny it was—a twisted and bitter kind of funny—to realize that this was just the kind of thing she had hoped to find. And now that she had, she wished she hadn't.

Where were they now, she wondered. Probably scattered to the four winds —or in this case the seven seas. More than likely with a considerable amount of extra cash in their pockets in return for keeping quiet about what they knew . . . or what they'd seen. And if Howard Hanks was right, what they'd seen was the tanker off-loading its cargo of crude oil onto waiting barges or into an offshore pipeline.

The crew had to have known what was going on—at least the officers definitely did. And the seamen would have recognized that it wasn't normal to off-load cargo within a day or two of leaving port, and then continue on empty.

And Remy understood that her chances of tracking down any of the crew were virtually nil. Maybe Howard Hanks had succeeded in talking to one of them. Maybe it was even where he'd gotten his proof of fraud. Or maybe he hadn't talked to any of them. If he had, surely he would have known whether the crude had been off-loaded onto barges or into a pipeline. He wouldn't have held out both as possibilities.

Maybe Gabe was right. Maybe Hanks didn't have anything more to go on than suspicion. Maybe he was trying to scare somebody into making a mistake . . . somebody like Cole.

She turned away from the thought and walked to the window, the night's darkness a mirror for the sudden desolation she felt. She looked out, directly at the glittering lights of Algiers. Below was the Spanish Plaza with its lighted fountain. And in between, the wide, black ribbon of the Mississippi made its sweeping crescent curve, outlined by the lights on both banks.

Then, on the river itself, she saw lights moving. At first she thought they belonged to the ferry that ran from the foot of Canal Street across the river to Algiers Point. Then she realized they were the running lights of a ship crawling steadily upriver, the vessel itself almost invisible from this distance—a black shape on a black river.

Suddenly she was seeing another darkened ship—close to her—enveloped in swirling fog, two men silhouetted at the rail, thick lines stretching toward her. It was a full second before she realized the image of the ship was in her mind. There was white lettering on the bow—white lettering that spelled out the name of the ship.

"Please, God, let me read it," she whispered.

CRESCENT DRAG—

"I don't care what you say." A woman's voice, bitter and accusing, broke over Remy, shattering that fragment of a memory. "She was dancing so close to you, it would have taken a crowbar to pry the two of you apart. It was disgusting."

She spun away from the window and stared at the open door to the corridor, for a fraction of a second frozen by the sound of footsteps. Someone was out there! Who? Why?

"What did you expect me to do? Shove her away?"

That voice—it was Lance's. Dear God, she couldn't let him find her here. She looked frantically around the lighted room for some place to hide. That side door—it had to lead somewhere, if only to a closet.

"You didn't have to look like you were enjoying yourself."

"Dammit, Julie! Do we have to go through this every time we go out for the evening?" Lance protested angrily as Remy ran to the desk. At the moment speed seemed as important as silence. She grabbed her purse off the top of the desk, slinging the strap over her shoulder and hugging the folder against her, hoping their voices would cover any sound she made.

"You should be flattered that after seven years of marriage I still care enough to be jealous."

Their voices were closer; they were coming this way. She darted for the side door. Just as she reached it, Remy heard a low, steady hum. The copy machine —it was still on.

"I have never liked green eyes, Julie."

Remy dashed over and turned the machine off, the click of the switch sounding much too loud. She raced back to the door and forced herself to turn the knob slowly, to ease back the latch. When the door gave, she opened it only wide enough to enable her to slip through. But when she tried to glide noiselessly through the narrow opening, her purse thwacked the frame.

"What was that?"

"What?"

Remy closed the door and flattened herself against it, shutting her eyes, longing to drink in great gulps of air, yet too afraid to breathe.

"I thought I heard something." Lance's voice moved along the corridor, accompanied by the sound of firm, long-striding footsteps. Right behind them was the tap-tap-tap of high heels.

Remy's eyes flew open. The file cabinets. She'd forgotten to lock them. It was too late. He was too close. Would he look? Would he notice? Would he blame it on a careless file clerk?

Dear heaven. Remy looked around her, suddenly realizing she wasn't in a closet. She was in somebody's office. Lance's? It couldn't be—could it? She spotted the door to the corridor and darted to it, pressing herself against the wall next to the hinges so the door would hide her if it was opened.

"Hello? Is somebody here?" He was directly outside; only the wall separated them. Remy sank her teeth into her lower lip, biting down on it hard to keep from betraying herself with a sound, a breath.

"It's probably the cleaning people, Lance," replied the woman, obviously his wife. "Nobody else would be working this late."

He was walking past the office door, continuing on toward the file room, his steps a little slower now—as if he was listening. Somehow she had to get out of here. If he started looking around, he'd find her. There was no place to hide.

"Lance—"

"Shut up."

Remy snuck to the other side of the door and very, very carefully turned the knob, then opened it, not a crack but a sliver. When she peered out, the corridor was empty—in both directions, as near as she could tell. They must be in the file room. Then came the metallic sound of a file drawer gliding that last inch before it shut. She must have left one partially open. How long did she have—maybe seconds?—before he opened the connecting door to this office?

She had one chance, and she took it, slipping out the door into the corridor and running swiftly and silently toward the reception area, totally exposed and expecting at every step to hear his shout of discovery. But it never came. As she rounded the corner, she threw one quick look down the hall. It was still empty. She dashed across the reception area to the door. He'd left it unlocked! She couldn't believe her luck as she banished the image of fumbling with the keys from her mind.

She opened the door and slipped outside, taking care this time not to hit her purse on the frame. She closed it as quietly as she could, then turned, glancing from the elevators to the door to the emergency stairs.

Not the stairs—they were too open, too exposed, too noisy; the slightest sound would echo. She ran to the elevators and punched the Down button, then waited, watching for an arrow to light up above one of them.

"Hurry, hurry," she murmured under her breath, then caught the faint whir of one coming. Suddenly it hit her—the bell, the damned bell would ding when it reached this floor!

It did—twice—as loud as any alarm to her ears. Remy cast one last glance over her shoulder at the office door, then darted inside the cage and pushed the Lobby button, and then the one marked Door Close.

In their own good time, they slid shut. She made her first-ever white-knuckle descent in an elevator, her hands holding the shoulder strap of her purse and the file folder in a death grip as she wondered whether Lance had seen or heard her—and whether security would be waiting for her when the doors opened.

But no uniformed guard was standing outside when the elevator reached the lobby. Remy hesitantly stepped out and was immediately engulfed by a laughing, loud-talking group streaming out of another elevator. One of them, a man, accidentally bumped into her.

"Oops, sorry," he said, as Remy noticed the security man at the desk—on the phone. With Lance? "Hey, you're a cutie, you know that?" The man draped an arm around her shoulders, his breath reeking of whiskey.

Remy saw the security guard glance at the group, and she carefully withheld any objections to the man's overt attentions. "Thanks," she said, letting the man draw her along with him as the group headed in the general direction of the doors.

"Whatcha been doing? Working late at the office?" he asked, looking at the folder she was carrying.

"Sort of."

"That's too bad. We've been partying."

"Really."

"Yeah, we been at the bar up on top."

"The Top of the Mart."

"Yeah, that's the name of it." He leaned closer and giggled. "Agnes lost her purse. She laid it down on the ledge, and the next minute it was gone. Did you know that bar revolves? About an hour later, there was her purse."

"How nice. I'm glad she got it back." They were directly level with the security desk.

"You wanna go party with us?"

"I don't know. Where are you going?"

He frowned. "Hey, Johnny!" He called to one of the men at the front of the group. "Where're we going?"

"Pat O'Brien's!"

"Yeah, Pat O'Brien's. I'll buy you one of those tornado drinks."

"Hurricane."

"What?"

"Never mind." They were out the door, walking into the sharp, cool night. She slipped free of his draping arm, offering a quick, "I've been to Pat O'Brien's before. Maybe another time."

She had to force herself not to run to the parking lot, recognizing that she was almost safe and that this was no time to draw undue attention to herself. As she neared the sleek bronze Jaguar, she hastily dug through her purse for the keys. She unlocked the driver's door and quickly slipped behind the wheel, depositing her purse and the folder on the passenger seat, then sinking back against the tawny leather seat. Safe. It was over. Or was it? Wasn't it just beginning?

"What have I gotten myself into?" she murmured. "I must be crazy."

But she wasn't crazy, and she hadn't gotten herself into anything. On the contrary, she'd probably been involved from the onset—perhaps knowingly, or perhaps not. One thing she was sure about: she had seen the *Crescent Dragon* tied up to a dock—in the mist and darkness of night. But what else had she seen? Or was the operative word *whom*?

She sighed in frustration and inserted the key into the ignition.

23

''GOOD MORNING.'' Remy breezed into the dining room, encompassing all at the table in her greeting.

"You seem remarkably chipper this morning," Frazier observed, from his chair at the head of the table.

"I had a marvelous night's sleep, that's why," she said as she crossed to the serving table and poured orange juice into the one remaining glass beside the crystal pitcher. "How was the party? I have to admit I didn't hear any of you come in."

"It was—" Gabe started to answer.

"Remy, what are you doing in those clothes?" Sibylle looked at her with something akin to concern for her sanity.

Remy plucked at the fawn-colored jodhpurs. "Isn't it obvious? I thought I'd go horseback riding this morning." Actually, she didn't know if she could ride a horse, but the jodhpurs, riding boots, and chocolate-brown corduroy jacket with fawn-colored suede patches at the elbows had been in her closet. Judging by the signs of wear on the inside of both the boots and the pants, she assumed she'd worn them for the use they were intended for and not simply for appearances.

"At Audubon Park, I suppose," Gabe said.

"Is that where I usually go? I wasn't sure." She walked over to sit beside him, her juice glass in hand.

"Remy, have you looked outside?" her mother protested.

"Yes." But she glanced over her shoulder again at the bleak gray overcast beyond the dining-room windows, then scooted her chair up to the table. "Depressing, isn't it? I decided it would be better to go out in it than stay in the house and have that gray gloom get me down."

"But it's cold."

"I prefer to think of it as 'brisk.'" She unfolded her napkin and laid it across her lap. "And I'd much rather go riding when there's a nip in the air than when it's warm and muggy. Besides, I'm dressed for it," she said, indicating the black ribbed turtleneck sweater she wore under the heavy corduroy jacket.

"What if it rains?"

"Mother," she said in a laughing voice. "I may have lost my memory, but I still have enough sense to come in out of the rain." But she mentally crossed her fingers, hoping the rain would hold off until later in the day.

"By that I take it you mean you haven't been able to remember anything else," Gabe said, studying her with a sympathetic look.

She hesitated, then deliberately hedged the truth. "Not really. A few times I've had vague déjà vu feelings that I've seen or done the same thing before, but I can't honestly say they were memories."

"You're home and safe with us again—that's what counts," Gabe assured her.

"I know." She took a sip of her juice, then asked, dividing the question between Gabe and her father, "Have you been able to find out anything about the *Dragon*?"

"Not yet," Gabe replied.

"I thought Uncle Marc might have learned something."

"He didn't." Her father's answer was curt, his expression closed and tight, making it clear this was not a subject he wished to discuss.

She would have dropped the matter, but another question occurred to her. "Has anyone come right out and asked Cole what his meeting with the insurance people was about? It seems to me that regardless of how strong his contract is, he's still accountable to the board."

She saw Gabe and her father exchange a quick glance, and then Gabe smiled at her. "Out of the mouths of pretty babes," he murmured, then shrugged. "I suppose we've all been so worried about you that we overlooked the obvious. It's definitely an option we should consider."

"I'll mention it to Marc at lunch today," her father stated.

This time the subject was closed for good as Nattie walked in with their breakfast. Remy breathed in the aroma coming from the tray and immediately guessed, "Pecan waffles."

"With honey butter, brown-sugar syrup, and sausage," Nattie announced, setting the first plate in front of Remy's mother. "It should stick to your ribs and give you some cushion when you fall off that horse."

But Remy had no intentions of going horseback riding. It was nothing more than an excuse to be absent from the house.

Remy parked along the edge of the levee road and stepped out of the Jaguar, the road's oyster-shell surface crunching beneath her riding boots. A few feet from the opposite shoulder, the levee's grassy eight-foot bank sloped away to level out beside the River Road, which followed the Mississippi's twists and bends.

She closed the car door, then glanced in the direction of the tank farm and pipeline terminal on the other side of the road. Some one hundred tanks, resembling giant steel cans painted a dull white, stretched away from her in orderly rows, the whole area enclosed by a towering chain-link fence. A sign on the gate identified it as the property of the Gulf Coast Petroleum Association, a name that meant nothing to her.

A commercial jetliner rumbled in the distance, making its departure climb from nearby New Orleans Airport. Remy watched it for an instant, then noted the hard, cold look of the clouds overhead and hoped again that they reflected only the gray of winter and not the gray of rain.

Turning, she faced the Mississippi River and the trio of petroleum docks that stood in the muddy brown waters some three hundred feet from the bank. Low, flat barges were moored to the downriver dock, but the middle one—the nearest one—had an oceangoing tanker tied alongside.

Was this the dock where the *Crescent Dragon* had taken on its last load of crude? Was this where she'd seen the tanker? She couldn't remember, and she'd found nothing in the company files that identified the location of the vessel's last berth—or, at least, if the information was there, she hadn't recognized it as such. And heaven knew, there were literally dozens of petroleum docks scattered along the Mississippi River, stretching all the way to Baton Rouge. Most of them, like this cluster, were located upriver or downriver from the city itself, away from thickly populated areas—or so the Port Authority had told her when she'd called them from a phone booth.

Unfortunately, that was about the only useful information she had been able to obtain from them. The man she'd spoken with had claimed he didn't know how to go about finding out where a specific vessel had been berthed more than five months before. He wasn't even sure the commission kept a record of such things, especially when there was no requirement for a vessel to notify them when it left port. He'd told her that the dock agent probably kept track of that type of information.

Which left her back at square one—which dock, and which dock agent?

With no crew available to question, the dock was her only starting point. If she'd been there when the *Dragon* was loaded, as she believed, she might have been seen by one of the dockworkers. If she could locate the men on duty that night, talk to them, maybe one of them could tell her what had happened, who'd been there, and what she might have seen.

It sounded possible . . . even logical. Remy smiled to herself, fully aware that it wasn't logic that had selected this particular petroleum dock as the place to begin asking her questions—it was simply the second one she'd come across.

The entrance to the first had been locked up tight, with no one on duty at the gate, and she'd been forced to drive on. She tried not to think about how many more like that she might encounter, and concentrated instead on this one.

A ramp, wide enough to allow the passage of a motorized vehicle, led out to the middle quay. Ignoring the sign that read AUTHORIZED PERSONNEL ONLY BEYOND THIS POINT, Remy walked onto the ramp and continued past the NO TRESPASSING and NO SMOKING signs posted at frequent intervals along the entire length of it.

The reek of petroleum fumes grew stronger as she neared the tanker. Stout mooring lines ran from the vessel to the bollards on the concrete dock, securing the ship to its berth, and a gangway stretched from the dock to the ship's weather deck. There was no sign of activity on the tanker itself, except for the three chick stands that connected the dockside pipelines to the ship's holding tanks.

Catching sight of two men on the dock, Remy angled toward them. For some reason she'd expected it to be busier than this, with more of the bustle she'd observed on the cargo wharves.

"Hey, lady!" a voice barked, directly behind her.

Remy stiffened, suddenly and unexpectedly feeling the cool breath of the river fog on her cheeks, smelling the dampness of the mist, and seeing darkness all around her—the darkness of night, that night. In that instant she knew she'd been surprised by someone that night—just like this.

She whirled around and stared at the bejowled bulldog of a man facing her. Not by him—she was oddly certain of that. He wore a plaid-lined jacket in a dark navy twill and a pair of pants in the same fabric that rode precariously low on his hips, the waistband dipping under his big beer-belly.

"What're you doing out here? Didn't you see the signs?" He jerked his thumb in the direction of the NO TRESPASSING placard behind him. "No one's allowed on this dock without authorization."

"I know. I was looking for someone who could give me permission. Can you?" She gave him her most winsome smile, but he didn't bat an eye.

"You'd have to see the director of operations, Tom Hayes, and he ain't here today."

"What about you? What do you do?"

"I'm in charge of loading and operations."

"Then maybe you can answer a few questions for me—"

"Look, lady. We don't give tours and we don't allow visitors. You'll have to leave now."

"At least you can tell me whether you're loading or unloading this ship," Remy persisted.

"Loading it," he said, and he pursed his lips and teeth to emit a loud, ear-splitting whistle. He followed it with a shout and motioning swing of his arm. "Charlie! Come over here!"

Both men on the dock turned at the sound of the shrill whistle, but it was the shorter of the two who broke away to answer the summons. As he trotted over, the jaunty tilt of his billed cap, the natural spring to his step, and the litheness of his build all gave a deceptive impression of youth. When he stopped in front of them, Remy noticed the deep lines that age and the elements had carved into his face, and she realized he was a great deal closer to sixty than to thirty.

He darted a curious, bright-eyed glance at Remy, then averted his gaze to the man beside her. "What'd ya want, Mac?"

"This lady needs an escort back to her car."

"My pleasure."

Remy started to protest, then recognized that she'd only succeed in antagonizing Mac further. As stubborn as that man was, he'd probably have her bodily carried off the dock if she refused to leave voluntarily.

As the man walked off toward the tanker's gangway, Remy glanced at her escort. "I'm sorry about this, Mr.—"

"Just Charlie," he insisted, grinning. "Everybody calls me that. And don't mind him. He snaps at everybody when he's under the gun to get a ship out. At times like this, he's our version of a Big Mac Attack."

She smiled wryly. "I do feel like I've been pounced on and chewed a bit." She saw the tanker's captain step to the rail of the bridge deck. Mac cupped his hands to his mouth and yelled something at him. The captain responded with an acknowledging salute and went back inside. "What was that all about?" she asked, and reluctantly moved toward the ramp.

Charlie lifted his shoulders in a light shrug. "Mac was probably letting the captain know he could go ahead and call for a river pilot."

"A river pilot." She looked at him with quick interest.

"Yeah, all ships on the Mississippi have to carry a river pilot licensed by the state, someone who knows the river, the locations of its shoals, the tricks of its currents, everything. The ships have to give the Pilots' Association a three-hour advance notice of their departure. Which is about how long it's gonna take us to finish loading this tanker. By then, with luck, the crew will have reported for duty, the pilot'll be on board, and down the river she'll go."

"Then a river pilot takes a ship all the way to the mouth." Unconsciously, Remy slowed her steps, forcing Charlie to shorten his loping stride to stay abreast of her.

"There's always a pilot on board, but not the same one. A Baton Rouge pilot gets on here and takes her down to around Chalmette. A Crescent River pilot gets on board there and helps guide her to Pilot Town. Another pilot takes her from there out to the sea buoy. From this dock, a tanker like that's got about a hundred and forty miles of river to navigate before it reaches the open waters of the Gulf. Kinda amazing, isn't it?"

"I don't think I realized it was that far," Remy murmured, thinking as well that no matter where the *Dragon* had been loaded, it must have had well over a hundred miles of river to navigate. And somewhere along that hundred-plus-mile stretch, the bearded Mr. Hanks claimed, the tanker could have off-loaded its cargo of crude onto waiting barges. If it had, the river pilot would have known about it. "Charlie . . . how long does it take to unload a tanker like that one back there?"

"We can do it in less than twenty-four hours."

"It takes that long." Remy stopped in surprise, twenty feet short of the end of the ramp.

He chuckled. "It wasn't that many years ago when we thought we were doing good to turn a tanker around in three days."

"Would it change any if you were unloading onto barges instead of a pipeline?"

"Not really. Your rate of discharge is the same."

"What about these river pilots?" These river pilots who were bound to keep some kind of log on the ships they guided. These river pilots who obviously lived in the area, who could tell her where the *Dragon* had been docked and whether she'd made any stops in her journey downriver. "How would a person get hold of them?"

"You just call 'em up."

"You mean they're listed in the phone book?" She nearly smiled at the fact that the answer could be so simple as they made the turn off the ramp toward her car.

"Yep. All you gotta do is look in the Yellow Pages under the Pilots' Association, and the office numbers for all three of them are there."

"Which means I can let my 'fingers do the walking' instead of me," Remy murmured to herself, this time letting the smile come, aware that she was no longer faced with the daunting and time-consuming task of going to all the petroleum docks, trying to locate the tanker's last berth. A couple of phone calls should tell her that—and give her the names of the pilots who had been on board the *Dragon* on her downriver trip.

"Sorry—what'd you say? I couldn't hear," Charlie said, flicking a hand at a small Toyota pickup truck that was accelerating to make the sloping climb onto the levee road.

"Nothing." She paused in front of her car to let the pickup go by. As the small white truck drew level with her, it suddenly applied its brakes, the tires digging into the shelled surface and skidding to a stop a half a length behind her.

The passenger door immediately swung open, and a man dressed in a dark business suit and tie, wearing a pair of attractive gold-rimmed glasses, stepped out and turned his frowning look on her. Judging by the deep perpendicular creases between his eyebrows, Remy suspected that he frowned a lot more than he smiled. She mentally braced herself to receive another lecture about unauthorized visitors.

"Remy. I thought I recognized you. What are you doing here?"

My God, she thought, he knows me. She hadn't expected that, and made another quick study of him, trying to find something familiar. He looked to be somewhere in his late thirties or early forties. His hair was dark and combed straight back from his face—a sternly pragmatic face, with no particularly distinguishing features, unless it was the thinness of his lips.

"This is a surprise. I didn't expect to run into you here," she declared, pretending to know him—a decision she hadn't been conscious of making.

"And I didn't expect to see you. So what brings you here?" He tried to smile, but the expression was foreign to him. Remy briefly thought that it was a shame; he could have been a good-looking man if it weren't for the permanent scowl etched in his forehead.

"What brings me here?" she echoed his question, certain that she couldn't tell him the truth. If he knew her, he must know her family, and she couldn't have him telling them what she was doing. She had to come up with some other reason—something innocuous. "A friend of mine is writing a book, and I offered to help her with some of the research. One of her characters is in shipping, and she thought I'd know about it."

"A friend of yours? Which one?"

"I don't think you know her. She works at the museum."

"I see." Was he convinced? Remy couldn't tell as she tried to conceal how uncomfortable she felt under his penetrating study. "Did you get all the information you needed?" His glance flicked to Charlie, as if guessing that he'd provided it.

"I think so." She produced the car keys from her jacket pocket and glanced pointedly at the pickup, its motor idling. "I won't keep you. I know you have things to do, and I have a date with a horse to keep."

"See you around, Remy." He hesitated a moment longer, then turned and climbed back into the cab of the pickup.

Remy waited until the truck pulled away, then looked at Charlie. "I hate it when that happens."

"What do you mean?"

"My mind's an absolute blank. I know him, but I can't remember his name."

"Him? That's Carl Maitland."

"Of course." She pretended to recognize the name. In truth, it was vaguely familiar, but she couldn't remember why or how. She held out her hand. "Thanks for escorting me to my car, Charlie—and for your patience in answering all my questions."

"No problem." His calloused hand briefly gripped hers, then released it. "And if your friend needs any more help with her book, tell her to call me. I got some stories about things that have happened on the docks that she wouldn't believe. They'd make a good book."

"I'll tell her."

As she walked around the car to the driver's door, he called after her, "Last name's Aikens. I'm in the phone book."

"Got it," she said, and waved a final good-bye.

Leaving the tank terminal and the petroleum docks, Remy followed the River Road for a short distance, then turned off and made the jog to intersect with Airline Highway. She stopped at the first pay telephone booth she saw. In the directory, just as Charlie Aikens had promised, were the numbers for all three river-pilot districts. She called the Baton Rouge district first and simply asked if someone could tell her which pilot had been aboard the tanker *Crescent Dragon* when it had left port in the early part of September last year. Within minutes a man came back on the line and said the pilot had been Pete Hoskins—no, he wasn't there right now. He was on a Russian grain ship and probably wouldn't be back for another five hours.

Her second call was more productive.

Thirty minutes later Remy was sitting in a booth in a Mid-City coffee shop with the *Dragon*'s Crescent River pilot, Gus Trudeau, a tall man of imposing proportions with a full head of sandy hair tinged with gray. She watched him take a long drink of the scalding-hot coffee, secretly convinced he had an asbestos-lined mouth.

Amazingly, he didn't breathe out fire, smoke, or steam when he set his cup down on the Formica-topped table and looked her squarely in the eye. "So you're a writer, eh?"

"That's right. I'm writing a follow-up piece on the *Crescent Dragon*, a retrospective story from the viewpoint of various people like yourself who had some involvement with what turned out to be her last voyage." Remy thought the cover was a good one—one that would arouse the least possible amount of suspicion about her interest in the tanker. "So tell me, Mr. Trudeau, what do you remember of her? Were there any problems? Did anything unusual happen?"

"No, it was pretty routine. When I took over from Pete Hoskins, the Baton Rouge pilot, I remember he told me that she answered pretty sluggish, so I kept that in mind on the trip down to Pilot Town. And I talked briefly with the captain, too, about the storm brewing in the Gulf."

"Then there weren't any stops—any delays along the way?"

"None."

"That was almost six months ago, Mr. Trudeau." Remy eyed him curiously. "How can you be so sure about that?"

"Like I told those other two who came around asking—"

"Other two?" She frowned. "What other two?"

"I don't remember their names, but one was a heavyset guy with a beard who came around asking questions about the tanker—musta been two weeks ago. Then a couple days before that, I talked to another guy. He was younger, probably in his thirties, tall, brown hair."

Gabe. She should have known her brother would do some checking of his own. "I'm sorry. I interrupted you. What was it that you told them?"

"Just that when a ship goes down in a storm three days after you've been on her, you remember that ship *and* that trip—*well.* You go over the trip in your mind, compare notes with the other pilots, and try to remember if there was something—anything—that might have indicated the vessel wasn't really seaworthy."

"And you did that. You talked with the other two pilots," Remy guessed.

"I did. And it was routine all the way."

"Did they have any stops or delays?"

"None. And I know that for a fact, because I saw copies of their log sheets."

She took a small sip of the still-hot coffee and wondered whether she should take his word for it or talk to the other pilots herself. "You don't happen to know where the tanker was docked, do you?" she asked curiously.

"Pete told me he picked her up at the old Claymore docks." He hesitated, then nodded. "That's right. She was berthed in the upper one. I remember Pete told me the current takes a funny twist there and can sometimes be a problem when you're pulling away from the dock. That's when he discovered how slow the tanker was to maneuver."

"Where are the Claymore docks?"

"Let's see." He leaned against the booth's red-vinyl back, a thoughtful, searching frown claiming his expression. "What mile marker are they located on?"

Remy immediately guessed that he was talking "river" miles. "No, I was wondering how I could reach them from land."

"I don't know if I can tell you how to get there by land," he said, absently scratching his head. "They're on the east bank, north of Kenner a ways. I'm sure you could get to 'em by the River Road."

She realized that she must have been close to them earlier that day. "How far are they from the tank farm and docks owned by Gulf Coast Petroleum?"

"Those *are* the old Claymore docks."

"What?"

"Those *are* the Claymore docks," he repeated.

She'd been there—at the very place where the *Dragon* had been berthed—and not known it, not recognized it, not remembered. "Wait. There are three docks there." And she'd been on the middle one. "Which one did you say the tanker was at?"

"The upper one."

She shook her head in confusion. "Which one's that?"

"The upriver one—that's why it's called the 'upper' dock."

She hadn't been on the right dock. Was that why nothing had seemed familiar to her? She didn't dare go back and risk running into that Carl Maitland again. And she doubted that "Bulldog" Mac would be any more cooperative the second time around. Then she remembered Charlie—dear, wonderful Charlie Aikens, so friendly and free with information. Was he one of the men who had loaded the *Dragon*? Had he seen her there that night? Wouldn't he have recognized her if he had? His number was in the phone book, he'd said. All she had to do was call and ask. And if he hadn't worked that shift, maybe she could persuade him to find out who had.

With an effort, she brought her attention back to the booth. "You said the trip downriver was routine, but—was there anything about the *Dragon*'s voyage that raised questions in your mind? In other words, when it went down, was it way off course? Or had it not traveled as far as you thought it would? Anything like that?" Even though the pilot had eliminated the possibility of the tanker off-loading its shipment of crude oil onto river barges or a pipeline downstream, there was still a chance it had hooked onto an offshore pipeline.

"No. According to the Coast Guard report I read, it went down about where you'd expect, given its course and speed and the strength of the storm. It sunk just a mile or two off the sea-lane. Fortunately, it's a well-traveled route, and the crew was able to signal a passing ship. And before you ask, no, we didn't run into much barge traffic."

"I beg your pardon?"

"The bearded guy asked a lot of questions about the barges that ply the Delta waters south of the city. But like I told him, about the only barges you meet downriver are the ones hauling trash and garbage out into the ocean."

"I see," she said, and went back to something he'd said just before that. "The Coast Guard issued a report on the sinking?"

"Yes."

She wondered why she hadn't found a copy of it in the company files. Had it been there, and had she somehow overlooked it?

She was still bothered by the question when she arrived home. She walked into the house and immediately caught the distinctive aroma of bay leaves and spices stewing in a gumbo pot. Her father was in the entrance hall, holding the telephone receiver to his ear. He hung up when he saw her.

"I was just dialing the stables to see if you'd left."

Remy faltered an instant in midstride, then recovered and smiled at him in mock reproof, trying not to think how close she'd come to getting caught in a lie. "Why would you be doing that? I told you I'd be home in time for lunch, and here I am," she said, then chided him as she paused to pull off her gloves. "I have the distinct feeling you're keeping closer track of me now than you did when I was a teenager."

"That's not true."

"Isn't it?" she challenged lightly.

"If it is, it's only because it's natural for us to worry after the way you disappeared before."

"I promise I'm not going to disappear again, so stop worrying."

"Remy." Her mother came out of the dining room. "I thought I heard your voice. I was just telling Nattie I didn't think you were going to make it back for lunch. How was your ride?" She inspected her daughter's appearance with a slightly puzzled expression. "I expected you to come back chilled to the bone, with your nose and cheeks all rosy-pink from the cold, but you look . . . fine."

"The Jaguar *does* have a heater. I warmed up on the way home." Remy glanced toward the dining room and deliberately sniffed the air. "Is that shrimp gumbo I smell?"

"Yes. I'll let Nattie know you're here. You'll want to change out of those riding clothes—"

"I'll do that later. Right now I'm starved."

Food was actually the furthest thing from her mind, but exercise was supposed to make a person hungry, and if she wanted to maintain the pretense that she'd spent the morning horseback riding, she had to feign an appetite.

An hour later, fresh from the shower, Remy sat in the middle of her bed, swathed in her satin robe, a towel wrapped turban-style around her wet head, and the folder containing copies of the documents from the company files lying open in front of her. Her first rifling search through the stack had failed to turn up a copy of the Coast Guard report. She started to go through the papers again, one at a time.

Two quick raps were the only warning she had. Frantically, she pulled the towel off her head and dropped it over the files to conceal them as the bedroom door swung open.

"Nattie," she declared in relief when the tall, spare black woman walked in. "You startled me." She laughed self-consciously and nervously combed her wet hair away from her forehead with her fingers.

"I knocked first."

"I know."

"Where're your boots?"

"In the closet. Why?" Frowning, Remy slid off the bed when Nattie immediately walked in that direction.

" 'Cause I'd better get 'em cleaned before they stink up the place," she said, opening the closet door and walking inside.

"You don't need to." Remy took a quick step after her, then stopped as Nattie emerged from the closet, boots in hand. Except for some white dust from the levee road's oyster-shell surface, the soles and heels of her riding boots were dry and unstained—as Nattie quickly saw. "I already cleaned them," Remy asserted.

Nattie shot her a skeptical look, then walked over and picked up the dark-brown corduroy riding jacket that Remy had laid over the back of the loveseat. "Just like you already brushed all the horse hairs off this jacket, I suppose."

"That's right." Why was she lying? Nattie didn't believe her, not for one second. But she couldn't tell her the truth. She wasn't even sure what the truth was. "Nattie, I—"

Nattie held up a hand to stave off the rest of her words. "Lies and rabbits both have a way of multiplying. I'll just put these boots back in the closet and hang up this jacket and leave it go at that."

"Thanks." Remy smiled a little in relief.

"I just hope you know what you're doing," Nattie muttered as she walked back into the closet.

"So do I," she replied over the faint rustle of clothing and hangers.

As soon as Nattie left, Remy lifted the covering towel off the open folder and began going through the individual copies again. Suddenly a name leapt out at her—Maitland. She stared at the invoice from Maitland Oil Company for the tanker's shipment of crude. Maitland Oil Company—as in Carl Maitland, the well-dressed man in the white pickup who'd addressed her by name? They had to be one and the same. Which meant that not only did he know her family, he also did business with the Crescent Line.

What if he ran into her father or her uncle? What if he mentioned seeing her at the docks—and the research she was supposedly doing for a friend? But she couldn't worry about that now. She'd deal with it when and *if* it happened. Maybe by then she would have found out something—or remembered something.

Right now she needed to look for that Coast Guard report. Later she'd call Charlie Aikens and see if he knew or could discover anything for her. She idly wondered what time he'd be home from work, then continued going through the sheaf of papers.

After the fourth ring, a familiar-sounding voice came on the line. "Yeah, Charlie here."

"Charlie." Remy glanced at the digital clock on her bedstand. Seven thirty-two. "I was beginning to think you were going to work all night."

"I stopped by Grogan's for a couple of beers. Who's this?"

"Remy. Remy Cooper." With the Crescent Line and the Jardins virtually synonymous to anyone on the waterfront, she'd realized that she'd have to use a different name. "I'm the one Mac had you escort off the dock today."

"Oh, sure," he said, as it dawned on him. "I remember you. How're you doing?"

"Fine. Listen, I was wondering if you could help me with some more information my friend needs for her book."

"I'll try."

"Do you remember the tanker the *Crescent Dragon*? She was loaded with a shipment of crude from your docks last September, probably the fifth or sixth."

"Hell—excuse my language, but we service so many barges and ships off those docks, I lose track of the names of 'em all."

"Yes, but this one went down in the Gulf during a storm."

"Yeah, there was a tanker that sank last year," he said slowly, thoughtfully. "And now that you mention it, I think I do remember hearing some of the guys talking about how she'd loaded out from our docks. But I didn't work on her."

"Could you find out who did? My friend would like to talk to them."

"No problem. I'll ask around tomorrow when I go in. Somebody's bound to remember something. Ships don't take up residence in Davy Jones's locker every day. What's your number? I'll give you a call tomorrow night and let you know what I've found out."

"I'd better call you. I'm not sure where I'll be."

"Carnival goes into full swing tomorrow, with wall-to-wall craziness, doesn't it? I steer clear of it myself these days. It's not like when I was young—not with all those gays strutting around dressed up like fancy showgirls. It used to be a wild time; now it's just plain crazy," he declared, then said, "You give me a call tomorrow night . . . 'bout this same time."

"I will." Remy said good-bye and hung up. With that in motion, the next thing on her agenda was to locate a copy of that Coast Guard report.

24

"SHE'S STARTED SNOOPING around asking questions."

He gripped the telephone's black receiver a little tighter and sat down in the chair behind the desk. "I don't believe you."

"I'm telling you she is. I know it for a fact," came the low, accusing reply. "Right now she's asking the wrong people the right questions. It's got to stop there."

He frowned, stunned, confused, and troubled. "But she can't remember anything. I know she can't."

"Maybe not, but she's damned well trying to. That insurance investigator Hanks can't cause us half as much trouble as she can, and we both know it. The last thing we need is somebody else going around asking questions. Do you hear me?"

"I hear you." The room suddenly seemed very stuffy. He reached up, loosened the knot of his tie, and unfastened the top button of his dress shirt. "Just let me handle it."

"I let you handle it the last time, and look what almost happened."

"But nothing did happen, did it?"

"And I'm not going to take the chance of something happening this time. I've gone too far, come too close. I'm not going to lose everything now."

"You won't. *We* won't."

"You're damned right we won't. Because I'm having her watched every time she leaves that house—and if I find out she's opening her mouth to anybody else, I'll persuade her to shut it."

"We agreed, going in, that there'd be no violence—no one would get hurt. You—"

"The ground rules have changed. Remy's changed them. No one's going to ruin me—not her, not you, no one. Do you understand?"

"Of course."

"Then do something about her, or I will."

There was a sharp click and the connection was broken. He held the receiver to his ear a second longer, then slammed it down and leaned back in his chair to stare at the ceiling, and not at the darkness that loomed outside.

Crowds lined St. Charles Avenue and filled the neutral strip in the middle. Small children sat perched atop stepladders in seat contraptions specially designed for the occasion. More youngsters were on the ground, gripping bags brought to hold the afternoon's booty. Some wore masks, others didn't, but all —young and old and everyone in between—stood with eager hands outstretched to the parade of riders in spangled costumes and the maskers on mountainous papier-mâché floats and screamed, begged, and cajoled—"Throw me something!" "I want the pearls!" "Over here!" Occasionally Remy heard someone erroneously call out, "Throw me something, *mister!*" as the all-female krewe of Iris, which by tradition always paraded on the Saturday afternoon before Mardi Gras, rolled by, launching the start of what amounted to a four-day weekend.

Carnival parades in New Orleans were never a spectator sport. The fun, the thrill, the excitement of them was in catching the prizes thrown from the floats —the plastic beads, the coasters, the toys, the aluminum doubloons. It didn't matter that today's treasure invariably became tomorrow's trash, not when the mask of adulthood was shed to reveal the child in everyone. But Remy didn't join the throng that surged against the barricade to catch the trinkets hurled at them by an obliging masker. Instead, she took advantage of a brief open space along the outer fringe and quickened her pace. During the mad scramble to retrieve necklaces that had fallen through ensnaring fingers to the ground, she reached the corner and turned, heading toward the river.

Away from the parade route, the congestion lessened along the sidewalks, if not on the streets. Traffic going into the city proceeded at a crawl when it moved at all. As Remy walked past cars inching their way along, she knew it would only get worse the closer she got to Canal Street and the Vieux Carré. There was no doubt in her mind that she'd made the right choice in leaving the Jaguar in the garage.

When she entered the doors of the International Trade Mart twenty minutes later, the quiet of the building was a welcome shock after the ceaseless din of the parade crowds, marching bands, blaring car horns, and tooting kazoos. She smiled at the security guard on duty at the desk and went straight to the elevators. She hadn't realized she was on edge until she felt the tension falling away as the elevator whisked her to the fifteenth floor and the corporate offices of the Crescent Line.

She stepped out of the elevator and glanced at her watch, mentally giving herself an hour to locate the Coast Guard report. From a zipper pocket in her purse, she took the shiny new key that an all-night locksmith had made for her, copied from her father's set, and inserted it in the lock. It turned easily under her hand. She stepped inside and locked the door behind her. She paused long enough to drop the key in her purse, then crossed the reception lobby and turned down the corridor toward the file room.

Voices. She heard voices. She stopped to listen, telling herself it was ridiculous—no one would be here on a Saturday, especially not the Saturday before Mardi Gras. She was probably hearing the shouts from the parade crowd on

Canal Street—or a band. On the fifteenth floor? No, the voices seemed to be coming from the wing of executive offices at the opposite end of the hall. There was definitely someone there—more than one "someone." Remy started to quietly retreat, then paused near the opening to the reception area.

That voice—its pitch, its rhythm—it sounded like Gabe's. That was impossible. He and her father had left the house about ten minutes before she had—to go to the krewe's float barn, they'd said. Then she heard the deep rumble of a second voice, and she frowned. Gabe was with Cole? Why?

Curiosity overcame caution as she slipped down the hall, hugging the wall, intent on getting close enough to hear what they were saying. Remy caught the sound of a third voice—its tone smooth, charming, disarming. Then Cole interrupted, and it was a full second before she realized that the third voice belonged to Marc Jardin. Her uncle was there too?

Farther along the corridor, a door stood partially open. She saw the ice-blue fabric on a side wall and instantly pictured the rest of the room. It was windowless, the expanse of cool color relieved by a single impressionistic painting of the New Orleans waterfront with the triple spires of St. Louis Cathedral rising in the background. A long table of pale pecan and eight chairs with seat cushions covered in a matching ice-blue fabric filled the rest of the room—the boardroom.

They were all in the boardroom. Remy stiffened, sharply recalling her conversation with Gabe at the breakfast table the day before, when she'd suggested they should ask Cole about his meeting with the insurance company instead of wondering what had transpired. Gabe had indicated that they'd consider it.

But they'd done more than consider it; they'd acted—acted and deliberately excluded her from the meeting, without even telling her one was scheduled.

Damn them, she thought, yet she wasn't at all surprised, only irritated at their overly protective attitude.

"The insurance company has you scared, Frazier. Why?" So her father was with them!

When Remy heard Cole speak, his words now as distinct as his deep voice, she discovered that she'd moved closer without even realizing it.

"The reputation of this company happens to be at stake," her father responded in a clipped and angry voice.

"Then you should want me to defend it, instead of insisting that I capitulate to their demands," Cole fired back, equally curt, and Remy immediately sensed the hostility in the air, a hostility that neither man seemed to be attempting to conceal.

Marc Jardin attempted to inject a measure of calm and reason. "I don't think you understand, Buchanan, how very damaging it would be for these accusations of fraud to become public."

"Damaging to whom? To you, Marc?" Cole challenged. "Are you afraid all the publicity might make your political friends decide you aren't the most likely candidate for governor in the next election? I don't know why they should mind—corruption and fraud aren't new to Louisiana politics."

"I won't pretend that isn't a concern of mine," her uncle asserted stiffly. "But it is hardly my only concern. Like the rest of the family, I'm thinking not only of myself but of the good of the company. There is no reason for any of this to become public. An amicable and *quiet* settlement with the insurance company can be negotiated."

"The Crescent Line is not repaying one dime of the claim. If you're all so anxious to hush this thing up, then I suggest you dig into your own pockets and buy them off with the money you've been siphoning from the company for years," Cole retorted. He paused and then added in a harshly amused and cutting voice, "Of course, if you did that, then you wouldn't have the funds to buy your election, would you, Marc? As I understand it, between the problems in the oil patch and Wall Street's Black Monday, you've taken a financial bath, Frazier. As for the good counselor and our genius with figures—the thirty-six-twenty-four-thirty-six kind—it must be hell not to be able to get your hands on all that money your granddaddy socked away in a trust fund for you."

"All of that is irrelevant and immaterial, Buchanan," Gabe spoke up. "The insurance company isn't looking to any of us. They're looking to the company for their money."

"They can look and threaten all they want. The company lost a ship that was fully loaded with a cargo of crude paid for in advance. We collected for that loss legally. And we both know, Counselor, that an anonymous phone call claiming there was no oil on board when the tanker went down and a signature on a receipt for plastic explosives hardly constitute incontrovertible evidence that a crime was even committed. And I'm not about to jeopardize the financial stability of this company simply because the board of directors is afraid of bad publicity. Look at the balance sheet." There was a thump on the table, accompanied by a whisper of paper. "To pay back even a portion of the claim would destroy the progress the company's made this past year and cripple it for the next five, if not longer."

"And if that happened, you wouldn't be entitled to the ten-percent ownership share your agreement calls for in the event that you succeed in turning the company around in three years, would you?" Lance inserted, his voice heavy with sarcasm. "You accuse us of having selfish motives, but you aren't looking out for the company's interest—only your own. You've always hated us, Buchanan. Half the reason you signed on was so you could show a bunch of rich bastards you were better than they were. Only you found out you weren't the wonder boy you thought you were, didn't you? That's why you came up with this insurance scam, isn't it? It brought in the working capital the company so badly needed before it could even hope to turn the corner. Plus you probably sold that shipment of crude on the black market and salted away six or seven million dollars in some Swiss account. There's no doubt, Buchanan, that you had the motive, the means, and the opportunity. Sooner or later that insurance investigator will prove that. And it galls me that by settling with the insurance company, we'll be saving your ass."

Stunned by the brutal logic of Lance's indictment, Remy discovered she was holding her breath, waiting for a quick, angry denial from Cole. But it didn't come. Instead, there was a long and heavy silence.

When Cole did speak, it was with a deadly calm. "That's the family line, is it? I figured it would be something like that."

"On Monday morning," her father began, "you will contact the insurance company and set up a meeting with them. Marc will handle the settlement negotiations—"

"No." Cole's flat, quiet refusal cut him off in midsentence.

"What?"

"No," he repeated, in an even firmer tone. "I'm still running this company, Frazier. There will be no settlement talks."

"I don't think you understood Lance. Either you work out a deal with the insurance company, or this board will be forced to demand your resignation."

"You can demand till hell freezes over," Cole snapped.

"I strongly advise you to reconsider," Gabe said quietly. "The insurance company's allegations and limited evidence of attempted fraud are sufficient cause for this board to question your conduct. If you refuse to resign, this board will remove you from office for malfeasance, and will terminate your contract."

"Try it," came Cole's quick and cold challenge, followed by the sound of a chair being pushed back. "You try it, and I'll file so many charges and counter-charges of malfeasance against this board that the Jardin name will make head-lines every damned day. If it's a fight you want, Frazier, you've got it."

"You can't win."

"Maybe not. But if I go down, you'll all go with me."

Without warning, the door was yanked the rest of the way open and Cole came striding out—not in a business suit and tie, but in a pair of soft, washed-out jeans and a bulky pullover of ecru that made him look rougher, tougher. There was the smallest break in his stride when he saw her in the corridor. Hostile gray eyes washed over her, their coldness a shock to her numbed senses.

"I assume you brought your rubber stamp," he muttered as he swept past her.

Realizing that he thought she approved of their decision, Remy whirled around to tell him that she'd had no knowledge of this meeting, then stopped. The things she'd heard—Lance's accusations, Gabe's warnings, Cole's threat—what did she think? Were they right?

"He's bluffing," she heard Marc say.

"Don't kid yourself," Lance snapped. "The bastard means it."

"Damn him," Gabe swore, and slammed a hand on the table. "Why can't he see it makes more sense to settle with the insurance company than to get involved in a long and costly legal battle? That was a perfectly sound argument, and he didn't even listen to it."

"You can't reason with a man like that," her father murmured tightly just as Remy heard Cole go out the front door.

"We've got to do something," Marc insisted. "Dammit, Frazier, we can't let him ruin us. My God, you know what will happen if any of this gets out."

It suddenly hit her what they were saying. They weren't solely concerned with whether Cole was guilty or innocent, or even with whether the fraud charges were true or false. Their approach was much more pragmatic: find a solution that would have the least damaging effect on the company overall. In their opinion, that solution was to negotiate a settlement with the insurance company before any further action was taken. Wasn't that the sensible thing to do? Couldn't the rest come later? Remy went after Cole.

When she reached the street, she caught a glimpse of him crossing Canal, heading for the Quarter, then immediately lost sight of him. The parade was over, and the crowds that had gathered to watch it pass along Canal Street now flooded onto the narrow streets of the Vieux Carré. She hurried after him, joining the streaming mass of revelers, tourists, and college kids as they saun- tered along, a look of anticipation on their faces, searching for something— they weren't sure what, but they were confident they'd know it when they found it.

Impatiently Remy threaded her way through the throng, trying to catch up to Cole. She barely glanced at the promenading drag queen in a gold-sequined body stocking complete with feathery tail plumes or at the couple in matching satin jackets with DETROIT AUTOMOTIVE written on the back, who nudged each other and gawked at her-him-it, unaware that it was only the first of many elaborate and outrageous costumes they would see as Carnival turned the Quar- ter's narrow streets into a bizarre bazaar indeed. At this point, the families who had earlier lined the parade route were nowhere to be seen.

A one-man band worked the corner of Chartres and Conti, blowing, strum- ming, and drumming an unusual rendition of "Mardi Gras Mambo." Remy spot- ted Cole as he shouldered his way around the crowd that had gathered to watch because it seemed the thing to do. She shouted his name, but he didn't hear her. Finally the cross-flow of strolling people on Royal slowed him down long enough for her to close the distance between them.

"Cole, wait!" she called, and she saw him look back, his eyes locating and then narrowing on her. For an instant she thought he was going to keep going, but he stopped, letting the crowd break around him. She pushed her way to his side, murmuring hasty excuses as she went.

"What do you want?" he said, and brushed off a hawker selling an assortment of gorilla, Dracula, and plain or sequined Lone Ranger–style masks.

"To talk." She felt his impatience, his rigid anger, and wondered how she was going to reach him.

"If you've come to repeat the family position, I've already had a bellyful of it."

"You don't understand—"

"I understand better than you do," he snapped, and he swung away to plow his way through the living stream to the other side of the intersection.

Remy was right on his heels, following in his wake. There was a slight thinning of people on the side street, enough to allow her to draw level with him as she quickened her steps to a running walk to keep pace with his long strides.

"Cole, my family's only thinking of what's best for the company."

"Like hell they are." He kept walking.

Now angry herself, she grabbed at his arm, feeling the hard bunching of muscles beneath the bulky knit of the sleeve. "Dammit, Cole, will you stand still and listen to me?"

He halted so abruptly that she shot past him and had to swing back to face him. "Listen to what?" he demanded. "More phony declarations that they're only thinking about what's best for the company? They're only worried about mud getting thrown on the Jardin name—and maybe leaving a stain that won't wash out."

"That's not true. Once the insurance company goes through with its threat to file both civil and criminal suits, the Crescent Line will spend a fortune in attorneys' fees fighting it. All they want to do is spend the money now to settle it before it gets to that stage. Big companies do it all the time. It isn't an admission of guilt on anyone's part. It's simply good business."

There was a sudden and sharp narrowing of his eyes. " '*Once* the insurance company goes through with its threat'? Why didn't you say '*if*'? You're assuming that the claim was fraudulently collected. Why?"

"I don't know why I phrased it like that," she replied uneasily, aware that it had been an unconscious slip on her part; made because she believed she knew something.

"Don't you? What proof could there be?"

"You mentioned something about plastic explosives."

"Which doesn't mean anything unless the insurance company can find some-one who can swear he saw them on board the tanker. And I was talking about the crude, not that. How could the *Dragon* have been empty when it went down?" he challenged, watching her closely. "I saw her being loaded at the docks. Roughly ten hours after she left the dock, she was at the sea buoy— that's within the normal range of trip time during low water. And the river pilots all swear the water was lapping at her Plimsoll line, indicating that the tanker was running fully loaded. Her course didn't take her close to any off-shore oil rigs or drilling platforms. And the Coast Guard found her wreckage floating less than two miles from her anticipated course. How could she have been empty when she went down? What happened to the crude oil? Do you know?"

"Of course I don't." But the facts he'd set forth bothered her too. Everything seemed to indicate that it was impossible for the tanker to have been empty. It was what made her doubt the insurance company's accusations.

"Then why is your family so anxious to get rid of me? Why are they setting me up to take the fall for this?"

She looked at him, seeing the bitterness and anger in his harsh features. He sounded paranoid. She remembered how much he despised her family and all it stood for. *Uptown*. How many times had he thrown that word at her? Why? Because he felt insecure? Inferior? Or was he asking her all these questions to make himself appear innocent?

"They only threatened to remove you from office when you refused to coop-erate."

"Is that why you're here—because their threats failed and now you hope to persuade me to accept the family line?"

"I'm trying to persuade you to be reasonable," she argued.

"No." He shook his head, disputing her claim. "You don't want me to be reasonable. You want me to be the patsy."

"That's not true."

But he wasn't listening. "I was a fool to believe I meant anything to you," he muttered thickly. "And I have the feeling you and your family played me for the fool all along. But not anymore, Remy. Not anymore."

When he walked away, Remy didn't go after him—but she wanted to. That was the crazy part. She ran a hand over her face, feeling confused, bewildered, understanding only a part of what was going on—the part that dealt with facts, not emotions, reactions, or relationships.

Was she overreacting? Was she seeing shadows that weren't there? What were the facts? A tanker had sunk in a storm, a tanker owned by her family's company. Had it been deliberate? Had it been loaded with crude oil when it went down? Or had the crude been off-loaded? Where? How?

Blindly she turned onto Bourbon at the corner and headed uptown, buffeted by the human current flowing in the opposite direction. Laughter, rebel yells, carefree voices swirled around her, occasionally competing with the wail of a jazz clarinet, the driving beat of a rhythm-and-blues tune, or the deep-voiced chanting from a group of rollicking college kids patiently urging a likely-looking wench at a gallery rail above them to "show us your tits," an echo of the very phrase scrawled across her T-shirt, offered all in good fun, if in questionable taste—proof that a trace of the pagan rites of spring lingered in the Vieux Carré during the ninety-six-hour day of Mardi Gras.

Remy walked around a barker posted in front of the open door to a topless bar, mechanically reeling off his spiel to the passersby. Heads turned to peer inside, but nearly everyone kept walking. On impulse Remy walked into the next bar she came to. Typical of most bars during Carnival, it was quiet, uncrowded. All the action was in the street, and bars were merely a place for revelers to buy another go-cup.

She went directly to the pay phone in a back hall by the restrooms. With a quarter in hand, she dug in her purse, found the number, and dialed it. There were too many answers she didn't have, too many questions that led her in circles, too many things that didn't make sense—especially Cole's part in all this. If there was a scam and he was involved in it, then why hadn't he immediately jumped on her family's recommendation to work out some kind of settlement with the insurance company—*before* their investigator came up with incriminating evidence? Why was he playing hardball?

"This is Remy Jardin," she said quickly, before she could question the wisdom of what she was doing. "I need to talk to you. Can you meet me in . . . twenty minutes at La Louisiane, in the lounge?"

The reply was affirmative.

In the quiet, softly lit lounge, Remy sipped at her whiskey-laced coffee and glanced over the rim of the cup at the burly man with the salt-and-pepper beard seated across from her, watching as he peeled off a ten-dollar bill and gave it to the bartender. When the bartender walked away, the insurance investigator lifted his Scotch and water in a toasting gesture.

"To surprise phone calls?" he suggested. Remy didn't respond. He noted her silence with another keen glance, then took a quick sip of his drink, barely moistening his lips. "You said you had some information for me."

"No. I said I wanted to talk to you." She set her cup down on the small cocktail table, keeping her voice calm and controlled. "I've come to the conclusion that the insurance company's charges of fraud are totally false."

"Is that right?"

"I think you know it too, Mr. Hanks. You must have learned that it takes roughly twenty-four hours to unload a tanker of the *Dragon*'s capacity. Given the time it sailed from the Claymore dock, the distance it traveled, and the location where it went down, it was physically impossible for the shipment of crude to be unloaded anywhere en route. And you have to agree that there isn't any percentage in deliberately sinking a fully loaded ship simply to collect the insurance. Hence there's no scam, and no fraud. You're on a wild-goose chase."

"Am I?" He regarded her thoughtfully. "I'm afraid I don't see it that way."

"What other way is there to see it?" she retorted. "You can't change the facts or the laws of physics. That crude couldn't have been off-loaded into pipelines or onto barges, as you suggested. There wasn't time."

"I admit that's bothered me some."

Remy laughed at that, sounding just a little brittle with nerves. "It should have bothered you more than 'some,' Mr. Hanks."

He looked at her, his mustache and beard moving near the corners of his mouth, obviously with a smile that she couldn't see for all the hairy growth. "You claim I'm on a wild-goose chase, Miss Jardin, but I think you're on a fishing expedition."

She hesitated a split second, then admitted, "I am. I honestly can't believe those charges are anything but false. Yet—you seem to believe otherwise. How can you, given the facts?"

"Have you ever seen a magician make an elephant disappear?"

Remy leaned back in her chair, impatient and a little irritated. "Please don't try to convince me it was all done with mirrors."

"Magic—it's all an illusion. The only time the hand is quicker than the eye is when you're watching the wrong hand. It's called misdirection. Football coaches design entire plays around that concept."

"I'm not in the mood for riddles." Especially when she was living one. "Say what you mean."

"I'm saying, what if it was all an elaborate hoax? What if that tanker never sank at all? What if the debris the Coast Guard found was nothing but a smoke screen? What if the *Crescent Dragon* is in some faraway port with a different name painted on her sides and fake registry?"

"But the crew abandoned ship," she protested in a stunned voice.

"*Did* they abandon it? Or was that another smoke screen so a different crew could take their place and sail off in the tanker?" he countered. "While everyone's looking in one place, the tanker is really somewhere else."

Remy shook her head, bemused and skeptical. "It's a very interesting theory, but I think you're reaching. If that's all you have to go on—"

"It isn't," he said, and he reached inside his tweed jacket.

"Yes, I've heard about the receipt for plastic explosives," she said as he pulled a square of paper from his breast pocket. Then she noticed there was more than one item in his hand. "But a receipt doesn't prove the explosives were ever taken aboard the tanker."

"Do you recognize this man?" He placed a black-and-white photo on the cocktail table, facing her.

Remy drew the picture closer and studied the man with his wide, staring eyes and thick, bushy brows. He had dark, slick hair, a swarthy complexion, and a sweeping handlebar mustache waxed to points at the ends.

She shook her head, answering honestly, "I don't remember seeing him before."

"What about this one?" He laid a second photo down beside the first.

The man in the second picture laughed out at her, his strong white teeth gleaming in the center of a dark, closely trimmed full beard. His hair was dark too, a little on the long side, and definitely curly. Remy stared at his thick, full eyebrows, then looked again at the man in the first picture.

"I don't know him, either, though I can see a similarity between the two—the eyebrows, the forehead, the swarthy complexion. Are they related?"

"This"—he tapped the first picture —"is Keith Cummins, the first mate aboard the *Dragon*. And this is Kim Charles," he said, indicating the second photo. "A Eurasian and known demolitions expert with one conviction for arson. A handwriting expert has examined the signatures of both Keith Cummins and Kim Charles. He insists they were written by the same hand."

"I see," she murmured.

"We have our link between the explosives and the tanker, Miss Jardin," he said, sweeping up the photos and tucking them back into his breast pocket.

"And where is this . . . Mr. Charles?"

"That's a curious thing about the *Dragon*'s crew. After they were rescued and their statements were taken, they all—every last one of them—disappeared, vanished, poof . . . like magic," he added deliberately. "Another curious thing —the last time Kim Charles, alias Cummins, was seen was approximately a week ago . . . in Marseilles, France. And who do you suppose was in Marseilles that same day?"

"Who?" Remy asked, even though she already knew the answer.

"Buchanan. He claims he was there on company business. The strange thing is that he arrived the night before, but didn't come into the branch office until late in the afternoon. And like our explosives man, he was seen on the waterfront in the morning. What do you suppose he was doing there? Meeting his cohort in crime, maybe?"

Why *had* Cole gone to Marseilles? The question was a hammer that kept pounding at Remy as she walked along Iberville, moving slowly but steadily away from the boisterous throngs that packed Bourbon and Royal streets. Until the bearded Mr. Hanks had tossed out those questions, she hadn't realized how desperately she had wanted to believe that Cole wasn't mixed up in this insurance fraud. She'd secretly been hoping that he'd say something different— something that wouldn't implicate Cole.

She sighed and lifted her gaze to the rosy afterglow the setting sun had painted on the sky, remembering Cole's warmth, his smile, his gentleness—and trying to forget the coldness that could come into his eyes, the almost obsessive dislike of her family, her friends, and the damning things that had been said.

It could have been just a coincidence that he was in Marseilles at the same time as that Kim Charles. Or he could have been trying to find him—to question him about the *Dragon*, as she would have done if she'd known the man was there. Remy sighed again, aware that she was attempting to justify his presence there.

And again she wondered why he was so adamantly opposed to settling with the insurance company. Was it greed, as Lance had suggested? Cole had said himself that returning any portion of the insurance money would jeopardize the company's profit potential for the next several years—and therefore his bonus of 10 percent ownership in the company as well. Was he trying to hold out for that? Wasn't the money he'd made from selling the crude oil on the black market enough?

Why would he have done it at all? Lance had said it was because he'd seen that he wouldn't be able to turn the company around without it. Was that it? To save his pride? His ego? Or was it solely for the money? Why, when he had nothing but contempt for her family and its wealth? Or . . . had he done it for her? Had he felt so insecure that he thought she couldn't love him unless he had a lot of money? Didn't he realize how much she loved him?

Yes, that was the problem—she loved him. Even knowing that he might have committed fraud, she still loved him. That was why the thought hurt so much. Right or wrong, guilty or innocent, she loved him. It was staggering to discover that she cared that deeply, that strongly for him.

She felt a tear on her cheek and hastily wiped it away, glancing around to see if anyone had noticed. But the few tourists strolling up the relatively quiet side street weren't paying any attention.

She heard footsteps quicken behind her. Automatically she tightened her grip on her purse and started to look back, angling closer to a stuccoed building.

Suddenly she was grabbed from behind, both arms seized by a pair of hands that jerked her to a stop. As she tried to cry out, a sweaty palm clamped itself over her mouth, smothering the sound. She felt the painful wrenching of her shoulders as her arms were pulled together behind her back, pinned by a hooking arm, and trapped by the solidness of a man's body.

There was a man in front of her, too, in a blue plaid shirt and faded jeans, a Halloween mask covering his face—a mask of a pig, with mean dark eyes and tusks protruding from the sides of its ugly snout. Remy had only a heartbeat's time to wonder why she'd never noticed how frightening a pig's face could be.

Then a voice growled in her ear, "This is the only warning you're going to get, little gal. Stop asking questions, and keep your mouth shut."

That voice. She'd heard it before. That night on the dock. This was the same man who'd grabbed her then, hurting her arm and calling her "little gal."

As she tried to see the face that was pressed so close to her ear, something slammed into her stomach. The pain—she couldn't breathe. The other man had hit her. She realized that as his fist slammed into her again. She tried to twist sideways and elude the third blow, but it struck her, causing knife-sharp agony.

There are people on the street, her mind screamed. Why don't they see? Why aren't they coming to help me? The hand was no longer covering her mouth, but she couldn't make any sound come out—she couldn't draw a breath. It was like a nightmare—trying to scream, wanting to scream, but having only silent screams come out.

She had a hazy glimpse of a blurred hand coming toward her face, then there was just the roaring in her head when it struck her jaw—again and again. Suddenly the ground seemed to drop out from beneath her. She felt herself sinking onto the sidewalk and tried to catch herself.

The man from the dock had let her go. They were both gone. Dizzily she looked up and saw them hurrying down the street. And she saw the other people, too, staring at her in frozen shock. She couldn't know that her eternity of terror had lasted no more than twenty seconds. She tried to stand up . . . but God, it hurt so much.

25

WITH EACH CAREFUL BREATH she drew, Remy smelled the sharp, antiseptic odors of the hospital. The pain had subsided to a throbbing ache in her face and stomach—as long as she didn't move too much or breathe too deeply. She focused her eyes on the cubicle's hospital-green curtains, which partitioned her bed from the rest of the emergency room.

"Is there anything else you can tell me about these two men? The color of their hair? Their eyes?"

She swung her gaze toward the uniformed policeman standing next to the bed and gave a very small shake of her head. "All I can remember . . . is the pig's face," she said slowly, her face stiff from the swelling along her jaw and cheek, "and how mean it looked with those big tusks sticking out—like a wild boar's, but the mask was painted pink . . . like Porky Pig." She made a weak attempt at humor. "Somehow I have a feeling I'll never think of Porky Pig as cute or funny again."

The officer nodded absently and went back to his questions. "What about the man who grabbed you from behind? You said he put his hand over your mouth. Was he wearing a ring?"

Remy closed her eyes, trying to remember if there'd been any sensation of metal. "I don't think so." She started to sigh, then winced at the sudden stab of pain that stole her breath. "His palm was sweaty, I remember that, and his fingers were rough—calloused."

"What about the second man, the one in the pig mask? Was he wearing rings, watches?"

She pictured that blurred image of his right hand coming at her face. "I'm almost sure there wasn't anything on his right hand, but . . . I don't know about the left."

He made a note of that, then flipped his notebook shut. "If you think of anything else, Miss Jardin, just call the station."

Again Remy gave a barely perceptible nod of her head in agreement, saying nothing about the warning that had preceded the beating. She couldn't—not without telling him about everything, including the insurance company's allegations of fraud. The first people to come to her aid afterward had been from out of state. They'd automatically assumed they'd witnessed a mugging—after all, this was big, bad New Orleans, and things like that happened here. By the time Remy had recovered enough to speak for herself, she'd realized it would be better to let everyone believe it *was* a mugging. And everyone had . . . without question.

As the green curtain fell back in place behind the departing policeman, Remy heard her mother's anxious voice demanding, "Is she all right? Where is she? I want to see her."

A second later the curtain was swept aside and Sibylle Jardin stepped quickly into the cubicle. If she'd been the hand-wringing type, her fingers would have been twisted in a knot, but she wasn't. She faltered briefly when she saw Remy lying there, one cheekbone red and swollen, a purpling under one eye, a bruise coloring the skin above her jaw. But her hesitation lasted only a fraction of an instant, and then she moved to Remy's side and lightly ran smoothing fingers over the top of her hair.

"Remy, my poor darling," she murmured, biting at her lower lip.

"I'm all right, just sore." Remy reached for her hand and gave it a reassuring squeeze.

Then Gabe was there, hovering on the other side of the bed, his look intense, angry, his face white under its tan. "Who did this, Remy? What'd they look like?"

She heard the tremble of rage in his voice, a brother's rage. "I don't know. They wore masks."

He half turned from the bed, then swung back. "What the hell were you doing in the Quarter, anyway? You said you were going to stay home and lie around the pool. Why didn't you? Dammit, why'd you have to go out?"

"Gabe." Sibylle silenced him with a look, giving her a reprieve from his questions, but Remy knew it was only a temporary one. Sooner or later she'd have to answer them.

"I'm sorry. It's just—" He raked a hand through his tobacco-brown hair, something helpless in the gesture.

"I know," her mother murmured.

"Is she going to be all right, Dr. John?" Her father stood at the foot of the bed, looking pale and shaken.

Remy glanced at the white-haired man standing beside him. She'd expected someone old, short, and irascible, but Dr. John was tall and proud, exuding competence—a Southern version of Marcus Welby, right down to the vacuous smile.

"I've consulted the resident who examined her when she was brought in. Her injuries, for the most part, are minor. The bruises on her face you can see, and we do have a cracked rib."

Remy heard that and observed dryly, "If *we* had a cracked rib, Dr. John, *you* wouldn't be smiling." He chuckled, and she added, "Or laughing."

"Listen to her. I think that proves my diagnosis, Frazier," he declared. "By Mardi Gras the bruises will have faded enough for makeup to cover them, and she'll be dancing at the ball—at least to the slow songs."

"Does that mean we can take her home?" Sibylle asked.

The doctor hesitated a full second before answering. "I'd like to keep her here overnight—strictly for observation. There is her recent ordeal in France to consider."

When she heard his announcement, Remy felt oddly relieved. She didn't want to go home and face a barrage of questions—not tonight, when she ached all over and just breathing was an effort. Tomorrow. She'd tell them about the warning tomorrow. She knew there'd be an argument, and she simply wasn't up to it.

"Yes, I think it's best for Remy to stay here tonight," her father agreed.

"I'll arrange for a private room," Dr. John said, then winked at Remy. "And one of our gowns—a Charity exclusive, guaranteed to repel muggers."

"Just what I need," Remy murmured, not at all amused.

An hour later she was in a private room, far removed from the hustle and bustle of the emergency room with its dinging bells and rattling gurneys, its urgent voices and moaning injured. She lay in the regulation hospital bed with eyes closed, not sleeping or resting, just aching, but aching undisturbed, without her mother offering to fluff her pillows to make her more comfortable or Gabe asking if she wanted something to drink. As long as she kept her eyes closed, they left her alone.

Her mother sat in a chair beside her bed. Remy could hear her idly flipping through the pages of a magazine. Gabe was at the window, alternately pacing and stopping, pacing and stopping. Her father had stepped out of the room several minutes before, maybe longer. She was losing track of time, and silently wondered how much longer it would be before visiting hours were over. They'd have to leave then.

What a contrast this was from Nice, when she'd been so desperate to have her family around her. Now they were here and she wanted to be alone so she could rest . . . no, that wasn't true—so she could think.

"Stop asking questions, and keep your mouth shut," the man had growled. Asking questions of whom? Who'd sent those men to beat her up? Not Cole. He wouldn't do that. She was sure of it. Did that mean she'd been wrong to think he was behind this fraud?

She heard footsteps in the corridor, approaching her room. Not the quiet, rubber-soled squelch of a nurse's shoes, but the firm sound of hard leather soles. They entered her room and paused.

"How is she?" The low question came from her father.

"Sleeping, I think." Gabe moved away from the window. Remy heard his footsteps stop somewhere near the door.

"Good. I spoke with Dr. John just now." His hushed voice was barely above a whisper, and Remy had to strain to catch his words. "He's making all the arrangements to have Remy flown by air ambulance to the clinic tomorrow morning."

She stiffened in instant protest, then breathed a little easier when she heard Gabe reply, "She isn't going to like that."

"She isn't in any condition to argue. She's lying to us, Gabe, and I don't like it. Something's wrong. We can't watch her every minute. She needs to be in a place where she can be monitored at all times."

"I agree," came Gabe's soft, hope-killing reply.

She wouldn't go. She *couldn't* go—not now. But how could she stop them? They'd override any protest she made. If she told them about the warning and the few things she could remember about the tanker and that night on the dock, they'd be more determined than ever to protect her and get her out of harm's way. And if she became too vocal in her objections, they might persuade Dr. John to give her something—and then when she came to, she'd find herself in the clinic, with the doctors there convinced that she'd lost her mind as well as her memory.

Dear God, what was she going to do? She had to think of something. She couldn't let them send her away.

She remembered the pig mask with its small, mean eyes and vicious-looking tusks. The man had said this was the only warning she'd get. If she stayed, if she asked more questions, if they found out. . . . Remy shuddered and immediately felt a stab of pain from the fractured rib.

"Remy." Her mother's voice reached softly out to her an instant before she felt the touch of a hand on her arm. Slowly she let her eyes open. "We're leaving now, dear. We'll see you in the morning."

She made a faint sound of understanding, then pretended to drift back to sleep.

Silence. Remy unconsciously held her breath and listened for the faintest whisper of sound in the hospital corridor outside the darkened room. Nothing. She could hear nothing. She hadn't heard any movement in a long time.

She folded back the thin blanket and the bed sheet, then used her hands and elbows, propping them under her, to carefully and gingerly ease herself into a sitting position. She wondered if she dared turn on the small wall-light above the hospital bed's metal headboard, then decided against it. She groped for and found the telephone on the stand next to the bed, picked it up, and set it on her lap.

There was just enough light from the window to allow her to see the numbers on the dial. Directory Assistance gave her the number, and she dialed it. "It's Remy," she said quietly, softly, keeping one eye on the closed door to the corridor. "I need a place to stay tonight, and I didn't know who else to call." She almost sighed in relief, but she knew it would hurt too much. "Can you come get me? I'm at Charity. . . . I'm fine," she insisted. "Just bruised up some. I'll explain when I see you. . . . No, don't come in. Wait for me outside."

She put the phone back on the stand, then half rolled and half slid out of the high bed, gritting her teeth against the waves of pain that every movement seemed to bring, despite the stretch bandage that bound her rib cage. She found her clothes in the closet, but changing into them was agony.

Once she was dressed, Remy leaned against the wall to gather her strength, then moved to the door and listened for footsteps and the stiff whisper of polyester uniforms. Nothing. Cautiously, she opened the door a crack and peered out. The corridor outside her room was empty. She opened the door a little wider to check the nurses' station. There were three of them there, talking softly among themselves, none of them looking in her direction. But to reach the elevators, she had to go by them, and she knew she didn't have a hope of accomplishing that unseen. Then she spied the fire stairs and silently blessed the architect who had unwittingly placed them so close to her room.

She counted to three and slipped out the door, pulling it almost shut behind her, unwilling to risk a sharp click of the latch. Not a single head turned in her direction. Cradling her right side, Remy darted across the corridor to the stairway door.

Five minutes later she walked out the front door of the hospital. She spied the car parked at the curb, its engine idling. She hurried to it, never once doubting her decision, which had been prompted by one single question: if she remembered what she'd seen on the dock, would she be safe anywhere?

26 ❧

THE CLANGING CRASH of the brass knocker had been replaced by a fist pounding at the door, the racket drowning out the sound of the cathedral bells ringing out their summons to morning Mass. "I'm coming!" Cole shouted a second time, padding across the living room in bare feet, fastening the snap of his jeans as he went. The hammering didn't let up. He threw the night bolt and started to jerk the door open, but it exploded inward and Gabe Jardin charged through, with Lance at his heels.

"Where is she? Where's Remy?" He looked wildly around the room, fury and desperation in his face.

"Remy?" Cole frowned. "What makes you think she's here?"

"Because she's disappeared from the hospital—as if you didn't know." He glared at Cole as if he were a roach to be crunched underfoot, then just as quickly waved a hand at the door to the kitchen, ordering, "You check in there, Lance. I'll look back here."

"Hold it." Cole grabbed Gabe's arm as he started toward the hall that led to the bedroom. "What was Remy doing in the hospital?"

"You mean she didn't tell you?" he jeered and tried to shrug off Cole's hand.

But Cole tightened his grip, easily outmuscling him as he surged forward to growl in his face, "Listen, bastard, you don't like me and I don't like you, but you're not taking one step in any direction until you tell me what Remy was doing in a hospital."

Gabe eyed him uncertainly but held his ground. "She was mugged yesterday afternoon in the Quarter. A couple guys in masks worked her over."

"Why?" Stunned by the announcement, Cole loosened his grip.

"How the hell should I know? Maybe they were a couple of crazies high on crack." He pushed past Cole as Lance came swinging out of the kitchen.

"She's not in there, Gabe."

"Come on. We'll look back here."

When the two of them headed toward the bedroom, Cole made no attempt to stop them. Instead, he turned away in troubled silence.

"Where is she?" He had a stranglehold on the black receiver, his hand—like his voice—trembling with fear and rage. "What have you done with her?"

"Who?"

"You know damned well I'm talking about Remy."

"Isn't she in the hospital?"

"No," he admitted. "She disappeared from there . . . sometime in the night." He gripped the phone even tighter. "Leave her alone—do you hear? If you touch one hair on her head, I swear I'll—"

"—kill me?" the voice taunted with contempt. "Don't make threats you can't keep."

"Dammit, I—"

"Don't give me any of this noble shit! You won't do a damned thing, and we both know it. You're all greed and no guts. You always have been."

"Where's Remy?"

"I don't know. But you'd better find her before I do."

Fog. A menacing white mist swirling thick and cool around her. Out of the night fog came an eerie yellow glow, dancing, wavering, coming closer and closer. Remy wanted to run from it, but her feet were rooted to the ground. The yellow light kept moving toward her, flaring, separating into two, three, then four towering columns of flame. Black faces loomed from beneath the dancing fire, black faces on black bodies wrapped in white rags, bodies dancing, gyrating, high-stepping, holding aloft their flaming torches, grinning at her, and rattling their tin cups in her face.

Flambeaux. Remy laughed in relief. It was a parade, a night parade, complete with black torchbearers to light the way. Riders emerged on snorting, sidestepping steeds, their rich costumes, knightly in design, all with plumed helmets and hooded faces, glittering in the mist. Then came the float, a dazzling display of bright, shining paint and sparkling glitter. Riding atop it was the god Comus, the chosen ruler of the parade, a silver and white specter of rhinestones and blinding white stones. He raised his jeweled goblet to her, and Remy clapped her hands together in delight, seeing gray eyes smiling at her from behind the full mask. Cole. Comus was Cole, the god ruler of—

Suddenly the mask changed shape, sprouting a snout and huge, gleaming tusks. Remy recoiled from the image. No—Cole couldn't be the man in the pig mask. She backed away, shaking her head in denial, as he kept pushing the goblet toward her.

Then she remembered that Comus was never the true ruler, not in the arcane society of the krewe. No, the true power in the krewe lay with the captain— one of the riders who had preceded Comus's float. She turned and ran through the thick fog after the disappearing riders. But her legs moved so slowly, so very, very slowly, that she couldn't catch up with them. She could see the streaming tails of the horses and the gleam of their polished hooves as the mist started to gradually swallow them.

"Wait! Wait!"

A rider stopped and turned in his saddle. Gone was the shimmering hood that concealed his face. In its place was a pig mask. Mean, glittering eyes fixed their accusing gaze on her.

Remy froze and whispered, "Who are you?"

"I told you to stop asking questions!"

All of a sudden the mist around her dissolved and she was surrounded by riders, riders in pig masks. In unison, they chanted, "You were warned. You were warned," and walked their horses toward her, tightening the circle.

"No! No!" She was screaming, but no one was listening. She could see the parade crowds along the street, their arms outstretched to the riders, but they weren't looking at her.

She felt hands on her and she struck out wildly, feeling the pain again, stabbing, slicing. . . .

"It's all right, girl," a voice crooned. "Sssh, now. You're safe here. Do you hear? You're safe."

She came awake with a rush, aching and disoriented, still half in the grip of the dream. She stared into Nattie's face, the dark and gently knowing eyes looking back at her.

"Nattie," she murmured, trying to swallow the fear that still choked her throat. "I—" She glanced around, seeing the rose-flowered paper on the walls, the white woodwork, the chintz curtains at the windows, and the old chiffonier against the wall, the top of it cluttered with framed family photographs and crystal atomizers. The spare bedroom at Nattie's house—that's where she was. She remembered now—Nattie had picked her up the night before at the hospital and brought her home to her small cottage-style house in the Channel. She felt the pressure ease from her shoulders and realized Nattie had been holding her down. ". . . I was dreaming, wasn't I?" She saw she was clutching at the sleeves of Nattie's chenille robe, and she let go of them to run a hand lightly over her cheek, feeling its soreness, its ache.

"The way you were thrashing around, I'd say it was more like a nightmare," Nattie declared as she rose from the edge of the bed.

"It *was* a nightmare." She relaxed against the feather pillow and felt the last of her terror drain away. "Has it only been five days that I've been home, Nattie? In some ways it feels like a lifetime." Nattie didn't comment as she walked over to the window and raised the shade, letting in a bright glare of light. Remy winced at it and lifted a hand to shield her eyes. "What time is it?"

"Going on eleven o'clock."

"It can't be." Remy started to sit up, but her injured rib raised an immediate and painful objection.

"Maybe it can't be, but it is," Nattie stated, then laid a brightly patterned velour robe over the spindled foot of the bed. "The bathroom's across the hall and the coffee's in the kitchen."

Ten minutes later Remy walked into the living room, a cup of black coffee in hand, wearing the caftan-style robe over the cotton shift Nattie had loaned her the night before. Nattie sat curled up in a colorful chintz armchair, the Sunday edition of the *Picayune* on the floor beside her, the section with the crossword puzzle folded open on her raised knees.

Nattie gave her an inspecting look, then said, "As soon as I get this puzzle finished, I'll get you some witch hazel for those bruises on your face. It'll take some of the swelling down and ease the sting."

"Thanks," Remy said, then hesitated. "I'll need to use your phone to make a call."

"If you want some privacy, there's an extension in the kitchen, or you can use the one in here." With a nod of her head, Nattie indicated the beige phone on the end table next to the sofa.

Remy glanced at the phone and wished she could wait until she'd drunk her first cup of coffee before making the dreaded call. But she knew that postponing it wouldn't make it any less of an ordeal. She crossed to the end of the sofa and sat down carefully on its hard cushion, then picked up the receiver and dialed the number from memory.

"Hello?"

"Mother, it's Remy—"

"Remy! Where are you? Are you all right?" she rushed the words, then turned away from the mouthpiece and called, "Frazier, it's Remy. She's on the phone." Then she was back. "We've been so worried about you. We didn't know what to think when the hospital phoned us this morning and said you were gone."

"Remy, is that you?" her father broke in with the demand.

"Yes, it's me. And I'm fine—"

"Where are you? We'll come get you."

"No." This time it was Remy who broke in. "I'm not coming home—not now. I'm only calling to let you know I'm fine and I'm perfectly safe where I am."

"But where are you?"

She hesitated an instant, then replied, "I'll talk to you later." And she hung up. She stared at the phone for several more seconds, then looked at Nattie. Her dark eyes regarded Remy with open curiosity, but she asked no questions —she hadn't even asked any the night before, when she'd picked her up at the hospital. Beyond telling Nattie that two men had beaten her up and flatly stating that she wasn't going home, Remy hadn't offered any other explanation —and Nattie hadn't demanded one. But she was entitled to know. "I'm sorry to draw you into the middle of this, Nattie, but they want to put me in some clinic outside of Houston. They were going to have me flown there this morning. That's why I snuck out of the hospital last night. I didn't know how else to stop them."

"That must be the same clinic they were talking about sending you to when you first came back," Nattie guessed.

"Yes. There's more, though, Nattie," Remy said, then briefly told her about the insurance company's claim of fraud over the sinking of the tanker, her belief that she'd witnessed something that night on the dock, and her attempts to find out what it was.

"Are you sure you should be telling me all this?" Nattie frowned warily.

"I have to. You see"—Remy paused and cradled her coffee cup in her hands— "before those two men beat me up, they warned me to stop asking questions and to keep my mouth shut."

"And you don't plan to do either one, do you?" Nattie folded her arms across her chest in a gesture that indicated both resignation and challenge.

"How can I? Somehow I have to find out what or who I saw that night. Until I do, how will I know whom to trust? Whom to believe? Obviously I'm a threat to somebody." She stared at the black coffee in her cup. "And the more I think about it, Nattie, the more convinced I am that there's a connection between the man I was seen struggling with in Nice and the two men who worked me over. Maybe they aren't the same men, but they must have something to do with the *Dragon.* It's too much of a coincidence for it to be anything else."

Nattie swung her feet to the floor and laid the crossword puzzle aside. "You're saying you think somebody followed you all the way to France and cornered you there?"

"It makes sense, Nattie. Whoever doesn't want me to talk now couldn't have wanted me to talk *then.* Maybe that's what we were arguing about when he struck me and I hit my head on that tree." She sighed at the irony. "He must have thought he was home free when I ended up with amnesia."

"And he couldn't have been too pleased when he found out you were asking questions."

"I know." She combed a hand through her hair and glanced at the room's small fireplace, framed in metal stamped with a design of entwined morning glories. "He probably thinks I'm close to remembering what happened. Who knows? Maybe I am."

"Or maybe you were just getting close to the truth with your questions."

"But I haven't talked to that many people. I met with one of the river pilots who guided the *Dragon*, and I talked to Charlie—Charlie. I was supposed to call him last night," she remembered, reaching for the phone.

"Who's Charlie?" Nattie frowned.

"Charlie Aikens. He works on the dock where the tanker was loaded. He was going to find out who was working the night the shipment of crude was loaded —or at least try to." Unfortunately, his number was in her purse, which the hospital had locked away somewhere for safekeeping when she was admitted. She had to get his number through Information.

On the fourth ring, a woman answered; Remy hadn't expected that. Somehow she'd gotten the impression from Charlie that he lived alone. Of course, that didn't mean he couldn't have company.

"Is Charlie there?"

"No, he isn't."

She caught the stiff, almost defensive tone in the woman's voice. "I'm Remy Cooper, and Charlie was getting me some information on shipping for a friend of mine's book. Do you know when he'll be back?"

"He won't . . . not ever." There was the smallest break in the woman's voice. "Charlie's dead."

Remy froze, every muscle contracted in shock and alarm. "When? How?" They were the only words she could get out.

"Yesterday. They told me there was a section of the dock that had been damaged a while back, and he was checking to see if it'd gotten worse. They think he got dizzy or slipped. He fell in the river."

"Are you sure? Did anyone see it happen?" She felt sick, sick with fear and guilt. She didn't even look at Nattie when she took the coffee cup from her hand and set it on the end table.

"They heard him cry out when he fell, but there was nothing they could do. The current swept him away." The woman kept talking, as if she needed to say all these things to believe them herself, her voice flat and thin with grief. "Charlie's my brother, the only family I had left. They recovered his body this morning. The funeral home said I should bring them a suit to bury him in. I thought he had one. Why does Charlie have to be buried in a suit?" she protested in a sudden burst of anguish. "He hated them—called 'em 'monkey suits.' Momma always used to make him wear one to go to church, and he'd argue with her. 'God don't care if I'm wearing a suit,' he'd say. Do you think I have to get a suit for him?"

"No. No, I don't think so," Remy murmured. "I'm . . . I'm sorry." Numb, she hung up the phone and turned to Nattie. "That was Charlie's sister. She says he's dead. If that's true—" She stopped and fought off the sudden surge of panic. "Was there anything in the paper about a drowning yesterday?"

"I think there was something, but I didn't read it."

They both got down on the floor beside the chair and went through the newspaper, section by section, page by page. Remy found the paragraph-long write-up on a back page of the B section. It gave the same account Charlie's sister had, with the added detail that it had happened in the morning, and said the search was continuing for his body. Remy sat back on her heels and stared at the article.

"I know exactly what you're thinking," Nattie announced.

"What if it wasn't an accident?" Remy finally said it out loud. "What if he didn't fall into the river? What if he was pushed? He was asking questions for me, Nattie." Still holding the folded page with the article, she got to her feet and started to pace, automatically hugging an arm to her bandaged ribs."I already know that the man who grabbed me that night on the dock was the same man who held me while his buddy hit me. I recognized his voice. He could have found out that Charlie was asking questions—and made sure I didn't find out his name." As another thought occurred to her, Remy stopped and swung back to face Nattie. "They had to know I'd find out about Charlie. Maybe they even wanted me to. Maybe they thought if the beating didn't scare me into shutting up, this would."

"It scares the hell out of me," Nattie said. "Just what could you have seen that night?"

"I don't know." Remy shook her head in frustration. "When I talked to Howard Hanks, the insurance investigator, yesterday afternoon, he had this theory that the tanker had never gone down at all—that it was an elaborate hoax to collect the insurance money. He thinks the *Dragon* is sailing around out there somewhere under another name. The debris the Coast Guard found, the crew in lifeboats—that was simply to make it look like the tanker had sunk in the storm. Instead, another crew came on board and sailed off in it."

Nattie's mouth gaped open in shock as she sagged back against the chair. "The man's crazy."

"I thought it was farfetched, too."

"It's more than farfetched; it's downright stupid," she declared in disgust, and clambered to her feet. "Do you realize how many people it would take to pull off a stunt like that? I don't know how many are in a crew, but let's say there's fifteen. With two crews, that makes thirty people. And how did that second crew get on board the tanker? A helicopter wouldn't have flown them out there —not in a storm. Which means they'd have to have gone by boat, and now you got more people involved. What happens if one of the thirty-five or forty people decides he doesn't like the split he got? Do you realize how many chances you've got of being blackmailed? And believe me, silence is golden, especially if you're the one paying somebody to keep his mouth shut. No." She shook her head. "If you're going to commit a crime, the fewer people who know about it, the better."

"You're right," Remy murmured, faintly stunned by the logic of it.

"Of course I am." Nattie sat back down in the armchair and laid both arms on its curved armrests. "If there were any switches pulled, it had to be at the very beginning. That's what you must have seen. Exactly how much do you remember?"

"Almost nothing," she admitted in frustration. "I saw the tanker moored to the dock, and then a man grabbed me. That's it. That's all I've been able to remember."

"Didn't you say it was foggy that night?"

"Yes—"

Nattie held up her hand. "If you've overlooked that detail, what others have you omitted? Think about it, picture it in your mind, and describe every thing you can recollect."

She started to say it was a waste of time, but—what if it wasn't? "All right." She closed her eyes. "It was dark and very foggy. The *Dragon* was tied up to the dock. I remember seeing the mooring lines and the gangway. There were two men at the rail—"

"What'd they look like?"

"It was too dark. All I could see was their silhouettes. One of them had a cigarette—" She opened her eyes with a snap. "He was smoking. There're No Smoking signs all over the place."

"I don't imagine smoking is one of the smartest things to do when you're loading crude oil on a tanker," Nattie remarked drolly.

"Then why was he smoking?"

"Maybe the tanker was already loaded."

"But it would still be too dangerous to smoke on deck."

"We'll get back to that later. Tell me what else you can remember."

Remy tried, closing her eyes again, but all she could picture was the black shape of the tanker in the mist and the two men at the rail. "Nothing." She shook her head impatiently. "It was too dark."

"Dark?" Nattie frowned. "The ship was dark? Weren't there floodlights? Ships loading at night are usually lit up like Christmas trees."

"Not this ship," Remy stated. "It was mostly dark, except for a few lights on the bridge deck." She breathed in sharply, suddenly remembering more, and instantly grabbed at her ribs as pain shot from them, nearly doubling her over.

Nattie was immediately at her side, curving a supporting arm around her shoulders. "When are you gonna learn you can't be doing things like that? You better sit down." She helped her to the sofa.

Remy clutched at Nattie's hand, drawing her onto the hard sofa cushion beside her. "I remember Cole was standing on the bridge deck with Carl Maitland and a man with a handlebar mustache—the man Howard Hanks said was a demolitions expert." She stared at nothing, the memory of that night coming back in a jumbled rush. "I'm not sure what happened next—after I saw Cole. I think maybe . . . I waved to him. That man grabbed me and said something like . . . 'Not so fast, little gal.' Then . . . something about snooping around. The walkie-talkie." She curled her fingers around Nattie's hand. "He had a walkie-talkie hooked to his belt. A voice came over it—a valve had broken, it said, and there was water all over the deck. Water, Nattie. That's it, isn't it?" Turning, she searched the woman's face—not with excitement or relief at remembering, but with a cold feeling. "That's the switch. The *Crescent Dragon* had no crude on board when it went down because its tanks had been filled with water." She laughed briefly, softly, in harsh remembrance. "And

Maitland explained it away by convincing me they were loading fresh water for bathing and drinking. I believed him."

"You probably did that night," Nattie said. "More than likely you didn't recognize the significance of it until later—when the insurance company started making all that noise."

But it was the bitterness of that memory that she was tasting—the bitterness and the ache it caused, not its significance. "Cole was there. He was with Maitland, watching the tanks being filled with water. He was part of it."

No matter how many times she'd considered the possibility of his guilt, she'd resisted believing it. Now she couldn't any longer. The memory of Cole on the bridge, his faced bathed in full light, with Maitland at his side, was too vivid, too clear.

"I know it hurts." Nattie patted her hand in comfort. "Every woman wants to believe her man is good. They seldom are, but that never makes it any easier to accept."

"No." Had Cole been the man in Nice? He'd claimed he was in New Orleans at the time. But she only had his word on that. She'd never checked. She could imagine how upset she must have been when she realized what he'd done— how hurt, how angry, how disillusioned. She would have argued with him, lashed out with the hurt and confusion of betrayal—a betrayal of both her trust and her family's. But the men who'd beaten her up—she couldn't believe he'd sent them. "Maitland. He saw me at the docks the other day. He saw me with Charlie. He sent those men to give me this warning." She touched the bruises on her face, oddly relieved to be able to shift the blame for them away from Cole.

"It wouldn't surprise me a bit if he had," Nattie responded. "Whenever he came to the house for one of your momma's dinner parties, that Maitland always reminded me of a barracuda, lurking in some dark pool, looking all small and innocent until you saw his teeth."

"Wait a minute. This doesn't make sense." Remy painfully pushed herself off the sofa again. "It's obvious why Maitland did it. He could sell the same oil twice. But what would Cole get out of it? The Crescent Line paid for that crude in advance. I've seen a copy of the cashier's check."

"You certainly don't have a criminal mind, Remy," Nattie said with a shake of her gray head. "He got money from Maitland. They probably worked out some percentage deal to share in the proceeds of that second sale. More than likely he got his money right out of that cashier's check."

"More than likely," she agreed, then sighed tiredly. "But how do we go about proving that?"

"An audit of Maitland's books would probably turn up some sizable checks written to companies nobody's heard of. The money might even have passed through a couple of those dummy companies before it got to Cole's hands." Nattie paused, then asked gently, "What are you going to do?"

"I don't know." Remy walked over to a window and lifted the rayon sheer to look out at the quiet Sunday morning. "I'm not sure. First I want to find out whether Charlie's death was an accident. Tomorrow I can check with the coroner's office and see what they can tell me." A little black girl skipped along the banquette in front of Nattie's house. She was wearing a pink ruffled dress and a dainty hat that was perched atop her braided hair and tied to her chin with ribbons. Remy wanted to go outside, take her hand, skip down the street with her—and feel again that innocent and carefree. Sighing, she turned from the window and met Nattie's gaze. "I have to know if this has gone beyond fraud, to murder."

SILENCE ECHOED THROUGH the house, a silence that said no one was home. Remy blinked sleepily and glanced around the living room, then crossed to the doorway into the kitchen, Nattie's pink scuffs slapping at her heels with each step. More silence waited for her in there, as the cat clock on the wall, with its moving eyes and swishing tail, chided her for sleeping late. Ignoring the hands pointing to nine o'clock, Remy headed toward the coffee maker on the counter, fighting the grogginess that came from too little sleep too late.

A note was propped against the glass carafe:

> Remy,
>   *Since you had to leave your purse at the*
>   *hospital, I thought you might need some walking-*
>   *around money.*
>   *Gone to work,*
>   Nattie

Paper-clipped to the back of it was a twenty-dollar bill. Remy slipped the bill into the slash pocket of the velour robe, also loaned to her by Nattie—like the slippers on her feet, the cotton nightgown she wore, and the new pancake makeup and mascara waiting in the bedroom to cover up her bruises. She smiled to herself as she poured a much-needed cup of coffee, but the smile faded when she saw the newspaper on the counter, folded open on the obituary notices. The very first one was for "Aikens, Charles Leroy, age 57."

She sighed, not really needing to be reminded of the cause for this flat feeling she had. Absently she combed her tousled length of hair away from the side of her face and reached for the paper, only to be distracted by the sound of a car pulling into the drive. Frowning, Remy lifted her head. Nattie wouldn't be coming home at this hour. She must have been mistaken—the car must have actually pulled into a neighbor's driveway instead.

But the slam of a metal door sounded close. Remy moved to the window above the kitchen sink and peered out. If there was a car in Nattie's drive, though, it hadn't pulled far enough forward for her to see it from the kitchen window.

The doorbell rang twice, in rapid succession, and she whirled around to face the living room. A salesman—it had to be. Nattie wouldn't have told her family she was here. She wouldn't. The doorbell chimed again, something strident and insistent in the sound. Another short interval of silence followed and Remy waited, poised, tense. Whoever it was would give up soon.

She nearly jumped out of her skin at the sudden pounding knock that replaced the chiming bell. She told herself he probably thought the doorbell didn't work. *"He"?* It had to be a he; a woman wouldn't knock that loud or that long—would she? Whoever it was, he couldn't be a friend of Nattie's, or he'd know she was at work.

Hearing the demanding rattle of the doorknob, Remy stiffened. Somebody wasn't taking "nobody-home" for an answer. She threw a look at the back door. Should she—silence. No rattling, no pounding, no ringing. For how long? Was he leaving?

She ran swiftly, lightly, to the living-room doorway, keeping to one side so she wouldn't be seen by anyone looking through the windows on the front porch. She snuck a glance at the front door, the glassed top of it curtained with gathered sheers. There was no dark shape on the other side of it—and nothing at the windows. And no sound of a car door opening and closing or an engine starting, either.

Then she saw it—her unstructured raspberry cardigan sweater lying in plain sight on the arm of the sofa. Anyone peering in the window would have seen it —and anyone who knew what she'd been wearing on Saturday would know she was here, or would at least be certain she'd *been* here.

She heard the telltale creak of the screen door behind her. My God, he'd come around back! She bolted out of the kitchen and ran for the front door. It was locked. She threw the security bolt and reached again to try the doorknob.

"Remy!"

She threw a half-panicked look over her shoulder. Cole halted inside the living-room doorway, his gray eyes narrowing sharply at the bruises on her face. Frozen by her memory of that night and her now-certain knowledge of his guilt, Remy stared at him, conscious of the throbbing in her side and the hard pounding of her heart. He looked nonthreatening in his double-breasted suit of navy wool and patterned tie. Had she thought he would be threatening?

Cole raised his hands in a calming gesture. "It's all right, Remy. It's me. I didn't mean to frighten you."

Frighten her. Had she been frightened? Of course she had. The specter of the pig mask was always there, hovering at the edges of her consciousness. She hadn't let herself think about it. She hadn't let herself think about the beating, the pain, the fear. She hadn't let herself imagine how they must have watched her, stalked her, then swooped on her without warning—in broad daylight, with people around, silently telling her she wasn't safe from them anywhere.

She felt the trembling start, the trembling of delayed reaction. Cole took a step toward her, his hands still raised, and Remy shrank against the door.

"I won't hurt you, Remy."

She wanted to scream at him that he already had—he'd cheated, he'd lied, he'd betrayed her belief in him, her love. But as if in a bad dream, she couldn't get any sound to come out.

"I swear I won't hurt you. I'd never hurt you." He sounded as if he were talking to a frightened child.

My God, that was what she felt like. She turned from him and leaned against the door, feeling the facade of bravery fall away as the first tears rolled down her cheeks. Those two men had forever shattered the illusion that she was inviolable. They had proved that she was vulnerable, that her status and the Jardin name were no protection. She hadn't wanted to face that. She'd denied it. But the seed of fear had been planted, and with Charlie's death it had taken root.

She felt his hands move onto her shoulders and stiffened in instant resistance. "No," she choked out the word, and tried to shrug away from them. "Don't touch me. Don't."

But his gentle grip persisted in turning her away from the door and toward him. Remy brought her hands up to keep from being drawn into his arms, struggling with all the proverbial weakness of a woman—knowing it and hating it.

"Sssh, it's all right," Cole murmured. "You're safe. I won't let anyone hurt you." The crazy part was that she did feel safe in the circle of his arms, with his shoulder right there waiting for her to cry on it. She tried to swallow a sob, and his hands pressed her closer. "Go ahead and cry, Remy," he urged softly. "After all you've been through, you need to. Only a fool wouldn't be scared. And you're no fool."

She stopped fighting the tears and sagged against him, weeping softly, brokenly, vaguely conscious of the comforting stroke of his hands on her back and her hair, mutely reaffirming that everything was all right. But she cried because nothing was all right, and never would be again—not her own feelings of security, not their love, and . . . not Charlie.

How long she cried quietly she didn't know. At some point she became conscious of Cole rubbing a lean cheek against the side of her hair, of the wet smell of wool from his jacket, and of the drained feeling of tears being used up.

"How—" Her voice sounded so choked and husky that Remy stopped and started over. "How did you know I was here?" She kept her head down, not ready to look at him, not ready to face him.

"I'd looked everywhere else." His voice was strained with emotion. "On my way to the office this morning, I remembered your endless Nattie-isms, and I took a chance." He turned his mouth to her hair, his arms tightening slightly around her. "When I told myself that it was over for us, that we were finished, I spent all Saturday convincing myself I didn't want you, I didn't need you . . . I didn't love you. Then your brother came charging into my apartment Sunday morning, thinking you were there. Why, Remy? Why would he think that? Why did you come here? Why aren't you at home with them?"

But she just shook her head, unable to answer him.

In the next second his mouth was near her ear and he was murmuring thickly, "It doesn't matter. I want to grow old and cranky with you, Remy. Do you understand what I'm saying?"

"Yes," she whispered, and she wondered, was it possible? Could they survive this? Unsure, she drew back from him, her hands resting on the lapels of his navy suit coat, her gaze fixed on them.

He tilted her head back and tactilely examined her bruises, first with his fingers, then with his lips. So light was the graze of his mouth that she wanted to cry again. It wasn't loverlike—it was pure loving.

She shut her eyes. "Cole . . . I remember. I remember that night on the dock. I know how it was done."

She felt the stillness of his hands, his body. She couldn't bring herself to look at him—not yet.

"What are you going to do?" His voice was low, his tone cautious.

"I don't know."

"Will you help me?" His hands tightened their grip on her arms in silent demand. "I need you, Remy."

She opened her eyes to stare at the knot of his tie, hesitating as she thought of Charlie. If Maitland had had him killed—and she was convinced that Maitland was the one, not Cole—maybe he'd acted without Cole's knowledge. But what did that change? Charlie was still dead.

Pushing away from him, she stepped free and shook her head. "I can't help you, Cole."

"Dammit, why not?" The explosion of anger instantly dissipated in a gusty sigh. "I know the answer to that, don't I? The family. I meant what I said. I'm not going to let them destroy me—even if it means I have to destroy *them*," he said—without the rancor she'd expected.

"Cole, you're destroying *yourself*," she protested, finally looking at him. "Why can't you see that? Maybe if you'd cooperate, it would go easier for you. If you'd just tell them—"

"I can't, Remy—not even for you."

"I don't want this, Cole. I love you. You've got to believe that."

His gray eyes made a slow search of her face, something sad and yearning in his expression. "Oddly enough, I do. But it's gone too far now. I can't turn back."

Charlie. He knew about Charlie. "Neither can I."

"Then there's nothing left to be said, is there?"

"No."

He held her gaze an instant longer, then opened the front door and walked out. He didn't look back to see her standing in the doorway.

The taxicab rolled to a quiet stop at the curb. Remy handed the driver the ten-dollar bill that was all she had left from Nattie's loan. "Keep the change," she said, and climbed out. She crossed the grassy verge to the scrolled iron gate, then stopped to study the white-pillared house and the two perfectly proportioned magnolia trees guarding its front lawn.

She pushed open the gate and stepped through, then closed it behind her and made the long walk up the banquette to the front door. As she'd expected, it was locked. She lifted the heavy brass knocker and dropped it twice, then waited.

Nattie opened the door, clad in her black uniform and snow-white apron. She took one look at Remy and sighed grimly. "You've been to the coroner's office. I was hoping you were wrong."

"So was I." Remy stepped inside and paused while Nattie closed the door. "Where are they?"

"In the solarium," she said with a nod of her head in its direction. "Mr. Marc's with them. They're beside themselves wondering where you are and what's happened to you."

"I know." She could hear the low, worried murmur of voices, yet she hesitated, unable to shake the feeling of dread. But it had to be done, and she had to do it. She was the only one who could.

Before she was halfway to the solarium door, Gabe saw her. "Remy!"

It was as though a torrent was being unleashed as their voices rained on her, sharp with anxiety and reproof, gentle with relief and concern. She let them wash over her, not listening, not letting them sidetrack her from the thing she'd come to do. That would be too easy.

"Do you have any idea how worried we've been about you?" Gabe led her to the sofa and gently sat her down on the soft cushions, sitting beside her and curving an arm around her shoulders.

"Where were you?" her father demanded. "And what was the idea of taking off like that? Don't you realize—"

"Don't scold her, Frazier. Can't you see how tired she is?" Her mother pressed a cup of tea into her unresisting hands. "Drink this."

She didn't. Instead, she stared at the amber-brown tea, watching the shimmer of its surface and the dark leaves at the bottom of the cup. "I remember being on the dock the night the *Dragon* was loaded." Her statement shocked them all into silence. "There was never any crude oil loaded onto the tanker. They filled it with water."

"Are—are you sure, Remy?" Gabe asked cautiously.

"Yes." She shot a quick glance at her uncle, standing stiffly near the end of the sofa. "Lance was right. Cole was part of it—he and Carl Maitland."

"Cole. . . . " Her father sat down rather abruptly in a side chair. "How do you know that?"

"Because I saw them on the bridge, watching the tanks being loaded with water. It was quite clever, really." She was surprised at how cold her hands felt. "Maitland gets paid for a nonexistent shipment of oil, then turns around and sells the same oil and shares the proceeds with Cole. Meanwhile, a demolition charge sends an aging tanker to the bottom, and the Crescent Line collects from the insurance company for the crude it paid for but never received and for a ship that had seen better days."

Marc whistled thoughtfully, then murmured, "I'd say it was damned clever."

"And you knew this." Gabe looked at her. Remy nodded reluctantly. "Why didn't you tell us before?"

"I don't know. Maybe I wasn't sure. Maybe I didn't want to believe Cole was mixed up in it. Maybe that's why I planned to go off by myself for a few days when we were in France. Maybe I was trying to decide what to do. I honestly don't remember." She tipped her head back and gazed at the high ceiling, fighting the rawness in her throat. "Now . . . I find myself wondering if Cole could have been the man I was arguing with. He says he was in New Orleans—"

"He told you that?" Gabe frowned.

"Yes." She felt suddenly confused as Gabe got up off the sofa and stalked over to the decanter of whiskey on the drink cart. "Wasn't he?"

"He was in Marseilles." There was a loud and brittle clink of ice cubes in a glass. He removed the crystal stopper and cast Marc a challenging look. "What's that—maybe a twenty-minute flight to Nice? Hell, he could have been there and back in the company jet without any of us ever knowing it—except Remy, of course."

"Maybe." She touched the purpling mark on her left cheekbone—the puffy swelling was gone, but the extreme tenderness remained. "But *this* was a warning from Maitland."

"Maitland." Gabe turned from the drink cart. "I thought you said you didn't know the two men who beat you up."

"Not by name. But I recognized the voice of one of them. He's the same man who surprised me that night on the dock. I'm sure he works for Maitland."

"What makes you think that?"

She told them about her recent visit to the dock area, about Maitland seeing her there with Charlie, and about Charlie's offer to obtain the names of the men who'd loaded the tanker and his subsequent "accidental" drowning. "Only it wasn't an accident. I saw the coroner's report this morning. He had a bruise on his cheek, like mine . . . like he'd been hit by something . . . like a fist. Of course, the coroner theorizes that he was struck by an object in the water. But I know he was knocked unconscious—or at least dazed by a blow—and thrown into the river."

"That would be difficult to prove," Gabe observed. "If there weren't any witnesses."

"There were two. But one saw him only *after* he was in the water, and the other was probably the man who hit him." She blocked out all emotion. It was the only way she could get through this.

"You *assume* he hit him, but you don't know that for a fact, do you?" Gabe said.

"Of course not."

"That's what I thought." He walked over and sat down beside her again, fitting his palm to hers and linking their fingers together. "Look . . . let us handle it from here. Stop trying to be a one-sister show."

She managed a smile of sorts and nodded, but she had to know. "What are you going to do?"

"To start with," Marc inserted, "you've given us the leverage we need to force a resignation from Buchanan. We can have him packed and gone before the day's over. Which will leave us free to negotiate a settlement with the insurance company."

"Wait a minute." Remy turned to her father and Gabe. "You aren't going to let them get away with it, are you?"

"You think we should file charges against them," Gabe guessed.

"Don't you?"

"In principle, yes. In reality, it would be a waste of time." He held her hand a little tighter, not letting her pull away. "It's a white-collar crime. There'd be a lot of headlines, a lot of scandal, but the chances of either one of them ever going to jail are slim to none."

"As much as I hate to admit it, Gabe is right," her father declared with a heavy sigh. "And then too, we can't overlook the fact that the Crescent Line would be drawn into any charge of insurance fraud. We would end up being a defendant—and we'd be found guilty."

"That kind of notoriety wouldn't be good for anyone," Marc put in. "There's nothing this town loves more than a scandal. It's something like what happens at the scene of an accident, with people driving by slowly, wanting to see how much blood there is and to watch somebody writhe and twist in pain so they can feel alive."

"But what about Charlie?" Remy protested.

"We'll look into that," Gabe said in reassurance. "But I'll be honest, Remy. The mere fact that he agreed to get some information for you isn't sufficient cause to file a murder charge against anyone, not without some corroborating evidence. A bruise isn't enough, especially when the coroner reached the conclusion that he was struck by an object in the water. A defense attorney wouldn't have to be F. Lee Bailey to get a man off with that kind of testimony. I'm sorry, but—"

"—that's the way it is," she finished the sentence for him, pulling her hand free of his entwining fingers and pushing the teacup onto the glass-topped coffee table, then rising to her feet in barely controlled agitation.

"I'm afraid it is."

"Remy, I have the feeling you're blaming yourself for this man's death," her father said gently as she moved toward the windowed wall, a confection of white wood and glass. "You're thinking he'd still be alive if you hadn't asked him to help you. But that's something none of us can know. Whether his death was an accident or a deliberate act, you're not responsible."

She wanted to challenge that, but instead she just stared at the shafts of sunlight piercing the canopy of an oak to shine in a broken pattern on the rosebush skeletons in her mother's prize garden. "And Maitland, what are you going to do about him?" She wrapped both arms around her middle. Not because her ribs were hurting, but because she felt vaguely sick.

There was a lengthy pause before Marc responded to her question. "Maitland . . . is a slightly different situation. However, he does live—and work—within our community. There are certain *subtle* pressures that can be brought to bear. We can promise you that, Remy."

"We know how to handle this problem," her father asserted. "You've done more than enough. It's our turn now."

"Of course." She turned from the window, avoiding their eyes. "If you'll excuse me, I think I'll go to my room. I feel like I've been living in these clothes. I need to change."

"You look tired, darling," her mother observed. "This has been such an ordeal for you. Would you like me to have Nattie bring a lunch tray to your room? I'm sure you'd like to rest."

"Yes, thank you," she murmured absently, and she left the room, sickened by her silence and by the token objections she'd raised to their plans to hush up this whole messy affair very quickly and very quietly. It was wrong, she knew that—even though common sense told her they were right. Even if Cole and Maitland were tried and convicted of fraud—after lengthy delays, postponements, and appeals—they'd probably get off with a suspended sentence and probation. And the insurance company would still look to the Crescent Line for restitution, and possibly even damages. All that scandal, all that publicity—for what? A slap on the hand.

Her family was merely following a common business practice by dealing with the problem themselves, in their own way. But she was going along with them for a much more selfish reason: she didn't want to see Cole punished. She was glad there was another way to handle it, a way that wouldn't dirty his name and brand him a criminal.

"Forgive me, Charlie," she whispered as she climbed the mahogany stairs to her room.

A breeze, chill and sharp, blew strongly through the open French doors onto the second-floor gallery. Remy hesitated, then set the tray bearing the remains of her lunch on the low table by the loveseat and walked over to close them. As she drew them together, a car pulled up out front and a man charged out of the driver's-side door.

Cole. Remy froze for an instant, staring as he swept toward the house with long, rigid strides. What was he doing here? The wide gallery quickly blocked him from view, and Remy turned, hearing the squeal of brakes from a second car as she started across the room, leaving the French doors partially closed and the lunch tray on the table.

The clangorous pounding of the brass knocker shattered the quiet of the house, and Remy broke into a running walk, reaching the top of the stairs just as Nattie arrived at the front door. Nattie barely had a chance to open it before Cole shoved his way inside.

"Where the hell is she? I want to see her—now!" His voice was like a distant and ominous roll of thunder.

"Cole—" Remy stopped halfway down the steps, stunned by the anger in his expression when he swung toward her, his jaw clenched, all the muscles in his face contracted, making him appear even more gaunt-cheeked and hard-edged.

As Cole moved toward the staircase, Marc charged through the door, looking all flustered and upset. He grabbed at Cole's arm. "Buchanan, I told you—"

"And I told *you* I wanted to hear her say it." Cole shook off his restraining hand and continued to the foot of the stairs, fixing his silver-black stare on her. "I want to hear it from you."

"What are you talking about?" Remy glanced uncertainly at her uncle.

"He doesn't believe—"

"Don't you put words in her mouth," Cole snapped. "Let it come from her."

"You mean—" she began.

"Tell me what you told them," he demanded, pushing the words through his teeth.

She closed her eyes for an instant, then opened them to meet his gaze, hurting for him and for herself. "I'm sorry, Cole, but I saw you with Maitland that night on the dock when you were loading the tanker with water."

"That's a goddamned lie!"

She flinched at the rage in his voice even as her uncle spoke, reminding him, "Buchanan, you've already admitted you were there with Maitland."

"Yes, dammit, I was, but—"

"Cole, stop," Remy protested. "Don't make this any harder than it already is."

He turned back to her, harshly demanding, "Was it hard this morning? You said you loved me. And was I supposed to believe that?"

"It's the truth. I do love you—"

"Save it for one of your Uptown friends," he said harshly. "Someone used to a woman saying she loves him in one breath and then stabbing him in the back in the next." He pivoted to face Marc. "You wanted my resignation—now you've got it. Tell Mrs. Franks to clean out my desk and drop my things by the apartment."

"Cole, wait." Remy started after him as he crossed to the door, but Marc caught her.

"Let him go, Remy." The door slammed shut. "It's better this way."

28 ⟿

MARDI GRAS NIGHT, and the interior of the Municipal Auditorium had been transformed into a splendorous setting worthy of the ball considered by many to be *the* social event of the year. Gleaming, swagged, and valanced draperies formed an elaborate backdrop for the dais of the ball's god-ruler and his court. Overhead, chandeliers glittered, the prisms dripping from their many tiers catching and reflecting the light. And below, a dazzling white carpet covered the floor of the dais, spilled down its steps, and spread over the entire stage. A stage that was now empty—the expectancy in the air growing.

Remy sat in the special "call-out" section near the dance floor, reserved for ladies, wives, mothers, friends, and debutantes of the members of the Mistick Krewe of Comus. She wore her hair piled atop her head in soft, smooth waves. Layers of artfully applied makeup completely concealed her bruises and created a kind of mask of calm composure, a mask that she was certain would crack if she smiled—though that was hardly a concern, since she found nothing to smile about.

She turned her head to catch something her mother said, the long multis-trands of emerald and blue beads of her earrings brushing the shoulder of her long-sleeved top, which was covered with teal-blue sequins. Sibylle's remark didn't require a reply, and Remy made none as she turned back to watch the opening of the gala event.

In the ancient tradition of the Old World *bals masques*, it began with a glit-tering processional led by last year's court in evening dress, followed by the members of the exclusive Carnival club in their beaded and plumed costumes. Remy sat through the mimed welcome by the hooded captain and managed to appear interested when this year's debutantes, in de rigueur white gowns, were presented.

During the tableau that followed, she absently played with the clunky jew-eled pendants on the gold chain belt she wore around the waist of her emerald-colored taffeta skirt, then forced herself again to pay attention to the introduc-tion of important guests to the masked god-ruler Comus, seated on the ornately gilded dais with his queen.

At the conclusion of it, the "call-out" dances began. Remy sat through the first one while her mother danced with her father and Gabe danced with his date for the evening. Her name was called for the second, and she took to the floor to dance with her father, her sequined top concealing her tightly girdled ribs. Her brother partnered her on the third. Then it was back to her chair. Shortly after that, the general dancing began—restricted to the krewe and their ladies only, of course.

She watched the swirl of taffeta, satin, chiffon, and silk, beaded, bangled, and rhinestoned in coral, saffron, azure, plum, turquoise, and, naturally, white, and longed to hear the band strike up "If Ever I Cease to Love," the official song of Mardi Gras, which signaled the meeting of Rex and Comus—and the end of the ball, a song played slowly and oh so very seriously. Thinking of it, the lyrics sprang into her mind:

> *If ever I cease to love,*
> *May sheepsheads grow on apple trees*
> *May the moon be turned into green cheese*
> *May oysters have legs and cows lay eggs*
> *If ever I cease to love. . . .*

This time she couldn't summon a smile at the incredible, forgettable lyrics.

She contained a sigh and sipped at the white wine Gabe had brought her, surrounded by music, laughter, and the susurration of gay voices. What was she doing here? she thought, then wryly wondered how she could have forgotten. Her family had insisted that she attend—to maintain appearances.

In the space of time between Rex's arrival by riverboat on the previous evening, Lundi Gras, and the Zulu parade on Mardi Gras morning, word had gotten out: Cole Buchanan had been ousted as president of the Crescent Line, the very man who had formed a liaison with Remy Jardin that had shown every indication of becoming a permanent one. If she failed to attend the ball, only one possible conclusion could be drawn by the family's very important friends: there was a severe split in the family over the decision.

Surely by now "appearances" had been satisfied. She'd been seen by everyone who mattered. Was it necessary to maintain this charade to the end? What difference could it possibly make if she went home early?

She left her seat and went in search of Gabe or her father—not to *ask* them, but to *tell* them she was leaving. Neither was on the dance floor, or among the chatting clusters at the edges. Remy guessed immediately where the two of them were—at the backstage bar, talking business, power, and politics in between comparing golfing, football, and hunting notes with some of their colleagues. An invitation to have a drink at the backstage bar was a privilege offered to few, but at the moment, Remy didn't even give a damn that it was off-limits to her sex. She was tired of their secretive, cliquish, little-boy rules and this endless concern for appearances.

She was stopped at the entrance by a krewe member. "Sorry, no one's allowed back here."

Remy had half a notion to point out that he was back there, but she said instead, "I need to speak to my father, Frazier Jardin. It's urgent."

He hesitated, then drawled, "All right, but you wait here, Miss Jardin."

At another time, in a more puckish mood, she might have followed him, but tonight Remy simply wanted to get out of there. As she started to turn away, she caught sight of Gabe backstage. She nearly called out to him, but then she saw the man with him—Carl Maitland. She dropped the wineglass and covered her mouth with her hand, smothering a cry of shock as she backed up a step.

It had been Gabe with Maitland that night! Gabe, not Cole. She remembered now that she'd seen Cole with Maitland earlier—in the daylight. That had to be why the image of them together had been so sharp, so clear. But that night it had been Gabe. Gabe. How could she have gotten it so mixed up? Suddenly she could almost hear the French psychiatrist saying that her memory could return chronologically or . . . out of sequence, in random bits that made no sense.

Gabe saw her standing there. His mouth started to lift in a smile, then a stunned look claimed his face and he turned pale. He knew. He knew she remembered. And Maitland—he knew too. She felt the glare of his eyes, then saw him take a quick, angry step toward her. Gabe moved forward to stop him. Remy had a glimpse of Maitland shoving him aside as she turned to run, like an animal scenting danger, with flight her only defense.

She tried to lose herself in the crowd fringing the dance floor, but a quick glance over her shoulder showed Maitland cutting directly toward the main exit. She couldn't make it, not before he was there to block it.

Changing direction, Remy darted out a side exit into the warren of corridors that ringed the main auditorium. She hesitated. What now? She couldn't think. Her mind was reeling—no wonder Gabe hadn't wanted to go to the police about Charlie, no wonder he hadn't wanted charges brought against Maitland, his partner in crime, no wonder he'd wanted to hush the matter up with the insurance company, no wonder he'd been so eager to pin the blame on Cole.

Cole. She spied a bank of pay telephones tucked along the wall of a small alcove. She ran over to them and picked up the farthest one. She had no change, so she dialed his number and charged the call to her home phone.

"Please be there," she whispered, closing her eyes as she listened to the ring.

"Yes." That low, abrupt voice—it was Cole.

"Cole, it's Remy. I—" There was a sharp and very definite click on the other end. She jerked the receiver away from her ear to stare at it in shock. He'd hung up on her! She hesitated, then hurriedly tried again. When he answered, she spoke in a rush. "It was Gabe, not you. I didn't remember that until just now, when I saw him with Maitland. Please don't hang up. I was wrong. You weren't involved. I know that now."

"Your confession comes a little late, Remy."

"No," she choked on the word. "It can't be too late. They know I remember what really happened. And they know I know about Charlie Aikens. I think Maitland had him killed. Now he's looking for me. I can't go to the police. Gabe would convince them I'm crazy. The amnesia, the beating, he'd have them believing I'd become paranoid, schizoid, something. The beating, Cole, that was Maitland's warning for me to keep my mouth shut. My God, I'm babbling." She swallowed a hysterical laugh and tilted her head back, fighting down the panic.

"Where are you, Remy?"

"At the auditorium, the Comus ball."

"Stay there. I'm coming right over."

"I can't. He's looking for me—"

"And it would seem that he has found you," a voice said as her wrist was suddenly seized and the receiver ripped from her hand. Remy turned and had a moment to see Maitland's cold, cold eyes, magnified by the elegant gold-rimmed glasses he wore, then her arm was jerked behind her back and twisted high. She gasped at the paralyzing pain. "Don't scream, Remy," Maitland warned in a dry, confident voice. "I would hate to bruise that pretty face of yours, especially when the other marks are healing so nicely. And it would be embarrassing to carry you out of here because you passed out from drinking too much. You understand what I'm saying, don't you?"

"Yes," she gasped again.

"Good. Now, we're going to take a little walk—very calmly and very quietly. Right?"

Remy nodded. The tuxedoed security men on duty at the entrance to keep the "wrong" people from getting in to the ball—did he think he could walk her past them? How could he explain manhandling her this way? Or did he expect her to meekly walk at his side? If she could create just enough doubt in their minds, enough to make him turn her loose—regardless of any convincing lines he might tell them—she could run.

He steered her out of the alcove and back into the side corridor. He didn't turn her toward the entrance, though, but rather forced her in the opposite direction. Where were they going?

A short distance down the hall, Remy had her answer. There was a side exit—a fire door, the kind that opened from the inside but not from the outside. He propelled her toward it, then reached around and pushed down on the metal bar, swinging the door open, his grip on her tightening rather than loosening.

He pushed her through the doorway ahead of him, the cool night air sweeping over her as she stepped out into the deep shadows of the building. She heard the whoosh of the automatic closure pulling the door shut, and felt the press of his body against her.

"Where are you taking me?"

"I thought we might go for a ride."

The parking lot. There'd be people in the parking lot. But again, he didn't turn her in the anticipated direction. Instead, he made her keep in the building's shadows, staying parallel with the wall. She heard the jingle of car keys, then spied a black BMW parked close to the building's service entrance. Her heart sank.

As if sensing it, he murmured, "I never guessed how convenient it would turn out to be."

"You'll never get away with this," she said tightly.

There was a mocking click of his tongue. "Really, Remy, that sounds like a line from an old B movie or a bad TV script."

"You won't," Remy insisted, trying not to sound as desperate as she felt. "First Charlie, now me. Won't that look too suspicious?"

"Did you read yesterday's paper? There was an article in there about a young coed from LSU who died from a drug overdose. She was an honors student, came from a good middle-class family—not the kind of girl you'd think would get mixed up with cocaine. It was just a small story. When I read it, I couldn't help thinking how different it would have been if she had been the daughter of a wealthy, prominent family. It might have stirred the police to take action against these drug dealers."

"My family would never believe that."

"They wouldn't have any choice," he said curtly, then returned to a smoother tone. "Besides, the family is always the last to suspect their child's on drugs—until they're faced with irrefutable evidence."

"No," she whispered in protest.

"It won't be so bad, Remy. Think how high you'll be flying when you go."

She couldn't get into that car with him. Somehow she had to get away. Then she realized that he'd either have to shift his hold on her or be forced to unlock the car with his left hand. In either case, that would be her chance—maybe her only chance.

He steered her to the passenger door and jerked her to a stop, then positioned her at right angles to the door. He wasn't going to switch hands; instead, he'd probably tighten his grip, as he'd done before. She'd have to block out the pain.

It stabbed through her shoulder as the keys jingled and he leaned toward the car. She sank her teeth into her lower lip and turned her head, focusing on his legs. She kicked as hard as she could, aiming for the side of his knee.

Remy felt his leg instantly buckle and heard his loud groan as his fingers loosened on her wrist. She spun free of him and broke into a run, grabbing up the front of her long taffeta skirt in one hand and ignoring the thousands of needles that seemed to be embedded in her other arm.

She heard him mutter, "You bitch," and then the slam of the car door. She looked back and saw him hobbling after her, the light from an auditorium window glinting on the lens of his glasses—and on the metal barrel of a gun.

She ran blindly. There were cars on the street. Should she try to flag one down? Would it stop? Would they help—or speed away? If she tried, wouldn't that give Maitland a chance to catch up with her—to catch her? She looked back. He was still coming after her, still favoring his leg, still slowed by it, still carrying the gun. She had to get away.

The park, with its twisting, dimly lit paths, its thick shrubbery and quiet lagoons—she could hide there. She could lose him there.

She ran away from the streetlights, toward the gaping darkness of the park, sobbing with each breath. She plunged into its blanketing shadows, her heels immediately sinking in the grass. She stumbled and fell, her lungs, her side, her whole body on fire. For a brief moment she simply lay there, fighting for breath, not certain she could get back up. But she did, pausing long enough to slip off her high heels before pressing on, slower this time, hugging the shadows and holding her full skirt tightly around her to keep the taffeta from rustling so noisily.

Someone cursed long and low. Remy froze. It had sounded close. How close? Where? She searched the shadows and caught a movement. Someone was over there. There was a gap in the bushes behind her. She started to back into it, one quiet step at a time. Would he see her? Would he catch the faint shimmer of her sequined top in the darkness?

As a hand grabbed her from behind, she screamed and whirled around, striking out blindly to free herself. Both arms were seized.

"Stop it, Remy. Stop it," someone demanded, shaking her hard when she persisted in struggling. "Do you hear? Stop it."

Something penetrated—the sound of that voice, the sensation of the hands, the flashes of images in her mind. Remy paused to look at the man's face.

"You." She recoiled from the sight of her father. "You're the one who hit me. You're the one I was arguing with at the Espace Masséna." She moved her head slowly from side to side, not wanting to believe it, not wanting to remember. "Why?"

"I didn't mean to," he murmured. "But you wouldn't listen. You wouldn't understand. We would have lost everything. Wall Street . . . the real-estate deals that went sour in Texas . . . what money we had, we'd gambled on Maitland's offshore venture. When it failed too, he had to pay it back. That's all we did. Make sure he had the money to pay back what he owed. The extra was just . . . interest."

" 'We'? You and Gabe. . . . " Then she remembered. "No, it was Marc and Lance too. It was all of you."

"For God's sake, no one got hurt."

"Only Charlie and Cole," she taunted.

"Buchanan's a cat. He'll land on his feet. Charlie . . . he was your fault."

"Oh, God." She bowed her head, unable to look at him as she strained to get as far away from him as possible.

The leaves whispered a warning. "Frazier," a voice said. Her father started to turn, relaxing his hold on her arm, and Cole stepped out of the shadows, his right hand swinging out of the darkness to clip Frazier Jardin's jaw. As her father reeled sideways, Cole caught her arm, his gray eyes smiling briefly at her. "I've wanted to do that for a long time." Then his hand was sliding around her waist, coaxing her along. "Come on. Let's get out of here."

"Maitland's out there somewhere. He has a gun, Cole."

The information elicited a few choice obscenities from him.

From a nearby street came the scream of police sirens. "Cole—"

"I called them before I left." He drew her with him as he moved slowly along the hedges. "Unfortunately, they're going to the auditorium. Maybe we can fool Maitland by doubling—"

At that moment Maitland stepped out of the bushes directly in front of them, the small but deadly-looking barrel of his gun leveled at them. "Look what we have here," he murmured coolly. "What do you suppose happened? A lovers' quarrel, maybe. In the rage of rejection, he shoots her, then commits suicide. Sounds plausible, doesn't it?"

Cole stepped a little ahead of Remy, placing himself between her and Maitland. "It's plausible *only* if you come close enough to leave powder burns. Why don't you do that, Maitland?" He wagged his fingers, urging him to come closer.

"Carl, no," came her father's strangled cry as he plunged out of the shadows a few feet from them, a frightened and panicked look on his face. "My God, she's my daughter. You can't do this."

"I suppose *you're* going to stop me," Maitland jeered in contempt. "How, Frazier, when you couldn't even stop her? I should have remembered that Jardins are notorious for never having the guts to finish what they start. Well, *I* do."

There was a noisy thrashing in the brush to his right. Maitland swung toward the sound and Cole lunged for the gun, driving his arm high in the air. A stab of flame shot from the barrel, accompanied by a small, explosive pop as Cole struggled to wrest the gun from Maitland. Gabe charged out of the bushes, and at the same second, Remy saw the gun arc through the air.

"Get it, Remy!" Cole shouted.

It landed somewhere in the grass. She ran to the spot where she thought it had fallen and frantically groped through the short, clipped grass. Then she felt the cool smoothness of metal beneath her fingers and quickly snatched it up. When she turned with the gun, Gabe was standing in front of her.

He hesitated a second, then held out his hand. "Give me the gun, Remy."

She took an uncertain step backward and shook her head.

"Dammit, Remy, I wouldn't have let him hurt you. I was trying to stop him. Now give me the gun."

Suddenly Cole was beside her, breathing hard and taking the revolver from her hand. Out of the corner of her eye, she caught the gleam of flashlights moving toward them: the police.

THE CATHEDRAL RANG the midnight hour, signaling the end of Mardi Gras and the beginning of the Lenten season, the time of fasting. Remy listened to it and shuddered faintly, staring heedlessly at the bare branches of a mimosa tree in the small brick-walled courtyard.

She heard a footstep on the flagstones and half turned as Cole stepped through the French doors and joined her on the private patio off his apartment. He silently offered her a glass of brandy. She took it and sipped it, then turned back to her contemplation of the night.

"I was coming to you. I was going to leave Nice the next morning," she said dully, the memory of it all now very clear. "When you accused my family of instigating this fraud and we argued so bitterly, I didn't believe you—even though I was nagged by the memory of that night when I saw Gabe's red Porsche parked on the levee road and stopped to see what he was doing there. I wanted to believe that the fresh water was for bathing and cooking. But when I confronted him—all of them—with it in Nice, they. . . ."

"I know," Cole said, studying the brandy in his own glass as he stood beside her.

"I listened to all their arguments—their justifications. The company was going to go bankrupt anyway, they said. And the way they looked at it, they had to get money out of it any way they could. They were destroying the Crescent Line—and they didn't care." She stopped in time to choke back a sob. "I thought I knew them, Cole. They're my family. To see them—to hear them . . . oh, God, it hurt."

"I know."

She breathed out a shaky sigh, realizing that it would never go away, that feeling of a faith betrayed—a trust, a love. "I . . . I knew I had to stop them. You and I had to take over the company. It was the only way to save it." She paused. "It still is."

"It won't be easy, Remy."

"Easy." She laughed at the word. "It will be ugly. Very, very ugly. But it has to be done."

He watched her with a sidelong look, his gray eyes quiet and measuring. "Now you sound like a Donovan."

She smiled faintly. "Maybe I do."

"You know, you could work a deal with your family," he said. "In return for their signing over their proxies to you and resigning from the board, you could withdraw the charges you filed against them tonight."

"I thought about that," she admitted. "But once you start compromising, where do you stop, Cole? And what justification would I use? Would I say it was to avoid a fight for control? Or to avoid a messy scandal and protect the Jardin name? Charlie died helping a woman he knew as Remy Cooper—not Remy Jardin. It's time the Jardin name stopped meaning so much."

"Or maybe it's time for it to mean more."

She looked at him and smiled. "Maybe it is."

He touched his brandy glass to hers, then lightly curved his arm around her and drew her into the crook of his shoulder.

Rivals

To Susie Correll—
    With gratitude and friendship for these past years
    working with you and the ones to come

1 ～

SOMEONE WAS WATCHING her. She could feel the weight of a pair of
eyes on her. It was hardly surprising in a room full of people—yet she had the
strongest sensation . . .

Twenty minutes earlier, Flame Bennett had arrived at the DeBorgs' twelve-room
aerie atop one of the gleaming towers on San Francisco's Telegraph Hill. Pausing in the marble foyer with her friend and associate Ellery Dorn, she'd hastily
begun tugging off her black Fendi gloves, one finger at a time, as she turned to
the waiting maid in her starched uniform. "Has Miss Colton arrived?"

"About fifteen minutes ago, Ms. Bennett."

The reply confirmed Flame's suspicion. They were late, later than even
fashion allowed. Tonight's party was more than just an exclusive gathering of
the San Francisco opera committee; it was a formal reception for the interna-
tionally acclaimed coloratura soprano Lucianna Colton, the guest diva in the
fall season's opening production of *Il Trovatore*. Not being on hand to welcome
her was the equivalent of being late for an audience with the Queen. It simply
wasn't done.

"What a pity we missed her entrance," Ellery murmured dryly as he handed
his topcoat and white silk scarf to the maid, then brushed absently at an invisible speck of lint on the sleeve of his black jacket.

Flame shot him a quick glance. His faint smile held a hint of mockery. That
was Ellery—cynical and urbane and elegant, with a wry mocking wit that could
be quite cutting. And, as always, he was impeccably groomed with not a single
strand of his light brown hair out of place.

"How typical of you, Ellery," she laughed as he stepped up behind her and
slipped the black fox jacket from her shoulders. "Your tears match your croco-
dile shoes."

"But of course." He gave the jacket to the maid, then tucked a guiding hand
under her elbow. "Shall we make our entrance?"

"We don't have any choice," Flame murmured with a trace of ruefulness he
didn't share.

Leaving the foyer, they passed through the reception hall and entered the
small sitting area beyond it. Her glance touched briefly on the sunny yellow
traditional sofa and black Regency chairs juxtaposed with a pair of eighteenth-

century oriental cabinets, the room's decor indicative of the genteel blend to be found throughout the spacious penthouse. But her attention was drawn to the bright chatter of voices interspersed with soft laughter coming from the main sitting room on the right.

Unconsciously she squared her shoulders as she paused in the arch to the claret-glazed room. Flame was accustomed to heads turning. Long ago, she had come to terms with the fact that her looks attracted stares, both the admiring and the envious kinds. It was more than being model tall and shapely or possessing a strongly beautiful face. No, what set her apart was that rare and striking combination of ivory fair skin, jade green eyes, and copper hair with just enough gold in it to tone down the red.

But the looks directed her way now held a hint of disapproval at her tardiness. She knew all the guests. Most were old family friends who had literally watched her grow up. Flame was one of the few at the gathering who had the distinction of being a direct descendant of one of San Francisco's founding families. And that very connection gave her entrée to the elite circles, an entrée that new money couldn't necessarily buy. As Ellery had once caustically observed, the color of a person's money wasn't nearly as important in San Francisco as the color of his or her blood. With the latter, one didn't automatically need the former.

Their hostess, Pamela DeBorg, a bright bird of a woman with feathery ash blond curls, spotted them and swooped over, the shawl scarf to her panne velvet Blass gown billowing out behind. "Flame, we had given up on you."

"It was unavoidable, I promise," Flame apologized. "The agency was filming a commercial at the Palace of Fine Arts. Unfortunately, we had some problems."

"Indeed," Ellery chimed in. "Our prima donna was a leopard—or should I say leopardess. I hope yours doesn't turn out to be as temperamental and uncooperative as ours."

"Lucianna is an absolute dear," Pamela declared, clasping her hands together in delight, the spectacular diamond ring on her finger flashing in the light. "You will love her, Flame. She is so warm, so affable . . . what can I say? You must meet her yourself. Come. She's in the Garden Room with Peter." She caught at Flame's hand, drawing her from the arch, then paused long enough to include Ellery. "You, too, of course." Then she was off, somehow managing to stay a half step ahead of Flame while turning to her, talking all the way. "Did I tell you she changed the entire travel schedule and flew here on a private jet instead? It was absolute insanity this afternoon trying to get everything rearranged." Flame smiled sympathetically, aware no other response was required. "And wait until you see her gown. It's gorgeous. But the necklace she's wearing —a fabulous diamond and ruby *bijoux* that will make you die with envy. Jacqui hinted that she thought it was paste," she added, dropping her voice to a conspiratorial level when she mentioned the chronicler of San Francisco's society doings, Jacqui Van Cleeve, a former socialite herself before her divorce. "But those rocks are definitely real, Flame. That necklace reeks of Bulgari's touch. Believe me, I know."

Flame didn't doubt that. It had been said that Pamela DeBorg's collection of jewelry could rival the Duchess of Windsor's, both in quantity and quality.

Just ahead, a set of French doors stood open, leading into the Garden Room. Pamela swept through them, then paused a fraction of a second. The lengthy expanse of glass provided the grandly spacious penthouse with its de rigueur view of the Golden Gate Bridge and the bay. Intimate groupings of plushly cushioned rattan furniture were scattered among a profusion of potted plants and Chinese urns.

In the middle of it all, holding audience, stood the dark-haired diva herself, stunning in a back-plunging gown of scarlet that hugged her generous curves. She turned, giving Flame a glimpse of the ruby and diamond necklace and her much-photographed face, too prominently boned to be considered beautiful, although it undeniably commanded attention.

She certainly was the center of it now, Flame thought, glancing at the committee members clustered around her, including their host, the sandy-haired financier, Peter DeBorg.

"There she is," Pamela said needlessly and pushed forward. "Forgive me for interrupting, Lucianna, but I have someone from the committee I want you to meet—Flame Bennett."

"How nice." Her glance swung to Flame, her dark eyes showing a perfunctory interest that matched her smile as she said, "It's my pleasure."

"I assure you it's all mine, Miss Colton. And I hope you'll accept my apologies for not being here to welcome you when you arrived tonight."

"Yes," Pamela rushed to explain. "Flame was filming a commercial and they had some sort of problem with a lion or leopard or something."

"You're an actress then."

"No," Peter DeBorg spoke up. "Flame works for Boland and Hayes, a national advertising agency with offices here in San Francisco."

"I'm not sure I understand." Her questioning look ran from one to the other. "Are you a model?"

Flame smiled faintly. "No. I'm a vice-president with the company."

"A vice-president." Her full interest was now focused on Flame, sharply reassessing. "How wonderful to meet a woman with power."

Flame acknowledged the compliment with a gracious nod, then half-turned, directing the attention to Ellery. "I'd like to introduce you to another officer of the company and my closest friend, Ellery Dorn."

"Miss Colton." Ellery stepped smoothly forward and took her scarlet-nailed fingers, raising them to his lips. "We are looking forward to your Leonora. Although, if I may be so bold to suggest, instead of having San Francisco at your feet as you do here—" With a sweep of his hand, he indicated the glitter of city lights beyond the glass panes of the penthouse windows. "—you will have them *on* their feet."

"Ellery, how very clever of you!" Pamela exclaimed, clapping her hands together.

"And flattering," Lucianna Colton added with a regal incline of her head.

"I prefer to think of it as a portent of things to come," Ellery insisted as more guests strolled into the Garden Room, not to admire the view of the storied city but to have a closer look at the famous lady in scarlet. Catching sight of them, Ellery lightly took Flame's arm. "As much as we would like to monopolize your time, Miss Colton, I'm afraid we must deny ourselves. There are too many others eager to shower you with the same accolades."

After exchanging the usual pleasantries, Flame and Ellery withdrew. Almost immediately their place was taken and Flame heard Andrea Crane gush, "I was at La Scala last year when you performed so divinely in *Tosca*."

As they crossed the threshold into the main sitting room, Ellery glanced back and smiled wryly. "Amazing."

"What is?" Flame eyed him curiously.

Drawing her to one side, he nodded at the collection of guests, some seated, some standing. "Tonight's guest list reads like the Who's Who of San Francisco society. Yet . . . there they are fawning over a woman from some little midwestern town just because she can hit a high F without screeching."

"It's a bit more than that," she replied, momentarily distracted by the odd feeling she was being watched. "She is an extremely talented artist."

"Artistic talent is the elevating factor, isn't it?"

That sensation of a pair of eyes on her persisted, stronger than before. "Is this going to turn into a philosophical discussion, Ellery? Because if it is, I don't think I'm up to it." She half-turned, trying to discern the source of the eerie feeling, and came face-to-face with a waiter, a hawk-faced man in his mid-forties. For an instant she was unnerved by the piercing study of his deep-set hazel eyes, hooded by a heavy brow. Then his glance fell as he stepped forward and extended the salver of wineglasses balanced on the palm of his right hand.

"Would madame care for a glass of chardonnay?" Not even the smooth, respectful wording could eliminate the rough edge to his voice.

"Thank you." She took one of the stemmed wine goblets from the tray, her glance running over him again. Had he been the one staring at her? Although she couldn't be sure, she suspected he was. Why had it bothered her? Why had she felt so uneasy? Men customarily stared at her—for all the usual reasons. Why should a waiter be different? He offered wine to Ellery, then moved on to another group of guests.

"Brown shoes and black pants." Ellery raised an eyebrow in disapproval. "The caterer should pay more attention to the dress of his help."

Flame glanced again at the retreating waiter, this time noting the brown of his shoes. Unexpectedly, he turned his head and glanced back at Flame. The instant he realized she was watching him, he looked away.

A hand touched her arm, then traveled familiarly down to cup an elbow. "I see you finally made it."

Recognizing the voice, Flame tensed briefly, then flashed a quick and warm smile at the man who was easily her most important and influential client. At fifty-six, Malcom Powell looked it, too—an imposing figure of only average stature but very powerfully built. His dark hair was leonine thick and shot with silver, but that touch of gray only added to the image of an iron man. Some said that was exactly the way he ruled his huge chain of department stores across the country, a family business that he'd inherited and on which he'd built his reputation, although they currently represented only a small portion of his vast holdings.

"Malcom, I didn't know you were back in town."

"I flew in last night." His gray eyes bored into her, seeking a reaction, then flickered with irritation when he found only calm. "I left a message with your secretary this afternoon, but you never returned my call."

"I was tied up all afternoon filming a commercial. I didn't have time to check with the office for messages. You surely don't think I deliberately ignored your call." She accompanied her reply with a bright smile. Long ago, she had learned that the best way to handle Malcom Powell was by not letting him intimidate her. Confrontation was always better—if done carefully.

"No, not really."

"What was it you wanted?"

His glance flicked to Ellery. "Get Flame another glass of wine." He took the crystal goblet from her and set it on the lacquered side table along the wall. "And make sure it's been properly chilled this time."

"By all means." Ellery bowed his head with an exaggerated respect. "I'll even corner the wine steward and express your dissatisfaction to him." To Flame, he added, "It shouldn't take more than five minutes."

When he strolled away, Flame turned to Malcom, the cornerstone to her entire career. She owed him a great deal, and he knew it. She hadn't been hired by the agency eight years ago because of her qualifications or her college degree. She had been window-dressing for the firm—with valuable connections and contacts, someone they could parade before a client during a presentation. That's when Malcom had seen her, over five years ago. Less than a year later— at his insistence—she had been put in sole charge of his account. Plus, he had directed other companies her way, especially ones he did business with. Within three years, she controlled several of the agency's largest accounts. Naturally, they had promoted her to a vice-president.

She let her gaze run lightly over his face, taking in the broad, square jaw, the jutting chin with its dimpled cleft, the deep set of his gray eyes, and most of all the power that was so indelibly stamped in every line. Gratitude, admiration, respect—she felt all those things . . . as well as a trace of resentment.

"Have dinner with me Monday night." The invitation fell somewhere between a demand and command.

"Have lunch with me on Tuesday."

"Have you already made plans for Monday evening?"

"Yes," she lied.

"No, you haven't. I had your secretary check when I called this afternoon. We'll have dinner together Monday night."

"We'll have lunch on Tuesday," she countered. Again that feeling of being watched returned, but she couldn't let it distract her.

"Why must we always fence over such trivial issues?" Malcom grumbled in irritation. "Why can't you simply agree to dine with me on—"

"Tuesday at lunch. We made some changes in the holiday layouts. I want to go over them with you."

The look in his gray eyes took on a wanting quality. "Do we always have to discuss business, Flame?" he asked, holding her gaze.

"You know we do, Malcom." The entire conversation was an echo of hundreds that had gone on before.

"So you say, but I'll argue the point with you further—on Tuesday," he replied, conceding to her with a final dip of his head. "I'll have Arthur pick you up at twelve-thirty sharp."

"I'll be ready."

"So will I."

Flame knew she'd be in for another contest of wills on Tuesday. And she had to admit, if only to herself, that there was a part of her that enjoyed these stimulating duels of theirs—and Malcom's always challenging company.

As Ellery came walking back, that sensation of someone watching her resurfaced. "Your wine, m'lady." He offered a stemmed glass. "Chilled to precisely thirty-six degrees Centigrade. Or was it Fahrenheit?"

"There is a difference, my fine friend," she answered as she covertly scanned the room. Just as she suspected, the brown-shoed waiter with the hawk face was on the other side of the room, this time carrying a tray of hors d'oeuvres.

As she started to look away, her glance was caught and held by another man standing on the far side of the room, a shoulder negligently propped against the claret-glazed wall. His hair was as black as the tuxedo he wore. And despite the languid pose, the overall impression was that of a lean and rangy black panther, coiled energy held in check, ready to spring at a second's warning.

He stared back. She took a sip of wine without tasting it, conscious only of the unexpected quickening of her pulse. She thought she knew everyone at the party, but who was he? She looked again, telling herself that her interest was strictly curiosity—and not believing a word of it. His gaze never left her as he nodded absently to the person with him and raised a crystal tumbler to his mouth. For the first time, Flame glanced at the petite blonde beside him. Jacqui Van Cleeve, the columnist. Who was he? Obviously someone of importance.

"The man with Jacqui, Malcom, do you know him?"

But Ellery replied first. "I believe I heard someone say he's here with Miss Colton."

"Then it must be Chance Stuart," Malcom concluded, still trying to locate the pair.

"I think I've heard that name." But Flame couldn't remember where or why.

"I should think so," Malcom declared. "In the last ten years, Chancellor Stuart has become one of the largest land developers in the country. He has an uncanny knack for being at the right place at the right time." His expression grew thoughtful. "He's building that new resort complex in Tahoe. I wonder what he's doing in San Francisco."

"I expect that is precisely what darling Jacqui is trying to find out," Ellery surmised.

"My reason for coming here is hardly a secret, Miss Van Cleeve." Chance Stuart let his glance slide briefly to the persistent blonde, recalling Lucianna's warning that the woman was known for three things: her sharp eyes, her sharp nose, and her sharp tongue. He had to agree—everything about her was pointed, including her questions.

"Call me Jacqui," she invited. "Everyone does."

"Then let me explain again, Jacqui. I was on my way to Tahoe to check on my project there when Lucianna mentioned she was coming to San Francisco. I suggested she fly with me since it wasn't that much out of my way."

"Then you aren't looking for more property?"

"I'm not here for that purpose, but I'm always looking." He absently swirled the Chivas in his glass, listening to the melodic clink of the ice cubes against the crystal sides. "If you were on vacation and a hot story landed in your lap, would you ignore it?"

"No," she admitted.

"Need I say more?" He lifted the glass to his mouth and tipped it, letting the cold scotch trickle and burn down his throat.

"You've known Miss Colton for some time, haven't you?"

"A long time, yes." He lowered the tumbler, his glance automatically straying to the stunning redhead across the room. She had stirred his interest from the moment she'd walked into the room with a stride that had in it the faintest hint of a swagger, with a quick rhythm that synchronized and turned graceful the supple movement of her body. And her shoulders, wide and straight, had been presented squarely in a manner that flaunted her serene confidence. She was a woman all the way through—all lace and legs.

"Would it be safe to guess that your on-again, off-again romance with Miss Colton is back on again?" the columnist queried slyly.

"I hate to disillusion you, Jacqui, but all this on-and-off business is the product of your profession. Over the years, our relationship has never changed."

"I suppose you're going to try to convince me that you're just good friends." She openly mocked the cliché.

"It doesn't make good press, does it?"

"Not if it's true."

Ignoring that, Chance raised his glass and gestured toward the far side of the room. "Isn't that Malcom Powell?"

All the photographs he'd seen of the august lion of the retail world had depicted a somewhat stout and stern man. In person, he had a commanding presence, physically vigorous and trim despite that barrel chest.

"Yes, that's Malcom," the Van Cleeve woman confirmed. "Truthfully, I didn't expect to see him here. Diedre told me that he'd returned from a business trip only last night."

"Diedre?" He arched her a questioning look.

"His wife."

"Is that her?" His gaze sharpened on the pair, irritation flickering through him.

"No, that's Flame—Flame Bennett." During the brief pause that followed, Chance could feel the columnist carefully monitoring his reaction. "Gorgeous, isn't she?"

"Definitely." He continued to lounge against the wall, for the moment content to enjoy his unobstructed view of the woman so aptly named Flame, conscious of the hot, smooth feeling that flowed through him.

"Aren't you going to ask me about her?" The instant the faintly challenging question came out of Jacqui Van Cleeve's mouth, Chance knew she'd give him a complete rundown on Flame Bennett. She made it her business to collect every scrap of information—whether rumor or fact—on every person remotely important. And when a person had that much information, they could never resist sharing it.

"I was always told it wasn't polite for a gentleman to ask questions about a lady," he countered smoothly.

Her short laugh had a harsh and grating ring to it. "I have heard you accused of many things, Chance Stuart, but being a gentleman was never one of them. Granted you have all the manners, the polish, the clothes of one, but proper, you're not. You're too damned daring. Nobody's sure what you're going to do next and you move too fast. That's why you make such excellent copy."

"I'll take that as a compliment."

Again he felt the speculation in her study of him. "It will be interesting to see how you fare with Flame."

"Why do you say that?" He glanced at her curiously.

"Because . . . she's a woman of such contrasts." Her attention swung away from him, centering on the subject of their discussion. "She can be as fiery as the red of her hair—or as cool as the green of her eyes—and that quickly, too. I suppose that's part of the fatal attraction she has for men. You always see them fluttering around her like moths. She lets them get only so close and no closer."

"Why?"

"I'm not sure, but no man seems to last with her. It isn't even a case of off with the old and on with the new. No one sticks around long enough to be old. But there again you have the contrast. These romantic flings of hers are too few and far between. Therefore, you can't call her wild. Her behavior is definitely unconventional." After a fractional hesitation, she added, "Of course she was married briefly about nine years ago. Supposedly, it was one of those young marriages that simply didn't work. At least that was the official line at the time."

"And unofficially?"

"Truthfully? I never heard anything to make me think otherwise," the Van Cleeve woman admitted. "A failed marriage has made more than one woman wary of trying again. It could be as simple as that or it could be her career."

"What does she do?" Currently, careers were fashionable among socialites. But in his experience, Chance had found that the women were rarely more than dilettantes, dabbling in photography or modeling, owning art galleries, antique stores, or exclusive little dress shops invariably managed by someone else.

"Flame's a vice-president with the Boland and Hayes advertising firm," she replied, then added, "Of course, it's common knowledge that she has to work for a living. Even though she comes from one of San Francisco's founding families, there is little or no money left. No doubt a humbling experience, but I can assure you she's never suffered any hardship as a result. Like anywhere else, it pays to know the right people."

"Like Malcom Powell," Chance guessed.

"She handles his advertising account personally. And—there's been a lot of speculation lately about what else she might handle *personally* for him."

He detected something in her voice that raised his suspicions: "You don't believe it."

"No," she admitted. "By the same token, I don't believe Diedre when she insists that Malcom takes a fatherly interest in Flame. But what else can a wife of thirty-five years say? Believe me, if a father eyed his daughter the way he does Flame, he'd be subject to arrest. He wants her, but he hasn't had her."

"How can you be so sure?"

"If Flame was having an affair with him, she wouldn't try to hide it. It isn't her style." Jacqui frowned, as if aware she wasn't making herself clear. "I guess what I'm trying to say is—if Flame cared enough to get involved with a married man, then she wouldn't let herself feel any shame or guilt."

"What about the other man with her? Is he her latest fling?"

"Ellery Dorn? Hardly." She laughed, then explained. "Ellery is every married woman's choice for a walker when her husband isn't available. He's handsome, witty, charming—and gay. Surprised?" She shot him a knowing glance. "Not to worry. Few people ever guess that about him. That's what makes him so ideal."

"Then he's nothing more than a safe escort." Mentally Chance filed that little piece of information away along with all the rest. The more he learned about Flame Bennett, the more intrigued he became.

"They're good friends as well. As a matter of fact, Flame is probably closer to Ellery than anyone else. Of course, he's a vice-president in the same agency, so I'm sure the fact they work together has something to do with that."

"Probably." With a little push of his shoulder, he straightened from the wall. "Speaking of walkers, Lucianna is bound to be wondering what happened to me. I enjoyed the chat, Jacqui."

"So did I. And from now on, I'll be watching your progress with more interest."

"Not too closely, I hope." He winked at her as he moved away.

WITHOUT BEING OBVIOUS, Flame watched as Chance Stuart leisurely wound his way through the guests. He was tall, taller than he'd first appeared. She found herself liking the way he moved, like an athlete, all smooth coordination and easy grace. He certainly had the body of one, wide at the shoulders and narrow at the hips, with lean, hard muscle in between.

As he drew closer, Flame was able to see clearly his face and the dark blue of his eyes. She decided it was the deep blue color that made the impact of his glance so much like a jolt of electricity. His features could have been hammered out of bronze, beaten smooth without taking anything away from the ruggedness of his cheeks or the hard break of his jaw. But there was something else there too—some indefinable quality that stamped him as dangerous, a man who could smile and draw a throaty groan from every woman in the room.

With a faint start, she noticed that he was angling away from her. He wasn't coming over. She hadn't realized how much she'd anticipated meeting him until she felt the sudden sinking disappointment. She struggled to contain it, feeling foolish and a little conceited that she'd taken it for granted that Chance Stuart would seek her out. She realized that she'd read too much into the eye contact, fallen victim to the "across-a-crowded-room" syndrome. It would have been laughable if she didn't feel so let down.

But there wasn't time to dwell on it as she encountered a glare from Diedre Powell. Such looks were nothing new. Most wives regarded her as a threat to their marriages, especially older women like Diedre Powell with husbands who had a history of having affairs on the side.

And like most, Diedre had kept her marriage intact by smiling and looking the other way—until one day she'd seen her reflection in the mirror and fear had set in. Now her skin was pulled smooth, the chin tucked, the jowls gone, the eyelids lifted, her Chanel gown of blue silk crepe flowing over a figure that had regained much of its former trimness. And her hair was once again a lustrous brown—except for the shock of white that streaked away from her forehead.

The woman was living in her own private hell. Flame wondered if Malcom knew it—and if he did, did he understand? She doubted it. That hungry, possessive look in his eyes plainly stated that he wanted her, but she also knew that didn't mean he wanted a divorce. In his mind, there was no correlation between the two.

"There you are, Malcom." Diedre glided over to them, a smile fixed brightly in place, the Powell sapphires glittering at her throat and ears. "Sid Rayburn was looking for you a minute ago—something about a meeting at the yacht club on Thursday?"

"Yes, I need to get together with him. Where is he?" With a lift of his head, he glanced beyond her to scan the room.

"When I saw him last, he was over by the dining room." She waved a beringed hand in its direction.

As Malcom moved away, he briefly touched his wife's shoulder in passing. She turned to Flame, a faintly triumphant gleam in her eyes. "It's good to see you again, Flame. How have you been?"

"Busy . . . as usual," she replied evenly, aware that they were both going through the motions of polite chatter, and playing their own separate games of pretend.

"So I've heard." Just for an instant she showed her claws, then quickly sheathed them to smile pleasantly.

A few years ago, Diedre's attitude would have bothered her, but not anymore. Her skin had thickened. Wives invariably blamed her if their husbands started paying attention to her, with or without encouragement. She supposed it was easier to blame the so-called other woman than it was to admit that the fault belonged with the husband and his roving eye. It wasn't fair, but what was in this life?

From the Garden Room, a musical laugh broke above the chatter of voices. The sound drew Diedre Powell's glance. "I do believe that's Margo with Miss Colton. We've been missing each other all evening." She started to walk by Flame, then paused and laid a hand on her arm, her fingers closing briefly in what passed for an affectionate squeeze, and smiled at Ellery. "You really should see that Flame doesn't work so hard."

Then she was gone, leaving the cloying scent of Giorgio in her wake. "Such caring, such concern. Amazing, isn't it?" Ellery declared in mock admiration. "I do enjoy intimate little gatherings like these, don't you? As a matter of fact, I enjoy them so much that I think I need something stronger to drink than this wine. How about you?"

"I'm fine, really I am," she insisted, and smiled as she lifted her glass to take another sip of the dry chardonnay.

"If you say so." He shrugged and went off in search of the bar.

Her gaze followed the slim set of his shoulders halfway across the room, then wandered absently to the dimly lit Garden Room beyond the set of French doors. Chance Stuart stepped through the opening, his gaze making a leisurely sweep of the room in front of him. For an instant, everything inside her went still. As yet, he hadn't noticed her standing to his left and Flame took advantage of it to study the strong, rakish lines of his face and the ebony sheen of his hair, clipped close as if to curb its unruly tendencies. There was a sleekness about him—a raciness that convinced Flame he should be wearing a warning label advising the unwary that here was a man highly dangerous to the senses.

Still perusing the other guests, he reached inside his black evening jacket and took a gold cigarette case from the inner breast pocket. He flipped it open, then hesitated, his head turning slightly as his glance swung directly to her.

"Cigarette?" He held out the case to her.

"Thank you, but I don't smoke." She accompanied the assertion with a slight shake of her head in refusal.

A faint smile tugged at the corners of his mouth. "Do you object if I do?"

"Not at all." With a brief movement of her hand, Flame indicated the crystal ashtray on the side table near her.

She watched his strong, tanned fingers as they removed a cigarette from the case and carried it to his lips, their line as masculine and well defined as the rest of him. A light flared, then disappeared behind his cupped hand as he bent his head, touching the cigarette to the flame. A thin trail of smoke curled upward. Flame followed it and again encountered the lazy regard of his blue eyes, all warm and glinting with male appreciation.

"I don't believe we've been introduced." He wandered over, a hint of a smile now deepening the creases in his lean cheeks. "I'm Chance Stuart."

"I know," she admitted and smiled back, aware of the unexpected—and almost forgotten—sensation of heat coiling through her body. It had been a long time since any man had had that effect on her.

An eyebrow lifted. "Then you have the advantage on me." His voice was pitched low, a hint of a drawl in its delivery.

"From what I've heard about you, Mr. Stuart, that seldom happens," she said, softening the slightly pointed remark with a smile and adding, "I'm Flame Bennett."

"Flame," he said, as if testing the sound of it, his glance sliding to the fiery gold of her hair. "That's much more original than Red."

"Perhaps, like you, Mr. Stuart, I'm an original."

"I won't disagree with that. In fact, it's the first thing I noticed about you." Chance had the distinct feeling that his every remark, his every look was being weighed by her. However receptive she appeared to be to him—and she was— her guard remained up, a guard apparently few men had ever penetrated. He thought back to Jacqui Van Cleeve's comment about Flame and Malcom Powell. Powell was a man who always got what he wanted, yet this woman had successfully resisted him.

"Really, that's the first thing you noticed about me?" A smile played at the corners of her mouth, drawing his attention to her lips, soft and full at the centers yet strong. "And what was the second?" There was a hint of challenge in her question.

"The second wasn't so much noticing as it was recognizing that I wanted to see more of you."

Her knowing look simultaneously taunted and encouraged him as she laughed softly. "I do believe you're making a pass at me, Mr. Stuart."

"No," he denied, "I'm merely stating my intentions. And the name is Chance."

He detected the faint break in her poise, a break that allowed him to see the pleased look that flared in her eyes, welcoming his interest before her long lashes veiled it. "Your reputation is obviously well earned. You do move fast, don't you, ... Chance?" She hesitated deliberately over the use of his given name, setting it apart and letting an added warmth invade her voice.

"Am I moving too fast for you?"

"That's a very leading question," she replied, deftly parrying it without committing herself to anything, although a definite interest remained in her eyes.

"That's why I asked it." He smiled, his eyes glinting with a wickedly mocking light.

"Will you be staying in San Francisco long?"

"Not this time. I have to fly out first thing in the morning." Chance regretted that as he studied the tumble of red-gold hair that framed her face in a mass of rippling waves. On its own, the color was striking enough, but it was made more so by the ivory fairness of her complexion. He wondered if her skin would be as smooth to the touch as it looked. He let his glance stray to the lace top of her dress, ashimmer with black seed pearls sewn onto its scrolling pattern. Here and there the fine mesh revealed a discreet hint of flesh. "I like your dress." Almost absently he trailed the tip of his finger down a long sleeve, feeling the heat from her body—and the sudden tension that claimed her. He lifted his glance to her eyes. They were alive to him, returning his look measure for measure. "I wonder what it is about black lace that stirs a man's blood?" he mused aloud.

"I should think you'd be able to answer that question more easily than I could since you are very definitely a man."

"You noticed."

She laughed softly. "Along with every other female in this room."

"Excuse me, sir." A waiter intruded. "You are Mr. Stuart, aren't you?"

"Yes." He reached over and stubbed his cigarette out in the crystal ashtray.

"You have a call, sir. There's a telephone in the reception hall." The man stepped back, still keeping his gaze downcast. "If you would follow me."

Chance's gaze ran briefly to Flame. "You will excuse me."

"Of course," she said, with just a hint of regret in her smile.

With a nod, he signaled to the waiter to lead the way. As they set out, Chance tried to think who would be calling him—especially here. He hadn't left word where he could be reached when he'd left the hotel. But Sam could have tracked him down.

Sam Weber carried the title of senior vice-president in the Stuart Corporation, but his role was much larger than even the title implied. Sam Weber was his right arm, his detail man, his backup—just as he'd been when they'd served together in Nam, then later in college and finally in business. Chance made the deals and Sam pulled the loose ends together.

It had to be Sam calling him. But if it was Sam, then something had gone wrong.

The waiter halted short of the hall's square arch and gestured at the contemporary side table standing against the wall to the right of the room's entrance. "The telephone, sir."

Chance immediately spotted the brown receiver lying on the table next to the telephone and nodded briefly to the waiter. Dodging the overhanging boughs of the bittersweet branches that sprouted from the celadon vase in the center of the room, he walked over and picked up the receiver. "Hello—"

Before he could identify himself, a voice on the other end of the line broke in. "It certainly took you long enough, Stuart."

Chance stiffened, instantly recognizing that distinctive, raspy-edged voice that carried both the sound and the sting of whiskey, its tone as critical and malevolent as always. "How are you, Hattie?" he murmured tightly, feeling the old slow burn of anger and bitter resentment. He had stopped calling her *Aunt* Hattie nearly thirty years ago.

"Obviously still alive," came the challenging retort. Without any effort, he had a mental picture of her standing before him, gnarled fingers clutching the gold head of her cane, black eyes gleaming with hatred, white hair curling about a face lined by years of embitterment. Not once could he remember Hattie smiling at him—or even looking at him with anything that passed for approval. "I'm at your hotel," she announced. "I'll expect you here in precisely thirty minutes."

The imperious demand was followed by a sharp click as the line went dead. For an instant, Chance remained motionless, frozen by the icy rage that swept through him. Then he quickly hit the telephone's disconnect switch, listened for the dial tone, and punched the numbers to Sam's private line.

The call was answered on the first ring. "Yeah, this is Sam. What have you got?"

"Sam, it's Chance."

"Chance." The surprise in his voice was obvious. "I was going to try to reach you as soon as I heard from—"

"Hattie just called me. She's here in San Francisco."

"So that's where she went," Sam murmured, the familiar loud squeak of his office chair coming over the line as he leaned back in it.

"What's going on out there?" Chance demanded.

"That's what I'm trying to find out," Sam replied, then sighed heavily. "I know she had a meeting with old Ben Canon this morning. She was closeted in his law office for about two hours. When her driver came to pick her up and take her back to Morgan's Walk, he was told she'd taken a cab to the airport. We've been checking the passenger lists of every flight that went out of Tulsa today." There was a slight pause. "I guess I don't have to worry about that anymore."

"How did she know where I am?" Chance frowned, giving voice to the questions going around in his head. "And—why would she want to see me?"

"And what's her meeting with Canon got to do with this trip?" Sam added. "Chance, I don't like the sound of it. I'd like to believe that maybe she finally wants to make peace, but I can't buy it."

"Neither can I." A grimness settled through him. "It could be Canon found out that I own the holding company that just bought up the Turner land."

"It would take a corporate genius to unravel that ownership and trace it back to you. Ben's shrewd, but his knowledge of corporate law is as antiquated as he is."

Chance couldn't disagree with that. "There's no point in speculating why she's here. I'll know firsthand in another twenty-five minutes," he said, checking his watch.

"Call me back as soon as you can."

"I will."

Hearing the click on the other end that signaled the breaking of the connection, Sam Weber slowly returned the receiver to its cradle, then leaned back in his swivel chair, ignoring its protesting squeak as he rubbed a hand across his mouth in troubled thoughtfulness.

"Well . . . where is she?"

Startled by the prodding question, he shot a glance at the apple-cheeked woman seated across the desk from him. For an instant, he'd forgotten that he wasn't alone. A smile pulled at one corner of his mouth as he realized that he could always count on Molly Malone, Chance's executive secretary and staunchest supporter, to remind him otherwise.

With a shift of his weight, Sam tipped the chair forward and lowered his hand. "In San Francisco."

"What? Why?" A rare scowl marred features that were inherently jovial in expression. Not that Sam had ever been fooled by her plump and jolly look. Behind those spaniel brown eyes was a mind as keen as a newly stropped razor. There were few who could ever put anything over on Molly. If she had any blind spot, it was Chance. She doted on him like a mother—and frequently pointed with pride to the strands of gray in her nut-brown hair, claiming that he had given her every one of them. "What's she doing there?"

"That's what I'd like to know." Sam pushed a wayward lock of his sandy hair off his forehead, combing it back with his fingers. But, like the rest of his cowlicks, it refused to be tamed and quickly fell back. "She called Chance and said she wanted to meet with him. He's on his way to see her now."

"That—I hesitate to even call that mean old biddy a woman. It's an insult to my gender," Molly declared huffily. "But you mark my words, she's up to something."

"I agree." Absently, he gazed at the framed photographs of his wife and children that cluttered his desk. "But what?"

Shortly after Chance left, Ellery strolled back. "I'm not going to ask if you missed me. I noticed you had company. Could it be that the inimitable Chance Stuart is responsible for the glow you're now wearing?" he murmured, raising an eyebrow. "Talk about 'only having eyes for each other.' "

"Must you always exaggerate, Ellery?" In truth she did feel passionately alive, but she hadn't realized it showed.

"Was I? You mean you weren't at all attracted to him?"

"Will you stop trying to put words in my mouth—my impossible friend!"

Flame demanded with affection. "I found him very fascinating and, at the moment, that's all there is to it."

"If you say so."

"I do." Smiling, Flame tried to keep an eye on the entrance to the sitting room, certain Chance would be returning any minute.

But her view of the archway was unexpectedly blocked by Lucianna Colton when she emerged from the Garden Room, surrounded by her coterie of admirers. She paused, looking about the room as if trying to locate someone. "I know Chance was here only a moment ago," she declared to no one in particular, then swung around to face Flame, her dark eyes piercing despite the smile on her lips. "Wasn't he talking to you a moment ago?"

Before Flame could say that he'd been called to the phone, Chance appeared in the doorway. "There he is, Lucianna." Pamela DeBorg drew the soprano's attention away from Flame.

His moving glance sought her out, lingered briefly, then shifted to Lucianna as she crossed the room to meet him. Reluctantly, Flame watched as Chance maneuvered Lucianna away from the others and spoke to her privately. She stared at the two dark heads bent so closely together. Lucianna smiled and nodded agreement to something Chance said, then reached up and lightly stroked her fingers down his strong jaw—as if it was her right.

When the couple rejoined the other guests, his hand moved across Lucianna's back-plunging gown and hooked itself to the side of her waist with the ease of long familiarity. Seeing that, Flame wondered if he'd meant any of what he'd said to her. Maybe it had all been a game to him, a way to pass the time. She didn't want to believe that, yet it seemed all too possible now. Perhaps her ego deserved it. There was one certainty, however, the pleasure she'd felt earlier was gone.

Dimly she heard them offer parting comments to their hosts. When someone protested that it was much too early for them to leave, Chance replied, "For you, perhaps, but you have to remember Lucianna is still on New York time. She has rehearsals tomorrow. And I know her. If she stays much longer, she'll talk herself hoarse. We can't have that."

There was one moment before they left when his eyes briefly locked with hers. But this time, Flame wasn't so foolish as to read something significant into it.

She drank the last of her wine and set the empty glass on the tray of a passing waiter. As she started to turn to Ellery, she noticed Diedre Powell looking her way. No doubt Malcom was somewhere in the vicinity, she thought, and sighed inwardly.

"Let's leave, shall we. It's been a long day and I'm tired." Oddly enough, it was true. She felt drained, physically and emotionally.

Ellery seemed about to make one of his cuttingly astute observations, then appeared to think better of it. "Yes, it has been a long day," he agreed. "Why don't you make our apologies to the DeBorgs while I get the car."

"All right," she smiled, a trace of weariness showing.

"I'll pick you up in the front of the building in, say . . ." He turned back the cuff of his jacket sleeve to look at his watch, then hesitated, his glance darting to something on the floor near her feet. "Is that slip of paper yours?"

"What paper?" Flame stepped back as Ellery reached down and picked up the square of paper folded neatly in half.

He flipped it open. "How cryptic," he murmured, an eyebrow arching.

"What is it?"

He hesitated, then handed it to her. "Perhaps it is yours after all."

"Now who's being cryptic?" she chided, then looked at the paper, tensing when she read the hastily scrawled message inside: *Stay away from him!*

"Short and sweet, isn't it?" Ellery murmured.

"Very," Flame agreed tightly and shot a sharp glance in Diedre Powell's direction. Yet it seemed too childish, even for her. But if not her, then who?

"I'm sorry." Concern darkened Ellery's eyes. "I shouldn't have let you see it."

"It doesn't matter." She closed her fingers around the paper, crumpling it into the palm of her hand. "Sticks and stones, Ellery, sticks and stones."

"Of course."

But both knew it was a child's cry. An adult knew better.

3

AS THE LIMOUSINE PULLED away from the curb, Chance gazed at the mist swirling outside the tinted windows and continued to puzzle over Hattie's unexpected arrival. There was no logical reason for her to fly halfway across the continent. It wasn't to see him. The Hattie Morgan he knew would rather see him in hell first.

A soft sigh was followed by a stir of movement next to him as Lucianna settled back against the plush velour seat. "I'm glad we were able to slip away from the party early, Chance." She reached for his hand, sliding her palm over his and lacing their fingers together. "Those affairs can be so tiring."

"Especially the endless compliments." He sent her an amused look.

"Not that." She poked at his arm in playful punishment. "That's the one part I like."

"That's what I thought, my prima donna."

She smiled and let that go, her expression turning thoughtful as she tilted her head back, resting it against the seat and exposing the long, creamy arch of her throat. "It's playing the role of the prima donna that's so tiring sometimes. You not only have to dress the part, but you must act it too—always pleasant, always smiling, pretending to be friendly, but never too friendly or you'll lose your mystique. But above all, a prima donna must be aloof to criticism. You have to smile and never let them see how it cuts you."

"You do it well." Chance studied the mask of self-assurance and confidence that had become a permanent part of her. There was little resemblance between the woman beside him and the hillbilly girl from the mountains of Arkansas he'd met for the first time fifteen years ago singing in a smoky piano bar—the same girl whose pastor once claimed was an angel singing in his church choir.

But she'd left all that behind long ago—along with the thick rural accent and the unglamorous name of Lucy Kowalski. Today few would guess at her background—as few guessed at his.

"Truthfully—" Sighing, she kicked off her satin pumps dyed to match the scarlet of her dress. "—I'm tired of smiling. I don't know which aches more— my cheeks or my feet." She turned her head to look at him, a coy appeal in her dark eyes. "Will you rub them for me?"

"Your cheeks?" Chance smiled, deliberately misunderstanding.

"What a stimulating thought, darling." She slipped her hand free and lightly stroked his cheek. "Why don't you start with my feet and work your way up?" she suggested and curled her legs under her to kneel on the seat cushion facing him. "That's what you used to do. Remember?"

"You never let me forget." But he didn't object as she shifted to recline lengthwise on the passenger seat and rested a stockinged foot on his thigh. Automatically he cupped his hands around it and began gently kneading its sole and running his thumb along its arch.

A low moan of pleasure came from her throat. "Mmmm, that feels so good, Chance." He smiled and said nothing. For minutes there was only silence. Then Lucianna murmured, "Was it nine or ten years ago that you pulled off your first really important deal—the one that netted you more than a million dollars?"

"Nearly ten." He lifted her foot off his thigh and placed it on the seat. Obligingly she raised her other foot for him to rub.

"I tried to be happy for you. In a way, I was." Her shoulders lifted in a vague shrug. "But I hated you, too. You were succeeding and I wasn't."

"I know." They'd gone their separate ways after that. No longer lovers, and jealousy straining even their friendship.

"Now I've made it, too." Satisfaction riddled her voice. "Chauffeured limousines, sable coats, designer gowns, my own personal hairdresser, everything first class—all the accoutrements of success are mine. I'm thirty-five years old. Thankfully, that's young for an opera singer. My voice will be good for another fifteen years—longer if I'm careful. But, do you know what's funny, Chance? I have everything I've ever wanted, yet, being with you again, I realize how lonely I've been."

"Lonely?" He arched her a skeptical look. "With your traveling entourage of maids, hairdressers, and accompanists? Impossible."

"It's true. I'm not close to them like I am to you. We should get married, Chance."

His thumb paused in midstroke halfway down her foot. Then he ran it the rest of the way to her heel. "And do what? Meet each other in airports? You know how much I travel. And you said you were booked for—what?—over a hundred performances next year alone. That wouldn't be much of a marriage, would it?"

"But don't you see, Chance, you understand how much this means to me. If I married anyone else, he would object to all the traveling I have to do. Maybe not in the beginning, but in time he would. I've seen it happen with too many other singers, male or female. But you wouldn't mind. You have to admit, Chance, that we are good for each other."

"You don't really want to marry me, Lucianna." But he understood what she meant. Over the years they had become comfortable with each other—the way two old friends could be. They slipped in and out of the roles of lovers because it was easy. He knew he could find comfort and affection in her arms—with no demands from her, no strings, no expectations to be fulfilled. "We know each other too well."

"Is that bad?" she chided. Yet the very absence of any hurt in her voice proved to him that he was right in what he said. "We are a lot alike, you and I."

"Be honest, Lucianna. Do you really want a husband who knew you when you were Lucy Kowalski, a nobody from nowhere with only pride and ambition to her name? We both started at the bottom and clawed our way to the top. We aren't the same people anymore. We've put all that behind us. I don't want to be reminded of it every morning. I don't think you do either."

"I couldn't stand it." Her voice vibrated with feeling as she turned her head away, presenting him with the power of her profile. "Although, it did sound like a good idea," she added, a little wistfully.

Looking at her and feeling the ease of friendship, he thought of Flame, the intriguing green of her eyes, the sculptured bones of her face, and the aloof calm of self-control, but, beneath, was an untapped well of emotion. She was a woman of strong will, perhaps even stronger than his own. That alone was a challenge to him, but that alone didn't explain her attraction for him, an attraction that had something to do with the awareness that lay between them. The few minutes he'd spent with her, she'd stimulated more than his desire.

Then he'd gotten the phone call from Hattie. What the hell did she want? A troubled frown darkened his expression.

The limousine made a wide turn into the private cul-de-sac of the hotel's entrance, its headlights piercing the wispy white fog. Roused from his thoughts, Chance gave Lucianna's silk-clad foot one last kneading squeeze and swung it off his leg. "Better put your shoes on. We're here."

"Must I?" Again there was that petulant note in her voice, but when Lucianna stepped from the limousine, her feet were once again wedged in red pumps.

Their individual suites were located on opposite ends of the same floor. When they emerged from the elevator, Lucianna paused, angling her body toward him and idly running her fingers up the edge of his jacket lapel, her dark eyes bold with invitation. "This business meeting of yours can't take much more than an hour, can it? I have a magnum of Taittinger's chilling in my room."

Chance let his gaze linger on the pouting fullness of her lips. She was a sensual woman, practiced in pleasing him. Two hours ago—maybe even less—it would have been a foregone conclusion that he would spend a satisfying hour or two in her bed. But he couldn't summon any interest in the thought now.

"Another time," he suggested.

A hint of regret was in her smile, yet her look was thoughtful. "There always is with us, isn't there?"

"Yes," Chance agreed, recognizing that each time they parted it was with the certain knowledge that they would meet somewhere again, sometimes by design, sometimes not.

"Till then." She rose up to kiss him, old patterns reasserting themselves in the warmly delving contact. Chance responded automatically, his mind preoccupied with his impending meeting with Hattie.

The instant he turned from Lucianna to walk down the corridor to his suite, he forgot her, his thoughts centering wholly on Hattie Morgan, dominating them as she had once dominated him. But no more. That had ended long ago.

Or had it? A wry smile tugged at the corners of his mouth as he realized that again she had commanded him to appear and he had obeyed the summons. This time, however, it had been voluntary. He had to find out what had brought her to San Francisco. He'd always believed that nothing short of death would ever persuade her to leave Morgan's Walk. Obviously he was wrong.

He inserted the key in the lock and gave it a turn. When he opened the door, he heard the soft music playing in the background, the soothing symphony of strings, like the lights left burning in the sitting room, courtesy of the night chambermaid. Stepping inside, Chance closed the door behind him and started to slip the room key into his pocket, then checked the movement.

Hattie sat in the room's wing chair, facing the door—and Chance. His glance skimmed her, taking in the mink-trimmed traveling suit from another era and the sensible low-heeled shoes on her feet. The blue-white of her short hair lay in soft waves about her face. At first glance, she looked like everybody's favorite aunt, but a closer look revealed the stiffness of her spine, the unbending set of her shoulders, and the gloved hand that gripped the handle of her cane like a royal scepter.

"You're late." It was more a condemnation than disapproval that threaded through her husky voice.

"So I am." A muscle flexed along his jaw as Chance remembered the eight-year-old boy who had once winced from the lash of her tongue, confused by the venom in it and the hatred that burned so blackly in her eyes. He glanced at the companion chair, angled to face Hattie's, then moved away from it, walking over to the suite's small bar. "It's obvious I'll need to have a talk with the concierge about letting strange women into my room." He picked up a decanter of brandy and splashed some in a snifter. "How did you manage it, Hattie? Did you convince him you were my sweet old aunt?" Chance mocked cynically as he scooped up the glass, cradling its round bowl in his hand.

"It was much simpler than that," she retorted. "I merely bribed the chambermaid to let me in. I've never had to resort to lies to get what I want. I'm not a Stuart."

He smiled at the gibe, feeling no amusement at all, only a cold anger as he wandered over to stand nearer to the room's center. "You have yet to tell me, Hattie: to what do I owe the displeasure of your visit?"

With satisfaction, he watched her lips tighten into an even thinner line. "You're very confident, aren't you?" she observed. "You think I have no choice but to leave Morgan's Walk to you."

"It galls you, doesn't it?—the thought of Morgan's Walk passing into the hands of a Stuart. But you're bound by the conditions set down in your own inheritance of the land. On your death, it must pass to a blood relative. If there is none, then it all becomes the property of the state of Oklahoma. But that condition doesn't come into play, does it?" Chance paused, taking a short sip of the brandy and letting its smooth fire coat his tongue. "It's a pity you didn't have children of your own, Hattie. Then you wouldn't be faced with leaving it all to a nephew you despise."

But both of them knew that she had never been able to have children as a result of injuries received in a riding accident in her youth. He had a dim memory of an argument between his father and Hattie. In it, his father had shouted obscenities at her and taunted that she was only half a woman, twisted with jealousy and bitterness because she would never have a child born of her flesh. It wasn't until he was much older that he knew what that meant. By then, he'd learned that Hattie's hatred went much deeper than that.

"Morgan's Walk means nothing to you." It was more an assertion of fact than an accusation.

"You're wrong, Hattie," he said softly. "I have many memories of the place where I lived for eleven years . . . the place where my mother died. Her body wasn't even cold before you threw us out."

"I threw out a range wolf and his cub. But for my sister, I would have done it much sooner." Not a flicker of remorse showed in her expression.

"And you never let any of us forget that either. You couldn't even let my mother die in peace," Chance recalled, along with all the bitterness.

"Others may be fooled by your fine clothes and fine airs—or your beguiling smile—but not me. They may marvel at your ability to spot a weakness and move in, but I am well aware that you were born with the cunning and the instincts of a wolf. Do you think I don't know what you intend to do with Morgan's Walk? A Stuart ultimately destroys everything he gets his hands on."

Chance slowly rotated the snifter in his hand and absently studied the swirling, amber-brown liquid in the bottom. "Some things deserve to be destroyed, Hattie," he said, neither affirming nor denying her accusation. "A place that's known only hatred is one of them." Lifting the glass, he bolted down the last swallow of brandy.

Her gloved fingers tightened their grip on the cane. "Morgan's Walk will never be yours," she declared in a voice hoarse with anger.

Amused, Chance cynically arched an eyebrow in her direction. "Short of murder, there's no way you can prevent me from getting it. Like it or not, Hattie, I am your only kin—your only choice for an heir."

"Are you?" There was a smoothness, a smugness in her expression that he hadn't observed before. "I wouldn't be too sure about that."

Chance was instantly wary, and smiled to hide it. "Is there some significance to that remark?"

"Merely that you may not be my last remaining relative."

"Am I supposed to believe that?" he mocked.

"It happens to be true." Her cool statement reeked of confidence.

He studied her with a long, considering look. "It's a nice try, Hattie. But if there was anyone else, you would have mentioned them long ago."

"Perhaps I just found out about this person myself."

He didn't wholly believe her, but he didn't like the gleam in her eyes either. He started to ask how she'd found out about this so-called relative, then remembered the meeting she'd had this very morning with the crafty old lawyer Ben Canon, and checked the impulse, asking instead, "Is that what—or should I say, who?—brought you to San Francisco?

"I thought you should be the first to hear the news . . . and I wanted to see your face when I told you. You see—" She paused again for emphasis and rose from her chair, briefly leaning heavily on her cane. "—I know how much you were counting on getting Morgan's Walk. I never underestimate the greed of a Stuart. You would be wise not to underestimate the determination of a Morgan to stop you."

"I'll remember that."

When she started toward the door, Chance walked over and opened it for her. The cane ceased its rhythmic tap on the floor as she paused short of the threshold, a hard satisfaction gleaming in her eyes. "This is one time when I have truly enjoyed seeing you, Stuart."

"Then you'd better enjoy the feeling while it lasts, Hattie," he returned, his mouth forming a cold smile.

"I intend to." Again the cane swung out in advance of her stride..

In three steps she was by him and out the door. For a grim second, he stared after her stiffly erect form, then closed the door on her. Turning into the room, Chance hesitated a split second, then crossed to the telephone and dialed the number to Sam's private line.

As before, the call was answered on the first ring. "Hello."

"Chance." He identified himself and glanced briefly at the door. "It looks like we may have a problem, Sam."

"Hattie," he guessed immediately.

"Right. She claims another relative exists, one who will be the heir to Morgan's Walk."

"What?! My God, Chance, you don't think it's true, do you?"

"I don't know, but I intend to find out."

"She could be bluffing."

"I can't take that gamble, Sam. The stakes are too high," he replied grimly. "Get hold of Matt Sawyer. Tell him to drop whatever he's doing and get on this right away. If there is a second legitimate heir to Morgan's Walk, then Canon's probably the one who tracked this person down. Tell Matt to start working on that angle."

"Will do."

Chance paused briefly, then asked, "Is Molly there?"

"Sitting right here," Sam confirmed, a smile in his voice.

His own mouth curved faintly in response to the image that flashed instantly into his mind of the sweet-faced woman who, only now at fifty-five, had started to count the strands of gray in her brown hair. Widowed and childless, Molly Malone had gone to work for him nearly fifteen years ago, starting out as a part-time secretary, girl Friday, and office cleaning lady. Somewhere along the line in those first few months, she had added mothering to her other duties. She ran his office staff now, some said with an iron hand, although she was still butter in his. Time clocks meant nothing to her. She worked all hours; "Whatever it takes" was her favorite line. She *lived* the Stuart Corporation—not out of loyalty to her job but because it was his. Chance knew that. Just as he knew that no woman could be more devoted to her son than Molly was to him—even to the extent of making his enemies her own. And of them she hated Hattie most of all—almost obsessively so.

He glanced at the gold Rolex on his wrist. "It's already after midnight there in Tulsa. I suppose she stayed to find out what Hattie wanted with me."

"You got it."

"Since she's there, tell her to get on the phone and start calling all the hotels in San Francisco until she finds the one where Hattie's staying. As soon as she does, relay that information to Matt. He's bound to have an investigating firm that he works with here on the West Coast. I want to know her every move—her every contact from the time she arrived to the time she leaves."

"You don't believe that Hattie flew all the way out there just to see you, do you?" Sam declared with dawning awareness. "You think this alleged long-lost relative might live out there."

"It's a possibility we can't overlook." Without a break, Chance continued, "I'm flying out to Tahoe first thing in the morning. I'll probably be tied up most of the day with the architect and engineer going over the design problems we have on the main hotel and casino structure. I hope we won't have to make any changes that will affect the companion ski lodge and chalets. But you know how to reach me if anything comes up. Otherwise, I'll be back in Tulsa late Sunday night. Tell Matt I'll expect him in my office nine o'clock Monday morning with a full report."

"Done."

As Sam's parting "Take care" faded, Chance hung up the phone. For a moment he stood there idly studying the empty brandy glass in his other hand. Then he turned and started across the room, loosening the knot of his black tie and unfastening the collar button of his shirt as he went. At the bar, he reached for the decanter again and poured half a shot of brandy into his glass. With his fingers curved around the bowl, he picked up the snifter, then paused. Swiveling at the hips, he turned, slanting his shoulders at the wing chair that Hattie had occupied.

"You didn't really believe it would be over so easily, did you, Hattie?" he murmured. "You should have remembered the promise that eleven-year-old boy made you. Maybe you've seen the last of me, but Morgan's Walk hasn't."

THE SATIN CAFTAN WHISPERED softly about her legs as Flame wandered into the black-and-white living room of her Victorian flat, absently nursing that first cup of morning coffee in both hands. With sleepy-eyed interest, she surveyed the casually intimate grouping of furniture around the zebra-striped wool rug, the eye-catching white-on-white motif of the overstuffed sofa repeated on the cushions of the dramatic horn chairs finished in gleaming black lacquer accented with solid brass.

There was an awareness that the room's decor was a subtle reflection of her own personality, the airy and open effect of white contrasted sharply by the dynamic and sensual impact of black. And Flame also knew that the sleekly contemporary look on the inside was at odds with the ornate gingerbread trim of the building's exterior. The turn-of-the-century house had supposedly been a wedding present from a doting father to his beloved daughter, like so many others that had been built on Russian Hill, so named after a cemetery for

Russian sailors that had occupied its summit during the city's early history. Twelve years ago, the mansion's many rooms had been converted into spacious, individually owned apartments.

Looking around her, Flame realized that this flat was the one good thing that had come out of her disastrous marriage. It was hers now. Although at the time, she would have willingly given it up along with anything else just to obtain a divorce. Fortunately, that hadn't been necessary.

The buzzing ring of the doorbell cut sharply through the morning stillness. Flame frowned at the black mantel clock above the white marble fireplace. It wasn't nine o'clock yet. No one came to visit this early on a Saturday morning. Her friends knew how much she relished her weekend mornings—waking up at her leisure, dressing when she pleased, and going out if she chose. During the weekdays she adhered to a set schedule of appointments, meetings, and business luncheons, but the weekends when she wasn't working on a rush campaign or on call, she spent strictly on impulse, shopping or sailing with friends, occasionally taking in an exhibit she wanted to see or simply lolling around the apartment and catching up on current novels. The evenings were different, usually with some private dinner party, social function, or benefit interspersed with concerts and theater performances.

When the buzzer rang again, more strident in its summons the second time, Flame set her cup down on the glass top of the black lacquer and brass occasional table and ran lightly from the living room into the foyer, her bare feet making little sound on the honey-colored parquet flooring. Out of habit, she glanced through the front door's peephole. On the other side stood an elderly lady, a pillbox hat of loden green perched atop a soft cloud of white hair. Despite the slight distortion from the thick glass, Flame was certain she didn't know the woman.

The woman started to ring the doorbell a third time. Flame pushed the tousled mass of her hair away from her face with a combing rake of her fingers and began unfastening the series of security locks and chains. In the midst of the third ring, she swung the heavy oak door open.

"Yes?" She glanced expectantly at the elderly stranger, certain she had come to the wrong address. Yet the avid stare from the elderly woman's brightly black eyes inspected every detail of her appearance, skipping over the purple and pink of her caftan to center on her hair. "Were you looking for someone?" she prompted when the silence threatened to lengthen.

For an instant she doubted the woman had heard her and briefly wondered if she might be deaf. Then an awareness seemed to enter the woman's expression.

"Forgive me for staring," she said, a pleasant huskiness in her voice. "But— your hair, it's exactly the same shade of strawberry blond as Kell Morgan's. His portrait hangs over the fireplace in the library."

"Who are you?" she challenged, a fine tension rippling through her as she suddenly realized why those eyes looked familiar. Her father's had been just as brilliantly black, always shining with life. But that was impossible. She didn't have any family left—no aunts, no uncles, no cousins.

"I'm Harriet Fay Morgan," she announced, a pleased smile curving her lips and emphasizing the tiny fracture lines that aged the parchmentlike fineness of her skin. "And you are undoubtedly Margaret Rose Morgan."

"Bennett." The correction was an automatic response.

"You're married?" A pepper gray eyebrow lifted in sharp question.

"Divorced."

"Yes, yes, I remember now. Ben told me that." Irritation briefly darkened her expression at the momentary memory lapse. And that hint of vulnerability prompted Flame to notice that—for all the woman's alertness—she had to be in her late seventies or early eighties . . . too old to be made to stand outside, especially when there were a dozen questions Flame wanted to ask.

"Won't you come in, Mrs. Morgan?" She swung the door open wider and stepped to one side, allowing her to pass.

"Thank you." With an unhurried dignity, the woman entered the foyer, her small shoulders square and straight beneath the jacket of her fur-trimmed suit, its cut reminiscent of a fashion popular twenty years ago. The cane seemed to serve as a prop rather than a support as she turned to Flame. "I must insist that you call me Hattie. I never married, but to be called 'Miss' at my age seems inappropriate."

"Of course." Flame led the way into the living room. "I have fresh coffee made. Would you like a cup?"

"I prefer hot tea if you don't mind."

"Not at all. Please, make yourself comfortable. I won't be a minute."

But it was closer to five minutes before Flame returned with a pot of tea, the attendant cream, sugar, and saucer of lemon as well as a teacup and saucer balanced on a tray along with a cup of coffee for herself. In her absence Hattie Morgan had enthroned herself on one of the horn chairs. Catching back a smile at the thought, Flame realized that there was a certain hauteur about Hattie that bordered on regal.

"Lemon, cream, or sugar?"

"Lemon, please," she replied, taking the delicate Sevres cup and saucer from Flame, her glance lightly sweeping the room. "This is pleasant," she observed, her attention returning to Flame as she lifted the dainty cup from its saucer. "Of course, it's nothing at all like Morgan's Walk."

"Morgan's Walk is your home?"

"Our family home, yes. It's stood for nearly a hundred years, and, God willing, it will stand for a hundred more."

"Where is that?"

"Oklahoma, about twenty minutes from Tulsa."

She volunteered no more than that, leaving Flame with the impression that Hattie was waiting for her to ask the questions. "You mentioned a man named Ben earlier. Who is he? For that matter, who's Kell Morgan?" Flame took her coffee and moved to the corner of the sofa nearest to Hattie's chair.

"Ben Canon is the family lawyer, and has been for years. It was through his efforts that I located you. And Kell Morgan"—again those bright eyes took note of the glinting red lights in Flame's hair—"was my grandfather. His brother was Christopher Morgan."

The latter was said with a sense of import, yet it meant nothing to Flame. "Should I know that name?"

"He was your great-grandfather." She sipped at her tea, eyeing Flame over the cup's golden rim. "You aren't familiar with your father's family history, are you?"

"Not very," she admitted, her frown thoughtful and wary. "All my father ever told me about his grandfather that I can remember was the story of how he'd come to San Francisco shortly before the turn of the century and fallen hopelessly in love with Helen Fleming, the daughter of one of the city's founding families. Within three months, they were married. Other than that . . ." Flame shrugged, indicating her lack of knowledge, and settled back against the sofa's plump white cushions and curled a leg underneath her. For all her relaxed poise, inside she was tense. "I know several of my friends have become deeply involved in tracing their family tree and finding out all they can about their ancestors. It's as if they must in order to have any sense of who or what they themselves are. I've never agreed with that. In my opinion, everyone has his own separate identity. Who my ancestors were or what they did has nothing to do with who I am today." But even as she made her slightly impassioned disavowal, she was aware that her own actions frequently contradicted that. Because of who her family was, she had a certain prestige. She hadn't earned it; her ancestors had. And even while a part of her resented it, she used it to open doors, to mix with the right people, and to further her own career. She stared at the coffee cooling in her cup, conscious of the silence and not feeling particularly proud of her accomplishments. "If I offended you, Hattie, I'm sorry. Obviously you share their interest in family trees or you wouldn't be here."

"Their interest, perhaps, but not for the same reason. And I'm certain we differed in our approach. You see, it was a living descendant of Christopher that I was anxious to find." But she didn't elaborate. "Believe me, that wasn't easy. Soon after Christopher Morgan left Morgan's Walk and went west all those years ago, the family lost touch with him. We couldn't even be sure he had kept the Morgan name."

"Why would he change it?" She frowned.

"Who knows?" Those sharply bright eyes never once left Flame's face, their burning intensity somehow mesmerizing. "It was hardly uncommon for a man who went west to change his name and take on a whole new identity. Frequently it was to conceal a criminal past, but sometimes it became a symbolic way to start a new life."

She understood such reasoning. After her divorce, she had elected to keep her married name, as if by doing so she was no longer a Morgan. But everyone knew she was.

"Tell me about yourself," Hattie urged. "I understand you work."

"Yes, I'm a vice-president and account executive for a national advertising company here in the city."

"A vice-president. You must be very intelligent."

Was she? Or had she finally gotten smart and stopped fighting the family name and started using it instead to get what she wanted? As a vice-president, she received an excellent salary, but even on that she wouldn't have been able to afford half of what she owned. Practically all the expensive furnishings in her flat and nearly her entire wardrobe of designer clothes she'd purchased from agency clients, but never at retail. No, she used her position, both with the company and in society, to obtain special discounts. That was the way the game was played, and she'd learned to be good at it. It was a form of urban survival today.

"It helps to know the right people, too," she replied, lifting her shoulders in an expressive shrug, a little uncomfortable with the compliment.

"I understand you are an only child."

"Yes."

"And both your parents are gone."

Flame nodded. "They were in an auto accident eleven years ago. My father was killed instantly. My mother was in a coma for several days. She died without ever regaining consciousness." After all this time, the sense of loss was still acute. Even now, she missed them. There were moments when she could almost hear her mother's laughter—and her dad's teasing voice. They had loved her. Not because of her bloodline or because she was beautiful, but for herself. Since she'd lost them, she'd learned just how rare that kind of love was.

"You and I are a lot alike, I think," Hattie observed. "We've both had to learn to be independent at an early age. My mother died a few hours after my baby sister was born. I was thirteen at the time—with a baby to take care of and a household to manage. Then I lost my father when I was nineteen. Suddenly Morgan's Walk was mine. I not only had a baby sister to raise, but an entire ranch to run."

"Morgan's Walk is a ranch?" Flame was surprised by that. "I thought it was some sort of an estate." Although what kind of estate there could be in Oklahoma, she had no idea. Certainly it had never occurred to her that it was a ranch.

"It's both. There's almost twelve hundred acres of land within its boundaries. Once it was twenty times that size, but time and circumstances have whittled away at it. Most of it is river valley, some of the lushest, greenest land you'll ever see." Where before Hattie's demeanor had been marked by a watchful reserve, there was now animation, a rapt excitement lighting her face and putting an even brighter glow in her eyes. "It's beautiful country, Margaret Rose, all rolling hills and trees unbelievably green against the blue of the sky. And the main house sits at the head of the valley. Oh, and what a house it is— three stories of brick with towering white colonnades. Your ancestor Christopher Morgan is the one who designed it before he came to California. All the bricks came from a kiln right on the property, and they used the land's red clay to make them. Wait until you see it. I know you'll love it."

"I'm sure I would." Flame smiled, touched by the woman's obvious love for her home. "Although it's not likely I will."

Hattie seemed startled by that. "Oh, but you will. You must. Morgan's Walk will be yours when I die."

For a stunned instant, Flame stared at her. "What did you say?" she managed at last, certain she had misunderstood.

"Morgan's Walk will be yours when—"

She didn't need to hear any more. "You can't mean that. You don't even know me," she protested.

"You're a Morgan. I knew that the minute I saw you. It was more than the red of your hair and the high cut of your cheekbones. It was the strength of pride and the determination to succeed that I recognized in you."

"That doesn't explain anything." She frowned. "It doesn't even make sense."

"But it does. You see, Morgan's Walk must pass to a Morgan. If there is no direct descendant, then the land becomes the property of the state. That's why it was so important that I find you. For a time I thought—" She caught herself up short, and dismissed the rest of the sentence with a shake of her head. "But I don't have to worry about that now. I found you."

It sounded logical. Almost too logical. Flame couldn't help being skeptical. People just didn't ring somebody's doorbell and announce that they were inheriting a ranch—in Oklahoma or anywhere else.

"Is this some elaborate con to get money out of me?" she demanded. "Because if it is, you're wasting your time."

"You're suspicious by nature. That's good," Hattie stated, a satisfied gleam in her eyes. "Morgan's Walk will definitely be safe in your hands. You won't let . . . anyone take it from you."

Flame caught that faint hesitation. "Is someone trying to get it from you?"

Hattie leaned forward and pushed her teacup and saucer onto the coffee table's glass top. "As I said, it's rich land. There will always be someone who wants it. People have fought over land since before the time of Moses, haven't they?" She smiled smoothly. "As for money—I won't pretend that Morgan's Walk is as prosperous as it once was. It isn't. At best, you'll receive only a small income from it after all its costs are paid. Of course, you may run into some sort of inheritance tax situation. You might want to check into that."

She kept talking as if the matter were settled. Couldn't she see how absolutely improbable it sounded? Flame tried to explain. "Hattie, I'm a city girl. I don't know the first thing about cows or ranching."

"I am eighty-one years old. You surely don't believe that I chase cows at my age. I grant you, I can still climb on a horse and ride out to look things over, but I have a foreman who oversees everything—a ranch manager, if you will. Charlie Rainwater is a good man—as honest and loyal as the day is long. You leave him in charge and you won't have a thing to worry about. In time, you'll learn from him everything you need to know. Now." She folded her hands together in a gesture that seemed to indicate it was time they moved on to more important matters. "How soon can you come to Morgan's Walk?"

That was the last question Flame expected to hear. "I don't know that I can. After all, I do have—"

"Forgive me," Hattie interrupted. "I didn't mean that you should drop everything and fly out with me today. I know that you have certain responsibilities and commitments you have to honor. But surely you can arrange to have a long weekend off and come for a visit. It's selfish, I know, but I want the chance to show Morgan's Walk to you myself."

Unwilling to commit herself, Flame said, "I'll have to check my schedule."

"You'll come," Hattie stated confidently. "You're a Morgan. And whether you want to admit it or not, your roots are buried deep in that land. It will pull you back."

"Perhaps," Flame conceded, although she personally wasn't certain she believed any of this.

With her mission complete, a few minutes later Hattie said her goodbyes and left for the airport. Flame offered to call her a cab, but Hattie said, no, she had a car and driver waiting outside for her.

Alone again, Flame returned to the living room. But the quiet of the morning was gone. In its place was a feeling of unreality—as if the last hour hadn't happened, that it had all been her imagination. Had it? No. The teapot was there on the tray next to the cup Hattie had drunk from. But that still didn't mean any of it was true. For all she knew, Hattie was just some crazy old woman. She probably didn't even own a ranch. No, it was all too farfetched.

Still . . . Flame looked around the room and felt a loneliness wash over her. It was all that talk about family. She hesitated, then walked over to the white lacquered bookcase and took down the family photo album. She hadn't looked at it in years, not since— She shook the memory aside and flipped the book open.

She smiled at the photo of a four-year-old girl, a new Easter bonnet perched atop her carroty curls, too fascinated by the shiny black of her patent leather shoes to look at the camera. Those were simpler times, happier times. She kept turning pages, pausing now and again to gaze at a snapshot of her with her mother or her father or the rare few when all three of them were in the same photo. They were all there, past Christmases and birthdays, ski vacations in the Rockies or the Sierras, sailing trips along the coast, her first dance recital, her first communion, eighth-grade graduation, dances, proms, boyfriends. And in every picture, there were smiles and laughter.

Tears welled in her eyes as she looked at the last photo. She was standing next to her father in front of a fiery red Trans-Am, a graduation present from her parents. It was jammed to the ceiling with her clothes and the thousand other things she was certain she would need at college. It hadn't mattered that she was only going across the bay to Berkeley. She had to take it all. Her father had his arm around her shoulders, laughing and hugging her close.

A tear rolled down her cheek. With the back of her hand, Flame scrubbed it away, sniffed back the runny wetness in her nose, then laughed softly, remembering the time when she'd been seven and taken a tumble on the slopes, banging her knee. She'd cried and her father had given her his handkerchief. She'd blown her nose, then asked him one of those impossible questions, "Daddy, why does my nose run every time I cry?"

He'd had an answer for her. He always did, not necessarily the correct one, but an answer just the same. "Maybe because it's sad that you got hurt."

"Then why doesn't my mouth run?" she'd wanted to know. "Isn't it sad, too?"

"Your mouth runs all the time. Jabber, jabber, jabber."

And she'd laughed and laughed. He'd always made her laugh.

A soft sigh trembled from her, wistful of that time when she'd been happy and loved . . . and so very sheltered. Although she hadn't known it at the time.

The next pages were missing, ripped from the book in a fit of wounded rage. She fingered the ragged edges of the stiff paper, not at all sorry they were gone. She didn't need photos to remind her of Rick.

The sudden loss of her parents had been a brutal shock. For days after their separate funerals, one after the other, she'd been too numb to feel anything. Then came the grief, the pain, the terrible loneliness. But more than that, she'd felt lost and alone, with no anchor and no direction. To have their love wrenched from her so suddenly had left an awful, aching void. She'd desperately needed to be loved again. She had started reaching for it, grasping for it everywhere and anywhere. On campus the talk had been that she was a little wild. Maybe it had looked that way, but she hadn't been, not really.

Then, at a frat party, she'd met Rick Bennett. That night he'd made her laugh—the way her father used to do. And he had dark eyes and dark hair, like her father. And he'd been handsome in a clean-cut all-American way that spoke of solidness, steadiness. Rick had taken her home that night, back to her sorority house, then called to say goodnight. He'd phoned the next morning, too, to tell her good morning.

Almost from the beginning, they'd been inseparable. The only thing they hadn't done together was attend the same classes. He'd been a post-graduate student in law, and she'd been only a lowly sophomore—majoring in Rick was always what she'd laughed and said then. Which had been the absolute truth.

In retrospect, it seemed appropriate that Rick had proposed to her on April Fools' Day. Of course, he had made it sound very romantic by claiming that he'd picked it because he was a fool over her. During their short engagement, he managed to pass his bar exam and persuaded Flame to introduce him to a very senior partner with one of San Francisco's most prestigious law firms, who was also a longtime friend of her family. Whether out of friendship or sympathy for Flame or an objective evaluation of his qualifications, he had subsequently invited Rick to join the firm.

Then came the wedding. Rick had insisted it be a lavish affair. Flame had argued against it. Without any family of her own, she hadn't felt right about it, but he'd urged her to remember her social position—and to be practical and think of all the wedding gifts they would receive, items they wouldn't have to buy to set up house. She could have told him that gifts of silver and Baccarat crystal would hardly be practical for a young couple, but in the end, she'd relented, and the guest list for the wedding had read like the Who's Who of San Francisco society.

On her marriage, Flame obtained absolute control of her parents' estate, which amounted to a little more than a quarter of a million dollars. The first purchase they'd made had been this pricey flat—no boxy condo in a concrete-and-glass high-rise for them. And second, they'd bought a Porsche for Rick. He'd always wanted one, and an aggressive young attorney needed to project the right image. And that image had meant clothes. Brooks Brothers suits hadn't been good enough for Rick; it had to be Cardin, Blass, and Lagerfeld.

Oddly enough, she had never minded the money they'd spent. The apartment was a good investment as well as a comfortable home. As for the car, she'd loved Rick and wanted him to have it because he'd always dreamed of owning one. And the clothes, she'd been just as guilty of wanting to wear only the best.

No, the money hadn't been their problem. As soon as they'd returned from their honeymoon in Greece, Rick had urged her to renew her family contacts and persuade some of her friends to recommend him for membership in the yacht club. Soon they were going out nearly every night—to this party or that dinner, a gallery showing or a ballet, a charity benefit or a gala opening. They'd dined only at the trendiest restaurants and partied only at the "in" spots.

In the beginning, she'd accepted his reasoning that it was important to his career for him to mix with the right people. San Francisco was full of brilliant young lawyers, but without influential contacts few of them would ever achieve their potential. And Rick had no intention of being a brilliant older lawyer still waiting to be made a partner in the firm. She'd agreed with him—and allowed him to organize her daytime activities, too—becoming involved in the "right" charities and civic organizations, lunching, playing tennis, or going shopping with wives whose friendships he wanted her to cultivate.

After seven months on that social merry-go-round, Flame had grown weary of it and rebelled. There had been some charity ball they were supposed to attend, but when Rick had come home from the office that evening, she hadn't been ready.

"Why aren't you dressed?" He looked at her with some surprise and glanced at the gold Piaget wristwatch she'd given him for Christmas. "You'd better get a move on or we'll be late."

"No, we won't." Ignoring his look of impatience, she went to him and firmly placed his hands on the back of her waist, then wound her own around his neck. "Instead of going to the ball, let's stay home and have a romantic evening together . . . just the two of us." She leaned up and nipped at his ear. "We haven't done that in a long time. And I have a bottle of Dom Perignon chilling in the fridge, along with some Beluga caviar. Later we can fix some fettucini, or maybe a steak. You slip out of that tie and I'll—"

As she started to loosen it, Rick stopped her. "I love the thought, darling, but we'll have to do it some other time. Tonight we have this charity thing. They're expecting us."

"You make it sound as if they'll cancel the ball if we don't show up. I assure you they won't," she teased with a cajoling smile. "So why don't we just skip it?"

"No." He set her away from him, a finality in his voice and his gesture that rankled.

Still Flame persisted. "Why not?"

"Because we said we'd be there and we're going."

"Rick, it's a charity ball, for heaven's sake. How many hundred functions like it have we attended these last six months? I'm tired of them. Aren't you?" She frowned.

"Whether I'm tired of them or not is immaterial," he retorted, yanking at the knot of his tie. "Affairs like this are important to me. I thought you understood that."

Stung by his tone, Flame was tempted to ask if they were more important than spending time with her, but she checked the angry impulse and turned away instead, feigning a shrug of indifference. "Then you go. I'll stay home by myself."

"Don't be ridiculous, Flame," he snapped. "You're a Morgan. You have to be there."

You're a Morgan. How many times had she heard him say that? She'd lost count, but this time, the phrase sunk in. She swung on him in full temper. "My name is Bennett. Or had you forgotten that little detail?"

He flushed guiltily. "You know what I meant."

"No." She shook her head in firm denial. "I don't think I do. Why don't you explain just how you see me? Am I your wife? Am I the woman you love? Am I your life's partner? Or—am I your social entrée?" she challenged, suddenly remembering the thousand little conversations that had taken place over the past months—and the way Rick had always drawn her family name into them. She realized that he knew more about the history of her family than she did.

From that point on, the confrontation had degenerated into a shouting match, insults and accusations hurled on both sides. In the end, Rick had stormed out of the flat, and for days afterward they'd been cold to each other. Eventually they'd gone through the motions of making up, but it had never been the same after that.

As the weeks wore on, Flame had gradually come to see that she'd unwittingly hit on the truth. If Rick loved her at all, it was because she was his passport into a world that would have otherwise barred him from entering. He didn't love her, not for herself. He never had. Two months later, she'd filed for a divorce.

She'd walked away from the marriage scarred but much wiser. She'd learned a valuable lesson, one that she found many occasions to apply. Over the years, she'd discovered that few people sought her company for its sake alone. Some, like Rick, saw her as a passport to power and prestige. Some were outright social climbers. Others were attracted by her beauty and regarded her as a prize to be paraded on their arm. And to others, like Malcom Powell, she represented a conquest that had eluded him. All of those people she had eliminated very quickly from her life, dropping them the instant she discerned their reason for wanting to be with her—which was much easier than most supposed. As a result, her circle of friends was small indeed. And, of them, she regarded only Ellery as her one true friend. He'd never asked anything of her and never once taken advantage of their friendship. On the contrary, Ellery had always given—of his knowledge, his understanding, his time, and his company.

Slowly Flame closed the photo album and hugged it tightly to her. That old need to love and be loved was still there, but of necessity, buried deep inside. Friends, a beautiful home, gorgeous clothes, and an unquestionably successful career weren't enough to fill the emptiness. Without someone to share them with, they meant little. But who?

Instantly an image of Chance Stuart flashed in her mind. Suddenly she could see again that faintly wicked glint in his blue eyes, the raffish charm of his crooked smile, and that aura of virility he wore so casually. She smiled, realizing that he'd made a very definite impression on her—and wondered if she would see him again or whether it had been a line, forgotten minutes after it was said. Probably.

Sighing, Flame returned the photo album to its place on the shelf, her fingers lingering for a moment on its worn, leatherbound spine. As she turned, her glance fell on the horn chair. That strange visit from Hattie Morgan had started this rush of memories with all her talk about family. How odd that it had taken a stranger to remind her.

THE BLACK MARBLE and glass of Stuart Tower loomed tall and proud, adding its own bold statement to the progressive skyline of cosmopolitan Tulsa. Like everything else Chance Stuart owned, it carried his name, emblazoned in gold leaf to gleam in the sun for all to see. More than one had suggested, not entirely in jest, that he should take that scrolled *S* and put a line through it, turning it into a dollar sign, because everyone sure as hell knew that the name Stuart and money were practically synonymous.

When the silver Jaguar wheeled into the entrance to the underground parking garage, the brash young attendant in the booth quickly sat up straighter, threw a one-fingered salute at the driver, then gazed after the car with a mixture of longing and envy. It rolled to a smooth stop in the space marked RESERVED, C. STUART. Chance stepped out and crossed to the private elevator. It made only one stop—on the twentieth floor, the offices of the Stuart Corporation.

The elevator whisked him silently to the building's top floor and opened its doors onto Molly's office, the private entrance allowing him to avoid the public reception area and the many offices of the company's various departments. As always, Molly was already seated behind her desk, guarding the door to his office, her chubby cheeks rounded in a smile of welcome when he walked out of the elevator.

"Morning, Molly. Has Matt Sawyer arrived?" he asked, heading straight for his office.

"Not yet."

"Show him in the minute he does." Chance opened the door, then paused. "And let Sam know I'm here."

"Right away." She reached for the intercom.

Without waiting, Chance entered his office and automatically closed the door behind him, then crossed the bleached wood floor to his desk in the corner. He glanced briefly at the stack of telephone messages and letters waiting for his attention on the desk's granite top. Turning his back on them for the time being, he walked to the smoke-tinted glass that enclosed two sides of the immense room.

His corner office overlooked buildings that represented some of the finest examples of the Art Deco architecture so popular in the thirties. Once those buildings housed the offices of such oil giants as Waite Phillips, Bill Sinclair, and J. Paul Getty. Chance studied them briefly then lifted his glance to the city sprawled over the rolling hills of Oklahoma's Green Country.

Many had questioned his decision to make Tulsa his headquarters when he could just as easily have picked Dallas or Denver if it was a central location he wanted. Few knew of the affinity he felt for this city. It had come a long way from its humble cowtown beginnings, a wide spot along a dusty trail—and from its wild and rowdy days as an oil boomtown. All its rough edges had been smoothed. Now it stood sleek and sophisticated with its alabaster skyline, a high-tech city in a high-tech world. He and Tulsa had much in common. It was more than a hometown boy coming back after he'd made good—much more.

There was a quick rap on his door followed by the click of the latch. Chance swung around expecting to see Sam walk in. But it was Molly, a steaming cup of coffee in her hand. "I knew I had missed something. Nobody makes coffee as good as you do, Molly."

"You're only saying that to make sure I don't go on strike and refuse to make coffee for you anymore." She crossed the room and set the cup on his desk, beaming at his praise, her round cheeks growing rounder, and reminding him of the time he had teased her about being his all-round girl—round cheeks, round eyes, round face, and round body. Then her look faded to one of faint disapproval and he knew he was about to be lectured on something. "One thing's certain. That Lucy woman—"

"Lucianna," he corrected, transferring his attention to the phone messages in his hand.

"Whatever she calls herself now, she didn't bring you any coffee in the morning."

"No. Room service did."

Molly ignored that. "You've known this Lucianna a long time, I know, but she won't make you a good wife. And it's time you got married."

"What can I do? I keep asking and you keep turning me down." He walked back to his desk.

"You're impossible." She pretended to be angry with him. "When are you going to wake up to the fact that you're thirty-eight years old? You not only don't have a wife, but you don't have any children either."

Sam strolled into the office, lanky and trim with a thatch of unruly light brown hair. "At least, none that you know about, Molly."

She turned. "If he had any, I'd know. Everyone would, because you can bet the mother would file a paternity suit."

"If it's a child you want, Chance, Patty and I will loan you one of ours. You can take your pick. Right now I think Patty would willingly give all four of them away. It was a bad weekend at home. I'm glad I spent most of it here."

Chance straightened from his desk, fully alert. "Did you come up with anything?"

Sam shook his head. "I've already filled you in on everything I know. Until Matt gets here . . ." He shrugged the rest.

"Molly, see if Matt Sawyer's here yet."

"Of course." Easily she slipped back into the role of the efficient secretary and left his office to return to her own.

Sam watched her go, then turned back to Chance, grinned, and shook his head in amusement. "She never gives up, does she?"

"Not Molly."

Sam wandered over to the desk and sat down in the charcoal suede chair that faced it. "Did you get everything worked out in Tahoe to your satisfaction?"

Chance smiled crookedly. "Let's say I got everything worked out. Whether it will be to my satisfaction remains to be seen." The Tahoe project was his most ambitious to date. When completed, it would be a year-round resort complex, with a palatial hotel and gambling casino adjacent to the marina and yacht club, and a luxury ski lodge coupled with chalet-style condominiums and an array of ski runs and trails.

"I talked to Kiley this morning," Sam said, referring to their construction manager on the project site. "He mentioned you had a little run-in with Nick Borrello."

"You could call it that," Chance conceded. "Among other things, he accused me of stealing his casino."

Admittedly he'd bought it from the man at a bargain price, but the casino had lost money the last three years—for a number of reasons. Poor management was one of them, and another was its location on the fringe of Tahoe's main gambling area. As a small, independent casino it couldn't compete with those operated by the big hotels and it couldn't siphon away enough of their trade.

As a casino alone, Chance wouldn't have been interested in it. But he'd looked at its lake frontage, the surrounding forest, the jutting mountain behind it and its proximity to the gaming centers, and knew immediately that the site was—in the argot of land developers—a "Tiffany location."

"He's certainly changed his tune, hasn't he?" Sam remarked. "Not six months ago, he was so happy to have you take it off his hands that he would have gladly kissed your feet." A smile spread across his face, boyish in its charm. "For that matter, most of your competitors were convinced you'd bought a lemon."

"I know." Chance smiled back, aware that he hadn't been quick to correct that impression either. Instead, he'd waited to announce his plans for the site until three days after the Nevada gaming commission had given him their nod of approval. At that point, he inked the lease he'd arranged with the Forest Service, giving him the mountain behind the casino. With that in hand, he held a press conference and announced his plans.

Suddenly everybody had sat up and taken another look at the deal he'd put together. That's when they realized that not only had he bought it at a rock-bottom price, but he also didn't have a dime in it himself. A major hotel chain anxious to get into the area had fronted all the money, and a national insurance company was waiting in the wings to fund the rest of the project. By the time the development was completed and in operation two years from now, his profit from it would be in the hundreds of millions. Most developers had walked away, shaking their heads and grumbling that they hadn't seen the same potential—and admitting, however grudgingly, that he'd pulled another rabbit out of the hat with typical Stuart style.

But not the former owner, Nick Borrello, who had initially bragged about the deal he'd made. Now he was screaming foul. But Chance was used to that.

The door to his office swung open, and Molly stepped in briefly to announce, "Mr. Sawyer's here." She moved to one side, allowing the man to enter.

Few people would look twice at Matt Sawyer, and fewer still would guess that the former FBI agent had left the Bureau to head one of the more reputable private security agencies in the country. He was a nondescript man of average height, build, and coloring, but his investigative skills were widely regarded. Five years ago, Chance had hired him for the first time to locate the owner of a small but vital piece of property, whose whereabouts were unknown. He'd had his own people on it for nearly a month. Matt Sawyer had located the man in less than forty-eight hours. Since then, Chance had employed his services on numerous occasions, and he'd proved himself invaluable more than once in tracking down much-needed information.

"Hello, Matt." Chance came around the desk to greet him, briefly gripping his hand, then motioning toward the small grouping of sofas and armchairs where he held many of his informal meetings. "What did you come up with?"

"Not a lot yet, but we're working on it." He gave his trouser legs a hitch as he sat down on the cerulean blue chair and placed his briefcase on his lap. "I did talk to Ben Canon's secretary. She was fairly cooperative, but there was a lot she either didn't know or wouldn't tell me." He snapped open the case and took out two folders. "She did confirm that Canon had a meeting with Hattie at nine on Friday, but she claimed she didn't know what it was about. She said Canon instructed her to hold his calls and closed the door to his private office so she didn't overhear any of the meeting. Which, according to her, lasted about ninety minutes. She was sure of the time because Canon had an eleven o'clock appointment and Hattie was gone before that client arrived." He passed one of the folders to Chance and gave the other to Sam. "Somewhere around nine-thirty—she wasn't certain of the exact time—Canon buzzed her on the intercom and asked her to make reservations for Hattie to fly to San Francisco that same day. And she also arranged for a cab to take Hattie to the airport. But, according to her, no explanation was given for the trip or the urgency of it."

"She has to know more than that." Chance tossed the folder and its detailed report on the coffee table without opening it, knowing that it would obtain merely facts and he wanted impressions as well. "She's his secretary. She sees everything that passes over his desk. She's bound to know what he's working on."

Matt shook his head. "Not the way Ben Canon operates. The way she described him, he keeps everything pretty close to the vest and never confides in her about a client. He opens all the mail himself and has a set of locked files in his office where he keeps any correspondence or paperwork dealing with current cases." He paused, a wry smile crossing his mouth. "And you aren't going to believe this. He has an old manual typewriter that he uses to type any important correspondence himself."

"Why does he even bother to have a secretary then?" Sam frowned.

"To answer the phone, I guess." Matt shrugged.

Chance continued to eye Matt closely. "You found out something from her, didn't you?"

Matt looked at him and allowed a rare smile to show. "In addition to answering his phones, she empties the wastebasket in his office. On Friday night she found a large manila envelope in it from a Whitney or a Whittier or a name similar to that. She noticed it because the return address was Salt Lake City and she has an aunt living there. She thought the man might be a doctor —a gynecologist maybe. She wasn't sure, but she remembered something like that being printed below his name. And I'm guessing that it didn't say gynecologist. Instead it read genealogist."

Sam sat up. "I'll bet you're right, Matt. I'll bet Canon hired him to try to locate anyone who might be related to Hattie."

"It's logical," Matt agreed. "They have amassed quite a collection of family records in Salt Lake City, second only to the archives in Washington, I understand. Anyway, if there is a genealogist named Whittier or Whitney there, he shouldn't be too hard to find."

"What about Hattie's stay in San Francisco?" Chance wanted to know.

"We weren't quite so lucky there. As you know, she stayed downtown at the Cartwright. By the time my associate in the Bay Area was able to get someone over there Saturday morning, she'd already checked out. A little after eight, the desk clerk said. The doorman remembered that she was picked up by a man driving a dark green sedan. He wasn't sure of the make or model, but he thought it had California plates. About two and a half hours later, a car matching that description dropped her off at the airport. The agent didn't get close enough to get the license number. Unfortunately, we don't know what she did, where she went, or who she might have seen in that two and a half hours between the time she left the hotel and arrived at the airport."

"No description on the driver?" Chance asked.

"None. But obviously either she or Canon knows somebody in San Francisco. I have a contact in the telephone company checking to see if either of them made any long-distance calls to the Bay Area in the last week." He closed the briefcase, snapping it shut with an air of finality. "Like I said, we don't have a lot of hard information for you right now, but I have a lot of things we're working on."

"This has to have top priority, Matt," Chance reminded him, the hard gleam in his eyes leaving the man in little doubt that he meant it. "If you can't find the information one way, then try another, but find it. Don't let locked files stand in your way."

"I understand." Matt nodded quietly, not needing any elaboration on that statement.

After he'd gone, Sam turned to Chance, his hands thrust deep in his pockets in a troubled and thoughtful pose. "It doesn't look like Hattie was running a bluff, does it? But you never thought she was. Why?"

"You didn't see her. She was like a cat still busy licking the cream off her whiskers." He picked up the report from Matt and carried it to his desk.

"I still don't believe it," Sam declared, raking his fingers through his hair. "To have some long-lost cousin wind up with Morgan's Walk . . . Chance, what are you going to do?"

"I'll buy it if I have to."

"What if this person won't sell?"

"Everybody has a price, Sam. That's where Hattie made her mistake. Whoever this relative is—he isn't going to give a damn about Morgan's Walk. All he's going to care about is how much he'll inherit."

"But if Hattie's already talked to him, she could have turned him against you already. And if she hasn't, you can damned well bet she will."

"It won't matter. We'll use a third party to make the deal. He'll never know he's selling it to me."

"I wish I could be as sure as you are."

"It's a hand we'll have to play when we find out who this relative is and get some background on him. Maybe by the time I fly back to San Francisco for Lucianna's opening night this Friday, we'll know. Which reminds me . . ." He picked up the phone and punched the intercom line to Molly's phone.

"Yes?" came the crisp response.

"Molly, I want you to send some flowers for me."

6

TENSION GRIPPED THE SMALL meeting room off the agency's graphic arts department as Flame studied the rough sketches spread across the long table in front of her. Proposed layouts for new print advertising lay side by side with storyboards for television commercials. A shirt-sleeved artist with rumpled brown hair shifted uneasily in his chair, the strain of waiting for a reaction from her finally showing. The movement drew a sharp but sympathetic look from the copywriter. Ellery ignored both, and Flame didn't even notice either, the whole of her attention focused on the concepts before her. Slowly and reluctantly she shook her head.

"You don't like it," Ellery concluded, his remark covering the half-smothered curse from the artist.

Flame breathed in deeply and released the breath in a regretful sigh. "Truthfully? No." She picked up the storyboard. "This idea for a new commercial is merely a slicker version of the one we've been airing."

"It's been very successful."

"I know it has, but we've been reworking this same theme for a year now. We need a new slant, something that will appeal to younger crowds. The results from the market research and demographic study we did this summer indicated that a very low percentage of people in their twenties shop at Powell stores. In my opinion, that should be our target market. The whole point of any advertising campaign is to increase sales and broaden the consumer base. If there's a segment of the market we're not reaching, then we go after it."

"Any ideas on how we might accomplish that?" Ellery walked over to stand beside her.

"Ideas are your province." A smile played at the edges of her mouth as she handed him the storyboard. "My job is to point you in the direction our client wants to go."

"Thanks," he murmured dryly.

The copywriter paused in her doodling and pushed her glasses higher on the bridge of her nose. "This survey you mentioned—did it say why they don't shop at Powell's?" She hooked an arm over the back of the chair, training her entire attention on Flame, her thoughts already focusing on the problem at hand.

"Basically, their reaction to Powell's fell into two categories. One, they saw Powell's as being too staid, too conservative. Second, and not too surprisingly, they thought it was too expensive." She paused to glance at Ellery. "I'll get a copy of those reports to you."

"That might be helpful."

"I think it will." She nodded. "The objective of this new campaign has to be to give Powell's a youthful, modern image—*without* alienating its established customers. I think you should begin to think about a new logo—something to relate to the nineteen nineties and the year two thousand. That will lead to new copy and new visuals."

"A piece of cake," the artist snorted, lifting his shoulders in a mock shrug of unconcern. "We can do that in our sleep, can't we, Andy?" he said to the copywriter. "Problem is, we're not going to get much sleep."

A knock at the door interrupted the discussion. Flame turned as the door opened and her assistant, Debbie Connors, poked her head inside, her long blond hair swinging forward in a mass of crinkly waves. "Sorry, Flame, but you asked me to remind you about your luncheon appointment with Mr. Powell. The car's out front now waiting for you."

Flame glanced at her watch and sighed. "Tell them I'll be right down."

"Mustn't keep the great man waiting," Ellery murmured dryly.

There was irony in the look she sent him. "You may be jesting, but it happens to be the truth." She started to the door. "I'll have Debbie drop those reports by your office. If there's anything you need clarified, we can talk after I come back from lunch this afternoon."

Ellery nodded, then added with a sly smile, "Have fun."

The sleek gray limousine, polished to a gleam, was at the curb waiting for her when Flame emerged from the building. The stocky chauffeur hurriedly tossed his cigarette aside and reached to open the rear passenger door for her.

"Afternoon, Ms. Bennett." He touched his cap to her, a smile wreathing his broad face.

"Hello, Arthur." She returned the smile and automatically handed the portfolio case to him. "How are the grandkids?"

"Just fine, ma'am." Pride widened his smile even further. "Growing like weeds, they are."

She laughed at that, partly because it was expected. "They have a way of doing that." She lifted her glance to the strip of blue sky visible between the towering canyon walls of the street's flanking high-rise buildings. "Gorgeous day, isn't it?"

"Indeed it is, ma'am. Indeed it is." His hand was at her elbow politely helping her as she bent to climb into the rear seat. He waited until she was comfortably situated then closed the door. The blare of traffic on the streets intruded briefly when he opened the front door and slid behind the wheel, laying the slim case on the seat beside him. Then there was silence, broken only by the whisper of the air conditioner as the car turned into the flow of traffic.

Leaning back in the plushly upholstered seat, Flame took advantage of the quiet to relax from an unusually hectic morning. Absently she gazed out the window at the rush of people on the crowded sidewalks, caught in the lunch-hour bustle.

On either side, skyscrapers stretched upward, walling in the streets. The agency's offices were strategically located on the fringes of both the city's financial district, referred to by many as "the Wall Street of the West," and the elite shopping area around Union Square with its high-fashion stores and deluxe hotels. Flame smiled, recalling an observation Ellery had once made concerning the proximity of the two areas, finding it singularly appropriate since on one side, the buildings were sky-high and on the other, the prices were.

"Where are we having lunch today, Arthur?"

With a turning lift of his head, he made eye contact with her reflection in the rearview mirror. "I don't know, ma'am. I was told to bring you to the store."

"I see." She sat back, briefly wondering at this break from the normal routine. Usually they lunched at Malcom's club. Still, she didn't mind. In a way, she almost welcomed it. A change of scene might satisfy some of this restlessness that had been bothering her these last few days.

A short five minutes later, Arthur let her out at the front entrance to the main Powell store from which all its many national branches had sprung. With portfolio case in hand, Flame entered the store, breezed past the perfume counter with its barrage of scents, and went straight to the executive offices located on the mezzanine level.

When she entered Malcom's outer office, the stern-looking brunette behind the desk glanced up and allowed a smile to cross her expression. "Go right in, Ms. Bennett. Mr. Powell's expecting you."

"Thank you." At the door to his office, Flame hesitated a split second, then walked in without knocking.

A Tabriz carpet covered the parquet flooring and every vertical inch was faced with hand-selected California pine that had been painted, laboriously stripped, then waxed, imbuing the expansive and imposing office with the aura of a captain's cabin. That feel of a mariner's room was subtly reinforced by the framed map of the China Seas that hung on the wall behind the massive antique desk at the far end of the room, a desk that failed to dwarf the man seated behind it, for all its size. Malcom rose from his chair as Flame approached, the tap of her heels muffled by the heavy Persian rug.

"As usual, you look lovely, Flame." His gray glance ran over her in swift appraisal. "I especially like that suit you're wearing."

"You should." Smiling, she briefly lifted a hand in a model's gesture to show off the Adolfo suit of turquoise blue knit. "It's from your fourth floor."

He smiled back, the cleft in his chin deepening. "I always knew you were a woman of discriminating taste." His look was covetous, revealing his desire to add her to his list of possessions.

Seeing it, Flame kept her smile in place and murmured a deliberate, "*Very* discriminating, Malcom, . . . in all things." She set the leather portfolio onto the seat of the stiff-backed chair in front of his desk. "Shall we go over these changes before lunch?" Assuming his agreement, she started to unfasten the metal clasp.

"Has Harrison approved them?" he asked, referring to his marketing director.

She nodded affirmatively. "I went over them with him last Thursday."

"Then there's no need for me to look at them. If he's satisfied, so am I."

His reply was unexpected. In the past, Flame had always gone over such things with him, however minor they might be. It had been a means of maintaining the guise that these were business luncheons, even though she'd known all along that business had nothing to do with his desire for her company. This change to something openly social, something personal—what did it mean?

She wasn't sure. Perhaps an increase of pressure from him to coerce her into a more intimate relationship.

Inwardly she was on guard, but outwardly she retained her easy smile as she relatched the case with a decisive click. "If you don't want to see them, that's fine with me, Malcom." Turning to him, she let her smile deepen. "I never argue with a client."

"That's very wise, Flame." His gray eyes were thorough in their close study of her. "Because the customer is always right. And if you don't believe that, try doing without him."

Was that a threat? It certainly had the sound of one, but the warm light in his eyes seemed to deny that. Flame chose to regard it as nothing more than a clever rejoinder.

"You should include that in your next company newsletter as a proverb by Powell. Coming from the CEO, it would definitely make good copy."

"I might do that."

"You should." She paused to pick up her leather case. "So, where are we going for lunch today? You haven't said."

"We aren't." He came around the desk to stand before her. "We're going to eat here. I decided it was time I made use of my private dining room for something other than dry and boring business luncheons. Do you mind?"

"Of course not." Flame didn't allow the faintest glimmer of misgivings to show, even though this was the first time she would be lunching with him at somewhere other than a public place. "At least we shouldn't have any reason to complain about the service today."

"Or the food, I hope," Malcom added, a glitter of rare humor in his look.

"With a chef as superb as yours is reported to be, I'm sure we won't have to live on bread alone."

"Shall we find out?"

Taking her by the arm, he ushered Flame into the anteroom he'd converted into a private dining room at a rumored cost of fifty thousand dollars, although it was too tastefully done to show. The wood-paneled splendor of his office was repeated in the anteroom. This time the decor's nautical feel was reinforced by a massive oil painting—a China clipper ship running before a sea storm—that hung above the Edwardian side table.

Irish linen covered the small round table in the center of the room, its leaves removed to more comfortably accommodate a party of two. But no candles gleamed and no roses bloomed from crystal vases, and the brass chandelier overhead was turned to full bright, eliminating any suggestion of romantic intimacy. Noting that, Flame breathed a little easier.

As soon as they were seated, a waiter opened a bottle of wine. Malcom waved aside the presentation of the cork and the offer to sample the wine, gesturing instead for the waiter to fill both glasses with the bottle's deep red wine. Malcom lifted his glass to her in a typically silent salute, then waited, watching as Flame sipped from hers.

"A cabernet," she said with approval.

"Do you like it?" The tone of his question implied that if it didn't meet with her approval, they'd have something else.

"It's excellent." Although many considered it fashionable to drink only the dry white wines, Flame had always preferred the full-bodied taste of a good red.

"It's fine." Malcom nodded to the hovering waiter, then finally tasted his own.

"Would you like me to begin serving now, sir?"

Again Malcom nodded affirmatively. The waiter withdrew to the serving pantry, then returned almost immediately with a salad of fresh spinach and strawberries for each of them. Flame smoothed the linen napkin over the lap of her turquoise blue skirt then reached for her salad fork.

"How was your weekend?" Malcom inquired.

"Quiet, thankfully. Which is just the way I like it." Using her salad fork, she folded a spinach leaf onto its tines. "Oh, but Malcom, I did have one rather bizarre visitor."

Briefly Flame told him about the elderly woman who had called on her Saturday morning, claiming to be a distant relative. When she mentioned the supposed inheritance of a ranch in Oklahoma, Malcom agreed that it was all too farfetched, that the old woman was probably delusionary—if not senile.

"What about your weekend?" she asked. "Did you have your usual complement of house guests?"

His wife's penchant for entertaining was legendary, and an invitation to the Powell family residence in the exclusive island community of Belvedere was highly coveted, both for the "in" status it implied and for the island's balmy climate and scenic vistas of San Francisco's skyline to the south and the famed Golden Gate Bridge to the west. Established by the old guard of affluent San Franciscans shortly before the turn of the century, to escape the summer fog, Belvedere had become renowned for its historic homes, narrow, winding roads, and beautiful gardens, and a life—typical of most island communities—that centered on the water, becoming the home of the elite San Francisco Yacht Club.

"Not this weekend," Malcom replied. "Like yours, mine was quiet. As a matter of fact, I took the boat out for a last sail." The vessel he so casually referred to as a boat was a sleek forty-foot sailing yacht that had competed in the America's Cup some years earlier. "The way my schedule looks these next few months, I probably won't have another opportunity to take it out again before winter sets in."

Sailing was a topic of mutual interest. Their conversation revolved around it through the salad course. The waiter returned with the entrée and placed it on the table before Flame. "Veal with a green peppercorn sauce, this is one of my favorites," she declared, directing a quick smile at Malcom.

"Don't you think by now I know what you like?"

At that instant, Flame realized the entire menu had been selected on the basis of her personal preferences, everything from the choice of wines and the salad to the entrée and—"Then we must be having chocolate soufflé for dessert," she guessed, trying to sound offhand to hide the fact she was impressed that he'd cared enough to notice her likes—that he'd wanted to please her.

"What else?" His look gleamed with confidence and satisfaction.

She laughed softly, aware that her mood had lightened considerably, much of her earlier tension gone. She decided it was the combination of the excellent wine and food, the room's rich, yet comfortable atmosphere—and, perhaps most important, Malcom's subtle attentiveness to detail.

Through the rest of the meal, both the anticipated chocolate soufflé for dessert and the coffee afterward, they chatted about business in general, with a few side trips into politics and the economy. It was this exchange of views and opinions, typical of most of their past luncheons together, that Flame enjoyed, the talk stimulating in a quiet sort of way and providing a diversion from the endless shoptalk at the agency—and the sniping gossip.

"More coffee?" Malcom started to reach for the silver pot the waiter had left on the table.

She refused with a faint shake of her head, then smiled. "Need I say that the luncheon was superb."

"I'm glad you enjoyed it." His glance ran swiftly over her, admiring in its assessment. "That particular shade of turquoise is an excellent color on you. It brings out the green of your eyes. You should wear it more often."

"If you always serve up flattery after a meal, we'll have to make it a point to lunch here more often, Malcom," she declared, smiling as she folded her napkin and laid it on the table.

"I'll remember that," he replied, then paused briefly. "Speaking of remembering, I have something I want to show you." Pushing his napkin onto the table, he rose from his chair. Joining him, Flame walked back into his office. "For some time, I've been considering expanding the line of furs we carry at our major stores." Malcom stopped to close the doors to the dining room. "Naturally I'm concerned about maintaining the Powell reputation for quality. That's why I'd like your opinion on this coat."

The request wasn't unusual. In the past, Malcom had frequently consulted with her on such things, reasoning that she represented both ends of his market —the working career woman and the socialite.

Her interest piqued, she followed when Malcom walked to the small conference table on the far side of the pine-paneled room. A luxurious dark fur lay across one of the chairs. He picked it up, then turned, draping it over his arm for her inspection. The instant Flame saw the dark, almost black, full-length fur, she felt as if the air had been snatched from her lungs.

"Malcom, it's exquisite," she murmured and reached out to touch it, then darted a quick, dawning look at him. "It's sable, isn't it?"

"Russian sable, yes. Try it on."

Needing no persuasion, Flame turned and let Malcom help her into it. As she ran her hands under the stand-up collar of the coat and down the front, letting her fingers slide through its thickness, she was certain there was no sensation quite like the sensual feel of a fur—soft, silken, and utterly luxurious. Nothing else could make a woman feel so feminine, so elegant—so incredibly alluring.

Impulsively she turned to Malcom. "It's stunning."

"On you, it is."

His response was hardly effusive, but the look that blazed in his eyes more than made up for it. She swung away knowing she shouldn't have invited him to notice, but feeling too recklessly glorious to care. She wrapped the coat tightly around her and hugged it, burying her fingers deep in its fur.

"I have a suggestion." The weight of his hands settled onto her shoulders. "Why don't you wear it to the opera Friday night?"

Briefly she allowed herself to be tempted, then sighed in regret. "I couldn't. It wouldn't be right," she said with a firm shake of her head.

She hadn't noticed the slight pressure that had drawn her back against him until she felt the warmth of his breath near her ear. She should have moved away from it, but she didn't.

"It couldn't be more right." The pitch of his voice was low and caressing. "It belongs on you, Flame." His lips moved against her hair, a feathery sensation gliding toward her neck.

Instinctively she turned her head to deny him access. "Don't." The protest sounded weak to her as his mouth found the shell of her ear instead, the sensitive nerve ends reacting to the unexpected contact and unleashing a cascade of shivers.

She hadn't realized how vulnerable she was—how susceptible. She shouldn't have spent so much time alone this past weekend, thinking and remembering how much she wanted to be loved, recognizing that there was no lonelier sound than laughter that was heard only by the one who laughed, that there was no hollower victory than the one celebrated by the victor alone. There was no such thing as independence when there was no one standing beside you; there was only loneliness. The touch of Malcom's hands and the brush of his lips against her skin were reminding her of that all over again.

"I want you, Flame." His breath heated the side of her neck. "I have from the moment you walked into this office five years ago. I vowed then to make you mine. You belong to me, Flame. It's time you admitted that."

She realized that she'd been ripe for this moment. And Malcom had set the stage perfectly with the wine and the food, the easy conversation and the sable coat that had reminded her she was a woman with normal, human needs. But could she trust him? Was it her needs he sought to fulfill? Or, like Rick, did Malcom want her to satisfy his own ends?

His hands glided down the fur sleeves, following the bend of her arms to enfold her while his mouth brushed tantalizingly over her cheek and ear. But it was less his caresses she responded to than the stroking words he murmured.

"Haven't I shown you how it can be with us? Quiet dinners together. Intimate evenings with just the two of us. It will be so very wonderful, Flame, if you'll just let it."

She wavered for the briefest of moments. "No," she said, then more decisively: "No."

In one quick step she was free of his arms, and in two more, there was distance between them. Hurriedly she shed the coat, then turned and thrust it back at him, holding herself absolutely rigid so he wouldn't discover how badly she was shaking inside.

"The fur is beautiful, Malcom, but I don't care for the conditions that are attached to it."

"You didn't offer any objections to them a moment ago," he reminded her, a confident gleam in his gray eyes.

Unable to deny that, Flame ignored it. "We've been through this before." When he failed to take the fur from her, she tossed it onto the back of a nearby chair. "I am not going to become your mistress," she insisted stiffly. "I won't be used like that."

"*You* won't be used." Anger flared, hardening the grim set of his features. "Who the hell do you think you are? Without me, you're nothing but another impoverished socialite with a lot of pride. Your job, your salary, your vice-presidency, your so-called career, I'm responsible for every bit of it!"

She'd pushed him too far and she knew it. But there was no turning back—even if she wanted to. "I never asked you for any favors, Malcom."

"But you were damned quick to accept them. I've bought and paid for you ten times over."

"When you wanted me to handle the Powell account, I made it clear that if you thought you were buying anything else, I wasn't interested. I promised you that your account would have my absolute priority. And it has. I have jumped every time you've called. The only place I haven't jumped has been into your bed—and I won't!"

His smile was anything but pleasant. "Even if it means losing the Powell account . . . and all the others I sent your way? I opened corporate doors for you, Flame, and I can close them just as fast—and make certain they stay closed to you."

"Is that an ultimatum, Malcom?" The thin thread that held her temper snapped. "Are you telling me that either I go to bed with you or you'll destroy my career? Do you want me so badly you don't care that I'd be hating you all the while you were making love to me? A hostile merger, is that what you want?"

"No, dammit, it isn't!" He half swung from her, raking a hand through the silver-tipped mane of his hair.

Flame stared at him, conscious of the rawness inside, and the trembling of hurt and anger. Abruptly she pivoted on her heel and walked stiffly to the high-backed chair in front of his desk. She retrieved her portfolio case from its sea cushion and started for the door. But Malcom was there waiting for her. She halted an arm's length away.

"I honestly don't think you can complain about the job I've done for you, Malcom. Or the agency, either. If you think you're entitled to more than that, then pull the account. Don't hold that threat over my head."

"I never intended to," he stated impatiently.

"No?" She smiled without humor. "It sounded remarkably like a power play to me."

In one stride, he closed the space between them and caught her arms. "Dammit, Flame, you're not indifferent to me. You proved that when I held you in my arms."

"I've never denied that I enjoy being with you. I've always admired and respected you, Malcom—and liked you, too. And that's precisely the reason I won't become your mistress."

"You're not making any sense."

"Aren't I? Malcom, I don't have any illusions that it would be anything more than an affair. Maybe I'm greedy, but I'm not interested in being some man's mistress—not even yours. I don't want a brief affair where I'm just another possession. I want more than that—something that offers me the promise . . . or at least the hope . . . of a lasting, fulfilling relationship with someone who cares about *me*." She looked at him, more conscious than ever of the void in her life. "Maybe you'd make me happy for a time . . . I don't know. But sooner or later, you'd get tired of me and it would be over. Then where would I be? We couldn't work together anymore. It would be too awkward—for both of us.

Ultimately you'd take your account to another agency. And I'd lose you—and it, too."

"You don't know that."

"Let's not kid ourselves, Malcom. That's precisely what would happen." She was still angry but now there was an icy edge to it. "Either way I'd be on the losing end. I've known that all along."

His hands relaxed their grip on her arms, then released her altogether. "You wouldn't lose, Flame, I can be very generous." The look in his eyes was just as strong with the desire to possess as it had been before. Nothing she'd said had made any impression on him.

"I'm not an object to be bought, Malcom. I thought I'd made that clear," she retorted, then gave up, recognizing further argument was pointless. "If you'll excuse me, I have to get back to my office."

He didn't argue. "I'll have Arthur bring the car around."

"I prefer to walk, thank you."

And walk she did, covering the dozen or so blocks between Powell's and the agency at a brisk pace, thinking she could walk off her anger. But it didn't work. By the time she reached her office, she was angrier than before—angry at Malcom for attempting to threaten her, and at herself for giving him the opening. How could she have been so stupid—so weak?

When she sailed into the small outer office occupied by her assistant, the young blonde looked up from her desk, a look of relief rushing across her face. "Am I ever glad you're back." Flame walked right by her and pushed open the door to her office, then froze in shock. "—The florist delivered some flowers," Debbie finished lamely.

Some flowers? They were everywhere! Not a foot of flat surface failed to have a vase on it, cascading with boughs of Phalaenopsis orchids. Haltingly, Flame entered her office, still stunned by the fragrant profusion of white orchids.

"Incredible, isn't it?" Debbie murmured from the doorway.

Flame turned, finally recovering her voice. "Who sent them?"

"There's a card on your desk." Belatedly, the girl realized that the top of it couldn't be seen for the orchids. "I put it on the phone."

As Flame crossed to the desk, it suddenly occurred to her that there was only one person she knew who would indulge in such extravagance. She snatched up the card and ripped it open, muttering under her breath, "So help me, if Malcom thinks—"

Then she read the message inside: *"Till next time we meet,"* signed *Chance Stuart.*

Stunned, she leaned against a corner of the desk and tried to catch back the incredulous laugh that bubbled from her.

"Who's it from?" Debbie asked as Ellery appeared at her shoulder.

"Is Flame back?" Then he saw the orchid opulence in the office. "Hello, what is this? Are you turning your office into a jungle paradise or did you get the FTD account?"

The telephone rang. "I'll get it." Debbie hurried back to her desk in the anteroom.

"Isn't it incredible, absolutely incredible?" Still faintly awestruck and almost at a loss for words, Flame trailed a hand under an arching bough, its whole length strung with exotic white blooms.

"Who sent them—Tarzan of the jungle or Merlin Olsen?" Ellery wandered into the room, his glance centering on the card in her hand.

"Chance Stuart." She was still trying to believe that.

Debbie poked her head in the doorway again. "Flame, there's a long-distance call for you from a Mr. Stuart. Line two."

For an instant, her glance locked with Ellery's. Then she turned and tried to find the telephone again amid the tangle of trailing orchids. Locating it at last, she picked up the receiver and punched the button with the blinking light, conscious all the while of the silly flutters of excitement in her stomach.

"Hello." She tried to sound natural, but who could when her office was inundated with flowers and the sender was on the line.

"Flame. Chance Stuart. How are you?" The rich timbre of his voice seemed to travel right through the wires, all lazy and warm with the potent smoothness of hot brandy.

Instantly her mind conjured up the image of his dangerous smile and his rakishly handsome face. "At the moment, I'm engulfed by cascades of orchids. They're everywhere—and they're beautiful."

"I'm glad you like them."

"I do."

"I called because I happen to have an extra ticket for the opera on Friday. It's an excellent seat in the parterre . . . right next to mine. Could I persuade you to use it and attend the opera with me?"

Hesitating, Flame glanced at Ellery, aware that she had planned to go with him, but she was more aware of the way her first and only meeting with Chance Stuart had ended. He'd left the DeBorgs' party with his arm around the opera's guest diva.

"What about Miss Colton?" she asked with forced casualness.

"Lucianna will be onstage singing, I believe. But whether she is or not, I'm still asking you. Will you come?"

"I have made other plans." She looked again at Ellery. He smiled wryly and motioned for her to accept. "But I think I can change them without any difficulty."

"Good."

After supplying him with her address and agreeing on a time, Flame echoed his parting words, "Till next time." Then she hung up, her fingers lingering on the receiver for a moment, his card still clutched in her other hand.

"Do you know"—Ellery tilted his head back to eye her thoughtfully—"you have the very definite look of a woman in love?"

"That's ridiculous." Yet her cheeks felt unusually warm. "I don't even know him."

"My dear Flame, love is not an opinion. It's a chemical reaction. Either something happens between two people or it doesn't."

"Are you talking about love or spontaneous combustion? Not that it really matters." She shrugged. "Both can blow up in your face." She'd had too much experience with such things to be guided by her own feelings. "I've found it's much safer to do a little testing first. It can save a lot of hurt."

"Careful, my dear. Your scars are showing."

"I'll cover them up with powder," she replied, then looked around the room at the profusion of orchids, again overwhelmed by the sheer number of them. "What am I supposed to do with all these?" she wondered out loud.

"Enjoy them, my dear," Ellery offered dryly. "Simply enjoy them."

Flame shot him a glance of wry amusement. "You know, Ellery, I'm almost convinced you're a romantic masquerading as a cynic."

He smiled and winked slyly. "Just like you."

His reply startled a laughing breath of instinctive denial from her. But Ellery paid no attention to it as he strolled out of her office. Flame shook her head in mock exasperation and turned to the nearest vase of orchids, a vague wistfulness for shattered illusions entering her expression as she breathed in their fragrance, the card from Chance still in her hand.

LANTERNS GLEAMED FROM the ornate wrought-iron gateposts that marked the entrance to the courtyard of the imposing War Memorial Opera House. Its towering arched windows blazed with lights, announcing to the world the fall opening of the opera. Outside, sleek limousines, Rolls-Royces and Mercedeses lined Van Ness Avenue, while notables gathered inside.

The cultural event signaled the advent of San Francisco's social season. Everybody who was anybody, along with those who wanted to be somebody, attended the gala. They came to see and be seen—to the eternal delight of every couturier around the globe. And they were all there, de Ribes silk brushing against the taffeta of Ungaro, Valentino velvet rubbing shoulders with the satin of St. Laurent. Adding to the dazzle of it all were the glittering diamonds, the gleaming rubies and sapphires, and the sparkling emeralds that adorned the fingers, wrists, throats, and ears of the opera's patrons.

When Flame arrived on the arm of Chance Stuart, notice was duly taken of the high sweep of her hair, the diamond clusters at her ears, and the strapless sheath gown of de la Renta ombre-beaded silk crepe topped by a matching bolero jacket with long sleeves and wide shoulders. But it was her escort, clad in black evening attire, who stirred their interest with his dark good looks, electric blue eyes, and naughtily wicked smile. For once Flame was the one who received the green glances of envy. And she accepted them with pleasure.

A flashbulb went off, its bright flare of light momentarily blinding Flame. She held up a hand to shield her eyes and blinked rapidly to clear them. "I think I'm going to be seeing spots in front of my eyes all evening, especially after the gauntlet of paparazzi we ran outside."

"I don't blame any photographer for wanting to add a picture of you to his private collection," Chance murmured, his glance running warmly over her.

Her smile mocked his highly flattering but untrue statement. "I have the feeling they were more interested in the devilishly handsome man I was with."

"Devilish—is that how you see me?" The grooves in his lean cheeks deepened, suggesting amusement but stopping short of a smile.

"In some articles I read about you recently, it was suggested that you have the devil's own luck . . . and, the way your smile can evoke the most wicked thoughts, it occurred to me you might have traded in your tail and horns for a black tuxedo tonight."

He held her gaze, his look becoming decidedly intimate, shutting out everything else around them. "Maybe that explains it, then."

"What?" She was surprised by how breathless she felt.

"A devil's always drawn to fire—the hotter the better." His mouth slanted in a smile. "This could prove to be one helluva night."

"Flame, darling." Jacqui Van Cleeve pounced from the crowd. Flame swung her attention away from Chance, more disturbed by his suggestive comment than she cared to admit, and focused it on the society columnist, dressed in a slightly outrageous charcoal and pink floral gown of silk damask with a back bustle that seemed singularly appropriate to Flame, considering how much Jacqui's tongue already wagged. "I missed you at the Guild's pre-performance dinner gala. Ellery assured me you would be here tonight. Of course, there's no need to explain your absence now. I can see why you weren't there," she declared, turning to Chance. "Welcome back."

"Jacqui." His dark head dipped in acknowledgment as he gave her one of his patented smiles. "You are very eye-catching this evening."

She laughed, the large bangled hoops at her ears swinging with her movements. "I definitely don't blend into the wallpaper—unless it's Victorian." She paused, her eyes sharpening on him with a knowing air. "I honestly wasn't sure San Francisco would see you again. I'm glad I was wrong."

"What can I say? I was drawn back like a moth," he replied, his glance sliding naturally to Flame, the glitter in it as much as his words indicating that she was the reason he'd returned.

She tried not to look as pleased as she felt. And she tried, too, not to let her expectations rise too high, something she'd fought all week. But it was proving to be very difficult, especially now that she was with him and discovering all over again that his company was every bit as stimulating as she remembered.

"I can see you deserve your reputation for moving fast," Jacqui observed in a low murmur.

"I've never found anything to be gained by waiting," Chance countered smoothly. "Have you?"

"No," she conceded, then cast a reporter's eye over the bejeweled crowd around them. "They really dragged out the rocks tonight, didn't they? It's amazing how easy it is to tell who's wearing the real thing. All you have to do is look for a burly bodyguard hovering nearby—one with an unsightly bulge in his jacket." She paused, a smile breaking across her face. "This reminds me of the time I attended some exclusive charity ball in Dallas. There was a woman there, positively draped in diamonds. I made some remark that I thought it was a bit much. And this sweet little Texas gal informed me in this drawling accent of hers, 'Jacqui, honey, when it comes to diamonds, less is not necessarily better.' If tonight's any indication, I'd say the sentiment seems to be universal. Look." She laid a hand on Flame's arm, drawing her attention to the slender blonde near the arched windows, dressed in a Lacroix creation that was all froth and chiffon. "There's Sandra Halsey. Isn't that a divine gown she's wearing?"

"It is," Flame agreed.

"She had it flown in on the Concorde for the occasion. Talk about conspicuous consumption," Jacqui declared, then paused, her lips thinning in faint disapproval. "I do wish someone would tell her to stop sprinkling her conversation with French phrases. It's so terribly déclassé."

"And déclassé isn't?"

But Jacqui Van Cleeve was completely impervious to the light gibe. "No. We stole it from the French too long ago. Now it's as American as sabotage. Would you both excuse me? I'd swear she's wearing the Halsey rubies and Claudia vowed they would never touch her neck. Wouldn't it be something if those two have finally settled their feud after all this time?" Then she was off, her bustle wagging like the tail of a bloodhound hot on a scent.

Smiling faintly, Flame turned to Chance. "In case you haven't noticed, the only difference between our Jacqui and an ordinary news hound is the diamond-studded collar she wears. Other people's secrets are her stock and trade, printable or not."

"No doubt many that people wished she didn't know."

"That's putting it mildly," she murmured, and wondered to herself what Jacqui knew—or thought she knew—about her.

It was a question that grew stronger when she noticed Malcom Powell coming toward them, his stride unhurried. She hadn't seen or spoken to him since she'd walked out of his office on Tuesday. She met his glance, conscious suddenly of the aura of power he exuded. He didn't like being denied anything he wanted. She watched as his gaze sliced from her to Chance, then back again, the look in his eyes hovering somewhere between a demand and an accusation.

"Hello, Malcom," she greeted him first, keeping her voice cool but pleasant.

"Flame." He inclined his head briefly, the strands of gray in his dark hair catching the overhead light from the chandeliers and giving it a silvery cast.

"I believe you met Chance Stuart last week—" she began.

"Yes, at the DeBorgs'," Malcom confirmed and extended a hand. "I wondered if you would fly back to catch Miss Colton's performance."

As they gripped hands, Flame felt the tension in the air—like that of two adversaries meeting for the first time and quietly sizing each other up.

"For that among other things," Chance replied.

"Oh?" There was a challenge in that single sound from Malcom but Flame missed it, distracted by the odd feeling that she was being watched.

"Where's Diedre? Isn't she with you?" Flame asked, instantly using the inquiry as an excuse to scan the crowd and locate the party staring at her.

"The wind mussed her hair. She went to the powder room to repair the damage."

But Flame only heard the first part of Malcom's explanation as her glance initially swept by the man in the navy suit, then came back to catch his watchful gaze fastened on her. His face, there was something familiar about its hard, pointy lines, yet she couldn't place who he was or where she had seen him before. Abruptly, almost guiltily, he turned and walked away. His lack of formal attire prompted Flame to wonder if he was part of the building's security. But security usually wore black suits.

Why was she letting it bother her? Strange men had stared at her nearly all of her adult life. She forced her attention back as Malcom said, "There's Diedre. If you two will excuse me . . ."

"Of course." Flame smiled, still slightly distracted. Just for a moment she let her gaze follow Malcom as he walked away.

"Your agency handles the advertising for his stores, doesn't it?" Chance remarked.

"Yes," Flame admitted, wondering if he'd heard the rumors about her alleged affair with Malcom. But there was nothing in his expression to indicate that the question was anything other than an idle one. "As a matter of fact, we've been working on the store's holiday ads and commercials for the past month. For us, Christmas starts well before Thanksgiving."

"That's getting into the Christmas spirit early."

Mockingly she corrected him. "Ah, but we're dealing with the commercialized version of Christmas—the one that promotes the belief it's more blessed to give than to receive, and inspires the ringing of cash registers instead of silver bells. Our advertisers tend to spell Christmas with dollar signs."

"Scrooge would be proud of them." He grinned.

Flame laughed at that and added, "Too bad no bah-humbugs are allowed. He'd fit right in now."

"What about you? Are you a bah-humbug person?" Chance asked, eyeing her curiously.

"Not really." She sobered slightly. "Although I admit, without any family left, Christmas has lost much of its meaning for me."

"You don't have any family?"

She shook her head. "I lost both my parents some years ago. And, since I was an only child . . ." She shrugged off the rest of the sentence and the twinge of loneliness that came with it, and switched the focus to him. "I suppose you're from a big family." None of the articles about him had contained any mention of family. In fact, Flame couldn't recall any reference to his background other than the mention of a tour of duty in Vietnam.

"No, like you, I'm an only child with both parents gone. And holidays don't mean much to me either." A smile curved his mouth, but it was the look of understanding in his eyes that touched Flame.

Sid Barker stood squarely in front of the pay phone and puffed impatiently on his cigarette, his right shoulder twitching in a nervous shrug. His gaze moved constantly, his hazel eyes darting restless glances at the well-heeled guests that passed him.

Uncomfortable among this moneyed crowd with their fancy airs and superior looks, he unconsciously rubbed the top of a brown shoe along the back of his navy trouser leg, trying to give some polish to its scuffed toe. He smoked the cigarette all the way down to the filter, then took a last drag and exhaled the smoke out the long beak of his nose.

As he started to stab the butt into the sand of the ashtray stand, the phone rang. He dropped the cigarette instantly and snatched the receiver from the hook before it could ring again.

"Yeah, it's me," he said, the roughness of the street in his voice. "What took you so long? . . . Right, I saw them together not five minutes ago. I think she made me though. . . . If you say so," he said, moving his head in disagreement. "But I don't think it's going to do much good. . . . If that's what you want, that's what I'll do. It's your money."

He hung up, cast a quick look around to see who was about, then turned and slicked a hand over his thinning hair, the twitch back in his shoulder. With another scanning look, he headed back to find the redhead, his mind racing to find a way to get her alone.

For once, luck was on his side. Just when he figured it would be hours before the right moment presented itself, there it was. She was standing to one side, listening but not appearing to take part in the conversation.

Moving as quickly as he dared without drawing undue attention, Sid Barker circled around and approached her from the side. He was two steps away when she finally noticed him, her glance at first startled, then probing. Maybe she hadn't recognized him after all. He stopped close to her and furtively slipped her the note from his pocket.

A frown flickered across her smooth forehead as her green eyes dropped their inspection of him to glance at the paper. Immediately he moved away and plunged into the thick of the elegant crowd.

"You'd better wise up before it's too late and stay away from him. You'll regret it if you don't."

Stunned by the threatening message scrawled across the paper, Flame stared after him, the phrase *stay away from him* echoing in her head. Those were the same words that had been written on the piece of paper at the DeBorgs' party last week. As the milling crowd closed in behind him and hid him from her view, she caught a glimpse of his brown shoes. The waiter with the hawk-like features, the one she'd caught staring at her so rudely—it was the same man.

But the message made no more sense than it had before. Stay away from whom? From Malcom? From Chance? And who could have sent it? If *him* referred to Malcom, then Diedre was the logical choice. But if it was Chance, then who? Lucianna Colton? Did she consider Chance her private property?

Or could it be . . . Malcom? He didn't like competition of any sort. The more she thought about it—and remembered the threats he'd made on Tuesday —the more it sounded like him. He wasn't above using intimidation to get what he wanted. Obviously nothing she'd said to him on Tuesday had made any difference. He wanted her. And her feelings, her future, didn't enter into it, no doubt rationalizing it all away with some vague thought of seeing to it that she was well taken care of.

"I think it's time we took our seats." The suggestion was accompanied by the touch of a hand on her back, both startling her. With a quick turn of her head, she encountered Chance's warm look, a look that immediately sharpened. "Is something wrong?"

"No." She smiled quickly, perhaps too quickly. "It just occurred to me that you'd probably like to go backstage and wish Miss Colton luck tonight."

Chance smiled and shook his head. "Lucianna goes into total isolation for at least three hours before a performance. Her hairdresser and the wardrobe lady are the only people she allows in her dressing room."

"You've known her quite awhile, haven't you?" There was something in the ease of his answer that had made her suspect that.

"Longer than either of us cares to remember." The hand at the back of her waist increased its pressure slightly, an altogether pleasant sensation. "Shall we go in?"

Smiling, she lifted her head a little higher, determined to let none of this spoil her evening. "I think that's an excellent suggestion, Mr. Stuart."

Shortly after they'd taken their seats, the house lights dimmed and the orchestra began the opening strains of the prelude to *Il Trovatore*. There were the last-minute stirrings and whispers as those who had lingered took their seats. Then the curtain lifted on a fifteenth-century setting of a castle and its gardens in Aragon surrounded by the mystery of night.

The captain of the guard, in a resonant bass voice, recounted to the retainers gathered around him the lurid tale of an old Gypsy woman, burned at the stake for the crime of casting an evil spell on one of the Count's two infant sons, and how, to avenge her mother's death, the daughter of the Gypsy steals the other child and, according to the story, throws it into the fire that had killed her mother, thus establishing Verdi's melodramatic plot of a Gypsy's vengeance.

At the end of the guard's tale came the ominous tolling of the midnight hour. Then Lucianna Colton made her entrance in the role of Leonora, a noble lady of the court.

As applause greeted her appearance, Flame stole a glance at the man beside her. In the darkened theater, the lights from the stage cast the angles and planes of his face into sharp relief, highlighting the prominent bones of his cheek and jaw, and hollowing with shadows his lean cheeks. She was conscious of the strength in his smoothly carved profile—and she was conscious, too, that he showed little reaction to Lucianna's appearance. She'd wondered if he would—if he'd had some sort of disagreement with the soprano—if he had invited her tonight in retaliation. Yet she could read nothing into his expression that suggested any of those things. He looked pleased by the applause Lucianna received, but no more than anyone would be when they knew the performer.

A little ruefully, Flame realized that it wasn't going to be so easy to put those obscure warnings out of her mind and simply enjoy the evening. As if sensing her gaze, Chance turned his head slightly to return the look. In that moment, she became conscious of the scant inches that separated them, their shoulders nearly touching. Fleetingly, she wished the opera was ending instead of just beginning, then forced her attention back to the stage as Lucianna Colton, staying in character, waited for the burst of applause to fade, then began her opening aria, a song of love and emotions awakened.

The second-act curtain opened to a dawn scene of the Gypsies' mountain encampment and the famous strains of the Anvil Chorus. When it faded, the Gypsy's daughter, now an old woman, began to sing her impassioned version of her mother's death at the stake.

Chance listened to the Gypsy's hatred and bitterness and the ringing cry to "Avenge Thou Me," but his attention ultimately strayed from the mezzo-soprano's aria. There was too much in the character that reminded him of Hattie, all twisted with a hatred that seemed to feed on itself.

He could have dealt with that but not the frustration that a week's worth of digging had failed to provide him with the name of Hattie's new heir, the one who would deny him Morgan's Walk. Matt Sawyer had learned the identity of the genealogist in Salt Lake City, a certain Bartholomew T. Whittier. Unfortunately, the man had gone to England to trace the ancestors of one of his clients. Matt had finally located him in some remote village in the north of England, but Whittier hadn't been much help. Yes, he'd remembered compiling the information on the West Coast branch of the Morgan family, but the attorney he'd dealt with in Tulsa had demanded that he forward all his notes along with the information he'd obtained. So, no, he didn't have any records. However, he was quite certain that the only living descendant of that branch had been a woman, although she had married and her name wasn't Morgan anymore. No, he couldn't remember what it was—not without his notes. But he could gather all the information again. This time it shouldn't take him so long since he knew many of the sources he'd used previously. Yesterday the genealogist had flown back to Salt Lake City, at Chance's expense, to begin the search for the Morgan descendant all over again.

Originally Chance had hoped that when he flew out here this weekend, he'd have the name of this long-lost Morgan. He didn't, but there was some consolation in knowing that he would be dealing with a woman. The odds were in his favor that a woman in California wouldn't be interested in owning a cattle ranch in Oklahoma, however romantic it might sound to her. Sooner or later the novelty of it would wear off, and he intended to make certain it happened sooner rather than later.

It would mean more trips to San Francisco, but—he glanced sideways at Flame—he had a feeling he'd be making more of them anyway. Why not combine business with what was certain to be pleasure?

AFTER THE PERFORMANCE, Flame accompanied Chance backstage and joined the throng of friends and admirers crowding into Lucianna Colton's dressing room to shower her with their plaudits. Flame couldn't disagree with a single one of them. The brilliant shading of the cadenzas, the wonderful coloring of the trills, the breathtaking use of rubato, and the free, liquid quality of her voice convinced Flame that she deserved them all.

She watched as Lucianna Colton, still in heavy stage makeup and gowned in an emerald green kimono, rushed to embrace Chance. "I was wonderful, wasn't I?" she declared with refreshingly honest arrogance.

"You were more than wonderful. And if fifteen curtain calls don't prove that, nothing will." Chance straightened from the embrace with a streak of scarlet lipstick on his cheek.

"It was glorious, wasn't it? They just kept applauding and applauding. I thought they'd never stop." She noticed the lipstick stain on his cheek and made a rueful little moue with her mouth. "Look what I've done. I've left my mark on you, darling." She reached up to wipe it away with her thumb, but succeeded only in smearing it.

"Don't worry about it." Using the handkerchief from his pocket, he wiped at the stain himself.

"I'm not," she murmured, a faintly smug smile curving her red lips.

"It was a brilliant performance, Miss Colton," Flame inserted. "Your name deserves to be spoken in the same breath with Callas, Sills, and all the other greats."

"That's kind of you." But the very coolness of her gaze made Flame wonder if the diva didn't resent her being with Chance. Immediately, Lucianna swung her attention back to him. "You will be at the party, won't you?"

"Maybe later."

"Lucianna, darling." A man burst into the room, throwing his arms open wide in exaggerated adoration. "You were divine, superb, truly nonpareil."

"Oscar," Lucianna cried in welcome and rushed to meet him. "You loved me?"

"Loved you? Darling, you made my heart cry," he exclaimed as Chance took Flame's arm and steered her through the crowd and out the door.

Lucianna's dark eyes watched him leave. Maybe later, he'd said. But she knew him too well. He wouldn't be coming to the party. He'd be with that redhead instead. And the thought turned her cold inside—the hot cold that burned. Why? She'd seen him with other women before. Yet some instinct warned her this one was different. Had she lost him?

No. She wouldn't accept that. They had been lovers—and friends—for too many years. No woman would ever love and understand him as well as she did. He would come back to her.

She tilted her chin a little higher and turned a bright smile on her own. "I am fabulous, aren't I, Oscar?"

Once clear of the adoring crush, Chance said, "I took the liberty of making a late dinner reservation for us. I hope you don't mind."

His announcement caught her off guard. She thought he intended to whisk her home after the comment he'd made to Lucianna about the party. "Not at all." She smiled quickly, brilliantly.

But obviously he noticed the split-second hesitation that preceded her answer. "If you prefer to attend one of the parties, I can cancel the reservation."

"No. Although I thought you might want to toast Miss Colton's triumph tonight."

"Why would you think that?" He arched a dark eyebrow in her direction, curiosity in his look.

"The two of you are close." She attempted to shrug off the answer. "That's common knowledge."

"You've been listening to rumors." He reached in front of her to open the door, then paused with his hand on the latch, his body angled toward her. "You, of all people, should know better than to put much stock in rumors."

It was said gently, with a mere hint of a chiding smile. And Flame realized instantly that he'd heard the rumors about her and Malcom Powell. He'd heard them and dismissed them. She smiled, suddenly at ease with both herself and him.

Those who elected not to attend one of the post-opera parties usually went to Trader Vic's or L'Etoile or one of the other currently popular gathering spots, assuming, of course, they were well enough connected to get a seat. To Flame's surprise, Chance had made reservations at none of those. Instead he stopped the Jaguar in front of an intimate little French restaurant with a reputation for serving excellent nouvelle cuisine.

"Do you approve?" he inquired as he helped her out of the car.

"Very much." Her glance skimmed the baroque doors that marked the café's entrance. "Although I wasn't aware it stayed open this late."

"It doesn't." A hint of a smile grooved his cheeks. "They made an exception tonight."

There was a flicker of disbelief, then amazement at the implication that he had arranged for the restaurant to open specifically for them. But when they walked through the doors, Flame saw that it was true. The tables beyond the foyer were empty, and lavish sprays of orchids cascaded from every vase in the foyer—Phalaenopsis orchids—the very kind he'd sent her.

"The florist had a few left over." His remark was one of those throwaway answers not to be fully believed, and Flame didn't. Every bit of this had obviously been planned in advance.

Before she could say anything, a slim man with the thin face and nose of a Frenchman glided forward to greet them. "Monsieur Stuart, Mademoiselle Bennett, welcome to François. The opera, you enjoyed it, yes?"

"Very much, Louis," Chance replied, giving his name the French pronunciation.

"Your table, it is ready. If you would follow me, please." He led them to a table for two, aglow with flickering candlelight. At Flame's place setting stood a crystal bud vase with a single orchid spray arching from it. After he had seated them, Louis stepped to the silver champagne bucket on its legged stand, removed the bottle being chilled in ice, and held it out to Chance for his inspection. "Carlton's Pêche, as you ordered, monsieur."

"Excellent, thank you, Louis," he replied, nodding his approval.

With practiced deftness, he uncorked the bottle of peach champagne and filled their fluted glasses with the effervescent wine, then withdrew. Chance lifted his glass.

"Shall we drink to the next time?" he suggested.

"Till next time," Flame echoed the message that had accompanied the orchids, and touched her glass to his. She took a sip of the refreshingly light yet heady wine, then laughed softly. "I think I'm a little overwhelmed. Orchids, a café to ourselves, imported peach champagne. Do you always go to such lengths to impress a woman?"

"Only when I consider it important." Again there was that gleam of amusement in his eyes that was so much more seductive than the lascivious looks some men gave that said they could hardly wait to get her into bed.

"I'm flattered." More than that, she was conscious of the bright sparkle of electricity between them, an electricity that gave new life to rare and half-forgotten feelings and evoked a desire to please, to share, to touch, and—to love.

But there was always the risk that these feelings were one-sided. Hadn't past experiences shown her that? There were any number of reasons Chance sought her company. Although she didn't think a desire to be seen with a beautiful woman was one of them. And if it was her contacts he was interested in, they wouldn't be here in this restaurant. But, he'd known about Malcom. For all she knew this could be some sort of power play. Maybe he wanted to take something he knew Malcom Powell wanted.

She hated these suspicions, but that wariness had spared her a lot of hurt in the past. Once burned had equaled two hundred times shy in her case.

"You don't look flattered," Chance observed. "If anything, you look troubled about something. What is it?"

"Nothing," she denied. "I suppose I was wondering why you did all this. It's wonderful, but—it wasn't necessary."

"That depends on your definition of necessary," he replied smoothly. "Take the orchids, for example. By surrounding you with them, I could be certain of having your undivided attention when I called to persuade you to change your plans and come with me tonight."

She laughed. "That is an understatement. You had more than my undivided attention; you had my interest totally piqued."

"And as for coming here—" He smiled. "—you'll have to admit that if we'd gone anywhere else, we would have been constantly interrupted by friends and acquaintances. Here, we can dine quietly, just the two of us. So, while all this may seem extravagant on the surface, it's really very logical."

Finding it impossible to argue with him, Flame lifted her glass. "To logic—Stuart style."

After that, Flame found it amazingly easy to relax and enjoy the champagne, the meal, and the company. There didn't seem to be any lack of things to talk about.

"You saw the new Franco Zeffirelli production of *Turandot*," she exclaimed with envy. "I've been dying to see it. I've heard the stage design is magnificent."

"It should be, considering the cost of it reportedly ran upward of a million," Chance replied dryly. "I've often wondered if the money wouldn't have been better spent getting some of the great name stars to appear at the Met."

"That's true," she agreed. "Now if you want to see them, you have to go to Europe."

"That's where the money is. They get paid more over there than they do here."

"I know, but it's still a shame," she said, then sighed wistfully. "I had tickets to see *Turandot* the last time I was in New York. Unfortunately, I wasn't able to go at the last minute and wound up giving them to a friend."

"Were you in New York on business—or pleasure?"

"Business. The agency's corporate headquarters are in New York and I was there for a meeting."

"Do you go there often?"

"Three or four times a year. What about you?"

"About twice that . . . sometimes more."

"Where do you stay?" she wondered curiously.

"At the Plaza." He tipped his head to one side. "Why do you ask?"

Smiling faintly, she swirled the champagne in her glass, watching the bubbles breaking at the surface. "I wondered if you stayed at your competitor's hotel."

"My competitor?" His gaze narrowed in puzzlement.

"Donald Trump." She grinned teasingly at him over the rim of her glass.

He smiled at that. "We may be in the same business, but I don't regard him as a competitor. I'm not interested in any development in Manhattan or Atlantic City. He's welcome to do whatever he's big enough to do there. I'll take the rest of the country for my territory."

The glint of amusement in his eyes eliminated any hint of arrogance from his statement and drew a soft laugh from Flame. "I'm surprised you didn't say the world."

"I have to leave room for growth," he chided, grooves dimpling his lean cheeks.

"Now why didn't I think of that?" she declared, feigning a sigh.

A discreet distance from the table, a waiter stifled a yawn. Flame caught the sudden movement of his hand and quickly looked away, wishing she hadn't seen it. She didn't want to be reminded of how very late it must be.

"What are you doing tomorrow—or perhaps I should say, today?"

Meeting his gaze, she noticed the quiet, masculine insistence of it. And she noticed a dozen other things at the same time—like the ebony sheen of his hair in the low candlelight and the innate strength of his tanned fingers curved so gently around the bowl of his brandy glass.

"The Museum of Modern Art has an architectural show by Mario Botta that I've been wanting to see. I'm told it's quite impressive."

"Could I persuade you to change your mind and drive down to Carmel with me for lunch?"

"I hope you don't intend to accomplish that by inundating me with orchids again," she declared laughingly. "I don't know what I'd do with more."

"I won't—if you'll agree to come with me to Carmel and, in the words of its famous mayor, 'make my day.'"

Laughing, she lifted her hands in mock surrender. "I'll come quietly."

"Good." His smile widened. "I have some calls to make first thing in the morning. I can pick you up—say, around ten-thirty?"

"Wonderful. We can take the scenic route along the coast highway and still be there in plenty of time for lunch."

The waiter returned to their table, trying his best to look alert. "May I bring you anything else? More brandy, perhaps?" he suggested, glancing at Chance's nearly empty glass.

"Not for me." He looked to Flame, but she shook her head, echoing his refusal. "That will be all, I believe."

His reply signaled the end of the meal and the evening. Much of the drive back to her Victorian flat was made in silence, an oddly comfortable one. At the front door to her flat, he held out his hand for the keys. "May I?"

Willingly she surrendered them to him and watched as he unlocked her door. When he turned to give them back to her, she knew—even without the sudden acceleration of her pulse to tell her—that the moment had come. There was a sameness to it, wondering if it would be awkward, if her expectations had been raised too high by the easy intimacy of the evening—if she would like being kissed by him.

As his hand glided onto the curve of her jaw, she tilted her head back in age-old invitation. His face was there before her, sculptured in bronze, his gaze moving slowly over her features.

A faint smile softened the line of his mouth. "Ten-thirty tomorrow."

There was promise in his voice, but not nearly as much as she found in his kiss as he rubbed his mouth lightly over her lips then came back to claim them in a sensual tour de force.

And the sensations lingered long after he'd gone.

9

AT QUARTER PAST TEN, the doorbell rang. Flame hurried to answer it, hastily tying the folded ends of the silk scarf into a knot beneath her hair in the back, and finishing just before she reached the door. When she opened it, there stood Chance. Her heart did a crazy little flip-flop at the sight of him.

Previously, he'd always been in evening clothes. This was the first time Flame had seen him in casual dress, with his shirt unbuttoned at the throat, revealing a smattering of dark chest hairs, and black denim pants fitting smoothly over slim hips and muscled thighs. A Windbreaker in the same shade of blue as his eyes hung over one shoulder, held by the hook of his finger. The result was less smooth sophistication and more rugged virility.

"I'm early." His mouth formed that now familiar smile as his gaze made a slow sweep of her. "You look rested and refreshed."

"I am." Although she wasn't sure how much sleep she'd actually gotten. Not that it mattered, since she'd wakened with the feeling that she owned the world. "Let me get my jacket and I'll be ready."

In the living room, she retrieved the matching jacket to her full skirt of stone beige twill. As she started back to the foyer, the phone rang. More than likely it was Ellery wanting to know how her evening had gone. Shrugging that she could talk to him later, she ignored the ring and walked swiftly back to the foyer.

Leather-bound tomes lined the bookshelves in the library at Morgan's Walk, their weighty presence adding to the room's somber tone. Behind the Victorian pedestal desk of mahogany, a museum piece itself, Hattie Morgan listened to the unanswered rings and impatiently tapped a finger on the leather arm of her chair.

"Where is that girl?" Angrily she pushed the receiver back onto its cradle, breaking the connection and stopping the irritating *brrings* in her ear. Turning, she cast a disgruntled look at the portrait of Kell Morgan hanging above the fireplace mantel. The accumulation of dust and grime over the years had muted the bright copper shade of his hair, but she remembered the oil's original color —and the number of times she'd wished that color had been her own. But that girl, Margaret, had it.

"I should have called earlier. I shouldn't have waited." She reached for the gold handle of her cane, propped against the desk within easy reach. Gripping it with her gnarled fingers, she pounded it once on the hardwood floor, venting her frustration and anger. "How did he find her so quickly? She'll see through him. She has to."

She struck the cane on the floor again, but the loud thud made the pain in her head worse. The prescription Doc Gibbs had given her would alleviate much of it, but she didn't like taking it. She didn't like the dullness that came with it, especially now when she needed to think.

Tucked among lush Monterey pines with the Pacific Ocean at its feet, Carmel-by-the-Sea had long been a favorite retreat of writers and artists drawn to the site by the simple charm of its village look and the wild beauty of its surroundings. Strolling along the sidewalk crowded with tourists, passing shop after quaint shop, Flame decided its true appeal was its wonderfully eccentric character. Here was a town that turned down its thumb at such things as billboards, neon lights, and large retail signs, and turned its back on such customary amenities as sidewalks and curbs on its side streets, then pointed with pride at its dearth of streetlights and traffic signals.

Yet, as she glanced in the window of a gourmet food shop, Flame knew the village community wasn't capable of supporting the one hundred and fifty—odd shops in the town, more than a third of which were galleries carrying the works of local artists. They had to rely on the tourist trade. Carmel wasn't adverse to progress—as long as it came on its terms. Maybe that's what she liked best about it, more than its charm or its picturesque setting.

"Look out." Chance's warning came simultaneously with the tightening pressure of the arm hooked casually around her shoulders.

In the next second, she was hauled against him and out of the path of a nine-year-old racing his bike. By the time Flame saw the boy, he was gone, and she was molded firmly to Chance's side, an altogether pleasant discovery.

Looking up, she saw the grooved smile he directed at her, all lazy and warm like the look in his eyes. "There's nothing more dangerous than a speeding nine-year-old."

"I don't know about that," she said, well aware that the rapid beat of her pulse had nothing to do with nearly being knocked down by a child. "I can think of one or two other things more dangerous."

"Can you?" His gaze strayed to her lips and lingered there. "I can only name one. We'll have to compare notes later and see if we agree."

"Or the ways we differ," she suggested, unconsciously staring at his mouth.

As his arm loosened its band around her, Flame recognized that there was no more reason for her hand to be braced against the rock-hard flatness of his stomach. Reluctantly she withdrew it and turned to resume their stroll down the busy street. But she continued to feel the comfortable weight of his arm draped around her shoulders when they began walking again.

"Hungry?"

She almost laughed at that leading question. The touch of him, the warmth of him, the feel of him beside her had made her hungry, ravenously so. But she couldn't tell him that.

"A little," she admitted instead. "If I remember right, there's a charming Italian restaurant a little farther down the block. We could go there."

"Why not?"

Her memory proved accurate, and after a five-minute wait, they were shown to a table in a corner of the room. Flame smiled when she saw the predictable red-checkered tablecloth and the Chianti bottle dripping with multicolored wax from the candle lodged in its neck.

"This place hasn't changed a bit," she said, recognizing a familiar print of Naples on the wall as she sat down in her chair. "The last time I was here, it was with a group of my sorority sisters just before spring break. Then two carloads of guys from the fraternity followed us down. We all came in here to eat. First someone threw a meatball, then we were flinging spaghetti in each others' hair. Before long, it turned into a food fight, Italian style. I'm surprised the place survived that. It's amazing the insane things you do when you're young and foolish."

"I guess it is."

"What college did you attend?" she asked curiously, then held up a hand to quickly check his answer. "No, let me guess. I used to be very good at this. It was in the Midwest, right?" He nodded, watching her with an amused look. She smiled. "I was positive it wasn't an Ivy League school. It was probably a Big Ten. Ohio?" she guessed.

"Wisconsin."

"I was close."

"Where did you go?"

"Berkeley." She knew her smile faded a little, but she had too few good memories attached to that time in her life. "My mother wanted me to go to her alma mater, Vassar, but I rejected that, insisting that I wasn't going to leave sunny California for the frigid East. I picked the Berkeley campus of the University of California instead—the home of the free spirit right across the bay. I think I chose it because even though I wanted to leave the nest, I didn't want to stray too far. I'm glad I didn't." She hesitated, then explained, "I lost both my parents in an auto accident the following year."

"It must have been a difficult time for you."

"It was. It's not something you ever really get over, but I've learned to accept it." And she'd accomplished that by not letting herself dwell on their deaths but, rather on their lives. "I wish you could have met my father. He was a wonderful man." She paused to smile. "I know. All daughters say that about their fathers, but in my case it was true. Every time I think about him, I remember that perpetual gleam of laughter in his eyes. Even in serious moments, it was there—just below the surface, ready to break through."

Picking up the new lightness of her mood, Chance observed, "And I'll bet one look from those baby greens and he gave you anything you wanted."

Laughing, she admitted, "Most of the time. What about you? What were you like when you were a little boy?" She had the feeling he'd probably been one of those charming rascals, full of the devil, in and out of mischief all the time.

An eyebrow lifted in mocking challenge. "Who said I ever was one?"

Before Flame could respond to that, the waitress stopped at the table to take their order. As she opened her menu, Flame began to wonder if Chance had actually been joking when he'd said that. Something—some underlying edge in his voice—suggested that the remark made in jest was the truth. Belatedly, she remembered that he'd told her his mother had died after a long illness. He'd been eleven at the time. Which meant she'd obviously been ill through much of his childhood. Perhaps he'd even helped to take care of her—as much as a seven-, eight-, nine- or ten-year-old could. It certainly wouldn't have been a happy or a carefree time.

Lunch turned into a long, leisurely affair as they lingered at the table over a cup of cappuccino, talking about everything and nothing. It was midafternoon when they finally emerged from the restaurant and headed for the beach to walk off the meal.

Seagulls wheeled and swooped over the rolling surf, tumbling headlong toward the shore. Idly, Flame watched their acrobatics as she wandered over the white sugar sand with Chance, his arm around her shoulders and her own curved to the back of his waist, a thumb hooked in the belt loop of his denim pants. There was wild, classic beauty to the setting with white-capped waves crashing onto the long, curving stretch of beach, a beach guarded by ancient Monterey cypress, all twisted and bowed by the ceaseless sea wind.

It was a place that appealed to the senses—the wind whipping at her hair, sharp with the tang of the ocean, the muted rumble of the waves rolling onto the beach, the diamond sparkle of the sunlight on the deceptively smooth waters of the bay. And all of it seemed to make her more aware of the man beside her, like the casual rubbing of his hip against hers with each stride they took, or the pervading warmth of his body heat. She was forced to admit that she was more conscious of Chance than she had been of any man in a long time.

"It's beautiful, isn't it?" she said, needing to break the silence no matter how mundane the comment.

"Very."

"I'm glad they haven't built a lot of hotels and condominiums along the beach. It would spoil the natural beauty of it." Her comment drew a low chuckle from him.

"And I'm glad not everyone shares that opinion, or I'd be out of business along with many other developers."

"That's what you do, isn't it?" she realized with a trace of chagrin. "Build fabulously large resort complexes. How did you get into that? There are so many other kinds of things you could have chosen instead—residential, industrial, retail centers."

"A combination of things, I suppose." He paused, his gaze turning thoughtfully to their surroundings, a seriousness in his expression that she rarely saw. "From the time I can remember, the importance of land was drilled into me. But the resort aspect came about while I was at college. Have you ever heard of the Wisconsin Dells?"

"Vaguely. I remember the name, but I don't know anything about it."

"It's a vacation area in Wisconsin, very scenic, very commercialized, and very popular with residents in the surrounding states. Seeing the Dells as a college student and being exposed to Playboy's famous resort at Lake Geneva made me realize that people love to play—young, old, rich, and poor—and everyone in between. Whether the times are good or bad, they still play. If anything, the need to escape becomes even stronger during the bad times—the wars and depressions. That's why they flock to the beaches and the mountains —or any place where they can be surrounded by beauty, atmosphere, and, preferably, luxury."

"Which is exactly what a Stuart resort provides," Flame guessed, then tried to remember: "How many resorts carry the Stuart banner now? Is it six?"

"Seven," he corrected, directing that lazy, lopsided smile at her again. "Plus the one in Tahoe under construction and two more in development."

"Very impressive," she murmured, dipping her head to him in mock homage. And it was, especially when she recalled from the articles about him that he'd built all of his multimillion-dollar resorts in less than twelve years, and considering that some had taken two years to construct, that was quite an accomplishment.

Abruptly, he halted their stroll. "Why is it that we always seem to be talking about me? What about you and your life?"

"Mine isn't nearly as interesting as yours."

"To you maybe, but not to me," he said, slowly shaking his head as he turned toward her, his hand automatically sliding under her jacket onto her waist. At the moment, Flame wasn't sure if she was more aware of the warm pressure of his hand on the curve of her waist or the hard feel of his ribs beneath her own. "There are a dozen things I've yet to find out about you." His voice was pitched low, faintly mocking yet provocatively challenging.

"Such as?"

"Such as . . . how did you manage to become a vice-president without becoming hardened by all the dirty infighting of corporate politics?" His gaze moved slowly over her face, blatant in its interest. "Who put that wariness there that I sometimes see in your eyes? How could your ex-husband have been so foolish as to let you go?" As she felt the brush of his fingers in her hair, he asked, "Does your hair always look like spun fire in the sunlight? Did your mother have lips like yours? And does every man find it as hard as I do to keep my hands off you?"

All sense of caution fled as she moved into his arms, her mouth lifting to meet his more than halfway. There was none of last night's sensual exploration. This time her lips rocked with his in need, tasting the trace of salty spray on them and discovering the hot satin of his tongue. Everything quickened and rose inside her, the blood rushing through her veins and suddenly heightening all her senses.

Her hands had long ago found their way under his Windbreaker and now splayed themselves over his back to feel the flexing play of its muscle. Arching, she leaned into him, letting him take all her weight and intensifying the soaring feeling. There was a dim recognition of his hands moving expertly over her body, but she didn't try to keep track of them. It was enough that they were spreading the intimacy of the kiss over her.

When his mouth rolled off her lips and began to trail a series of warm, wet kisses over her face, Flame felt herself tremble, a passion she had always known she possessed but that had gone too long unused, surfacing. Who had been the last to ignite it? She couldn't remember. But she had the feeling that no one had ever aroused it as thoroughly or as quickly as Chance had. Did she want that? Could she afford it? She felt his mouth at the corner of her lips again and turned into it, her mouth opening to take his tongue and let the hot, soft sensation of it fill her.

Then came the jarring blare of rock music from a ghetto-blaster, drowning out the undulating rumble of the heavy surf. She sensed a matching reluctance as Chance disentangled his mouth from hers and pulled away. The sea wind felt suddenly very cool against her kiss-heated lips. She kept her face turned to him, catching that flash of irritation in the look he threw at the trio of giggling girls, sauntering down the beach darting glances over their shoulders at them. But there was no sign of that irritation when his glance came back to her, the blue of his eyes darkened by the thing that had happened between them—something too private, too intimate to be continued in such a public place. Yet his arms stayed around her, not letting her go immediately.

"Do you have any plans for tonight?" he asked, a faint huskiness in his voice.

"I don't know," she replied softly, the smallest of smiles curving her lips. "Do I?"

The grooves in his hard, lean cheeks deepened. "Indeed you have. Dinner with me and . . . whatever else happens to follow it."

The desire to bed her was in his eyes and he made no attempt to conceal it, silently letting her know that the final decision was hers to make. For her to take that step, emotions had to be involved. But weren't they already? Why couldn't she be honest with herself and admit that she felt a great deal more than mere lust? She wanted to trust. She wanted to believe, especially now that she already cared.

"In that case, maybe we should start back," she said, smiling lightly and moving away from him. "I'd like to shower and change before we have this special dinner."

In silent agreement, Chance turned to head across the heavy sand already marked by the indentations of their previous footsteps. He kept an arm around her, drawing her with him to again walk at his side. For a time, Flame studied the twin set of tracks before them, one large and one small, noticing how closely together they were and thinking how right it looked.

Then she lifted her gaze to the clump of cypress ahead of them, their gnarled trunks gracefully bowed by the wind. At the base of the nearest one stood a man in a tan Windbreaker, smoking a cigarette and . . . watching them. She was sure of it. Abruptly he dropped the cigarette, briefly stepped on it, then swung away and started walking in the same direction they were going. But when he'd turned, his hawklike profile had been clearly outlined.

It was the waiter with the brown shoes, the same man who'd delivered that message of warning last night. Stunned, Flame faltered slightly, breaking the ambling rhythm of their steps and throwing Chance offstride as well.

"Careful." His arm tightened in support as if he thought she had stumbled over something. She felt his glance move to her and quickly tried to eliminate the look of shock from her expression. But obviously not quickly enough. "Is something wrong?" he asked.

"No." She couldn't very well tell him that some man had followed them all the way to Carmel—especially if, as she suspected, it turned out to be Malcom who was paying this man to tail her.

"Are you sure?"

"Of course." She gave him a wide smile. But she wasn't sure he believed her.

10 ✐

IN THE DIMLY LIT LOUNGE, a small combo played a dreamy ballad, all soft and bluesy with longing. A handful of couples moved slowly around the handkerchief-sized dance floor frequently described as intimate. Flame fully agreed with the description as she danced with Chance, not a breath of space between them, their feet moving indifferently to the rhythm, their heads bent together, with Chance now and then turning his mouth against her temple or cheek in discreet caresses.

Idly, she ran her fingers along the corded muscles at the back of his neck, letting them glide into the clipped ends of his black hair. There was a wonderful forgetfulness in his arms that allowed her to block out the memory of the dark green sedan that had followed them back from Carmel three cars behind —and the memory of the same car parked at the corner when Chance had picked her up. None of that had any place here, not with his arms around her and the dreaminess of the music drifting through her.

As his mouth lightly rubbed against her forehead, Flame smiled. "Walks along the beach, candlelit dinners for two, orchids by the jungleful, soft music, soft lights, and cheek-to-cheek dancing—I have the feeling that I'm being very thoroughly romanced," she whispered, and felt his mouth curving into a smile.

"It couldn't possibly be because you are," he murmured dryly, the huskily low pitch of his voice as caressing as the hand on her back.

"Then you admit it?"

"When subtlety fails, bold moves are required."

"And you know how to move boldly, don't you?" The teasing lightness in her voice was simply a part of the verbal game they played—a way of masking the mounting tension, a tension that was both exciting and stimulating. "I do believe you're trying to take advantage of me, Mr. Stuart."

"Wrong." His head moved faintly in denial. "I'm trying to persuade you to take advantage of me." Drawing back to watch her reaction, Chance studied the strong, pure lines of her face, knowing how the mere sight of her moved him, a feeling intensified by the softly rounded shape of her body pressed so easily against him.

For the first time, he saw no wary hesitation shadowing the green of her eyes. They looked back at him bright and clear, shining with a promise that nearly broke through his restraint. He managed to check the impulses that pushed at him, and obeyed, instead, the instincts that had warned him from the beginning that this wasn't a woman who could be forced into giving or swayed by lavish compliments and passion-filled kisses.

He was a man of the land. He always had been. And land taught a man patience, a virtue necessary to give something the time it needed to grow and ripen. Not even buildings sprung up overnight.

"That's an intriguing thought," she murmured softly and his glance fell immediately to her lips, faintly parted. Today, at the beach, he had come close to tasting the fullness of their response. And Chance knew that he'd never be satisfied with anything less than all of it. "Taking advantage of *the* Chance Stuart."

"Interested?" He raised their linked fingers and lightly rubbed his mouth over hers.

She watched him, a half smile forming as if secretly amused by some thought that had just occurred to her. "There's this little voice inside my head that keeps saying, 'Take a chance.'"

"I like that voice. Maybe you can persuade it to speak a little louder."

"I don't need to. I want to take a chance." She raised her head to him, her upturned lips seeking his mouth.

He had barely tasted the honeyed gloss of her lips when the band stopped playing and a scattering of faint applause broke around them. Chance pulled back slightly, breaking the contact but not letting her go. "Why don't we continue this at a place that's less crowded and infinitely more private than here? Like my suite."

"I think that's an excellent idea."

Chance unlocked the door to his suite, then stepped back to let Flame precede him. Without hesitation, she walked by him and wandered into the sitting room, then paused and turned back to him with a model's grace, the tiered flounces on the skirt of her slim black silk dress briefly flaring out. The collar of her fur jacket was high around her throat, the sooty black of it contrasting sharply with the copper-gold of her hair.

Deliberately she looked around the room, then brought her glance back to him, something playful about the soft line of her mouth. "I thought I might find a room full of orchids waiting for me again. Or, at the very least, peach champagne on ice."

He went to her, a smoothness inside him that wouldn't last any longer than it took to touch her. "We don't need those props, Flame," he said, his hands gliding along her jaw and into the hair behind her ears. "Not when we have this."

He kissed her with a long, slow warmth that gradually took possession of both of them. For him, he knew there could be no orchid half as fragrant as the perfumed scent of her hair, and no wine half as intoxicating as the taste of her on his tongue.

This time there was no hesitation, no testing to see if the ground could support what was being built. Instead it was a meeting of two forces, each strong in its own right, and in the silent probing of the other's strength, uncovering feelings that didn't require passion to achieve intimacy.

As she leaned into his kiss, Chance felt the heaviness of her body settle against him, the thickness of the fur preventing him from feeling the womanly shape of her. Reluctantly he straightened, his hands sliding down to slip the jacket from her. He gave it a toss onto the closest chair, his gaze never leaving her face, all the while highly conscious of the nameless feelings that surged through him, powerfully aroused yet oddly tender, too.

For an instant, he searched for something to say, but all of it had been said before—in some other hotel room, to some other woman. He didn't want to use those same words with Flame. There was a flicker of surprise at the realization that he wanted it to be different with her.

But there was a pattern to things that couldn't be changed, and he recognized that, too, as he picked her up, cradling her in his arms, and carried her into the bedroom. There, he set her down and kissed her again, rediscovering the earthy and stimulating pressure of her lips.

When he pulled back to loosen his tie, she held his gaze with an eloquent ease and raised her hands, reaching behind her neck to unfasten the top hook of her dress. Leaving his tie half undone, Chance turned her around and slowly slid the zipper all the way down to the base of her spine, watching with interest the back of her dress separate and reveal the creamy white of her skin and the lacy black of her teddy. He slid the dress off her shoulders and down her arms, stimulated by the silken texture of her skin. As he bent to nibble at the white bareness of a wide, straight shoulder, the dress fell the rest of the way to the floor in a rustling whisper.

While his fingers edged the thin straps of her teddy off her shoulder, his mouth followed its ridge to the base of her neck. Her head was thrown back and to the side, allowing him to explore at length the rapidly pulsing vein in her neck. He was conscious of the disturbed, shallow breaths she took, and the faint tremors she tried to contain. He wanted more, so much more.

He turned her into his arms and found himself confronted with the rest of the racy nothingness of her teddy. "Black lace," he murmured, gazing at the wispy pattern of dark threads that so thinly veiled the slow but agitated rise and fall of her breasts.

"You said black lace on a woman did things to a man's blood." There was a disturbed edge to her voice that reached out to him. "And I wanted to affect you that way."

"You do." His own voice vibrated from some place deep inside him.

With infinite care, he dispensed with the fragile garment, prolonging the moment to heighten the anticipation for both of them. Anticipation became realization as she stood naked before him, pooled in the light coming from the doorway to the sitting room. For a moment it was enough just to gaze at the picture she made, her lips faintly parted, her eyes on him, the light shining on the rounded contours of her body and shadowing its hollows. Then he had to touch and prove that this statuesque figure was real.

He started at her neck, his fingertips gliding down the slender arc of her throat to the hollow at the base of it. Separating, his hands moved along twin paths to the jutting roundness of her breasts, their fullness a wondrous and lusty surprise to him as they spilled over the cup of his hands. He felt her breathe in sharply, deeply, then hold it, her lashes fluttering down. He rubbed his thumbs over the erect points of her nipples, drawing a tremor from her, followed by a sound that fell halfway between a sigh and a moan, a purring quality to it that matched the way she arched her body toward him. He let his hands trail lower, onto the flatness of her stomach, muscles contracting inwardly at his touch. Then he spread them over the cradling protrusion of her pelvic bones and around, onto the firm cheeks of her bare bottom, and drew her to him.

There was no more doubt now. She was very real, the outline of her rounded breasts pressed firmly to his chest, the sensation of them penetrating through his clothes. She was all heated flesh moving under his hands as she came to him, her lips seeking his and breathing their drugging sweetness into his mouth. He gathered her in, briefly giving way to the pressures inside. Her lips parted under the stroke of his tongue, her own mating with his, hot and soft, tasting of wine and some other intoxicating flavor uniquely her own. At last, he set her away from him and his own clothes made a pile on the floor next to her, her admiring eyes watching him all the while, their look heavy-lidded with desire.

As he lifted her for the last time, her arms wound themselves around his neck. There was silence between them, their eyes, their hands, their bodies communicating much more eloquently than mere words could have done. Chance carried her to the bed, the covers already turned invitingly back. The mattress dipped under his weight centered on the point of one knee as he laid her down, then followed after her.

She rolled to him, her slim hand gliding across his bare chest, and running its fingers through the curling hairs, then sliding up to the back of his neck. The pull of her parted lips brought his mouth down to them, open and hot, eating at him with need.

He slid a leg between her thighs and instantly felt her push against it as he cupped a breast in his hand and played with its nipple, rolling it between his thumb and forefinger and marveling at its high erectness. Shifting his attention from her lips, he explored the perfumed hollow behind her ear. Taking her delicate lobe between his teeth, he nipped at it gently, then nibbled his way down the long cord in her neck. She was all motion against him, her hands running over his shoulders, neck, and back, her body straining toward him, her hips arching in a rubbing rhythm until he was surrounded by heat, pressure pushing at him from inside as well as out.

With the thigh he had wedged between her legs, he lifted her higher in the bed, bringing her luscious breasts within easy range. Her fingers tangled with his hair, digging and flexing as his mouth moved from the hollow of her throat to a tautly erect nipple and traced its round tip with his tongue. Her back arched, her body urging him to take all of it, but he needed no such coercion as he drew it in. Aroused by the deep-throated sounds that came from her and the quickened rate of her breathing, Chance let his hand move lower, abandoning its fondling of her other breast to wander over the flatness of her stomach, pausing to investigate her navel then finally sliding into that silken nest of auburn-gold hair pressed so tightly against his thigh.

He wanted her. God, how he wanted her—right now—this minute. He almost let himself be swept away by the force of that need, then finally controlled it. This was their first time together and he wanted it to be theirs, together. He didn't question the why of it—not now—and concentrated instead on prolonging the pleasure for both of them and reveling in the taste, the touch, the smell, the sound—the sight of her in his bed.

When the pressure became an agony neither could endure, he shifted onto her, his weight briefly pinning her. With no barrier to break, he was absorbed into her and she was all tight and warm around him. He brought his mouth down, slanting it across her lips as he lifted her hands high above her head and linked her fingers with his. The need to hurry fled. This was a moment to be enjoyed to the fullest. He moved slowly, making each thrust long and deep, and feeling the rise of her hips match each stroke.

As the tempo increased, seemingly on its own, there was only sensation—the feel of her tongue licking away the beads of perspiration that had formed on his upper lip, and the rake of her teeth across his shoulder before she bit into his muscle, smothering the moaned cry of his name, the urging press of her hands running over his back and buttocks, and the soft, wild suppleness of her body melded so completely with him. There was an illusion of the world spinning and he wrapped his arms tightly around her, not letting her go any-where without him.

Unable to sleep, Flame carefully eased Chance's arm from her and slid noise-lessly from the bed. She paused to look back and make sure she hadn't wakened him. In sleep, there was even more strength in his features, a kind of hard pride that was usually masked by a smile. She stared for a moment, remembering again that absolute rawness of emotion, so powerful and so beautiful . . . much more than excitement, much more than exquisite release.

She turned from the sight of his face and the clean, male lines of hard muscle and flesh. At her feet lay the white of his dress shirt. She hesitated briefly, then picked it up and put it on, smiling at the sleeves that were much longer than her arms. She rolled back the cuffs to her wrists and padded silently into the darkened sitting room, fastening two of the front buttons along the way.

She drifted over to the window and gazed at the night lights of San Fran-cisco that gleamed back at her from the inky darkness. Absently, she turned up the collar of his shirt and buried her face in it, breathing in the heady fragrance of his masculine cologne.

When she'd come to his suite, she hadn't known one moment of doubt. She'd wanted him to make love to her. She'd wanted him, and she'd had no desire to hide those feelings. For too long she'd kept her own natural passion suppressed.

But she'd never expected his lovemaking to unleash this torrent of feeling. It was a little frightening—this depth of feeling she had for him now. She shied from the word *love*. To use it would mean he had the power to hurt her. But, dear God, if she didn't see him again after tonight, that would hurt, too.

"There you are." As his voice came to her from the darkness, Flame stiff-ened, suddenly sensing that he was very near. When she felt his hands settle onto the looseness of the shirt's sleeves, she turned before they could actually close around her arms. There was a lazily possessive look in his eyes. "I was beginning to think I dreamed you."

"I couldn't sleep." Seeing him standing there with that look in his eyes, she felt that swell of incredibly tender feelings again. As his hands curved onto the sides of her waist, she smoothed her own over the hard, flat muscles of his chest, the contact reminding her of his strength—and his gentleness. "Chance, I—"

But he cut in before she could explain the cause of her sleeplessness. "It's scary as hell, isn't it?"

Stunned that he could know exactly what she was thinking, she offered no resistance when he drew her closer, cradling her hips against his. "How—"

"—did I know?" He finished the question for her and smiled. "Do you think you're the only one it happened to? In case you've forgotten, I was there, too."

"You very definitely were," she admitted. "But I didn't know if it had the same impact for you."

"It did." He gathered her the rest of the way into his arms and rubbed his cheek and mouth against her hair. "Tomorrow is going to come whether we like it or not, Flame. And when it does, I'll have to leave."

"I know." Pride kept her from clinging to him.

"We'll both have our share of nights to sleep alone. I don't want tonight to be one of them."

There was no mocking inflection in his voice, no teasing, no making light of it; he was completely serious. Moved by that, Flame gazed at this man who fit her as comfortably and warmly as a second skin.

"Neither do I," she said, certain now that getting through the lonely nights ahead would be difficult as long as she had the stirring memories of this night to keep her company.

"Then come back to bed with me."

The urge was strong to say something ridiculously romantic, like "I'd go anywhere with you." Instead Flame shifted slightly in his arms and curved an arm around the back of his bare waist to turn him toward the bedroom, letting her actions say what would have sounded too foolish coming from her lips.

Back in the bedroom, Flame slipped out of his shirt, and turned to the bed. Chance was already there, his long frame stretched out full length on the mattress, the covers down around his waist revealing the male torso that was all hard, flat muscle and bronze flesh. She paused for an instant, knowing that he was looking at her and knowing, too, that he liked what he saw.

As she climbed into bed, Chance rolled onto his side and reached out to snare her and draw her firmly to his side. His face was inches from her. She watched his gaze idly follow the track of his hand as it glided over her rib cage to cup the underswell of her breast, giving rise again to those initial stirrings of desire.

Then his gaze came back to wander over her face in a thoughtful study. "I can't seem to make up my mind," he murmured.

"About what?" She ran her hand over his arm, feeling the bunched muscles.

"If this is where you belong—or where I belong? There's a part of me that wants to put a brand on you and claim you as my private and very personal property," he said, then paused. "And there's another part of me that feels very humble. And *that* is a feeling entirely new to me."

"For me, too," she whispered.

"Flame." That was all he said before his mouth opened on her lips taking them whole and devouring them with a bold sensuality that she easily matched.

That intense hunger was something she understood too well, and she returned it with equal aggression.

This time when they made love, she was struck by the wild harmony of it, like the fury of a storm that comes, unleashes its torrents, then passes, leaving in its wake the earthy and invigorating feeling of clean, fresh air.

11 ~

CHURCH BELLS PEALED the call to morning worship as Chance pulled up in front of her flat. At the same moment, Flame saw Ellery coming down the steps of the Victorian mansion. She waved briefly to him, and ignored his halt of surprise as she turned to Chance.

"There's no need to walk me to the door." She didn't want to prolong the goodbye that had to be said.

"I'll call you."

And with Chance, that wasn't a line. He never said anything he didn't mean. She'd learned that about him, as well as many other things. "If you don't reach me the first time, don't give up. Wherever I am, I'll be back."

"I don't give up on anything." His hand tunneled under her hair, cupping the back of her neck and pulling her to his mouth. Flame responded to the heated kiss that was packed with feeling and promise. When he released her, she felt warm all the way through. The glittering darkness of his blue eyes added their own promise to the kiss as he murmured, "Till next time."

"Till next time." She echoed the phrase that had become almost a talisman to her, then reached for the door handle.

When she climbed out of the sportscar, she was faintly surprised at how clear-eyed she felt, with no sting of tears, no painful tightness in her chest. All because of that wonderful certainty that there would be a next time. Leaving the car she crossed to the base of the steps, then turned to watch Chance drive away.

"Since you're so terribly overdressed for church, this is obviously the morning after a glorious night before." Ellery came down two more steps to stand behind her.

"What makes you think it was only the night before that was glorious?" She was a little surprised by the lightheartedly smug feeling that prompted her to tease him back. It had been so long since she'd been in love that she'd forgotten how good it could make a person feel.

Ellery drew his hand back, his eyes widening slightly and that eyebrow arching as she turned to climb the steps. "We are feeling a little cocky this morning, aren't we?—if you'll excuse the expression."

His remark didn't immediately register, her attention distracted by the sight of the dark green sedan that pulled into the empty parking space on the opposite side of the street. "Ellery, without being obvious, take a look at that dark green sedan—a Ford, I think—parked about halfway down the hill. Can you see the driver?" She kept her back to the street—and the sedan—and pretended to look through her evening bag for the door key.

"Not very well," Ellery said after a brief pause. "Why?"

"Do you remember that waiter with the brown shoes at the DeBorgs' party last week? He had a big hooked nose."

"I remember." A silent question remained in his voice, waiting for an explanation for all this.

"Look closely at the driver and see if it's the waiter."

"He's too far away. All I can see is the shape of a man's head on the driver's side."

"Never mind." She shrugged in irritation and took the key from her bag. "Let's go inside."

Frowning, Ellery glanced one last time at the car, then followed Flame as she ran lightly up the steps to her door. "What's this all about? Why would you think that's the waiter?"

"Because he's the sender of that nasty note—or more correctly the deliverer of the note." She inserted the key in the deadbolt lock and gave it a quick turn, then pushed her weight against the door to open it.

"How do you know that?"

"Because—" She breezed into the foyer, leaving Ellery to close the door behind them, then paused at the door to the hall closet and slipped off her fur jacket. "—he had another message for me at the opera Friday night. That one he delivered in person."

"Another message?"

"Yes. The gist of it was the same as the first—stay away from him. Only this time there was an added warning that if I didn't, I'd be sorry." She was conscious of the brittleness beneath her offhand manner, but she couldn't pretend anymore that it didn't bother her. "On top of that, he followed me everywhere I went all weekend." Stiffly she draped the jacket onto its shouldered hanger and hung it in the closet.

"Everywhere?"

"No, not everywhere—thankfully." In spite of her tension or maybe because of it, she glanced at Ellery and laughed, again conscious of her newfound feelings. "And don't raise your eyebrow at me, Ellery Dorn."

"Would I do that?" he declared in mock innocence.

"You do it all the time."

"At least now I know why I wasn't able to reach you all weekend. Although I must admit at the moment I'm more interested in finding out who the *him* is in the 'stay-away-from' messages. Was the second more enlightening than the first?"

"No," she admitted. "But it has to be Chance."

"And the sender?"

She hesitated as she briefly let her glance lock with Ellery's. "I think it's Malcom. Who else is there? Initially I thought it might be Lucianna, but she strikes me as the kind who would come at me with her claws unsheathed if she thought I was taking her man." She paused, her shoulders sagging in vague discouragement. "After that . . . disagreement . . . I had with Malcom the other day, I know he isn't above making threats. And this business of having me followed—it could be his way of impressing me with the lengths he'll go to for what he wants."

"What are you going to do about it?" This time Ellery was just as serious as she was.

"I know what I'd like to do. I'd like to threaten him with a sexual harassment suit."

"But you don't dare," Ellery guessed.

"Not if I want to continue as a vice-president of Boland and Hayes." A wry smile pulled at one corner of her mouth. "Besides, a suit like that would do more damage to my reputation and career than it ever would do to his. What agency would want to hire me after that kind of headline? And what client would want to work with me? None. So . . . I don't have any choice but to tough it out with him and show him that I won't be intimidated, not by him or anyone else."

Ellery set his attaché case on the floor, freeing his hands to applaud her mockingly. "Marvelous speech, darling. Stiff upper lip and all that."

She threw him a look of mild exasperation. "If you're quite through, you can tell me what you wanted to see me about. This obviously isn't a social visit or you wouldn't have brought that along." She gestured at the leather case by his feet.

"My timing may be questionable, but I have with me some new ideas for the Powell holiday ads." His mouth twisted in a ruefully apologetic line. "I thought it would be a good idea if we went over them privately, then, if you shoot them down the way you did before, you won't completely demoralize my staff."

"You're right, Ellery. Your timing is very questionable."

"If you'd rather wait—"

"No. Just give me a few minutes to shower and change—and to forget that without a great deal of effort I could learn to heartily dislike Malcom." She started down the hall to her bedroom, adding over her shoulder, "Feel free to make some coffee."

The aroma of freshly brewed coffee permeated the air when Flame came out of her bedroom, dressed more casually in a pair of brown slacks and an oversized beige sweater. She hadn't bothered to dry her hair, instead slicking it back from her face, the wetness of it bringing out the red lights. She found Ellery in the living room with all the roughly sketched layouts and storyboards spread over the coffee table.

"I poured you some coffee." With a wave of his hand, he indicated the cup sitting on the glass top of the occasional table.

"Thanks." Retrieving it, she sipped at the steaming hot liquid, the smell and the taste of it reminding her of the breakfast she'd shared with Chance in his suite mere hours ago. She'd eaten most of hers while sitting on his lap, all because she had tried to decline any food, insisting that she couldn't eat in the mornings. Chance had taken it as a challenge, pulled her onto his lap, and proceeded to feed her bites of a pineapple Danish. In retaliation she had done the same to him with a raspberry one. Before it was over they had ended up licking the filling from each other's fingers and kissing it from the other's lips, the flavors of raspberry and pineapple mingling together in the process. It had been the most enjoyable breakfast she'd ever had.

She glanced at the black lacquered mantel clock, deciding Chance was probably at the airport by now. Possibly he could have even taken off already. Idly, she wondered when he would call.

"Well?" Ellery prodded her for a reaction. "Are any of these the slant you wanted?"

With a start, Flame realized that she'd been looking at the sketches without seeing any of them. "Sorry, I—" The ringing of the telephone interrupted her, and she jumped to answer it, certain it was Chance calling from the airport.

But the whiskey-rough voice on the other end of the line didn't belong to Chance. "Is that you, Margaret Rose? I've been calling all weekend. This is Hattie Morgan."

"Hattie." Belatedly Flame remembered the proud old woman who had come to see her with that wild story about being related and leaving a ranch in Oklahoma to her. She'd thought she'd heard the last of her. "Where are you?" she wondered.

"At Morgan's Walk, of course," came the snapped answer.

"Of course. I should have guessed." She felt a twinge of pity that the poor woman was still clinging to her fantasy. More than likely she was at some nursing home, and all this was just a lonely attempt to reach out to somebody. "Hattie, is there someone there I could talk to? An attendant or a nurse?"

"A nurse?! No, there is not!"

"It isn't that I don't want to talk to you, Hattie." Flame tried again. "I merely want to—"

"You don't believe me, do you?" came the accusation. "You think everything I said was the ramblings of a senile old woman. I'll have you know that my mind is as sharp as yours."

"I'm sure it is—"

"No, you aren't. But I can prove everything I said to you. Do you have a paper and pencil?"

"Yes." A notepad and pen lay next to the telephone.

"I'm calling you long distance from Oklahoma. Mark this number down." With a sharp, staccato rhythm, she reeled the numbers off, then commanded: "Now, read it back to me."

Flame couldn't help smiling as she repeated the numbers she'd hastily jotted on the pad. The woman was indeed sharp—sharp enough to know that she could have pretended to write them down. Now Hattie knew she had.

"Good," came the clipped response. "Now I'm going to hang up and I want you to call me back at that number."

"Hattie—"

"No. I don't want you to have any doubt that I am calling from Oklahoma. You can check the telephone directory yourself and see that I've given you the area code for Oklahoma."

"I know that—"

"Then do it and call me back. Reverse the charges, if you like." There was a sharp click, then the line went dead.

Frowning with sudden doubt, Flame slowly lowered the receiver to stare at it. Had she misjudged this Hattie Morgan? Was it possible she had been telling the truth?

"Is something wrong?"

Ellery's question deepened her frown. "I don't know." She depressed the disconnect switch, held it down for a short span of seconds, then released it and waited for the dial tone. When it came, she pushed the "O" button for the operator. "Yes, the area code for Oklahoma, please," she requested as soon as a voice came on the line. "The Tulsa area. . . . Nine one eight," she repeated while staring at the same set of digits she'd written on the pad. "Thank you," she murmured automatically as she hung up the phone.

"Who was that call from?" Ellery was now on his feet. "What's going on?"

She half-turned to him, still trying to sort through it all herself. "Do you remember my telling you about that elderly woman who showed up at my door last week with that preposterous story that I was her last living relative and she was going to leave me her ranch in Oklahoma? That's who just called me."

"What did she want?"

"She wants me to call her back—and the number she gave me has an Oklahoma area code." She exhaled a silent laugh of disbelief and doubt. "You don't suppose all that was true? I thought she had slipped away from some nursing home or private care center. I mean, she could have easily read somewhere that my maiden name is Morgan—or that my Morgan ancestors married into one of the founding families in San Francisco." She stared at the phone, remembering how casually she had dismissed the whole incident. "It seemed so logical that a lonely old woman with no family of her own would want to pretend that she was related to me, especially when she saw that I had red hair, the same color as some grandfather of hers."

"You don't really believe she intends to leave you some cattle ranch in Oklahoma?" Again there was that high arch of an eyebrow from Ellery, conveying skepticism and question.

"I don't know what to believe," Flame admitted and picked up the telephone again, dialing the number Hattie had given her. "But if she answers, at least I'll know she told me the truth when she said she lived in Oklahoma."

The first ring had barely ended when a voice demanded, "Hello?"

"Hello—Hattie?" She felt oddly tense.

"Yes," came the clipped response, followed by an even sharper demand: "Is that you, Margaret Rose?"

"Yes, it is."

"You certainly took your time about calling me back."

"I did as you suggested and confirmed that the area code you gave me was for Oklahoma."

"Then you should be satisfied on that score." No attempt was made to mask the indignation and irritation in her voice.

"I am." Flame tried to remain tolerant.

"I intended to ask how soon you would be able to visit Morgan's Walk, but it's become quite apparent to me that you neither believe in its existence nor that we are related."

"Hattie, you surely have to realize how it would all sound to me."

"I do. Although I thought I had convinced you of the truth of my claim when we talked. After all the searching I did to find you, I—But that is beside the point, isn't it? My word is not enough. You obviously require proof, and it's probably best that you do. Keep that wariness, Margaret Rose. It is better that you don't trust anyone too much."

"You said something to that effect before," Flame recalled.

"And it's true . . . as you'll find out. But—be that as it may—since it's proof you need, it's proof you shall have. I'll arrange immediately for copies to be sent to you documenting that you and I are of the same Morgan lineage. They should be in your possession no later than the end of the week."

"Hattie, that isn't necessary—"

"Oh, but it is. It's very necessary. You must learn that everything I tell you will be the truth—and everything can be supported with proof."

"I believe you," she insisted with fading patience.

"No. Not yet you don't, but you shall. In the meantime, I would prefer that you take nothing on blind faith. Now, when you receive the papers, study them over carefully. Then we'll talk about your trip to Morgan's Walk."

"What is it that you're not telling me?" Flame demanded, giving way to her growing suspicion. "There's something I should know, isn't there?"

"There are many things you should know now that Morgan's Walk will be yours when I'm gone. Too many to discuss on the phone. We'll go over everything when you come here."

"But—"

"There is one other thing I must know, Margaret Rose, and it's very important."

Flame pressed her lips tightly together, irritated by the way Hattie had sidestepped her question. As the pause lengthened, she realized a response was expected. "I'm listening, Hattie," she challenged somewhat sharply.

"I was beginning to wonder," she retorted. "Now, tell me, have you mentioned my visit and our . . . little discussion to anyone—anyone at all, even in passing?"

"Yes. Was it supposed to be a secret?" She frowned.

"How many people did you tell? Think carefully."

"Only two."

"Are you quite sure?"

"I am very sure," Flame replied, allowing a trace of impatience to enter her voice. "It wasn't something I went around telling everyone I met."

"These two people, who are they? And please, you must accept that if it wasn't important, I wouldn't ask."

Flame paused, wondering whether she might have been right about Hattie Morgan all along. All this cross-examination and talk of proof was becoming a bit much. "One was a very close friend of mine, whom I have known for years —a Mr. Ellery Dorn. And the other was a client and friend, Mr. Malcom Powell."

"Those are the only ones you told? No one else?"

"No one. I've already said that." She tried very hard to remember she was talking to an elderly woman—and apparently a slightly paranoid one at that.

"In that case, I want your word of honor that you will not discuss this further—with anyone. And when you receive the copies of the documents I'm sending you, don't show them to anyone . . . unless, of course, you wish to take them to your attorney to verify their authenticity. But no one else. Do I have your word on that?"

"Why this secrecy? When you were here, you weren't concerned about who I might talk to."

"I didn't see the need then. Now I do. I have my reasons, Margaret Rose, and I will explain them to you when you come to Morgan's Walk. As I said, I will tell you everything then. And you will understand perfectly why I must ask for your word now. Do I have it?"

She sighed, knowing that this was the only answer she was going to get. "Yes, you have my word."

"You won't regret it. Goodbye, Margaret Rose. We shall talk again next weekend, after you have had an opportunity to study the papers."

"Goodbye, Hattie." She hung up the phone, still trying to fathom the entire conversation.

"That sounded like a rather bizarre conversation," Ellery prompted.

Flame turned, lifting her arms in an expressive shrug. "I'm not even going to pretend I understand. Although I have the feeling that I just took a blood oath not to divulge our conversation to anyone, including you."

"Why?" His frown was halfway between amusement and amazement.

"I don't know." She shook her head. "It's all terribly mysterious and hush-hush. So hush-hush, she won't tell me. Maybe it's a ploy to get me sufficiently intrigued so that I'll fly out there."

"Intrigue. That's a curious choice of words."

"And maybe more accurate than I know."

12

AS HATTIE RETURNED the receiver to its cradle, she heard the creak of a floorboard in the great hall outside the study door. For an instant she held herself motionless, listening. After eighty-one years, she knew every creak and groan in this old house, and the sound she'd just heard hadn't been one of its natural grumblings.

"Who's there?"

There was no answer to her demand. Her mouth tightened into a thin line as she grabbed up her cane and pushed out of the worn leather chair. With the tap of the cane giving her walk a three-beat tempo, she crossed to the arched opening, the double set of pocket doors flush to the carved frame. Her sweeping glance searched the area to her right, then homed in like an arrow on the stout, gray-haired woman.

"I knew there was someone out here," Hattie declared. "You were eavesdropping on my telephone conversations again, weren't you, Maxine?"

The woman turned, indignantly drawing herself up to her full height, her already ample bosom managing to appear considerably larger as she pushed her chest out. "With all due respect, Miss Hattie, I have better things to do with my time than listen in on your conversations."

"Then what are you doing out here and why didn't you answer when I called out?" Hattie's gaze narrowed suspiciously on her, not believing a word of that disavowal, however exemplary it sounded.

"I didn't answer because I thought you were talking to someone on the telephone. I didn't realize you expected me to reply."

"Then you admit you knew I was on the phone."

"Yes, I knew. And I also knew that this dusting needed to be done. Which is precisely what I was doing."

Hattie had a moment's uncertainty as she tried to find a flaw in the house-keeper's explanation, but the sudden stabbing pain in her head eliminated it as she paled at the excruciating pain and started to lift a hand to her head, feeling the blackness press in on her.

"You didn't take your pill, did you?" Maxine Saunders accused. "I'll get it for you."

"No. No pill. I don't want it." Hattie fought back the blackness, winning another battle with it.

"You know what the doctor said—"

"Such touching concern, Maxine. One would almost think you cared," she taunted bitterly.

"After spending the last thirty years of my life taking care of Morgans, it's become a habit, Miss Hattie," she retorted, almost as sharply. "I've tried to give it up many times. Maybe one day I'll succeed."

"Thirty years, is that what it's been?" Hattie struggled to recall despite the throbbing in her head. "Yes, that's right." She slowly nodded. "You were always making sugar cookies for . . . that whelp. Said they were his favorites."

All expression left the woman's face. "He was a little boy."

Hattie harrumphed at that, then stepped back and pulled the pocket doors closed, eliminating the possibility that the housekeeper would eavesdrop on future conversations. The cane swung with each stride, hitting the floor a beat off from her footsteps, as Hattie walked back to the large swivel chair behind the mahogany desk and sat down.

Again she picked up the telephone, this time to dial Ben Canon's home number. The housekeeper answered and she waited impatiently for Ben to come on the line.

When he did, Hattie came straight to the point. "Make copies of the documents and the summary that man from Utah sent us and get them off to Margaret Rose right away. But be certain you don't make any mention of Stuart. Include my sister's death if you think it's necessary, but not her marriage or the child that came from it."

"That may not be a wise thing to do under the circumstances, Hattie," he replied. "She's seeing Stuart—"

"Yes, yes, I know," she interrupted impatiently. "You told me."

"You need to talk to her, Hattie."

"I have. That's why I want you to send those documents to her."

"No, I mean, you need to warn her about Stuart."

"I can't. She already thinks I'm a senile old woman who doesn't know what she's talking about. She's not entirely convinced we're even related. She thinks I made it all up. Heaven knows why. If I told her the truth about Stuart and tried to warn her that she's walking into a trap with him, she'd never believe me. More than likely, she'd be convinced I was crazy. Worse than that, she'd go to

Stuart with the story. He'd twist things around and sweet-talk her into turning against me. No, I need to have her here when I tell her. I need to convince her that what I say is the truth."

"How do you know Stuart hasn't talked to her?"

"She would have told me if he had."

"You can't be certain of that," Ben argued.

"Yes, I can. She would have confronted me with any story he might have told her, but she didn't. She swore she mentioned my visit to only two people, and neither of them was Stuart."

"He's playing it very cool, isn't he?" Ben murmured. "I'd still like to know how he found out about her so quickly. We've got a leak somewhere, Hattie."

"When will you have my new will ready?" she demanded. "I know Stuart. He'll contest the handwritten one we did in your office."

"I'm typing up the last of it right now, here at home. I'll bring it out for you to sign as soon as I'm finished. I thought it would be best if no one in my office knew about it."

"Good. And be quick about those copies, Ben. I'm running out of time."

"I know, Hattie. I know."

Then he rang off and once again she was surrounded by the companionable silence of the house. This time she could draw no comfort from it, not when she knew the very walls around her were threatened. Her glance strayed to the pair of antique oval frames that sat on the desk next to the telephone. Silver filigree surrounded a photograph of her parents taken on their wedding day. But it was the picture in the second frame that claimed Hattie's attention. She stared at the photograph of a young, dark-haired girl with big, trusting eyes, her face shining with innocence.

"This is your fault, Elizabeth." The tenderness of love softened her voice and added an unspoken forgiveness to the words as Hattie reached out and lightly stroked an arthritically crooked finger over the cheek of the girl in the picture, her baby sister.

Elizabeth Morgan had been sickly almost from the day she was born. Countless days and countless nights Hattie had nursed her fragile sister through bouts of colds, fevers, pneumonia, and influenza. At times, it had seemed that delicate little Elizabeth had caught every sickness that went around, but with her it had always been worse than anyone else had. Often Hattie had wondered whether her sister might have been stronger if their mother hadn't been so ill before she was born. She gazed at the photograph and the aura of fragility it had captured forever.

"Why did I send you into town that day? Why?" It had been an innocent errand to pick up a few nonessential supplies that could have waited for another day, but Elizabeth had wanted to go—she'd wanted to be helpful instead of always a burden. And Hattie had let her go alone.

Elizabeth was late—later than she should have been. Hattie's imagination worked overtime, envisioning dozens of dreadful reasons—but she couldn't know how dreadful. Cranky with worry, she jumped on Elizabeth the instant she returned.

"Where have you been? Do you realize how late it is? How could it possibly take you this long to run a simple errand?"

Elizabeth laughed at her questions, as usual, not at all bothered by their sharpness. "Don't fuss at me like I was one of the hired hands, Hattie. I would have been back sooner, but halfway home, I had a flat tire."

"A flat tire." Her glance sliced to the car, noticing for the first time that the tire on the left front wheel was darker than the others—and minus the clogs of dried red mud that marked them. "You couldn't have changed it yourself." Elizabeth wasn't strong enough to either jack up the car or remove the lug nuts, and Hattie knew that.

"No. A man on a motorcycle stopped and changed it for me or I'd still be there."

"Not one of those hoodlums in a black leather jacket." She shuddered inwardly at the thought of her Elizabeth in the company of one of those toughs with their disgustingly long hair.

"He was nice, Hattie. And he wears the leather jacket to protect him from flying gravel and things like that."

But Elizabeth didn't tell Hattie the way he'd looked when he took his jacket off—or the way his muscles had bulged beneath that thin T-shirt when he'd been changing the flat—or the way his shiny black hair had gleamed in the sunlight—or the way he'd swaggered a little when he walked—or the way he'd looked at her as if she was a piece of candy he wanted to eat. At twenty-seven, Elizabeth hadn't had much experience with men, seldom dating in high school partly because she'd been sick much of the time and partly because Hattie had been strict about when she could date—and who. But mostly because she was painfully shy.

And she knew that Hattie wouldn't approve of this boy at all. Although he wasn't a boy; he was a man in his early twenties, younger than she. She'd been a little scared when he first rode up. Everyone knew that the guys who rode motorcycles had a reputation for being fast. But it had been a little exciting, too. That's why she had let him coax her into trying on his black leather jacket. She had liked that—and the way he had smoothed his hands down her arms once she put it on.

"Have you ever ridden a motorcycle?" he'd asked.

"No."

"Come on. I'll take you for a spin on mine."

"I—can't." She knew she shouldn't even be talking to him, let alone trying on his jacket and definitely not riding his motorcycle. Yet he made her feel so daring—and pretty. She wasn't of course. She was plain—a dark mouse and not vibrant and strongly handsome like Hattie. "I'll be late as it is."

"Where's home?"

"Morgan's Walk."

"You live there?" He looked again at the car, then back at her.

"Yes."

"What's your name?"

"Elizabeth. Elizabeth Morgan."

He'd lifted an eyebrow at that. "You must be the dragon lady's baby sister."

"You shouldn't call her that." For an instant, she regretted letting this conversation begin.

"I'm sorry." He smiled, and it was the kind of smile that made her want to melt. "If she's your sister, then she can't be all bad."

"She isn't. She's wonderful." But guilt set in. "I'll have to go. She'll be worried about me." Hurriedly she removed his jacket and gave it back to him.

"You aren't going to run off, are you?" he protested when she moved to the car and opened the driver's door.

"I—Thanks for stopping to help . . . and changing the tire for me." Yet the way he looked at her, Elizabeth had the feeling it was more than thanks he wanted. "I . . . please, let me pay you something—" She reached for her purse on the car seat.

"Keep it," he said. "I don't take money for helping a lady in distress, especially such a beautiful lady."

No one had ever told her she was beautiful. No one.

But she didn't mention any of that to Hattie—or the feeling that her knight in shining armor had just ridden up on a motorcycle. It would have sounded too silly, especially when she didn't know his name.

For days afterward, Elizabeth lived in secret hope of seeing him again. She made up excuses to go into town, thinking she might run into him. Finally, at the Columbus Day Parade, she found him again. And when he asked her again to go for a ride on his motorcycle, she got up enough nerve to go with him. She loved every minute of it—the racing down the highway at ninety miles an hour, the wind roaring in her ears competing with the wild pounding of her heart, and the hugging him tightly most of all. He turned off on some country road and stopped along a quiet riverbank. There, with the sun glittering on the water and a canopy of autumn red and gold leaves overhead, he kissed her.

Afterward, with her whole body still tingling from his kiss, she whispered, "I don't even know your name."

"I don't want to tell you," he murmured against her neck. "When you find out who I am, I'll never see you again."

"No. How can you say that?"

"Because—" He lifted his head, his gaze burrowing straight into her—all the way to her heart, it seemed. "—I'm Ring Stuart."

For a moment, Elizabeth felt cold with fear, knowing what would happen if Hattie ever found out whom she was with. It didn't matter to her though, not now that he'd kissed her. "I don't care what your name is, Ring Stuart," she declared fervently, and he'd kissed her again, reminding her why she didn't care.

In the weeks that followed, she arranged to meet him whenever and wherever they could, but never often enough or long enough. Yet the very infrequency and shortness of their meetings gave each one an intense sweetness.

Immersed in the fall ranchwork, Hattie didn't guess what was going on, not until she insisted that Elizabeth ride with her out to one of the pastures and check on the winter graze. Charlie Rainwater, one of the ranch hands, rode along with them. He was the one who drew Hattie's attention to the change in her younger sister.

"Does Miss Elizabeth have herself a fella or something?" he asked.

"No," Hattie denied immediately, regarding the idea as ludicrous. Not that she was against Elizabeth's having a beau. She had simply given up on her younger sister ever marrying, convinced that she was destined to be a spinster like herself. After all, Elizabeth was twenty-seven years old and had never had a steady beau. Hattie didn't think it was all that surprising. As much as she loved her, she recognized that Elizabeth was too plain, too thin, too shy, and too sickly—hardly wife material. Yet Charlie's comment troubled her. "What makes you think she has a boyfriend?"

He shrugged his shoulders and nodded his head in Elizabeth's direction. "Just watchin' her over there, hummin' to herself and pickin' them bouquets of dry weeds—and lookin' dreamy-eyed as a doe. You put that together with all the trips she's been makin' into town lately, and I figured she had a fella stashed away somewheres."

Hattie didn't miss the implication of that comment—the implication that her Elizabeth was meeting someone on the sly. Her little sister wouldn't do something like that. If Elizabeth had a boyfriend, she'd bring him to Morgan's Walk so Hattie could meet him. Wouldn't she?

She started noticing things after that—little things like the flimsy excuses Elizabeth made to justify her trips to town, the flush that was in her cheeks when she came back, and the shininess in her eyes. Finally, hating the suspicions, Hattie ordered Charlie Rainwater to follow Elizabeth the next time she went to town and find out once and for all whether she had anything to worry about.

"Ring Stuart?! You mean Jackson Stuart's boy?"

"That's the one," Charlie confirmed when he reported back to her.

"You must be mistaken." Her Elizabeth wouldn't be with a Stuart.

"There's no mistake, ma'am. It was Ring Stuart, all right. I didn't want to believe it either. That's why I made sure. I didn't think there could be two people who walked down the street like they owned it—like the way he does. And there isn't."

"What do you mean—she *met* him?"

"Just that, she met him. She took that blouse back to the store like she said she was gonna do. Then she went over to this park, and there he is waiting for her."

"Maybe it was just a coincidence that he was there."

"It's possible, ma'am," Charlie conceded, shifting his weight from one foot to the other and staring down at the pointed toes of his boots.

"But you don't think so," Hattie guessed.

"No, ma'am."

"Why?"

He seemed reluctant to answer that, then finally glanced at her from beneath the brim of his battered hat. "When she saw him standing there, ma'am, she ran right into his arms like she was comin' home after bein' away a long time."

At that moment, her shock had shown—her shock and that sense of ultimate betrayal. "That will be all, Charlie." She dismissed him, unable to ask more, not wanting to hear more—not wanting to know how completely Elizabeth may have betrayed them all . . . with a Stuart!

"I knew you'd react like this, Hattie," Elizabeth said when Hattie confronted her. "That's why I never told you. I didn't keep it from you to hurt you. I just knew you wouldn't look at Ring and judge him for himself."

"He's a Stuart."

"That's his name, yes. But what does that mean?"

"How can you ask that? You know—"

"All that happened years and years ago, Hattie. I wasn't alive then and Ring wasn't either. You can't hold him responsible for something his father did. Ring's different."

"He's a Stuart. He's cut from the same cloth, and it's bad cloth."

"That isn't true. Ring is good—"

"Good for nothing like all the rest of them."

"Stop talking like that. You don't even know him."

"I know all I need to know about him."

"How can you condemn him just because his last name happens to be Stuart? Why does that automatically make him bad? Why can't you forget something that happened over fifty years ago? It didn't happen to you."

"But I saw Stuart after he was released from prison. I was there when he confronted our grandfather. I heard what he said—and saw the hate in his eyes—" Just as she saw the indifference in Elizabeth's face. None of it mattered to her sister. She was convinced those long-ago threats had nothing to do with her. Hattie knew just how wrong she was. She tried another tactic. "Have you seen where this Stuart boy lives?"

"No," Elizabeth admitted, somewhat subdued.

"It's a shack, hidden away in the hills at the end of a long dusty road. When he was a boy, that shack was a haven for every gangster from Clyde Barrow to Pretty Boy Floyd. And during the war, when cowboys from this very ranch were dying on the beaches of Normandy, a black market business was operating from there. Ring Stuart comes from a fine, upstanding family, wouldn't you agree?"

"That doesn't mean he'll be like his father."

"He was raised by him."

"But Ring has plans, wonderful plans—"

"To get his hands on Morgan's Walk, just like his father tried to do."

"That isn't true."

"Isn't it?"

Hattie was wise enough to see that no amount of arguing, threats, or reasoning on her part could sway Elizabeth from her misplaced belief in this renegade. Romantically and foolishly, her naïve little sister saw herself and Ring Stuart as star-crossed lovers irresistibly drawn together despite the long-standing rift between their families—in the fanciful tradition of the Montagues and the Capulets. His faults and his failings didn't matter to her, convinced as she was that her love would change him. Hattie knew better. People didn't change no matter how much they might want to—not on the inside where it mattered.

Wisely she stopped short of forbidding Elizabeth from seeing Stuart again, recognizing that much of this was her fault. She'd protected her baby sister too much from the harsher side of life, trying to make life easier for her than she'd had it. She'd kept her in innocence even as she'd envied it—and used it as vicarious means of escaping from the stressful responsibility of Morgan's Walk.

No, the way to put a stop to this disastrous relationship before it went any farther was not to prevent Elizabeth from seeing Stuart again, but to pay a little visit on the one who had taken advantage of her sister's trusting innocence.

* * *

A crow cawed the alarm and swooped off an oak branch, black wings flapping as Hattie negotiated the car over the rutted track. A squirrel abandoned its search for nuts among the fallen leaves and raced to the nearest tree, chattering noisily at her, when she went by. Ahead, the thick tangle of brush and woods crowding both sides of the narrow lane retreated to form a clearing, a clearing cluttered with rusting car bodies, empty oil drums, and piles of worn tires strewn among the yellowed weeds. The landscaping matched the tumble-down house that sat in the middle of it, all the paint long since peeled from its boards, leaving them a dirty weathered gray.

In front of the house, looking distinctly out of place, stood a hopped-up cycle, a black and shiny machine of sleek power. Kneeling on the ground beside it, tinkering with the motor, was Ring Stuart. He straightened slowly to his feet when Hattie drove in and parked her car ten feet from the big Harley cycle.

When she got out of the car, he took a couple steps forward and idly wiped his greasy hands on an equally greasy rag. With a steely calm she looked him over, not at all surprised by what she saw. A pair of faded jeans blatantly hugged his narrow hips, leaving little to the imagination for a knowing eye. A dirty T-shirt clung to every muscled contour of his chest, its short sleeves rolled up to the points of his shoulders, the right one bulging over a pack of cigarettes. Her glance touched briefly on the revolting tattoo of a knife dripping blood from the blade tip that ran down his left biceps. Then she examined his face. The devil had given him his lean, handsome looks and hell-black hair, as well as a pair of lightning blue eyes to go with them.

"Well, well, well, if it isn't the duchess herself." His lip curled in a sneering smile. "I kinda figured you'd be paying me a visit, only I expected you to come yesterday."

"You did," she murmured, disliking him even more intensely than she'd expected.

"Yeah." He sauntered a few steps closer, his weight balanced on the balls of his feet, giving a cocky spring to his walk. "I spotted that cowboy you had following Elizabeth right off. You should have seen his eyes bug out of his head when he saw the way she kissed me—and kept kissing me."

"You're disgusting."

His smile widened. "Elizabeth doesn't think so. As a matter of fact, she's crazy about me. She likes it when I kiss her . . . among other things."

Hattie stiffened at his deliberately suggestive remark. "You know I'm not going to allow this to continue."

"There's nothing you can do about it, duchess," he said, his head tipped arrogantly back. "She's old enough to know her own mind. She doesn't need your consent or approval."

"How much?"

"How much?" he repeated on a note of amusement. "Man, you really are something, duchess. You know I've often wondered what it would be like living in that big house with people waiting on you, serving you coffee in dainty china cups and fetching the morning paper for you. It must be real fine living."

"How much money do you want, Stuart, to leave my sister alone?"

"You really think you can buy me off, don't you, duchess?"

Pointedly she swept her glance over the weed-choked clearing and the dilapidated house with its front porch askew. "What's your price, Stuart? Name it."

"I've already got what I want. I've got Elizabeth. She's mine and you can't take her away from me. If you thought you could, you wouldn't be here talking to me now." He paused, his confidence growing. "She was real shy with me at first, but she isn't shy anymore. It kinda surprised me at first. But after meeting you, I'm convinced that she's got all the passion in your family. What kind of sister are you, anyway? She loves me and here you are trying to make me give her up."

"It would never work between you. Never."

"Why? Because you think I'm not good enough for her?"

"I know you aren't."

"She doesn't agree with you. Y'see, the difference is she believes in me, and that means more to me than all the money you could pay, duchess."

"I'm warning you—"

"No, I'm warning you—you'd better watch how you talk about your future brother-in-law or I just might take your little sister away from you for good."

She held his gaze for a long minute, then said, "You're a fool, Stuart," and turned on her heel and walked back to the car.

Driving out of the clearing, she could see his reflection in the rearview mirror as he stood in the middle of the track, watching her leave and looking cocksure. At a midway point, the long lane to the shack widened. There, Charlie Rainwater waited in the ranch pickup along with a half-dozen hands from the bunkhouse. Hattie pulled up alongside the truck.

"He wouldn't listen, Charlie," was all she said.

"I figured as much, Miss Hattie." He turned the key in the truck's ignition, the engine grinding slowly to life. "Reasonin' with a Stuart is a lot like talkin' to a mule. First, you gotta get their attention."

He shifted the pickup into gear and the vehicle lurched forward onto the rough trail. Hattie sat in the car and waited, listening to the lonely sigh of the wind in the trees. Fifteen minutes? Twenty? She wasn't sure how much time passed before she heard the rumble of the pickup making the return trip.

Charlie drove up beside her, a cut on his lip and a bruise swelling his cheek, but there was a smile on his face that went ear to ear. "He wasn't able t'do much talkin' when we left him, Miss Hattie, but I can guarantee that he got the message."

When Hattie returned to Morgan's Walk that day, she said nothing to Elizabeth and went about her work as usual. Late in the afternoon, Elizabeth received a phone call from one of her girlfriends. Unbeknown to Hattie, Ring Stuart had called Sally Evans and persuaded her to phone Elizabeth with a message. Sometime after midnight, Elizabeth slipped out of the house and met Ring Stuart. Hattie didn't discover she was missing until morning. She looked for her, but she found no sign of either of them. The next day, Elizabeth called to say that she and Stuart were married, and asked if they could come home to Morgan's Walk.

"You can come home anytime, Elizabeth, but not with him. I won't have a Stuart sleeping under this roof."

"Then neither one of us can come, because I'm a Stuart now, too."

Two months went by, two miserable and bitterly lonely months for Hattie with memories of Elizabeth haunting every room. She made no attempt to contact her, certain that in time she would come to her senses and see what a terrible mistake she had made. Then came the phone call from Ring Stuart informing Hattie that Elizabeth was ill.

Piles of dirty dishes with food caked on them covered the kitchen counters. Empty beer bottles spilled over the sides of the wastebasket and sat next to every chair and butt-filled ashtray in the filthy shack. The thought of her Elizabeth living in this germ- and dirt-infested dwelling sickened Hattie as she followed Ring Stuart down a dingy hall to one of the back bedrooms.

In the bedroom, Hattie stepped around the dirty clothes strewn on the floor. Bedsprings squealed noisy protest under Ring Stuart's weight as he sat down on the edge of the bed and took Elizabeth's hand.

"Honey, Hattie's here."

She stopped two feet short of the bed and fought back the bitter tears that stung her eyes when she saw Elizabeth, her wan face as pale as the pillow slip beneath her head. "This place is a pig sty. How can you live in this filth?"

"I'm sorry. I know it's a mess." Her voice was barely more than a whisper. "I haven't been feeling too well lately, and—"

"—and he's too lazy." Hattie hurled the contemptuous accusation at Stuart.

"Hattie, it isn't man's work," Elizabeth chided gently.

"I never thought he was a man, and now that I've seen the way he takes care of you, I know he isn't." She moved to the bed and laid the back of her hand against Elizabeth's cheeks, feeling for a temperature, and completely ignoring the glare from Stuart.

"That isn't fair, Hattie," Elizabeth protested. "Ring has tried, he really has. But he can't keep a job and look after me, too."

"He's certainly done a fine job of looking after you, hasn't he?" she murmured caustically, unable to suppress the rage she felt at her Elizabeth being forced to live in these wretched surroundings. "Have you called the doctor, yet?"

"I saw him yesterday." Elizabeth caught at her hand, a frailness in the attempt to clutch at Hattie's fingers. A smile fairly beamed from her face. "Hattie, we're going to have a baby. So you see, I'm not really sick. I'm pregnant."

For several long seconds, Hattie stared at the girl she'd raised since birth, inwardly revolted by the prospect of her sister having a child sired by a Stuart. She wanted to scream at her and demand to know if she realized what she had done—the terrible consequences of this.

Instead, she swung on Stuart. "I want to speak to you. Now!" She turned on her heel and marched from the room. The instant she reached the living room, she whirled to confront him. "I'm taking her out of this pig hole you call a house, today."

"She won't go without me, duchess," he said confidently. Hattie lifted her head slightly, eyeing him coldly. "Looks like my daddy was right all along, doesn't it? A Stuart will have Morgan's Walk."

"Not you. It will never be you," she vowed.

"But my son will."

"God willing, the child will never live to cry its first breath. But you'd better pray that when Elizabeth loses it, she doesn't lose her life as well."

"Damn you, I love her!"

"Do you? Or is it merely convenient to love her?"

"I love her," he insisted angrily.

"But not enough to give her up—not enough to do what's best for her. You deliberately got her with child. You knew how fragile her health is yet you risked her life by impregnating her."

"Everything will be all right. You'll see."

"It had better be, Stuart. Otherwise, you'll answer to me."

Although bedridden through most of her pregnancy, Elizabeth carried the baby to term and gave birth to a remarkably strong and healthy boy. Yet the ordeal seemed to have taken its toll on her own health. As the months went by, she grew weaker. Anemia was the initial diagnosis, but when she failed to respond to treatment, she was admitted to the hospital for tests.

Returning from a consultation with the doctor, Hattie found Ring in the library, his feet propped on the desk and blue smoke curling from the cigar in his mouth. "Are you wondering what it's like to run Morgan's Walk? If you are, you're wasting your time. You'll never find out," she declared, jerking off her gloves.

He didn't move from his relaxed position as he smiled at her through the smoke. "You can't be sure of that, duchess. After all, you aren't going to live forever."

"I swear I will see you in hell before I let the day come when a Stuart has the right to sit behind that desk. Now get out of my chair."

He pulled his feet off the desk top and bowed his head in exaggerated respect as he slowly stood up. "I return your throne to you."

"It probably doesn't interest you at all, but the results from the tests came back."

Reluctantly she observed the leap of concern in his eyes. "How's Elizabeth?"

Coldly, with no more emotion left, Hattie replied, "Your wife has leukemia." Before her eyes, Stuart crumbled in shock.

"My poor darling Elizabeth," she whispered to the girl in the silverframed photograph, then slowly drew her hand away and pushed out of the chair. The loneliness of the old house seemed to press in on her, its weight combining with the tiredness of battling for so long. This time she leaned heavily on the cane as she crossed to the portrait above the fireplace.

"I regret but one thing in my life—that I told them to stop after they had given him a good beating. I should have had him killed." She bowed her head. "The fault was mine. It was never Elizabeth's. She didn't know what she was doing, but I did. I should have put an end to it then."

13 ∽

THE MORNING SUN PEERED through the smoked glass windows of the Stuart Building's top floor, spreading its refracted rays over the small group gathered around the circular burl conference table in the executive office. A slight man with cherubic features and soft spaniel eyes held the floor, his usual reticence forgotten as he spoke about the one field in which he was an acknowledged expert; he was considered by many to be one of the best, if not *the* best, civil engineer in the country.

"When I passed these preliminary drawings for the dam by Zorinsky at the Corps, he saw a problem in only one area." Fred Garver riffled through the pages of blueprints on the tall easel until he found the one he wanted, then flipped back the ones in front of it to reveal a cross section of the proposed dam. "He felt the concrete keys should be another three feet deep to eliminate any possible undermining of the dam itself. If we do that, we're probably talking about an additional cost of another half million dollars—depending." He paused to shoot both Chance and Sam Weber a quick look. "Without test borings of the site, I can't be sure what we'll run into once we start excavating. I don't know if we'll hit rock, sand, clay, or what. All the construction figures I've given you are just rough estimates. And I mean rough."

Sam expected Chance to acknowledge that comment. When he didn't, Sam darted a quick glance in his direction and frowned slightly at Chance's obvious absorption with the scribblings he was making on the notepad resting on his knee. He had been preoccupied through much of the meeting—a meeting he had called to get an update on Garver's progress. Yet he hadn't asked one question or shown any interest in the engineer's drawings. That wasn't like him. That wasn't like him at all.

"Yes, we understand that, Fred," Sam inserted to fill the void.

"As long as you do." The engineer shrugged his acceptance and turned his attention back to the cross section. "Personally, I don't think it's necessary to increase the depth of the keys. Although if we do incorporate Zorinsky's recommendation, then we would probably be assuring ourselves of a quick approval from the Corps. The way I see it we have two choices: we can either make this change now or wait until we get to do some test borings to know what we're dealing with. How soon will you be taking title to the property so we can get on it and do our preliminary site work?"

Sam looked again at Chance, wishing he would field that question, but there was no indication that he'd even heard it. "We can't give you a date yet." He didn't think it was his place to admit that Chance might not get title to it at all, not the way things were going.

"Do you want us to just sit tight for a while or go ahead with the change?" Damn, but he wished Chance would speak up. This wasn't the kind of decision he normally made when a project was in its preliminary stage. Looking at Molly, her chair positioned at an unobtrusive distance from the table, Sam wondered what he should do. She grimaced faintly and shrugged her shoulders, unable to offer any suggestion to him. He shifted uncomfortably in his seat and nervously cleared his throat. The sound seemed to rouse Chance, his attention lifting somewhat abstractedly from the notepad before him.

Still, Sam doubted that Chance knew the question. "Why don't you give us a couple days to think it over, Fred, and we'll get back to you with our decision?" he suggested, trying to cover for Chance's inattention to the entire discussion.

"That won't be necessary." Chance contradicted him. "Make the changes in the design. When the time comes, I'll want to move on this project fast. I don't want anything holding us up." He shoved his notepad onto the table and rolled to his feet. "Leave a set of the drawings so I can study them later, and send us a copy of any changes. We'll stay in touch."

As if pushed by some inner restlessness, he left the conference table and walked to the window. His back remained to them, abruptly but effectively bringing a quick end to the meeting.

Sam exchanged another troubled look with Molly, then helped Fred Garver and his young associate gather their materials together, and made certain a full set of the preliminary drawings remained behind. With Fred reverting to his reticent ways, there was little conversation as Sam walked him to the door. No mention had been made of Chance's inattention during much of the meeting, but Sam felt obligated to offer some sort of explanation in his defense.

"Don't mind Chance," he said at the door. "He's had a lot on his mind lately."

"I guessed as much." Fred nodded, throwing a brief glance over his shoulder in Chance's direction, his mouth curving into a smile of understanding when he looked back at Sam.

After they'd left, Sam hesitated a moment at the door, then turned and walked back to the conference table. Chance was still at the window, staring out, his hands idly shoved in the side pockets of his trousers. Molly quietly gathered up the dirty coffee cups and set them on the serving tray.

Sam picked up the rolled set of blueprints and turned it in his hands. "Do you want me to leave these here for you or put them on the drafting table in my office with the others?" But his question drew only more silence, and his concern and bewilderment at Chance's behavior gave way to exasperation. "Dammit, Chance, you haven't heard one word anybody's said in the last hour, have you?"

"No, he hasn't," Molly stated quite emphatically as Chance half-turned to give them both a blank, preoccupied look. "He's been doodling on that pad of his. Whenever he starts doing that, you can be sure he isn't listening to anyone."

"Sorry." Chance frowned. "I guess my mind is elsewhere."

"My God, that's an understatement," Sam muttered, shaking his head. "Your mind has been *elsewhere* ever since you got back from San Francisco. Exactly what happened out there?"

"It's that Bennett woman, isn't it?" Molly guessed, eyeing him with wondering interest. "The one you sent all those orchids to."

Chance held her gaze for several seconds, his look distantly thoughtful and his silence seeming to confirm her statement. Then he turned back to the window. "It just may be that you're going to get your wish after all, Molly."

For a stunned instant, she couldn't say anything, then she asked, somewhat tentatively, "Are you saying that you're thinking about marrying her?"

Like Molly, Sam stared at Chance, not entirely convinced that he really meant to imply that. Chance swung away from the window, his glance briefly touching each of them as a wry smile tugged at his mouth.

"The thought has crossed my mind," he admitted, as if amazed by it, too. "Is there any coffee left in that pot?"

"I—I don't think so."

It was obvious to Sam that she was practically bursting with questions about this woman who had managed to capture the heart of the man she loved like a son. For that matter, he was, too. In all the years he'd known Chance, he couldn't remember him ever seriously contemplating marriage to anyone. He always said he was married to his work, that the company was the only mistress he needed. Sam always thought that if anyone got Chance to the altar, it would be Lucianna. His relationship with her went back a good fifteen years. Nothing lasted that long unless there was some strong feeling on both sides. So who was this Bennett woman?

"Get a fresh pot for us, Molly. I have some things I want to go over with Sam. And bring me the notes of the meeting with Garver as soon as you have them typed." The decisive tone sounded more like the old Chance, the one who placed business first and everything else a distant second.

Molly heard it, too, and reluctantly smothered her curiosity. "Right away."

As she left the office, carrying the tray and her stenopad, Chance turned to him and gestured at the roll of blueprints in his hands. "Is that the set Garver left with us?"

"Yes." Sam nodded, unable to make the lightning switch in conversation. "Chance, were you serious a minute ago about this girl in San Francisco?"

"Woman," he corrected. "Woman, Sam. Intelligent, sensitive, warm . . ." He paused, his expression taking on a faintly rueful look. "I can't seem to stop thinking about her. And no woman has ever intruded on business before."

"Are you going to marry her?"

"I don't know." He seemed reluctant to go that far. "I only know I keep remembering what it was like being with her. Not just being in bed with her, but being with her." This time the shake of his head was more definite as if he was trying to rid his mind of the memory of her, at least temporarily. "This isn't getting us anywhere. Unroll the site map. I want to see where Garver thinks the shoreline will be once the lake forms behind the dam."

Sam spread the sheet with the site drawn to scale on the table, anchoring two of the ends down with the sugar bowl and creamer Molly had left. "It hasn't changed much from his original drawing, except maybe over here on the north side where the waterline doesn't come up as high on the bluff as he first estimated. Otherwise, it's the same as before—with virtually all of Morgan's Walk under water." Including the house, but Sam didn't say that.

"That bluff area shouldn't have much effect on Delaney's master plan of the project," Chance remarked, barely looking up from his study of the site drawing as Molly reentered his office with an insulated pot of fresh coffee. "All the same, you'd better make a copy of this and send it over to his office," he said, referring to the architect and land planner on the proposed resort complex. Then he tapped a finger on the northwest corner of the manmade lake. "We're definitely going to need the Ferguson property. What's the status on it? Have they agreed to an option yet?"

"They insist they won't sell—at any price. Their son's farming the land for them now and they plan on turning all of it over to him and moving into town this next year. It's the same story with the MacAndrews place."

"Who holds the mortgages on their farms?"

"One of the savings and loan companies, I can't remember which one right now. I'd have to check the reports."

"Buy the mortgages."

"Chance, we're probably talking somewhere in the neighborhood of a half a million dollars to do that," Sam protested.

"We need those parcels. We'd pay more than that if we could buy them outright."

"That's not the point." Sam hesitated. "Chance, you have to be realistic. Right now—the way things stand—we can't even be sure you're going to get Morgan's Walk. And without it, we can't build the dam—and without the dam, we don't have a lake—and without the lake . . . Let's face it, without Morgan's Walk, we don't have a project. We've spent all this money on adjoining land, site plans, and designs for nothing."

"We'll get Morgan's Walk. One way or another."

"I know you keep saying that—and you're probably right. But don't you think it would be wise if we waited at least until Matt tracks down this new heir of Hattie's before we invest any more cash in the project? We've got a ton of money tied up in it now."

"You're getting conservative on me again, Sam," Chance chided.

"Dammit, somebody has to around here."

"Buy the mortgages, Sam, and stop worrying about Morgan's Walk."

"Stop worrying, he says," he muttered, catching Molly's eye and shaking his head.

"If Chance says not to worry, then you shouldn't." Molly was prepared to expand on that thought, but she was interrupted by the long beep of the telephone. Automatically she turned to the extension sitting on the rosewood credenza next to the conference table. "Mr. Stuart's office," she said, once again assuming that crisp, professional air. Then her glance flashed to Chance, a sudden high alertness entering her expression. "Yes, he's here. Just a moment." She pushed the hold button and extended the receiver toward Chance. "It's Maxine. She says she needs to talk to you."

His head came up sharply at the mention of the housekeeper from Morgan's Walk. In two quick strides, he was at Molly's side, taking the phone from her.

"Hello, Max. How are you?"

"Truthfully? There are times I'd like to strangle her. She's been impossible to live with lately."

"What happened?" He knew something had or she wouldn't risk a call.

"I overheard a telephone conversation she had with some woman she called

Margaret Rose. It has to be the one, because she was talking about sending copies of documents that prove they're related."

"Just Margaret Rose. That's all?"

"Yes." A sigh of regret came over the line. "If she used a last name, I didn't hear it."

"When was this?"

"Last Sunday. I would have called sooner, but she's been watching me like a hawk. Every time I came up with a reason to come into town, she sent somebody else. Finally I had to break my reading glasses. That's where I am now—at the optical company getting them fixed."

"When the time comes that I can, I'll make all this right, Max," he promised.

"Whether you do or don't doesn't matter. I'm not doing this for any reward, Chance. I'm doing it because Morgan's Walk should rightfully go to you when she passes on—not to some stranger in California. It's what your mother would have wanted—God rest her soul. Hattie's just doing this to be mean and spiteful. Of course, she always was that, but it's gotten worse lately."

"How is she?"

"She's in a lot of pain all the time now. She tries not to let on, but I can tell. I think she's forgotten I was a registered nurse long before I was a housekeeper. Knowing what she's going through, sometimes I can't help feeling sorry for her. I'm convinced that half of what she's doing now is because she's crazy with the pain. She's like a mortally wounded animal, wanting to take something with her when she goes."

"With your help, maybe she won't succeed."

"I hope not."

"Was there anything else?"

"Nooo." She dragged out the word, as if none too certain of that. "She did make another call after she'd talked to this Margaret Rose woman. Probably to Ben Canon, although I don't know that for sure."

"Why do you think it was Canon?"

"Because he came to the house later that afternoon. When I answered the door, he said she was expecting him."

"Do you know why he was there?"

There was a pause before she answered, "I think it was to have a new will signed. I know they called old Charlie Rainwater and Shorty Thompson into the library, probably to witness it. I asked them later, but those two are so closemouthed I couldn't get anything out of them other than a grunt."

"I can't say that I'm surprised," he admitted grimly. "If anything, I thought she would have had a new will drawn up right after she learned about this Margaret Rose."

"I thought you would probably anticipate that," she said, then paused again. "I'd better hang up. She sent Charlie into town with me. He could walk in any minute and I'd rather he didn't see me on the phone."

"You take care of yourself, Max—and thanks for the information."

"You know I'll help any way I can. Be good, Chance."

"I will." He hung up.

"Hattie's made a new will, has she?" Sam remarked in a grimly troubled voice.

"Yes." Chance turned to look at him thoughtfully, then glanced sideways at Molly. "Get Matt Sawyer on the phone for me," he directed, then commented idly, "At least we have a first name to give him. I wonder how many women named Margaret Rose there are in the San Francisco area—specifically ones with a residential phone. A computer search of the phone company's records should be able to provide us with such a list."

14

COPIES OF BIRTH CERTIFICATES, baptismal records, marriage licenses, church registers, obituary notices, death certificates—they were all there—spread across her desk top. In between bites of the seafood salad she'd ordered from a local deli, Flame checked the names against the ones that appeared on the ancestral chart Hattie had included in the packet of documents. Although she hadn't had time to verify everyone, the evidence seemed irrefutable. She and Hattie Morgan were related, albeit distantly.

A quick rap on the door pulled her attention from the papers on her desk. "Yes?"

Almost immediately the door opened and the blond-haired Debbie Connors stepped inside, her look anxious and agitated. "I'm sorry, Flame, but Mr. Powell's outside. He wants to see you. I didn't know what to tell him." The words tumbled from her in a rush.

"He's here?" Flame questioned, as stunned as her assistant was.

"Yes, I—" The door behind her started to move, pushing Debbie along with it. She stepped hastily out of the way as Malcom Powell walked through the opening.

Flame rose from her chair, unsure what to make of this unexpected visit. Surely he had to know that by coming here, the mountain had moved. "Malcom," she said in greeting, then added coolly, "you should have let me know you were coming."

He paused in the middle of the room. A hand-tailored gray suit, the same iron-dark shade as his hair, smoothly fit over his powerfully built chest.

"I see I've interrupted you in the middle of a late lunch," he observed, his sharp eyes flicking a glance to the partially eaten salad on her desk.

"I'm finished." In truth, her appetite had fled when he walked in the door. She picked up the salad container along with its plastic flatware and paper napkin and deposited them in her wastebasket. When she turned back to Malcom, Flame caught Debbie's frantic what-do-you-want-me-to-do look. "That will be all, Debbie. Let me know when Tim Herrington arrives."

"The instant he comes," she promised and hurried out the door, this time closing it tightly behind her.

"This is the first time I've ever been in your office," Malcom remarked, looking around him with curious interest, his glance skimming over the white lacquered desk and attendant chairs, upholstered in a textured fabric of pale cerulean blue, and lingering on the abstract painting behind her desk, the Art Deco sculpture on the occasional table, and a set of needlepoint pillows in a geometric design on the small sofa.

"What did you want to see me about, Malcom?" She could think of only one reason for his unannounced visit as she gathered together the documents on her desk and slipped them back into their manila envelope.

He walked over to the window. "I almost called and had Arthur pick you up. Then I thought better of it." He stood with his hands clasped behind his back in a pensive pose. "After our luncheon last Tuesday, I had a feeling you wouldn't react well to such a summons. You would have come, but only because you felt you had no choice. You would have resented that. And it isn't resentment I want from you."

Flame very carefully avoided asking him what he did want. She knew the answer to that. She always had. Remaining by her desk, she waited for him to continue, a fine tension threading through her nerves and matching the slow simmer of her anger.

"I think you should know where I stand, Flame. The Powell account is yours as long as it is handled satisfactorily. I won't hold it over your head."

Provoked by the tone of largess in his remark, she challenged, "Am I supposed to thank you for that?"

He half-turned to look at her. "You should," he said, his eyes defiantly narrowed in their penetrating study of her. "Those were brave words you said last Tuesday, but that's all they were. I know you won't admit it, but I could use the account to get what I want from you."

"Don't bet on it," she snapped.

Malcom merely smiled. "I don't think you realize just how vulnerable you are to that type of pressure." Then he shrugged, dismissing it. "But it won't be applied. A victory under those circumstances would be hollow indeed. Which is not to say I'm giving up," he inserted quickly, a subtle warning contained in the firm advisory. "I'm only saying that when you come to me, it will be of your own free will."

Ignoring his latter statement, Flame tilted her head at an aggressive angle and demanded, "Does that mean you'll be calling off your bloodhound?"

"I beg your pardon." He turned the rest of the way around, his eyebrows lowering to form a thick bushy line that hooded his eyes.

"You amaze me, Malcom," Flame murmured with a touch of sarcasm.

"What are you talking about?"

"I'm talking about the man who's been following me for the last week, the one you hired," she retorted, her anger showing, although tightly controlled.

"I didn't hire anyone to follow you. Why should I?"

Both his denial and confusion seemed genuine. She frowned. "Either you have acting talents you haven't used—or you're telling the truth."

"It is the truth," he insisted. "Who's following you and why?"

She hesitated, still watching him closely. "A man. I saw him for the first time at the DeBorgs' party for Lucianna Colton. He was a waiter, in his middle to late forties with brown hair and a large, hooked nose. He drives a dark green sedan, a late model Ford." There was nothing in his expression to indicate the description meant anything to him. "And twice he's passed on messages warning me to stay away from Chance Stuart. I assumed . . . you were behind them. But you weren't, were you?"

"No." His gaze narrowed on her sharply. "Have you been seeing a great deal of Stuart?"

"When he's been in town, yes," she admitted.

"Are you serious about him?" A muscle flexed visibly along his strong, square jaw.

She waited for a twinge of doubt to come, but none did. "Very serious," she stated, amazed by the buoyantly content feelings within that had surfaced with the admission.

Malcom paused, then laughed abruptly. "My God, I didn't realize I could still feel jealousy." A slight frown creased his forehead as he gazed at her in thoughtful study. "I don't know why that should surprise me. With you, it's always been different. Perhaps, in the beginning it was the chase and the conquest that appealed to me, but that changed long ago—"

"Stop it, Malcom," she warned.

He looked at the sparkle of temper in her eyes and smiled. "You excite me the way no other woman has—including my wife."

"I don't care, Malcom! Your feelings are a problem *you'll* have to deal with— not me. I am not going to be the solution to them." She struggled to keep her voice down and her temper in check.

Moving away from the window, Malcom crossed to the side of her desk, that aura of power emanating from him and reminding her that he was a force to be reckoned with. She faced him squarely, conscious of the possessive look in his eyes and the slow skim of his gaze as it traveled the length of her.

"Stuart's not the man for you," he announced.

Infuriated by his arrogant assertion, she snapped, "That's for me to decide!"

"Right now your eyes are filled with him. But it won't last. You'll come to me . . . in time."

Momentarily shaken by the certainty in his voice, she fought to dispel it. "You have forgotten one very important detail, Malcom. Whether Chance Stuart is in my life or not, my answer to you would be the same as it's always been —no."

He didn't like her answer, but a knock at her door checked his reply. Aware that anger had flushed her cheeks, Flame turned, welcoming the interruption as Tim Herrington, the head of the agency's San Francisco branch, walked in.

"Sorry to bother you, Flame," he began, then paused in feigned surprise when he saw Malcom Powell. "Malcom, I didn't realize you were here." He crossed the room, a hand outstretched in hearty greeting, his eyes big and dark behind the bottle-thick lenses of his gold-rimmed glasses.

"Hello, Tim. How are you?" Malcom responded perfunctorily.

"Fine, just fine. And you? No problems, I hope." His glance ran to Flame as if addressing the remark to her, concerned that there might be trouble with the agency's biggest client.

"None at all," Malcom assured him.

"Good." He seemed to visibly relax, the falseness of his wide smile diminishing.

The two of them chatted about business in general a few minutes longer, then Malcom brought the conversation to a close. "You'll have to excuse me,

Tim, I have another appointment." He looked at Flame. "We'll have lunch next week. I'll have my secretary call and let you know the day," he said, taking it for granted that she would make room on her schedule to accommodate him. Which, of course, she would.

Alone in her flat that evening, Flame again went through the sheaf of documents Hattie had sent her. When she came to the photocopy of her own birth certificate, she paused, her attention centering on her given name of Margaret Rose. A smile touched her lips, softly edging the corners. Her mother had been the only one who ever used that name. To everyone else, she'd always been Flame. But not her mother. Never her mother.

Her glance strayed to her purse lying open on the glass-topped occasional table next to her chair. She hesitated then reached inside and pulled out the small compact that had been a gift from her mother on her thirteenth birthday. A special occasion called for a special gift, her mother always said. And this one was special indeed. Done in cloisonné art, the design depicted a vase holding a bouquet of daisies and roses. Somewhere, sometime, her mother had read or heard that in French Margaret meant daisy. At the time, her father had joked that the design should have been a candle with a tall flame, but her mother hadn't found his remark all that humorous.

Flame suspected that her mother believed she would outgrow her nickname someday. Once—Flame couldn't remember exactly when anymore—her mother had told her she'd picked the name Margaret Rose because it had a certain ring of pride and dignity about it that she liked. Of course, Flame had thought it sounded dreadfully old-fashioned and used to cringe whenever her mother called her Margaret Rose. Now no one ever did—no one, that is, except Hattie Morgan.

The telephone rang.

"Speak of the devil," Flame murmured, as she reached for the phone. She cradled the receiver against her shoulder and slipped the compact back into her purse. "Yes, hello."

"Flame? It's Chance."

"Chance, this is an unexpected pleasure." She brought the phone a little closer, holding it with both hands.

"I hope so." There was the suggestion of a smile in his voice. "I had a few minutes before I have to be at a meeting, so I thought I'd call and see if you have any plans for the weekend."

"I hope I do—with you, that is." She smiled, finding it impossible to play it coy with him. "Are you flying in?"

"Long enough to pick you up."

"Where are we going?"

"That's a secret."

"That isn't fair," Flame protested, intrigued just the same. "How will I know what to pack? You have to give me some kind of clue. Will I need snow skis or a swimsuit?"

"A swimsuit. And maybe something simple for the evening and a light wrap."

"Is that it?"

"You can fill in the blanks from there."

"In that case, I'll bring something lacy and black." She smiled into the phone.

"Or you could opt for nothing at all," Chance added suggestively, then said, "I'll have a car pick you up at work at four o'clock. Is that all right?"

"I'll be ready."

"So will I."

15

AS THE LIMOUSINE DROVE onto the concrete apron, a fuel truck pulled away from a sleek, white Gulfstream jet, with the distinctive "S" logo of the Stuart Corporation emblazoned in gold on its fuselage. Flame spotted Chance almost immediately, standing next to the wing with one of the flight crew. There was a turning lift of his dark head when he heard the limousine. A high alertness held him motionless for a split second, then he said something to the stockily built man with him and moved away to meet the approaching limo.

He was at the door when she stepped out. Again, she felt the jolting impact of his blue-eyed glance, followed by the heady warmth of his mouth moving onto hers in a slow, claiming kiss. As he drew back, Flame gazed at the rakish angles of his face, so smooth and yet so rugged. She had wondered if she would experience the same rush of feeling when she saw him again or if a week's separation would have changed that. It hadn't. Her pulse was behaving just as erratically and that vague breathless feeling of excitement was still there. But those were physical reactions, easily identified. What was harder to name was the strong pull of emotion, that elated feeling of having come home—the one that had to fit under the heading of love.

The creases in his lean cheeks deepened, suggesting a smile even though there was little movement of his mouth. "Hello again."

She was amazed at how much meaning could be conveyed in that softly murmured greeting. "Hello again," she whispered back. She would have gladly gone back into his arms but his glance to the side reminded her they weren't alone.

Half-turning, Flame saw the chauffeur as he lifted her two pieces of luggage from the trunk and handed them to a second man in a flight uniform, younger and slimmer than the first with a definitely Latin look.

"Juan Angel Cordero," Chance identified the man for her, giving his name the full Spanish pronunciation. "But we call him Johnny Angel. He'll be flying the right seat. Johnny, meet Flame Bennett."

"Glad to have you aboard, Ms. Bennett," he acknowledged in flawless English, his dark-eyed look warm with appreciation.

"Thank you."

"And our pilot in command, Mick Donovan," Chance said, directing her attention to the man walking up to them, the one he'd been talking to when she'd arrived. "Flame Bennett."

"Hello, Captain." She noticed immediately that his strong, broad features seemed to be permanently etched in calm, unruffled lines. He had the kind of face that inspired confidence, and the touch of premature gray in the sides of his close-cropped hair merely added to the image.

"Ms. Bennett." A faint smile of welcome lifted the corners of his mouth, gentling the crisply pale blue of his eyes. "I just received the latest weather report. Looks like I can promise you a smooth flight."

"To where?" she asked, her own curiosity about their destination resurfacing.

He hesitated, sliding a brief glance at Chance, then smiled. "To paradise, Ms. Bennett—Stuart style."

"You still aren't going to tell me where we're going, are you, you devil!" She flashed a mildly accusing look at Chance.

"I'm saving it for a surprise." He smiled back at her, then turned to the pilot. "Everything set?"

"As soon as Johnny gets Ms. Bennett's luggage stowed, we'll be ready to leave whenever you are."

"Then let's go." His hand moved to the small of her back to guide her to the waiting jet.

As she turned, Flame thought she caught a glimpse of the hawk-faced man who'd been following her for the last ten days. She looked again at the man heading toward the office of the private aviation company. At this distance, she couldn't be sure it was the same man, yet a feeling of unease ran through her. She had previously dismissed the man as an irritating annoyance, thinking Malcom was responsible for the tail. But he wasn't. She had no idea now who was behind it. Maybe no one. The city had its share of crazies, and, for all she knew, this man could be one of them. And that possibility was a more frightening one.

When she got back, she'd have to do something about him, but not now. She didn't want anything or anyone intruding on her weekend with Chance. She reminded herself that she couldn't be sure it was even the same man. She could be seeing ghosts where none existed. After all, no dark green sedan had followed her to the airport. Of that, she was certain. Smiling, she walked with Chance to the jet's stairway.

A certain amount of luxury was to be expected in a corporate aircraft, but Flame wasn't prepared for the scale she found when she entered the stylishly appointed cabin. Leather suede in a pale ivory color covered the walls. The same shade was repeated in the upholstery on the swivel chairs, this time with the addition of threads of sea-foam green accented by French blue. The entire color scheme served to enhance the array of sculptures scattered through the cabin and invisibly secured, works of Brancusi, Giacometti, and Moore. The collection represented a veritable Who's Who of twentieth-century sculptors. Yet there was no sense of being overpowered by it. Instead, the effect was one of restrained elegance.

"Like it?" Chance was directly behind her, his hands warm on her arms, his breath stirring the edges of her hair.

"I love it. It has the feel of a . . . small sitting room in a private home—comfortable, beautiful, a place to relax and enjoy."

"This is—for all intent and purposes—my second home," he admitted. "If the truth was known, I probably spend more time in this one than I do at my house in Tulsa." Behind them came the grinding hum of the steps being retracted, followed by the closing of the hatch door. "Sounds like we'd better take our seats," Chance remarked. "Once Mick gets the green light, he doesn't like to dawdle. After we're airborne, I'll take you on a tour of my home-away-from-home."

"I'd like that."

As good as his word, shortly after the jet leveled off at its flying altitude, Chance showed her through the aircraft. The interior design was a marvel of understated luxury, compactness, and high tech. Fine leather, the same creamy pale shade as the suede walls, covered a low coffee table that—at the push of a button—became a conference table. In addition to a full entertainment center, there was also a work station with a microcomputer that allowed Chance to transmit information to his Tulsa headquarters by modem and remain in constant touch with his business operation.

And the small galley, Chance informed her, was capable of serving a full-course meal for eight. The galley cabinets, covered in the same ivory leather as the tables in the main cabin, contained a complete setting of Italian china and silver, as well as an appropriate quantity of linen.

The powder room had the same combination of suede and leather with its accents of sea-foam green and French blue, plus a carpet of gold on the floor.

Last, Chance took her into the rear compartment, sectioned off from the galley and main salon area by a door. As she looked around the small executive compartment, Flame noticed a double-width closet built into the wall next to a leather-topped desk, also built in. Impelled by curiosity, she opened its doors. Inside, there were hanger after hanger holding men's suits, sportcoats, blazers, and slacks.

"I keep a complete wardrobe on board," Chance explained.

"How convenient." She swung the doors closed, then turned to survey the plush sofa covered in a velvety fabric of French blue.

"It saves a lot of packing and unpacking," he agreed dryly, then added, "The sofa makes into a double bed."

"How *very* convenient," Flame mocked suggestively, smiling as she rejoined him by the doorway.

"On international flights, it can be." His gaze took on an intimately possessive look as he lifted his hands, tunneling them under her hair to lay on either side of her neck. "I can't believe how much I've missed you."

The husky pitch of his voice made it easy for her to admit, "And I can't believe how much I've missed you, too."

As she tilted her head back, his mouth found hers with unerring accuracy. Instantly, Flame was conscious of the warm feeling that sprang to life inside her, a feeling he could arouse so expertly without their bodies even touching.

With obvious reluctance, he shifted his attention to the corner of her lips. "I should have arranged to make this a longer flight. We would have had time then to see if that bed could be put to a more satisfactory use than sleeping."

"Does that mean we're almost at our destination?" She slipped her hands inside his suit jacket and spread them over his shirt front, feeling the heat that emanated from his lean, hard body.

"We probably have another hour to go yet, maybe more," he admitted, then forced himself to pull away, as if the temptation of her nearness was more than he could resist. "But after waiting a week to be with you again, I'm not interested in a quick romp. I want to take my time making love to you."

"I admit a quick romp would merely be an appetizer," Flame conceded, eyeing him with a playfully deliberate, seductive look. "But don't you usually serve your guests an appetizer before you offer them the main course?"

"Yes, but I like everything served in one sitting." His mouth slanted in a one-cornered smile.

Sighing, she lowered her gaze to his shirt front and slid her fingers under his silk tie to trace the line of buttons. "I don't suppose there's any way you can get this plane to fly faster."

"I wish." He chuckled softly, bringing his hands down to capture hers by the wrists and end their tantalizing exploration.

"It never hurts to dream," she said, offering no protest when he gently directed her back to the main salon area. Then recalling the hurt of previous lost illusions, she qualified that, "Almost never, anyway."

"You have to dream," Chance said. "Otherwise you'll never have a dream come true."

"Have your dreams come true?" she wondered curiously.

"Some of them have. I'm still working on others."

"Such as?" she asked, trying to imagine what he might dream about.

"Getting this jet to fly faster."

She laughed in full agreement.

16

THE SUN WAS RIDING low in the sky, setting fire to the clouds on the horizon, when the jet touched down at the private landing strip along the western coast of Mexico. That much Flame had guessed from the southerly route they'd taken from San Francisco, keeping the coastal mountains on their left and the Pacific Ocean on their right. Chance confirmed they were in Mexico but he wouldn't enlighten her further.

Alongside the runway stood a small open-air building set amidst a stand of palm trees and rampant mounds of lavender bougainvillea. As the jet taxied onto the tarmac, Flame had a glimpse of the sign on what was obviously the terminal building. But the glimpse was too brief and her knowledge of Spanish too limited. She still didn't know where they were. Not that it bothered her. On the contrary, this aura of mystery merely heightened her interest and added a further touch of excitement to her weekend away with Chance.

A car waited for them on the tarmac. On the driver's door was the now familiar logo of the Stuart Corporation. In the time it took Flame and Chance to walk to the car, her luggage was transferred from the plane to the limousine's trunk. Less than five minutes from touchdown, they were driving away from the inland airport, following a paved road that wound over the mountain toward the ocean beyond.

As they approached a scenic overlook, Chance spoke to the driver in Spanish. Immediately the car slowed and pulled onto the graveled roadside, stopping well short of the viewpoint.

"Do you still want to know where we're going?" Chance arched an eyebrow at her, his sidelong look glinting with faint challenge.

She sensed his desire to show her, a desire that seemed to be couched in a pride and a need to share. That, coupled with her own curiosity, made it easy for her to answer quickly. "Yes, yes, yes," she declared, grinning back at him.

He helped her from the car, then led her to the edge of the overlook, his hand firmly hooked around the side of her waist, keeping her close to his side.

The Pacific sprawled before her, the slanting rays of the sun laying a long golden trail across it. At the end of the sun's trail was a small bay surrounded by a dazzling blaze of gold that spread up the mountain slopes. Flame breathed in sharply at the sight, stunned by the discovery that the golden glitter came from the buildings stairstepping the slopes in tier after tier. Here and there, she saw ruby splashes of cascading red flowers and the emerald fronds of tall palm trees.

"Welcome to Cuidad d'Oro de la Stuart . . . Stuart's City of Gold."

"Chance, it's phenomenal." She stared at the golden tower of a multistoried hotel that stood near a pearl white beach, its balconies strung with more ruby garlands of red flowers. "The buildings, they actually look as if they're gilded. They aren't, are they?"

"No. After six months of testing, we finally developed a stuccolike compound composed mainly of a micalike substance that reflects the sunlight. It's most effective at this time of day."

In Flame's opinion, that was an excessive understatement. "I have the feeling I'm looking at the fabled city of gold."

"Wait until you see it at night when it catches the silver of the moon and the stars."

Back in the car, they resumed their journey down the winding mountain road to the secluded resort complex, driving past the bay with its yacht harbor and marina crowded with charter boats for deep sea and sport fishing. A strolling mariachi band played for the bathers still lingering on the beach to catch the last rays of the sun.

For those who shunned salt water, the high-rise hotel offered an oversized swimming pool—although Flame hesitated to call it a pool when it resembled a meandering tropical lagoon complete with a cascading waterfall and rock ledges. Across from the hotel, a small shopping village with fountains and an arbored square offered familiar Mexican wares. The tiers of buildings on the surrounding slopes were a combination of condominiums and private villas. It was to one of the latter that the driver took them.

As they drove onto the gated and walled grounds of the villa, Flame was immediately enchanted by its lushness. Bougainvillea grew rampant, its multitude of red and purple blooms nearly overpowering the fragrant scarlet hibiscus and the tall graceful palms. A golden fountain sent a continual spray of water into the air, a spray the sunlight turned into diamond droplets.

Her enchantment grew when she entered the house itself. Built in the grand manner around a coral rock courtyard, the interior abounded with architectural and visual vignettes—recessed window seats, intricately carved cathedral ceilings, antique wooden doors, coral stone fireplaces, and floors of Spanish tile and pegged oak. Scattered discreetly throughout were works of Aztec and Oaxacan art, some like the terra-cotta pot tucked among the tropical greenery that added to the open-air feel of the cool and spacious villa, and others, like the magnificent hammered bronze sun disk, boldly displayed to dominate the room.

The loggia off the master suite overlooked the mosaic-inlaid swimming pool, surrounded by a deck of travertine marble. Beyond gleamed the bay, reflecting now the scarlet hue of the sky.

"Will this do for a weekend hideaway?"

At the sound of Chance's lightly mocking question, Flame turned from the loggia's panoramic view and tried to match his bantering tone. "It's . . . simple, but nice." She feigned a shrug, then found she couldn't maintain the pretence of indifference, not even in jest, and wound her arms around his neck, clasping her hands behind his head. "It's beautifully perfect and perfectly beautiful, Chance."

"I'm glad you think so, my love."

The intensely intimate look in his eyes was answered by the darkening sparkle in her own. As his hands settled naturally onto the curve of her waist, she started to step into his arms, then checked the movement when she spied the stout Mexican housekeeper approaching the opened glass and wrought-iron doors to the loggia.

"Excuse me, Señor Chance." She halted in the opening, a short round woman made shorter and rounder by the stiffly starched white apron tied around her black uniform. Shy dark eyes glanced briefly at Flame in silent apology. "Señor Rod is on the telephone. He asks if you have arrived. Do you wish to speak to him now?"

Chance hesitated, arching a look of regret at Flame. "Yes, tell him I'll be with him in a moment, Consuelo. I'll take the call in the study."

"Sí," she murmured and retreated from the room.

"Sorry," he said to Flame. "Rod Vega is my man in charge down here. I shouldn't be long. Why don't you go ahead and freshen up or whatever, and I'll meet you in the main salon in—say, thirty minutes?"

"That long," she complained, her lower lip jutting in a playful pout.

"That long." He smiled.

Again she had to settle for a warm, but brief kiss. She lingered on the balcony a moment longer after he'd left, aware that he'd be back and confident the evening would be theirs. She turned to the view, and breathed in the sharp clean tang of the sea air. Paradise, Stuart style, Captain Donovan had called it. It was definitely that and more.

She heard the door to the master suite open and realized that if she intended to change and freshen up, thirty minutes wasn't all that long. She walked back inside and found the housekeeper had returned.

"Ramon has brought your luggage," the woman said, indicating the two cases lying atop a richly carved luggage rack. "Would the *señora* wish me to unpack for her?"

"Please." Flame walked over to the rack and retrieved her makeup case from the smaller bag. "And when you come to the blue chiffon outfit, would you lay that out for me? I want to change into it."

"*Sí, señora.*"

Nearly thirty minutes later, Flame exited the master bedroom, the free-floating chiffon of her blue print skirt swishing softly about her ankles. She caught a glimpse of her reflection in a hall mirror and smiled at the deep plunge of the blouse's softly ruffled neckline. The effect of the loose-fitting blouse of the blue-dotted chiffon was subtly risqué, an effect emphasized by the sleeking of her fiery hair into a classic chignon. She loved the wickedly alluring feeling the combination gave her.

As she walked down the wide hall, her high heels clicking across its tiled floor, ahead she could see the march of pillared arches that surrounded the main salon, giving it a galleried look. When she was nearly to it, she heard the explosive *pop* of a champagne cork. Smiling, she quickened her steps, realizing that Chance was already there waiting for her.

With her chiffon skirt wafting about her in a rippling sweep, Flame passed through the first arched opening into the salon. Chance turned to meet her, holding a fluted glass of champagne in each hand. She observed with satisfaction the quick lidding of his eyes as his surveying glance went no lower than the neckline of her blouse that revealed all of her cleavage. When he dragged his glance back up to her face, the flare of desire was strong in the darkened blue of his eyes—the very reaction she'd hoped to arouse.

"You look ravishing," he murmured when she halted before him.

She took the glass of champagne he handed her, giving him a coy look of mock disappointment. "And I hoped that I looked like a woman about to be ravished."

He arched a black eyebrow at her. "The evening is young."

"Promises, promises," she taunted playfully and took a sip of the sparkling wine. The instant it touched her tongue, she recognized its distinctive flavor. "Peach champagne."

"Of course." He smiled and took a drink of his own.

She deliberately looked about the salon, like all the rooms in the villa designed in grand proportion and superb symmetry. "What? No orchids?"

"I'm glad you mentioned that." He reached inside his jacket and pulled out a long narrow jewelry case. "Here."

She looked uncertainly at the jewelry case he'd given her, then lifted her gaze to the lean, rakish lines of his face, unable to conceal her vague astonishment. "What's this?"

"Open it," was all he'd say.

Flame hesitated an instant longer, then set her glass down and lifted the hinged lid. Light blazed from inside with sparkling brilliance when she opened it. She gasped audibly at the sight of the magnificent diamond brooch designed in the shape of an orchid spray and flanked by a pair of matching diamond earrings.

"Now you'll always have orchids."

She stared at the brooch, tears welling in her eyes, moved as much by the sentiment of the gift as she was by the magnitude of it.

If all he'd wanted to do was give her an expensive present, he could have picked up any bauble. But he hadn't. No, he'd chosen with thought and care, wanting to give her something special, something that signified their personal relationship.

She didn't resist when he took the case from her numbed fingers and removed the brooch from its bed of purple velvet. As he pinned it to her blouse, she looked up at him, the blur of tears softening all the hard edges of his face. With no hurry at all, he unclipped the drop earrings she wore and fastened the diamond pair in their place. When he'd finished, he surveyed the results, his hands settling warmly on the tops of her shoulders, a gentleness and a simmering ardor in his look and his touch that affected Flame as deeply as his gift.

"Beautiful," he pronounced in a husky murmur.

"Oh, Chance, I—I don't know what to say," she admitted, for mere words failed to describe her astonishment, her joy or her appreciation.

"Then don't say anything."

She didn't. Instead she wrapped her arms around his neck and kissed him, letting her hands, her lips, and her body show him how much his gift meant to her. His arms gathered her close, his hands moving in a restless and needy exploration over her shoulders, spine, and hips, their heat penetrating the filmy fabric of her blouse and skirt. The color and texture of their embrace quickly changed as Flame responded to the unleashing of emotions and desires held too long in check on both sides. She strained closer, arching to him, her fingers sliding into his hair, pressing and urging until the kiss became rough with need, lips, tongues tangling together. But it wasn't enough. Maybe it would never be enough. She dragged her lips from his and ran them over his face, lipping the high bone of his cheek and nuzzling at his ear, taking all the liberties with him that he did with her, conscious all the while of the high tension of her body and the loud heart thud in her ears.

"Do you have any idea how much I want you—now—this very minute?" Chance murmured thickly, his heated breath stirring against her ear and sending delicious shudders cascading down her neck. "I had this entire evening planned—champagne, a candlelight dinner, easy conversation, a stroll in the moonlight . . . a stroll that would ultimately take us to the bedroom. Now, I want to skip everything in between and take you straight to the bedroom—to hell with the rest."

Flame smiled against his cheek, his feelings and desires echoing her own, but with a difference. "Where is it written that a woman can't be wined and dined and taken on moonlight strolls—*afterwards?*"

"Where, indeed?" he murmured, drawing back an inch or two to study the swollen softness of her lips and the green of her eyes, heavy-lidded with desire. "Long ago I learned the value of improvising."

"Did you?" She trailed the tip of a nail down the line of his jaw.

"Yes." In one fluidly smooth movement, he picked her up and cradled her in his arms. "And with you, I always seem to be improvising."

"I love the way you improvise . . . among other things," Flame added as she began to nibble on the corded muscles in his neck.

In the master suite, all the raw urgency, all the need for haste that had brought them to the bedroom fled. They stood facing each other, less than three feet apart, bathed in the pool of light from the single lamp. Without either saying a word, they slowly began to undress, peeling off layer after layer. It was more than their clothes they stripped away and more than their bodies they bared to each other. As they looked, really looked at each other, they exposed their feelings, their hearts, and their minds to the other.

When he held out his hand to her, she felt a lump rise in her throat. There was something so beautiful in the moment and the gesture she wanted to cry. As she gave him her hand, they moved toward each other, meeting in the middle of the space, their bodies touching. At last she could feel the heat of his body, the hard muscled wall of his chest, and the powerful columns of his thighs. Reaching up, he pulled the pins from her hair and let it spill onto her shoulders as she ran her hands over him, his smooth skin like hot satin to the touch.

He held her gaze, his thumbs idly stroking the hollows behind her ears. "I love you." The declaration was a low rumble of intense feeling all wrapped up in a single phrase.

"I love you, too," she whispered back as she rose to meet his seeking lips.

Later, much later, they opened another bottle of peach champagne, dined by candlelight, and strolled beneath the stars, ending up again in the master suite and rediscovering all the delights of making love.

17

THE GLASS DOORS to the balcony stood open, letting in the freshness of the morning breeze. Chance paused in front of them, watching the stout Mexican woman as she added a bowl of fresh fruit to the breakfast table set up on the balcony. His glance strayed to the twin place settings, drawn by the cozy look of matching crystal glasses, china cups, and gleaming flatware silently facing each other. Breakfast for him was usually black coffee and occasionally juice; he rarely sat down to a meal. But this morning was different. He wouldn't be eating alone. He would be with Flame. It was amazing how appetizing that sounded.

He fastened the clasp on his watch, then turned his head slightly to bring Flame into view. She sat on the damask-covered bench in front of the lighted vanity mirror, robed in a kimino of peacock blue silk, a matching band catching the hair away from her face while she applied the last of her makeup.

Looking at her, Chance felt again a powerful surge of nameless tender feelings all wrapped up with the need to touch and protect. A thousand times he had attempted to identify those feelings, but they were too elusive. Being with her was like stepping outside after a summer rain into a world that was suddenly clean and invigorating, livening all the senses. Yes, when he was with her, he felt good, very good.

"It seems we're having breakfast outside this morning," he remarked when she caught him looking at her.

"I suggested it to Consuelo while you were in the shower. You don't mind, do you? It's such a beautiful morning." She turned back to the mirror and raised the mascara wand to her lashes.

"And in here, too." He wandered over to stand behind her and study her reflection in the mirror, admiring anew her bold, vibrant beauty.

Her glance met his in the mirror, a hint of demurring amusement in the greenness of her eyes. "It will be . . . in just a few more minutes." She returned the mascara wand to its container and laid it on the vanity table.

Amidst the collection of lipstick, creams, and shadows, Chance noticed a flat cloisonné case. "This is an unusual piece." He picked it up to take a closer look at the intricate design depicting a vase of flowers.

"Isn't it?" Flame said in an agreeing tone, laying down a cotton swab and picking up a tube of lipstick. "My mother gave it to me on my thirteenth birthday—when I was finally allowed to wear makeup. Powder, lipstick, and mascara, to be precise."

"Is this lettering on the vase?"

"My initials—M.R.M.—with the 'M' in the center, of course." She pressed her lips together, spreading the lipstick evenly, then reached for a tissue to blot them.

"M.R.M.?" Everything inside him went still, his gaze riveted to the lettering.

"Margaret Rose Morgan. That's what I was christened. Daddy's the one who gave me the nickname Flame when I was about a year and a half old. It stuck." Smiling, she reached up and slipped the band from her hair, giving her head a shake to let the fiery strands spill forward. "My mother always thought I'd outgrow it in time."

Her glance flicked to his reflection, expecting to encounter his answering smile. Instead, his expression seemed frozen, the muscles along his jaw tightly corded. Bewildered by his reaction, Flame turned sideways on the bench.

"Is something wrong, Chance?" She noticed the way his hand closed around the compact, his knuckles white. She wasn't certain he'd heard her. Then his gaze shot to her face, all icy blue and cold. "Chance, what is it?"

Immediately he looked down. "I just realized—I have nothing of my mother. Nothing at all." He held the compact an instant longer then gave it back to her.

The compact had always been special to her. Yet, it was only now, with some invisible hand squeezing her heart, that she realized how very precious it was.

"Chance, I . . ." But she didn't know what to say.

His mouth quirked faintly in an attempt at a smile. "It doesn't matter," he said, his expression now shuttered. His hand touched her hair, lightly fingering a red lock as if he was somehow distracted by its fiery color. A light rap on the door broke his absorption. "Yes?" There was a sharpness in his voice, making Flame aware of the hard tension hidden just below the surface.

"The telephone, Señor Chance," came Consuelo's partially muffled and heavily accented reply. "It is for you. Señor Sam is calling. He say is *muy importante* he speak to you."

"I'll take the call in the den." He continued to study her hair for another full second before letting their eyes meet. Again his expression was unreadable. "It shouldn't take long."

"All right," she agreed, striving for lightness, recognizing that he didn't want sympathy. "It'll take me a few more minutes to finish dressing anyway."

He let the lock of hair slide from his fingers, then drew his hand away, lightly touching her cheek in parting before he turned and walked from the master bedroom. Flame looked down at the compact her mother had given her those many years ago.

Rage, resentment, and the wretched irony of the situation all seethed inside him as Chance strode across the Spanish tiled floor to the massive teakwood desk. Dammit, he didn't want it to be Flame. She was the one untouched thing in his life. With her, he could almost forget everything. Dammit to hell—it wasn't fair! But when had life ever been fair to him? He looked at the jet-black phone on the desk and forced his fisted hand to unclench and reach for it.

"Yeah, Sam," he said into the mouthpiece, deliberately shutting out all emotion.

"Chance, I'm sorry to call you like this, but . . . you have to know. We've learned the identity of Margaret Rose. Chance, it's Flame."

"I know."

"You do? How? When?"

"It doesn't matter." He rubbed a hand across his forehead, his mind racing now that he had refused to feel anything.

"Does she know who you are? Did she confront you with it? What has Hattie told her?"

"Obviously nothing." He went through everything Flame had ever said to him. There was nothing that even hinted she was aware of his connection to Hattie. Why? Considering how much Hattie hated him, why hadn't she tried to poison Flame with it? He could think of only one reason: she hadn't had the opportunity yet. Which meant he had to make sure Hattie didn't get it.

"Could it be that Hattie doesn't know you've been seeing her?" Sam ventured.

"How could she?" He doubted that Flame would have mentioned him to Hattie. She wouldn't have any reason to. In this short period of time, it was logical to assume that any conversation between Hattie and Flame hadn't touched on private matters.

"Chance, what are you going to do? She's bound to find out."

"Maybe not. Maybe I can prevent that."

"How?"

But it was something he needed to think through first. "I'll talk to you later, Sam."

He stood at the wrought-iron rail of the loggia overlooking the bay and the golden resort far below. His stance was that of a man lost in thought, his head drawn back, his gaze fixed on some distant point at sea, and his hands buried deep in the pockets of his slacks. Flame paused, wondering if he was still thinking about his mother, then continued to him. He didn't hear the dull click of her sandaled heels when she walked up behind him—completely unaware of her presence until she touched his arm.

Then he turned, that familiar, lazily intimate look immediately darkening his eyes the instant he saw her—that look that always caused those crazy tumblations of her heart. She smiled, realizing that everything was all right again.

"Your phone call must not have taken very long."

"No." His gaze wandered over her face as if intent on memorizing every detail. Then he bent his head, his mouth brushing over her lips before settling onto them with a driving need that had her leaning into him, supported by the encircling crush of his arms. She felt an edge of desperation somewhere—whether from her or from him, she couldn't tell. But it was there, a part of this desire to be absorbed wholly into one another. When the strain for closeness became too much, his mouth rolled off her cheek to the lobe of her ear, his breathing as heated and heavy as her own. "How long have we known each other?" he murmured.

She had to think—which wasn't easy when all she wanted to do was feel. "Three weeks."

He lifted his head, framing her face in his hands. "Yet I can't imagine my life without you in it."

"I know. I feel the same." She was a little surprised by how easy it was to admit that.

"Are you as certain of your feelings as I am?"

She searched and found not a trace of doubt. "Yes."

"Then marry me. Now. Today."

If she had bothered to try, she could have come up with a dozen valid reasons not to rush into another marriage. But none of them—not the short time she'd known Chance, not her career—was strong enough, singly or combined, to override the fact that she loved him and, more important, he loved her.

"Yes," she said simply.

"You're certain." He studied her closely. "I know women like to have big, elaborate weddings. If you want to wait for that—"

"No." She shook her head, as much as his cupping hands would allow. "I've had the white satin gown and veil before. I don't care about the trimmings this time, Chance. Your love is more than enough."

"I do love you, Flame," he stated firmly. "Promise you'll remember that."

"Only if you promise to remind me," she teased.

"I'm serious, Flame. I've made my share of enemies over the years. No matter what anyone might tell you about me, I do love you. And I intend to go on loving you for the rest of my life."

"Darling, I'm going to hold you to that—and to me, for the rest of *our* lives," she declared confidently, joyously.

Sid Barker kept the pay telephone pressed tightly to his ear as he mopped away the perspiration on his forehead and upper lip with his already sodden handkerchief. Damn this tropical heat, he thought, and wished for a tall, cold beer. At the continued silence on the line, he started to swear at the Mexican operator for not putting his call through, then he heard the muted *brrring* on the other end, answered immediately by a familiar voice.

"Yeah, it's Barker," he said and darted a quick glance at the door not ten feet away. "I managed to locate them in Mexico—finally. But you've got a problem. I'm here at some sort of government building—and they just got married." He anticipated the shocked and angry response he received—and the doubt. "It's true, I swear. I was standing close enough I could have been a witness. . . . How could I stop it?" he shot back in sharp defense. "I didn't know what was going on until it was too late. I thought he was just taking her on a little sight-seeing tour of the village to show her how the other half lived—the ones who clean his expensive hotel rooms and wait on his rich guests." The resentment faded as his voice grew more thoughtful. "Maybe I should have guessed something was up when I got word his private jet had taken off. Less than three hours later, it was back. I figure now that he had them pick up a ring for her. You should see the rock she's wearing." There was movement at the door as a pair of beaming government officials escorted the newlyweds out of the room. Barker cupped his mouth to the receiver, speaking in a hushed rush. "They're coming out now. I've gotta go."

Without waiting for a reply, he hung up and walked briskly from the building to his rental car, guarded by a pair of enterprising Mexican boys.

The heavy damask drapes at the bedroom windows were partially closed, shutting out much of the afternoon sunlight. Maxine paused inside the doorway, struck by the unnatural stillness in the room. Unconsciously she held her own breath as she listened for the sounds of breathing on the ornately carved four-poster. The pink satin of her quilted bed jacket trimmed with eyelet lace emphasized the pallor of her crepey skin, pinched and gray with pain. Pity swept through Maxine, followed by an instant hardening. Hattie Morgan was getting just what she deserved.

Moving silently, the thick rubber soles of her sturdy work shoes making little sound on the hardwood floor, Maxine approached the huge bed that dominated the small room. Hattie had slept in this room ever since she'd left the cradle more than eighty years ago, even though the spacious master bedroom right next door had gone unused for more than sixty of those years. Maxine had always wondered at that.

She glanced hesitantly at the woman, then picked up the brown plastic container of prescription pills from the nightstand. She checked the capsules inside, trying to decide how many, if any, were gone.

"You're always snooping around, aren't you?" The caustic accusation shattered the stillness.

Maxine turned toward the bed. "I thought you were resting." With forced calm, she set the container back down on the nightstand.

"Then what are you doing in here?" A glaze of pain clouded the usually sharp eyes. "I heard the phone ring. Who was it?"

"Mr. Canon. He's still on the line. But I didn't want to disturb you if—"

Hattie released a scornfully loud breath of disbelief and held out an age-gnarled hand. "Give me the phone, then leave the room." With lips pressed tightly together, Maxine lifted the phone from the nightstand and placed it on the bed next to Hattie, then turned away. She stiffened in resentment at Hattie's parting shot: "And I'm not so drugged that I won't be able to tell if you listen in on the extension."

As the housekeeper moved away from the bed, all Hattie could see was a shadowy dark figure. She could feel the excrutiating pressure at the back of her eyes obscuring her vision. She was frightened by it and the dimness of her new world. As she waited to hear the door close behind Maxine, she wondered which was the hardest to bear—the pain or the fear. Interminable moments passed before Hattie heard the distinctive click of the downstairs extension being hung up. She felt for the telephone beside her, fingers closing around the receiver and lifting it to her ear.

"Yes, Ben, what is it?" She spoke harshly, fighting to keep the inner panic at bay.

"They're here in Tulsa," came the reply. "He brought her back with him."

"It's true then," she said, her voice strained by the fervent hope he would deny it.

"Yes. She married him."

"She promised me—" Hearing the frantic edge in her voice, Hattie abruptly broke off the rest of the sentence, realizing it no longer mattered what Margaret Rose had promised her. "We'll just have to see what we can do about it, won't we?" she said with forced bravery.

"Right," Ben Canon replied, an offer of encouragement in the response.

A few minutes later he rang off and the line went dead. Briefly Hattie felt that way inside as she hung up the phone. But she couldn't quit. She couldn't let Stuart win, not when she'd fought so long and so hard—not when she'd come so close. She groped for and found the old-fashioned bell pull next to the bed. She yanked on it impatiently and called, "Maxine. Maxine!"

Almost immediately she heard the muted sound of running footsteps in the hall outside her room.

The door burst open. "Are you all right, Miss Hattie?" Concern laced the housekeeper's voice. "Shall I call the doctor?"

"No," Hattie snapped. "Get me Charlie Rainwater."

"But—"

"Now!" She snapped again. When the door swung shut with a resounding click, Hattie sagged back against the pillows and muttered dejectedly to herself, "How could you be such a fool, Margaret Rose? I thought you were smart enough to see through him." She closed her eyes and pressed a hand against them, trying to suppress the blinding pain in her head.

Her position remained unchanged until she heard the scuff of booted footsteps approach her door nearly fifteen minutes later. She brought her hand down and lifted her chin up, jutting it forward at an aggressive angle.

"Come in," she responded in answer to the rap at her door, not letting any of the pain or fear creep into her voice. Pride wouldn't let her permit Charlie to see that she might be beaten. He believed in her. He had all these many years.

He paused beside the bed. "Maxine said you wanted to see me."

"Yes." She wished his face wasn't so blurred to her, but it was enough just to hear the soothing drawl of his voice and smell that mixture of saddle leather and tobacco that always clung to his clothes. "We have trouble, Charlie. She did marry him." She caught the sound of his half-smothered curse and smiled faintly before going on to explain about the call she'd just received from Ben Canon.

"What do you want me to do?"

When she felt his work-roughened fingers brush over her hand, Hattie caught at them briefly. "He's brought her back to Tulsa with him, Charlie. I knew he'd be arrogant. And that is his mistake."

"Then you don't think it's too late."

"It can't be." She clung desperately to that. "But we'll have to be ready to act at a moment's notice. We don't have much time."

"You can count on me, Miss Hattie." He squeezed her hand tightly, emotion thickening his voice.

"I know I can." She nodded, feeling the same tightness and the same vague regrets.

"We'll make it."

"Of course we will," she said, more confidently, drawing strength from his belief in her . . . just as she always had in the past. She let go of his hand and lay back, listening to the burring spin of the telephone dial as he placed her call to Ben Canon.

"Hello, Ellery? It's Flame." She sat crosswise on Chance's lap, idly and possessively fingering the short strands of his thick black hair.

"How was your weekend of sizzle in the sun? Or was it sizzle in the sack?" came Ellery Dorn's dry reply. "From the sound of your voice, I'd say you're still floating on cloud nine."

She laughed at that, her glance straying to the plane's porthole windows and the puffy white clouds beyond them. "Actually I am—literally and figuratively."

There was a pause, then a puzzled "Where are you?"

She partially covered the phone's mouthpiece with her hand and looked at Chance. "Where are we?"

"About thirty thousand feet over Dallas." A faint smile edged the corners of his mouth as he continued to idly massage the curve of her hip bone.

When Flame relayed the answer to Ellery, he responded with a droll "I sincerely hope you're in an airplane."

"I am, I am." She laughed again, recognizing that she was so happy she could laugh at anything.

"If you're flying over Texas now, that means it will be another two and a half hours or more before you reach San Francisco."

"That's what I'm calling you about, Ellery." There was a part of her that was bursting to tell him the news—and another part that wanted to drag out the moment. "I won't be flying back to San Francisco—at least, not tonight."

"Why not? Where are you going?"

"To Tulsa." She couldn't keep it to herself any longer. "Chance and I got married."

"What?"

She laughed at the surprise in his voice. "It's incredible, isn't it?" She ceased playing with Chance's hair and held up her left hand to gaze at the interlocking wedding band and five carat marquise-cut diamond ring set in platinum that now so beautifully adorned her ring finger.

"Incredible isn't the word for it," Ellery replied. "Flame, are you sure you know what you're doing?"

She looked once more at Chance. The deep blue of his eyes mirrored all the love that she felt. "Very sure," she murmured, swinging the mouthpiece of the receiver out of the way and leaning closer to kiss him, letting their lips cling together for several precious seconds.

"I hope so," came Ellery's sotto voce reply.

But it was enough to bring Flame's attention back to the matter at hand. "Would you mind doing me a favor, Ellery? Talk to Tim in the morning and let him know I won't be in the office for a couple of days. Explain that I'm taking a short honeymoon. And let Debbie know, too, so she can cancel any appointments I have."

"When can we expect you back?"

"Chance has to leave on a business trip—when did you say? Wednesday?" He nodded in confirmation. "I'll fly back then. Which means I'll be in the office on Thursday morning. Okay?"

"Your honeymoon is obviously going to be as short as your engagement," Ellery observed. "Oh, one more thing, Flame—"

"Yes."

"Congratulations and happiness, my dear."

"Thank you, Ellery."

"And tell Stuart I hope he knows what a lucky man he is."

"I will. Talk to you Wednesday night." She returned the phone to its console concealed in the cabinetry next to the couch, then faced Chance, linking her hands together behind his neck. "Ellery insisted that I remind you what a lucky man you are."

"Extremely lucky," he agreed smoothly.

"So am I." Silently she studied his face, admiring its bronze angles, so strong and clean from the slanting cut of his jaw to the unbroken line of his nose. She noticed the look in his eyes, that look that spoke of a pride of possession. She smiled, feeling it, too. They belonged to each other now, and how very wonderful that was. Idly she smoothed a strand of hair away from his wide brow. "How long before we reach Tulsa?"

With an effort he dragged his gaze from her face and looked out the window. "That looks like the Red River below us, which means we're crossing into Oklahoma. We'll probably be landing in another twenty minutes or so."

"So soon," she murmured in mock disappointment.

"Yes." There was more than a trace of regret in his voice as his glance slid to her lips. Then he breathed in deeply. "We probably should move back to the main cabin. You'll have a better view from there of your new home when we fly in."

"That's a shame when I'm so comfortable sitting here," she declared softly and brushed her lips across the ridge of his cheek, breathing in the earthy fragrance of his cologne.

"We aren't there, yet," he reminded her as he turned his head, seeking and finding her lips.

Ten minutes later they were interrupted by the buzz of the intercom. It was the pilot, Mick Donovan, notifying Chance that he was about to begin his descent into Tulsa. With some reluctance, Flame traded her comfortable seat on Chance's lap for one of the richly upholstered chairs in the main cabin.

With her seatbelt securely fastened, Flame leaned forward, angling her body to look out the window at the wide open landscape of rolling hills below. The long slanting rays of the setting sun set fire to its autumn hues, intensifying the shades of its golds, rusts, and reds and giving a richness to the land.

Somewhere out there, she remembered, Hattie Morgan lived. She'd have to give her a call while she was here—assuming, of course, that she'd have the time to spare on this short trip.

Then Chance's arm curled around her waist and all thought of Hattie fled as he leaned forward to look out the window with her. "There's my city," he said. "Daring and dynamic Tulsa."

Etched against the fiery backdrop of the sunset's red sky, she saw the gleaming towers of the city itself, rising out of the surrounding hills and seemingly throwing them off with a mighty shrug of its shoulders. She stared at the tall sleek buildings, their proud stance reminding her somehow of Chance.

"Well, what do you think?"

She felt the brush of his chin against her hair, and hesitated briefly, wondering how she could tell him that her first impression of Tulsa was of something powerful and aggressive—something lean, tumultuous, and restless—the very things she sensed in him sometimes.

But the feeling was too elusive to put into words. She chose a safe middle ground instead. "I like it already. It's vigorous and alive."

"That black building to the right is the Stuart Tower, where my company's headquartered." He pointed it out to her just before the plane banked away to make its approach to the airport. Chance kept his arm around her as they both sat back in their seats. "In the morning, you can come into the office with me. I want you to meet Sam and Molly."

"I'd like that, darling." From the few things he'd said about them, she had gotten the feeling that these two people were the closest thing he had to a family. "I just hope they like me."

"They will. Although I probably should warn you that Molly may come off like a mother-in-law."

"Ah, a potential ogre—any suggestions?"

"Just tell her how wonderful you think I am and you'll have her eating out of your hand." He grinned, certain that Molly would love her as much as he did and refusing to consider the friction that would arise if she didn't.

And Flame laughed. "You mean you aren't eating out of my hand?"

"If you think I am, that's all that counts."

She sensed the shift in his mood to something more serious, more intimate. "What about Sam? How do I get him to eat out of my hand?"

"Ask him about cars. The man's crazy about anything with four wheels and a motor—a little like I am about you." He kissed her, and Flame wasn't aware of the jet's wheels touching down.

18 ∽

SAM LEANED AGAINST the corner of Molly's desk, one hip resting on top of it. He took another deep drag on his cigarette and glanced anxiously at the doors to the private elevator, then swung his gaze to Molly, watching as she fussed over the fresh floral arrangement on the credenza behind her desk. She stepped back to survey the result, then nodded in mute satisfaction even though Sam couldn't see that she'd changed the placement of a single flower. Turning, she ran the same critically inspecting eye over the room. When he saw it fall on the serving tray with its precise arrangement of china cups and saucers, the requisite creamer and sugar, lacking only fresh coffee to be poured in its decorative urn, his nerves snapped.

"So help me, Molly, if you touch those cups on that tray one more time—"

"I wasn't even thinking of that," she denied, flashing him an impatient look. "I was wondering if I should have had the bakery send up some Danish pastries. Watch your ash. It's going to drop on the floor."

"God forbid," he muttered, cupping one hand under the cigarette as he swung it to the ceramic ashtray on her desk, then pulled it back to tap the buildup of ash into the gleaming bottom. "You'd probably call maintenance and have them bring up a vacuum cleaner."

"I would not." Immediately she picked up the ashtray and emptied it into the wastebasket under her desk, then snatched a tissue from the box she kept on the credenza and wiped the last speck of ash from the ceramic tray. "Molly, will you stop this fussing?" He stabbed his cigarette out in the ashtray the instant she set it down. A bundle of nerves himself, Sam impatiently pushed away from her desk.

"I just want to make the right impression," she retorted, grabbing the ashtray again.

"Where are they anyway?" He pushed back the cuff of his jacket to check his watch. "Chance said they'd be here by ten-thirty. It's past that now."

"You didn't expect them to be on time, did you?" Molly chided. "After all, they are newlyweds." Then she sighed, her eyes crinkling at the corners, matching the curve of her lips. "I can hardly wait to meet her."

Sam shook his head is disagreement and rubbed at the tension cording the back of his neck. "I'm afraid I can't say the same."

Molly looked at him with some surprise. "Why not?"

"Because . . ." Sam hesitated, but he'd held it inside too long. It had to come out. "—I have bad feelings about this marriage," he said, turning to face Molly as he brought his hand down, fisting it in helpless frustration. "Dammit, I don't understand why he married her—why he didn't talk over his plans with me first?"

"He loves her." As far as Molly was concerned, no other explanation was necessary.

"But don't you see, Molly, that's the point. This is one time I don't think Chance thought things through too clearly."

She shook her head, unwilling to listen to his criticism. "He knows what he's doing."

"Does he?" Sam challenged. "Let's forget the fact that he didn't have her sign any prenuptial agreement, and concentrate instead on what's going to happen when she finds out about Hattie and the ranch. Do you know that he hasn't told her anything about Hattie? And when I talked to him after they got back last night, he informed me he wasn't going to tell her."

"Why should he?"

"Because sooner or later, she's going to find out. And if he keeps it a secret from her, think how it's going to look."

"When the time comes, Chance will handle it. He always does," she stated with supreme confidence. "You worry too much, Sam."

"Maybe." But the boyish features continued to wear a troubled look as he combed the lock of hair from his forehead, unaware that it fell back. "I don't know, Molly. I just can't help thinking this is all my fault. Chance relied on me to know what Hattie was up to and I let him down. If only I'd paid more attention to those meetings she was having with Canon, but I thought she was trying to find some legal loophole to avoid willing the land to Chance. I'd already checked that out eight ways to Sunday and knew it couldn't be done. But I never dreamed she was tracking down another heir. It never even occurred to me there might be one. If I had known—if I'd had her followed that day she went to Canon's office, I'd have known about her trip to San Francisco—who she saw—everything. And Chance would have known—going in—that Flame was Margaret Rose. It's for sure we wouldn't have all these complications we're faced with now."

"You are such a pessimist, Sam." Molly clicked her tongue at him. "You see Chance's marriage as a complication, but I see it as the perfect solution." The elevator light flashed on, indicating it was in use. "Here they come." Molly hurriedly sat down in her chair and grabbed up a pen and notepad, then patted the sides of her peppered gray hair. "Quick. Look busy," she admonished Sam.

"Busy?" He frowned in confusion. "But they're on their way up."

"I know. But we don't want to look like we've been standing around waiting for her to arrive."

"Why not? That's what we've been doing for the last twenty minutes."

"We can't let her know that." Her glance fastened itself on the front of his suit jacket. "There's cigarette ash or lint on your lapel."

Sam brushed it off with a flick of his fingers, amused by her anxious flutters to have everything neat and in order despite his continued concern over the situation. "I'm surprised you don't want me to spit on my fingers and slick down my cowlicks," he murmured.

A faint ding accompanied the swish of the elevator doors gliding open, checking any answering retort Molly might have made as she directed a beaming smile at the emerging couple. Sam took one look at Chance's bride and understood completely how this woman had succeeded in stealing Chance's heart when so many others before her had failed. In one word, she was a knockout. Gorgeous, subtly sexy—especially in that sweater dress of kitteny soft angora—yet . . . the more Sam studied her, the more traces of Hattie he saw behind that warm and glowing look she wore. Just little things, like the proud way she held her head, the sharpness in her green eyes, and that confident squaring of her shoulders. Trite or not, he had a feeling she had a temper to match the fiery color of her hair—and all it would take to spark it was someone trying to pull something over on her. He hoped to hell Chance knew what he was doing.

"Am I allowed to kiss the bride?" he asked after the initial flurry of introductions and acknowledgments were over.

"Of course." The words of laughing assent came from Flame.

Sam darted a quick look of surprise at Chance and struggled to hide the surge of misgivings as he brushed his lips across her proffered cheek, breathing in the spicy fragrance of her perfume. Chance seemed to think nothing of the assertion by Flame, but in Sam's opinion, those were words of warning that here was a woman who knew her own mind and didn't let others do her thinking.

"I have fresh coffee made," Molly volunteered. "Would you like a cup?"

"We'll have it in my office," Chance inserted, then arched a questioning look at Sam. "You'll join us, won't you?"

"Of course. Which reminds me—" he began, following after them as Chance led Flame into his office. "Patty asked me to invite the two of you for dinner on Sunday. She's anxious to meet you."

"Dinner on Sunday." Chance looked at Flame, his gaze intimately warm and possessive in its run over her face. "We should be back by then."

"Back? From where?" Sam frowned, then remembered. "That's right. You have to fly to Padre Island on Wednesday."

A vague nod confirmed it, leaving the impression that Chance was too distracted by his new bride to give the whole of his attention to anything or anyone else. "While I'm there, Flame's going to fly back to San Francisco and tie up all her loose ends. Which means you'll need to make reservations for her, Molly, on Wednesday's flight, but only one way. I'll meet her on Friday and we can fly back together."

"I'll make a note of it."

Not liking the sound of Chance's plans, Sam immediately spoke up. "And I need to go over some things with you, Chance." He glanced apologetically at Flame. "You'll have to forgive me for stealing him away so soon. But it's business. You understand?"

"Of course. No problem."

"I promise I won't keep him long."

"Molly, why don't you take Flame on a tour of the offices and introduce her around?" Chance suggested. "Just remember to have her back by noon. We have a luncheon date."

"I think I can manage that with no difficulty."

His arm tightened briefly around Flame's shoulders, a smile tugging at his lip corners. "Molly's convinced I'm perfect. Try not to disillusion her too much."

"How could I, when I agree with her completely?" she countered, matching his mocking tone.

"I like her already, Chance," Molly declared.

"I knew you would." But his smile was directed at Flame, a familiar pride of possession in his look.

"Come on. We'll leave these two to their business."

Sam noticed the way Chance's gaze stayed on Flame as Molly trundled her off, as if he was reluctant to let her out of his sight—although not for the same reason that Sam had. When they turned down the hallway, Chance forcibly turned his attention back to Sam.

"Let's talk in my office," he said, taking Sam's agreement for granted as he crossed the room to the heavy walnut door. Sam followed him inside and closed the door behind them. Chance went directly to his desk and began leafing through the messages that had accumulated in his absence. "What's on your mind, Sam?"

"For starters, I don't think it's a good idea for you to let her go to San Francisco alone. What if Hattie tries to contact her while she's there?"

"I've already considered that possibility. I want you to get hold of Sawyer and have him waiting at the gate when she arrives on Wednesday. I want someone watching her twenty-four hours a day and a tap on her phone. If anyone—Hattie, Canon, that detective Barker—tries to talk to her, I'll expect Sawyer to make sure they don't succeed. By Friday, I'll be there."

"And what about from now until then—or after you get back? You can't be with her every minute, Chance," Sam argued.

"When she's at the house, Andrews can screen all incoming calls. And if she goes out anywhere—to shop or to play tennis—it will probably be with Patty. She won't know anyone else here. And, until she gets settled in, she won't be seeing anyone other than people I introduce her to."

"You make it sound so simple—so cut and dried—but it's not that way, Chance." He lifted his hand in a silent appeal. "What if it's the other way around? What if Flame's the one who contacts Hattie? She could, you know. She's bound to have her phone number. What's to stop her from calling Hattie, getting directions, and driving out to see her?"

"She'd say something to me about it first."

"What if she didn't? What if she did it on the spur of the moment?" Sam leaned both hands on the granite top of the desk, trying to press home his point and penetrate that aloof unconcern. "How would you know?"

"I'll know." Chance dropped the sheaf of his messages onto his desk, letting them scatter from the orderly stack as he faced Sam across the desk top, his control snapping from the strain of the last two days—the strain of living half the time in heaven and the other half in hell. "I'll know if I have to bug my own house and have her followed everywhere she goes from now on. Dammit, Sam, I know I can't eliminate the risk but I can minimize the exposure." The level of his voice didn't change, but rather the tone of it deepened to a forceful pitch. "And that's precisely what I intend to do."

"I'm sorry," Sam began hesitantly, drawing back from that tautly controlled anger. "It's just that—"

"I know," Chance cut him off abruptly and swung away, moving to the window and inhaling a deep breath, regretting the anger he'd turned on Sam. "I found out this weekend just how greedy I am, Sam," he said, staring out the window at the sprawl of the city beyond the glass panes. "I want Flame and I want that land. I'll do whatever I have to do to make sure I don't lose either one."

"I understand."

"Do you?" He smiled wryly, unsure that he did.

The beeping ring of the telephone intruded. "I'll get it." Sam reached across the desk and picked up the receiver. "Yes, this is Sam Weber." Almost immediately he lowered the phone, placing his hand over the mouthpiece. "Chance, it's Maxine."

Pivoting sharply, Chance reached for it. "Let me talk to her." He took the phone from Sam's hand. "Yes, Maxine." A tension kept him motionless as he listened to her hurried message. "Thanks for letting me know." Slowly he carried the receiver back to its cradle.

"Letting you know what?" Sam asked, watching him closely.

He let his hand stay on the telephone. "It's Hattie. According to Maxine, she's very ill. She doesn't think she can hold on much longer."

Sam let out a long, slow breath. "I'm not sure I believe it. And I feel guilty for hoping it's true."

"I don't."

"It looks as if everything's going to come to a head sooner than I thought. It's going to get real touchy, Chance."

"I know."

19

SUNLIGHT FLASHED ON the marquise-cut diamond on her finger, sending prisms of light dancing across the car's dash. Absently, Flame turned her gaze out the window at the still unfamiliar scenery of big and bold Tulsa. She had yet to explore it—or get used to the huge canopy of pale blue sky that seemed to stretch forever, unmarred by ocean-born cloudbanks or blanketing fog.

It was moments like these, when the strangeness of her surroundings made itself felt, that it all seemed unreal. She touched the ring on her finger, the one Chance had placed there. It was physical proof this wasn't a dream. She was his wife.

Flame Stuart. She smiled, liking the sound of it.

Even though she was resigning from the agency, she planned to continue with her career here in Tulsa. Not right away, of course. She wanted to spend as much time as possible with Chance these next few months. Later she'd see about obtaining a position with some local agency. Or maybe she could work with Chance in his company, handling the ad campaigns on his various projects. Either way, she knew she would ultimately want the challenge and mental stimulation of work again.

She smiled to herself, realizing that this was a fine time to be thinking about all this. But it had all happened so suddenly—the marriage ceremony coming right on the heels of his proposal, then less than twelve hours later flying here with a new husband to a new home. And what a gorgeous home it was, a 1930s mansion styled after a gracious Palladian villa. She remembered that moment on their arrival when Chance had carried her over the threshold into the marble foyer with its grand, curved staircase—and later, when he'd taken her to the special master suite. Sighing, she ran her fingers into her hair and flipped it behind her ear with a combing toss of her hand, the enormity of the step finally hitting her. My God, she was giving up her home, her job, her friends—everything that had ever meant anything to her. But she'd known that when she'd married Chance. It hadn't mattered then because he was with her, right at her side.

Overhead, the contrails of a passing jet streaked the sky, reminding Flame that Chance was halfway to Texas by now. She wished he was in the car with her so she could take hold of his hand and have the physical reassurance that she wasn't alone in this. Instead, she fingered her wedding ring and sighed her longing.

"Is something wrong?"

Startled by the question that came from the silence, Flame glanced at the man behind the wheel, momentarily at a loss for an answer. She couldn't very well admit to Sam Weber that she was having a slight case of postwedding jitters, not when she knew that deep down she didn't really have any doubts about her decision to marry Chance.

"No. I was just thinking about all the things I have to do once I get to San Francisco." Conscious of his close scrutiny, she turned her attention to the freeway traffic in front of them. "Is it much farther to the airport?"

"Ten minutes, more or less. Which means—" He paused to glance at the clock on the car's dash. "—we'll be there a good forty-five minutes before your flight leaves."

"I don't know why Chance insisted that you take me to the airport. I could just as easily have gotten a cab or had Andrews drive me. It wasn't necessary for you to do it. I'm sure you have more important things you could have been doing."

"You're not going to hear any complaints from me." Sam took his eyes from the road long enough to flash a boyish grin her way. "As far as I'm concerned this is a very pleasant break."

"Well, good, Sam." She hoped he meant that.

At odd times, she'd had the feeling that Sam wasn't particularly happy about her marriage to Chance. It was nothing he'd said. No, it was more the way he looked at her sometimes, as if questioning her reasons. She supposed Sam thought she might have married Chance for his money. She hadn't, of course. His wealth didn't matter to her at all, but Sam couldn't know that.

"I'm sorry Chance had to leave so soon after the wedding," Sam remarked, genuine regret tinging the glance he sent her. "The two of you should have gone off on a long honeymoon."

"I don't mind," Flame insisted with a dismissing shake of her head. "I've known from the beginning that his work demands a lot of travel. Maybe it's best our marriage starts out as it will go on."

"Maybe. But I still believe newlyweds need some time alone. I told Chance before he left that Molly and I were going to take a look at his schedule and see if we can rearrange to give you those three or four weeks together. It shouldn't be too difficult—barring any emergencies, of course."

"Sam—" Flame began, touched by his thoughtfulness and wondering if she had misjudged him.

But he didn't give her a chance to say more. "You'd better start thinking about where you want to go, otherwise Molly will have it all planned for you," he warned, humor twinkling in his hazel eyes. "She's already told Chance that she thinks he should take you to Venice."

"Is that right?" Flame smiled, amused by the conspiracy that had been going on behind the scenes.

"Yes." Then Sam seemed to hesitate. "Molly can be quite bossy at times, especially where Chance is concerned. But she means well. I hope you know that."

"Chance told me the same thing." Her smile widened as she recalled, "Actually, he told me that Molly was the closest I would come to having a mother-in-law."

Sam chuckled. "That's true enough. As a matter of fact, you know that old cliché about believing the sun rises and sets on someone. As far as Molly's concerned, Chance is the sun. And nobody had better dare to cast a dark shadow over his life or they'll answer to her."

"I did get that impression. Truthfully, though, I like her."

"It's impossible not to like Molly. She's quite a woman. Once you get to know her better, you'll understand what I mean." He paused to slide Flame a sideways glance, a boyish grin pulling up one corner of his mouth. "I hope I have half of her energy and spunk when I'm her age. Do you know that she was in her forties before she went hunting and fishing for the first time? On top of that, her first time out she bagged a trophy buck. I know. I was there. In fact I was the one who took her hunting. She's something else," he declared, then added, "and independent as the day is long. When she first went to work for Chance, she was taking a night school course in auto mechanics. She'd decided that the local garage was taking advantage of her because she was a woman and didn't know anything about cars. Speaking of cars, remind me to show you my vintage Porsche when you and Chance come for dinner on Sunday."

"He mentioned that your hobby was restoring classic sportscars."

"Patty would tell you it's my passion." Again there was a flash of boyishness in his grin. "I don't know that I'd go so far as to say that, but I do enjoy tinkering with cars. I always have. For me, it's a great way to relax and—it's a hobby I can share with my sons along with hunting and fishing. Patty and I have four boys. The youngest is eleven and the oldest is sixteen. Right now we're in the process of rebuilding a 'seventy-six Corvette for Drake, our oldest." The brake lights on the car directly in front of them flashed red as the traffic on the freeway began to bunch up. "Hello, what's this?" Sam frowned as he applied the brake and reached for the stick shift to gear down. "This is the wrong time of the day to be having a tie-up."

But a tie-up it was, as the traffic slowed to a crawl, then came to a stop altogether another hundred yards farther.

Flame thought she heard the wail of a siren. "Do you suppose there's been an accident?"

"Maybe." With a tilt of his head, Sam peered into his side mirror. "Here comes a motorcycle cop. I'll see what I can find out." He rolled down his window and flagged the policeman slowly wending his way between the stopped cars. "What seems to be the problem, officer?"

"A tractor-trailer rig jackknifed on the overpass," came the reply, half-muffled by the revving of the cycle's engine. "There's a tow truck on the scene, so it shouldn't be much more than ten minutes before they get a lane cleared."

"I hope not." Sam glanced at his watch. "We have a plane to catch."

Trapped between freeway exits, they had no choice but to wait it out. Ten minutes turned into fifteen, then twenty. Finally, nearly twenty-five minutes later, the traffic started moving again.

When Sam pulled up to the curb in front of the airport terminal, Flame had barely fifteen minutes to make her flight. "With luck, your departure will be delayed. They usually are," he said as he hurriedly retrieved her luggage from the trunk. "Just the same, we'd better check your bags at the gate to make sure they're on the same flight with you."

As they started toward glass doors, an airport security guard stopped them. "I'm sorry, sir, but you can't leave your car parked here. This is an unloading zone only."

"Five minutes, that's all I'll be. I swear," Sam argued, but he argued in vain. Sighing in defeat, Sam turned to her. "It looks like you're going to have to go ahead to the gate while I park the car. He won't listen to reason. Can you carry your bags? He claims there are luggage carts inside."

"I can manage," Flame assured him.

"Okay." Reluctantly he transferred the two cases to her. "I'll meet you at the gate as soon as I can."

"That's not necessary, Sam—"

He cut her protest short. "I'll be there anyway—just in case you miss the flight or it's delayed."

Recognizing it would be a waste of time to argue, Flame gave in. With a bag in each hand for balance, she entered the terminal building and walked directly to the monitor screens listing the departing flights and their respective gate numbers.

As Flame scanned the screen for her flight, a gentle drawling voice intruded: "Beggin' your pardon, ma'am." She glanced absently at the man who had stopped beside her, an aging cowboy in a suit of brown polyester with the distinctive yoked front of the western cut. "You're Margaret Rose, aren't you?" A pair of rheumy blue eyes lifted their glance to her hair. "Miss Hattie said I'd know you straight off by the red of your hair."

"Hattie Morgan." Momentarily she was startled to hear him speak the woman's name. "I had planned to call her when I came back," she said more to herself than to the aging cowboy. "Do you know her?" she said, then smiled, realizing she had asked the obvious.

"Yes, ma'am." As if suddenly remembering his manners, he doffed the cream-white Stetson and held it in front of him revealing a head of wispy thin white hair, flattened by the hat. "Miss Hattie said she'd mentioned me to you. I'm Charlie Rainwater, the foreman at Morgan's Walk."

"She did, yes. It's a pleasure to meet you, Mr. Rainwater." Just for an instant, Flame eyed him curiously, taking in his wiry slim body, the half-moon shape of his white mustache, and the deep tan of his skin, leathered by years of sun and wind. He had a strong, lean face—and a kind one, innately gentle, like his eyes.

"How did you know I'd be—" But her question was interrupted by an announcement over the airport's public address system. "That's my flight. I have to go. Please tell—"

"You can't go, ma'am." He lifted a hand as if to stop her. "Miss Hattie needs to see you."

"But—"

"Ma'am, she's dying," he inserted firmly over her half-formed protest.

"What?" Stunned by his blunt statement, Flame stared at him.

"It's true, ma'am. I wish it weren't, but wishin' don't make it so."

"But . . . I talked to her only last week. She sounded fine on the phone." She struggled to shake off the sense of shock. "What happened? Did she have a heart attack?"

"No, ma'am." A dip of his head briefly concealed his expression. "She has a brain tumor. The doctors told her last spring there wasn't anything they could do."

"No," she whispered, remembering the desperation she had sensed in the elderly woman, a desperation she had blamed on loneliness. But that hadn't been the cause at all.

"She's been asking for you, Miss Margaret." His watery eyes made their own silent appeal. "Will you come to Morgan's Walk with me? I promised her I'd find you and bring you back. If the good Lord's willing, we won't be too late."

"I—" Flame glanced uncertainly at the monitor screen. The flashing number indicated her flight was in the boarding stage. But it wasn't imperative that she return to San Francisco on this particular flight. She could catch another . . . later. She turned back to the white-haired ranch foreman and smiled faintly. "I'll go with you."

Deep gratitude welled in his look. "It will mean everything to Miss Hattie. Thank you." He pushed his hat back onto his head and picked up her suitcases. "I have a car waiting outside. If you'll come with me . . ."

She hesitated, the thought occurring to her that perhaps she should wait and advise Sam of her change in plans. But the anxious look on the foreman's lined and weathered face revealed his eagerness to be on his way back to Morgan's Walk. And time was of the essence. Nodding her assent, Flame turned and walked to the glass doors.

Approached by a winding road and circular drive, the stately Georgian mansion of red brick stood atop a knoll overlooking a long golden valley flanked by a ridge of hills painted in the gold, scarlet, and rust of autumn. Some one hundred yards to the right of it, nestled in a pocket of oak trees, were the ranch's outbuildings, the rustic simplicity of the utilitarian buildings in sharp contrast to the subtle grandeur of the manor house.

Through the car window, Flame gazed at the imposing three-story structure with its pillared entry and gleaming white shutters. This was Morgan's Walk, designed by her great-grandfather, Christopher Morgan. She frowned, suddenly wondering why he'd left it. Why had he gone to San Francisco? Hattie had never explained that. In truth, she had never thought about his reasons, believing that San Francisco was obviously preferable to the vast nothingness of Oklahoma. But, at the time, she hadn't known he'd left something this special behind. Why?

The Lincoln pulled up behind two cars already parked in the circular drive. Before the engine died, Charlie Rainwater was out of the car and opening the rear passenger door for Flame. Picking up on his sense of urgency, she wasted no time stepping out to join him.

"Doc Gibb's still here. I hope that's a good sign." He nodded in the direction of the car directly in front of the Lincoln, then tucked a hand under her elbow and guided her to the mansion's pillared entrance.

"I hope so, too," she murmured, gripped by the memory of another hurried trip following the car crash that took her father's life and ultimately her mother's.

Inside, afternoon sunlight streamed through the leaded glass windows and laid a golden pattern across the rich parquet flooring of the spacious reception hall. Absently, Flame scanned the ornate ceiling moldings, the glittering crystal chandelier, and the hall's period furnishings, recognizing that the mansion's interior filled the exterior's promise of gracious formality within. Yet it was the silence, the stillness, of the house that made the greatest impression. She turned to the aging foreman as he removed his hat and ran combing fingers through his thin white hair, rumpling its flatness.

"I'll bring in your bags directly, ma'am, but it'd be best if I took you straight up to Miss Hattie."

"Of course."

He led her to the gleaming oak staircase that curved in a grand sweep to the second floor. As Flame climbed the steps, she trailed her hand along the smooth banister, its finish darkened by the oils from the many hands that had touched it before hers . . . Morgan hands. Again she felt a sense of the past, a curiosity about the ones who had lived here.

"Your roots will pull you back." That's what Hattie had told her. Was that what was happening to her? Hattie would say so. Hattie. Flame lifted her glance to the second-floor landing, her thoughts now turning to the woman.

At the top of the stairs, she glanced expectantly at the set of double doors that obviously led to the mansion's master suite, but Charlie Rainwater directed her to the right with a wave of his hat.

"Miss Hattie's room is over here," he said.

This time he led the way. A tightness gripped her throat almost the instant she stepped inside the room—a tightness that came from the sudden rush of fear. All the drapes were closed, shutting out the afternoon sunlight and throwing the corners of the room into deep shadow. A lamp on the dresser cast a feeble pool of light.

"Why is it so dark in here?" She wanted to fling the drapes open and rid the room of this feeling that death lurked in its black corners.

"The light hurts her eyes." The answer came from a tall, harried-looking man standing to her right, the cuffs of his dress shirt rolled back and the vest to his suit stretched tautly around his protruding middle.

"This is Doc Gibbs, ma'am."

Even before the foreman introduced him, the stethoscope around the man's neck had identified him for Flame. A smile touched the corners of his mouth, conveying sadness and regret. "You must be Margaret Rose," the doctor said, his voice soothingly low and quiet. "I'm glad you could come. She's been asking for you."

Flame stared at the inert figure lying in the four-poster bed, half in shadows. "Shouldn't she be in a hospital?"

"There's very little that can be done for her now." The admission came reluctantly, betraying a frustration at his own helplessness that, for all his medical skills, he couldn't deny. "And this was Hattie's wish—to be here in her own home—in her own bed." He touched the medical bag on the dresser beside him, a syringe lying at the ready. "I wanted to give her something for the pain, but she wouldn't hear of it."

"She wanted to be lucid when you arrived, Mrs. Stuart." The third voice came from the shadows. Momentarily startled, she turned as a short, round man stepped forward into the dim light.

Something about him reminded Flame of a leprechaun. Maybe it was his small height at barely five foot two or the white socks he wore with an old suit or loud green tie or the shiny pate of his balding head partially ringed with a fringe of brown hair or the jovial roundness of his face. Yet he had the shrewdest pair of brown eyes she'd ever seen.

"This here's Ben Canon, Miss Hattie's attorney," Charlie Rainwater explained.

"Mr. Canon," she murmured the acknowledgment.

As he nodded in return, a thin, thready voice came from the four-poster, "Who is it? Who's there?"

As if commanded by the faint, demanding cry, the wiry foreman moved swiftly to the bedside. Leaning down, he gently laid his hand on top of hers. "It's me, Miss Hattie. Charlie," he said, a touching warmth in his voice. "She's here. I fetched her just like I promised."

There was a sigh, followed by an agitated, "Maxine?"

"Ssh," the aged cowboy murmured in an effort to quiet her. "I sent her home this morning; told her she needed to rest after sitting up with you the past two nights."

"Good." A weak nod of approval accompanied the comment. Then her voice seemed to gather strength as she commanded, "Bring her to me, Charlie. Bring Margaret Rose to me."

The foreman looked at Flame, then hesitated, his glance slicing to the physician standing beside her. "What about Doc, Miss Hattie?"

"Tell him . . . tell him to leave." She made a feeble attempt to grip the foreman's hand. "You and Ben, I want you to stay."

"We will." With a jerk of his head, he directed the doctor to the door, then motioned for Flame to approach the bed.

The physician looked none too pleased with the request, but he didn't argue. "I'll be right outside if you need me, Charlie."

As he slipped quietly from the room, closing the door behind him, Flame walked slowly to the bed, gripped by a vague sense of déjà vu. The surroundings, the circumstances, the individuals were all different. This was not a hospital room. It was not her mother lying in the bed. There had been no accident. Yet the poignant feeling was the same—the feeling that this was going to be the last time she would see Hattie alive.

Charlie Rainwater stepped to one side, making room for her as Flame came up to take his place next to the bed. The shadows seemed to lift, allowing a clear view of the woman, her head and shoulders propped by a mound of feather pillows. That cloud of white hair was the same, but the face looked older, much older than Flame remembered. That parchment-fine skin was furrowed with lines of pain, lips pinched and pale. And the deathly white of her face was only intensified by the pink satin of her old-fashioned quilted bed jacket.

Swallowing to ease the constriction in her throat, Flame smiled faintly. "Hello, Hattie. It's me—Margaret Rose."

Her eyelids fluttered open, revealing a pair of dark, nearly black eyes that tried to focus on her. "Margaret Rose?" A deep frown creased her already lined brow. "Come closer. I can't see you." Obligingly, Flame sat on the edge of the bed and leaned toward the woman. Those dark eyes brightened, relief shimmering through them. "Your hair." A gnarled hand lifted briefly, as if to touch Flame's hair, but she lacked the strength, and the hand fell weakly back. "It is you." She breathed the words, softly, faintly.

"Yes." Flame covered the bony, age-spotted hand with her own and squeezed it lightly.

Anger suddenly blackened Hattie's eyes, turning them sharp and accusing. "You promised me. You gave me your word. How could you do it?"

"Do what? I don't understand." She frowned, recalling a promise of some sort, but it was all too vague.

Hattie's head moved against the pillows in obvious agitation as she ranted on, giving no sign that she'd heard Flame's reply. "You swore you wouldn't do anything until we talked. How could you let yourself be taken in by him? I thought you were smarter than that. I tried to warn you about him. I tried."

"What are you talking about? *Who* are you talking about?" Flame demanded, half-convinced the pain was making Hattie delirious.

"Why did you have to go and marry him?" Her fingers closed fiercely around Flame's. "Why didn't you see through him?"

"Chance? You're talking about Chance?" She stiffened in disbelief.

"It isn't too late, Margaret Rose." Dark eyes fastened on her. "We can get your marriage annulled. Ben can get it annulled."

"I don't want an annulment." Flame pulled her hand back and shot a quick look at the wiry foreman. "She doesn't know what she's saying."

"Listen," he urged quietly, the white curl of his long mustache moving slightly with the sympathetic smile that lifted the corners of his mouth.

"He's using you, Margaret Rose." That rasping voice reached out to her again. "Stuart only married you so he could get control of Morgan's Walk."

"That's nonsense." Flame stood up, her whole body rigid with denial.

"It's true, I tell you." For an instant, there was hard force behind her voice, then Hattie subsided weakly against the pillows, more pain twisting through her face. "It's true," she whispered. "He thought I would have to leave it to him when I died. But I fooled him. I found you." Her eyes closed. "He found you, too, though. I don't know how. You can't let him have Morgan's Walk. You have to stop him, Margaret Rose." Her head moved from side to side against the pillows, her voice growing fainter. "I promised my grandfather on his deathbed that no Stuart would ever get his hands on this land. You must keep that promise. Do you hear me?"

"Yes, I hear you." The woman was mad. It was the only possible explanation that made any sense to Flame at all. Chance loved her and she loved him. That was the basis for their marriage—not all this nonsense about Morgan's Walk. But why did she keep going on about it? What could she mean?

"Don't . . . don't ever trust him. The Stuarts are a ruthless breed. They'll do anything . . . even murder to get what . . . they want." She was slipping deeper into the blackness of pain. She seemed to know it as she made one last valiant attempt to fight it off. "Ben will tell you. Ben and Charlie. They have the proof. They'll show you. Won't you? Ben? Charlie?" An edge of fear crept into her voice for the first time.

"We're here." The old foreman quickly stepped to the bed, the brightness of tears in his eyes as he reached down to cradle her hand between his callused palms. "Ben and me, we'll explain everything just like you would have done."

"The pain, Charlie." There was a hint of a sob in her voice. "I don't think I can take it anymore."

"You don't have to, Miss Hattie." With a turn of his head, he looked over his shoulder at the attorney standing well back from the bed. In a voice husky and thick, he said, "Take Miss Margaret Rose down to the library, Ben, and have Doc Gibbs come back in."

"Of course." Stepping forward, the diminutive attorney lightly touched her arm. Frozen inside with a mixture of grief, disbelief, and confusion, Flame let herself be led from the room.

20

THE LIBRARY OCCUPIED a secluded corner of the mansion's first floor, its tall, small-paned windows looking out onto the tree-shaded rear lawn. Rich paneling of black oak lined three sides of the room, while bookshelves stretched from floor to ceiling on the fourth. A pair of wing-backed chairs, covered in burgundy leather and studded with brass, flanked the imported marble fireplace, the pair of them mates to the chesterfield sofa that faced them.

Alone in the room, Flame wandered over to the large mahogany desk that took up one whole corner. Yet she couldn't escape the sensation that there were eyes following her. She pivoted sharply and faced the portrait that hung above the mantel. There he was, glaring at her in silent accusation. No matter where she went in the room, it was the same.

She stared at the man in the painting. Over the years, an accumulation of smoke and grime had dulled its colors, but it hadn't lessened the impact of that strong-jawed face or those piercing black eyes. And the hair visible beneath the wide brim of his western hat had a definite red cast to it, although Flame wasn't ready to concede that originally it might have been the same fiery gold color as hers.

"Hattie frequently stared at the portrait like that, too." The remark came from the library's arched entrance with its set of sliding pocket doors. Flame swung toward them, startled to see the attorney in the opening, his short arms laden with a large tray holding a silver coffee service and china cups. "Imposing, isn't it?" He walked into the room, the thick rubber soles of his oxfords making little sound on the hardwood floor.

"I assume that's Kell Morgan." Her teeth, her nerves, and her temper were all on edge.

"Hattie told you about him?" He sent her a questioning look as he awkwardly set the tray down on the occasional table next to the wing chair, rattling the china cups against each other in the process.

Again Flame observed the innate shrewdness of his eyes and reminded herself that this little man was not as jolly or as harmless as he appeared. "She mentioned that her grandfather's portrait hung above the fireplace in the library."

"Yes, of course." He wrapped a pudgy hand around the silver handle of the coffee service and picked it up. "I know you said you didn't use it, but I brought some cream anyway. Charlie made the coffee earlier, and—around here—cowboys like their coffee black and thick. So you might want to dilute yours with a little cream."

But Flame wasn't interested in talking about coffee or cream. She wanted answers to those ridiculous charges Hattie had made. "What was all that nonsense Hattie was saying about Chance?"

Ben Canon hesitated a fraction of a second, then finished filling one of the cups with coffee. "I'm afraid it wasn't nonsense."

"You're wrong." He had to be. "In the first place, Chance would never have expected to inherit Morgan's Walk, even if he knew about the place. She must have been delirious when she said that. She told me that it had to pass to a direct descendant."

"Your husband is Hattie's nephew."

"But—how can that be?" She'd always understood that Chance had no family—none at all.

"His mother was Hattie's baby sister." The lawyer glanced at her, a knowing gleam lighting his eyes. "Obviously he didn't tell you that."

"No." Why? Why hadn't he told her? Why had he kept it a secret? Had he done it deliberately? Or, like her, had he simply not gotten around to mentioning Hattie?

"I'm afraid there are a great many other things that he has failed to tell you as well."

"That's what you say," she charged. "But I don't believe you. I don't believe any of this. Where's all this supposed proof Hattie was talking about? Show it to me—if you can."

He held her gaze for a long, considering second, then shook his head. "I prefer to wait until Charlie joins us."

"Why? What difference does it make whether he's here or not? Or is he your proof?" Flame challenged, armed by the memory of Chance saying, "No matter what anyone tells you, remember that I love you." "You surely don't expect me to accept his word for this, because I won't."

As if on cue, she heard the clump of booted footsteps in the hall outside the library. Flame glanced at the doorway as Charlie Rainwater appeared. Grief bowed his shoulders and shadowed the faded blue of his eyes.

"Hattie?" That was all Ben Canon said, just her name, but that one word was loaded with question. Flame unconsciously held her breath, bracing herself for the old foreman's answer. However much as she might resent Hattie's unfounded accusations against Chance, she couldn't pretend, not even to herself, that she wouldn't be touched by the old woman's passing.

The droop of his mustache lifted slightly as Charlie Rainwater made an attempt to gather himself. "She's resting for now," he said. "The doc's gonna sit with her."

The attorney nodded, but made no comment as he turned to the serving tray on the table. "I brought in some of that coffee you made, Charlie. Would you like me to pour a cup? I seem to have been elected by default to do the honors."

"I sure would," he accepted readily, his long legs carrying him into the room, the thud of his heeled boots echoing hollowly in the high-ceilinged room and increasing the feeling Flame had that they had gathered here to keep a lonely deathwatch.

"Would you like to change your mind, Margaret Rose, and have a cup with us?" the attorney offered again, the spout of the coffee server poised above the third cup.

"No. And please stop using that name. My mother's the only one who ever called me that." Her mother—and Hattie.

"That's right. You're known as Flame, aren't you?" Ben Canon recalled, his sharp eyes sliding to the red of her hair. "A most descriptive sobriquet."

"I'm really not interested in your opinion, Mr. Canon—only in the explanation you promised to give me once Mr. Rainwater joined us."

"Yes, so I did." He took a sip of his coffee, and peered up at the considerably taller foreman. "It seems her husband failed to mention that he was Hattie's nephew."

"He is. That's true enough, ma'am." Charlie Rainwater took a hurried and noisy slurp of coffee, then wiped at the clipped ends of his mustache with the back of his forefinger. "He was born right here in this house—in the room right next to Miss Hattie's. If you don't believe me, you can ask Doc Gibbs. He was the one who brought him into this world." Pausing, he stared into the black of his coffee. "A sad day it was, too. I don't reckon any of us expected to see the day come when there'd be a Stuart in this house."

"But his father—"

Charlie never gave her a chance to finish as he looked up, a cold fire blazing in his eyes. "Ring Stuart was a lazy, no-good hoodlum. He didn't give a hoot about Miss Elizabeth. He just wanted the easy life Morgan's Walk could give him. Miss Hattie tried to tell her that, but Miss Elizabeth wouldn't listen. Her eyes were so full of him, she couldn't see anything else." He gave a wry shake of his head, but there was little humor in the slant of his mouth. "That really ain't so surprising, I guess. Them Stuarts always did have more charm in their little fingers than most men got in their whole body. So what does Miss

Elizabeth do, but run off and marry him. With her being of legal age, there wasn't much Miss Hattie could do about it. She tried. We all tried. But once Miss Elizabeth married him, Miss Hattie had no choice but to turn her out. That hurt her. That hurt her bad. She loved that girl. Raised her from the time she was born, and she was just a kid herself."

"But how could Chance have been born here if Hattie threw his mother out?"

" 'Cause she took her back. Miss Elizabeth got real sick and there he was not taking care of her like he should. Miss Hattie couldn't stand that, and Stuart knew it. I warned her that she was playin' right into his hands when she brought them both back to Morgan's Walk, but she said it was better to have the devil close so she could keep an eye on him and know what he was up to. We all knew what he figured. With Miss Hattie being so much older than Miss Elizabeth, he thought she would die first and his wife would get Morgan's Walk —and he'd have control of it. But it didn't work that way. Miss Elizabeth got blood cancer. Many's the time you could see it workin' in his mind to hurry Miss Hattie's demise along, but he couldn't twitch a hair without somebody seein' it. That's when he started drinking—out of frustration mostly." He cupped both leathered hands around the delicate china cup. "I reckon he had reason to be frustrated, 'cause he sure didn't get Morgan's Walk like he wanted —like he tried to do."

"Let me see if I understand this," Flame murmured tightly. "Simply because his father married to get control of this ranch, you have tarred Chance with the same brush. Is that your proof?"

"There's more to it than that . . . Flame," Ben Canon inserted, hesitating fractionally over the use of her name. "Much more. As a matter of fact, the trouble with the Stuarts goes all the way back to *his* day." He half-turned to look at the man in the portrait.

"I suppose this has something to do with the deathbed promise Hattie referred to." She caught a jeering note of sarcasm in her voice. Part of her regretted it, yet mockery seemed her only defense at the moment. She couldn't allow herself to take any of this seriously.

"I think it would be closer to say that this addresses the events that led up to it." His smile failed to conceal the hard scrutiny of his glance. "Perhaps it would be best if I began by telling you a bit about the founding of this ranch, and the history of this area. After all, Morgan's Walk will pass to you on Hattie's death. It's only fitting that you should know something about it—out of respect for Hattie, if nothing else."

At the mention of the woman's name, she felt a twinge of guilt, realizing how callous she must sound to him. She wasn't. There were simply too many emotions pulling her in different directions—anger, confusion, pity, sadness, and—however much she was unwilling to admit it—fear. Fear that Hattie might be right—that maybe she was being used by Chance. Because of it, the urge was strong to flee the room and this house so she wouldn't have to listen to any more of their lies about him. But she stayed. Like it or not, she had to know.

"You're quite right, Mr. Canon," Flame stated, tilting her chin a little higher. "If Morgan's Walk is to be mine, I should know more about it."

"Good." He nodded in approval.

Without thinking, she glanced at the portrait and froze, an eerie chill running down her spine. Those eyes—the eyes of the man in the portrait—they'd lost their accusing glare and now regarded her with a pleased look. Flame tried to tell herself that she was imagining it, that her mind was playing tricks with her, yet the impression persisted.

Shaken by it, Flame walked over to the coffee tray. "I think I'll have a cup after all."

"Help yourself, by all means." The lawyer waved a hand in the direction of the silver pot as he crossed to the fireplace.

The coffee was every bit as black as he'd warned her it was, but she didn't dilute it with cream, for the moment preferring the strong brew. With cup in hand, she sat down in the nearest wing chair. Following her lead, Charlie Rainwater settled his wiry frame into its mate, both of them angled to face the diminutive attorney. He stood to one side of the blackened hearth, the top of his head barely reaching the marble lip of the tall mantel. She fixed her gaze on him, refusing to let it stray to the portrait that dominated the room and, currently, her thoughts.

"As you know from the documents I forwarded to you on Hattie's behalf," the attorney began, "Kell Morgan—christened Kelly Alexander Morgan—was born in eighteen sixty on a small farm—although a southerner would call it a plantation—outside of Hattiesburg, Mississippi. When the Civil War broke out, his father, Braxton Morgan, joined the Confederate Army and sent his wife and young son off to New Orleans to stay with his sister and her family. When that city fell into Union hands, she took her son and fled to an uncle's farm near Dallas, Texas. Approximately six months after the war ended, Braxton Morgan rejoined them . . . minus an arm and with a crippled leg. Needless to say, circumstances forced them to continue living with his wife's family. A year later, your great-grandfather, Christopher John Morgan, was born."

"That was eighteen sixty-six," Flame said, recalling the year that had appeared on the baptismal record.

"Yes." He moved away from the fireplace, his short legs setting an ambling pace as he wandered toward the bookshelves that lined one full wall of the library. "Much has been written about the Reconstruction years in the South, so it should suffice to say that they were rough times for children like your great-grandfather and his brother to be growing up. I don't know if you read between the lines in that obituary notice I sent you from a Dallas newspaper regarding the death of Braxton Morgan, but it seems he was killed during a drunken brawl —no doubt still defending the honor of the South. That was eighteen sixty-nine. Two years later, his wife died, probably from exhaustion and overwork. To her uncle's credit, he kept both boys and raised them. Then, in eighteen seventy-five, Kell Morgan struck out on his own at the tender age of fifteen— although I suppose we should keep in mind that in those days that made him nearly a grown man."

When he turned to gaze at the portrait, Flame's glance was drawn to it as well. She searched but couldn't find that stern and forbidding quality she'd first seen in his expression. Looking at the man in the painting now, she could see only the pride and strength of an indomitable will stamped in his hard, angular features . . . that and those dark eyes boring into her as if trying to press their will on her.

"He signed on as a drover to take a herd of longhorns north to the railhead at Wichita, Kansas," Ben Canon went on. "That was back in the heyday of the great cattle drives north. Which isn't to say that Texas cattle hadn't been driven to northern markets before then. They had—as far back as the eighteen fifties. Most of them were brought up the Shawnee Trail, called the Texas Road by some. It cut right through the eastern half of the state and stretched from Texas all the way to St. Louis. And a wide road it was, too. It had to be, to accommodate the military supply caravans, freight wagons, and the settlers' schooners that traveled over it.

"But it was the Chisolm Trail Kell Morgan went up that spring. It wasn't until late fall when he was heading home that he saw this part of the country for the first time." Canon stared at the portrait, absently studying the man in the painting. "I've often wondered what he thought when he topped that ridge of hills and saw this valley before him—lush with the autumn gold of its tall grass and bright with the silver shimmer of the narrow river running through it. With only three years of schooling he could barely read or write, so his impressions were never committed to paper. But he told Hattie the sight of the valley was an image that lived in his mind from that day on."

Charlie Rainwater spoke up, nodding his head at the portrait. "According to Miss Hattie, that painting didn't do him justice—not like seeing him in the flesh. He stood six foot one in his stockinged feet—and she claimed he had a pair of shoulders that were just about that wide. She said that every time she saw him he reminded her of a double tree standin' on an upright shaft. And nobody ever called him Red—at least, not twice. No, he was always known as Kell Morgan." His glance darted briefly to Flame. "I never had the privilege of meeting him, you understand. He passed away long before I ever came to work here. But everybody I ever talked to said he was a hard man, but a fair one. As long as you were loyal to the brand, he'd stick by you right or wrong. Miss Hattie said he never smiled much—that he did all his talkin' with his eyes. When he was mad, they'd be as black as hell, but when he was happy, they'd glow . . . like they was lit from inside. And he loved this land, too. He was out riding it and checkin' cattle right up to the day he died. Sixty-five, he was."

The painting lost much of its one-dimensional quality, the smoky blue haze of its background now projecting the tall, redheaded man in western clothes from the canvas. And that dark glow Charlie mentioned was in his eyes, those eyes that seemed to look directly at her.

"Although uneducated, Kell Morgan was an innately intelligent man—and a keen observer, too," Ben Canon inserted, again taking charge. "When he returned to Texas, he started noticing the changes in the making. The era of the open range was drawing to a close. Every year more and more fences were going up. And the long drives north to the railheads took valuable weight off cattle. Four years in a row, he made the long, arduous trek north with somebody else's longhorns. And each time, he stopped to look at his valley—and stayed longer on every trip.

"Now you have to remember that all this land belonged to the Creek Nation. And I use that term *nation* advisedly. The Creek land was a separate entity with its own boundaries, governed by its own laws. Back in the eighteen thirties, the federal government, or more precisely, President Andrew Jackson, decided with typical arrogance that it would be in the best interest of the Five

Civilized Tribes—the Creeks, the Cherokees, the Choctaws, the Chickasaws, and the Seminoles—to give up their lands in the South that had been their home long before the first white man set foot on this continent, and move west to escape the corrupting influence of the whites. Through a series of nefarious treaties, they succeeded in removing them to this area.

"Now, according to Creek law and tradition, no individual held title to any given parcel of land. It was all owned in common. Which meant it was impossible for Kell Morgan to buy his valley outright. But during his trips here and his sojourns in the neighboring Creek village of Tallahassee, which the cowboys on the trail dubbed Tulsi Town, he became acquainted with a politically influential mixed-blood Creek named George Perryman. Through him, Kell Morgan succeeded in leasing his valley. With the money he'd put aside from his wages, he managed to buy one hundred head of scrub cattle, drove them north to his valley, wintered them on the rich grass, and made the short drive to market in the spring." He paused, a certain slyness entering his grinning smile. "That may not sound like much of a start to you unless you consider that he bought them at a price of seventy-five cents a head and sold them for over fifteen dollars a head. With his profits, he leased more land, bought more cattle, and repeated the process with the same results.

"By eighteen eighty-two, Kell Morgan was justly considered a cattle baron. Three years earlier, the U.S. Postal Service had opened its *Tulsa* Station, subtly changing the town's name once again. And by eighteen eighty-two, the Frisco Railroad had extended its line into Tulsa. No longer did Kell Morgan have to drive his cattle to the railhead; it had come to him."

Without a break in his narrative, the balding attorney turned and scanned the rows of books on the two shelves directly in front of him. "During all this time, he hadn't forgotten his little brother, Christopher, back in Texas. By then, Christopher wasn't little anymore. He was a strapping lad of sixteen. With his newly acquired wealth, Kell sent him off to college in the East, determined that Christopher would have the education circumstances had denied him." He extracted a wide volume from the shelf and flipped it open as he swung back toward Flame. "When Christopher finished college with a degree in engineering, he returned here to Morgan's Walk. In that interim period, Kell had been adopted by the Creeks. Now with full rights to the valley—as full as any Creek had—he had Christopher design and build this house. Prior to that, the only structures had been a dog-trot cabin and a log bunkhouse for his cowhands." Pausing beside Flame's chair, he handed her the leather-bound volume, an old photo album. "Hattie thought you might like to see some pictures of your ancestors. Here's one of your great-grandfather, Christopher Morgan."

His finger tapped the thick black paper directly above an old sepia print pasted on the page. A young man sat in a stiff pose, one large hand resting on his knee and the other holding a dark, wide-brimmed hat. He wore a dark suit and vest, the jacket opened to reveal the looping gleam of a watchfob and the white of a starched shirt collar tight around his throat. Although unsmiling, the expression on his smooth-shaven face conveyed an eagerness and a love of life. It wasn't closed and hard like the man in the portrait, although the strong, angular lines of their features were very similar. Their hair color was different, of course. In the brown-tinted photograph, Christopher Morgan's appeared to be a light shade of brown with even lighter streaks running through it.

"You can tell they were brothers," Flame remarked idly as she turned the page, curious to see more of the old photographs.

"Miss Hattie said back then they were as close as two brothers could be," Charlie Rainwater declared with a faintly envious shake of his head. "They weren't a lot alike, though. About as different as daylight and dark, I hear. But just like daylight and dark go together to make a whole day, that's the way it was with them."

"In your great-grandfather's case, it was probably hero worship for his older brother," Ben Canon added. "And Kell Morgan probably saw in his younger brother the educated man he wished he could be. I understand there was a good deal of mutual sharing of knowledge—Christopher teaching Kell about history and philosophy, and Kell giving him lessons in range lore."

The next pages in the album contained photographs of the house under construction, some posed and some not. Flame was able to pick out Christopher Morgan in two of the pictures. Then she found a third photograph of the brothers. Side by side, the differences in their personalities were obvious—Kell Morgan looking impatient and uncomfortable, and Christopher, happy and smiling.

"I don't understand." Flame turned her frown of confusion to the attorney. "If they were so close, why did Christopher Morgan leave and never come back?"

"I'm coming to that," he assured her.

Impatiently she flipped to the next page, irritated by this air of mystery and dark secrets. She wished he'd get to the point of all this and stop dragging it out. Then her glance fell on the lone photograph on the facing page of black paper.

It was a picture of a young woman in period dress. Dainty and refined were the two adjectives that immediately sprang into Flame's mind. She looked as fragile as a china teacup, and Flame could easily imagine the elegant curl of her little finger when she sipped from one. Her dark hair was swept up at the sides, ringlets peeking from beneath the small brim of her high-crowned hat trimmed with ostrich feathers and shiny ribbons. Her heart-shaped face appeared ivory smooth and pale, needing no artifice of makeup to enhance its doll prettiness.

"This woman, who is she?" Flame glanced expectantly at the attorney.

He answered without looking at the photograph. "Ann Compton Morgan, Kell Morgan's wife. You see, after the house was finished and all the furnishings arrived, Kell decided it was time he took a wife. Naturally, not just any woman would do. He had a shopping list of requirements his future bride needed to fulfill. First of all, he wanted a woman with refinement and breeding, someone with culture and education, possessing style and grace—preferably pretty, but attractive would do. But, above all, she had to be the daughter of a family active in either politics, banking, or railroads. In short, his wife had to be a lady and a valuable liaison." Observing the disapproving arch of her eyebrow, Ben Canon smiled. "As crude and chauvinistic as that might sound to you, you must remember that Kell Morgan was a pragmatic man. Christopher was the idealist."

"Obviously," she murmured.

"In the fall of 'eighty-nine, after the first great land run opened the so-called Unassigned Territory to homesteaders the previous spring, giving birth to the towns of Guthrie and Oklahoma City, Kell Morgan went to Kansas City to find his bride."

"And his list went right out the window when he met Ann Compton," Charlie Rainwater declared, punctuating it with a faint chortle of amusement as he pushed out of his chair and walked over to the tray to pour himself some coffee. "Fell for her like he'd been shot out of the sky, he did," he said, winking at Flame.

"Is that true?" Flame turned to the attorney for confirmation, not so much doubting Charlie's word as being surprised by it. Kell Morgan seemed the type who would make a loveless marriage of convenience.

"Indeed, he fell hopelessly in love with her. And from the standpoint that her father was a socially prominent physician in the community, but without any important business connections in his family, she failed his major requirement in a wife. The fact that he married her anyway after a month-long whirlwind courtship merely proves that, like most men, Kell Morgan had his weaknesses."

He walked back to the bookshelves and removed a slim volume, bound in rose-colored cloth, its edges threadbare and worn. "In every other respect, however, she was exactly what he'd wanted in a wife—an educated woman, well versed in arts and literature, trained in the social graces, and extraordinarily pleasing to the eye. When you read the diaries she kept, you'll see that Kell Morgan swept her off her feet. Although what girl wouldn't be if she was ardently pursued by a handsome and rich cattle baron with a grand and stately mansion on the prairie waiting for the warmth of a woman to transform it into a home. There are frequent passages in her diary that deal with the romantic ideas she had about life on the frontier. She expected it to be an exciting adventure. And it would seem that Kell Morgan had made little effort to dispel those notions. He was too intent on winning her affections—and her hand in marriage."

When he paused to draw in a deep breath, Flame had the feeling he was doing it purely for effect. "Later, much later, he blamed himself for her disenchantment. Their first few months of married life here at Morgan's Walk were deliriously happy ones—according to her diary. Then, I suppose, the newness of her surroundings wore off. Nothing had prepared her for the tedium and isolation of ranch life—or the long hours, sometimes days at a time, she spent alone while her husband was out on the range. Growing up in the city, she was used to a constant round of teas, socials, cotillions, or friends stopping by to call. Here, she had no friends; visitors were few and far between; and her nearest neighbor was half a day's buggy ride away. She had nothing in common with the sun-browned women who lived around her. Most of them had never seen a parasol before she came and knew nothing about the classics or chamber music. Naturally, Tulsa was the closest town of any size, but the activities it offered—other than an occasional church social on a Sunday afternoon or parties at private homes—were geared more for the cattlemen in the area, eager to blow off steam on a Saturday, drink, gamble, and cavort with the town's soiled doves."

Flame absently smoothed her hand over the diary's cloth cover. She, oddly, was reluctant to open the book and read the young woman's innermost thoughts. Somehow it seemed an invasion.

"From everything you've told me about her, I have the impression that she had a great deal more in common with Christopher than she did her husband." As she voiced her thoughts, it suddenly occurred to her. "Is that what happened? Is she the reason he left and never came back?" Then she frowned, even more confused than before. "What does all this have to do with the Stuarts?"

A smile of amused tolerance rounded the attorney's plump cheeks. "You're getting ahead of me again, Flame."

"It strikes me that Annie Morgan would never have been happy here." Charlie Rainwater crossed to the fireplace and stood with one leg cocked and a hand propped on the smooth marble face as he gazed up at the portrait. " 'Course, he always believed that she would have come to love it if she hadn't gotten with child that first year they were married."

"Yes, the confinement of her pregnancy coupled with the loneliness and boredom she already felt merely added to her unhappiness," Ben Canon agreed. "Not even the joy of giving birth to a healthy baby the following year made up for it. That boy, by the way, was Hattie's father, Jonathan Robert Morgan," he added in an aside, then continued. "Naturally little Johnny had his own way of keeping Ann close to home, even though she was able to find a wet nurse for him. Kell did his best to keep her happy. All these books, the ebony piano in the parlor, a buggy of her own, and a matched team of high-stepping grays to pull it—he gave her everything but the one thing that might have helped: his company. As she frequently states in her diary, a son is no substitute for a husband. And by the early fall of eighteen ninety-three, you get a very real sense of her loneliness, dissatisfaction, and . . . desperation, I suppose." He gestured briefly at the closed diary Flame held. "Hattie has marked the page where the story begins."

Flame hesitated, then glanced at the slim volume in her hands, belatedly noticing the thin, age-yellowed tassel draped over the back cover. A chainstitch of thin threads connected it to a hand-tatted bookmark inserted between the pages near the back of the diary. She resisted the attorney's subtle urging to read the woman's private journal, then realized this was part of the proof Hattie had promised.

Reluctantly she slid her fingers along the bookmark and opened the diary to the prescribed page. For a moment she stared at the small, neat handwriting, each letter precisely and perfectly formed. Then she began to read.

21

AUGUST 29, 1893

I am going! Kell has finally consented to let me accompany him when he takes the herd of horses to Guthrie to sell to the homesteaders who have gathered there to make the Run into the Cherokee Strip. He didn't say, but I know it was Chris who persuaded him to change his mind. He was so adamant that I must remain at Morgan's Walk the last time we argued, insisting that such events attracted the worst as well as the best, that I despaired of him ever permitting me to go. How fortunate I am to have Chris for a brother-in-law. If he had not championed my cause, I am quite certain I would have gone mad if I had been forced to stay in this house all alone for two weeks.

My darling Johnny will have to remain here with Sarah. I shall miss him dreadfully, but the journey overland would be too much for a three-year-old. It's terrible to be pulled like this, wanting so much to go, yet hating so much to leave my son behind. But it will only be for two weeks.

It should be an experience quite beyond compare. Papa writes that his patients have talked of little else but the opening of the Cherokee Strip to settlers. I have heard that people are pouring in from all parts of the country to take part in the Run. Some are estimating that there may be as many as one hundred thousand people on the starting line when the gun goes off. One hundred thousand! And here I am, hungry for the sight of one.

SEPTEMBER 9, 1983

At long last, we have arrived in Guthrie. There were times when I despaired we would ever make it. The heat was—and is—unbearable. It has not rained all summer and the dust is so thick it coats everything. All my traveling clothes are covered with it. I know I resembled a walking powder puff when I arrived at the hotel. Each step I took, dust billowed about me. I fear the rigors of outdoor life shall never be for me. I have been bounced and jarred, jolted and rattled until I marvel that all my bones are still connected. Chris knows how I suffered on that journey, but I dared not say a word to Kell. He would have sent me back to Morgan's Walk on the spot and I would have missed all this excitement. (Although I assure you I shall be making the return by train.)

Excitement there is in great abundance, too. The street outside our hotel window is crowded with people in every kind and type of conveyance imaginable. Many of the wagons have clever little sayings written on their canvas covers. We passed one that read:

"I won't be a sooner, but I'll get thar as soon as the soonest."

And another said:

In God we trusted.
In Texas we busted.
But let 'er rip
We'll make 'er in the Strip.

The determination—the fervor that is on the faces of these people—is something to see. Kell calls it land fever. It is definitely contagious, for I feel the same restlessness of spirit. Kell has forbade me to leave the room unless he or Chris accompanies me. He says there are too many desperados, gamblers, and swindlers in town, come to fleece these poor, unsuspecting homesteaders of their precious savings, and he fears for my safety should I venture out alone. Yet when I look out the window of our hotel room, I see whole families jammed in their wagons, young men on blooded horses, boys on ponies, old men on ambling gennets, and women—yes, women, here to make the Run all alone! The thought staggers me. Yet the ones I've seen seem to be a decent sort—not at all the type one might expect to find.

As a matter of fact, a woman stopped us just as we were about to enter the hotel. She looked to be in her late twenties and, despite the layers of dust that clung to her, I could tell she was stylishly dressed. . . .

"Please, will you buy my hat?" The woman fumbled momentarily with the lid to the hatbox she carried, then lifted it and produced the hat from inside for Ann's inspection. "It came all the way from Chicago and I've only worn it twice. You can see it's just like new."

At first Ann drew back from the proffered hat and the strange woman accosting her on the sidewalk. Not that she could possibly be in any danger, not when she was flanked by two tall, strong men, with Kell on one side of her and Chris on the other. Then she saw the hat—red felt trimmed in red velvet and adorned with feathers and gray satin ribbon. It was the perfect thing to wear with her pearl gray dress.

"It's beautiful," Ann declared, then looked again at the woman, conscious all the while of the firm pressure of Kell's hand at her elbow and his rigid stance of disapproval, but she wouldn't be hurried inside. "Why on earth would you want to sell it?"

"I . . ." The woman pushed the receding line of her chin a little higher, asserting her pride. ". . . I need another five dollars to pay the filing fee when I make my claim."

"Where is your husband?" Kell demanded, much to Ann's embarrassment. "I have none."

A spinster. Ann looked at her pityingly, then realized what the woman was saying. "You aren't making the Run yourself?" This was no sturdy farm woman with a complexion turned ruddy and coarse by the sun. Both her manner and style of dress spoke of gentility and education.

"Indeed I am," she stated. "I intend to have a place of my own—become a woman of property." Then she explained that she'd been a teacher for the last eight years in the backwoods of Texas, obliged to board with the parents of her pupils. "I want to sleep in my own bed, have my own curtains at the window, and cook my meals on my own stove. And this is my one chance to do it. Please, will you buy my hat?"

. . . Kell bought the hat for me, although afterward he said he shouldn't have encouraged her to go ahead with her foolhardy plan. He says that it will be a stampede when that gun goes off to start the Run. I'm quite sure he's right. I wonder at the daring she has. I know I could never be so bold as to do such a thing. Yet I understand the desperation I saw in her eyes, that need to break from a way of life she despises before it crushes her spirit completely.

It is nearly four o'clock and I am to meet Chris in the lobby on the hour. I think I shall wear my new hat.

There is so much more to tell. I hope I shall remember it all to write down later, but Chris awaits and I am anxious to be out of this room and among people again.

From the stairs' bottom step, Ann scanned the jumble of people crowded into the hotel's small lobby. With the red felt hat perched atop her freshened curls and a closed parasol in hand, she idly fanned her face with a lavender-drenched kerchief, and dabbed occasionally at the perspiration that gathered so readily on her upper lip. A fan turned overhead, yet it seemed to accomplish little beyond circulating the oppressive heat. She looked, but there was no sign of Chris. Usually he was easy to spot in a crowd, like Kell, standing a good inch over six feet, which put him head and shoulders above nearly everyone else. It wasn't like him to be late. Perhaps he'd stepped outside for some air. Ann decided to check.

Skirting the crowded lobby, Ann made her way to the double doors, propped open to admit any breeze that was stirring. Outside the hotel, the spectacle of the street greeted her once again. She had never seen anything like it in her whole life—cowboys mounted on snorting, half-tamed broncs, dudes in their checked suits and square-crowned bowlers, and women in their poke bonnets and worn gingham dresses riding on buckboards and prairie schooners crammed with all their possessions. The constant stream of traffic churned the dust and created a cloud that hugged the ground. And the rumble of wagons, the rattle of trace chains, the thunder of hooves, the creak of leather, the crack of the whips, the shouted curses of the drivers all combined to assault the ears, just as the stench of sweating bodies, man and animal, combined to assault the nose.

Ann pressed the lavender-scented kerchief close to her nose and looked about the boardwalk outside the hotel's entrance for Chris. But there was only one man in front of the hotel. Dressed in a black waistcoat and black hat, he stood at the edge of the walk facing the street. He was tall, but not as tall as Chris. Nor were his shoulders as wide. And his hair did not possess the gold streaks the summer sun had put in Chris's. Rather, it was black, that deep shining black of a raven. He turned his head to look at something up the street, giving her a side view of his clean-shaven face. Then, as if sensing her gaze, he turned the rest of the way, the satin brocade of his gray vest gleaming between the parted front of his waistcoat.

Excitement fluttered in her breast. He was quite the handsomest man she had ever seen—and a gentleman, too, judging by his dress. But it was definitely improper for a married woman to be staring at a strange man. With a guilty flush, Ann looked away and attempted to cover her momentary confusion by opening her parasol. As she extended it to one side of her, a stout man in a tweed suit and bowler hat chose that moment to exit the hotel. He walked right into it, knocking it out of her hands.

With her mouth open in dismay, Ann watched it land on the sidewalk practically at the man's feet. She saw him look at it, and observed the faint smile that tugged at one corner of his mouth—and wanted to die of pure mortification. She rushed to retrieve it, ignoring the profuse apologies offered to her by the man who had knocked the parasol from her grasp.

Before she could stoop to pick it up, a black-sleeved arm reached down. "Allow me." The warm, low pitch of his voice seemed to vibrate right through her.

Immediately she straightened to stand erect and struggled to regain her composure, succeeding to a degree. Her opinion of his looks didn't change when they finally faced each other. If anything it intensified when she encountered the deep blue of his eyes, darkly outlined by thick, male lashes as black as the wings of his brow.

"Thank you." She held out her hand for the parasol.

But he didn't immediately give it back to her. Instead, he opened it first, then returned it, angled to shade her face from the late afternoon sunlight. The look in his eyes was much too familiar as his gaze wandered over her face.

"It would be a sin, indeed, for the sun to damage skin such as yours. I have not seen the likes of it since I was in St. Louis a year ago." Unexpectedly he reached up and lightly trailed a finger across her cheek. "It's as creamy white and smooth as a magnolia petal."

She knew she should object to such effrontery. At the very least, she should be shocked by it. But shock didn't accurately describe her tingling reaction. Thankfully, she had the good sense not to comment on either his remark or his feathery caress of her cheek. And she hoped her silence on the matter would correct any wrong impression she might have given.

"Are you here to make the Run?" he asked.

"Gracious, no." She laughed, mostly to release some of the unbearable tension that gripped her. "My husband is here to sell some of our horses to the settlers."

"I am envious."

"Sir?" She blinked at him in confusion, then fought the sensation that his gaze was absorbing her whole.

"I would be envious of any man who has the honor of calling such a rare and beautiful flower his wife."

Flustered, she lowered her gaze and attempted a cool "You flatter me, sir."

He cocked his head at a denying angle. "Truth is never flattery. And it is the truth when I say that you are a rare and beautiful flower, one that a man doesn't expect to find out here on the prairie."

Nor did she want to be here. She hated its emptiness, its isolation, and its rustic society. She longed for the lawn parties, the literary teas, and the cultural pleasures she'd left behind in Kansas City. Once more she wanted to sit at a dinner party where the guests didn't belch or tuck the napery over their shirts or talk about cows and shipping rates or the bank panic.

Suddenly aware of the lengthening pause, Ann murmured a quick "I suppose not," then smiled with forced brightness. "I shall tell my husband that when I see him. I'm sure he'll find your observation quite interesting."

"You're meeting him?"

"No. That is, his brother is meeting me here. Kell . . . my husband will join us later for dinner."

"Kell. That's his name?"

"Kell Morgan, yes. Do you know him?" she asked curiously.

"I know *of* him," he replied, carefully qualifying his answer. "But then, there are few in the territory who have not heard of Morgan's Walk. That is your home, isn't it, Mrs. Morgan?"

"Yes." She held her breath for an instant, wondered if she dared to ask. "And you are?"

"Jackson Lee Stuart." He touched the brim of his hat. "At your service . . . anytime."

A trio of riders raced up the street, whipping their horses and ki-yipping at the top of their lungs as if the race for land on the Cherokee Strip had begun. Distracted by the commotion, Ann glanced at the street and immediately spotted Chris riding toward the hotel. Regret swept through her, sharp and poignant. She knew his arrival would signal the end of her meeting with Mr. Jackson Lee Stuart and she didn't want it to be over—not yet.

She forced a bright smile onto her face. "There comes my brother-in-law now."

Jackson Stuart looked over his shoulder, then turned back to her. "Now that you have another protector to look after you, I will take my leave."

"It has been a pleasure, Mr. Stuart." Automatically she offered him her hand in parting.

"If the fates are kind, we'll meet again." Her heart skipped a beat or two as he bowed slightly and carried her gloved hand to his lips, his blue eyes holding her gaze. Instead of kissing the back of it, he turned it over and pressed a kiss into the very center of her palm. She was quite breathless with shock—and that guilty feeling of forbidden pleasure—when he straightened and released her hand. "Let us hope that they are."

She couldn't agree to that, not out loud. Tipping his dark hat to her, he moved off, joining the stream of pedestrians on the boardwalk. With an effort, Ann tore her gaze from him and crossed to the edge of the walk to greet Chris as he dismounted.

"At last you're here," she declared gaily. "I was about to decide you'd forgotten me."

"Never." Smiling, he looped the reins around the hitching rack and gave them a quick tie, then joined her on the walk. "But what are you doing out here? I thought we agreed to meet in the lobby."

"We did." She switched the parasol to her other shoulder as she linked her arm with his. "But you weren't there when I came down so I stepped outside to look for you."

"That wasn't wise, Ann. Didn't I see a man talking to you when I rode up?"

She had difficulty meeting his gaze, and chided herself for feeling so absurdly guilty. She had done absolutely nothing to be ashamed of.

"Yes," she admitted, quite openly. "He retrieved my parasol after some passerby had knocked it from my hand. He was very polite."

"Just the same, you shouldn't venture out alone. This town is filled with unsavory types. Kell's right."

"I'm sure he is." Just for an instant, she was angry. She turned on Chris, unleashing her frustrations on him as she always did. "But I didn't endure that horrid trip just to trade one prison for another. You might as well know that I have no intention of spending my entire time here in that hotel room alone. I want to get out and see things—and do things. So much is happening . . . there's so much excitement. I want to be part of it, Chris."

"I know." He covered the hand that gripped his forearm and gave it an understanding squeeze.

Ann looked up, realizing that she could always count on his sympathy. Dear, wonderful Chris, so like Kell in looks, yet so unlike him. Both had the same strong features and dark eyes, but on Kell they were hard and cold, whereas on Chris they had a gentleness, a sunniness that matched the dark gold of his hair. She could tell him anything and he would understand.

"Kell worries about you, Ann," he said. "You can't blame him. He loves you."

"I know." She lowered her gaze, realizing that she could tell him anything, but not necessarily everything, and definitely not about Jackson Stuart.

How odd that such a brief meeting should linger in my mind this way. I wonder if I shall see Mr. Stuart again. Is it wrong of me to hope that I do?

I must end this. Kell calls me to bed.

SEPTEMBER 14, 1893

The horses are selling well now that Kell has moved the herd twenty miles north to the small town of Orlando. That is where the registration booth is located for this area, so all the settlers have gathered there to sign up for the Run. Kell keeps the horses groomed and grained, so they look sleek and fast. Already he has sold all but ten of the one hundred horses he brought. Which is truly remarkable when one considers that he sells them for two hundred dollars each. Six months ago he asked thirty dollars a head for the same stock!

Now that the horses have become such valuable steeds, guard must be kept on them at all times. And with literally thousands of people crowded into that small community, there are no accommodations available, so I have been obliged to remain here at the hotel in Guthrie. Either Chris or Kell rides the twenty miles back every night so that I at least have company for breakfast and dinner.

I chafed so at being forced to rely on newspaper accounts to know what was happening outside my hotel door that Kell finally consented and allowed me to accompany him to Orlando today and see for myself the spectacle of all the "strippers"—that is what the newspapers are calling the settlers intent on making the Run onto the Cherokee Strip.

I admit that within minutes of embarking on the journey to Orlando, I questioned the wisdom of it. The temperature soared to one hundred degrees in the shade—if one could find any. And a wind blew constantly, as hot and dry as everything else. Need I mention that the dust was unbearable. I can still feel the grit of it on my skin.

But the sight I beheld at the end of the morning's journey staggers my mind even now. Tents were pitched everywhere, transforming the prairie into a sea of brown canvas that rippled like waves in the incessant wind. And there were vehicles of every shape, size, and description—buckboards, covered wagons, buggies, pony carts, even a racing sulky. I read that there may be as many as ten thousand people camped at Orlando. To me the number seemed much larger than that. Add to all that teeming humanity their animals, and the entire scene becomes one beyond words.

Most pitiful of all, however, were the hundreds upon hundreds of people waiting in line to register. Some had been in line for as much as forty-eight hours. They dared not leave or they'd lose their place in line. And it was a line that grew by the hour instead of diminishing as the ones in front received their certificates. How they could stand there hour after hour in that infernal heat with gale winds swirling that choking dust around them—with not a speck of shade to offer them a respite from the blazing sun—I shall never know. Many succumbed to the heat, collapsing into the dust where they stood. It was a sight that would have torn at my poor papa's heart—especially the women. One was the woman who sold me her hat. She had changed so that I barely recognized her. . . .

Ann pulled back on the buggy reins and stared at the woman in the torn and bedraggled gown. Her face was black with a mixture of dirt, sweat, and tears that had caked, melted, and caked again. Her hair hung in a lank, tangled mass about her shoulders. Ann couldn't believe it was the same woman. But it had to be. That brightly beaded reticule, clutched tightly in both hands, was the same as the one into which the woman had put the five dollars that Kell had given her for the hat. It was doubtful that there could possibly be two like it.

The woman turned her head and stared at the hooded buggy with blank, bloodshot eyes. Then, as Ann watched, the woman's pupils rolled back and she sank to the ground in a heap. Ann gasped in horror, and that horror increased when she realized that no one was going to risk losing their place in line to come to the woman's aid. Hastily she wound the reins around the whipstand, gathered up her skirts, and clambered from the buggy, not taking the time to call to the cowboy Kell had detailed to escort her.

She ran to the woman and knelt in the dirt beside her, for the moment mindless of the heat and the blinding dust. She tried to lift her off the hard ground and cradle her in her arms, but the woman was too heavy for her.

"Please." She scrambled to her feet and appealed to the others in line. "Someone get a doctor. There must be one in town. She's fainted from the heat. She needs help."

"Here." The man in front of her shoved a dirty blanket into her hands. "Wad that up and stick it under her head. She'll come around in a few minutes."

Stunned by his callous indifference to the woman's plight, Ann stared at him, but he turned his back on her and shuffled forward as the line moved a foot at a time. Ann turned to the next man as he started to walk around her and rejoin the moving line.

"No." Impulsively she caught at his arm. "You can't walk by like that."

He glared at her with red-rimmed eyes. "Yo sure as hell ain't gonna stop me, missy. An' yo ain't gonna steal her place in line neither. If yo want to register, yo can just git yore fancy ass to the back of the line." His talonlike fingers dug into her shoulder and gave her a rough push toward the rear, the suddenness and the violence of it sending her sprawling hands first into the dirt.

Shocked as much by his vulgarity as by his roughness, Ann lay there for a stunned instant, then pushed up on her knees just as a big black stallion slid to a prancing stop not three feet from her. A man vaulted from the saddle. Her heart somersaulted at the sight of Jackson Stuart, jacketless in the heat with just a thin cotton shirt, wet with perspiration, covering his arms and torso.

He was at her side in a stride, catching her by the shoulders and pulling her upright as if she weighed no more than thistledown. "Are you all right, Mrs. Morgan?" His hat was pulled low on his forehead, its brim shading the gleaming bronze of his face and intensifying the sharp blue of his eyes.

"I'm . . . fine." She nodded shakily, aware that her hat was askew and her beautiful gown was smudged with dirt. As she reached down to brush uselessly at the dust, Ann noticed the holstered gun strapped to his hip. She was surprised to see him wearing one. Kell, yes—a gun fit him as naturally as the hardness of this land—but not Jackson Stuart. It was the moment's pause the gun gave her that kept her from mentioning the unconscious woman lying on the ground only a few feet away.

And in that moment, Jackson Stuart spun around and grabbed the man who had shoved her. "I believe you owe the lady an apology." There was a coldness in his voice that stunned Ann, but the man just looked at him with torpid eyes, his senses too dulled by the heat to catch the threatening tone. In a lightning move the gun was in his hand, the muzzle pressed under the point of the man's chin and the hammer back. "I said—you owe the lady an apology, mister."

Suddenly everything was still around her except the wind-swirled dust. Someone up the line called out, "Better do it, Joe. That's Blackjack Stuart."

What did that mean? Was he some sort of desperado? Ann stared at him in confusion, barely noticing at all the poor settler's wide-eyed look of alarm as he stammered out an apology.

"That's better." Jackson Stuart smiled smoothly and gently eased the hammer down, then released the man and holstered his gun all in one fluid motion. When he turned to Ann, his look was warmly apologetic. "Sorry. Sometimes they need to be reminded of their manners."

"Of course," she murmured, not knowing what else to say. "Please, there's a woman over here suffering from heatstroke. We need to get her out of the sun —and to a doctor if there is one."

"There's a tent down the way that passes for an infirmary. We can take her there." He crouched down on one knee beside the unconscious woman, his hands tunneling under her shoulders and her skirts to pick her up.

"Put her in my buggy," Ann instructed as her escort came riding up.

"Sorry, Mrs. Morgan. I didn't see you stop." The cowboy grabbed at the creased front of his hat brim in a quick gesture of respect, then struggled to control his mount as it shied away from the flapping skirts of the woman Jackson Stuart carried. "What happened?"

"This woman collapsed. We're taking her to the doctor."

Jackson Stuart nodded in the direction of the black stallion, standing quietly with its reins dragging the ground. "Tie my horse to the back of the buggy. And if you've got any water in that canteen, we'll need it."

"Yes, sir." He untied the canteen from his saddle and handed it to Ann, then walked his horse over to the stallion and scooped up the trailing reins.

Ann climbed into the buggy unaided, then turned to help Jackson maneuver the woman onto the seat. She was limp as a rag doll in Ann's arms. Then Jackson Stuart crowded onto the buggy seat and relieved her of the heavy burden.

"Open the canteen for me," he said.

Ann removed its cap and handed it to him, watching as he held it to the woman's parched and cracked lips, tipping it slightly to let the warm water trickle into her mouth. He was so gentle with the woman that Ann found it difficult to conceive that a moment ago this same man had held a gun to a man's head. He didn't look at all sinister. In fact, were it not for the absence of a jacket, he had the appearance of a polished gentleman—and an extraordinarily handsome one at that.

"Here." He gave her back the canteen, then loosened the yellow neckerchief from around his throat and pulled it free. "Wet this for me. We'll see if we can't cool her down a bit—and get some of this dirt off her face."

The smile he flashed her was the sharing kind that made her feel warm inside—just like the sound of "we." It was the two of them helping, but Ann hadn't thought of it that way until he'd said it. Quickly, she moistened the cloth, then gently bathed the woman's face with it.

The woman stirred, roused perhaps by the coolness of the water on her hot skin or the shade of the buggy's protruding hood. "Where . . . where am I? What happened?" Feebly, she lifted a hand, her eyes still glazed.

"Sssh. You fainted," Ann explained softly, glancing briefly at Jackson as he reached forward and unlooped the buggy reins with one hand, giving them a slap. The buggy lurched forward. "We're taking you to the doctor. You'll be fine."

"No," she moaned, her head rolling from side to side. "I can't. My place . . . I'll lose my place. . . . No," she sobbed, her arms reaching, her body lifting with its last bit of strength to get back to the line.

"Stop it. You're in no condition to go back there." Half-frightened by the woman's crazed reaction, Ann tried to make her lie still, pushing her back against the buggy seat.

The woman tried to resist, but the effort was too much. Instead her dirty-nailed hands clutched at Ann's gown. "My land," she whimpered, her shoulders shaking with great, silent sobs. "I was so close . . . so close." Her voice was so faint Ann had to strain to hear it above the hot, blowing wind and the constant din of the settlers' camp. "It would have . . . been my turn."

Ann pried herself loose from the woman's clutches and poured more water from the canteen onto the already damp cloth, the rolling bounce of the buggy causing her to spill some of it on her skirt. She darted a quick look ahead of them, then swung it to Jackson. "How much farther is it?" She was a doctor's daughter, but she'd never had to cope with a sick person. "She's out of her head, raving on about losing her place in line and her land. She needs quiet and rest, but I can't make her calm down." There was an edge of panic in her voice, part of it picked up from the woman and part of it from her own sense of helplessness.

"Here." He took a slip of paper from his pocket and handed it to Ann. "Give her that. It'll quiet her."

"What is it?" Ann frowned at him.

"A registration certificate." He whoaed the gray, stopping the buggy in front of an open-sided tent. "That's what she was standing in line to get so she could legally make the Run on Saturday." He wrapped the reins around the whipstand and swung to the ground, then turned back.

"But—" She remembered the line of people standing in the blazing afternoon heat, a line that got longer instead of shorter. "—it's yours."

His mouth twisted in a quick smile as he reached to lift the semiconscious woman from the buggy. "I'll get another."

He hefted the woman from the buggy seat and cradled her limp weight in his arms. Belatedly, Ann stoppered the canteen and scrambled down to join him, fighting her layers of skirts and ignoring the outstretched hand of her dismounted escort rider. The precious slip of paper was still clutched in her gloved hand when she reached Stuart's side.

"How will you get another?" she repeated. "You surely aren't going to stand in that line?"

His glance moved over her face, taking in the concern for him. The sight of it pleased him, and he toyed with the idea of letting her worry a little longer, then decided against it.

"It isn't necessary, not if you have the cash to spare to buy one. You'd be surprised how many people in that line sell their certificate after they get it, then go back and do it over again."

"Why?" She couldn't imagine anyone enduring the agony of that line.

"To make extra money." He carried the woman inside the tent and laid her on an empty cot. Mumbling more protests, she tried to rise, but he gently pushed her back onto the cot, then took the slip of paper from Ann and folded the woman's fingers around it. "Here's your certificate."

With an effort the woman focused her reddened eyes on it. Relief cracked through her dirt-streaked face as all resistance went out of her.

"Thank you," she whispered, her body shuddering with dry sobs, but there was no welling of tears in her eyes. She had none to spare.

"I'll put it in your bag." He loosened the beaded, drawstring pouch looped around her wrist and tucked the certificate inside, then placed the reticule in her hand, closing her fingers around it. She clutched the small bag tightly to her breast and closed her eyes.

A man with shirt sleeves rolled and a checked vest straining to surround his protruding belly wandered over to the cot, mopping the perspiration that streamed down his bewhiskered jowls. With an air of disinterest, he looked down at the woman.

"Sunstroke," he grunted, then looked at the two of them. "Are you kin?"

"No," Ann replied. "I believe she's here alone."

"Another single woman." He grimaced tiredly. "It's hardest on them. Chivalry vanished out here after the first day. Now it's everyone for him—or her—self." He ran the sweat-damp handkerchief around inside the collar of his shirt. "What's her name?"

"I don't know," Ann realized with a trace of chagrin.

He sighed and shook his head, something wry and cynical in the smile that twisted his mouth. "I had a man die of sunstroke earlier today. We're still tryin' to find somebody that knows his name." Then he seemed to gather up some energy. "Well, you done your share. Now I'll do what I can for her. Won't be much. I haven't got any help here. Nobody does. They all quit to make the Run and get a piece of land of their own—or die tryin'."

He took hold of the woman's wrist, locating her pulse as he pulled a gold watch from his vest pocket and flipped it open. His air of unconcern chilled Ann. Where was his compassion? His solicitude? Sapped from him by this sweltering prairie as it had been from the others in the line?

"He's right, Mrs. Morgan. There's nothing more you can do for her." Jackson Stuart's hand lightly gripped the back of her arm, its faintly insistent pressure urging her to leave.

She let him steer her from the tent, then halted outside its supporting poles, still within the shade of its canvas. The buffeting wind pushed at her, its breath hot like the blast from a furnace. Settlers plodded by, their heads bowed, their shoulders hunched against the wind, and their faces blurred by the haze of dust.

"All these people," she murmured. "Half of the ones I saw in the line looked like they belonged in the infirmary. How do they endure these conditions?"

"I've been told it's worse along the Kansas border at Arkansas City. Two, maybe three, times as many settlers are gathered there. In just one day fifty collapsed from the heat, and six of those died before nightfall."

She turned to him. "Why? Why do they do it?"

His gaze was turned outward, thoughtfully surveying the scene. At her question, he directed his look to her. "For a piece of land to call their own, what else?" The corners of his mouth deepened in wry amusement. "You should see them at night, sitting around their campfires, pouring over maps of the Strip, studying every wind and bend of a river or creek, deciding which plot of ground they're going to claim, tracing a route to it, then memorizing the terrain around it so they can find it once the race begins . . . assuming, of course, that someone else doesn't get there first. It's all they talk about—all they think about —all that keeps them going."

"But why?" She remembered the woman he'd just carried inside—dirty, bedraggled, half-dead from the heat, yet she'd been frantic to get back in that line. She hadn't cared about her disheveled appearance or the grime and sweat that blackened her face or the agony of standing hour after hour in the full sun —not as long as she got that silly scrap of paper. "Why does it mean so much?"

He gave her a long, considering look, then once again faced the dusty scene before them. "You're looking at the losers of this country, Mrs. Morgan, the losers and the dispossessed. Former slaves from the South, and Johnny Rebs who came back to burned-out homes and Reconstruction, and the people who came west too late to get the rich lands in Iowa, Kansas, and Missouri—or else tried and failed. This is the only cheap land left for them, the only place where a man or a woman can file a homestead claim on as much as one hundred and sixty acres for as little as one dollar an acre depending on the location of their claim. This is the only chance a store clerk, a schoolteacher, or a livery boy has to own a piece of land. This whole Territory is being settled by losers. They have nowhere else to go, and they know it. If they don't get their chunk of ground here, they likely never will. That's why they're so desperate—why they cling so tenaciously to those certificates." He paused briefly. "It's no place for the faint of heart, though."

"No," she murmured in absent agreement, recognizing that she was one of them. She hadn't been faint of heart, not in the beginning. When she'd married Kell, she had been as eager and excited as these people were about her new life on the frontier, thinking it would be one long adventure. "But they don't know what it's like here. They don't know how isolated, how monotonous—how very primitive it is," she declared, inwardly longing for the life she'd left behind in Kansas City.

Jackson Stuart wasn't surprised by the undercurrents of dissatisfaction and despair in her voice. He'd pegged her from the start as an unhappy woman left too much alone. And the interest—the curiosity—she'd shown toward him outside the hotel that afternoon in Guthrie had merely confirmed it. A contented woman might have cast an admiring glance his way, but she wouldn't have been curious. More than that, she wouldn't have had that hunger for attention in her eyes.

No, the mistress of Morgan's Walk was a very lonely and unhappy woman. Which raised some very interesting possibilities.

"Why are you here?" Ann stared, recognizing that he wasn't like the others. He was too aloof, too detached from all this. Yet he'd had a registration certificate. "Is it the land you want, too?"

"It's the sport of it that's drawn me here, I guess. The high-stakes gamble of it. It's a race of sorts—with the prize going to the fleetest, the cleverest, and the luckiest. And, it's going to take all three—a fast horse, smart riding, and Lady Luck on our shoulder—to claim the choice sites, especially the town lots." He carefully avoided mentioning that nearly every would-be settler had brought his life savings with him—and that the sack in his saddlebags contained nearly two thousand dollars he'd managed to glean from them in the past two days during friendly games of chance.

"Is that what you want? A town lot?"

"Yes."

"What will you do with it?"

"More than likely sell it to someone who arrived too late to claim one for himself—at a profit, of course."

"Then you won't build on it?"

"No."

"Exactly what is it that you do, Mr. Stuart?" She tilted her head to one side, regarding him curiously. "Back there, some man referred to you as 'Blackjack' Stuart."

"I'm a gambler by profession, Mrs. Morgan, and vingt-et-un, better known as blackjack, is my game . . . hence the name."

"I see," she murmured.

"I doubt that you do, Mrs. Morgan. A gambler's life is a lonely one. It isn't without compensations, however, for I have traveled the length and breadth of this country. St. Louis, San Francisco, New Orleans, New York . . . I've been to them all at one time or another—stayed at the finest hotels, dined at the best establishments, smoked imported cigars, and supped the best wines. Diamond stickpins, suits from a St. Louis tailor—I even own the fastest horse in the territory." He nodded his head in the direction of the black stallion tied behind the buggy, impatiently pawing at the ground. "But all of life's luxuries are meaningless if you have to enjoy them alone."

"I . . . I have heard that said before." She tried not to let him see how much his words echoed her feelings.

"It's been my fate to be extraordinarily lucky at cards, but a woman's love has always eluded me."

"I find that very difficult to believe, Mr. Stuart. Forgive my boldness, but you are a handsome man. I'm quite sure you could have your choice of women."

"But it's been my misfortune that when I have found a woman I could love, she already belongs to someone else."

. . . And he was looking directly into my eyes when he said that. It flustered me so, that I must admit I could think of no suitable reply. Although he didn't actually say that woman was I, his meaning was unmistakable. Under the circumstances, I had no choice but to take my leave of him. To stay might have led him to think I would welcome his advances. Which I do not. I am, after all, a married woman. Yet I did feel pleasure that another man—a stranger— could be attracted to me. I expect that is terribly vain of me to say, but it's true all the same.

SEPTEMBER 16, 1893

The most exciting thing has happened. Kell has secured seats for us on one of the passenger coaches. I shall get to see the start of the great Run after all. There has been so much confusion and rumor of late, saying first the trains will run, then they won't, then they will but only settlers with certificates can board—that I began to doubt I would witness the launching of these hordes of settlers. What a bitter disappointment that would have been too, after spending this entire week here in Guthrie, caught up in the contagion—the madness—of the pending land rush, then not to see this moment in history.

Now I shall. Unfortunately, Kell wasn't able to arrange for us to have a private car. They aren't allowed for some reason. I expect the authorities fear the owners of the private cars would profit from them by selling space to settlers and, thus, deprive the railroad company of revenue. Nevertheless we are going. I wonder if I shall see Jackson Stuart.

Cordoned from the crush of fellow sightseers by a human wall of a half-dozen cowboys from the ranch, Ann sat on the very edge of her seat, facing the train's open window. She was certain that nothing in the annals of history could compare with the sight before her. Covered wagons, light buggies, two-wheeled carts, sulkies, horses and riders, heavy wagons drawn by oxen, and a few foolhardy souls on foot stretched in a ragged column as far as the eye could see—and each one positioned so close to the other that there wasn't space to walk between them.

On the train itself—three locomotives strong with forty-two cars in tow—there was barely room to breathe, let alone move. Settlers bound for the Strip literally packed the cattle cars, with more hanging off the slatted sides and piled on top of the cars. Not two windows from her seat, a man clung to the window-sill, his feet on a crossbar.

Just recalling the insane scramble that had ensued when the settlers had been allowed to board the train drew a shudder. It had been a veritable stampede, with everyone pushing and shoving, grabbing at anything and tearing clothes, knocking people down, then trampling on them, in ruthless disregard of age or sex. And there had been naught the poor trainmen and officials could do but stand back or be bowled over.

Now they all waited as the sun steadily climbed higher in the sky. Stationed in front of the endless long line, troopers of the U.S. Cavalry sat on their horses, standing guard until the appointed hour. Although, according to Kell, their presence hadn't been particularly effective the night before when hundreds of so-called sooners had eluded the cavalry patrols and illegally slipped across the line under the cover of darkness to lay claim on the choicest parcels "sooner" than anyone else.

"It's almost time, isn't it, Kell?" She gripped the fingers of his hand a little tighter, unable to take her eyes from the scene. So many people, yet all of them so still, so quiet, so tense, bodies and hearts straining—she could feel it. Unconsciously, she held her breath.

"Almost," he confirmed.

At precisely high noon, the eight million acres known variously as the Cherokee Strip or the Cherokee Outlet would be thrown open to settlement. The morning newspaper claimed that over one hundred thousand settlers would enter the Strip from various gathering points along the northern and southern boundaries.

In the unearthly silence of the moment, the pounding of her heart sounded louder than the puffing chug of the idling train. Here and there an impatient steed pawed the ground or champed restlessly on the bit in its mouth. Noises that once would have been lost in the din of the thousands gathered here now sounded unnaturally loud, jangling nerves already thin with stress. Again, Ann scanned that long ragged line, certain that Jackson Stuart was among them somewhere—but where?

A hundred yards distant, a horse reared and lunged ahead of the column, the bright sunlight glinting on its shiny black neck, wet with sweat. The man upon its back effortlessly wheeled the anxious animal back into line—a man wearing a black hat and a gun strapped to his side, like so many of the other riders. Although she had only a brief glimpse of him before he was swallowed up by the line, Ann felt certain it was Jackson Stuart. She leaned closer to the window, trying to locate him again.

As the trumpeter blew the first sweet, swelling notes on his bugle, the staccato crack of rifle fire broke all the way up and down the line. Instantly the jagged line erupted, bursting forward in a seething rush of humanity. The thunder of thousands of pounding hooves, the rumble of rolling wheels, the rattle of moving wagons, the shriek of the locomotive's whistles, the neighs of panicked horses, and the yells, shouts, curses, and screams of the settlers all melded together into one terrific roar—a roar of agony and madness suddenly unleashed on the world, frightening in its fierceness and stunning in its volume. Red dust rose in a mighty cloud, momentarily enveloping the stampeding horde that left in its wake overturned wagons, fallen horses, and downed riders.

Paralyzed by the sight and sound of it, Ann stared. For an instant she was certain that all had been swept away by the billowing red sand. Then a scattered line of horsemen broke from the devilish cloud and raced with the wind ahead of it. And one of them—yes, one of them was Jackson Stuart. The fear that had knotted her nerves dissolved in a rush of relief. He was safe. More than that, he was in front, streaking across the prairie on his swift black stallion.

More and more wagons and riders emerged from the settling dust cloud and fanned across the empty plains, the horrendous din from their numbers fading to a rumble dominated by the fierce chugging of the train. Talk broke behind her in a flurry of awed comments.

"So many dreams racing across that prairie," Chris murmured.

"But more than dreams will die before this day is over," Kell replied in a hard, dry voice.

Jackson Stuart wouldn't be one of them. He was there in front, leading the way. He would succeed. Others might fail, but not he. Swept by a feeling of elation, Ann swung from the window to face her husband.

"It was glorious, Kell. Simply glorious. A sight never to be forgotten. An experience I wouldn't have missed for the world." So much danger and excitement—observed from a safe distance, it was true, yet she'd been part of the moment, feeling the heat and the wind, the heart-pounding tension and strain, the thunderous roar of the masses and panicked need for speed.

"Then I'm glad I brought you with me." His mouth curved slightly in one of his rare smiles. "Tomorrow we'll head home—back to Morgan's Walk—and enjoy a little peace and quiet for a change."

He looked at me with so much love in his eyes that I felt ashamed of myself for wishing, even briefly, that we didn't have to return. What is wrong with me? I long to see my son again and hold him in my arms, yet I loathe the thought of spending day after day in that house again.

22

A BLOTCH OF INK stained the remaining third of the page, giving Flame the impression that Ann Morgan had cast the pen down in agitation and frustration. She felt the same tormented mix of emotions, the same sense of dread. She had no desire to read more, certain she could guess the rest of it.

As she started to close the diary, she was pulled sharply back to the present by Ben Canon's remark: "Interesting reading, isn't it?"

"Yes," she responded automatically, suddenly aware of the cheery crackle of the fire blazing brightly in the fireplace and the pungent aroma of pipe smoke drifting through the air.

Windowpanes, darkened by the shadows of evening beyond them, reflected the light from the lamps that had been turned on. From some other part of the house came the muted *bong* of a clock, slowly tolling the hour. Flame wondered if Ann Morgan had listened to that same bell mark hour after hour in this house.

"Would you like another cup of coffee, Flame?" The attorney stood next to the massive marble fireplace, a brier pipe loosely cupped in his hand. He used the chewed stem to point to the silver coffee service. "I made a fresh pot, so I can guarantee it won't be as strong as the last."

A smile rounded his shiny cheeks, but the bright twinkle in his eyes had a sly look to it. Each time she looked at him, Flame expected to see pointy ears poking through the fringe of hair that ringed his bald crown. It was a bit of a surprise when she didn't.

"If you're gettin' hungry," Charlie Rainwater volunteered, comfortably ensconced in the twin to her chair, positioned close to the hearth, "they'll be bringin' sandwiches over from the cook shack in another hour or so."

"No, I don't care for anything." She glanced down at the partially closed diary on her lap, the pages held apart by the finger she'd wedged between them. "And I don't think it's necessary to read any more of this journal. Obviously she abandoned her husband and ran off with this Jackson Stuart."

"Nothing is obvious," Ben Canon asserted with a certain knowing quality. "I suggest you read a little further. If you've passed the part about the land rush, then skip ahead to the month of—November, I believe it was, somewhere around the tenth."

Irritation rippled through her. "Wouldn't it be quicker and simpler if you just told me what happened back then, Mr. Canon?"

"Yes," he agreed quite readily. "But, under the circumstances, *Mrs. Stuart*, it would be better if you learned about it from a source other than myself. I wouldn't want to be accused of bias or prejudice."

Flame responded to his smile with a glare, then directed her attention back to the diary. Fighting this strange sense of foreboding she had, she opened the book again and flipped ahead to pages bearing a November date.

NOVEMBER 9, 1893

Two absolutely wonderful things happened today! This morning at breakfast, Kell announced that we will go home to Kansas City for the holidays! I have longed for this, hoped for this, prayed for such a trip almost from the day I arrived here. That first year, we couldn't go because I was anticipating the arrival of my precious Johnny. And the second and third year, he was much too small to take on such a trip—and I couldn't leave him. And I don't think Papa would have welcomed me if I had come without his grandson. But this year, Johnny is a sturdy three-year-old, and we are going, all three of us. Kell has already made arrangements for us to have a private car for the journey. We will leave on the third of December and spend at least a month there.

The holiday season in Kansas City . . . I can hardly wait. There will be so many parties and gatherings, so many festivities to attend, such a gay and glorious time we'll have.

But what to take and what to wear? Living out here, I fear my dresses have become hopelessly outdated. I will have no choice but to peruse at length my most current issue of "Harper's" and see if I can rectify the problem. There is time to do nothing else, and I refuse to go back and have all my friends regard me as a country bumpkin.

I had no opportunity to do anything about my wardrobe today because . . . we had a visitor. And you will never guess who it was. I could not believe my eyes when I saw him. After Johnny had awakened from his nap, I took him outside to play. It was such a warm and bright afternoon— the finest autumn weather—that I thought the fresh air would be good for him. Heaven knows, in another month that dreadful north wind will come howling across this country, bringing along those dreary gray clouds filled with ice and snow—and it will be much too cold to venture out.

Anyway, by pure happenstance, while Johnny was frolicking with the puppies of one of Kell's hunting dogs, I wandered onto the front lawn. Why? I don't know. It's as if I was drawn there by some mysterious force. When I glanced down the lane, I saw a man leading a lame horse. From his manner of dress, I knew instantly it was not one of our cowboys or a neighbor. And I also knew, even though at that distance I couldn't see his face, that the man was Jackson Stuart. How often I have thought of him these past weeks and wondered how he had fared that day of the great Run. The newspapers were filled with accounts of those murdered in apparent disputes over land claims. Some were "sooners" and deserved no better fate, but others were legitimate settlers like Mr. Stuart. So many times, I had hoped he was alive and well—and there he was.

Mr. Stuart was on his way to Tulsa when his beautiful stallion went lame. Fortunately, he remembered he was near Morgan's Walk. Considering the lateness of the hour, I knew he wouldn't reach Tulsa before dark and suggested to Kell that Mr. Stuart spend the night with us and continue his journey in the morning on one of our horses. Naturally, Kell agreed with me. . . .

Dinner that evening was easily one of the most enjoyable—if not *the* most enjoyable—Ann had experienced since her arrival at Morgan's Walk. Rushed as she'd been trying to prepare everything for their unexpected, but much welcomed, guest, she hadn't been able to spend as much time at her toilette as she would have liked. But judging from the frequent, appreciative glances Jackson

Stuart sent her way, he obviously found a great deal about her appearance to admire. She felt like a flower blossoming under the sun of his attention.

Naturally, the topic of conversation at the table centered around the great land Run into the Cherokee Strip, an experience they had all shared in, either as a participant or observer. For the first time, Ann felt free to chatter away, recounting her many and varied impressions of the start of the race.

"The din was quite deafening," she said. "I have heard that others likened it to a mighty artillery barrage. I really couldn't say if that was so or not, but I do know that the noise was so great that one felt completely consumed by it. I cannot imagine how it must have sounded to be in the middle of it. Was the start of the race truly as dangerous as it looked? You were there in the midst of all that chaos, Mr. Stuart. Tell us what it was like."

"Insanity. Everyone on that line was of one mind—to get in front quickly and escape the crush. But in those first few jumps after the gun went off, wheels locked, horses bolted, wagons overturned, riders collided."

She remembered that scene of horror, and shuddered expressively. "All for the dream of owning a piece of land. I can't imagine risking your life for a dream."

"What is life without a dream?" Jackson Stuart challenged lightly. "Mere existence, Mrs. Morgan, with no hope for anything more. And there has to be more. Otherwise, why go on?"

"What is your dream, Mr. Stuart?" Chris inquired.

Jackson Stuart leaned back in his chair and looked around the dining room with its long cherrywood table and glittering chandelier overhead. "To own a house as fine as Morgan's Walk someday, to travel and see the sights."

"That's a tall order," Kell observed.

"Why dream small, Mr. Morgan?" Stuart reasoned. "You didn't."

Dinner that evening ended much too soon for Ann. She wished she could linger at the table another hour and enjoy more of Jackson Stuart's stimulating company, but when Kell rose, she had no choice but to follow his lead. Hardly had she made the first movement to rise, but Jackson Stuart was there to pull out her chair. She acknowledged his assistance with a faint nod of her head, conscious of those black lashes screening a look that was much too bold in its admiration, screening not from her but from her husband. Trying to control the sudden pitter-patter skip of her pulse, she turned to Chris and walked with him from the dining room, the lampas skirt of her golden brown bengaline gown whispering softly with the gliding movement.

"What was the situation in the new territory when you left it, Mr. Stuart?" At the inquiry from Kell, Ann suppressed a sigh. Business. Sooner or later, the conversation always turned to cattle and crops or politics.

"There were still a large number of disputes over the ownership of various claims. It will probably be months before all that's settled. But the rest of the homesteaders are looking to spring. If you have more horses to sell, especially work animals, you'd find a ready market for them, Morgan. After the race, it's been hard to find a horse in the territory that isn't windbroke."

"That might be a good idea, Kell," Chris spoke up. "We probably have a dozen or so head we could spare from our haying teams. Maybe keep the younger stock and sell off the older animals."

"It's something to consider," Kell agreed, typically noncommittal.

At the drawing room arch, Ann paused and turned back, her glance automatically running to their handsome guest. "If you gentlemen will excuse me, I'll leave you to your brandy and cigars."

For an instant, Jackson Stuart seemed taken aback by her announcement, but that brief flicker of surprise was quickly smoothed from his expression. "In all honesty, Mrs. Morgan, I wish you wouldn't. I noticed the piano earlier and had hopes you might play this evening. You do play, don't you?"

Modesty prevented her from admitting that she was a competent pianist. "A little, yes."

"Then, may I impose on you to play for me? It's been a long time since I've heard anything other than someone pounding on a bar-room piano."

"I—" She glanced at Kell, but she could read no objection in his bland expression. "—I should be delighted to play for you, Mr. Stuart."

"You do me honor, Mrs. Morgan." He bowed slightly from the waist, the gleam in his eyes most stimulating.

Aflush with pleasure, Ann entered the drawing room and walked directly to the ornate piano of elaborately carved ebony. She sat down on its bench and arranged the fall of her skirt, then reached for the sheets of music propped on its stand.

Conscious of the crystal clink of the brandy decanter and the subdued murmur of voices behind her, Ann glanced over her shoulder. "Was there a particular selection you would like to hear, Mr. Stuart?"

"No," he demurred, briefly lifting his brandy glass to her. "I'll leave the choice to you."

"Perhaps something by Bach, then." She chose a concerto filled with suppressed passions and began to play, all the while conscious of her audience and determined to acquit herself well.

Stuart applauded briefly when she finished. "Beautiful, Mrs. Morgan. Simply beautiful." She glowed under the praise that was in both his voice and his look. "But I beg you not to stop now."

"Yes, play some more, Ann," Kell urged as he pushed out of his chair, rolling fluidly to his feet. "If you'll excuse me, Mr. Stuart, I'll leave you in my wife's capable care. I have considerable paperwork waiting for me in the library." He turned briefly to Chris. "I'll need to talk to you before you turn in tonight."

Ann started to protest his departure, then firmly pressed her lips together, recognizing that it would do no good. It never had. That's what was so vexing. He'd spend all day riding over his precious ranch, then most of the evening hunched over its ledgers and account books, leaving scant time for her.

She turned back to the piano and began to play, unconsciously choosing a particularly volatile piece. Halfway through it, she saw Chris leave the room, tossing a quick smile in her direction that promised he'd be back. She doubted it, not once Kell got his hands on him. But what did it matter? Jackson Stuart was here. She smiled, aware that at least she had his undivided attention.

Chris Morgan walked into the library. "I just realized who that is in there, Kell." Unconsciously he lowered his voice to conspiratorial volume. "That's Blackjack Stuart. He's supposed to be connected with the Dalton gang."

Kell showed no surprise at the news as he briefly looked up from his ledger, each entry made in a labored scrawl. "That connection was obviously broken last year when the Dalton gang was wiped out in Coffeyville."

The Indian Territory had long been a haven for outlaws. Emmett, Grant, and Bob Dalton had lived in Tulsa most of their lives. The locals rarely commented on the presence of the notorious in their midst. Too much time and trouble was involved in reporting them to the nearest federal authorities in Fort Smith, Arkansas, one hundred miles away—three days by horseback or one by train. And usually by the time a U.S. marshal would arrive on the scene, the outlaws would have been warned and gone. Judge Parker, the so-called Hanging Judge, had done his best to bring law and order to the Territory, but he was only one man with seldom more than forty marshals at any one time to police an area that easily required twenty times that number to do the job adequately.

Chris stopped before the big mahogany desk. "You've known who he is all the time, haven't you?"

"Yes."

A frown creased his forehead as he half-turned from the desk, running a hand through the streaked gold of his hair. "If you knew, then why did you invite him to stay the night? Blackjack Stuart supposedly funneled information to Dalton on gold shipments and the like. Maybe he's doing it for someone else now."

"Ann invited him. Under the circumstances, I couldn't very well turn him away and risk offending him. The Daltons may be gone, but Stuart still has friends. And we don't have enough men at this time of year to mount a night guard on the cattle if he decided to retaliate for some imagined slight."

Chris couldn't argue with that logic. For years there'd been a gentlemen's agreement of sorts between the locals and the marauding element. Asylum was offered in return for protection. In theory, it worked. In practice, banks were still robbed, travelers were still waylaid, and cattle were still rustled, not always by outlaws taking refuge in the area. The general lawlessness of the area contributed to the current agitation to have the land of the Creeks brought solely under the jurisdiction of the United States government, and bring an end to the current system of dual authority.

"Do you think you should say something to Ann? It may be more than a coincidence that his horse went lame so close to Morgan's Walk."

"Maybe," Kell conceded. "But he isn't the first man with a questionable past to stop here. We've even had some work for us. I don't see any point in saying anything and causing her needless worry. Stuart will be gone in the morning." He returned the pen to its desk holder and nodded at the chair in front of his desk. "Sit down and tell me how the meeting went today."

Chris paused, drawing in a deep breath and making the mental switch in topics, then took a seat in the leather-upholstered armchair. "About the way we expected. The Creeks aren't changing their position. They refuse to have any discussions with representatives from the Dawes Commission. Fortunately, or unfortunately, depending on your point of view, the Dawes Act that was signed into law last March calls for *negotiations* with the Five Tribes to reach an agreement for the extinction of their communal titles to the land and the allotment of one-hundred-and-sixty-acre parcels to individual heads of families. The Creeks aren't going to negotiate. Like the others, they're going to fight it."

"Where does that leave us and Morgan's Walk?"

"In the middle," Chris said, lifting his hand in a helpless gesture. "We both know it's inevitable that the tribal lands will be broken up. The way they swarmed over the Strip shows just how land hungry people are. And for all the thousands who made the Run, there are that many and more who missed out. Now they're looking in this direction. The government has already said that all the excess land will be sold to settlers."

"I intend to keep this valley, Chris." It wasn't so much a statement as a vow.

"I know." Sometimes Chris had the feeling that Morgan's Walk meant more to his brother than life itself. "We'll just have to make certain we're first in line —and that we have a lot of friends in high places."

When Christopher Morgan remained absent midway through the third piece, Jackson Stuart wandered over to the piano and lounged against it, still absently nursing the brandy in his glass. Ann found his nearness most disconcerting, especially the sensation of his gaze examining every detail about her, from the ornate tortoiseshell comb in her hair to the bengaline front of her corsage. She stumbled briefly over a particularly difficult passage, then completed the piece without another error.

"Beautiful," he murmured. "Absolutely beautiful."

Conscious that his gaze had never left her, Ann had the very warm feeling that he wasn't referring to the music. She drew her hands away from the keys and forced them to lay serenely together on her lap. "I'm glad my playing pleases you." She lifted her glance, a breathlessness attacking her throat when she encountered the full force of his gaze.

"It's more than your playing that pleases me." The smoothness of his voice was like the caressing stroke of a hand. "The first time I saw you outside that hotel in Guthrie—amidst all that coarse mob of settlers—I sensed instantly that you were out of your element. This is the setting for you—a richly furnished drawing room, surrounded by a host of admirers." He paused, his glance making an idle sweep of the room before coming back to her, humor glinting in the blue of his eyes. "At the moment, I'm afraid it's a host of one."

"I should be angry with you for saying such things," she declared, showing a hint of a smile. "But I find it quite impossible."

"That's because I speak the truth. You were not born to this wild, uncouth land, Mrs. Morgan. Your manner of dress, your taste in music, your air of refinement, all speak of a more cultured environ."

"That's true." Ann didn't attempt to deny it as she rose from the piano bench, the damasklike fabric of her dinner gown settling about her in a whisper of richness. "Kansas City is my home."

"You must miss it very much."

"At times, yes." Pride wouldn't allow her to admit how unhappy she often was here. "The parties, the theater . . . Have you ever been to Coates Opera House? Oh, it's magnificent," she declared without giving him a chance to answer. "I do hope a production will be staged while Kell and I are there in December. I so dearly long to see one."

"You . . . and your husband are going to Kansas City?"

"Yes, in December for a monthlong visit." She swung to face him, all her joy at going bubbling through. "We shall be spending the holidays with my father."

"You must be very excited."

"Oh, I am. I haven't been home in more than four years—although at times it has seemed much longer than that."

"When do you leave?" He absently swirled the brandy in his glass, watching her with contemplative interest, his mind already scheming.

"The third," she answered blithely.

Chris returned to the drawing room, and Jackson Stuart immediately begged to be excused. "It's late and I have imposed on your good company long enough. It's time I turned in before I wear out my welcome."

"You could never do that, Mr. Stuart," Ann assured him, quite sincerely.

"I hope not." He took her hand and, for a moment, lightly held her fingers. "I will be off early in the morning, long before you arise, so I will pay my thanks to you now, Mrs. Morgan. This has been an evening I will long treasure. Thank you." He lifted her hand to his lips and kept it there an instant longer than was proper.

There went her heart again, fluttering madly against her breast at the pervading warmth of his lips and the boldness of actions in front of Chris. "Your company has been most welcome, Mr. Stuart," she replied, fighting the breathy quality in her voice.

With a nod to Chris, he left the room. Ann listened to the sound of his footsteps moving toward the staircase, then turned, feeling Chris's eyes on her. Their look was much too penetrating.

"He's such a polite man, isn't he?" she remarked, striving to sound offhand.

"He's a stranger, Ann," he reminded her.

"But a very charming stranger."

True to his word, Jackson Stuart was away before Ann finished her morning toilette. From her bedroom window, she watched him ride away from Morgan's Walk on one of their sturdy brown cow ponies. She tried to tell herself it was foolish to feel such a sense of loss at his leaving. But foolish or not, she did.

Four days later, Jackson Stuart returned to pick up his stallion. Ann was in the dining room, helping Cora Mae polish the silver. A loathsome task, but it was the only way to insure the lazy woman removed every trace of tarnish. When she heard the uneven tattoo of a horse's hooves drumming on the lane's hard clay, Ann frowned and crossed to a front window, certain it was much too early for Kell to be returning.

She caught back a breath at the sight of the black stallion coming up the lane, lunging at the bit in an attempt to break out of a trot. Jackson Stuart sat astride the horse, a dark figure in his black waistcoat and hat, the silver brocade of his vest flashing in the sunlight. Again she was struck by the handsome, dashing figure he made as she watched him rein the restless stallion in and dismount at the foot of the front steps.

He was coming to the door! She swung from the window and took one eager step toward the entry, then stopped abruptly, looking down in horror at the work apron tied over her house dress of striped brown wool—and the gloves on her hands, blackened by tarnish. From the foyer came the rapping thud of the brass knocker rising and falling against the front door.

"Cora Mae, answer the door—quickly!" she snapped to the black maid as she hastily stripped the gloves from her hands, silently praying the grime hadn't penetrated the cloth.

"Yes'm." The slim black woman hurried from the dining room, glad to leave the hated task.

Ann pulled off the apron and tossed it, along with gloves, onto the table, then ran to the doorway, stopping short of its carved oak frame to smoothly pat the upswept sides of her hair and make certain no strands had escaped. When she heard Cora Mae open the door, she pinched her cheeks to put color into them. Although she wasn't sure it was necessary, as flushed with excitement as she felt. Then, straining to appear serenely composed, she glided into the reception hall.

"Who is it, Cora Mae?" she called cheerily.

The colored woman held the front door open, but remained squarely before it, denying admittance as she looked back at Ann. "It's a Mister Jackson Stuart. He's asking for Master Kell, but I told him he ain't here just now."

She moved quickly to the maid's side and dismissed her with a curt nod, then turned a warm smile on the man standing outside the door, conscious of the heart thudding in her chest. Immediately he removed his hat in her presence, revealing the gleaming black of his hair.

"Mr. Stuart, what a pleasant surprise," she declared. "Won't you come in?" She swung the door open wider to admit him.

But he smiled and shook his head in refusal. "I think not, Mrs. Morgan." Yet there was no mistaking the regret in his voice and his expression as his glance moved over her with that familiar covetous look. "Your housemaid informed me your husband isn't at home, and I wouldn't want to compromise your reputation if some neighbor should happen by and think you were entertaining an admirer in your husband's absence."

"You're right, of course." She felt hot all over, realizing that was exactly what she did want—not the neighbor part, but the other, the stimulation that came from entertaining a male admirer, the fending off of compliments in a way that encouraged more, the pretending that a hand hadn't been held too long— that whole thrilling aura of anticipation. After four years of marriage, all that had gone from her relationship with Kell. In truth, her husband had never looked at her the way Jackson Stuart did—as if he longed to ravish her.

"Will you pass along my thanks to your husband for the loan of a horse and the care for my stallion?" Jackson Stuart asked.

"Of course," she agreed, much too brightly.

"Then I'll bid you adieu, Mrs. Morgan."

As he started to bow over the hand she automatically extended to him, she felt a panic grip her throat. "Will I—we—ever see you again, Mr. Stuart?"

His lips barely brushed the back of her hand before he straightened. "I have the feeling our paths are destined to cross again, Mrs. Morgan—if Fortune is with me."

As he rode down the lane, Ann fervently hoped he was right, realizing— quite shamelessly—that she wanted to see him again.

23 ❧

KANSAS CITY—THE NOISE, the gaiety, the bustle, the crowds—Ann couldn't get enough of it. Horse-drawn carriages battled with cable cars and vendors in their pushcarts for the right-of-way on the paved streets. Wood and stone buildings—three, four, and five stories high—towered on either side, stout and sturdy buildings, not the flimsy false-fronted kind they built in Tulsa. People crowded the sidewalks, hirsute men in top hats or bowlers and women in their fur-trimmed coats and muffs. And everywhere the clang of cable cars, the cries of boys hawking newspapers, the rattle of carriage wheels, and the clamor of a city on the move.

The first four days were one round after another of shopping, lunches, afternoon teas, dinners, private receptions, and parties. By the fourth day, Ann talked as knowledgeably as her friends about the fantastic electric light display at the Chicago Exposition, had memorized the words and music to "A Bicycle Built for Two," and wondered how she had ever survived at Morgan's Walk all this time without a telephone.

Garbed in a long dressing sacque to cover her combination, petticoat, vest, and her new evening corset elaborately trimmed with lace frills and rosettes, Ann stood beside the bed and studied the two gowns laid out for her inspection. She vacillated between the two, holding up first the *ciel* blue damask, then the Nile green China crepe. Hearing the firm tread of footsteps in the hallway, she turned toward the door, her unbound hair swinging freely about her shoulders. Her look of heavy concentration lifted as Kell walked into their private suite of rooms in her father's house.

"I'm glad you're back," she declared, turning away as he gave his hat a toss onto a swan chair and absently ran a hand through the waving red of his hair. "I need your help." She stepped back to frown thoughtfully at the two gowns again. "Which do you think I should wear to the Halstons' dinner tonight?"

"We aren't going out for dinner again tonight, are we?" A frown sharply creased his forehead, drawing his auburn brows together in a thick, disapproving line.

"To the Halstons', yes. I told you about the invitation this morning." She picked up the damask gown and held it against her, then turned to look at her reflection in the freestanding full-length mirror. "The color of this one suits me, don't you think?"

"Ann, do you realize that we have been here four days, and not once have we had dinner with your father?"

"Of course we have," she insisted, not taking her eyes from the mirror. "He was at the Taylors' and the Danbys'."

"That isn't the same as having dinner here."

"Perhaps, but Papa understands," she retorted, aware that her husband had already tired of this constant round of social affairs. But she didn't care. After four miserably lonely years on that ranch, she was entitled to one month of fun and she wasn't going to let Kell spoil it for her.

"He would understand a great deal more if you spent an entire evening with him."

Ann ignored that as she critically studied the style of the five-year-old gown. "The color's fine, but the bustle—it protrudes much too far. I wish my new gown was ready," she complained. "Everyone will take one look at me in this and know it was part of my bridal trousseau. If only there was some way to alter it—but I don't dare take it to the seamstress. Her tongue's as fast as her needle. In two days all of Kansas City will know it's an old dress I've had restyled." She chewed at her bottom lip, trying to think how the dilemma could be salvaged. Then she remembered her father's housekeeper. "Mrs. Flanagan, of course. She's excellent with a needle. I'll have her look at the dress."

With her problem solved, she tossed the damask gown onto the bed and picked up the China crepe. She heard the quick set of footsteps in the hall outside their door and started to turn, then decided, no, she'd speak to Mrs. Flanagan tomorrow. If it was to be the Nile green gown, she needed to choose her accessories. Perhaps the feathered fan of rose and white, with the matching aigrette for her hair.

The bustling footsteps came to a quick stop outside their door and a sharp, demanding rap, rap, rap followed. Ann paused briefly in her silent debate as Kell walked to the door and opened it. The short, chubby Irish woman stood outside, a white ruffled cap covering red hair that the years had thoroughly shot with silver.

" 'Tis sorry I am to be disturbing you, Mr. Morgan, but this wire just come for you. And I be thinking yourself would want to be reading it straight away."

"Thank you, Mrs. Flanagan." Kell took the telegram from her.

"No trouble, Mr. Morgan. No trouble at all." With a dismissing wave of her hand, she was off, scurrying away on some other urgent business.

"A telegram," Ann repeated, mildly curious. "Who's it from?" She glanced indifferently at Kell's frown of concentration as he struggled to read the message.

"Chris," he answered, then appeared to grow impatient with his own slowness in reading the words and handed it to her. "Read it for me."

She was a bit startled by this rare admission that his reading skills were less than adequate. Usually he was too proud to acknowledge his lack of education —at least in front of her.

" 'HIT BY RAIDERS STOP HORSES STOLEN STOP LITTLE BILLY AND CHOCTAW DEAD STOP THREE WOUNDED STOP NEED HELP STOP.' . . ." Slowly Ann lowered the telegram, a dread filling her as she spoke the message's last line: " 'CAN YOU COME STOP.' "

She had never seen his face so stony grim before or his eyes so hard. Even before he said it, she knew what was coming. "We'd better start packing."

"No." Her fingers curled around the telegram, crumpling it into her palm, but she wasn't aware of it as she swung away from Kell, fighting the hot tears that stung her eyes. "I won't go! You promised we'd stay a month. It's only been four days."

"Ann, someone has stolen our horses and murdered two of my men—and wounded three more. For all I know, Chris might be one of the wounded."

That possibility gave her pause, but still she insisted: "I don't care."

"You don't mean that. You can't," he snapped. "And you can't expect me to stay here and go to your dinners and parties when I'm needed at Morgan's Walk!"

"Then you go!" she hurled at him, then faltered, realizing that she had stumbled on the answer. Turning, she repeated it with less anger. "You go, Kell, and let me stay here." She went to him, now all appeal, tears running unchecked down her cheeks, her fingers gripping the lapels of his frock coat in silent entreaty. "Please, Kell. Please let me stay. There's nothing little Johnny or I could do there."

He gazed at her upturned face, her dark eyes shiny with more tears. She was his weakness. He'd never been able to refuse her anything. And he couldn't now.

Kell caught the next train south by himself. Ann remained at her father's house in Kansas City with their son.

The bon ton of Kansas City filled Coates Opera House for the special performance of *Manon*. Between acts, they mingled to see and be seen, to talk and be talked about. Men in their black evening dress gathered in groups, striking negligent poses of elegant ease and puffing on their Havana cigars while they bragged about their latest business coups and groused about the failing banks, often taking malicious delight in the economic fall of a competitor. Women in their best silks and satins glided about, whispering behind their fans about this person and that and lavishing compliments on one another.

"Ann, how good to see you again." A blond-haired woman glided up to her, dressed in a gown with lace and feather trimming that was so tightly corseted Ann wondered how she could breathe. Not that she cared. Helen Cummings was not a friend—not since she had stolen Ann's beau five years ago, then compounded the offense by marrying him.

"Helen, how are you?" She smiled politely and prayed that the woman was miserably unhappy.

"The same—deliriously happy." She waved off the question with a sweep of her lace and feather fan. "I heard only yesterday that you were back for a visit. When did you arrive?"

"A week ago."

"That explains it," Helen declared. "Bobby and I were away."

"Yes, I believe someone mentioned that you were in New York."

"I don't need to ask how you're managing in the wilds of the territory. You look simply ravishing in that gown," she remarked, somewhat grudgingly. "I was admiring it earlier and someone mentioned it was a Worth."

Actually it was patterned after an illustration Ann had seen of a gown designed by Worth, but if Helen Cummings chose to think it was an original, Ann wasn't about to correct her. In truth, she knew that her gown of Parma violet damask was the most elegant gown of any worn that night—and distinctive, too. The corsage was pointed in front and trimmed all around the low neckline with white tulle and lace. A double garland of beads sewn on tulle with delicate crystal pendants curved from the bust to the right side of the waist, fastened there by clasps in the shape of St. Jacques shells. Similar garlands of beads and crystals were strung diagonally across the damask skirt above a flounce of embroidered lace. She wore her dark hair parted in the middle and drawn back in large waves to form a high coil, then adorned it with twists of beads to match the gown.

Helen Cummings was clearly envious of the result, and Ann intended to keep it that way. "It is beautiful, isn't it? My husband saw it and insisted that I have it, regardless of the cost," she lied. Kell had cast only a cursory glance at the illustration and hadn't laid eyes on the finished gown yet. She'd gotten it from the dressmaker's only this afternoon—after much screaming and railing on her part.

"Speaking of your husband, where is your wealthy cattle baron?" the blonde inquired with a touch of snideness.

"He was called away—on some sort of urgent business." Ann shrugged, pretending she didn't know what it was all about.

"You surely aren't here this evening by yourself?" Helen looked properly shocked.

"No." Ann smiled smoothly. "Papa brought me."

"Your father—it's been ages since I've seen the good doctor. Where is he? I must say hello."

"He's—" Ann glanced toward the end of the room where the men were gathered in small clusters, a miasma of cigar smoke hanging over them. Her gaze immediately became riveted on a man dressed in a single-breasted waistcoat in black, a small white bow tie around his neck and studs marching down the front of his stiff shirt. He stood with one leg slightly cocked, his hair gleaming blackly in the flickering gaslight and his eyes—his blue eyes . . .

"My dear, you're gaping," Helen chided. "Who is it that has so caught your eye?"

Ann recovered her surprise and astonishment at seeing Jackson Stuart, and broke into a smile. "Why, it's a dear friend," she replied, stretching the truth a little. "I had no idea he was in the city."

To her immense delight, Jackson Stuart noticed her and immediately made his way toward her. She could hardly wait to introduce her dashingly handsome acquaintance to Helen Cummings and watch the woman's envy. Then she experienced a moment's unease and shot an anxious look at the petite blonde, the daughter of one of Kansas City's oldest and most influential families—and the daughter-in-law of another. If Jackson Stuart showed so much as the slightest interest in her, Ann swore she'd never speak to him again.

But he took no notice of Helen as he halted before her. "Mrs. Morgan. I wondered if our paths would cross during my sojourn in Kansas City." He bowed over her hand, holding her gaze with his warm look.

Helen Cummings stirred beside her, fluttering her fan to gain his attention. Ann knew the woman was just panting to be introduced to him, but she deliberately ignored her. "It seems Fortune was kind to both of us, Mr. Stuart."

"Indeed." He straightened and bestowed on her that faint smile that somehow managed to be so incredibly sensual. "How quickly time passes. It seems such a short time ago that I stayed with you and your husband at Morgan's Walk, but already a month has passed." Then he paused, his glance flickering elsewhere. "Is your husband somewhere about? I don't remember seeing him."

"No, Kell's away on business. It will probably be a week or more before he returns."

"Really?" Jackson Stuart pretended he hadn't known that . . . just as he pretended he didn't know the cause for Morgan's absence. But his money belt bulged with his share of the proceeds from the sale of the stolen horses to a less than scrupulous trader in the Cherokee Strip. Thanks to the fleetness of his black stallion, he'd made it back to Tulsa in time to see Kell Morgan get off the train—alone. He couldn't help feeling a certain smugness that his plan was working so well. He vaguely regretted that it had been necessary to kill those two cowboys, but it had been the only way he could make sure Kell Morgan came back—and that he might consider it too dangerous to have his wife and son return, in the event the night raiders struck again, going for the cattle herd. He'd been certain Ann Morgan would agitate to remain in Kansas City—and he'd obviously been right.

"Helen, may I present Mr. Jackson Stuart, late of the Oklahoma Territory." As Ann Morgan introduced the blonde woman with her, Jackson caught the slight edge in her voice and noticed she failed to identify the woman as a friend. "Mrs. Helen Cummings. We both attended the same finishing school."

"Mrs. Cummings." He acknowledged the introduction with a polite bow and nothing more.

"Mr. Stuart, it is such a pleasure to meet a friend of Ann's . . . especially such a handsome one," the woman declared, looking at him through the long sweep of her top lashes.

Although it went against his nature, he didn't flirt back and, instead, merely smiled. Out of the corner of his eye, he observed the flicker of satisfaction that fleetingly crossed Ann's expression, and knew she approved of his aloofness.

But Helen Cummings wasn't to be put off. "What is it exactly that you do, Mr. Stuart?"

"I dabble in many things—blooded horses, cattle, land . . ." He let it trail off as if his interests were too many to mention.

"What brings you to Kansas City?"

He was spared from answering that as an older man walked up to them. "There you are, Ann. I've been looking for you."

"Papa, I'm so glad you're here. There's someone I want you to meet." She quickly hooked her arm with her father's and drew him forward.

Jackson Stuart looked with interest at the next obstacle he had to overcome as she introduced him to her father, Dr. Frank Compton. He was somewhere in his fifties, a little below average height. Gray silvered his dark hair at the temples and streaked the mustache and goatee he wore. His eyes were the same brown-black color as his daughter's and his features possessed a certain benign softness that befitted his profession. Although, at the moment, he appeared somewhat distracted, as if he had other things on his mind than meeting Jackson Stuart—despite the fact that Ann Morgan implied that he was a longtime personal acquaintance of her husband, an implication that couldn't have fitted better with his plans.

"Delighted to meet you, Mr. Stuart, but I'm afraid you'll have to excuse us," he declared, politely but briskly.

"Papa, what's wrong?"

"I'm sorry, child, but I'm afraid we must leave." He patted the hand that clutched at his arm. "It's Mrs. Stanhope's time. Their carriage is waiting out front for us."

"But—must we leave now? The opera isn't over yet," Ann protested plead-ingly. "There is still the last act to come. There is such a beautiful aria in it, can't we stay? What will another hour matter?"

"A great deal to Mrs. Stanhope," her father chided, an indulgent smile lifting the corners of his mouth.

"Must I go too?" There was a decidedly petulant droop to her lower lip.

"You know it wouldn't be proper for you to stay. An unescorted lady. Unless, of course, Mrs. Cummings and her husband—"

Jackson Stuart broke in before the doctor could suggest that Ann join the Cummings party. "With your permission, Dr. Compton, I would be honored to serve as Mrs. Morgan's escort for the remainder of the evening." He did his best to appear harmless and respectful under the doctor's sharply assessing look. "As a matter of fact, I would welcome the opportunity to repay the accommoda-tions and hospitality your daughter's husband has extended to me in the past."

"How very thoughtful of you to offer." Ann fairly beamed at him, not taking her eyes from him as she said to her father, "I assure you, Papa, Mr. Stuart is a most honorable man. Were Kell here, I'm sure he would vouch for him as well."

The good doctor hesitated, then smiled. "In that case, it would be churlish of me to refuse your offer, Mr. Stuart. I leave my daughter in your capable care."

"I promise you won't regret it."

"I'm sure I won't," he replied and turned to his daughter. "Advise Mrs. Flanagan that I likely will be very late, but I hope to be home before morning."

"I will."

Well before the final act began, they took their seats in the private box, with Jackson Stuart occupying the one that had previously been taken by her father. Although she pretended not to notice, Ann knew they were the cyno-sure of all eyes. The whole house was atwitter, fans spreading as everyone speculated about the handsome stranger sitting next to her. She loved the attention. She'd gone too long without it. The last time she'd created such a stir among her friends had been when Kell had courted her—another stranger, but one with red hair . . . a rich cattle baron from the Indian Territory. Not a single one of her friends had thought she would marry so well—not after losing Robert Cummings to Helen Thurston. She'd proved them wrong. Now, with Jackson Stuart sitting beside her, they would all wonder what her life was like at Morgan's Walk. Not for anything would she tell them the truth. She preferred to have them think she commonly entertained the likes of Jackson Stuart.

As far as Jackson Stuart was concerned, the evening couldn't have turned out better if he had planned it. During the ride in the closed hansom cab to her father's residence, Ann inquired about the length of his intended stay in the city.

"That will depend on how much I find to keep me here," he replied. "I had thought about traveling on to Chicago, or New York—or maybe south to a warmer clime, like New Orleans. And you? You will be staying—what? Another three weeks?"

"At least," she confirmed.

"Then perhaps I will, too." He smiled at her undisguised glow of pleasure at his answer.

"The Throckmortons are having a reception tomorrow afternoon. If you have no plans, perhaps you'd like to attend."

"If it means having the pleasure of your company, I'd be delighted."

The cab waited while he walked her to the door and chastely kissed her gloved hand. When he walked back to the hansom, he silently congratulated himself on his luck. She couldn't know that she was playing right into his hands.

"Where to now, mister?" the driver asked from his perch behind the cab.

Jackson Stuart looked up at a night sky so black that it seemed to possess a velvet shine. And scattered across it, like crushed and loosely strewn crystals, were the stars. The night was young and he was on a winning streak. Long ago, he'd learned to ride it for all it was worth.

"I've heard Madam Chambers has a blackjack table," he said idly, then smiled at the driver. "Fourth and Wyandotte." The address was squarely in the heart of the city's bon-ton block of sin. He climbed into the cab, wondering if Annie Chambers, the madam of the swank and exclusive brothel, would remember him.

24

DURING THE NEXT ten days, Jackson Stuart became her constant companion, escorting her everywhere and anywhere she went—shopping expeditions, skating parties, dinner receptions, and gala holiday balls. There were only two places he didn't take her—to church . . . and to bed. But the latter would come . . . in due time. Everything was progressing exactly the way he'd anticipated, including the familiar usage of their given names, begun almost a week ago—at her behest.

"I have never seen you look more beautiful than you do tonight, Ann," he declared as he swirled her around the ballroom, holding her close, no longer concerned about keeping the proper distance between them. Neither was she, he noticed, aware that she frequently invited the brush of his lips against her temple and cheek when they danced.

"Nor have you looked so handsome." She flirted with him openly now—if discreetly.

"If you were the only woman to think so, I would forever be content." Deliberately he inserted a seriousness into his manner, then observed the quick breath she drew before she melted closer to him.

He said no more as he gazed into her eyes and guided her steps through the last few measures of the song. When the music stopped, an immediate flurry of voices rose to fill the silence. He was slow to lead her off the floor, then halted at the edge of it and let his glance sweep the ballroom, decorated with garlands of holiday greenery trimmed with red velvet bows.

"Do you remember what I said to you that evening at Morgan's Walk?" He continued without allowing her an opportunity to respond. "After seeing you here in this setting, I am more convinced than ever that you don't belong in the Territory." He held up a hand to stave off the comment she was about to make. "It's true, Ann. You're a precious jewel wasted in that nothingness, hidden by that dulling red dust. But, here, tonight, the fullness of your luster and sparkling brilliance shines for all to see and admire. This is where you should be, always —in a setting like this, with chandeliers glittering and violins playing."

"I wish it could be so." She attempted to mask the hint of longing in her voice. "But Morgan's Walk is my husband's home . . . and mine." Belatedly she linked herself to the man whose name she now carried.

"So?" Jackson shrugged. "Let it remain your home—your wilderness retreat. There's no reason you have to spend every day of your life there. Your husband can—as many others have done—install a manager to run the place for him. Or better yet, leave his brother, Christopher, in charge while the two of you travel. That's what I would do if I was in your husband's place."

"You and I are so very much alike, Jackson," she declared wistfully, then grimaced prettily in regret. "I only wish Kell thought as we do. But he would never consider leaving Morgan's Walk for any length of time. He loves that place." A bitterness crept into her low voice as she averted her glance, a shimmer of tears in her eyes. "Certainly more than he loves me."

"Ann—"

Her head swung back, a rare defiance glittering in her eyes. "Morgan's Walk is far from here and much too boring a topic. Dance with me, Jackson."

Again he took her into his arms and swept her onto the floor, secretly smiling in satisfaction. Yes, it was all going perfectly.

Close to midnight, they joined the throng of departing guests leaving the ball. Sometime during the evening, it had begun to snow. A mantle of white covered the ground while more soft, fat flakes fell as they made their way through the snow to the hired carriage and Jackson assisted her inside, then climbed in himself and spread the fur robe over the skirt of her evening cloak.

As the carriage pulled away from the mansion still ablaze with light, the trilling voices of other departing guests faded into the stillness of the snowy night. Despite the crunch of the carriage wheels in the fallen snow and the jingle of the team's harness bells, a magical, hushed quality permeated the air. Ann could almost believe they were the only two people in the world.

Bundled warmly in her evening cloak of black satin, its hood and cape trimmed with black marten fur to match the muff she carried, Ann leaned forward to gaze out the carriage window, her breath rising in wispy puffs of vapor. "Look, Jackson. See how white the snowflakes appear against the black of the night. Have you ever seen anything so beautiful?"

"I know of only one thing that rivals it."

She turned her head and discovered he was right there, looking out her side of the carriage, his face only inches from hers. She was instantly conscious of the rapid palpitations of her heart . . . and the thready rush of excitement she felt as his gaze moved over her face.

"What's that?" she asked, fully aware a compliment was coming—and aware, too, that she had invited it.

"The pure white of your skin against the velvet dark of your hair, it's perfection." His voice was as soft as a caress.

Yet there was perfection, too, in the noble straightness of his nose, the rise of his cheekbones, and the sculptured slant of his jaw. Secretly she thrilled to the intimate messages his eyes so frequently sent her. He made her feel things she shouldn't. She was a married woman. Yet, looking at the well-shaped line of his mouth, she understood why the apple had looked so very tempting.

"Ann." That was all he said—just her name. But how many times had he said it just that way and made her feel that she was the most desirable woman on earth? Wicked thoughts she had. Wicked, wicked, wicked thoughts. But, oh, they felt so good.

She wanted to be kissed. He saw it in the tension of her, the motionlessness. The signal was always the same whether given by the most proper of ladies or the most pocked and painted of whores. All women were at the mercy of the same signals. Most men expected a difference, but Jackson Stuart knew better.

Her lips felt cool beneath his, chilled by winter's breath. As he went about warming them, he felt her hesitation and that vague, never completely formed impulse to turn away, but she stayed with the kiss. Soon she was reaching into it, bending like a supple willow, her lips all eager and soft. He pressed the advantage, taking her beyond herself, taking her farther than she wanted to go, until she broke away suddenly heavy, her gloved fingers clutching at the front of his coat, her face averted from him.

"No." Her faint protest was near a moan. "You mustn't—we mustn't."

"I know." He sought her temple, grazing his lips over it. Satisfaction, smooth as the best whiskey, ran through him at the swiftly indrawn breath she took. "That's what I've been telling myself for days now, but it doesn't change the way I feel." He continued to brush his mouth over her, speaking all the words against her skin and feeling the faint tremors of longing. "Ann, you must know—you must have guessed—that I came to Kansas City because you were here. I wanted to see you again, talk to you—if only for a moment. I couldn't believe my luck when you said your husband was away. But was it luck, Ann?"

"I don't know," she whispered.

"Neither do I. I only know that I've fallen in love with you."

"No."

He ignored her faint protest, his hands tightening to check her feeble attempt to pull away from him. "It's true. I love the look of you and the glow of your smile. I love the fragrance of your skin and the perfume of your hair. I love the sound of my name on your lips and the beat of your heart next to mine. I love the feel of you and, yes, the taste of you. Ann, my sweet, my darling."

There was such agony, such aching intensity in his voice that she was enthralled by it. These last days he had flirted with her often and said bold things, but she never dreamed she had inspired such a depth of love. The discovery was heady and thrilling, just as his kiss had been. She turned her head slightly, letting him find her lips again, no longer frightened by the desire that had flamed within her, now welcoming the forbidden feelings and the excitement of them.

His mouth was all over her lips, not like the last time with a tenderly persuasive ardor, but with hunger—tasting, eating, devouring until she felt wholly consumed by his kiss. But what a delicious feeling it was—so beyond her experience, leaving her completely bereft of thought and breath, her heart pounding until she was quite weak.

When he lifted his mouth from hers, she sagged against him and rested her head against his shoulder, limp with feeling and aware that it had never been like this with Kell—never. The band of his arms remained tight around her, keeping her close while his restless, kneading hands moved over her shoulders and back, alternately pressing and caressing.

"What am I to do, Ann?" he murmured, his lips brushing the elaborate coil of her dark hair. "I can't bear the thought of letting you go back to Morgan's Walk. I know how miserable and lonely you are there. Yet, how can I ask you to come away with me when I have nothing to offer?" A groan of despair came from his throat. "When I think of the fortunes that have passed through my hands at the gaming tables, I curse myself for not realizing the day would come when I'd meet an enchanting creature like you. What money I have is enough for me, but not enough to lavish you with the beautiful gowns, the jewels, the furs you deserve to have—or to take you to all the beautiful places you deserve to go. I would give anything to have your husband's wealth—anything but my heart, for you already have that. Ann, Ann." He murmured her name in husky urgency as he lifted her head, cupping her cheek in his hand and gazing at her. Her face had a dreamy sensuousness, her lips parted, eyes heavy. He'd won her over. "What a fool Morgan is. What a fool."

"I wish—" She was afraid to say the rest, afraid to admit she had chosen wrong when she married Kell. He loved her, and, in his way, he had been good to her. It was selfish of her to want the life Jackson had described—and it was sinful of her to enjoy his kisses, but, oh, she did. She did.

"I wish it, too, my love," he declared. "But I can't ask you to leave your husband when I can offer you so little. But—if I should find a way—tell me that I have cause to hope."

"You do, yes." She couldn't deny it.

Again she was swept away by his kisses, carried off by their languorous heat that produced such feverish longings. All too soon the carriage stopped in front of her father's house. One more time they kissed within the shadows of the closed carriage, then Jackson walked her to the door and bid her a proper goodnight.

She swayed toward him, not wanting him to go, but he stayed her with a smile and a promise. "Till tomorrow."

"Yes, tomorrow," she whispered, and watched him walk away amid a swirl of falling snowflakes. In that instant, she was convinced there was no feeling stronger than the sweet ache of love.

The next two days were the happiest Ann had ever known, filled with secret looks, whispered words of love, and stolen kisses—and every moment heightened by the risk of discovery. But that only served to make the rest that much more exhilarating. Truly it was an enchanted world.

But on the morning of the third day, the spell was broken—shattered—sending Ann into a thousand scattered pieces. Distraught, she hurried down the hotel corridor, checking the room numbers on the doors and constantly glancing over her shoulder, fearing that she might be seen—or worse, recognized, despite the veiling net of her hat. At the door marked twenty-two, she paused and looked down the hallway once more, then rapped lightly and quickly.

"Just a moment," came the muffled but impatient reply, the voice unmistakably Jackson's.

She waited anxiously outside the door, the seconds ticking by with interminable slowness before she heard the approach of his footsteps. She leaned toward the door in nervous eagerness as it swung open.

"Yes, what is it?" The instant he saw her, Jackson Stuart halted in the middle of pulling on his white linen shirt. "Ann?!"

He sounded as shocked at seeing her as she felt at seeing him in a state of partial undress. She stared at the smattering of dark chest hairs, then turned her head away, hot with embarrassment at the prurient thoughts that raced through her mind.

"I—I shouldn't have come." She made a halfhearted move as if to leave, but he stopped her, catching at her arm and drawing her back.

"Don't go. Come inside before someone happens by."

She didn't resist when he pulled her into his room and closed the door. The front of his shirt swung together, hiding his naked chest, but she continued to keep her eyes downcast, her heart pounding like a mad thing.

His hands gripped her arms near the elbows, just below the exaggerated pouf of her coat's velvet sleeves. "Ann, you're trembling. What is it? What's wrong?" He bent his head to look under the brim of her hat and through the screen of its black veil to her face.

"I—I didn't know what to do." She hesitated, then pulled the folded telegram out of her muff. "This came early this morning. It's from my husband." He released her to take the telegram, a stillness coming over him. She didn't wait for him to read the message. "He arrives on the afternoon train." The raw feeling of desperation that she'd managed to hold in check thus far now broke from her. "I had to let you know. I couldn't let you come to take me to the Willets' reception and find Kell there. I had to see you. I had to—"

"I know," he said, stopping the rush of words.

She looked up, her gaze clinging to his. "I won't be able to see you anymore, Jackson."

He smiled lazily, unable to believe she was actually here in his hotel room. Although why he doubted his luck, he didn't know, considering the way he'd bucked the tiger last night and walked away from the faro table a big winner.

"What time does his train get in?"

"It's scheduled to arrive at two-ten this afternoon."

"Then we have three hours." He tossed the telegram onto the floor, then loosened her veil and rolled it over the brim of her hat. "Let's not waste them with words, Ann."

The hat soon went the way of the telegram, to be followed shortly by the muff and the long velvet coat. Dispensing with her dress of striped changeable silk was easy, too, as long as his lips stayed close enough to smother the beginnings of any vague protest.

She felt drunk with his kisses, a dreamy looseness taking over all her limbs. She clung to him for support, letting the arm hooked around her tightly corseted waist take all her weight and thrilling to the feel of his muscled flesh beneath the linen of his shirt.

As he continued to shower her eyes, cheeks, and lips with kisses, his fingers moved to the lace-trimmed throat of her high corset cover. When the top button sprang free at his touch, Ann caught back a breath, aware that his deft fingers had already moved on to the next. She had never been assisted out of her clothes by anyone except her personal maid. Not even Kell had taken such liberties. At finishing school, she'd been taught that a woman of gentility didn't expose her private areas to a man, not even her husband. Voluminous night-gowns with long sleeves and high necks satisfied the need for modesty in the marrige bed, however awkward and cumbersome they sometimes proved to be.

But she would have no such protective garment with Jackson. She went hot at the thought, aware that just to be seen in her petticoats by a man was considered scandalous. Worse, the heat she felt wasn't embarrassment. What a wicked woman she was to want to expose herself and excite him further. But that was exactly what she desired. Exactly.

The corset cover hung loose about her. She moaned softly as he pushed her arms down to the side, then slipped the silk garment from her, his hands smooth against her skin, not callused and rough like Kell's. Unerringly his fingers moved to the laces at the back of her corset. Some distant part of her idly marveled that the workings of a woman's undergarments held no mysteries for him. Then she was drawing her first unfettered breath, a breath that ended in a tiny shudder.

With the corset vanquished, he untied the strings to her rose-colored petti-coat of quilted satin and let it fall about her legs in a rustling whisper. When he picked her up and lifted her out of it, she felt as weightless as a babe. Held close to him, she made another discovery. The fine muslin of her combination and its frills of torchon lace proved to be no barrier against the sensation of his hard-muscled body pressed against her flesh. She could feel every flexing ripple through the thin fabric as he carried her the few feet to the bed. There, he slowly lowered her feet to the floor, turning her to face him as he did so and letting her body slide upright against him, making her aware of every masculine contour in the process.

She could hardly breathe, her senses assaulted on all sides by him. And the affliction wasn't eased by the quick claiming of her lips in another intimately delving kiss. Its power was such that at first she wasn't aware of the deft manipulations of fingers at the front opening of her combination. Then she felt the touch of his hand against her bare skin. Reaction splintered through her in needle-sharp tingles of surprise and delight. She sagged against him, letting him take all her weight, but he sank under it to sit on the edge of the bed, drawing her with him to stand between his spraddled legs.

Dazed, she looked down, her hands clutching at the ridges of his shoulders for balance. A tension gripped her as she watched him spread the front of her combination open, starting at her stomach and gliding up through the valley between her breasts, then branching to expose the bones of her shoulders. She brought her arms down to her sides so he could slip it off, her breath now running shallow and fast, matching the ragged, quick-hammer beat of her pulse.

As he pushed the one-piece garment over her shoulders, the fine muslin briefly caught on the hardened points of her breasts, then sprang free of them. She saw the way his eyes devoured her breasts, and closed her own, a melting heat starting somewhere in her midsection and spreading. She waited to feel the caress of his hands as he slowly pulled the combination chemise and drawers down her arms. Just below her elbows, he stopped and gave the back of the garment a twist, pinning her arms out straight behind her, throwing her shoulders back and her breasts forward.

Startled, Ann looked down, her lips parting in a question that she never had a chance to form as he spread a hand over her flat stomach and moved it up, up, up, then finally reached the underswell of a breast. He glanced up and saw her watching him. The darkening light in his eyes almost made her want to swoon, but she didn't want to miss any of the delights his eyes promised. And delight there was as he began to nuzzle her breasts, kissing and licking at their nipples until Ann quivered in reaction, an ache coiling ever tighter and centering ever lower in her stomach.

With one final pull of the garment, he freed her arms. Immediately she dug her fingers into his hair and pressed his face to her breast, ending the teasing of his lips. She bowed her head against the awesome pressure that continued to build inside her. Through heavy, half-closed eyes, she watched him tug his shirt off and give it a fling across the room. Then his hands were back on her, rolling the undergarment down over her hips. She was aware of his actions, yet she wasn't. As in a dream, everything blurred together, things happening without her paying attention to the how of them—like the way she ended up on the bed.

Yet, as in a dream, too, certain things stood out very sharply, a single moment held in time—like the way he had left her to strip off his trousers and drawers, then came back to fill her vision. She had never seen a man unclothed before. She stared at his wide shoulders and leanly muscled chest with its smattering of curly dark hairs. Her glance drifted lower to the hard flatness of his stomach, then lower to his stiffened organ. A breath caught in her throat. She hadn't known a man's body could be so beautiful. Some distant part of her wondered if Kell looked like that beneath the long nightshirt she'd always insisted he wear to bed.

But the thought no more than registered when it vanished as Jackson lowered himself onto her, using his legs to wedge hers apart. The fever that had heated her body cooled somewhat under the settling weight of him on top of her and the sensation of his bony hardness against her inner thigh. This part she knew all too well. She felt the first twinge of disappointment as his lips teased the corner of her mouth, his warm breath rolling across her skin. But there was no positioning of her hips, no awkward, probing attempt at entry. Instead, his hands were busy touching and stroking, moving over her with wayward ease, their path unencumbered by any voluminous nightgown. Ann began to relax and enjoy once more, taking advantage of the chance to run her hands over the bareness of his muscled arms and shoulders and revel in the sensation of skin against skin.

When his mouth transferred its attention from her lips to her neck and the hollow of her throat, she moaned in soft pleasure, liking the little shivers his nibblings sent dancing over her flesh. And she arched in eagerness when he bent his head to suckle at her breasts again. But they didn't seem to satisfy his hunger for the taste of her skin as his grazing mouth wandered lower, feeding on each curve of her ribs. When his moist lips traveled onto her stomach, her muscles contracted sharply, that curling ache intensifying until she wanted to cry out at the tormenting sweetness of it. And Jackson was doing nothing to ease it. On the contrary, his only interest seemed to be in kissing every inch of her.

When she realized his exploring kisses were taking him into a forbidden area, she made a panicked attempt to stop him. "Don't. You—" Jolted by the sudden hot sensation that swept through her, Ann jammed a fist into her mouth and tried to bite back the animal sound that rose from her throat.

A wildness claimed her. Unable to control it, she abandoned herself completely to it, writhing and twisting with eyes closed, fingers digging at the bedcovers beneath her, a sheen of perspiration breaking out all over her. When the pressure within built to an intolerable level, suddenly he was on top of her again, sliding effortlessly in and burying himself deep. This time she didn't even try to check the soft cry—or any of the other raw sounds that rolled from her as he began to move inside her.

Sprawled across the bed, a bedsheet halfheartedly draped across her hips, Ann felt gloriously limp and empty. Still faintly dazzled by the wonder of the experience, she turned her head to look at the man who had shared it with her. He was watching her, the glint in his eyes holding both a trace of satisfaction and amusement. She rolled onto her side and arched close to him, feeling like a purring cat as she threaded her fingers through the silken hairs on his chest.

"Proud of yourself, are you?" she murmured, peering at him through the tops of her lashes. "Now that you've had me."

Reaching out, he snared her waist and pulled her closer still. "Aren't you?"

"Deliciously so." She rubbed her head against his shoulder, feeling even more like a contented feline. "I didn't know it could be like that." She smiled, convinced she'd discovered the most incredible secret.

"All you needed was a man to show you."

She sighed an agreement to that, recognizing that her husband certainly never had. By nature, Kell wasn't a demonstrative man, his feelings invariably contained behind that hard wall of reserve. She thought back to the times she'd lain with him, remembering the tender restraint of his kisses and his touch. Never once had he attempted to take her out of herself—not the way Jackson Stuart had. In fact, she'd always had the impression that Kell never expected her to enjoy any of it—that he got it over with quickly out of deference to her.

But was that her fault? she wondered, recalling their wedding night and how rigid with fear she'd been. Kell had showered her with ardent kisses that night; the caress of his hands had been eager and bold, but she'd been stiff and completely unresponsive. Too many of her married friends had hinted at how awful it was. Even her father had lectured her on her wifely duty to submit to her husband's demands, implying that his exercise of conjugal rights was something to be endured. And that terrible, ripping pain had confirmed everything they'd said. Afterward, she had cried and cried, resisting all of Kell's attempts to console her, hating to feel even the touch of his hands, let alone to be taken in his arms.

Perhaps it wasn't surprising that her husband had become something less than an ardent lover. It was what she'd wanted. She didn't want to think about Kell—not now. But she had to. He'd be arriving this afternoon.

Suddenly she was assailed by a whole host of doubts and uncertainties. "Jackson, will I—will I see you, again?" The possibility that she wouldn't seemed unbearable.

He tucked a hand under her chin and lifted her head from his shoulder, his gaze warmly possessive as it moved over her face. "Do you think I could stay away from you now—after this?"

The tension left her in a faint tremor of relief. "I didn't know. I wasn't sure," she admitted, smiling at her doubts. But the smile faded as a new thought occurred to her. "But how? With Kell here—"

"Not here. Not Kansas City." His fingers moved caressingly over her face, stroking her cheek and her lips, tracing their curves and hollows in loving detail. "When your husband arrives this afternoon, I want you to convince him that you're tired of the city, that you miss the peace and serenity of Morgan's Walk—that you're eager to go home."

"He'd never believe me." She turned from his hand, loathing the thought of going back there, but Jackson wouldn't let her pull away.

"He'll believe you," he stated confidently. "He'll believe you because it's the very thing he desires."

"How can you ask me to go back there when you know how much I hate it?"

He smiled at the shimmer of resentment in her eyes. Not once had she suggested leaving her husband for him. If the thought had crossed her mind, Jackson Stuart was certain she would have instantly dismissed it. It was something her pride wouldn't allow. She was a doctor's daughter who had married above herself. No matter how miserable or wretchedly unhappy she was, Ann Morgan wasn't about to give up her newfound wealth and status—not for love, especially when he'd told her that he had nothing else to offer her. In her own way, Ann Morgan was just as greedy as he was.

"I want you to go back, my darling, because it's the safest place for us to meet," he said.

Confusion darkened her eyes. "The safest? How? If you start coming to the house—"

"Not the house. We'll meet in Tulsa. You make trips into town twice a month for mail and supplies, don't you?"

"Yes."

"And when you're there, don't you usually take a room at the hotel so you have a place to rest and freshen up?" He already knew the answer to that. In fact, he was certain he knew her habits better than she did.

"Yes."

"Then, we'll meet there in your room—where we can be alone."

"But—what if we're discovered?"

"We won't be. The desk clerk's a friend of mine. He'll warn us if anyone comes. And don't worry, my love. We won't have to meet in secret for long . . . just until I can find a way for us to have the kind of life we want," he said against her lips, then claimed them in another long, drugging kiss. He was already sure of the way, but until he was sure of her, he wouldn't take the final steps.

Ann was at the train station to meet Kell when he arrived that afternoon. And, just as Jackson Stuart had predicted, she had no difficulty convincing her husband that she was homesick. Three days later, the entire Morgan entourage boarded the train to return to Morgan's Walk.

Ten days later, she went to town and took a room at the Tulsa House as usual. She barely had time to remove her dust cloak and hat when she heard a furtive tap on the door. With heart pounding, she hurried to open it. Less than a minute later, it was once again closed and locked and she was in Jackson Stuart's arms.

25 ✒

MARCH 27, 1894

I fear Chris has found out about us. I shouldn't have gone into town when I was there only last week, but another seven days seemed such a long time to wait before seeing Jackson again that I had to go. Rarely can we spend more than an hour together, but those stolen hours are what have made my life bearable these last few months. What a wanton woman I have become, yet I feel no shame—only guilt at the way I must deceive Kell.

And now fear as well that Chris may convey his suspicions to Kell. I know he must suspect something. He looked at me so strangely when I opened the door to admit him. And well he should have, for my clothes and hair were all disarranged from my haste in dressing, and my chin was reddened by the sharp stubble on Jackson's face. Next time I must insist that he shaves immediately before he meets me. Next time. I pray there will be one, and that all my fears are foolish imaginings and that Chris's odd silence during the ride home meant nothing. Yet I'm certain that, as quickly as Chris arrived after Jackson had left, he must have passed him in the hall. Did he see him leave my room as well?

He said nothing to me. He didn't even comment on my state of disarray. Naturally I explained away my appearance by claiming that I had been weary from the long ride into town and had lain down to rest. I'm not sure he believed that.

Whatever he thinks or suspects, I know he has had no opportunity to speak to Kell, as Chris didn't dine with us this evening. After he had escorted me safely back to Morgan's Walk, Chris left again almost immediately—to go to one of the neighbors, he said. Kell seemed to know about it, so perhaps that truly is where he went.

What a long, trying evening this has been for me. As usual, Kell shut himself in the library with his precious account books shortly after dinner concluded, and I have been alone with my thoughts.

I sit here by the window of our bedroom and look at the rising moon and the first glitter of stars. Somewhere I know that Jackson sees them, too. I wonder if he thinks of me as I think of him.

—How odd? I see a horse and rider approaching the house through the trees in the back.

Who could be coming to call at such a late hour? And why doesn't he ride up the lane? It can't be Chris. He was astride his palomino when he left, and this horse looks black, as black as

The sentence was left unfinished. Curious, Flame turned the page, but it was blank—as were all the rest of the pages in the diary. She looked up and found Ben Canon watching her with speculative interest. That bright gleam in his eyes seemed to gauge her reaction, trying to determine the extent of her curiosity. She felt a ripple of irritation at the way she had been maneuvered into caring. But that was immaterial now. She had to find out the rest of it.

Yet she didn't want to give him the satisfaction of knowing how thoroughly she was hooked. With false calm, Flame closed the diary and laid it on the cherrywood table next to the plate of cold sandwiches.

Flame avoided stating the obvious, aware that Ben Canon had to know precisely where Ann Morgan's diary left off. "I assume the rider she saw was Jackson Stuart."

"It was." With one hand, he removed his reading glasses and slipped them inside the breast pocket of his jacket, drawing her attention to the thick booklet held open in his other hand.

"What happened then?" She studied the age-yellowed pages, fairly certain the booklet wasn't another diary yet unable to make out what it was.

Unhurried, the attorney wandered over to her chair. "I think it would be best if you learned the answer to that by reading a transcript of your great-grandfather's testimony at the trial."

"What trial?" Frowning, she hesitantly took it from him.

"The trial of Jackson Stuart for the attempted murder of Kell Morgan."

Inwardly she faltered at his announcement as her glance raced to the portrait above the mantelpiece. Maybe she should have expected something of the sort, but she hadn't. Attempted murder, Ben Canon had said. That meant Stuart hadn't succeeded. Had it been a deliberate attempt on Kell Morgan's life or had it been the result of an accidental confrontation? From Ann Morgan's diary, Flame assumed that she had recognized her lover and slipped out to meet him. Looking at the hard, proud man in the painting, she could easily imagine the rage, the humiliation, and the hurt he would have felt if he'd caught his beloved wife in the arms of another man. Honor would have demanded a challenge. Was that what had happened?

The answers to her questions were in the opened transcript she held. She forced her gaze away from the portrait and brought it down to the nearly hundred-year-old document in her hands.

Q. Please state your name for the record.
A. Christopher Morgan.
Q. You are the brother of the intended victim, is that correct, Mr. Morgan?
A. Yes, sir.
Q. And you reside at the ranch known as Morgan's Walk along with your brother, is that correct?
A. Yes, it is.

Q. Will you please tell the court where you were on the evening of March 27th of this year?

A. In the early part of the evening, I was at a neighboring ranch—the Bitterman place. It was late when I got back to Morgan's Walk. Probably between ten and eleven o'clock.

Q. Will you describe to the court what happened when you returned to Morgan's Walk? And may I remind you that you are under oath.

A. Yes, sir. As I said, it was somewhere between ten and eleven. I'd unsaddled and turned my horse into the corral. I was on my way to the house. I noticed there were lights still burning in the library. I realized Kell—my brother—was still up working on the account books. So I came the back way to the house—through the trees. The library's located on that side of the house. I thought I'd check in with him since I hadn't talked to him all day.

I was probably a hundred and fifty feet from the house when I saw somebody prowling around outside. It was close to payday, and I knew we had more cash on hand than we usually keep at the ranch. The thought crossed my mind to raise the alarm, but I couldn't be sure there wasn't someone inside holding a gun to Kell, so I slipped closer. . . .

With gun drawn, Chris moved through the trees, then froze against the trunk of an oak as a large patch of white floated across the ground toward the dark figure of a man. It was Ann, a dark shawl thrown over the top of her nightgown. He felt sick inside. All the fight went out of him as he lowered his gun and slumped against the tree.

A hundred times he'd told himself that he was wrong about that afternoon—that Ann was too fine and too good to get mixed up in some illicit affair. She'd been so anxious to go to town that day. There was some lace that she absolutely had to order right away, she'd said. Then when they got there, she hadn't gone to the mercantile store; she'd gone straight to the hotel "to freshen up." When she hadn't come out an hour later, he'd gone to see what was keeping her. He wanted to get back to the ranch and over to the Bittermans'.

He hadn't been surprised to see Blackjack Stuart in the hall. The gambler had hung around Tulsa all winter. When they passed each other, Chris had caught the smell of some flowery fragrance and had smiled, guessing that Stuart had just passed a pleasant hour or two in the company of a woman.

When Ann had opened the door to him, he'd smelled the exact same perfume on her. And she'd had the disheveled look of a woman who had just stepped out of some man's arms. She said she'd been resting, but her eyes had been overly bright, her face glowing with the look of a woman who had just been thoroughly satisfied. And he'd seen what a man's whiskers could do to a woman's delicate skin.

He hadn't wanted to believe. He'd fought against it, but there she was, running into Stuart's arms. Somewhere back in the trees, a horse snorted in alarm and moved skittishly, rustling the remains of last year's fallen leaves.

Chris looked toward the house, his gaze drawn to the lights shining through the glass-paned doors to the library. Kell was there. How could he tell him about his wife? How could he possibly keep it from him? His gut felt all twisted inside, an anger clawing at his throat. He wished he'd never found out.

He wished he'd never gone to that hotel room. He wished anything that would mean he didn't have to face Kell with Ann's betrayal.

Jackson Stuart heard the whisper of movement a second before his stallion snorted the alarm. In a half crouch, he whirled to face it, leveling the long muzzle of his revolver at it, then cursed his luck when he saw Ann running across the grass to him. In another minute, he would have had the angle that would have made her a widow, a very rich widow.

He lowered his gun, but didn't holster it, catching her with his free arm as she flung herself at him. "My darling, I can't believe you're here," she whispered, pressing a hundred kisses over his neck and jaw as he drew her deeper into the shadows, keeping one eye on the library all the while. "How could you take such a risk? But I'm glad you did. I needed to see you. I've been so worried."

But he didn't listen, wishing to hell she'd shut up so he could think how to salvage this. Yet over and over, he kept thinking that he should have known his luck had changed—he should have known last night when he lost four straight hands at blackjack. He would have lost the fifth if he hadn't palmed an ace. Then he'd nearly got caught. He'd walked away from the table, unwilling to push what was left of his luck any farther.

He should have made his move against Morgan sooner, but he'd wanted to make sure they had the ranch payroll on hand. He could have killed Morgan a dozen times from ambush, but he'd wanted to make it look like a robbery. He didn't want any suspicion thrown on him when he later married Morgan's widow.

The money was there in the library, according to Ann, locked in a cashbox Morgan kept in the bottom drawer of his big mahogany desk. And Morgan was in there, too. Dammit, he'd come so close to making it all work, he couldn't give up now. Tomorrow. He had no choice but to wait until then now that Ann had seen him. Damn her.

Suddenly he tensed, catching a movement in the library. Then Morgan appeared at the set of doors, his tall, broad frame nearly filling them. He opened one of them and stepped outside. Alerted by the scrape of his boot on the brick walk, Ann looked over her shoulder and emitted a faint, strangled cry of alarm, briefly pressing closer to Jackson. For an instant Jackson stared at the perfect target Morgan made, silhouetted by the lights from inside. His luck hadn't changed, he realized, as he raised his gun, thumbing back the hammer.

When Chris saw Kell step outside, his glance immediately raced to the embracing lovers. Not even the depth of the night's shadows could conceal the white of her gown. Sick with dread, he knew Kell was bound to notice it. Then he caught the gleam of moonlight on the barrel of a gun. Cold fear shafted through him. Kell wasn't armed. He always unbuckled his gun belt the minute he walked into the house.

"Is that you, Chris?" Kell called out, followed by a questioning, "Ann?"

Thrown into action by the sound of his brother's voice, Chris brought his gun up and yelled, "Look out, Kell! He's got a gun!"

Stuart squeezed the trigger just as the full-throated cry of warning shattered the night's stillness, the explosive report drowning out most of it. Ann's scream barely registered as his glance stayed long enough to watch Morgan go down, lost in the dark shadows close to the ground. Then Stuart swung toward that voice out of the night, blood pumping high and hot through him, a steely calm guiding his every move. Morgan's brother stepped out from a tree into the full light of the moon, his gun leveled, looking for a clear shot. Exultant at the thought that he could eliminate both Morgans, he pushed Ann from him, not wanting her endangered by a stray bullet, and simultaneously snapped off two quick shots.

He pulled back the hammer on the third and caught Morgan's gun flash. He heard its barking report as the bullet slammed into his right shoulder, the impact spinning him to the side and sending his own shot wild. There was no pain, only a hot, burning sensation. He tried to come around and bring his gun to bear on the younger Morgan again, but Ann came out of the shadows, crying his name and throwing herself at him amid the sound of more gunshots and shouts of alarm. Off-balance, he couldn't absorb the sudden weight of her against him, her momentum driving them both to the ground, the fall jarring the revolver from his hand. Swearing viciously he tried to push her off him and grope for the gun, pain knifing through his shoulder.

A boot came down hard on his wrist, pinning it to the ground. Stuart looked up—into the muzzle of a gun. A handful of half-dressed cowboys stood around him, some with suspenders drooping around their pants and others with belts and holsters buckled around their red flannels. He let his head fall back against the earth's hard pillow. His bid for Morgan's Walk was finished. He'd lost.

In a kind of dazed shock, Chris walked over to them and stared at the dark wet stain that spread slowly from the small hole in the back of Ann's white nightgown. He looked at the gun in his hand. The bullet that had made that hole had come from it. Repulsed by the cold feel of it, Chris let go of the gun, letting it fall to the ground, then crouched down next to Ann. She lay slumped and motionless—like a rag doll partially draped over the man whose life she had tried to save.

"Ann." Tentatively he reached to touch her. "I didn't mean to. I didn't see you. Why? Why?"

"What'd he do?" one of the cowboys spoke up. "Use her as a shield?"

Chris didn't answer, letting them think what they liked and hoping his silence might protect Kell from the dishonor his wife had brought him. He started to pick her up, gently and tenderly, not wanting to hurt her, mindless that she was beyond hurt.

"Don't touch her."

There was such hoarseness in that voice that Chris hardly recognized it as Kell's. When he looked up, his brother towered over him, his left arm hanging limply at his side, blood dripping steadily off the tips of his fingers.

"Boss, you're hurt," someone said.

But no one took a step toward him, frozen by the look of stark, white grief that had turned his face to stone. Chris backed away from the body, his mouth and throat working convulsively as he searched for the words to tell his brother how sorry he was. But he couldn't find them and he had a feeling Kell was beyond hearing them.

He watched in a silent agony of his own as Kell sank to his knees beside his wife's body and picked her up with his one good arm, cradling her against his chest and burying his face in the dark cloud of her unbound hair. Those big shoulders heaved, racked by grief, but no sound came from him—nothing at all.

Vaguely Chris was aware that Stuart had been dragged to his feet but he paid no attention to him until one of the men asked, "What about this guy? Want us t' string him up?"

For an instant, he was tempted to give the order. For an instant, anger boiled inside him. For an instant, he wanted to blame Stuart for Ann's death, reasoning that none of this would have happened if it wasn't for him. But hanging Stuart wouldn't erase the guilt he felt. He'd been the one who pulled the trigger, not Stuart. And he couldn't pretend otherwise.

"Tie him up and lock him in the tack room," he said. "And, Gus, ride into town and get a doctor for my brother. While you're there, tell the sheriff to wire the marshal and tell him we've got a prisoner for the tumblewagon."

"She was killed," Flame murmured absently, a touch of sadness in her voice. "The poor woman."

"It was ruled accidental." The attorney held a match to the bowl of his pipe and puffed deeply, drawing the fire into the tamped tobacco. "Conjecture is—" He shook out the match and tossed it into the fireplace. "—she saw that Stuart was hit and went to his aid, inadvertently stepping into the line of fire. I find it much more logical and more in character than the supposition that she might have been nobly sacrificing her life to save him."

Having read Ann Morgan's diary, Flame agreed with that, although she doubted Kell Morgan would have found much consolation in the knowledge. As her glance swung to the portrait, she noticed there were no doors along the outer wall, only a window.

"This room doesn't have any doors to the outside."

"Not anymore." Charlie Rainwater waved a leathered hand at the paneled wall to the left of the fireplace. "They used to be there, but about a week after his wife's death, Kell Morgan ordered them walled in and the brick path outside torn up. I figure the sight of 'em probably haunted him, makin' him remember that night and relivin' her death all over again." He tipped his head back and gazed at the portrait. "From all accounts, he took her dyin' pretty hard. It's not surprisin', I guess, when you think how much he adored her."

Ben Canon grunted an agreement to that, then removed the pipe stem from between his teeth to add, "I doubt if his grieving was made any easier by Stuart's brag from his jail cell in Tulsa about how close he came to having everything that belonged to Kell Morgan—from his money and his house to his wife." He arched a glance at Flame. "Which is what prompted Kell Morgan to insert the condition that the property must pass to a blood heir or revert—at that time—to the Creek Nation. Later, after statehood was granted in nineteen-o-seven, he changed it to the state of Oklahoma."

"I see." Flame bowed her head briefly, her glance falling on the transcript in her lap. "What happened to Jackson Stuart?"

"He was tried before Judge Isaac Parker in Fort Smith and found guilty of attempted murder. With typical harshness, the judge sentenced him to thirty years at hard labor. Ten or fifteen years earlier, Parker would probably have ordered him to be hanged, on the theory he was guilty of somebody's death, even if he hadn't succeeded in his attempt on Kell Morgan's life. But times had changed, and Parker was no longer the final authority in the Territory. Too many of his decisions had been appealed to the Supreme Court and reversed." A smile rounded his shiny cheeks, ruddy in the fire's glow. "I suppose you could say that Stuart's luck had returned. A prison sentence was definitely better than a hangman's rope."

"And Chris Morgan, my great-grandfather?"

"He left Morgan's Walk shortly after the trial was over—never to return. I'm sure you can appreciate the guilt and remorse he felt over Ann Morgan's death. However inadvertent or accidental, it was a bullet from his gun that killed her. And, as Charlie said, Kell Morgan took her death very hard. But it wasn't something he verbalized. In the code of the western man, he held his grief inside and went off by himself for days on end. With the responsibility he felt for her death, Chris Morgan believed—rightly or wrongly—that his presence was a constant reminder to his brother of that night. So, he left." The attorney paused, gesturing briefly with his pipe in the direction of the mahogany desk. "There is a letter from him to that effect if you'd like to read it."

"No, it isn't necessary." She refused with a silent shake of her head, convinced there was, indeed, such a document to support his statement. Gathering up the photo album, the diary, and the transcript, Flame rose from her chair and carried them over to the desk, placing them on top of it, then turning to confront the two men. "I admit this was a very interesting story—" she began.

"Oh, but it isn't the end of it, Mrs. Stuart," Ben Canon broke in, again that gleam of supreme confidence lighting his eyes. "In a way, it could be called the beginning. You see, Blackjack Stuart was released from prison after serving twenty years of his thirty-year sentence. By then little Johnny Morgan had grown up into Big John Morgan. Unfortunately he inherited not only his mother's dark hair and eyes, but many of her rashly impetuous tendencies as well. At the tender age of sixteen he was obliged to marry the daughter of a neighboring rancher. Hattie was one of those miracle babies, born six months after the wedding."

"But she was a chip off the *old* block," Charlie Rainwater inserted. "A Morgan through and through. And old Kell spotted that right off. By the time her legs were long enough to straddle a saddle, he was taking her everywhere with him. Some of the old-timers used to tell me about watching this five-year-old tyke out hazing cattle with the best of 'em, cuttin' out a steer or chasin' back a cow that broke the herd. She was Kell Morgan's shadow, all right, and closer to him than she ever was to her pa."

The foreman made no attempt to disguise the admiration in his voice when he spoke of Hattie Morgan. The mention of her turned Flame's thoughts to the woman lying upstairs—and the accusations she'd made against Chance. She felt her wedding ring, twisting it about on her finger, suddenly impatient again with all this talk that had nothing to do with him.

"I hope this is leading to something." Pushed by a restlessness and vague irritation, she crossed to the fireplace.

"It is," Ben Canon assured her. "As I mentioned earlier, Blackjack—or Jackson Stuart, as Ann Morgan preferred to call him—was released from prison in nineteen fourteen. He returned to an Oklahoma vastly different from the one he'd left. It was no longer a territory. In nineteen-o-seven it had joined the

Union as the forty-sixth state. The discovery of the Glenn Pool oilfield in nineteen-o-five and the Cushing field in nineteen twelve had transformed Tulsa from a dusty cowtown into the oil capital of the world. The city's streets were paved; electric streetcars provided public transportation; and modern 'skyscrapers'—five and six stories tall—had sprung up all up and down Main Street. There were shops and stores of every kind and description, offering the biggest and best selection there was to their customers.

"And Morgan's Walk . . ." As the attorney paused for dramatic effect, his gaze rested heavily on Flame. "With statehood, Kell had finally acquired title to the twelve hundred acres that comprise this valley. He owned another two thousand acres of adjoining land besides that, and leased the grazing rights on another five thousand, making Morgan's Walk the largest cattle ranch near Tulsa. It was a showplace for the entire area. The newly oil-rich looked at this house—one of the finest examples of Georgian architecture west of the Mississippi—and built their mansions to rival it."

Smiling to shift the mood, he went on. "So it was on a fine spring day in early May that Kell Morgan took his seven-year-old granddaughter to Tulsa so she could pick out her birthday present, an occasion made doubly memorable by the fact that he allowed her to sit on his lap and drive his touring car, a Chevrolet, to town. . . ."

Young Hattie Morgan kept a firm hold on her grandfather's hand as she walked proudly along the crowded sidewalk. But each time they passed a store window, she couldn't resist stealing a glance at her reflection in the glass and admiring the well-dressed girl that looked back at her. Everything she wore was new— from the shiny patent leather slippers with tailored bows on her feet to the leghorn straw hat adorned with flowers and ribbons on her head, but especially the polka-dot dress with its full skirt and lace-trimmed ruffles. Her grandfather had declared she was the prettiest girl in Tulsa in her new outfit. And she felt certain he was right. He'd never been wrong about anything. Either way, these new clothes were at least as wonderful as the hand-tooled saddle he'd given her for Christmas.

Suddenly his hand tightened with punishing force, bringing her to an abrupt stop and pulling her back to his side.

"Well, what a surprise! If it isn't the great Kell Morgan himself." A stranger stood squarely in their path. Hattie tilted her head back to look at him from beneath the floppy brim of her new hat. White streaked the hair beneath his hat and his face had a hardened, gaunt look about it, but it was the darkly bright gleam in his blue eyes that caught and held her attention. There was something about it that wasn't nice, despite the wide smile that curved his mouth. "I wondered when I'd run into you, Morgan."

"What are you doing in town, Stuart?" The tone of her grandfather's voice was chilling. Hattie knew he only talked like that when he was really angry.

She decided this stranger named Stuart couldn't be very smart, because he just kept smiling, too dumb to know how he was riling her grandfather. He'd be sorry.

"The same as you, Morgan—walking wide and free," he replied. "Although I notice you don't throw as big a shadow as you used to, not with all these oil moguls around here now."

Frowning in bewilderment, Hattie turned to her grandfather. "What's a mogul, Grandpa?"

The stranger immediately turned the inspection of his blue eyes onto her. "And who do we have here?" He crouched down in front of her, a hand reaching out to flip the lace ruffle on her bertha. "Aren't you a pretty little lady."

"I'm Harriet Morgan," she informed him coolly and importantly. "But my grandpa calls me Hattie."

"Hattie. That's a very pretty name." The man straightened, again turning his gleaming gaze on her grandfather. "So she's your granddaughter, is she? I heard your son was raising girls out there." Then he winked at her. "Maybe I'll just have to wait until she grows up and then marry her."

"It wouldn't do you any good, Stuart. It wouldn't get you Morgan's Walk—not anymore."

"Yeah, I heard about the change you made—that it has to pass to a blood kin." His smile widened. "You'd be surprised what a patient man I am. I'd be just as happy to see it pass to my son."

Her grandfather was getting angry. She could see the vein standing out in his neck. "That will never happen, Stuart."

The man's smile faded. Suddenly he looked dangerous. "Maybe it will be over your dead body, Morgan, but I swear to you the day will come when a Stuart owns Morgan's Walk."

"Approximately a month later, Stuart married a widow about twenty-five years his junior. She had a hundred-and-sixty-acre farm back in the hills that her late husband left her. It wasn't much of a farm, with only about sixty acres of tillable bottom land, the rest rock and trees. The speculation was that Stuart had married her thinking there was oil on the place, especially when drilling rigs moved onto the property six months after he married her. Six wells were drilled, but they were all 'dusters'—dry holes. The widow, however, ultimately gave him a son—Ring Stuart.

"Yeah," Charlie spoke up. "And the threat that Miss Hattie had lived with all her life suddenly became very real when her baby sister Elizabeth ran off and married Ring Stuart." He paused, then added, as if to make sure Flame understood the significance of all this, "Ring Stuart was your husband's father."

"And that's it?" she challenged. "That's the extent of your proof against Chance—a threat that was made seventy-odd years ago? Because he married me, you think he's after Morgan's Walk."

"Not just because he married you," the attorney denied, then hesitated a split second, surveying her with a considering glance. "There are other factors. For instance, how long have you known him?"

"A month, more or less." She tilted her chin a fraction of an inch higher, fully aware that it sounded like a very short time.

"What a remarkable coincidence," Ben Canon declared with mock wonder. "It was approximately a month ago that we learned of your existence and Hattie informed Chance that he would not be her heir."

"Did she specifically name me?"

"No. But for a man with Stuart's sources—and resources—it wouldn't be too difficult to learn your identity."

Unable to deny that, Flame chose to ignore it. "What makes you so certain he wants this ranch? With his money, he could buy a hundred—a thousand—like it."

"No doubt he could," Canon agreed. "That's a question you'll have to ask him. And when you do, ask him why he's bought or optioned all the property adjoining Morgan's Walk to the south and east. Even for him, that's bound to represent a tidy investment of capital. Make no mistake about it, Flame, he wants this land."

She wanted to deny it, to argue with him, but he sounded much too confident and that made her very cautious. "Why?"

"You mean he didn't show you his plans for this property when you went to his office Monday morning?"

"What plans?" she demanded, struggling to hold her temper.

"His plans to dam the river and turn this entire valley into a lake, complete with marinas, resort hotels, condominiums, and luxurious lake homes. It's a very impressive project, I understand."

"I don't believe you." She shook her head in quick, vigorous denial. "You're basing all your accusations against Chance on the fact that a Stuart once tried to get control of Morgan's Walk through marriage. Even if Chance wanted this land—which I'm not convinced he does—there are other ways he could obtain it. He didn't have to marry me to get it."

"True," the attorney conceded. "For instance, he could have tried to buy the land from you. Although he couldn't be sure you would be willing to sell it. Which would mean he would have to bring a variety of economic pressures to bear to force you to sell. Or he could use his considerable political influence to have the land condemned. Or he could have contested the will. But any one of those options might take years—with no guarantee that at the end the land would be his. But marriage—think how much quicker, how much more certain that must have seemed to him."

"And I suppose you think it's impossible he might actually love me." A bitterness crept into her challenge.

"Forgive me, I certainly don't mean to suggest that you are without considerable attractions. I'm sure he found it very convenient to love you."

She hated him for saying that. She hated to think that she was being used. "I don't believe you," she repeated tautly.

"Well, believe this, Flame. He intends to destroy Morgan's Walk. If he has his way, all of this will be under a hundred feet of water. You are the only one who can stop him."

Footsteps approached the library, their tread heavy and slow. Flame turned toward the doorway as Charlie Rainwater rose from his chair, a tension gripping him and freezing him in place.

The doctor appeared in the opening and paused, his glance sweeping all three of them before it fell. "She went quietly. There was no pain, Charlie."

26 ～

CHANCE CHARGED OUT of the private elevator before its doors had fully opened. His gaze sliced to Molly as she started to rise from her chair, her customary wide smile of welcome missing, in its place a look of anxiety and regret. Chance took no notice of either as he issued a sharp "Has anyone located her yet?" He caught the faint negative shake of her head and didn't wait to hear the actual words. Without a break in stride, he swept past her desk to his office door, snapping over his shoulder, "Get Sam and tell him I want him in my office—now."

Anger pushed at him as he crossed to his desk, an anger that had a hot spur of desperation to it. At the sound of footsteps, Chance swung back to face the door. Sam walked in with Molly right behind him.

He approached the desk, looking harried and rumpled, as if he'd been up half the night—which he had. "I'm sorry, Chance—" he began.

But Chance had heard all the apologies at three o'clock in the morning when Sam had called to tell him Flame was missing. He'd had a bad feeling when he hadn't gotten an answer last night at her flat in San Francisco. But Sam had initially assured him there was nothing to worry about; he'd checked with Matt Sawyer and found out that her flight had been delayed in Dallas with a mechanical problem and she wouldn't arrive in San Francisco until well after midnight Pacific time.

"Dammit, Sam, we both know where she is." Pivoting sharply, he turned to the smoked-glass windows, fighting the rage and frustration he felt at coming so close to having it all, then having it literally snatched from him at the last minute. "She's at Morgan's Walk."

"We can't be sure of that," Molly offered in placation. "She could have changed to another flight in Dallas or decided to spend the night there and catch a morning plane. There are any number of possible explanations—"

"No." Chance dismissed them all with a firm shake of his head as he stared grimly at the bleak gray clouds that hung over the city. "Somehow Hattie got to her."

"Jesus, Chance, what if she's found out? What if she knows you want the ranch?"

His control snapped at Sam's worried question. He spun on him. "She wouldn't have found out a damned thing if you had done your job and stayed with her! Hattie wouldn't have been able to get near—Flame!"

She stood in his office doorway, rigid as a statue, gripped by an icy fury that swept all remaining doubt from her. She completely ignored his two cohorts in the deception and focused the whole of her attention on the man who had tricked her, used her—betrayed her.

Recovering quickly from his initial surprise at seeing her, Chance faltered barely an instant, then started around his desk to come to her, his expression making a lightning transition from shock to relief. "Where on earth have you been? We've been turning half the country upside down looking for you." Once, the sight of that intimately possessive look in his eyes would have sent her straight into his arms. Now it failed to move her at all. "I've been half out of my mind thinking something had happened to you."

"I overheard how worried you were, Chance," she replied coolly, watching as he came to a stop, a good twenty feet still separating them, his head lifted in wary caution. She started toward him, taking slow and deliberate steps. "What exactly was it that you were afraid I'd find out? That Hattie Morgan is your aunt? Or that you stood to inherit Morgan's Walk before I appeared on the scene? Or that when I did, you decided the most expedient and expeditious course of action to regain control of the land was to marry me?"

His narrowed gaze was quick in its study of her, taking in the icy green glitter of her eyes and the faintly contemptuous curl of her lips. "Flame, I know how it must look—how it must sound," he began carefully. "But that's not the way it is."

"Isn't it?" Her challenging voice trembled with an anger she no longer tried to conceal as she stopped in front of him. "What a pushover I must have seemed to you, lapping up all your lies and coming back for more, honestly believing that you loved me and that I could trust you—turn on the charm and sweep me off my feet. That was your game plan, wasn't it?"

"You're wrong, Flame."

"No, you're the one who's made a mistake." She had come here this morning, certain that if she could talk to Chance, he'd clear away all her doubts. He had, but not in the way she'd expected. With a wrenching twist, she pulled off her wedding rings and held them up for Chance to see. "These don't mean any more to me than they do to you." Coolly she opened her fingers and let them fall to the floor, taking pleasure in the brief flare of anger in his expression. She started to turn away, then paused. "I suppose I should inform you that your aunt died at twelve-forty-two this morning. Unofficially, I am the new owner of Morgan's Walk, and I swear to you, Chance, that you will never possess so much as one inch of that land."

This time when she turned to walk away, he grabbed her and hauled her back to him, his fingers digging into the soft flesh of her arms. "Dammit, Flame, will you listen to me?"

She didn't flinch from him or attempt to pull free. "What's the matter, Chance? Have you decided that charm won't work so now you're going to resort to violence? Hattie said you'd do anything to get Morgan's Walk."

He released her abruptly, his jaw clenched, eyes cold. He didn't try to stop her when she walked away. At the doorway, she paused to look back at him.

"The funeral's Saturday morning. Don't come. You won't be welcome." Then she was gone, closing the door behind her.

He stared at it, then scooped the rings from the floor and held them in his palm. The diamond's sparkling brilliance seemed to taunt him—just as she had. He closed his fingers tightly around them and turned to walk back to his desk.

"Aren't you going after her?" Sam frowned. "You can't just let her walk away like that. You've got to talk to her—make her understand."

"Not now. She's in no mood to listen." He had never seen her like that—so angry, so hurt, all closed to him, and ready to throw his words back in his face.

"Chance is right." Molly spoke up quickly in his support. "Right now she feels hurt. And all she wants to do is hurt back. You can't reason with someone in pain. You have to wait—give her a couple of days for it to ease, then talk to her."

"I hope you're right," Sam said, clearly not sharing her certainty.

"I am." She smiled confidently. "She loves you, Chance. I'm as sure of that as I am that the sun comes up in the morning."

"But what if you're wrong?" Sam murmured, shaking his head.

"She isn't," Chance asserted, holding up the hand that clenched the wedding rings. "I'll have these back on her finger. It may take me some time, but they'll be there. I'm not going to lose her—or Morgan's Walk."

But Sam wasn't to be consoled as he ran a hand through his rumpled hair and sighed. "This is all my fault."

The phone rang, the blinking light indicating the call was coming in on Chance's private line. "I'll get it," Chance said as Molly started to answer it. "It's probably either Maxine or Matt Sawyer calling to let us know about Hattie." He picked up the phone.

"Chance, darling, it's Lucianna." The familiar melodic trill of her voice came over the line. "I hope I'm not calling at a bad time, but there's this ridiculous rumor going around that you got married without letting your friends know a thing about it. Is it true, darling?"

He looked at the rings in his hand. "That seems to be open to argument at the moment."

A SHROUD OF COLD gray clouds covered the late afternoon sky, casting its gloom over the imposing three-story brick mansion and adding to its bleak, cheerless look. Dead brown leaves tumbled across the lane in front of Chance's Jaguar, chased by a brooming wind out of the north.

He slowed as he approached the house. There were no cars parked in front of it, indicating that if any of the neighbors had stopped after the funeral, they'd already left. Which meant Flame would be there alone.

He'd debated long and hard about the wisdom of coming out here today. According to Matt Sawyer, Flame was scheduled to fly back to San Francisco tomorrow. He wondered if he should have waited to contact her after she had returned to the city where they'd met, but he didn't think so. The timing now was ideal, too. Sobered by the ritual of the funeral this morning and the opportunity to reflect afterward, she was bound to be more receptive than she might be another day. And, dammit, he wanted to see her. She was his wife.

He parked the car in front and climbed out. The brisk north wind whipped at his hair and sent more leaves scurrying across the lawn as Chance stared at the house he'd once lived in. A black wreath hung on the front door. There had been a wreath of mourning on the door the last time he'd stood in front of the house—at almost this very spot. That time it had been for his mother.

Suddenly he was a little boy again, fighting the tears he was too old to cry and feeling the choke of a child's hatred in his throat. His father's hand was hard on his shoulder, the reek of whiskey strong on his breath.

"Did you see her face when you told her someday you'd be back? White, she went. White as them pillars. And you will, boy." His father's fingers dug into the ridge of his shoulder, the grip hurting him. "Look at it. Look at it and remember, because that house and all this land is gonna be yours. And there's nothing that bitch can do about it. Nothing."

"I hate her." The words came from the back of his throat, pushed out by all that bitterness and hot emotion. "I hate her and I hate that house. When it's mine, I'm gonna burn it down."

"Now you're talking stupid. Bricks don't burn." He turned Chance away from the house and pushed him toward a dusty pickup. "Come on. Let's get out of here."

"Where are we gonna live, Pa?"

"We'll find us a place. Don't you worry."

They'd found a place all right—an old shotgun house in Tulsa, a ramshackle relic from the boom days when the oil companies had built cheap housing for their workers. The house had been freezing in the winter and sweltering in the summer, and most of the time it stank of his father's vomit. But the rent had been cheap, just about what he'd earned every month on his paper route that year. His father had worked sporadically then, enough to keep food on the table, clothes on their back, and a bottle of whiskey by his bed. By the time Chance turned fourteen, he'd stopped doing even that much. Enough for a cheap bottle of booze, that was all he'd cared about—that and raving drunkenly about Hattie and reminding Chance that all this was just temporary. Two years later he'd finally succeeded in drinking himself to death.

Hattie had done that to his father—taken his pride and self-respect and ground them under her heel. When they'd lived here at Morgan's Walk, Chance had watched his father slowly crumble under the constant lash of her tongue. He'd hated her for that. Oh, he had yes-ma'amed her and no-ma'amed her, but never with respect in his voice—only defiance.

That was a long time ago. Yet, standing here, it didn't seem all that long. Breathing in deeply, Chance mentally shook off the memories and walked to the front door. He lifted the brass knocker and dropped it twice, the wind carrying off the hollow thuds.

Maxine opened the door to him, her look of surprised recognition quickly turning to quiet welcome. "Chance. I've been thinking about you so often these past two days, and here you are."

Stepping inside, he took both her hands and smiled at the stout house-keeper who had been his only friend. "How are you, Maxine?"

The puffiness around her eyes told of the tears of grief she'd already cried, and the brightness of them now indicated more were held at bay. "She could be

such a cruel woman at times, Chance, but she suffered so at the last that I—"
She bit back the rest as her chin quivered. She forced a smile. "It's hard to
believe she's gone. I expect any minute to hear her yell for me."

"I know." His glance swept the grand foyer, finding it exactly as he remembered it, right down to the celadon vase on the round table. More than that, he
could feel Hattie's presence, the stirring of old hostility.

"It isn't fair, Chance," Maxine murmured. "I always thought the next time
you walked through that door, it would be for good. Now . . ." As her voice
trailed off, she glanced sideways in the direction of the main parlor.

Instantly Chance knew Flame was there. "I'm here to see Mrs. Stuart, Maxine."

"She won't see you." She shook her head sympathetically. "She gave strict
orders that if you called or—"

"Maxine, I thought I heard—" Flame halted in the parlor's framed arch, her
gaze locking on him. She wore a long-sleeved black dress, very plain and very
elegant, and her red hair was swept back in a classic chignon. No jewelry of any
kind adorned her, and only a minimum of makeup. Yet she had never looked
more strongly beautiful to him than at that moment. He released Maxine's
hands, letting her step back from him and ignoring the housekeeper's guilty,
worried look.

"Hello, Flame."

"What are you doing here?" Perhaps it was the trace of hoarseness in her
voice or the faint lines of tension around her mouth that alerted Chance to her
fatigue and the stress she was under. He wasn't sure. In any case, he could see
that she seemed tired and, he hoped, vulnerable.

"I came to see you." He moved away from the door and Maxine, angling
toward Flame. "You are still my wife."

"You'll be hearing from my attorney about that."

Even though he'd expected something of the kind, he still felt an anger at
actually hearing the words. "By your attorney, I assume you mean Ben Canon."

"Does it matter?" She was angry, too, but it was the cold kind she'd shown
him at his office. "Whatever reason you thought you had for coming no longer
exists. Please leave or I'll have you thrown out."

"Why are you so afraid to talk to me, Flame?"

"I'm not!" Her temper flared ever so briefly before she shuttered it. "And I
don't have to stand here and listen to you to prove that."

"Hatred is a very contagious thing. It permeates the very walls of this
house." He wandered past her into the parlor, his glance skimming over the
room's familiar furnishings—the ebony piano, the Victorian sofa and chairs, and
the silk rug on the floor that held traces of the tea he'd spilled on it long ago.
"The place hasn't changed," he mused, then angled a glance over his shoulder at
her. "I lived here as a boy. Did Hattie tell you that?" She nodded, almost warily.
"I wasn't allowed in the parlor except on very rare occasions, but I used to sneak
in here when she wasn't around. She caught me once, jumping off the piano,
and took her cane to me. I probably deserved that. But she had no right to
refuse to let me see my mother for three days." Chance paused, remembering, a
bitter cynicism pulling at a corner of his mouth. "It's odd, but it never made any
difference to Hattie that my mother was a Morgan. I was born a Stuart, and

because of it, she made my life hell. If there's any justice in the hereafter, that's where she is now."

"Am I supposed to feel sorry for you now?" Flame mocked from the archway, her arms folded in front in a challenging stance. "Is that what you hoped to accomplish with that poor, abused childhood vignette? Do you know what's sad, Chance?" She walked over to him, never losing that hint of defiance. "If you had told me that before—if you had been honest with me—I probably would have believed you . . . and made an even bigger fool of myself. I suppose I should thank you for that."

He faced her, now wary himself. "I made a mistake—"

"A big one. You used me. You used me as a quick and easy means to get Morgan's Walk. I will never forgive you for that or forget it."

"You're wrong. When we met, I didn't know you had any connection to Hattie."

"It doesn't matter when you found out—before or after you met me. The point is, you didn't tell me. On the contrary, you deliberately kept it from me."

"I admit that was wrong. Maybe I didn't think you would understand. Maybe I wanted us to have more time together first. But it wasn't a lie when I told you I loved you."

She laughed—a harsh breathless sound. "I can't believe this. After what you've done, do you really think you can come here and tell me how much you love me, and I'll just fall into your arms? Do you really think I'm so stupid—so gullible—that I'll let myself be taken in by you again?"

There was an ominous tightening of his mouth, a muscle leaping along his jaw. "I expect you to listen to reason."

"Whose reason? Yours? You make me sick, you lying bastard." She turned from him, hating him as violently as she'd once loved him.

"Dammit, Flame." His hand snaked out to seize her arm. She halted, turning rigid at his touch, and stared coldly at the hand on her arm, saying nothing. The silence stretched for several tense seconds, then he removed his hand from her arm. "You've been infected by the hate that lives in this house, haven't you?"

"Is that why you're so determined to destroy it and build your grand development on it—because you see it as a place of hatred?" Flame caught the faint start that Chance wasn't quite quick enough to conceal at the mention of his proposed development. "Did you think I didn't know what you planned to do with Morgan's Walk—and all the rest of the land you've bought?"

"Whatever use I may or may not have considered putting this land to has nothing to do with why I'm here."

"Doesn't it?" she mocked. "You mean you didn't come here to win me back? I'm curious, Chance. How were you going to convince me to flood this valley and destroy Morgan's Walk? Were you going to wait a couple of months, then come to me and say, 'Darling, I have this great idea to take that land you inherited and turn it into a fabulous resort complex—think of the millions you'll make from it, so much more than you would ever realize if you maintained its current ranching operation'? Maybe you'd add an incentive—'We'll do it together, darling—work side by side as partners.' Naturally, I'd be so blindly in love with you that I'd agree. That's the way you thought it would work, isn't it?"

"Why should I answer that when you wouldn't believe me anyway?" he challenged quietly.

"You're right. I wouldn't."

Reaching out, he gently took hold of her arms. Flame stiffened instinctively, ready to resist if he should attempt to force himself on her, but he didn't. She was almost sorry. There was a part of her that was so raw it wanted to lash out—to kick and scream and claw. But the undemanding warmth of his hands didn't invite it.

"I've hurt you, Flame. I know that." There was a persuasive pitch to his voice now, softly serious and subtly soothing. "You have every right to be angry with me—"

"I have your permission to hate you—how nice," she murmured caustically, deliberately striving to shatter the spell of his voice.

"Dammit, I came here to apologize, Flame—to tell you that I love you—I need you."

"You need Morgan's Walk—which I now own," she fired back and watched his head recoil, his eyes narrowing in a probing study.

"Such a sharp tongue you have," he murmured. "Who is it you're trying to convince that you don't love me anymore—you or me? If it's me, I'm not buying it, because I know you still care."

She felt her first twinge of uncertainty, conscious of the way everything had quickened inside her moments ago, her pulse accelerating, her senses heightening—coming to battle-readiness, she thought. Yet, she managed to meet his gaze coolly. "As conceited as you are, I'm sure you believe that."

"Love can't be turned off with the flick of a switch—as much as you might want to convince me otherwise."

"That all depends on the circumstances," Flame asserted, but Chance shook his head, rejecting her claim.

"No, the feelings you had for me are all still there—hidden behind a wall of anger and hurt pride. You may prefer to deny it, but you want me every bit as much as I want you."

When she felt the pulling pressure of his hands, her first impulse was to forcibly resist. Flame instantly rejected that, realizing that only by showing complete indifference would she prove anything to him. As he drew her into his arms, she steeled herself not to react. When his mouth moved toward hers, she waited until the last second, then turned her head aside, letting his lips graze her cheek.

Undeterred, Chance simply transferred his attention to the pulsing vein in her neck. Suddenly it all felt achingly familiar—the sensuous nibbling of his mouth, the caressing splay of his hands, and the hard, lean shape of him. She had to force her hands to remain at her sides as she fought the memory of how it had been between them. The child in her wanted him to hold her tightly and kiss away all the hurt. But it required the innocence of a child to believe that kisses would "make it all better." And she had lost that innocence long ago. Physical love—no matter how enjoyable and satisfying—was a momentary thing. It couldn't right the damage that had been done. He'd used her; and by using her, he'd betrayed her. She couldn't trust him anymore.

She closed her eyes against her inner tremors of longing, not entirely sure how much she could trust herself. "Are you through?" She injected all the iciness she could into her question.

She felt him pause, then slowly straighten to look at her, but she carefully kept her face averted, unwilling to let him see how fragile her defenses against him actually were.

"For now," he said, that lazy edge back in his voice. "But you're not as indifferent to me as you'd like me to believe. I'd prove it to you, but if I did, you'd hate me for it. And it isn't your hate I want, Flame. It's your love."

Stung by his arrogance, she lifted her head sharply to glare at him. "Hattie was right. I'm only now beginning to realize how right she was. You'd stoop to anything, wouldn't you? You'd lie, cheat, steal—whatever is required to get your hands on Morgan's Walk." She shrugged off his hands and stepped back, unable to bear the touch of him. "I think you'd better leave, Mr. Stuart. You're not welcome here—ever."

For a long second, he made no move at all—said nothing. Just when she thought she might have to summon Charlie Rainwater and some of the boys from the bunkhouse, Chance slowly nodded. "I'll go. But I'll tell you the same thing I told Hattie. I'll be back. This isn't finished between us."

"That sounds remarkably like a threat." She tilted her head a little higher, letting him see that she wouldn't be intimidated.

His lips curved in a smile that was anything but warm. "I never make threats, Flame. I thought you knew me better than that."

She stayed exactly where she was, not moving as he walked around her to the foyer. When she heard the front door close, she pivoted slowly to stare after him. Seconds later she heard the growling rumble of his car starting up. Then she was surrounded by the unsettling silence of the house. Made restless by it, Flame ranged over the parlor, then stopped at a window and studied the rolling tumble of dark gray clouds beyond the glass panes.

That was exactly the way she felt inside—dark and churning with a violent turbulence. These feelings had been there, seething below the surface for the last three days. She'd managed to block them out, but seeing Chance again had unleashed them. Flame finally admitted to herself what she'd instinctively known all along: it would never be over between them. Morgan's Walk made it impossible.

If she'd had any doubts that he still wanted the land, his coming here had eliminated them. He was as determined as ever to get it. Hattie had warned her about that very thing before she died. But how could he succeed? Hattie had left it to her.

Flame turned from the window, suddenly troubled. Ben Canon had told her something. She pressed a hand to her forehead, trying to remember what he'd said. He'd mentioned something about Chance contesting the will and—yes, something about applying financial pressure to force her to sell. But he'd talked about a third alternative. Her frown lifted as she slowly brought her hand down —remembering. "He could try to get the land condemned." That's what Ben had said.

Why have it condemned? The lake, of course.

She had to stop him. But how? What was this development of his? If she was going to fight him and win, she had to know more about his plans. Against a man like Chance, she needed specific knowledge. Otherwise, she could never hope to block any attempt he made. She couldn't constantly be on the defensive. She had to find a way to take the fight to him.

The instant she thought it, Flame realized that it wasn't enough to merely prevent him from getting Morgan's Walk. If it was the last thing she did, she had to make him pay, for her great-grandfather's sake as well as her own. It was time a Morgan got even, and she was the one who was going to do it.

It was odd the hot calmness she felt, the rawness—the rage—that had consumed her these last three days now finding a channel, a direction. It didn't matter that at the moment she didn't know how she would go about exacting a fitting retribution. That would come. First she had to learn all she could about Chance's plans for the land.

But how? Ben Canon had indicated there were drawings or blueprints of it in Chance's office. How could she get a copy of them? Chance would never volunteer a set. If there was some way she could get into his office . . . She drew in a quick breath, suddenly realizing that maybe there was.

She'd have to act quickly. Tonight, in fact. And clothes, she'd need evening clothes, something ultra-dressy. Nothing she had with her would do. She'd packed for a weekend in the sun, not an autumn week in Oklahoma. The dress she had on she'd bought yesterday for the funeral. Did she have time to go buy something? She glanced at the ancient grandfather clock that stood beyond the parlor doors in the foyer. It was nearly five. Would there be shops open that carried the type of evening dress she needed? And where were they? Flame railed at the time she'd lose looking for one, especially when she knew there were at least three suitable outfits hanging in her closet in San Francisco.

Closet. That was it. Hattie's closet, jammed with an entire wardrobe of clothes for every occasion. If she could find something that worked, it didn't matter how old it was. The style of evening clothes rarely changed. As for size, with a little tucking and pinning, she could make it fit.

As Flame walked swiftly from the parlor, Maxine entered the foyer. "I heard Cha—— Mr. Stuart leave. Would you like me to start supper now, Mrs. Stuart?"

After faltering briefly, Flame continued to the staircase. "You don't need to cook anything, Maxine. I'm not hungry tonight."

"Oh, I don't have to cook. The neighbors brought enough casseroles and salads to last a week."

"I'd forgotten that." Flame halted momentarily at the base of the stairs and turned back to the housekeeper. "If I want anything to eat later, I'll get it myself. There isn't any need for you to stay. It's been a long day all the way around. I'm sure you'd like to go home."

"I am tired and . . . ." Maxine hesitated. "If you're sure you don't need me anymore this evening, I think I will go back to my place."

"When you leave, would you stop by the bunkhouse and ask Mr. Rainwater to come to the house?"

"Of course."

With that minor detail handled, Flame started up the steps to put the rest of her plan in motion, her thoughts racing ahead as she tried to recall what evening wear she'd noticed in Hattie's closet.

28

FROM THE STREET BELOW, Flame couldn't see any lights shining from the windows of the Stuart Tower's twentieth floor. On a Saturday night, it wasn't likely anyone would be working—unless it would be a cleaning lady. Just the same, she drove slowly around the block for another look.

A quick drive through the underground garage confirmed no Jaguar was parked in the space reserved for Chance. Satisfied that all was safe, Flame drove the ranch's Lincoln around to the building's front entrance and parked at the curb. She gripped the steering wheel with both gloved hands and breathed in deeply, trying to settle the clamoring of her nerves, heart, and senses.

Before she could question the wisdom—or indeed the sanity—of her actions, she stepped out of the car and nervously smoothed a hand over the hipline of the coffee-brown satin gown. Its slim line suggested something out of the midfifties, but the simplicity of its style made it almost ageless, and definitely suitable for her purpose since society's critical eye wouldn't be reviewing it. She reached inside the car for the matching evening bag and the full-length fox coat. The fur coat had been an absolute find. It wasn't in the best condition, its sleeves and collar showing wear, but it was exactly what she needed.

She draped it around her shoulders and unconsciously cast a furtive glance down the street, but all was quiet, with few cars moving about in the downtown area. She turned toward the building's glass entrance and the lobby within, brightly lit with fluorescent lights. Pausing, she felt the front of her gown and made sure the orchid brooch of diamonds was securely pinned at the center of its V-shaped neckline.

Thank God she needed to appear anxious, agitated, and upset, because that was exactly the way she felt as she hurried to the doors, moving as quickly as the gown's front-slit skirt would allow. At the doors, Flame stopped and rattled them and tapped repeatedly on the glass. Finally the uniformed guard behind the lobby's security desk looked up, a Hostess Twinkie halfway to his mouth. Flame gave him her most appealing smile and rattled the locked door again.

He hesitated a split second, then laid the Twinkie on its cellophane wrapper, and hastily wiped the crumbs from his mouth with a backhanded scrub, got up, and walked around the desk. The guard was somewhere in his early sixties, the gray hair beneath his cap cut close to his head in a short butch, and his double chin hanging over the collar of his shirt, the same way his beer belly hung over the belt of his pants. But it was the noisy jingle that caught Flame's attention as he approached the doors, a large metal ring strung with keys dangling from his hand.

On the other side of the door, he stopped and searched through the keys. Flame glanced anxiously over her shoulder, certain that Chance would drive up any second and she'd be caught in the act. Powerless to hurry the guard along, she waited, mouth dry, nerves screaming with impatience while he separated one key from the rest, and inserted it in the lock. The instant a crack showed, Flame darted inside.

"Is something wrong, miss?" He eyed her curiously, tipping his head down to look at her through the top of his black-rimmed bifocals.

"You don't know how relieved I am to see you." She clutched at his arm, drawing him with her as she moved from the door toward the bank of elevators. "I was afraid there wouldn't be anyone here to let me in. I didn't know what I was going to do. The most awful thing has happened." Near the security desk, she let go of his arm and unfastened the jeweled clasp of her evening bag. She started to reach inside, then stopped and looked at him as if just realizing. "You have no idea who I am, do you? And here I am rattling on. I'm Flame Stuart—Chance Stuart's wife."

He immediately brightened, his jowled cheeks lifting in a smile. "Of course, Mrs. Stuart. The whole building's been buzzing with the news of your marriage to Mr. Stuart," he declared. She'd counted on that—just as she'd counted on the slowness of the word getting around that she'd left him. "Everybody said Mr. Stuart found himself a beautiful redhead and they certainly were right about that."

"Aren't you so kind, Mr.—" She glanced at his nametag.

"Dunlap. Fred Dunlap."

"Mr. Dunlap. Let me explain my problem. As I said, the most awful thing has happened," she rushed on, reaching into her purse again, this time taking out one of the diamond earrings that matched the brooch. "I've lost the mate of this earring. Chance—Mr. Stuart—gave them to me as a gift, along with this pin. I'm supposed to meet him in an hour and he expects me to be wearing them. I've searched everywhere. Then I remembered that I was wearing them the day we came here. Is there any way you can let me into my husband's office so I can see if maybe I left it there? I can't bear the thought of telling him I lost it."

"I sure can, Mrs. Stuart. It's no trouble at all." He shifted his heavy bulk toward the elevators, again going through the many keys on his ring. "You just come with me and I'll take you up."

"You have no idea how grateful I am, Mr. Dunlap. I've been half out of my mind with worry over this." She was certain she sounded like a babbling fool, but she couldn't seem to stop talking as she followed him to the elevators. "I know the set must have cost him a fortune. But it's more than that. It was the first present he gave me. Well, not the first. He sent me orchids first. That's why he had this pin and these earrings designed in the shape of orchids, because they were actually the first."

Flame wasn't even sure the security guard was listening as he used a key to open some sort of utility panel and flip some switches inside. The Up arrow blinked on above the elevator directly in front of her and its doors silently glided open. She practically ran into the cage, then waited again for the lumbering guard to join her. He punched the button for the twentieth floor. Seconds ticked by with unnerving slowness before the time-delayed doors finally slid shut.

As she watched the light above the doors blink on the ascending numbers of the floors, the silence seemed worse than her previous chatter. "I never realized how slow these elevators were," she declared in utter truthfulness.

"It's always like that when you're in a hurry. Nothing ever moves fast enough."

"I guess not," she said and laughed nervously.

Finally the elevator came to a stop on the top floor. With stomach churning, Flame waited in its dimly lit lobby while the security guard went to turn on the office lights. Again the seconds seemed to drag forever before he came back and led her down the wide hall to Chance's office. There she had to wait again for him to find the key and unlock the door.

When he followed her into the office, Flame wanted to scream at him to leave. Instead, she forced herself to smile. "Thank you so much, Mr. Dunlap," she said, turning to face him, letting her body language indicate to him that his presence was no longer required.

He hesitated uncertainly. "I'd be happy to help you look for that missing earring, Mrs. Stuart."

"That isn't necessary," she rushed. "I mean, you've done so much already and I wouldn't want to take you away from your desk. After all, you do have a job to do. It wouldn't be right for me to take you away from your duty."

"I suppose not." He nodded a grudging agreement. "If you should need me, though, you just call thirty-one thirty-one. That's my extension and I'll be up here in no time."

"I'll remember that. Thank you, Mr. Dunlap." She remained where she was, watching as he turned and left, not drawing an easy breath until she heard the distant *ding* of the elevator. Then she hurried over and closed the door—just in case he decided to come back and check on her.

Turning, she swept the long fox coat off her shoulders and scanned the room, trying to decide where to begin her search for the preliminary drawings of the proposed development. She started with Chance's desk, specifically the long credenza behind it. But none of the papers on top of it contained any reference to the project, and a search of the drawers and doors proved equally fruitless.

Aware that time was against her, Flame moved quickly to the built-in cabinetry along the wall in the informal sitting area. Behind one set of doors, she found a bonanza of blueprints. She wasted precious minutes going through them and, again, came up with nothing.

Where were they? She fought down the momentary panic and widened her search to the bookshelves near the conference table. Nothing. My God, what if they weren't here? What if they were in Sam's office instead?

Then she spied the long cardboard tubes in an upright rack next to the credenza on the other side of the burl table—the kind of tubing blueprints and drawings were kept in! Struggling to control the leap of excitement, Flame went to investigate, flinging the fur and the brown satin evening bag onto one of the conference chairs.

Ten minutes later, three of the tubes had offered up detailed drawings of site plans, preliminary blueprints for the proposed dam, and artist's renderings of the luxury hotel, marina, condominiums, and town houses. And the credenza had yielded an assortment of information—everything from an environmental impact study to a feasibility report. Plus Flame had found copies of several memos outlining the status on additional land purchases Chance was trying to make.

She was stunned by the amount of time, effort, and money that had already gone into the project. Which seemed to prove how confident Chance had been that he would get Morgan's Walk—one way or another. Nothing in Ben Canon's remarks had given her the impression that Chance's plans for the development had progressed this far. She wondered if the attorney knew.

Sobered by the discovery, Flame went through all the drawings, blueprints, and reports again, searching for duplicates, gathering them in a stack to take with her, and returning the rest to their original places. She doubted that Chance would ever notice there were copies missing. Fortunately, there were duplicates of everything with the exception of the colored renderings, an initial engineering report, and an overall topography map. But there were black-and-white copies of the renderings, a subsequent engineering report that appeared to contain much of the same information as the first, and a contour map showing natural water drainage.

Suddenly, from the outer office, came the muffled *ding* that signaled the arrival of the elevator. She froze. The private elevator—the one that came from the underground parking garage—the one that required a key to operate—the one Chance used! She went cold, her heart leaping into her throat and lodging there.

With discovery imminent, she looked frantically around the room for a place to hide. But there was no obvious place—no closet, no darkened alcove, no shadowy corner hidden from view. The office was too open, too exposed. She couldn't crawl under his desk; he was bound to go there. Hiding behind the sofa was out, too; he'd see her crouching behind it when he walked by.

There were footsteps in Molly's office. She had to act fast. With speed more important than silence, she scooped up the stack of information she'd gathered and dumped it in the corner, hoping it wouldn't be noticed, then grabbed the fur coat and the evening bag off the chair and dragged them with her as she scrambled under the round conference table and frantically pulled the chairs in closer, hoping the forest of legs would obscure her.

As the door to Chance's office opened, Flame tried to make herself as small as possible and pressed close to the center pedestal. She didn't dare move—or even breathe—for fear the satin of Hattie's gown would rustle and betray her presence.

But it wasn't Chance who entered. It was a woman. Flame could see her reflection in the office's smoked-glass windows. She almost breathed a sigh of relief, thinking it was the cleaning woman. With her, she could talk her way out of this situation. Then she recognized Molly Malone and knew she didn't have a prayer of convincing Chance's secretary that she was under the table looking for her supposedly lost diamond earring.

"Honestly, these cleaning people," Molly grumbled aloud. "Heaven knows how long these lights have been on. If they had to pay the electricity bill here for a month, they wouldn't be so free with them."

There was a click, then darkness—except for the light shining through the doorway to Molly's office. In the reflecting windows, Flame saw Molly's silhouette briefly outlined in the doorway before she walked through and pulled the door shut behind her, throwing Chance's office into near-total darkness.

Flame breathed out shakily and relaxed a little. For the moment she was out of danger—but she was also trapped. She couldn't leave until Molly did. What was she doing here on a Saturday night? How long before she left? What if the security guard came up to see if she'd found the earring? What had made her think she could get away with this in the first place? Why had she taken so much time looking through everything? Why hadn't she simply grabbed what she could find and left? If she had, she would have been out of here and safely on her way back to Morgan's Walk.

She listened to the sounds of Molly moving about in the outer office, file drawers sliding open and clanging shut. A short span of silence was followed by the rapid tappity-tap of the typewriter. Helpless, Flame sat on the floor under the table, surrounded by an increasingly weighty darkness.

But the sound of the typewriter didn't last long. Then a desk drawer shut and a chair squeaked noisily. Again there were footsteps and more indistinct movement.

How long had Molly been here? Five minutes? Ten? Twenty? In the darkness, Flame had no conception of time, but it seemed an eternity went by before she finally heard the bell-like signal of the elevator doors. Then, all was quiet—except for the loud thudding of her own heart. After making certain no crack of light was visible beneath the door, Flame groped her way out from under the table.

This time she didn't dally, but moved as quickly as the darkness would allow, gathering up the papers and plans and clutching them in her arms along with the fur coat and bag. Feeling her way along the wall, she found the door. It opened at the turn of her hand. She stepped quickly into Molly's equally darkened outer office.

Somehow she managed to make it to the hall without bumping into anything. From there she could see a faint light shining at the far end and knew it came from the dimly lit elevator lobby. She caught up the coffee-brown skirt of Hattie's long gown and ran all the way. It wasn't that far, yet when she reached the elevators she felt winded and weak, her heart rocketing against her ribs. Panic, that's what it was.

She forced herself to drink in deep gulps of air and breathe out slowly, taking the few necessary, precious seconds to calm herself. Then she laid the fox coat on the floor and placed the jumble of reports, plans, and drawings inside it. She wrapped the coat around them, paused long enough to push the button to summon the elevator, then picked the coat up, papers and all, and held it in front of her, doubling the coat nearly in half, draping it over her arm and hopefully hiding the bundle it contained.

When the elevator doors opened, she stepped quickly inside and pushed the button for the lobby floor, then caught a glimpse of her reflection in the wall's mirror and turned to survey her appearance. My Lord, but her face looked strained and pale. Hurriedly she pinched her cheeks to put color into them, then noticed the bareness of her earlobes. The earrings: they were still in the evening bag. Awkwardly she clutched at the unwieldy fur-wrapped bundle with one arm and unfastened the purse's clasp to rummage inside for both diamond earrings. She clipped the second one on her ear just as the elevator doors opened on the lobby floor.

Cautiously, Flame looked out, making certain the security guard was alone at the desk. Then with a bright smile she breezed over to him.

"I found it. Can you believe it?" She turned her head from side to side, letting the diamond earrings flash their fire at him.

"That's wonderful, Mrs. Stuart."

"It is, isn't it?" she declared, hugging the fur tightly to her and turning flirtatiously pleading. "Would you mind not saying anything to Mr. Stuart about this? I'd rather he didn't know I'd misplaced it even for a moment."

"Don't worry, Mrs. Stuart." The man grinned and winked conspiratorially at her. "It will be our little secret. My lips are sealed."

"Thank you, Mr. Dunlap. You're an absolute dear," she said, already moving away from the desk toward the front doors.

She had to wait for him to unlock them again, then practically ran to the Lincoln parked at the curb. She opened the door, tossed the precious fur bundle onto the passenger seat, and hurriedly slipped behind the wheel. Her hands were shaking so badly she could barely insert the key into the ignition lock. When she turned the key in the switch, the motor growled to life. The guard stood at the glass doors, watching her. She waved to him as she pulled away from the curb onto the empty street. He waved back.

She felt weak, a mass of jangled nerves, exhilarated and relieved all at the same time. When she glanced at the digital clock on the car's lighted dash, she realized that only twenty-three minutes had passed. She'd been certain she'd been in the building at least an hour. She'd done it, though. She'd swiped the plans right from under Chance's nose. She started to laugh and couldn't stop.

29

EARLY SUNDAY AFTERNOON, Flame emerged from the jetway at the San Francisco International Airport and walked straight to the waiting Ellery, receiving his welcoming kiss on the cheek. As usual, he asked no questions. He didn't need to. By the time they reached her Russian Hill flat, she'd told him the whole galling mess.

Her suitcases stood in the hallway to her rear bedroom, exactly where Ellery had set them down when they walked in. But the long box she'd brought back with her had been sliced opened and its contents spread over the glass coffee table.

Flame poured more champagne into her fluted glass. The sparkling wine, a gift from Ellery, had been intended to toast her state of newly wedded bliss, but it had become, instead, a means to cool the seething anger that continued to churn inside her. She turned to Ellery, so casually elegant in his lavender cashmere sweater as he lounged against the white sofa.

"More champagne?" she asked.

He waved his partially full glass in absent refusal. "Do you know this is the first time I've drunk champagne at a marital wake? It's a rather novel experience." But his sardonic smile faded, his glance turning thoughtful and sympathetic as he directed it at her. "You sounded so blissfully happy when you called last Sunday, I must admit I never dreamed—"

"Neither did I." She cut him off before he could actually say the maddening words.

He leaned forward to study the black-and-white renderings on the coffee table in front of him, resting his elbows on the knees of his precisely creased trousers. "This is some development he wants to build." Then he lifted his head, suddenly curious. "How did you manage to get all these plans and reports?"

"I have them. What does it matter how?" Flame shrugged.

He responded with a wry smile. "Why did I bother to ask? It's obvious that under the circumstances, he wouldn't have given them to you. Which means you must have purloined them—to put it delicately."

"They're copies. He'll never miss them."

Ellery made no comment to that, and let his attention return to the array of paperwork and plans before him. "The thing that puzzles me is—why Tulsa? Why Oklahoma? This project has to run into the multimillions. Why would he invest that kind of money in this area?"

"You haven't looked at the feasibility and market study." Flame walked over and pulled it from the stack. She flipped it open to a map of the United States with the project site marked and a circle radiating out from it. "If you'll notice, the development is within a four-hundred-and-fifty-mile radius—approximately a day's drive—of every major metropolitan area in the Midwest: Dallas, Houston, Kansas City, St. Louis, Denver, Memphis, New Orleans—and Chicago falls a fraction of an inch outside of that magic line. Nearly one-third of the nation's population lives within that circle. He could easily turn this into the vacation mecca of the Midwest."

"I believe you're right," he said, faintly startled by the discovery. "My God, what a shrewd bastard."

"But he needs Morgan's Walk to do it." She riffled through more of the drawings until she found the site plan. "Because the dam that makes his lake is right here—on what is now *my* land. If Chance has his way, nearly every acre of it will be under water."

"Exactly what do you intend to do with all these plans and blueprints? Obviously you could pin them to a wall and throw darts at them—or fashion them into an effigy of Stuart and burn it. But other than that . . ."

"I'm going to a reputable engineering company and have them review them for me."

"Why?" Ellery frowned, an eyebrow arching. "You know what they are."

"But that's all I know. I'm not an engineer. I can't read a set of plans. Maybe there's something here that I'm not seeing . . . some way that Chance can get my land."

"You keep talking as if you believe he'll try to go through with this project. Surely that's impossible now that you've inherited the land. If you won't sell it to him—and I assume you won't—then he'll have to give it up and count his losses."

"Will he?" she countered. "You don't know how ruthless he can be. It's bred in his bones. Don't forget he married me thinking it would give him control of the land. He wants Morgan's Walk, Ellery." Her fingers tightened around the fluted champagne glass, her voice vibrating with her tautly controlled anger. "His reasons go beyond the time and money he has invested. No, with Chance, it's strictly personal. He hates Morgan's Walk. That's why he searched for and found a way to destroy it. The fact that he'll make millions in the process is merely a bonus. He'll try, and he'll keep trying, Ellery. That's why I have to find a way to stop him."

"This whole thing reeks of a vendetta," he observed, again with that wry movement of his mouth. Flame stiffened, catching the hint of mockery in his voice. "Revenge is sweet and all that."

"No, Ellery, you're wrong," she declared in an icy calm. "Revenge is everything."

30 ✓

MOLLY MALONE EYED the man standing before her desk suspiciously, which she covered with one of her patented, pleasant smiles. "I'm sorry. Mr. Stuart isn't in yet. He plays squash on Thursday mornings, which means he'll be late getting to the office." She pretended to check the day's appointment calendar, which by now she had memorized. "Unfortunately, when he arrives, he has to go straight into a meeting. I'm afraid he'll be tied up all day. What did you need to see him about? Perhaps I can help you."

"I don't think so. It's personal." His tan raincoat was stained and worn, a button missing from the front, and the polyester suit under it didn't look any newer, yet the man carried himself with a quiet authority.

"I see," Molly murmured and took another look at him, trying to guess his age. Somewhere in his early fifties, she thought. And despite the string tie around his neck and the cowboy boots on his feet, she was certain he was neither a rancher nor a farmer. His face didn't have the dark ruddy tan of a man who'd spent his life outdoors, and his eyes didn't crinkle at the corners from squinting at the sun all day. "In that case, why don't you let me make an appointment for you?" she suggested.

"That won't be necessary." The saclike pouches under his eyes and the turned-down corners of his mouth gave him the look of a weary yet extremely patient man. "I'll wait until he comes."

"But he has a—"

"That's all right." He swept aside her objection with an indifferent flick of his hand. "I won't take more than a couple minutes of his time, and I'm sure he can spare me that much before his meeting."

Molly clamped her mouth shut, recognizing that short of having the man thrown out, he wouldn't be persuaded to leave. She turned in a faint huff and busied herself with some papers next to her typewriter, watching him out of the corner of her eye as he wandered over to study a painting on the wall.

"Molly?" Sam called to her from Chance's office, a perplexed note in his voice.

As she rose from her chair, she shot the man another suspicious look, then went into Chance's office. Sam was over by the conference table, a bundle of blueprints under his arm. He turned when she entered the room.

"Some of these plans are in the wrong slots." He frowned. "The architect's drawings are where the blueprints for the dam should be, and the dam blueprints are— It doesn't matter where they are. But somebody's been in them and mixed them all up. I know Chance wouldn't do it. And I certainly didn't. Who else could have gotten into them?"

"They're all there, aren't they?"

Sam nodded affirmatively. "That was the first thing I checked."

"It was probably the cleaning people, then. They pick the oddest places to be thorough in their dusting, then leave cobwebs in the corners for everyone to see." She shrugged it off as unimportant and glanced over her shoulder toward the partially closed door to her office. Lowering her voice, she said, "There's a man out there who insists on seeing Chance when he comes in. He won't give his name or state his business, but I'd swear he's a process server. I can smell them."

Sam's frown deepened. "You think someone's suing the company?"

"What else?" She lifted her hands in an empty gesture, then added, "I think you should go down and warn Chance before he gets on the elevator. He should be here any minute."

"I will." He shoved the rolled blueprints at her. "Take these and put them in my office."

Two of them threatened to unroll when he handed them to her. Molly juggled them for an instant, then they both heard the bell-like *ding* of the elevator. They looked at each other, realizing it was too late.

"Chance Stuart?" came the man's inquiring voice.

"Yes?"

"This is for you." The announcement was followed by the sound of footsteps leaving the outer office to enter the hall.

Molly turned to face the door as Chance walked into his office, scanning the legal-looking document in his hands, his forehead creased in a troubled frown. "A process server," she said to Sam. "Didn't I tell you I could smell them?"

But Sam wasn't interested in the accuracy of her guess as he tried to read from Chance's expression the seriousness of this new occurrence. "We're being sued, I take it. By whom?"

Chance flashed him a quick look, a killing coldness in his eyes, the muscles standing out sharply along his jaw. But he didn't immediately answer the question, striding instead to his desk and tossing the papers on it, then moving to the window behind it and staring out, his head thrown slightly back and his hands thrust into his pockets.

"We're not being sued, Sam," he said curtly. "Flame has petitioned the courts to have our marriage annulled."

"Damn," Sam swore softly.

"Oh, Chance," Molly murmured sympathetically as she took a few uncertain steps toward him. "I'm sorry.."

He pivoted sharply, his glare running to both of them. "I never said I was accepting this as her final answer."

"Of course not." Molly stiffened immediately, lifting her head to show him her total support and confidence.

"Who's her attorney?"

"Guess," Chance countered sarcastically.

"Ben Canon," Sam murmured, then sighed heavily. "You're right. I should've known that." He glanced hesitantly at Chance. "When you saw her on Saturday, did she give you any inkling at all that she was going to do something like this?"

"Yes. But I didn't believe it would come this quickly."

"What are you going to do?" Sam frowned. "What can you do?"

"Stall," he said, and shifted his attention to Molly. "Get Quentin Worthy on the phone and tell him you're messengering over this petition. And tell him to find me the best damned divorce lawyer there is, and I don't care where he has to go to get him. In the meantime, I want any action on this petition postponed. Explain to him that I'm trying to get my wife to agree to a reconciliation."

"You don't really think she will, do you?" Sam questioned skeptically.

"Of course she will," Molly spoke up. "She's hurt and angry and upset right now, and it's all that Morgan woman's fault. But she loves Chance. I know she does. She'll realize that herself. You wait and see—absence will make the heart grow fonder."

Sam shook his head at her eternal optimism. "If you're going to start tossing out clichés, Molly, don't forget: out of sight, out of mind. And there is half a continent between them. You can't get much more out of sight than that."

"If the two of you are finished trading clichés, then I'd like to know if there are any appointments on my calendar for tomorrow that can't be postponed," Chance broke in.

Molly flashed him a guilty look of apology and replied, "You're supposed to have breakfast with the governor in the morning—at the governor's mansion in Oklahoma City—but as far as the rest are concerned, they could easily be switched to another day. I don't recall anything else that's pressing."

"In that case, after you get in touch with Quentin Worthy, call Mick Donovan and advise him that we'll be flying to San Francisco when we leave the capital tomorrow."

31 ❧

MALCOM POWELL'S DRIVER had the umbrella at the ready, its ribbed canopy opened to shield her from the Thursday afternoon drizzle, when Flame stepped from the car. "Thank you, Arthur." She flashed him a hurried smile as she took the umbrella from him and held it over her head.

He touched his cap to her. "See you next week."

She nodded a brief acknowledgment to that and moved away from the car, cutting across the flow of scurrying pedestrians to reach the entrance to the office building. Ellery was there, holding the glass door open for her, obviously just returning from lunch himself.

Under the shelter of the entrance's overhang, Flame paused long enough to lower her umbrella and release the catch to close it. Ellery sent a glance after the limousine pulling away from the curb.

"I see you had lunch with the Great One today," he observed.

"Yes."

His eyebrow lifted at her clipped answer, but she ignored it as she brushed past him to enter the building. In two strides, Ellery drew even with her again, matching her brisk pace to the elevators.

"That bad, was it?"

"I beg your pardon." She pretended she didn't know what he was talking about.

"You're still gritting your teeth. Which would suggest your luncheon with Mr. Powell was something less than a pleasant experience."

She started to deny it, but what was the point? Ellery knew her moods too well. "Unfortunately, Malcom wasn't as tactful as other clients and co-workers have been."

"Asked you a lot of questions about your breakup with Stuart, did he?" Ellery guessed.

"That's one way of putting it, yes."

It had begun almost the moment she'd walked into his office, her long paisley velvet skirt swinging about the calves of her boots. She hadn't crossed the length of the room to the massive antique desk where Malcom stood; instead, she'd stopped midway and deposited her handbag on a chair.

"I'm sorry I'm late, Malcom." She'd talked at him as she tugged off her gloves and unbuttoned her poncho-style raincoat, careful to avoid the probing study of his gray eyes. "Debbie—my assistant—is home with the flu. I have a temporary in her place. When they rang up to say Arthur was waiting for me downstairs, I was on the phone with another client. And she never passed the message on to me before she left on her lunch break." She'd sent him an apologetic smile as he moved out from behind his desk, angling toward her.

"I understand." But the smoothness of his reply had failed to conceal the underlying edge of irritation in his voice, reminding Flame that Malcom Powell wasn't a man who liked to be kept waiting.

When she'd squared around to face him, she'd been confronted by the power of his presence. She'd stared at the muscular swell to his chest, arms, and neck that was impressive, and the broadness of his square jaw and the forceful thrust of his dimpled chin that spoke of his iron will. She'd wondered how she could have possibly forgotten in two short weeks.

The hard gleam in his gray eyes had been difficult to meet. "Although I must admit I had started to suspect that you'd run off again with your lover. Or —should I say your husband?"

Stung by his probing taunt, Flame had let her gaze drop and masked it by sweeping off her cape and draping it on the chair with her purse. "That was a mistake." She'd fallen back on what had become her stock answer these past few days. "One that I've taken steps to correct as soon as possible." She'd feigned a smile of indifference and deliberately glanced at the pocket doors to Malcom's private dining room, slid open to reveal the table set for two within. "We're having lunch here. How nice."

"I told you Stuart wasn't the man for you."

No one else had pursued the subject, taking her reply as the final word on the matter. But not Malcom.

"So you did—and you were right," she'd admitted, more sharply than she'd intended. "But if you asked me here today to gloat—"

"Not to gloat, but simply to remind you that I'm here." His gray glance had wandered over her in an assessing fashion, the look in his eyes turning warm. "My feelings toward you haven't changed, Flame . . . nor my desires."

"I think you should be able to appreciate that after making one mistake, I'm not about to make another."

"And I think . . . that whatever happened between you and Stuart must have been a bitter blow to your pride."

"It was more than my pride he hurt!" She'd flared immediately, then abruptly turned away, struggling to regain control of her emotions. "If you don't mind, Malcom, I'd rather not discuss any of this," she'd insisted curtly.

"I can see that," he'd murmured. "But I can't help being curious. I've never seen this much anger in you, Flame—not even when you've lost your temper with me."

"Maybe I have cause."

"Maybe you do," he'd said in a considering way. "And maybe a glass of your favorite chardonnay will cool it a little."

They'd gone into his private dining room then, but that hadn't been the end of it. Several times during the course of the meal, Malcom had alluded in some way to Chance and her breakup as if he knew, or guessed, that there was a great deal more to the story than she was telling.

"I think Malcom hoped I'd weep on his shoulder," she said to Ellery as they joined the crowd of workers waiting in front of the elevators. "But I don't need his shoulder—or anyone else's."

"Speaking of shoulders, we'll have the artwork finished on the Shodderly ad next week." Interrupted by the arrival of an elevator, Ellery waited until they'd wedged a space inside, then picked up where he'd left off. "Do you want to take a look at it a week from Friday?"

"It would have to be first thing. I have an appointment in Oakland that afternoon."

"What's in Oakland?" Ellery frowned.

"Thorgood Engineering."

"I've never heard of them. When did the agency acquire that company for a client?"

"They aren't a client. I'm seeing them on a personal matter." The elevator came to a stop at the agency's floor. "Excuse us, please." She squeezed her way through the jam of people to the open doors, with Ellery right behind her.

"This is about those plans of Stuart's, isn't it?" he said.

Nodding an affirmative answer, Flame walked by the receptionist's desk and into the hall that led to her office. "If nothing else, they can tell me the steps Chance would have to take in order to have my land condemned for his lake."

"Time is definitely not lying idle in your hands, is it?" Ellery murmured.

"No. And you can bet he isn't wasting any either. Which is why I can't afford to sit back and wait to find out what his first move will be. . . ."

He caught her arm, stopping her short of her assistant's office and eyeing her with a knowing look. "Why do I have the feeling that you already have some scheme in motion? And I don't mean this engineering thing."

Flame smiled, with just a hint of smugness. "When I talked yesterday to Ben Canon—my attorney in Tulsa—I asked him to find out whether Morgan's Walk met the criteria for a listing in the National Register of Historic Places. If it does, there might be some objection to having such a house sitting on the bottom of a lake."

"Very good." Ellery inclined his head in approval.

"I thought so." But she also knew it was much too early to be congratulating herself. Still, she couldn't help feeling a little pleased as she turned and entered her assistant's office. "Did any messages come for me while I was gone, Miss Austin?" She didn't trust the temporary to automatically pass them on to her after this noon's fiasco.

"Just two." The bright-eyed brunette promptly plucked them from her desk top and handed them to Flame, then wasted a sidelong glance at Ellery.

"Thank you." Flame scanned the pair of messages as she crossed to her office door.

"Oh, Ms. Bennett, wait." The brunette's anxious call turned her around. "I forgot," she said guiltily. "There's a man waiting in your office for you."

"In my office? Who?"

"I believe his name was Stuart. He said you knew him."

Too furious to speak, Flame longed to strangle the girl. Instead she swung on Ellery. "I know." He held up a hand, staving off any need for words. "I'll call the service for you and have her replaced."

"Did I do something wrong?"

As Flame swept into her office, she heard Ellery say, "I think that's a safe assumption, Miss Austin."

Chance stood at the window, his back to the door, when she came through. He looked back, angling his wide shoulders at her, then slowly turned to face her. Just for an instant, under the full impact of his gaze, she felt the tear of old feelings. Just as quickly she blocked them out, and pushed the door shut behind her.

"What are you doing here?" she demanded.

"I believe you asked the same thing the last time we saw each other." The grooves on either side of his mouth deepened in a mock smile. "And my answer is the same—I came to see you."

"I thought I made it clear that I didn't want to see you." Flame crossed to her desk.

"I can't accept that." He wandered over to stand in front of her.

"You have no choice," she snapped. "And what do you mean coming into my office and making yourself at home as if—"

"—as if I was your husband?"

"That isn't what I was going to say!"

"No, it probably wasn't," he conceded with a slight dip of his head. "I decided it would be better to wait here than in the outer office where any number of your co-workers might see me. I thought it might spare you a lot of needless questions."

"Such consideration would be touching if it came from anyone other than you." She sat down behind her desk and began going through the stack of mail on top of it, pretending to scan the letters although not absorbing one word.

"Flame, I didn't come here to make you upset or angry—"

"Then why are you here?" She finally lifted her glance to his face, taking in the familiar sight of its smooth, rakish lines, so very strong, so very compelling.

"I came to talk to you."

She arched him a scornful look. "Don't you mean—to talk me out of Morgan's Walk?"

"No, I don't." There was a quietness to his voice that she couldn't ignore. "You've condemned me without hearing me out. I'm not saying that when you do, you'll change your mind. But you owe me that much, Flame."

"I don't see it that way," she replied stiffly.

"Maybe you don't, but what harm will it do to listen? Have dinner with me tonight."

She started to reject his invitation hotly, then another thought occurred to her and she wavered, covering her hesitation by rising from her chair and moving away from the desk and Chance at right angles. "Where are you staying?"

"The Carrington."

She wheeled to face him, still gripped with indecision and unwilling to act impulsively a second time. "Let me think about it and call you later at the hotel."

Chance sensed she was on the verge of agreeing to meet him. But he also had the feeling that if he pushed her, she'd refuse. He backed off.

"All right." He nodded slowly in acceptance. "I'll wait to hear from you."

She was surprised that he'd given in so easily. She'd expected him to press her for an answer. She wondered why he hadn't as he walked out of her office. Was he that confident she would ultimately accept? Did it matter if he was? He couldn't possibly have guessed the reason she was contemplating meeting him.

Chance had barely left her office when Ellery walked in. His glance ran over her, quick with concern. "Are you all right?"

"Did you think I wouldn't be?"

"I wasn't sure."

"I promise you, Ellery, I'm not about to fall apart simply because I saw him again." She walked back to her desk.

"What did he want?"

Her mouth twisted in a humorless smile. "He wants me to have dinner with him tonight so we can talk."

"You refused, of course."

"Not yet."

For several seconds, Ellery was silent, studying her with a probing eye. "Some devious wheels are turning in that head of yours."

Flame smiled. "He's made his first move. He's going to try to win me back. He convinced me once before that he loved me, why shouldn't he think that he could do it again? What would happen, Ellery, if I let him think he might succeed?" she wondered aloud.

"Do you know what you're saying?"

She ignored his question and continued to talk out her stream of consciousness. "If I strung him along, he wouldn't dare contest the will—or make any overt move to get control of Morgan's Walk. And think of the time it would gain me."

"Stuart isn't a man to be easily tricked."

"I know." She shrugged that off. "But he'll also expect me to play hard-to-get. And that won't be difficult at all."

"This isn't a game," Ellery warned.

She turned her overly bright green eyes on him, the devil of malice in them. "Yes, it is. It's called 'deceit'—I learned it from an expert."

Flame deliberately waited until nearly six o'clock to call Chance and accept his invitation. When he offered to pick her up, she refused. "We can dine at your hotel," she said. "I'll meet you in the restaurant at eight."

In the hotel's multitiered dining room, Chance observed Flame's approach as the maître d' escorted her to his table. He paid little attention to the way heads turned when she passed, for he was wholly absorbed by the striking picture she made coming toward him, dramatic in a high-necked black-and-white suit in a spotted silk moire. The lofty way she carried her head and the confident swing of her square shoulders came naturally to her, like the fiery gold color of her hair. That they created a stir and caught the eye was purely incidental. She'd done more than that to him, though. She'd settled much of his restlessness of spirit, she'd aroused his masculine instincts to possess and protect. He hadn't realized how much of either until she'd walked out. He wanted her back. He had to have her back. Chance was as single-minded in this as he was in getting Morgan's Walk.

When she neared the table, he stood to greet her. Her glance swept him coolly as she murmured a greeting, then let the maître d' seat her in the chair opposite him. The waiter arrived instantly to ask if she would like something from the bar. Her hesitation was momentary, her glance running to the glass of scotch before him, then she ordered a glass of chardonnay.

Once they were alone at the table, she finally met his gaze with a look of studied indifference. "I believe this is a first," she said. "No peach champagne and no orchids."

"I didn't think it would be appropriate." He scanned the strong modeling of her features, looking for a break somewhere in the reserve she'd thrown up against him. But he couldn't penetrate the green mystery of her eyes, so cool and aloof to him now. He would have preferred to face the fire and temper she'd shown him in her office rather than this air of tolerance and disinterest.

"You were right. It wouldn't be." Then her attention was pulled away from him as the waiter returned with her wine. She thanked him with a smile—the first Chance had seen on her lips since he'd kissed her goodbye the morning he left for Texas—the morning that had signaled an end to the rare happiness he'd known. When she faced him again, all trace of the smile was gone. He felt a sweep of hot anger and immediately clamped down on it, recognizing it would get him nowhere with her.

He lifted his glass of scotch in a toast. "Thank you," he said.

"For what?" She held her wineglass, as if unprepared to sip from it until she knew the answer.

"For coming tonight."

"Chance Stuart—humble?" she mocked. "I find that extremely difficult to believe."

He took a drink of his scotch, the burn of it in his throat matching his own emotional rawness. But he'd learned long ago not to let such feelings show. "I received my notice that you're seeking an annulment."

Now she took a sip of her wine. "I suppose you intend to fight it."

"If I thought it would do any good, I would." By his definition, stalling was not the same as fighting.

The cool curve of her lips challenged. "Don't you mean—if you thought it would get you Morgan's Walk, you would?"

"Flame, I didn't ask you here tonight to talk about Morgan's Walk."

"Really?" Skepticism riddled her voice.

"I want to talk about us."

"There is no 'us,' if you're referring to you and me." She paused, a glint of derisive amusement appearing briefly in her eyes. "Of course, by 'us' you could also be referring to me and Morgan's Walk."

"Once before I told you I made a mistake in not telling you Hattie Morgan was my aunt—and that Morgan's Walk would have been left to me if she hadn't learned about you. And I made a mistake in not telling you I wanted that land. But that wasn't my biggest mistake," he said, carefully choosing his words. "My biggest one was wanting both. I was greedy, Flame. When I said I loved you, that wasn't a lie. If there wasn't a Morgan's Walk, I'd still want you for my wife."

Something quick and surprised momentarily flickered in her expression, then a wary doubt set in as she eyed him steadily, searching his face. Within seconds, her glance fell to the wineglass, a cynicism edging the corners of her mouth.

"That's a safe thing to say, isn't it, Chance? It almost sounds convincing. There's just one problem—there *is* a Morgan's Walk. There always will be. So that situation will never arise." She lifted her glass, her eyes mocking him. "Aren't you lucky?"

"How can I be when I lost you both?" he reasoned smoothly.

"Perhaps you're right," she conceded, her glance running over him again. "But it isn't over, is it? You can still contest Hattie's will. Who knows? Maybe you'll even win."

He sat before her, dark and elegant in his tailored navy pinstriped suit and pale silk tie, the soft candlelight throwing the planes and hollows of his sculptured face in sharp relief. Tonight, perhaps more than any other night, he had the look of a gambler, a man who dared to do what others only dreamed. He was a man who lived on the edge of danger and enjoyed the view. But she wasn't swayed by that as she'd been before, reminding herself that gamblers were notorious for cheating and conning people.

"I don't plan to contest the will, Flame. It wouldn't accomplish anything for either of us, except to tie up the title in the courts for years and cost a fortune in attorney fees."

She relaxed a little, aware that a court fight was a battle she couldn't afford to wage. That was the advantage Chance had over her; he could outspend her ten thousand to one and not miss a penny of it. At the same time, she didn't dare trust that he truly meant what he said.

"Plans can always change, though, can't they?" she challenged, aware that her only hope was to be able to stall Chance long enough to give Ben Canon time to get the estate settled, a process the Oklahoma lawyer was doing his best to expedite.

"It's possible," he agreed, "but highly unlikely."

"I notice you didn't rule out the possibility," she said.

"I don't rule anything out. And I'd like to persuade you to do the same."

"Me?" She frowned, unsure what he meant by that.

He looked at her, something strong and vivid—and unsettling—in his gaze. "Hasn't it occurred to you that I might be telling you the truth, that I might honestly be in love with you, and I would have wanted you for my wife whether you'd been Hattie's heir or not?" As she started to reply, he cut her off. "I don't want you to answer that, only to consider it as a possibility. Nothing more. Otherwise we'll end up arguing all night. Why don't we call a truce? I won't try to convince you to change your mind about me if you won't bring up Morgan's Walk and the way I tried to deceive you over it. Agreed?"

Flame hesitated, not entirely sure that was wise. Yet to refuse might indicate a vulnerability on her part. "Why not?" she said. "At least it will guarantee a quiet dinner."

Chance smiled at that. "I think we'll be able to find something to talk about." He picked up the menu. "Speaking of dinner, why don't we decide what to order. I'm told the rack of lamb here is excellent."

Dinner proved to be more of an ordeal than Flame had expected. She'd forgotten how incredibly persuasive Chance could be when he set out to charm. More than once she'd caught herself responding to that seductive smile of his or that lazy glint in his eyes. Habit, that's all it was—an ingrained reaction to the same stimuli. But there was danger in that, even though such inadvertent responses also served her purpose by letting him think that, with persistence, he might succeed in winning her back.

When Chance suggested an after-dinner drink, Flame refused. Once she would have lingered, wanting to prolong their time together, but not anymore. Instead, she made her excuses to leave, explaining that she had an early day tomorrow and some work to finish tonight in preparation for it. She doubted that he believed her. Not that it mattered. If he chose to think she was running from him, that was all the better.

But Chance didn't make it easy for her to escape, insisting that he see her safely into a cab. She was obliged to wait while he summoned the waiter and signed the check. As she crossed the lobby with his hand resting lightly on her lower back, Flame was reminded of the time she'd gone up those elevators with him to his suite. She felt sick and angry all over again when she remembered the way she'd been taken in by all his smooth lies. Never again.

Outside in the night-cool, the doorman whistled for a taxi. But it was Chance who stepped forward to open the door for her when it drove up.

"Thank you for dinner," she said and started to climb in.

The touch of his hand on her arm checked that movement. "I want to see you again, Flame." It wasn't a request or a plea, merely a statement of his desires.

She looked at him, conscious of the quiet intensity of his gaze that had once made her believe he cared deeply about her. "I don't know."

"I'm flying to Tahoe in the morning—to check on my project there," he said. "Will you come with me?"

"In your jet? So you can spirit me off to some faraway place for a wildly romantic weekend? No thank you," she declared with a firm shake of her head. "I've been through that before."

"Then join me there," he persisted.

She hesitated, then drew away from him and slid into the cab. Inside, she glanced back at him. "I'll think about it."

He didn't like her answer, but, as she expected, he didn't press her for a more definite one.

The mirror-smooth lake reflected the sapphire blue of the sky and the snow-capped peaks of the Sierras. But the postcard-perfect setting was marred by the belching roar of machinery and the rattling whir of riveters' guns as the construction raced to get the steel superstructure up and closed in before the first heavy snows of winter fell.

In a hard hat, Chance walked among the customary construction rubble on the high-rise hotel site, flanked by the structural engineer and the architect, and trailed by his on-site construction manager, the steel contractor, and his foreman. He stopped to watch a crane swing a steel beam into place, then questioned the architect about the number of cars that could be accommodated beneath the hotel's porte cochere, shouting to make himself heard above the racket.

A steelworker hot-footed it across the site, waving an arm to get their attention. Spotting him, Chance paused and waited for the man to reach them.

The steel contractor stepped forward to intercept him. "What's the problem?"

He looked at Chance and motioned over his shoulder in the direction of the office trailer. "There's a lady here wantin' to see Mr. Stuart," he yelled his answer.

Chance lifted his head sharply and glanced at the trailer, everything tensing inside him. Flame. She'd come. Without a word, he walked away from the others and headed for the trailer, his stride lengthening and quickening as he neared it. He pulled the door open, his image of her vivid and bright, all his acute hungers revived.

He stepped inside and stopped short. "Lucianna." He was angry, frustrated, the bitterness of disappointment strong on his tongue. "What are you doing here?"

"I came to see you, of course." All warm smiles and glowing eyes, she came to him. He caught at her, his arms stiffening to prevent the kiss she wanted to give him. "Sam told me you were here. Now, don't be angry with him. He was thinking of you. This is a time when you should be with friends."

"You should have called first," he said tightly. "I've asked Flame to join me here."

"Wonderful." Lucianna shrugged her lack of concern and smiled. "When she comes, I promise I'll disappear without a trace."

But Flame didn't come.

32

THE OATMEAL KNIT of her long jacket flared slightly from the matching shaped turtleneck dress as Flame swept aggressively into Karl Bronsky's office at Thurgood Engineering, an eagerness in her stride that she didn't even try to contain. Her glance darted automatically to the drafting table in the corner, then fell on the rolled plans lying on the desk and finally lifted to the thin, tanned man coming around the desk to welcome her.

"It's good to see you again, Ms. Bennett. Please have a seat." Karl Bronsky was a freckle-faced man in his midforties with mild eyes and a habit of nodding with each spurt of talk, as he did now. "The traffic on the Bay Bridge must have been murder. It always is on a Friday, with everybody racing to get out of the city for the weekend."

"It was." But she wasn't interested in wasting time exchanging pleasantries about the traffic or the weather. "When I talked to you this morning, you indicated you had finished your review of the plans I left with you."

"I did." Again there was that sharp nod of his head as he circled back around his desk.

"What did you think of them?"

"What did I think? I think it's one helluva ambitious project—if you'll pardon my language—the kind every engineer dreams about being a part of."

"Then . . ." She paused, choosing her words carefully. ". . . you didn't see any flaw in them."

"You have to understand, Ms. Bennett, these are in the preliminary stage. They aren't finished working drawings. Which isn't to say a lot of thought hasn't gone into them. Obviously it has. In my opinion, it's definitely a viable project."

"I see." She tried not to let her disappointment show.

"Now you asked me specifically to look at the plans for the dam." He began going through the stack of rolled blueprints and drawings on his desk. "As you know, none of these contains the name of the firm responsible for drawing up the plans—or any reference to its location."

"I know." She'd made certain all such references were removed before she'd given them to him for review. She hadn't wanted to run the risk that someone in Thurgood Engineering might know someone with the engineering firm Chance had used. Fields of business tended to be small worlds, and she didn't want word accidentally getting back that she was in possession of these plans.

"Anyway, I don't know who engineered the plans on the dam, but he seems to be a highly competent individual—or group of individuals." He unrolled one of the sets and anchored the corners down with a paperweight, pencil holder, stapler, and desk pen set. "As a matter of fact, I only question him on one area. Which isn't to say I think he's wrong. It's impossible to second-guess somebody when you aren't in possession of all the facts."

"What did you question?" Flame noticed that he'd unrolled the overall site plan.

He leaned over it, a faintly puzzled look clouding his sunny freckles. "You did say that you owned this valley and these people had come to you with the proposition for this massive project."

"Yes."

"The thing I can't figure out—at least not without more information—is why they chose this particular site for the dam and why they would want to flood the entire valley."

"What do you mean?" She tried to check the sudden leap of hope, reminding herself it was too premature. "Where else could they build it?"

"Again, you have to recognize, Ms. Bennett, that I haven't seen the actual site. I'm just going by these plans. But when I look at this, the most logical location for the dam would seem to be this neck of hills here—" He pointed it out to her on the plan. "—well north of the present site. Which would leave this entire south section of the valley intact."

Which was also where the house and all the ranch buildings were located, Flame realized. She stared at the map, too stunned for an instant to react.

"Think of the golf course and country club that could be built in this valley —and what a complement it would be to the rest of the development. It would definitely be an improvement over that rolling dervish of a course they show winding through the hills now." He raced on with his thoughts. "Naturally, it would change the shape of the lake—send it into this valley to the northwest. To me that would be a better location for the marina and hotel with these hills sheltering it from high winds. Changing the dam site opens up a whole new set of options. You could put in a landing strip for private aircraft, and, Lord knows, a development like this is going to attract the kind of people who have their own planes. The way it stands now, you'd have to flatten a hill to put an airstrip in, and cost-wise it probably wouldn't be feasible."

"Then, why—" But she knew why. Chance hated Morgan's Walk. He wanted to destroy it. He wanted it at the bottom of the lake.

Karl Bronsky straightened, regret bringing two thin lines to his forehead. "I shouldn't have gone on like that. Again, I have to stress that the engineer who did this work and chose this site over the one I suggested may have very sound reasons."

"Such as?"

"Test borings could have shown him that this location wouldn't support a dam without costly subshoring. Maybe here he can anchor it to bedrock for a fraction of the money." He shrugged, indicating a multitude of possibilities. "Without inspecting the site and doing the necessary tests, I'm only guessing, Ms. Bennett."

"Mr. Bronsky." She spoke slowly, playing with all the possibilities in her mind, even the outrageous ones. "Is it possible that sometime within the next two weeks you could fly to Oklahoma with me and look at the property yourself?"

"Oklahoma—is that where it is?" he said, then breathed in deeply, considering her suggestion with obvious interest. "I suppose I could arrange my schedule to free up a couple of days."

"Good, because I'd like to know if it's absolutely necessary for all of my land to be flooded." She smiled faintly. "It's not that I don't trust the work of this engineer. I'd just like a second opinion."

"I don't blame you. In fact, it's probably the smart thing to do."

The traffic light ahead turned red and the limousine eased to a smooth stop at the crosswalk. From the rear seat, Flame watched as a cable car clanged across the intersection. Idly, her glance swung to Malcom's driver, Arthur, separated from the rear passenger area by a sliding glass partition. He'd turned the radio to an easy-listening station and the soothing music of an old André Previn tune came softly over the stereo speakers.

Turning her head on the back rest, she looked at Malcom and smiled faintly. "If I closed my eyes, I think I could fall asleep."

The cleft in his chin deepened slightly, amusement glinting in his eyes. "I thought you had."

"After that marvelous lunch, can you blame me?" Her smile widened, but the wonderfully lethargic feeling remained, making her feel all lazy and replete. "Right now it wouldn't take much persuasion to turn me into an advocate of siestas."

With customary keenness his gaze examined her face. "You do look tired."

She didn't deny that she was. "I've been on the go constantly for the last ten days trying to get everything caught up so I can leave tomorrow for Tulsa. This is the first time I've been able to sit back and truly relax in days—and I have you to thank for it."

"Tulsa. That's Stuart territory you know," he challenged, closely watching her reaction to Chance's name.

Flame smiled with a degree of cool unconcern. "He doesn't have an exclusive on it, Malcom."

"Do you intend to see him while you're there?" he asked, aware that she'd met with him before.

"Possibly." Although she had agreed to see Chance, that didn't mean she would. She'd canceled meetings with him before. "It depends on my schedule. There are a lot of legal matters that I need to clear up regarding the settlement of Hattie's estate—documents to be signed, that sort of thing."

She didn't mention that the engineer Karl Bronsky would be flying the day after she arrived to meet with her and look over Morgan's Walk, specifically the proposed dam site and his alternative. She had yet to confide in Malcom the reasons behind her split with Chance or the battle ahead of her to prevent Chance from acquiring control of the land he'd married her to get.

Malcom frowned thoughtfully, his gaze narrowing. "I don't understand why you see him when you keep saying you're through with him."

She smiled away his remark, a playfully chiding light entering her eyes.

"You make it sound as if he's been my constant companion, Malcom. I've only met him twice. And contrary to recent rumors, there is no reconciliation in the works."

There wasn't a trace of doubt in her voice. Was she over him? Malcom wondered. It was true she no longer reacted hostilely to the mere mention of Stuart, but a vindictive gleam appeared in her eyes each time his name was brought up.

The traffic light turned green and the limousine rolled forward with little sensation of motion to its passengers. "How long will you be in Tulsa?"

"Just over the weekend. I'll be back the first of the week." She glanced at him curiously. "Why?"

"I was wondering what your plans are now that you've become a woman of property and independent means." He smiled to conceal the fact that he didn't like the idea of Flame going to Tulsa, even for a brief time—any more than he liked the idea that she might be meeting Stuart while she was there. "Is this preliminary to a permanent move?"

The possibility she might move out of easy reach . . . beyond his influence . . . had concerned him ever since she'd told him about her inheritance of a large ranching estate in Oklahoma.

"*Modestly* independent means," she corrected lightly. "Certainly not enough to induce me to resign from the agency."

"Good." Malcom smiled in disguised relief. "That means I won't have to work with a new account executive."

She gave him a look of mock reproval. "Next, you'll be trying to convince me you're only interested in my mind."

"I admit your company is mentally stimulating," he replied, matching her bantering tone, then paused, letting his gaze travel slowly down her curved figure. "Unfortunately I haven't had the opportunity to discover how stimulating you can be in . . . other ways."

She released an earthy laugh. "You never give up, do you, Malcom? If persistence was a virtue, you'd be the most virtuous man I know."

His smile widened. "It's called wearing down the opposition."

"You're definitely an expert at the game," Flame declared, a hint of amusement remaining in her voice.

His look grew serious and wanting. "Does that mean I'm finally making progress?"

She started to deny that, then paused to look at him, suddenly recalling how comfortable and at ease she had been with him these last two hours. Wasn't that rare—as rare as the heady excitement she'd known with Chance?

Giving him the most honest answer she could, she said, "I don't know, Malcom."

He said nothing to that, simply took her hand and lifted it up to press a kiss in its palm as the limousine came to a stop in front of the agency's building. Arthur stepped out and opened the passenger door for her, extending a hand to help her out. She withdrew her fingers from Malcom's grasp and climbed out of the car, then turned back.

"Thank you for lunch . . . and for your company, Malcom."

"We'll talk again next week after you get back from Tulsa," he promised, the possessive light in his gray eyes even bolder than before.

Slowly and thoughtfully, Flame turned and walked to the building's entrance.

33 ✦

SUNDAY MORNING, Flame walked the freckle-faced Karl Bronsky to the front door of Morgan's Walk, his preliminary inspections of the land completed. Charlie Rainwater waited outside to drive him to the airport.

"Thanks again for the hospitality," he said. "I didn't mean to impose."

"You didn't," she assured him. "We'll talk when I get back to San Francisco."

"Right." Then he was out the door.

Flushed with a feeling of victory, Flame closed the door behind him and turned, barely able to contain her excitement. Then she saw Maxine standing in the foyer watching her.

"Is Mr. Bronsky leaving already?" The housekeeper frowned.

"Yes." She was instantly alert, recalling the foreman's warning that Hattie had long doubted Maxine's loyalty. According to him, she'd never made it a secret that her sympathies were with Chance. If there was any leak at Morgan's Walk, the housekeeper was the likely source. "Charlie's taking him to the airport to catch his flight."

"It seems to me it was hardly worth his time to fly out here," the woman declared. "The two of you arrive in time for supper last night, then he takes off with Charlie first thing this morning and stays gone most of the day. He couldn't have spent more than an hour with you. That's a funny way to treat your host, if you ask me."

"Karl's a city boy. He's never been on a working ranch before and he was fascinated by it. Maybe he always dreamed of being a cowboy when he grew up." Flame shrugged to indicate her lack of concern.

"What does he do for a living?" Maxine asked curiously.

"What does anybody do who lives in a city? He works in an office surrounded by four walls."

If Maxine noticed her avoidance of a direct answer, she gave no sign of it. "Ben's waiting in the library to see you."

"Will you bring—"

"I already took him a pot of coffee, and I included an extra cup for you."

"Thank you, Maxine. That will be all." With long, swinging strides, Flame crossed the foyer and walked down the hall to the library, her spirits lifting again with that inner sense of triumph.

She entered the library, then turned, with hardly a break in motion, and drew the pocket doors closed. A fire blazed in the hearth, the cheery crackle of its flames matching her ebullient mood as she crossed to the desk. Ben Canon sat behind it, his diminutive frame dwarfed even more by its massive size. She stopped short when she saw the coffee tray and the spread of legal papers before him.

"The plans. Where are they?"

"I rolled them up and set them in the corner." With a swing of his balding head to the right, he directed her attention to the plans propped against the bookshelves behind him, half-hidden by the walnut stand supporting a world globe.

"Maxine didn't see them, did she?"

"No. I already had them put away when she brought the coffee."

"Good." Flame relaxed a little then.

"Did your engineer friend get off all right?"

She nodded absently as she retrieved the site plan and spread it out on the desk. "Charlie's taken him to the airport. I'm afraid Karl walked poor Charlie's legs off today." A hint of a smile touched her mouth. "To hear him tell it, Karl tramped every foot of the hills at both locations, and even climbed down to inspect the riverbanks. Just before he left, Karl told me his visual inspection hasn't given him any reason to believe that the dam couldn't be built on the north site. I've authorized him to do whatever test borings are necessary—and I also told him to bring in a crew from the coast, not to use anyone locally. I don't want Chance to find out what we're up to."

"What *are* you up to?" Ben Canon rocked back in the desk chair and folded his pudgy hands across his chest to study her with a puzzled, penetrating look. "As your attorney, don't you think I should know?"

"I want to prove this second dam site is viable. You've already warned me about the political power and influence Chance wields. If we have to fight a condemnation attempt, this might be a weapon for us—an alternative to his proposal that will, at least, save the house and part of the valley."

She had another idea, too—one she'd been toying with ever since Karl Bronsky had brought up the possibility of another dam site—but she didn't mention it to Ben Canon. She knew how crazy, how impossible, it would sound to him. It probably was, but she hadn't been able to totally convince herself of that yet.

"It might work." He nodded slowly in thoughtful approval. "Is that it?"

"I was curious about something else," she admitted, and moved the site plan over in front of him. "This valley on the northwest side, it doesn't appear that Chance owns it—or has optioned it. I'd like to find out who owns it."

"It's probably the Starret place, but I'll stop into the county courthouse and check the tax rolls to make sure."

"I think it would be better if you didn't do it yourself, Ben. If Chance finds out, he might wonder why you're interested, and we don't want to tip our hand to him."

"You sound remarkably like Hattie," the lawyer observed, then humphed a short laugh. "She's probably turning circles in her grave knowing you've invited him here to dinner tonight."

"Maybe," Flame admitted as she began rolling up the site plan. "And maybe she'd approve." This would mark the third time since their separation that she'd met with Chance, and the first time it wouldn't be at a public place. That part didn't concern her. She was confident of her ability to handle him, even if sometimes she momentarily let herself be attracted to him again. No, not to him, she quickly corrected that thought. She was attracted by the memory of how it had been between them before she'd discovered he was only using her. That sense of loving and being loved had been powerful then.

Ben Canon rocked forward in his chair, a rare grimness pulling at the corners of his mouth. "I wish you could persuade Stuart to tip his hand."

Aware that the crafty old lawyer never made idle comments, Flame glanced at him sharply, noting the look of heavy concentration that creased his brow as he studied the papers before him, the ones he'd been going over when she came in. "You had a reason for saying that, Ben. What is it?"

"As you know, the inventory and appraisal of all of Hattie's assets has been completed—along with compilation of all the outstanding debts, mortgages, and bank notes. While I was going over them to establish the worth of her estate, I came across something that bothers me."

"What?"

"The bank sold the mortgage on Morgan's Walk last spring."

She immediately tensed. "To whom? Chance?"

"I don't know, and that's what bothers me. I have the name of a corporation that's the new mortgage holder, but I can't trace the true owner. Which makes me suspect that I'd find Chance at the end of the maze of holding companies and private trusts. Unfortunately I can't prove it."

Flame turned away, bitterly realizing just how hollow and fleeting that sense of victory could be. "He knows how to stack the deck, doesn't he?"

"You could say that."

"I suppose he can call the entire mortgage due."

"He can and—more than likely—he will."

"What about the money from Hattie's life insurance policy?"

"There's enough to pay the estate tax and give you about six months' operating capital. I'm afraid the only way you're going to be able to pay off the mortgage to Chance is to find yourself another lender. And, I have to be honest, Flame, that isn't going to be easy."

"Why? The ranch is worth it."

"The value's there, yes. But good management and the ability to repay— that's what a lender will look at very hard, especially these days with so many family farms and ranches going under. And you know next to nothing about the ranching business."

"I don't, but Charlie Rainwater—"

"—is old. Old enough to draw Social Security. It's time reality was faced, Flame." He handed her a sheaf of papers. "Morgan's Walk is something of a white elephant—especially this old house. As you can see from those cost/ income statements, the ranching operation itself has shown marginal profits the last few years. And nearly every bit has gone into the maintenance and upkeep on this building." He paused, regret entering his expression. "I know how much Hattie loved this place, and, in my own way, I fought as hard as she did to keep it from falling into Stuart's hands. But realistically speaking, if this house wasn't out here in the country, I'd recommend that you donate it to some local histori- cal society for a museum—anything to get out from under its costs. I don't mean to sound like the prophet of doom, Flame, but if the cattle market should go down or the calving losses in the spring are high or Charlie's health goes bad and your new manager isn't as sharp as he is, you could be in trouble. I'm telling you all this to make sure that you see you're going to have a tough time of it all the way around . . . especially with this mortgage business."

"I see," she murmured, then added wryly, "At least I'm beginning to." She stared at the papers in her hand. "May I keep these and look them over?"

"By all means," Ben nodded. "Those are your copies." He set his briefcase on top of the desk and flipped it open. "I have some documents that require your signature." He laid them out for her and gave her a pen. "With luck, and no interference from Stuart, by the end of next week Morgan's Walk and everything on it will officially be yours."

"Good," she said, although at the moment she was beginning to wonder about that.

"Oh, and something else." He reached inside his briefcase again and took out a newspaper clipping. "This was in a Reno paper recently. I thought you might like to see it—just in case Stuart decides to give you any problems about the annulment."

The newspaper photograph showed a smiling Chance and beaming Lucianna, and the caption beneath it read: "Real estate magnate Chance Stuart and diva Lucianna Colton back together again. Seen at a recent fund-raiser for the performing arts." Flame didn't read any more, going cold, then hot with rage. All that talk about how much he loved her and needed her, how much he wanted her back—for herself—it was all more lies. And he was coming here tonight to tell her more.

After dinner, Chance stood in front of the parlor's fireplace, a brandy glass in his hand, and stared at the new flames dancing and darting over the seasoned logs in defiance of any pattern. It should have been a cozy setting—brandy and coffee for two, the flickering glow of the fire, the easy quiet of the house, the low lights of the room.

A single floor lamp burned, its dome-shaped, fringed shade diffusing the lights from its bulb and casting a soft amber glow on the wing chair where Flame sat, her body angled sideways, knees drawn up. Turning his head slightly, Chance surveyed her with a sidelong look.

Like a contented cat, she looked, all curled up in the chair, the sleeves of her intarsia sweater pushed up, the loose fit of her white slacks clinging softly to her long legs. Her mane of red-gold hair ran faintly lawless back from her lovely and proud face. The mere sight of her stirred him profoundly.

Yet, as he looked at her, it wasn't Flame he thought about. His mind kept playing back the discussion he'd had with Sam today in his office.

"Chance, a whole month has gone by. Don't you think it's time we did something?" Sam argued, exasperation and frustration showing on his features. "We haven't contested the will. If we don't do something in the next couple days, the court's going to hand Morgan's Walk over to her. You realize that, don't you?"

"Tying up the title to that land isn't going to accomplish anything, Sam. I'm not going to fight her on it, and that's final."

"You're not going to fight her on that, and you're not fighting her on the annulment either. Dammit, Chance, I know you love her and you want her back. I understand that, but—what about Morgan's Walk?"

"What about it?"

Sam lifted his shoulders in a helpless gesture. "It just seems to me that you're counting an awful lot on getting Flame back. I mean, you're not making any other move to get the land."

"If I take any action against her now, I can forget persuading her to come back to me. She'd be convinced all I want is the land."

"Maybe so." Sam sighed, a heavy, disgruntled sound. "But I worry about the amount of time going by. I'm not saying you should call the mortgage due, but you could hassle her a little by demanding financial statements and a review of the loan. Put some pressure on her and maybe shake her up a bit."

"You don't shake Flame up; you just make her mad."

"I think it's a mistake to do nothing, Chance. How long can we afford to sit on our hands?"

"As long as it takes."

Sam looked at him. "Are you making any headway with her? Or is she just stringing you along?"

He hadn't had an answer for that—and he didn't now as he swirled the brandy in his glass, then tossed down most of it.

"More brandy?" The softness of her voice reached out to him, stirring his senses, but it was the politeness of her inquiry that registered.

"No." He turned the rest of the way around to face her chair, letting his gaze move over her. She seemed vaguely restless by it, her guard lifting, shuttering the green of her eyes and masking her expression with a blandness. "During the last—almost four—weeks, we've had dinner together, talked, and occasionally even laughed together. So why do I have the feeling that I'm not getting through to you—that you're just going through the motions?"

With an unhurried grace, she uncurled her legs and rose from the chair, her hands sliding into the slanted side pockets of her slacks as she wandered over to the fireplace. "I think you've forgotten these meetings were your idea, not mine."

"I suppose they've meant nothing to you—that you've regretted every unguarded smile you gave me," he taunted, lifting the glass halfway to his mouth and speaking over the top of it. "And you have given them to me. Granted, they happened at weak moments—when you forgot to hate me."

"Then they must have been rare indeed," she returned coolly.

He smiled at that and finished the rest of his brandy, then walked over to the coffee table and set his empty glass on top of it. He didn't turn back.

"What do you want from me, Flame?" Every sense was sharpened as he waited for an answer that didn't come. He spoke again with a rising energy, his anger close. "Am I supposed to crawl? Beg? What?"

"I want nothing from you, Chance. Absolutely nothing."

When he turned, she had her back to him, facing the fire. He stared at the tall, willowy shape she made against the firelight.

"I don't believe you've stopped caring, Flame." As he walked up behind her, he saw her stiffen in sudden alertness, defending herself against the steady beat of his presence.

"And I don't care what you believe."

"I've made you laugh. I've made you smile. I've made you angry. And, no doubt, I've made you cry."

"While you're enumerating your list of accomplishments, don't forget that you've also made me hate you."

"But you care. You're not indifferent to me, any more than I am to you." He touched the soft points of her shoulders, his hands settling gently onto them, remembering the feel of her—and feeling the tensing of her body. Drawn closer by her nearness, he brushed his lips against her hair, breathing in its clean scent. "I've missed you." He hadn't meant to say that, but now that it was out, he said the rest, too. "I've always believed that a woman had to be every-thing to a man—or nothing. You are everything to me, Flame. Everything." He let his hands trail down her arms and follow the bend of her elbows to cross in front of her, drawing her back against him. She tipped her head to the side, as if away from him, but he found the slender curve of her neck and the vein that throbbed there. "I never knew anything about family or love—not growing up here, in this house. But you taught me . . . you showed me how it could be."

"No." She wasn't sure what she was saying no to—to him, to her memories, to the physical response he evoked? His words, his voice, his touch were all working on her, undermining the barriers she'd put up against him. She offered no resistance at all when he turned her into his arms.

"Yes." His glance ran quickly over her.

This close, Chance noticed the long sweep of her lashes and the curvature of her mouth—and the small lines at the lip corners, which made her—when she chose—look willful and steel-proud. Her breasts were pressed to his chest so he could feel the quick beat of her heart and the quick in-and-out run of her breathing. Her face was set against him, yet he sensed she was disturbed and uncertain—she who seldom was. There was no doubt in his mind, though. He needed her. For him, she was the softness and the endlessness, the fire and the green, cool depths.

"I need you, Flame," he murmured and kissed her, his mouth coming down hot and firm. Taken by surprise, or suddenly willing—Chance wasn't sure—but she kissed him back, deeply.

Then she pulled herself away and backed up, moving out of his reach. "You're good, Chance," she declared, her voice still husky with the level of her disturbance. "You're very good." She wondered how she could have forgotten, even for a moment, that the man was an expert at seduction. "But it isn't going to work, not a second time. Because I know it isn't me you need; it's Morgan's Walk."

"That's a separate thing."

"Is it?" She took the newspaper clipping from her pocket—the one with the photograph of Chance with Lucianna—and handed it to him. "I can see how heartbroken you are over losing me."

He shot a look at it, then brought his gaze straight back to her. "This means nothing. Lucianna is an old friend. You know that."

"Then let her console you. I'm sure she's good at it."

"Dammit, Flame—" He took a step toward her.

She brought him up short with a cold "I think you'd better leave, Chance.

You've had your dinner and you've had your conversation, but you're not going to have me."

He hesitated. She saw the indecision warring in him, the impulse to press his point—and to take advantage of the vulnerability she'd shown him. Then he appeared to change his mind, crumpling the newspaper clipping and tossing it into the fire.

"I'll go," he said. "We'll settle this another time."

She knew better—because there wasn't going to be another time. But she didn't tell him that. She let him walk out of the parlor believing that she would meet him again somewhere, sometime. But there was no more need for that. She'd gained the time she wanted.

When she heard the front door close behind him, she turned to the fireplace and watched the flames leap greedily to consume the crumpled paper. For an instant, the grainy photograph of Chance and Lucianna, arm in arm, stood out sharply. In the next second, it was all black char.

34

TWICE AFTER SHE RETURNED to San Francisco, Chance attempted to contact her again, but Flame had been tied up in meetings on both occasions and hadn't bothered to return his calls. She knew that sooner or later he'd realize she was deliberately avoiding him, but she hadn't had time to concern herself with that.

Every spare hour—every spare minute—of her days had been taken up by meetings, phone calls, and long discussions with Karl Bronsky and an associate of his, Devlin Scott. The results from the test borings had come back, proving the northern dam site was definitely viable. But Flame no longer regarded it as a weapon with which to fight any condemnation proceedings initiated by Chance. The northern dam site had become the cornerstone for a daring new plan—a plan she had discussed with no one except Karl Bronsky and Devlin Scott, a plan she had constantly reviewed and refined on her own until she felt it was ready. Even now she hadn't told Karl all of it—certainly not the most critical part.

Deciding that she was as fully prepared as she would ever be, Flame made the final call that would either set her plan into motion or put her back to square one.

"Hello, Malcom. It's Flame."

"If you're calling to cancel our lunch on Thursday, you realize this will be the second week in a row you've done that."

"I'm not." Their Thursday luncheon was the farthest thing from her mind. "I have a business proposition I'd like to discuss with you."

"A business proposition." A note of alertness entered his voice. "Regarding what?"

"It's personal. It has nothing to do with the agency," she said. "And I'd prefer to show you, rather than try to explain it over the phone."

"When would you like to meet?"

"Anytime," she said. "In fact, the sooner the better."

"What about this evening?" Malcom suggested. "I have a six o'clock meeting, but I should be free by eight. I'm spending the night at my apartment in town rather than drive home to Belvedere. We could meet there at, say, eight-thirty."

With no hesitation, Flame replied, "Eight-thirty it is."

When she hung up, her assistant contacted her on the intercom. "You have a call on line two, Flame, from a Mr. Canon in Tulsa. Do you want to take it or shall I tell him you'll return the call later?"

"I'll take it." She immediately picked up the phone and pushed the button on the blinking line. "Hello, Ben."

"I just received a call I thought you might be interested in."

"From whom?" She frowned curiously, certain Chance wouldn't be calling him.

"A local real estate agent. He wanted to know if there was a possibility the new owner of Morgan's Walk would consider selling it. It seems he has a party in Texas—Dallas, supposedly—who's interested in the property."

"Really?" she murmured, suddenly angry. "You can bet Chance is behind this." It irritated her that Chance would think she was too stupid not to see through this ruse.

"I'm sure of it," Ben agreed. "He knows you would never sell to him. More than likely he's hoping you'll sell the land to somebody else to spite him— especially if the offer is generous. Which I'm sure it will be."

"What did you tell the agent?"

"Basically nothing."

"Call him back and tell him—" She checked her first angry impulse in favor of another thought. "Tell him you don't think the new owner is interested in selling, but to have his Dallas party contact me personally, and indicate you think I could be persuaded if the price was right."

"If that's what you want, I'll do it."

"It is." She smiled faintly. "There's more than one way to string Chance along."

Malcom Powell's town apartment on the eighteenth floor of the sleek steel-and-glass high-rise was small by society's standards, but definitely luxurious. A single spacious room combined the living and dining areas with an elaborate entertainment center. The decor was modern in its approach while possessing classical overtones—Malcom collected marble obelisks and Biedermeier wood furniture. Done in a study of grays, the color scheme was designed to draw the eye to the panoramic view of the city and its glitter of night lights.

But Flame took little note of either when she arrived at the apartment promptly at eight-thirty. After inquiring politely about his earlier meeting, she wasted no time on pleasantries.

"Do you mind if I use the table for these plans?" Without waiting for his reply, she crossed the floor of pearl-gray marble to the lacquered dining table.

"Not at all." Malcom followed at a more leisurely pace, then watched with curious eyes as she removed a set of drawings from her large leather portfolio case and spread them on the table. "Can I pour you a drink?"

She started to refuse, then noticed the glass in his hand. "Gin and tonic." When he returned with it, she set the drink aside without taking so much as a sip from it, and opened her attaché case instead, taking out the booklet that contained the summary and analysis of Chance's proposed development.

"After I talked to you this morning"—Malcom observed her actions but didn't step up to the table to look at the material she set out—"I initially thought you wanted to talk to me about setting up your own agency, but something tells me I was way off the mark."

"You were." She threw a quick smile at him. "As you know, I recently inherited some property in Oklahoma. This—" She indicated the site plans and drawings on the table. "—is what Chance Stuart planned to do with that land."

Moving up to stand beside her, Malcom glanced briefly at the plans, then angled his shoulders toward her, his gaze intent in its study of her. "As I recall, you inherited the property *after* you left him."

"That's true." It wasn't easy, but she managed to meet his gaze squarely, pride asserting itself despite the bitter blow it had been dealt. "And I think it's obvious by the amount of thought and work that's gone into these drawings he had planned this project long before he met me. As you can see from this site plan, he's already in possession of these parcels. All he lacked was the valley."

"And that's why he married you."

"Yes." There was no reason to deny it, and at this point Malcom deserved to know the truth about Chance—about everything. "I'd like you to look this over for me, Malcom, and tell me what you think honestly of the project."

He looked at her at length, as if trying to discern the motive behind her request. Finally he simply nodded. "All right."

When he took a pair of steel-rimmed reading glasses from the inside pocket of his charcoal gray business suit, Flame picked up her glass and wandered over to the living room area, leaving him to study the information without looking over his shoulder. Oddly enough, she didn't feel nervous. Impatient, yes. Determined, definitely. But nervous, no. She knew precisely what she wanted, why she wanted it, and what she would do to get it—with no second thoughts and no regrets.

She resisted the urge to pace the room and sat down instead on the soft leather sofa facing the dining table and Malcom. She sipped at her drink, tasting none of it. She made a concerted effort not to stare at him, yet she was aware of his every move, the recessed lighting overhead reflecting off the streaks of gray in his dark hair with each tilt of his head.

The waiting became unbearable. Still, she didn't move from the sofa, the ice in her drink turning to water. When she thought she couldn't stand the tension anymore, Malcom took off his reading glasses and paused to take one last look at everything on the table, then turned in her direction.

"Well?" She prodded him for some comment without budging from the sofa, unconsciously holding her breath.

"I think Stuart would probably have set the real estate world back on its heels again—and pocketed millions in the process," he said, then paused. "Or am I assuming too much when I said 'he would have'?"

"No, you're not." She got up from the sofa and walked over to the dining table. There, she opened the portfolio and took out another set of drawings. "This is the development I want to build." She spread them out on the table, covering the ones she'd taken from Chance's office and ignoring the sharp look of surprise Malcom gave her. "As you can see, the concept is virtually the same as his. The placement of various things has been changed. The dam site is located farther north on the river, opening this valley, which lends itself perfectly to a thirty-six-hole course and a hotel/country club with ample room for condominiums and town houses to be built around it, as well as a landing strip for private aircraft. Changing the dam site also necessitates a change in the location of the resort hotel and marina, moving them over to this area. Actually, it's a better location than the one he had, since it gives the marina protection from the prevailing winds in the area. And"—she had difficulty keeping satisfaction from creeping into her voice—"changing the dam site also means that most of the land Chance owns is left—literally—high and dry."

"You're serious about this," Malcom realized.

"I have never been more serious about anything in my life," Flame stated. "However, I should point out the site for the resort hotel and marina is outside the boundaries of Morgan's Walk. Seven individually owned parcels make up the site, including the valley area that will be flooded once the dam's in place. Naturally, that land will have to be acquired as quickly as possible."

"Why are you doing this, Flame?" he asked quietly—almost too quietly. "It's more than the money you might make, isn't it?"

"Chance still wants my land. The mere fact that he married me to gain control of it proves how determined he is to get it. He isn't going to stop just because that attempt failed. He'll try and keep trying until he succeeds. He already holds the mortgage on Morgan's Walk. I received a call from my attorney today advising me that I'll probably be receiving a very lucrative offer to buy the ranch—supposedly from an investor in Dallas. There's no doubt in my mind that Chance is behind it. When I turn that down, he'll simply call the mortgage due. If I should be successful in obtaining a loan somewhere else—which won't be easy—more than likely he'll buy it up, too. He's going to do everything in his power to squeeze me out. If all I do is fight a holding action, ultimately I'll lose. Which leaves me one alternative," she concluded. "I have to beat him at his own game."

She caught the glimmer of new respect and admiration that appeared briefly in Malcom's look. Then he smiled, ever so faintly. "And maybe get a little revenge in the process."

"That's part of it, too," she admitted with candor.

"And this business proposition you mentioned on the phone—where do I fit in your scheme of things?"

"I need a partner." She didn't bother to add that he had to be someone with power and financial credibility, regarding that as a given. "I *might* be able to put this development together by myself, but we both know how difficult—if not impossible—it would be, especially if Chance finds out. But with the Powell name and money behind me, even Chance Stuart would find it hard to go up against you."

"But why should I back you, Flame? Aside from the money that could be made, what do I get out of it?"

"Me," she replied evenly.

His smile was faintly sardonic. "I knew that's what you were going to say." Flame experienced her first moment of unease. "However tempting the proposition is—and it is very tempting—I'm not sure I like the idea of being used by you to get back at Stuart."

"We have always been honest with each other, Malcom," she said, choosing her words. "I'm not sure you realize how rare that is. I know I didn't. Never once have you implied to me that you desired anything more than an affair. In fact you openly admitted that you had no intention of ever leaving your wife. I've learned to appreciate that honesty—and many other things as well. I have always respected and admired you, Malcom, both as a businessman and a man. And we enjoy each other's company, too. As you once pointed out to me, we get along well together. What better basis for a relationship is there than a mutual admiration and respect?"

He breathed in deeply, a trace of wariness in his expression. "I want you, Flame—more than I've ever wanted any other woman. I want you so much that I almost believe what you say. You're very convincing."

"And I want you. Revenge is part of it, Malcom. I'm not denying that." Moving slowly, she closed the space between them until she stood mere inches from him. Still, she made no move to touch him. "But it isn't all of it. I'm tired of being alone. I'm tired of being lonely. I want someone I can share things with, whether it's work or play. Is that really so difficult for you to believe?" she argued quietly.

"No."

"Then . . . can we be partners?"

In answer, his hands closed on her arms and drew her the last few inches to meet his descending mouth. She responded to his kiss, although admittedly without the passion and intensity of feeling that she once had given Chance. But she'd learned the painful way that it was better to love wisely, safely, than to be swept away by emotion. She swayed against him and wound her arms around him, answering the forceful pressure of his kiss.

When he led her into the bedroom, another quiet composition in gray, a part of her regretted that, in the order of things, they next had to make love. As she undressed beneath his heated glance, she reminded herself there would be time enough later to discuss strategy and options. Now there was this. It was not a passive lover he wanted, and she knew that. She sincerely tried to give what he did want. She met his force with her own and urged him to drive away her memories. After all, it was part of the bargain.

If his hands and lips were not as quick to seek out and find her pleasure points—if he relied more on strength than finesse to show his desire—if the satisfaction from their coupling was less than what she'd known before—she blocked it out. Afterward, lying in his arms, her head resting on his powerfully built chest, she felt a measure of contentment and ease. That was enough for her.

35 ✒

SAM WALKED OUT of his office and threw a quick glance at the closed doors to Chance's suite, then hesitated and went over to Molly's desk. "Is Chance busy?"

"Busy?" She sighed and glanced at the lighted button on the telephone indicating one of the lines was in use. "He's in there trying to get hold of Flame again."

"And all he's getting is the usual runaround, right?" Sam guessed and shook his head, joining Molly in her troubled sigh. "In the last two months, he's spoken to her exactly once, and I'd be willing to bet that was an accident. If she'd known he was calling, she would never have picked up the phone."

"He worries me, Sam," Molly declared. "Have you noticed the weight he's lost? And he isn't sleeping nights, either. It's no wonder he's so irritable and—"

"—impossible to talk to." He finished the sentence for her.

"Why is she treating him like this? Doesn't she know what she's doing to him?"

"You're as bad as Chance," Sam murmured, looking at her with a mixture of sadness and disgust. "It doesn't seem to occur to either one of you that she just might not give a damn."

"Maybe I was wrong about her." Such a concession coming from Molly bordered on the monumental, and Sam knew it. "She seemed to be genuinely in love with him. Maybe it was an act. That's the only explanation that makes sense."

"There might be one or two others." But Sam didn't go into them. Molly would never admit that part of the blame for Flame's present attitude might belong to Chance for the way he'd deceived her about Morgan's Walk. As far as Molly was concerned, she should have forgiven him for that.

"I thought that Hattie woman was cruel and heartless," Molly said, an anger showing in the tight working of her jaw. "Now I'm beginning to think it runs in the family. The amount of suffering those two women have brought into his life . . ." She sighed again and looked at Sam. "What are we going to do?"

"I don't know about you, but I have to go in there and tell him that I finally heard from J.T. If he's in a bad mood now, it's only going to get worse."

"What happened?" she asked, then immediately guessed. "She refused to sell."

"Something like that." He walked over to the doors and knocked once.

But Chance didn't hear it as he slammed the receiver down, cutting off the voice on the other end of the line as she started to explain that Ms. Bennett was in a meeting and couldn't be disturbed, an excuse he'd heard too many times to believe anymore. No woman had ever rocked and torn at him like this, until he could think of nothing else but having her back. She was like a hammer beating at his strength. Cursing under his breath, he ran a hand through his close-cropped hair as he leaned on his desk, his shoulders hunched against the ache that wouldn't go away.

"Chance?" Sam's voice intruded, bringing his head up sharply.

"What is it?" he snapped, turning his chair away while he fought to regain his composure.

"I just finished talking to J.T. in Dallas."

He spun the chair back around. "Has he met with Flame?" He checked the impulse to ask how she was and demanded instead, "What did she say? Has she agreed to sell Morgan's Walk?"

"No." Sam paused briefly. "Her exact words to him were—and I quote—'Tell Chance Stuart that Morgan's Walk isn't for sale at any price.' Naturally J.T. denied that you were in any way involved in the offer. But I guess she just smiled and showed him the door."

"Damn." The curse was barely more than a whisper.

"Don't you think it's time we took the gloves off, Chance?"

He leaned back in his chair and reached in his jacket pocket, taking out the set of wedding rings he'd carried with him every single day since Flame had dropped them at his feet. He closed his fingers around them, feeling the edges of the diamond cut into his palm.

"Call the mortgage due," he said, then slowly pulled open the center drawer of his desk and dropped the rings inside. He pushed the drawer shut, and wished he could be as successful in shutting Flame from his mind. "Cut off all credit to Morgan's Walk. Call in every favor and apply whatever pressure you have to, but get it done. I want to drain her cash, and leave her nothing to operate on. While you're at it, hire away all the ranch help you can."

36 ✒

HEARING THE TURN of a key in the lock, Malcom lowered the newspaper and took off his reading glasses, his glance turning to the entrance hall in his apartment. The closing of the door was followed by the firm tap of high heels on the marble floor as Flame strode into view, still dressed in the brown-and-white wool Adolfo suit she'd worn earlier in the day, a combination made all the more striking by the red of her hair.

"I expected you an hour ago."

"I know, darling." She gave her wool and alpaca coat a toss, flinging it onto one of the chairs, then crossed to the back of the sofa and bent down to give him a quick kiss. "I'm sorry. My meeting with Ellery took longer than I thought. There were simply too many things to go over. Would you like me to freshen your drink?" she asked, reaching for his glass.

"Please," he said as she crossed to the liquor cart, his glass in hand.

"I have to spend most of tomorrow at the agency." Using the tongs, she plucked cubes from the ice bucket, dropped some in his glass and the rest in hers. "I'm not going to have any choice, unfortunately. I have too much work backed up."

"You're spreading yourself too thin. It's time you gave the agency notice."

Watching as she splashed more whiskey into his glass, Malcom could see she didn't look the least bit tired, mentally or physically. On the contrary, he'd never seen her look so vibrantly alive, driven by a restless energy. The impression was reinforced when she turned back to him, giving him the direct effect of her green eyes. In that moment, he saw her then as she was to him, the shape and dream of beauty, the image of a still fire burning in the night, perfect and pure-centered with a white heat. He wanted to believe he was responsible for that bright glitter in her eyes. But he knew better, and her next words confirmed it.

"I can't, not for a while yet. I don't know how closely Chance is watching me. If I quit the agency, he'll start wondering what I'm going to do." She walked over and handed him his drink. "And we can't risk arousing his suspicion too soon." She kicked off her alligator pumps and sat down on the sofa cushion beside him, curling her silk-clad feet under her and angling sideways to face him. "Besides, my work load with the agency isn't that heavy now that I've managed to turn most of my clients over to other account execs in the firm—with the exception of Powell's, of course." She reached out to touch him, her fingers tracing the lobe of his ear then trailing over the square line of his jaw.

"Of course." He smiled automatically while silently wondering if he'd ever cease resenting the way every third sentence of hers contained some reference to Stuart. The man was an invisible presence constantly with them. The bed was the only place he didn't appear—and Malcom wasn't entirely certain about that. Endless times he'd found himself wondering if he pleased her in bed as fully as Stuart once had. His virility had been something he'd never doubted . . . until now. Over and over he reminded himself that Flame was with him—not with Stuart. Yet he couldn't shake the feeling that she would never have come to him if it wasn't for her desperate thirst for revenge. He probably should be grateful to Stuart, but he was beginning to despise the man as much as Flame said she did. In truth, he was eager to tangle openly with Stuart and prove who was the better man.

"Speaking of Chance—" The ice cubes in her drink clinked against the sides of the glass as she idly swirled the gin and tonic. "—the notice came last week calling the mortgage due. I have sixty days to come up with seven hundred-odd thousand dollars."

"Last week." Malcom frowned. "You never said anything about it."

"I forgot what with all the meetings we had with the engineers and the land planners. We have plenty of time to come up with it so it really doesn't matter. And I have no intention of paying it until the very last minute. I'm sure he believes he's created a problem for me and I want him to go on thinking that."

"You're a cunning woman, Flame." At the same time that he realized that, he also recognized that her every thought, her every move were dictated by what she expected Stuart's response or reaction to be.

"It's going to take cunning—and an element of surprise—to beat him." Again her restlessness surfaced as she uncurled her legs and rolled gracefully to her feet, avoiding his gaze. "Which reminds me—did Karl drop the new site plan by your office? He said he'd have it ready today."

"It's on the table."

"Are there many changes?" She walked over to study it for herself.

"A handful, but they're all minor ones." Malcom hesitated, then set his glass down on the coffee table and joined her in the dining area. "He has the plans for the dam finished as well. I gave Karl the name of my contact in Washington and told him to fly there next week so he can look them over."

"Aren't you being premature—"

"No." Malcom overruled her. "If we're going to run into any major snags, it will be with the dam. And I want to know about them as soon as possible."

She shrugged her acceptance of his decision, but he could tell she didn't completely agree with it. "Has your attorney heard anything further from any of the real estate agents in Tulsa?"

Malcom had instructed his attorney to utilize the services of seven different real estate agencies to buy the seven parcels where the resort hotel and marina were to be built. "Not as of yesterday."

"I wonder what the problem is. It bothers me that we've been able to acquire options on only three of them. They've been working on it almost a month now."

"Has it ever occurred to you they might not be anxious to sell?" he chided.

"But I'm anxious to buy," she stated, then glanced at him. "Malcom, do you realize that you have never seen Morgan's Walk? These site plans and drawings are all you've ever seen of the property. Why don't we arrange to fly out there for a couple days?"

"I suppose I could rework my schedule." It was the idea of having Flame to himself for two or three days that appealed to him more than looking at the development site itself.

"We could meet with the real estate agents while we're there and find out what the holdup is. If it's a matter of price, we can authorize them to increase the offer. If it's something else, we can figure out a way to deal with it," she said, thinking out loud. "I think the trip is definitely a good idea. The last time I talked to Charlie he mentioned he was having some problems. He's lost most of his help on the ranch," she added in a quick aside. "And there was some difficulty with the feed store. Maybe I can get that ironed out too while we're there."

"It's always business with you, isn't it?" Malcom murmured, realizing that very little about their relationship had changed.

For an instant, she went absolutely still. Then she turned, all the stiffness flowing from her. "No, not always." A smile played with the corners of her mouth. With a supple lift of her arms, she draped them around his neck and let a finger play with a strand of dark hair at his nape. "I distinctly remember numerous occasions when business was the farthest thing from my mind. Don't you?" Lightly she brushed her lips across his, then brought them back, letting the tip of her tongue moistly trace their unyielding line.

For an instant, he resisted, then he pulled her roughly against him and crushed her lips in a hard kiss, hoping this time to block the sensation that there was someone else with them.

37

EVERYTHING IN THE latest status report indicated that his Tahoe project was progressing well ahead of schedule, but Chance could find little satisfaction in the figures and construction projections. They didn't fill the empty places in his body and his spirit, the wild and lonely ones that bred his restlessness and short temper. He felt the stir of memories and firmed his jaw against it. She wasn't coming back to him. He'd accepted that—just as he'd accepted that the rest of the days would have an emptiness, haunted by the memory of the time he'd had with Flame. It was something he couldn't change. He had no choice but to live with his bitter regrets.

Without warning, the door to his office opened. Chance looked up from the report, made irritable by the intrusion. "Dammit, Molly." But it wasn't Molly who posed briefly within the frame, then boldly entered the room. "Lucianna." He stood up, rankled by her unannounced arrival and showing it. "What are you doing here?"

"That's no welcome, Chance," she chided. She was dramatically clad in a leopard print cashmere coat trimmed at the collar, sleeves, and hem in fox with a matching fur toque covering the black of her hair. Casually, she deposited her purse on a chair and came around his desk. "You should say: 'Lucianna, darling, what a wonderful surprise to see you here.'"

When he failed to kiss her, she slowly withdrew her hands, skillfully covering whatever rejection she might have felt with a proudly indifferent expression. "I've come to take you to lunch. And don't tell me you're too busy. I've already checked with your dragon lady and you have no appointments for the next two hours. As a matter of fact—" A knowing smile curved her wide mouth. "—your schedule is relatively free for the next four days—no trips, no important meetings, nothing. Which will take us right into the weekend, maybe beyond."

"I thought you were supposed to be in Europe this month."

"I was," she admitted, almost too casually, and turned away from him to stroll to the window. "But there is a small problem with my throat. The doctor has told me I must give my voice a complete rest for three months—and I told him I would cancel all engagements for *one* month only."

Catching the hint of fear in her voice, Chance relented. "Three months," he said. "They'd have to put you in a straitjacket and tape your mouth shut, wouldn't they?"

She swung back to him, her dark eyes turning soft at his understanding. "That's what I told him," she said, then lifted her hands in an empty, helpless gesture. "But here I am with an entire month. And I said to myself—who better to spend it with than you? It will be like old times, won't it?"

He looked at her, recalling the high passion that had once filled their days together, and recalling, too, the loneliness of his life now—and how grim that loneliness was. "Maybe it will," he conceded, then smiled faintly. "In any case, you're welcome to stay."

Not pressing the point, Lucianna drew back, her expression confident and warm. "Where are you going to take me for lunch?"

"As I recall, you were taking me."

"In that case—" She walked over and hooked her arm with his. "—I'll have to find some place *very* cosy and *very* quiet."

As she started to draw him away, Sam barged into the office. "Chance, I—" He stopped short, frowning in surprise at the woman on Chance's arm. "Lucianna. What are you doing here?"

She sighed in mock exasperation. "The welcomes I receive here leave a great deal to be desired. I expected better from you, Sam."

"I'm sorry, I—" A look of chagrin briefly raced across his expression, only to be replaced by the troubled frown he'd worn when he came in, his attention swinging once again to Chance. "Fred Garver just called me and wanted to know what was going on. His friend Zorinsky, with the Corps, claims there's another set of plans for the dam being circulated in his department."

"That's impossible." Chance automatically dismissed it. "Somebody probably saw a similarity in place names and confused the two."

Sam nodded, "That's what I said. Fred did, too, but Zorinsky swears it isn't the case—that he triple-checked to be sure before he called Fred. The plans call for a dam to be built on Morgan's Walk, but this dam is located almost a mile north of our site. The house and most of the valley won't be flooded."

"What?" Chance frowned, suddenly wary, his skepticism fading as he unconsciously slipped free from Lucianna's hold. "Where did these plans originate? Did Fred find that out?"

"They were done by an engineering firm called Thurgood. Fred's pretty sure it's a West Coast company. That has to mean Flame's behind it." He paused, then went on with rising energy. "A lot of things are starting to make sense, Chance—like some of the comments that filtered back to us from the ranch hands we hired away from Morgan's Walk. Remember they said some men had been there taking soil samples? At the time I shrugged it off, figuring she'd contacted some oil and gas companies and arranged to have their geologists come out to see if there was the potential for any oil or gas on the property, but obviously—"

"—they were doing test borings for the dam." Chance finished the sentence for him.

"Exactly." Sam punched the air with his finger, emphasizing the point. "And something else is adding up, too. Fred said that with the dam moved up the river, more of the land to the northwest will be flooded. Remember the rumors we've been hearing about a lot of real estate activity going on there? Somebody's buying up—or trying to buy up—that hill land. And we thought somebody had gotten wind of our development and was doing some speculating. We also said almost the same thing when we heard those rumors about a big resort development going in somewhere in the Midwest. We thought they were talking about *our* project. But I'll bet you anything she's got something in the works along the same line."

"There's a problem with that theory, Sam," Chance said. "She hasn't got the money to do it. We've seen her financial statement. Excluding Morgan's Walk and her apartment in San Francisco, she has a personal net worth of only about twenty thousand dollars that she can get her hands on readily. She might have used some of the proceeds from Hattie's life insurance to have the plans drawn up for the dam, but, Sam, she hasn't been able to raise the money yet to pay our mortgage demand. So where is she going to get the money to buy all this property?"

"From Malcom Powell." Lucianna sat in the chair next to Chance's desk, holding her compact open with one hand and applying a fresh coat of lipstick to her already red lips with the other, her purse lying open on her lap. Briefly she met the glance he shot her. "He's the logical choice, darling, since the two of them are in the midst of a torrid affair."

"That rumor was thick when I met her," he replied impatiently. "Their relationship is purely business. She handles his advertising account with the agency, and that's all."

"It may have been all *then*." Lucianna shrugged with feigned idleness and recapped the tube of lipstick. "But it's a fact now. Oscar told me they've been seen together almost constantly."

"I told you she handles the account for his stores," he snapped. "Naturally she has to meet with him."

"Naturally." She smiled at him in a look of mock acceptance. "And I'm sure that's the reason he gave her a key to his apartment in town—so they could have private business conferences in the bedroom instead of the boardroom."

"I don't believe you," he murmured coldly.

"About the key or the fact that they're lovers? They are, you know. But you don't have to take my word for it." She returned the compact and lipstick to her purse and closed it with a definite click of the clasp. "Call Jacqui Van Cleeve—or read her columns these past few weeks. That woman doesn't print anything that isn't the absolute truth. And believe me, she has a network of spies that are the envy of the KGB."

He looked at her for a long, challenging moment, demanding that she admit she was wrong—that she had exaggerated. She looked back at him, in her dark eyes a sadness, a hint of pity, and regret that she'd been the one to tell him. Then it hit him. She was telling the truth. A hot swell of jealousy ripped through him. He turned from both of them, his hands doubled into tight fists, wanting to strike out at something, anything—but there was nothing, just a hard pressure squeezing at his heart.

"Chance, I—" Sam began tentatively.

Chance stiffened, then turned slowly. "Call Fred back, will you? Tell him if he can't get a copy of those plans, I want him to draw his best guess of the new lake's location. And I want it now," he ordered, conscious of the flatness, the deadness, in his voice.

"Right." Sam nodded, backing toward the door.

He pushed the intercom button. "Molly, will you come in here?"

From her chair, Lucianna murmured, "I have the strange feeling our lunch has been canceled."

He ignored that as Molly entered. "Get hold of Kelby Grant. Tell him to get over here. I have some land I want him to buy for me—yesterday," he said grimly.

"Yes, sir."

"And Sam," Chance called him back before he got to the door. "Tell Fred I want a finished set of drawings on our dam site as fast as he can get them done for me. And I want the Corps' stamp of approval on them the day after—and I don't care how he gets that done."

"But he can't complete the plans without doing test work on the site itself," Sam protested.

"Tell him to get a crew out there and get it done."

"But we don't own the land." He looked at Chance as if he'd taken leave of his senses.

"Haven't you ever heard of trespassing, Sam?" he replied tiredly. "As soon as you get Fred lined out, call Matt Sawyer. Tell him I want everything he can get me on Malcom Powell."

"Will do."

Molly was on Sam's heels when he exited the office. "Sam, what's all this about? What happened?" In the briefest of terms, he explained it to her. When he'd finished, Molly looked properly outraged. "What does she know about building a development? Malcom Powell's money or not, she'll never succeed."

"I don't know about that Molly. From everything I've read about Malcom Powell, he could match Chance dollar for dollar. If that isn't bad enough, it's old money. Chance doesn't have the phone numbers of half the people Malcom Powell calls by their first name. With him backing Flame, this is going to turn into one helluva war. And Morgan's Walk is going to be the battleground for it."

"She's got to be stopped."

"How?" he asked, and shook his head over the lack of an answer.

"Well, someone has to try," she insisted.

"I know." A troubled sigh broke from him. "I can't help feeling this is all my fault, Molly. If I hadn't let Chance down—if I'd kept a closer watch on Hattie, we would have found out about Flame right from the start. Then maybe none of this would have happened."

"Wishing won't change the past," Molly replied curtly. "So don't waste valuable time dwelling on it. Concentrate instead on finding a way to stop her. Which reminds me—" She turned to her desk. "There was a note in today's mail from Maxine. The new duchess of Morgan's Walk will be arriving on Thursday —with two guests. It will be interesting to find out who they are."

38

EXHILARATED FROM THE brisk gallop back to the barns, Flame walked back to the imposing brick manor house of Morgan's Walk with her arm around Malcom's waist and the weight of his resting possessively around her shoulders, a quickness and a lightness to her steps that matched her new mood. As they approached the front door, she drew apart from him and waited, allowing him to open the door for her, then swept into the entrance hall. There she stopped and turned back to him, pulling off her riding gloves as he closed the door behind them.

"What a marvelous ride," she declared, leaning into Malcom when he returned to her side, curving his arm to the back of her waist and asserting his claim on her once more. "How about a drink to top it off?"

He shook his head. "I think I'll shower and change instead. Why don't you join me?"

"Not this minute, but I'll be up directly," she promised. "I want to check with Maxine and see if there were any calls, then find out what Ellery's doing."

Ellery called from the parlor, "Do I hear my name being bandied about?" Flame pressed a quick kiss on Malcom's cheek in parting, then moved to join Ellery in the parlor. "I see the Lone Rangeress and her powerful companion have returned. Hi Ho Silver and all that," Ellery observed dryly, lounging with his usual ease on the sofa in front of the fireplace.

"And it was wonderful, too," she stated, ignoring his jesting remark. "There was a blush of green over the whole countryside. I had the feeling that any moment every tree and bush was going to burst into leaf. We rode up to the dam site and I showed Malcom where the lake will be." She walked over to the drink cart and poured some tonic water in a glass, adding some ice cubes from the insulated bucket. "You should have come with us."

"No thanks. When I go riding, I prefer to have the horses under the hood of a car."

Something crackled. Belatedly, Flame noticed the daily paper lying open on his lap. "You've been reading the newspaper," she accused. "You said you didn't want to go because you wanted to work on the sketches for the golf course."

His eyebrow lifted at the hint of impatience in her voice. "I can't make up my mind whether this project of yours is turning you into a shrew or a slave driver."

"A shrew?" She frowned, faintly indignant. "How can you say that, Ellery? I have never behaved like a shrew."

"Really?" His eyebrow arched even higher. "I think you've forgotten how rudely you berated those poor people on the phone this morning."

"You mean those real estate agents?" She remembered that earlier sharpness of her tongue—without regret. "They deserved it. The ones who weren't waiting to hear back on the offers they'd made were waiting for a little time to go by before making another offer—so they wouldn't appear too anxious and drive up the price. Why should they care? They aren't buying the land. I am. Ben warned me that people were laid back around here, but this morning was ridiculous."

"We are testy, aren't we?" Ellery murmured.

She started to snap an answer at him, then sighed. "Sorry. It still irritates me when I think how much time has gone by—all because they didn't want to look as though they were trying to pressure anybody to sell. Believe me, they aren't going to be concerned about that anymore." She took a quick drink of the iced tonic water, then wandered over to the fireplace. "You managed to avoid my question about the sketches. Did you get anything done on them?"

"Even though this was supposed to be a pleasure trip, yes, I did sketch for my supper," he mocked. "They're on the table by the window."

Flame walked over to look at them. Altogether there were six different views—all in pencil—of the valley, its pastureland and shade trees turned into the manicured green of a golf course.

"Ellery, these are very good," she declared as she went through them again.

"Then I won't have to go hungry tonight."

She turned, smiling at him in amused exasperation. "Will you stop that? I'm trying to pay you a compliment." .

"Thank you." He bowed his head in mock docility.

Shaking her head at him, she laid the sketches down, mentally reminding herself to show them to Malcom later. "Seriously, Ellery, they are good. Sometimes I think your talent is going to waste in the art department of Boland and Hayes."

He dismissed that with a careless shrug. "Speaking of art—" He picked up the newspaper in his lap. "—have you seen today's paper?"

"I haven't had time to look at it. Why?"

"There's a small piece in here I found interesting."

"What's that?" She crossed to the sofa and glanced over his shoulder, her attention drawn first to the article near his right thumb. "You mean the story about the tenor Sebastian Montebello guesting in the Tulsa production of *Otello*? I think I saw a poster about that some—" She faltered, her eye caught by the photograph in the left-hand corner, a photograph of Chance Stuart and Lucianna Colton. Flame stared at the warm and lazy smile on Chance's face, a smile she'd once believed he reserved exclusively for her. Now Lucianna was the recipient of it. The caption beneath mentioned a minor throat ailment that had sidelined the renowned coloratura and stated her intention of attending *Otello*—in the company of real estate magnate Chance Stuart—to see the performance of her dear friend, Sebastian Montebello.

"I wonder if it's too late to get good seats," she murmured.

"You're surely not thinking of going?"

"Why not?" she challenged. "I'm certainly not going to stay away simply because he'll be there."

"Heaven forbid," he murmured.

"If Malcom and I can get seats, do you want to go?"

"My dear Flame, I wouldn't miss this for the world."

Arriving patrons of the opera filled the foyer of Chapman Music Hall, the subdued chatter of their voices punctuated by an occasional trilled greeting. From the hall itself, Chance could hear the muted and discordant notes of the last-minute tuning of instruments by the orchestra. He took another deep drag on his cigarette and exhaled the tangy smoke in a rush.

Not for the first time, he wondered why he'd agreed to come. He glanced at his watch. Eight more minutes before the overture was scheduled to start.

Beside him, Lucianna caught the slight movement of his wrist, and his downward glance at his watch. "You aren't too bored, are you, Chance darling?" she murmured soothingly.

"No," he lied.

"I'm sorry I had to drag you here tonight," she said, explaining again. "Unfortunately Sebastian found out I was in Tulsa. He would never have forgiven me if I hadn't come tonight. I wouldn't care, but I have to sing *Aïda* with him this fall. And I shudder to think the hell he could create for me on stage if he chose to be spiteful. It's bad enough putting up with his endless practical jokes."

"And you're the perfect victim for them, aren't you?" Chance guessed. "You approach everything with such intensity, even rehearsals, completely immersing yourself in the role, you open yourself up to it."

"He does it to destroy my concentration so he looks good and I look bad," she declared, then sighed, casting him a sideways glance. "As much as I don't want to, I have to go backstage before the performance and wish him well. Will you come with me?"

"Of course. Only I think you're about to be waylaid," he said, spotting the tall, anorexic brunette making a beeline through the crowd toward them and realizing that he should have known Gayle Frederick would be waiting to descend on Lucianna the instant she saw her. The woman fancied herself a patron of the arts. Which meant she was too rich to be called a groupie.

"Chance, how wonderful to see you." She sailed up to him and kissed him on both cheeks with typical theatrics.

"Gayle," he murmured in acknowledgment.

"And Miss Colton," she gushed, turning to Lucianna. "You don't know what a thrill it is to meet you. What a night this is going to be—Sebastian Montebello on the stage and Lucianna Colton in the audience."

"How very kind you are," Lucianna smiled, putting on her "diva" face.

"Not at all," she insisted. "If anything, I'm lucky. Although not as lucky as you," she added, sliding a quick look at Chance. "I mean, here you are with the throb of every heart in Tulsa."

"I am lucky," Lucianna agreed, her hand tightening ever so slightly on Chance's arm.

Catching the minor stir of activity at the entrance, Chance glanced in that direction. A fine tension, different from the impatience and irritation he'd felt before, held him motionless as he found himself looking at Flame. The months and days since their first meeting at the cocktail party seemed to drop away. Again he was staring at her from across a crowded room, drawn by that arresting combination of red-gold hair and jade green eyes.

Yet, tonight she looked untouchable—somehow distant and aloof. Frowning at the change, Chance studied her closer. She was wearing her hair differently. Instead of cascading in a luxuriant mass around her face and shoulders, it was smoothed back and caught in a wide clasp at the nape of her neck. The style wasn't severe, yet its effect was to subdue the fire with high sophistication. That wasn't Flame. Neither was the strikingly chic and elegant suit of quilted copper lamé that she wore, unrelieved by any jewelry. The straightness of its long jacket completely hid the ripeness of her figure, giving Chance the impression that she had gowned herself in a suit of copper armor.

Someone moved into his vision, blocking his view of Flame. For an instant Chance tried to look through the man, then the cleft chin, the square jaw, and the iron eyes registered. It was Malcom Powell—her new lover. Chance looked at the glowing tip of his cigarette, a tightness coiling through him.

When he lifted his glance again, he caught the smile she gave Malcom . . . so warm, so admiring, so damned intimate. He had tried to convince himself that she had turned to Malcom out of spite—that it had been a means of getting back at him . . . maybe even an attempt to make him jealous. But the way she looked at Powell . . . With a hint of savageness he turned and stabbed the end of his cigarette in the ashtray, burying it deep in the fine white sand.

"Look, Malcom Powell and his party have arrived," Gayle Frederick declared as Chance straightened and turned back. He stiffened in alertness when he saw they were coming directly toward them, although he doubted Flame had seen him yet. "Didn't I tell you this was a night," the brunette added, her low voice riddled with excitement. "You know him, don't you, Chance?"

"Yes."

Lucianna's fingers dug into his arm. "Perhaps—" she began. But Chance, anticipating her suggestion they leave before Flame and Powell reached them, silenced her with a faint shake of his head. The anger in him wanted a confrontation with Flame.

"He's visiting friends in the area." Gayle issued the quickly whispered aside even as she turned to snare the approaching party that included, Chance noticed, Ellery Dorn. "Mr. Powell, how delightful to have you with us this evening. Let me be—if not the first, then the most recent—to welcome you to Tulsa."

"Thank you . . . Mrs. Frederick, isn't it?" Powell replied with a suggestion of a bow.

"Yes," Gayle confirmed, preening a little at his recognition. "And I believe you know the marvelous diva, Lucianna Colton, and—of course—Chance Stuart."

"Indeed." The gray eyes turned on him, iron-smooth and blatantly measuring.

"Powell." Nodding once, Chance returned the look and briefly gripped the man's hand, aware of the strength and power that lay in more than just Powell's hand.

Continuing with the introductions, Gayle said, "And this is Flame Bennett from Morgan's—"

But Flame broke in. "Mr. Stuart and I have met before."

Her coolness grated at him as Gayle swung toward him, red firing her cheeks. "Oh, dear," she murmured, remembering precisely who Flame Bennett had been.

"It's all right, Gayle," he said, masking his anger with a smoothness. "The ex–Mrs. Stuart has a habit of bringing up a past that is better forgotten." Deliberately Chance held Flame's gaze. She tried to conceal it, but he saw the flash of anger in her green eyes.

"I am so sorry—"

"Don't apologize, Mrs. Frederick," Flame inserted coolly. "It isn't necessary. Mr. Stuart isn't known for the accuracy of his memory."

Chance turned to Powell. "Is it business or pleasure that's brought you to

Tulsa?" he inquired, letting his glance slide back to Flame, and catching her slight tensing.

"I believe you could call it a working vacation," came the smooth reply.

"Flame takes care of the advertising for you—doesn't she?" he said, pausing fractionally. "Among other things, I understand."

His pointed barb completely escaped Gayle Frederick as she pushed her way back into the conversation. "I do hope you're considering Tulsa as a location for one of your stores, Mr. Powell. With Neiman-Marcus and Saks here already, all we're missing is a Powell store."

"We'll see," he replied as he took Flame firmly by the arm, a complacent and confident gleam in his eyes asserting the closeness of his relationship with her. "Shall we go, Flame darling? Ellery?" Then, to Chance: "If you'll excuse us, I think it's time we took our seats."

As they moved away to join the line of people drifting into the theater, Gayle sighed. "How awful. I never did get to meet the handsome gentleman with them. Is he someone important, do you know?"

Chance ignored the question, turning his attention instead to Lucianna. "You said you wanted to go backstage."

"How good of you to remember that," she murmured somewhat archly. "Especially when I thought you'd forgotten all about me."

"There's nothing wrong with my memory, Lucianna." Although at the moment, he wished there was.

Flame tried to concentrate on the tenor's performance, but her glance kept straying from the lighted stage to the rows of silhouetted figures in front of her. Covertly she scanned them again. She wished she knew where Chance was sitting. The way the back of her neck was prickling, she was almost certain he was somewhere behind her.

Again she asked herself why she had let that newspaper photograph of Chance and Lucianna goad her into coming here tonight. Had she wanted Chance to see her with Malcom so he would know she had a man in her life? Or had she wanted to see for herself if all the gossip in the papers about his affair with Lucianna Colton was true—that his alleged *good* friend had become his lover again?

If it was proof of the latter she'd wanted, she'd certainly gotten it. The way Lucianna had been molded to his side, as if they were connected at the hip, and that arrogantly triumphant gleam in her dark eyes that said "He's mine"—and the possessive curve of his arm around her waist—all of it had combined to make the intimate status of their relationship blatant to the most casual observer. Had Lucianna been his lover all along—even when he'd been pursuing her? Flame went cold at the thought, hating both of them now.

Applause broke out around her. Belatedly Flame joined in as the house lights slowly came up, signaling the start of intermission. She feigned a casual glance over her shoulder. But too many people were moving about, standing, stretching, turning to chat to someone, or wending their way to the aisle. If Chance was back there, she couldn't see him.

Squaring around, Flame hesitated, conscious of an enveloping tension, then stood up, tucking her lizard purse under her arm and smiling briefly at Malcom. "I think I'll get some fresh air."

Malcom started to warn her that she'd likely run into Stuart out there, then he realized she knew that—just as she'd known Stuart would be at the opera tonight. He nodded instead and said nothing, remaining in his seat and smoldering in his own private hell. Oh, he had her, but he had never really had her.

Outside, the wind had died to a whisper and the night was warm with the promise of spring. The city lights of downtown Tulsa had blurred the stars to a dusting of pale specks overhead, too faint to compete with the bright lights shining from the windows of the monoliths that loomed in front of the Performing Arts Center.

In the distance, a horn honked, but there were few cars on the downtown streets. The only hum of traffic came from far away. Flame breathed in the quiet of the night, feeling its calmness smooth over her as she gazed across the precisely landscaped green of the Williams Center.

"I've been hearing some rumors lately." The lazily seductive drawl of Chance's voice seemed to reach out from the night and stroke her.

The calm fled, leaving a high alertness. Somehow Flame managed to restrain the impulse to spin sharply around and, instead, continued to gaze into the night. "Have you?" she countered, certain he was alluding to her relationship with Malcom.

"Yes." A soft footfall warned her that Chance was directly behind her.

She took a quick breath and caught the fragrance of his cologne, earthy and masculine. Slowly she turned to face him, recognizing that not only was she ready for this confrontation, she was also looking forward to it.

He stood before her, dark and elegant in his black evening attire. "Very interesting rumors, they are, too."

"Really?" She tried to read his expression, but it was too bland, too hooded.

"Yes, all sorts of talk about dams, resort hotels, marinas."

She stiffened, her heart rocketing. That was the last thing she'd expected him to say. How had he found out so quickly?

As if reading her mind, he said, "Did you think I wouldn't hear about your project? Sometimes it really can be a small world, Flame."

"So it would seem," she murmured tightly.

"You don't really think you're going to succeed, do you?"

"You surely don't think you're the only one capable of building it, do you?" she challenged.

"Initially I didn't put much stock in the rumors—until I found out who your partner was." He tipped his head at a considering angle. "You got into bed with Powell literally as well as figuratively, didn't you?"

Angered, she asserted, "It must gall you to know that I'm going to build the development you planned and still keep nearly all of Morgan's Walk intact."

"Assuming you succeed." His smile mocked her.

"I will."

"Will you? You've dealt yourself into a game with the big boys, Flame. And in cutthroat competition, there aren't any rules."

"Is that supposed to frighten me?" Flame taunted.

"You've already made a beginner's mistake. You should have bluffed—pretended that you didn't know what I was talking about until you found out for sure how much—or how little—I knew about your project. But you admitted it." There was a wry and lazy slant to his smile. "You tipped your hand, Flame."

"That makes us even," she retorted. "Because now I don't have to wonder anymore whether you know what I'm doing. You've told me."

"This is the only warning you're going to have, Flame," he said quietly. "For your own good, you'd better get out while you can."

"And let you take over Morgan's Walk? I'll see you in hell first," she declared with a faint but defiant toss of her head.

He dismissed that with a vague, shrugging motion. "I've been there most of my life anyway." He paused. "When you see Powell, tell him there's nothing to be gained by waiting. He might as well write me out a check for the mortgage balance. I never did like to spend my own money. I might as well use his to stop you."

"You'll get it when it's due and not before."

"Suit yourself." He started to turn away, then swung back. "Speaking of Powell. Is he enjoying the bedroom benefits of your partnership as much as I did?"

Stung by that remark, she struck hard at his face, the impact jarring every nerve in her arm. Instantly she was seized, his fingers digging into the quilted fabric of her copper sleeves and bruising her arms. Refusing to struggle and give him the satisfaction of overpowering her physically, Flame stood silent and unyielding, meeting the icy glitter of his blue eyes.

"Does he make you furious like this?" he demanded.

"You'll never know." She observed the brief flexing of the muscles along his hard jaw and knew her gibe had gotten through.

"Won't I?" he mocked. "You're too cool. Which tells me he doesn't ruffle you at all. You don't *feel* anything with him, do you?"

"I trust and respect him—which is more than I could ever say about you," she hurled bitterly.

But Chance just smiled. "Trust. Respect. Those are lukewarm things. Not like this."

He hauled her against him, his mouth coming down on her lips before she could turn away. The angry and demanding passion of his kiss drove at her. Despite all the twisting and turning of her head, she couldn't elude its heated force. Then came the shocking recognition that some part of her didn't want to end this moist, rocking together of their lips. Pride wouldn't let her respond, but a hunger inside wouldn't let her break it off.

Abruptly Chance pushed her from him. Dragging in a deep breath, she threw back her head to look at him, taut-jawed and grim-lipped. Could he see the brightness of her eyes? she wondered. Did he know it was caused by hot tears?

"Do you realize how ironic it is, Flame?" he challenged, a harshness tightening his voice. "You condemned me for using you to get Morgan's Walk. Yet you can justify the way you're using Powell because he's your means of keeping it."

She trembled, angered that he would dare to make such a comparison. She wanted to shout at him that it wasn't the same at all. There was no pretense of love in her affair with Malcom—not on either side—and no attempt at deception either. Theirs was an arrangement that suited both of them. But Chance had already walked away from her. She glared after him, watching as he disappeared inside the building, and hating him for trying to paint her with his own devil-black brush.

Turning her back on the lighted hall, she drank deeply of the night air and fought to cool her temper. Why did she let him rile her like this? Why didn't she simply ignore his pointed gibes? There was no truth in them.

"Have you had all the fresh air you want?" Malcom tried but he couldn't keep the accusing edge out of his voice.

It wasn't the fresh scent of the night air he caught when he halted behind her, but the heady tang of a man's cologne that mixed with her perfume. Swinging around at the sound of his voice, she faced him, all heat and fire. He had the satisfaction of knowing that whatever Stuart had taken, it had been without her consent. Yet he was irritated, too, by the deep emotion Stuart had succeeded in arousing, when he himself had barely created a ripple in all this time with her.

"He knows, Malcom." Her voice was made tight by her attempt to keep all feeling from it.

"He knows about what?"

"Our development."

"You told him?" He eyed her in surprise.

"I told him nothing that he didn't already know." She gripped her small purse with both hands, her knuckles whitening with the pressure. "This changes things, Malcom. He'll be out to stop us now."

"I'll handle him. Don't worry. As soon as we get back, I'll get Bronsky moving on an approval for the dam—and place a few calls of my own to clear the way for it. I have the financing for the project virtually in place now. I can't think of any obstacles he can throw in our path that will stop us."

"But you don't understand," she insisted urgently. "He's going to come after us with everything he has. This isn't a fight we can win by waging it at long distance. One of us will have to stay here in Oklahoma from now on. Obviously, that has to be me."

He disagreed with her logic, but he didn't think logic had anything to do with her decision. She claimed to hate Stuart, yet she wanted to be here to do battle with him. Silently, he studied her—so rigid and proud. He wanted to kiss away that stiffness, but he doubted that he would like the taste of another man's lips.

"That's what you've wanted all along isn't it? To move out here," he said with a certain fatalism.

"No," she denied, as if stunned he should even suggest it.

"That's what you planned to do when you married him."

"Well, I'm not married to him now," she replied angrily.

"Yes, I know. But I wondered if you remembered that." He took her arm. "Let's go back inside. The night air doesn't seem to be agreeing with either one of us."

39 ~

IN LESS THAN a week's time, Flame flew to San Francisco, packed her things, notified the building manager of her intended absence for several months, arranged for her mail to be transferred, resigned her position at the agency, cleared her desk, and caught a flight back to Tulsa. Fortunately, she had been grooming Rudy Gallagher to take over the Powell account, the only major client she had continued to handle personally the last few months, so the actual transference of her accounts had been the least time-consuming of her tasks. The rest had been hectic and harried, every minute crammed with something that needed to be done.

And the pace hadn't slowed up when she arrived back at Morgan's Walk. Friday morning the freight service delivered the boxes of personal items she'd arranged to have shipped to her. She sorted through them, separating the three marked with the letter *P*, indicating they contained either her paperwork or office supplies, and carried them into the library. The rest she gave to Maxine to unpack.

Weary from jet lag and too little sleep in the last five days, Flame stood in the middle of the library and stared at the three boxes, then shook her head at her inability to decide which to unpack first. What did it matter? Ultimately she had to unpack all three.

Using the scissors from the desk, she cut through the packing tape and unfolded the cardboard lids. From the grand foyer came the pounding thud of the front door's brass knocker. At almost the same instant, the telephone rang.

Hearing the rapid clumping as Maxine hurried down the stairs, Flame called out, "I'll answer the phone." Leaving the opened box on the floor, she crossed to the desk and picked up the phone on the second ring. "Morgan's Walk, Flame Bennett speaking."

"I know what you are trying to do." Startled by the strange-sounding voice on the line, Flame pressed the receiver closer to her ear and frowned. "You had better stop or you will be very sorry."

"Who are you?" she demanded angrily. "*What* are you?"

But the line went dead. She held the phone away and stared at it. Something about the threatening call was vaguely reminiscent of the hastily scrawled messages she'd received in the past. The hawk-faced man—she hadn't thought about him in weeks. But that had all happened back in San Francisco—before she married Chance. Had he followed her all the way to Tulsa? If so, why had he broken the pattern and called her instead of leaving her another one of his menacing little notes?

That voice, it had sounded alien . . . mechanical—like a robot's. It was definitely not made by a human. No, some kind of voice synthesizer had been used, obviously to protect the identity of the caller. But she'd never heard the hawk-faced man speak. She couldn't have recognized his voice.

She mentally shook the whole thing away and returned the receiver to its cradle, telling herself that she was making too much out of it. More than likely the call was some adolescent's idea of a prank. As far as she was concerned, a very unamusing one.

"I see I've caught you in the midst of settling in."

Flame spun around and stared for a blank instant at Ben Canon standing in the doorway, materializing out of nowhere, like the leprechaun he resembled.

"Maxine said you were in here." His gaze narrowed sharply on her, his remark reminding her there'd been someone at the door when she answered the phone. "Is something wrong?"

"No," she denied quickly, then gestured toward the phone. "Some crank called. That's all," she said, shrugging her shoulders in an attempt to dismiss the threatening phone call. "Come in, but you'll have to excuse the mess. As you can see, I have moved in, bag, box, and baggage."

"Yes, I noticed part of it in the foyer." He smiled in sympathy as he walked over to a wing chair.

"What brings you all the way out here?"

"I have some good news." He set his briefcase on the chair.

"I could use some." Especially in the wake of that phone call, but she didn't say that as she skirted the box at her feet and joined him in front of the fireplace, conscious as always of the portrait that watched her.

The lawyer took a letter from his briefcase and handed it to her. "Morgan's Walk has received preliminary approval to be listed as an historic place. I stress preliminary. It could still be rejected. Unfortunately we can't claim Will Rogers slept here—or that Edna Ferber wrote part of *Cimarron* in one of the guest bedrooms. We could be certain of acceptance then. Still, I think this is a good sign."

"So do I." As Flame started to glance through the letter, Maxine walked into the library, carrying a coffee tray, the thick rubber soles of her orthopedic shoes making almost no sound on the hardwood floor.

"You didn't say, but I figured you'd want coffee," she declared, throwing a pointed look at the attorney.

"That's thoughtful of you, Maxine."

She sniffed at his compliment. "I decided it was better to bring it now than get all the way upstairs and have you holler for me to get it." Just as she set the tray down on the cherrywood table, there was another knock at the front door. The housekeeper left the room, muttering, "This house is turning into Grand Central Station."

"Are you expecting someone?" Ben glanced at her curiously as he helped himself to a cup of coffee.

"No. But I wasn't expecting you either."

Almost immediately, Maxine was back. "It's some real estate man named Hamilton Fletcher." She handed Flame his business card. "He asked to talk to you, but he wouldn't say about what."

Flame recognized the agency name on the card as one she'd commissioned to buy land for her. Ignoring Maxine's probing look, she said, "Show him in."

With a white straw Stetson in hand and gleaming black cowboy boots on his feet, Hamilton Fletcher looked the part of a gentleman rancher, quiet and unassuming, with a thin, almost scholarly face. "I don't mean to be barging in on you like this, Mrs. Bennett," he apologized immediately, talking in a soft drawl. "We've talked on the phone, but we've never met. I'm Ham Fletcher . . . with the Green Country Real Estate Agency."

"Of course, Mr. Fletcher. I remember you," Flame replied, then introduced him to Ben Canon, whom he already knew.

"I've just come from the Crowder place, the one you wanted me to try to buy for you," he said. "Since I was so close, I thought I'd stop and see if I couldn't straighten something out. After I talked to you on the phone last week, I went to see the Crowders and made them another offer. When I stopped by today, they said they weren't interested in selling . . . and that they'd already told the other fella that."

"What other fella?" She frowned.

"That's what I was wonderin'," he replied with a troubled smile. "If you've got someone else trying to buy their land for you, it'd be best if I backed off and not muddy up things. I know you were upset that I was taking so much time—"

"Mr. Fletcher," she interrupted, "I don't have anyone else trying to buy the Crowder place for me."

He lifted his head, his hazel eyes rounding slightly. "In that case, ma'am, there must be somebody else who's wanting to buy that land, too."

"Then let me suggest that you go back to the Crowders and make another offer—a substantially higher one," Flame stated crisply.

He hesitated, slowly turning his hat in his hand. "The last offer I made them was a hundred dollars an acre more than the land's worth."

"Then make it five hundred," she replied. "I want that land, Mr. Fletcher."

He drew back his head. "I don't think there can be any doubt about that— not with that high of an offer."

"Good. Then if there's nothing else, Mr. Fletcher—" she murmured, raising an eyebrow at him.

He took the hint. "I'm on my way to the Crowders. I appreciate your time, Mrs. Bennett. Mr. Canon." He nodded to both and left.

The agitation and impatience she'd managed to contain in Fletcher's presence broke free the instant he walked out of the library. She whirled from the doorway and started to pace. "Chance has found out I need that valley."

"I think that's a safe bet." Ben Canon nodded.

"And I think I know how," she said grimly, turning to face him. "The day before I left San Francisco, I met with Karl Bronsky. It seems our application and plans for the dam have mysteriously disappeared. We have to submit everything all over again. If Chance doesn't actually have our original plans in his possession, then he has copies of them. Which means he knows everything." Just as she had once known everything about his project. "Which is why he has someone out there trying to buy the rest of the valley before we can. Thank God we already have three of the parcels under option. But that Crowder piece is pivotal. We have to have it."

"I'm sure Stuart knows that, too."

"What do you know about the Crowders, Ben?"

He gave her an empty look and shook his head. "They're just a name on a county plat to me. You need to ask Charlie that question. He knows everything about everybody living within twenty miles of Morgan's Walk."

Spring was a busy time of year at Morgan's Walk. Between the demands of Charlie's schedule and hers, Flame wasn't able to talk to him until the following day. Then she went to him, joining the foreman at the corrals—ketchpens, Charlie called them—where the ranch hands were ear-tagging, vaccinating, and branding the young calves and castrating the bull calves.

Charlie stood at the fence, his arms draped over the top rail and his boot hooked on the bottom one. When she walked up to stand beside him, he glanced sideways at her and nodded, the white of his mustache lifting in a quick smile.

"You gettin' all settled in Miss Flame?" he drawled, not bothering to raise his voice above the bawl of the white-faced calves and their mothers.

"I'm getting close." She watched a cowboy on the ground prodding at a bewildered calf, urging it farther into the narrow chute. "How are the new men doing?"

Charlie made a sound of contempt. "Most of 'em are about as worthless as tits on a boar." Then he quickly shot her an apologetic look. "Beggin' your pardon, Miss Flame, but that's what they are. I gotta watch 'em every minute or I'll find 'em sittin' on their brains." Red dust swirled as a calf charged past them, newly released from the chutes. Charlie instantly straightened and yelled impatiently at one of the cowboys. "Holstener! You let that calf go without taggin' his ear. Run him back through." Then he relaxed again in his negligent pose against the fence and muttered sideways at Flame, "See what I mean?"

"Yes."

"Don't you worry about it, though. I'll get the work out of 'em."

"I know you will." She paused briefly, then asked, "Charlie, what do you know about the Crowders?"

"Which ones?"

"The Crowder family that owns that valley farm north and west of us."

"Old Dan Crowder and his wife, you mean." He nodded. "Yeah, they're still livin' there on what they call the homeplace. Although I hear their daughter and her husband are doin' most of the farmin' since ol' Dan took sick. They had two boys, but they're both dead now. They lost the oldest when he was just a pup. The other boy was killed in an automobile accident . . . must have been ten years ago. Now they've got just the girl. 'Course, she's got three young'uns. I can't remember what her name is . . . Martha . . . Mary . . . Marjorie. It's something like that."

"You said Mr. Crowder's ill?"

Charlie nodded. "Operated on him last year for throat cancer. That family's had a rough time of it, one way or another. But they're good people—honest, hardworking. Makes you wish folks like that had a decent place to live."

"The farm's not worth much?"

He shook his head. "The soil's too poor. Sittin' in the valley like that, you'd think it'd be good bottomland, but it ain't. They probably make enough from farmin' to keep their heads above water and that's about all."

"You'd think they'd sell it and buy somewhere else."

"You'd think so. But there's been a Crowder workin' that land since before this territory became a state. 'Course, there was already a Morgan here when they came."

"Hey, Charlie!" a cowboy shouted. "Reckon we can have the cook fry us up a mess of mountain oysters for supper tonight?"

Charlie shouted back, "At the rate you boys are movin', we'll still be here come daybreak."

"I'll let you get back to your work, Charlie," Flame said, encouraged by the information he'd given her about the Crowders. The father's recent illness and surgery had to have placed the family in some financial straits. She felt certain they'd find her generous offer for the farm much too tempting to resist.

But a phone call to the real estate agent, Ham Fletcher, later that day failed to provide her with an answer—good or bad. He said he'd left the offer with Mrs. Crowder and planned to call back the first of the week if he didn't hear from them in the meantime. He promised he'd call her the minute he had an answer one way or the other.

But Sunday came and went without a phone call from him.

Flame frowned in her sleep at the blaring ring that tried to waken her. She tried to shut it out. For a time, she was successful. Then it came again, louder and shriller than before. With a groan, she rolled over, certain it couldn't be morning already. She felt as if she'd just fallen asleep. Then her grogginess faded as she realized it wasn't the alarm going off; it was the telephone ringing.

She groped for the pull-chain to the lamp by her bed and peered blearily at the green-shining numbers on her digital alarm clock: 11:36 P.M., they read.

"Malcom, there's a two-hour time difference," she moaned and lifted the receiver, carrying it to her ear. "Hello," she said, trying to force the sleep from her voice.

"You did not listen to me," came that strange mechanical voice over the line, its monotone oddly distorted and tinny. Flame sat bolt upright in the bed, fully awake. "I warned you. You had better stop now or you will be sorry."

"If this is supposed to be funny," she declared angrily into the phone, "I am not amused."

But there was no reply, nothing but the hollow sound indicating the connection had been broken. Flame gripped the receiver an instant longer, then slammed it down. Who was doing this? The hawk-faced man? But why? First he had warned her to *stay away from him*. By that she had assumed he meant Chance. Had he? Now he was warning her to *stop*. Stop what? It didn't make any sense. The two didn't seem to connect.

But if it wasn't the hawk-faced man, then who? Chance? He had tried to warn her off that night at the opera, hadn't he? Was this some tactic of his to scare her away? Perhaps. Yet, try as she might, she couldn't imagine him deliberately frightening her like this.

On Wednesday, Flame sent Maxine home early. Twenty minutes after she left, the telephone rang. Flame stiffened instantly, a high tension leaping through her nerves. She stared at the phone on the desk and listened to it ring a second time, reminding herself that she hadn't received any threatening calls in the last three days. Did that mean they had stopped? Or was this one?

Hating her jumpiness, she picked up the phone. "Who is this?" An instant of silence followed. "I—"

"Flame? Is that you?"

"Malcom." She recognized his voice and immediately felt foolish for sounding so combative. Those calls had bothered her more than she realized. "I'm sorry. I didn't know it was you."

"Who did you think it was?"

"It doesn't matter." She didn't want to go into it just now. There were too many other—more important—things she had to talk to him about. "I'm glad you called. I was going to try to reach you later tonight. How are you? Is everything all right there?"

"Everything's fine . . . although lately my luncheon meetings have become very dry and boring affairs."

"It must be the company you're keeping nowadays."

"I'm sure of that," Malcom replied.

"Listen, I have some good news. We've been able to secure an option on another parcel. At least, it's verbally secured. Ben's drafting the agreement now and I'm having dinner with him tonight to go over it. Hopefully we can telex it to you in the morning."

"Why don't you bring it with you when you fly back on Friday? One more day shouldn't hurt anything."

For a moment she didn't know what he was talking about. Then she remembered she'd originally said she would fly back this weekend to wrap up any loose ends. "I won't be able to come, Malcom. I'm sorry. I have too many things to do here."

"It's amazing, Flame," he said in a tone that revealed his ill humor. "You were too busy to see me before you left. And now you're too busy to come back. In all the times we've talked this last week, I have yet to hear you say you miss me. We made an agreement, Flame, and this long-distance communication wasn't part of it."

"Believe me, I don't like it either. I do miss you, Malcom. Maybe I haven't said it, but you don't know how many times I've wished you were here. I need you, and there's so much we need to talk about. It appears we're going to have a problem acquiring the Crowder property. They turned down our last offer. I know they need money. They don't have medical insurance and they owe the hospital a small fortune for the operation Mr. Crowder had last year. With the doctor bills and the ongoing treatment he needs, they have to be deeply in debt. I'm trying to find out how much they owe. That's one of the things I wanted to go over with you. Maybe if we offer them enough money to pay off all their bills and have a little nest egg left, we might be able to induce them to sell. What do you think?"

"It sounds logical," he replied, cynically thinking that she missed talking to him all right—about business. Why couldn't she have said she missed him— and left it at that?

"It means we'll be paying more than the farm's market value. But that land is so crucial to us I think ultimately it will be worth whatever we have to pay." There was a slight pause, then she said, "Malcom, why don't you fly here? Once I get all the figures together, it will be so much easier to go over them with you in person than trying to do it over the phone."

"It certainly would, wouldn't it?" he murmured dryly.

"This isn't a decision I want to make without you, Malcom. Can you come?"

"Not this weekend. I have a board meeting to attend Saturday morning."

"What about the following weekend?"

Malcom hesitated. Opening Day was the following weekend, signaling the start of the yachting season in San Francisco. In all the years he'd been married, he and Diedre had never failed to participate in the event, frequently holding a party on their boat. But he wanted to see Flame. Out of all those years, what harm would it do to miss one Opening Day?

"I might be able to arrange that," he said at last.

"Wonderful. We can turn the air conditioner on and spend a cosy evening in front of the fireplace with lights turned down low and a fine old brandy I found."

She sounded happy. Malcom wondered if Diedre was right when she said he was getting cranky and difficult to please. After all, Flame had asked him to come. And she'd never been the helpless, clinging type. That was part of what had attracted him to her in the first place—her pride and independent spirit.

"Where can I reach you later tonight?" she asked.

"What time?"

"I don't expect my dinner meeting with Ben to last much longer than a couple hours. I should be back at Morgan's Walk by ten at the latest. Ten o'clock Central time, that is."

"Which means eight o'clock here, and I'll be at the DeBorgs' having dinner. Why don't you call me in the morning at my office?"

"First thing," she promised. "And try to come next weekend, if you can, Malcom."

"I will. I want to sample that brandy by the fire . . . and you."

40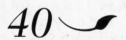

WHEN FLAME WALKED OUT of the downtown restaurant, her glance went automatically to the towering black monolith in the next block. The ebony gleam of its marble façade seemed to loom over her, the distinctive gold *S* of the Stuart logo taunting her with its presence. Abruptly, she turned and waited for Ben Canon to join her.

"Thank you for dinner," she said. "I enjoyed it."

"After all the evening meals you've had alone at Morgan's Walk, I thought it might be a pleasant change."

"It was." She opened her purse and took out her car keys. "I'll call Malcom in the morning and advise him that you'll be telexing the final draft of the option agreement first thing."

"I'm going back to my office right now and make those few minor revisions we discussed tonight," he replied, holding up the folder in his hand that contained the document. "Where did you park? I'll walk you to your car."

"I'm in the lot across the street." She nodded in the direction of the light blue Continental parked directly beneath a light. "You don't need to walk me over there, especially when your office is in the opposite direction."

"Just trying to be a gentleman." He shrugged indifferently, accepting her refusal of his company.

"Be my lawyer instead and get that option agreement finalized before Chance slips in and buys that land out from under my nose."

He chuckled at that. "You're sounding more like Hattie every day. Goodnight, Flame."

He waved the folder at her and set off with a jaunty stride. Smiling absently, she watched him for a moment, then angled across the street to the parking lot. A security light cast its bright glow over the sky blue Lincoln parked next to its tall pole, banishing all the night's shadows.

As Flame paused in its light to unlock the driver's door, she felt a prickle of unease, that odd, uncomfortable—and much too familiar—sensation that she was being watched suddenly claiming her. She hadn't had that feeling since she'd left San Francisco—back when the hawk-faced man had been following her. She looked around, scanning the lot and the street, half-expecting to see the hawk-faced man shrink out of sight. But there was nothing—no one walking along the sidewalk, no one sitting in a parked car, no dark shape lurking in the shadows of the buildings nearby.

Almost angrily she tried to shake off the feeling, blaming it on those threatening phone calls that had her imagination working overtime, as she unlocked the car door and quickly slipped behind the wheel. Yet it remained, cloaked in the need for haste that had her accelerating out of the parking lot onto the street.

Four blocks from the restaurant, the rearview mirror reflected the glare of bright headlights behind her. Flame immediately tensed. Where had that car come from? She was certain there'd been no vehicle waiting to turn at the last intersection. How had it appeared like that—as if out of nowhere? Then she realized how paranoid that sounded and chided herself for seeing a threat in something so innocent as a car behind her on a public street. The entrance ramp for the interstate was just ahead, for heaven's sake. Naturally there'd be more traffic around it, even in this quiet downtown area.

Flame honestly tried to ignore the car behind her, yet she was aware that it turned onto the interstate when she did. But, so did a second car behind it.

The fifteen-mile stretch of highway to her exit seemed much longer tonight. Along the way, she passed slower-moving traffic and other vehicles passed her, yet the glare of headlights in her rearview mirror remained constant. Over and over again, Flame told herself that it didn't necessarily mean it was from the same car.

When it took the same rural exit she did, she began to wonder if her first instinct had been right—that the car was following her. It was five miles to Morgan's Walk from here—five miles on a narrow, two-lane highway that carried very little traffic, especially at night.

With her uneasiness growing, Flame slowed the Lincoln, trying to force the car behind her to pass. But it slowed down, too. When she speeded up, it did, keeping the same close distance behind her. Her palms began to sweat. The hawk-faced man had never been this obvious when he'd tailed her before. Why now? Then she realized that whoever was back there wanted her to know she was being followed—he wanted her to be worried . . . frightened. The worst of it was—he was succeeding.

Straining, she tried to see beyond the bright beams of her headlights into the blackened night, searching for a landmark that would tell her how much farther it was to the turnoff for Morgan's Walk. Ahead, the highway curved sharply to the right. From that point, Flame knew it was less than a mile to the ranch's drive. She flexed her fingers, trying to ease their knuckle-white grip on the steering wheel, as she slowed the Lincoln to make the curve.

But the car behind her didn't, its headlights suddenly looming closer, the reflection of their glare nearly blinding her.

"Are you crazy?" Flame cried out. "Don't you know there's a curve up ahead?"

A second later it slammed into her from behind, the impact jolting her, pitching her forward against the steering wheel, and sending the Lincoln shooting into the curve. She was going too fast! The car would never hold the curve!

As she braked frantically, the Lincoln briefly skidded sideways, crossing into the other lane. She fought desperately to control it, fear tightening her throat, nerves screaming. But she couldn't hold it on the road. The car careened wildly into the ditch on the opposite side. There was a split second of terror when she thought it was going to roll. Somehow the Lincoln righted itself and plunged up the other side of the ditch, bouncing and roughly tossing her from side to side.

It came to a shuddering stop in an open pasture twenty yards from the road. Flame sat there for a full second, her fear-frozen hands gripping the steering wheel. Then the shaking started, tremors of relief vibrating through her as she realized how very close she had come to disaster. She sagged against the seat back, then stiffened, remembering the car that had forced her off the road. All she could see of it was the red of its taillights in the distance.

She had no idea how long she sat there with the engine idling, the transmission in park—something she had no memory of doing—waiting for the shock to subside. Finally, on shaky legs, she got out and inspected the damage. All she found were some dents in the chrome bumper and clods of earth and clumps of grass caught here and there.

Aware that there was little hope of anyone driving by at this hour, she realized that she either had to walk for help or drive out of there and back onto the road herself. She chose the latter option.

That mile to Morgan's Walk was the longest she'd ever driven in her life, her arms, her shoulders, her neck aching from the banging about she'd taken. She was certain she'd wind up with several lovely bruises, but at least that was all. It could have been much worse—and that was the scary part.

The telephone started ringing the minute she walked into the house. She stopped short, dread sweeping over her as she stared at the beige telephone on the foyer table. Slowly she walked over and picked it up.

"Hello," she said, a wary tension in her voice. That alien voice replied in its eerie monotone, "You were warned. You may not be so lucky next time."

Flame gripped the phone, unable to speak, unable to move—paralyzed by the significance of that message. As the line went dead, she could feel every aching bruise and strained muscle in her body . . . and the fear rising again in her throat.

Fighting it, she quickly depressed the button and heard the familiar hum of the dial tone. Hurriedly, she punched a set of numbers, but in her haste, she inverted two of the digits and had to start all over again.

"Ben." She held the receiver with both hands. "Someone . . . someone deliberately ran me off the road."

"What? When?"

"Just now. On my way back to Morgan's Walk. It was deliberate, Ben. Somebody's trying to kill me."

"Flame, where are you? How do you know it was deliberate? What makes you so certain?" The questions came rapid-fire, the shock in his voice evident.

"I'm here . . . at Morgan's Walk. I just got a phone call telling me—" She stopped, catching the edge of panic in her voice, and started again, forcing a calmness. "—telling me that I'd been warned—and that I might not be so lucky next time."

"What?" Ben sounded as stunned as she had been. "Who was the call from?"

"I don't know."

"Was it a man's voice? A woman's?"

"It was a robot's," she replied and laughed nervously, trying to shake off her fear.

"What? Be serious, Flame."

"I am. Somebody's using some sort of voice synthesizer to make these threatening calls."

"These calls," Ben repeated. "There have been others?"

"This makes the fourth—or maybe it's the fifth. I can't exactly remember now."

"Dammit, Flame, why didn't you tell me about them?"

"I didn't think they were important. I thought they were a prank. Now . . ." She breathed in deeply. "Now I think I should notify the police."

"I'll do it. You stay there and I'll bring a detective out to talk to you. As soon as you hang up from me, call Charlie. I don't want you alone in that house."

She started to protest that such a precaution wasn't necessary, then thought better of it and agreed to call Charlie.

"I'll be there in thirty minutes—forty at the outside," Ben promised.

Flame sat in the parlor with both hands wrapped around her third cup of the strong black coffee Charlie had made for her when he arrived. Time and the potent brew had managed to push most of the fear to the back of her mind, and enabled her to regain control of her emotions, allowing her to go over the events again and again and again with the detective from the Tulsa police department.

"No. I told you I couldn't see what kind of car it was," she repeated her previous answer. "He followed too close. The glare of the headlights—"

"*He?* The driver was a man?"

"That was merely a figure of speech," Flame insisted, her patience waning at this endless picking over every little detail. "I couldn't see the driver. I don't know if it was a man or a woman."

"And there weren't any other cars on the road?"

"None," she said, shaking her head. "Not before or after I was forced off the road."

"Let's go back over these threatening calls you say you've been receiving."

"Again?" she murmured, sighing in irritation.

"Yes, ma'am, again," he confirmed, his voice remaining unmoved and continuing its stubborn and polite run. "What did the caller say?"

"He—" Flame caught herself. "—*it* warned me that I'd better stop or I'd be sorry—or a variation of words to that effect."

"Stop what?"

"I don't know!" As the answer exploded from her, she took a quick breath and tried to control her rising temper.

"You must have assumed something," the detective persisted.

"I *assumed* the calls were a prank." She shoved the coffee cup onto the end table and rose from the sofa, too agitated to remain seated any longer. She crossed stiffly to the fireplace, ignoring the throbbing protest of her right knee at the renewed activity, then turned back to confront the detective. "Somebody tried to kill me tonight, Mr. Barnes, and I want to know what you're going to do about it!"

He leaned back in the chair, resting his head against the rose brocade upholstery. "Who would want to kill you, Ms. Bennett?"

Flame hesitated a fraction of a second. Abruptly, she turned her back on the detective and stared at the ornate fireplace screen. "I moved here only a few weeks ago. I don't know many people here." She hesitated again and turned back to face him. "I'm not sure if there's any connection, but—before I moved here—when I was in San Francisco, I was followed by this man. Twice he slipped me threatening messages."

The detective looked at her with sharpened interest, his pen poised above his small black notebook. "What did he look like? Can you describe him?"

"He was . . . of average height and build, in his late forties. I think he had brown hair and I believe his eyes were hazel. And there was a very pronounced hook to his nose. I always thought of him as the hawk-faced man."

"And these messages, were they the same as the phone threats you've been receiving?"

"No, they were different. That's why I'm not sure if it means anything. The hawk-faced man was always warning me to—I quote—'stay away from him.' "

"Who were you to stay away from?"

"I—"

"Excuse me," Ben Canon spoke up. "I think I can clear up this matter. You see, on behalf of my late client Hattie Morgan, I engaged the services of a private detective in San Francisco—a man by the name of Sid Barker—first to locate Ms. Bennett, then to . . . look out after her."

Flame swung around to stare at him. "You hired him to follow me?" she demanded, reacting with a mixture of shock and outrage.

His smile was meant to calm. "You were the heir to Morgan's Walk at that point. And Hattie was anxious that . . . nothing happen to you." His deliberate hesitation made it obvious to Flame that Hattie had been trying to warn her away from Chance.

"Why didn't you tell me this before?" But it was too late to be angry about it, especially when she knew how right Hattie had been to warn her about Chance.

"It never occurred to me," Ben said ruefully. "I'm sorry."

"Then who's making these calls? Who's trying to kill me?" She didn't want to think Chance was behind all this. But, with the hawk-faced man eliminated, who else could it be?

"There must be someone, Ms. Bennett," the detective insisted. "An ex-husband, a former boyfriend, a jealous lover, an angry wife—someone."

Diedre. Did Malcom's wife feel so threatened by her affair with him that she would do something this drastic? No, it wasn't possible. She was in San Francisco; that was much too far away. The same was true with Lucianna . . . unless she or Diedre hired someone. But Flame rejected that possibility, too, unable to visualize either woman actually hiring someone to kill her.

She lifted her head in challenge. "My ex-husband is Chance Stuart. Does that help you?"

He breathed in deeply at that. "Stuart, eh."

"Yes," she said, her voice clipped and sharp, betraying her strained nerves. "Tell me, Mr. Barnes, exactly what are you going to do about the attempt on my life tonight?"

His shoulder lifted in a vague shrug. "Check your car over, see if the lab can pick up any traces of paint from the other vehicle that might help us identify at least the make of it." He paused briefly. "But to be perfectly honest with you, Ms. Bennett, even if we are lucky enough to track down the owner of the car, it still doesn't mean he or she was the driver of it. And even if we could, it's doubtful that they could be charged with anything more than reckless driving."

"But what about the phone calls? The threats on my life?" she demanded. "You can't simply disregard them."

"To make a case for attempted murder, we'd have to be able to prove the driver of the car made those phone calls. We could put a tap on your line and monitor all your calls, but—from what you've told me—the caller never stays on the line for more than fifteen or twenty seconds. Which means there wouldn't be time enough to trace the call."

Flame read between the lines, a fine tension gripping her. "And if you could, what then?"

The detective had the grace to look uncomfortable as Ben Canon spoke up. "The caller would probably be charged with a misdemeanor."

"A misdemeanor," she repeated in a stunned voice.

"That's assuming we can't prove the caller was the driver of the car that tried to run you down," the detective explained. "I'm sorry, Ms. Bennett, but until a felony is actually committed—"

"You mean until—this person—actually kills me, there's nothing you can do," Flame accused, trembling now with an anger born out of this awful feeling of helplessness.

He said nothing to that, instead closing his notebook and slipping it into his jacket pocket. "If you think of anything else that could be useful, you have my card. You know how to get hold of me. And if you receive any more threatening calls, mark the time and the exact message, and keep me informed."

Ben stood up. "I'll see you to the door, Mr. Barnes."

"That isn't necessary." The detective rose from the wing-backed chair and nodded politely to Flame. "I can find my way out."

There was silence in the parlor, broken only by the sound of his footsteps in the entrance hall, then the final click of the front door closing behind him. Flame was conscious of both Charlie and Ben watching her.

"I think it's obvious the police aren't going to be much help in this." She tried to sound nonchalant, cynical, but the words came out stiff and brittle.

"You think it's Chance, don't you?" Ben said.

"I don't know what to think," she replied, agitation putting a sharp edge on her answer. She didn't want to believe it was Chance even though he was the only one it could be. He had vowed to stop her. Yet she couldn't imagine him resorting to violence to accomplish it. Could she be that wrong about him?

"Flame, I—" Ben began.

Briskly, she interrupted him. "I'm sorry, but I don't want to talk about this anymore. I'm tired and I . . . just want to get out of these clothes." And forget, she thought to herself, but she knew that was impossible even as she walked from the room.

41 ◡

WITH THE EASE and deftness of long experience, Charlie Rainwater reached down and unlatched the pasture gate without dismounting from his horse. Flame waited on her mount while he swung it open for her. She rode through the opening, then reined in her horse on the other side and watched as he swung his horse through and closed the gate, again from horseback. Satisfied it was securely fastened, he straightened in his saddle and looked for a moment at a pair of white-faced calves cavorting about under the contented eyes of their Hereford mommas.

"That's a sight these old eyes of mine never get tired of seein'," Charlie declared as he turned his horse away from the gate and walked it up to hers. His faded blue eyes studied her thoughtfully. "Are you really goin' through with your plans for that development?"

"If I can." Assuming she didn't get killed first, Flame thought, the memory of her near brush with death too fresh yet.

These last five days, she'd thought of little else, becoming tense and on edge—and suspicious of everyone. She'd sworn Charlie and Ben to secrecy, extracting their promise not to mention the threatening phone calls or the attempt on her life to anyone—not even Malcom. If he found out, she knew he'd insist that she return to San Francisco. In her mind, to run from these threats would be the equivalent of giving up, and she wasn't about to do that.

Neither could she totally discard the possibility that Malcom's wife might be the one behind them. Or Maxine, who had looked after Chance as a child and believed he should have inherited Morgan's Walk. Or Lucianna Colton, who might want Flame completely out of Chance's life. Or some crazy environmentalist who didn't want the river dammed and made into a lake. Dammit, it could be anybody. It didn't have to be Chance.

Frustrated and confused, Flame pointed her horse toward the imposing brick mansion that crowned the gentle knoll and overlooked the entire valley—the mansion her great-grandfather had designed and built. Suddenly it hit her. Morgan's Walk had to pass to a blood relative! All along Chance had been the obvious suspect, but now she realized that he had an even better reason to want her dead—Morgan's Walk would automatically pass to him. The facts seemed inescapable: he was the only one who stood to gain if she either gave up the fight—or was killed.

Yet, when she remembered the times she'd been with him, the tender strength of his arms, the loving stroke of his hands, Flame couldn't imagine, no matter how she tried, that Chance actually would hurt her, not physically. He was trying to scare her. That's what he was doing. He thought he could frighten her off. She was angry then, angry that he thought she could be intimidated by the threat of violence. But why should that be a surprise? It wasn't the first time he'd underestimated her.

She was so engrossed in her own thoughts, that she barely heard Charlie when he said, "Every time I look at those Herefords scattered across that green pasture, I try to picture a bunch of rich folks riding around in those electric carts chasin' a dimpled ball. But it just won't come to me. I just keep seein' the river, the trees, and the cattle." His horse snorted and pricked its ears in the direction of the house. "Looks like you've got some company, Miss Flame."

"What?" Frowning, she gave him a blank look.

"I said you got company." He nodded in the direction of the dusty pickup parked in front of the house.

"I wonder who it is?" Someone was at the front door—a woman. Maxine appeared to be arguing with her. Flame lifted her horse into a trot and cut across the front lawn, the thick grass reducing the echo of hoofbeats behind her to a dull thud as Charlie followed.

Nearing the house, she heard the woman's voice raise in angry challenge. "I know she's in there. You just march right back and tell her that I'm not leaving until I see her!"

"But she isn't here," Maxine protested. "She went—" She stopped, catching sight of Flame riding up with Charlie.

The woman turned, giving Flame her first good look at her as she reined her horse to a halt short of the portico steps. Somewhere in her early thirties, she was a tall woman, a solid woman, dressed in a pair of polyester knit slacks, the kind with the elastic waistband and stitched-in creases, an overblouse of print cotton giving her upper body an extra heaviness. Her light brown hair was cut short and curled in a tight frizz that required little care. She faced Flame in tight-lipped anger.

"What seems to be the problem, Maxine?" Flame swung down from her horse and passed the reins to Charlie.

"This woman—" Maxine began but never got a chance to finish.

"So you're the Bennett woman—the new duchess of Morgan's Walk," the woman spat with contempt. "This place was big enough for Hattie. Why isn't it big enough for you?"

"I don't believe we've met."

"No. You're too high and mighty to come yourself. You send that agent of yours instead to dangle all that money in front of us." She took a step closer, her broad face taut with resentment. "And in case you haven't guessed, I'm Martha *Crowder* Matthews."

"The daughter," Flame murmured, unintentionally out loud.

"Yes, 'the daughter,' " the woman snapped. "And I'm telling you to your face that our farm isn't for sale! I don't know who you think you are to come around here waving money in our face and thinking we'll snatch at it. Four generations of Crowders have farmed that land, and someday my sons or daughter will work it. My great-grandfather and my grandfather are buried there, and when my father passes on, he'll be buried there, too. Everybody's wondering what's happening to the family farm when it's people like you who are destroying it."

"Mrs. Crowder—Mrs. Matthews," Flame quickly corrected herself. "I'm not trying to destroy—"

But the woman wasn't interested in listening. "I sent that real estate agent of yours packing this morning. If he ever comes back to badger my father again about selling, and making him feel bad because he can't take care of his family the way he'd like, you're going to answer to *me!* Now, I'm warning you to stop— and you'd better listen."

Flame stiffened, the phrasing almost an exact echo of the threatening messages she'd received. Was this woman the one who'd made all those calls? And ran her off the road? Remembering those terrifying seconds when the car had been bearing down on her, Flame grew angry.

"Don't threaten me, Mrs. Matthews."

"I'm not threatening anything—I'm telling you!" she said and stormed off the portico, straight to the pickup truck coated with a film of red dust.

Spinning tires spit gravel as the truck lurched forward under a heavy foot. Flame watched it speed away from the house.

"Looks like you aren't going to be able to get the Crowder land," Charlie observed, leaning loosely on the saddlehorn.

She flashed him a sharp glance, any sympathy she might have felt toward the woman banished by yet another threat. "We'll see about that."

"What's he talking about?"

At Maxine's probing question, Flame turned, realizing the housekeeper had overheard everything. "Nothing that concerns you," she said curtly, and climbed the portico steps, removing her riding gloves. "Have you cleared away all those boxes from upstairs? I don't want that mess there when Mr. Powell arrives tomorrow evening."

"No, ma'am, but I will."

Thunder rumbled in the far distance, nearly masking the sound of the car's engine as Charlie drove the ranch's Lincoln around to the front of the house. Crossing the foyer, Flame glanced out the window at the ominous black clouds that darkened the sky. As yet, it hadn't begun to rain, so she left her raincoat draped over her arm and her umbrella closed.

She stopped at the foot of the staircase and called up, "Maxine, I'm leaving to pick up Mr. Powell at the airport. When you're through laying out the extra towels, you can go home."

A muffled reply came from one of the upstairs rooms, acknowledging the message. As Flame started for the door, the telephone rang. She hesitated, then walked over to the table and picked it up.

"Morgan's Walk."

"You have been warned," the mechanical voice intoned. "Why have you not listened?"

"You don't frighten me," she retorted angrily, but as usual, the connection had already been broken. She slammed the receiver down and stood there, vibrating. Why had that Matthews woman called again? Did she think she hadn't made herself clear yesterday? Then Flame grew still, realizing it was an assumption on her part that the Crowders' daughter was the one behind the threatening calls. She had no proof. Again she felt the rawness of anger. Who was doing this to her?

"Ms. Bennett?" Maxine stood at the top of the stairs, frowning in surprise. "I thought you'd left."

"Not yet." She glanced sideways at the phone. "Maxine, . . . have you taken any . . . strange calls?"

"Strange? What do you mean?" She started down the stairs, studying Flame with a puzzled look.

"Peculiar-sounding voices—or maybe they hang up as soon as you answer."

"No." She shook her head without hesitation. "There haven't been any calls like that." She eyed Flame a little closer. "Are you sure you feel all right, Ms. Bennett?"

It almost sounded as if she thought Flame was losing her mind. "I'm fine," she retorted and crossed immediately to the door.

Charlie Rainwater was coming up the steps as she walked out. "There you are," he said. "I wasn't sure you heard me drive up with the car. Here's the keys."

"Thank you." She took them from him, and started to walk to the car, then hesitated and turned back to him. "Charlie, do you know what kind of car the Crowders have?"

"They don't have a car—leastwise not anymore. They sold it last fall to pay some of Dan's medical bills. All they got now is that pickup their daughter was drivin' yesterday." Then he frowned. "Why?"

"Just curious." She shrugged off the question and resumed her course to the Lincoln, more troubled than before. Maybe she hadn't seen what kind of car had almost run her down, but she was positive it hadn't been a pickup truck. Assuming the woman had borrowed a neighbor's car, that still didn't explain how she'd known Flame was at that restaurant—unless, of course, she'd followed her there. Yet that didn't seem logical—not for a woman with a husband and children at home and a sick father to care for. And why hadn't the Matthews woman confronted her as she had yesterday instead of trying to run her down? That was backwards.

Flame sighed heavily as she slid behind the wheel of the Lincoln. If she eliminated Martha Crowder Matthews as a possibility, that left Chance again.

Halfway to the airport, the clouds opened up and sent down cascading sheets of rain. Terrific claps of thunder mixed with jagged bolts of lightning to show Flame the awesome power of a Midwest storm.

The violent rain cell delayed the arrival of Malcom's private jet. Flame used the time to contact Detective Barnes at the police department and inform him that she had received another threatening call, giving him the exact time and the brief message. As she returned to the lavishly furnished waiting room in the F.B.O. Building, she cynically wondered why she had bothered to call him. There was nothing the police could do about the threat, except to file it away. She sat down in one of the leather chairs and listened to the hammer of the rain on the roof and the ominous rumble of thunder.

The rain came down in sheets, drenching Chance as he dashed from the silver Jaguar to the covered entrance of his Tulsa mansion. He paused long enough to shake off the excess water, then reached for the door. But it was opened from the inside as his houseman Andrews appeared, clad in a raincoat, with a black umbrella in hand.

"Mr. Stuart. I was on my way out with the umbrella." The somberly competent man gave Chance a look of mild reproval for not waiting.

"I don't need it now," Chance replied briskly.

"Obviously," Andrews murmured, stepping back to admit him and observing the water that dripped from him.

"Where's Miss Colton?" Automatically he handed his briefcase to the houseman, his glance sweeping the marble foyer of his Tulsa residence. "I didn't notice the Mercedes when I drove in."

"She returned from shopping about forty-five minutes ago, sir." Andrews took a handkerchief from his pocket and wiped the bottom of the case before setting it on the imported marble floor. "She was caught in the rain as well and went upstairs to change. I'm relieved you made it back safely, sir. With this violent storm in the area, I thought you might be delayed several hours."

"We landed about an hour before it moved in." He ran a quick hand through his hair, combing the wet strands away from his face with a rake of his fingers.

"You've been back that long," Lucianna accused from the grand, curved staircase, pausing in a dramatic fashion midway down then descending the rest of the way, the long, tunic-style jacket to her satin lounging pajamas flowing out behind her. "Why didn't you call and let us know you were back? You have no idea how worried I've been thinking you were up there in those clouds with all that thunder and lightning. Where have you been all this time?"

"I had some things I needed to go over with Sam and Molly." His quick smile at her approach failed to erase his vaguely preoccupied air.

Ignoring it, Lucianna started to slide her hands around his neck, then felt the dampness of his suit jacket and drew back. "Darling, you're soaked to the skin."

"It's raining outside—remember?" he murmured, an ironic twist to his mouth.

Lucianna turned to the houseman. "Andrews, draw Mr. Stuart a nice hot bath," she instructed peremptorily.

"Don't bother, Andrews," Chance said, vetoing her order. "Just lay me out some clean, *dry* clothes."

"Very good, sir," the houseman replied, inclining his head in a movement that fell somewhere between a bow and a nod.

"Are you sure, darling?" Lucianna murmured softly, sidling closer to him while taking care not to let her satin lounging suit come in contact with his wet clothes. "I was going to volunteer to wash your back . . . among other things." She slipped her hands inside his jacket and smoothed them over his custom-made shirt as Andrews silently climbed the staircase to the master suite.

Chance caught her hands and set them away from him. "Maybe another time," he said, rejecting both her advance and her suggestion.

Momentarily taken aback, she laughed to cover it and took him by the hand to lead him to the stairs. "You'll regret that someday, Chance Stuart. I don't make offers like that very often." When he failed to respond with some equally teasing rejoinder as they started up the bleached oak staircase, Lucianna eyed him thoughtfully, trying to fathom this oddly preoccupied mood he seemed to be in. After all these years, she thought she knew his every mood, but this one puzzled her. She finally asked, "Is something wrong, Chance?"

"Of course not. What makes you think there is?" he shot back, the very abruptness of his answer making it ring false.

"This feeling I have that something's bothering you."

And the guarded look he gave her, masked by a lazy smile, heightened the feeling. "Woman's intuition, I suppose."

"Darling, you can't deny I'm a woman. And my instincts tell me that something's upset you and put those lines of tension around your mouth," she replied confidently, her glance flicking to the unusually thin line of his lips.

He looked at her, for a moment neither denying nor confirming her observation. Then a loud clap of thunder vibrated through the house, setting the wall sconces' pendants of Nesle crystal to tinkling.

"Blame it on the storm then—and the violence in the air," he said.

Suddenly she knew that, whatever was bothering him, it had something to do with Flame. Rage flashed through her, jealous rage. She looked away, aware that it was useless to confront him. Flame Bennett was one subject Chance refused to discuss with her—not even in the most general terms. Had he seen her? Talked to her? But that was impossible. He'd come directly from the airport. No—he'd met with Molly and Sam before coming home. Then the meeting must have been about her. She had never hated anyone as much as she hated that woman. But she knew how to make Chance forget her. It merely required setting the proper scene.

Twenty minutes later, Chance stood beside the king-sized bed and tucked the tails of his striped shirt inside the waistband of his Italian slacks. Outside, the storm had subsided to a steady rain. Lightning flashed, drawing his glance to the rain-washed window.

In his mind's eye, he saw again the jagged bolt of lightning that had lit up the night sky as he'd been leaving the airport after meeting with Sam and Molly —the bolt of lightning that had revealed the light blue Lincoln in the parking lot and the woman walking away from it, an umbrella tipped against the sheeting, wind-whipped downpour. The long shape of her, the familiar way she moved—it was Flame; he'd known it immediately even though he couldn't see her face. There was only one possible reason for her to be at the airport: Malcom Powell was flying in to spend the weekend with her.

From the adjoining sitting room came the distinctive *pop* of a champagne cork, shattering the mental image of that rainy scene. Abruptly Chance turned away from the bed where she'd slept with him for those few precious nights as his wife, turning his back on those memories just as she had spurned him.

A set of double doors led into the sitting room. He crossed to them and pulled them open. Andrews glanced at him briefly, then continued to pour champagne into the two fluted glasses, a serving towel deftly wrapped around the bottle to absorb the bubbly foam. When Lucianna saw him, she undraped herself from the brocade sofa she'd been lounging on and assumed a seductive pose, her hands gripping the plump edges of the sofa cushions, her shoulders hunched forward, and her head thrown back.

"Feel better, darling?" Her dark gaze slithered admiringly over him.

"Drier," Chance replied and strolled the rest of the way into the room as she picked up the two glasses and rose from the sofa to cross to him. "Champagne. What's the occasion?" he said, taking the glass she handed him.

"Darling, when has there ever had to be an occasion for us to drink champagne?" she challenged, and touched the rim of her Baccarat crystal glass to his.

Chance lifted the glass to his mouth, but the effervescent wine had barely touched his lips when he jerked the glass away. "What the hell—" He bit off the rest of the expletive, flashing a furious glance at Lucianna.

She laughed at his reaction. "It's peach champagne, darling, not poison."

He swung on the houseman as he folded the towel neatly around the bottle nestled again in its bed of ice in the champagne stand. "How much more of this do we have, Andrews?"

"You instructed me to purchase two cases when—"

"Throw it out. All of it!"

Andrews blinked at the appalling waste. "But, sir—"

"I said—get rid of it!" Chance set the fluted glass on the contemporary acrylic table with such force the crystal stem broke, spilling champagne on the ecru rug and sending the rest of the glass shattering to the floor. Yet he seemed mindless of it as he strode to the door.

"Chance. Where are you going?" Lucianna called, still stunned and confused.

He stopped at the door and turned. The look in his eyes was cold—so cold it burned. "To the library." Then his glance cut to Andrews. "Hold my calls. I don't want to be disturbed."

Lucianna flinched at the loud slam of the door when he pulled it shut behind him. Slowly she focused on the peach champagne in her glass. "He told you to buy this when he brought *her* here to live, didn't he, Andrews?" She murmured the accusation.

There was a slight pause before the houseman answered, "It may have been around that time, yes, ma'am."

She walked over to the champagne stand and poured the contents of her glass onto the ice, then glared at him. "Why are you standing there? You heard Mr. Stuart. Get rid of it. Now!" She swung away from him and folded her arms tightly in front of her, still holding the empty champagne glass.

There was a rustle of movement, then the almost silent click of the door latch. Alone in the room, Lucianna looked at the glass in her hand. In a fit of rage, she hurled it at the wall and shut her ears to the sound of the expensive crystal shattering into fragments.

42 ⟋

AS MALCOM STEPPED out of his Learjet, Flame went forward to meet him at the bottom of the stairs. When he reached her, she quickly shifted the umbrella to cover both of them from the downfalling rain and gave him a quick kiss in greeting, which he immediately lengthened into something warmer.

"You're definitely all in one piece." She smiled at him. "I wondered if you would be."

"So did I," Malcom replied.

"Was it very turbulent up there?" she asked, surveying him with some of her earlier concern.

"We were able to fly around the worst of it."

"Good. My car's in the lot," she said. "We'll come back for your luggage."

"Come back? From where?"

"We were supposed to meet Ben Canon and Ham Fletcher ten minutes ago," she said, water splashing about their feet as she hurried him across the tarmac to the parking lot across from the F.B.O. Building. "Ham Fletcher's the real estate agent who's been trying to buy the Crowder land for us—with absolutely no success. He insisted it was important that he talk to us. I started to meet him by myself, but I thought it would be better if you hear firsthand whatever it is he has to say rather than for me to try to repeat it."

"Where are we meeting them?"

"At the hotel here by the airport."

Irritation rippled through him as Malcom ducked inside the car and settled in the passenger seat. "I fly all this way—just to step off the plane straight into another meeting. You know this isn't what I expected, Flame," he challenged. "What happened to that fine old brandy and our cosy evening in front of the fire—the one you described to me over the phone?" And the one that had persuaded him to come out here.

"I'm sorry, darling, but I promise we'll do it another night," she said, then immediately started telling him about the latest development with the Crowders. Malcom pretended to listen, but he didn't hear any of it. He remembered the perfunctory kiss she'd given him when he'd stepped from the plane. With a touch of irony, he recalled the way he had always imagined an affair with Flame—that it would bring passion and an escape from stress into his life. Instead it had brought him more pressure. He talked business sixteen hours a day as it was. And he'd flown all this way to do more of the same. He laughed silently at himself, realizing that he'd given up a rare leisurely weekend on his boat for this.

His smile faded as he recalled Diedre's reaction when he'd told her he wouldn't be there for Opening Day. He'd waited until two days ago to tell her. He wasn't sure why. Maybe to make the trip sound more urgent. But he hadn't fooled her for a second.

"This Friday. That means you won't be here for Opening Day," she'd said, her acute disappointment plainly visible.

"I'm sorry, but it can't be helped," he'd insisted.

"Where do you have to go?"

He'd hesitated a fraction of a second before answering. "Tulsa."

In that instant she'd known exactly who he was meeting and why, although she hadn't said a word. The hurt that flashed so briefly in her eyes had said it all. She'd turned away from him then, her shoulders hunching slightly as if to hold in the pain.

"If you have to go, you must," she'd said, with an attempt at lightness. "There'll always be next year." Then, in the tiniest of voices, she'd asked, "Won't there?"

"Of course." He'd been gruff with her—gruff to hide that twinge of guilt. He wondered what she was doing now.

"Here we are," Flame said, rousing him from his thoughts. "Ben arranged for us to use one of the hotel's meeting rooms. He said he'd meet us in the lobby."

A glass pitcher of ice water and four glasses sat on a tray in the middle of the long table. Next to them on a separate tray was an insulated carafe of coffee, Styrofoam cups and packets of sugar and powdered creamer. The rest of the table was taken over by opened briefcases, notepads, and ashtrays.

Malcom sat back in his chair at the head of the long table, his fingers linked together across his middle. At the opposite end, smoke spiraled from the brier pipe clenched between the attorney's teeth. Like Ben Canon, Malcom mostly watched and listened as Flame conducted the meeting, exhibiting a hard intensity and determination. She reminded him of a corporate tiger, seizing on any point that might give her the end she sought.

"But, Mr. Fletcher, you just said you believed Mr. Crowder would like to sell."

"I know what I said," the agent replied. "But his daughter won't let him."

"What right does she have to tell him whether he can sell or not? The title is in his name. He doesn't need her permission."

"Yes, he does. She has control of everything."

"That's ridiculous. She's his daughter," Flame said, with considerably more than a trace of impatience.

"I don't know how it works exactly. Maybe Mr. Canon can explain it better, but she's . . . I guess you'd call her his legal guardian. They set it up when he went in for that cancer surgery last year. And that's still the way it is. The poor man can barely make himself understood, and he's so sick and weak most of the time from that medication he has to take that he can't write more than a word or two at a time, then he has to rest. And Mrs. Crowder, she's beside herself, worrying over him and all the bills, not knowing how they're going to pay and what's going to happen."

"What is wrong with that woman?" Flame pushed to her feet. "Can't she see that if she would accept our offer, then her parents could have some peace and security in their last days instead of all this worry over bills? Instead of being so concerned about where he's going to be buried when he dies, she should be thinking about how he's going to live."

"You'd think so," the agent agreed. "But she's determined to hang on to that farm no matter what."

"This guardianship—or whatever it is," she said, turning to Canon. "Can it be revoked?"

"Possibly." He took the pipe from his mouth to answer. "You'd probably have to take her to court and prove she was unfit to do it. And you're talking time there. Mr. Crowder might be dead by then."

"What if he signed a sales contract, agreeing to sell at our price, could we make them honor it?"

"I doubt it."

"They aren't going to sell, Mrs. Bennett," the agent stated. "I think you'd better accept that. And if you have thoughts of making them another offer, you'll have to find yourself another man to take it to him. She came after me with a shotgun the last time I was out there, and she was crazy-mad enough to use it. Next time she might. And no commission—regardless of the amount—is worth my life. I'm sorry, but that's the way it is."

"I understand." But her look called him a quitter.

He stood up, closed his briefcase, and picked up his cowboy hat, holding it respectfully in front of him. "I wish you luck."

"Thank you." She remained standing, her gaze following him as he walked from the room.

Ben Canon thoughtfully poked at the charred tobacco in his pipe bowl and sent an upward glance at Flame. "There's one consolation in all this. If she won't sell to us, she won't be selling it to Stuart either."

She turned on him roundly. "That isn't good enough. We have to have that land. It's absolutely essential to the development. Which means we have no choice," she declared firmly. "We have to buy their mortgage and force them out."

"Why?" Malcom studied her with critical eyes, catching her stunned glance that quickly flared into bewildered anger.

"What kind of a question is that?" she demanded. "You know very well why."

"Do I? I wonder." All of his business life he'd heard statements very similar to hers. Yet he resented hearing such ruthlessness coming from her. "Those people want to keep their land. But you're going to force them off it."

"I am not that cold-blooded, Malcom," she said, her indignation rising. "I want to buy their mortgage and force them to *sell*, not throw them off the land without a penny. We'll pay them much more than the land is worth."

"Is that how you justify it?"

"What is going on?" she demanded. "If you have another alternative, tell me, because I can't see that we have any other choice except to give up. And if we do that, Chance—"

"I wondered how long it would be before Stuart's name was mentioned," he murmured.

"Malcom, whom do you think we're fighting? Who do you think is out there trying to get Morgan's Walk—any way he can?"

"And who do you think is becoming just as ruthless as Stuart?"

"I have to be!" she cried in anger. "It's me he's trying to destroy."

"And that makes it all right for you to destroy the Crowders' lives."

"I am not—*we* are not—destroying their lives. Ultimately, we're helping them," she argued.

"And you're going to *make* them accept that *help* whether they want it or not . . ."

"When did you become so righteous?" she demanded. "How many stores have you forced out of business or into bankruptcy? How many companies have you taken over? The iron man isn't exactly lily white."

"That was business. With you, it's purely vengeance. It's taken me a while to realize that everything you do revolves around getting even with Stuart. Maybe I didn't want to see it before."

"That isn't true," she denied, made restless and impatient by his accusation.

"Isn't it?" Malcom replied, a little sadly. "The only reason you're with me, Flame, is because I can help you get back at Stuart. You're using me . . . in much the same way he used you."

"How can you say that?" The fullness of her temper moved darkly over her face, clouding the green of her eyes.

"Because it's the truth. And I've discovered I don't like it." He got to his feet, amazed that all he felt for her at the moment was pity. "Go ahead and buy the mortgage, force the Crowders into selling. Do whatever you like, Flame. You've changed. You've become vindictive, twisted by your desire for revenge. And I want no more part of it."

When he started for the door, she demanded, "Where are you going?"

He paused near the door and turned back to her. "Back to San Francisco—to spend the weekend on my boat with my wife. And believe it or not, I'm looking forward to it."

She stiffened, her chin coming up. "Are you pulling out on me, Malcom? I thought we were partners."

A smile tugged at the corners of his mouth. "You once told me that you wanted our relationship to be strictly business. You've got what you wanted. The next time you need to meet with me, call my secretary. She'll schedule an appointment for you."

Flame spun away, not watching him walk out the door, her hands gripping the back of a chair, his accusation ringing in her ears. She felt Ben Canon's eyes on her.

"He doesn't understand," she insisted defensively, but it was too late to explain to Malcom about the threatening calls she'd received.

"I can see that," he replied, idly puffing on his pipe.

She grabbed up her things and started for the door. "You heard what he said. Buy the mortgage on the Crowder farm—the sooner the better."

Still smarting from Malcom's remarks, Flame swept out of the room and down the hall to the hotel lobby. She had a brief glimpse of his familiar profile, the silver tips in his dark hair flashing in the light, as he slid into a cab. Resentment, hot and galling, raced through her again. She'd been honest with him. She'd told him from the start that getting even with Chance was part of this. Hadn't he believed she was serious? Had he thought it was some game she'd get tired of playing in a few weeks? Was that why he had twisted everything around and tried to make it sound as though she had somehow deceived him? She hadn't, not once. She suspected that the real truth was their relationship hadn't lived up to his fantasy of it, so—with typical arrogance—he blamed her. Let him.

She pushed through the lobby doors and paused long enough outside to drape her raincoat over her head, not bothering with the umbrella, and ran through the rain to her car. With windshield wipers slapping at the steady rainfall, she drove out of the hotel lot, onto the street, heading for the freeway entrance a block away. Driving down the on-ramp, she spotted a gap in the blur of red taillights and accelerated quickly to highway speed to fill it.

There was a release in the speed and power at her command—a release from the anger and frustration that had no other outlet. She gripped the wheel, fingers clenching and unclenching, her lips pressed tightly together as she stared through the pouring rain at the gleaming taillights in front of her.

A car came up behind her, its headlights on full bright. Flame winced at the painful glare of them in her rearview mirror, a brightness that seemed to be magnified by the rainy, black night.

She muttered irritably at the unseen driver, "Didn't anyone ever tell you it's common courtesy to dim your lights when you're behind another car?" She flashed the Lincoln's headlights from low to high beam and back again, then gestured in the rearview mirror for the car behind her to do the same, but the driver didn't get the message. "Dammit, will you dim them?"

In an attempt to escape them, Flame swung the Lincoln into the passing lane. But the other car swerved with her, staying right on her tail. She switched back to the right lane and slowed down, hoping it would pass her. But the full, reflected glare of its blinding headlights were there again, directly behind her.

This time Flame realized, all her previous irritation and anger fleeing as alarm surfaced, that she was being followed . . . more than likely by the same person who had forced her off the road before. And just as before, whoever was back there wanted her to know he—or she—was there.

"Dammit, who are you?" she cried in a mixture of fear and frustration.

She tried, but between the sheeting rain running down her rear window and the harsh brightness of its headlights, she couldn't see what kind of car it was—if it was Chance's silver Jaguar or something else. Flame spotted the interstate sign indicating an exit one mile ahead—and the one after it promising gas, food, and lodging at the exit . . . and, more important, help.

She pushed her foot down on the accelerator and raced for the exit. Her stalker stayed right with her. She didn't slow down or signal her intention as she neared the off-ramp. Instead, she waited until the last possible moment then swerved the Lincoln onto the exit, and began to brake.

She was surrounded by darkness and pouring rain. The glare of the headlights—they weren't there anymore! The car hadn't followed her. With a quick turn of her head back toward the interstate, Flame tried to catch a glimpse of the car before it disappeared.

But she couldn't see it. It wasn't there. At the same instant, she had that eerie feeling she was being watched. Some sound, some motion, some instinct told her the car had pulled alongside her on the wide off-ramp. She automatically slammed on the brake as she turned to look.

There was a faint, explosive sound as her windshield fractured into a glass mosaic of a thousand tiny pieces. She couldn't see!

Fighting the waves of panic, Flame brought the car to a full stop. That's when she noticed the two small holes in the windshield—bullet holes—and the corresponding holes that had also shattered the glass in the driver's window.

The next day, the sky was blue and clear, the sun shining brightly, the water puddles standing around Hank's service station at the interstate exit offering the only lingering evidence of last night's storm. But the nightmare of it was very real to Flame as she watched a man from the police lab measuring the diameter of the bullet holes in the windshield of the sky blue Continental.

When she shuddered uncontrollably, Charlie touched her arm. "Are you okay?"

She thrust her chin a little higher, but carefully avoided looking at him. "Somebody's trying to kill me, Charlie," she murmured tightly. "Hattie warned me he'd stop at nothing—not even murder. But I didn't believe her."

43

RUNNELS OF PERSPIRATION streamed down his face and neck, plastering the cotton T-shirt against his chest. Drawing the racket back, Chance channeled all of his strength into his swing at the fast-flying ball and rocketed it back at the wall. Immediately he moved back, shifting to a ready stance, totally intent on the ball yet aware of his opponent, one of the trainers at the gym. The man made a diving swing at the careening ball—and missed. Game point.

Chance straightened, lowering his racket, muscles relaxing, the wind drawing in and out of him deep and even. He looked at his opponent lying sprawled on the squash court floor. Slowly, tiredly, he pushed to his feet and glanced at Chance, shaking his head.

"That's it. I've had it," he said, admitting defeat. "Man, I don't know who you're mad at, but you're out for blood."

The image of Flame came to Chance's mind, proud and strong, the flare of icy defiance in her green eyes. He dropped his glance and turned away to get his towel. "Hard day at the office, I guess."

"I guess," came the answering echo of full agreement. "Remind me never to play you at the end of the day again."

His mouth moved in a semblance of a smile as Chance scooped up his towel from the corner and rubbed it over his face and neck, letting its thickness sop up the sweat. Out of the corner of his eye, he caught the movement of the door to the court swinging open and turned, in absent curiosity. When Sam walked in, Chance checked the downward stroke of the towel along his neck, an alertness coursing through him, then continued to wipe at the perspiration.

"What's up?" he asked.

But Sam glanced at the trainer. Taking the hint, the man lifted his towel in a parting salute and headed for the door. "See ya."

Chance lifted his head in an acknowledging nod, then brought his full attention to bear on Sam, noting immediately Sam's unwillingness to meet his gaze. "What happened?"

"I was three hours late." Grimness and guilt moved over his boyish features. "She's locked up the Crowders' mortgage. The bank said she was there this morning to sign all the papers."

"Damn that woman," he swore in frustration, throwing back his head to glare at the ceiling and bringing his hands to rest on his hips, the racket against his side.

"I thought we had her when we managed to buy those two parcels this last weekend, but they aren't vital to her project. We needed the Crowder piece," Sam said, his glance finally seeking Chance's eyes. "She's won, hasn't she?"

"Not if I can help it." He pulled the towel from his neck. "Get Donovan on the phone and tell him to get the jet ready. I'm flying to Washington tonight and push for an approval on our dam myself."

"It's no good." Sam shook his head, then explained. "I talked to Molly before I came over here. That's how I knew where you were. Fred called to say he'd heard from Zorinsky. Morgan's Walk has been listed on the National Registry for Historic Places. He says there's no way you're going to get an approval now."

This time Chance said nothing. He stood there silent and staring, his mind racing. She'd blocked him.

Sam shifted uneasily. "Do you want me to wait?"

"No." His voice was hard and flat. "I have some thinking to do."

Sam hesitated then left him standing alone in the court.

44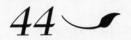

DARKNESS PRESSED ITS black hands against the library windows. Flame held the telephone firmly to her ear and waited for that voice to finish its threat, an anger like ice freezing her motionless. When a faint *click* signaled the connection was broken, she hung up and pushed the rewind button on the tape recorder she'd hooked to the phone. There was a quick whir of the tape, then a snap as the machine shut itself off. She played back the message, making sure she'd recorded all of it, then rewound the tape, and picked up the phone again, dialing the number in her address book.

"Yes? Stuart."

That hard, impatient voice belonged to Chance. She smiled coldly. "Isn't it amazing? You must have been sitting on top of the phone to answer it so quickly. Or maybe you just finished making a call."

"Flame?" Surprise ringed his voice.

"You didn't expect to hear from me, did you?" she murmured smoothly. "I thought I would call and tell you I know exactly what you're doing. But it isn't going to work, so you can stop making your threatening calls. You aren't going to get Morgan's Walk even if you succeed in killing me. I've seen to that."

"Kill you? What are you talking about? What calls?"

Her smile widened. "I didn't expect you to admit anything. After all, you were the one who told me I should have bluffed and pretended I didn't know what you were talking about."

"Dammit, I don't know," came the angry retort. "What threats? What calls?"

"Maybe this will refresh your memory." She held the telephone to the tape recorder and played the message for him, a slight shiver of dread breaking through her control as the alien-sounding voice spoke in its flat monotone: "Your luck has run out. I will stop you for good."

"My God, that voice—what is it?"

"It certainly isn't yours, is it?" she retorted. "And much safer than trying to disguise your own. But it isn't going to save you. The police will receive a copy of this tape. They know about the other attempts on my life. And if anything happens to me now, Chance, the police will come directly to you. And I'll have the satisfaction of knowing that you'll never get Morgan's Walk." She paused slightly, recalling the message. "You aren't going to stop me for good. I'm going to stop you."

She hung up, surprised to discover that her hand was trembling. She gripped it for a minute, then ejected the tape from the recorder and took an envelope and a sheet of paper from the desk drawer. Not letting her mind think, she swiveled her chair around and slipped the paper into the portable typewriter she'd brought with her. With an eerie detachment, Flame noted the pertinent details: the time of the threat, its content, her subsequent call to Chance, and her current action. She took the paper out of the typewriter, signed and dated it, then slipped it along with the tape into the envelope and sealed it shut.

With an odd feeling of finality, she laid the envelope aside and leaned back in the chair, gazing at the portrait of Kell Morgan above the mantel. "I promise you," she murmured, "a Stuart will never have Morgan's Walk."

She felt flat, drained, no emotion left. She'd fought so hard against believing Chance would want to harm her that finally accepting it had taken everything out of her. She realized that, deep down, she'd actually believed that he'd cared for her, despite his deception and trickery. But he hadn't. She knew that now. The last illusion of his love was gone.

She continued to stare at the painting. "It was the same for you as well, wasn't it?" she realized. "Ann didn't love you either. And, like me, you ended up alone in this house. Your parents had died years before, and you'd driven Christopher away with your pain and hatred the same as I—" She closed her eyes, a tightness gripping her throat. "The same as I drove Malcom away with mine."

My God, what had she become? A cold, bitter woman, obsessed with revenge. She remembered the Crowder family and the daughter's determination to keep their land—and her own fierce determination to get it from them. Malcom was right—she had become ruthless and vindictive. She hated Chance, but was she any different from him?

It was funny, she felt dead already—beyond feeling, beyond caring. There were things she should be doing, but they seemed unimportant as she sat and stared at the portrait.

The dull bonging of the grandfather clock in the foyer, chiming the hour, finally aroused her. She sat up and rubbed a hand across her forehead, then picked up the report from Karl that she'd been reading when the phone had rung. But she couldn't seem to concentrate on it.

From the rear of the house came a creaking sound, like the hinges of a door squeaking. Flame paused, listening for an instant, then dismissed the noise as the normal groans of an old house. But it heightened her sense of hearing, making her conscious of a dozen other sounds—from the loud thudding of her heart to the soft whisper of the paper in her hand.

When something rustled in a bush outside, she started at the noise. There was a face in the window! Chance. In shock, she stared into the glowering blue of his eyes, the expression on his hard, lean face lined with impatience and anger. Then she saw the gun in his hand. Her glance flew to the portrait above the mantel and saw the fear in Kell Morgan's eyes. She looked back at Chance. He shouted at her and pushed at the window, but the thick glass muffled his voice.

The report forgotten, she grabbed the phone and tried to reach Charlie at the bunkhouse, but there was no dial tone. She beat at the disconnect switch. It was no use. The line was dead. As she scrambled out of the chair, he pounded at the window, trying to get in. Her legs felt like leaden weights, and the desk seemed to grow bigger and wider as she tried to run from behind it and get to the doors.

He yelled, this time loud enough that she could hear, "Flame, no!!!"

She faltered no more than a split second to glance at him, then turned back to the hall doors. A figure, clad all in black, blocked the opening, a gun in her hand. Flame had that one glimpse, then something slammed into her. Dimly she heard an explosion and the crash of breaking glass as she fell down . . . down . . . down . . . into a swirling black abyss.

45 ✒

STRONG FINGERS SQUEEZED her hand, the warmth of them penetrating, causing her to stir. She surfaced slowly as if wakening from a deep sleep. She opened her heavy eyes, focusing them on the figure of a man standing next to the hospital bed.

"Ellery, I thought—" She had a fuzzy memory . . . that figure in black . . . the gun . . . Chance had tried to kill her. She was in the hospital. She remembered a nurse smiling over her and saying she was out of surgery, that she was going to be fine. She looked at the IV bottle on the stand beside her bed, a tube running to her hand, then frowned at Ellery. "How did you get here?"

"Ben called Malcom, and Malcom called me. I caught the red-eye flight, and here I am." His usually cynical mouth curved into a tender smile. "You gave us quite a scare, but you're going to make it. The bullet nicked an artery, but no vital organs. You lost a lot of that San Francisco blue blood, but the doctor tells me you'll probably be up and around in a couple days."

"Did they . . . did they arrest Chance?" She forced the question out, needing to know yet not wanting to.

"Chance?" An eyebrow lifted in momentary bewilderment. "Why should they?" His expression took on a wryly gentle look. "Or is it a crime in Oklahoma for someone to save your life? Because, my dear, if it wasn't for Stuart you would have bled to death before the ambulance got there."

"But—" She frowned, trying to make sense of this. "He was there, Ellery. He had a gun. I saw him."

"Poor Flame." Affectionately he gripped her hand a little tighter, a pitying light in his eyes. "You thought he was in it with her, didn't you? He wasn't. He was there to stop her."

"Her?" Her confusion deepened as she searched his face, wanting to believe him, yet afraid. "Who are you talking about?"

Her mind raced. Was it the Matthews woman—or Maxine? But if it was true that Chance had come to stop one of them, then how would he have known of her intent . . . unless he had plotted with her? Could it have been Lucianna? But why would she want her dead? Chance didn't love her, . . . did he? There was so much fragile hope in those two little words that Flame felt the aching start all over again. If it was true he'd saved her, didn't that mean he still cared? Oh, God, she wanted him to.

"I'm talking about Stuart's secretary, Molly Malone," Ellery replied, his voice again marked with gentleness.

"Molly?" Shock splintered through her, followed by even more confusion. "But why? Why would she want to kill me? I never did anything to her."

"Not to her—to Stuart."

She breathed in sharply at his answer, the memory instantly flashing into her mind of Chance saying, "Molly's the closest you'll come to a mother-in-law" —and Sam's remark that Chance was the sun in her life and her world revolved around him, that his enemies were her enemies.

Ellery went on. "From what I understand, she believed that Morgan's Walk rightfully belonged to Stuart—and by eliminating you, she'd be rectifying the situation. And, at the same time, she'd be preventing another Morgan woman from hurting him anymore."

"Like Hattie," she murmured and pressed her head back against the pillow to stare at the ceiling, the sting of tears burning her eyes.

She remembered Hattie's hatred for him—and the number of times Ben Canon had told her she sounded just like Hattie. She recalled the one occasion Chance had talked about his childhood—the day of Hattie's funeral—telling her how cruel Hattie had been to him, and how it hadn't made any difference to her that his mother was a Morgan, he carried the Stuart name, so she hated him. And her own reaction had been bitter scorn.

"I've made such a mess of things, Ellery. Just look what I became." She gazed at him through the wash of tears and tightened her hold on his hand. "It makes me wonder why he bothered to stop her." She tried to smile at her question, but the quivering of her chin made it a futile attempt. "How did he even find out what she planned to do?"

"Evidently you called him and played some sort of tape that sounded like a talking computer his company recently acquired for a blind office worker. First he tried to reach Molly to ask her about it, then came out to Morgan's Walk. When he discovered her car parked a half mile down the lane . . ." Ellery paused, smiling crookedly. "Actually the whole thing sounds like a Dashiell Hammett novella."

She made another feeble attempt at a smile. "I guess it does."

He squeezed her hand. "They told me I could only stay for a couple minutes. I'm afraid my time's up."

"You'll come back?"

"Tonight, after you've had some rest." He lifted her hand and pressed her fingers against his lips, then hesitated, holding her gaze. "Stuart's outside. In fact, the nurses tell me he's been camped out there ever since they wheeled you back from surgery. He wants to see you."

She caught back a little sob of joy and tried to not let her expectations get too high. "I'd . . . I'd like to see him."

"I'll send him in."

When Chance walked through the door after Ellery left and Flame saw the hard, smooth lines of his face, faintly shadowed by a night's beard growth, she wanted to cry. But she had too much control, too much pride, even now when she realized how wrong she'd been. He came to the side of the hospital bed and stopped near the foot of it, his blue eyes hooded and dark. She noticed his right arm was in a sling.

"You were hurt."

He glanced at the sling as if he'd forgotten it was there, then touched it briefly with his other hand. "A minor flesh wound. This will come off tomorrow, if not sooner."

"I'm glad." She hesitated, conscious of the tension, the strain, the awkwardness that was between them, and wishing there was a way to erase it. "I'm sorry about Molly. I know how close you were to her."

"You know, then." His gaze probed her expression, a hint of anguish and regret surfacing in his eyes.

She nodded. "Ellery told me. He said you saved my life. I—"

"It was my fault you were in jeopardy in the first place." Guilt—was that what he felt? She couldn't tell as he moved a step closer, briefly bowing his head before lifting it again to look at her, his jaw-line held rigid. "Flame, I want you to know that . . . Morgan's Walk is yours." She felt her hope start to crumble at his words. Again it was the land. "There will be no more attempts by me to take it from you. I swear it was never worth your pain—and God knows it was never worth your life to me." Conviction vibrated through his voice, deepening its timbre.

"But I don't want it either," she protested, a little stunned to discover she meant it. "There's been too much pain, too much bloodshed, too many wrongs committed in its name—on both sides."

"I came to the same conclusion last night," he said, nodding slowly and watching her.

"In a day or two," she said, thinking out loud, her gaze clinging to him, "I'll talk to Ben about possibly deeding it to the state . . . maybe for a park."

"Tell him that . . . that I'll lend any support he needs."

"I will." It seemed the final break. Without Morgan's Walk between them, she'd have no other excuse to see him. And she wanted to see him. Dear God, she still loved him.

A nurse walked in, her starched uniform rustling crisply. She smiled politely but firmly at Chance. "I'm sorry, but you'll have to leave now."

As he looked at her one more time, then turned to go, Flame knew she couldn't let him walk out. "Chance." Her fingertips caught at his hand. He turned back, his thumb coming down to hold on to her fingers, something stark and painful flashing over his face. "Is . . . Is it too late for us, Chance?"

Just for an instant there was a bright flare of blue—that same warm look he used to give her. Then he glanced down at her hand curved over his. "It's never too late, Flame, if we don't want it to be."

Behind his guarded reply, she detected the emotion-charged tightness in his voice and hope soared. "I don't want it to be."

He looked at her as if to make sure she meant it. "And I never have," he declared huskily.

Wordlessly she pressed her hand more tightly onto his and watched his mouth curve into that lazy warm smile that had always tugged at her heart. For the first time, she honestly believed it wasn't too late.

The nurse interposed again, "I'm sorry, sir, but—"

"I'm going," Chance said, his gaze remaining fixed on Flame, that warm glint in his eyes. "But I'm coming back." He leaned down and pressed his lips against her forehead, then whispered against her skin, "Till next time."

"Till next time." As she echoed his words, she felt a strong, rich eagerness. There was hope, dear God, there was more than hope.

Heiress

Part One

1

SUNLIGHT PIERCED THE THICK canopy formed by the branching limbs of the oak trees and dappled the century-old marble monument that laid claim to this section of the Houston cemetery as the Lawson family plot. Cut in the shape of an ancient obelisk, the monument had been erected more than one hundred years ago to watch over the graves of the first Lawsons to be buried in Texas — and to commemorate the Lawsons who had died far from their East Texas home while proudly serving the Confederacy. Again mourners had gathered, and the hallowed ground was opened to receive the body of yet another member of the family, Robert Dean Lawson, Jr., known to all as Dean.

The suddenness of her father's death — for Abbie, that had been the hardest. An accident, the police had said. He'd been driving too fast and missed a curve. Ironically, he'd been on his way home from the airport, returning from a business trip to Los Angeles. Killed on impact, Abbie had been told, as if that made his death easier to accept.

It hadn't. The pain, the regret came from not having the chance to talk to him one last time, to tell him how very much she loved him, and maybe . . . just maybe . . . hearing him say that he loved her. It sounded so silly, so childish to admit that, yet it was true. She was twenty-seven years old, but she still hadn't outgrown the need for her father's love. No matter how she had tried to get close to him, something had always stood between them, and years of battering hadn't broken down the wall.

Numb with grief, Abbie lifted her glance from her father's closed casket, draped in a blanket of Texas yellow roses, and scanned the crowd massed around the grave for the services. Admittedly the turnout wasn't as large as the one at her grandfather's funeral nineteen years ago. Even the governor had come to it. But that was to be expected. Her grandfather R. D. Lawson had been one of the pioneers in the petroleum industry. He was the one who had refilled the family coffers after they had been virtually emptied during those terrible years of Reconstruction that had followed the Civil War. Bold, shrewd, and very sure of himself — that's the way Abbie remembered him, even though she'd been a child, barely eight years old, when he died. Judging from the stories she had heard, he had been a colorful and charming character, and occasionally ruthless about getting what he wanted. In those early days in the oil business, sometimes a man had to be.

But the Lawsons weren't oil millionaires. Whenever people insinuated as much to Abbie — christened Abigail Louise Lawson after her grandfather's mother — she loved to steal her grandfather's famous line: "Not oil, honey. We made our money in mud." The startled expressions on their faces always made her laugh. Then she would explain that *mud* was the term given to drilling fluids that were pumped into a well to soften up the ground for the drill bit, carry off the tailings, and maintain pressure to prevent a blowout. In the early days of rotary drilling in the oil fields, a mixture of clay and water — literally mud — was pumped into the hole. Later, additives such as barite and bentonite were included in the mixture to increase its weight. In the late 1920s, after working in the booming Texas oil fields, R. D. Lawson came up with his own formula for "mud" and marketed it himself, starting a company that he eventually built into a multimillion-dollar corporation.

Following her grandfather's death and the subsequent sale of the company by her father, the Lawson family's role in Houston had changed considerably. No longer were they members of the vast petroleum industry. Without the company's power base, their influence on the oil community was minimal, reduced to long-standing friendships with former associates of R.D. However, with the family's wealth and heritage, they had remained a major part of the Houston social scene, as evidenced by the number of prominent Texans among the crowd of mourners.

Looking at all the well-known faces, Abbie thought it was odd the way one took note of such things at a time like this, as if the living needed an affirmation of the importance of the loved one who had died — an affirmation that could only be measured by the number of influential people who came to the funeral.

Catching a movement out of the corner of her eye as her mother slipped a silver lace handkerchief underneath the black veil of her hat and dabbed at the tears in her eyes, Abbie started to turn to her. At almost the same instant, she noticed the young woman standing near the memorial obelisk, a woman so eerily familiar that Abbie had to take a second look. She stared at her in shock, the blood draining from her face. The resemblance was uncanny.

"Now let us pray," the minister intoned, bowing his head as he stood before the closed casket. "O Lord, we have gathered here today to lay to rest the body of your servant, Dean Lawson, beloved husband and father . . ."

Abbie heard the minister's call to prayer, but the words didn't register. She was too stunned by the sight of the woman in the crowd. It isn't possible. It can't be, she thought wildly, suppressing the shudder caused by the chills running up her spine.

As the woman stood with her head slightly bowed, a breeze stirred the mass of lustrous nut-brown hair about her face — the same rich shade of hair as Abbie's. But it was the color of the woman's eyes that had Abbie completely unnerved. They were a brilliant royal blue, fathomless as the ocean depths — the same vivid color as her own. "Lawson blue," her grandfather had called it, boasting that it meant their eyes were "bluer than a Texas bluebonnet."

Abbie had the distinct feeling that she was looking into an imperfect mirror and seeing a faintly distorted image of herself. It was a strange sensation. Unconsciously she raised a hand to her own hair, verifying that it was still sleeked back into its French twist and not falling loose about her shoulders like the woman's across the way. *Who was she?*

With the question echoing over and over again in her mind, Abbie leaned closer to Benedykt Jablonski, the manager of the Arabian stud farm at River Bend, the Lawson family home southwest of Houston. Before she could ask him about the woman who was virtually her double, a murmured chorus of "Amens" signaled the conclusion of the graveside services, and the previously motionless throng of mourners began to stir. Abbie lost sight of the woman. One second she was there, and in the next she was gone. Where? How could she disappear so quickly? *Who was she?*

As the minister approached their chairs, her mother stood up, the black veil screening her wet eyes. Abbie rose to stand beside her, as always feeling protective toward this slender reed of a woman, her mother, Babs Lawson. Like her father, Abbie had made it a practice, from the time she was a child, to shield her mother from anything unpleasant. Babs just couldn't cope with problems. She preferred to look the other way and pretend they didn't exist, as if that would make them miraculously vanish.

Not Abbie. She preferred to confront situations head-on and usually led with her chin, mostly due to that Lawson pride and stubbornness that she had inherited in abundance. Just as now, unable to shake the image of that woman from her mind, she scanned the faces of the people milling about the grave, vaguely aware of the words of condolence offered by the minister to her mother, but intent on locating the woman who looked so much like her. She had to be here somewhere.

Instinctively she turned to Benedykt Jablonski, seeking his help as she had done nearly her entire life. Dressed in a tweed suit that was nearly as old as he was, he held his small-billed cap in front of him. His thick, usually unruly iron-gray hair was slickly combed into a semblance of order.

Age had drawn craggy lines in his face and faded his dark hair, but it hadn't diminished the impression that he was a bulwark of strength. Nothing ever seemed to faze him. Considering all he'd been through during World War II, with the Nazi invasion and occupation of Poland and the immediate postwar years under Soviet control, perhaps that wasn't so surprising.

Now, standing next to his solidity, Abbie recalled the way she used to say that everything about this man was square: his jaw, chin, shoulders — and his attitude. Yet Ben had been the steadying influence in her life. It was to him she'd gone as a child with all her questions and problems.

A solemn man who seldom smiled, he studied her briefly, reading her body language the way she'd seen him do so many times with a young Arabian colt in training. "What is wrong?" His voice carried the guttural accent and the lyrical rhythm of his native Poland.

"A moment ago, there was a woman standing near the family marker. Did you see her?"

"No," he replied, automatically glancing in the direction of the monument. "Who was she?"

"I don't know," Abbie replied, frowning as she again skimmed the faces of the people milling about. She knew she hadn't imagined the woman. Absently she ran a hand across her waist, discreetly smoothing the black Chanel dress, the crepe de Chine soft and silky to the touch. Determined to find the woman, she turned back to Ben and said, "Stay close to Momma for me, Ben."

"I will."

But Abbie didn't wait to hear his reply as she moved out among the grave-side gathering, pausing to speak with this person, accepting the press of hands in sympathy from another, nodding, smiling faintly, murmuring appropriate responses — all the while looking for the woman she'd seen so briefly.

Just as she was about to decide the woman had left the cemetery, Abbie saw her standing on the fringe of the crowd. Again she felt unnerved by the striking resemblance between them. Next to her stood the gray-haired Mary Jo Anderson, her father's longtime legal secretary, who had more or less run his limited law practice single-handedly over the years. Shocked and confused, Abbie stared at the two of them. What was Mary Jo doing with her? Did she know her?

Fingers closed around her arm as a man's deep voice came from somewhere close by. "Miss Lawson? Are you all right?"

"What?" Turning, she looked blankly at the tall, dark-haired man now beside her gripping her arm.

"I said, are you all right?" His mouth quirked slightly, lifting one corner of his dark mustache in a faint smile that was both patient and gentle, but his narrowed eyes were sharp in their study of her.

"I'm . . . fine," she said, mentally trying to shake off her abstraction as she stared at his rough-hewn features, conscious that there was something vaguely familiar about him.

Remembering the woman, she glanced back over her shoulder to locate her. The man curved a supporting arm around the back of her waist. "You'd better sit down." He started guiding her in the opposite direction.

Abbie stiffened in resistance. "I told you I'm fine." But she was propelled along by his momentum to a nearby folding chair. There she took a determined stand and blocked his attempt to seat her. "I feel fine," she insisted again.

Eyeing her skeptically, he cocked his head to one side and let his hands fall away from her. "You don't look fine. As a matter of fact, Miss Lawson, a minute ago, you looked like hell."

It was his bluntness more than the sight of Mary Jo Anderson walking away from the gravesite alone that caused Abbie to center her whole attention on him. She thought she had learned to hide her feelings over the years. Perhaps she hadn't — or maybe he was just more observant than most.

Either way, Abbie tried to cover her previous reaction. "It was probably the heat."

"It is hot," he acknowledged with a faint nod of his head, but Abbie suspected that he didn't think the stifling afternoon heat was to blame. As his gaze moved lazily over her face, its look still sharp and inspecting, the action reinforced the feeling that she'd met him somewhere before — and he'd been just as thorough in his study of her that time, too.

"I am all right, though. Thanks anyway for your concern . . ." She paused, unable to supply his name.

"Wilder. MacCrea Wilder." The name didn't ring any familiar note with her and he seemed to sense that. "We met briefly this past spring, in your father's office."

Her memory jogged, Abbie suddenly could see him taking up most of the big leather armchair in her father's private office, the look of irritation that had crossed his face when she had barged in unannounced, interrupting their meeting, and the way he'd leaned back in the chair and watched her while absently rubbing a forefinger back and forth across his mustache and upper lip. That afternoon he'd been dressed in a khaki shirt with the cuffs turned back and the collar unbuttoned at the throat, revealing a faint smattering of chest hairs. She remembered the ropes of muscles in his forearms, the slick look of bronzed skin, and the breadth of his shoulders. But there had been something else, too. She frowned, trying to recall the thing that eluded her. She breathed in and accidentally inhaled the musky fragrance of his masculine cologne.

"Oil." Mixed in with the aroma of her father's pipe tobacco had been the smell of the oil fields. "Wasn't that what you were talking to my father about?"

"Indirectly. I'm flattered you remember."

"Are you?" Somehow he didn't seem to be the type to be influenced by compliments one way or the other.

"Who wouldn't be flattered to have a beautiful woman remember him from a chance meeting?"

"I could name a few." Abbie wasn't fooled by his smooth charm, any more than she was fooled by hard muscles. She was usually good at sizing up people.

"Your ex-husband, for instance?"

Automatically Abbie covered the bare ring finger on her left hand. The platinum wedding rings, dominated by a brilliant three-carat sapphire encircled with diamonds — the very set she had chosen at Tiffany's after she and Christopher John Atwell had romantically breakfasted outside the Fifth Avenue store in New York — no longer adorned her third finger. Ten months ago, she had thrown them at him and watched the intertwined pair tumble to the floor and break apart — like their disastrous six-year marriage. She had walked out of their home on Lazy Lane in Houston's River Oaks section that very afternoon, moving home to River Bend and taking back her maiden name. Certain things in her life she regretted, but the end of her marriage wasn't one of them.

Still, she resented his trespass into her personal life. "You seem to know a great deal about me, Mr. Wilder," she replied, challenging him ever so faintly.

"As I recall, you had received your final divorce decree that day and wanted to celebrate. A man doesn't exactly forget when a young — and strikingly attractive — woman announces her availability."

Until now she had forgotten the reason she had barged into her father's office that day. "You remember?" she said, her tone softening. "I'm flattered."

"Are you?"

She looked at him with new interest, surprised at the quick way he had picked up the cue and turned her own words back to her. A part of her felt alive for the first time since she had received the news of her father's death, but only briefly. She couldn't escape the soberness of this occasion, not with her father's closed casket still visible and the oppressively hot air heavy with the sweet scent of roses.

MacCrea glanced at the brass-encrusted coffin. "I want you to know how sorry I am about your father's death."

Abbie regretted the return to trite phrases — and equally trite responses. "Thank you. And thank you for caring."

The instant he walked away she felt his absence, but she didn't have an opportunity to dwell on it. Someone else was waiting to offer her more words of sympathy, and Abbie began making the rounds once more, but her gaze was always moving, searching for that woman, still wondering who she was.

Rachel Farr watched her from a distance, observing the grace and assurance with which she moved through the crowd. It was that expensive little black dress that did it, Rachel decided — so simple yet so elegant, with its black satin accents at the cuffs, placket, and mandarin collar. Or maybe it was the way she wore her hair — all swept up in that sophisticated French twist that made her look so stylish and poised. She certainly didn't appear to be suffering from the heat and humidity the way Rachel was. Her dress wasn't sticking to her skin and her hair wasn't damp with perspiration like Rachel's. Rachel had expected the heat, but not the humidity. Texas was supposed to be dry, brown, and flat. Houston was flat, but lushly green and obviously wet.

Rachel glanced down at the single red rose she held clutched in her hand. Its velvety petals were already drooping from the heat. She'd bought it at the flower cart in the terminal of Houston Intercontinental Airport shortly after she'd arrived from California yesterday afternoon. She wanted to place it on Dean's coffin as a symbol of her love for him, yet she was afraid to make this one simple gesture.

Last night she'd gone to the funeral home, but she hadn't found the courage to go inside, fearing the family's reaction and reluctant to cause a scene. And today, she'd sat outside the church while they held services for Dean inside, wanting to be there, yet oddly feeling too unclean to attend. Finally, she had followed the procession of Lincolns, Mercedes, Rollses, and Cadillacs to the cemetery on the edge of town.

Over and over she kept thinking that if his secretary hadn't telephoned her, no one would have notified her of Dean's death. It might have been days, weeks, perhaps months before she'd found out otherwise. She had tried to express her gratitude to Mrs. Anderson, but she had sensed how awkward and uncomfortable the woman felt with her at the funeral.

It wasn't fair. She had loved Dean, too. Surely his family could understand that she wanted to grieve with them and share the pain of their mutual loss. She'd had so little of him and they'd had so much. She would place the rose on his coffin. She didn't care what they thought.

Not giving herself a chance to have second thoughts, she set out quickly, walking blindly along the narrow strip of ground that separated the rows of graves. Her low heels sank into the thick carpet of grass that covered the ground as she moved in and out of the dappling shade cast by the towering oak trees that stood guard over the dead. It seemed as though she was traveling in a vacuum, encapsulated by a grief that dulled her senses, the sights and sounds of her surroundings making little impression on her.

Yet, despite all the hurt and suffering she felt, Rachel was conscious of the irony of the moment. Since she'd been able to have only small pieces of his life, it was fitting somehow that she was only allowed a small piece of his death. But just as she had railed at the inequity of the former, she cried over it now. There was nothing she could do that would change it. Dean was the only one who had possessed the power to do that, and he was dead.

Suddenly the casket was before her, draped in a blanket of sun-yellow roses. Rachel stopped beside it and hesitantly laid the wilted red rose on top of it. The bloom looked so forlorn and out of place she wanted to cry. She blinked at the tears that stung her eyes and trailed her fingers over the edge of the casket in a last good-bye as she turned away. When she looked up, she saw Abbie standing a scant fifteen feet away, staring at her with a confused and wary frown. For a split second, Rachel was tempted to hurry away, as if she were guilty of something. She wasn't. So why should she run? Gathering her fragile pride, Rachel lifted her chin a little higher and started forward at the same instant that Abbie did.

They met midway. Abbie spoke first. "Who are you? Should I know you?" Her voice was lightly laced with a soft Texas drawl, like Dean's. Rachel noticed that she was taller than Abbie by a good four inches, but it didn't make her feel superior in any way, only awkward and gauche.

"I'm Rachel. Rachel Farr from Los Angeles."

"From Los Angeles?" Abbie's frown deepened. "Daddy had just returned from there."

"I know." Realizing that Abbie had absolutely no idea who she was, Rachel suddenly felt very bitter and hurt. "Dean used to say we looked a lot alike. I suppose we do, in a way."

"Who are you?" she demanded again.

"I'm his daughter."

Abbie recoiled in shock and anger. "That's impossible. *I'm* his daughter, his only child."

"No, you're —"

But Abbie didn't want to hear any more of her preposterous lie. "I don't know who you are or what you're doing here," she declared, struggling to keep her voice down, "but if you don't leave now — this very minute — I'll have you thrown out of this cemetery."

BARELY ABLE TO SEE through her tears, Rachel bolted from the grave, making her long legs carry her quickly away. She wished she had never come to the funeral. It had been a mistake — an awful mistake.

How had she expected Abbie to react when she met her? Had she thought Abbie would throw her arms around her and greet her like the long-lost sister she was? Half-sister, at any rate. Had she hoped that Abbie would invite her home? No, that would have been awful.

She could imagine nothing worse than seeing all the trophies Abbie had won competing in horse shows on Dean's horses. Rachel had long ago begun haunting the Los Angeles Public Library, going through its magazines and out-of-town newspapers to satisfy her hunger to find out more about the father she saw so seldom. What did he do when he wasn't with her? Where did he live? How did he live? Over the years River Bend had been featured in several magazines, mainly those dealing with Arabian horses, but a few society-type publications as well. Dean had rarely mentioned any of them to her, but in them she'd seen too many photographs showing Abbie astride some gorgeous Arabian with Dean standing proudly at its head.

She'd seen pictures of the family's Victorian mansion, and of the expensive fashions worn by his wife and other daughter when they attended their lavish parties and balls. She'd read all about Abbie's formal coming-out in the society columns of the Houston newspapers: she didn't want to look at pictures of her, stunning in an elaborate white gown, dancing with Dean at a debutante ball. Abbie, so beautiful and daring — and looking so much like her it hurt.

She couldn't bear the thought of hearing about Abbie's travels with Dean to England, Europe, and the Middle East; she had never gone anywhere with Dean except to Disneyland and Catalina Island.

All her life she'd been filled with envy, knowing that Abbie had Dean with her all the time. He was there to tuck her into bed at night. He was there for every holiday, every Christmas morning when she got up. He was there for every important occasion, from piano recitals to graduation. But Rachel had been lucky, especially since her mother died, to see him four times a year.

It was obvious whom he had wanted to be with, whom he had loved. She doubted that she had ever been more than an embarrassing burden to him, an unwanted complication. She thought she'd put all that pain and bitterness behind her. After graduation from UCLA, she had tried to make a life for herself without him. She had a good job and a promising career as a commercial artist with a large advertising firm in L.A. But today, all the old wounds had been opened again. And the hurt went deep — deeper than ever before.

She paused, trying to get her bearings and locate her rental car. Just as she spotted the tan Firebird, a long black limousine pulled onto the shoulder of the cemetery lane and parked in the space behind her car. A uniformed driver hopped out and opened the rear passenger door. Absentmindedly Rachel stared at the silver-haired man who stepped out.

The man said something to the chauffeur, then walked away from the limousine, striding briskly toward Rachel and the gravesite behind her. Something about his strong facial features reminded Rachel of Dean. He was in his middle fifties — about the same age as Dean. She wondered whether his eyes would crinkle at the corners when he smiled the way Dean's had.

A moment later she saw that they did as he noticed her and smiled quickly. "How are you?" The warmth, the sincerity in his voice gave meaning to the question, changing it from an offhand phrase of greeting. Rachel was startled to find herself shaking hands with him in the very next second.

"Fine, thank you." Hurriedly she wiped away a tear that had slipped onto her cheek, certain she probably looked awful, her eyes all bloodshot and puffy. But the kindness in his look told her he was too much of a gentleman to notice.

"The services are over, aren't they?" he asked instead. "I'm sorry I was late, but I . . ." He paused, a frown flickering across his expression. "Excuse me, but you aren't Abbie, are you?"

"No. I'm not." She wanted to die when she noticed the way he unconsciously drew back from her. All her life she'd fought against this sense of shame. She'd done nothing wrong, yet she had never been able to escape this feeling of guilt. Trembling with agony of a different kind, Rachel turned to leave.

"Wait. You must be . . . Caroline's daughter."

She paused, tears of gratitude welling in her eyes. At last she'd been recognized by someone, someone who could truly understand the deep loss she felt. "You . . . knew my mother?" Hesitantly she faced him.

"Yes." A smile of understanding crinkled the corners of his eyes. "Your name is Rachel, isn't it?"

"Yes." She smiled for the first time in days. "I'm sorry," she said, shaking her head a little vaguely, too choked with emotion to say much more. "Your name?"

"Forgive me. I took it for granted that you would know me. My name is Lane Canfield."

"Mr. Canfield. Yes, Dean spoke of you often. He . . . thought a great deal of you."

There were some who claimed Lane Canfield owned half of Texas — and the other half wasn't worth buying. According to newspaper accounts Rachel had read, his holdings were vast and widely diversified, ranging from real estate developments to luxury hotels and giant petrochemical plants. Photographs had rarely accompanied the articles. Rachel seemed to remember hearing that Lane Canfield shunned personal publicity.

"To be truthful, the feeling was mutual. Dean was a remarkable man, and a loyal friend. He will be missed by many people."

"Yes." She bowed her head with the grief his words elicited.

"Do you still live in Los Angeles?" Gently he directed their conversation to a less emotional subject.

"Yes. He'd just been out to visit me. His flight back was delayed. He was late. He was hurrying to get home when . . . the accident happened." Hurrying back home, to Abbie, the daughter he loved.

"Will you be staying in Houston long? Maybe we could have lunch, or dinner, together. I think Dean would like that, don't you?"

"You don't have to do that." She didn't want to be a duty, an obligation, to anyone.

"I don't *have* to do anything. I *want* to do it. What hotel are you at?"

"The Holiday Inn, the one near the Astro," Rachel heard herself answer.

"I'll call you tomorrow after I've had a chance to check my schedule."

"All right."

After their good-byes were said, Lane lingered to watch the young woman as she walked away. The resemblance between father and daughter was strong. She was tall and slender like her father, with his thick brown hair and incredibly blue eyes. Sensitive and vulnerable — yes, she was very much like Dean.

Abbie didn't waste any time locating her mother, convincing her that it was time to leave, and hurrying her off to the waiting limousine. She didn't want to take the chance that her mother might run into this woman who claimed . . . It didn't matter what she claimed. The very idea was ludicrous, absurd. The woman was obviously crazy.

The snarl of departing cars on the narrow cemetery lane slowed all movement to a crawl. Her nerves tense and brittle, Abbie leaned back in her seat, wondering how many of their friends that woman had talked to, told her lies to. Texans dearly loved a scandal.

Covertly she glanced at her mother. "Babs—that's short for babbling brook"; supposedly that was the way R. D. Lawson had frequently referred to her, partly in jest and partly seriously. Abbie had to admit that it was a singularly apt description of her mother. Her mother was bubbly and bright, flitting from this thing to that. She could chatter for hours and not say anything. Her life seemed to be nothing more than one long stream of parties. She loved giving them as much as going to them.

Abbie felt that two people could not have seemed less suited for each other than her parents. Yet Babs had absolutely adored Dean. She didn't make a single decision, no matter how trivial, without consulting him. She believed in him totally. Any and everything he did, she thought was perfect.

Not quite everything, Abbie thought, frowning slightly as she recalled arguments that had taken place behind closed doors: her mother's shrill voice and the sound of crying, her father's angry and determined, yet pained, look when he stalked out. Her mother always remained in the room, sometimes for hours, emerging pale and drawn, unusually silent, her eyes puffy and red. Some of the early memories were dim, yet Abbie had the impression that their arguments were always over the same thing—and that *thing* was somehow connected to the frequent business trips her father made to California to see one of his clients.

Once, shortly after she had gone off to college at the University of Texas, Abbie had suggested to her mother that she accompany him to Los Angeles. "After all," she had reasoned over the telephone, "now that I'm not at home anymore, why should you stay in that big house all by yourself? This is the perfect opportunity for you to start going places and doing things with Daddy."

She could still remember the strangled yet adamant *no* that had come over the line.

"Momma—"

"I hate California," had come the retort, with uncharacteristic bitterness.

"Momma, you have never even been there."

"And I don't care to ever go, either." Abruptly Babs had changed the subject.

With anyone else, Abbie would have demanded to know why. She could become incredibly stubborn when confronted with a wall of any kind. If necessary, she'd take it apart brick by brick just to find out what was on the other side. But it had been obvious this was something Babs didn't want to face. Now Abbie wondered why.

That Rachel woman had said she was from Los Angeles, Abbie recalled unwillingly. Of course, that was just a coincidence—like the distinctive blue of her eyes. Lawson blue. Made uneasy by the thought, Abbie frowned, haunted by the memory of the way her father used to stare at her when he thought she wasn't watching, his expression vaguely wistful and pained, a look of sadness and regret in his eyes, eyes the same shade of deep blue as her own—and that Rachel Farr woman's.

She had always thought he looked at her like that because he wished she had been a boy. What man didn't want a son to carry on the family name and tradition? None, she was sure. He had tried to love her. And she had tried desperately to gain his love without ever fully succeeding.

Maybe that was her fault. Maybe if she hadn't argued with him so much . . . Half the time she had picked a fight with him just to make him look *at* her instead of *through* her. They had fought over everything from horses and homework to pot and politics. Their last major confrontation had been over her divorce.

"Abbie, I think you're being too hasty, as usual," he'd said when she told him she had left Christopher. "Every married couple has problems. If you would try to be a little more understanding —"

"Understanding!" she had exploded. "Tell me just how understanding a wife is supposed to be when she discovers that her husband is having affairs — even with women she knows!"

"Now that doesn't mean —"

"What do you expect me to do? Condone it? Are you suggesting that I should look the other way while he makes a fool of me in front of all our friends? I won't be humiliated like that — not again."

"I can understand how you would be hurt by his . . . indiscretions." He had chosen his words with care and slowly paced in front of his desk as if presenting his case to a panel of jurors. "I doubt that he meant for it to happen. Things like that can begin so innocently. Before he knows it, a man can find himself more deeply involved than he ever intended to be. It wasn't planned. It just happened."

"Is that the voice of experience talking, Daddy?" she had caustically shot back at him, only to notice the way he blanched and turned quickly to avoid her gaze. He had looked guilty. Never one to miss an opening that could give her the advantage, Abbie had charged in. "Have you been unfaithful to Momma? Is that why you are siding with Christopher against me, your own daughter? Don't you care that I'm unhappy?"

"Of course, I do," he had insisted forcefully.

"Do you? Sometimes I wonder." She had turned away from him, struggling to control the bitterness she felt. "Daddy, I know you think I should forgive and forget what has happened. But I can't — and won't. I can't trust him. Without trust, there's no love. Maybe there never was any. I don't know anymore, and frankly, I don't care. I just want out of this marriage and Christopher out of my life."

"Dammit, Abbie, no Lawson has ever gotten a divorce."

"In that case, I'll just have to be the first, won't I? It's time somebody set a precedent." On her way out of his study, she had paused at the door. "But don't worry, Daddy. I won't ask you to represent me. I'll get some other lawyer — one without your high scruples."

The subject was rarely broached again after that. Yet Abbie knew he had never truly reconciled himself to the divorce. She had returned home, conscious of the new tension between them and determined to outlast it. Only she hadn't. He had died first. She felt a choking tightness in her throat and tears struggling to surface.

Beyond the tinted glass of the limousine's rear windows, Abbie saw Rachel Farr standing among the gravestones. Had her father had an affair with another woman in the past? Was Rachel Farr the result of it? Was the possibility really as preposterous as she'd first thought?

Too many half-forgotten memories were making it seem more than just a string of coincidences. Snatches of arguments she'd overheard between her parents, the constant trips to Los Angeles, four and five times a year, the way he used to look at her as if seeing someone else — things she had never regarded as pieces to a puzzle were all fitting together now. Devoted husband and father. Had it all been an act? All these years, had he kept another child hidden away in Los Angeles?

Struggling against a sense of betrayal, Abbie stared at Rachel, again considering the startling similarities: the hair color, the shape of the face, and the blue eyes. The prepotency of the sire — that's what Ben would have called it, in horsemen's terms. The ability of a stallion to stamp his offspring with his looks.

It felt as if her whole world had suddenly been turned upside down and shaken hard. Everything she had ever believed to be true, she now questioned. All these years, Abbie thought she knew her father. Now he almost seemed like a stranger. Had he ever really loved her mother — or her? She hated the questions, the doubts . . . and the memories now tainted with overtones of deception.

"Abbie, look!" her mother exclaimed. Abbie instantly stiffened, certain her mother had noticed Rachel Farr. "Isn't that Lane Canfield?"

So consumed with Rachel, Abbie hadn't paid any attention to the man she was talking to. It was Lane Canfield, her father's closest friend. She hadn't seen him since her wedding six years ago, but he had changed very little. He was still trim, still a figure of authority, and still managed to look cool and calm in the afternoon heat despite the suit and tie he wore. If anything, his hair — always prematurely gray — now had more white in it, giving it the look of tarnished silver.

But what was he doing talking to Rachel Farr? Did he know her? He acted as if he did. If all this was true, wasn't it logical that her father would have confided in Lane? That logic became even more damning when Abbie remembered that her father had named Lane Canfield the executor of his will.

"It is Lane." Her mother pushed at the switch on the armrest, trying to open the limousine's automatic windows. Finally the window whirred down, and the humid heat of the June afternoon came rolling into the car. "Lane. Lane Canfield!"

Hearing his name, Lane turned then walked over to greet them. "Babs. I'm so sorry I wasn't able to get here sooner. I was at a meeting in Saudi Arabia. I didn't receive the news of . . . the accident . . . until late yesterday. I came as quickly as I could," he said, warmly clasping her hand.

"It's enough that you're here. Dean valued your friendship so much, but I'm sure you know that." Babs clung to his hand. "You will ride back to the house with us, won't you?"

"Of course. Just give me a minute."

As he walked away, Abbie wondered if he was going after Rachel. But no, he walked to a black limousine parked several cars ahead and spoke to the driver, then started back. She felt numb, not wanting to believe any of this.

When Lane Canfield climbed into the back of the limousine and sat in the rear-facing seat opposite her mother, Abbie saw the way he looked at her, taking note of her every feature and obviously making the comparison with Rachel. He didn't seem surprised by the resemblance between them — which meant he must have expected to see it, Abbie realized.

"You will stay for dinner tonight, won't you, Lane? The Ramseys and the Coles will be there, and several others said they'd be stopping by. We'd love to have you join us," Babs insisted.

"I'd love to." With difficulty, Lane brought his attention back to Dean's widow, still an attractive woman at forty-eight. "Unfortunately I'll have to leave early. I have to get back to town tonight and attend to some business."

"I understand." Babs nodded, her voice quivering. For an instant, she appeared to be on the verge of breaking into tears, but she made a valiant effort to get hold of her emotions as she turned to Abbie. "Lane was best man at our wedding. But I guess you know that, don't you, Abbie?"

"Yes, Momma."

"I don't think I will ever forget that day." Babs sighed, her face taking on a nostalgic glow. "Do you remember, Lane, how our car wouldn't start? Dean must have worked on the motor for nearly an hour. He had grease all over his tuxedo, and I just knew we were going to have to leave on our honeymoon in that carriage. He tried everything, but he just couldn't get that car to run."

"I believe there were a few parts missing." Lane smiled, recalling how he and his cohorts had sabotaged the vehicle.

"No wonder." Babs laughed, a merry sound still infectious after all these years. "You loaned us your car, I think."

"Yes." He reminisced with her aloud as his mind wandered back to the start of that long-ago day.

GUESTS HAD BEGUN ARRIVING at River Bend long before the wedding ceremony in the garden was scheduled to begin. Everything was pristine white for the occasion. The stately mansion, the ornately carved picket fence, the elaborately scrolled gazebo — all sported a fresh coat of whitewash, as did every building, barn, and fence on the place.

No expense had been spared: even the Spanish moss that naturally adorned the towering oak and pecan trees on the grounds had been sprayed with silver dust, leaving the guests in no doubt that R. D. Lawson whole-heartedly approved of his son's marriage to Barbara Ellen Torrence, the daughter of an old Texas family reputed to have the bluest blood despite the fact that financially they were in the red, victims of the stock market crash of '29; and leaving the guests in no doubt that the Torrences were not too proud to let the nouveau riche R. D. Lawson pay for this lavish and elaborate wedding. As far as R.D. was concerned, no other setting would do but River Bend, restored, virtually rebuilt, to its former glory.

Located on the Brazos River less than twenty miles southwest of the very center of Houston, River Bend was surrounded on three sides by croplands and rice fields, the flatness of the coastal prairie unbroken except by the occasional farmhouse or tree. But the one hundred acres that remained of River Bend conjured up images of the Old South. Here, the strongest and tallest of the oaks, pecans, and cottonwoods that grew in the thick woods next to the river were left standing, towering giants bearded by the lacy moss and strung with wild grape vines.

Set back from the main road, nearly hidden by the trees, the main house was a magnificent fourteen-room Victorian mansion. A wide veranda wrapped itself around three sides of the house, outlined by a handsome balustrade repeated as a parapet around a narrow second-floor balcony. A cupola crowned the third story, which contained R.D.'s billiard room, and provided a center balance point for the corner turrets.

Once this mansion had been the heart of a thousand-acre plantation founded back in the late 1820s by a Southern cotton planter, Bartholomew Lawson, who was drawn to the area, like so many others of his kind, by the rich alluvial soil along the Brazos River bottom. As R.D. liked to remind everyone, there was a River Bend long before there was a Houston. Lawson slaves were in the fields back in 1832 when a pair of land speculators from New York were peddling lots in the tract of land they had bought on Buffalo Bayou.

River Bend flourished for nearly half a century, but the Civil War and the abolition of slavery changed all that. During the years of Reconstruction, large parcels of the plantation were sold to satisfy old debts and claims for back taxes. When R.D. was born at the turn of the century, only three hundred acres of the original plantation were still in the family; not a trace remained of the slave quarters near the river that had once been home to nearly a hundred blacks; and the mansion was a hayshed, its vast lawn and surrounding pecan grove a pasture land for the cattle and hogs. R.D. — his momma called him Bobby Dean — lived with his parents in the cottage that had been built to house the overseer and his family.

At the age of fifteen, R.D. went to work in the Texas oil fields. That's where the big money was. It made sense to him that if he was going to dig in the dirt, he might as well get paid for it. He got hired on by a man with the wishful name of "Gusher" Bill Atkins, who owned a rotary drilling rig. His first job was working in the mud pits. Eventually he graduated to a "roughneck," working on the floor of the drilling rig, handling the pipe. Within a few years, he'd tried his hand at nearly every job on the rig.

Those were the wild, freewheeling years of the oil business. The whole nation was certain the country was on the verge of running out of oil. Dire warnings were regularly issued by the government in the late 1910s and early 1920s, accompanied by statistics that showed production and consumption of oil were increasing at a considerably faster rate than new reserves were being found. The rush to find new fields was on, led by the "wildcatters," the independent oil men. For the most part, the major oil companies, who had the pipelines, the refineries, and the distribution market, sat back and watched, letting the wildcatters take the risks in a new area. Once oil was found, it was a simple matter for them to step in and buy up leases on adjoining land, or buy a piece of some wildcatter's action, or simply purchase the crude oil he produced.

It didn't take much money to drill a well back then, and little scientific knowledge was required. New drilling sites were selected on a basis that was pretty much "by guess and by golly." The only way to know for sure whether there was oil beneath a particular formation was to drill.

More than once, R.D. had been tempted to raise some money and drill his own well. But he'd heard too many stories and seen too many wildcatters who were rich as Croesus one year lose it all in a string of dry holes the next. The only ones consistently making money, other than the majors, were the men supplying materials and equipment.

Maybe because it was his first job, or maybe because he'd been raised a dirt farmer, R.D. was fascinated by the drilling mud used in the hole. All he had to do was scoop up some in his hand and he could tell by the feel and the texture of it — sometimes by the taste or smell of it — whether it was the right consistency for the job, or if it needed to be thinned or thickened.

After six years of working in oil fields, R.D. recognized the many functions mud performed. It did more than soften the formation the drilling bit was cutting through, more than bring the bit's cuttings to the surface for disposal, and more than sheathe the wall of the hole to stabilize it so it wouldn't cave in. If the mud was the right weight, it exerted more pressure than any gas, oil, or water formation the bit encountered, thus preventing the blowout of a well. Over the years, he'd seen his share of blowouts — lengths of pipe, the drill, and other equipment thrown high in the air and turning into lethal missiles. Whenever a blowout was caused by natural gas, invariably there was fire. A gusher was nothing more than a blowout caused by oil. As spectacular as they were, they were still dangerous and a colossal waste of oil.

As his fascination with mud grew, R.D. began experimenting with different mixtures and ingredients, picking the brains of geologists and chemists in the oil fields, and learning terms like *viscosity*. In 1922, he came up with a formula that seemed to be consistently successful. That same year his father died, killed when his horse bolted and overturned the wagon he was riding in.

R.D. found himself back at River Bend, faced with a difficult decision. His mother, Abigail Louise Lawson, better known as Abbie Lou, couldn't work the farm by herself, and they couldn't afford a hired hand. But how could he stay and run it when his heart was in the mud pits of the oil fields? To make matters worse, that skinny little neighbor girl, Helen Rae Simpson, had grown into a doe-eyed young woman while he was gone, and R.D. found himself in love.

Determined to do the right thing, he stayed to farm River Bend and follow in the tradition of his ancestors. He married Helen, and a year after their wedding, Robert Dean Lawson, Jr., was born. He should have been happy: he had a son, a lovely wife, a home, and a farm that was producing enough for them to get by. For three years R.D. tried to convince himself that a man couldn't ask for more, but he just couldn't stop talking about mud.

Abbie Lou Lawson recognized her son's discontent. One December night at the supper table, she — who had given him her dark hair and blue, blue eyes — offered him a solution that would provide him with the means to achieve his dream. They would sell the roughly two hundred acres of River Bend's cropland and keep the rest. The old mansion was a white elephant nobody would buy, and the one hundred acres of pasture wouldn't bring much either. The money from the sale would start him in the mud business and she would keep the books, the same as she had for the farm.

Within three months, the plan became a reality. R.D. applied for his patent and began peddling his products, making the rounds of the various oil fields and calling on drillers. But it was hard to make sales. Few were interested in such revolutionary ideas. Only the drillers in trouble with stuck drill pipes or cave-ins were willing to listen. Most of them were skeptical, but desperate enough to try anything. However, his successes usually only guaranteed him that the next time the driller was in trouble, he would call R.D.

Those first years were discouraging. And that discouragement was compounded by the stock market crash and then the death of his wife. A few times he would have given up, but his mother wouldn't let him. She encouraged him to expand, to set up a laboratory to test new products and equipment, and to hire field representatives to sell the company's products and educate the drillers on their use. The world might be suffering a depression, but the oil industry wasn't. Within ten years, he went from being a one-man operation to having seventy people on the payroll. He started buying up smaller companies, taking over their patents, quadrupling the size of his business. Suddenly he was a millionaire several times over.

Thanks to the woman who believed in him: Abigail Louise Lawson. R.D. gazed fondly at the gilt-framed photograph of her taken a year before her death. Blue eyes smiled back at him from a face crowned with snow-white hair swept atop her head in a mass of curls, a pair of chandelier drop earrings dangling from the delicate lobes of her ears.

"Real diamonds, they are, too." R.D. winked at her, as he had the day he'd given them to her. "You and me, we made 'em sit up and look, didn't we? Hell, we never did do what they expected. They all figured we would buy us one of those big fancy homes in River Oaks, but we fixed up River Bend instead — and reminded them all that Lawsons had been here long before most of them were. This time Dean's the Lawson who's foolin' 'em, marryin' that Torrence girl. And a damned fine wedding it's going to be, too."

The gold mantel clock chimed the quarter-hour from its perch on the carved walnut shelf above the fireplace. As if he could hear her reprimand, R.D. grimaced faintly and faced the mirror above his dressing table once more.

"I know I left this getting-ready business a bit late." He made his third attempt at tying the black bow tie. "But I had to go down to the barns and make sure they had the mares all harnessed up right and the carriage ready. Remember that fancy horse carriage I bought you so you could ride in that parade we sponsored to get people to buy war bonds? That's what the bride's gonna arrive at the wedding in. She's over at the cottage with her family, gettin' ready."

He paused for a minute to stare at his reflection. He just didn't feel like a man about to turn fifty, despite the gray spreading through his thick hair. His face had the look of smooth leather with permanent creases worn across his forehead and around his mouth and eyes. There was no sagging skin along his strong jawline, although maybe just a little under his jutting chin, emphasized now by one end of the tipsy-tilted bow tie.

Exasperated, R.D. yanked it loose and started over again, absently resuming his conversation with his mother's photograph. "You should see that carriage. Garcia has it covered with white flowers. Lilies of the valley, gardenias, and apple blossoms. It reminds me of those buggies they use in the Rose Parade. I'm having it pulled by those two matched gray Arabians. White as milk, those two mares are now. I've got 'em in the black harness with white plumes. That young Pole polished the leather on that harness until it shines like a pair of patent-leather shoes on a fancy nigger. I like that Jablonski boy." He nodded decisively. "He definitely has a way with horses. And he knows a helluva lot about the breed. Although, half the time I can't understand him, his accent is so damned thick." Again the bow tie sat askew. "Hell, I never could tie these damned things," R.D. muttered and ripped it apart. "Dean!"

His booming voice sent the silver-lead crystals on the master suite's chandelier jingling as he stalked out of the room, dressed in the required tuxedo with the tie dangling around his neck, but minus his shoes. He padded down the hall toward his son's turret bedroom, his feet making little sound on the hardwood floor of heart pine.

The bedroom door was ajar. R.D. started to push it open, but he paused when he caught sight of his son in the room. Dean was every bit the gentleman R.D. had hoped he'd become. Well aware of his own rough edges and lack of formal education, R.D. had been determined his son would have it better. The rough-and-tumble days were gone — the days when a handshake was all it took to make a deal. That's why he sent Dean to Harvard Law School after he'd graduated from the University of Texas. Ever since the boy was ten years old, R.D. had worked him every summer in the company, making him learn the business from the ground up. He sent him to the best schools and made him learn about the arts and manners. That's what it took in today's world. And, from the beginning, R.D. had been grooming Dean with one thought in mind: that someday he'd take over the reins of the company.

And there was the result, lounging on the arm of an overstuffed chair, totally relaxed and comfortable in his formal attire and smiling affably at his former college chum at Texas, his best man for the wedding, Lane Canfield. Dean was tall — although not as tall as R.D.'s six feet — and good-looking, with the Lawson eyes and thick, brown hair. His face still had the smooth, fresh look of a boy without a care in the world. But when had he ever had to worry about anything? Sometimes R.D. wondered if he hadn't given the boy too much, made life too easy for him. But then he remembered how he had worked him every summer while most of his friends played.

If R.D. could change one thing about him, he wished Dean had some of Lane Canfield's gumption. From what he'd been able to learn, Lane had taken over much of the operation of his family's petrochemical plant in Texas City and almost single-handedly put it in the black. Rumor claimed that he planned to enlarge the facility.

So far, Dean simply hadn't shown R.D. he could be that aggressive. But he hadn't had a chance to, either. All that was going to change now that Dean was coming on board full-time — as soon as his honeymoon was over, that is.

A door slammed somewhere in the house. As Dean glanced over to the door, R.D. hesitated a split second, then pushed it open the rest of the way and walked into the room.

"I think you forgot your shoes, R.D." Dean grinned.

"I've been fighting with this damned tie for twenty minutes."

"Let me tie it for you, Mr. Lawson." Lane walked over to him and took the mangled ends of the tie and adjusted the two to the proper length.

R.D. tilted his head back to give him room and eyed his son, still calmly perched on the chair arm. "I expected to find you pacing up and down, pawing the ground like an eager stallion at the trying bar."

"That's what Lane keeps telling me, but there'll be time enough for that when the ceremony's over," Dean replied with a negligent shrug of one shoulder, then rolled gracefully off the arm of the chair and stood up. "Lane and I were just going to have some of that champagne Jackson brought up. Care to join us and toast the end of my bachelor days?"

"Sure, but don't pour me any of that champagne. I'd just as soon have some bourbon and branch water, if you got any handy."

"Coming right up."

When Lane finished tying the bow tie, R.D. inspected the result in the dresser mirror. The knot was squarely in the center and the bow was perfectly straight. "I'll be damned if I can ever get it to look like that."

"Practice. That's all it takes," Lane assured him.

"I suppose. It's for sure I never had much cause to get duded up like this when I was a young man. Formal attire wasn't the required dress in the oil fields." Smiling, R.D. turned from the mirror. "Some of those old boys would get a real belly laugh if they could see me now."

"To hear him talk, you'd think he didn't like getting all dressed up. But believe me, Lane, he loves it," Dean said, coming over to hand them their drinks and remaining to lift his glass in a toast. "To my last hour as a free man."

After a clink of glasses, they all took a sip, then R.D. raised his. "I think we should drink to havin' a woman in the house again to make this place come alive."

"Hear, hear," Lane agreed, not quite certain whether Dean's hesitancy had been imaginary or not.

Ever since R.D. had entered the room, Dean's behavior had changed. True, they had been laughing and cracking jokes before, but it had been a way of easing the wedding jitters. Dean had been nervous — plucking at upholstery threads on the chair and smoking cigarette after cigarette. But all that had vanished the minute his father walked in. Dean had thrown his guard up, become subtly reserved and aloof, and disguised it with his teasing banter. Although Lane would never say as much to him, it was obvious Dean was intimidated by his father.

"I stopped by the cottage a little while ago to make sure there weren't any last-minute hitches," R.D. said.

"Did you see Babs?" Dean inquired, ever so casually.

"No, but I heard her, tittering and tee-heeing away in the back bedroom."

"That sounds like Babs." His mouth quirked in a half-smile as Dean reached for the champagne bottle to refill his glass.

R.D. watched him closely, his forehead puckering in a frown. "This is probably going to sound like a dumb question, but . . . you do love the girl, don't you?"

"If I didn't, I wouldn't be marrying her." But one look at his father warned Dean that such an offhand reply wouldn't suffice. He wanted to know more. R.D. wanted him to open up and tell him how he really felt. That had always been difficult, if not impossible, but Dean tried. "I'm not sure I can explain it, but . . . when I'm with her, it's like the sun's always shining. She . . . makes me feel important — like I was someone special."

"Well, you damned well are. You're a Lawson."

Realizing that his father didn't really want to hear the truth, Dean recovered and managed to force out a laugh. "I meant in the way a woman can make a man feel important and special." Which was to say that, around his father, he sometimes felt like something less than a man. Lord knew he tried to be the son his father expected him to be, but too often he fell short.

A few minutes later, R.D. finished his drink and left the room. "Your father's quite a guy," Lane remarked.

"Yes. He is," Dean agreed. He loved him. That's what made it so hard, knowing he failed to measure up to R.D.'s standards. Lane was the kind of son R.D. should have had. "Yesterday he took me over to the company and showed me my new office. It's right next to his. He's really been looking foward to the day when I join the company full-time."

There wasn't any way Dean could disappoint him. But he knew in his heart he was no more cut out to be the head of a mud company than he was to be a lawyer. More than once he had wished that if R.D. wanted him to manage something, why it couldn't be the Arabian breeding operation here at River Bend. The horses were Dean's real love, and the one common bond he had with his father.

It all began when R.D. bought him a pony-sized horse, reputed to be Arabian, for his seventh birthday. The mere thought that he had a horse just like the one Valentino had ridden in *The Son of the Sheik* had been enough to capture Dean's imagination totally. He promptly dubbed his new horse Araby. As he galloped Araby beneath the pasture's moss-draped pecan trees, he used to pretend they were in the desert, racing across the sands. He even used to steal sheets from the clothesline to wrap around himself in an attempt to mimic the flowing robes Valentino had worn in the movie. No more did he have to ride that broken-down old mare and wear his legs out trying to kick her into a trot. He had a horse that could run like the wind — and followed him around like a puppy dog.

But R.D. had been impressed by that combination of spirit and docility — and remarkable stamina. While he was on the road, he started tracking down previous owners of the gelding and discovered that the horse was sure enough a purebred Arabian, sired by a stallion named Hamrah, imported from the desert by a man named Homer Davenport — a fact that absolutely thrilled Dean.

R.D. had bought the gelding on impulse, drawn by the claim it was Arabian. Years ago, when he was learning to read, his mother used to sit him down at the kitchen table and have him read aloud to her while she fixed the evening meal. They didn't have many books. As a change from the Bible, she used to let him read from the yellowed pages of an old journal kept by an ancestor, dated in the late 1850s. In one part, this Lawson ancestor had extolled the virtues of a young racehorse recently purchased from a man named Richards in Kentucky, marveling at its ability to gallop for miles and miles without showing any sign of tiring, boasting of its blazing speed, and admiring the beauty of its head, the largeness of its dark eyes, the proud arch of its neck, and the high carriage of its tail. The horse was an Arabian.

R.D. never knew what happened to that horse, but he suspected that like so many other things, it had been a casualty in the ensuing Civil War. So he'd bought Dean the small Arabian gelding and told him the story about the previous Lawson who had owned an Arabian, too.

But buying the horse had revived his own childhood interest in Arabians. During a business trip to the California oil fields, R.D. heard about the Kellogg Ranch and decided to attend one of their regular Sunday shows for the sole purpose — he thought — of obtaining a photograph of Jadaan, the gray stallion ridden by Rudolph Valentino in *The Son of the Sheik*, for his son. But R.D. was totally captivated by the horses he saw, especially the stallions Raseyn and Raswan. He had to have them — or if not them, then their offspring. At the time it meant nothing to him that both were imported from the Crabbet Park Stud in England, both sired by the Polish-bred stallion Skowronek. He just knew he liked what he saw.

Less than six months after Dean's seventh birthday, four more horses arrived at River Bend: three fillies and a stud colt. R.D. hadn't planned to get into the horse-breeding business, especially with his company currently suffering from growing pains, but he was. He reasoned that this way he was putting that one hundred acres of pasture land to productive use. Besides, it was just four horses, not counting his son's gelding. Little did he realize that in the early 1930s there were less than a thousand purebred Arabian horses in the whole United States, making his five rare indeed.

But the first time his friends saw R.D.'s dainty-boned, delicate-faced Arabian horses, they broke out in laughter. Texas was Quarter horse country. Next to those compactly built, powerfully muscled animals, his horses looked like pissants. By then R.D. had done some reading up on Arabians, but his friends weren't interested in his explanations that Arabian horses weren't a breed but a subspecies of horse with distinct anatomical differences, whereas the Quarter horse was a man-made breed, formed by the mixture of different blood types, including Arabian. Nearly all light horse breeds traced back to the Arabian: Thoroughbreds, Morgans, Saddlebreds, Tennessee Walkers, Standardbreds, and Quarter horses.

But the ribbing didn't stop. In defense of his Arabians, R.D. began riding them as soon as they were old enough and competing in open horse shows against their Quarter horses, usually entering nearly all the classes to prove the Arabians' versatility and stamina, frequently placing and occasionally winning. He let Dean ride them in the junior classes as well, to show that despite their spirited looks, they were gentle enough for a child.

Dean loved the show ring. And he loved the horses. They were his best friends, his playmates and confidantes. Riding them was the one thing he was good at; the proliferation of ribbons from those first shows and from subsequent all-Arabian horse shows proved it. Arabian horses were one thing he didn't have to take a backseat to his father on. In fact, he thought he knew more about them than R.D. did.

Over the years, the Arabian horse population at River Bend had grown from five to thirty-five, the bloodlines heavily weighted in favor of Crabbet imports of Skowronek and Mesaoud lineage. In Arabian horse circles, River Bend Arabians had earned the reputation of being among the best in the country. If R.D. would just give him the chance, Dean knew he could turn River Bend into the top Arabian horse farm in the country — maybe even the world.

True, he had received his law degree and passed the bar exam, and as of yesterday, he had been made a vice-president in the company. But those were meaningless titles. He wasn't a lawyer or an executive; he was a horseman. He wondered if he'd ever be able to get R.D. to understand that.

Lane lifted aside the French cuff of his shirt sleeve and checked his watch. "It's time we were going down. One of the duties of the best man is to make sure the groom doesn't keep the bride waiting."

"Knowing Babs, she'll keep *us* waiting." But Dean started for the door anyway, the thought of his bride-to-be bringing a smile to his face. In the back of his mind, though, he was wondering how he was going to convince Babs that they should cut their honeymoon in New York by a couple of days so he could stop in Illinois on their way back and look at some of the Egyptian-bred Arabians at Babson Farm.

A picket fence surrounded the small yard of the overseer's cottage, which was built in the same architectural style as the mansion but on a smaller and less elaborate scale. A pecan tree, gnarled and twisted with age, spread its broad limbs above the small house, its canopy of leaves providing shade from the unrelenting Texas sun.

A pair of white horses hitched to a carriage decorated with white flowers came to a prancing halt on the narrow dirt lane in front of the cottage. Their coats gleamed like ivory satin, a contrast to the ebony sheen of their hooves.

Benedykt Jablonski cast one last inspecting glance at them as he hopped down from his seat beside the driver, a stable groom decked out in a top hat and tails for this auspicious occasion. Ben struggled not to smile when he glanced back at him, certain he looked equally strange in the footman's uniform his employer, Mr. R. D. Lawson, had insisted he wear.

Ever since the actual preparations for the wedding had begun the day before, Ben had watched it all with growing awe. It had always been his understanding that only royalty went to such extravagant lengths, but here it was in America, on a grander scale than he'd ever seen. But how much had he seen in his twenty-five years of life? How much besides war, with its devastation and hunger, and the oppression of foreign occupation?

That was Poland; that was the past. This was America; this was his present. He was free, and his life here was good. Again he was being allowed to work with his beloved Arabians. And he was part of the young master's wedding, however small his role.

With shoulders squared, he strode through the gate to the front door of the cottage and rapped loudly twice. A heavyset man in formal clothes opened the door, glowering at him like an intruder.

Nervously, Ben cleared his throat. "For the bride, we wait."

The man stared at him blankly, the frown on his forehead deepening as if he didn't understand what Ben had said. Then he noticed the carriage waiting by the front gate and turned, calling to someone in the cottage — in a heavy Texan accent that Ben found equally difficult to understand — "Betty Jeanne, the carriage is here. Are you about ready in there?"

In the back bedroom, Babs Torrence anxiously turned to view her reflection in the mirror. "Momma, is it that time already? Am I ready? Have I forgotten anything?"

No. It was all there: the veil of Brussels lace, "something old" from her grandmother; the wedding gown of white satin, "something new"; the pair of pearl and diamond earrings, "something borrowed" from her mother; and the cerulean ribbon around her bridal bouquet, "something blue."

"You look lovely, darling. Absolutely lovely." Betty Jeanne Torrence discreetly shooed the maid out of the bedroom, then finally called an answer to her husband. "Tell them we'll be right there, Arthur, dear. And don't get yourself all in a dither. You know how it makes your face red."

But Babs didn't hear a word her mother said as she looked worriedly into the mirror. The satin gown, a Dior original, was the essence of femininity, with its high lace collar and heart-shaped neckline, the satin material curving snugly in to hug her waist, making it look no bigger than a minute, then flaring out into a floor-length skirt.

"Momma, this Merry Widow is hooked too tight. I just know it is," Babs complained for the fifth time about the strapless undergarment that was a combination of brassiere, corset, and garter belt.

"Nonsense," her mother retorted as she busily poked another pin through the veil to hold it more firmly in place, smoothing a stray strand of Babs's ash-blonde hair as she did so.

"It is," Babs insisted. "I just don't dare take a deep breath or I'll pop right out of it."

"Honey, if you have room to take a deep breath, then it's not tight enough."

"If this is a dream, I wish someone would pinch me," Babs declared and turned from the mirror, the gown and the petticoats beneath it making a soft rustling sound. "I can't believe Dean Lawson is really marrying *me*. Do you think he truly loves me?"

"He's marrying you. That's what matters," her mother insisted brusquely, then tempered her callousness with a smile. "You're going to take his breath away when he sees you coming down the aisle on your father's arm. Now, you remember what I told you about tonight?" Babs nodded, desperately wishing her mother wouldn't go on about her approaching wedding night. "It will all seem strange and awkward at first, but . . . you'll get used to it. And don't worry. I'm sure Dean will expect a few tears."

Her father appeared in the doorway. "Betty Jeanne. They're waiting for us." Smiling quickly, Babs turned, welcoming the interruption.

"And it will be worth it," she declared, gazing with pride at her daughter.

"I'm ready." Babs picked up the front of her skirts and hurried from the room at a running walk, brushing a kiss across her father's florid cheek as she went by. "Hurry, Daddy. We don't want to be late." As she emerged from the cottage, she stopped to stare at the carriage lavishly adorned with bridal-white flowers. She was reminded instantly of the Confederate Ball that marked the opening of Houston's debutante season. That night she had made her debut. That night she had met Dean. He had been the handsomest man there. She couldn't believe her luck when he asked her to dance, not once but twice. It wasn't until after the second dance that she found he was *the* Dean Lawson. By then, it didn't matter that her parents had been anxious for her to marry well; she was already in love.

She felt exactly like Cinderella about to climb into her coach drawn by white horses and ride off to marry her Prince Charming. All that was missing was the glass slipper. But she didn't care. She was about to become Mrs. Robert Dean Lawson, Jr.

There was a smattering of applause from the guests seated in the rows of chairs spread across the lawn when the carriage pulled up to let its precious passengers out. The lawn had been transformed into an English garden, with huge pots of white azaleas competing for attention with equally large tubs of yellow roses. Dividing the rows of chairs into two sections was a carpeted runner of pure white that led to the altar in the gazebo, its white trellises laced with more flowers. A stringed orchestra played the "Wedding March" as Babs started down the aisle on her father's arm with yellow rose petals strewn in her path. She could just as easily have been walking on air.

The wedding ceremony was merely a prelude to the lavish buffet reception on the lawn that followed. The four-tiered wedding cake was an architectural wonder, each layer separated by frosted columns of white, stairstepping to the top tier where the figures of a bride and groom stood inside an exact replica of the gazebo. After the ritual cutting of the cake, the new Mr. and Mrs. Dean Lawson toasted each other. Glasses were raised by the guests, filled with either champagne from the silver fountains or, for those who preferred, hard liquor from the bars set up on the lawn.

The newlyweds posed endlessly for the official photographer, then mingled with their guests, always together, Babs clinging proudly to Dean's arm, reveling in her new status, the princess to her prince. As she deferred nearly every inquiry about their future to him, Dean seemed to grow taller by inches. "Whatever Dean wants," "I'll let Dean decide," "You'll have to ask Dean about that," were beautiful words to him.

Twilight was settling over River Bend as Dean and Babs, she in her pale pink traveling suit, made their dash amidst a pelting shower of rice to his car — a car that wouldn't start, creating hoots of laughter among the onlooking guests. All sorts of advice was shouted to Dean, which he largely and wisely ignored as he raised the hood and checked the wires. When Dean attempted to enlist Babs's aid in starting the car, the typical husband-wife interchange created more peals of laughter.

"Dean, you know I can't drive," Babs protested.

"You don't have to drive. Just start the car. Now, when I tell you, turn the ignition and pump the gas pedal."

"Which one's the gas pedal?"

"The one on your right."

"This one?"

"Yes, honey, but . . . not now. I'll tell you when." After several attempts failed, Dean suggested, "Use the choke."

"What's that?"

Dean told her, and Babs promptly turned on the radio. In the end, Lane took pity on them and gave Dean the keys to his car so they could leave to spend their wedding night in the Houston hotel suite before boarding the train for New York the next day.

4

AS THE WHITE BOARD fences that outlined the boundaries of River Bend came into view, Lane was momentarily disconcerted by the feeling he had been literally transported back in time. It was as if the same horses were grazing beneath the sprawling limbs of the oak and pecan trees, their satiny coats shimmering in metallic shades of bronze, copper, silver, and gold. Beyond them, he expected to see the grounds clogged with cars, the wedding guests still lingering.

After watching Dean and Babs drive away, he remembered turning and finding the usually brash and robust R. D. Lawson standing silently beside him, his look distant and thoughtful. Then R.D. had glanced sharply at him, as if suddenly realizing he was there.

Lane remembered that he'd said, "Well, they're off. They looked happy together, didn't they?"

R.D. had stared after the car. "I wonder about her," he had said, then added hastily and forcefully, "I like the girl. But if she keeps acting helpless and dumb, pretty soon she's going to believe it. It's a damned shame she never knew my mother. Now, there was a woman," he had declared and slapped Lane heartily on the back, clamping his hand on Lane's shoulder. "Come on. There's still some partyin' left to be done."

At the time, Lane had regarded R.D.'s description of Babs as unfairly demeaning. But after more than thirty years, Babs still possessed that endearing childish quality. She still reminded him of a little girl who needed someone to look after her. Babs, who loved parties and beautiful clothes. Lane wondered if R.D. had been right. Had she been playing a role? Had that role become reality?

Covertly, Lane studied the Babs before him, the face behind the veil still relatively unlined, her hair still femininely styled in soft curls, its color still the same shade of dark blonde — whether naturally or artificially retained, he didn't know. The sad, lost look in her hazel eyes, however, was poignant and real.

"Dean never tired of their antics," Babs remarked when a half-dozen yearlings bolted away from the fence in mock fright as the limousine passed by. They streaked across the pasture with their tails flung high, and fanned out among the ancient oaks to watch the vehicle traveling up the driveway. "Beauty in motion, he called them. Living art."

"Indeed." But he couldn't help thinking that even in death, she was clinging to him.

The limousine rolled to a stop in front of the house. Lane waited until the driver assisted Babs out of the car, then he stepped out to join her. From the stable area, the shrill, challenging whistle of a stallion shattered the late-afternoon quiet. Drawn by the sound, Lane absently noticed all the improvements

Dean had made since he'd taken over at River Bend following his father's death some nineteen years before.

The old barn had been torn down to make room for the large stable complex with its attendant paddocks and support facilities, a complex that covered more than twice the area of the original. All the new structures mimicked the gabled roof and cupola of the mansion. In the distance, a bay stallion strutted along a high fence, its neck arched and ebony tail flagged, its small, fine head lifted high to drink in the wind's scents. Lane guessed that he was also the source of the shrill call that had rent the air a moment ago.

"That's Nahr El Kedar." The statement came from Abbie Lawson, the first words he'd heard her speak since they'd left the cemetery. "You helped Daddy import him from Egypt."

"I'd forgotten all about it. That was a long time ago." Somewhere around twenty years, if he remembered correctly. His participation in the project had been relatively minor, mainly consisting of putting Dean in touch with some of his contacts in the Middle East to facilitate the handling of all the red tape of importation.

"Would you like to see him?" There was something challenging in the look she gave him. Lane suspected that Dean would have described it as one of his grandmother's "You-come-with-me, and-you-come-with-me-*now*" looks.

"Abbie," Babs began hesitantly.

"Don't worry, Momma. I won't keep him long." Without waiting for his assent, she set off confidently toward the stud pen. Lane found himself walking along with her.

After matching her for several strides, he realized that she wasn't as tall as he'd thought. The high heels she wore gave the illusion of height, plus she carried herself as if she were tall, but she was actually several inches shorter than he was. That seemed odd. He remembered . . . Lane caught his mistake. It was Rachel who had been his height.

"I saw you talking with her at the cemetery."

Lane was momentarily taken aback by Abbie's remark, coming as it did directly on the heels of his own thoughts. "You saw me . . . talking with whom?" he said, aware that he was treading on delicate ground.

"I believe her name is Rachel Farr." She turned the full blaze of her blue eyes on him. "She claims that Daddy was her father. Is that true?"

Lane didn't relish being the one who removed that last element of doubt. But it was equally pointless to lie. "Yes." Immediately she began staring at some point directly ahead of them and kept walking, but with a new stiffness of carriage that revealed the inner agitation she was trying desperately to control.

"But why would he —" The instant Abbie heard the naïveté of her question, she cut it off. She had already experienced firsthand the infidelity of a husband, with no real cause, no adequate justification . . . and no flaw in their sex life. Yet the idea that her father had been unfaithful to her mother — it shook Abbie. "I always thought my parents were happy together."

Only now when she tried to remember how they had acted together did she realize how very little they had in common. Her father had been all wrapped up in the horses, but her mother took little interest in them, except to attend the social events at major shows. And their conversations: her mother never talked about anything but parties, clothes, new room decor, gossip, and, of course, the weather. Abbie hated to think how many times she'd heard her mother brightly declare, "I never discuss politics, business, or economics. That way I never show my ignorance." And she didn't. If any conversation took a serious turn, she either changed it or moved on. But that was just Babs. She was funny and cute, and engagingly frivolous. Everyone loved her.

Heavens, there were times when Abbie had wanted to shake her. She had never been able to run to her mother with any of her childhood problems, no matter how trivial. She wanted more than her mother's pat answer, "I wouldn't worry about it. Everything always works out for the best." Too frequently, her father hadn't been available either. Abbie had invariably poured out all her troubles to Ben.

Was that what her father had sought in a mistress? Someone to talk to? Someone who would listen and understand? Someone who was more than a decoration on his arm? Someone to stimulate him intellectually as well as sexually? Almost immediately, Abbie shied away from such thoughts that smacked of disloyalty to her mother. Even if her mother was a disappointment to him in some ways, her father had no right to take another woman. He had betrayed her. He had betrayed them all.

As Lane and Abbie reached the stud pen, she walked up to the stout white boards. The dark bay stallion, his satin coat the color of burnished mahogany, strutted over to her, snorting and tossing his head, then arched his neck over the top board and thrust his finely chiseled head toward her.

A picture of alertness, the stallion stood still for an instant, his graying muzzle nuzzling her palm, his large dark eyes bright with interest, his pricked ears curving inward, nearly touching at the tips, his nostrils distended, revealing the pink inner flesh of their passages. For all the refinement of his triangularly shaped head tapering quickly to a small muzzle, the width between his eyes, and the exaggerated dish of his face, there was a definite masculine quality about the horse.

Abruptly the stallion lifted his head and gazed in the direction of the broodmares in the distant pasture, ignoring Abbie as she raised her hand and smoothed the long black forelock down the center of his forehead, the thick forelock concealing the narrow, jagged streak of white. With a snaking twist of his head, the stallion moved away from her and wheeled from the fence to pace its length.

"Kedar's in remarkable shape for a stallion twenty-two years old," Abbie said, just for a minute wanting the distraction he provided.

"He's a fine-looking animal," Lane agreed.

"His legs aren't all that good. He's calf-kneed and a little down in the hocks. But he has an absolutely incredible head, and Daddy always was a headhunter. As long as an Arabian had a beautiful head, he assumed it had four legs. Arabians of straight Egyptian bloodlines are noted for having classic heads. That's why all the Arabians on the place trace directly back to Ali Pasha Sherif stock — all, that is, except for that two-year-old filly over there." Abbie gestured to the silvery-white horse standing at the fence in the near pasture. "Her dam was the last of the Arabian horses my grandfather bred. I wouldn't let Daddy sell her when he sold off all the others after Granddaddy died. Daddy gave me her filly last year."

"You've obviously inherited your father's love for horses."

"I suppose." When the stallion came back to the section of the fence where they were standing, Abbie idly rubbed his cheek. "If I wanted to spend any time with him, I didn't have much choice."

Immediately she regretted the bitterness in her statement, especially since it was only part of the story. Horses had been her companions and playmates all her life. She loved working with Arabians and being around them — not just because of her father, but because of the feeling of satisfaction it gave her.

Blowing softly, the stallion nuzzled the hollow of her hand. Abbie returned to the subject that was really on her mind. "My mother must have known about this all along. Why did she put up with it?" Abbie didn't really expect an answer, but Lane gave her one.

"I think . . . they reached an understanding."

"Momma does have a knack for ignoring anything remotely unpleasant," Abbie admitted, wryly cynical. But his answer explained why she had childhood images of her mother shutting herself in her room for hours and coming out with red and swollen eyes whenever her father left on a "business" trip to California; yet in recent years, Abbie could only recall her mother being unusually silent right after he'd gone. "How many other people knew about Daddy's . . . affair?"

"Initially there was some gossip, but it pretty well died out a long time ago."

"And this woman, the one he had an affair with — what happened to her?"

"She died several years ago. Rachel's been pretty much on her own since she was seventeen."

"You expect her to be named as one of the beneficiaries in Daddy's will, don't you?"

"I think it's logical to assume he would have included her."

"And if he didn't, she could contest the will and demand her share of his estate, couldn't she?" Abbie challenged, voicing the fear that had been twisting her insides all during the long ride from the cemetery — a fear that filled her with anger and deep resentment. River Bend was her home. It had been in the Lawson family for generations. This Rachel person had no right to any part of it.

"That will depend on how the will is written. Dean may have directed the bulk of his estate to go to his widow, Babs, or he may have set up a trust, giving her a life estate on the property and providing for it to pass on to his heirs upon her death."

" 'Heirs'? If you're going to use the plural, shouldn't it be 'heiresses'?" she suggested stiffly.

"Until the will is read, Abbie, I don't think we should be anticipating problems."

"I'm not like my mother, Lane. I prefer to face every possible contingency. And you can't deny that this might end up in a long and messy court battle."

"It's possible."

Looking away from him, Abbie gazed out over the shaded pastures all the way to the distant line of trees that hugged the banks of the Brazos. She knew every foot of River Bend, every bush and every tree. The horses out there — she could call them all by name and list their pedigree. This was her heritage. How could Lane stand there and tell her not to feel that it was threatened?

"Who was his mistress? What was she like?" She sensed his hesitation and swung back to face him. "I want to know. And don't worry about sparing my feelings. It's better if I know the truth after all these years. Momma probably doesn't know what it is anymore. You're the only one who can give me that."

After studying her thoughtfully for several seconds, Lane began telling her all he knew. "Her name was Caroline Farr. She was from somewhere in the East, I believe. Dean met her at a private showing of an art exhibition at the Museum of Fine Arts here in Houston."

HOT AND TIRED, Dean tugged at the knot of his tie as he climbed the grand staircase to the second-floor suite he shared with his wife. He wished to hell he could shed all the pressure and frustration of the office as easily as he could shed the business suit and tie he wore to it. For three damned long years he had tried, but he just didn't fit the mold. Whereas making business decisions was so easy for R.D., Dean would agonize for days before recommending a course of action, and even then, most of the time he hadn't considered half the options R.D. raised. He had never felt so inadequate.

A long gallop before dinner, that's what he needed, Dean decided as he pushed open the door to their bedroom and walked in. He paused when he saw Babs, clad in a dressing gown and seated at the vanity table, primping in the beveled mirror.

"There you are, darling." Her reflection smiled at him from the mirror. "How was your day?"

"Rotten." Dean pulled the loosened tie from around his neck and closed the door behind him.

"That's too bad. But tonight you can relax and forget all about it and just enjoy yourself," she declared airily and waved a hand in the direction of the four-poster bed with its delicately carved maple posts ending in ornate finials and its Marlborough feet. "I had Jackson lay out your clothes, and your bathwater is already drawn."

Dean stared at the evening suit so precisely laid out on the peach and green floral-striped spread and began to tremble with anger. "What's going on? Don't tell me. Let me guess. It's another one of your damned parties." He couldn't hide the disgust he felt. Night after night, there was always something: a formal dinner invitation, a charity benefit — or if they stayed at home, they invariably had company over to dine, when they weren't the ones giving the party.

"Darling." Babs partially turned around to look at him, her hazel eyes widened by the look of hurt surprise he had come to know so well after nearly three years of marriage. "Tonight they're holding that private showing at the museum. When I asked, you said you wanted to go."

Maybe he had. He didn't remember. Too many other things were on his mind. "I've changed my mind, and we're not going."

"But everyone's expecting us to be there."

"Just once, can't we have a quiet evening at home?" "And talk," he wanted to add, but he had already learned that Babs didn't want to listen. Every time he tried to express the doubts he had about his role in the company and the dissatisfaction he felt, she brushed them aside with some variation of "It's hard now, but I know you'll work it out. You always do." He tried to tell himself that it was wonderful to have a wife who believed in him, who believed he could handle it. But he couldn't handle it. What would she think of him when she found that out?

"We'll stay home if that's what you want. I honestly didn't know that you didn't want to go tonight. I'm sorry. Truly I am." She rose from the peach velvet cushion covering the seat of the carved maple bench and crossed the room to cup his face in her hands. "I want to do whatever you want. So if you don't want to go, neither do I."

She smiled brightly, but he knew it was a lie. She loved all these social functions. It gave her the chance to be a little girl again and play dress-up. He felt guilty for depriving her of that. Just because he was miserable, that was no reason to make her evening miserable, too.

"We'll go." He caught one of her hands and pressed her fingertips to his lips. "You're probably right. I need to go out and take my mind off the office."

"I know I am." Raising on her tiptoes, Babs kissed him warmly. "Now, hurry and take your bath before the water gets as cool as rain."

Minutes later, Dean was stretched out in the long, claw-footed bathtub, letting the tension float away and sipping on a bourbon and water Babs had thoughtfully fixed for him. He listened with only half an ear to Babs as she chatted away to him from the other side of the door to their private bath.

"You're just going to love the new gown I'm wearing tonight, Dean." There was a slight pause before she continued. "Remind me to wear these stiletto heels the next time we're going to a party where there will be dancing. They are positively deadly. Once and for all I'm going to cure that left-footed Kyle MacDonnell of stepping on my feet. Oh, talking about cures, that reminds me . . . I was talking to Josie Phillips the other day, and she told me that if I wanted to guarantee myself of getting pregnant that we needed to make love on a night when there is a full moon."

"What?" The water sloshed around him as Dean sat bolt upright in the tub, hoping his hearing had deceived him.

"A full moon. Isn't that the wildest thing you've ever heard? But Josie swears that all four of her children were conceived when she and Homer did it on nights when there was a full moon outside. I checked the calendar, and there won't be a full moon again until the middle of this month."

In a flash, Dean was out of the tub. He was still dripping water as he opened the connecting door and walked into the bedroom, absently tying the sash of his terry-cloth robe around his waist.

"Babs, just how many people have you told that you haven't been able to get pregnant?"

She gave him a blank look, then shrugged. "I don't know. It's hardly a secret. People aren't blind. They can see for themselves that I'm not going to have a baby," Babs declared, smoothing a hand over the close-fitting waistline of her off-the-shoulder evening dress in a black-on-white floral silk. "What am I supposed to say when people ask when we're going to have a baby? That we don't want one yet? You know we do. And you know how anxious poor R.D. is for us to have one."

"I don't think it's something you should be going around telling every Helen, Mary, and Jane about." He had enough trouble without having to face friends who knew he couldn't even manage to get his wife pregnant. "If you want to talk to someone about it, talk to a doctor."

"I have." She slipped on a long white-kid evening glove, carefully fitting the snug material between each finger. "He said I was just being too anxious and that what we needed to do was stop trying. Have you ever heard anything so preposterous? How in the world does he expect me to get pregnant if we don't do anything?" She reached for her other glove. "You really need to hurry and get dressed, honey. R.D. is already waiting for us downstairs."

At the private showing of the art museum's latest acquisitions, Dean viewed the new paintings with indifference. A low hum of voices surrounded him, the volume mostly subdued, although occasionally a cultured laugh rose above it. Despite the setting, there was a sameness to the gathering — the same people, the same conversation, and the same high-fashion look that made up nearly every affair Babs insisted they attend.

He wished now he hadn't given in and agreed to come. He could have been home at River Bend with the horses. There was a show in two weeks and he wanted the half-dozen Arabians they were taking to be in top condition. Not that he really needed to worry about that — not with Ben on the job. He envied Ben being able to work with the horses every day, all day. All he could manage was an early-morning ride.

When Babs wandered on to another painting, Dean drifted along with her, managing to appear interested even though he wasn't. The work was some surrealist thing, an incongruous mixture of colors and images. R.D. joined them, with the MacDonnells in tow.

"Amazing work, isn't it?" Beth Ann remarked, studying the painting as if mesmerized. "So full of power and energy, don't you think?"

Dean nodded and wished he had a drink.

"I think" — Babs paused as she contemplated the painting a little longer — "he must have really liked red."

For an instant, there was absolute silence. Then R.D. burst out laughing. "Babs, you're just too precious for words," he declared, wiping the tears from his eyes. "I swear, those are the first honest words I've heard tonight. Come on." He hooked a big arm around her small shoulders and herded her toward another painting on the other side of the room. "You've got to see this one over here."

A slightly embarrassed Beth Ann trailed after them dragging Kyle along with her, but Dean stayed behind and pretended to study the painting on the wall. Right now he wasn't in the mood for his father's company.

"Do you like it?"

Dean glanced sideways at the woman who had come up on his right. He was faintly surprised to discover he didn't know her. That in itself was a novelty, but so was the woman. She wasn't dressed like Babs or any of her friends. Instead she wore a plain black sheath and absolutely no jewelry. Her dark hair was lifted back from her face, then allowed to fall in a thick cascade onto her back — a style that didn't remotely resemble the curls of Babs's Italian cut.

As unusual as the woman's appearance was, Dean wasn't interested in making idle conversation with a stranger. "I find the painting very interesting," he said and started to move on.

"Then you don't like it," she stated flatly.

"I didn't say that." Dean frowned.

"No," she agreed. "You said it was 'very interesting.' That's what everybody says when they don't really like something."

"In this case, it isn't true. I happen to like surrealism," he replied, mildly irritated by the hint of censure in her voice, and tired of others believing that they knew what he liked or wanted.

"This isn't true surrealism, not like Dali." She continued to study the painting, her unusually thick eyebrows drawn together in a slight frown. "It's too coherent for that. This is more like a picture puzzle."

She spoke with such certainty and authority that Dean found himself drawn in by it. "What makes you say that?"

"Because . . ." And she went on to explain the symbolic use of numerals to represent mankind and the human intellect set against the blazing red of the sun, the vivid green of the land, and the swirling blue of water, creating an allegory of man and his relationship with nature.

Dean followed only part of it. Somewhere along the way, he became fascinated by her intensity — an intensity that was both serious and passionate. It was there in her gray eyes, the dark gray of the clouds on the leading edge of a thunderstorm, clouds shot with lightning and jet black in the center. It seemed perfectly natural to shift his attention from her eyes to her mouth. She had soft, full lips, the lower one pouting in its roundness — blatantly sensuous, not at all dainty like the sweetheart shape of Babs's. Dean started wondering what they would look like if she smiled.

"Do you work here at the museum?"

"No, I don't."

"You spoke so knowledgeably that I thought . . ." He shrugged off the rest of it.

"I've studied art extensively and spent two years in Europe going from museum to museum, poring over the works of the old masters."

"Are you a collector then?" Although he had never been good at judging a woman's age, she seemed young — young for an art collector, anyway. Dean doubted that she was any older than he was.

"No." She looked at him with a kind of amused tolerance. "I'm an artist."

"You are. Don't tell me this is one of your paintings." Dean stared at the oil she had lectured about so intelligently only minutes ago.

"No." She smiled for the first time — just a curving of the mouth, her lips together. "My style is much more turbulent, more emotional, not landscapes of the mind like his." As she gestured at the painting, Dean noticed her hands, the long fingers and the short nails. The hands of an artist, graceful and blunt.

"What's your name? I have the uncomfortable feeling that I'm going to be embarrassed when I find out who you are."

"I doubt it." Again there was that little smile. "I'm what is known as a struggling artist. I don't think the name Caroline Farr is going to mean anything to you. Maybe someday, but not now."

"I'm Dean Lawson." As he formally shook hands with her, Dean noticed the strength of her fingers and the firmness of her grip. He also noticed that his name didn't mean a thing to her. More than that, she didn't seem all that impressed by him. It pricked his ego just a little bit. Between his looks and his name, Dean had never had any problems attracting women, but Caroline Farr was obviously different. "I'd like to see some of your paintings sometime."

"I should warn you they're not surrealistic."

"My wife will be glad to hear that. She doesn't care for it at all."

At that point their conversation returned to a discussion of art, and the inability of many to appreciate its different forms and styles. More precisely, Caroline talked and Dean agreed.

"Your accent . . ." Dean tried to place it and failed. "You're from somewhere in the East, aren't you?"

"Connecticut."

"Are you just visiting here in Houston?"

"Not really. Right now I'm staying at a friend's summer house in Galveston." When she said that, Dean automatically began to scan the milling guests, trying to remember which one had a beach house on Galveston Island. "It doesn't belong to anyone here."

"Was I that transparent?" Dean smiled.

"Yes."

"Sorry. But, since you're not from here, you're obviously someone's guest."

"Why?"

"Because this affair tonight is by invitation. The collection doesn't go on public display until tomorrow."

"Tomorrow I'll be in Galveston. I wanted to see it tonight."

"My God." Unconsciously Dean lowered his voice. "You mean you crashed this? You just walked in?" He hovered between incredulity and stunned admiration of her audacity.

"Of course." She was very matter of fact about it and indifferent almost to the point of arrogance. "This isn't someone's home. It's a public museum. Why should it be open to one — privileged — class of people and not to all?"

"That's a good point." He tried not to smile. "However, most if not all of these guests are patrons of the museum."

"Because they have donated works of art or money, does that entitle them to special treatment?" she countered in a challenging tone.

"They think so."

"I don't."

"Obviously." Dean had never met anyone like her before. He'd heard that artists were a proud, temperamental breed. Wealth and status supposedly meant nothing to them. Dean found that hard to believe, even though this Caroline Farr seemed to feel that way. "You know, I really would like to see some of your paintings."

She gave him a long, thoughtful look. "Most afternoons you can find me on the west end of the beach."

Someone came up to speak to him. When Dean turned back, she was gone. He was surprised to find that he wanted her still to be there — that he wanted to talk to her and learn more about her. He was intrigued by her seriousness and her passion, the intensity that emanated from inside her and charged the air around her. He caught sight of her across the room, tall, statuesque, dramatic in black. He wanted to go over there to her, but he didn't. He'd already been seen talking at length with her. It wouldn't look right if he sought her out again. Dean smiled faintly as the thought occurred to him that Caroline Farr would probably mock such a conventional attitude. She wasn't bound by the rules that restrained him. He wondered what it would be like to feel free to say and do what he wanted, without worrying about whether he was living up to someone else's expectations: his father's, his wife's, or his friends'.

A seagull swooped low in front of his car as Dean drove along the deserted beach, the window rolled down to admit the stiff breeze blowing in from the Gulf. His jacket and tie lay over the back of the passenger seat. The sleeves of his shirt were rolled up and the collar unbuttoned. He felt like a kid playing hooky for the first time — a little guilty because he hadn't returned to the office or gone home after the meeting, and a little excited because he was doing something he shouldn't.

But the farther he drove on the tideline's hard-packed sand, the more his excitement faded. For the last half-mile, he hadn't seen a single soul, not even a surf fisherman. She had told him he could find her here "most afternoons," but obviously not this one. Admittedly it was late, Dean thought as he squinted into the glare of the sun hovering low in the western sky. He wondered if maybe it was just as well that Caroline wasn't here. He'd be better off if he forgot all about her. Of course, he'd tried that, but he just hadn't been able to get her off his mind these last four days.

More than once, Dean had questioned why, out of all the women he knew, he was constantly thinking about Caroline. Her looks were striking, but he could name any number of women who were more beautiful. And his marriage was basically a happy one. Sure, there were times when he wished he could talk to Babs about some of the things that troubled him, but that didn't change the way he felt toward his wife. That was just silly, lovable Babs, and he really didn't want her any other way.

As he thought about Babs, Dean realized that he had no business being out here. He was about to turn the car around, when he saw Caroline about fifty yards ahead on the edge of the sand dunes. In that second he forgot everything: vows, loyalty, and convention. It was all gone, lost in the excitement of seeing her again.

Intent on the canvas propped on her easel, Caroline didn't even look up when he stopped the car a few yards away and climbed out. Dean walked over to her slowly, taking advantage of the chance to gaze at her unobserved.

Her hair was caught up in a ponytail secured with a string of red yarn, but the strong sea breeze had tugged several long, dark strands loose and now lashed them across her face — a face that was a study of concentration, her gray eyes narrowed, flicking their glance sharply from the canvas to the scene she was trying to capture, then back again, her dark eyebrows drawn together, and the line of her mouth pulled taut in determination, her full lips pressed firmly together. There was a paint smudge on her cheek, and another on the point of her chin.

More paint was splattered on the man's plaid shirt she wore with the tails tied in a knot at her waist. The looseness of the shirt failed to hide the outline of her breasts, thanks to the breeze that shaped the cotton material to her body. A pair of snug capri pants was stretched over her full hips and emphasized her long, slender legs. She was barefoot, her toes half buried in the sand. Somehow Dean had guessed she would have beautiful feet.

"The artist at work," he said.

"I'll be finished here in just a . . . few . . . short . . . minutes." Each pause was filled with decisive strokes of the brush.

"Do you mind if I look?"

"Not at all," she replied, shrugging her indifference but not taking her concentration off the painting except to dab her brush in more paint from the palette she held in her left hand.

Dean circled around to stand behind her left shoulder. Flames radiated from the canvas, a core of red-orange spreading to yellow-orange, then gold, and yellow-white to tan. Swirled in amidst them from both sides came shades of light blue and dark green. The fiery turbulence of the painting made such a visual impact that Dean didn't immediately see the image of a late-afternoon seascape with the waves reflecting the long trail of light cast by the setting sun.

"It's very powerful," he said quietly.

The Sun and the Sea, she called it as she paused to study it critically. "I like to take subjects that have been painted endlessly by artists and see if they still can move us."

"I think you've succeeded." Dean didn't pretend to be an expert, but he was impressed with the sensation of intense heat and light that the painting evoked.

"Maybe. Either way, I'm losing the sunlight effect on the water that I want." Smoothly, efficiently, she began cleaning up and stowing her paints and brushes away. "Care to join me for a drink?"

"Sure."

The summer house sat off by itself in a sandy meadow of sea oats. Supported by a network of pilings that protected it from high water, it resembled a large square box with legs. Once the house had sported a coat of sunshine yellow, but long ago the sun had bleached it to a shade of cream.

During the short drive to the house, Caroline had explained that it belonged to the parents of a friend, a fellow teacher. Caroline, it seemed, was a struggling artist rather than a starving one, who supported herself by teaching art classes in elementary school. She devoted all of her summer vacation to her own artwork.

"What made you pick Galveston?" Dean took the easel out of the backseat and followed Caroline up the driveway of crushed seashells.

"It was a place to live rent-free. Truthfully, it was more than that. I'd never stayed on this side of the Gulf Coast before. Just around Sanibel Island on the Florida side." She climbed the flight of wooden stairs to the wide porch that ringed the beach house. From the porch, the shimmer of sunlight reflected on the rolling water of the Gulf could be seen. "I've always been drawn by the sea. As a child I lived in a house only three blocks from the Sound. Maybe that's why I always want to be close to it. It's so . . . primordial. We all come from it. Even the fluids in our bodies have a high saline content. Without salt, we'd all die. So maybe my need is much more primitive than just being used to living near it." As Caroline pulled the screen door open, Dean caught it and held it open for her, then followed her inside.

The kitchen, dining, and living area was all one big room, starkly furnished with the bare essentials of table, chairs, and sofa. The rest of the space had been turned into a temporary art studio. Caroline walked directly to it and propped the partially finished painting on an empty stand.

"You can set the easel by the door," she said. "There's cold beer and part of a bottle of wine in the refrigerator. Help yourself."

"What would you like?" Dean hesitated for an instant, then set the easel against the wall by the door and went into the kitchen.

"I prefer wine. A holdover from my sojourn in France, I suppose."

After she finished putting her paints and equipment away, she washed the paint from her hands and face in the kitchen sink. But she didn't attempt to freshen up any more than that, neither brushing her windblown hair nor applying new makeup to her clean face. Not that Dean thought either was needed to improve her appearance, but he was slightly taken aback by her lack of vanity. As she sat on the couch next to him, curling one long leg beneath her, Dean silently admired her strong self-confidence.

They talked, covering a variety of subjects. One drink led to two, and two led to three. In many ways they were so different, coming from totally diverse backgrounds and lifestyles, yet Dean couldn't remember a time when he'd enjoyed a woman's company so much.

Caroline drank the last of her wine and reached down, setting the glass on the floor. There was no end table. She turned back to face him, sitting sideways on the couch with an elbow propped on the backrest near his head.

"I wasn't sure I wanted you to come here," she admitted, letting her gaze wander over his face.

"Why?" He suddenly didn't feel too sure of his ground, not with her.

"Because I was afraid you were going to be one of those insufferable bores who brags all the time about how much he's worth and what he owns." She smoothed the lock of hair at his temple, then let her fingers trail into his hair. "I'm glad you're not."

"So am I." Reaching up, Dean cupped his hand over the nape of her neck and slowly drew her face closer.

The moment was inevitable. It had been since he met her on the beach. This was what he'd come for, what he wanted. Caroline did as well. He could see it when he looked into the velvety depths of her gray eyes.

As he kissed her, her lips opened and Dean groaned at the silken feel of her mouth, taking him in, wanting all of him. He felt as if he'd been swept into one of her paintings, fiery-hot and turbulent, his need for her consuming him, primordial as the sea.

In one sinuous movement, she uncurled her body and turned to lie sideways across his lap, never losing contact with his mouth. Her body was there for him to touch and explore. As his hands roamed over her, cupping a breast, stroking a thigh, curling over a hip, she was all motion beneath them, her soft buttocks rubbing across his stiffening joint in exquisite torture.

She nuzzled his ear, the darting of her tongue creating more excitement. "I want to undress you, Dean," she whispered. For one split second he was too stunned to react. Jesus God, he thought. He'd heard artists were uninhibited.

He tried to imagine Babs saying something like that to him, but even drunk, she would be incapable of it. "I want to see your body."

Everything from that point on had the quality of a dream: Dean standing motionless while she removed his clothes, piece by piece, the touch of her hands on his naked skin setting off a wildness he had never known, the bright glow that had leaped into her eyes when she saw his erection, and the sound of her low voice telling him there was nothing more beautiful than a man's body. Her own clothes seemed to disappear in the blink of an eye. In that instant, Dean knew there was nothing more beautiful than this woman's body, with its firmly shaped breasts, slender waist, and wide hips made to cradle a man.

Then he was holding her, loving her, rolling his tongue around her taut nipples while she writhed against him, her hands urging, her body exhorting, her legs twining around to draw him inside. There was no sanity, only hot sensations rocking through him, carrying him to a depth of passion, a stormy rapture.

Afterward Dean surfaced slowly, knowing he had never been loved nor given of himself so completely. This incredible woman in his arms had reached into his soul and brought out emotions he hadn't known he could feel.

By the time he could make himself leave Caroline, it was late. That night when he got home, he made tender love to Babs, letting his body beg forgiveness for his adultery, knowing he would do it again and again.

From that night on, Dean saw Caroline whenever he could, stealing an hour here, two hours there, sometimes an entire evening. It meant he had to lie, to make up fictitious appointments and invent excuses for coming home later than usual. He shied away from pretending he had to work late, fearing that his father might begin to question that. Most of the time he used Lane Canfield, claiming he had a meeting with him or he'd run into him somewhere, knowing that because of his long friendship with Lane, such an excuse wasn't likely to arouse suspicion. Other times it was an Arabian horse somebody had that he'd gone to see.

Dean tried not to think about the double life he was leading: on one hand, the devoted, loving husband, maintaining the routine of married life as if everything were normal, and on the other, the eager lover, cherishing every second spent with his mistress. Not once did he let himself wonder how long it could go on. There was only now. Nothing else mattered.

With Caroline, Dean felt free to be himself for the first time in his life — sexually free, confident that nothing would shock or offend her; and emotionally free, certain that he could talk openly about his feelings and know that she would understand.

At the same time that he told her about his dream to someday turn River Bend into the top Arabian stud farm in the world, a contemporary rival to the legendary Crabbet Park Stud in England or Janow Podlaski in Poland, he admitted the mixed feelings he had about working in his father's company, wanting to please him while knowing he lacked the ability ever to run the multimillion-dollar corporation.

"He's wrong to expect you to follow in his footsteps, Dean," Caroline stated in the black-and-white way she had in her opinions. "No one can do that — and shouldn't. You are an individual. His way will never be yours. You need to tell him that. Make him understand what you want. Just because the company is his life's work, that doesn't mean it has to be yours. He probably won't like it when you tell him that, but what can he do? He has to respect you for taking a stand. And he has to know that you didn't reach this decision without ever trying to see if it was something you could do."

Although Dean was willing to concede that she was right, he was hesitant to take such a giant step. Caroline had never met R.D. She had never seen him tear someone's logic to shreds, then piece it back together, creating a totally different conclusion. But he did sit down with R.D. and discuss his desire to take a more active role in the breeding operation and relieve R.D. of some of that responsibility. R.D. agreed to it almost immediately. Dean felt that if he could prove himself with the Arabians, his father would be more receptive to the idea of Dean dropping out of the company.

Life suddenly seemed very good to him — complicated, perhaps, but good just the same. Everything seemed to be within his reach: Caroline, the horses — everything.

Whistling a catchy tune he'd heard on the car radio driving home, R.D. crossed the living room's parquet floor of light chestnut and dark walnut boards and paused in the archway leading to the hall to do a mock little sashay, then proceeded to the staircase. He paused at the bottom and hollered up, "Babs, girl! I'm ready to go do a little dancin' if you are!" He started whistling again as he waited for her to come down. When he failed to hear the sound of her footsteps in the upstairs hall, he stopped and cocked his head to listen. Nothing.

"Babs?" he called again, then started up the stairs. It wasn't like her to be late for a party, and certainly not when it was gonna be a good ol' Texas barbecue.

When he reached the second-floor landing, he turned and walked over to the door to the bedroom suite that belonged to Babs and Dean. R.D. paused outside to listen and heard a faint noise that sounded like Babs was sniffling. He knocked once and reached for the doorknob. She was standing at the window with her back to the door when he opened it. A lace shawl was draped around her shoulders, covering the Mexican-style peasant blouse that went with the bright full skirt.

"Babs, are you ready to go?" R.D. frowned at the startled way she jumped when she heard his voice then hastily wiped her nose with a wadded handkerchief. He wasn't sure, but he thought she dabbed quickly at her eyes before she turned away from the window.

"I'm sorry, R.D. I guess I didn't hear you." Her voice was tremulous as she went through the motions of looking around her. "I know I laid my clutch purse somewhere."

"Here it is." R.D. picked it up from its resting place on the marble-topped side table by the door. "What's the matter? Are you coming down with a summer cold?"

"Maybe a little one." But she avoided looking at him as she walked over to get her purse from him.

She looked unnaturally pale. When she got closer, R.D. could see the telltale redness of her eyes. "I don't think you've got a cold. Those look like tears to me."

"Nonsense." She airily tried to brush aside his comment, but R.D. had never been one to be brushed aside easily.

"I know tears when I see them. Now either you've been peeling onions or something's the matter. Why don't you tell me what's bothering you, girl?"

"I — Oh, R.D., I don't know what to do." After a faltering attempt to deny anything was wrong, she started to cry again.

"There, there." He put an arm around her shoulders and guided her over to the apricot-colored chaise longue. There he sat her down and gave her his clean handkerchief. "It can't be as bad as all that."

"That's what I keep telling myself." Babs sniffled. "But what if it is?"

"Why don't you stop this boo-hooing for a minute and tell me what this 'it' is?"

"I — it's Dean." She lifted her tearful glance to his face. "I . . . think he's seeing . . . another woman."

He felt first disbelief, then a kind of dazed shock as he looked back over the last two months and saw a pattern to Dean's absences. Still, to Babs, he denied it. "Whatever gave you that silly notion?"

"He's been late so much and . . . and . . . Tomi Fredericks told me this afternoon that he's been seeing a woman in Galveston." She rushed the awful words in her haste to get them said. "Some . . . bohemian artist," Babs added, as if that made it worse.

"Now how in the name of Sam Houston would she know?" R.D. wondered aloud.

"She said that . . . Billie Joe Townsend saw them together on the beach last Friday night when Dean said he'd gone to look at a horse. According to him, Dean kissed her right there in public and then . . . they went walking off down the beach together, so close that you couldn't have got a slip of paper between them. And Tomi claimed that . . . others have seen them, too."

"And you call that proof?" R.D. chided. "Somebody saw somebody who looked like Dean. Did any of them talk to him?"

"I don't think so," she admitted.

"Well, then it seems to me your so-called friend Tomi is just trying to stir up trouble."

"But what if she isn't? What if it's true? He's been so different lately — so preoccupied. Tonight he said he was going to have a drink with Lane and meet us at the barbecue. But what if he isn't? What if he's really with her?"

"And what if cows fly? There's about as much chance of that as there is of Dean leaving you for some other woman. And that's the truth." He'd see to it. "Now, when I take a girl to a party, I expect her to be smiling and happy. So you go wash away those tears on your face and meet me downstairs in" — R.D. made a show of looking at his watch — "five minutes."

"Five minutes." She gazed at him with a glimmer of a grateful smile on her face. "I just love you to pieces, R.D." She pressed a wet kiss firmly on his cheek.

"You'd better behave yourself, girl, or folks'll start talking." He winked at her and smiled.

But the smile faded from his face as he went downstairs and closed the pocket doors in the library before he reached for the telephone.

* * *

The next morning, Dean stifled a yawn as he entered the office of his secretary, Mary Jo Anderson. "Late night?" She smiled and peered knowingly at him over the tops of her horn-rimmed glasses. Trained as a legal secretary, she had joined the company six years ago and knew more about the mechanics of the company than he did. Bright and efficient, she had covered his mistakes many times.

"That's putting it mildly." He stopped at her desk to pick up his telephone messages. "If it had been left up to my wife, we still would be dancing. Luckily the band packed up their instruments and went home at two in the morning."

"There's a message there from Lane Canfield. He wanted you to call him back as soon as you came in. He said it was important."

"Will do." He separated it from the others and put it on top, then continued on to the connecting door to his private office, smothering another yawn. "Better bring me a cup of coffee, Mary Jo," Dean said over his shoulder as he pushed open his door.

"Black with lots of sugar?"

"You've got it." Leaving the door open, he walked straight to his desk and picked up the phone. After dialing Lane's number, he settled himself in the swivel chair behind his desk. Directly in front of him on the opposite wall hung the painting Caroline called *The Sun and the Sea*. Every time he looked at it, it was like having her there with him. "Lane," Dean said when his voice came on the line. "How the hell are you?"

"Busy as usual. And you?"

"The same. Mary Jo said you wanted to talk to me right away. What's up?" Just at that moment, she walked in bringing his coffee.

"I had a strange phone call from your father last night," Lane said. Dean froze. For a split second he couldn't think. He couldn't even breathe. "Dean? Are you there?"

"Yes." He felt the first rush of panic as Mary Jo set his coffee cup on the desk. "Yes, just a minute." Covering the receiver's mouthpiece with his hand, he held it away from him and struggled to keep his voice pitched normally. "Would you mind closing the door on your way out, Mary Jo?"

"Of course."

Dean waited until he heard the click of the latch before he uncovered the mouthpiece. "Sorry, I'm back now. You said R.D. called? What did he want?"

"He was looking for you. He had the impression we were supposed to be together."

"What did you tell him?" Dean felt himself breaking into a sweat. He should have guessed that sooner or later something like this would happen, and been prepared for it. But he hadn't.

"I wasn't sure what to say. So I . . . gave him a story that I had gotten tied up with some last-minute paperwork and we were supposed to meet later."

"Thanks," Dean said, exhaling the breath he'd unconsciously been holding.

"He didn't leave any message. Just said he'd talk to you later." Lane paused expectantly, but Dean couldn't fill the gap. "Would you mind telling me what's going on?"

After carrying on a silent debate with himself, Dean realized he had to tell somebody. He couldn't keep it to himself any longer. And he knew he could trust Lane. Dean started talking and didn't stop until he had told Lane practically everything about Caroline and his relationship with her. "I know this probably sounds trite, but Caroline is the most incredible woman I've ever met. I love everything about her." Dean paused, and smiled self-consciously. "I guess I kinda got carried away with my answer, didn't I?"

"A little."

"I want you to meet her, Lane." It suddenly seemed very important to have his best friend meet the woman he loved. "I've got an appointment in Texas City late this morning. Caroline is going to drive up to meet me for lunch. Are you free? Could you join us?"

"I had planned to drop by the plant this afternoon. I probably could get away from here a little earlier than that."

"Try," Dean urged.

Lane promised that he would.

Initially, Lane had been prepared to dismiss Dean's voluble praise as the rantings of a married man enjoying his first taste of forbidden fruit. But after seeing Caroline and him together at the small café, communicating with a look or a touch, and completing each other's sentences, he knew he was wrong. This wasn't some infatuation that would eventually burn itself out. It was much more serious than that.

Lane could even understand what had attracted Dean to Caroline in the first place. She was intelligent and articulate, serious and dedicated. Nothing was ever halfway with her—not even love. She either loved something or someone totally and completely, or not at all. She was the antithesis of Babs.

As he watched them, he had the feeling he was looking at a pair of star-crossed lovers. No matter how much in love they were, Lane could see that they had nothing in common. Their clothes typified it, Dean in his Brooks Brothers suit and Caroline in her black pants and shirt. Their attitudes and their outlooks were nowhere near the same. Saddest of all, Lane recognized that, individually, they couldn't—and wouldn't—change.

As the three of them left the café, Lane started to say his good-byes and leave, but Dean stopped him. "You can't go yet. Caroline has something for you."

Curious, Lane followed them over to her vintage Chevrolet. A framed and mounted canvas sat in the backseat, carefully separated from a clutter of rags, easels, and boxes. With Dean's help, Caroline lifted it out and presented it to Lane.

Shades of gray, white, and black swirled out at him, shot with splinters of silver-gold. Within the enveloping mists of the painting, Lane had the impression of spires, tall cylinders, and a long vertical shaft.

"Do you recognize it?" Dean asked, his eyes alight as he watched Lane's face.

"There is something familiar about it," Lane admitted, but the images were too faint, hidden too well by the swirl of white and gray.

"It's the San Jacinto Monument with the tank farms and chemical plants in the ship channel in the background, shrouded in the early-morning fog and the smoke and fumes from the chemical plants."

As soon as Dean explained it, Lane was suddenly able to discern the faint outline of the lone star, the symbol of Texas, atop the monument's limestone shaft. "Yes, of course."

"I call it *Progress*," Caroline said.

A somewhat cynical observation, Lane thought, then decided that he was becoming too sensitive over anything that even implied criticism of the pollution around the ship channel. He also recognized that she could have depicted a scene much worse than the reality of the acidic haze and smoke that blanketed the area. She could have painted the waterway itself on fire.

"I like it, Caroline," Lane stated, after studying it a little longer, then he smiled. "And if I was supposed to get a message, I did. I'll hang it in my office just to remind me."

"Dean said you wouldn't be offended." As she looked at him with approval, Lane couldn't help wondering if he had just passed some test. "I have to be going," she said and turned to Dean.

Lane quickly interjected his good-bye and carried the painting to his car so the two lovers could have a degree of privacy. As Caroline drove out of the lot, Dean rejoined him.

"Didn't I tell you she was talented and wonderful?"

"You certainly did," Lane agreed.

"I'm glad you like the painting. You know, she won't let me buy her any presents. I should say, expensive presents. Canvas, paints, brushes — those she'll accept. But she just isn't interested in material things like clothes, jewelry, or perfume. Can you imagine meeting a woman like that?"

"No — at least, not until today."

As Dean gazed in the direction she'd gone, his faint, musing smile changed into a vaguely troubled frown. "I keep wondering why R.D. never mentioned anything about calling you when I talked to him at the barbecue last night."

"Maybe it just slipped his mind."

"R.D.?" Dean retorted skeptically. "He has an elephant's memory."

To play it safe, Dean had stayed close to the office and home for the next three days, but his need for Caroline outweighed caution and he'd finally had to see her, just for a little while. Even so, the fear that his father might suspect something forced Dean to look at his present situation and try to decide what he wanted to do about it. He loved Caroline and he wanted to spend every minute of his time with her, yet he still cared for Babs — not as deeply as he did for Caroline, but just the same, he didn't want to hurt her. She was completely innocent. She was a good wife, a loving wife. None of this was fair to her. But he also knew that he'd never be able to give Caroline up. Selfishly, what he wanted was for things to go on the way they were.

As he looked over the new crop of foals grazing in the near pasture with the mares, Dean felt an empathy with the foals. Right now, their world was perfect — their mothers right there by their sides offering comfort, protection, and a ready supply of milk — but soon they would have to be weaned. The separation of mare and foal would cause suffering. If Man didn't do it, Mother Nature would. It was unavoidable. Dean knew he was personally faced with a similar situation. It was unrealistic to pretend things didn't have to change. The trauma of a separation was inevitable, but a separation from whom? That's what he'd kept asking himself when he'd gone to see Caroline after work that afternoon.

Sighing, he pushed away from the fence and walked toward the house. Not a breath of air stirred the leaves of the ancient oaks and pecans that shaded the lawn. The hot, sultry weather of an East Texas early August had settled over River Bend with a vengeance. By the time Dean climbed the veranda steps, his cotton shirt and jeans were sticking to him, the denim material drawing tightly against his legs with each stride.

Some claimed that air-conditioning was man's greatest gift to Texas. Dean wholeheartedly agreed with that as he stepped inside and paused a minute to let the coolness wash over him. Intent on a shower and a change of clothes, he headed for the stairs, the heavy thud of his cowboy boots on the foyer's heart-pine floor echoing through the house with its fourteen-foot-high ceilings. But before Dean reached the massive staircase, R.D. walked into view and paused beneath the curved archway to the library.

"Would you mind stepping in here, Dean? I need to talk to you." R.D. turned and walked back into the library. Dean hesitated a minute, then followed him inside the room lined on two walls with glass-enclosed bookcases of heavy walnut. As R.D. rounded the curved hunt desk that faced the fireplace, he glanced back at Dean. "Close the doors."

Suddenly uneasy, Dean backtracked and pulled the pocket doors shut, then turned around and moved hesitantly forward. "Is something wrong?"

"That's what I'd like to know." R.D. sat down on the walnut-framed swivel chair padded with navy-blue leather and tilted it back to fix his gaze on Dean.

"I don't follow you." Frowning, Dean shook his head slightly, all the while feeling more uncomfortable.

"I think you do," R.D. stated and rocked his chair forward to rest his arms on the desk in front of him. "Where did you go after you left the office tonight?"

"Why?" Dean struggled not to look guilty, well aware that inside he was squirming just like he had when he was a kid, caught doing something he shouldn't. "Did something happen?"

"Just answer the question."

Lying had become second nature to him. "Babs has a birthday coming up. I . . . was out looking for a present for her."

"Like you met Lane the other night?"

Dean tried to laugh. "I don't know what you're talking about."

"Dammit, boy! Don't lie to me!" R.D. brought a hand crashing down on the desktop. Then he stood up and breathed in deeply, making a visible effort to control his temper. "You know damned well what I'm talking about. You've been seeing some woman in Galveston, so don't bother to deny it. She's an artist, I understand — no doubt the one who did that yellow painting you've got hanging in your office."

"Her name is Caroline Farr."

R.D. snorted. "I wish she was Farr — far away."

"I'm in love with her." It was almost a relief finally to admit that to his father.

For a moment there was only silence in the room as R.D. looked away, his face expressionless, as if he hadn't heard what Dean had just said. "It's one thing for a man to get a little somethin' strange on the side now and then, but it's another to let himself get involved." He swung back to glare at Dean. "Have you forgotten you're married? That you've got a wife upstairs?"

"I haven't forgotten." Dean couldn't meet the accusing look in his father's blue eyes.

"She knows. You do realize that?"

"How?" Dean frowned.

"You've been seen and the talk's gettin' around."

"I didn't know." He hung his head, realizing just how complicated the situation had become — and how much worse it could get.

"Tell me one thing, Dean. Just what do you plan to do about it?"

"I'm not sure. I —"

"Well, you can be sure of one thing. There has never been a divorce in the whole history of the Lawson family. And there isn't going to be one now. That little gal upstairs is your wife and you married her 'for better or worse.'"

"I know that."

"Well, if you know it, then you bring this little affair of yours to an end — and damned quick."

"You don't understand, R.D." Dean raised his hands in a helpless and angry gesture of frustration. "I'm in love with Caroline."

"I'm truly sorry about that," R.D. stated. "But I don't see where that changes anything."

A fan whirred in the corner of the beach house, slowly wagging its head from side to side, the blades spinning to circulate the air. But Dean hardly noticed its refreshing draft as he sat slumped on the living-room couch with his head resting on the seat back, his legs stretched out in front of him, and Caroline's dark head pillowed on his stomach. He was glad of the silence. A half a dozen times in the last hour, he had tried to get the words out that would tell her it was better if they didn't see each other again, but every time they'd become lodged in his throat. Regardless of what R.D. said, no matter how he tried, he just couldn't imagine life without her.

"I like your nose. It has a very noble line."

Dean glanced down to find Caroline watching him with her dissecting artist's eye. "It does, eh?"

"Yes." She shifted her position slightly, changing the angle of her head on his stomach to give herself a better view of his face. "Have you ever wondered what a child of ours would look like?"

"No, I haven't." Such talk was painful to him. It spoke of the future, and Dean wasn't sure they had one. "I think I'll get another beer." He slid a hand under her shoulders and gave her a little push off of him. Obligingly she swung her feet off the couch and sat up. "Want anything?" Dean asked as he walked over to the refrigerator.

"No."

He took a long-neck out of the refrigerator and pried the top off with the opener that was lying on the counter beside the cap of his last bottle. Turning, he took a swig of beer and saw Caroline standing by the counter island, her hands stuffed in the side pockets of her shorts.

"I'm going to have a baby, Dean."

"You're . . . you're what?" After the first shock of disbelief passed, Dean started to laugh — happily, uproariously. This changed everything. Even R.D. would have to agree to that. There was no other choice now except for him to divorce Babs and marry Caroline. He couldn't allow a child of his to be born illegitimately. The bottle of beer sat forgotten on the countertop as Dean lifted her off the floor, holding her high in the air, and spun around the room.

"Dean, stop. This is crazy," Caroline protested, but she was smiling, too.

"Crazy. Wonderful. It's all that and more." He kissed her shoulder, her neck, and her lips before he let her feet touch the floor again.

"I'm glad you're happy about it."

"Happy? I'm delirious!" He gazed at her, certain she had taken on a new radiance. "How long have you known?"

"A couple of weeks."

"A couple of weeks? Why didn't you tell me before?"

"I wanted to be sure this was what I wanted. I've always liked children, but I've never seriously thought about having one of my own before. My paintings were always my children. But I had to face the fact that I'm twenty-nine years old. In a few more years, I'll be too old. It's a case of now or maybe never." When she paused to look at him, she lost her serious expression and smiled. Dean was relieved. She had sounded so coldly logical that it had scared him a little. "And besides, I happen to love the father of this baby very much."

"And I love you, Caroline." He drew her into the circle of his arms and held her close, shutting his eyes tightly as he rubbed his cheek against her hair. "We'll get married as soon as I can arrange the divorce, but I promise you, it will be before the baby is born."

She seemed very still in his arms. "And then what, Dean?"

"What do you mean?" He nuzzled her hair, wondering whether it would be a boy or a girl. He still felt a little dazed at the prospect of becoming a father. A father.

"I mean" — gently but firmly she pushed away from him, creating some space between them — "what will we do? Where will we live?"

"At River Bend, where else? I'll breed my Arabians and you'll raise our baby — and maybe one or two more — and paint. Maybe we can talk R.D. into turning his billiard room on the third floor into a studio for you."

"I don't think so." She turned out of his arms and walked a few feet away.

"It's worth a try. Give him a grandson and R.D. will probably give you the moon." Dean laughed.

"I meant that I don't think that would work." Caroline twined her long fingers together, revealing an agitation that was totally foreign to her. "I love you, Dean. I'll always love you. But I would *hate* living there."

"You don't know that," Dean protested, stunned by her statement and its implications. "Wait until you see it. It's a beautiful old home with turrets and bay windows . . . the design of the parquet floor, you'd fall in love with it. The craftsmanship of the woodwork —"

"The beautiful furniture, the crystal, the china, the elaborate clothes and the entertaining that goes with them — I don't like that kind of life, Dean. Please try to understand that's not the way I want to live," she said insistently.

"You're being emotional right now. It's the baby." Dean grabbed at any excuse rather than accept what she was saying.

She sighed heavily with a mixture of exasperation and despair. "Could you live anywhere else than River Bend? Would you be happy for the rest of your life living in a house like this one, without all the fine and beautiful things you're used to?"

"I . . . could try." But he just couldn't imagine it.

"I won't ask you to, Dean. I don't expect you to give up your life for me and I can't give up mine for you. Just the same, I'm glad that you wanted to marry me."

"What are you saying?" He stared at her, icy fear clutching at his throat.

"I love you, but I won't marry you." She turned her back on him and faced the table strewn with brushes, paints, cleaning fluids, and rags. "I was offered a teaching post at a private school in California. I've decided to accept it." Her shoulders lifted in a little shrug. "After all, I've never seen the Pacific Coast. I'll be leaving in ten days."

"You can't! You're going to have my baby."

"I can have it in California as easily as I can have it here." She sounded so callous.

"If you love me, how can you leave me?" As he caught hold of her arm and turned her around, he saw the tears in her eyes. "Dear God, Caroline, I don't think I can live without you."

"Don't — " Her voice broke. "Don't make this any harder for me than it already is."

"Then stay."

"I can't."

No amount of cajoling, demanding, begging, or arguing on Dean's part could persuade her to change her mind. In the following ten days, he tried time after time with no success. She was going to California. "If you want to see me, you can come there," she said and gave him the address and phone number of the school in Los Angeles. When he tried to give her some money, she shoved it back in his hands and informed him that she would not accept any financial support from him. If he wanted to pay part of the medical expenses he could, but she insisted that she was more than capable of raising the baby without his help.

That first week Caroline was gone, Dean went through hell. Twice he called the number she'd given him; both times he was told she hadn't reported in yet. When he was almost driven crazy with the thought that she'd disappeared from his life for good, she called. She'd had car trouble in Arizona. No, she was fine. She'd found an apartment in Malibu, near the beach. The Pacific was so different from either the Gulf or the Atlantic, she could hardly wait to start painting it. And she missed him.

Life suddenly seemed worth living again. Dean started making plans to fly to California and see her as soon as Babs was feeling better. Two days ago she had collapsed at a charity luncheon. The doctor was certain it was merely a case of exhaustion brought on by the heat and a slight case of anemia. With a couple of weeks of rest and a well-balanced diet, she would be on her feet again.

As soon as he arrived home that night, Dean went upstairs to see her. She was reclining in the chaise longue, wrapped in a ruffled silk robe of mint green. A bed tray was across her lap, but Dean noticed the food on it had barely been touched.

"You're supposed to be eating," he admonished as he bent down to drop a kiss on her forehead. "Doctor's orders."

"I don't want it."

Dean glanced at the food on the plate. "You've always liked spinach omelettes. Surely you can get down a few more bites."

"That tastes like . . . squashed meat."

"How about if I have Justine fix you something else?"

Babs turned away to look out the window, but she couldn't turn far enough to hide the quivering of her lower lip. "I don't care."

"Babs, what's wrong? This isn't like you." He sat down on the edge of the chaise and took her hand in his.

"You don't really care," she retorted, sniffling and lifting her chin a fraction higher.

"I certainly do." Dean frowned.

"I know you don't love me anymore."

"Babs —"

"It's true. You think I haven't noticed the way you've been acting this last week. Well, I have. You've been mooning around here like — "

Never once had Babs accused him of being unfaithful, even though, as R.D. had told him, she knew. Grateful for that, Dean tried now to ease her mind a little. "She's gone, Babs." He heard her quick little intake of breath. "She left last week. I never meant for you to be hurt. I'm sorry."

"Then" — she gazed at him hopefully — "you're going to stay?"

She was so vulnerable, so childlike, constantly needing assurance. How had he forgotten that? "Yes."

"I need you so much now." She clutched at his hand, a wondrous smile breaking through the tears. "Darling . . . we're going to have a baby."

Babs's pregnancy was a complicated one, and toxemia had kept her bedridden for the last few months of her term. Dean managed to squeeze in two short trips to Los Angeles in the next few months to see Caroline and assure himself that all was healthy and normal for her. He didn't like the garage apartment she had rented, but Caroline insisted it was adequate for her needs and flatly refused to move into a five-room house he found. But as Babs grew closer to term, Dean was too concerned about her health to leave her, trusting that healthy and self-sufficient Caroline would somehow manage, as she claimed.

Two weeks before Babs's due date, her doctor decided to take the baby by caesarian section. Dean sat out the operation in a private waiting room with R.D.

The doctor walked into the waiting room, still clad in his surgical gown and cap. "It's a girl, Mr. Lawson. Five pounds ten ounces and bawling her head off."

Dean came to his feet as R.D. stopped pacing. "Babs — how is she?"

"She's going to be fine," the doctor assured him. "They have taken her to Recovery. She should be coming out of the anesthesia fairly soon."

"I'd like to see her."

"Of course. Come with me," the doctor said.

"Here." R.D. reached inside his jacket. "Have a cigar."

Dean was there when Babs came to. She was groggy and a little silly, but for Babs, that was normal. Relieved, Dean joined his father at the nursery window.

"There she is." R.D. pointed to a red-faced, squalling infant wildly waving her little fists. A downy mass of black hair covered her head. "Strong little tyke, isn't she? And a Lawson through and through. Look at her yellin' her head off, lettin' the world know she's here. And those eyes, too, they're Lawson blue."

"All babies have blue eyes when they're born, R.D." But Dean smiled at the obvious pride his father took in the child. He felt it, too.

"Not blue like that. Are you still going to name her after your grandma?"

It had been Babs's suggestion to name the baby after the woman who had raised both himself and R.D. if it was a girl. Dean had agreed, knowing how much it would please R.D. "You're looking at Abigail Louise Lawson."

"I like that." R.D. nodded approvingly, a softness entering his expression before it slowly turned thoughtful. "When's the other one due?"

Dean was surprised by the reference to Caroline. R.D. had rarely mentioned her since that day last August when Dean had informed him Caroline was going to have his baby. R.D. hadn't said much except to remind him that a father had as much responsibility as a mother to see that a child was properly brought up, provided for, and educated. But the lecture had been unnecessary. Dean knew he could never abandon Caroline or the child born of their love.

"Soon," was all he said in reply.

At the Lawson Company headquarters the next morning, Dean waded through a gauntlet of backslapping congratulations on the birth of his daughter before he reached the haven of Mary Jo Anderson's outer office. "Sorry." He held his suit jacket open to show the emptiness of his inner pockets. "I'm fresh out of cigars. Those guys out there got them all. At this rate, I'm going to have to buy them by the case."

"I don't mind. R.D. would probably have a heart attack if he walked in here and saw me smoking a cigar anyway. Congratulations, just the same." But she didn't seem as enthusiastic as everyone else. Dean wondered if it was because she knew about Caroline. He'd had to confide in her. As his private secretary, Mary Jo screened all his mail and phone calls, and handled a lot of his personal bills. In an emergency, Caroline had to be able to reach him. Where else was safer than here at the office? And someone had to know where to reach him when he went to California, especially when Babs had been so ill during her pregnancy.

"She's a beautiful baby, Mary Jo. We decided to name her Abigail Louise after my grandmother, but we're going to call her Abbie." Feeling self-conscious about the way he was carrying on, Dean walked over to her desk and picked up the previous day's messages. "Have a dozen yellow roses sent to Babs at the hospital, will you?"

"Of course." She paused a moment then said, "You had a phone call yesterday that's not with your messages."

Tense with anticipation, Dean looked up from the now unimportant pieces of paper. "Caroline?"

"Yes. She had a baby girl yesterday morning. Rachel Ann."

Yesterday. The same day that Abbie was born. Stunned by the coincidence, the terrible irony, Dean was speechless.

THE BAY STALLION SNORTED restlessly and tried to elude her hand, but Abbie continued to hold him there and rub his cheek. She needed this excuse to avoid looking at Lane. She didn't want him to see the tears that smarted in her eyes.

"I remember stopping by his office one day," Lane said, continuing with his story. "You would have been . . . probably four or five years old at the time. Dean was sitting behind his desk, reading a letter. There was a color snapshot on his desk of a little girl with big blue eyes and long dark hair . . . pulled in a ponytail, I think. She had on a swimsuit, and there was sand in the background. The little girl stood there smiling shyly at the camera. I thought it was you and said something to that effect to Dean. He corrected me.

"'That isn't a picture of Abbie,' he said. 'It's Rachel. It's amazing, isn't it, how much they look alike?' I must have picked up the photograph, because I remember Dean took it from me and stared at it. 'And both born on the same day, too,' he said. 'Every time I look at Abbie, I see Rachel. It's almost like having both of them with me all the time. When I go places and do things with Abbie, I can almost believe that Rachel is there, too.'"

When Lane paused, Abbie sensed he was looking at her, probably seeing the striking resemblance again. She hoped he didn't expect her to say anything, because she couldn't. The muscles in her throat were so achingly tight, she couldn't even swallow.

As the silence threatened to lengthen, Abbie realized Lane was leaving it up to her to break it. "And Momma — when did she find out? About his other child, I mean."

"I'm not sure, probably a couple of years after you were born. With all the trips Dean was making to Los Angeles, she became suspicious that he was seeing Caroline again. When she confronted him, he told her about Rachel. How much, I don't know. I do know he promised Babs he would never leave her, even though he was deeply in love with Caroline and intended to visit her and Rachel whenever he could. I'm sure your mother didn't like it, but she accepted the situation. After all, she was desperately in love with him, too." Lane paused, a frown gathering on his forehead. "By that, I don't mean to imply that Dean didn't have any feelings for her. He did care about Babs very much."

"If that's true, then he wouldn't want her hurt any more than she's already been. I hope you'll agree that there isn't any reason for Momma to see the entire contents of the will if it can be avoided. She has suffered enough, I think. Surely as the executor of Daddy's will you can arrange that."

"To a degree. However, the will has to be filed with the probate court. It will be a matter of public record."

"I see," she said tightly.

"I'm sorry, Abbie."

"I know. Everybody always is." She couldn't help sounding cynical and a little bitter. That was the way she felt.

"Abbie," Lane began, "I hope you can appreciate how difficult, mentally and emotionally, it must have been for your father. He was in an extremely awkward situation and he handled it the best way he could. It's the most natural thing in the world for a father to want to love and protect his children, and to spare them from unnecessary hurt. And it's just as natural that he would want to provide for them in the event anything should happen to him."

"What about . . . Caroline?" Abbie questioned, only now struck by the possibility that she, too, might be one of his beneficiaries.

"She died several years ago — from an aneurysm, I believe."

Several years ago. "I see," was all that was left for her to say. A misting of tears blurred her vision as she lightly stroked the stallion's soft nose. "I appreciate your frankness, Lane. You'd probably better go to the house now before Momma starts wondering what's keeping you."

"Aren't you coming?"

"I'll be there soon."

The stallion attempted to pull away from her again, but Abbie kept him there until Lane had walked away. Then she let him go and watched him, her father's favorite, as he galloped around the small pen and stopped at the far end to call to the mares in the pasture, his sleek body quivering in anticipation. But his love call went unanswered.

Abbie turned and walked blindly away from the stallion run that butted up to the stud barn. The gray filly nickered plaintively to her, but Abbie's misery was so great she was unaware of the horse. She felt the tears coming and had to find a place where she could be alone and cry.

She sought refuge in the building that housed a reception area for visitors as well as the manager's office, the tack room, and her father's private office. Attached to the main stable by a breezeway that her grandfather had always called a dogtrot, it commanded a view of the stables, the stud barn, and the pastures. A black wreath hung on the door. Another time Abbie would have been moved by the gesture of the stable help to show their grief over her father's passing, but she didn't even look twice at it as she pushed through the door and headed directly to her father's private office, pulled by memories of the times she'd spent with him there . . . memories that now seemed so false.

Once inside, she closed the door and leaned against it to look around the room, her throat tight, her chin trembling. Sunlight, filtered by the pecan trees outside, streamed through the window onto the richly paneled walls covered with trophies, framed photographs, and show ribbons. A heavy oak desk sat in front of the window, strewn with papers, notes, and breeding charts. To the right of it stood antique file cabinets that contained the papers, pedigrees, and breeding files for every horse at River Bend. Behind the glass doors of the corniced and columned oak bookcase, shelves held books on equine ailments, horse husbandry, and genetics. Along the near wall stretched a chesterfield sofa upholstered in Madeira-brown leather and trimmed with brass nailheads. Partners to it were the wing chair and ottoman.

Abbie walked around to the big leather armchair behind the desk and ran her hand over the hollow curved into the headrest. She remembered how hard she had tried to please her father — to make him proud of her. Abruptly she turned away from his chair, fighting the writhing anger and hurt inside.

She almost regretted asking Lane to tell her about her father and Caroline. Before, she'd at least had her illusions. Now she didn't even have those. But she had asked for the truth and she got it. It wasn't Lane's fault that it wasn't what she'd expected.

She thought he'd tell her that it had been some cheap, meaningless affair; that her father had made a regrettable mistake he'd had to pay for for the rest of his life; that some tramp had tricked him into getting her pregnant then blackmailed him with the child; that . . . somehow, he'd been trying to protect the family honor and spare them his shame.

Instead, she'd heard a story of tragic love — of two people from different worlds, deeply and passionately in love with each other, but destined to remain apart — and the child born from that love.

No wonder she'd never been the daughter he wanted. She was the wrong one. All she'd ever been was a look-alike stand-in, a double, right down to having the same birthday.

Abbie longed to scream and release all the pain she felt inside, but what would that change? Nothing — nothing at all.

With hands and teeth clenched, she moved away from the desk and fought to convince herself that she didn't care that he hadn't loved her. She wasn't a child anymore. She didn't need his love. But Abbie didn't think she could ever forget — or forgive him for — the years of deception. As a hot tear rolled down her cheek, she blinked to clear her burning eyes, and wondered how she could have been so naïve all this time.

On the wall in front of her was an old photograph of her grandfather, R.D. Lawson, taken at the Scottsdale Arabian Horse Show the year he died. He stood there beside the two-year-old gray filly, River Wind, named Champion Filly of the Scottsdale Show — the dam of Abbie's filly, River Breeze. A Stetson hat concealed the iron gray of his hair, but it didn't hide the proud smile that wreathed his face and softened its hard angles. The picture showed a robust man who carried his years well.

As Abbie stared at the photograph, memories came flooding back. She was finally forced to admit that she hadn't been blind to what had gone on all these years: she had simply refused to see it. Innumerable incidents had contained clues, but she had ignored them all.

She remembered the last time she'd seen her grandfather alive. He'd gone to the airport to see them off on what Abbie regarded as a family vacation. In actuality, it had been combined with a business trip her father was taking to check on the company's overseas offices and to look over Arabian breeding stock in other countries for possible purchase and importation. She had been all of eight years old at the time, so the reasons for the trip hadn't mattered to her. They were going: Abbie, her parents, and their black maid, Justine, brought along to look after Abbie.

LONDON WAS THE FIRST stop on their overseas tour. Abbie, with her boundless energy, fueled by excitement, didn't suffer from jet lag and didn't understand why the first full day of their vacation in a new city had to be spent so quietly. She wanted to go out and explore this town where people drove on the wrong side of the road and talked so funny she could hardly understand them. She wanted to ride on one of those red double-decker buses and see the palace where the queen lived.

"Babs, why do I have the feeling she is going to hound us until we agree to do something?" Dean caught hold of Abbie's hands and forced her to stand still in front of his chair.

One look at her father's tolerantly amused smile and Abbie knew she had him. "Ben says it's because I'm just like my grandpa. I won't quit no matter what."

"Ben just may be right," Dean conceded, aware that at times, his daughter's persistence bordered on sheer bullheadedness — a trait tempered by a naturally warm and outgoing nature. Not at all like the shy and sensitive Rachel, Dean thought, recalling the way she watched him with those haunting blue eyes of hers. Rarely did they sparkle and dance the way Abbie's did now.

"Ben's always right," she announced pertly.

"Most of the time, anyway." Affectionately he tweaked her nose, then glanced over at Babs, still clad in her Italian palazzo pajamas, and propped up with a cushion of pillows on the sitting-room sofa. "Let's take the child for a walk, Babs. The fresh air and sunshine will do us good."

"I doubt it, honey." She groped for the cup of coffee sitting on the end table, the last that remained from the late morning breakfast they'd had served in their hotel suite. "This is worse than the mornings after one of the MacDonnells' barbecues. My eyes feel like a pair of peeled grapes full of pits. And I know I must weigh two hundred pounds, as heavy as I feel."

"If she's gained that much weight, then she really does need to exercise, doesn't she, Daddy?" Abbie grinned slyly.

"She certainly does."

"I have a better idea," Babs said, pausing to take a slow sip of her coffee. "You and Abbie go for a walk and let me stay here and rest."

"No." Abbie pulled free from Dean's hands and walked over to the sofa to take the coffee cup out of her mother's hands. "You have to come with us. This is our vacation and we're supposed to have fun."

After a considerable amount of joint prodding and coaxing, an hour later the three of them were strolling down the London streets. At least, Dean and Babs were strolling. Abbie was skipping ahead, eager to experience the sights and sounds of this city that was so new to her.

Abruptly she turned and started walking backward, a perplexed look on her face. "Why isn't there any fog today? Isn't there supposed to be fog in London?"

"Not every day," Babs said. "It's like at home in Texas. Sometimes it will roll in at night, or early mornings. And sometimes it will just hover on the river, like it does on the Brazos, sneaking around the trees on the banks and spooking into the pastures."

"It gets scary then." But Abbie's eyes were bright with excitement at the thought.

"Turn around and watch where you're going before you run into some-body," Babs admonished.

"And don't get too far ahead of us," Dean added when Abbie started to take off at a run. "You'll get lost."

"Yes, Daddy." Unwillingly she slowed down.

If that was Rachel, Dean knew she'd be right at his side holding on to his hand, especially when they were at some public place with a lot of people around. She said it was because she didn't want to get separated from him, but Dean suspected that Rachel was a little too timid and insecure to venture off by herself. Abbie, on the other hand, didn't even know what a stranger was. Night and day, his daughters were, regardless of how much they looked alike.

"I forgot to tell you, Babs, before you were up this morning, I made ar-rangements with the concierge for a guide to take you and Abbie around London tomorrow and show you the sights. I'll probably be tied up the rest of the week handling things with the company office here."

"Abbie isn't going to be too happy about that." Neither was Babs, but she wasn't about to admit it.

"She'll have too much to see and do to notice I'm not around. Look at her." Dean smiled. "Her head's swinging from side to side like one of those dogs on the dashboard of a car."

During the next three days, Babs and Abbie took in all the must-see sights, accompanied by the unobtrusive Justine and their guide, Arthur Bigsby. They watched the ceremonial Changing of the Guard in the forecourt of Buckingham Palace, but Abbie was disappointed that she didn't get to see the queen — and she didn't think the palace was as nice as their home at River Bend, although she did concede it was bigger. She was impressed by the glittering array of Crown Jewels and royal regalia at the Tower of London. She argued with Arthur when he tried to tell her Big Ben was the large bell in the Clock Tower of the Houses of Parliament in Westminster. Everyone in Texas knew Big Ben was the clock.

Westminster Abbey was all right. She couldn't imagine why anybody would want to be buried in a church, especially kings. That's what cemeteries were for. She fed the pigeons in Trafalgar Square and laughed when one sat on her head.

When they met Dean for lunch, her array of observations and the questions they raised was endless. Why wasn't there a circus at Piccadilly Circus? Why did they call cookies biscuits? Why did they call supper high tea? If there was high tea, what was low tea?

Dean finally pointed at her plate and said, "Eat."

"Poor Arthur should have tried that," Babs said. "She absolutely wore the man out. And me, too."

"Well, tomorrow will be different. I thought we might drive down to Crabbet Park and look at their Arabians."

"Really, Daddy? Are we honest and truly gonna go there tomorrow?" Abbie asked excitedly.

"Yes. I thought we'd leave bright and early in the morning so we can spend as much time there as we want."

"You and Abbie go. When it comes to horses, I can't tell a gelding from a stallion."

"Momma, that's easy. Ben says all you have to do is —"

"Abbie, it's not polite to interrupt." Dean tried to look stern and not laugh.

"I'm telling you, Dean, some of the things she knows would make Justine blush," Babs declared, then went on with what she had been about to say before Abbie interrupted her. "Anyway, I want to go to this boutique in Chelsea called Bazaar. Some new designer named Mary Quant has it. Her clothes are supposed to be all the rage now. I haven't had a chance to do any shopping yet."

"I'd like to go shopping," Abbie said wistfully, then quickly added, "But I'd rather go to Crabbet Park with you, Daddy."

"Is there any reason why we can't go shopping after we finish our lunch? I haven't had a chance to do any shopping either." And he wanted to send something to Rachel from England — something nice.

"I have an appointment to have my hair done," Babs said. "I can't very well cancel it if you expect me to look presentable tonight when we have dinner with your London manager and his wife."

"In that case Abbie and I will go, and meet you back at the hotel later."

A taxi dropped them off at the main entrance to Selfridge's Department Store. Usually Dean had trouble choosing something for Rachel, especially when it came to clothes; he was never sure she'd like it or whether it would fit. With Abbie along, he hoped to solve at least part of the problem.

As they entered the children's wear department, Dean spied a girl's dress in lavender-checked gingham trimmed with white lace. "Abbie, do you like that one?"

"It's okay." She wrinkled up her nose. "But I don't like lavender. Look at this blue dress, Daddy. Isn't it pretty? I'll bet it just matches my eyes."

"It sure does. Why don't you try it on? And the lavender one, too."

"Daddy," she protested at his first choice.

"For me. I want to see what you look like in it."

"Okay," she declared with an exaggerated sigh of agreement.

A few minutes later Abbie emerged from the fitting room, wearing the gingham dress. "See, Daddy." She did a slow pirouette in front of the mirror. "It doesn't do a thing for me."

Dean was forced to agree that it didn't suit her at all, yet looking at her, he could see the quiet and reserved Rachel wearing it, her dark hair tied up in a ponytail with a matching lavender ribbon. "Take that one off and try the blue one on." As Abbie disappeared into the fitting room again, he turned to the sales clerk. "I want that lavender dress, but I'd like to have it shipped, please."

"But your daughter —"

"I'm not buying it for Abbie."

"Very good, sir. We'll be happy to ship it wherever you like."

After the blue dress, Abbie tried on a half-dozen other outfits ranging from sport clothes to party dresses. Finally she chose three that she just couldn't live without. As Dean was paying for the purchases, Abbie noticed another sales clerk wrapping the lavender gingham dress in tissue. She pulled Dean aside.

"Daddy, I told you I didn't like that dress."

"You mean the lavender one?" He pretended not to know. "I think some other little girl is getting it."

"Oh, good." She rolled her eyes ceilingward in a dramatic expression of relief. "I was afraid you were buying it for me." As the clerk handed Dean the packages and receipt, Abbie hovered at his side. "Where to next?"

"Wherever you want. Although it is getting late. Maybe we should head back to the hotel."

"But I thought you wanted to do some shopping." Her eyebrows arched together in a bewildered frown.

"I already have." He held up the packages as evidence.

"Oh, Daddy." She broke into a wide smile. "I love you."

Back at their hotel suite, Justine took charge of the packages and Abbie, and informed Dean that Mrs. Lawson hadn't returned from her beauty appointment yet. Checking his watch and mentally calculating the time difference, he walked into the master bedroom and closed the door. The telephone sat on the nightstand between the twin beds. Dean picked up the receiver and dialed the operator.

A very British voice came on the line. "May I help you?"

"Yes, ma'am. I'd like to place an overseas call to California." After supplying the needed information, Dean waited through the innumerable clicks and cracklings before finally hearing the dull ring on the other end of the line. Then, above the faint hum of static, he heard Caroline's voice. As always, it brought that same soaring lift of his spirits.

"Hello, darling." He tightened his grip on the receiver as if that could somehow bring her closer.

"Dean." Her voice was filled with surprise and delight — with just a trace of confusion. "But . . . I thought you were —"

"I'm calling from London. I'm missing you so much I just had to hear your voice. How are you? You sound wonderful." Swinging his legs onto the bed, he reclined against the pillowed headboard and gazed at the room's high ceiling, but saw her face in front of him.

"I'm fine. So is Rachel. As a matter of fact, she's standing right here, tugging at my arm. I think she wants to say hello."

"Put her on."

There was a moment of muted voices in the background, then Rachel came on the line. "Dean, is it really you? You are calling from England?" Amid the excited rush of her questions, there was a touchingly tentative quality to her young voice.

But that didn't cause the quick twinge of pain Dean felt. It was the use of his given name. Rachel never called him Father or Papa or Daddy — always Dean. Caroline had insisted on that from the start, just as she had insisted on Rachel knowing about her illegitimacy from an early age. Caroline didn't believe in hiding from Rachel the truth that her parents were neither married nor divorced like those of other children. Her classmates and friends were bound to ask questions and make remarks that would ultimately hurt, but not as much if they prepared her for them. In Caroline's opinion, the use of his given name gave Rachel a degree of protection from unwanted questions about her father and allowed her to decide what she wanted to tell about him. Although Dean was forced to agree with Caroline, he didn't like it. He hated the fact that Rachel knew about his other family, his other daughter. He hated the questions she asked about them — and the guilt he felt.

"Yes, it's me, calling from England." But it was a struggle for him to keep the light, happy tone in his voice. "I bought you something today. It's being sent, so you probably won't get it for a few weeks."

"What is it?"

"I can't tell you. It's a surprise. But I think it's something you'll like very much. By the way, guess where I'm going tomorrow?"

"Where?"

"To Crabbet Park. Remember the book I sent you for Christmas about Lady Anne Blunt? We sat and read parts of it when I was there in January."

"Oh, yes!" she cried excitedly, animation taking over her voice. "About how she traveled with her husband, riding on horseback to Persia and India, and all through Arabia and Mesopotamia and Egypt, and crossing flooded rivers and deserts way back in the eighteen hundreds. She lived with the Bedouins and learned to read and speak their language. And she learned all about the Arabian horse and bought the best she could find so they wouldn't become extinct. The Bedouins called her 'the noble lady of the horses.' And even though she had a home in England, she loved the desert and horses so much that she went back to Egypt to live. And that's where she died. But her daughter in England loved Arabians, too, and she kept them all and bred them and raised the finest horses in the world." Rachel finally paused and released a dreamily heavy sigh. "It was a wonderful story. I've read it over and over."

"I can tell." Dean smiled, feeling a sense of pride that she was developing a love for Arabians, too.

"Mommy has to help me with the words sometimes."

"I'm sure she does." There were some Arabic ones even he couldn't pronounce. "Anyway, tomorrow I'm going to the stud farm that was owned by her daughter, Lady Wentworth."

"Are you? Oh, I wish I was going, too."

"So do I, honey," he said tightly. "So do I. But maybe someday." Yet try as he might, he couldn't imagine the day ever coming when he could openly take Rachel with him on trips like this.

"Yes." She didn't sound too hopeful either, but she quickly tried to hide it. "I forgot to tell you, Dean: I convinced Mom to let me take riding lessons this summer. I had my first one yesterday. My riding instructor says I have a natural seat and good hands. Of course, I told him that you've taken me riding before and shown me some things."

"It sounds like I'd better start looking for a good horse suitable for a new, young rider."

"I'd like that, Dean, more than anything," she declared, the fervor in her voice eliminating any doubt that she meant it.

"I'll see what I can find when I get back." He talked with Rachel for a few more minutes, then spoke again to Caroline. Much too quickly Dean heard the door to the suite open, signaling Babs's return. Hastily he said his good-byes to Caroline and hung up.

Don't let her know, don't let her see, don't let her hear; just let her pretend none of it existed. That was his agreement with Babs. He did his best to keep it and not cause her any more anguish.

After a short drive south of London through the Sussex countryside on the way to Brighton, they arrived at the famed Arabian stud farm founded in 1878 by Lord and Lady Blunt on his ancestral estate. Even though the land wasn't Texas-flat, the lush green pastures, the big old trees, and the beautiful Arabian horses in the paddocks reminded Abbie of her home at River Bend. She hadn't realized how much she missed it until she saw Crabbet Park.

"Grandpa says the horses here are relatives of ours." Abbie scanned the sleek horses, searching for one that might remind her of River Rose, River Sun, or River Magic.

"Some of them, maybe," her father agreed as they followed one of the stable hands across the thick grass of the manicured grounds that had been the site of the famous annual Sunday parades during Lady Wentworth's days.

"I wonder if they'll show us Skowronek's stall. That's the way you pronounce it: Skov-ro-neck. Ben says that in Poland all the *w*'s are pronounced like *v*'s. That's vhy he talks the vay he does." She longed to hear his voice and listen to his endless stories and the fascinating things he knew about horses, especially Arabians.

"I know."

"Did you know that when Skowronek first came to England from Poland, he was used as a hack? Can you imagine a famous stallion like that being used as an ordinary riding horse and rented to people? Ben says that's what a hack is."

"But he wasn't famous at the time. And remember, there was a war going on. World War I. So people had other things on their minds beside Arabians."

"Ben says it was lucky that Skowronek was here because Communist soldiers stole the horses from the farm where he was born. And when the stallion that was his father — Ben says he'd always been a very gentle, well-mannered stallion — started to fight the soldiers that were trying to take him out of his stall, they shot him. Isn't that terrible?"

"It certainly is."

"Anyway, like Ben says, it's a good thing Lady Wentworth saw him and recognized what a great stallion he was. He was pure white, you know. They call him a gray 'cause he had black skin underneath like all Arabians, except where they have white markings, then the skin is pink. But Skowronek looked snow-white. Both Ben and Grandpa said that's very rare."

"That's true."

"Look, Daddy." Abbie spied the clock below the roof peak of the arched entrance to the Coronation Stables, built of brick, the muted color of terra-cotta. "Ben says the main stables at the stud farm in Poland where he worked had a clock tower. We should put a clock in ours at River Bend so we can be famous, too."

"It takes more than a clock, Abbie." Dean smiled down at her. "You need a stable full of outstanding broodmares and two or three really great stallions."

"But we have that, don't we?"

"Not yet, but we will."

"Are you going to buy some of these Arabians?"

"Maybe. First we have to look at what they have and see if it's what we want."

They spent the better part of the day looking over the Crabbet Arabians available for sale, walking around each horse to study its conformation from all angles, observing its action at a walk, a trot, and an airy canter, and studying it close up. Everything from yearling colts and fillies to Arabians under training to aged broodmares was paraded out for their inspection. Iridescent chestnuts, flashy bays, dappled grays, all slickly groomed, their coats glistening in the sunlight — Abbie wanted to buy nearly every one of them.

Although Dean found it difficult to fault the majority of them, none had aroused more than a passing interest. He couldn't define exactly what it was he was seeking — a look, an aura that made one horse stand out from all the others, something that would spark the gut feeling, "this is the horse."

As they drove away from the stables, Abbie felt the sting of tears in her eyes. One part of her hated to leave the familiar surroundings and the other part of her just wanted to go home to the real thing: River Bend.

"I think Grandpa would have liked that gray filly. She looked a lot like River Wind, and he loves her." Just talking about her grandfather made her feel worse, but she couldn't admit to feeling homesick for fear her father would not take her with him on another trip. "How come you didn't buy any horses? Didn't you like them?"

"I liked them, but they weren't quite what I wanted. Maybe we'll be luckier next week in Egypt," he replied, his mouth twisting in a crooked smile of wry hope.

"It's gonna be a while before we go home, isn't it?" Abbie asked. "I'll bet Grandpa and Ben are really missing us."

Teeming Cairo: a city of cacophonies, with its honking of horns, babbling of Arabic tongues, braying of donkeys, chanting of the muezzin, and bellowing of camels; a city of contrasts, with its modern buildings sharing the skyline with minaret-topped mosques, its cars and trucks traveling the narrow streets with donkey carts, caleches, or camel herds on their way to the slaughterhouse, and its people in Western attire walking along the crowded sidewalks with those in the more traditional robe and headdress; a city of extremes, with its abject poverty and limitless wealth, and harsh desert edges and verdant river bottoms.

Cairo was chaos after the quiet order of England. Babs hated it and refused to set foot outside their Western hotel. Justine was terrified of the strangeness of this city inhabited by heathens. Stuck in the hotel with nothing to do, Abbie grew all the more homesick.

After much persuasion, her father convinced her mother that she at least had to make one excursion out of the hotel to see the Pyramids of Giza on the outskirts of Cairo. Elaborate arrangements were made through their guide, Ahmed. When they arrived at Giza, a pair of horses was waiting for Abbie and her father, all saddled and bridled, ready to take them closer to the Great Pyramids.

Despite Ahmed's insistence that the horses were true steeds of the desert, Abbie was quite certain these skinny, narrow horses were not Arabians. She climbed on just the same and cantered her placid mount alongside her father's. Together they rode beneath the blazing sun toward the Pyramids that stood out starkly against a sky of pure blue. Abbie was just a little bit disappointed to discover that the ancient Pyramids looked just like the pictures she'd seen of them, only older maybe and more crumbled.

Near the base of the Pyramids, they rendezvoused with the car bearing Ahmed and her mother. The horses were taken away and replaced by a camel that its driver called Susie. All of them had to take a ride on this groaning, moaning "ship of the desert." Both Abbie and her father broke into laughter as her mother shrieked and grabbed at the protruding horn of the strange saddle when the camel rolled to its feet in a slow lurch. However, Abbie didn't think it was at all funny a few minutes later when she tried to pet the camel and it spit at her, literally ending their excursion on a sour note.

At dinner that night, her father suggested that Abbie accompany him the next day to visit the El Zahraa Arabian stud farm. She leaped at the chance, her head filled with visions of another Crabbet Park — another River Bend.

Located outside the city limits of Cairo in Ein Shams, the stud farm occupied sixty acres of desert. Before the overthrow of King Farouk, it had been known as Kafr Farouk and run by the Royal Agricultural Society. But with the recent ascension of Nasser to power, its name had been changed to El Zahraa and its governing board now went by the more democratic name of the Egyptian Agricultural Organization. Prophetically, perhaps, the neighboring land to El Zahraa stud farm had once been the site of the Sheykh Obeyd, the Arabian stud farm established by Lady Anne Blunt in Egypt.

A dust as fine as powder enveloped the car as they traveled down the long driveway lined with palms leading to the main stables of El Zahraa. Beyond lay sandy, grassless paddocks. Abbie saw immediately that this was not Crabbet Park or River Bend. There wasn't an oasis of green here, just more dry sand and hot sun.

At a distance, the horses in the paddocks looked positively skinny to her. Up close, she found out they didn't look any better. They had the delicate heads, arched necks, and high tail carriage typical of Arabians, but where were their satiny coats, and why did they look so lean?

When she put the question to her father, he replied, "The Egyptians like their horses slender. They think ours have too much flesh on them. Their favorite saying is 'We ride our horses, we don't eat them.'"

In Abbie's opinion, this was a wasted trip. She was certain there couldn't possibly be anything here that her father would be interested in buying to ship back to River Bend.

But Abbie was wrong. After more than three hours of walking, looking, and reviewing, Dean saw *the* horse he'd been looking for all this time. As they approached a group of yearlings, munching on a pile of berseem hay in a paddock, a bay colt lifted his head to gaze at them. The colt had the most incredibly classic head Dean had ever seen, his profile showing almost an exaggerated dish and his eyes large and dark. Dean stopped and just stared.

Here was the horse of his dreams — here in the desert sand beneath a blazing blue sky, surrounded by shimmering waves of heat. For a moment, Dean was afraid he was looking at a mirage. If he blinked, the colt might disappear. His eyes began to water. Unwillingly he did blink, but the colt was still there.

"I'm telling you, Babs, that colt had the most gorgeous head I've ever seen on an Arabian." Dean stood in front of the dresser mirror, tying his tie while Babs continued to add the finishing touches to her makeup in front of the mirror in the bathroom.

"I didn't think he was all that great," Abbie inserted, not caring that she hadn't been asked. Already dressed for dinner with Justine's help, she wandered about her parents' bedroom in the hotel suite, pausing now and then to twirl about and watch the full circle the skirt of her new blue dress made.

"I don't have any idea how much they want for him, but with a colt like that, price doesn't mean anything. You talk about charisma. This colt has it and then some. El Kedar Ibn Sudan, that's what they call him." Dean pulled the knot tight and adjusted it to sit squarely in the center of his shirt collar. "The head man wasn't there today. I'm going to have to call tomorrow and arrange to see him. They wrote his name down for me. I've got it here somewhere." As he reached for his tie tack, he scanned the items lying on top of the dresser. "It must still be in my jacket pocket. Abbie, my jacket's on that chair by you. Will you bring it here?" She scooped the wheat-tan jacket off the arm of the chair, letting it dangle upside down, and whirled around so her skirt would flare out.

"Careful," Dean warned. "You're going to dump everything out of the pockets."

Abbie stopped just as a postcard slithered out of a pocket to the floor, landing facedown. "Did you send Grandpa a postcard?" Bending down, she picked it up and started to read the writing on the back of it. "Dear Rachel—"

"It's not polite to read other people's mail, Abbie." Dean took it from her before she could read more.

As he walked over to slip the postcard into the pocket of his dinner jacket, Abbie tagged after him, frowning curiously. "Who's Rachel?"

He darted a quick glance at the open bathroom door, then smoothed a hand over the top of her head and smiled, "Just somebody I know, okay?"

"Okay." Shrugging, she moved off to inspect her reflection in the mirror vacated by her father. She stared at the dark-haired, blue-eyed girl, wearing a new blue dress, white patent-leather shoes, and lace-edged anklets, then wiggled her hips to watch the skirt swing out.

Busily clipping on a diamond earring, Babs emerged from the bathroom, the pink silk chiffon of her Empire-style evening dress whispering about her. "Do you think I should wear the necklace, too, Dean, or would it be too much?"

"I'd wear it."

"Would you? You'd look positively silly in it," Babs replied, her hazel eyes twinkling outrageously, but her expression otherwise perfectly serious. Dean laughed.

Catching their playful mood, Abbie wanted to join in. "Momma, guess what?" She danced over to her and glanced slyly over her shoulder at Dean. "Daddy's sending a postcard to a girl named Rachel."

Silence. Absolute silence came crashing down as the smile faded from her father's face. Sensing that something was dreadfully wrong, Abbie turned to look at her mother. She was white with shock, her expression almost pained as she stared at him.

"Babs . . ." He took a step toward her, his hand reaching out.

"Abbie, leave the room." The words came from her mother with a rush, yet there was something desperate in the tone of her voice, as if something terrible was about to happen.

"But . . ." A little frightened, Abbie stared at her mother, so motionless, never taking her eyes off her father.

"Leave the room now!"

Abbie recoiled instinctively at the sudden movement her mother made when she swung around, turning her back on Abbie to face the highboy against the wall, her body so rigid it was trembling. Abbie felt the touch of her father's hand on her shoulder.

"Go find Justine, and have her brush your hair." Firmly but gently, he steered her toward the door to the suite's sitting room.

Once there, she turned back to him. "Daddy, I —"

"I know, honey, It's all right." He smiled at her.

But Abbie knew it wasn't. She didn't understand what she'd done wrong. She'd only been teasing when she mentioned that postcard. Didn't they know it was a joke? She was just trying to have fun like they were, teasing each other.

As the door started to swing closed, shutting her out, Abbie heard the taut accusation that burst from her mother, her voice low and barely controlled. "How could you, Dean? How could you let her find out?"

"She doesn't know anything. I swear it."

"How can you be sure? What did you tell her?"

"Nothing."

The door latched tightly shut, muffling the rest of their argument. Abbie slowly turned away from the door and moped over to one of the chairs. Fighting tears, she slumped onto the cushions and stared at the blue skirt of her dress. She didn't like it anymore.

The telephone in the sitting room rang once, then twice. On the third ring, the tall, slender Justine came out of the adjoining bedroom to answer it. Abbie didn't even look up. More than ever she wanted to go home to River Bend.

"Lawson suite, Justine speaking. . . . A call from America? Yes, I'll stay on the line."

Abbie looked up. "If that's Grandpa, I want to talk to him."

But Justine waved a shushing hand at her, then pressed her fingers over her other ear, shutting out any sound but that from the telephone. "Hello? This is Justine. . . . Yes, Miz Anderson, he's here. He and Miz Lawson are getting dressed for dinner." Discovering that it was only her father's secretary, Abbie slumped back in the chair. "Why, yes, Miz Anderson, I'll get him right away." Justine hurriedly laid the receiver down next to the phone and almost ran to the master bedroom door, her dark eyes wide with a look of concern. "Mr. Lawson?" she called his name as she knocked loudly.

"What is it, Justine?" Despite the muffling door, the impatient snap in his voice came through. Abbie sank a little lower in the chair.

"It's your secretary on the phone. She has to talk to you right away. There's . . . been an accident."

"I'll take it in here."

"What kind of an accident?" Abbie wanted to know.

But Justine just looked at her without answering and walked back to the telephone. After making sure the bedroom phone had been picked up, she placed the black receiver back on its cradle, then stood with her head bowed in an attitude of prayer.

Abbie frowned. "What happened, Justine?"

At that instant, she heard a wailing cry come from the bedroom, dissolving into terrible sobs. She scrambled out of the chair and dashed to the connecting door, hesitating only a second before pushing it open and running into the room. Abbie paused when she saw her father holding her crying mother tightly in his arms. He looked stunned, and close to tears himself.

Haltingly, she moved toward them. "Daddy . . . what's wrong?"

"Abbie." His look of pain intensified as he loosened his hold on her mother. Together they turned toward her, Babs making a valiant effort to check her crying.

Their hands reached out to her, but Abbie was almost afraid to go to them. She wanted to turn and run before this terrible thing claimed her, but her legs carried her forward within reach of her mother's clutching hand.

"Darlin', it's . . . your grandpa," her mother said, then quickly covered her mouth, as more tears rolled down her cheeks, smearing the makeup she'd so carefully applied.

Abbie didn't want to ask, but she couldn't stop herself. "What about Grandpa?"

"There's been an accident, honey," her father said, briefly closing his eyes before looking at her again. "He was crossing the street and . . . stepped in front of a car."

Frightened, she looked from one to the other. "He's going to be all right, isn't he?"

Her father simply shook his head. "I'm sorry, honey. I'm truly sorry." He tightened his grip on her hand, making her fingers hurt. "I know how much you loved him."

"No." Abbie shook her head, not wanting to believe they were trying to tell her he had died. "He'll be all right. You'll see. When we get home, you'll see."

Her mother turned and hid her face against her father's shoulder, crying softly, brokenly, as he pulled Abbie closer and put his arm around her, too. But Abbie wouldn't cry, afraid if she did, it might really be true.

"I wanta go home, Daddy."

"We are, honey. We are."

The funeral was big, even by Texas standards. Everybody came, including the governor. But Abbie didn't cry, not at the funeral. The tears didn't come until later, after they had returned to River Bend and she'd run off by herself. Ben had found her in River Wind's stall, crying herself sick. It had taken a long time for him to convince her that she wasn't somehow to blame for her grandfather's death.

His death changed many things. Within a year, Dean had sold the drilling fluids company R.D. had founded and made a return trip to Egypt to purchase the Arabian colt of his dreams. In addition, he bought three fillies. With all the paperwork involved, the lengthy sea voyage, and the sixty days of quarantine in the U.S., it took nearly a year before the new horses finally arrived at River Bend.

In the meantime, the old barn was torn down and a new stable under construction — the first step in an expansion program that created many more new facilities at River Bend during the next ten years. The practice established by R. D. Lawson of using "River" as a prefix in the names of all the Arabians foaled at River Bend was altered somewhat by Dean. He registered his newly imported Egyptian-bred Arabians with the prefix "Nahr" attached to their names — the Arabic word for "river." El Kedar Ibn Sudan thus became Nahr El Kedar.

Buying trips to Egypt became annual events. Abbie didn't go with him again until she was in her teens, but she was never able to share his enthusiasm for the lean, narrow Arabians bred in Egypt, nor his fascination with the barren desert. Nor did she agree with his decision, when the stallion Nahr El Kedar turned five, to sell all the Arabians at River Bend bred by her grandfather, regardless of their worth or championship potential, and breed solely Arabians with newer Egyptian bloodlines. It was as if he were rejecting everything her grandfather had built — first the company and now the horses. Loving him as she did, Abbie tried to understand and not regard his actions as being even remotely disloyal.

Truthfully, she didn't have a lot of time to dwell on his possible reasons. Too many things were happening in her own young life to claim her attention. In addition to the Arabian horse shows that she continued to participate in, and the preparations for them, there were school, friends, and dates. Without any false sense of modesty, Abbie recognized that she was becoming a strikingly beautiful girl, extremely popular with her male classmates. Of course, she also recognized that having wealthy and prominent parents didn't hurt her popularity either.

With the advent of her senior year in high school, Abbie's life truly became hectic. Following in her mother's tradition, this was the year she would be one of the debutantes presented during the Houston season, which meant she would require a lavish haute couture wardrobe in addition to the formal presentation gown in the requisite debutante-white. Babs insisted that nothing less would do.

The selecting of some fifteen ballgowns, the fittings, the shopping for accessories, the planning for parties — it all seemed so endless to Abbie. She'd lost five pounds and the season hadn't even started yet. It had sounded like a lot of fun, but it had turned out to be a lot more work than she thought.

"That was good." Babs nodded approvingly as Abbie gracefully straightened from the full court bow, her taffeta underskirts rustling beneath her ankle-length skirt. "Now do it again. A little lower this time."

Abbie groaned. "Lower? Now I know why they call this the Dallas Dive."

The traditional forehead-to-the-floor curtsy performed by all Texas debutantes went by many names: the Dallas Dive, the Texas Dip, and naturally the Yellow Rose curtsy. When done correctly, with grace and dignity, the deep court bow was a thing of regal beauty. But a misstep, a slight imbalance, and it could be the ultimate in ignominious disasters.

"If you practice it enough now, it will become second nature to you. It will be all one fluid motion, sweeping and grand — and easy."

"It will never be that," Abbie muttered into her skirt as she dipped her upper body as low as it would go, practically sitting on the floor in the process, the muscles in her legs and ankles screaming with the repeated strain on them.

"Now, turn around and practice it in front of the full-length mirror. And remember, one long, flowing motion." Babs proceeded to demonstrate what she meant.

"You're cheating, Momma. You have on pants," Abbie retaliated, a little envious of the smooth, effortless bow executed by her mother.

"Most girls make the mistake of practicing in pants or shorts or regular skirts. Then they're thrown by all the yards of long material in the skirts of their ballgowns." A laugh broke from her. "I remember at one ball, Cissy Conklin caught her heel in the hem of her gown and went sprawling headfirst on the floor. It was so hilarious seeing her spraddled there on the floor like a dressed-up duck on a platter, I laughed 'til I cried. She was such a know-it-all little snob that I was glad it happened to her. Of course, when she saw me laughing, she had a hissy-fit right there on the spot."

"Momma, I'm surprised at you," Abbie teased. "That wasn't nice."

"Neither was she. Not that it mattered." Babs shrugged. "Her daddy gave a new meaning to the word *well-oiled*. He had more pumpjacks on his land than ticks on a cow's back."

"I'll have to remember to tell Christopher that one. He thinks you come up with some of the funniest phrases." Abbie stepped in front of the full-length mirror and smiled a shade triumphantly. "All the girls turned positively emerald green when I told them that Christopher is going to be my escort at the Confederate Ball."

"Which is just three days away," Babs reminded her. "So practice."

"Oui, Mama." Mockingly obedient, Abbie swooped low to the floor and held the pose to glance at her reflection.

Behind her stood the scrolled iron bed, enameled in shiny white with brass and alabaster finials topping the end posts, and covered by a floral bedspread of blue cornflowers, a match to the blue walls in her turret bedroom. To the right of the bed was a doorway to the second-floor hall. A gray-haired Jackson, the black houseman hired years ago by R.D., appeared in the opening, as always very reserved and proper. Delicately he cleared his throat, letting his presence be known.

"Yes, Jackson." Abbie straightened, turning with a little flourish.

"Miss Lawson, Mrs. Lawson," he said, acknowledging both of them with a nod. "Mr. Lawson asked me to let you know he was home. He's in the library."

"Thank you, Jackson," Babs replied.

He retreated, as soft-footedly as he'd appeared. Abbie stared after him for a minute. "Do you know . . . in all these years, he's never slipped — not once — and called me Abbie."

"And he never will either. Jackson takes a lot of pride in what he considers to be his role in this household. Part of that is keeping his distance. I admit, I've always felt he's the authority here. He runs the house, and us, very well."

"That's true." But Abbie's interest in Jackson faded, replaced by the information he'd relayed to them. "I'm going downstairs and show Daddy my progress in the Texas Dip. Maybe I can talk him into brushing up on his waltz steps."

Quickly she was out the door before her mother could insist that she practice more. At the stairs, she gathered up her long skirt and the voluminous taffeta slip and ran lightly down the steps. Halfway down she heard the phone ring, but it was quickly silenced. Since there was no summoning call to the telephone for her, Abbie swung around the carved newel post at the base of the staircase and headed for the library.

The pocket doors stood closed. Gripping the fingerholds, she slid them open wide and stepped into the room. Her father was behind the desk, the telephone in his hand. She had that one glimpse of him as she went into her full court bow, briefly feeling like a princess paying homage to her king and wanting to laugh.

But as she straightened to walk to his desk, he held up his hand as if to stave off her advance, turning his face away and hunching over the telephone. She sensed something was wrong — very wrong.

"Daddy, what is it?" She watched as he hung up the phone, gripping the receiver tightly — so tightly Abbie expected it to snap in two. "Daddy?"

When he stood up, he seemed to be in a state of shock. He walked blindly toward the door without even looking at her. His face, his eyes, everything about him looked haunted. Worried, Abbie went after him.

"Daddy, are you all right?" She caught his arm as he entered the foyer.

He looked at her, but she didn't think he could really see her. "I . . ." His mouth moved wordlessly for several seconds. "I have to . . . go. I . . . I'm sorry."

As he pulled away from her and headed toward the front door, Abbie saw her mother coming down the stairs. "Momma, something's wrong with Daddy. He got a phone call and . . ."

Babs ran the rest of the way down the steps and hurried to his side. "Dean." She had never seen him look so lost and broken before — not even when R.D. had died so suddenly. "What's happened? Tell me."

He gripped her arms, his fingers digging into her flesh, but she was afraid to tell him he was hurting her, afraid he'd let go. "Oh, God, Babs." The words came from some deep, dark well, wrenched from his soul. "I can't believe it. I can't. Please, God, she just can't be dead."

Babs stiffened, something inside her hardening in the face of his shock and grief.

"Momma, what is it?" Abbie questioned, not standing close enough to have heard.

"There's been a death. An old . . . friend of your father's in California." She looked at Dean, tears stinging her own eyes. "I'm afraid he'll have to go out there. Would you . . . leave us alone, Abbie? Please."

Vaguely Babs was aware of Abbie slowly climbing the stairs, but all her attention was on Dean. It tortured her to see him this way.

"You do understand, Babs. I have to go," he said brokenly. "I have to be there."

"Yes. I know you do," she stated flatly.

When he released her arms, her flesh tingled painfully. She walked with him to the front door and watched as he hurried down the steps to the car parked by the front gate. Slowly she closed the door and leaned against it, sobbing softly. Caroline's name hadn't passed between them, but she knew he'd lost the woman he so deeply loved.

"I'm glad," she whispered, and buried a fist against her mouth. "God forgive me, but I'm glad she's dead."

ABBIE REMEMBERED HOW hurt and upset she'd been when she learned her father wouldn't be returning in time to present her at the Confederate Ball. She hadn't understood why he couldn't come back for it. Why he had to remain in California just because someone he'd known for a long time had died.

The Confederate Ball was the most important event in her life. It was her launch as a debutante. He was supposed to present her and dance the first waltz with her. She couldn't walk out there alone: it wasn't done. Of all the hundreds of parties and balls that would follow, why did he have to miss this one?

Her mother had tried to console her by assuring Abbie that any number of their friends would be happy to stand in for her father. Lane Canfield was out of the country, but Kyle MacDonnell or Homer— But Abbie had stormed out of the house, insisting that if her father wouldn't be there, neither would she.

She had saddled up one of the Arabians and gone tearing down the lane, galloping across the hay fields and drained rice fields of the neighboring Hix farm, making a long, wide circle that brought her to the banks of the Brazos, and following it back to River Bend. Ben was waiting for her when she returned to the barns. She remembered the silent disapproval in his expression as he inspected the sweat-lathered mare.

"I'm sorry. I'll cool her out."

"Yes, you will," Ben had replied. "We both will, and you will tell me what this is all about."

Most of her anger had been spent in the ride, but not her hurt and bitter disappointment. As always, it had been so easy to pour out all of her troubles to Ben.

"I told Momma I wasn't going to the Confederate Ball and she could just cancel everything. It's all a lot of nonsense anyway. This is nineteen seventy-one, for heaven's sake. Who cares about being a debutante in this day and age?"

"You do, I think."

She had desperately wanted to tell Ben that that wasn't true, to insist that she was a liberated young woman and all this parading before Houston society like a slave on an auction block was sexist. Maybe all the pomp and pageantry was silly, but it was her moment in the spotlight, when all the eyes of Houston would be on her.

"I'm not going to be presented by some friend of Momma and Daddy's," she had stated forcefully, again close to tears. "If Grandpa were alive . . . but he isn't. Can you understand, Ben? I don't want just anybody presenting me. It's got to be somebody—" She had started to say "like my father" just as she had turned to look at Ben. "—somebody like you." Someone who knew and loved her; someone who had always been there when she needed him; someone she cared about. "Ben, do you know how to waltz?"

"Me?" He had been so startled Abbie had laughed.

"Yes, you. Would you present me?"

"Me? But I am only . . ." He had started to gesture at the stables, but she had caught his hand.

"You're the only man I'd walk out there with other than my father." She had caught a brief glimpse of tears in his eyes as he bowed his head and stared at the hand clutching his.

"You honor me." His voice had been husky with emotion, one of the rare times she ever remembered Ben showing any. Then he had shook his head, as if to refuse.

"There's nothing to it, Ben. All you have to do is walk out with me when I'm introduced and the announcer talks about my Confederate ancestors. Then we'll dance the first waltz until my escort cuts in. We'll have to rent you a black tux and white tie . . . and gloves. You'll look so handsome. And I'll tell everyone you're our dearest, dearest friend from Europe. With your accent, they'll go crazy over you." When he wavered, Abbie had pressed her advantage. "Please, Ben. At least come to the rehearsal with me. They'll walk you through everything."

"I have not waltzed since I was a young boy."

"Let's see how rusty you are." Still holding the mare's reins, Abbie had placed his hand on her waist and raised the other one. "Ready? One, two, three. One, two, three." While she hummed a waltz tune, they had started to dance, haltingly at first, then with increasing ease. "You see, Ben, it's just like riding a horse. You never really forget how." They had waltzed across the stable yard, leading a tired and bewildered mare.

The night of the Confederate Ball, Abbie, arrayed in an off-the-shoulder antebellum gown of white satin designed by St. Laurent, her hair piled atop her head in dark ringlets, arrived at the country club in a horse-drawn carriage that was met by a member of the Albert Sidney Johnston Camp of the Sons of Confederate Veterans, the sponsor of the Confederate Ball, dressed in full Confederate regalia. To strains of "Lorena," an erect, square-shouldered Ben, completely transformed by the white gloves, white tie, and black tuxedo he wore, walked proudly at her side as she was presented and made her full court bow to an applauding, cheering throng of guests. After all the debutantes were presented, Abbie danced the "Tennessee Waltz" with him until her escort for the evening, Christopher Atwell, cut in and fastened a corsage on her wrist, an act that traditionally symbolized her assumption of responsibility for her social destiny.

Even though it wasn't the same as if her father had been there, Abbie had fond memories of that evening—because of Ben, ill at ease, yet going through it for her.

By the time her father had returned after a week's absence, Abbie had been too caught up in the whirl of parties, teas, and balls to take more than passing notice of his apathy. Now, hindsight enabled her to see that he had been a man bereaved by the death of the woman he loved.

Abbie remembered it all so clearly, the brooding silences, the faraway stares, the pained look in his eyes. Her lips felt wet and she pressed them together to lick them dry, tasting the salty moisture of tears . . . her tears. She could feel them running down her cheeks, one after the other.

No wonder she'd never been able to be the daughter her father wanted.

No parent ever loves his children equally, no matter how he might try or pretend. There is always one that is the favorite, one that is special. But it hadn't been her. Never her. Obviously it had always been Rachel, the daughter of the woman he had loved for so long. Yet all this time he'd let her believe she was the only one; all this time she'd wondered what was wrong with her, certain that something had to be — otherwise he'd love her. Hurt and angered by the deception, Abbie dug her fingernails into the palms of her hands, needing the physical pain to ease the emotional one.

Behind her the office door opened. Instantly she stiffened, opening her eyes wide to try to clear them of the stinging tears.

"Your mother asked me to find you."

Abbie slumped at the quiet sound of Ben Jablonski's voice. She didn't have to hide her feelings from him. "Ben, did you know about the woman and child Daddy kept in California?"

There was a long pause before he answered. "I heard some talk . . . among the help."

"It was more than talk. It was true." She poured out the whole agonizing story to him, and its obvious conclusions. "Why, Ben?" She choked on a sob, as always demanding from him the answers she couldn't find. "Why?" She felt the light pressure of his big hand on her shoulder and swung around to face him. "Why couldn't he love me, too?"

"Ssssh, baby." Gently he gathered her into his arms and crooned to her in Polish.

She leaned against his shoulder and doubled her hands into tight fists. "I hate him for what he did, Ben. I hate him!"

"No. You don't hate him." He smoothed her hair with a gentle touch. "It hurts so much because you loved him."

Abbie cried, this time for herself.

THE DISTINCTIVE SKYLINE of downtown Houston soared above the flatness of the sprawling Texas city. Coming from Los Angeles, Rachel hadn't expected to be impressed. In her opinion, city downtowns were all alike — a collection of skyscrapers crowded together to form concrete canyons jammed with traffic — a place you only went if you absolutely, positively had to.

But as she turned down Louisiana Street, she was radically revising her opinion. Initially she was struck by the high-rise buildings themselves, each one unique, like an architectural signature written against the sky. Contemporary in design, their individual use of shapes, angles, and glass was unusual, if not controversial. She couldn't help marveling at the progressive mixture that combined to make a single statement of dynamic growth.

She felt the energy and vitality that surrounded her. In almost any direction she looked, construction was under way on a new tower. She couldn't shake the feeling that she was driving through an outdoor gallery devoted to architecture. Yet the wide streets, the short blocks, and the building setbacks gave the downtown a sense of space. In fact, when she stopped looking up at the bronze and silver reflecting towers and noticed the small plazas, the spraying fountains, and the sculptures scattered about, Rachel caught the mood of the city center: vital yet leisurely, with a kind of laid-back energy, Texas-style.

Nowhere was the impression stronger than when she turned off Louisiana Street onto Dallas and approached the landscaped entrance to the Hotel Meridien, where she was to meet Lane Canfield for lunch. Designed in the form of an elongated trapezoid tapering to a sharp point at its western end, the building was faced entirely with bronze glass, echoing the color theme of the off-white concrete and bronze used so effectively in adjacent structures. But the severity of its form was broken by the zigzag construction of its front that faced the plaza entrance and added dimension to the hotel.

Although Rachel hadn't inherited her mother's creative talents with a brush, only a technical skill, she had acquired an appreciation for art from those early years of constant exposure to it. To her mother, art had been everything. It was her great love. After that came Dean. Rachel had never been sure where she ranked with her mother, but it had been somewhere down the line. Caroline had loved her, but when a choice had to be made, art had always come first. She had lived her life the way she wanted, compromising for nothing and no one.

It was a selfish attitude that Rachel had frequently resented when she was growing up, especially when she learned that Dean had wanted to marry her mother. She was certain her life would have been very different if they had married. She wouldn't have grown up so lonely, feeling unwanted and unloved — and ashamed of who she was. During those first years in elementary school, she had learned very quickly that being a love child wasn't the wonderful thing her mother had claimed, and that *love child* wasn't the term ignorant people usually used to describe her. The feeling had never really left her, even now, in this supposedly enlightened age.

Maybe that's why she'd always had this vague fear of drawing attention to herself. She wanted to blend in, be like everyone else. It was almost better to be a wallflower; then people wouldn't be whispering behind her back.

But when she parked her rental car and entered the hotel, Rachel felt uncomfortably conspicuous. The California layered look of her dirndl skirt, knit top, and belted overblouse didn't fit the understated elegance of the hotel's French-flavored decor. Too self-conscious to approach the clerk behind the genteel reception desk, Rachel approached a bellman and asked him for directions to the hotel's Le Restaurant de France.

Inside the restaurant's entrance, she hovered uncertainly. This formal atmosphere was the last thing she'd expected to find in Texas. Texas was supposed to be barbecue and boots, cowboy hats and chili peppers. Despite the restaurant's name, she hadn't dreamed Lane Canfield had invited her to a place like this for lunch. All her life, she'd wanted to have a meal in surroundings like these, but she'd never gone to a fancy restaurant, certain that she'd end up feeling out of place.

And she did — from the top of her long, straight hair to the bottom of her sandaled feet. As the maître d' approached her, wearing a uniform that had the unmistakable stamp of custom tailoring, Rachel realized that even he was better dressed than she was — a fact he noted in one sweeping glance at her.

"May I help you?"

She felt intimidated and struggled to suppress it. "I'm supposed to meet Mr. Lane Canfield here for lunch."

"Mr. Canfield." An eyebrow shot up, then quickly leveled as he smiled respectfully. "This way, ma'am."

Seated at a secluded table for two, Lane Canfield sipped at his bourbon and water and stared absently at the empty chair opposite him. Idleness was unnatural to him. Usually every minute of his day was crammed with business: meetings, phone calls, conferences, or reports of one kind or another.

Lane frowned absently, trying to recall how long it had been since anything had taken precedence over his business. There'd never been time in his life for anything — or anyone — else. Sex wasn't even a diversion to him. He hated to think how many times he had arranged for one of the prostitutes from his carefully screened list to come to his penthouse apartment, then screwed her while he mentally plotted out some new corporate strategy. Why? What did he want? What was he killing himself for? More money? More power? Why? He was millionaire a hundred times over.

Dean's death had affected him in ways he hadn't expected. He wondered how he could fairly say he'd been Dean Lawson's friend. Yes, he had interrupted his busy schedule to attend his funeral, but in the last ten years, how many times had he seen or talked to Dean? Eight, maybe nine times. No more than that. Yet Dean had made him the executor of his will.

And what had he done? Turned the paperwork over to one of his staff to handle — too busy, his time too valuable for him to get involved with any of the details beyond the contents of the will.

Reaching up, he felt the front of his suit jacket, making sure the letter was still in his inside pocket — the letter that had been addressed to him marked PERSONAL: ONLY TO BE OPENED IN THE EVENT OF MY DEATH, with Dean's name signed below.

It had been buried among the papers, bills, and documents collected from Dean's law office by his secretary, Mary Jo Anderson. He had assigned the task of sorting through them to his own personal secretary, Frank Marsden. Frank had found the sealed envelope and delivered it into Lane's hands late yesterday afternoon. This morning, its contents had been verified.

Lane knew it was the letter in his suit pocket that was partly responsible for all his soul-searching. The opening lines of the letter haunted him:

Dear Lane,

    I hope you never have to read this. I promised myself long ago that I would never tread on our friendship. But now I find myself in a situation where I must ask a favor of you. There's no one else I can trust. It's about my daughter, Rachel, Caroline's child. . . .

Trust. The word nagged at Lane. He had done so little to deserve it. What troubled him more was the doubt that there was anyone among his own circle of friends whom he could trust with something so very personal in nature. Not a single name came to mind. The people he dealt with and called friends were not that at all. It was a sobering discovery at the age of fifty-six to realize you had no one you could turn to.

But whom did Rachel have? Motherless. Now fatherless. No blood relative who wanted her. Abbie had made that clear. Since meeting her at the cemetery, Lane had thought about Rachel often: the sadness, the hurt in her blue eyes, haunting him at odd moments. He wondered if she had suffered much from the stigma of illegitimacy while growing up. He doubted that she could have escaped it entirely, considering how thoughtless and cruel other children could be at times.

Roused from his reverie by the sound of approaching footsteps, Lane glanced up and saw Rachel following the maître d' to his table. As he rose to greet her, he noticed how stiff and tense she appeared.

"Hello, Rachel."

"Hello. I'm sorry I'm late." Immediately she sat down in the chair the maître d' pulled out for her, then awkwardly helped him move it closer to the table.

"You're not late." Lane resumed his own seat. "I was able to leave the office sooner than I planned. It gave me a chance to relax and have a drink."

She seemed self-conscious and ill at ease, her glance skittering away without even meeting his as she opened the menu in front of her. "I know how busy you are and I'm grateful that you could spare the time to have lunch with me."

Her cheeks looked flushed to him, and he doubted it was rouge. She wore very little makeup, but with her skin and eyes, he didn't think she needed any. "It's my pleasure. It isn't often that I have lunch with an attractive woman."

She glanced briefly around at the other customers in the restaurant, her glance lingering on one or two of the more fashionably dressed women in the room. "You're very kind, but I doubt that, Mr. Canfield."

"You shouldn't. It's the truth." Belatedly he realized she was embarrassed about the way she was dressed. He blamed himself for not saying something when he had suggested meeting here, but it hadn't occurred to him. "Would you like something to drink before we order lunch?" he asked as the waiter came up to their table.

She hesitated briefly. "Perhaps a glass of white wine."

"A chardonnay or Riesling? We have a very nice —"

"The chardonnay will be fine," she interrupted.

"We'll trust your judgment on the vineyard and the vintage," Lane inserted to stave off the anticipated inquiry from the waiter, guessing — he was sure correctly — that Rachel wasn't knowledgeable about wines. "And I'll have another bourbon and water."

"Very good, sir."

"This is a beautiful restaurant," she remarked as the waiter left.

Personally, Lane regretted his choice, observing how uncomfortable she was there. He'd assumed that Dean had taken her to places like this in Los Angeles. Maybe not, though. Caroline certainly wouldn't have been impressed by it.

"It's a little stuffy, but the food is excellent."

"I'm sure it is."

Dammit, he felt sorry for her, although he suspected his pity was the last thing she wanted. He had intended this lunch to be something personal. He felt he owed that to Dean. More than that, he felt Rachel deserved it. He didn't want this to become a business discussion about the contents of Dean's will and the letter in his pocket. That had to be dealt with, but not now. After their drinks arrived and they ordered their meals, Lane started asking her questions, trying to get her to talk about herself and her work as a commercial artist, and relax a little. He discovered it wasn't easy to draw her out of her shell, but he persisted, responding to the challenge.

"Are you still living in Malibu?" he asked after his questions about her work gained him only meager responses.

"No. I have an apartment in the hills near the riding stable where I keep my horses."

"You have horses?" He remembered how involved Abbie was with the Arabian horses at River Bend. He should have guessed that Rachel would pick up Dean's obsession for them as well.

"Well, only two, actually. Ahmar is the gelding Dean bought me when I was twelve. He's the first horse I ever owned. Before that I had a pony — a Welsh-Arabian cross. Ahmar is nineteen years old now, but you'd never guess it. He still loves his morning gallops and gets jealous if I take my filly Simoon out instead."

"Ahmar. He's an Arabian, of course," Lane guessed.

"Of course," she laughed for the first time. He liked the warm spontaneity of the sound. "A fiery red chestnut. In Arabic, *Ahmar* means 'red.' He's my very best friend."

A horse for a best friend, Lane thought, noticing that she appeared embarrassed by her admission. If that was true, then her life must be lonelier than he'd thought.

The waiter returned with their food order: a lobster salad for Rachel and duck terrine for himself. He let it absorb her attention for a few minutes.

"You said you have another horse," he prompted.

"Yes, Simoon, a three-year-old filly. Dean gave her to me as a yearling. She's out of one of the mares he imported from Egypt a few years ago, and sired by his stallion Nahr El Kedar." Rachel described her at length, for a little while completely forgetting herself. It was a different Rachel that Lane saw then, warm and glowing, that wall of reserve lowered, but only briefly.

"What about boyfriends? I'm sure there's someone back there in L.A. waiting for you."

"No." She picked at the remains of her lobster salad. "Between my job and my horses, I don't have a lot of free time for dating. I go out once in a while, but not often."

Lane could tell by her expression that the experiences left a lot to be desired. As sensitive as she was, there was no doubt in his mind that she'd probably been hurt at one time or another. And the old saying "once burned, twice shy" was probably more than apt for her.

After Rachel had refused both dessert and coffee, Lane asked for the check. "I enjoyed the lunch very much. You were right. The food was excellent." She laid her napkin on the table and picked up her purse. "Thank you for asking me."

"Don't leave yet," Lane said, checking the movement she started to make. "I thought we might take a walk in the park across the street. There are a few things I want to talk to you about."

With a hand at her elbow, Lane guided her across the street to Sam Houston Park. They strolled together across the rolling green, past historical St. John's Church and the gazebo to the rushes growing along the bank of Buffalo Bayou. There Rachel turned and looked back at the modern skyscrapers of downtown towering over the small park.

"The architecture here fascinates me." A gusting wind blew her long hair into her face. She combed it out of the way with her fingers and held it, the pose pulling the loose blouse tautly across her breasts. Lane was not so jaded that the sight failed to arouse him. Rather, he felt a healthy stirring of desire in his loins, and had to remind himself that she was the daughter of a friend — not that he was entirely sure what difference that made. "I guess I get that from my mother. I don't know." She shrugged absently. "When I think of all that Los Angeles is doing to try to revitalize its downtown area and then . . . see this. I mean, there's construction going on everywhere."

"Counting cranes is Houston's favorite pastime," Lane said, referring to the giant construction cranes that poked their long necks from nearly every building site. "Some people want to declare them the state bird."

"I can believe it."

"If you want a better vantage point of the downtown buildings, we can walk over to Tranquility Park. It's just a block or so from here."

"I know you're busy. And I can't keep taking up your time. . . ."

"It's my time." With a wave of his hand, he pointed out the direction they would take. "Before you leave for California, you should take a drive around Houston. There are high-rise buildings clustered miles apart on the outer loops with architectural styles that rival what you see here."

As they walked across the park with the sun beating down on them and the wind tugging at their clothes, Lane did something he hadn't done in years — decades, maybe. Impulsively he took off his tie, unbuttoned his shirt collar, and removed his jacket, hooking it over his shoulder on his finger. It was as if a weight had been lifted from him. He felt lighter, freer — even a little younger as he directed Rachel across the street again to the futuristic Tranquility Park.

Named after the Sea of Tranquility on the lunar surface, the park was built as a Bicentennial tribute to the Apollo flights to the moon, and constructed atop the concrete deck of a multilevel underground garage. As they wandered past the reflecting pools, Lane explained some of the symbolism in the park's design, with its grassy knolls representing lunar mounds, and the fountains, ascending rockets.

"I'm told it's beautiful in the late afternoon when the angle of the sunlight hits the fountains just right and turns the water golden," he said, then admitted, "Actually, this is the first time I've ever been here."

"It's peaceful here."

"It certainly is."

She walked over to a bench and sat down, gripping the edge of the bench with her hands. "You said you wanted to talk to me about something."

"Yes." Lane joined her. "I'm sure you must have guessed that Dean's will has been read. He named me as the executor of his estate."

"I see."

"Rachel." The rest was hard for him to say, even now. "There was no mention of you in the will. Legally, you could contest it . . . and probably be awarded a third of his estate. At this time, I can't tell you what that amount might be, but —"

"No." She shook her head, her expression sadly fatalistic. "I won't do that. River Bend, the house, the horses — all that is theirs. It never belonged to me. I won't claim part of it now."

"Rachel, I'm sorry." He could tell she was hurt.

"Don't be," she insisted with a tight little smile, trying to pretend she didn't care. "I think I always knew I'd be left out. I mean, why should anything change just because he's dead?" She bowed her head. "That sounded bitter. I didn't mean for it to."

In her place, Lane thought he would have been more than bitter. Even in death, Dean hadn't publicly acknowledged her existence. "I don't want you to misunderstand me, Rachel. Your father didn't forget you. It seems that shortly after you were born, he set up an irrevocable trust fund in your name. Today, between the contributions he made into it and the accumulated interest, the fund totals over two million dollars."

"What?" She stared at him incredulously.

Lane smiled. "The exact figure is something like two million, one hundred and eighty-seven thousand dollars, plus change. The way the fund was set up, the money was to come to you when you reached the age of thirty — or in the event of his death . . . unless of course you were under twenty-one at the time."

"I can't believe it." Tears swam in her eyes, but her expression was joyful. "Daddy — Dean did that for me?"

"Yes." Moved by her poignant display, he smiled even wider, more gently. As her hands came up to cup her nose and mouth and catch the tears that spilled from the inside corners of her eyes, Lane swung away the suit jacket he'd carried and reached out to draw her into his arms. "Child," he murmured, but she felt like a woman against him.

At first, she simply let him hold her and comfortingly pat her shoulder while she cried softly. But the tears seemed to wash away some invisible wall she'd built around herself. Soon she was leaning against him, letting him support her, her face buried in the crook of his neck, her fingers clutching the front of his shirt. Lane rubbed his cheek and jaw against the silken top of her head, wondering when he'd last felt as deeply as she did. His own emotions had been buried too long in his work.

"I don't believe it." She sniffed at the tears that wouldn't stop and wiped at her nose and eyes, trying to regain her control. "He must have really loved me.

Sometimes, I —" She pulled back, gazing at Lane with haunted eyes. "Is this another of his presents to buy off his guilty conscience?"

"I think he loved you very much. And, like any father, he wanted to provide you with some financial security for the day when he couldn't look after you." That much Lane believed was true, but he wouldn't speculate on whether Dean's concern had been motivated by a guilty conscience.

Maybe Dean had lavished presents on her in the past to make up for the time he couldn't spend with her. Thousands of people did that. Was that a guilty conscience or an attempt to buy a child's love? Was either one really wrong? Lane had never been a parent. He couldn't say.

"I will tell you this, Rachel. He wouldn't have been much of a father if he hadn't taken steps to provide for your future."

"He *was* good to me — always." She moved away from him a little as she finished wiping the last of the tears from her face. Then she smiled wryly at him. "I can imagine what you think of me, falling apart like that."

"I think . . . you're beautiful." And he'd never meant a statement more. Impulsively he leaned forward and lightly kissed her lips, briefly feeling their softness and tasting the salt of her tears. Then it was his turn to wonder what she thought of him. But the look in her eyes seemed to be one of trust. He was stung by the possibility that she had regarded his kiss only as a fatherly peck.

"I'm not really sure any of this is happening to me." She shook her head vaguely. "Yesterday, I was wondering how I was going to keep both my horses. Dean always paid the boarding fees on them. I was going to look for a cheaper apartment when I got back. Now, with that much money, I can live anywhere I want, do anything I want."

"Indeed you can."

"It's staggering. I always knew Dean was wealthy, but I never dreamed I would ever have that much money. I'm not even sure what to do with it."

"What have you always wanted to do? No, seriously," Lane encouraged, observing her show of reluctance. "What's something you've always dreamed about having or doing if you had the money?"

Glancing down, she fingered her blouse. "I've always wanted to have a closet full of beautiful clothes — and a real home. But my dream . . ." She hesitated, glancing sideways at him, her self-consciousness returning. "This is going to sound silly and childish to you, Mr. Canfield."

"I'll only answer that if you call me Lane."

"Lane. Practically all my life, I've dreamed of owning an Arabian horse farm. Simoon — the filly Dean gave me — she was going to be my start. I've been saving money for the stud fee so I could breed her next year. Then I could sell the foal and use that money to buy me another broodmare, and slowly build a herd that way. I've been trying to find some land I could buy or lease, but it's all so expensive in California I can't afford it on my salary. And I never could bring myself to ask Dean to help me. He already had a farm, and, even though he never said so, I know he would have been uncomfortable if I got into the Arabian horse business, too. He knows all the top breeders everywhere in the world. How would he have explained me? And, of course, there was his family."

"You don't have to worry about any of that now. Money can't alter the past or make you happy, but it can help you to realize your wildest dreams. So go ahead and dream, Rachel. That's what it's for."

"It is, isn't it?" she mused. "Back in my apartment in L.A., I have the barn all designed for my dream farm. I mean, it's complete right down to the dimensions of the foaling stalls, the veterinary lab, the video equipment, everything — even the materials to be used in the construction."

Lane listened to her dream and remembered the way he had talked, back in the beginning when he was getting started. Those were the good days, when he'd had time to rejoice in his successes and savor the sweetness of them. Now, he was too busy. Watching her, he realized how much he missed the excitement of dreaming. He envied her the feeling.

"Have you given any thought to where you would like to build this?"

"I always assumed it would have to be California. Which is fine. Most of the major breeders are located in either California or Arizona. But where would I *like* to build it?" She paused, a slight ruefulness twisting her mouth. "Dean always talked so much about Texas."

"You will have to spend quite a bit of time here — at least initially. There's going to be a considerable amount of paperwork involved in transferring the funds into your name. Naturally you're going to need someone you can trust to advise you on the best way to invest a sum that size. I'm sure there are qualified people in California who can help you, but I think your father would have wanted me to assist you in making such decisions. You don't put over two million dollars in a savings account to draw interest. You can, but it isn't wise."

"I can't even comprehend that amount," Rachel admitted. "And I would like you to advise me. I know how much Dean trusted you. And how could I be sure I'd find someone else like you? But I hate the thought of bothering you —"

"Rachel, I would be happy to do it. I would never have volunteered myself otherwise. Have we got that settled?"

"Yes." She smiled and Lane felt warmed by it.

"Now, back to your dream farm. Tell me how you would go about accomplishing it." He encouraged Rachel to expound on her plans, enjoying the animation in her face, the free play of expression, and the total absence of the air of reserve behind which she'd hidden her feelings earlier.

"To start with, I'd like to find three or four really good mares," she began. "Ideally, I'd buy older broodmares — twelve or thirteen years old probably — proven producers. That way I could have better quality mares for a lower price. Even though their most productive years would be over, I could still hope to get three, maybe more good foals from them. If I could be lucky enough to buy broodmares already in foal, I'd have the choice the following year of selling the foals as weanlings to start generating an income or keeping the really good ones to build my own herd."

She continued to talk, telling him all her plans, her breeding theories, and her ambitions. Occasionally Lane would insert a comment or question, but mostly he just listened. For one so young, in his eyes, she had impressive knowledge of horses and various bloodlines. Then he remembered the way Abbie had talked, and decided that maybe it wasn't so surprising after all. Like father, like daughter.

"Look at the fountains." Rachel halted in surprise to stare at the molten-gold cascading water. "Have we talked that long?"

"We must have." Lane was surprised that he'd so completely lost track of time, as well. Appointments usually made him a prisoner of the clock. Yet he hadn't glanced at his watch once since he'd been with Rachel. He realized it was a good thing he'd told Frank to clear his calendar of all appointments this afternoon.

Rachel hastily stood up, smoothing the front of her skirt and withdrawing behind her wall of reserve again. "I'm sorry for boring you like that."

"My dear, you could never bore me." Lane straightened, reluctant to part from her. Rachel had awakened desires in him that he'd forgotten he'd ever felt. They were more than mere sexual urges, easily gratified. Their makeup was more complex, evoking a longing to arouse and please, to cherish and protect, to give and delight in the giving. Sobering feelings — all of them.

"It's kind of you to say that, Lane, but I know I did." Her lips curved faintly in a smile of regret, then she glanced down the street. "I left my car parked at the hotel."

"I'll walk you there." He swung his suit jacket over his shoulder again and curved his arm around the back of her waist, trying to keep the contact casual, as they set out of the park. "What are your immediate plans?"

"I've . . . made reservations to fly back to Los Angeles tomorrow morning." But she seemed to question whether she should cancel her plans.

"I'm sure there are plenty of things you need to take care of there as well as here. All the document signing and paperwork for the trust account can wait until next week. It isn't going to vanish between now and then."

"That's true. I could fly back here the first of the week."

"If you're short of funds, I'll be happy to advance you some money."

"No, I . . . I can use my savings. There's no reason not to now, is there?" She still seemed a little dazed by the news. "It's hard to think of myself as being rich, an heiress to a fortune."

"That's exactly what you are. Let me know what day you'll be coming back. We'll have dinner. I still haven't shown you that painting of your mother's I mentioned at lunch."

"I'd forgotten all about that."

"I hadn't." Any more than he'd forgotten what it had been like to hold her in his arms and kiss her as he'd done a little while ago. "Would you have dinner with me next week?"

"I'd like to, yes, but —"

Lane didn't want to hear another self-effacing comment about taking up his busy time. He cut in to stop her: "Then let's consider it a date," realizing that he meant it in the strictest old-fashioned sense.

"All right." She nodded in agreement, smiling faintly as if pleased, yet afraid something would happen to change it. Lane wondered how many times Dean had made a promise to her that he hadn't been able to keep. He didn't like the impression he had that Rachel was preparing herself to be disappointed. No one should be that insecure. He vowed to change that.

10

THE SOUND OF ABBIE'S footsteps on the stairs disturbed the stillness that enveloped the house. There'd always been an empty feeling to it whenever her father was gone. Now that feeling would be permanent. Abbie paused near the bottom of the staircase and glanced at the closed doors to the library. They had always been kept shut when he was away.

Not needing such a reminder, Abbie ran down the last three steps and crossed the foyer to slide the doors open, then paused to stare at the neat, tidy top of his desk, not at all the way he'd left it.

This past week she'd gone through the room, cleaned out his desks — both here and at his office in the stables — and sent what few pertinent documents she'd found to Lane Canfield. But there hadn't been any letters, photographs, or mementos that pertained to his mistress and child in California. If there were any, Abbie suspected that he'd probably kept them at his law office. That was Mary Jo Anderson's province.

There had been many things to do this past week, things her mother hadn't been up to doing: notifying the accountant to send her father's records to Lane, forwarding the bills to him, cleaning out her father's drawers and closet, throwing out his old clothes and packing the rest into boxes for distribution to local charitable and religious organizations, sorting through personal articles such as jewelry and toiletries and deciding which ones to save and which ones to discard. It hadn't been easy to remove the physical traces of him from the house.

Even though they were gone now, he still haunted it. Somewhere a clock ticked, marking time against the low hum of the central air-conditioning and echoing the feeling of expectancy that permeated the house, as if any second he was going to walk through the front door. But he wasn't . . . not now, not ever!

Abbie pivoted sharply and strode across the foyer to the living room arch, letting the heels of her riding boots strike the polished boards of the heart-pine floor as hard as they wished in an attempt to chase away the ghosts — and the nagging fears.

From her chair near the bay window, her mother looked up from the stack of sympathy cards that surrounded her. "Is something wrong, Abbie?" Babs frowned quizzically.

She resisted the impulse to say yes. How could she tell her mother that, despite the fact that Rachel hadn't been mentioned in the will, and despite the fact that Lane had informed her that Dean had made separate provisions for Rachel and it was extremely unlikely she would contest the will, she still felt uneasy about it? Until the estate was actually settled, the possibility remained. And she couldn't ignore it.

"Nothing at all," she lied. "I just wanted to let you know I'm headed for the stables. I thought I might work River Breeze a little."

"The way you came marching in here, it sounded like we were being invaded by the whole Russian army or something."

"Sorry. I'll be outside if you need me."

"Don't forget: the Richardsons are coming for dinner tonight at seven."

"I won't."

Abbie turned and left the room, more quietly than she'd entered it. Outside, the summer sun had begun its downward slide and the oak trees in the front yard cast long shadows across the lawn. Abbie paused in the shade of the wide veranda and turned her face toward the cool breeze that came whispering through the trees, letting its freshness calm her nerves.

A battered old pickup truck was parked in front of the stables. Abbie recognized it instantly. No other truck was in such sorry shape in the entire county. Her father used to joke that rust was the only thing holding it together. It belonged to Dobie Hix, who owned the neighboring farm to the west of them. Abbie smiled wryly, guessing that his brand-new pickup was probably parked in his garage. He rarely drove it, except to town. He didn't want to get it all beaten up bouncing over the rutted lanes to his fields, so he drove the old one most of the time.

Ever since Abbie could remember, he'd always been like that: buying something new, then never using it until it was old. It didn't matter that he could probably afford ten new trucks. Between the land he owned and the acreage he leased, he farmed close to fifteen hundred acres. More than once Abbie had heard her mother insist that Dobie was tighter than the bark on a tree with his money. His tightfisted hold on a dollar had become almost a standing joke in the area. Abbie had laughed about it once or twice herself, but never in front of him.

She wondered what he was doing here at River Bend. He sold them the hay they used to feed the horses, but the hay shed was practically full. Her curiosity aroused, Abbie headed over to the stables.

As she neared the breezeway, she saw Ben standing in its shade, talking with Dobie. "I am certain you have nothing to worry about, Mr. Hix."

"I figured that." Dobie nodded his head in agreement, the rolled brim of his straw cowboy hat bobbing up and down with the motion. As usual, he was dressed in an old pair of faded Levi's, a plaid shirt, and a leather belt with his name stamped in fancy letters across the back of it. "I've always known Lawson was good for it. It's just —" He spied Abbie and halted in midsentence. "Hello, Abbie." Quickly he swept off his hat and self-consciously ran his fingers through his fine strawberry-blond hair, trying to comb it into some kind of order.

"Hello, Dobie." She glanced at the sprinkling of freckles that gave him such a boyish look despite the fact that he had to be, at least, thirty-five. "What's the problem?"

"No problem," he insisted, smiling. "Leastwise, nothing that you need to worry your pretty head about." Then he ducked his head as if regretting the compliment he'd paid her.

More than once since her divorce, Abbie had gotten the impression that, with the least little encouragement from her, Dobie would renew the suit he'd pressed throughout almost her entire senior year of high school, particularly at the Gay Nineties debut party held here at River Bend, the Victorian mansion providing the theme and backdrop. It had been an elaborate bash thrown by her parents. All the invitations, bearing a tintype photograph of Abbie dressed as a Gibson Girl, had been hand-delivered by uniformed messengers wearing flannel trousers, bow ties, and straw skimmers, and riding a bicycle built for two. A carnival had been set up on the grounds, transforming it into Coney Island, complete with a midway — and a kissing booth. Dobie Hix had been very free with his money that day, Abbie recalled, buying up all the tickets when she was selling kisses. Her mother had insisted that they couldn't leave him off the invitation list, when he was their closest neighbor. Truthfully, Abbie hadn't objected — until she had to endure the embarrassment of his monopoly on her kisses, and later his broad hints about their lands adjoining and the advantages of combining them.

Nearly every time she'd gone riding after that, she'd run into him somewhere: down by the river, along the fence line, by the road. She'd had the feeling he hung around and watched for her. He hadn't really given up until she announced her engagement to Christopher Atwell. But she'd never been frightened of him, only irritated by his persistence.

His hands dug into his hat, crumpling the brim. "I saw you at the funeral. I would have come over, but . . . I want you to know how sorry I am about your daddy. He was a fine man."

"Thank you, Dobie."

"If you ever need anything — anything at all — remember, I'm just up the road. You let me know if I can help in any way."

"I appreciate that, but I can't think of anything right now. Ben and I have things fairly well under control, I think."

"I'm sure you do." He glanced at Ben, then hesitantly back at her. "Maybe the next time you're out riding, you can stop by the farm and visit." But he didn't wait for a response to his invitation. "Well, I'd best be gettin' along." With a bob of his head, he moved by her toward the rusty pickup, shoving his hat onto his head as he went.

As the truck rattled out of the yard, Abbie turned to Ben. "What did he want?"

"He came about the hay bill. When he delivered the last load, we had not yet paid him for the winter hay."

"Daddy must have overlooked it. Make a note of the amount and send it to Lane so he can make sure it's paid with the rest of the bills." But Abbie frowned, aware this wasn't the first inquiry they had received regarding past-due bills.

"I will see that he receives it."

With that settled, Abbie glanced toward the paddock where her silver-gray filly was kept. "I thought I'd lunge Breeze. She's had it easy this last week."

"It would be good . . . for both of you. You go," Ben prompted gently. "I will bring the halter and line."

She smiled at him, briefly acknowledging his gesture, then headed for the paddock gate. The filly trotted forward to meet her with an effortlessly floating stride — gliding over the ground, all delicacy and grace, head up, neck arched, her silvery tail erect and streaming behind her like a banner in the wind. As

Abbie came through the gate, the filly nickered a welcome and impatiently nuzzled her arm.

Laughing softly, Abbie turned and caressed the filly, rubbing her favorite place just above the right eye. The texture of the filly's coat was slick as satin beneath her hand. Here and there, a smoky dark hair was hidden among the dominant white coloring, but beneath, the filly's skin was as black as the hair-cloth tents of the Bedouins in which her desert-bred ancestors had lived. The mares were prized above all others by the nomad raiders of the sand.

"Lonely, were you?" Abbie crooned, watching the filly's small ears move to catch every inflection of her voice. "And I suppose there was no one around to give you any attention. Well, you don't have to fret anymore. I'm back now."

She embraced the filly, hugging her neck, feeling the affection returned, the warmth of another body. The sense of being wanted — needed — was strong. Abbie responded to it, talking, sharing, and never minding how silly it might sound, not until the filly alerted Abbie to Ben's presence at the fence.

"I think she's happy to see me." She took the halter from him and slipped it on the young horse.

"She missed you."

"I missed her." She buckled the throatlatch and snapped on the lead rope as Ben opened the gate.

The silver-gray horse came prancing through the opening behind Abbie, animation and eagerness in every line, yet, for all the show of spirit, there was still slack in the lead rope Abbie held. Ben studied the filly with a critical eye, looking for any faults or imperfections.

"She reminds me of Wielki Szlem. What a magnificent stride he had."

"That's when you were at Janow?" Janow Podlaski was the famed state-run Arabian stud farm in Poland where so many of the great Arabian stallions had stood: Skowronek Witraz, Comet, Negatiw, and Bask.

Ben nodded affirmatively as a faraway look came into his eyes. "I was fifteen when they hired me to work at Janow." He'd been talking about the past more and more of late, Abbie noticed. "That was before the war with Germany, when many of Janow's grooms were drafted into the army."

Many times Abbie had heard the story of his experiences in Poland during World War II: the dramatic flight to evacuate the valuable stallions and brood-mares in advance of the invading German army, only to be turned back by Russian forces; the horses that were left at farms along the way; the ones confiscated by the Russians, including the great Ofir, sire of Wielki Szlem; the years of occupation by the Germans; the horrors of the Dresden bombings that claimed the lives of twenty-one prized horses; the valuable bloodlines that died out; the maneuvering that had enabled the Janow stud to come under British jurisdiction immediately after the war; and Ben's eventual immigration to the United States entrusted with the care of a stallion that subsequently died of colic on the long sea voyage. As a child, Abbie had thrilled to his tales. Even now, when she thought of him leading a horse through Dresden in the midst of an air raid, with bombs exploding all around, it raised chillbumps.

From the stud pen an elegent bay stallion, an inbred son of Nahr El Kedar, nickered shrilly at the gray filly Abbie led. Ben cast a contemptuous glance in the stallion's direction. "Racing, that is the test of a stallion. It is not how pretty he looks. Look at that one. Does he have heart? Does he have courage? Does he possess the stamina and disposition to endure the rigors of training and competing on the racetrack? Will he pass it on to his get? Who knows?" He shrugged his shoulders. "Many times I argued with your father on this, but never would he listen to me. The horse has a pretty head. That was all he cared about."

"I know." Just as she knew that Benedykt Jablonski based his opinions on the breeding practices in Poland, where racing played a vital role in the selection process of breeding stock. And Abbie had agreed with him even though it put her at odds with her father.

Ben had always disapproved of her father's practice of close inbreeding. "Incest breeding," he called it when Dean bred father to daughter or brother to half-sister. It set the good traits — the big eye, the dished profile or long neck — but it often exaggerated the faults — slightly sickle-hocked hind legs became severe, or a hint of calf knees became decidedly such. Abbie didn't like it either, especially when she saw that the overall quality of the River Bend Arabians had declined because of it.

She led the young filly into the work arena. Inside the solidly fenced area, she switched the lead rope for a lunge line and took the whip Ben handed her, then walked the horse to the center.

Having been raised on the farm, surrounded by horses, with no neighbor children her age living nearby, Abbie had naturally turned to horses as friends. They had become her companions, her playmates, and her confidants. But more than loneliness had drawn her. Any affection or loyalty shown by them was genuine. Unlike humans, they weren't capable of pretense, and they'd never betray her trust.

Most of the other girls Abbie knew had gone through a horse phase sometime in their early years, but hers had carried over into adulthood. When she was with horses, she felt good about herself. That had never changed.

After Abbie had succeeded in getting the filly to relax and trot smoothly in a counterclockwise circle around her, she saw Ben Jablonski leave the arena fence and head in the direction of the barns. She smiled faintly while keeping her attention focused on the filly. Once Ben would never have allowed her to work a young horse unsupervised. Compliments from him were rare, and when they came, they were invariably stated by his actions, as now.

Rachel slowed her car as she approached the entrance to River Bend, marked by a white signboard, the name written in black scrolled letters with the black silhouette of an Arabian horse below them. She stared at the horses grazing beneath the huge, moss-draped trees in the pasture, none of them close enough for her to see clearly.

She had driven here straight from the airport, returning to Houston a day earlier than she had planned. During the short time she'd spent in Los Angeles, she'd managed to quit her job, pack and store everything she didn't bring with her, and sublet her apartment to one of her co-workers. Everything had gone so smoothly that Rachel was even more convinced that her decision to move to Texas was the right one. As soon as she found a place to live, she would have her horses shipped from California. Except for them, that life was behind her, a part of the past.

Flexing her grip on the steering wheel, Rachel hesitated, then turned the car onto the narrow lane and followed its winding path through the trees. Ever since Dean had given her Simoon, she had wanted to see the filly's sire and dam in person, not just pictures of them. And she wanted to look over the facilities at River Bend that she had read so much about.

As the car neared the heart of River Bend, the trees parted — like an honor guard before their ruler — and revealed the towering mansion with its gables and turrets, its skirting veranda and parapet. It was a stately, elegant home. Yes, *home* was the word, Rachel realized. There was nothing cold or austere about it for all its grandness. It looked like a place filled with hidden delights and wrapped in a warm invitation to come and explore.

Staring at it, Rachel remembered the spare apartments of her childhood, cluttered with her mother's paintings and permeated with the smell of paints and thinners. This home could have been hers. The thought swelled inside her — a bitter, choking thing.

Almost unwillingly, Rachel recalled when her mother had died, so suddenly, so unexpectedly. She'd come home from school and gone upstairs to the studio loft — and found her mother lying on the floor in front of an unfinished painting. When she had failed to get her mother to respond, Rachel ran to a neighbor's for help. After that, everything was a blur. She remembered being at the hospital and some man in green telling her that her mother was dead. She no longer knew whether Dean had arrived that night or the next day. But he had come. And she had cried and cried and cried in his arms.

At some point, either before the funeral or after, Rachel wasn't sure now, she had asked, "What's going to happen to me?" She'd been seventeen at the time, but she'd felt like seven — left alone and frightened.

"I've made arrangements for you to stay with Myria Holmes," he'd said, mentioning one of her mother's artist friends. "She offered and —"

"I don't want to live with her!" She had almost cried, "I want to live with you," but she'd stopped herself before the words came out. It had been so painful to realize she had secretly hoped all along that Dean would take her back to Texas with him; that he wouldn't be able to bear the thought of leaving her here alone, with no one; that he loved her too much to go away without her. She had been crushed to learn that she wasn't going to be leaving with him.

"It won't be for long," he'd hurried to assure her. "Next year you'll be going to college and living on campus with your friends."

But he'd never understood that she didn't have any friends, not really. They'd come in and out of her life, some staying longer than others, letting her believe that maybe this time she had a best friend she could trust, but each time she'd been disillusioned. Now that her mother was gone, no one loved her or wanted her around all the time — not even her own father.

God, how she longed to be wanted and loved — and feared it would never be. Her horses, that was all she had. And she told herself they were all she needed. Their affection, their companionship was enough.

Just ahead, a lofty oak tree split the lane into two branches, one leading to the white mansion and the other veering off to the huge stable complex. Rachel swung the car to the right — to the horses.

* * *

After a twenty-minute workout, Abbie led the silver-gray filly out of the work arena, the perimeter of which was solidly boarded to eliminate outside distractions. Snorting and blowing, the filly paced alertly beside her. As they approached the stables, Abbie felt a tug on the lead rope. Mistaking the pull for a show of eagerness to reach her stall and receive her evening measure of grain, Abbie glanced sideways at the filly, chiding, "Worked up an appetite, did you?"

But the dainty ears and huge dark eyes were trained on the car parked near the stables' office annex. Abbie didn't recognize the late-model car. One of the grooms approached from the direction of the annex.

"Who does the car belong to, Miguel?" she asked curiously, not immediately seeing any stranger in the vicinity. "Is it just someone wanting to look at the horses?" Visitors — some prospective buyers, some not — frequently stopped at River Bend to look at their Arabians.

"Si. She wanted to see El Kedar. I pointed out his pen to her. I was just going to get Señor Jablonski."

By then Abbie had already seen the tall, dark-haired woman crossing to the reinforced stallion run. She was nondescriptly dressed in a natural gauze blouse and tight-legged jeans minus any distinctive label, her long hair worn straight, sweeping past her shoulders. Rachel. Abbie recognized her immediately, and every muscle in her body suddenly grew taut.

"Never mind getting Ben," she told the groom. "I'll handle this one." She pushed the lunge line, lead rope, and whip into his hands. "Take Breeze to her stall and see that she gets a good rubdown before she's fed."

Without waiting for an acknowledgment, Abbie set off for the stud barn and its adjacent runs. Somehow she wasn't surprised that Rachel was here, but she seriously doubted that Rachel had come to look at the inheritance she was giving up. It was probably just the opposite.

Rachel stood pressed against the heavy rails, gazing admiringly at the aging bay stallion on the far side of the paddock, who was suspiciously testing the air to catch the scent of this stranger. At first she wasn't even aware that Abbie had joined her. Then she darted a quick glance at her and self-consciously drew back from the fence.

"He's magnificent," she said, a slightly nervous edge to her voice as she turned her attention back to El Kedar.

"My father thought so." Abbie wasn't sure why she'd said that, except in some way, she knew she wanted to challenge Rachel and assert her claim to him — to River Bend, to everything that she had once thought of as solely hers.

"At his age, I expected him to be heavier . . . thicker-necked, maybe, and stoutly muscled. But he looks lean and fit."

"We've always had trouble putting weight on him, especially during the breeding season. He was born and raised in Egypt. They don't believe in putting flesh on them. He was a three-year-old when he finally arrived here at River Bend — practically skin and bones after the long sea voyage and the quarantine. He'd never seen a blade of grass, let alone walked on it or ate it. And he'd never had room to run free." In a paddock separated from El Kedar's, a bay stallion similarly marked trotted boldly up to the fence and whistled a challenge to his older rival. "That's Nahr Ibn Kedar, his son."

"He doesn't have El Kedar's presence, does he?"

Abbie was briefly surprised by Rachel's observation. She hadn't suspected that she was so knowledgeable about Arabians. "No. El Kedar has never reproduced himself." Abbie paused, fighting a tension and an anger she couldn't quite understand. "Exactly why have you come here?"

Again she noticed Rachel's hesitation, that trace of uncertainty and nervousness in her expression. "I've only seen pictures of El Kedar. I've wanted to see him in person ever since Dean gave me his daughter, Nahr Simoon, out of Nahr Riih."

Abbie stiffened, remembering the filly, one of the best of El Kedar's daughters — the filly her father had supposedly sold. But that was yet another lie he'd told. She couldn't admit that, certainly not to Rachel.

"You called him by his first name?" she said instead.

"Yes. It was my mother's idea. She thought it would create fewer questions than if I called him Father or Daddy." Just for an instant, a wryness, faintly sardonic, crept into her voice and expression. But it was gone when Rachel turned from the fence and swept the stable area with a glance. "I was hoping I might tour the facilities here."

"Why?" Abbie wondered. To appraise its worth?

"I . . . I just wanted to see it. I've heard so much about it."

"I'm sure you'll understand that a tour isn't possible." Pushed by some territorial compulsion, Abbie wanted only to get her away from there, off of River Bend, *now*. Rachel had no right here, none at all. "River Bend isn't open to the public. And it won't be again until the estate is settled."

"Surely it wouldn't hurt anything if I just . . . looked around," Rachel suggested tentatively.

Over my dead body, Abbie thought, trembling with the rage she felt inside, not really knowing where it came from — and not really caring. "I can't allow that." She managed to keep the pitch of her voice calmly even and firm, but it wasn't easy.

"I see." Rachel held herself stiffly, looking a little hurt. "In that case, I guess there isn't much point in my staying here any longer."

"I guess not."

"Thank you for at least letting me see El Kedar."

"You're welcome."

As Rachel walked back to her car, Abbie felt the tears burning in her eyes. She was afraid, and it was the first time in her life she could remember feeling fear. So much had happened. She'd lost her father. She'd lost her illusions of the past. She couldn't stand the thought of losing even one small part of River Bend.

Surely Rachel hadn't really believed she would blithely show her around. Did Rachel really think she was so stupid that she hadn't guessed she intended to claim part — maybe even all — of it? Abbie wondered as she watched Rachel slide behind the wheel of her car and close the door. Well, she was wrong if she did.

Abbie started to turn and walk back to the stables. Out of the corner of her eye, she caught a movement along the fence and glanced over, expecting to see Ben. But the tall, dark-haired man in a wheat-tan sports jacket and crisp new jeans bore no resemblance to the elderly Pole.

She breathed in sharply, fighting to bring her emotions under control, as she stared at MacCrea Wilder. She wondered how long he'd been standing there. How much had he heard? She saw his glance follow Rachel's car as it pulled out of the yard. When they'd met at the cemetery, Rachel had been involved that time, too, Abbie remembered.

"Mr. Wilder. I didn't hear you walk up." She studied his angular face, noting the aggressive jut of his chin and jaw. Despite the smooth darkness of his eyes, his was a hard face, she realized.

"I guessed that." Unhurriedly, he moved toward her. When he reached the approximate place where Rachel had stood, he stopped. "Did I understand right? She's your half-sister?"

Abbie didn't have to wonder anymore about how much he'd overheard. "Do you know anything about horses, Mr. Wilder?"

His mouth quirked in a little smile, lifting one corner of his mustache. "I know which is the back end."

"In the Arabian horse business, the term half-sister is restricted to fillies foaled by the same mare. Rachel Farr and I share the same sire."

Idly MacCrea studied her, catching the glitter of moisture in her blue eyes. He frowned briefly, realizing that he'd unwittingly touched a sore spot. She had looked so calm and poised to him before, completely in control, that he hadn't noticed the fine tension emanating from her. He could see it now in the firm set of her lips and the almost rigid lines of her jaw.

"Sorry. I guess I put my foot in it, didn't I?"

"All the way up to your boot tops," she retorted curtly.

"But I couldn't know that, could I?" he reminded her, squarely meeting her gaze and holding it until hers fell away.

"I don't suppose you could," she admitted grudgingly, leaving him with the impression that she would have preferred to battle it out with him and let him be the scapegoat for her anger. But a fight with Dean Lawson's daughter was the last thing he wanted. "Is there something I can do for you, Mr. Wilder? I presume you didn't come out here just to eavesdrop on a private conversation."

"I stopped by to see your mother."

"You'll find her at the house."

"I figured that. But I wasn't sure she was receiving visitors yet, so I stopped by the stables to check. That's when I saw you."

Abbie believed him. She didn't want to, but she did. "I was just on my way to the house to change for dinner. If you'd like, you can walk along with me."

"Thank you, I will."

11 ⤳

"MOMMA." ABBIE ENTERED the foyer, conscious of MacCrea Wilder following her — just as she had been conscious of him during the walk to the house. She'd forgotten what it was like to be physically aware of a man, to be alive to the close swing of his arm next to hers, the inches it would take before they accidentally brushed. When had the sensitivity been buried? During her years of marriage to Christopher? Had she taken a man's nearness so for granted that she'd become indifferent to it? Maybe familiarity did dull the senses, she decided. Practically every man she'd dated, both before her marriage and the few afterward, she'd known for years. Maybe that's why it was different with MacCrea. She didn't know anything about him, not his background, or his tastes—or even the way he kissed. Abbie smiled at herself, amused that she even had such thoughts, considering all the things she had on her mind. Yet she almost welcomed the diversion he offered.

"Someone's here to see you, Momma." She led the way into the living room.

As she turned, she caught the sweeping glance he gave the room before he focused his attention on her mother. Despite his seeming casualness, Abbie suspected that he had noted every detail. She doubted that those ever-watchful dark eyes missed much.

But she wondered how he'd seen it, as she looked around the room, taking in the wainscot's striped pattern of alternating chestnut and walnut boards that matched the parquet floor, the walls painted a cool shade of blue above the wainscot, the elaborately carved walnut molding around the fireplace, the neo-Victorian tufted velvet sofa and swan chairs, and the lace curtains at the tall windows. She wondered whether he liked it, then almost laughed. What did it matter whether he liked it? This was her home, not his.

"I haven't had the pleasure of meeting you before, Mrs. Lawson. I'm Mac-Crea Wilder," he said, shaking hands with her mother.

"Mr. Wilder. I'm happy to meet you." But she threw a questioning look at Abbie.

"After meeting you in person, I can honestly say that the photograph your husband kept on his office desk doesn't do you justice."

"You're obviously a Texan," Babs laughed, beaming at the compliment. "Only a Texan can tell tall tales like that and get away with it."

"It's no tale. I promise you," MacCrea chuckled, the sound coming from low in his throat. Abbie was warmed by it.

"Now I know it is," Babs declared, and waved a hand at the sofa and chairs. "Make yourself comfortable, Mr. Wilder. Jackson?" As she turned to summon their houseman, the ubiquitous Jackson appeared in the archway, carrying a tray of iced drinks. "Oh, there you are. And you brought extra glasses of iced tea."

"Yes, ma'am. I heard the gentleman and Miss Lawson come in," he replied, walking in and pausing to offer each of them a glass from the tray. "Will there be anything else, ma'am?"

"I don't think so, Jackson. Thank you." As the black houseman withdrew, they each found a place to sit, Abbie on the blue-flowered velvet sofa with her mother and MacCrea in a pale-blue swan chair, but she noticed he waited until they were seated before he sat down himself.

Abbie also noticed that the swan chair didn't suit him at all, with its gleaming walnut arms carved in the shape of swans with necks bowed and wings curved back to form the chair's sides. With his broad shoulders and lean hips, he was much too masculine to look natural in such an ornate chair. Abbie remembered that her robust grandfather had referred to the twin chairs as the "bird seats" and claimed he always felt ridiculous sitting in them, but he sat in them anyway. Like MacCrea, he didn't let them bother him or make him uncomfortable.

"You knew Dean?" Babs prompted.

"Not well. My relationship with him was mainly business." Crossing his legs, MacCrea hooked his hat on the bend of his knee. "He was helping me with a project of mine."

"Are you involved with Arabian horses, too?" Babs guessed, influenced by the boots, the hat, and the jeans, even though they were fairly standard dress in Texas.

"Mr. Wilder's in the oil business," Abbie inserted. "He's one of those wild-catters." In her opinion, he fit the mold of the independent oil men — a bit of a gambler with shrewd instincts.

"Not exactly," MacCrea denied smoothly, meeting her glance. "I'm a drilling contractor by trade, although on occasion I have taken a small piece of action in a well."

"Then what was your business with my father?" Abbie had assumed her father had been putting together a limited partnership to raise the capital for some new well, a fairly common practice of his.

"Truthfully, I was hoping he had talked to you about it, Mrs. Lawson," he said, shifting his gaze to her and watching her expression closely.

"Dean knew better than to discuss business with me," Babs declared. "What I know about it wouldn't fill a beanpot."

Abbie caught the look of disappointment that flickered briefly in his eyes, then it was deftly smoothed away, leaving only the grim set of his jaw to indicate that her reply wasn't the one he had wanted to hear.

"What kind of project was Daddy helping you with?" Abbie leaned forward, her curiosity thoroughly aroused.

He hesitated, as if trying to decide how much to tell her . . . or how much she'd understand. "With the help of a computer friend of mine, I've come up with a system that can test the downhole performance of drilling fluids. Without getting too technical, it will allow an operator to better determine what kind of drilling fluids he might need."

"You mean mud." Abbie smiled.

His mouth crooked in response. "Yes. The Lawson name is somewhat legendary in the mud industry. I grew up hearing the old-timers telling stories about your grandfather."

"R.D. was a character," Babs recalled fondly, her expression taking on a reminiscent glow. "He never did anything small. With him everything had to be big — and I mean Texas-big. This house was so alive when he was here. He just filled it up. Not that he was noisy, although his voice could boom when he wanted it to. He said it came from all those years he spent in the oil fields, trying to talk above the racket going on. But when he was home, you just felt like you could relax 'cause everything was going to be all right. He'd see to that." She paused to sigh. "I always thought it was a shame Dean sold the company R.D. worked so hard to build and took such pride in. Was your family in the oil business, too, Mr. Wilder?"

"My daddy was a drilling contractor. He was born in the Permian Basin area west of Abilene on the family ranch. That's where he caught the oil fever." MacCrea didn't bother to add that the ranch had been lost in a foreclosure sale during the depression, making his father's venture into the oil fields to find work a necessity.

Nor did he consider it advisable to talk about his own childhood. By Lawson standards, it would probably be regarded as rough. His mother had died when he was barely three years old. He had traveled with his father after that, living in whatever drilling site the rig was sitting on, playing in the mud pits, and eating with the crews. Texas, Arkansas, Oklahoma, Kansas, Wyoming, Louisiana — he'd gone to school all over the country and started working in the fields when he was twelve. When he'd turned eighteen, his father had made him a full partner and changed the signs on the trucks to WILDER & SON DRILLING CONTRACTORS. They were going to make it big together. John Thomas Wilder had been more than his father; he'd been his partner and buddy, too.

"Your father: is he . . ." Abbie hesitated over the question.

"He's dead. Killed in a freak drilling accident several years ago." Thirteen years ago, to be exact, he remembered, conscious of the hard flatness in his voice and the effort it took to suppress that memory and keep it locked in the past with his feelings. He took a sip of the cold tea, then lifted the glass in the widow's direction. "This is good tea, Mrs. Lawson. Some people make it too sweet for my taste."

As MacCrea Wilder raised the iced-tea glass, Abbie noticed the effeminate crooking of his little finger. The mannerism struck her as being totally out of character with his otherwise ruggedly masculine presence.

"The secret is not the amount of sugar you add, but the amount of lemon. Even with something sweet, you like that hint of tartness," Babs replied.

"That's the way Grandpa always said he liked his women," Abbie recalled, guessing it was MacCrea's reference to him that made her remember that.

"Your grandpa knew what he was talking about." He looked at her when he said it.

Abbie wondered whether he intended it merely as a response or as a personal reference to her. More than once, she'd been accused of having a sharp tongue. She had to admit that, earlier at the stables, she'd hardly been cordial to him. He drank down the rest of his tea, curling that little finger again.

"It was kind of you to let me take up your time this way, Mrs. Lawson. But I don't want to keep you any longer." He set his empty glass down on the tea table beside his chair, picked up his hat, and rolled to his feet, all in one slow, fluid motion. "Thank you. For the tea as well."

"It was our pleasure, Mr. Wilder." Babs stood up to shake hands with him.

He held on to it. "I meant to tell you how sorry I am about your husband."

"Thank you." There was the faintest break in her composure.

Abbie covered for her. "I'll walk out with him, Momma."

"There's no need for you to do that," MacCrea inserted.

"I don't mind." She shrugged. "You left your pickup parked by the stables, and I have to go there anyway."

With the good-byes over, Abbie left the house with him. She couldn't help noticing how preoccupied he seemed to be as they went down the porch steps to the sidewalk.

"You never did say exactly how my father was helping you."

He glanced at her absently, still giving her the impression that his thoughts were elsewhere. "He had talked about possibly becoming involved financially, but mainly he was going to put me in touch with the right people. Even though he wasn't in the business anymore, he still had contacts. That's why I went to him."

"Why?" Abbie frowned, not following him. "I mean, what was the purpose in introducing you to these contacts?"

"Right now, all I have is a prototype of the testing equipment, so I could get a patent on it. But that's all it is — a prototype. Working models have to be built and extensive field testing done. I'm not in any position — financially or otherwise — to develop and market it by myself."

"So what are you trying to do? Sell the patent?"

"Only as a last resort. It's my baby. I've worked on it a long time. I don't want to let it go completely if I don't have to. But maybe I won't have a choice." He shrugged to conceal the anger he felt at finding himself back at square one. All the groundwork he'd laid with Lawson was wasted time and effort. He had to go out and do it all over again. He was beginning to wonder if it was worth it.

"Grandpa always said, 'Houston attracts people who make things happen. You can't keep 'em down, no matter what.'" She smiled carelessly at him. "So, at least you came to the right place."

"Maybe so." He couldn't help noticing the wide curve of her lips, their expression of warmth, and their soft fullness.

The first time he'd seen her at Lawson's office, he'd been aware of her striking looks, that unusual combination of rich, dark hair and incredibly blue eyes. He was a man capable of being aroused as readily as any other by a beautiful, well-built woman, but that day he'd been turned off by her brittleness and demanding ways — phony and spoiled, with nothing behind that beautiful window dressing. At the funeral, he'd seen she could be vulnerable. And now . . . now, he wondered if he'd been mistaken about her. Maybe she wasn't the spoiled, shallow woman he'd thought she was.

"What will you do now?" she asked.

"Start over."

"I might know some people you can talk to." Lane Canfield was the first name that came to her mind. "I'll make some calls and see what I can find out. Is there someplace I can reach you?"

He took a business card out of his pocket and scratched a telephone number on the back of it with a ballpoint pen. "You can get ahold of me at this number," he said, handing it to her. "Don't pay any attention to the one on the front of the card. It's an answering service."

"What's this, then?"

"The phone at the drilling site south of here in Brazoria County. You can reach me there day or night."

"Don't you ever go home?"

"That is home. Once we start making hole — drilling, in layman's terms — I'm there around the clock," he explained, glancing at her sideways, a lazy gleam in his eyes challenging her. "Have you ever seen a rig in operation, Miss Lawson?"

"Lots of times. This is Texas," Abbie asserted, then smiled in mock chagrin. "Of course, I've seen them all from the road."

"For a Texan — and R. D. Lawson's granddaughter — your education has been sadly neglected."

"I suppose it has," she conceded lightly, feeling oddly invigorated by his company — really alive for the first time in a long while. She wondered if he felt the same. But he had a face like her grandpa's. It only revealed what he wanted it to.

"Want to correct that with a tour?"

"With you as the guide?"

"You guessed it. If you're not busy after lunch tomorrow, come out to the site. I'll show you around." He supplied her with concise directions as they reached the cab of his truck. "You can see the mast from the road, so you can't miss it."

"It doesn't sound like it. I'll see you tomorrow, then."

He nodded and climbed into the dusty black truck and pulled the door shut. As he started the engine, Abbie stepped farther back and lifted her head in acknowledgment of the casual, one-fingered salute he flicked in her direction. Then he reversed the truck away from the stables and swung it toward the lane.

"Another visitor?" Ben Jablonski spoke beside her.

Abbie turned with a start. The noise of the truck's engine had drowned out the sound of his footsteps. She hadn't heard him walk up behind her. "Yes," she replied absently and glanced back at the dust being churned up by the departing truck, then realized what Ben was implying by his phrase "another visitor." "You saw her," she stated.

"Yes."

"Why do you think she came here?"

"Perhaps she was curious."

"Maybe." But Abbie doubted it, the feeling again returning that her world was being threatened. As the grimness and tension came back, she turned toward the stables. "I think I'll go check on Breeze."

The oil industry had changed considerably since its early boom days when the famed Spindletop gusher turned Houston into a city and a center of the oil industry with its inland port, oil refineries, and petrochemical plants. Technological and scientific advancements had brought more sophisticated equipment and techniques into use. Environmental and federal controls had reduced pollution and waste, and increased costs. Demand and deregulation of oil and natural gas prices had sent the world price of crude oil soaring in 1980 to more than thirty dollars a barrel, with predictions of future prices reaching fifty, sixty, maybe even seventy dollars a barrel.

One factor remained constant: the key role played by the independent oil men, the wildcatters. They still drilled the vast majority of test wells in the exploration for new fields, as high as nine times the number drilled by the giant oil companies. The wildcatters were responsible for some 80 percent of the gas and oil discoveries in the United States.

Few, if any, wildcatters absorbed the full cost of drilling. They spread their risk, selling off percentages of ownership to the majors or other independents, giving up percentages to the landowner or the drilling contractor or both, and selling limited partnerships to private investors. The successful ones were cautious and conservative gamblers.

MacCrea Wilder might call himself a drilling contractor, but Abbie knew better. She'd listened to too many discussions between her ex-husband and his banker father not to know that most financial institutions were reluctant to speculate on newcomers. They wanted to look at a wildcatter's track record and examine his staying power. With his small deals here and ownership percentages there, MacCrea was establishing a performance record in wildcatting and generating royalties that were both an asset and an ongoing cash flow. His drilling company gave him an independent income and a business history, as well as knowledge and experience in the field.

When everyone from mail-order promoters to lease brokers called themselves wildcatters, Abbie wondered why MacCrea played it so low-key. She smiled at herself, amused by her own curiosity about him. There was no doubt that the man had thoroughly aroused her interest.

In every direction she looked, the scenery was all sky, a blue dome towering over the flat coastal prairie of cropland, broken now and then only by a ground-hugging farmhouse occasionally shaded by a lonely tree. A crop-dusting plane swooped low over a rice field, releasing its white misty trail of pesticide or herbicide, then buzzing her red Mercedes convertible before climbing higher, giving the pilot an eyeful of the dark-haired beauty behind the wheel, dressed in a simple backless sundress in royal purple, belted at the waist with a chain of silver conchos, lizard-skin sandals on her feet.

Still smiling thoughtfully, Abbie returned the pilot's wave and continued down the road, speeding by a pasture scattered with slow-bobbing pumpjacks rhythmically drawing crude oil from completed wells. She watched the horizon to her right, looking for the distinctive iron skeleton of an oil derrick. According to MacCrea's directions, she should see it any minute now.

Suddenly there it was, poking its head up about a mile off the main road. She slowed the car, anticipating the turnoff that would take her to the drill site. Less than a quarter-mile ahead, a gray-white strip converged on the highway at a right angle. Abbie turned onto the road spread with oyster shells and followed its straight line to the iron-ribbed tower in the distance.

The tall derrick dominated the drill site from its perch atop the substructure platform. Sprawled at its feet were the support components: the diesel engines that powered the rig, the racks of pipe stacked in layers, the mud pumps and pits along with their auxiliary equipment, the fuel tanks, and the onsite office trailers. All were interconnected by a system of walkways and stairs.

More than a half-dozen vehicles were parked in the clearing that surrounded the drilling rig. Abbie parked her Mercedes in the space next to MacCrea's black pickup. The steady roar of the diesel engines covered the slam of her car door as she paused to look around. Several workers were in sight, but none of them seemed to notice her arrival. Without the cooling draft of the moving car, the heat became oppressive. She tucked her hair behind her ears, grateful for the turquoise sweatband across her forehead.

As she started toward the nearest office trailer, MacCrea stepped out, dressed in a pair of blue-green coveralls and a hard hat. Right behind him came a second man, dressed in street clothes — a print shirt and tan trousers — but wearing the requisite hard hat.

"Hello." She walked over to MacCrea, glancing questioningly in his companion's direction. "Have I come at a bad time?"

"Not at all," he replied and introduced her to the on-site representative of the major oil company that had contracted the drilling of the well. "Like me, Chuck lives on the site," MacCrea explained, gesturing over his shoulder at the trailer behind them. "I promised Miss Lawson I'd give her a tour of the operation."

"Be my guest. Anyone who's been in the business any length of time at all has heard about your grandfather. Here." He removed his safety helmet and offered it to Abbie. "You'll need this."

"Thanks." Like them, she had to speak louder to make herself heard clearly above the steady din from the power plant and the equipment in operation.

After MacCrea had adjusted the inner band of the hat to fit her and set it on her head, they started out along the walkway. He took her by the mud pits first, showing her the heavy gray-brown fluid that had been the basis of her family's fortune. He explained how the mud was pumped from the pits through a discharge line to the vertically mounted standpipe on the near leg of the derrick (properly called a mast, since it needed no assembly), and from there it entered the kelly hose down the kelly, the drill pipe and collar exiting at the bit at the bottom of the hole. Abbie discovered that, with all the noise in the background, it was easier to understand everything he said if she read his lips, too.

From the mud pits, they traveled down the elevated walkways to the steel pipe that carried the mud and bit cuttings circulating out of the hole and dumped them onto a vibrating screen called a shale shaker. He pointed out the raised earthen pits behind it where the cuttings were dumped after being extracted from the mud. The mud was recycled back to the pits after passing through some other processes that Abbie didn't follow completely — although that was only indirectly MacCrea's fault. He introduced her to the mud engineer on the site, and when he learned that he was talking to R. D. Lawson's granddaughter, his explanations became very technical.

"You made a big impression on him," MacCrea observed dryly as they headed for the stairs leading to the rig's raised platform. "He'll be bragging to everybody how he explained modern drilling-fluid methods to R. D. Lawson's granddaughter."

"Too bad I didn't understand any of it."

At the bottom of the narrow set of stairs, MacCrea paused and let her go in front of him. As Abbie mounted the steps, she was conscious of the beads of sweat forming above her upper lip — and of the curious glances from the crew when she reached the top. She paused to let MacCrea take the lead again.

"The floor of a rig isn't the cleanest place in the world. There should be an extra pair of coveralls in the doghouse." He directed her to the small storage shed atop the platform a short distance from the stairs. Inside the storehouse, he took a pair of blue-green coveralls, like his, off a hook and handed them to her. "They aren't the latest fashion, but at least they'll keep your clothes from getting dirty."

Abbie could tell just by looking at them that they were too big and too long, but she put them on anyway and rolled up the pant legs. She felt like one of those clowns in baggy pants, and judging by the gleam in MacCrea's eyes, she looked like one, too.

But he was right: the floor of the rig around the hole was slopped with the grayish mud. There was relatively little activity at the moment. MacCrea introduced her to the driller, who operated the drilling machinery from his control console and supervised the work of the other floormen. She met a couple of the rotary helpers, too, known as roughnecks in the old days.

MacCrea attempted to explain some of the equipment and its uses, but by the time he got done talking about monkeyboards, catheads, ratholes, catwalks, and mouseholes, Abbie wasn't sure whether she was on a drilling rig or at a zoo.

Her head was pounding from the noise, heat, and mental confusion when they finally descended the steps back to the ground. She felt the guiding pressure of his hand between her shoulders and glanced up, wondering what he could possibly want to show her now. He pointed at the near trailer. She walked to it gladly.

As he opened the door for her, she felt the blessed coolness of air-conditioning and practically ran inside. There she paused and gratefully swept off the hot helmet and her sweatband, shaking her damp hair loose with a toss of her head. As the door closed behind her, muffling most of the rig's noise, the telephone on the desk started ringing. Abbie stepped out of the way as MacCrea walked over to answer it.

"Wilder Drilling."

Abbie unzipped the protective coveralls as she glanced around the Spartan office. A pair of filing cabinets stood against the wall behind his desk. A Naugahyde sofa that showed the abuse of the drill site faced it from the opposite wall. Two straight-backed chairs completed the furnishings. The paneled walls were blank except for a framed photograph propped against the paneling on top of a filing cabinet.

"Yeah, Red. Just a minute." MacCrea covered the phone's mouthpiece with his hand. "There's not a lot I can offer you in the way of refreshments, but there's a little kitchen through that door. The coffee in the pot is probably black syrup by now. If you want to make fresh, go ahead. There's beer in the refrigerator and a jar of instant tea in the cupboard. Help yourself."

"Thanks." Abbie stepped out of the coveralls and laid them across one of the straight chairs, her own clothes sticking to her skin.

The trailer rocked slightly as she crossed to the door, already partway ajar, and pushed it the rest of the way open. The cupboards, range top, and sink took up one short wall in the compact kitchen, with the refrigerator against the opposite wall. A table and two chairs took up the rest of the floor space. Beyond the kitchen a door leading to the rear of the trailer stood open. Unable to resist the opportunity to explore, Abbie peeked to see what was back there.

A bed, its covers all rumpled, hugged one wall. Opposite it was a built-in dresser next to a closet. Beyond it the door to a small bathroom stood open. She realized MacCrea had been serious when he said he lived here.

In the kitchen she fixed herself a glass of iced tea, then, on impulse, made one for MacCrea, adding sugar to both, and carried them into the office. He smiled his thanks when she handed it to him and took a long drink before continuing his conversation on the telephone.

Sipping at her own, Abbie wandered over to take a closer look at the photograph on the filing cabinet. A much younger MacCrea smiled back at her, minus the mustache he now wore. She was struck by the differences between the MacCrea she knew and the one in this picture. An occasional lazy gleam had replaced the laughter shining out of the dark eyes in the photograph. The same lean, strong features were in the picture, but they hadn't been honed to a hardness yet; the lines and creases were missing. She had no impression of determination or inner toughness when she looked at this younger version of MacCrea. This one had the world by the tail, and was ready to whip it into shape.

Curious, she shifted her attention to the older man who MacCrea had his arm around. He, too, grinned proudly at her, almost hiding the tiredness in his weathered face. Abbie saw the resemblance between them, and realized the older man had to be MacCrea's father. The love between them was obvious to anyone looking at the photograph. Abbie felt a sudden stab of envy, followed by a twisting pain from her own loss — a loss rooted in more than just the death of her father, but in the bitter discovery and disillusionment that came after as well.

"Yeah, I'll talk to you later, Red." MacCrea hung up the phone, the chair squeaking as he pushed out of it. Abbie continued to stare at the photograph, giving herself time to control that sudden surge of resentment.

"That's your father, isn't it?" The ice cubes clinked in her glass as she used the hand holding it to indicate the picture.

"Yes. It was taken a month before he died." Taking a drink from his tea, MacCrea turned away from the filing cabinet and the photograph. Again, Abbie noticed the total lack of emotion in his voice when he referred to his father or, more specifically, his death. She sensed it was something he didn't like to discuss. "Sorry about the interruption. That was my toolpusher on another site, filling me in on their progress."

"A toolpusher." She felt inundated by the flood of new terms she'd heard in the last two hours. She was amazed by how much she'd thought she knew about the oil business, when she actually knew practically nothing.

"A toolpusher is in charge of the entire drilling operation and coordinates everything with the company man. That's temporarily my job here," he explained. "My regular man is in the hospital with a broken leg. Normally I'm not tied to one site like this."

Abbie caught herself watching his lips when he talked. Slightly disconcerted that she had allowed the practice to carry over from the tour of the drilling operation, she quickly averted her glance, focusing it instead on the iced-tea glass in his hand. Immediately she noticed the peculiar crooking of his little finger, its suggestion of daintiness completely at odds with the smooth toughness conveyed by the rest of him.

"Why does your little finger bend like that?" She thought it might have been broken at some time.

"This?" He glanced down at it, his mouth quirking, tilting one side of his mustache as he lifted a shoulder in a shrug of indifference. "I was born with a shortened tendon in the first joint. It's a family trait."

"I wondered," she admitted, smiling.

The trailer door opened behind them, letting in the noise from outside. As

Abbie turned toward it, one of the roughnecks poked his head inside. "We got a kick, boss."

In the next second, MacCrea was brushing past her, shoving his tea glass on the desktop and grabbing up his hard hat as he went by. "Does the company know?"

"Not yet," the roughneck replied, pulling back as MacCrea charged out the door.

"Tell him," MacCrea ordered, his tone sharp and abrupt.

She didn't understand what was going on. Why had he sent for the company man? Had they hit oil? Intrigued by the possibility, she hurried to the door before it swung shut, reaching it in time to see MacCrea bounding up the steps to the rig floor, covering them two at a time. Abbie started to run after him, then remembered she didn't have her safety helmet on. When she went back for it, she saw the coveralls on the chair. She hesitated briefly, then pulled them on over her clothes and hurried out the door, still struggling with the stubborn zipper.

By the time she reached the raised metal platform, MacCrea was standing off to one side, holding a conference with the company man, Kruse, and the mud engineer. Everyone else seemed to be just standing around, waiting. Then Abbie noticed that the level of noise had fallen off and saw that the rotary table wasn't turning. She realized they'd stopped drilling. But she still didn't know what that meant.

She walked over to MacCrea to ask him. None of the three men paid any attention to her at first, too intent on their discussion, which was totally beyond her limited knowledge. MacCrea glanced briefly in her direction, his brow furrowed in concentration as he kept his attention focused on the mud man.

Suddenly he shot another look at her, and recognition turned into anger. "What the hell are you doing here?" In two strides, he had her by the arm.

"I was just—" Abbie tried to explain as he roughly spun her around and propelled her toward the stairs.

"You get back to that trailer and you stay there! Do you read me, lady?"

"Yes, I—" She was stunned by the anger that seethed from him, as palpable as the sun's burning heat.

"Then get going," he snapped, shoving her down the steps.

Abbie grabbed at the rail to stop herself from falling, wrenching the muscles in her left shoulder and arm in the process. When she regained her footing, MacCrea was gone. Embarrassed that others had witnessed her rude eviction from the premises, Abbie ran the rest of the way down the steps and walked back to the trailer, holding herself stiffly erect.

The minute she set foot inside the trailer, she rubbed her aching arm and nursed her wounded ego, her embarrassment turning to indignant anger. She stripped off the coveralls and the hard hat, dumping them both on top of his desk. She started pacing about the room, letting her anger build.

Abbie had no idea how long she waited in the trailer before he returned, but she knew it was a long time—more than enough time for her to have cooled off, but she hadn't. She was boiling mad when he opened the door and walked in.

She didn't even give him time to shut it before she launched into him. "Just who the hell do you think you are, pushing me around like that?" He looked tired and hot, sweat making dark spots on the front of his coveralls and under his arms, but she didn't care.

"You had no business being there," he muttered, shouldering his way by her, barely even glancing at her.

"And just how was I supposed to know that?" She followed him, addressing her demanding question to his back as he swept off his hard hat and combed his fingers through the curly thickness of his dark hair. "You never said anything to me. You just barged out of here without so much as a word to me."

MacCrea swung around, glowering at her. "Dammit, you heard Pete say we had a kick!"

"You had a kick." She longed to give him one. "Hasn't it occurred to you that I don't know what that is? And I still don't. But did you bother to explain? No. You —"

"So it's another damned lesson you want, is it? Well, honey, you damned near got more than that. A well 'kicks' just before it blows out. Have you ever seen a well blow?"

Taken aback by his explanation, and the danger it implied, Abbie lost some of her anger. "No. But I've heard —" she began, considerably subdued.

"You've heard," he mocked sarcastically. "Well, honey, I've *seen*. And let me tell you, it isn't a pretty sight. You don't know what's down in that hole — gas, saltwater, or oil — or maybe all three. And you don't know how much pressure it's packing. Whether it's got enough to blow you and your rig sky-high. Or if it's gonna be a ball of fire. You could have been standing on a damned powder keg out there."

"Well, I obviously wasn't," Abbie retorted. "I'm still standing here. Nothing happened."

"Nothing happened." He repeated her words through clenched teeth as he seized the undersides of her jaws, the heel of his hand pressing itself against her throat. For an instant, Abbie was too startled to resist. "I ought to —"

"Wring your neck" was what she expected him to say, but it never came out as he suddenly crushed his mouth onto her lips, brutally grinding them against her teeth, shocking her into immobility. After interminable seconds, the pressure eased. Short of breath and with racing heartbeat, Abbie waited for his mouth to lift from hers. But it lingered there, motionless, maintaining a light contact but nothing more. Cautiously, she looked at him through her lashes. He was watching her, the fiery blackness in his eyes reduced to a smoldering light that strangely bothered her more than his anger.

Then he broke all contact and turned, stepping away from her. He stopped with his back to her and sighed heavily, his hands resting on his hips. "Would it make any difference if I apologized?" he asked, almost grudgingly.

"Only if you choked on it." She was trembling, but she was faking her anger now.

"Good." He swung around to face her, his features set in grim lines. "I won't have to say something I don't mean. The method I used to get you off the drilling floor might not have been polite, but you have to admit it was effective. And I didn't have to waste a lot of time on explanations — time I couldn't afford. As for kissing you —"

"That wasn't a kiss."

"Maybe it wasn't," he conceded. "But you wouldn't have liked the alternative any better. I have enough problems right now out there without getting the riot act read to me by you all because of your damned ignorance and hurt pride. So if you'll excuse me, I have a lot of work to do."

As he turned and opened one of the file-cabinet drawers, Abbie walked blindly out the door, stung by the things he'd said and hating him for making her feel so wretched, when he'd been the one at fault.

12

AWED BY THE EXPENSIVE decor in the penthouse, Rachel wandered into the spacious living room, artfully done in a subtle blending of gray, peach, and cream. It was like something out of the decorating magazines, everything precisely arranged with an eye for symmetry and balance. Nothing gaudy or overdone, just an understated elegance.

Her glance was drawn to the large windows that overlooked the city. Rachel walked over to them, anticipating the panoramic view of Houston at sunset, the glass-walled towers reflecting the sky's fuchsia hues, and the first dull glow of the streetlights far below.

"What do you think?" Lane came to stand beside her.

"Breathtaking," she said, then looked at him and smiled. "And fitting, too, to have Houston at your feet."

"I don't know about that last part," he replied.

His modesty was sincere. During the few times she'd seen him, Rachel had discovered that was one of his traits. Sometimes it was difficult to remember that this was only the third time she'd seen him, counting the funeral. The feeling was so strong that she'd always known him. She admired that confidence he exuded, never overtly, always calmly. She liked him. Sometimes she worried that she liked him too much.

"You've been so kind to me, Lane." She didn't want to misinterpret that kindness, to build her hopes too high.

"It is extremely easy to be kind to a beautiful woman, Rachel. Don't misunderstand me. I didn't invite you to dine with me this evening out of any sense of obligation to your father. I wanted your company."

Rachel believed that. The first time he'd asked her to have lunch with him, she had thought he'd invited her to fulfill some duty he felt he owed her father. The first may have been an obligatory gesture, but not the second. She could tell he wasn't patronizing her. His interest seemed genuine. Truthfully she was flattered . . . and a little thrilled that a man of Lane Canfield's standing would want to spend his time with her. It made her feel important.

That's why her minor shopping expedition into Houston today had turned into a major one. None of the clothes in her closet had looked suitable; all of them were too casual, appropriate for California maybe, but not for dinner with

Lane Canfield. She'd spent the better part of the morning and early afternoon combing the shops in the Galleria, looking for something sophisticated yet simple, this time not letting price sway her.

Finally she'd found this white linen suit with a matching camisole top on a sale rack. Its lines were simple and timeless, yet the epaulets of pearls on the padded shoulders gave it that touch of elegance Rachel had wanted.

After buying the evening suit and the accessories to go with it, she'd gotten up enough nerve to take the final plunge and stopped at the Neiman-Marcus salon to have a complete makeover done by one of their beauty consultants. A woman named Karen had shown her how to use makeup to soften her features, add fullness to her lips, and bring out the blue of her eyes. She had her hair cut to shoulder length and styled to curl softly about her face. For the first time in her life, she felt sophisticated and confident enough about her appearance to accompany Lane to the most exclusive restaurant in Houston. But what could be more exclusive than his penthouse apartment in Houston's Magic Circle?

"I have to confess, Lane, that I didn't accept because you were a friend of Dean's. I came because . . . I like being with you." Rachel felt bold saying that, but she wanted him to know her true feelings.

"It's mutual, Rachel. I can't begin to tell you how much I enjoy being with you. If I did, you'd start thinking I was a lecherous old man."

"No. Never that." She didn't like it when he talked about himself that way. She had never felt so comfortable with any man before. The men she'd dated seemed like immature boys in comparison — not that she had ever dated all that much.

"It's a curious thing, the way the aging process works. Chronologically the body gets older, but the mind — well, I think and feel about twenty years younger." He smiled, his eyes crinkling at the corners the way she liked. "To put it in your vernacular, when I'm with you, I feel like a young stallion."

She laughed softly. "I hope not. Young stallions can behave so foolishly at times."

"Maybe that's what worries me, Rachel. That I am being foolish where you're concerned."

Behind the quiet statement, there was a question. Rachel heard it and felt the sudden skittering of her pulse in reaction. She wasn't any good at being coy and flirtatious. Abbie probably was, but Rachel couldn't think of anything flattering or witty to say. She had to resort to the truth.

"I don't think you are." She practically whispered her reply, conscious of how much she was admitting about her own feelings toward him. She gazed at his face, liking the lines that gave it so much character. They told so much about the man he was: his strength, his confidence, and his sense of humor — although there was little evidence of the latter in his expression at the moment as he studied her intently.

"I hope you mean that," he said.

She felt the light grip of his hands on her arms, bunching the thick shoulder pads of her boxy jacket. He drew her gently toward him. The warm touch of his lips was firm and persuasive, not demanding a response, yet seeking one.

Hesitantly she returned his kiss, letting her lips move against his while controlling her ardor, not wanting to appear gauchely eager to a man as experienced and worldly as Lane Canfield. Tentatively she let her hands touch the sides of his waist, the rich fabric of his jacket feeling like silk beneath her fingers.

His hands glided onto her back, his arms folding around her to draw her closer still, and his kiss now spoke to Rachel of need and want, two emotions she felt in abundance. She answered him, warmth spreading through and filling her body. As her breathing deepened, she inhaled the masculine fragrance of his cologne. It was neither musk nor spice nor citrus, but some exotic blend that made her feel almost giddy.

Someone in the room coughed delicately, but the sound hit Rachel with all the shattering force of a lightning bolt as she realized they weren't alone. She jerked from the kiss and averted her face, hot with embarrassment. Lane loosened the circle of his arms while retaining a light hold on her.

"Yes, Henley. What is it?" Lane sounded tolerant, not the least upset by the intrusion of his butler. Then Rachel recalled that he'd introduced Henley as his houseman, although the man's aloof bearing, his cordial impassivity, had reminded her of a butler.

"A telephone call, sir. I believe it's somewhat urgent."

"I'll be there directly." Lane dismissed him and returned his attention to Rachel.

She didn't know what she was supposed to say or do in a situation like this. Then she was doubly mortified by the discovery that her fingers were clutching his jacket. She would have looked ridiculous if he'd tried to leave just then. Hastily she let go as her face felt as if it had caught fire. Lane tucked a finger under her chin and gently turned her face toward him. Rachel tried to look at him, but her glance skipped away from the amusement that glinted in his eyes.

"You blush beautifully," he murmured.

"I'm sorry." She felt dreadfully inadequate. She had tried so hard to appear sophisticated so he would like her and respect her, but she had failed miserably. She always did.

"Why?"

"You must think I'm naïve."

"Because you were embarrassed when Henley walked in right in the middle of our kiss?"

She nodded.

"My dear, I would have been disappointed if you weren't. I considered that kiss to be special and private — not something to be shared with others. You obviously did, too, and I'm glad."

He started to kiss her lightly, but their lips clung moistly together, unwilling to part. Rachel wanted it to go on, to recapture that warm feeling that had just started to grow inside her when the last kiss was so abruptly halted, but she couldn't block out the image of formal and proper Henley hovering somewhere out of sight, waiting, knowing what he'd seen and what their silence meant. Reluctantly she drew back.

"Your telephone call," she said.

"Ah, yes." With a rueful smile, he let her go. "I won't be long."

"Is he there?" Babs Lawson anxiously hovered close to Abbie's shoulder.

"Yes. He's being called to the phone right now." Absently she twisted the receiver cord around her fingers, her impatience growing with the lengthening delay. "Before I forget, tell Jackson we'll need another place setting for dinner tonight, Momma. Dobie Hix will be joining us."

"He will? Why?"

"Because I invited him," Abbie snapped, then sighed, realizing that she'd been snapping at everyone since she'd come back from the drilling site. "He came by the stables this afternoon and I decided to ask him to stay for dinner." She didn't mention the broad hints Dobie had made . . . or the unpaid hay bill.

"If we're having company, maybe I should have Jackson get out the good china. What do you think?" She made it sound as if it were a major decision that required discussion.

"I doubt that Dobie would know the difference. Do whatever you want, Momma." She had too much on her mind to be bothered with such trivial things. Distracted by her mother, Abbie almost missed hearing the voice on the other end of the line. "Hello. Lane?" She tightened her grip on the receiver.

"Yes."

"This is Abbie Lawson." She didn't waste time apologizing for bothering him at his home but went straight to the point. "We've been receiving quite a number of phone calls from creditors wanting to know when they'll get their money."

"Give them my office number and tell them to call me. I'll handle it." His response was too pat. It irritated her; nearly everything did.

"That's what we've been doing. But . . . how long will it be before they're paid?"

There was a lengthy pause at the other end of the line. Abbie sensed that, at last, she had his full attention. "Why don't I come out to River Bend on Thursday," he finally said. "That way I can sit down with both you and your mother and explain the situation to you."

"The sooner the better."

"Yes. I'll see you then. And give Babs my regards."

"I will." But the line had already clicked dead. Abbie frowned and replaced the receiver on its cradle, wondering why she didn't feel relieved. That long pause, the strange tone of his voice before he'd hung up — they troubled her.

"What did Lane say?"

Abbie shot a brief glance at her mother. "He sent you his regards and . . . said he'd be down on Thursday to talk to both of us."

"I'm glad. This is all so embarrassing — the phone calls and the questions."

"I know, Momma." Abbie nodded.

As good as his word, Lane was back within minutes of leaving her alone in the living room. But Rachel noticed immediately how preoccupied he looked, not anything like the smiling, jaunty man who'd left the room.

"Is something wrong?" Her question seemed to startle him out of his reverie.

Quickly he fixed a smile on his face, but she noticed that it didn't extend to his eyes. "No. Nothing at all. Just a business matter." He reached to take her hand. "Henley informed me that dinner can be served whenever we're ready. Are you hungry?"

"Yes." She let him lead her into the dining room.

The table was set for two, replete with white candles burning in silver holders and champagne chilling in a silver ice bucket. On one of the china plates lay a long-stemmed red rose. Henley pulled the chair away from the table directly in front of it and held it for her.

"See how optimistic I was tonight?" Lane said as Rachel scooted her chair closer to the table with Henley's assistance. "Candles, champagne, roses, and privacy." Henley popped the champagne cork from the bottle with a practiced *whoosh*. Lane glanced at him, then back to Rachel, and smiled faintly. "Well, almost privacy."

Rachel tried to hide her smile, even though Henley gave no indication that he'd heard a single word Lane had said. He filled their glasses with champagne, then retreated from the room via a side door.

"To a beautiful evening, and a beautiful lady." Lane lifted his wineglass and Rachel touched hers to it, the melodic tinkle of crystal ringing softly in the air. She sipped the champagne, noticing over the rim of her glass how thoughtful Lane had become again. This time he caught himself. "I was just thinking — wondering is probably a better word — whether you'd like to have dinner with me again this Friday night. I'll be tied up probably all of Thursday at River Bend. Otherwise —"

"I'd like to, yes." Rachel rushed her acceptance, still debating whether she should mention her own visit to River Bend. She decided against it, unwilling to recall how unwanted — and uncomfortable — she'd been made to feel.

13

AFTER BEN HAD BROKEN the news to the half-dozen stable hands, Abbie stepped forward to explain the situation to them. She knew she was in an awkward position, and their stunned, quizzical looks didn't make her task any easier. She slipped her fingers into the side pockets of her jodhpurs, trying to appear relaxed and in control despite the tension she felt.

"We want you to know that your layoffs are temporary. It's obvious that we need help to take care of all these horses. Unfortunately, until my father's estate is settled, we don't have the cash available to pay you. It's legally tied up by the court." Abbie doubted that they understood the judicial system or the inheritance laws any better than she did. "We can't ask you to continue to work at the farm and wait until later to receive your wages. We know you all have families." Still, she had her fingers crossed that some of them would volunteer to stay on.

"How long do you think this will be before we can get our jobs back?" Manny Ortega inquired in his heavy Spanish accent, his brow furrowed in a troubled frown.

"I don't know." Lane Canfield had been reluctant to speculate on that when he'd spoken with Abbie and her mother that morning. She saw the discontented shakes of their heads. "Maybe six weeks," she held out hopefully.

But their expressions didn't change as they nervously fingered the pay envelopes Ben had passed out to them. Three of the stable hands glanced at Manny, looking to him to be their spokesman. "You will let us know when to come back, no? Señor Jablonski will call us?"

"Yes, he'll call." Nettled by their reaction, Abbie watched them as they shuffled off to their vehicles, where they congregated briefly to talk among themselves, then went their separate ways.

"How bad is the problem?" Ben stood beside her.

"It's just a temporary situation," she insisted. "Nearly all Dad's personal and business accounts are frozen." Lane had explained it in more detail, but that was the gist of it. "We knew we were short on funds, but we expected to get a check from the insurance company. Now, we've learned that Dad cashed his life insurance policy last year and neglected to tell anyone."

"Why was this done?"

"I don't know. It's spilt milk now." Abbie shrugged. "We don't have it and we're not going to get it. And what with Dad's law practice, the farm, and his personal finances, things are in a tangle. Lane says it's going to take longer to sort them all out than he first thought. The loss of the insurance money is just frustrating, that's all. We'll make it . . . in spite of them." With a jerk of her head, she indicated the vehicles driving out of the yard.

"What did you expect them to do?"

"I thought Manny would stay. He's worked here for six years steady."

"He has a family to feed," Ben reminded her with his usual tolerance, but he recognized the signs that indicated her mood was turning argumentative. From the time she was a child, she reacted this way when things went wrong. It was as if she had to pick a fight with someone to release her pent-up anger and frustration.

"Maybe. But it just proves to me that a man's loyalty is bought." At the moment, Abbie didn't care how angry or cynical she sounded.

A pickup drove into the yard, dust swirling around it like an enveloping fog. At first glance, she thought it was Manny's truck, that he'd changed his mind and come back. But that hope came crashing down when she recognized MacCrea Wilder's black pickup even before he stepped out of it.

All too clearly, she remembered the way he'd treated her the last time she'd seen him. She felt her temper rising and didn't even try to control it as she strode across the stable yard to confront him. He paused beside the truck's tailgate to wait for her, letting her come to him — which irritated Abbie even more.

"Afternoon, Miss Lawson." His words were polite, but his look was icy-cool.

"Don't tell me you've reconsidered and decided to apologize for your rude-ness — or should I say 'crudeness' — the other day," she chided, sarcasm in her voice as she relished the opportunity to make him squirm.

"You mentioned the other day you might know some people I could talk to about the computerized test system I've developed. I came by to get their names from you, if you have them."

The man's gall amazed her. "A couple of them did call me back this last week," she informed him, although she had deliberately not mentioned his project to Lane Canfield. "But I'm not about to give their names to someone like you. I don't help someone who has manhandled me. I thought you would have guessed that."

MacCrea breathed in deeply, then released it slowly, eyeing her coolly all the while. "So you still think I owe you an apology? All right. I'm sorry I was even remotely concerned for your safety. As you pointed out, nothing happened. Of course, if the well had blown, you'd be thanking me for saving your life even though you were 'manhandled' in the process."

Abruptly he pivoted and walked back to the cab of his truck, leaving her standing there, struggling to come up with some cutting retort, but she couldn't summon any of her previous venom as he climbed in the cab and slammed the door. As much as she hated to admit it, MacCrea was right. If the outcome had been different, she would have been grateful.

He didn't even glance in her direction as he drove away. Abbie lingered, watching until his truck disappeared down the winding lane. Then, slowly, she walked to the house.

With twilight only a couple of hours away, the shadow racing beside Abbie's Mercedes was long. A sheet of paper with the names and phone numbers of two men who had expressed an interest in MacCrea's invention lay on the passenger seat next to her.

The turnoff to the drill site came quicker than she expected. Abbie braked sharply to make it, the front tires grabbing at the oyster shells as the rear end started to fishtail on the loose surface, but she made the turn.

When she reached the drill site, the activity there appeared normal. She knew, even before MacCrea had told her, that once drilling was started, three separate crews worked round-the-clock shifts until the contracted depth was reached. She parked her car beside MacCrea's pickup in front of his office trailer, picked up the paper from the passenger seat, and stepped out.

Still dressed in her jodhpurs and riding boots, she paused in front of the trailer door and took a deep, steadying breath. She had never found it easy to swallow her pride. Most times she preferred to choke on it. She knocked twice on the metal door, then opened it, doubting that her knock could be heard above the noise from the drilling operation.

As she walked in, she saw MacCrea sitting behind the desk, a bottle of beer in front of him. She hesitated, then pulled the door shut behind her. He rocked back in his chair, staring at her with his dark, impenetrable eyes, his features showing no discernible expression. Then his attention shifted to the bottle of beer as he picked it up.

"What do you want here?"

What had she expected? Abbie wondered. A red carpet rolled out for her? She gripped the paper a little tighter and crossed to his desk.

"I brought you those names you wanted." She managed to inject an air of bravado into her answer as she held out the paper to him.

"Just lay it on the desk." He took a swig of beer and turned the chair sideways, then rolled out of it to walk to the file cabinet, as if dismissing her.

She felt a surge of anger and clamped down on it tightly, reminding herself that she had come to apologize, not to clash with him again. She glanced down at the scatter of papers and reports on his desk.

"Just anywhere?" Abbie challenged.

"Yup. I'll find it." He opened a metal file drawer and started riffling through its folders.

As she started to lay the paper on his desk, she noticed the rough draft of a lease agreement for the mineral rights to a piece of property. She'd seen too many of those forms at her father's law office not to recognize it. She laid her sheet down and picked the document up.

"What's this? Are you planning to drill your own well?" She skimmed the first page, noting that the legal description referred to a piece of property in Ascension Parish in Louisiana.

The trailer shook slightly under the force of the single, long stride Mac-Crea took to carry him to her side. "My plans are my business," he said curtly, taking the document from her and laying it back down on the desk. "Now, if you're through snooping, the door is behind you."

"I didn't come here just to bring you those names." She touched the edge of his desk, hating the awkwardness she felt. "I could have easily mailed them to you."

"Why didn't you?"

Stiffening at the challenging tone of his voice, Abbie tipped her head back to look at him. No matter how she might try, her pride wouldn't let her appear humbly contrite.

"I came to apologize," she retorted. "I know that this afternoon, and the other day, too, I behaved—"

"—like a horse's ass," MacCrea broke in, his mouth crooking in a humor-less smile. "Remember, I told you I knew that end of a horse when I saw it."

Abbie forgot her carefully rehearsed speech as anger rushed in. "Dammit, MacCrea, I'm trying to apologize to you. You're not exactly making it easy."

"No easier than you made things for me."

It didn't help to know that he was right. Somehow she managed to get her temper under control, however grudgingly. "All right, I was an ass today—"

"I'm glad you agree."

Swallowing the angry response that rose in her throat, Abbie glared at him. "For your information, just before you arrived today, I had to lay off all our stable help and most of our servants at the house because we don't have the cash to meet their payroll until my father's estate is settled. Now, maybe that doesn't excuse the way I behaved to you, but I wasn't in the best of moods when you showed up. I know it was probably wrong to take my frustrations out on you, but . . . that's what I did. And I'm sorry," she finished on a slightly more subdued note, not really understanding why she had told him about their financial problems except that he'd provoked her.

"I didn't know."

Uneasy under his contemplative gaze, Abbie stared at the desktop. "How could you? Any more than I could know there was any real danger the other day. You could have explained it a little better. You know, you're not exactly a saint either, MacCrea."

"I never claimed to be," he reminded her.

"Look, I came here to apologize, not to get into another argument with you. I hoped—" What had she hoped? That he'd understand the vagaries of her temper when no one else did, not even herself? That maybe he'd feel sorry for her because financially they were having problems? That maybe they could start fresh without this hostility? "I hoped you'd accept that."

For an unbearably long second, there was only silence. Then MacCrea offered his hand to her. "Apology accepted, Abbie."

She hesitated a fraction of a second, then fit her hand into the grasp of his and watched as it became lost when his fingers closed around it, leaving only her thumb in view. His skin was brown as leather, a contrast to the tanned, golden color of her own. The calloused roughness of his fingers reminded her of the pleasant rasp of a cat's tongue against her skin. She looked up to discover his eyes watching her closely. Something in their depths made her pulse quicken.

"How about a beer to wash the bad taste from your mouth?" A smile tugged at the corners of his mouth.

Abbie smiled back, discovering that even though the apology had been difficult to get out, it hadn't left any sour aftertaste on her tongue. "I'd like one."

"Make yourself comfortable while I get your beer." He gestured at the tan Naugahyde sofa.

As MacCrea disappeared into the trailer's compact kitchen, Abbie settled onto the sofa, turning to sit sideways on the cushion and hooking a booted toe behind her right knee. When he returned, he held an empty glass and the long necks of two bottles of beer. Unconsciously she studied him as he approached her, taking in the width of his shoulders and the narrowness of his hips. His dark, almost black hair was thick and wavy, a little on the shaggy side, but that seemed to suit him. Yet it was his face, with its hard strength stamped in the sculpted bones of his cheek and the carved slant of his jaw, that she found so compelling. She kept wanting to describe the bluntly chiseled angles and planes of his features as aggressive, arrogant, and impassive, but she was never able to define that quality about them that attracted her.

As he set the glass down on the end table closest to her and poured beer into it, she let her curiosity again direct her gaze to the narrow line of his hips, then glanced up quickly when he straightened and moved to sit on the other side of her.

"There you go," he said, folding his long frame onto the sofa cushion.

"Thanks." Abbie lifted the glass, briefly saluting him with it, then took a sip of the cold beer, conscious of his arm extended along the sofa back, his hand resting inches from her shoulder.

"What will you do now that you don't have any help to take care of the horses?" MacCrea's question touched a wound that was still sore.

"Naturally Ben is still there. He's practically family. Between the two of us, we'll manage." But Abbie didn't know how they would. Ben might look like an ox, but he was an old ox. Even though there was still a lot he could do, much of the heavier work would fall to her, she knew. "I'd rather not discuss it."

"Why?"

"Because . . ." She caught the sharpness in her voice and paused to sigh heavily. "I guess it bothers me that none of the stable help volunteered to stay on. Most of them have worked for us for several years and never once missed a paycheck. You'd think they would trust us to pay them as soon as we got the money from Daddy's estate."

"Maybe they knew their landlords and bill collectors wouldn't trust them. A lot of people around here live from paycheck to paycheck. If you've never lived like that and tried to raise a family, then you can't appreciate what it's like."

"I know," Abbie admitted, recognizing that she'd never had to worry about money her whole life. There had always been plenty of food on the table and clothes in her closet. The material necessities of life she'd known in abundance; it was the emotional needs that she hadn't always had met. But she didn't want to talk about that either.

"Financially, it can be rough after someone dies. Wilder Drilling Company owned five rigs the day my father was killed when a well blew out. The insurance check was sitting on his desk, waiting for his signature. Two other workers were injured in the same accident. I wound up losing everything but one rig. It wasn't easy, but I managed to build the business back up." MacCrea studied the long-necked bottle of beer in his hand, staring at the brown color of its glass as he remembered that he'd only been two short years away from getting his degree in geology when he'd had to quit college, and how he'd struggled through those early years on his own when few companies wanted to hire a young, untried contractor to drill their wells.

"Your father was killed when a well blew?" she repeated, stunned by the news. "No wonder you reacted the way you did with me. If I had known . . . Why didn't you tell me?" she demanded.

"You didn't give me much of a chance," he reminded her dryly.

"I guess I didn't." She paused briefly. "What happened? Do you know?"

"Yeah, I was there. He'd made me a toolpusher that summer — his man in charge on the site. Of course, he covered himself by putting his top men in my crews. It was my second well. He'd stopped by to see how I was doing. I went to get the company man. He was up there, joking with the driller while the guys were tripping in a length of pipe. I heard somebody yell and turned around just as a ball of flame engulfed the mast." He shook his head, seeing it all again — the human torches leaping off the raised platform of the rig's floor, trying to escape the inferno. One of them had been his father. "He was killed."

He took a swig of beer, then set the bottle down on the side table and rubbed his hand down the top of his thigh to wipe off the bottle's moisture. Abbie observed the action. She wanted to tell him she understood his pain. She'd lost her father, too. Then she noticed his hand as it lay flat on his leg. His little finger rose prominently above the others, bent while the others lay straight. A family trait, he'd said.

"Your finger really is crooked, isn't it?" She leaned forward to examine it more closely. "Won't it lie flat at all?"

"If you hold it down it will. Go ahead. Try it."

Abbie hesitated. "Does it hurt?"

"No."

She reached out and tentatively pushed the first joint down with her fore-finger. There was no sense of resistance as she held it down, but the instant she lifted her finger, it popped back up again. "I've never seen anything like that."

"It runs in the family."

The little finger appeared perfectly normal except for its jutting angle. As Abbie started to study it again, a lock of hair swung forward into her eye. Before she could reach up to push it back, she felt the brush of his fingers across her brow and temple as he lifted her hair back. She looked up, feeling the warm tingle as his fingers lingered to caress her cheekbone lightly. The intensity of his gaze, heavy-lidded, revealed a man's interest. Abbie recognized it instantly, and it ignited a breathless excitement in her.

"You have the bluest damned eyes," he murmured.

"I know."

His hand slid to the cord in her neck where blood throbbed in her vein. The pressure was light yet insistent, guiding her to him. But Abbie didn't need its direction as she moved to meet him, closing her eyes when his mouth was finally too close to see. The soft hairs of his mustache tickled the sensitive edges of her lip an instant before his mouth covered hers.

She explored the gentle contours of his mouth in the most tactilely stimulating way, satisfying the curiosity that had merely been whetted by the brief meeting of their lips several days earlier. His kiss was more than she'd expected, warm and firm, persuasively arousing in its devouring investigation of her own lips. Desire was building inside her, her breathing deepening, and her body straining to move closer still. Abbie realized how easily this could get out of hand, and she wasn't entirely sure that's what she wanted yet.

With an effort, she broke away from his spellbinding kiss and pushed herself back a few inches to bring his face into focus, discovering that at some point she had braced her hands against his chest for balance. She was beset by a whole new awareness of him — the natural heat of his body burning through the cotton of his shirt, the faint ripple of powerful muscles drawing breath into his lungs, and the heavy thud of his heart beating beneath her hands. Then she felt the weight of his hands on her, one resting idly on her lower ribs and the other absently massaging her upper shoulder.

It was crazy. All this time she thought she'd been in control of everything that was happening. Only now did she realize how totally absorbed she had been by the kiss. She studied the strong lines of his face in wonder, stunned by her response to him. His gaze traveled over her face.

"Now that was a kiss." Her voice sounded just a little throaty to her ears, as she subtly reminded him of the violence of their previous encounter.

"I wondered if you would notice the difference." His husky voice was like a caress.

As his dark eyes focused their attention on her lips, a faint tremor of want quivered through Abbie. "This is much better, MacCrea," she murmured as his hands exerted pressure to draw her back to him — not that she needed their coercion.

Her lips parted when they met his mouth, inviting the full intimacy of his kiss. When it came, she drank him in, letting his tongue mate with her own and probe the recesses of her mouth, a rawness sweeping hotly through her that made her ache for more. A storm of sensations buffeted her — the taste, the smell, the feel of him — and she let them engulf her.

His hands shifted their hold on her, now gripping and pulling. Abbie felt oddly weightless, boneless, as he effortlessly lifted her onto his lap. She slid her hands around his neck and into his thick hair, unable to remember the last time she'd felt so alive. Ever since her father had died, she'd been filled with so much pain and bitterness. Now that was gone, and it was as if she was being reborn in MacCrea's arms, her senses awakened again to all the exquisite pleasure of life and living — of love and giving.

How long had she ached to love and be loved? It was happening to her now. Each caress, each response, each demand she made was diminished by the magnitude of his. And Abbie didn't care why. If it was merely lust, it didn't matter. Selfishly, she wanted to feel more of these sensations — of being needed and wanted.

His arms bound her tightly to him, fitting her snugly into the cradle of his body, while his hands stroked her body, exploring the curves and hollows of her, the roundness of her hips, and the firmness of her thighs — always stimulating, always arousing, always urging closer contact. And all the while, the kiss went on and on, their breath rushing hotly together, their throats swallowing the intoxicating taste of each other.

When at last he moved his mouth from her lips and brushed it along her jaw to the sensitive hollow behind her ear, Abbie exulted in the low groan that came from his throat and turned her head slightly to allow him to kiss her neck. Quivers of sheer pleasure danced along her nerve ends as he nibbled at her skin, taking exciting little love bites. She felt his fingers at the buttons of her blouse and breathed in sharply when the pleasing roughness of his hand met her bare skin and cupped her breast. Desire seemed to throb through every inch of her body. It was like being consumed by a fever that heated every inch of her flesh, and MacCrea offered the only relief.

"You know where this is leading, don't you?" His thickly spoken question was slow to penetrate her sensation-riddled consciousness. MacCrea lifted his head to look at her face, resisting the pressure of her hands to pull him back to her.

She wasn't sorry he'd partially broken the spell of passion to question her intentions. It would have happened at some point, mentally if not verbally. Very early in her sexual experiences with men, Abbie had recognized that it was invariably the woman who controlled the situation and determined the degree of intimacy. Most men went no farther than the woman let them, stopping, however reluctantly or angrily, wherever she drew the line. Abbie had never made love to any man unless it was what she specifically wanted.

His question hovered in the air. Abbie bridged the space between them and nuzzled his ear, lightly rubbing her lips over its inner shell. When she answered him, her voice was barely a whisper. "I hope it's leading to the bedroom." She darted her tongue into the dark opening and smiled at the raw shudder that quaked his body, enjoying her ability to arouse him sexually.

A second later, his fingers dug into her arm as he forced her away from his ear. Desire had darkened his eyes to black, yet amusement lurked in them, too. "You do, do you?"

"Yes. Don't you?" she murmured.

"It would be a helluva lot more comfortable than this."

"I agree." She touched his face, exploring the high ridge of his cheekbone and tracing the slanted line of his jaw, then directing her fingertips to his mouth, which fascinated her so.

He caught hold of them and pressed them to his lips, then gently scooted her off his lap onto the sofa. As he stood up, he kept hold of her hand, as if unwilling to break contact. Abbie wondered if he thought she was going to back down. She wasn't. Once she made up her mind about something, she never changed it. But she let her actions tell him that as he pulled her up to stand in front of him, actions that she regarded as neither wanton nor brazen, but merely a reflection of her feelings.

His arm circled the back of her waist, drawing her against the length of his body and lifting her onto the toes of her boots as he bent his head to reach her mouth. She leaned into him, arching her back and pressing her hips against his thighs, conscious again of the difference in their heights, but more conscious of the differences in their bodies.

After kissing her thoroughly, MacCrea straightened and let her rock back onto her heels. Turning, he kept an arm around her waist to draw her along with him, and guided her toward the bedroom.

Abbie paused, aware of MacCrea behind her, and started to undo the rest of her buttons, the ones he hadn't bothered to unfasten. This was always the awkward time, the moments spent apart undressing. It always took the bloom from her passion and turned it into something calculated.

"No, you don't." MacCrea caught her by the arm and turned her around to face him. Startled, she looked at him in confusion, then he pushed her other hand out of the way and unbuttoned the last two buttons of her blouse. "I'll have this pleasure, thank you."

Abbie doubted that he intended to undress her fully. Maybe the blouse and her brassiere, but after that, he'd become too impatient. Strip and hop into bed, that had been her experience — and that of her friends as well. It didn't matter. This was more than she usually got.

He pushed the blouse off her shoulders, taking the bra straps with it, and bent to nuzzle her neck and the ridge of her shoulder. Abbie shivered at the delicious shudders that raced through her body, ignited by his nibbling kisses. Slowly, he pulled the blouse down her arms, caressing her skin as he went. Then it was free. She caught a flash of white out of the corner of her eye as he tossed her blouse onto a chair.

Then he turned her away from him, but the exciting nuzzling didn't stop. She felt his fingers at the hook of her brassiere and unconsciously held her breath, waiting for its release. It came a second later and her breasts hung free. As the brassiere went the way of the blouse, one of his large hands glided around her ribs and cupped the weight of one breast in its palm. The second one was quickly claimed by his other hand. Abbie couldn't stop the sighing moan of pleasure that rose from her throat.

Fighting the weakness that attacked her limbs, Abbie leaned against him and turned her face toward his chest as his thumbs drew lazy circles around her nipples, stimulating them into erectness. Her stomach muscles tightened, and a hollow ache started low and spread quickly.

All of a sudden she was lifted into the air and turned. Abbie wanted to scream in frustration, knowing this was when it would stop, that his own desire demanded consummation at this critical point when her arousal had just begun. So certain was she about his intentions that she wasn't surprised to find herself seated on the edge of the bed.

When he picked up her leg and started to tug off her riding boot, she stared at him, not knowing what to think. The second boot hit the floor soon after the first one. Her heavy socks followed them, each slowly peeled away, allowing him to caress her feet in the process. Until that moment, Abbie had never considered her feet to be a part of her body that she wanted caressed, never regarding them as particularly sensual. MacCrea showed her otherwise.

After that, she didn't know what to expect from him. He pulled her upright, then spanned her waist with his hands and lifted her up to stand on the bed. As his hands slid to her breasts, she breathed in sharply and deeply, then couldn't quite release it as he nuzzled one of her breasts, rubbing his lips over its roundness and across the nipple, his tongue darting out to lick it and making it harden even more. Moaning at the exquisite torment, Abbie dug her fingers into his thick hair and urged him closer.

As his mouth opened to take in the point of her breast, a searing pleasure rocketed through her. She forgot all about his hands until her lower stomach muscles contracted sharply with their contact with his flesh. He'd unzipped her jodhpurs. Shot with frissons of raw passion, Abbie knew she'd never felt so weak with desire in her entire life. He pushed the pants off her hips and the weight of the material slid them partway down her thighs. A boneless feeling nearly overwhelmed her as his hands glided over her bare bottom and paused to knead the soft cheeks, then moved on, down the backs of her legs, dragging the jodhpurs with them. She felt her knees start to buckle under the warmth of his hands. When he swung her off her feet, Abbie instinctively wrapped her arms around his neck and curled her body against him. One final tug stripped the jodhpurs from her.

Totally enraptured, she studied his profile, his face so close to hers she could see every pore in his leather-tan skin, his hair all rumpled and furrowed by her fingers, and his mustached mouth still moist from sucking her breasts. The slanted angle of his forehead continued along the straight ridge of his nose and ended with the natural thrust of his chin. Despite all the aggressive lines, MacCrea suddenly seemed incredibly handsome to her.

She watched his gaze wander over her nakedness. When he turned his head to look into her face, she saw the desire that darkened his eyes and weighted their lids. She wanted him. She wanted all of him. Slowly he set her onto the floor, his hands trailing over her skin as if reluctant to release her.

"Now, it's your turn." His voice was low and deep, its huskiness belying an otherwise even pitch. "This is the part I enjoy."

For a split second Abbie didn't catch his meaning, then realized she was supposed to undress him. Her own desire was so strong at that moment that she wanted to protest the delay in consummation. But she knew she wasn't being fair.

Trying to speed up the process, she practically ripped the buttons from his shirt, but when she bared his chest, she was overwhelmed by the need to touch him, to press her own body against his muscled torso and feel the wall of his chest flatten her breasts. She discovered how exciting, how stimulating it could be to run her hands over him, to let her lips explore his hard flesh, and to taste the faint saltiness of his skin.

As she slid his shirt down his arms, she began to appreciate the sensual joy to be found in unveiling him a little at a time, feeling for herself the bulge of his biceps and the sinewy cords in his forearms. She could tell that he was enjoying it, too, by the faint tremor that shook him when she unfastened his jeans and unzipped his fly.

At last the moment came when his Jockey shorts were the only article of clothing that remained. She was conscious of the trembling of her hands as she slid her fingers under the elastic waistband and pushed them slowly down.— conscious, too, of his erection straining against the confining cloth. Her throat was tight as she watched it spring free when she slid his shorts down.

Bending, she continued to pull the shorts down his legs, not stopping until he stepped free of them. She straightened and lightly, very lightly ran her fingers down the underside of his shaft, smiling at the convulsive leap it made into her hand, and the hiss of his indrawn breath that muffled his half-curse.

He grabbed at her hand and yanked her against his body, naked and hard, the heat of his flesh firing her skin. "Who taught you that?" he growled.

"You did," she whispered. "Just now."

Abbie wondered if he realized just how much he had taught her. Before this moment, she'd never known so much pleasure could be derived from exploring a man's body, that it was something to be enjoyed as much as the kisses and caresses.

With a twisting motion, MacCrea lowered her onto the narrow bed and followed her down to lie along her side. She turned to him eagerly. "Make love to me, MacCrea," she urged, more than ready for him, she thought, only to have him show her how wrong she was as he kissed, fondled, and caressed her body, building the aching tension inside her until she was raw with need, while he resisted the stimulation of her hands and the urging of her lips.

At last, when the throbbing ache was almost unbearable, he shifted his weight onto her and entered her as smoothly as a blade into its sheath. A storm of sensations drew her into its vortex, everything centering lower and lower, the fusion culminating in a glorious explosion that sent her soaring, for a few shattering seconds transported to a purely physical plateau where all was sensation.

Then it was over and she lay nestled in his arms, her head on his chest. After all that she'd learned about MacCrea in the last hour, she wasn't surprised that he continued to hold her instead of rolling over to light a cigarette or climbing out of bed to get dressed. This intimacy after the act was part of making love, too. She was so content she wasn't sure she ever wanted to move.

But she rubbed her cheek against his chest and sighed. His chin moved against the top of her head. "You know you are damned near perfect, Abbie?"

"And I thought I was perfect," she mocked, smiling.

"Maybe if you were a little taller."

Like Rachel, she thought and immediately wished that name had never come to her mind. All her contentment seemed to flee, as if a moment ago it hadn't even existed. Abbie stirred restively, her peaceful mood gone.

"What's the matter?"

Abbie pretended to glance at the curtained window and the blackness of nightfall beyond it. "It's later than I thought. I'd better be going." She left the warmth of his arms and swung out of bed, reaching for her clothes scattered around the room.

"There's no hurry, is there?"

"Momma doesn't know where I am. I don't want her to worry." She finished tugging on her jodhpurs and sat down on the edge of the bed to pull on her boots. The mattress shifted as MacCrea sat up.

"She'd probably be more worried if she knew."

"Probably." Abbie smiled at him.

He combed the hair back from the side of her face. "I still say you have the bluest damned eyes."

So does Rachel. Dammit, Abbie railed silently. Why was she thinking about her? Trying to block out the unwanted thoughts, she leaned over and kissed him. She waited for him to say something, to indicate that he wanted to see her again. But he made no response.

She left the trailer a few minutes later without knowing whether she'd ever see him again.

14 ～

ONE MORE BALE of hay would do it. Pausing to gather the needed strength and breath, Abbie wiped the sweat around her mouth onto the sleeve of her blouse, every limb trembling from her overworked muscles. But no matter how sore and weary she was, the horses had to be fed.

Bending her aching back, Abbie slipped her gloved fingers under the baling twine and attempted to heft the heavy bale onto the flatbed with one mighty swing. But she rammed it against the edge of it instead, unable to lift it high enough, and quickly used her body to pin the bale against the flatbed. Then grunting and straining, she struggled and shoved to push it over the edge. Almost immediately, she collapsed against the flatbed trailer, letting it support her, too exhausted to stand on her own and too tired to cry. She didn't even feel human anymore, just an itchy mass of hay chafe glued together with sweat.

"Why do you not wait for me to help with those bales?" At the sound of Ben's scolding voice, Abbie hastily straightened to stand erect. "What you think? That you are Superwoman?"

In no mood to be lectured about her strength or lack of it by an irritable old man, Abbie swung around to snap at him. But one look at his tired and wan features reminded her that these last six backbreaking days had taken their toll on him as well. They were both cranky and out of sorts from the mental and physical strain of trying to take care of all these horses, working practically from dawn 'til dusk. Even then there'd been tasks they'd had to neglect, like the training of the yearlings and two-year-olds, and the cleaning of the empty stalls in the barns.

"I was trying to save time." Abbie lied rather than hurt his pride by telling the truth, that he was too old to stand up under this kind of heavy labor. "How is Amira's foal?"

Problems just kept coming their way. One of the new foals had come down with a severe case of scours, a relatively common occurrence when the dam came back into season. They had isolated the pair immediately to avoid the risk of spreading the diarrhetic condition to other sucklings in the pasture.

"She is not good."

He needed to say no more. Abbie knew how critical it was. Foals had little reserve. If the lost fluids weren't replaced, the resulting dehydration could kill them or weaken them so badly they'd contract other diseases.

Abbie glanced toward the house. "Maybe we should call Doc Campbell."

"We will see."

She opened her mouth to argue with him, then closed it, deferring to his judgment. If Ben didn't believe the foal's condition was critical enough to warrant calling in the vet, there was no point in questioning his decision. He had years more experience than she did. And, Lord knows, they probably already had a huge outstanding veterinary bill that had accumulated over the spring foaling and breeding season.

Judging by the barrage of phone calls they'd received in the last few days, they owed practically everyone in the whole county. Abbie sighed dispiritedly. Nothing could be done about any of that until the estate was settled, so there was no use thinking about it, not when they had so many horses to feed before dark.

In an attempt to cut down on the amount of time spent distributing hay and grain to all the horses, they had turned most of them into the pastures for mass-feeding from wooden troughs. This meant that some of the horses would be bullied out of their portions by the more dominant members of the herd, but it couldn't be helped.

"We might as well get on with this." Abbie turned and faced the flatbed trailer and laid her hands on its wooden floor, preparing to jump onto it, but her weary muscles simply refused to make the effort. "Will you give me a leg up, Ben? I can't make it." She didn't even try, and instead stepped onto the cupped hands he offered and let him boost her onto the trailer. As he walked toward the tractor hitched to the flatbed, Abbie stopped him. "I meant to ask you if they're going to deliver that grain tomorrow. We don't have much left."

"They wanted to speak about the bill to your mother first."

"That's right. You told me that." Abbie frowned, irritated with herself for forgetting. "I meant to call them this afternoon. As soon as we get done here, I'll phone Mr. Hardman at home tonight."

And this time she vowed she wouldn't forget. She let her legs dangle over the side of the hayrack and leaned against the bale behind her, too grateful for its support to mind the bristly stalks that poked her back. The tractor roared to life and jerked the flatbed after it, briefly jarring Abbie, but she didn't move, conserving her energy for the moment when she'd have to hop off the back and scurry around to open the pasture gate.

She couldn't remember ever being so tired and sore. Every bone, muscle, and fiber in her body ached. The only thing that kept her going was the certain knowledge that this situation couldn't last much longer. The estate would be settled. There was a light at the end of the tunnel. But why did she have the feeling it was a train?

Above the noisy engine of the tractor, she heard the rumble of a pickup truck. She felt a little leap of anticipation in her heart, hoping it was MacCrea's. She hadn't seen or heard from him since that night. Maybe . . . She sat up and tried to swallow the bitter disappointment when she recognized the rusty old pickup that belonged to Dobie Hix. He pulled in front of the pasture gate and stopped, blocking the entrance. She had a pretty good idea of why he'd come.

As the tractor lumbered to a halt, Abbie jumped off the back of the flatbed and charged around to the front to confront Dobie as he climbed out of the truck. "If you've come about the money we owe you, we still can't pay it. Nothing's been settled yet. There's your precious damned hay." She gestured wildly at the hayrack behind her. "Go ahead and take it!"

A look of shock crossed his face as he swept off his battered straw cowboy hat and held it in front of him. "That's not why I came, Abbie. I don't want that hay. You all need it for your horses. It's yours. I just came to give you a hand. I know you don't have any right now and—"

"Dobie, I . . . I'm sorry." She was miserably ashamed of the way she'd unjustly lashed out at him. Feeling incredibly tired and defeated, she ran a gloved hand over her face, wondering why she'd said those terrible things. "There was no excuse for what I said."

"You're tired. This isn't work for you to be doing. Those bales are heavy even for a man to lift." He waved his hat in the direction of the flatbed. "Let alone a gal as little as you."

"I'm stronger than I look," she flared.

"I know you are, but it still isn't work you should be doing."

What other choice did she have? How else were all these horses to be fed? Was she supposed to let Ben do it all? What if he suffered a heart attack? What was she supposed to do then? Somehow Abbie managed to keep all those angry questions to herself. No matter how illogical and chauvinistic Dobie's statements were, she recognized that he was merely trying to be thoughtful.

"We appreciate your offer, Dobie. Thanks."

"That's what neighbors are for." He shrugged. "I only wish you had let me know that you were shorthanded. I would have been over to help sooner."

"You will stay for dinner."

"There's no need in that."

"I insist." She didn't want him or anyone else to think they didn't have enough food in the house to eat. Their present straitened circumstances were temporary, and she didn't want anyone imagining otherwise. "I'll tell Momma to put another plate on the table." And she'd make that phone call she'd forgotten earlier.

As she started for the house, Dobie climbed back into his pickup and moved it out of the way. Abbie listened to the sound of its engine, wondering how she could have mistaken its clattering roar for MacCrea's. She guessed she'd simply wanted it to be his, even though she'd known when she'd left his trailer that night that he probably wouldn't come around again. Why should he? After all, she hadn't made that a condition for going to bed with him.

MacCrea was a wildcatter, a gambler, hardly the type she could expect to have an ongoing relationship with. He was the kind who was here one day and gone the next. It wasn't as if she'd lost anything that she hadn't expected to lose, so why was she still thinking about him? But the answer to that was easy. With him she had felt alive and whole, possibly for the first time in her life. It wasn't a feeling she could easily forget.

She entered the house through the back door and stepped into the kitchen. Her mother turned toward the door, a slightly panicked expression on her face, and quickly placed her hand over the mouthpiece of the telephone receiver she held.

"Abbie. I'm so glad you're here," she rushed. "It's a Mr. Fisher on the phone. Long distance from Ohio or Iowa—I can't remember which. He's calling about some horses he sold to your father last year, but he says he never got paid for them. Abbie, I don't know what to say to him. You talk to him." She pushed the receiver at her.

"Just give him Lane Canfield's number and have him call there. Lane knows more than we do," she insisted wearily.

"I can't. You tell him, Abbie."

Stifling her irritation at her mother's inability to cope with something so simple, Abbie took the telephone and barely listened to the story the man recited. Her response was the same as the one she gave to all the recent callers: a referral to the man handling the settlement of the estate. Afterward, she hung up the phone and stood facing the wall, feeling mentally, physically, and emotionally drained.

"It's all so upsetting when they call like that, Abbie," her mother declared. "I never know what to say to them."

"I told you to leave the telephone off the hook," Abbie said tiredly, wondering why she had to deal with everything.

"But what if our friends tried to call and couldn't get through?"

What friends? Abbie thought, wondering if her mother had noticed how few had called since word had gotten out about their present financial straits. Maybe she should have expected it, but it still rankled. After all, they weren't broke. This was just a temporary situation.

She picked up the telephone and dialed the home number of the owner of the local feed-and-grain company. As soon as she identified herself as a Lawson, she had no difficulty convincing him to send out another load of grain, despite their outstanding account. She sighed as she hung up, relieved that the Lawson name still carried some weight.

"Before I forget, Momma . . ." Abbie turned and saw her mother standing at the sink, peeling potatoes—a sight that still seemed foreign. In the past when her mother had puttered in the kitchen, it had usually been to supervise the meal preparation, adding a touch here and changing something there, but never to cook herself. Now, she had no kitchen help to supervise. No one except Jackson, and cooking and cleaning were two things he assisted with only grudgingly, considering both to be beneath him. The brunt of the housework and meal preparation had fallen on her mother. ". . . we're having company for dinner tonight. Dobie Hix came by to help with the horses, so I invited him to eat with us."

"In that case I'd better peel more potatoes, and maybe fix another vegetable. Perhaps some broccoli . . . with cheese sauce."

Abbie left her still mulling over ways to stretch the evening meal to feed four and returned to the stables. With Dobie lending Ben a hand to feed the horses, Abbie set out to clean some of the stalls.

All the doors and windows in the stable stood open to allow crossventilation, but little of the evening breeze reached the interior. Abbie paused to wipe the sweat from her face, then laid the pitchfork across the wheelbarrow and gripped the handles to roll it to the next stall.

"Let me do that for you, Abbie." Dobie came up behind her just as she lifted up on the handles.

"I can manage." Once she got it balanced and rolling, it practically pushed itself. It was just a matter of getting it started. She strained forward, pushing with all her weight. It moved an inch, then Dobie's hands were gripping the wheelbarrow as he shouldered her out of the way.

"It's too heavy for you to be pushing." He rolled it effortlessly to the next stall.

"How do you think it got this far, Dobie?" Abbie muttered, but she really didn't object to letting him push it. It was heavy and she was tired.

She swatted absently at a fly that buzzed around her face, then reached for the pitchfork. She didn't dare stop to rest. She was afraid if she did, she wouldn't be able to get herself moving again, like the wheelbarrow.

"I'll get another pitchfork and give you a hand. We'll have these stalls cleaned in half the time."

"Thanks, but Ben wondered if you could lend him a hand over at the stallion barn when you were finished with the hay. The stallion kicked out a couple boards in his stall. Ben thinks one or two others might be weak." She would gladly have traded places and let Dobie finish cleaning the stalls. Unfortunately carpentry wasn't one of her talents. Abbie knew she was more apt to smash a thumb than pound a nail.

"I'll get that fixed and come back to help you."

"Thanks." She smiled absently in his direction and scooped up a pile of manure from the stall's straw bed, then swung the pitchfork over to the wheelbarrow to dump it.

The rhythm took over: scoop, lift, pitch, scoop, lift, pitch. Abbie didn't even hear Dobie leave the stall. In the background, the radio played some twangy country tune. A radio was always going in the barns, tuned to a music station to soothe the horses and keep them company. But Abbie had stopped listening, thinking, feeling, and smelling a long time ago. Like a robot, she simply scooped, lifted, and pitched.

As she swung another forkful of manure and soiled straw into the wheelbarrow, out of the corner of her eye she saw a man leaning against the stall door. She stuck the pitchfork under another pile, then realized the man was Mac-Crea. She froze, her heart suddenly lurching against her ribs. She turned and looked again to make sure she wasn't seeing things.

"Hello, Abbie." His deep voice felt almost like a caress.

"MacCrea." She was flustered. Her heart was pounding as hard as a galloping horse. She felt all shaky inside, and she didn't like it. She didn't like wanting anyone this much. It left her too exposed. She shifted her grip on the pitchfork handle and bent again to her task, but this time she slowed her rhythm way down, making a project out of sifting the horse apples from the straw.

MacCrea watched her, the way he'd been watching her for the last several minutes, stimulated by the sight of her lissome body, remembering the way it looked without clothes, the way it had taken him and drained him. All week she'd haunted his trailer. Everywhere he'd looked, he'd seen her — on the sofa, by the door, in front of the sink, and most of all, in his bed. Each phone call, each rumble of a car, he'd expected to be her.

"It's been a week since I've seen you," he said.

There was the smallest break in her action as she swung the pitchfork over to the wheelbarrow. With a practiced twist of the handle, she dumped the manure onto the growing pile, then let the tines rest on the top and glanced in his direction, her look guarded. "You knew where to find me."

He wanted to walk over to her and pluck the wisps of straw from her dark hair, but MacCrea knew he wouldn't stop there. "I finally realized that you weren't going to get in touch with me."

"It was your move." The straw rustled as she once again turned and searched for more waste. "If you only wanted a one-night stand, I wasn't about to make any demands on you, MacCrea."

Too damned much pride, MacCrea suspected and wondered why her back wasn't bowed by the weight of it. But he knew he admired it. Abbie was different from other women he'd known. It *had* been his move, but none had ever let him make it. They'd always arranged to bump into him accidentally or made up an excuse to see him or call him. Abbie had a ready-made excuse to do that. She could have gotten in touch with him to give him more names. But she hadn't. And here he was.

"I never had any intention of seeing you again." That's what he'd told himself when Abbie left that night. He'd enjoyed her, but it was over, and that was the end of it. How many times had he said that this past week? Every time he remembered her, and that was too often.

"So why are you here?" She paused, her back still to him, both gloved hands gripping the pitchfork, then she laughed, a short, hollow sound. "That's right. I forgot. You wanted names from me."

"Yes, I wanted that." He didn't like talking to her back, and he didn't like not having her full attention. He pushed away from the frame of the stall door and crossed the space between them in two long strides. Startled, she didn't try to resist when he took the pitchfork from her hands and tossed it aside. He dug his fingers into her arms, feeling the heat of her body flow through them, and turned her to face him. Everything seemed to go still inside him as he stared down at her, taking in the glistening sheen of her complexion, the parted softness of her lips, and the boundless blue of her eyes. "But that's not why I'm here and you damned well know it."

"I do?" It sounded as if she breathed the words, as her expression became all soft and warm.

For a split second, he was furious with himself for not staying away. He had no business getting involved with her. He couldn't afford the distraction of an affair just now. Between running his drilling company, trying to get this lease locked up and the capital raised to drill a well on it, and getting this new computerized testing process of his off the ground, he didn't have the time to devote. Hell, in his line of work, he was never in one place that long. And he wasn't in a position yet to settle down and run his operation from behind a desk. He'd learned by experience that long distance invariably killed a relationship. But he just couldn't get Abbie out of his head. She'd meant more than a one-night stand, whether he wanted to admit it or not.

"Don't play dumb, Abbie. You knew I'd come."

"I knew . . . if you felt anything at all, you would."

He was taken aback by her candor. He had expected a denial, not a frank admission of tactics. But when hadn't she been full of surprises? He felt the touch of her hands on his stomach and his control snapped. Raising her the necessary few inches, he covered her lips with his mouth, tasting, drinking, and eating their softness, driven by a hunger that hadn't been fed for a week.

But a kiss didn't come anywhere close to satisfying his hunger. He broke it off, aware of how rough and labored his breathing had become, and how hard he'd grown. He started to rub his cheek against her hair, but a straw poked him. Impatiently, he plucked it from her tousled hair.

Her arms tightened around him as she pressed her head closer against his chest. "I'm a mess," she said, her voice partially muffled by his shirt.

"Funny, you don't feel like a mess." He ran his hands over her, remembering the feel of her body and the way she'd fit him as snugly as a glove. He molded her to him, pressing her against his hips, trying to ease the aching in his loins.

She moaned softly, "Oh, MacCrea, I want you, too." Shifting in his arms, she drew him down to her lips and arched her body even closer to him.

He'd heard all he needed to hear. Neither the time nor the place meant anything to him as he loosened the tail of her blouse to touch the heat of her flesh. She turned her lips away from his mouth, murmuring, "Not here," but he ignored her faint protest and nibbled at her throat. She pushed away from his chest in forceful resistance. "No." This time her voice was stronger.

A man's angry, drawling voice came out of nowhere. "Take your hands off of her!"

The warning had barely made an impression on MacCrea when someone grabbed his arm and jerked him around. He had a split second to focus on his assailant before a fist filled his vision. A long-ingrained fighting instinct took over as MacCrea jerked his head back to avoid the blow and it glanced off his jaw.

The sandy-haired man in the battered straw cowboy hat swung wildly at him and yelled, "Run, Abbie!"

MacCrea blocked the fist with an upraised arm and quickly jabbed the man in the stomach, but not before his head was snapped back by a third swing that found its target. But the jarring contact didn't stop him; it only made his heart pump faster and speed the flow of adrenaline through his system. His blurred vision saw only his opponent. He slammed his fist into the man's midsection again and followed it with a left to the jaw and another right to the head that threw the man backward against the wall, knocking his hat off. Bareheaded, he slumped against it, his legs buckling as he tried to shake off the blow.

MacCrea went after him. He'd been in too many brawls to quit when his opponent went down. This was the time to finish him off and make sure he didn't get up again. Suddenly Abbie was in his way.

"Stop it, MacCrea!" she shouted angrily. "Can't you see you've beaten him?" He paused, dragging in a breath to fill his laboring lungs, just starting to get his wind and to feel good. Abbie turned to the other man and crouched beside him. "Dobie, are you all right?"

"Yeah." But the man didn't sound at all certain of that. MacCrea started to smile in satisfaction, then winced instead, for the first time feeling the cut on the inside of his lip. That stinging sensation was followed instantly by the ache in his hands, his knuckles sore from their jarring contact with the man's face. MacCrea flexed them and tried to shake out the stiffness.

It irritated him the way Abbie was fussing over the other guy. "Just who the hell is this character?" He pressed his fingers against his split lip and explored the extent of the cut with his tongue, tasting a trace of blood.

The man looked at him as if realizing just that second that MacCrea was still there. He made a move toward him, but Abbie pushed him back. "It's all right, Dobie. He's . . . a friend." The man she called Dobie relaxed, but Mac-Crea noticed that his expression remained hostile. If anything, it became more so as he straightened to his feet, shrugging off Abbie's attempt to help him.

"I'd like you to meet MacCrea Wilder. MacCrea, this is Dobie Hix, our neighbor. He's been coming over to help Ben and me with the horses."

"Hix." MacCrea acknowledged the introduction with a nod of his head, and the man mumbled something in reply, but didn't offer to shake hands.

MacCrea noticed the look Hix darted at Abbie. It would have been obvious to a blind man that Hix was crazy about her. Or maybe it was just obvious because he recognized the symptoms. Just when he thought Hix was going to leave and he'd have Abbie to himself again, the old man appeared in the stall doorway. His sharp eyes seemed to take in the situation in a flash, although his stoic expression never changed.

"Your mother says we should clean up for supper now," he informed Abbie.

"Thanks, Ben." Then she turned expectantly to MacCrea. "You will join us, won't you?"

This was his chance to bow out, to leave before he became involved any deeper with her. Common sense told him to clear out, but MacCrea heard himself accepting the invitation. All during the long walk to the house with Abbie and her two cohorts, MacCrea cursed himself for being twenty kinds of fool.

The very minute Abbie set foot in the house, she left him to cool his heels in the living room. He spent a good fifteen minutes listening to Babs Lawson chatter away about nothing while avoiding the staring match Hix kept trying to instigate.

He was about ready to make his excuses and leave when Abbie sailed down the staircase into the room and the sight of her blocked all other thoughts from his mind. Her skin glowed with a scrubbed freshness and her wet hair was skimmed back from her face and plaited in a single braid, the severe style softened by wispy curls around her temples and neck. She had changed into a simple cotton frock in a vivid shade of green with a row of white buttons down the v-neck front. She breezed past him, leaving in her wake the clean smells of soap and some sexy perfume. MacCrea watched her, staring at the way her breasts strained against the material of the snug-fitting dress top.

He stayed. She sat next to him at the dining room table, their chairs crowded close together, her thigh brushing against his. It was unquestionably the longest meal MacCrea had ever had to sit through, trying to participate intelligently in the table talk.

"No, thanks." MacCrea refused the second cup of coffee Babs Lawson tried to pour him and pushed his chair away from the table. "The food was good — too good. As a matter of fact, I'm afraid I'm going to have to walk some of it off. Join me, Abbie?"

"Thanks." Abbie slipped her hand into his, squeezing it lightly. He started for the back door, but she paused next to Ben's chair. "We'll check on the foal."

Ben nodded, then glanced at Dobie's downcast expression as the door clicked shut behind them. He liked their neighbor. Dobie Hix was an honest, hardworking, God-fearing man, but Ben knew that he did not have the strength of will to handle a spirited, headstrong woman like Abbie. He had the gentleness but not the firmness. She would walk all over him.

As for this MacCrea Wilder, Ben wasn't sure about him. He'd seen him only a few times, yet he'd sensed a restlessness about the man. Other things pulled him. Abbie needed someone strong and dependable so she could remember how to be soft and trusting. This man was strong, but Ben questioned how long MacCrea Wilder would be around.

"I think I'll get some fresh air, too." Dobie Hix rose abruptly and headed for the door. He grabbed his hat off the hook, then paused. "That was a lovely meal, Mrs. Lawson. Thank you."

"You're more than welcome, Dobie."

Ben wasn't certain whether Dobie intended to add to his collection of barely visible bruises, so he pushed back his chair. "I will join you, Dobie."

He followed Dobie onto the veranda and stood beside him at the top of the steps. The sun was down and moonlight silvered the grounds — and the couple walking body against body across the clearing. Dobie stared at them and impatiently tapped his hat against the side of his leg.

"Maybe it isn't my place to be saying this, but I don't like him, Ben." He shoved his hat onto his head and pulled it low.

Ben wondered if Dobie noticed that the pair was headed for the office annex, not the broodmare barns where the sick foal was. "She is a woman grown."

"Yeah, I guess so." Dobie clumped off the porch. "I'd better be getting home. See you in the morning."

"Good night, Dobie." Ben remained on the porch.

As they entered the dark annex, MacCrea attempted to turn Abbie into his arms, but she eluded him and caught hold of his hand to pull him deeper into the shadows. He followed reluctantly.

"Where are we going?"

"Here." A doorknob turned, a latch clicked open, and he breathed in the smell of leather. "It's my father's private office." She led him inside, then released his hand. He could barely make out the myriad of shapes, distinguishable mainly by their differing shades of darkness. "Wait here."

He could hear her footsteps as she moved confidently into the room. There was a snapping sound and the soft glow of light from a small green-shaded desk lamp spread over the room. He glanced quickly around the room, noticing the desk and chair, the paneled walls covered with pictures and trophies, and the leather sofa, its cushions empty and inviting. He looked at Abbie, partially backlit by the desk lamp, then glanced at the ribbons and trophies on the near wall.

"That's some collection."

"Yes." Abbie looked at them briefly. "I won most of them, the ones in the English pleasure and park classes."

"You must be quite a horsewoman."

"I can ride with the best of them." Her smile gave her reply a totally different meaning.

"So I've discovered."

"The door has a lock," she said.

MacCrea shut the door behind him and turned the lock. This time they wouldn't be rudely interrupted by her neighbor or anyone else. She was still standing in front of the desk when he turned back into the room. He walked over to her, paused, then ran his hands over her bare collarbones and up her neck to cup her face. Bending, he kissed her, taking little bites of her lips and feeling the rapid beating of her heart. At last he came up for air, and a tremor shook him. She looked into his eyes, and he had the feeling she could see all the way into his soul.

"You have the bluest damned eyes." He kissed their corners, closing them, and slid his hands onto her shoulders, his thumbs caressing the hollows. Conscious of the slight rise and fall of her breasts, he let his gaze travel down to them and center on that hint of cleavage behind the first white button. Then his fingers were around it without his being aware of moving his hand.

"No." She stopped him before he could free the button, and stepped back from him. "I'll do it."

A protest formed, but MacCrea never got it out as he watched the swift deftness of her hands reveal that she wasn't wearing a bra under that dress. Christ, she wasn't wearing a damned thing! he realized as the dress slithered to the floor and she stood completely nude before him, bathed in the soft lamplight.

He swore and she laughed. Then he had her in his arms. After that, it all became a blur of raw passion: the shedding of his clothes, the entwining on the leather couch, the kissing and fondling of bodies, the rhythmic rocking in unison, their climax, which forever trapped in his memory images of her nipples so erect with arousal, the side-to-side turning of her head, the arching thrust of her hips, and the look of raw wonder on her face.

MacCrea and Abbie lay nestled together on their sides like two spoons, the narrow couch not giving them any room to sprawl in contentment. He felt a tingling in the arm that pillowed her head, the warning of the nerves that they were going to sleep, but he didn't move. Hell, he didn't want to move from her.

Frowning, he absently studied the top of her mussed hair, the dark strands pulled loose from the single braid. He tried to analyze his feelings and understand why, with her, everything seemed different. True, Abbie went out of her way to please him, but so had other women, and succeeded as well. So what did she give him that others didn't or hadn't? Maybe it was the way she loved him with more than her body. All her emotions, her passion, went into it. She gave him everything — every part of her. But there wasn't any room in his life right now for a wife and family.

Marriage. My God, was he really thinking about marrying her? He concealed his shock and felt Abbie rub her cheek against his arm like a purring cat.

"After Daddy's funeral, I came here to think. Until that day, I didn't know he had another daughter. All along I thought I was the only one. It was hard for me to accept. It still is," she mused. "She was his favorite."

"How do you know that?" He felt her shrug a little.

"I know," was all she said. "You've seen her, MacCrea . . . you've seen Rachel. You know how much I look like her." He was struck by her phrasing: "I look like her" and not "she looks like me." "Every time Daddy looked at me, he saw her. Do you?"

"No." Until she'd mentioned it, he'd completely forgotten she had a half-sister, let alone the resemblance between them.

As Abbie turned in a tight circle to face him, needle-sharp pains shot through his arm. Wincing, MacCrea shifted onto his back to ease the pinching in his arm and pulled Abbie partially onto his chest. Using her forearms to prop herself up, she searched his face, her own expression warm and loving. He didn't want to notice that, any more than he wanted to notice the rounded contours of her breasts hanging full before him.

"I'm glad we made love here, MacCrea." She leaned forward and kissed him, her lips soft, her breath fresh. He felt himself growing hard again and tried to will it to stop. "Now when I come here, I'll remember this. I'll remember how good it was." She laid her head on his shoulder, pressing her firm breasts against his chest.

"Abbie." He knew he wanted to go on seeing her. But if he ever had to choose between his business future and her, he knew Abbie would lose. He wouldn't sacrifice his ambitions, his dreams — his life — for her. She'd give and he'd take. Wrong or not, that's the way it was going to be. But it wasn't necessary to make that choice yet. Maybe it never would be.

She made a protesting sound and snuggled closer to him. "I know it's late and I have to get up early in the morning, but I wish we could stay here all night."

"What are you going to be doing this next week?"

"Lane is supposed to come. Hopefully, he'll have this mess straightened out with Daddy's estate." Her mood changed. MacCrea sensed her restlessness.

"That's your days. What about your nights? Are you free?"

"No, I'm very expensive." She sat up, her smile mocking him.

"Are you, now?" The lightning change of topic and tempo kept him alert. She stimulated him mentally as well as sexually.

"Yes. And don't you forget it." She picked up his pants and tossed them to him.

15 ✒

BUT LANE CANFIELD DIDN'T come to River Bend until the end of the week. Now that he was there, sitting in the living room, Abbie felt uneasy, her nerves on edge. She didn't know what was going to come out of this meeting with him, but something had to. This waiting and all the attendant uncertainty was becoming a strain on everyone.

As she listened to her mother chattering away, playing hostess, she wanted to scream at her to stop, but she couldn't. Her mother had been in such good spirits all morning that Abbie dreaded the moment when they would vanish.

Which they surely would. She had noticed that Lane hadn't touched either the coffee or the pecan tart he'd taken. Abbie had trouble convincing herself that he simply wasn't hungry or thirsty.

"Now, Lane, what was it you wanted to talk to us about?" Babs smiled and sipped at her coffee, blithely indifferent to the tension that was twisting Abbie's stomach into knots.

"Unfortunately, what I have to tell you isn't good," Lane began, setting his cup and saucer on the end table by the tasseled arm of the sofa.

"What are you trying to say?" Abbie demanded. "Is Daddy's estate going to be tied up in some litigation?" All along she'd suspected Rachel would contest the will and demand a share of the estate. Now it was happening. Abbie was sure of it.

"No. Nothing like that." He appeared to dismiss the possibility out of hand.

"Then what?" She frowned.

"It's taken some time to get a clear picture of exactly what the financial condition of the estate is. And I'm afraid it's worse than was first thought."

"What do you mean?" Mentally Abbie braced herself as she watched him closely.

"I'm sure you know that when Dean sold his father's company, he received a very large sum of money—"

"Twelve million dollars," Abbie remembered.

"Taxes, commissions, and various other costs had to be paid out of that, so actually he netted less than that," Lane stated. "Over the years, he has repeatedly dipped into that capital. Even though he borrowed money to build the improvements at River Bend — the new stables, et cetera — the actual breeding and showing of his horses was a constant cash drain. His law practice operated in the red as well. Add to that some unwise investments and an extremely high standard of living, and . . ." He paused, as if unwilling actually to voice the rest.

"You're saying there isn't any money left?" Abbie asked, hoping it wasn't true.

"I'm saying he was heavily in debt. His mortgage payments to the bank are past due. Property taxes are owed. There is virtually no source of income."

"You mean we're broke?" She doubted she understood him correctly.

"I'm sorry. But the assets will have to be sold to satisfy the claims against the estate."

"What has to be sold?" Abbie questioned, dreading the answer, yet needing to know precisely what he meant. "The horses? Some of the land? You just can't mean we'll have to sell River Bend."

"I'm afraid I do."

"No." Abbie couldn't believe it. She darted a stricken glance at her mother. Babs looked white. "Momma." She didn't know what to say to her.

"Is it that bad, Lane?" Babs watched him anxiously.

"Yes, Babs, it is." His expression was grim, regret evident in the way he avoided her gaze. "You know I'll help in any way I can."

"I know," Babs said dejectedly.

But Abbie still couldn't believe it was true. Things couldn't be that bad. She stared blindly at the papers Lane took from his briefcase, physical proof of his claim, evidence in black and white of monies owed, complete with names, dates, and figures. Her mind reeled with the words that sprinkled his conversation: mortgages, overdue loans, past-due bills, property taxes, delinquent payments.

All the talk of liabilities and indebtedness was followed by a discussion of terms such as "appraisal of assets," "inventory of stock and equipment," and "estate auction." But once Abbie waded through the business and financial language, she saw that Lane was saying they had to sell the only home she'd ever known, the beautiful Arabian horses she loved, the little corner of the world she lived in. Everything that was familiar to her, everything she'd ever loved, had to go under the auctioneer's hammer. River Bend was to be sold, the home that had been in her family for generations. This was her life he was talking about so coolly and unemotionally. Didn't he see that? She listened to him in frozen shock, rooted in her chair, unable to think, with the constant whirl of questions spinning in her head.

What was going to happen to them? What about Ben? Where were they going to live? What would they do? Where could she find a job? Doing what? Where would they get the money to eat? How could they move all this furniture when they didn't know where they were going? Why had this happened? How could her father have done this to them? How could he have done it to her mother?

But Lane never offered answers to any of her questions as he kept talking, now using phrases like "possible proceeds left after satisfying the creditors." He was so calm and matter-of-fact about it all that none of it seemed real. This wasn't happening to them. It couldn't be.

"Don't worry about anything, Babs," Lane insisted. "I'll handle all the details. Someone will be out in a couple of days to take a complete inventory and estimate the fair value of everything. I promise you we'll get the best prices we can."

"Promise. How can you promise anything?" Abbie angrily protested the way he kept trying to assure them everything was going to be all right. It wasn't all right. "How can you sit there and tell us not to worry? It isn't your home that's being sold! It isn't your world that's being turned upside down!"

"Abbie." Her mother was stunned by her outburst.

"I don't care, Momma. We're about to lose everything, and he's telling us not to be upset about it! Well, I am!" She couldn't take any more of his bland pap and bolted from the house.

Hot tears burned her eyes as she ran blindly to the stables. All she knew was that she had to get away and think — off by herself, away from everyone and everything. She grabbed a hackamore from the tackroom wall and ran to the paddock, hounded by the pounding questions in her head, driven to panic by the desperation and uncertainty. Somewhere there was an answer, a solution, a way out of all this — and she had to find it. They just couldn't lose everything. It was all a mistake, a dreadful mistake.

Her fingers were deft and sure even in her present turmoil as she hurriedly buckled the hackamore on the silver head of her filly and led her out of the paddock. She looped the reins over the Arabian's arched neck, grabbed a handful of mane, and swung herself onto the filly's back. With a prod of the heel and a pull on the reins, she turned her silver-gray horse toward the gate to the large back pasture.

Vaguely she was aware of Ben running toward her and shouting, "Abbie, what are you doing? Where are you going with that filly? Come back! Too young, she is!" Nothing he said registered. It was just more words, none of them having any effect on her overwhelming need to run as fast and as far as she could.

Somehow she opened the gate without even being aware of doing so. One minute it blocked her path and the next, the long pasture was before her. She urged her mount into a gallop, unconsciously whipping the reins across the marbled flank. The surprised filly leaped forward and stretched into a run.

Everything was a blur to Abbie: the startled horses scattering out of their way, the trees standing motionless, and the water running in the creek that fed into the Brazos River. She saw nothing beyond the pricked ears in front of her, felt nothing other than the wind whipping her long hair, and heard nothing beyond the pounding hoofbeats. Faster and faster they ran.

The filly stumbled, breaking stride and throwing Abbie forward. As she clutched at the sleek neck in an effort to regain her balance, Abbie felt the wetness, the slime of lather, and realized what she was doing. Pulling back on the reins, she managed to slow the winded and excited filly to a stop, then hurriedly slipped off her back, dragging the reins with her.

"Easy, girl. Easy, Breeze. It's all right now." Abbie tried to quiet the filly as she danced nervously away from her, dark nostrils flaring wide to show the red inside, gray sides heaving, black skin glistening wetly through the silver neck hairs.

Another set of hooves pounded the ground behind her. Abbie turned as Ben rode up on the old gelding they kept as a stable pony. He dismounted, stiff with anger, and strode over to her. "What you think you do, Abigail Lawson?" But his eyes were already focusing on the young Arabian horse. "You want to ruin this filly? Too young she is to be ridden so hard."

"I'm sorry, Ben." She watched anxiously as he ran a practiced hand down the filly's slim legs, all the while crooning softly in Polish. When he straightened, Abbie searched his stern expression. "Is Breeze all right?"

"Now you worry," he snorted in disgust. "Why you not worry before?"

"I'm sorry. I wasn't thinking."

"No, you think. You think only of yourself. Always when you get angry and hurt inside you make someone else suffer. To you it does not matter. It is only that you want to feel better. You do not deserve such a filly as this one."

"Maybe I don't." Her throat tightened. "But she's mine. She belongs to me." She wrapped her arms around the filly's quivering neck, unable to hold back the tears anymore. They streamed down her cheeks. "Breeze is all right, isn't she, Ben?" She turned to look at him.

"Yes." He relented slightly from his hard stand. "I felt nothing. It is lucky you weigh so little. The bones of a two-year-old have not finished their growing. This you know. We ride them little bits. We do not racing around the pasture go."

"I know."

"You will walk her to the barns. You will not ride her. And you will rub down her good."

He was lecturing her as if she were still fourteen years old and didn't know any better — as if she didn't know how to take care of a horse. But the flare of resentment quickly died as Abbie was forced to admit that her actions hadn't shown she did.

Dejectedly she gathered up the reins and turned to lead the filly back to the barns. Yet when she looked over the pasture at the horses she'd known since they were foals, the creek where she had played as a child, and the trees she'd climbed, she was overwhelmed by a terrible sense of loss. Soon she'd have to leave all this, she realized — leave everything she'd always known and taken for granted. To go where? To do what? It still didn't seem real.

"Why all the tears, tell me?" Ben asked.

"We have to sell out. Daddy owed too many people when he died. There isn't any money to pay the debts. It all has to be sold to pay the creditors. Everything has to go — including us."

"Is this true?" He frowned.

Abbie nodded. "Lane told us when he came. We're bankrupt. I knew there were problems, but I never thought . . . I never dreamed it was this bad." She looked at Ben, the old man who'd rode out all the previous storms with her and given her strength. "What's going to happen to us? What's going to happen to you? You've been the uncle I never had. What am I going to do without you?"

"Child." He gathered her into his arms. Abbie wanted to cry some more, but now she couldn't. This time he couldn't reassure her. It wasn't going to be all right. "Your poor momma," he said. "How frightening for her."

"Momma." She hadn't even considered what effect the news would have on her mother. Her own shock had been too great. In a vague way, she'd recognized that this meant she was her mother's only means of support now. She not only had to look after herself, but her mother, too. It wasn't fair, but whoever said life was fair? "River Bend, the horses, they're all to be sold. All except River Breeze. She belongs to me." She pulled away from Ben and turned to the filly.

"She will be a good mare on which to build a new broodmare herd."

"Don't, Ben." Abbie nearly choked on the lump in her throat. "This is no time for foolish dreams. Right now I've got to worry about finding a roof for our heads and food for our table. And Momma. I've got to worry about Momma, too."

Babs pressed her fingertips against the throbbing in her temple, then lowered her hand and pushed herself out of the chair. Instinctively she wanted to forget everything Lane had said, pretend the situation wasn't as bad as he had portrayed it. But she couldn't. Not this time. No one was going to make it all right for her — not Dean, not R.D. She had no one but Abbie.

As the front door opened, Babs turned toward the foyer, recognizing the familiar tread of Abbie's footsteps. But Abbie walked past the living room and started up the stairs.

"Abbie," Babs called after her and heard the hesitating footsteps and the sound of their return.

Then Abbie appeared in the archway, looking all windblown and tired, still wearing that troubled frown.

"I was worried about you. You were so upset when you left." She had seen her daughter angry before, but never so distraught. "I wanted to be sure you were all right."

"I guess I am." She shrugged vaguely. "I just had to get away by myself and sort things out." Her dark hair was all snarled and tangled, and Babs could see the tear streaks on her cheeks and the lost look in her eyes as Abbie wandered into the living room, looking around her as if she had to memorize every detail. She reminded Babs of a frightened little girl — her little girl. "I can't believe we have to sell River Bend. This is our home. If we sold the horses and all the land except for the little piece the house is on, why wouldn't that be enough?"

"Don't you remember, Lane explained about the large mortgage on the house?" Babs's heart went out to her daughter.

"There has to be a way we could assume it. This is our home." Behind all the anger, there was despair. Then Abbie sighed bitterly. "How could Daddy do this to us, Momma? I don't understand. Did he really hate us that much?"

Babs breathed in sharply. Never once in all these years had she suspected that Abbie felt she was unloved, too. How was it that she could have a daughter and know so little about her feelings? Babs wanted to reach out to her now and reassure her that it wasn't as bad as she thought, but she wasn't sure how.

"I believed Lane when he said that, had your father lived, he would have obtained the funds to pay all these debts. In his own way, he cared about us." She couldn't say "love." Any love Dean had felt for her died long ago. He had stayed out of duty, guilt, and probably pity. Babs had never wondered whether Dean actually loved Abbie. She'd simply assumed he did. If he hadn't, maybe she was to blame for that. He didn't love her, so maybe he couldn't love the child she had given him either. But it accomplished nothing to dwell on the past. Babs knew she must think of Abbie now.

"As for this house, you would have left it again someday, Abbie, when you found another man you loved and wanted to spend your life with. You would have married him and moved away . . . to a home of your own, just as you did with Christopher. It isn't as if you would have lived here all your life if this hadn't happened."

"But you would have. What about you, Momma? You love this house. The curtains, the wallpaper, the furnishings — you picked out everything. This is your home. How can you leave it?"

"I don't mind, really." She said it to reassure Abbie, but almost the instant the words were out of her mouth, Babs realized they were true. "After R.D. died, all I ever knew here was loneliness. I don't think I want to live with the memory of that around me all the time."

"Momma, you can't mean that."

"I do." She was equally surprised by the discovery. "It's a drafty old house, impossible to heat in the winter and impossible to cool in the summer. It's always damp and miserable. The plumbing is bad and the windows are always warping shut." There was so much wrong with the house it was a wonder she'd never noticed it before.

"But . . . where will we go? What will we do?"

"I don't know." She forced a smile and fell back on the phrase that had always been her talisman. "Everything will work out for the best. It always does."

"I hope so." But Abbie couldn't be as confident. She didn't have her mother's optimistic attitude. A snap of the fingers wasn't magically going to produce a job or a place to live. She'd have to go out and look for them . . . and, at the same time, keep the farm going, get the horses in sale condition, and prepare for the auction. Everything had to be in tiptop shape if they hoped to get good prices.

16 ～

SILENCE ASSAILED HER when Rachel entered the steakhouse. Pausing, she glanced at the sea of white tablecloths and empty chairs in the dining area. A faint murmur of voices came from the adjacent lounge. Rachel glanced hesitantly at the doorway to the bar.

She knew she was early for her dinner date with Lane, but she hadn't been sure how long it would take her to find the restaurant. With Houston's lack of any zoning laws, she'd already discovered that restaurants, or any type of business, could be located in the middle of some small residential area.

Even though she hadn't noticed Lane's car parked outside, Rachel decided to check in the lounge to see if he was there. As she moved toward it, she nearly walked right into a man coming out. His hands came up to catch hold of her arms and stop her.

"Sorry, miss. I'm afraid I wasn't looking where I was going."

"No, it was my fault," she insisted, her pulse racing at the near collision.

Embarrassed, she stepped back, freeing herself from his hands and darting a quick look at the man dressed in black denim jeans and a loose-fitting white shirt open at the throat and gathered at the shoulder seams. A low-crowned cowboy hat sat on the back of his curly brown hair, hair the rusty color of cinnamon. Young and brashly good-looking, he stepped aside with a little flourish, his glance skimming the jade-green jersey wrap dress she wore. Self-consciously Rachel walked by him into the nearly darkened lounge, avoiding contact with the interested gleam in his hazel eyes.

Two men stood at the bar and one sat at a back table. All three looked up when Rachel entered the room. None of them was Lane. Feeling their speculative stares, Rachel abandoned any thought of waiting in the lounge until Lane arrived. Never particularly adept at turning aside unwelcome advances, she hurriedly retreated to the foyer.

The man in the cowboy hat walked out of one of the swinging doors that led to the restaurant's kitchen. Again Rachel felt his interest centering on her when he noticed her standing at the entrance to the dining room. Guessing that he must work there, she gathered her courage as he approached.

"Excuse me, but . . . would it be all right if I sat down at one of the tables?"

All in one sweeping glance, he took in her, the empty restaurant, and the entrance to the lounge. "The restaurant part won't open for another ten minutes yet. I don't think the boss would mind if you sat down."

"Thank you." She smiled politely, not quite meeting his eyes as she started to walk past him.

"Could I bring you anything to drink? A cold beer? A glass of wine?" he asked.

Rachel hesitated, but since he'd offered, she decided it couldn't be an imposition. "A glass of white wine, please."

"Coming right up." He sauntered off toward the lounge.

She watched him a moment, the way he was dressed making her wonder if he was the bartender. She hadn't noticed one behind the bar—not that she was interested in what he did for a living. It meant nothing to her one way or the other. She entered the dining room and chose an empty table by the wall.

She had barely sat when the man in the cowboy hat reappeared. She glanced at the wineglass in his hand and unfastened the clasp on her shoulder purse to search out her wallet, using it as a distraction to avoid his gaze. "How much do I owe you?"

"It's on the house."

"I can't let you do that."

"It's the boss's way of apologizing for the fact that he couldn't seat you right away. He likes to keep his customers happy." He offered her the glass, holding it by the stem. There wasn't any way she could take it from him without touching his hand. She reached for the glass, her fingers barely brushing his, but even that brief contact made her feel awkward and ill at ease.

"Thank him for me, please. But this wasn't really necessary. I'm the one who came early, before the restaurant opened." She clasped the wineglass tightly in both hands and stared at the pale, nearly colorless liquid.

"I think he wanted to make sure you stayed." He continued to stand there, watching while she sipped nervously at the wine, anxious for him to leave. "My name's Ross Tibbs, by the way."

"How do you do, Mr. Tibbs."

"No, that isn't the way it's supposed to work. You see, I tell you my name, then you tell me yours. Let's try it again." He smiled, and two very attractive dimples appeared in his smooth cheeks. "My name's Ross Tibbs."

"Rachel. Rachel Farr," she responded, not knowing what else to do.

"I thought to myself, what big blue eyes you have."

"That's very flattering of you, Mr. Tibbs." But his compliment made her feel all the more uncomfortable.

"Ross," he insisted. "I'll bet your nickname is Blue Eyes."

"No. Just plain Rachel."

"You're not plain by a long shot. I could write a song about you. I'm a songwriter and singer. I play here on the weekends, give the place a little atmosphere and class. Of course, that'll only be 'til the end of July. After that, my agent's booking me into Gilley's. See, there's a good chance Mickey Gilley's going to record one of my songs on his next album." He said it all with a kind of pride and modesty that didn't make it sound like he was bragging.

Now that she knew he was a performer, she understood why he could talk to her with such ease, and say exactly what he was thinking. She envied that lack of reserve with strangers. At the same time, she wished Lane would come. She felt so much safer with him.

"That's wonderful." She was glad for him, even though she knew her voice lacked sincerity.

"I don't start singing until around eight o'clock, but I always come early to grab a bite to eat and give my food a chance to digest before I have to perform. Why don't you join me? I'd like the company, and there's no need for you to eat alone either. It makes for a long meal."

"Thanks, but I'm waiting for someone. He should be here anytime."

"That's just my luck." Ross Tibbs smiled ruefully. "The pretty ones are always spoken for."

"You're very kind." She wished he'd stop saying things like that.

"I'm not kind. Envious is more like it." His admiring look flustered her even more. "And, listen, if the guy is stupid enough not to show, the invitation stands. Okay?"

"He'll be here," Rachel asserted with more conviction than she felt.

There was always the possibility that Lane might not be able to make it. As busy as he was, a hundred other things might have come up that were more important than having dinner with her. He might be tied up at the farm, unable to get away. That had happened to her before with Dean — too many times to count. He had constantly made plans to see her, then broken them at the last minute. She wished she hadn't arranged to meet Lane here, at a public restaurant. It would be so embarrassing if he called and canceled.

Just as she was getting anxious that he wouldn't come, Rachel saw Lane enter the restaurant. "Here he is now," she said to Ross Tibbs, as Lane approached her table. "Hello." She watched his eyes light up with that special look that made her feel as if she was the most important person in the world to him, a look reserved for her alone. It gave her confidence and assurance. She could say or do anything and he'd still feel the same. "I was afraid you might not make it."

"Nothing would have kept me from you." He kissed her lightly on the cheek, the heady fragrance of his expensive cologne washing over her. "If necessary, I would have moved heaven and Texas to get here."

"And I'll bet you could." She laughed, proud that it meant so much to him to be with her. After all, he was Lane Canfield.

"I hope I didn't keep you waiting long." His attention strayed from her, and she saw his gaze narrow ever so slightly on Ross Tibbs.

"No. I was early," she said, and unwilling to have Lane think she might have something to hide, she added, "Lane, I'd like you to meet Ross Tibbs. He's the singer here. He was kind enough to keep me company while I was waiting for you to come. Mr. Tibbs, this is Lane Canfield."

"Mr. Tibbs, I'm in your debt." Lane held out his hand.

Ross took it and stared at him. "Lane Canfield. *The* Lane Canfield?"

"The same," Lane admitted with neither apology nor pride, just a mere statement of fact.

Ross released a low whistle under his breath and shook his head, obviously impressed. "It is an honor to meet you, sir. Everybody in Texas knows who you are."

"I doubt that everyone does." Lane smiled politely, then glanced at Rachel. "I see you already have a drink. I could certainly use one myself."

Rachel noticed the look of curious speculation on Ross Tibbs's face, as if he was trying to guess what her relationship to Lane was. For the first time she was aware of their age difference — a young woman with an older man. She hated the idea that people might think it was something sordid and cheap when it was nothing of the sort. Lane Canfield was a wonderful man and he meant a great deal to her. His age had no bearing on that. Why did people have to judge others and turn something special into something dirty? she wondered as Ross Tibbs moved away from the table, retreating toward the lounge. All her life they'd done that to her. It wasn't fair.

"He's a good-looking young man," Lane remarked. "You probably should be having dinner with him instead of me."

"Don't say that, please." It hurt, and she blinked at the tears that so quickly stung her eyes.

"Rachel." He sounded surprised and bewildered as he reached over and covered the hand she rested on the table. "I was only joking."

"You weren't, not really." She knew better. "You feel self-conscious about being seen with me in public. I'm sure you're concerned that people will think you're foolish."

"I don't give a damn what people think. I never have, Rachel, or I would never have built the companies I have," he insisted sternly. "Only one person's opinion is important to me and that's yours. I know you deserve someone young, with his whole life still ahead of him — not someone like me, who's used up most of his. My feeble attempt at a joke was my way of acknowledging how lucky I am that you are with me and . . . it was also my way of saying that I would understand if you ever decided to choose him, or someone like him, instead of me."

"I won't. I'm sure of that." She saw the way he smiled at her, almost patronizingly. "I suppose you think that's amusing."

"No. I was just remembering when I was your age, I was that sure about things, too. Now I'm older, and I know better. You can't be sure of anything, especially what the future holds."

She longed to deny that and swear that he would always be special to her, but she was afraid such a declaration would sound childish and silly. "I know it's true, but I wish you wouldn't say that."

"Now is enough, Rachel," he said gently. "When you think about it, all anyone has is now. The past and the future don't really matter. Let's enjoy tonight and worry about tomorrow when it comes."

"If it comes."

"If it comes," Lane conceded, then released her hand as a waitress approached their table. Rachel missed the warm pressure of his fingers. As he ordered a drink, she wondered if she would ever be able to explain to him the void he filled in her life. "So tell me, did anything new and exciting happen today?"

"Yes. Or, at least, I think it's exciting. As of this morning, Simoon and Ahmar are on their way here from California. I've made arrangements to board them temporarily at a private stable until I get a place of my own. It's going to be so good having them here. I've missed them," she stated simply.

"When will they arrive here?"

"In three or four days. The driver's going to take it in easy stages so the long haul won't be too much of a strain on them."

"You've talked so much about them, I'm looking forward to finally seeing them."

"I want you to meet them. But . . . I know how busy you are, and this isn't really very important in comparison." She hated the idea that he might have suggested it just to humor her.

"It's important to you. That makes it important to me." Lane leaned forward and laid his arm on the table, extending his hand to her. Rachel slid her hand into his palm and his fingers closed around it, the pressure warm and reassuring. The waitress returned with his drink, but this time Lane didn't let go of her hand. When the woman set the drink before him, he thanked her absently and dismissed her with an indifferent nod. "As I was saying before we were interrupted, I'm interested in everything about you, Rachel."

"I know you say that."

"It's true." He understood her hesitation. He'd had trouble coming to terms with it himself. In the beginning, he'd tried to convince himself that his interest was motivated by a sense of responsibility and compassion. But it was much more complicated than that. Other women had wanted him, but Rachel actually *needed* him: his knowledge, his guidance, and his affection. The butterfly was slowly emerging from her cocoon, and Lane knew he was responsible for her transformation. Watching it, he felt renewed himself — strong and vital again, losing his jaded outlook. Out of all the women he'd known, she was the first to arouse the man in him, both emotionally and sexually. "How many times do I have to tell you that before you believe me?"

Warmth flowed from his hand. It seemed to fill her up until she thought she would burst with happiness. Not a wild kind: the feeling was more contented, like sitting in front of a fire on a cold night, close enough to feel all toasty and warm inside, but not so close that the heat burned.

"Maybe a thousand," Rachel teased.

His eyebrows shot up, amusement deepening the corners of his mouth. "I believe you're flirting with me."

She laughed shyly. "I guess I was."

"Don't stop. I like it."

"Now you're flirting with me."

"I know. I like that, too." He picked up his glass. "Shall we drink to our mutual flirtation?" Lifting her wineglass, she touched it to his, then sipped at the dry Chablis, her eyes meeting his over the rim. There was something warm and intimate about the moment that gave her confidence.

"I wish we were alone." She wanted to be held and kissed — loved.

Lane took a deep breath, then seemed to have trouble releasing it as an answering darkness entered his eyes. "I think we'd better change the subject," he murmured as he reluctantly released her hand and leaned back in the chair, putting more table between them. "What else did you do today?"

She was tempted to test the full extent of her ability to disturb him, but she was afraid she might find out it wasn't that great. "I spent the biggest share of today riding around looking at various properties for sale with that realtor you recommended. She must have shown me ten different parcels outside of Houston. Unfortunately none of them was what I had in mind."

"What are you looking for?"

Another River Bend, but Rachel couldn't bring herself to admit that. Ever since she'd gone there that afternoon, the sight of it had lived with her. Nothing she'd seen since had come even close to being comparable.

"I'd like to find about a hundred acres with some buildings already on it, not farther than an hour out of Houston. It sounds easy, but something has been wrong with every piece of land I've looked at: either the price is more than I want to pay, or it's too far out, or it's too heavily wooded and the cost of clearing it and turning it into pasturage is too high. I don't know." She sighed, all her insecurities and feelings of inadequacy flooding back. "Maybe the whole idea is impractical. After all, who am I? A twenty-seven-year-old woman with two million dollars and no practical experience in breeding Arabians. I not only have to buy land and horses, but I need to hire a qualified manager, trainers, and grooms as well. I'm just dreaming if I think I can do it."

"Dreams are never practical, and they shouldn't be. But they do come true. Hold on to it, Rachel. You can make it happen if you try, but only if you try."

"Do you really believe I can do it?" No one, not even Dean, had ever encouraged her so totally. As her glance swept over his thick, silvered hair and strong face, Rachel finally identified the thing that attracted her so. The look of eagles — that was the quality a person sought in a stallion, a rare blend of nobility, pride, and strength. And Lane had it.

"Yes."

"Deep down, I think I can, too. I know it won't happen overnight. It takes time to establish a breeding program and prove that it works. A lot of it is trial and error. Dean taught me that. The knowledge I gained from him is going to be very useful. Look what he accomplished on a hundred acres, how successful he was. There's no reason I can't do the same." Rachel saw the frown that flickered across Lane's face, erasing the smile of interest and encouragement that had been there seconds ago. "What's the matter? Don't you agree with that?"

"I do." The smile came smoothly back, yet Lane seemed slightly distant.

But she wasn't reassured. She knew she must have said something wrong. Why else would he frown? But what could she have said? She tried to recall exactly what she'd been talking about when Lane reacted. It was something about Dean and River Bend. River Bend . . . Lane had been there today. Was that it? Had she unconsciously reminded him of something that had happened there? Had she reminded him of Abbie?

Resentment rose in her throat, but she forced it down. She'd had to accept that all her life. Why should she think it would be any different now?

Somehow she managed to get through the meal without letting on how hurt she felt — hiding it just as she'd done so many times in the past with Dean. As she left the steakhouse with Lane, she caught a glimpse of Ross Tibbs in the lounge, singing and accompanying himself on the guitar. She remembered how much she had been looking forward to spending the evening with Lane — and realized how anxious she was now for it to end.

Lane followed her back to her hotel in the Galleria. When he suggested having coffee in her hotel suite, Rachel wanted to plead tiredness, but realizing how kind he'd been to her, she felt too guilty to refuse.

Lane was standing at the window of the suite's luxurious living room, looking at the light-studded nightscape of Houston, when room service arrived with the coffee. Rachel poured each of them a cup and carried them over to the window. As usual, their conversation was centered on her plans for an Arabian horse farm. Rachel couldn't help wondering if that was the only subject Lane could think of to talk to her about.

"Have you ever considered taking on a partner?"

"What do you mean?" She frowned.

"I mean, why don't you and I become partners in this farm of yours?"

"What?" Rachel couldn't believe she'd heard him correctly. "Why would you want to become involved in it?" If it was only to help her, she knew she couldn't let him.

"Everyone knows that breeding operations are excellent tax shelters if managed properly. In my position, I can certainly use the write-offs. So you see, it's to my advantage to become involved. It would be a joint venture, with you overseeing the operation and me contributing part of the capital."

"You're serious."

"I am very serious."

"Are you sure this is what you want to do?" Rachel clutched at his hand, hardly daring to believe him.

"Only if you want me for a partner."

"There isn't anyone else I'd rather have than you, Lane." Inside, she was exploding with happiness. She couldn't imagine anything more wonderful than always having Lane there to turn to whenever she had a question or a problem. All her life she'd wanted to share this dream with someone. Doing things alone was no fun. She'd done them that way all her life and she knew. She wanted to plan with someone, work with someone, and share success with someone. "You can't know how happy you've made me, Lane."

"I'm glad. I want you to be happy."

"Earlier tonight, I had the feeling you had something on your mind." She'd been so certain it was Abbie, but now . . . "This was it, wasn't it?"

"I . . . have been giving the idea considerable thought lately."

But Rachel caught the slight hesitation. All her life she'd been sensitive to such things, quick to pick up the smallest nuance of phrasing — the careful wording that made a statement neither the truth nor a lie.

"I thought I might have said something wrong or maybe . . . there were problems at River Bend." Watching him closely as she voiced her suspicions, Rachel saw the faint break in his expression.

"Why should you think that?"

She wasn't fooled by his smooth smile. "It was River Bend. Something happened today that you don't want me to know." He was keeping things from her, shielding her the way Dean had, and she hated that. "What is it?"

"Yes, there are some problems there, but I'd rather not talk about them right now. After all, we have plans to make, critical things to decide . . . such as what are we going to name our farm?"

Rachel tried to go along with him. "South Wind." She'd picked out the name years ago. "According to legend, the Prophet Mohammed claimed that Allah summoned the south wind to him and the angel Gabriel grabbed a handful of it. From that, God created the Arabian horse." But she couldn't muster her usual enthusiasm for the subject.

"I like it."

"It's no good, Lane," she said. "If you don't tell me what happened, I'll just wonder about it. Did they say something about me?"

"No, Rachel, it isn't that at all. I didn't want to talk about it now because this is a big moment for you. I want you to enjoy it."

"So do I." But there had never been a single occasion in her life that hadn't been shadowed by Dean's other family. And it seemed that nothing had changed. "But I have to know."

"All right." He sounded grim. "It seems your father was heavily in debt when he died. He was behind in his payments. Everything is heavily mortgaged. It will all have to be sold to pay his creditors."

"But" — Rachel stared at him in disbelief — "how could that be? It's impossible. He couldn't have been broke . . . not with all the money he left me."

"That money was tied up in a trust for you. He couldn't touch it."

"Abbie, her mother — what about them?"

"I'm confident that after the assets are sold off and the accounts settled, there will be enough money left to enable them to find a new home and carry them for a while."

"River Bend is to be sold." She couldn't imagine such a thing happening. "Dean loved that place." Even more than he'd loved her mother, refusing to leave it for her. "It's been in his family for generations. It doesn't seem right that someone who isn't a Lawson should have it." The instant the words were out of her mouth, the thought flashed in her mind. "I'm a Lawson — by blood." She turned to him eagerly. "Lane, let's buy it."

"What?" An eyebrow shot up in surprise.

"Don't you see? It's perfect. Not only can we keep it from falling into a stranger's hands — someone who wouldn't love it and care for it the way Dean did — but we'd also have all the facilities standing there ready for use. There wouldn't be the expense of building. Plus River Bend already is a recognized name in the Arabian horse world. Time won't be lost establishing a reputation for ourselves. It's so obvious I'm surprised it didn't occur to you."

"Obvious, perhaps, but is it wise? That's something we need to think about."

"What is there to think about?" Rachel argued, not understanding why he didn't agree with her. "It's logical, practical, and sound. Even I can see that." Then she guessed his reason for hesitating and stiffened. "You're worried about how they'll react to me buying River Bend, aren't you?"

Lane set his coffee cup aside and took her gently by the shoulders. "All I'm saying is that we should think it through carefully. River Bend was Dean's home. It's natural that you would feel a special attachment to it. And I love you for wanting it to stay in the family. But I don't want you to make an impulsive decision that you may later regret. Right now, your reaction is mainly an emotional one. It isn't imperative that you make up your mind tonight. River Bend won't be sold for several more weeks yet. You have time and I want you to take it. Will you do that for me?"

"Yes," she agreed reluctantly, and turned away from him to stare out the window. "But I know I'm not going to change my mind. I don't care what they think. Maybe that sounds heartless, but . . . River Bend is going to be sold anyway. They're going to lose it, so what possible difference could it make to them who buys it? At least if I do, it will still be in the family. They should be grateful for that."

"Maybe. But let's sleep on the idea for a few days and talk about it then."

"All right." She breathed in deeply and nodded.

"I meant what I said a few minutes ago."

"I know. And I will think about it."

"I wasn't referring to that." Lane smiled faintly, his gaze running over her profile in a caress.

"Then what?" With so many other thoughts crowding her mind, Rachel didn't try to guess.

"I meant it when I said I love you."

He said it so softly, so gently, that for a full minute, its meaning didn't register. When it did, Rachel was stunned. "Lane," she whispered and turned to touch his face in wonder that a man like him could love her.

As he kissed her long and deep, she wrapped her arms around him and slid her fingers into his thick hair. That he should love her was such an amazing thing that she was afraid to believe it.

"Lane, are you sure?" She ached inside that it might be so.

"You are the woman I love," he insisted and smoothed the hair away from her face, then kissed her brow, nose, and cheek with feather-light touches of his lips.

"But I'm illeg—" His lips silenced the rest.

"You're a love child," he murmured against them.

Her breath caught in her throat. She drew back to stare at him. "My mother always said that."

"She was right. You were born out of love and intended for love. And I'm going to show you that."

The proof was offered by his lips and hands, caressing and arousing a desire in her that Rachel hadn't known she could feel. When Lane's hand stroked her breast, it was as if in adoration of her shape, and Rachel reveled in the feeling.

"I love you, too, Lane." Delicious shivers danced over her skin as he nibbled at her neck and ear.

"Do you?" He drew back, bringing her face into focus. "I want to believe that, but I'm older than you—much older. Are you sure you don't see me as a father figure?"

"Why do you have to say things like that?" she protested, hurt and angry that he should doubt her. "I look up to you, yes. But is it wrong for a woman to look up to the man she loves?"

"No, it's not wrong, if that's what it is."

"Why are you trying to put doubts in my mind?" She hated the way he was making her question her feelings. For her, it was enough that she felt them. Emotions weren't meant to be analyzed.

"Have you ever been in love before?"

"No." Twice she'd been close, but love had always eluded her—always.

"Then how can you be sure you know how it feels?" he reasoned. "I'm going to be out of town for a couple days. When I get back, we'll see how you feel then. If it is love, examining it won't hurt it . . . or change it." Shifting his hold on her, he hooked an arm around her shoulders and turned her away from the window. "Walk me to the door before I decide to take advantage of your moment of weakness."

Rachel almost wished he would. When he kissed her good night, she couldn't recapture her earlier pleasure in his touch. He'd given her too much to think about: her feelings for him and River Bend.

At nine-thirty, MacCrea saw the flash of headlights through the trailer windows. On the phone earlier, Abbie had told him she'd be there by nine. He started for the door, then turned abruptly and walked into the kitchen instead, irritated by how much he wanted to see her and hold her. After she'd made him wait this long, he'd be damned if he was going to run out there to her like some lovesick swain. He pulled a bottle of beer out of the refrigerator and waited for the trailer door to open.

When she walked in, everything else went out of his mind. She was slim and petite, but filled out in all the right places, as the low neckline of her peasant blouse revealed. Her dark hair lay thickly about her shoulders, all loose and soft, the way he liked it.

"Hello." That was all she said.

"I was beginning to wonder where you were." As he moved toward her, MacCrea noticed the tiredness in her eyes and the faintly troubled look in her expression despite the smile she gave him.

"It took longer than I thought. We have another sick foal. Ben thinks it might be pneumonia."

She slid her arms around his middle and tipped back her head for his kiss. MacCrea was happy to oblige. She responded, but not with the fervor and greedy passion he'd come to expect. She seemed unnaturally subdued. Something was on her mind and it wasn't him. A little annoyed, he released her and walked over to the kitchen counter.

"How about a cold beer?" He popped the top off his bottle with an opener.

"No. The last thing my head needs right now is alcohol." She sounded discouraged or angry, MacCrea wasn't sure which—maybe both. She turned toward the table. "What's this? Flowers?" She touched the spray of wildflowers in the amber glass as if assuring herself that they were real.

"I decided the place needed a man's touch." He moved over to stand next to her, breathing in the shampoo scent of her hair.

"They're beautiful." But her smile was barely more than a movement of the mouth.

"Careful. You might get carried away by so much excitement," MacCrea taunted.

"I'm sorry." She sighed, her glance sliding off him. "I guess I'm tired tonight."

That wasn't tiredness he saw; it was tension. Abbie was wound up tighter than a spring. Talking wasn't what he'd had in mind when she arrived, but until she relaxed a little, something told him she'd just go through the motions of making love. MacCrea didn't want that and decided, if they had to talk, it might as well be about a subject that interested him.

"You said Canfield came today. Did everything go all right?" He started to raise the bottle to his mouth, but he stopped in midmotion as Abbie turned abruptly away from him, suddenly agitated and angry.

"He showed up all right." Her voice vibrated with the effort of holding her feelings in check. Then just as abruptly as she'd turned away, she turned back and headed for the refrigerator. "I think I will have that beer you offered."

Curious, MacCrea watched her. While she took a cold bottle of beer out of the refrigerator, he opened the overhead cabinet and took down a glass. He watched as she snapped the cap off with the opener. The sharp popping sound seemed to release some of the built-up pressure inside her as well.

"What happened?" MacCrea pushed the glass across the counter toward her.

Abbie hesitated, then poured the cold beer into the glass, the foam rising thickly. "It's hardly a secret, I guess. In a few days, the whole damned state of Texas is going to know about it. You see, MacCrea," — she paused, the bitterness in her voice thicker than the foam on her beer — "we're broke. That's what Lane had to tell us today."

"What do you mean by broke?" He frowned, aware that different people had different definitions of the word.

"Broke as in head-over-heels in debt. Broke as in everything has to be sold to pay off the debts. Broke as in penniless — homeless." She gripped the bottle of beer tightly, her hand trembling with the vehemence and anger that had come from her.

"I think I get the picture," MacCrea said quietly, feeling a little stunned by the news.

"I doubt it," she retorted caustically. "Everything has to be sold: the house, the farm, the land, the horses, everything. I had a feeling we were going to have problems with Daddy's estate, but I thought they were going to come from Rachel. I thought she'd contest the will or make some sort of trouble. But I never expected this. Not once."

"It's rough." He knew better than anyone that right now words were meaningless. Abbie wasn't listening.

"I'll bet she knew all along. Lane must have told her. No wonder she didn't try to get a share of the estate. She already knew there wasn't anything to get." She picked up the glass of beer and drank down a quick swallow, then stared at the glass. "You know why there isn't any money, don't you? It's because he spent so much on her and that mistress of his. He probably showered her with expensive presents — like that filly he gave her."

"She was his daughter."

"So am I!" Abbie exploded. "But she always got everything! Did you know he was killed while he was on his way back from seeing her?"

"No."

"Not me. It was never me." She looked close to breaking, her voice choking up. "I had nothing of him when he was alive. Maybe it's fitting that I have nothing of his now that he's dead." She lifted her shoulders in a vague shrug, showing her helplessness. "I just don't know what to do."

It wasn't like her. But MacCrea could appreciate her dilemma. She'd never faced anything like this before. Other people's problems rarely had any effect on him, but this time was different. He couldn't be impervious to her situation. He took the glass from her hand and gathered her into his arms, struggling inwardly with the protective instinct she'd aroused. She leaned against him and rested her head on his chest, absently rubbing her cheek against him.

"There's so much to do I don't know where to start," she said miserably. "Somewhere I've got to find a job and a place to live, but doing what and where?"

"The last part's easy. You can move in with me." The idea of having her here all the time appealed to him.

"What about Momma and Ben? I don't think this trailer could accommodate four people. And there's Jackson. He was going to retire as soon as he received the bequest Daddy left him."

"I wasn't thinking about them."

"But I have to. At his age, Ben isn't going to find another job. And Momma has never worked a day in her life." Her arms tightened around him as she pressed herself closer. "Hold me, MacCrea. Just hold me."

That was all she asked. He cradled her to his body and swayed gently, rocking her ever so slightly. MacCrea didn't say anything. There was nothing he could say.

17

AS ABBIE SKIMMED the list of horses that had been compiled from the records by Lane Canfield's assistant, the name of her filly River Breeze stood out sharply among the Arabic names her father had given the rest. She stared at it first in surprise, then puzzlement. Obviously it was a mistake — one that needed to be corrected immediately.

With the list in hand, she left Ben's office in the stable annex to look for Lane or his assistant, Chet Forbes. Both were somewhere on the premises along with three other members of his staff, taking a complete inventory of everything on the place. The current plan called for two separate estate auctions to take place, the first to be a dispersal sale of all the horses, their tack, and related equipment, and the second, the sale of River Bend itself and its individual items.

Hearing voices coming from the tack room, Abbie crossed to its doorway and paused to glance inside. A portly man in shirt sleeves lifted four show halters off their wall hook, Ben identified them, and another man marked them down on his clipboard sheet — a tedious, time-consuming project.

"Four show halters," the man repeated as he wrote it down.

"One of those is silver," Ben corrected. "It is most expensive."

As the heavy-set man examined the halters again, Abbie explained, "It's tarnished. We'll have to polish it before the auction." She made a mental note of yet another thing that had to be done. The list was getting long. "Have you seen Lane or Chet Forbes?"

"Yeah, they're in the other office." A chubby hand motioned in the direction of her father's private office.

"Thanks," Abbie said, already walking away, striding quickly to the office door. She knocked sharply twice, then reached for the doorknob as a muffled voice invited her inside. Lane stood behind the desk going over some papers, with the man in wire-rimmed glasses, Chet Forbes, seated in the chair. Both looked up when she walked in. "Excuse me, but I was just going over the list of horses you gave me. You have River Breeze included. That's the filly *I* own. Daddy gave her to me last year."

"I wonder how that happened." The pale young man took the list from her and glanced at it briefly, then began going through the folders on the desktop. "I used the owner registration papers and the foaling records to compile the list."

"You probably saw my registration papers on Breeze in with the others, caught the name Lawson, and added it to the list without looking at it any closer."

"That's possible." Chet Forbes opened the folder and deftly leafed through the clipped papers, scanning the names as he went. "Here it is. River Breeze." After carefully examining both the front and back of the certificate, he looked up triumphantly. "I was right. The horse is registered to Dean Lawson and nothing has been filled out transferring the ownership to any other party."

"That can't be." Abbie took the folder from him and looked at the back of the certificate, but her name didn't appear on the line reserved for the buyer of the horse. "He gave River Breeze to me."

"Did he say he was signing the registration over to you?" Lane walked around the desk to look at it.

"That was last year. I don't remember exactly what he said. But you don't give somebody something and keep the title in your own name," Abbie insisted.

"Did you ever ask about the owner registration?"

"No. I assumed he sent it in. I never gave it another thought. I mean, it would have come here and . . . Daddy would have put it away for me. If I had wondered about it at all, that's what I would probably have thought happened." She looked at Lane, suddenly made wary by his questions. "She is mine."

"I don't know what to say, Abbie," Lane said, stalling. "You don't appear to have anything in writing to back up your claim to the horse — nothing with Dean's signature. The registration papers are still in his name. Legally, it would appear that the horse belongs to his estate."

"No." She choked on the angry denial.

"I'm sure Dean got busy and overlooked it. I'll see what I can do, if anything," Lane promised. "But you must understand this horse is a valuable animal — a valuable asset, if you will, not that much different from a building. You wouldn't expect a claim to a building to be regarded as valid if you had no title or documentation to back it up. I'm afraid the law will look at this in the same way."

"And Rachel: I suppose Daddy signed over the papers on the filly he gave her." Abbie couldn't keep the bitterness out of her voice.

"I couldn't say." Lane took the folder from her and handed it back to Chet.

"We matched up all the horses on the farm to the registration papers in the file. There were two baby horses—" Chet began.

"Foals." Abbie snapped out the correct term.

"Yes . . . two foals that needed some forms filled out for registration, but other than that, we found no discrepancies between the papers we had and the horses on the place," he finished.

"I believe you," she replied tightly, her voice shaking with the anger and resentment boiling inside her. "But she still belongs to me."

Lane met her challenging stare. "I'll do everything I can to make sure you keep your horse, Abbie."

"Please do." As she started toward the door, Lane accompanied her.

"Chet and I were just talking about hiring some extra help to get the horses ready for the sale."

"We'll need it," Abbie stated, walking out of the office and heading for the outer door to the breezeway. "Ben and I can't get all the horses trimmed and groomed by ourselves. As it is, we won't be able to get them in top show condition in a little over a month."

"I'll see that you have the help you need," Lane promised as they emerged from the annex.

"Thanks." But Abbie was distracted by the sight of MacCrea's black pickup parked next to Lane's car. She hadn't expected to see him until later that night, their late-evening rendezvous becoming almost routine. When she saw him coming from the house, she quickened her step, breaking into a welcoming smile. "MacCrea, what are you doing here? You didn't say anything about stopping by today."

"I thought I'd surprise you." Pausing in front of her, he regarded her in that lazy way he had that made Abbie feel warm all over.

"You did."

"Good." Possessively, MacCrea curved an arm around her shoulders and pulled her against his side with an apparent disregard for Lane's presence. Then he bent his head, as if to nuzzle her hair, and whispered, "I missed you." He straightened to smile crookedly at her, knowing she couldn't say the same without being overheard. Abbie made a face at him, secretly smiling, and Mac-Crea chuckled.

As Lane joined them, Abbie turned. "Lane, I'd like you to meet MacCrea Wilder. MacCrea, Lane Canfield."

MacCrea removed his arm from around her shoulders to shake hands with Lane. "It's a pleasure to meet you, Mr. Canfield."

"Mr. Wilder."

"I don't know if I've told you anything about MacCrea or not, Lane, but I meant to." Many times, Abbie realized, but each time she'd seen Lane, too many other things had cropped up. "He's a drilling contractor as well as a wildcatter. And he's come up with a new invention — some sort of a testing process. MacCrea can explain it better than I can."

"I doubt that Mr. Canfield is interested in hearing about it, Abbie," Mac-Crea inserted as he calmly sized up the older man. "It isn't exactly in his line."

"Daddy was going to put him in touch with some people he knew who could help MacCrea develop and market it. You know a lot of people in the oil business, Lane," Abbie reminded him. "Maybe you could arrange some meetings for him."

"I might be able to," he conceded. "It certainly never hurts to look at something. Maybe we could get together sometime and you can explain it all to me."

"Why don't I give you a call at your office the first of next week and set up a meeting?"

Abbie didn't hear Lane's response as the battered pickup owned by Dobie Hix came rattling into the yard. She frowned, wondering what he was doing there at this time of day. It was too early to feed the horses. But she was even more bewildered when she saw her mother sitting in the cab of the truck with Dobie.

"Excuse me." She turned away from Lane and MacCrea with only an absent glance in MacCrea's direction and headed for the pickup.

"Abbie, the most wonderful thing just happened." Her mother clambered out of the cab, all astir with excitement. "I've found a place for us to live."

"You did?" Abbie glanced sharply at Dobie Hix as he walked around the hood of the rusted truck. Hurriedly, he pulled off his hat. As the sunlight flashed on his hair, bringing out the red in its strawberry-blond color, Abbie wondered what he had to do with all this.

"Yes, and it's perfect," Babs Lawson declared. "Dobie just showed it to me. It's small. We'll have to get rid of some of our furniture, but we really don't need anything bigger. There's even a room for Ben."

"Where is this house?" Abbie didn't mean to sound skeptical, but she wasn't sure her mother understood all the things that had to be considered in selecting a place to live.

"It's over at my place," Dobie answered. "Some of my hired hands live on the farm with their families. I furnish them living quarters as part of their salaries. But this particular house is vacant now, and I thought if you wanted, you could live there. It ain't much — not like what you been used to, but —"

"Dobie, I don't know what to say." Abbie shrugged helplessly.

"I'll have to charge you rent for it. But it'll be fair. I need something to cover the costs of the utilities."

"If you didn't let us pay, we wouldn't even consider staying there." She wasn't about to accept charity from anyone, even a close neighbor.

"I know that, Abbie. But I think you'll like the house." Dobie gazed at her earnestly, anxious to convince her of the fact. "And I don't keep much livestock anymore, so the barn's practically empty. You can keep your horse there at no charge. It's just standing empty anyway."

"Do you see what I mean, Abbie? It's perfect for us," her mother declared happily.

"It sounds like it," Abbie was forced to agree. But she didn't understand why she didn't feel more relieved that a solution may have been found for the problem of where they would live. After all, it meant one less thing she had to do. She should have been happy that her mother had taken it upon herself to look into it. Instead she found herself wanting to find fault with the choice.

"If you want, I can run you over so you can look at it," Dobie offered.

"Maybe later. I'm busy now."

"Sure." Dobie glanced in the direction of Lane and MacCrea and reluctantly nodded. "Anytime you want to see it, you just come over."

"Thanks, Dobie. I will."

"Well." He smiled and played with his hat. "Guess I'd better get going."

"Dobie, thank you for taking me over to see the house." Babs reached out to shake his hand. "Don't worry, I know Abbie is going to like it as much as I do."

"I hope so." He pushed his hat onto his head and headed around the truck to the driver's side, saying over his shoulder, "See y'all later."

The truck's engine sputtered uncertainly, backfired, then chugged to life. Still struggling with the mixed feelings she had about the house, Abbie watched while he reversed away from the fence and aimed the truck down the farm lane.

"Wait until you see it, Abbie." Babs was still excited about the house and obviously proud that she had found it. "I know it's smaller than we're used to, but we don't need all the room we have now."

"I know. Maybe tomorrow morning we'll have time to go look at the house together." She started to turn away and rejoin MacCrea and Lane.

"This is certainly our day for company, isn't it? Who do you suppose that is?" Babs wondered.

As Abbie glanced down the long driveway to the road, Dobie's pickup took the shoulder of the narrow lane to let the other car pass. Abbie stopped abruptly, all her muscles and nerves growing tense.

"Probably somebody to look at the horses." Like last time, Abbie thought as she worked to keep her voice calm and evenly pitched. "Why don't you go up to the house and fix us some iced tea, Momma? And ice that cake you baked this morning. Lane would like that."

"That's a good idea."

With her mother successfully sidetracked, Abbie walked quickly toward the car slowing to a stop in the yard. She felt almost rigid with tension when Rachel Farr stepped out, a picture of freshness untouched by the hot afternoon sun. Resentment simmered near the surface as Abbie looked into the face that was so like her own.

"What are you doing here, Miss Farr? I thought you understood that you weren't welcome here." She blocked Rachel's path, realizing MacCrea and Lane were standing a few feet away only after Rachel darted a quick glance in their direction.

"I know, but I had to talk to you."

"My God, you're . . ." The barely whispered words came from behind Abbie. As she swung around, she caught the stricken look Babs turned on her —a look of shock at the resemblance between the two.

"Momma, I told you to go to the house." She hated seeing her own mother look at her that way. She had tried to spare her this. Why hadn't she listened?

"I'm Rachel Farr, Mrs. Lawson."

Abbie turned on her. "Why don't you just leave? We don't want you here."

"If you'd let me explain—" Rachel began again.

"We aren't interested in anything you have to say."

"Rachel." Lane came up to her.

"No, Lane. I told you that I've thought this through very carefully the way you asked," Rachel told him quietly, her tone firm despite a nervous tremor in her voice.

Abbie stared as Lane took Rachel's hand and clasped it warmly. "All right," he said.

There was an intimacy in the exchange, a sense of closeness, that left Abbie shaken and confused. She had guessed Lane and Rachel had talked before. But she had always assumed their meetings had dealt with her father's will, just as Lane's meetings with her and Babs had. Yet that look, the way he held her hand

and stood beside her — he was obviously more than a family friend. What made Rachel so special? Why did Lane like her better, too?

"Lane has explained to me the financial situation you are in . . . with all the debts," Rachel began hesitantly. "And I know the prospect of River Bend being sold at public auction can't be pleasant. Rather than have it all go up on the sale block, I'd like to buy it."

"With what? My father's money?" Bitterly Abbie recalled that Lane had told her that Dean had made separate provisions for Rachel.

"Most of the money will come from a trust fund he established for me, yes," Rachel admitted.

"Most of the money," which meant Rachel had received a sizable fortune, Abbie realized. River Bend had been appraised at well over two million dollars. And Rachel wanted to buy it. Even at his death, her father had made sure Rachel had money, even though he'd left them with nothing. Did she need any more proof than that, that her father hadn't loved her?

Abbie felt something snap inside, unleashing a torrent of hatred and anger. "I'd burn River Bend to the ground before I'd let you have it! Now get out of here! Go before I have you thrown off! Do you hear? Get out! Get out!" She couldn't think straight. She couldn't see. She wasn't even aware of the rising note of hysteria in her voice as she screamed at Rachel, watching her shrink against Lane for protection.

Suddenly MacCrea was between them, his hands digging into her arms with punishing force. "You've made your point, Abbie."

She trembled with the violence that raged inside her and choked her voice. "Just get her out of here."

But it was Lane who walked Rachel to her car and helped her inside. A diamond-bright trail of tears streaked Rachel's cheeks, but Abbie knew her own pain went deeper than tears. Glancing at her mother, she saw the drained and broken look on her face.

As the car pulled away and Lane started back to them, Babs turned weakly away. "I think I'll go to the house," she said.

"Yes, Momma," Abbie said tightly, then sagged a little herself when Mac-Crea released her arms. As Lane rejoined them, she eyed him suspiciously, now fully aware of where his loyalties were.

"I'm sorry you feel the way you do, Abbie," he said. "I know that Rachel was anxious to have River Bend stay in the family."

"She was anxious over that, was she? How very noble of her to be concerned about the family home. What about Momma? How do you think she feels knowing that Daddy left Rachel enough money to buy River Bend, but Momma didn't get a thing? Hasn't she gone through enough hell knowing that Daddy didn't love her? Did she have to be reminded that he had provided for his mistress's child, but not for his own wife and daughter?" Abbie raged bitterly.

"I know how you must feel —"

"Do you? I doubt it. Because now I feel the way Momma does. I can't stand this place. I can hardly wait until it's sold and everything on it."

Abbie walked away from them, aware that MacCrea hadn't said a word. But she didn't care what he thought — not right now. She hadn't realized it was possible to hate so much.

18 ～

"AND SIGN HERE." Lane flipped to the last page of the partnership agreement and indicated the x-marked line that required Rachel's signature. Rachel signed her name in the blank and straightened from the massive walnut desk in his office. "That's the last one." He stacked the copies of the agreement together as she laid the gold pen on his desk. "Here's your copy," he said, handing the top one to her. "Happy?"

"To have you for a partner, of course." Rachel smiled and turned to look out at the city, knowing that only one thing could make her happier: owning River Bend.

"We'll have to have dinner together tonight and celebrate."

His voice sounded closer, and she realized that Lane had left his desk and joined her. Rachel smiled at the thought that his plushly upholstered desk chair was too expensive to squeak. She looked around his office, admiring its clean, contemporary look. Like the building, the spacious executive office was done mostly in glass and chrome, its corner setting giving it a wide view of downtown Houston. She liked the symmetry and style of the room, everything in proportion, including the huge desk.

"I'd like that." She turned to him, then paused. "You haven't said whether you've talked to Abbie since . . ." She let the sentence trail off unfinished, knowing she didn't need to remind him of the disastrous encounter with her the previous week.

"I called yesterday to let her know we were sending her the proofs on the sales catalogue so she can check it for errors. The names of some of those horses would twist any man's tongue and send him scrambling for a dictionary . . . Arabic, of course." When she failed to smile at his attempt at humor, Lane sighed. "You haven't changed your mind, have you? Even though you know how they're going to feel?"

"No. I still want us to buy it." When she closed her eyes, she could still see Abbie's face, the contempt and rage that had been on it. If anything, it only made her more determined to have it. "I suppose you think that's wrong of me."

"No. No, I don't." Lane seemed to consider his next words before he spoke. "As a matter of fact, after you left that day, Abbie informed me that she and her mother hated the farm. She said she couldn't wait for it to be sold."

"She really said that? How could she?" Rachel was at once astounded and angry by the statement she regarded as blatant disloyalty. "River Bend is Dean's legacy. His family has owned it for a hundred and fifty years. How could she want to see it sold to some stranger?"

"I don't know. But that's what she said."

"Well, I'm not going to let it happen. I can't." She glanced down at the newly signed document in her hand. "I know you think I'm being silly and sentimental. Maybe we should just tear up these partnership papers, because I know you don't approve of buying River Bend—"

"You're wrong." He folded his hand around her fingers, tightening her grasp on the document. "I see no reason why we shouldn't buy it, especially when you want it so much."

"Do you mean that?" She searched his face anxiously.

"How could I look into those blue eyes and say no?" he chided.

"Lane." She breathed his name in an exultant laugh, then kissed him, pressing her lips ardently against his, loving him more at that moment than she ever had. Through the thin silk fabric of her dress, she felt his hands traveling along her back and arching her against the shape of his body. She wanted to hold on to this moment, with its heated closeness and consuming happiness. The world was hers now. If there was one dark spot in it, it was knowing that Abbie had been the one who had succeeded in convincing Lane to buy River Bend when she had failed.

Gently Lane tugged her arms from around his neck as he reluctantly withdrew his mouth from her moist, clinging lips. "I have yet to seduce a beautiful woman on my office couch," he said thickly, "but if we keep this up, you'll be the first."

Her own pulse racing, Rachel noticed the answering desire that darkened his eyes and weighted their lids. She felt like a temptress. One curl of her finger and she could get him to do anything she wanted. She reveled in the feeling even as he firmly set her away from him.

"I'm quite sure that I'm the happiest woman in the whole world right now, Lane. I not only have you, but soon, River Bend will be ours, too. Sometimes I wonder if this isn't all a dream . . . that maybe none of this is happening . . . that you didn't kiss me a minute ago."

"I found it very real. Everything else is, too, I promise you." He gazed at her for a long moment, then walked over to his desk, as if needing to put more distance between them. "I'll arrange for an agent to bid for us at the auction."

"Speaking of auctions, when I glanced through the list of broodmares to be sold, I saw several that I think we'd be interested in acquiring. Of course, I'm basing that strictly on their bloodlines. I've never actually seen them. Naturally, I would want to before we bought them."

"You're saying you want to attend the horse auction," Lane guessed.

"Yes. But considering the way Abbie behaved the last time I was there—ordering me off the premises—you know she isn't going to want me there."

"She can't bar you from it. It's a public auction, open to anyone, and that includes you."

"Maybe you should remind her of that the next time you talk to her."

"I will. Now, I don't mean to chase you off, but I have another meeting in"—he paused and glanced at the gold Piaget watch on his wrist—"five minutes. I'll pick you up at seven for dinner."

"I'll be waiting." She walked over and gave him another kiss, sensing that he wished it was longer and more passionate than the chaste kiss she bestowed.

On her way out of his office, Rachel collected her alligator purse from a chair. Over and over she kept reminding herself that soon she would be the new mistress of River Bend and Abbie would be out. She would have Dean's home. She would carry on the family traditions. And she would run the River Bend Arabian Stud. She felt an exhilarating sense of power. For the first time in her life, she felt she could do anything, be anything. Nothing could stop her: not the shame of her past, not Abbie — nothing.

As she swept through the outer office, she barely glanced at Lane's secretary and the man standing at his desk. In the lobby, she pushed the "down" button for the elevator and waited for it to come. She was still waiting when she was joined by someone else. She glanced absently at the man and instantly recognized him as the one who had intervened the other day with Abbie. According to Lane, Abbie had been seeing him regularly.

"You're MacCrea Wilder, aren't you?" she said, recalling the name Lane had told her.

"That's right." He nodded briefly, something hooded in his glance — or maybe she got that impression from the hat brim that shaded his dark eyes.

Rachel found it impossible not to compare him physically to Lane. Wilder was taller, broader in the shoulders, and more narrow in the hips than Lane. His thick hair was dark and wavy; Lane's was silver and straight. Lane was smooth-shaven and Wilder wore a full mustache, but he lacked that distinguished air that Rachel found so appealing in Lane. It was obvious to her that Abbie preferred the rugged, virile type.

"Lane mentioned that you've been seeing Abbie."

"I have," he confirmed, looking straight into her eyes.

She had expected him to scan her face and take note of the features she shared in common with Abbie. But he didn't. It was as if he saw no resemblance at all. For some reason she was thrown by that and fought to rid herself of that resurfacing sense of inferiority.

"Our elevator's here."

With a small start, Rachel noticed he was holding the doors open for her. She quickly stepped into the empty elevator, followed closely by MacCrea. She watched him punch the ground-floor button. Belatedly, she recognized the combination of tan blazer and blue jeans as being the same as that worn by the man in Lane's outer office.

"Were you the one talking to Lane's secretary when I came out of his office?" she asked as the doors slid shut.

"Yes."

"He said he had a meeting. Was that with you?" If so, it had certainly been a short one.

"No. I was making an appointment to talk to him later in the week."

"About Abbie?" she guessed.

"No. It's a business matter."

"I remember: Lane said you wanted to talk to him about some invention of yours. It had to do with drilling oil wells, I think he said."

"That's right."

"I know he sounded very interested in it," Rachel recalled thoughtfully, remembering that Lane had indicated he might become personally involved in the development financing and marketing of it. "Would you object if I sat in on your meeting with Lane, Mr. Wilder? This might be something I'd like to get into — purely as an investor."

"I don't mind, as long as Lane doesn't."

"He won't mind," she stated confidently, fully aware that Abbie would. Rachel smiled, discovering that she liked the idea.

19 ✧

THE COOL OF THE central air-conditioning greeted Abbie as she entered the kitchen through the back door. A roast baking in the oven was redolent of the tang of cooked onions. She picked her way through the boxes stacked by the door, all of them bearing the meticulous scroll of her mother's handwriting, identifying the cartons as containing sale items. Abbie searched the counter by the wall telephone, but the day's mail wasn't in its usual place.

Impatiently, she pushed open the connecting door to the formal dining room and checked the table and bureau top for the mail, then continued into the living room, her boots clumping loudly, then softly, then loudly again as she went from hardwood floor to area rug to hardwood floor again.

"Abbie, is that you?" her mother called from the upstairs landing.

"Yes, Momma." She crossed to the foot of the staircase. "Where did you put today's mail? Ben said there was a packet from Lane's office in it."

"It's on the table in the foyer." Babs came down the steps, dressed in a pair of slacks that looked like relics of the forties, with a scarf tied around her head like some Aunt Jemima character.

Abbie didn't know where her mother was finding the clothes she'd been wearing lately, but she suspected they were coming from the old trunks her mother had dragged out of the attic. She walked over to the side table and started leafing through the mail.

"I'm so glad you're here, Abbie. Which bedroom do you want for yourself at the other house? You never did say when we went over to the Hix farm to look at it," she reminded her as Abbie ripped open the manila envelope bearing the return address of Lane Canfield's office and pulled out the printed sales catalogue. "I'm trying to decide which dresser sets to keep and which to sell. Yours will fit in one room but not in the other. Same for mine, but the guest bedroom set will work in either."

On the third page of the catalogue, Abbie found River Breeze's name listed in bold type. Even though she had suspected that the filly would be included despite her claim of ownership, something died inside her when she actually saw it in print. Two days ago, Lane had called to inform her that the probate court seemed to be taking the position that the filly was too valuable to be regarded as a family pet. Yet Abbie had hoped.

"Abbie, did you hear me? Which bedroom do you want?"

"I don't care." She let the pages of the catalogue flip shut, then dropped it on the table with the rest of the mail. "You choose the one you want and I'll take the other."

"Is something wrong, Abbie?" Frown lines creased her forehead as Babs glanced from her to the catalogue and torn envelope on the table.

"Wrong?" Abbie shook her head vaguely. "I'm not sure I know what's right or wrong anymore, Momma." She reached for the front doorknob. "I'll see you later."

Abbie walked out of the house onto the wide porch feeling beaten. Everything was going from bad to worse, it seemed, and she wondered when it was going to stop. When was something good going to happen to her?

As she reached the top of the steps, she heard the hinges creak on the picket gate and looked up. MacCrea was striding toward her, tall and vigorous, a smile splitting his strong face. Here was something good, she realized and suddenly became aware of the bright shining sun and the blue of the jay on the lawn.

She practically ran down the steps, but by the time she reached the last one, he was there. And that step eliminated his height advantage and put her on just the right level to throw her arms around his neck and kiss him long and strong, putting everything she had into it. After a startled instant, he responded in kind, returning the driving pressure of her lips and wrapping his arms tightly around her and molding her to his body.

When she finally dragged her lips from his mouth, she was trembling. "I've missed you, Mac," she murmured. "I haven't seen you for two days. Where have you been?"

"If this is the kind of welcome I get, I'm going to leave more often." His low-pitched voice was a little husky.

"You hadn't better." She needed him. Abbie hadn't realized how much until now.

"I've got some good news. As of this morning, a major drilling-fluid company in Houston has agreed to field-test my computerized system for checking the downhole performance of mud — and market it, if it proves successful. The financing and everything has all been arranged."

"Are you serious?" For a split second she hardly dared to believe him, but the glint of satisfaction in his eyes told her it was true. "That's wonderful! Mac, it's fantastic!"

"You're damned right it is. And you and I are going out on the town and celebrate, starting now," he declared.

"This minute?" But she realized that was exactly what he meant. "MacCrea, I can't. I've got a thousand and one things I have to do this afternoon. Later, after the horses are fed tonight —"

"We're going now." His half-smile was lazy and confident.

"You're crazy. I can't leave all this work for Ben." Abbie tried to push away from him, but his arms were locked together behind her back.

"He'll manage. And if some of the horses go hungry tonight, it's not going to hurt them. You're coming with me and that's final."

"I am not — and that's final!" She didn't like his high-handed attitude. It smacked of dictatorship, and no one told *her* what to do, not even MacCrea.

His smile faded. "If that's the way you feel," — he paused, and she felt his arms loosen their hold on her, his hands retreating to her waist as he took a step backward — "I guess I'll just have to take matters into my own hands."

Suddenly she was being lifted. Abbie tried to struggle, but it all happened too fast. One minute her feet were on the steps, and the next she was slung over his shoulder like a sack of grain.

"MacCrea Wilder, you put me down this minute," she ordered through gritted teeth and pushed at his back, trying to lever herself off his shoulder, but he had a viselike grip around her thighs. Abbie held herself stiffly, refusing to kick and beat at him like some hysterical female.

"Sorry."

"You're not the least bit sorry," she spat, bobbing against his shoulder as he climbed the porch steps. "And just where do you think you're taking me?"

"To get you cleaned up. You smell like a horse."

"And you smell like a . . . a . . . ." She couldn't think of anything vile enough as he paused to pull the front door open wide, then carried her inside. "Dammit, MacCrea, will you please put me down now?" She wanted to hit him, but she knew how ineffectual any resistance would be.

"If I do, will you go upstairs and get ready?"

"No."

"That's what I thought." He shifted her to rest a little higher on his shoulder and headed for the staircase. "Hello, Babs," he said calmly.

Abbie twisted around to see in front of him. Her mother was halfway down the steps, staring at them in shocked bewilderment. "Momma, make him put me down," she demanded.

"I'm kidnapping Abbie and taking her out for a night on the town, but first I have to get her cleaned up." The lazy confidence in his voice made it easy for her to imagine the look on his face. "If you could just tell me which bedroom is hers, I'd appreciate it."

"The second door on the right at the top of the stairs."

"Momma!" Abbie was shocked at her betrayal.

"It will do you good to go out. You've been working too hard lately." Babs smiled at her as she walked by, continuing down the stairs.

"See? Even your mother agrees with me."

"My mother—"

"Careful," MacCrea cut in. "After all, she is your mother. It's not nice to call her names." At the top of the stairs, he turned right and headed for the open door to her bedroom.

"How dare you lecture me on manners?" Abbie protested angrily as he kicked the door the rest of the way open with his foot. "That makes about as much sense as some urban cowboy telling a real one how to crease his hat." Once inside the bedroom, MacCrea still didn't set her down or stop. "This is getting ridiculous," she muttered through her clenched teeth, the blood rushing to her head. "Will you just put me down?"

"In a minute."

Suddenly she had a glimpse of another doorway coming up — the one to her bathroom. "MacCrea, what are you doing?" she yelped in panic.

He swung her off his shoulders and set her down in the shower stall. "I told you, I'm going to get you cleaned up," he reminded her complacently.

Certain he was bluffing, Abbie faced him squarely. "You and whose army?"

The taunt was barely out when he swung her around to face the shower head and reached for the faucets. "MacCrea, no! Don't!" She grabbed at his hand, trying to stop him from turning the faucet on. "My clothes, you can't!" She screamed in shock as a full blast of cold water sprayed down on top of her. Sputtering with anger and a mouthful of water, Abbie groped for the faucet handle and finally managed to turn it off *after* she was already drenched to the skin.

Her hair was plastered in a wet sheet covering her eyes. She pulled it apart in the middle to glare at MacCrea, standing safe and dry outside the stall, his arms folded across his chest and his expression disgustingly smug.

"Now you'll have to get cleaned up and change clothes."

"Ya wanna bet?" She threw him a killing glance as she shook the excess water from her hands, but it didn't help. More just ran down from her wet blouse.

MacCrea reached out a hand and rested it on the shower faucet, his towering bulk effectively blocking her exit from the shower. "Honey, I'll even give you odds," he drawled. "Believe me, I would enjoy scrubbing you from head to foot. Truthfully, that idea isn't half-bad."

Just for an instant Abbie let herself fantasize that MacCrea was in the shower with her, his hands massaging the soap into her skin, lathering her breasts, and rubbing over her pubic bone. "Is that a threat, or a promise?" she countered, challenging him to go through with it at the same second that Jackson appeared in the bathroom doorway.

The usually unflappable houseman stared at them, his lips parted in astonishment. "Jackson," Abbie whispered, suddenly realizing that her wet blouse was virtually transparent — and she wasn't wearing a bra.

MacCrea glanced over his shoulder. "Did you want something, Jackson?" Inching sideways, Abbie shifted to hide behind MacCrea, feeling oddly embarrassed — for both herself and Jackson.

"I . . . I thought . . . I heard a scream."

"It was just Abbie," MacCrea explained. "Nothing for you to worry about. I'll handle it."

"Of course, sir," Jackson replied, recovering his poise and withdrawing with just a hint of a bow.

"Poor Jackson," Abbie said sympathetically. "I've scandalized him totally." As MacCrea laughed under his breath, she glared at him. "It's your fault. You're a bastard, do you know that?"

"And you're an ill-tempered bitch." His mustache twitched with his half-hearted effort to contain the mocking smile that played upon his lips. "It looks like we were made for each other." Straightening, he took his hand away from the faucet. "Now get out of those wet clothes and get cleaned up."

As he walked out of the bathroom, he closed the door behind him, leaving her alone. She stood there, dripping in the shower, unable to think about anything except that one remark he'd made. She wondered if he meant it . . . if he really believed they were made for each other, or if he had merely said it in jest. She didn't want it to be an idle joke. On the heels of that realization came the recognition that she was definitely in love with him — more in love than she'd ever been in her life. She felt suddenly afraid and defensive. She wasn't sure she wanted to love anyone this completely. It left her exposed and vulnerable.

Hurriedly she peeled off her wet clothes and stepped under the shower again. As she ran the soapy sponge over her body, she couldn't rid herself of the thought that its pleasing roughness might have come from MacCrea's caressing hands if Jackson hadn't shown up. She tried to tell herself it was just as well, but it didn't ease the ache she felt.

She stepped out of the shower and toweled herself dry, then wrapped another towel around her head and one around her body, sarong-fashion. As she walked out of the bathroom, Abbie saw the lacy underwear lying on her bed: bra, panties, slip, even a pair of sheer silk stockings. Then she heard the scrape of wire hangers being pushed along a clothes rod, the sound coming from her walk-in closet. Frowning, she walked over to it and saw MacCrea inside, going through her clothes.

"What are you doing?"

"Trying to find something for you to wear tonight." He pulled a red strapless dress of silk chiffon, layered in ruffles, from the rack. "This isn't bad."

"I'll pick out my own clothes, thank you." Abbie took it from him and hung it back up, nagged by the thought that maybe he'd done this with other women he'd known in the past. She was surprised by the surge of jealousy and possessiveness she felt. She couldn't stand the idea of MacCrea being with anyone else.

"Not that feathered thing, though," he said, slipping his arms around her middle, crossing them in front of her waist and pulling her back against him. The towel came untucked, but his arms held it in place. "You smell like a woman now," he murmured. "All you need is a little touch of perfume here." As he nuzzled the ridge of her bare shoulder, Abbie instinctively arched into a caress. "And here." He nibbled at the pulsing vein in her neck, sending chills of pleasure dancing over her skin. "And maybe a dab . . . here." His hand slid up between her breasts and hooked a finger over the towel, dragging it farther down as he traced a line down the center of her cleavage.

When he lifted his head, breaking off the stimulating nuzzling of her neck, Abbie turned within the circle of his arms to face him, the towel slipping more. "Don't stop now. I was just getting warmed up."

"Aren't you ever satisfied?" He gazed down at her with easy confidence.

"Did I imply I wasn't satisfied? I am, you know . . . at least most of the time," she added deliberately to tease him.

"Only most of the time?" He arched an eyebrow in amusement. "That's not how I remember it."

"Maybe you need to refresh my memory." She started unbuttoning his shirt.

"If I don't walk out of this bedroom in five minutes, especially now that the shower's not running, what is your mother going to think? And Jackson?" His eyes darkened perceptibly as his gaze traveled rapidly over her face, her bare shoulders, and the ever-lower-drooping towel.

"Momma is a woman. She understands. As for Jackson, I've already scandalized him. Besides" — she paused and slid her hands inside his shirt, spreading it open to expose his muscular chest — "it doesn't usually take longer than five minutes, does it?"

"You little witch." His voice rumbled from deep inside his chest, richly laced with humor. "You are going to eat those words."

"I'd like to," Abbie said, looking up at him with half-closed eyes, their lids weighted with passion. She reached for the buckle on his belt and MacCrea swore softly, achingly.

Two hours later, they were seated at a table in the crowded steakhouse, waiting for their drinks to arrive. Abbie opened her menu and glanced over the selections.

"Don't tell me you're still hungry," MacCrea mocked.

"For food," she retorted. "Dessert comes later."

"Now that's a proposition if I ever heard one," he chuckled as his glance strayed from her. "It looks like I'm about to have competition. Who is he? An old flame of yours?"

Abbie turned, expecting to see someone she knew, but she didn't recognize the man in the dark cowboy hat banded with silver conchos. Yet he was grinning at her like a long-lost friend.

"Hello, there. Remember me?"

"No, I don't think so." Abbie stared at him, searching for some resemblance to anyone she knew.

"Ross Tibbs. I sing here in the lounge. We met —" He stopped, uncertainty flickering across his face. "You're not her, are you? Across the room, I thought for sure — Man, you look enough like her to be her twin."

"Well, I'm not," she replied stiffly, fully aware that he must have mistaken her for Rachel.

"I'm sorry. I know I probably sounded like I was giving you the oldest line in the book, but you really do look like this lady I met named Rachel."

"Don't worry about it, Mr. Tibbs. It's happened before." She was thinking about her father when she said that, remembering how many times he'd stared at her with that strange look in his eyes . . . as if he was seeing someone else.

"I can sure understand that," the singer replied, smiling ruefully. "Again, I'm sorry I bothered you, Ra —" He caught himself and laughed self-consciously. "I guess I can't call you that, can I?"

"The name is Lawson. Abbie Lawson."

"Say, you wouldn't happen to be related to the Lawsons that have that Arabian horse farm outside of Houston?"

"Yes. River Bend is owned by my family." But only for a little while longer, she remembered, feeling again the emotional tear over losing it.

"I've been by the place a time or two. You've got some beautiful horses there. Didn't I see a notice somewhere that you're having an auction to sell them off?"

"Yes. Next week." She didn't even have to close her eyes to see River Breeze's name on the list.

"I might see you there," Ross Tibbs declared. "I always wanted to own an Arabian. Not that I could afford one, no matter how cheap they might sell. But a man can dream." As the waitress arrived with their drinks, he stepped to one side. "Listen, I . . . won't bother you any longer. If you get a chance after dinner, stop by the lounge and catch my act."

"We'll see," MacCrea inserted.

"Enjoy your dinner," he said, moving away from their table.

Aware of the way MacCrea was quietly studying her, Abbie tried to shake off her brooding thoughts. Forcing a smile, she lifted her glass to him. "Since this is supposed to be a celebration, don't you think we should drink to your success?"

"I do." He touched his glass to hers.

Abbie took a sip of her bourbon and water, then cupped the moist sides of the glass in both hands. "You know, you still haven't told me any details about how this all came about — or who all you're dealing with. I know you met with Lane last week. Did he set the whole thing up?"

For a fraction of a second MacCrea seemed on guard, his glance sharp, then the impression was gone. "Yes, he was involved in it from the start."

"Maybe I was wrong about him," she conceded absently.

"What do you mean?"

"He was trying to find some way I could keep my filly, but she's being sold with the rest. I questioned how hard he really tried to help, but, considering what he's done for you, maybe there wasn't any way he could arrange for me to keep River Breeze."

"So what happens now?"

"I don't know." Abbie shook her head, frustrated by the blank walls that seemed to surround her. "I'm not sure I can afford to buy her. A filly always brings more than a colt, unless you have an outstanding stallion or show prospect. And with her looks and bloodlines, she's bound to bring anywhere from ten to twenty thousand dollars — maybe more." She tried to smile. "We'd better talk about something else. This subject is too depressing."

"Did I tell you my regular toolpusher reported back to work the first of the week? He's on crutches, but he gets around pretty good. Which means I won't have to be on the site twenty-four hours a day."

"I like the sound of that already."

20

"WHAT DO YOU MEAN, she wants to come to the sale?" Abbie demanded, trembling with anger. "She —"

Lane held up his hand to stop the tirade. "Before you fly off the handle, remember that this auction is open to the public. She has every right to come if she chooses to do so and you can't stop her. I am only advising you of her plans because I hope to avoid any ugly scenes such as the one that occurred the last time she was here."

Recognizing that he had a valid point — it was a public auction — Abbie made an effort to control her temper, but she was almost choking on her own gall. "Why? What possible reason could she have to come to it?"

"She's interested in buying some horses," Lane replied.

Everything went still inside her. She was afraid even to draw a breath. "Which ones?"

"She didn't say."

What if one of them was River Breeze? Her anger turned ice-cold. For the first time since Lane had announced Rachel's plans to attend the sale, Abbie was thinking clearly, sharply, her mind racing swiftly to find some way to keep her filly from ending up in Rachel's hands.

"I'd like to know what you're going to do, Abbie," Lane said.

For a split second, she thought he was asking about the filly, then realized he was referring to Rachel. "Like you said, Lane, it's a public auction. Just tell her to stay away from my mother and me. Is there anything further we need to discuss?" she asked, an icy calm dominating her attitude.

"No, I think we've gone over everything."

"Good. I have work to do." Turning on her heel, Abbie pivoted away from him and walked briskly toward the stables. She had an idea, but she was going to need help to carry it out.

She found Ben in one of the foaling stalls, doctoring a minor cut on the foreleg of a young stud colt. "You are a clumsy boy," Ben said to the colt, the soothing tone of his voice belying the chiding words he spoke. "You must learn not to run into things or you will hurt yourself very badly sometime."

"I need to talk to you, Ben," she said when he released the colt. The horse charged across the large box stall to hide behind his mother, then peeked around her rump to eye Ben warily as he moved to the door.

"That one is what your father called an accident waiting to happen." Ben stepped unhurriedly out of the stall and slid the door shut. "Always he is cutting and scraping himself."

But Abbie wasn't interested in discussing the accident-prone colt. "We only have four days before the auction. Lane just told me that the grooms he hired will be arriving the day after tomorrow. Before they come, I want to get River Breeze out of here."

"Get her out of here?" His gaze narrowed sharply. "What are you saying?"

"I'm saying I don't want her anywhere on the farm when they arrive."

"What is going on in that head of yours?" Ben asked suspiciously.

"I've thought it all through," Abbie said. "When the Germans invaded Poland at the start of World War Two, what did you do? You evacuated all the horses from the stud and tried to find a safe place to hide them. That's what I want to do with River Breeze. If she isn't here, she can't be sold at the auction."

"It is not the same, Abbie. There is no war. If you would take the filly from here, you would be stealing her. That is wrong."

"Wrong. How could it be wrong to steal my own horse? And River Breeze is mine. You know that Daddy gave her to me, regardless of what the ownership papers say," Abbie reasoned, maintaining her calm. Anger never got her anywhere with Ben.

"This is true," he admitted reluctantly, still troubled by her proposal.

"Then how can I be accused of stealing my own horse?" She could tell he was wavering. "I need your help, Ben, but I'll do it alone if I have to."

"Where will you take her?" he asked gruffly.

"To Dobie's. He's already said I could keep her in his barn once we move. Momma has already taken some of our things over to the house. We can simply tell him that we want to bring River Breeze over there now so we don't have to deal with moving her later. He doesn't have to know anything different."

"You would lie to him?"

"No. I simply wouldn't tell him the whole truth."

"What do you think you will accomplish by doing this?" Ben tipped his head to the side and watched her closely.

So far he'd been satisfied by her answers, but Abbie knew this one was critical. On it, he would base his decision. If she didn't obtain at least his tacit approval, she doubted that her plan would succeed.

"I'll buy time," she said. "You know that I don't have much hope of outbidding anyone at the auction. If I can keep her hidden until after the sale, maybe I'll be able to buy her on terms. Or maybe we'll make enough money off the sale to pay off the creditors and she won't have to be sold. Don't you see, Ben, I have to take the chance that there will be a way?"

There was a long pause before he answered, as if he were mulling over all her arguments in his mind. "We should move her tonight . . . after it is dark."

Relief broke the iron control she'd exercised over her emotions. Abbie threw her arms around him and hugged him tightly. "I love you, Ben. I just knew I could count on you to help me."

A crescent moon hovered above the eastern horizon, a curved blade of silver against a midnight sky studded with stars. Beyond the pool of light cast by the tall yardlight next to the broodmare barn, a dark-colored pickup truck with a two-horse trailer in tow was parked.

Ben stood in the shadows of the vehicle, holding the lead rope attached to the filly's halter while Abbie smoothed the navy-blue horse blanket over the filly's back, concealing the silvery coat that stood out so sharply against the night's darkness. She fastened the belly strap and loosely buckled the chest strap, then drew the top of the blanket up to the arched crest of the filly's neck and fastened it securely under the throatlatch. The filly nosed Ben's shoulder as if seeking human reassurance about this unusual nighttime activity.

"That night we left Janow under the cover of darkness, the horses seemed to understand the need for silence, as this one does," Ben recalled, speaking in a hushed voice. "We left at night so the German Luftwaffe could not observe our flight. Mr. Rhoski, the manager of Janow, led the way in his carriage. Then my group, we followed with the stallions, riding one and leading another. After us came the mares, foals, and other young horses, most of them tied to carts carrying fodder for the march, pulled by the half-Arabians at the farm. It was a sight to see, Abbie. Two hundred fifty of Poland's best Arabians streaming out of Janow to be swallowed by the night.

"All along the road that night, we met hundreds — thousands — of our fellow countrymen from western Poland, fleeing from the Germans. They told us of the bombings by the Luftwaffe of the highways, the planes diving and shooting their machine guns at the people trying to escape. We did not go near the highways, but stayed on the country roads. When dawn was near, we hid the horses in the forests. We hid there all day. I was tired after traveling all night, but I could not sleep. I kept listening to the roar of the German planes, wondering if they would see us in the trees. When darkness came, we marched again, but that night the stallions were not so eager to travel. They did not prance and push at the bit as they did when we left Janow. I think they knew that the road to Kowel was a long and dangerous one — and that they would need all of their great stamina and courage to reach the safety on the other side of the Bug River."

"All set. We can load her in the trailer." Abbie patted the filly's withers and stepped back. Cloaked in the dark horse blanket, River Breeze blended in with the shadows, only her silver-gray head and tail visible against the darkness. But in the dark trailer, that little bit of white would barely be noticeable.

"Open it and I will lead her in." Ben shortened his hold on the lead rope.

As Abbie stepped out from behind the trailer and moved to the tailgate, a pair of headlight beams laid their long tracks on the winding lane. "Wait," she whispered to Ben, her nerves screaming with tension as he started to lead the filly out from the shadows. "Someone's coming. Stay there until I find out who it is."

"Maybe it is Dobie come to find out why we are so late." The filly pricked her ears at the sound of a running engine and Ben cupped a silencing hand over her muzzle.

"Maybe." But the vehicle didn't sound like Dobie's truck. Her mouth felt dry and her palms sweaty. Abbie tried to summon some saliva as she stepped away from the horse trailer and wiped her hands on the hips of her jeans, waiting for the vehicle to come under the tall yardlight next to the house. "It's MacCrea." She hadn't been aware of how scared she'd been until her knees almost buckled with relief when she recognized his truck.

"Do you realize you were supposed to meet me almost two hours ago?" MacCrea slammed out of the truck. "I couldn't figure out what happened to you, whether you'd had an accident, your car broke down, or what. Then I call the house and your mother says you're still here."

"Something important came up and I . . . forgot. I know I should have called you. I'm sorry." There wasn't anything else she could say.

"You forgot? Well, thanks a lot." He stopped inches in front of her, his hands on his hips in a gesture of anger and disgust. Then he shook his head, as if unable to believe any of this. "This happens to be a first, you know. I've never been stood up before. Naturally you would be the one to do it."

"I didn't do it on purpose. I honestly forgot."

"What came up that was so important?" he demanded.

Abbie was conscious of Ben standing only yards away in the shadow of the horse trailer, holding River Breeze. "One of our horses went down. We were afraid it was colic."

The filly picked that moment to snort. Abbie stiffened as MacCrea glanced toward the horse trailer. "Did you hear that?"

"What?" But she knew playing dumb wouldn't work. "It was probably one of the horses in the barn."

"This isn't where you usually park the horse trailer." MacCrea studied her suspiciously. "What's it doing hitched up to the truck?"

"We were using it today." A second later she heard the restless shifting of hooves as the filly grew tired of standing quietly. She knew MacCrea had heard it, too. She was almost relieved when Ben came walking out from behind the trailer, leading the blanketed horse. She was trapping herself in a snare of lies and she wanted it to end. "So we decided we might as well haul River Breeze over to Dobie's place before we unhooked the trailer." She walked over to the trailer and unlatched the endgate so Ben could load the filly.

"Wait a minute. I thought she was being sold at the auction." MacCrea frowned. "Was Lane finally able to arrange for you to keep her?"

"Something like that." She was reluctant to tell him of her plan. The fewer people who knew about it, the better chance she had to keep the horse hidden.

"All right, Abbie." He caught her by the wrist and forced her to turn around and look at him. "What's really going on here?"

"I told you. We're taking River Breeze over to the Hix farm," she replied, trying to appear tolerant of his supposedly stupid question.

"It's nearly midnight."

"A few minutes after eleven is not midnight."

"That clever little mind of yours is at work again, isn't it?"

"I don't know what you're talking about," Abbie declared.

"You know exactly what I'm talking about." But he turned to Ben when he emerged from the trailer after tying the filly inside. "Maybe you'd like to explain to me what's going on here?"

"It is for Abbie to say," Ben replied, but his look prodded Abbie to tell the truth.

"It's simple, MacCrea," she said, her voice becoming curt. "If the filly isn't here, she can't be sold."

"I should have guessed," he said grimly. "There are bound to be questions. Horses don't just simply disappear. How are you going to explain it?"

"Horses get loose all the time. A fence was down or a gate was left open and she got out. There are any number of ways she could get away." The strain of secrecy and the stress of lying followed by the forced admission all combined to make Abbie feel defensive.

"In the meantime, you're going to have her hidden away."

"That's right — until after the sale, when I can arrange to buy her."

"And what happens if someone finds out what you're doing?"

"They won't find out unless you tell them." The questions, the tension became too much. "Look, Rachel is coming to the auction to buy some horses. She isn't going to get River Breeze!" She twisted her wrist free of his hand and swung the endgate closed, then slid the locking bolt into place, shaking inside with emotion. Finally she turned back around to confront him. "Well, Mac-Crea?"

"I take it you're in this with her, Ben," he said.

"The filly belongs to her. Sometimes risks must be taken to do what is the right thing."

"Are you going to tell Lane?" Abbie needed to know where he stood.

"Why should I?" MacCrea countered.

"You think we're doing something wrong —" she began.

"I never said that. I think it's a damned-fool stunt, and you two are going about it like a pair of amateurs. I'm surprised you aren't dressed in black and have grease smeared on your faces. It would have been a helluva lot less suspicious if you'd simply ridden the horse over there and had your redheaded friend drive you back. Just how much does your friend know about this?"

"Nothing." She knew she had MacCrea's support even though he hadn't said it in so many words. She felt her confidence return. "I've let him assume that Breeze belongs to me, and any question about it has been resolved."

"Once you report the horse missing, what happens if someone asks him whether he's seen it?"

"That won't happen, because I'm not going to report that she's missing until the morning of the sale. With the pressure of getting all the horses ready for the auction, there won't be time to organize anything. Ben and I can pretend to look for her." So far he hadn't asked her a question that she couldn't answer. Confident that she had every contingency covered, Abbie grew impatient with the delay. "Everything's set. It's too late to change the plan now. Dobie is waiting for us, and if we waste any more time here, he's going to start asking questions. Come on, Ben. Let's go." As Ben headed for the driver's side, Abbie walked the length of the trailer to the passenger door, aware that MacCrea followed her. The interior light flashed on when Abbie opened the cab door. MacCrea held it as she climbed onto the seat, then turned to look at him. "I'll see you when I get back. You'll be here, won't you?"

"No. I'm coming with you, so move over." He climbed into the truck, barely giving Abbie time to scoot to the middle.

Leaving the headlights off, Ben drove slowly away from the stables with the horse trailer in tow. As soon as they were beyond the illumination of the yardlights, he slowed the truck to a crawl and sat hunched over the wheel, staring intently ahead to keep the truck and trailer aimed down the center of the narrow lane, with only the dim starlight to show him the path in the darkness.

"There usually isn't much traffic on the road at this hour of the night, but we don't want to take the risk of someone driving by and seeing us leaving here with the horse trailer," Abbie explained to MacCrea.

"They're liable to take more notice of you because you aren't running with lights." He grabbed the dashboard in front of him. "Watch the ditch on the right!"

Ben swerved the truck away from it and drove even slower. "It was like this in Poland. The night was so dark you could not see the ditches by the road. And so many people, too, fleeing with what possessions they could save. Wheels of the carts were always sliding off the road into the ditch."

"Ben took part in the evacuation of the Arabian horses from the Polish stud farm during World War Two when the Germans invaded Poland," Abbie explained in a quick aside to MacCrea.

"It took us three nights to reach a place where we could cross the Bug River, traveling only after dark and hiding the horses wherever we could during the day. German planes filled the sky over Poland like flocks of birds when autumn comes, but they did not fly beyond the Bug River. After we crossed it, we could travel during the day. We were maybe two days from Kowel, our destination, when we heard the artillery fire and learned that the Russians had invaded eastern Poland. So close we came, only to turn around and make the long trek back to Janow. We all agreed if the horses were to be captured, we would rather have them taken by the Nazis."

"In the First World War, the Soviet armies overran the stud farms and slaughtered nearly all the horses," Abbie added.

"When we returned to Janow Podlaski, the Germans were there." Ben turned onto the road and continued to drive without lights. "The commandant ordered us to move all the horses to the Vistula River, which was another hundred and fifty kilometers west of Janow. The horses needed rest. They had marched far and long, and the manager refused. It would have been better if we had gone, but we did not know the Germans and Soviets had made a treaty. Everything east of the Vistula was to be under Russian occupation. We tried to save the horses from them, but the Germans surrendered the studs to the Russians. It was only a few weeks later, the line was changed to the Bug River, but when the Soviet forces left Janow, they took with them the horses—spoils of war. That is how the great Ofir arrived in Tersk, a war prize stolen from Poland."

"Fortunately for the Arabian horse world, some seventy horses, too exhausted, lame, or too young to endure that first evacuation attempt, had been left in the care of farmers along the way. The Polish stud was able to recover most of them, including Balalajka, the dam of Bask, probably one of the greatest stallions since Skowronek," Abbie explained as the truck rumbled over the old bridge that spanned the creek.

"Yes, the owner of Balalajka was given sugar and alcohol in trade for her. We were able to obtain many horses in this way, so we could start breeding Arabian horses again."

"We're coming up on the intersection," MacCrea warned, then added dryly, "This is Texas, Ben, not Poland. I think it would be safe to turn on your lights anytime now."

"We are away from the farm now. It would be okay, I think." Reaching down, he pulled the knob that activated the lights. As the beam illuminated the road ahead of them, the truck picked up speed.

"This is more like the second time Janow was evacuated, isn't it, Ben?" Abbie smiled at him, his craggy face now bathed in the faint glow from the dashboard lights.

"That time we went by train. Thirty-one boxcars it took to carry all the horses. That was in 'forty-four. The Soviets had driven the Nazi armies out of Russia and were marching into Poland. It was a good thing we were able to escape with the horses. Much heavy fighting occurred around Janow Podlaski. The barns were destroyed by the artillery shelling, and some houses at Janow, also."

"What about Dresden and all the bombings there? You were in Dresden then. It was probably just as bad if not worse than Janow," Abbie said.

"I have the feeling you know the story better than Ben does," MacCrea mocked.

"I should," she retorted, smiling. "When I was a little girl, they were my bedtime stories. I was raised on his exploits during the war."

"We are here," Ben announced as he swung the truck and trailer onto the dirt driveway that went a quarter of a mile back to the headquarters of the Hix farm.

"Dobie waited up for us. There's a light on in the house," Abbie observed. "We might as well go straight to the barn, Ben."

A porch light flashed on as they drove past the main farmhouse to the old wood and stone barn, nearly dwarfed by the large machine shed next to it. Ben made a looping circle and parked near a side door. Abbie climbed out of the truck after MacCrea, then waited as Dobie loped across the farmyard to meet them.

"I figured you'd be here an hour ago. Did you have problems?" Dobie darted an accusing look at MacCrea as if convinced he was the cause for Abbie being late.

"We got tied up with a few things that took longer than we expected. I'm sorry you had to wait so long for us to get here, Dobie."

"I've got a place all fixed up for your filly in the barn," Dobie said.

The area was large and roomy, nearly twice the size of the box stalls at River Bend. A short partition in the middle divided one side into two open, double stalls complete with mangers and feed troughs. Abbie led River Breeze inside. The blanketed filly stepped daintily across the straw-covered floor, snorting loudly and breathing in all the new smells.

Abbie tied the lead rope to one of the manger rings, then removed the blanket and handed it over the manger to Ben. After she made sure the filly knew where the water bucket was located, she put some grain in the feed trough and turned her loose to investigate the new surroundings.

"I think she likes it," Dobie said as the filly nibbled at the grain, appearing to relax a little.

"She will." Abbie was concerned about that. "Thanks for letting me keep her over here."

"Now or later, it doesn't really make much difference." Dobie shrugged. "Do you want me to turn her out in the morning?"

"No, don't do that," Abbie said, conscious of MacCrea's taunting glance. "I think it would be better if she stayed inside . . . . at least until she gets used to her new home."

"If that's what you want."

"It is." She gave the filly a final hug and crawled over the manger to join the others. "It's late, and all of us have to work in the morning. Thanks again for everything, Dobie."

"If there's anything else I can do for you, you just ask."

As they walked out of the barn, MacCrea muttered close to her ear, "That poor fool would jump off a cliff if you asked him to."

"And you wouldn't," she guessed.

"No."

"That's what I thought." But she really didn't mind.

21 ❧

ON THE SURFACE, the scene at River Bend appeared to be one of confusion, but the pother was organized. In the center aisle of the broodmare barn, a horse stood tied and waiting while one of the grooms curried another. Farther down the aisle, a second groom combed out the tangled mane and tail of a third horse. The low hum of a pair of clippers came from the stud barn where a third groom worked, trimming the bridle path, fetlock feathers, whiskers, and any excess hairs under the jaw of another horse. Outside, the local farrier hooked the foreleg of an already groomed and trimmed mare between his legs and snipped away at an overgrown hoof while his young helper held the mare's head.

Abbie checked, but the mare's halter had no yellow tag tied to it, indicating she was to remain barefoot. In the assembly-line system they'd established, once the horseshoer was finished with a horse, it would be taken to the stud barn and bathed by the fourth groom, then confined to a stall.

The gusting wind riffled the sheets of paper attached to the clipboard Abbie carried. Impatiently she smoothed them down, then checked the list again for the name of the next horse. Somewhere a horn blared, breaking across the whinnies and snorts of the horses, the buzz of the clippers, and the rasp of the farrier's file. It sounded again and again, a sense of urgency accompanying the tooting blasts. Frowning, Abbie looked up as Dobie's old pickup came roaring up the driveway.

It squealed into the yard, the nearly bald tires spitting back the loose gravel. Impelled forward by a sense of foreboding, Abbie started toward it, then broke into a run when it rattled to a stop and Dobie poked his head out the driver's window.

"There's been an accident!" he shouted. "Your horse is hurt. You better come quick!"

"My God," Abbie whispered. Fear, cold as an icy finger, shivered down her spine. She stopped and whirled toward the barn. "Ben!" she yelled for him just as he emerged from the stud barn to learn the cause of all the commotion. "It's River Breeze! She's hurt!" She spun back to Dobie. "Have you called the vet?"

He shook his head with a vagueness that indicated it hadn't occurred to him. "I came straight here."

She tried to check the panic welling up inside her. Grotesque images of the filly down, thrashing in agony, flashed before her mind's eye as she raced around to the other side of the truck, yelling over her shoulder at the horse-shoer, who had stopped work. "Call the vet and tell him to get over to the Hix farm right away! It's an emergency!"

She scrambled into the cab with a winded Ben right behind her, hauling himself onto the high seat beside her. Before Ben could get the door closed, Dobie stepped on the accelerator and the pickup shot forward, its spinning tires spending up a fresh storm of gravel.

"What happened?" Ben asked the question Abbie hadn't been able to voice, afraid of the answer she might hear.

"I don't know. I'm not sure," Dobie said. "I had hooked up the windrower to the tractor and drove it out of the shed. Maybe it was the noise — all the clanging and rattling from the tractor and windrower. I was already past the barn when I heard this scream. I looked back and —" He cast an anxious glance at Abbie. She stared at him intently, waiting for the rest of the words that would finish the scenario running in her mind, feeling as if her heart was lodged somewhere in her throat. "I'm sorry, Abbie." He looked to the front and tightened his hold on the steering wheel with a flexing motion of his fingers. "She was laying on the ground, kicking and struggling. The bottom half of the

Dutch door was sprung open and cracked at the top. I'd left the top of the door open so she could get some air and see out. I guess she spooked at the noise and tried to get out."

"No." She didn't want to believe the accident was as bad as Dobie had described. She was sure the filly wouldn't have tried to jump the half-door; the opening was too small. A bad sprain, some cuts and bruises, that's probably all River Breeze had suffered.

"I think she broke her leg," Dobie added hesitantly.

"You don't know that," Abbie retorted. "You didn't check."

"No. I left her with one of my hired hands and came for you."

"Can't we go any faster?" Outside the truck windows the fence posts were a blur, yet the nightmarish feeling persisted that no matter how fast they traveled, the farm was still far away — and getting farther instead of closer.

All the way, Abbie kept remembering how close the machine shed had been to the barn. Except for a tractor, the filly had never been around farm machinery before. Naturally she would have been frightened by the banging clatter of such strange contraptions. Abbie wished she had thought of that, but she had been too concerned about secreting her horse.

By the time they drove into the yard, Abbie was frantic. She strained for a glimpse of the filly, hoping against hope to see River Breeze on her feet. But her silver-gray Arabian was on the ground. Abbie didn't even hear the cry of anguish that came from her throat. She practically pushed Ben out of the truck in her haste to get to the filly. Her legs were shaking so badly she wasn't sure they would support her as she ran to the downed horse, taking no notice at all of the man standing next to River Breeze.

The filly nickered and lifted her head when Abbie reached her. Abbie took one look at the dark eyes glazed with pain, the neck dark with sweat, and the tremors that quivered through the filly, and knew her horse had gone into shock.

"Quick! Get a blanket," she said to the hired man, then saw the rifle in his hands. She stared at him with a mixture of outrage and shock. "What are you doing with that?"

"The horse needs t' be put out o' its mis'ry. Ain't nothin' you can do fer it. Her front leg's busted." He gestured with the rifle, directing Abbie's attention to the filly's bloodied chest and legs.

Abbie's stomach was heaving convulsively as she almost threw up at the sight of the grotesquely twisted leg, lying askew like some ragdoll's. She fought off the nausea that left her knees weak and her skin cold and clammy with sweat.

"You're not going to shoot her. You don't destroy horses anymore just because they break a leg, so take that rifle and hang it back on your rack. And get a blanket like I told you." She knelt on the ground beside the filly and cradled the horse's head on her lap. "The vet will be here soon, girl," she crooned, reassuring herself as much as the filly. She concentrated on soothing the horse while Ben examined the extent of the injuries. The man left, but it was Dobie who came back with the blanket to cover the filly. Ben draped it over River Breeze, then straightened. Abbie looked up to search his face.

"The cuts are minor," he said. "Already the bleeding has stopped. One, maybe two are deep enough to leave a scar."

But his failure to comment on the broken leg was a telling omission. "Breeze is young and strong. She'll make it," Abbie said, sounding calm and determined even though, inside, she was scared — terrified that she might lose the filly she'd fought so hard to keep. "She'll make it. You'll see. She is descended from the great war mare Wadudda. After a desert raid, she was ridden over a hundred miles without stopping once. Her right leg was injured during the raid, yet she covered that distance in eleven hours. River Breeze has that same courage and heart. I know she does." Abbie clung tenaciously to that thought. She could build her hopes on it. She wasn't going to give up until the filly did.

"We will see what the doctor says," Ben replied.

Abbie refused to hear the doubt in his voice as she sat cradling the filly's head in her lap and brushing away the buzzing flies, mindless of the growing numbness in her legs, her heart twisting at every grunt of pain from the filly. She maintained her vigil, suffering along with River Breeze, while an eternity passed before the veterinarian arrived.

After a cursory examination, he was no more encouraging than Ben had been. Straightening, he looked at Abbie and simply shook his head.

"Broken legs can be set on a horse. They do it all the time," she insisted, challenging the vet to deny it.

"The break in the leg is too high. Supposing that I could get the bone set, I don't see how I can immobilize that shoulder area. I'm sorry, Abbie, but it doesn't look good," he stated reluctantly.

"But there is hope." Abbie grabbed at the slim straw he'd let slip.

"If this was a gelding, I wouldn't hesitate a bit in recommending putting the horse away. If by some wild chance the break healed, the horse would be a cripple the rest of his life. But I hate the thought of destroying a young valuable filly like this one with all her foal-producing years still ahead of her. But I'll tell you like I've told your father, I don't believe in prolonging an animal's agony when I know nothing can be done for it."

"But you don't know that," she argued. "How can you when you haven't even tried? You can set her leg and we'll rig up a sling to keep her off it until it can heal."

"Don't you be trying to tell me my job, young lady."

"Somebody should," she raged in desperation. "Just because this is an animal, that doesn't make you God, holding power of life and death over it."

"In the first place, setting a broken leg and rigging up a sling doesn't solve anything. That's when the problems start. Horses aren't people. You can't strap them in a bed and rig them up in traction and expect them to sit still for it. They're animals — dumb animals. And an animal in pain usually goes berserk. They panic and start kicking and lashing out, and usually wind up doing more damage to themselves. Sure, you've heard stories about horses with broken legs that have recovered and lived useful lives. But you haven't heard the stories about all the ones that didn't make it, that went crazy and had to be destroyed — like that Thoroughbred filly, Ruffian, a few years back."

"But we don't know River Breeze will do that."

"We'll see what we can do, Abbie, but don't get your hopes up."

The rest of the morning and afternoon was a living nightmare for Abbie, helpless to do anything but watch and wait. Since the front leg was injured, transporting the filly to Doc Campbell's clinic in town was out of the question. There was too great a risk that more severe damage would occur on the journey. After a half-dozen phone calls, Doc was able to locate a portable X-ray unit. When it finally arrived at the farm, the resulting X rays showed both front legs were broken. The left foreleg had suffered only a hairline fracture, but both the ulna and the radius bones were broken just below the shoulder joint in the right leg.

Abbie sat with the filly while Doc Campbell got on the telephone again and consulted with several fellow practitioners whose opinions he trusted. He came back with a course of action, admittedly radical, and sent Ben back to River Bend to fetch the farrier and Dobie to the welder in the machine shed with a hastily sketched diagram of the splint he wanted made. A Thomas splint, he called it, explaining to Abbie that it was an appliance frequently used on dogs and cats with broken front legs. By then, she was too numb inside to object that River Breeze was a horse, not a dog or cat. Reaction had set in, and all she wanted was for him to do something for her filly — anything.

Propped against a corner of the stall, Abbie sat huddled in a wool blanket — the same blanket that had covered the filly earlier. Exhausted from the long ordeal, she let her head roll back against the rough boards and closed her eyes just for a minute. A faint sound, a rustle of straw, and she snapped them open, instantly ready to spring to her feet.

But the filly was motionless, her gray head hanging listlessly, still under the lingering influence of the anesthesia. Both front legs were encased in plaster, with a pair of long metal splints curving in a high hoop up the gray shoulder and extending down to the hoof, attached to the shoe. A belly sling, fastened to a crossbeam overhead, supported most of the filly's weight.

Even though River Breeze had always been gentle and well-mannered, Abbie realized that it would take a horse with the tolerance of Job to put up with all those contraptions. Maybe she was wrong to put the filly through all this stress and pain. Maybe she should have let Doc Campbell put her to sleep. She stubbornly rejected the thought, determined that her filly would live no matter what it took.

She heard a footstep and called out softly, "Dobie, is that you?"

"It's me," MacCrea answered, coming around the corner of the stall's partition, his tall shape backlit by the bare bulb overhead.

"How —" She was suddenly too choked for words.

"I called your house earlier to let you know I was a man short on the afternoon shift and would be tied up tonight." He moved quietly over to crouch down beside her, sitting on his heels. "Your mother told me what happened. I'm sorry I couldn't get here any sooner."

"There wasn't much you could have done anyway, except maybe given Dobie a hand welding the splints." She was just glad he was here with her now.

"How's she doing?" He nodded at the filly.

"She's going to make it," Abbie asserted, again feeling that swell of determination.

"What are you going to do now?"

"Stay with her." She stared at the young filly all trussed up in the sling and splints, a sorry-looking sight. "I have to. A lot of horses go crazy with the pain and trauma and try to destroy themselves. I have to make sure that doesn't happen."

"That's not what I meant," MacCrea said. "Everybody knows the horse is here."

She hadn't thought of that. "So help me, MacCrea Wilder, if you say 'I-told-you-so,'" she threatened angrily. Too many times today she'd wondered whether an accident like this would have occurred if she hadn't brought River Breeze over here. All day she'd lived with the terrible irony of knowing she had done it to keep the filly and might lose her as a result.

"I'm not. I'm only wondering how you're going to handle the situation now."

"I don't know. Who would buy a cripple? Doc Campbell warned me that even if she makes it, there's no telling how well the bones will knit. There's a chance her legs will never be strong enough to support the weight of pregnancy."

"Make a full disclosure of everything the vet said and put the filly in the auction," MacCrea said.

"What?" She stared at him, regarding his suggestion as tantamount to betrayal.

"You said it yourself: Who'd buy her now? You should be able to pick her up cheap."

"I could," Abbie mused, then sighed. "The auction is only a day away. There's so much to be done yet. I know Ben can handle it, but I should be there to help." She was tired and confused, torn by responsibility. Too much had happened today, and it left her feeling drained and numb inside.

"You look tired. Why don't you get some sleep?"

"I can't." She shook her head, weighted with weariness. "I have to stay here and keep an eye on Breeze."

"I wasn't suggesting you should leave. Move over." The straw on the stall floor rustled with their movements as MacCrea wedged himself into the corner and shifted Abbie inside the crook of his arm, nestling her against his shoulder. "Comfortable?"

"Mmmm." She snuggled more closely against his side, drawing the blanket over both of them. Absently she rubbed her cheek against his cotton shirt, soothed by the warmth of his body and the steady beat of his heart. "I suppose you think I'm crazy for sitting up with a horse."

"Would you sit up with me if I was hurt?"

"Probably not." She smiled.

"That's what I thought." His voice rumbled from his chest, warm with amusement. Then she felt the stroke of his hand on her hair, lightly pressing her head more fully to the pillow of his chest. "Try to rest, Abbie."

Obediently she closed her eyes and felt the tension, the need for watchfulness, slipping away. MacCrea was here and she could relax.

Slowly, gradually, he felt her grow heavier in his arms and the rhythm of her breathing deepen. He tried to ease the cramping in his muscles with a flexing shrug of his shoulders, but there was no relief from the hard boards pressing into his back. He didn't know why Abbie hadn't chosen to keep watch from the soft comfort of a haystack instead of this damnable corner of the stall.

A scrape of metal against the cement floor of the stall was followed by the sound of hooves shifting in the straw. MacCrea glanced at the silvery horse. Her head was up, her ears were pinned back, and the white of one eye showed in alarm. Twisting her neck around, the horse made a weak attempt to bite the splint's iron hoop that rubbed against her shoulder.

"Hey, girl. Easy," MacCrea crooned. Her ears pricked at the sound of his voice as she swung her head around to look at him, blowing softly. "She's sleeping. Don't wake her up."

After a few seconds, the horse let her head droop again, the listlessness returning. MacCrea watched her closely for several more minutes, but the horse made no further attempts to fight the immobilizing makeshift harness. As Abbie stirred against him, he gently smoothed the top of her head and drew her closer still.

22

ALTHOUGH THE AUCTION wasn't scheduled to begin for another hour yet, an assortment of parked cars, pickup trucks, and horse trailers already filled the farmyard, a few overflowing onto the shoulder of the narrow lane, when Rachel arrived. She found a space between two vehicles parked near the house and maneuvered her car into it.

As she stepped out of the car, a hand touched her arm. Startled, Rachel turned sharply, half expecting to be confronted by Abbie. Instead she found herself gazing into Lane's smiling eyes, happy lines fanning out from the corners like so many rays from the sun.

"Lane." She breathed out his name in a mixture of delight and relief.

"Surprised?" He kissed her lightly.

"And glad," she admitted as he drew back to run an admiring glance over her, sweeping her from head to toe.

She met it confidently, aware that her choice of attire was both casual and elegant, as well as practical and feminine. Padded at the shoulders and graced with a high stand-up collar and turned-back cuffs, her ivory blouse was done in a softly draping silk charmeuse. A wide brown leather belt circled the shaped waistline of her camel skirt, which then fell gracefully full to midcalf. Instead of shoes, she wore a sophisticated version of flat-heeled riding boots. A silk scarf, the same ivory shade as her blouse, held her hair back at the nape of her neck. Her only jewelry was a pair of heavy gold earrings, sculpted in layers.

Since she'd moved to Houston, she'd thrown out or given away all her clothes and bought a whole new wardrobe. No more inexpensive California casual for her: now that she had some money, it was Texas chic, thanks to the helpful and instructive suggestions she'd received from clerks at several of Houston's more exclusive department stores — clerks vastly different from the disinterested, gum-chewing salespeople in the stores where she used to shop. Knowing what to wear, how to wear it, and when to wear it — and knowing that because of it she always looked her best — had done wonders to improve her self-image.

"You look stunning, as usual," Lane declared, then tucked a hand under her elbow and guided her toward the idly milling crowds near the stables.

"I didn't know you'd be here today. You never said anything about it when we talked on the phone last night." She looked at him curiously.

"Under the circumstances, I decided it would be wise for me to come and ensure that there wouldn't be any problems." He didn't say "with Abbie," but Rachel knew that's what he meant. "And, as Dean's executor, I felt I should be on hand to see how the auction went."

"Of course." A small crowd had gathered at the rail of the riding arena to watch a horse and rider working in English tack. Rachel paused with Lane to observe the pair, her attention first drawn to the flashy bay mare, then shifting to the rider. It was Abbie, dressed in jodhpurs, riding helmet, and white shirt, minus the customary jacket, her dark hair pulled back in a low bun. As she rode along the near rail, Rachel noticed that her face looked haggard and she had dark hollows beneath her eyes. "Did you see her, Lane? She looks awful." The words were out before she realized how tactless the remark was. She tried to cover them. "Is she ill?"

"No, I think she's just tired. She hasn't had much sleep lately, I understand." He hesitated, then added, "Her horse was injured in a freak accident a couple days ago. Both front legs were broken. She's been sitting up nights with her ever since."

"What happened?"

"The way it was explained to me, the horse got out of the pasture sometime in the night and strayed onto the adjoining farm. The neighbor caught her the next morning and put her in his barn, then called here to let them know the horse was safe. Before they could go get her, the horse was frightened by the noise from some farm machinery and tried to get out of the barn."

"How terrible." Rachel shuddered to think of such a thing happening to her mare.

"Yes. . . . I think Chet needs to talk to me about something," Lane said, indicating the man motioning for him. "Do you want to come along?"

"No. I think I'll wander through the barns and look over the horses." Rachel took the sales catalogue from her purse and folded it open to the page containing the names and sale numbers of the three mares she was interested in buying.

"I'll catch up with you later. You'll be all right?"

"Of course." She smiled, liking the way he was so protective of her. It made her feel secure and loved.

More than a dozen prospective buyers were scattered along the wide corridor, surveying the horses in the stalls, when Rachel entered. Inside, she checked the sale numbers of the horses on her list again, then started down the cement walkway, pausing in front of each stall long enough to read the number on the horse's hip. Along the way she caught snatches of conversation.

"This mare should nick well with our stallion. Her breeding —"

"— pretty head, but her legs are —"

"— always said, if you don't like the looks of a horse in the stall, don't buy it."

Rachel stopped in front of one of the last stalls in the row. The flaxenmaned chestnut mare stood at an angle that made it difficult for Rachel to tell if the last number on her hip was a five or a nine. As she moved to try to get a better view of the number, someone else came up to the stall to look at the horse. She paid no attention to him until he spoke.

"Hello, beautiful."

At first she thought the murmured words were addressed to the mare, although his voice sounded vaguely familiar. Idly curious, she glanced sideways at the man and encountered his gaze. As he pushed the dark cowboy hat with the concho-studded band to the back of his head, Rachel recognized the curly-haired singer, Ross Tibbs.

"Mr. Tibbs." She was surprised at how clearly she remembered him.

"I thought we agreed that it was Ross to you." He smiled, looking at her as if nothing and no one else existed, the sensation distinctly unnerving. "It's been so long since I've seen you, I was beginning to wonder if I hadn't dreamed you."

She was disturbed by the flattery inherent in his remarks. "I never expected to run into you at a horse auction. Why are you here?"

"Same reason you are, I expect. I came to look over the horses. I've always wanted to own an Arabian. I was kinda hoping I might be able to pick one up for a song." He winked at her, then smiled ruefully. "That was a joke. A poor one, I admit. Singer . . . song."

"Of course." She laughed uneasily.

"From the looks of all these folks that've shown up, there's not going to be much chance of me picking up a bargain. But, it never does any harm to window-shop now and then." Turning, he braced an arm against the stall, his head resting on a board near her head. She'd noticed how dark and thick his eyelashes were — long like a woman's. "I'd like to take you out to dinner after the auction's over."

"I can't." She was surprised and briefly embarrassed by the invitation.

"Why?"

"I'm . . . with someone." She stared at the open collar of his shirt, her eyes on the smooth, taut skin of his throat and neck.

"Who? Lane Canfield again?"

"Yes."

"Just what is he to you? Your sugar daddy or what?" He sounded almost angry, and the muscles along his jaw tightened visibly.

"No." Rachel didn't like the connotation of that term. It implied she was his mistress, his plaything. But what was she to him? "We're . . . friends. That's all."

"Friends, eh? That can cover a lot of ground, you know." Ross swung partially around, trapping her against the wall of the stall. "He's too old for you, Rachel."

"He isn't old," she insisted, but she recognized the shakiness of that argument. "Besides, maybe I like older men."

"I'm pushing thirty. I fit that category." He leaned closer and she felt smothered by his nearness, unable to breathe. Reaching up, he lightly traced the curve of her cheekbone with the tip of his forefinger, following it all the way to the lobe of her ear. "You remind me of Sleeping Beauty still waiting to be awakened by a kiss from her prince. I never read any fairy tale that had a prince with white hair in it."

She felt hot all over as her heart beat rapidly. He was staring at her lips and Rachel could almost feel the pressure of his mouth on them. She was frightened by the things she was feeling. Was this how her mother had felt with Dean — so overwhelmed by emotion that she abandoned everything, including her pride and self-respect? That wasn't going to happen to her. She wouldn't let it.

"Don't say things like that." She pushed away from the stall and hurriedly brushed past him, not stopping until she'd put several feet between them. Against her will, Rachel looked back.

"I'm sorry." He lifted his hand in a helpless, apologetic gesture. "I didn't mean any harm."

"Please, just leave me alone." She walked out of the barn and nearly ran into Lane on his way in.

"I was just coming to look for you." His initial smile faded slightly as his interest in her sharpened. "Is something wrong?"

"Of course not. What could be wrong?" Rachel forced a smile, surprised that she could do it so convincingly, and linked her arm with his to steer him away from the open barn doors before he could catch sight of Ross Tibbs.

She didn't want Lane to know she'd been talking with Ross or he'd guess why she was upset. Knowing that a moment sooner and Lane would have found them together made it all the more imperative that he not find out. At the same time, Rachel didn't understand this feeling of guilt just because for a brief instant she'd been attracted to — and tempted by — Ross. After all, nothing had happened.

"I thought Abbie may —"

"I haven't seen her." She began to breathe easier as his smile came back.

"The auction is scheduled to start in another ten minutes. I think we'd better head over to the sales ring if you want a good vantage point."

"Yes, we probably should."

As they walked toward the sales ring, they were joined by others converging on the same destination. Rachel noticed the looks Lane received and heard the murmurs of recognition. The first few times she'd been out in public with him, the stares and whispers had bothered her, but she'd grown used to the attention he attracted — the respect, admiration, and envy with which he was regarded. In fact, she was actually beginning to enjoy it.

"Testing: one, two, three. Testing. Testing." The auctioneer's voice came over the loudspeakers. "Well, folks, it looks like we're ready to start. We've got some fine horses for you today. And we'll start with Lot Number One. Coming into the ring now is the incredible stallion, Nahr Ibn Kedar, the five-year-old son of the stallion imported from Egypt by the late Dean Lawson himself. This magnificent stallion is being shown under saddle by Dean's daughter, Abbie Lawson."

Recognizing that he was dealing with a knowledgeable group of buyers, the auctioneer wasted little time extolling the pedigrees and show records of the Arabian horses that entered the ring one after another. And rarely did he interrupt his rhythmic chant to exhort higher bids from the participants. The quickness of his hammer to declare a horse sold instilled a feverish pace to the bidding and allowed few lulls between bids.

As Abbie rode out of the sales ring on the final horse to be shown under saddle, Ben waited to take the reins. She flipped them to him and dismounted, feeling exhausted. The heavy humidity from the moisture-laden clouds overhead was taking its toll on her, as well as the tension of trying to get the best out of every horse she rode.

"It goes well." Ben patted the mare's neck, then turned to lead the horse to the barn. Abbie fell into step beside him. "The auctioneer does not give them time to think how much they are bidding. We get good prices."

"I noticed." She should have been pleased about it, but she wasn't, and she blamed the indifference she felt on her tiredness. "Is the next lot ready for the ring?"

"Yes."

She spied the bale of hay shoved up against the stable door. It offered an escape from all the hubbub and confusion going on inside the barn. "If you don't need me, I think I'll just sit and rest for a minute."

"We can manage," Ben assured her.

"Thanks." She smiled wanly and angled away from him, walking over to the lone bale.

As she sank onto the compressed hay, Abbie removed the hot riding helmet and laid it on the bale, then leaned back against the barn door. For a time, she stared at the crowd gathered around the sale ring and idly listened to the auctioneer's singsong voice calling for higher bids on the mare and foal in the ring.

Then her attention wandered to the barns, the white-fenced pastures, and the old Victorian house — the place, the land, the buildings that comprised her home, the only real home she'd ever known. Suddenly it was all a blur as tears filled her eyes. Tomorrow it would be sold and a new owner would take possession of it.

Leaning forward, she scooped up a handful of dirt — dirt that turned into thick gumbo when it rained. She rubbed it between her thumb and fingers, feeling its texture and consistency, the way she'd seen her grandfather do a hundred times or more. When she'd ask him why he did it, he'd put some in her hands and say, "Now, feel that. It's more than just dirt, you know."

"It's Texas dirt," Abbie would reply.

"It's more than that. You see, that dirt you're holding, that's pieces of Lawson land." Then he would hold it up close to his face, smell it, and taste it with the tip of his tongue.

"Why did you do that, Grandpa?" she would ask.

"Because it's good for what ails you. Remember that."

Abbie remembered, closing her hand into a fist and squeezing the dirt into a thick clump in her palm.

"Mind if I join you?"

Startled to hear MacCrea's voice, Abbie sat up and brought her hands together, hiding the dirt clutched in her palm. "What are you doing here?"

"I had an errand to run in town, so I thought I'd stop by and see how the sale was going." He moved the riding helmet to one side and sat down next to her. "There's a lot of people here."

"Yes." Uncomfortable under his inspecting glance, she looked down at her hands.

"Are you all right?"

"I'm fine," she assured him with a quick nod. "Just tired, that's all." She said nothing to him about the dirt she held so tightly, doubting that he'd understand. From the little she'd learned about his childhood, she knew he'd never stayed in any one place long enough to form any deep attachment to it. He couldn't appreciate the strong bond she felt for River Bend, her home, her heritage.

Ben emerged from the stables and walked over to them. "I wanted to remind you that he will sell your filly after this mare leaves the ring."

"Thanks." Abbie pushed to her feet and headed directly for the sales ring. MacCrea walked with her, but she paid no attention to him. She worked her way through the crowd and reached the edge of the ring just as the auctioneer rang the hammer down, selling the mare and foal to the high bidder.

"The next filly to be sold — number twenty-five in your catalogue — was unfortunately injured in a freak accident two days ago," the auctioneer explained. "The veterinarian's report, which I have in front of me, states that both front legs were broken. Both have been successfully splinted and cast, and the veterinarian expresses a guarded optimism over the filly's chances of recovery."

Practically rigid with tension herself, Abbie closely observed the crowd's reaction to his announcement. Most shook their heads skeptically and a few turned away from the ring. No one appeared to be even slightly interested in River Breeze, not even Rachel, whom Abbie spotted standing on the opposite side of the ring, talking to Lane.

The auctioneer then went into a lengthy description of the filly's breeding, concluding with, "Regardless of this filly's injuries, I think you will all agree she has the potential to make an outstanding broodmare. Now what do I hear for an opening bid?"

Abbie held her breath as he and his assistants scanned the throng, but silence greeted them. Anxiously she waited until his second call for a bid was met with silence, then she signaled a bid of a hundred dollars.

"I've got a bid of one hundred dollars right over here. Who'll gimme two? Who'll gimme two?" The chanted call rolled off his tongue. As soon as it became apparent there were no takers at two, he halved it. "I've got one. Who'll gimme one-fifty? One-fifty?"

As MacCrea had predicted, no one wanted the injured filly. Within a scant few minutes after the bidding started, it was over.

"Breeze is legally mine now." Abbie turned to him, a smile lifting her tired features.

"So are the vet bills," MacCrea reminded her.

"I don't care," she declared, blithely defiant of such practical considerations. "She's worth it — and more." She still held the dirt in her hand, sweat turning it into a ball of mud. But she wouldn't let it go.

23

ALL MORNING LONG, ominous gray clouds loomed over River Bend, casting an eerie half-darkness over the tree-shaded grounds. Distant rumbles of thunder, like deep-throated growls, threatened rain. The auctioneer's podium stood on the veranda of the great house, facing the striped tent that had been erected on the front lawn to shelter the bidders in case it rained.

All day long, Rachel had watched people traipsing through the house, faces peering out at her from turret windows, children racing around behind the second-floor parapet, and hands tapping at wood to check its solidness. But she had yet to venture inside herself. When she set foot inside that house for the first time, she was determined not to be surrounded by irreverent gawkers.

A hush settled over the crowd gathered under the tent as the auctioneer announced the next item to be sold: River Bend itself. Rachel felt her stomach lurch sickeningly. All this waiting, the tension, the uncertainty had worn her nerves raw. She glanced anxiously around for Lane and saw him talking with Dean's widow. Twice Rachel had seen her and that Polish stud manager who had worked for Dean, but she had yet to see Abbie on the grounds.

A boom of thunder reverberated through the air, chasing those on the outer fringes farther under the canvas roof. Behind her, Rachel heard a man say, "I wouldn't be surprised if that isn't R.D. up there, pounding his fist on a cloud. You know he's looking down on this — and not liking it one whit."

Just for an instant, Rachel took the remark as a personal slur against her, then reminded herself that the man couldn't know she intended to buy River Bend. As the auctioneer continued with his legal description of the property and its buildings, she tried to locate the man Lane had pointed out to her earlier — the one who would actually do the bidding for them. But she couldn't find him in the crowd. The last time she'd seen him, he'd been smoking a cigarette near the old carriage house that had been converted into a garage.

Panicking at the thought that maybe he didn't know the bidding was about to start, Rachel caught Lane's eye and signaled him to join her. She waited impatiently as he worked his way through the crowd to her side.

"Where's your man Phillips? I don't see him."

"He's on the far side of the tent. I saw him there just seconds ago. Stop worrying." He took her hand and gave it a reassuring squeeze.

"I can't help it." She held on to his hand, locking her fingers through his, today needing his strength and his confidence.

When the auctioneer called for the first bid, it started to rain — at first just making a soft patter on the tent roof, then turning into a steady drumming. The sky seemed to grow darker.

The woman in front of Rachel turned to her companion. "Let's go find Babs and tell her we're leaving," she said in a low, subdued voice. " I don't want to stay for this. It's like all of Texas is crying."

Rachel tried not to let the woman's comment demoralize her. Those were just rivulets of rainwater running down the windowpanes of the mansion, not tears. This was the moment she'd been waiting for all her life . . . even though she hadn't always known it. Nothing and no one was going to spoil it for her.

"I haven't seen Abbie," she remembered. "Is she here?"

"She didn't come today," Lane replied.

Finding out that Abbie had stayed away from this auction made Rachel feel that she'd won a minor victory. Her dream was well on its way tò coming true, in a way she had never dared to imagine. Yesterday she had acquired three broodmares, all with foals at their side and checked in foal to Nahr El Kedar, increasing the number of Arabians she owned. And today, River Bend itself would belong to her. Now she would have that part of Dean's world that had always been denied her. She wanted to hug herself and hold on to that triumphant feeling, but she was too nervous, too anxious. Instead she gripped Lane's hand a little harder and listened to the bidding.

Higher and higher it went, finally narrowing the field to three bidders, their agent among them. When Rachel realized the price had climbed to over a hundred thousand dollars more than Lane had expected River Bend to sell for, she started to worry. Then the agent, Phillips, dropped out of the bidding. Pierced by a shaft of icy-cold fear, Rachel wondered if she had come this close, only to lose it after all.

"Lane, why isn't he bidding?" she whispered, afraid of the answer.

"He doesn't want to drive the price up more."

She realized it was some sort of strategy, but the suspense was almost more than she could stand. But when the gavel fell, knocking off the final bid, the auctioneer pointed to the bald-headed agent as the successful bidder. Weak with relief, Rachel sagged against Lane.

"Happy?" Lane smiled at her with his eyes.

"Not yet. I think I'm afraid to be," she admitted, aware that she must sound terribly unsophisticated to him, but it was the truth.

"Maybe it would seem more real to you if we went inside and looked around your new home."

"Not now. I'd rather do it later . . . after everyone leaves." She didn't want any strangers wandering through the rooms when she explored the house. She wouldn't feel that it really belonged to her if they were there.

"If that's the way you want it, we'll wait."

Late that afternoon, the last of the cars headed down the long driveway, carrying the auctioneer and his staff. The rain had stopped, but drops of water continued to plop down from the wet leaves of the giant trees in the yard. Overhead the clouds lingered, forming a charcoal-colored canopy over River Bend.

Nervous and excited, Rachel felt as giddy as a teenager as she waited for Lane to unlock the front door. When he held it open for her, she glanced hesitantly inside, in her mind seeing Abbie's apparition standing in the doorway, ordering her away.

But this was no longer Abbie's home. From now on she would do the ordering. Rachel walked inside to take possession of it. In the large foyer, she paused and gazed at the impressive staircase with its balustrades of ornately carved walnut. She tried to visualize Dean walking down those steps to welcome her, but the image wouldn't come.

Hiding the bitter disappointment she felt, Rachel followed Lane through the rest of the house, so huge compared to the apartments she'd always lived in. In every room, the wood of the parquet floors, the richly carved door and window moldings, the wainscoting, and the fireplace mantels gleamed with the patina that came from years of loving care. Yet the bare walls and windows seemed to stare back at her. With no furniture, curtains, or paintings in the house, their footsteps echoed with a stark, lonely sound.

"Once all the paperwork is finalized and you officially take possession, you can have an interior decorator come out," Lane said as they climbed the staircase to the second floor. "I'm sure there will be changes you want to make."

"Yes," Rachel said absently, but she doubted it would be anything drastic. She wanted to keep the house just the way it was. She planned to limit any decorating to choosing curtains, rugs, and furniture.

But when she entered one of the bedrooms on the second floor and felt prickles crawling up the back of her neck, she changed her mind entirely. She knew without being told the room had belonged to Abbie. Her Dior perfume still lingered in the air.

She crossed to the French doors that opened onto the narrow balcony within the parapet and pulled them open, letting the rain-freshened air sweep into the room. She paused there a minute, staring at the high limbs of the towering ancient oaks, some stretching out their arms so close to the house she had the feeling that she only had to reach out her hand to touch their shiny leaves. Drawn by the stillness, the peace of the view, Rachel wandered onto the railed balcony. Through the trees, she could see parts of the winding lane, the stable complex and paddocks, and the empty pastures.

As she leaned against the parapet, Lane walked up to stand beside her. "You haven't said very much."

She turned to face the house, half sitting and half bracing herself against the rail. "I guess I'm still finding it hard to believe this all belongs to me — to us," she corrected quickly.

"Yes, to us," he said thoughtfully. "I've been wondering . . . ," Lane began, then started over. "Have you ever given any thought to making our partnership a permanent one?"

"What do you mean?" Rachel frowned. "I thought it was. All the documents we signed, didn't they —"

Lane smiled ruefully. "I'm putting it badly, I'm afraid. I wasn't referring to our business partnership. I meant you and me. I think you know that I love you, Rachel. But do you love me?"

"Yes." She thought he knew that. Lane Canfield was everything a woman could ever wish for in a man. He was so good *to* her and *for* her — not just because he was fulfilling her dreams, but because he'd made her feel that she was someone very special.

"Do you love me enough to marry me and be my wife?"

"Do I!" She nearly went into his arms, but she checked the impulse, suddenly wary. "You mean it, don't you, Lane? This isn't some joke, is it?"

"I couldn't be more serious." The gravity in his expression convinced Rachel of that. "I've never proposed to another woman in my entire life. You would eliminate a lot of the misery I'm going through right now by simply telling me yes or no."

"Yes." Gazing at him, Rachel wondered if he knew how much he had given her: first a belief in herself and her dreams, then River Bend, and now the respect and legitimacy of his name. No man had done so much for her before — not even Dean.

In the next second, his arms were around her and his mouth was on her lips. She reveled in the adoring ardency of his kiss, overwhelmed by the knowledge that of all the women he could have chosen, Lane Canfield wanted to marry her. At last she drew back a few inches to look at his face, so strong and good and gentle. "I do love you, Lane."

"I suppose we should make this official." He reached into his jacket pocket and pulled out a ring. Rachel gasped as fire leaped from the circlet of diamonds that surrounded the large sapphire. Lane took her hand and slipped it onto her ring finger.

"It's beautiful." The words sounded so inadequate, but she couldn't think of anything else to say.

"I've been carrying that ring around with me for the last two weeks, trying to convince myself that it wouldn't be a mistake to marry you. You deserve to be happy, Rachel. If you'd be happier with someone else . . ."

"No one could make me as happy as you do," she insisted, refusing even to consider the possibility. "I am going to be so proud to be your wife. Mrs. Lane Canfield. I love the sound of it."

"So do I. Now about our wedding . . ."

"We can fly to Mexico tonight and elope if you want." Rachel almost preferred that. She didn't want to be reminded that she had no father to give her away, no family and few friends to invite.

"No. I want you to have a wedding with all the trimmings. Nothing elaborate, you understand. Just a simple ceremony and a small reception afterward with a few of our close friends in attendance. I want you to come to me in a bridal gown, all white satin and lace."

"Whatever you say, Lane."

"I'll do my best to make you happy, Rachel. I want you to know that. There will be times when my work will take me away from you, maybe for several days in a row, and for one reason or another you usually won't be able to come with me. You understand that, don't you?"

"Of course."

"I know how lonely your life has been. I don't like the idea that as my wife, you may be lonely again."

"I'll have a lot to keep me busy, between the horses and turning this into a home for us." As long as it was only his work that kept them apart, Rachel could accept the separations. What was really important was that she had his love.

"You're a remarkable woman," he murmured, drawing her into his embrace once again. She kissed him while secretly doubting she was all that remarkable, but it was important that he believed she was.

"Lane." She kissed him fervently, straining to give back part of the joy he'd given her. When she finally drew away from him, she knew she had aroused him. The evidence was there in the disturbed light in his eyes and the quickened rate of his breathing.

"It's moments like this that make me wish this was our wedding night," he whispered and set her slightly away from him.

Rachel was touched by the way he refused to anticipate their wedding night. She considered his attitude wonderfully old-fashioned and proof he was worthy of her trust. Yet in another way it bothered her. Sometimes she thought there was something wrong with her, that she wasn't desirable enough. Otherwise, if he loved her as much as he claimed, he'd be tempted to take her. But she didn't press the issue even now, fearing his rejection as well as his possible discovery of her own inadequacies at making love.

24

THE HEADLIGHT BEAMS raced ahead of the car as Abbie sped down the highway, the overlapping tracks of light a blur in front of her eyes. Instinctively she was running — running like a child trying to escape from the unkind taunts of her playmates. But no matter how far or how fast she went, she could never get away from the hurtful words.

For the last ten days, she'd listened to the swirl of rumors going around, speculating on the identity of River Bend's new owner. It was common knowledge that the man Phillips, the successful bidder at the auction, had been acting on behalf of an unnamed client. Today, when she and Babs had gone to Lane's office to receive a final accounting on her father's estate after all costs and debts were paid, she had learned the truth.

As she had feared all along, Rachel now possessed River Bend. But what Abbie hadn't known was Lane's involvement. The two of them owned it jointly. More damning than that, he had blandly announced that he and Rachel were getting married in September. At that point Abbie had walked out of his office, unable to endure his presence a second longer.

Lane Canfield. A trusted family friend. He had turned against them and joined with Rachel. It seemed that no matter which way she turned, she was faced with betrayal. She should have known the day of the funeral when he'd told her about Dean's long love affair with Caroline Farr exactly where his sympathies lay. She should have seen when he leaped to Rachel's defense that day at River Bend that he wasn't looking out for their interests. Rachel came first with him — just as she had with her father.

Maybe she could have eventually learned to live with the fact that her father had another child. Maybe she could have even accepted the fact that he had loved Rachel more than he ever had her. But the fortune he had left Rachel, while she had received nothing from him, the ownership of River Bend going to

Rachel, and Rachel's impending marriage to a man who was supposed to be a trusted family friend — combined, they were all more than Abbie could tolerate. Her initial resentment of Rachel had grown into a consuming hatred.

If Rachel thought Abbie was going to move away from the area and start a new life someplace else, she was wrong. And if she thought Abbie was going to forgo any further involvement in the breeding and showing of Arabian horses because Rachel was getting into it, she was wrong there, too. Whether Rachel realized it yet or not, she had a rival almost literally in her own backyard. There hadn't been anything Abbie could do to prevent the things that had happened. But now she intended to fight Rachel every step of the way, reminding Rachel by her presence alone that she was the intruder, the interloper, in Abbie's world.

A mile before she reached the drilling site, Abbie could see the glow from the platform's floodlights lighting up the night sky. It shone like a beacon guiding her to a safe haven, the way growing brighter the closer she got. Finally the clearing was directly in front of her car, the bright lights from the derrick spilling onto the dusty trailers and the pickups parked at the site.

After parking in front of MacCrea's office trailer, Abbie stepped out of her car and walked directly to it. She didn't bother to knock, knowing she wouldn't be heard above all the noise. Instead, she walked right in.

There was no one in the front half of the trailer. When she looked toward the rear, she saw MacCrea sprawled across one of the single beds, fully clothed and sound asleep. She walked back to where he lay and, for a moment, simply watched him. She had never seen him asleep before. His dark, wavy hair was all rumpled; his shirt, pulled loose from the waistband of his pants; and his muscles, lax. His chest rose and fell with the even rhythm of his breathing. Abbie smiled at the scowl on his face.

Things had gone badly for her lately. But watching him, she realized that she'd been so caught up in her own problems she'd forgotten that MacCrea had lost nearly everything after his father died. Yet he had battled the odds and built the company back up. She knew it hadn't been easy, especially at the beginning.

To be honest, her own situation wasn't as bad as it could have been. Besides River Breeze, she had her own reputation in the show ring. This last week, she and Ben had contacted several of the small Arabian horse breeders in the area and let them know their services were available to condition, train, and show outside horses. With the fall show season approaching, quite a number of the breeders expressed a definite interest in hiring them.

And they weren't totally broke. Babs would receive almost fifty thousand dollars from her share of the estate, money left over after all the creditors were paid from the auction receipts. If Abbie had stayed instead of walking out of Lane's office in such a huff, it might have been more. But her mother had insisted that Jackson receive the full amount of his bequest, and instructed Lane to take the amount necessary from her proceeds to make up the difference. It was a grand and noble gesture, one that Abbie had difficulty arguing with. Still, she didn't think it had been necessary for her mother to be *that* generous.

So, her mother had a small nest egg. Abbie had River Breeze, and after a bout with a fever, the filly was improving. Plus she had Ben for a partner. And, most of all, she had the man lying before her, frowning in his sleep, ready to fight some more.

Slowly and carefully she lowered herself onto him, letting her weight settle gradually. She gently smoothed the furrowed lines from his forehead with her fingers, not letting her touch be too light, to avoid tickling him. As she rubbed her lips over his mouth, letting them trace its outline, she felt him stir. His hand moved hesitantly to the small of her back, then glided along a familiar course up to her shoulders. Abbie knew he was awake even before he began to lip at her mouth and draw it to his. She kissed him, receiving a languorous response, like a flame slow to kindle and long to burn, heating her more thoroughly than any passionately demanding kiss could.

Finally MacCrea shifted onto his side, drawing her with him so her head rested on the same pillow facing him. "Hello," Abbie said softly.

"Now that's how a man likes to be woke up." His voice was still husky with sleep. He looked deep into her eyes, so deep that Abbie felt certain he could see all the love she felt for him. "I've missed you, Abbie." Emotion charged his words, and she felt her breath catch in her throat, hearing in the admission how much he cared for her even though he hadn't actually used the word *love*.

"I've missed you, Mac," she whispered.

His hand exerted pressure on her back a second before his mouth moved to claim hers. Abbie gave to him all the feelings she'd held inside, her heartbeat quickening and the blood running sweet and fast in her veins. There was nothing hurried about the long, full kiss; no sense of urgency pushed them. Abbie sensed that he, too, found something warm and satisfying in this closeness and sought only to enjoy it.

The loud racket from the drilling rig suddenly flooded the trailer. MacCrea pulled back, frowning.

"Hey, boss!" a rigger in a hard hat called as he stepped into the small kitchen, stopping short when he saw Abbie lying on the narrow bed with MacCrea. His head dipped as he looked hurriedly away. "Sorry. I didn't know ya had company." He retreated a step, uncertain whether to stay or go.

"What is it, Barnes?" Partially rising, MacCrea propped an elbow beneath him. Abbie lay beside him, not at all upset by the interruption, wrapped in the comforting feeling that she had the right to be there in his bed.

"We could use you out on the rig for a minute, that's all," he mumbled and turned to leave.

"I'll be right out," MacCrea told him. When the door closed, shutting out the noise from the rig, he looked down at her, a dark glow shining in his eyes, and added softly, "Much as I'd like to stay right here."

"And much as I'd like to keep you here, I won't." Levering herself up, she brushed a kiss across his cheek, then swung her feet onto the trailer floor.

MacCrea was only a step behind her when she entered the kitchen. She moved to the side to let him pass, her gaze following him as he grabbed his hard hat off the table and stepped to the door.

"I shouldn't be long." He smiled briefly in her direction, but Abbie could tell his thoughts had already shifted from her to the rig. "Put on some fresh coffee, would you?"

It was hardly a question since he was out the door by the time she said, "Okay."

Minutes later the electric percolator bubbled merrily, the wafts of steam rising from its spout sending the aroma of coffee throughout the trailer. Abbie tidied up the kitchen, then poured herself a cup of the freshly brewed coffee and carried it into the front office area of the trailer. Drawn by the photograph of MacCrea and his father, she wandered over to the filing cabinet and, for a time, studied the picture propped against the wall on top of it. The love, the deep bond, between father and son was so obvious that she couldn't help feeling a sharp pang of envy.

Fighting it, she turned away and walked over to MacCrea's desk, suddenly needing his closeness, the reassurance of his love. Impulsively Abbie sat down in the worn swivel chair behind his desk, its cushion and padded back long since fitted to the shape of his body. She rocked back in it, sipping at her coffee as she absently perused the papers and file folders scattered across the desktop.

One of the folders bore the label "CTS documents." CTS was the acronym for MacCrea's computerized testing system, Abbie remembered. Out of idle curiosity, she slipped the folder out of the stack and opened it to glance through the papers. She knew the project meant a lot to him, yet he'd never discussed the deal he'd made. As she leafed through some sort of partnership agreement, one of the signatures on the last page leaped out at her: Rachel Farr. Abbie stared at it in shock, certain there had to be some mistake. MacCrea couldn't . . . MacCrea wouldn't . . . She straightened slowly, the pages clutched tightly in her hands, her gaze riveted to the name Rachel Farr.

The trailer door opened and MacCrea walked in. Abbie turned her head, unable to speak, unable to think, unable to do anything except stare at him, frozen by the damning evidence in her hands. But he didn't seem to notice as he removed his helmet and gave it a little toss onto the sofa.

"I told you I wouldn't be long." A lazy smile lifted the corners of his mustache as he paused beside the desk, then glanced briefly at the papers in her hand. Without a break in his expression, he turned and walked into the kitchen area, saying, "The coffee smells good."

"What is this, MacCrea?" Abbie pushed out of the chair and followed him to the door, then stopped, still in the thrall of a shock that deadened her senses.

"That?" Half glancing at the papers in her hand, he lifted a cup of steaming hot coffee to his mouth, but didn't drink immediately from it. "It's a joint ownership agreement on the patent for the CTS."

"I know that." She shook her head and wondered if he had deliberately misunderstood. "I'm not talking about his signature. What is hers doing on it?"

"By 'hers' I assume you mean Rachel's." His voice was calm and even, the name coming from his lips with ease. "Since it's a list of owners, naturally Rachel's name is on it."

His casual announcement shattered the numbness that had kept all her emotions in check. Now they raged through her. "What do you mean, 'naturally'?" Half-blinded by anger, Abbie couldn't even make out the hated name on the list. "Are you saying she's one of your investors? That you — you —" She searched wildly for the words that would express the absolute betrayal she felt.

"That's exactly what I'm saying." MacCrea sipped at his coffee.

"You took money from her." She trembled violently as she made the accusation, hating him for standing there so calmly, as if he'd done nothing wrong. All along she thought he truly cared about her, but it was obvious he didn't. "How could you?" Abbie stormed.

"Simple. I wanted to get this project off the ground and out to the drilling sites. I never made a secret of that."

Abbie knew he hadn't, but admitting that just made everything worse. Infuriated by his phlegmatic attitude when he had to know what this was doing to her, Abbie slapped the coffee mug from his hand, mindless of the arcing spray of scalding liquid and the loud crash of the cup as it struck the opposite wall and broke.

"And you didn't care who you got the money from either, did you?"

"Not one damned bit!" MacCrea flared, her anger at last penetrating.

"Now I know why you didn't tell me anything about your *deal*." The contempt she felt matched the violent anger that quivered through her whole body. "You were very careful not to let me know who all was involved, weren't you? You did it *knowing* how I would feel about it. How could you?"

"Easy. This was business," MacCrea stated emphatically.

"Business. Is that what you call it?" She had another name for it: betrayal, the ultimate betrayal. "All that time you spent in Houston, you were meeting with her, weren't you?" She felt sick to her stomach just thinking about the two of them together. She could imagine how Rachel must have gloated over it, knowing she had stolen someone else who had supposedly belonged to her alone.

"There were others involved in those meetings," he snapped. "I wasn't alone with her, if that's what you're implying. I told you: it was business."

"Am I supposed to believe that?" Abbie taunted.

"I don't give a damn whether you do or not!"

"That's obvious." She could tell that he had no intention of altering the situation, a situation that meant he would have continued contact with Rachel. "And it's equally obvious that you don't give a damn about me either!"

"If that's the way you want to look at it." There was no yielding in his hard stand. There wasn't even a glimmer of regret in his expression, not even a hint of apology for his actions.

"This invention of yours was always more important to you than I was. I was a fool not to see that. Well, now you've got it!" She hurled the papers at his face and stalked quickly to the trailer door. Gripping the handle, she glanced over her shoulder, consumed by the pain, jealousy, and anger that were so firmly intermixed she couldn't tell them apart. "I hope they keep your bed warm at night from now on, because I won't!"

She charged out of the trailer into the floodlit night, fighting the tears and trembling that threatened to overwhelm her. She could still see him standing there, towering over the strewn papers and broken pottery shards from the mug, his expression thin-lipped and angry. But she had crossed that fine line, now hating him with all the passion with which she had once loved him.

In the trailer MacCrea stared at the door, his fingers curling with the urge to go after her and shake her until her teeth rattled out of her head. Instead he turned, the papers crackling underfoot. He glanced at them, then, in a burst of frustration, he rammed his fist into a cabinet door, the pressed wood cracking and buckling under the force of the blow.

25

ABBIE LOOKED ON AS the filly stood quietly while Ben cleaned and applied disinfectant to the large ulcerated sore under the foreleg caused by the rubbing splint. So far, River Breeze had adjusted well to the splints and lately had managed to hobble a few steps with them.

As Ben straightened to his feet, the messy task finished, the filly nuzzled Abbie's shoulder. The affectionate gesture seemed to be one of gratitude. Smiling, Abbie cradled the filly's silver head in the crook of her arm and lightly rubbed the arched neck with a small circular motion to imitate the nuzzling of a mare on her foal.

"You know we're doing all of this to help you, don't you, Breeze?" Abbie crooned, her chest tight with the pain of betrayal that just wouldn't go away. It was as fresh this morning as it had been two nights ago when she'd left Mac-Crea's trailer for the last time. If anything, the anger, hurt, and bitterness had grown stronger. When Ben left the stall to dispose of the soiled gauze pads, she pressed the side of her face against the filly's sleek neck. "You would never do that to me, would you, girl?" She drew comfort from that knowledge.

"Looks like she's healing real good."

Startled by the sound of Dobie's voice, Abbie stiffened. She hadn't heard him walk up to the stall and wondered how long he'd been standing there.

"Yes, she's coming along nicely." She gave the filly one last pat, then stepped away, feeling the strain of trying to behave normally so no one would guess that she had broken off with MacCrea. She couldn't talk about it — she didn't want to talk about it yet. "I planned to talk to you today about renting this barn and that section of pasture along the Brazos."

"But I already told you that you were welcome to use both. Neither one of them is of any use to me."

"But that was when we were talking about keeping only my filly here. Several local breeders have contacted us about training and showing their Arabians this fall. So far it looks like we're going to have about a dozen horses. Since Ben and I are going to have to rent facilities somewhere, I thought it would be much more convenient and more logical if I could work out some sort of arrangement with you to keep them here."

"If that's the case, I don't see why not," he replied with a falsely indifferent shrug. As tight as Dobie was with money, Abbie had been certain he wouldn't turn down the opportunity to make an extra dollar. She hadn't misjudged him. "Course" — he glanced around at the interior of the old barn — "this place isn't in very good shape."

"Ben and I can fix it up. We'll pay for the improvements." With what, she didn't know. But that was a worry she'd leave for another time. Maybe by then she'd have sold her Mercedes. "But we would expect a break on the rent because of it."

"I promise I'll be fair with you, Abbie. Anything is better than the nothing I'm getting for it now."

"I suppose that's true."

Knowing that now it was simply a matter of dickering over the price, she felt a little more relieved. It would be good to wake up in the mornings and once again hear the whinny of horses. She had missed that since leaving River Bend. And she could imagine how much harder it must have been on Ben. For nearly all his sixty-odd years, he'd been surrounded by horses — Arabian horses. The care and training of them were both his vocation and avocation. Without them, he felt useless and lost.

The side door of the barn banged shut. Abbie turned, expecting to see Ben. Instead it was MacCrea coming toward her, his long, lazy stride eating up the space between them. Stung, she felt all the hurts coming back, that terrible ache, and the rawness of wounds too fresh even to have begun to heal.

"What do you want?" She heard the brittleness in her voice — rigid and cold like a thin shell of ice. That's the way she felt. She looked him in the eye, taking care to ignore the probe of his dark gaze and not to let her glance slip to the heavy brush of his mustache to watch his mouth when he spoke.

"I want to talk to you."

Beside her, Dobie took a step toward the door. Abbie stopped him. "You don't have to leave, Dobie. I'm not interested in hearing anything he has to say." Pivoting sharply, she swung away from MacCrea.

"I had hoped you would have cooled off enough by now to let me explain a few things to you."

She swung back to face him, cold with rage. "There's no explanation you could give that would justify anything."

When she started to walk away from him, MacCrea grabbed her arm. "Dammit, Abbie —"

"Take your hand off me!" Burned by the contact, she exploded in anger. Releasing her arm, he drew back. "Don't touch me, MacCrea. Don't ever come near me again. Do you hear? I don't want to see — or hear from — you. Just get out! And stay out!"

MacCrea looked at her for a long, hard moment, then snapped, "With pleasure."

In the next second, Abbie was staring at his back as he walked out of the barn. She continued to tremble, but it was more in reaction than anger. Mac-Crea was gone. She kept reminding herself that she should be relieved to have him out of her life. But why wasn't she? With the exception of Ben, the men she'd known had never brought her anything but grief, from her father to her husband and all the way to MacCrea. She swore she wouldn't be any man's fool again.

Dobie came over to stand beside her. "Are you okay, Abbie?"

"Of course," she answered sharply.

"He wasn't right for you. I always knew that," Dobie said. "The man's a wildcatter. His kind are never in one place very long — always moving on to find the next big strike. A woman like you needs a home — a place you can sink your roots in and raise a family. You need a man to look after you and —"

"I'm perfectly capable of looking after myself. I don't need any man to do that." More specifically, she didn't need Dobie. And she could almost guarantee where he was leading this conversation. "If you'll excuse me, I have work to do — and I'm sure you do, too."

"Yeah, I . . . I do." He nodded, then glanced at her hesitantly before he turned to walk to the door. "I'll talk to you later about the rent for this."

"Fine."

After coming to terms on the rental, Abbie had insisted that a lease agreement be drawn up, covering both the barn area and pasturage, and the house they were living in. Although she doubted that Dobie would go back on his word, she preferred not to take anything on trust.

For the next two weeks, with the help of a laborer to do the heavy work, she and Ben had repaired the barn, fixed the fences, built small paddocks, and spray-painted everything in preparation for the arrival of their new charges. Even then, the facilities were barely adequate to fill their most basic needs — certainly nothing to compare with what they'd had at River Bend.

But the hard physical work left Abbie too exhausted to think about anything — not her former home or its new owners nor even MacCrea. With the approach of noon, Abbie trudged to the house while Ben went to the barn to check on the filly one more time. Every bone and muscle in her body felt bruised, but she had the satisfaction of knowing they had accomplished the impossible. When the first of the horses arrived tomorrow, the place would be ready and presentable.

Pushing open the back door, Abbie walked into the small kitchen, but no cooking odors met her. Babs always had lunch ready for them when they came in at noon. But this time her mother sat at the chrome table in the kitchen, holding the receiver from the wall-mounted telephone to her ear with a raised shoulder while jotting down something on the notepad in front of her.

"Yes, that sounds fine," she said into the phone. When she heard Abbie push the door shut, she started to turn around, then grabbed for the phone to keep it from slipping off her shoulder, the coiled cord pulled taut. "What? . . . All right. Let me call you back after I've had time to check on this." She told the party on the line good-bye as she walked over to hang up the phone. "I didn't realize what time it was, Abbie. This morning has just slipped through my fingers like butter." Hurriedly she began gathering up her papers and notebooks from the table. "I'll have lunch ready in just a few minutes. I'm afraid it'll have to be something cold."

"That's all right. I'll set the table for you."

"Just sit down and rest. You've worked all morning as it is."

Abbie was too tired to argue and gladly sat down in one of the chrome dinette chairs. "Who was that on the phone?" But Babs had her head buried in the refrigerator. She came out of it juggling bowls of potato and macaroni salad and a pitcher of iced tea.

As Abbie was about to repeat her question, Babs finally answered, "You've been so busy lately I haven't had a chance to tell you that Josie Phillips called me last week and asked if I'd help her plan a party for Homer's birthday next month. Her youngest daughter is in the hospital and Josie has a houseful of grandchildren. So I said of course I would."

"It should be fun for you." Abbie smiled wanly, vaguely resenting the fact that her mother's friends called only when they wanted something from her.

"She's . . . she's offered to pay me, the same amount it would have cost her for a professional party consultant for something this size: fifteen hundred dollars. And I'm in charge of arranging and coordinating everything."

"Fif — Momma, that's wonderful. But are you sure you want to do that? I mean, isn't it going to be awkward working for your friends?"

"Men do it all the time in business," Babs insisted logically. "Ever since Josie called me last week, I've been thinking: what is the one thing I am really good at? Giving parties. Your father and I used to give three or four really large parties every year, and who knows how many little dinner affairs? When I think of how much money we spent a year just on entertaining . . . why, your wedding alone came to almost five hundred thousand dollars. If your father had only said something to me — but how could he? I never wanted to discuss business or finances."

"You can't blame yourself, Momma. I don't think Daddy realized what kind of situation he was in financially." Or if he did, she doubted that he would have admitted it.

"I've never talked about it, but I think you know that my family didn't have very much when I married your father. It wasn't the money. I would have married him if he was as poor as a wetback. But suddenly I didn't have to worry about whether we could afford to buy a new dress or coat — or anything, for that matter. It was like playing with Monopoly money. There was always more if you ran out. Sometimes, I was even deliberately extravagant because I knew he was spending money on —" She stopped abruptly, catching herself before she referred to Rachel or her mother by name. "Anyway, that's all over. And I'm looking at this birthday party for Homer as sort of a trial run. If it works out the way I think it will, then I'm seriously considering going into business for myself."

"You mean that, don't you?" Abbie said as she realized it was true. As preposterous as the combination of Babs and business sounded to her, she couldn't laugh at it.

"I most certainly do. In the last thirty years, I've probably had more experience at it than any professional consultant in Houston. I know all the caterers and suppliers personally. And I can track down anything, no matter how unusual. That's no different than a scavenger hunt. And look at the people I know — people who have been to my parties in the past. They already know what I can do."

"Momma, you don't have to convince me," Abbie laughed. "I believe you can do it, too."

"For now, I can work right out of this house. I know you've been talking about finding a job in addition to your work with the horses, and I was wondering whether . . . you'd like to go into business with me — assuming, of course, that this works and I'm offered more parties."

"I'll help all I can. And I have the feeling you're going to need it. With the holidays and the debut season only a few months away, I'll bet you'll be flooded with jobs the minute the word is out."

"That's what I'm hoping, too." As the back door opened, she started guiltily.

"Here's Ben already and I don't have lunch on the table yet." She hurried back to the refrigerator to bring out the sandwich makings.

"How was Breeze?"

"She was fine. Just a little lonely, I think." He walked over to the sink to wash his thick, stubby hands.

Babs opened the top cupboard door next to the sink and began taking down the glasses and plates from the shelves. "I meant to ask you, Ben, when you went to the lumberyard yesterday, did you happen to drive by River Bend?"

"Yes, I did," he admitted slowly, darting a look at Abbie out of the corner of his eye. She tried to pretend she wasn't listening. She even made an effort to concentrate on something else — anything just so she would be reminded that River Bend no longer belonged to them.

"When I was by there the other day, I swore they were taking down some of the trees by the lane."

"They have chopped down several." Ben nodded affirmatively.

"But why?" The protest was torn from Abbie. Those old, twisted pecan trees and ancient oaks had been there forever.

"I was told they are widening the lane. I was also told they are making many changes in the house. Painters and workmen, they are everywhere."

Feeling sick to her stomach, Abbie pushed out of her chair and mumbled some excuse about changing out of her dirty clothes before lunch. But the truth was, she didn't want to hear any more. It hurt too much.

During the next two weeks, it became impossible for Abbie not to learn about the activities of her neighbors. The morning edition of the *Houston Chronicle* carried a story about the wedding of Rachel Farr and Lane Canfield. The article described the wedding and the reception that followed as a small but elegant affair attended by a few intimate friends of the bride and groom. The article didn't identify any of the guests by name, but Abbie was willing to bet that MacCrea had received an invitation to it.

The newspaper briefly mentioned, as well, that after the couple returned from their European honeymoon, they would be dividing their time between their Houston residence and their new country home, presently being renovated.

The latter was just about the only thing anyone wanted to talk about — from Dobie and the owners of the Arabian horses she and Ben had under training, to Josie Phillips and the various service companies they were dealing with in connection with the party. The only time she escaped it was in the mornings when she worked with Ben, training and exercising the horses.

She didn't try to pretend she didn't know about the changes going on at the farm, but neither did she initiate the subject in conversation. Sometimes she suspected people brought it up in front of her just to watch her reaction. And sometimes it was difficult not to let the bitterness and resentment show. Especially when she learned the gazebo was being torn down to make room for a swimming pool, and carpet was being laid on those beautiful parquet floors. But what could she expect from someone who cut down centuries-old trees just to widen a road?

According to the latest word she'd heard in Houston that afternoon while running some errands for her mother, the Canfields had returned unexpectedly, cutting their honeymoon short due to some pressing business matter. Their early arrival had apparently thrown everything into an uproar at River Bend. The renovations that were supposed to have been finished by the time they returned were nowhere close to being complete.

As she drove back, surrounded by the night's blackness, the windows rolled down to let the fresh air rush in, she tried not to think about any of it. Yet there was an awful sinking sensation in her stomach. She'd been dreading the time when Rachel would actually take up residence in her former home. She was back now, and that moment was only days away from becoming a reality.

As the newly erected entrance pillars to River Bend came into view, a lump rose in Abbie's throat. She glanced through the break in the trees, a break that hadn't existed until they had chopped down some of the old giants. She could just barely make out the white rail of the balustrade and part of a two-story turret. Her home — once.

Then she noticed the unusual storm cloud that blackened the sky beyond the house. Summer storms rarely came out of the north. She slowed the car and peered through the windshield. A yellow-orange light flickered in one of the turret windows. At first, Abbie wondered if some of the workmen were putting in overtime to get the job done, then she caught the acrid smell of smoke.

"My God, no." Instinctively she slammed on the brakes to make the turn into the newly widened driveway.

As she sped up the freshly black-topped road, the smell of smoke became stronger. She could see it rolling out from under the porch roof. Stopping the car short of the picket fence, she stared at the yellow tongues of flame licking around the front windows.

She climbed numbly out of the car and hurried to the porch, but the heat from the flames and the choking black smoke forced her back. She stepped back, staring in horror at the fire consuming her home, completely helpless to stop it. She had to get help. She raced back to the car and drove as fast as she could to the Hix farm. Once inside, she ran straight to the phone and dialed the number for the rural fire department.

"Abbie, what's wrong?" Babs hurried to her side. "You look white as a ghost. Were you in an accident?"

"No —" Abbie started to explain when she heard a voice on the other end of the line. "Hello? This is Abbie Lawson. I want to report a fire . . . at River Bend." She clutched the receiver a little tighter, conscious of her mother's horrified look. "I just drove by there. The whole first floor of the house was on fire."

"No!" Babs gasped.

"We're on our way," the man said and hung up.

Slowly Abbie replaced the receiver, then looked at Ben, who had come to stand next to her mother. "They'll never make it in time to save it." She made the pronouncement with an odd feeling that she couldn't explain. It was a strange mixture of guilt, sorrow, and apathy. "It's funny, isn't it? I would have done anything to prevent her from moving into that house, but not this. I never wanted it to burn down, Ben. I really didn't."

"I know." He nodded.

"Do you think we should go over and see if there's anything we can do to help?" Babs asked uncertainly.

"No. Momma. There's nothing we can do." Abbie walked over to the window that looked out in the direction of their former home. She could see the smoke billowing up like a dark cloud to block out the stars. Beneath it, there was a faint red glow. She didn't know how long she stood there before she heard the distant wail of a siren, but it seemed like an eternity. By then, the glow was brighter and the cloud was thicker.

When morning came, the pall of the fire hung over the countryside, tainting the air with the smell of charred wood and smoke. The greenbroke bay filly snorted and sidestepped nervously as Abbie swung into the saddle, but the young horse quieted quickly when Ben rode up alongside on the plump chestnut mare. She shortened the length of rein. "Ben, I want to ride over to River Bend."

"I thought you would," he said. "We can ride across the fields."

Both horses were fresh and broke eagerly into a canter without any urging from Ben and Abbie. With only two gates to negotiate, the mile that separated the Hix farmyard from her former home was quickly covered. But the burned-out devastation was visible when they were less than a quarter of a mile away.

The stallion barn was the only building still standing, but it hadn't escaped damage. Its roof was blackened, and its sides, once painted a pristine white, were now scorched brown and smudged with dark smoke. All that remained of the stables, office annex, and the equipment shed were blackened timbers and charred rubble.

The brick chimney stood like a tombstone over the mound of ash that had once been her home. But the trees, the beautiful old ancient oaks that had graced the yard — Abbie wanted to cry when she saw their seared and withered leaves and charred trucks.

The fence between the two properties was down. Abbie waited until Ben had walked his mare across the downed wires, then let the filly pick her way over them. The water-soaked ground was a mire of trampled grass and ashen mud. The young filly shied nervously from the burned remains of the house and edged closer to her older companion, not liking anything about this place.

Abbie reined the filly in, halting the young Arabian well away from the rubble. Several vehicles were parked on the other side of the smoke-blackened picket fence. Some men were over by the barns, poking through the timbers, a few of which were still smoldering. Three more men were going through the ashes of the house, with its blackened porcelain sinks, bathtubs, and toilets. She stared at the large, gaping hole gouged out of the lawn in the backyard: the site of the new swimming pool. It reminded Abbie of an open grave waiting to receive the remains of the house.

"It's worse than I thought it would be," she remarked to Ben.

"Yes."

"Hey, Ben! I thought I recognized you." Sam Raines, one of the volunteer firemen, came trotting over to them. His glance skipped away from Abbie to look back at the chimney. "It didn't leave much. By the time we got here last night, the whole place was in flames."

"We could see it. It looked bad."

"Sparks were flying all over. When that hay caught fire, I thought we were going to lose everything. We probably could have saved the stable, but we ran low on water. We had to concentrate what we had left on the one you see. You know, it's ironic. If they'd gotten the pool in, we probably would have had enough for both."

"Do you know what started it?"

"That's what they're trying to figure out now." He gestured to the men picking through the charred rubble of the house. "As near as we can tell, it started in one of the back rooms where the painters kept their thinner and paint rags. Who knows?" He shrugged. "The wiring in that house was old. There could have been a short, or somebody could have dropped a cigarette near those thinner rags. These old houses are fire hazards. I say it's a darned good thing no one was living in it. I'll bet it went up fast."

There was almost nothing left of the place she'd known from childhood: the house was burned to the ground, the stables and sheds completely destroyed. She could deny many things, but not the ache she felt inside.

The hinges on the picket fence gate creaked noisily in the stillness. At first Abbie was struck by the ludicrous sight of the silver-haired man holding aside the gate for the stylish brunette in a white silk blouse and pleated tan trousers. They started up the walk together, looking like a couple coming to call, but the sidewalk led to ash and rubble. When the woman turned her head, Abbie saw her face, white with shock and dismay. It was Rachel, a strikingly different Rachel. The coiffed hair, the clothes that had "designer" written all over them, the scarf around the neck, the bracelets on her wrists — she looked like some willowy fashion model.

Rachel saw her and stopped abruptly, then started across the muddy lawn toward her. Lane attempted to stop her, but she pulled away from him and continued forward. Abbie could tell Rachel was angry to see her there. Yet she was surprised at how calm she felt.

As Rachel approached head-on, the nervous young filly started to swing away, but Rachel grabbed the reins close to the chin strap and checked its sideways movement. "You did this," Rachel accused, her voice vibrating. "You started the fire."

"No!" Startled, Abbie tried to explain that she had been the one who turned in the alarm, but Rachel wasn't interested in hearing anything she had to say.

"You threatened to do this. There were witnesses, so don't bother to deny it. You couldn't stand the thought of me living in this house, so you set fire to it." She was trembling, her hand clenched in a fist. "God, I hate you for this. I hate you. Do you hear?" Her voice rose, attracting the attention of the men going through the burned rubble. Rachel roughly pushed the filly's head to the side, starting the horse into a turn as she released the reins. "Get out! Get off my land and don't you ever come here again!"

Angry and indignant, Abbie opened her mouth to defend herself, but Ben touched her arm, checking her denial. "She will not listen," he said. "We go now."

But Abbie wasn't content to leave it at that as she collected the reins. "Believe what you like, but I didn't do it!"

She reined the Arabian filly in a half-circle. It moved out smartly, eager to leave this place, with its heavy smell of smoke and currents of angry tension. Abbie held the young horse to a prancing walk and kept her own shoulders stiffly squared and her head up as she followed Ben across the downed fence.

Not until they were well out of sight did she give the filly her head and let her break into a gallop.

As they raced across the stubble of the mowed hay field, the wind whipped away the tears that smarted in her eyes. She knew the accusation would stick. No matter what the official cause of the fire was determined to be, people would still look at her as somehow being responsible. It wasn't fair.

26 ~

MacCrea stepped down from his truck to the sound of pounding hammers and whining saws. In front of him, like the phoenix bird rising from the ashes, stood the partially framed skeleton of a Victorian-style house similar to the one that had once occupied this same site. The house now under construction was like it in every detail, from the wraparound porch and balustrade to the twin turrets and cupola — except it was half again as big.

Simultaneous with the construction of the house was the erection of a huge barn in the same architectural style a hundred yards away. The one building not destroyed by the fire had been razed to make room for this new, massive structure. Nothing remained that had been there before except for the few old trees that had managed to survive the ravages of the fire.

The place crawled with carpenters, other laborers, and tradesmen. Mac-Crea stopped an aproned carpenter who walked by, balancing a long wooden plank on his shoulder. "Where can I find Lane Canfield?"

The man jerked his bandaged thumb toward the house and walked on. MacCrea took a step, then paused as a slender woman with dark hair emerged from the structure. Just for an instant, he was thrown by her resemblance to Abbie, and felt the stirring of old feelings. Grimly, he clamped his mouth shut and forced his gaze to the man behind her, Lane Canfield. Silently he cursed the fact that this happened every damned time he saw Rachel, certain he would have forgotten Abbie months ago if it weren't for her.

Lane lifted a hand in greeting, then Rachel claimed his attention. She seemed upset about something, but MacCrea couldn't hear what she was saying until the couple came closer.

". . . shouldn't wait to hire a night watchman. I want one now," she was insisting forcefully. "You know as well as I do that she's just waiting until the construction is further along before she does something."

"Rachel, there is no proof that she started the fire." There was a tiredness in Lane's voice that indicated this discussion was an old one.

"I don't need proof. I know her. She hates me." She seemed frustrated by her failure to convince her husband and turned to MacCrea in desperation. "Ask MacCrea. He'll tell you."

"Don't drag me into this," he said, shaking his head. "I don't get involved in personal disputes. I'm out of it and I want to stay out of it." But for him, the expressions of loathing and distrust, of resentment and anger, were echoes of the past. The difference now was that they came from Rachel instead of Abbie.

"I don't care if either of you agrees with me or not. I want somebody on guard here at night to make sure nothing happens." But she was no longer demanding; she was pleading with Lane. "Surely that isn't asking too much. After all, this is going to be our home."

"All right." Lane gave in, seemingly incapable of refusing Rachel anything she wanted. "I'll have the superintendent hire one right away."

"I'll go tell him for you. Thank you, dear." She gave him a quick peck on the cheek, then hurried away, heading back to the house to find the superintendent.

More than once MacCrea had observed the lack of passion in their relationship. Admittedly there were displays of affection between them — touching and hand-holding — and they seemed happy enough together. But as far as MacCrea could tell, there was something missing. Maybe he just remembered the way it had been with Abbie: whenever he was with her, he didn't want her to leave, and whenever he wasn't with her, he wanted to be.

Obviously Lane and Rachel were satisfied with something less. He wondered whether their age difference had anything to do with that or if it was simply a reflection of their personalities. Lane was very businesslike in his approach to things, and Rachel was somewhat reserved and quiet, although more and more she seemed to be coming out of her shell.

Either way, it wasn't any concern of his, MacCrea decided, and glanced at Lane. The man looked vaguely troubled as he watched his wife disappear inside the partially framed structure.

Sighing, Lane turned back to MacCrea and said, almost reluctantly, "She's been like that ever since the fire. She's obsessed with the idea that Abbie's to blame for it. Of course, it isn't as if she hasn't had cause to think that way. Abbie has . . ." Lane paused and smiled ruefully. "But I didn't ask you to come by to talk about her."

"No." He reached inside his windbreaker and took the papers from his pocket. "Here's the proposal. I think you'll find it pretty much the way I outlined it to you over the phone yesterday."

He handed him the papers and watched Lane's face as he skimmed the first page. Not that he expected to see a reaction: Lane was too canny for that.

But he did raise an eyebrow at MacCrea. "Are you certain your testing system doesn't work? This offer could be just a way of squeezing you out."

"I thought of that. But when negative reports started coming in from the field tests, I went out on test sites and checked it myself. It doesn't work. But they still like the concept. Rather than risk a possible infringement suit sometime in the future, they want to buy the patent rights on it now." MacCrea didn't mention that the drilling fluids company had initially suggested that he stay and work with the project. But he wasn't a scientist. Besides, he knew the longer he stayed around here, the longer it would take him to get Abbie out of his system once and for all. "In my opinion, I think we should accept the offer."

"You're probably right," Lane conceded.

"I know I am."

"So what will you do now?"

"I've acquired the mineral rights to some property in Ascension Parish. I plan to put a deal together and drill a development well there."

"From what I've been able to gather, the land men with a lot of big oil companies have been trying to get their hands on the oil and gas rights to that property for years now. How did you manage to get it?" Lane asked curiously.

"The old lady that owns it took a liking to me." MacCrea didn't think it was necessary to inform Lane that the old woman had once taken care of him when he was a child, sick with a bad case of bronchial pneumonia.

"I wouldn't mind getting in on it," Lane said. "I'd consider backing you on this, assuming, of course, that we can agree on a split."

Covering his surprise over the unexpected offer, MacCrea shot back quickly, "It all depends on how greedy you are."

"Or how greedy you are." Lane smiled. "Think it over and give me a call. We'll sit down and talk numbers and percents."

"I don't have to think about it. You have the money and I have the lease, the drilling rig, and the crew. I'm ready to talk a deal now. Maybe you need to think it over."

"Tomorrow, be at my office at ten. We can talk privately — without all this confusion." Gesturing, Lane indicated the construction going on around them.

"I'll be there," MacCrea promised.

27

As Abbie turned River Breeze loose in the small pen, the half-dozen horses in the adjacent corral crowded against the fence and nickered for the gray filly to come over and talk to them. The filly hesitated and swung her head around to look at Abbie as if reluctant to leave her.

"Go ahead." Abbie petted the silvery neck. "I have to leave anyway."

She stepped away from the filly and ducked between the board rails to join Ben on the other side of the pen. The filly moved haltingly over to the fence, her gait stiff and awkward. The casts had been off for a month now. Each day, her legs had gotten stronger, her coordination was better, most of the sores had healed, the swelling was reduced. Abbie knew the filly would have a permanent limp and there would always be some disfiguring enlargement of the forelegs but that didn't matter. Watching her move about on all four legs was the most beautiful sight Abbie had ever seen.

"She's going to make it, isn't she, Ben?"

"Yes. She will improve every day." He nodded.

"Do you think by this spring she'll be strong enough that we can get her bred?"

"I think so."

"We'll need to start deciding on a stallion. I want her bred to the best. I don't care how much the stud fee is." Then she sighed. "There's always the possibility she won't be fertile. We've had to give her a lot of drugs."

"We will have to wait and see."

"Yes." But she wished, just once, that he would offer an opinion. "Nobody expected Breeze to get this far. I want to start making a list of stallions that will nick well with her, Ben. We're going to breed her in the spring." She said it with confidence and determination, yet she had the uneasy feeling she was daring fate to intervene.

But when she saw the smile of approval that broke across Ben's lined and craggy face, she knew he shared her optimism. "The list I have already begun. It is God's miracle that she walks. We must believe that in His time, she will also become in foal."

Abbie smiled faintly. "Sometimes I wish I had your faith, Ben." It was mostly grit that carried her. She couldn't trust blindly. She hadn't been able to do that for a long time, she realized with a sigh, and pushed away from the fence. "I'd better get ready. I promised Momma I'd give her a hand at the party tonight."

Every tree and shrub along the driveway leading to the private estate in River Oaks was etched with tiny fairy lights. The sprawling house with its Spanish architectural details was decked in its holiday finery, too. Garlands of greenery strung with lights draped the porte cochere that welcomed the arriving party guests. With Thanksgiving barely over, this was the first party of the holiday season.

A Christmas tree, nearly twenty-five feet tall, dominated the glass-ceilinged *gran sala*. There, Rachel gave her mink jacket to a waiting maid and lightly grasped Lane's arm as they joined the rest of the guests milling throughout the expensive and lavishly decorated house.

Briefly she touched the Van Cleef and Arpel's diamond-and-emerald brooch that anchored the plunging sweetheart neckline of her gown, assuring herself it was still firmly in place, at the same time conscious of the weight of the matching earrings pulling on her lobes. Ever since their marriage, Lane had showered her with presents: clothes, jewelry, furs, expensive perfumes, and other trinkets. At first she had felt uncomfortable with all the gifts, remembering too well the way Dean had tried to buy her love and ease his conscience with them. But Lane took such joy in bringing her big or little gifts that Rachel thought it unfair to question his motives. Yet the doubt remained.

A waiter offered them a glass of champagne from his silver tray. Rachel took one, needing something to occupy her hands, but Lane declined. "I think I'll get a drink from the bar. Will you excuse me?"

"Of course." Invariably he left her alone at these social gatherings, though not always intentionally. Usually he ran into a business associate or someone he knew, and she was forgotten while he stopped to talk. To her regret, Rachel had quickly learned it was always business with him. That was his idea of a good time.

Meanwhile, she had to suffer through these evenings as best she could. She looked around, remembering that MacCrea was supposed to be here. At least he was someone to talk to. But she saw few familiar faces as she glanced around the room. She was still a stranger among them, not totally accepted yet.

When women had discussed her in various private powder rooms, they had accused her of being aloof and unapproachable. Little did they know that she didn't say much, unless the subject was art or Arabian horses, because she didn't know the people or the events they were talking about. Rather than show her ignorance, she said nothing. And there were some, she knew, who were covertly hostile to her — mainly those still loyal to Abbie and her mother. But they couldn't cut her, not Lane Canfield's wife. Rachel tilted her head a little higher. Whether they liked it or not, she belonged here as much as, if not more than, they did. She'd show them. In time, they'd have to accept her as one of them.

The soft strumming of a guitar came from one of the rooms that opened off the grand entry. Rachel gravitated toward the sound, taking advantage of the diversion it offered so that it wouldn't appear as obvious that she had no one to talk to.

In one corner of the spacious family game room, a small country band played for the couples dancing on a cleared area of the terrazzo floor. As Rachel wandered into the room, the singer stepped up to the microphone. She felt a little shock go through her when she recognized the slim man in the black tuxedo. Even at this distance, the black cowboy hat with its concho-studded band that had become Ross Tibbs's trademark was unmistakable. She should have guessed he'd be the entertainment tonight. Ever since the song he'd written had climbed to the top of the country charts, he'd become a minicelebrity in Houston, despite the fact that the song had been recorded by another artist.

She knew she should leave, walk right out of the room, but his clear baritone voice, rich with feeling and warmth, reached out to caress her and draw her closer. She moved along the wall until she found a place she could stand and watch him safely, inconspicuously.

But when the song ended, he turned to acknowledge the applause and looked directly at her. For an instant he was completely motionless, staring at her as if he was seeing her in a dream. Rachel wanted to look away, break the eye contact, but she couldn't . . . any more than she could control the sudden fluttering of her pulse.

Again he stepped up to the microphone. "I'd like to do another song for you that I wrote. As a matter of fact, I'll be recording it myself next week when I go to Nashville. It's called 'My Texas Blue Eyes' and goes something like this." He nodded to the band to begin, then glanced directly at Rachel and said softly into the microphone, "This is for you, my own Texas blue eyes."

Her skin felt as if it had suddenly caught fire. She looked around to see if anyone else had noticed that he'd dedicated the song to her, but all eyes were on him. Then he started singing:

> *Tell me, boys, have you ever seen her,*
> *The lady with those eyes of Texas blue?*
> *She'll steal your heart if you ever meet her,*
> *And leave you all alone and lonely, too,*
> *My blue eyes, my Texas blue eyes.*

> *I want to listen to your sighs*
> *And feel your body next to mine,*
> *But you're too far away to touch.*
> *Why do I love you, oh, so much,*
> *My blue eyes, my Texas blue eyes?*

The sweet longing in his voice, full of the passion and pain of loving, pulled at Rachel. She didn't want to feel the sensations he was evoking. They were too strong — and too wrong. Abruptly she turned and blindly picked her way through the crowd that had gathered to listen. At last she emerged from the room and paused to draw a calming breath and stop the pounding of her heart.

But his voice followed her:

> *I know that she will always haunt my dreams,*
> *That lady with those eyes of Texas blue.*

Moving as swiftly as she dared, Rachel crossed the atriumlike *gran sala* and went in search of Lane. When she didn't find him near the bar, she checked the formal dining room, with its stunning cut-crystal chandelier presiding over a long buffet table. She stiffened in surprise when she saw Abbie on the far side of the room, speaking in a hushed voice to one of the waiters.

Dressed in a peplumed jacket of quilted gold silk, belted at the waist and heavily padded at the shoulders, and a black velvet skirt, Abbie looked like one of the guests. For a split second, Rachel questioned how Abbie had received an invitation to the party. Then she remembered that Abbie and her mother hired themselves out to oversee all the arrangements for parties such as this one. Rachel couldn't help smiling a little as she watched the waiter acknowledge an order given by Abbie with a discreet nod of his head before she moved away.

On her way to the bar to double-check the liquor supply, Abbie stopped one of the maids and directed her to some dirty plates on a coffee table. As her mother explained their role to prospective clients, their duties were to assume all the responsibilities of the hostess, leaving her completely free to mingle with her guests. They would see to it that there was an ample supply of food and drink at all times, and make certain that ashtrays were regularly emptied and soiled plates and empty glasses quickly cleared away. Every facet — from valet parking so the driveway wouldn't be clogged with cars to the checking of wraps at the door, from the policing of the men's and ladies' rooms to keep them tidy and clean to the handling of belligerent guests who had had too much to drink, and from the initial planning of the party to the cleaning up afterward — became their obligation.

But assuming the role of hostess didn't mean that they physically did anything themselves. Still, when Abbie noticed an empty champagne glass set on the pearl-inlaid top of an antique Moroccan chest, she picked it up and carried it to the bar with her. Babs was elsewhere in the house making her own inspection tour of the rooms. Abbie usually worked behind the scenes, handling the food and drink, and rarely ventured out of the kitchen. But she'd just learned from the liquor caterer that he'd inadvertently brought only two cases of bourbon. Knowing her fellow Texans' capacity for the whiskey made with fermented corn mash, she was concerned that they might run short and wanted to check on how the supply was holding up.

She set the empty champagne glass on the counter and waited for the head bartender to finish talking to the guest at the opposite end of the long bar. When he finally turned away from him, Abbie suddenly had a clear view of the man.

MacCrea. She felt as if she'd been stabbed, the pain — the longing — was so intense. She stared at his face in profile, so compellingly masculine with its blunt angles and powerful lines. Every detail, every feature was achingly familiar to her, from the dark brush of his mustache to that curled lift of his crooked little finger.

She tried to blame her reaction on the shock of seeing him after all this time. What had it been, around three and a half months? She didn't understand how she could still love him after what he'd done. "Out of sight, out of mind" . . . she thought she had succeeded so well at that. Now she realized he'd never been out of her heart. But was it really any different from the way she had been with her father — loving him even when she hated him?

The head bartender walked over to her. "Did you need something, Miss Lawson?"

"Yes." But she momentarily forgot what it was as she saw MacCrea watching her, his gaze half-lidded, but not concealing the intentness of his stare. Unwilling to let him know how much seeing him again had affected her, Abbie assumed a businesslike attitude and focused her attention on the bartender, but out of the corner of her eye, she saw MacCrea push away from the bar and walk toward her.

"Hello." His low voice caressed her. She didn't even have to close her eyes to remember the feel of his rough hands stroking her skin.

She made a determined effort to ignore him. "How is the bourbon holding out?"

"Just fine," the bartender replied.

"Good." She refused to look at MacCrea. It didn't matter. All the rest of her senses were focused on him. She was aware of every sound, every movement he made. Finally gathering her composure around her like protective armor, she turned to face him. "Was there something you wanted?"

"You," MacCrea said calmly, matter-of-factly.

A thousand times she had turned aside similar remarks from men without batting an eye, but this time she couldn't — not from MacCrea. And she wasn't going to let herself be hurt again. He'd already proved she couldn't trust him. She turned sharply and walked swiftly away from the bar, not slowing down for anything until she reached the dining room.

"Going somewhere?" MacCrea said. Abbie swung around in surprise. With all the noise and confusion of the party, she hadn't heard him following her. But there he was, towering in front of her, studying her with a glint of satisfaction.

"I'm busy," she insisted stiffly, angered that he was making an issue out of this when he knew she didn't want any more to do with him. She turned her back on him and began fussing with the garnish around the bowl of pâté.

"You're not as tough as I thought, Abbie," he drawled.

"I don't particularly care what you think — about me or anything else."

"You're afraid of me, aren't you?"

"Don't be ridiculous," she snapped.

"Then why did you run away just now?"

"It certainly wasn't because I was afraid of you."

"Prove it."

"I don't have to." She was trembling inside with anger as well as his nearness. "Go away and leave me alone."

"I can't. I'm a hungry man." He spread his hand over her back, then let it glide familiarly down to her waist.

She couldn't remain indifferent to his touch, so she picked up the bowl and turned around with it, breaking the contact to face him. "Have some pâté then."

Smiling faintly, he took the bowl from her and set it back in its garnish nest, then braced a hand on the table behind her and leaned toward her. "Is that any way to talk to a fellow guest?" His breath smelled strongly of whiskey.

"You've been drinking."

"Of course. This is supposed to be a party, isn't it?" His glance swept the other guests milling about the area before coming back to her. "People usually drink at parties, don't they?"

"Yes." She looked away, angry and hurt that he was here saying all these things and stirring up her emotions because he'd had too much to drink — not because he still cared or because he wanted to make amends, but just for the hell of it.

"It's too bad you don't feel like joining me. You'd have a lot to celebrate. You see, my downhole testing system failed to pass its field tests."

She experienced a mixed reaction to his news. Although she was glad Rachel had lost the money she'd invested in it, she felt sorry for MacCrea. She knew how much the system had meant to him, and how hard he'd worked on it.

"What, no cheers?" he mocked. "I thought you'd be happy to hear it."

"I am," she said because it was what he expected her to say.

"Happy enough to have a drink with me?" MacCrea challenged, arching an eyebrow.

She hadn't realized how hard it would be to resist him, knowing she couldn't trust him, but somehow she managed it. "I'm not paid to fraternize with the guests. If you'll excuse me . . ." But when she tried to brush past him, he caught her arm.

"What do you mean by 'paid'?" A deep crease pulled his brows together as his gaze narrowed on her in sharp question.

"I happen to be a working woman with the responsibility of this party on my hands." She could feel the heat of his hand through the quilted silk of her jacket. She felt burned by the contact, and the memory of his pleasantly rough caresses. "I believe I told you once before to leave me alone. I hope I don't have to repeat myself." She hated the betraying tremor in her voice.

"I remember," he said smoothly, slowly taking his hand away, his level gaze never leaving her face. "I remember a lot of things, Abbie. More than that, I think you do, too."

Not trusting herself to respond to that, Abbie turned and retreated to the seeming chaos of the kitchen. The meeting with MacCrea had left her shaken — more shaken than she cared to admit. She tried to busy herself with something, anything that would get her mind off him . . . the way he had looked, what he was doing there, and why he had spoken to her at all. She wondered if he was regretting having done so. It hurt to think he might.

She picked up a silver coffee pot from the counter and carried it over to the tall stainless-steel urn to fill it, ignoring the constant comings and goings of the uniformed maids and waiters. As she turned away from the urn, she saw Rachel standing in the doorway, watching her.

Abbie stared at the elegant woman before her, taking in her dark hair skimmed back to emphasize the perfect oval of her face, the sparkling earrings of teardrop emeralds surrounded by glittering diamonds, and the figure-hugging gown of forest-green panne velvet that bore the unmistakable mark of Givenchy.

Suddenly Abbie was painfully conscious of her surroundings — and the coffee pot in her hand. She had known all along that sooner or later Rachel would be a guest at one of the parties. But why did it have to be tonight? And why did she have to come face to face with her in the kitchen, of all places?

Or had Rachel sought her out here deliberately? Abbie was almost certain she had. What better way for Rachel to remind her that they were no longer on equal footing? What better way to humiliate her? If that was her intent, she had succeeded, but Abbie was determined not to let her see that.

"Did you want something, Mrs. Canfield?" she inquired, icily polite.

"I was looking for the powder room, but I must have taken a wrong turn somewhere. Perhaps you could direct me."

Abbie longed to challenge that lie, but she smiled instead. "I would like to, but, as you can see, I'm busy," she said, indicating the coffee pot she was holding. "However, I'm sure one of the maids would be happy to show you where it's located." She called one of them over and instructed her to guide Mrs. Canfield to the powder room.

"How thoughtful of you," Rachel said coolly. "But then, you do seem to be very thorough in your work. The next time Lane and I decide to have a party, perhaps I'll give you a call."

Abbie felt the digging gibe and reacted instinctively. "Something tells me we'll be booked."

Rachel laughed softly, a low taunting sound, then turned with a graceful pivot and walked down the hall, a bewildered maid trailing behind her. Abbie's face felt hot, and she knew the flush wasn't caused by the heat of the warming ovens.

When Rachel rejoined the party, she drifted aimlessly from the fringes of one group to another, listening in on conversations without taking part except to smile or nod whenever her presence was noticed. Careful to stay well away from the family game room where Ross Tibbs was singing, she wandered over to the long bar and saw MacCrea at the far end, nursing a cup of coffee.

"Coffee, MacCrea? Haven't you heard this is a party?" But she felt no more festive than he obviously did.

"I never listen to rumors," he replied dryly, lifting the coffee cup to his mouth and taking a sip.

"Have you seen Abbie yet? But of course you have. You spoke to her earlier, didn't you?" Rachel said, watching closely for his reaction.

"Briefly." He nodded, his expression never losing its brooding look.

"Abbie and her mother are in charge of this party tonight. You'd think it would be awkward for them to work for people who were once their friends. I understand, though, that they've traded considerably on those friendships in order to get these parties. You'd think they would have more pride."

"Maybe pride doesn't pay the rent," MacCrea suggested.

"Maybe it only burns down houses that don't belong to you anymore," Rachel countered, the anger and bitterness over the destruction of the original Victorian mansion at River Bend resurfacing. "Excuse me. I'm going to look for Lane."

As she walked away, she saw Ross Tibbs coming toward her. She paused uncertainly, then realized there was no way to avoid meeting him.

"I was beginning to think you'd left. I'm glad you didn't," he said, looking at her in that warm way that always made her feel uncomfortable.

"I thought you were singing."

"Just taking a break between sets. This is quite a place, isn't it?" He glanced around the high-ceilinged room tastefully decorated with garlands and wreaths for the holiday season.

"Yes."

"You'd think with all these Christmas decorations there would be some mistletoe hanging somewhere, wouldn't you? But I've yet to see any. Have you?"

"No. No, I haven't. Excuse me, but I'm looking for my husband."

As she started to walk by him, he said, "I'm glad you liked the song I wrote for you, Rachel."

She stopped short. "What makes you think I did?"

"Because it made you so uncomfortable you had to leave the room."

She wanted to deny it. She wanted to tell him that it hadn't affected her at all. It was just another song — like so many other country songs. But the words wouldn't come. Instead she walked away, almost breaking into a run.

A little after midnight, Babs walked over to Abbie in the kitchen. "The party will be breaking up in another hour or so. If you want to go ahead and leave now, I'll finish up here. I know you've been up since six this morning, working with the horses."

"I am tired," Abbie admitted, conscious of the pounding in her head that just wouldn't go away. "If you're sure you can manage . . ."

"I'm sure. You run along home."

Ten minutes later Abbie left the house by the service entrance and walked along the path to the garage where she'd left her car parked. It seemed strangely quiet outside after all the clinking and clanking in the kitchen and all the laughter and noise from the party in the rest of the house. There was a faint chill in the early December air, but it felt good. She was almost to her car when she noticed the man leaning against the black pickup, one long leg negligently hooked over the other. Abbie stiffened in surprise as MacCrea casually straightened and came forward to meet her.

"I was beginning to wonder how much longer you'd be," he said.

But Abbie didn't respond. She didn't trust herself to talk to him. Instead she started for her car, walking briskly and clutching the key ring like a talisman.

"I've been waiting for you to come out." His breath made little vapor clouds in the air.

"If I had known you were here, I would have called a cab." She stopped beside the car and fumbled to locate the key to unlock the door, her fingers numb and cold.

"No, you wouldn't." He stood beside her, his hands in the pockets of his jacket. "You aren't the kind that runs, Abbie."

"You don't know me as well as you think you do." She tried a key but it wouldn't fit in the lock.

"Don't I? Right now, you're hating yourself because you still want me."

"You're wrong!" she insisted, stung into denying it.

"Am I?" He caught her by the arm and pulled her away from the car, toward him. She gripped the folds of his jacket, feeling the tautly muscled flesh of his upper arms, and tried to hold herself away from him. She could feel the mad thudding of her heart as she looked up at him, torn by conflicting emotions. "I don't think so, Abbie. I really don't think so."

She saw the purposeful gleam in his eye and knew she didn't have a hope of fighting him. He tunneled a hand under her hair and cupped the back of her head in his palm. As he covered her lips with his mouth, Abbie tried to remain passive and show him that she didn't care anymore. But it had been too long since she'd felt the warm pressure of his lips. She'd forgotten how good his kiss could make her feel. She missed the sensation of having his arms around her . . . of being loved.

Yielding to him at last, she returned his kiss and slid her hands up to his shoulders, no longer trying to keep him at arm's length, instead seeking the contact with his hard, lean body. As his arms gathered her close, she rose on tiptoe, straining to lessen the difference in their heights. All the passion and emotion were back, but with them, too, came the knowledge that they wouldn't last — they couldn't last.

When he dragged his mouth from her lips, Abbie pressed her head against his chest, trying to hold on to this poignant moment a second longer. "Tell me now I was wrong, Abbie," he challenged huskily. "Tell me you don't still care."

"The way I feel doesn't change anything. You still can't understand that, can you?" she said.

"Because of Rachel, I suppose."

She heard the grimness in his voice. It hurt. "Yes. Because of Rachel." She kept her head down as she pushed away from him, but he caught her by the shoulders.

"I thought by now you'd be over this stupid jealousy of yours," he muttered.

"It may be stupid to you, but it isn't to me," Abbie flared bitterly. "As long as you have anything to do with her, I'll have nothing to do with you. And don't try to tell me you didn't talk to her at the party tonight or that you don't go to River Bend to see her, because I've seen your truck there several times."

"And when you have, it's because I had business to discuss with Rachel *and* Lane. But, yes, you're right in your way of thinking. I was with her. Do you know what I think about when I'm around her? What goes through my mind?" he demanded. "You. Always. And you don't know how many times I wished to hell that it wasn't so. What makes it even crazier, she's not like you at all."

He sounded so convincing . . . or maybe she simply wanted to believe him. "I don't know what to think anymore." She was tired and confused. Too much had happened all at once, and she knew that right now she wasn't in control of her emotions. They were controlling her.

"There's no reason for you to be jealous of her. There never was, except in your head. Put it in the past where it belongs. All that's over now." His hands tightened their grip as if he wanted to shake her, then they relaxed, their touch gentling. "And if you have to think about something, Abbie, think about this. I love you."

For a split second, she resented him for telling her now. It tipped the balance of her emotions. Yet the rest of what he said was true, too. His business with Rachel was over. His testing system had failed. There was no more reason for him to have anything to do with her.

"I love you, too, Mac," Abbie murmured. "Don't you know that's why it hurts so much?"

"Abbie." As he lifted her off her feet, Abbie wound her arms around his neck and hung on to the man who had given her so much joy and pain — the man she loved. She kissed him fiercely, possessively, thrilling to the punishing crush of his arms and the driving pressure of his mouth as he claimed her as his own. She was sorry when he let her feet touch the ground again, but the look in his eyes made up for it. "You're coming with me."

But as he started to walk her to his truck, she suddenly remembered. "Wait. What about my car?"

"To hell with your car." MacCrea didn't break stride. "I'm not letting you out of my sight. I'm not going to take the chance that between here and my place, you'll change your mind."

Abbie wondered whether she would have second thoughts if she had time to think about it. It felt so right walking beside him, his arm around her, that she doubted she would. He loved her. With Rachel out of the picture, maybe they could start over. And this time they could make it work.

When they climbed into the truck, MacCrea insisted she sit next to him. Abbie happily snuggled against him, feeling like a teenager out with her boyfriend, stimulated by the close contact with him and the kneading caress of his hand, his arm around her, close enough to steal a kiss now and then as they made the drive to his trailer.

The drilling site was pitch-dark: not a single light shone in the clearing that once had been brightly lit at night. The truck's headlights briefly illuminated the dismantled rig loaded on a long flatbed behind a snub-nosed truck cab.

"You've finished drilling here?"

"Yep. We went to depth and came up dry."

But he wasn't interested in discussing the well as he stopped the truck, then proceeded to carry her into the trailer and all the way to the bed. There wasn't time for anything except making love — now — immediately. It was as if the months of separation lent a sense of haste and urgency to the consummation . . . that only through the coupling of their bodies could they bridge the angry pride and bitter jealousy that had driven them apart before.

Later they took the time to explore and enjoy each other all over again: a lovemaking filled with all the kisses, caresses, and fondlings that had been missing from the first. The climax was a long time coming, but when it arrived, Abbie knew it had never been so good between them before.

Afterward she lay in his arms, feeling wonderfully relaxed and content.

From the sound of his deep, even breathing, she guessed MacCrea was asleep. Smiling faintly, she closed her own eyes and started to turn onto her side and join him.

His encircling arm tightened around her and pressed her back onto the mattress. "Don't leave," he said in a voice heavy with sleep. "Stay with me tonight."

"I can't leave, silly." Abbie's smile widened as she turned her head on the pillow to look at him, his face a collection of shadows in the darkness of the trailer. "You wouldn't let me drive my car here, remember?"

His response was a throaty sound that indicated he'd forgotten she was dependent on him for transportation. "I should have carried you off like this weeks ago."

"Is that right?" she teased.

"Mmmm." The affirmative sound was followed by a long silence. Abbie thought he was drifting back to sleep, but then he spoke again, his voice a low rumble coming from deep in his chest. "I'm leaving for Louisiana this next week. I want you to come with me, Abbie."

"I don't see how I can," she said, feeling a sharp pang of regret.

"Why not?" Slowly he let his hand wander over her rib cage, letting the persuasion of his caress work on her resistance. "I'm sure we can find some minister in the parish willing to marry us."

"Are you proposing?" She couldn't believe her ears.

"Only if you're accepting. If you're not, I take it all back." He sounded amused, and Abbie didn't know whether he meant the proposal or not.

Afraid of taking him seriously, Abbie chose the middle ground. "I want to go with you. You have to believe that, Mac. But I just can't pick up and leave the way you can. I have responsibilities and commitments here."

"Like your mother, I suppose."

"Yes. Plus Ben, and I have contracted with several owners to train and show their Arabians." It didn't bring in a lot of money by the time all the costs were deducted, but she'd managed to earn enough to pay the high veterinary bills on River Breeze. The rest she planned to save to pay for the filly's stud fee. But she didn't go into all that with him. It didn't seem necessary. No matter how much she loved him or wanted to go with him, she just couldn't right now. "Do you have to leave next week? Can't you postpone it? What's in Louisiana? Why are you going there?"

"Oil. What else?"

"You can find that right here in Texas," she argued. "You don't have to go to Louisiana, do you?"

"I've acquired the oil and gas rights to a hot piece of property there."

"But it's still going to take you time to raise money to sink the well."

"Not this time. I have a financial backer."

"Who?" She felt suddenly tense.

MacCrea hesitated just a little too long. "It's no secret. Lane Canfield's putting up the money."

Abbie sat up and flipped on the wall light at the head of the bed so she could see his face and make sure this wasn't some cruel joke. MacCrea threw up a hand to shield his eyes from the sudden glare, but she saw there was no smile, no teasing light in his eyes. "You're serious, aren't you?"

"Would I lie about something like that?" He frowned.

"No. You never lie," Abbie said as she realized it, the anger rising in her throat like a huge, bitter lump. "You just let me think things that aren't true. The way you let me think you were through with Rachel — that you weren't going to have anything more to do with her."

"Are we going through all that again?" he asked grimly.

"No. No, we're not." Stiff with anger, Abbie swung out of bed and began grabbing up her clothes.

MacCrea sat up. "What the hell are you doing?"

"Can't you guess?" she shot back. "I'm leaving. I'm not going to stay around here and listen to any more of your half-truths. I've trusted you for the last time, MacCrea Wilder. Do you hear me? For the last time!"

"You haven't got a car, remember? You can't leave."

"Just watch me." Hurriedly, she pulled on her skirt and silk jacket, not bothering with her nylons. Instead she wadded them up in her hand as she started for the door.

"If you walk out that door, Abbie, I won't come after you again," he warned.

"Good." She reached for the handle.

"That damned jealousy is destroying you, Abbie. Why can't you see that?"

She stepped into the night and slammed the door on his angrily shouted words, then hurried to his truck. The keys were still in the ignition. She climbed in and started the engine. She saw MacCrea in the sweep of the headlights as he came charging out of the trailer. She gunned the engine and whipped the truck in a tight circle, driving away before he could stop her.

28

THAT NIGHT, ABBIE DREAMED about MacCrea. They had gotten married, and after the ceremony he had led her under some moss-draped trees toward a small white cottage where he said they were going to live. The front door stood open. Then Abbie saw Rachel waiting inside, and MacCrea told her that she lived there, too — that all three of them were going to live together "happily ever after." Abbie had broken away from MacCrea and started running, but MacCrea had chased her. At first she'd been able to run fast enough to keep him from catching her, then he had started growing taller and taller — and his arms got longer. Soon they were going to be long enough to reach her. She could hear Rachel laughing with malicious glee.

A hand touched her shoulder and Abbie screamed. The next thing she knew she was sitting bolt upright in bed, completely drenched in sweat. "I don't know about you, Abbie, but you just scared the life out of me." Babs stood beside the bed, clutching a hand to her breast and laughing at the sudden shock to both of them.

"I . . . I was having a nightmare." A nightmare steeped in reality. Still a little dazed, she glanced at the sunlight that streamed through her bedroom window. "What time is it?"

"A few minutes before nine. I thought I'd check and see if you wanted to go to church with Ben and me this morning."

"I think I'll skip church this morning."

"I'm sorry I woke you." Her mother moved away from the bed. "Go back to sleep if you can. And don't worry about Sunday dinner. It's in the oven."

As the door shut behind her, Abbie slid back under the covers, but she knew she couldn't go back to sleep. She wished desperately that she could forget last night. She'd almost gotten over all the pain and bitterness from the last time. Now it was back, more potent than before.

At least she had the consolation of knowing MacCrea was leaving the state. She wouldn't run the risk any longer of accidentally running into him, or seeing him somewhere with someone else — or with Rachel. He'd be out of her life, this time for good.

Abbie stayed in bed until she heard Ben and her mother leave the house. Then she went into the small bathroom off the hall, where she washed her hands and splashed cold water on her face, trying to get rid of that dull, dead feeling. She opened the mirrored door to the medicine cabinet over the sink and started to reach for her toothbrush, but she stopped short at the sight of the flat plastic case on the bottom shelf — the case that contained her diaphragm.

Especially during the first years of her marriage to Christopher, she had wanted a baby very much but had failed to conceive. Christopher claimed that his doctor had found nothing wrong with him and said their childlessness must be her fault. It was shortly after she'd begun taking fertility pills that she'd found out he was cheating on her. Initially Abbie had blamed herself, thinking that her inability to get pregnant had driven him to seek other women. Christopher had sworn that he loved her and that the others had meant nothing to him, and promised to be faithful. She waited, continuing to use birth control, unwilling to risk starting a family while their marriage was on such shaky ground — only to catch him playing around again.

Nearly certain that she was sterile, she had taken precautions with MacCrea only during the most crucial times. Now, with a sudden sinking sensation, Abbie calculated where she was in her cycle. Lately she'd paid little attention to it; it hadn't seemed important, since she wasn't going with anyone. She never dreamed last night would happen.

Now she was forced to face the very real possibility that she was pregnant. She pressed a hand to her stomach, feeling frightened and half-sick. After all this time, she was about to find out whether the problem *had* been Christopher's, or hers . . . only it wouldn't be Christopher's child growing in her womb. It would be MacCrea's.

She didn't want to think about it. She didn't even want to consider the possibility that she had finally gotten pregnant. But she had to. If she was pregnant, what was she going to do? What did she want to do? What was right? What was best? She reeled from the endless questions that hammered through her mind, finding no easy answers to any of them.

* * *

Before long, the possibility became more than just a fear as Abbie started waking up in the mornings plagued by a queasy feeling in her stomach. Several times she wasn't sure she was going to make it through the morning workouts, but she always did. When Babs remarked on her pallor, she blamed it on tiredness and overwork. But she knew she couldn't hide the truth much longer. Sooner or later people were going to guess, if they hadn't already.

The flashy gunmetal-gray gelding she was riding snorted at the tractor chugging across the adjoining cotton field. Abbie slipped a hand under his cream-white mane and petted his arched neck, speaking softly to the young horse to quiet him as she glanced at the man bouncing along on the tractor seat. Dobie waved to her. She lifted a hand briefly in response, then turned the Arabian gelding toward the barn, less than a quarter-mile distant.

During times like these, when she wanted to be alone and think, she was glad Ben believed horses should be ridden as much as possible over open country and not endlessly worked in arenas, traveling in circles all the time. He claimed nothing soured a good horse quicker than arena work, insisting it became just as bored as the rider with the monotony of it. Abbie agreed with his philosophy, although today her reasons were slightly selfish.

As Abbie rode into the yard, she saw Ben in the small work pen they'd constructed next to the barn. He was working with a yearling filly being trained to show at halter. A marvel to watch, he relied on none of the more severe methods she'd seen some trainers use — no chains under the jaw, no head jerking, and no harsh whipping. Instead, he used a long buggy whip to get the horse's attention, cracking it behind the filly's back feet, and rarely ever actually striking her with it. Most horses quickly learned that as long as they paid attention to Ben, the whip was silent. Once Ben had the horse's attention, it was a relatively simple matter to teach her to face him and to direct her movements by altering his body position, creating a conditioned response.

Abbie dismounted near the barn and watched from the sidelines as she unsaddled the gelding. As usual, Ben kept the training session short, preferring not to tax the horse's attention span. He finished at the same time Abbie started to rub down the gelding.

After he turned the filly back in with the other horses, he joined her. "The ride was good? Akhar went well for you?"

"Yes." Abbie paused at her task and pushed up the sleeves on her heavy sweater, conscious of the tenderness in her breasts.

"Do you feel better now, after the ride?"

"I feel fine. I did before I left," she insisted defensively, aware of the intent way he was studying her. In the last couple of days, she'd caught Ben watching her closely several times. She thought he suspected something, but maybe she was just becoming paranoid.

"When a person has problems, it is good to go riding sometimes."

"Problems? What makes you think I have any? No more than usual anyway. I'm just tired, that's all." But more so than normal. She felt she could sleep for a week and not be rested.

"It is natural for you to be," he said, and Abbie darted a wary glance at him. His usually impassive features wore a troubled frown of concern. "You have the look of a female when—" He stopped abruptly as if suddenly hearing the words coming out of his mouth.

There was no point in keeping the truth from him, Abbie realized. He'd already guessed. With a sober wryness she faced him squarely. "I hoped since I wasn't a horse, you wouldn't be able to tell by looking that I was pregnant. I should have known I couldn't fool you."

"It is true then?"

"Yes. MacCrea Wilder's the father." She knew Ben would never ask. "He was at the party we hostessed in River Oaks early this month." It seemed a lifetime ago instead of a little less than three weeks. "I thought . . . It really doesn't matter what I thought. I was wrong."

"Does he know?"

"No," she answered quickly, forcefully. "And he's never to know, Ben. No one is. I want your word that you'll never tell anyone, not even my mother, who the father is."

"If this is what you want, I will do it," Ben agreed, but with obvious reluctance. "But what will you do?"

She'd thought it through thoroughly, considered all her options, and reached her decision. "I'm going to keep the baby, of course." No matter what else in her life had changed, she still wanted a baby. In the end, it had been as simple as that.

"But a young woman with no husband, you know what people will say," he reminded her sadly.

"Then I'll just have to get myself a husband, won't I?" Abbie declared, feigning an insouciance that couldn't have been farther from her true feelings. At the sound of the tractor chugging in from the field, she turned and glanced at the driver. "He's a likely candidate, wouldn't you say?"

"He has asked you?" Ben questioned.

"No, but that's a minor detail." She shrugged that aside, the same way she shrugged aside her feelings. If she sounded hard and uncaring, it was because she had to be. With a baby on the way, she had to be practical. She couldn't afford the luxury of personal feelings—neither her own nor Dobie's. "I can handle him."

"But do you want a husband you can handle?" Ben frowned.

"I don't want any husband at all," Abbie declared somewhat hotly. "But since I have to have one, I might as well marry someone I can manage."

"You would not respect such a man."

"I don't have to respect him. I just have to marry him." But she didn't mean to sound so scornful of Dobie. "Besides, Dobie would be a good father."

Late that afternoon, after the horses were fed, Abbie walked by the machine shed on her way to the house. When she saw Dobie inside, tinkering with some part on the tractor, she hesitated. More than anything, she wanted to go to the house and lie down for a while, but this project of hers wasn't something that she could afford to postpone. Altering her course, she entered the machine shed.

"Hello, Dobie."

He straightened quickly at the sound of her voice and hastily wiped his greasy hands on an oil rag. "Hello, Abbie." He smiled at her warmly. "I saw you out riding this afternoon."

"I saw you, too." She returned the smile, then came to the point. "I was wondering if you're busy tonight. I'd love to go somewhere to have a drink and maybe dance a little. But I don't want to go by myself. It wouldn't look right. I thought . . . maybe you'd like to come, too."

For a moment he was too surprised to speak. "I'd love to," he said finally as he pushed the battered Stetson to the back of his head, revealing more of his strawberry-blond hair. "Maybe we can leave early and have dinner somewhere first."

"That sounds good," she said, agreeing readily.

"I'll pick you up about seven. How would that be?"

"Fine. I'll be ready."

When Dobie picked her up that night, he was driving the brand-new pickup he usually kept parked in the garage under a protective dust cover. Dobie was all slicked up himself in a western-cut jacket, a sharply creased pair of new jeans, and shiny snakeskin cowboy boots. Even his red-gold hair had the sheen that said it had been freshly shampooed.

The evening didn't turn out to be the trial Abbie had expected. She couldn't have asked for a more attentive escort. Dobie was always opening doors for her, holding her chair, and fetching her drinks. Over dinner, they talked mostly about his farm and the current commodities market. At a local country bar, they two-stepped and slow-danced, but he was always careful not to hold her too close. Abbie decided that she had rejected his attentions a few too many times in the past, making him leery now.

On the way home, she actually felt guilty for the way she was using him. She almost wished Dobie wasn't such a gentleman. But this was something she had to do, for the sake of everyone concerned.

She waited as Dobie came around to help her out of the pickup. He opened the door and reached for her hand. "Well, here you are back again, safe and sound."

Abbie climbed out of the truck, then continued to hold his hand once on the ground. "I want to check on Breeze before I go to the house. Would you like to come along?"

"Sure," he agreed cautiously, as if uncertain about what she expected of him.

She released his hand and started walking toward the barn. "I really enjoyed myself tonight. I hope you did, too, Dobie."

"I did," he assured her, lagging about a half a step behind her. "It's been a while since I've been out, too."

Reaching ahead of her, he opened the Dutch door. Abbie stepped inside and flipped on the light switch. Several horses snorted and thrust their heads over the mangers to gaze inquiringly at them. Abbie passed all of them as she walked down the aisle to her filly's stall. River Breeze nickered a welcome and pushed her velvety-soft nose into Abbie's hand. "How are you, girl?" Abbie crooned and scratched the hollow above one of her big liquid brown eyes.

"She really likes you." Dobie watched from the side. "I've never had much to do with horses myself — not since I got bucked off of one as a kid and broke my leg. We took her to the sale barn and sold her that very next week."

"You should have gotten back on." She turned slightly, angling her body in his direction. "After your leg healed, of course. Just because you got hurt once doesn't mean you'd get hurt again."

He looked at her, then down at the floor, and shifted his weight from one foot to the other. "Some things just aren't worth the risk."

"Why haven't you ever gotten married, Dobie? You have so much to offer a woman, besides a home and this farm. There must be dozens of girls who are just waiting for you to ask them."

"Maybe," he conceded. "But I've never wanted any of them." Hesitating, he glanced at her. "There's only been one girl I ever wanted to marry. I think you know that."

"You could have also changed your mind."

"I haven't." His voice sounded thin.

"I'm glad." She had to make herself smile encouragingly. She kept telling herself that everything would be all right if she could just get this over with.

He moved hesitantly closer and leaned a hand against the stall partition near her head. He looked at her for a long moment, then swayed uncertainly closer, and carefully pressed his mouth against her lips for a very few seconds. As he started to move away, Abbie cupped the left side of his jaw in her hand.

"I'm very glad, Dobie," she whispered and brought her mouth against his lips, moving it over them, gently persuading.

For an instant, Dobie was too startled by the initiative she'd taken to respond. Then his arms went around her and she was gathered against him. He kissed her roughly, fiercely, almost frightening Abbie with his unbridled ardor, like a man too long without water and guzzling down the first glass given to him.

Abruptly he broke it off. "I'm sorry, Abbie. I —"

"Don't be." She pressed against him when he started to pull away from her.

"I've wanted to . . . kiss you and . . . hold you for so long. And now — Why now, Abbie?" he questioned.

"Sometimes, Dobie, you get so used to having someone around you that you . . . don't notice them." Abbie chose her words carefully. "You know they are good and kind and wonderful, but . . . you just take them for granted. You don't appreciate all the really good things about them. I guess that's the way I've been with you."

"Is it?"

"Yes." She nodded affirmatively. "Ever since my divorce, I think I've been afraid to trust a man again. But these last few months, living here and seeing you every day — I guess it's opened my eyes."

"I figured I never had a chance with you."

"You were wrong." She laid her head against his shoulder, unable to look at him anymore and lie. "You were very wrong, Dobie."

"All this time, I —"

"I know." With a lifting turn of her head, she sought his mouth and closed her eyes tightly when he kissed her.

She felt like a cheat. But she firmly reminded herself that she wasn't. Dobie was getting what he wanted, and that was her. Maybe she wasn't all that he bargained for, but that's just the way life was.

As one kiss led to another, his caresses grew bolder. Soon it was a simple matter for Abbie to draw him down onto the pile of straw next to the manger. She hadn't realized seduction could be so easy — or that she'd feel so empty and sick inside afterward.

As tears pricked her eyelids, Abbie turned her back on him as she sat up and pulled on her blouse. She could hear him dressing behind her, the rustle of straw, the thump of boots being pulled on, and the race of a zipper. She buttoned her blouse slowly in an attempt to delay the moment when she'd have to face him and pretend how much she'd enjoyed it.

"Abbie." He knelt on the straw beside her. "Are . . . are you sorry?"

That was the last question she expected. She wanted to scream at him for being so damned considerate. "No, of course not," she replied.

And it was the truth. She'd do it all over again if that's what it was going to take to get a wedding ring on her finger. She wasn't going to subject herself to the embarrassment and humiliation of having an illegitimate child. The county had talked enough about her family. They weren't going to talk about her. By the time she had this baby, she was going to have a husband.

With renewed resolve, she turned to Dobie. "Are you sorry?"

"No." His smile, his whole expression, was filled with adoration. "I could never be sorry. I love you, Abbie."

"You have no idea how much I wanted to hear you say that," she declared fervently.

Three more times in the next few days, Abbie arranged to be with Dobie. Finally, on the day before Christmas Eve, she convinced Dobie that marrying him would be the most wonderful present she could have. That afternoon they were married by a justice of the peace and spent their wedding night at a Galveston motel.

When they drove back to the farm that gray and drizzly Christmas morning, Abbie was legally Mrs. Dobie Hix. She had the ring on her finger to prove it. But if anyone bothered to look closely at it, they could see it was only gold-plated, like her marriage.

29

LOW CLOUDS SHROUDED the windows of Lane and Rachel's Houston penthouse, obscuring the view of the city beyond. MacCrea stared at the thick clouds a few more minutes, then moved restlessly away and prowled about the living room. Over twenty minutes ago Lane had been called to the telephone by his houseman. MacCrea glanced at his watch, wondering how much longer Lane was going to be tied up. Irritable and impatient, he tried to blame his short temper on the damp and gloomy weather that had blanketed the Gulf Coast for more than a week and turned his drilling site into a swampy quagmire.

A key rattled in the door. MacCrea turned as the door swung open and Rachel walked in. The midnight-blue raincoat glistened from the droplets of moisture that beaded on the water-repellent material. As she started to unbuckle the wide belt that cinched the raincoat tightly around her waist, she noticed him standing there.

"MacCrea, this is a surprise. Lane didn't tell me you were coming."

"He probably forgot."

Unobtrusively the houseman appeared to take Rachel's raincoat and closed umbrella. "Did you receive the Christmas package we sent you?" She surrendered them automatically, with barely more than a nod at the quiet servant.

"Yes, and thanks for the sweater. I liked it." In truth, MacCrea couldn't even recall what color it was. Christmas had been just another rainy day to him, spent alone, without a tree or decorations like those that still adorned the Canfields' apartment.

"I'm glad." She glanced around the living room. "Where's Lane?"

"A long-distance call came in for him. He shouldn't be much longer." MacCrea hoped he wouldn't be. He was uncomfortable with Rachel and the memories of Abbie she evoked. "How's the house coming?"

"Luckily they got it all closed in before the rains started, so it's coming along fine." As she wandered over to him, there was something catlike in the way she studied him. "Have you heard the news yet?"

"News?" He arched an eyebrow, a little voice warning him that this news had something to do with Abbie.

"It seems my neighbor eloped over Christmas."

"Eloped. You mean she got married?" He reeled inwardly. Of all the things he'd braced himself to hear, that wasn't one of them. After the shock came anger. "Who to?"

"That redheaded Hix boy."

"That little —" MacCrea clamped his mouth shut on the rest, clenching his jaw so tightly his teeth hurt.

"You know why she married him, don't you?"

"No." Hell, she didn't love that little wimp. She couldn't.

"She did it to get back at me."

"How?" He frowned, not following her jealous logic.

"Practically all the land those Hix brothers own was once part of the original Lawson homestead. She only married him to get her hands on that land. You know how much she hates it that Lane and I have River Bend. Now she's going to see that we don't get our hands on any more of the family's former holdings."

"I see." It made sense to him. It was just the sort of twisted little plan Abbie would come up with. He knew just how eaten up with jealousy she was. Rachel was the reason Abbie had refused to marry him and destroyed everything good they had; now she was the reason Abbie had married Hix. "The stupid little fool," MacCrea muttered to himself.

"What did you say?"

"Nothing." Absently he shook his head, not wanting to believe the news. She was married now. He tried to tell himself that he was well rid of her, and all her stupid jealousies and hatred. He could almost convince himself of that. Almost.

30

ABBIE WAITED UNTIL the second week in January to go to the doctor and obtain a medical confirmation of her pregnancy. When she told Dobie, he was ecstatic. He insisted they go over to her mother's house and tell her the good news. His absolute joy when he told Babs and Ben was almost more than Abbie could cope with. At the first opportunity, she escaped from the living room and slipped into the kitchen on the pretext of making coffee.

Ben came in. "Are you not feeling well?"

"I'm fine," she insisted impatiently, tired of all the questions about her health. She had answered too many of Dobie's already. From the living room came the sound of his laughter, rich with jubilance, but it just irritated Abbie more. "Listen to him. I never dreamed he would be so proud and happy."

"It is a wonderful thing to be having a baby."

"Yes, but the way he's acting you'd think he was the father."

"Is that not what you wanted him to think?"

For a fraction of a second she paused, then hurriedly pried the lid off the coffee cannister. "Yes." But she wondered how MacCrea would react if he knew about the baby — whether he'd be bursting at the seams the way Dobie was. But she'd never know, because he wouldn't find out about it. That's the way she wanted it — for herself and the baby.

Later that night, Abbie lay in the double bed with her back to Dobie. She knew he wasn't asleep. He was like a little boy on Christmas Eve, too excited about Santa's impending arrival to close his eyes. She felt the mattress shift under his weight as he turned toward her. His hand moved over the top of the covers to touch her arm.

"Please, Dobie, I'm tired." She couldn't bear the thought of him making demands on her tonight.

"I know, honey. I was just thinking that from now on you need to take it a little easier."

"Yes." She didn't feel like talking, certainly not about the baby anymore.

"I've already told your mother that she'll have to find somebody else to help her with the parties 'cause you won't be able to."

Stunned by his announcement, Abbie rolled over to face him in the darkness. "You did what?"

Ever since they'd gotten married, he'd been hinting that it wasn't necessary for her to work anymore. She was his wife now, and she should be content to stay at home and cook and keep house for him. He'd give her whatever spending money she needed. Considering the way he squeezed a dollar, Abbie knew that wouldn't be much. For the most part, she had simply ignored him, believing that in time, he'd get used to the idea of his wife working.

"I told her you couldn't work like that anymore and stay up 'til all hours of the night at those parties. You need your rest now. And tomorrow you'd better call the owners of those horses you've been keeping here and tell them to come get them."

"I will do no such thing! The Scottsdale Show is less than three weeks away, and I've promised two of the owners that I'll show their horses there. It's one of the biggest Arabian horse shows in the whole country. And I've worked long and hard to get these horses ready for it. The stalls have already been reserved, the entry fees have been paid, and a hauler has already been lined up to take them there. Even if I could find somebody else qualified to show them at this date, I wouldn't."

"You aren't really taking off to Arizona for two weeks and leaving me here alone? You're my wife now." Even in the shadowed darkness of the bedroom his disbelieving frown was visible.

"Yes, I am going. You knew all along I planned to," she reminded him. "You're welcome to come." But she doubted that he'd be willing to leave the farm for that length of time — or spend the money to go.

"But with a baby on the way, you shouldn't be bouncing around on those horses."

"In the first place, Dobie Hix, I don't bounce. And in the second, I'm not going to quit working with the horses — or my mother. So you might as well get that out of your head right now."

"I'm only thinking of you. You need to stay home and take care of yourself," he argued.

"No, I don't," she stated emphatically. "I am a normal, healthy woman who is pregnant. It isn't an illness, Dobie. As a matter of fact, the doctor said that as long as I exercise and eat sensibly, everything should be fine. Until he tells me differently, I'm going to keep working. Besides, I'd go stark, raving crazy if I had to sit around this farmhouse day in and day out." That was the truth, but she hadn't meant for it to come out so harshly. "And there's Ben to consider. Those horses are his source of income."

"He could always work for me on the farm."

Abbie knew Ben would hate that. "If he couldn't work with horses, I think he'd die. They're his life, just like this farm is to you."

Dobie rolled onto his back and stared at the textured ceiling, his frustration almost palpable. "I swear I just don't understand you sometimes, Abbie," he muttered. "What are people going to think? You're my wife, and here you are working — and gallivanting all over the country."

"I don't care what they think. I'm going to keep working, and that's final. I don't want to discuss it anymore." She turned on her side and punched the pillow into shape, then lay her head on it and determinedly closed her eyes. When he started to say something, she cut him off with a sharp "Good night, Dobie."

* * *

But the topic became a running argument between them. At one point Dobie reminded her that *he* owned the farm, and if he didn't want horses on it, that's the way it was going to be. Abbie had quickly pointed out that he had signed a legal agreement, leasing her the barn area and pasture. And if he chose not to renew the lease when it expired in seven more months, then she'd find somewhere else to keep the horses.

When he brought up the parties, she asked him exactly how he expected her to pay the stud fee to have River Breeze bred in the spring. Was he going to give her the ten or twenty thousand dollars it was going to cost — plus boarding and transportation expenses? In his opinion, it was a stupid waste of money.

The situation between them didn't improve when he saw all the cocktail and evening dresses she was packing to take to Scottsdale. She was supposed to be going to a horse show. Abbie tried to explain to him about the gala parties that were an integral part of the Scottsdale Show scene. But he didn't think his wife should be going to parties — not even with Ben as her escort. By the time she set out to drive to Arizona with Ben, she and Dobie were just barely on speaking terms.

In Arabian horse circles, the Scottsdale Show at Paradise Park was considered one of the most prestigious, and some claimed expensive, shows in the country and the premier sales arena in the nation. The giant parking lot next to the showgrounds was jammed with horse trailers and vans bearing license plates from all four points of the compass, from as far away as Canada. The trailers ranged in size from a simple single-horse trailer to luxury models capable of hauling six horses with room left over for living quarters.

Arriving a day before the show actually started, Abbie and Ben checked into an inexpensive motel a couple of miles from the park, her small single room a vast change from the plush condo she had usually stayed in when she had attended the show with her father. But many things had changed in her life.

The first two days of the show were hectic ones, getting the horses settled in, clipped, and groomed, with more exhibiters arriving all the time, florists delivering huge potted plants to various stables to aid in the transformation of common stalls into showcases, and carpenters and electricians swarming all over the place like so many flies in a barn. Outside the main show ring, the bazaar area was growing as more booths opened for business, selling everything from syndicate shares to fried ice cream, horse tack to mink coats, and oil paintings to tee shirts.

But those first days were fun days, too, for Abbie. At every turn, she ran into someone she knew. All of them had heard about her father's death, and the subsequent sale of River Bend and its Arabian stock, but it didn't seem to matter to them. They were glad to see her, glad to see she was still competing, even if it wasn't on horses her family owned.

After competing in a late afternoon class, her first in the show, Abbie telephoned the horse's owners and informed them that their mare had made it through the first elimination round, then grabbed her dress bag and overnight case and hurried over to the ladies' shower trailers to get cleaned up. Desert Farm Arabians was holding an aisle party that evening to present their stallion,

Radzyn. Abbie was anxious to attend and see the stallion that she regarded as a top choice for her young mare.

When she saw the striking blood bay stallion, he was all she had hoped he would be and more. Despite the crowd that had gathered around him, partially blocking her view, she was impressed by his regal arrogance as he stood with his head held high and his ebony tail flagged.

"What do you think of him, Ben?" She glanced at the elderly man beside her, still wearing his same serviceable tweed jacket. His one concession to the party had been the tie he added.

He studied the horse critically. "He does not have the classic *jibbah* I would like to see," he said, using the term that referred to the prominent forehead, a distinctive feature on an Arabian horse.

"Breeze does. And Radzyn has the level croup and well-sloped shoulders. Breeze has the classic features, the long hip and short back. Where Radzyn is weak, she's strong — and vice versa. They should make a good nick, I think."

Slow to make up his mind, Ben finally nodded. "I think so, too."

"Good. That much is decided anyway." She hooked an arm with his, her dress sleeve of scarlet silk jacquard at odds with his worn tweed sleeve with its suede elbow patch. The other guests were wearing everything from tee shirts and jeans to sables and Gucci. "Now all we have to figure out is how we're going to pay the stud fee. They want fifteen thousand for a live foal guarantee or ten thousand without it."

She steered him toward the buffet table, a familiar hollow feeling in her stomach. It didn't seem to matter how much she ate anymore; she just couldn't seem to satisfy the ravenous appetite she'd acquired with her pregnancy.

"We will find a way. Do not worry," Ben assured her. "You will see when April comes."

"I hope so," she sighed and began piling the daintily cut sandwiches on her plate, adding a dollop of caviar on the side.

On the opposite side of the buffet table, a woman nudged her companion. "Look. Isn't that the new owner of River Bend?" she said, using a toothpick-speared meatball to point to her.

Abbie turned around to look in the direction the woman had indicated. There stood Rachel, a snow-white ermine stole draped low on her arms, revealing a black lace dress studded with sequins over a strapless underdress of rose satin.

"What's she doing here?" Abbie felt first cold, then hot. "She doesn't have any horses competing here, does she?"

"No. But I have heard that she has come to buy."

"The sales. Of course, she'd be here for them," she said.

And Abbie was also painfully aware that her own name wouldn't be on any of the invitation lists. Even if she was able to wangle a ticket from someone to attend one of the major sales — extravaganzas that rivaled any Broadway production — it would be in the bleachers. She certainly wouldn't be able to sit in the "gold card" section, the way she used to. Gaining admission to that favored area required a financial statement worthy of a Rockefeller — or Lane Canfield. But Rachel would be there, diamonds, ermine, and all.

* * *

For the rest of the show, Abbie was haunted by Rachel. No matter where Abbie went, she was there: in the stands, on the showgrounds, or at the elaborately decorated stalls of the major horse breeders. And she was always in the company of some important breeder — several of whom Abbie had once regarded as her friends. Finally, Abbie stopped going to the parties just to avoid being upstaged by Rachel.

Still, she wasn't able to escape all the talk about her. She had gone on a buying spree, purchasing some twenty Arabians either at the auctions or through private treaty. In the process, she had spent, some claimed, two million dollars . . . and became the new "darling" at Scottsdale.

Even though Abbie managed to come away with placings in two of the classes, she was glad when the show was over. Her pride had suffered about all it could stand. She needed to go home and lick her wounds.

Home. Looking around the old farmhouse, Abbie found it hard to think of it as home. River Bend was home. In her heart it would always be. But she tried not to think about that as she unpacked, because that meant thinking about Rachel.

At least her return had brought one consolation. Dobie didn't seem inclined to renew their argument. Although she sensed that he still totally disapproved of her activities, Abbie hoped he had finally realized she wouldn't change her mind. She was never going to be the stay-at-home, dutiful little wife and mother he thought she should be. The sooner he accepted that, the better their lives would be.

"Abbie! Hello? Are you here?" her mother called from the front part of the house.

"I'm back here in the bedroom." She scooped the pile of dirty clothes off the bed and started to dump them in the hamper, but it was already filled to the top with the two weeks' worth of Dobie's dirty laundry. Abbie dropped them on the floor beside it, wistfully recalling the days when there were maids to cope with all this.

"Are you resting? I . . ." Babs paused in the doorway and stared at the luggage and garment bags strewn about the room.

"Not hardly. I'm just now getting around to unpacking." She snapped the lid closed on the empty suitcase and swung it off the bed. "It took me all morning to clean the kitchen. Did you see the dust all over? It must be an inch thick. When Dobie lived here by himself, he used to keep this house neat as a pin. But he marries me and he suddenly becomes completely helpless around the house."

"Men can be like that."

"Totally uncooperative, you mean," Abbie muttered, trying to hide her irritation. "I hope business picks up some more. I can hardly wait until I can afford to hire a housekeeper."

"Couldn't you talk to Dobie about it? Surely he —"

"— would pay someone else to do the work he thinks I should do as his wife? No, Momma. I'm not going to waste my breath trying."

"I know that . . . you and Dobie have been having some problems. Most couples do when they're first married. There's always an adjustment period when two individuals start living together under one roof. Lately I've realized that it can't be easy for Dobie having his mother-in-law living next door."

"He'll get used to it." Abbie removed her evening dresses from the garment bag and inspected them for stains before carrying them over to the closet to hang up.

"Perhaps. But while you were gone, I found a small, one-bedroom condominium in Houston. I talked with Fred Childers at the bank and showed him what I've managed to earn from the parties. Of course, I'll have to use some of the money I received from Dean's estate to make the down payment, but the bank is willing to loan me the balance."

"Momma, you aren't moving," Abbie protested.

"I think it's best."

"For whom? And why? Whose idea is this? Yours or Dobie's? Momma, I'm going to continue to work with you. And if Dobie doesn't like it, that's his problem." She needed a source of income, more than what she could earn training and showing horses for others, if she was ever going to have the funds to pay the stud fee and buy more broodmares. She had every intention of building a breeding operation that would not only rival Rachel's but eventually surpass it. Rachel had it all now — the horses, the power, the money, the influence — but Abbie vowed that her turn was coming. Someday, all of Scottsdale was going to be talking about her.

"Dobie had nothing to do with my decision, although I honestly believe you two will get along better if I'm not popping in and out all the time. Besides, it will be much more convenient and practical for me to live in Houston. There won't be the time and expense of driving back and forth, not just for the parties themselves but to meet with the caterers and the suppliers, too. And I won't have all those long-distance charges on my telephone bill."

Abbie couldn't argue with any of that. Yet she smiled. "I wish you could hear yourself, Momma. Babs Lawson, the businesswoman." She had always loved her mother, but now that love was coupled with a new respect and admiration. "I'm proud of you, Momma. I really am."

"Look at who I had for a partner." Babs smiled, then paused, her expression turning thoughtful. "The truth is, both of us have changed a lot these last several months — for the better, I might add."

Reaching out, Abbie warmly grasped her mother's hand, finding that they were on equal ground.

Within two weeks, Babs had moved to her condominium apartment in Houston. For Abbie, it was a strange feeling to have her mother out there in the world — on her own. She had more difficulty adjusting to this new independence of her mother's than Babs did.

31 ~

THE RUSTY OLD PICKUP truck with a single-horse trailer in tow labored up the long incline, shuddering in the strong draft of each car that whizzed by it. On both sides of the wide swath the highway made through the mountains, the landscape was an arid and unfriendly collection of rock and sand, dotted with the scrawny clumps of sagebrush, prickly pear, and scrub grass.

Driving with the windows down, a pair of sunglasses shielding her eyes from the glare of the sun, Abbie kept glancing at the temperature gauge, waiting for the truck to overheat again. A hot wind, laden with dust from the Arizona desert, blew in and whipped at her ponytail, tearing loose strands of dark hair and slapping them against her face. She ignored it, just as she ignored the throbbing ache in her lower back and the uncomfortable soreness of her full breasts, intent only on coaxing the truck to the top of the grade. She glanced in the rearview mirror, checking on the horse trailer in tow and the gray filly traveling inside it.

As they topped the rise, Abbie shifted out of low gear and sighed in relief. "It should be all downhill from here," she said to Ben, riding on the passenger side. Within minutes the desert community of metropolitan Phoenix came into view, sprawling over the mountain-ringed valley before them, a collection of towns all grown together. "I guess we don't have to wonder anymore whether Dobie's old pickup will make it this far. I just hope we don't have to make a return trip in the heat of summer. It's hot enough now in April." She doubted the pickup would be able to negotiate many of the mountain passes when summer temperatures sizzled over one hundred degrees.

"We will drive only at night then," Ben replied, unconcerned.

"I should have thought of that." Abbie smiled ruefully, recognizing that she was mentally as well as physically tired from the long trip.

Four days it had taken them to make the journey from Texas, stopping frequently along the way to avoid putting too much stress on the filly's legs and giving her a chance to rest and graze along the roadside. Except for some stiffness and minor swelling, River Breeze had weathered the trip well so far, better than Abbie had expected. Trailering long distances was hard on any horse and doubly so for a crippled filly like River Breeze.

In retrospect, Abbie was glad now that she hadn't been able to afford the cost of hiring a professional hauler to transport the filly to the stud farm in Scottsdale. He probably wouldn't have made the trip in stages the way she and Ben had, nor would he have taken the extra care they had.

The trip was definitely worth the time and trouble it had taken. No part of it had been easy. Right from the start, she'd had the problem of trying to find a horse trailer she could borrow. She didn't have a trailer hitch on her car, nor the extra money to buy one and pay to have it installed.

When she had tried to talk Dobie into letting her take his new truck, he had refused, then told her she was welcome to take his old one, fully expecting her to turn that down rather than take the risk of the beat-up old truck breaking down on the road somewhere. Out of spite, and sheer stubbornness, Abbie had accepted it. She knew he would worry about her, and it served him right. Maybe he'd learn someday that nothing was going to stop her.

After driving since before dawn, they had stopped at a truck stop late that morning so Abbie could shower and change into her last set of clean clothes. Now that she was entering her fifth month of pregnancy, she couldn't squeeze into her regular clothes anymore and only had three maternity outfits to her name. She'd saved the nicest of the three for today, an embroidered tunic top with a pair of matching blue maternity slacks.

As they entered the outskirts of Phoenix, the traffic became heavier. "This is almost as bad as Houston." Abbie felt for the map on the seat and handed it to Ben. "Here's the city map. I've marked the route we need to take to get to Charlie Carstairs's farm. With all this traffic, you're going to have to watch for the signs and tell me where to turn."

Circulating fans whirred, maintaining a constant air flow through the stallion barn. At the far end of the double-wide aisle, a stable hand hosed down the brick floor to further cool the barn.

But all eyes were on the black bay Arab that had been led out of its box stall for their inspection. Rachel watched intently as the stallion arched its swanlike neck and danced on its back legs. Keeping a snug hold on the lead shank, the groom led the stallion around in a circle, then brought the animal to a stop directly before her.

The sight of him was so magnificent it nearly took her breath away. A faint thrill coursed through her veins as she stared at the black fire that burned in the stallion's velvety eyes, then lifted her gaze higher to the small ears, shaped like half-moons, pricked in alertness. Rachel inhaled the strong scent of him, a scent headier than any expensive perfume Lane had ever bought for her.

The large nostrils flared as the dark stallion lifted his small, refined head and trumpeted a call that quivered with longing. When she heard the answering neighs coming from the mares in the nearby barn, Rachel understood, feeling an odd twinge of envy.

Turning to Lane, she smiled faintly. "I think I recognized Simoon whinnying just then. I wonder if she knows she was answering her future lover."

"Somehow I doubt it," he replied dryly, his look one of gentle tolerance and amusement for her fanciful thought.

Rachel knew it was probably a foolish notion, but she wished, just once, he would go along with her. Then she immediately regretted being even faintly critical of him. From the very beginning, Lane had indulged her every whim when it came to horses, regardless of the cost or inconvenience. Just like this trip. Even though he had assured her he had some business to take care of in Phoenix, Rachel knew he was coming along to please her. He gave her so much that often she felt guilty she had so little to give him in return.

"Well? What do you think of Basha 'al-Nazir, Rachel, now that you've seen him close up?" Charlie Carstairs stood with his arms folded across his barrel chest, the large gold nugget he wore on a chain around his neck winking in the light as he angled his shoulders in her direction.

"He's truly magnificent." But in her mind, she was imagining the foal that would come from this union.

"You can put him back in his stall." Charlie gave the order to the manager of his stud farm, Vince Romaine. With a wave of his hand, the short, thin man passed the order on to the groom holding the stallion, as spare with his words as Charlie was voluble. "Every time I see that stallion I wonder if I really want to sell him," Charlie declared with a shake of his head. "But with Radzyn winning the championship here at Scottsdale, I've talked myself into concentrating my breeding program more on Polish-bred Arabians. That seems to be what the market wants today. And Radzyn has a lot of Polish blood in his breeding. As a matter of fact, Patsy and I are planning to go to Poland this fall and attend the sale at Janow. I'd like to pick up some good broodmares there to breed to Radzyn. The horse business is crazy, Lane. Five years from now everyone will probably be wanting Egyptian, and I'll be kicking myself six ways to Sunday for selling Basha. Then again, it may be Spanish- or Russian-bred Arabians."

"Don't ask for my opinion," Lane said, curving an arm around Rachel's shoulders as they all started toward the door leading outside. "Rachel is the expert on horses in our family."

"I just know what I like," she replied.

"And I'm not about to fault your tastes. After all, you picked me for a husband," Lane teased.

"Careful," Charlie warned, "or she's liable to start thinking she's made a mistake."

Even though she knew he was only joking, Rachel felt honor-bound to deny his remark. "I'd never think that. I couldn't."

"That's what she says now, Lane, but wait until some handsome young stud walks by. You mark my words. She'll start wishing she was single. You should have seen my Patsy carry on the other night over that new singer, Ross Tibbs. He's playing at one of the clubs in Phoenix. That's where we met him. Then he came out to the farm to look at the horses. Why, the way Patsy acted, you'd have thought he was God's gift to women."

After an initial start of surprise, Rachel struggled not to react to the news that Ross Tibbs was in town. She cast a furtive glance at Lane out of the corner of her eye, but there was no indication that the singer's name meant anything to him. Why should it? For that matter, why should she let it mean anything to her? He was just someone she'd met — a man who'd made a pass at her. Others had and she'd forgotten them. She would have forgotten him, too, if he hadn't started making a name for himself in the music business, she told herself as they emerged from the shade of the barn into the hot glare of the desert sun.

"What d'ya say we go to the house and have a drink. Patsy makes a mean margarita," Charlie declared, rubbing his hands together in a gesture of anticipation.

"Maybe we should wait." With a nod of his head, Lane indicated the pickup truck with a horse trailer in tow coming up the driveway. "It looks like you have more visitors arriving."

The pickup was an old model that showed its age in the rusted-out fenders and rust-splotched door panels. A thick layer of dust hid its true color, making it impossible for Rachel to tell if it was dark green or dark blue. As it pulled to a stop in front of the adobe building that housed the farm's offices, the battered old truck looked pathetically out of place against the well-manicured backdrop of the horse farm, where even the sandy ground outside the stalls was raked in a herringbone pattern.

"More than likely it's some backyard breeder with a mare to be bred. We get them from all over the country. I've seen them arrive hauling the horse in the back end of a pickup. You should see some of the nags they bring. Ewe-necked, Roman-nosed, and apple-rumped . . . it's a crime to have such animals registered as purebred Arabians," Charlie complained bitterly. "The worst of it is, is that most of them think that by breeding that excuse of an Arabian to one of my stallions, they're going to get a top-quality foal. Once in a while, they'll end up with a mediocre foal, maybe even a good one. But those recessive genes are still there, and sooner or later, those bad traits are going to sprout up again. Usually in the next generation. But you can't tell them that. The old plug is probably the only horse they own — the only one they can afford. The back-yard breeder may be the backbone of our industry, but, damn, I wish they'd be more selective in what they breed."

Fully aware that a year ago she would have been one of those backyard breeders Charlie was talking about, Rachel kept silent. She could have been the one climbing out of the pickup truck instead of that woman in the blue pants and matching top with her dark hair pulled back in a ponytail and wearing sunglasses.

"Go take care of them, Vince," Charlie ordered.

"Right." Separating himself from them, the stud manager walked swiftly toward the parked truck and trailer.

Rachel watched as the woman took a step toward them, then stopped and waited for Vince Romaine to come to her. The woman handed the manager some papers from her purse, but she was too far away for Rachel to hear what was being said. It was easy to imagine herself in the woman's place. There was even a slight resemblance between them, Rachel thought. Then the woman turned, presenting her with a side view that made her pregnant state obvious.

As the silvery mare was led out of the trailer, Charlie said in disgust, "Look at that mare. She's crippled in front. What did I tell you? We see everything here."

Rachel barely had a chance to look at the horse before Lane called her attention to the stocky, square-shouldered man holding the lead rope. "That old man . . . doesn't he remind you of Ben Jablonski?"

In that instant, everything clicked into place: the old man, the crippled filly, the dilapidated pickup, and the dark-haired woman. It was Abbie. As the realization shot through her, it was like a scab being torn off a newly healing wound and the sore stinging afresh. She glared at the woman who had always been the bane of her life.

"What is she doing here?" Rachel protested under her breath.

But Charlie heard her and turned sharply. "Do you know them?"

She was spared from answering as Vince Romaine came walking back. "They've brought a young mare they want bred to Radzyn, and they've got cash money to pay the stud fee. They didn't book in advance. So I thought I'd better check and see what you wanted me to do," he said.

"Did she give her name?" Lane asked.

"She said it was Hix," the manager replied. "She claims she knows you."

"I thought so." When Charlie glanced inquiringly at Lane, he explained, "She's Dean Lawson's daughter."

"You're kidding." He stared at the pregnant woman standing next to the battered truck. "I didn't realize she was having such a hard time."

"Maybe it's what she deserves." The retort was out before Rachel even realized she'd spoken. She could guess how heartless she must have sounded to her host, but she wasn't about to retract the statement. As far as she was concerned, it was the truth. "Excuse me, please. I'm going to the house."

As she walked away without waiting for a response, she heard Charlie say, "Find an empty stall for the mare."

Shock gave way to cold disbelief when Abbie noticed the silver-haired man standing next to the tall, heavy-set Charlie Carstairs. It didn't seem possible it could be Lane Canfield—not here. At this distance, she couldn't make out his facial features clearly, but there was a definite resemblance. And that mane of white hair was so distinctive she didn't see how it could be anyone else. That had to be Rachel with him. Instinctively Abbie knew she was right.

When Charlie Carstairs turned to confer with Lane and Rachel, Abbie braced herself for a fight. She knew if Rachel could find a way to deprive her of something she wanted—like having River Breeze bred to Charlie Carstairs's stallion Radzyn—she'd do it.

Abruptly Rachel split away from the others and started walking toward the large adobe ranch house. Abbie wasn't sure if it meant she had succeeded in her attempt or failed. Then Vince Romaine approached her again, and Abbie was forced to divide her attention between the stud manager and Rachel.

"Is there a problem, Mr. Romaine?" she demanded before he could say anything.

"No. Bring your mare and I'll show you where to put her. We keep all outside mares isolated from our home herd. Less chance of spreading disease that way."

Abbie didn't like the possibility that had just occurred to her. She started moving away from the short, thin man. "Excuse me. Ben, take Breeze and go with Mr. Romaine. I'll be right there," Abbie promised over her shoulder, then moved quickly to intercept Rachel.

But Rachel saw her coming and stopped. "What do you want?"

"Nothing," Abbie snapped, just as crisply. "I'm leaving my mare here to be bred. And if anything happens to her, I'll know you're responsible."

She'd invested more in the filly than just money. There was all the heartache and worry, all the hopes and dreams tied up in her, too. Abbie knew she couldn't stay and guard the young mare, protect her from Rachel. Rachel had taken or destroyed everything else that had ever belonged to her. River Breeze represented the future. She couldn't let anything happen to her.

"I have no intention of going anywhere near your mare. That's something you would do," Rachel stated coldly, then stared at her contemptuously. "The smartest thing MacCrea ever did was to walk out on you."

Abbie struck out blindly, slapping her hard across the face. For a split second she thought Rachel was going to react in kind. Abbie wished she would.

But Rachel didn't retaliate. Instead, she turned away and walked briskly toward the ranch house. Abbie watched her go, the anger draining.

Rachel had it all wrong about MacCrea. She had been the one to walk out on him. Yet it had hurt to hear Rachel speak his name. The very fact that Rachel had referred to him with such familiarity was proof of all her suspicions.

That evening, Rachel sat in front of the vanity mirror in Charlie's guest bedroom, raking the brush through her hair until her scalp tingled. She still smarted from Abbie's insinuation that she would harm her mare to get even for the fire.

She heard a shoe hit the floor and glanced at Lane's reflection in the mirror. He sat on the side of the bed, one leg crossed while he untied the laces of his other shoe. His expression was thoughtful as he looked up, meeting her glance in the mirror.

"You never did tell me what caused that scene with Abbie this afternoon."

After faltering for an instant, Rachel roughly pulled the brush through her hair again. "She was just being spiteful. I'd really rather not talk about it, if you don't mind."

"I wouldn't be too upset about it, if I were you. Women in her condition tend to be quicker to . . . take offense, shall we say?" He dropped the other shoe on the floor. "I must admit, though, I had no idea until I saw her today that she was expecting a baby. Did you?"

"No, I didn't. But as sudden as that wedding of hers was to Dobie Hix, I wouldn't be at all surprised if she had to get married." She knew that was a catty thing to say. She also knew Lane didn't like to hear her talk that way. When she sought his reflection in the mirror, she was surprised to see he was smiling. She turned sideways to look at him. "Did I say something amusing, Lane?"

"What?" For a moment, the sound of her voice seemed to startle him, then he recovered. "No, not really." He started unbuttoning his shirt.

But it had been something . . . something to do with Abbie. Rachel was positive of that. She had to find out why thinking about Abbie would make him smile like that. "Why were you smiling just then?"

"I was thinking about her husband — how proud and thrilled he must have been when he found out he was going to be a father."

His tone of voice was very calm and matter of fact, yet Rachel thought she had detected something wistful in it. Was it possible that he envied Abbie's husband? With a start, she realized that in all the months they'd been married, they'd never once talked about having children, not even when they were going over the new plans for the house. The extra bedrooms had always been referred to as guest rooms.

Somehow she'd had the impression that Lane didn't want children. It was nothing he'd said. She had simply assumed he didn't want any.

Truthfully, she'd never examined her own feelings on the subject. She supposed that, in the back of her mind, she'd always thought she'd have children someday just like any other person. But her dreams, her desires, had always centered on raising prize Arabian horses. Getting pregnant and having a baby was something she'd never tried to imagine. She shied away from the picture in her mind of Abbie, her figure all distorted by her pregnancy, her belly swollen almost to the size of a watermelon, and her breasts large and heavy.

But her feelings weren't important. It was Lane's she wondered about. "Would you like it if we had a baby?"

He paused in the act of pulling his shirttail free from his pants and stared at her with sudden alertness. "Are you trying to tell me something?"

"No." She laughed self-consciously and turned back to face the dressing table, certain she hadn't imagined that bright glint in his eye. "I was just wondering if it would bother you. You've always been so sensitive about the difference in our ages that I thought maybe it might."

Slowly he walked over to stand behind her chair. Rachel watched him in the mirror as he gently and caressingly placed his hands on her shoulders. When he lifted his glance to study her reflection in the mirror, his expression was impassive and unreadable.

"Would you like to have a baby, Rachel?"

"Only if you would." She couldn't honestly say she did. At this point, she was happy with things the way they were. But, if it would please Lane . . . if he wanted a child . . . after all he'd given her, she owed him that. "If you wouldn't be happy about it —"

"Not happy? I've always considered becoming a father to be the happiest moment in a man's life," he declared. Then his face crinkled with a smile that was warm and deeply affectionate. "You have no idea how much it means to me that you would want to have my child. But at my age . . . I'd be a doddering old man by the time a child of ours graduated from college. That wouldn't be fair — not to you or our child."

"Are you sure? When you talked about Abbie —"

"I probably sounded a little envious. I admit that when I first saw her, for a split second, I let myself imagine it was you. But I also know it wouldn't be right." He paused to study her image in the mirror. "Do you mind? I assumed that you regarded the horses as your children, that they could fill that part of your life."

"In a way, that's probably true." She'd never thought about it and didn't now. Turning, she grasped the hand that rested on her left shoulder and gazed up at him. "I just want to make you happy, Lane."

"Darling, I am. You're all I need for that." Bending, he kissed her warmly and firmly as if trying to convince her that he meant it. But Rachel didn't believe him. "It's late," he said as he straightened. She recognized that ardent look in his expression. "Don't you think you should be getting ready for bed?"

"Of course."

Avoiding his eyes, she gathered up her toiletry case and went into the adjoining bathroom. She set the case on the marble-topped counter next to the sink and turned on the faucets. Letting the water run, she opened the case and reached for the jar of cleansing cream inside. She hesitated when she saw her container of birth-control pills. Not once had Lane denied that he wanted a child. She remembered the look on his face when he'd referred to Abbie, admitting that he'd wished Abbie had been her.

Silently vowing that that would never happen again, Rachel pushed the pills out of their cardboard holder one by one and flushed them down the toilet.

* * *

Every morning, Rachel went to the stables to check on her mare, Simoon. Finally, the day before they were scheduled to leave, the charcoal-dark horse did not lay back her ears or squeal and kick when she was led alongside the padded trying bar that separated her from the "teaser," a stallion of slightly inferior breeding quality used for trying mares and determining which were in season. This time, Simoon responded to the teaser stallion's interested nicker-ings and leaned against the protective bar. Standing with her hind legs apart, the mare lifted her nearly black tail and urinated, showing a definite "winking" of the clitoris. The mare was ready to be bred.

When the dark-gray mare was led into the indoor breeding yard, Rachel was as nervous, excited, and apprehensive as she had been on her own wedding night. Initially she felt self-conscious about being present, but none of the handlers paid any attention to her as they prepared the mare, wrapping a bandage around her tail to keep the hairs out of the way, attaching the covering boots to her hind feet, and finally washing her vulva, hindquarters, and dock with antiseptic solution.

Suddenly the shrill trumpet of a stallion rang through the barn. With a quickening pulse, Rachel turned toward the doorway leading into the enclosed yard as Simoon nickered an answer. The black bay stallion seemed to explode into the yard, all fire and animation at the end of the groom's lead. With the water-dampened sand floor muffling the sound of his hooves, the stallion ap-peared to float above the ground, his legs lifting high, his neck arched, and his long tail streaming behind him like a black plume. The groom led the stallion in a tight circle and shook the whip at him as a reminder.

When the groom finally walked the snorting, plunging stallion toward the mare, Rachel experienced a faint shiver of anticipation. She remembered read-ing somewhere about an Arab sheikh who had invited guests to his tent to witness the mating of his prize war mare with a stallion of a valuable strain.

Standing on the sidelines, watching the courting stallion's sniffings and nuzzlings of the mare, she felt the same sense of moment. Amidst all the squeals and nickerings, she had the feeling she was about to observe the consummation of a royal union. All the ceremony was there: the ritualistic preparing of the bride, the grand entrance of the groom, and the presence of all the attendants.

Staring, Rachel waited for the moment when the stallion was fully drawn, not looking away or closing her eyes the way she did with Lane. This time she had to see everything. The instant the stud groom observed the tensing of the back muscles, the full erection, and the absolute readiness of the stallion, he allowed the eager stud to make his jump onto Simoon, the stallion instinctively swinging into position behind her as he did so.

Simultaneously, the handler on the other side grasped the mare's dark tail and held it out of the way, cautiously avoiding the stallion's hooves, while the man at Simoon's head checked her initial forward movement, preventing her from moving more than a step or two away from the mounting stallion. Rachel tensed in empathy and talked to the mare in her mind, mentally offering all the assurances she would have spoken to Simoon if she could.

Easy, my beauty. Don't be frightened, she thought, unconsciously straining against the imagined invasion, yet knowing it had to come. I know it hurts but it won't last long. He knows what he's doing. It'll be over soon. It always is. Just hold on a little bit longer. That's the way, my Simoon. As if hearing her thoughts, the dark-gray mare stood passively beneath the humping stallion. Rachel felt a quickening rush as the stallion's long tail flailed the air in an up-and-down motion, signaling his ejaculation. Yes. Yes, accept his seed, she told Simoon silently. Let it in now. You won't be sorry. I promise. Just let it come in. There, now, it's over. It wasn't really so bad, was it?

The bay stallion rested a moment atop the mare, then swung off. Rachel felt oddly flushed as the stud groom led the stallion away from Simoon and rinsed the stallion's sheath with a specially prepared wash. When she turned back to her mare, a handler unbuckled the boots on her hind feet and walked the horse out of them. As they started to remove the white bandage wrapped around her tail, Rachel noticed the man in a cowboy hat standing on the other side of the indoor yard.

In that stunned instant, when she recognized Ross Tibbs, she felt as if she had just touched an electric fence. Even though she had known he was in Phoenix, she had thought . . . she had *hoped* she wouldn't see him.

"Mr. Tibbs, what a surprise to see you here." She put on the brightly fixed smile she'd acquired since attending so many social functions with Lane.

"Mrs. Canfield." He mimicked her formality — deliberately, she suspected. "I read in yesterday's society column that you and your husband were here. It's been a long time since I've seen anyone from home. It gets lonely on the road after a while. You get to where you'd give anything just to see a familiar face."

Loneliness was something she'd known all her life, but she couldn't admit to it — not to him. A groom led her mare over to the exit. "Excuse me. They're taking my mare back to her stall. I want to see her settled in."

"Mind if I come along?"

She did, but she found it impossible to refuse. "Not at all."

Ross fell in step with her as she crossed the sandy yard, following behind the darkly dappled rump of the charcoal-gray horse. "I really like the look of your mare. I've been thinking about buying that stallion, Basha 'al-Nazir, off Charlie. But with the price he's asking, I'm not sure I can swing it yet, even though he's offered me some good terms."

"You were really serious when you talked about wanting to buy some Arabians last year." At the time, she thought he'd just been saying that to make an impression on her.

"Serious? Hey, it's been one of my dreams for . . . I don't know how long," he declared with an expansive wave of his hand. "Don't get me wrong. Music is my life, and always will be. But horses are my love. I can't explain it. That's just the way it is."

"I understand." Completely. The only difference for Rachel was that horses were her life as well as her love.

He asked her about Simoon's breeding, then about the other mares she owned. One question led to another. Rachel didn't remember leaving the stud barn or passing the broodmare barn or entering the separate facility where the outside mares were stalled. It was as if she had been magically transported from one place to the other. Although Lane had always willingly listened to her expound on her favorite subject — Arabian horses — she discovered it was different talking to someone who shared her obsession with the breed. Even when she and Ross disagreed on the attributes of a particular type or bloodline, it was enjoyable.

Once Simoon was back in her stall, together they looked over the other mares in the stable. As they approached the iron grate of one of the stalls, a mare the color of silver lifted her head and blew softly, her large, luminous dark eyes gazing at them curiously. Unconsciously, Rachel stopped short of the stall's partition.

"Now this one's a beauty," Ross declared, walking up to the stall to look over the barred top.

She stared at the mare that belonged to Abbie, watching the flare of the large nostrils as the young Arabian tried to catch their scent. Every time she'd come into the barn, the mare had nickered to her. Once Rachel had walked over to the stall, but the instant the mare had smelled her hand, she turned and hobbled to the far corner of the corral. Rachel hadn't gone near her since then.

Ross peered over the top of the stall, then turned back to Rachel, frowning in surprise. "Her front legs . . . she's crippled."

"Some freak accident, I heard." She didn't want to talk about the mare or her owner.

"That's too bad."

"Yes." Rachel walked on to the next stall, without waiting for him. A moment ago, she had been so relaxed with him. Now, she was all agitated and tense again.

"Remember the last time we were in a stable together?" The pitch of his voice changed, becoming more intimate.

"Please," she said in protest, remembering too clearly how she had felt when he'd touched her that day.

She felt the probing of his gaze, but she refused to meet it. "Charlie tells me that all Canfield knows about a horse is that it has four legs, a head, and a tail. What do you have in common with someone like him?"

"Please don't talk that way, Ross."

"You'll never convince me that you love him. You couldn't."

Out of the corner of her eye, she caught the movement he made toward her and turned sharply to face him.

"What do you know about it? You don't know me and you don't know Lane," Rachel protested in a voice choked with her warring emotions. She briskly walked away from him, breaking into a near-run before she reached the barn doors.

32

A BOOMING CLAP of thunder from the May storm drenching Houston rumbled through the office building as MacCrea Wilder entered the reception area, his dark hair glistening from his dash through the rain, its wave more pronounced. "I know I'm late, Marge." He held up a hand to stave off any comment from Lane Canfield's secretary. "The traffic's backed up all the way to the airport this morning."

"You should have seen it when I came to work," the redhead sympathized and reached for the intercom to announce him as she waved him to the inner door. "Go right in. He's expecting you."

"Thanks." He crossed the space with long, loping strides and pushed open the door to Lane's office. Lane was just getting up from his desk when MacCrea walked in. "Sorry I'm late."

"With this storm, I wasn't even sure your plane would be able to land." Lane came around the large desk to shake hands with him. A sheeting rain hammered the windows behind him, obscuring the rolling, black clouds that darkened the sky over Houston.

"Neither did I." MacCrea shrugged out of the damp linen blazer and tossed it over one of the two armchairs in front of Lane's desk. Hitching up his trouser legs, he sat down in the other, uncomfortable in his rain-soaked silk shirt. "I have some good news to report. Just before I left this morning, I got word that the number three well came in. So far, we're batting a hundred and it looks like it's just beginning."

"Well, it appears congratulations are in order all the way around." Smiling widely, Lane reached back and picked up a wooden box containing hand-rolled cigars and held it out to MacCrea. "It may be a few months early for a proud father to be passing out cigars, but have one anyway."

Surprised by the announcement, MacCrea halted in the act of taking a cigar. "A father?"

"Yes." The smile on his face seemed to grow wider. "Rachel's expecting a baby." After MacCrea had taken a cigar, Lane snipped off the end for him, then struck a match and held the flame under the cigar to light it for him.

"I'll be damned," MacCrea said between puffs.

"That's what I said," Lane chuckled. "Rachel's been deathly sick for nearly two weeks now. She thought she had a bad case of the flu. Finally, three days ago, I convinced her to see the doctor. He suspected she was pregnant, and yesterday, the lab tests confirmed it."

"When's the happy event to take place?" Recovering from his initial surprise, MacCrea settled back in the thickly cushioned armchair and studied his financial partner, vaguely amused by Lane's obvious pride and delight. His reaction seemed totally out of character for the no-nonsense man MacCrea had become accustomed to dealing with. Maybe he'd act the same way if he found out he was going to be a father.

"The latter part of January. Imagine me . . . a father after all these years." Lane shook his head in amazement and walked back around his desk and sat down. "Most men my age are awaiting the birth of their first grandchild. And here I am, about to become a father for the first time in my life. I have to admit I've never been so excited about anything in my life."

"Congratulations — to both of you. Or maybe I should say all three of you," MacCrea suggested wryly.

"Thank you. Rachel is as happy about it as I am, I'm glad to say. Of course, this morning sickness has really gotten her down." When he glanced at the photograph of his wife on his desk, MacCrea's attention was drawn to it. As always he was unsettled by that initial resemblance to Abbie: the dark hair, the facial structure, and especially the deep-blue eyes. "She's anxious about her horses and the work going on at the farm."

"How's it coming?" He tapped the ash from his cigar into the crystal ashtray on Lane's desk, the question dictated by politeness rather than any desire to know.

"The contractor expects the house to be completely finished by November. Which means we'll be able to spend the Christmas holidays there. Rachel is really looking forward to that."

"Then you haven't had any more problems?"

"You mean with Abbie?" Lane guessed.

Dammit, MacCrea cursed silently, knowing that was exactly who he had meant. Before he'd left Louisiana this morning, he'd sworn to himself that he wasn't going to ask about her.

Taking his silence as an affirmative response, Lane said, "You know she's expecting a baby, too . . . sometime in early fall, I think."

Abbie pregnant — with that farmer's child. "No. No, I didn't know." He suddenly felt sick inside. He couldn't explain it, not even to himself. He just knew he wanted to get this damned meeting over with and get back on that plane and fly the hell out of here, fast. It was over. Any lingering doubts he may have had vanished in that instant.

It was one thing when she had another man's ring on her finger. But when she carried another man's child . . . MacCrea laid the cigar down in the ashtray and let it smolder. Sooner or later, it would burn itself out. "You said you had some papers we needed to go over," he said, reminding Lane of the purpose of his visit.

Part Two

33 ✒

THE WIND-DRIVEN DUST swirled about the legs of the brightly festooned Arabian horses and whipped at the tassels and fringes that adorned their fancy bridles, breast collars, and long saddle blankets — elaborate trappings that were rivaled only by those of their riders, dressed in native costumes of flowing kuffieyahs and abas. The crowd outside the entrance to the main arena on the Scottsdale showgrounds parted to let the prancing horses pass.

"Look at all the beautiful horses that are coming, Mommy," Eden said excitedly.

Quickly, Abbie grabbed the hand of her five-year-old daughter and pulled her out of the path of the oncoming horses. "I swear I'm going to put a lead rope on you if you don't start listening and stay right beside me like you've been told."

Inadvertently Abbie glanced down at Eden's hand . . . and the crooked little fingers that curled ever so slightly higher than the others — from her father, from MacCrea. She had inherited the trait, along with her wavy hair, from him. Abbie wished she hadn't. She wished she could forget Eden had any father other than Dobie. She didn't want to be reminded that MacCrea Wilder even existed, but this had become impossible. His oil strike in Louisiana almost five years ago and his subsequent successes had placed his name on the lips of practically everyone in Houston.

"But I can't see," Eden pouted.

Abbie could appreciate that for a child, this crowd must seem like a forest towering around her. "You can see. The horses are going to pass right in front of you."

Single file, the horses and riders paraded by them, a glitter of gold, silver, and copper ornamenting costumes of brilliant red, blue, purple, and shiny black. With a swing of her dark ponytail, Eden turned to look up at Abbie and pulled at the sleeve of her blouse.

Obligingly, Abbie leaned down so Eden could whisper in her ear. "Windstorm is more beautiful than these horses, isn't he, Mom? If we dressed him up like that, he'd win for sure, wouldn't he?" she said, referring to the five-year-old stallion out of Abbie's mare River Breeze.

"I bet he would, too." Abbie smiled and winked in agreement.

"He's the best horse in the whole world," Eden asserted without a trace of doubt.

"Maybe not the best horse." Although deep down she believed that, too.

"He is, too." Eden stubbornly refused to listen to such disloyal talk.

"We'll see." Only Abbie knew how close that statement was to being the truth. All the top stallions in the country were here at Scottsdale to compete in the prestigious show. Windstorm had already won several regional championships, but a win here would give him the recognition he deserved.

It had been a long, expensive road just to get this far. But she was well on her way to having the high-quality Arabian breeding operation she'd dreamed of owning. She had leased more land from Dobie, built a new broodmare barn and a stud barn, purchased ten well-bred broodmares, and leased three more plus a stallion. And she'd done it all with money she'd earned herself, either from the thriving party business or from the high prices she had received from the sale of each year's crop of foals. She'd sold them all except Windstorm and a full sister to him foaled last year.

Abbie remembered all too clearly that trip to Scottsdale six years ago: sleeping in the back of that rusty old pickup truck in sleeping bags, eating cold sandwiches, hauling her crippled mare in a borrowed horse trailer, and watching every penny to be sure they'd have enough left to pay for the gas home. This time, she had a healthy bank account . . . and an Arabian stallion that just might win the championship. And she'd done it all the hard way, with no help from anyone except Ben — not even Dobie.

Sometimes she suspected Dobie resented that as much as he resented the success she'd had. She knew that secretly he had hoped she would fail. And his pride was hurt, too, by the amount of money she had made from the sale of the foals. He wouldn't let her spend a dime of it on Eden or the house, insisting it was horse money and that he alone would support his family. Abbie didn't argue.

It had stopped being a marriage a long time ago, if it ever had been one. She and Dobie lived in the same house, shared the same bed, and occasionally used each other to satisfy their physical needs. That's all it was. That's all it ever would be. Sometimes Abbie wished there were more to it, but, as long as she had the horses and Eden, she could manage to forget that something was missing from her life.

"Come on." She took Eden by the hand as the last of the horses and riders in the native-costume class went by. "Let's go find Ben."

"Where is Ben?" Eden hurried anxiously ahead, pulling at Abbie's hand. "Do you think he's lost?"

"I doubt it. He's probably waiting for us in front of the stallion barn."

Abbie guided Eden through the milling crowd on the showgrounds. The atmosphere was circuslike, with its array of sparkling costumes, brightly colored tents, and fast-food booths, all set against a backdrop of desert blue sky and waving palm trees. Exhibiters, owners, and trainers dressed in riding costumes, tee shirts and jeans, or the latest designer creations mingled with the sightseers: the tourists, curious townspeople, and horse fanciers, old and young, out for an afternoon's outing and a close-up look at the equine descendants from the Arabian desert right here in their own desert country. And a look they got, along with all the glamour and mystique that surrounded the Arabian breed.

As they approached the first stallion barn, Abbie spied Ben standing in the shade, waiting patiently. Bending down, she pointed him out to Eden. "There he is. See him?"

In answer, Eden tugged her hand free and ran ahead to meet him, her ponytail bouncing up and down and sideways. Smiling, Abbie watched her young daughter, clad like a miniature adult in riding boots, jodhpurs, and a string tie around the collar of her white blouse. She remembered the times when she had run to Ben with that same eager affection her daughter now showed. And Ben was as patient and gentle with Eden as he had been with her, if slightly more indulgent. There was no doubt about it in Abbie's mind, Eden had him wrapped around her little finger. Her crooked little finger, Abbie remembered, sobering with the thought.

"Mommy, Ben knew we would come here," Eden declared when Abbie joined them. "Ben knows everything, doesn't he?"

"Everything." Even the identity of your real father, Abbie thought, recognizing that over the years, he had been the trusted keeper of many secrets.

She lifted her glance to him and felt the tug of memories, old and new. Always he'd been her rock, square and stalwart, constant as the tides. While everything changed around him, he remained the same. There was hardly any evidence of the passing years in his craggy face. Abbie conceded that his gray hair had turned a little whiter, and she noticed that when he walked now, his feet shuffled a little, no longer striding out with their former firmness of step. His age was definitely catching up to him. She hated to see it. It was funny the way she could accept her mother's graying hair, but expected Ben to stay young forever.

"Will I ever know as much as you do, Ben?" Eden frowned.

"Someday, perhaps." He nodded sagely.

"Shall we go inside and have a look at Rachel's would-be contender for the championship?" Abbie suggested, knowing that if they waited until her daughter ran out of questions, they'd be here a month or more.

The long exhibition hall was lined with lavish showcase stalls the entire length of the building on both sides. Each farm represented had rented three, four, or more stalls, only one of which was used for the stallion on show. The rest were transformed into extravagant booths, each uniquely furnished and decorated, to promote the breeding farm and its stallions.

As they passed one that had been draped and roofed in black cloth to resemble the tent of a Bedouin sheikh, Eden tried to drag Abbie inside so she could investigate the plush cushions with the gold-tasseled corners. Another had been turned into a library, complete with rich walnut paneling and shelves of books lining the walls around a mock fireplace. Others were sleekly contemporary in their decor, making use of glitz and glamour to attract the eye of the passerby. The people strolling past the booths looked and marveled at the elaborate displays, but the real stars were still the stallions.

Halfway down the row, Abbie spotted the large booth that looked like a Victorian parlor, right down to the period antiques and silver tea service, and the dainty canapés offered as refreshments to visitors. Abbie scanned the dozen or so occupants of the River Bend booth, recognizing the farm's manager and several others, but Rachel wasn't among them. With all the big sales and exclusive private parties held in conjunction with Scottsdale, Abbie hadn't expected Rachel to spend much time in the farm's booth.

Nearly everyone in the River Bend booth sported the scarlet satin jacket emblazoned with the name Sirocco, the stallion Rachel had in the halter competition. Abbie had lost count of the number of people she'd seen on the showgrounds wearing those jackets. The farm was giving them away to anyone who would agree to wear it around the showgrounds. An expensive promotional tool, but a very effective one. The jackets were so plentiful, it was as if a scarlet tide were sweeping through the Scottsdale.

Rachel was sparing no expense to win the crown for her stallion. For months now, her advertisements of Sirocco had littered every major Arabian publication. The cost of this campaign had to run in the hundreds of thousands of dollars. Abbie couldn't hope to compete against Rachel financially, and she knew it. She wasn't poor by any means, but she didn't have the limitless wealth that Rachel had.

Abbie skirted the activity in the booth itself and went directly to the whitewashed stall emblazoned with the words RIVER BEND'S NAHR SIROCCO. A scroll of iron grillwork topped the upper third of the stall. Beyond the curved bars, Abbie caught the gleam of a blood-red coat. Before she could get a closer look at the stallion everyone was predicting to be supreme champion of the show, Eden yanked at her hand.

"I want to see, Mommy."

"Come on, short stuff." Bending down, Abbie picked up her daughter and swung her onto her hip, groaning as she did so. "I hope you realize how heavy you're getting."

"I know. That's 'cause I'm getting big. Ben says someday I'm going to be taller than you are."

"I wouldn't doubt it," Abbie agreed, inadvertently recalling that MacCrea was a tall man. Determinedly she turned to study the blood bay stallion in the stall.

As if aware of his audience, the stallion turned, presenting them with a side view of his magnificence. His long black mane and tail rippled in shiny waves, and the black of his legs glistened like polished ebony. In contrast, the deep red of his satiny coat gleamed like a banked fire. His head was small and fine, held high as he looked on them with disdain.

Previously, Abbie had seen only photographs of the stallion — taken in the winner's circle. In all the competitions Windstorm had won, her stallion had never come up against her archrival's. Rachel had campaigned Sirocco almost exclusively on the West Coast under the skilled tutelage and handling of Tom Marsh, universally considered the best in the business, and who charged his clients accordingly.

Two other small but successful breeders like herself came up to the stall to view the stallion that was the talk of Scottsdale, even though he had yet to appear in his first class. Abbie eavesdropped intentionally.

"I have to admit Sirocco is impressive," one said reluctantly. "He has that air that says 'Look at me.'"

"Oh, he'll win. There isn't much doubt about that," the other replied. "Even if there were a better stallion in the class, he'd still walk away with it. Everyone tries to pretend that judges aren't influenced by somebody's money or reputation. Once they see Tom Marsh lead this stallion into the arena with all of Canfield's millions behind him, I say they'll mark the champion on their cards right then."

"You're probably right."

"I know I am. They're never going to let a stallion from some small farm win. And I don't care how great the horse is either."

As the pair moved away, Abbie tried to convince herself that all their talk was just so much sour grapes. Windstorm had as good a chance of winning as Sirocco. It took a lot of money to show a horse, but money still couldn't buy a victory. A loss didn't necessarily mean the better horse had won. Usually it was a matter of opinion. Some judges put emphasis on different things.

"I don't like him," Eden decided, the corners of her mouth turning down. "He looks snooty, don't he, Mommy?"

"Doesn't he," Abbie corrected her grammar automatically.

"Doesn't he?"

"A little, I suppose." But she found it difficult to fault the stallion's look of arrogance. In its own way, it was very compelling, although she much preferred Windstorm's look of noble pride — that rare "look of eagles" that evoked a sense of both power and gentleness.

"Windstorm will beat him, won't he, Mom?" As far as Eden was concerned, Windstorm was a wonder horse. It was understandable in a way. She'd been around the stallion all her young life, hiding behind his legs to play peek-a-boo as a toddler and riding on his back at the age of three whenever Abbie led the stallion to and from the pasture. Abbie even had a snapshot of Eden curled up asleep using Windstorm as a pillow.

"We'll see," Abbie said and turned to Ben, seeking a less prejudiced opinion. "What do you think of him?"

"Handsome, proud, the classic head, flat croup, well-set tail. He would be many people's ideal Arabian."

"Yours?" Abbie didn't want to hear praise for the stallion.

Ben gave a faint, negative shake of his head. "For me, his neck is too long. With it, he may look pretty, but it makes his balance not good. Too, he is a little sickle-hocked and the bone, it is weak. He could break down easy, I think. But, a man who knows what he is doing could disguise that in the show ring so the leg would not look so straight."

"How does he stack up against Windstorm?" She was beginning to feel the strain of her daughter's weight on her arm and hip. She swung her to the ground to relieve the pressure. "Just stand here for a while," she told Eden when she started to protest.

"Some will think his neck is too short." Ben shrugged. "Others will think sixteen hands is too tall for an Arabian. Some will not like Windstorm because he is a gray."

"I know." Abbie sighed. In the end, it all boiled down to opinion. And nobody knew whose was right.

"Mommy, can I go watch television over there?" Eden pointed to a booth across the way where a television was playing back a tape of that particular farm's stallion.

Abbie hesitated, then decided there wouldn't be any harm in it. Eden would be close enough that she could keep an eye on her. Besides, it might keep her active daughter entertained for a little while. "All right, you may go over there and watch it. But no farther, do you understand? And don't bother anybody, either."

"Yes, Mommy," she promised solemnly, then took off at a run.

Abbie watched to make sure Eden did exactly as she had promised. Once Eden had plunked herself down on the carpeted floor in front of the television set, Abbie felt sufficiently assured that she turned back to Ben, dividing her attention between him and the blood bay stallion in the stall.

"I've heard Sirocco's disposition isn't all that good." Abbie knew that anyone who'd seen how gently Windstorm behaved with Eden, a five-year-old child, couldn't question her stallion's temperament.

"I wonder what this one knows about being a horse. What has his world been? Horse trailers, stalls, lunging at the end of a rope, and being paraded around an arena with people all around him whistling and shouting. When do you suppose he ran free in a pasture the way Windstorm does when he is home? Or when has anyone ridden him across the country just for the fun of it, the way you do with Windstorm? Always for him, it is shows and training. Would you not get sour, too?" Again Ben shook his head. "I do not blame the horse for being ill-tempered. I have never yet seen a show horse that was not a little bit crazy in the head."

"That's true." Although she didn't have Ben's years of experience, Abbie had seen some horses, mostly fillies, that had come off of successful careers in the show arena. They'd been around people so much they couldn't relate at all to other horses. Some had even been terrified when they were turned loose in a pasture with other horses.

"Somewhere is that stallion they imported from Russia this winter. I want to see him, too." Ben turned to survey the other booths down the line.

"I think it's on the other side, about three down. I'll get Eden and meet you there."

But Eden wasn't ready to leave. Before Abbie could insist on it, a couple who had purchased one of River Breeze's foals saw her and stopped to show her the latest pictures of the filly, now a classy-looking two-year-old, entered in the Futurity Filly class at the show. It was a proud moment for Abbie, since it meant two of her mare's offspring would be competing at Scottsdale: Windstorm and this filly, Silver Lining.

"Where's Ben?" Eden wanted to know.

"I thought you were watching television." Abbie frowned, surprised to find Eden at her side.

"Ahh, it's a rerun," she complained.

"Do you remember my daughter, Eden? These are the Holquists, Eden. They bought that filly you used to call Pepper, remember?"

"Yeah. Hi. Where's Ben?"

"He's looking at another horse."

"Can I go find him?"

"No. You stay right here." Abbie ignored the face Eden made to protest the order and resumed her conversation with the Holquists, knowing their success with this filly made them likely candidates for the purchase of a future foal. "I'm planning to have her bred again this spring. We tentatively have her booked with a son of Bask, but Ben wants to look at that new Russian stallion they've imported before we commit ourselves."

"There's Ben. I'm gonna go see him." Eden dashed off before Abbie could grab her.

"I don't know if it was such a good idea to bring her along or not," Abbie sighed as she watched her daughter disappear in the crowd, not altogether certain that Eden had seen Ben, but trusting that she had. "She's been like this ever since we arrived."

"There's so much excitement and so many things to see, you can hardly blame her," Mrs. Holquist replied.

"I suppose not. There's one consolation in all this, though. She will go right to sleep tonight."

The woman laughed. "She probably will. I just wish I had half her energy."

"Me, too." Abbie thought she recognized Ben at the far end of the row, but with so many people wandering about, she couldn't get a long enough look at him to be sure. "I'd better go after my daughter. We'll catch you later, maybe when we come by to see your filly."

"Good luck."

"Thanks. Same to you." She hurried off to search for her elusive daughter and Ben.

MacCrea walked into the long barn and paused to look around. Idly he started down the wide corridor, joining the meandering flow of people that hesitated here and stopped there. Oddly, MacCrea felt in no hurry to reach the booth and find Lane Canfield. He wondered at the impulse that had brought him here. His meeting with Lane hadn't been dictated by necessity. He could have postponed it for a couple of weeks, even a month with no harm done, but that would have meant meeting Lane in Houston. Maybe that was what he had wanted to avoid. It had been nearly three years now since he'd been back. Sometimes it seemed a lot longer — and sometimes it didn't seem long enough.

Someone bumped against his shoulder. "Sorry."

"It's okay." MacCrea paused, but the man walked on. He felt something pull at the pant leg of his jeans. Glancing down, he saw a little girl looking up at him. Her eyes were big and blue . . . and held the faintest shimmer of tears.

"Mister, can you see my mommy?"

"Your mommy." MacCrea was surprised by the question.

"Yes. You see, I'm afraid she's lost," the little girl explained with a worried look.

"It's your mother who's lost. For a minute there, I thought it was you," MacCrea said, amused by her unusual view of the situation.

"No. I left her over there when I went to see Ben." The little girl pointed to her left. "Only I couldn't find Ben, and when I went back, Mommy wasn't there. Can you help me find her?" Again she tilted her head way back and turned those round blue eyes on him.

Of all the people walking around, MacCrea wondered why on earth this kid had picked him to help her. What he knew about kids wouldn't fill the container for a core sample. But he couldn't resist the appeal of those beguiling blue eyes. He crouched down to her level and tipped his hat to the back of his head.

"Sure, I'll help. I always was a sucker for blue eyes." Smiling, he tweaked the end of her button nose, then scooped her into the crook of his arm and straightened, lifting her up with him. "We'll see if we can't find someone to make an announcement over the loudspeaker. How does that sound, midget?" He looked at her, conscious of the small hand that rested on his shoulder. She gazed back at him solemnly.

"I'm not a midget. I'm a little girl."

"Is that right?" MacCrea replied with mock skepticism. "How old are you?"

"I'm five-and-a-half years old."

"What's your name?"

"Eden. What's yours?"

"MacCrea Wilder," he answered, amused by the rapid comeback.

"MacCrea is your first name?" She frowned at him as he walked toward the barn's main entrance to look for an official of the horse show.

"Yup."

"That's a funny name. So is Eden, though. My daddy says it's the name of a garden and it's a silly name to give a girl. Mommy says I shouldn't listen to him."

"Well, I agree with your mommy. I think Eden is a nice name for a girl."

"Do you really? Mommy says people say things sometimes just to be nice, but they don't really mean them."

"Your mother sounds like she's a very smart woman."

"She is. Smarter than my daddy, even."

"And I'll bet that's really saying something."

"Naw." Eden wrinkled her nose. "My daddy doesn't know anything about horses. He's nice though."

"That's good."

"Where do you suppose my mommy is?" Eden half turned in his arm to look behind them.

"I have the feeling she's probably frantically looking for you."

"Maybe we should go back and see if we can find her." She squared around to gaze at him earnestly.

"I think it will be quicker and easier if we just have her paged over the loudspeaker and let her find us." Feeling her intent stare, MacCrea glanced sideways at the child. "Something wrong?"

"How come you have a mustache?"

"I suppose because I didn't shave it off."

"Does it tickle?"

"I've had a few girls tell me that it does."

"Can I see?"

Surprised by the request, MacCrea stopped. He wasn't sure whether to laugh or not as he looked at the bold little mite in his arms. He could see she was totally serious. "Go ahead." He shrugged.

He watched her face as she tentatively reached out to touch the ends of his mustache. It was a study of concentration and intense curiosity. Then he felt the faintest sensation of her small fingers moving over his lips as she ran the tips over the bluntly cut hairs of his mustache. A smile of amazement broke across her face as she pulled her hand back.

"It did tickle a little, but it was kinda soft, too. How come?"

"I don't know." MacCrea frowned. "Tell me, are you always like this with total strangers? Hasn't your mommy ever told you that you shouldn't trust people you don't know?"

"Yeah," she admitted, unconcerned. "She says I talk too much, too. Do you think I do?"

"Far be it from me to contradict your mother," he said dryly.

"What does 'counterdick' mean?"

"It means telling someone the exact opposite of what someone else has told him. In other words, if your mother told you something was good and I said it was bad, I'd be contradicting her. That wouldn't be nice."

"Oh," she said with a long, slow nod of her head, but MacCrea doubted that she'd actually understood.

He shifted his hold on the child, boosting her to ride a little higher within his encircling arm. "Come on. Let's see if —"

"Eden!" The frantic call came from behind them.

"Wait," Eden ordered as she looked back. "There's my mommy!"

Turning, MacCrea spotted the slim, dark-haired woman just breaking free of the crowd. When she saw him, she stopped abruptly. A kick of recognition jolted through him. Abbie. For an instant he forgot everything, even the child in his arms, as he stared openly, drinking in the sight of her after all these years — two months over six, to be exact.

He was surprised to find she had changed so little in all that time. She wore her dark hair shorter now, the ends just brushing the tops of her shoulders. Even though the voluminous folds of her split riding skirt disguised the slimness of her hips, the wide belt that cinched her small waist revealed that she had retained her shapely figure. And her eyes still held that blue fire that he remembered so well. If anything, the years had added a ripeness and strength to her beauty that had been missing before.

The shock of seeing him had drained the color from her face. MacCrea watched it come back in a hot rush. "Where are you taking her? What are you doing with my daughter?" Before he knew what was happening, she was grabbing Eden out of his arms and clutching her tightly.

"I didn't know she was your daughter." He was still slightly dazed by the discovery. "I suppose I should have guessed when I saw those blue eyes."

"We were going to have the man call your name over the loudspeaker, Mommy," Eden said, momentarily claiming Abbie's attention. "I'm so glad we found you. I was starting to get worried."

"She thought *you* were lost," MacCrea inserted, feeling the impact of her glance as it swung again to him. God, but he wanted to hold her again. He didn't realize how much until this very minute, when the ache was so strong, he actually hurt inside. But her wary look made him hold himself back.

"Why didn't you stay with me the way you were told? Then none of this would have happened," Abbie scolded, her accusing glare indicating very clearly that it was this meeting with him that she wished had never happened.

"But when I couldn't find Ben, I came back and you were gone," Eden asserted, pouting slightly at Abbie's censure.

But Abbie wasn't interested in her explanation. "Why was she with you?"

MacCrea exhaled a short, laughing breath. "It wasn't my idea. She came to me. I don't know why. Maybe I looked like someone she could trust."

"Unfortunately she's too young to know any better." The bitterness in her voice dashed any hope MacCrea had that time might have altered her opinion of him.

"His name is MacCrea. Did you know that, Mommy? It's a funny name, but I like it. He thinks my name is nice, too. Don't you?"

"Yes." He found perverse satisfaction in knowing that Abbie's daughter liked him.

"Why are you here?" A second after she asked the question, Abbie glanced in the direction of the River Bend display, guessing the answer. The line of her mouth thinned even straighter. "Somehow I doubted that you had acquired an interest in Arabians."

"We have an Arabian stallion," Eden told him excitedly. "He's the most beautiful horse ever. Would you like to see him? His name is Windstorm."

"Yes, I would, Eden." Accepting the invitation, MacCrea smiled lazily in the face of Abbie's grim, angry look.

"I'm sure Mr. Wilder has better things to do than look at our horse, Eden. He's a very busy man."

"But he said he wanted to," Eden insisted, then smiled proudly. "It isn't nice to counterdick someone, Mommy."

"You mean contradict," Abbie corrected automatically.

"That's what I said. Counterdick."

"She's a clever girl . . . just like her mother," MacCrea observed. "Where is this horse of yours, Eden?"

"He's in a different barn. We'll take you there, won't we, Mommy?"

"Maybe another time, Eden." Her glaring look warned MacCrea not to insist. "Right now we have to go find Ben. Mr. Wilder understands. Don't you, Mr. Wilder?"

"No." He wasn't about to let her out of the invitation so easily.

"Look —" she began, barely controlling anger, only to be interrupted by the old man who came shuffling up behind her.

"Good. You have found her." He laid a gnarled and age-spotted hand on Eden's shoulder. "We were worried about you, child. How many times has your momma told you not to run off like that, eh?"

Abbie was irritated that Ben should pick this minute to arrive, but he was so relieved to find Eden with her that it was difficult for her to be angry with him. Yet she had to make him aware of the situation. "You remember Ben Jablonski, don't you, Mr. Wilder." As Ben stared at MacCrea, Abbie saw him appear flustered and unsure for the first time.

"Of course. Hello, Ben. It's good to see you again." MacCrea stepped forward to shake hands with him.

Ben glanced questioningly at her. Abbie gave a faint shake of her head to let him know that, as yet, MacCrea did not know her secret. "How do you do, Mr. Wilder." Stiffly Ben shook his hand.

"He wants to see Windstorm, Ben." Eden turned excitedly to Abbie. "Now that Ben's here, we can take him to our barn now, can't we, Mommy?"

Abbie longed to tape her daughter's mouth shut. Failing that, she appealed to MacCrea, hoping that he'd stop being stubborn and accept the fact that she didn't want him around at all. "We wouldn't want to take up your time uselessly, Mr. Wilder."

"I'll be the judge of that."

"Very well, we'll show you the horse." She was unwilling to create a scene with Eden looking on, and she realized that MacCrea knew that. The alternative was to get this over with as quickly as possible. She swung Eden to the ground. "You're too heavy to carry."

"She can ride on my shoulders," MacCrea offered.

"No." She refused too quickly and tried to temper it, knowing that she couldn't risk MacCrea being that close to Eden. "It'll do her good to walk and burn up some of that energy." She pushed Eden at Ben. "We'll follow you and Ben. Be sure and hold tight to his hand."

As Eden skipped alongside Ben to take the lead, Abbie fell in with Mac-Crea. But she couldn't look at him. She couldn't even breathe. She had never guessed seeing him again would be so painful. In so many ways, he looked the same as she remembered. Maybe his face looked harder, carved by a few more lines. But the lazy smile was the same, and that charm that both mocked and challenged.

She'd been terrified when she'd seen him holding Eden — terrified that he'd somehow found out she was his daughter and intended to take Eden away from her. Even now she was frightened by the thought. And that fear was stronger than any other feelings seeing him had aroused.

"We sorta skipped all the pleasantries," MacCrea said as they walked out of the stallion barn into the brilliant Arizona sunlight. "Maybe we should start over. How are you, Abbie?"

"Married."

"So I heard. Is your husband here with you?"

"No." The last thing she wanted to discuss with MacCrea was her farce of a marriage. "He's at home. It's a busy time at the farm. He couldn't get away." She felt as if she was sitting astride a horse with a hump in its back — all tense and waiting for it to explode in a bucking spree, not knowing when it was going to happen or which way it would jump first, but knowing it was coming and knowing she had to be ready for it or she'd end up being thrown.

Eden turned around and said, "That's our barn, isn't it, Mommy? That's where Windstorm is staying, isn't it?"

"Yes, honey."

"Wait until you see him, MacCrea. He's the most beautiful horse there ever was," she declared.

"His name is Mr. Wilder, Eden." Abbie couldn't bear to hear her daughter address him so familiarly.

"She can call me MacCrea. I don't mind."

"I do. And I'll thank you not to interfere when I'm correcting my daughter," Abbie retorted.

Quickening her steps, Abbie crossed the last few yards of sand and entered the dark shade of the barn's interior ahead of MacCrea. Ben released Eden's hand and she ran ahead to a stall a third of the way down on the left side. "Windstorm, we're back. And we've brought you a visitor."

In spite of herself, Abbie smiled when she saw the stallion lift his head and nicker at the child running toward his stall. In her opinion, Windstorm was as close to perfection as any horse she'd ever seen, but of all his attributes, she considered his gentle spirit to be the most precious.

While the stallion had all the fire and flash of an Arabian, it seemed to come from a joy of life and a love of freedom rather than from any sense of wildness. And every one of his first crop of foals out of grade mares had inherited not only a lot of his look but also his disposition, including one out of a dam that was notoriously ill-tempered. The real test of any sire was his ability to pass many of his good traits on to his get. Abbie had the feeling that she was the owner of just such a prepotent stallion.

Abbie walked over to the stall to admire her stallion, something she was unashamed to admit she never tired of doing. At five years, Windstorm had grayed out to an almost pure white, with only a few streaks of silver-gray still visible in his long mane and tail. The blackness of his skin was revealed in the darkness of his muzzle and around his eyes, making them seem even larger.

"How's my man?" Abbie crooned as the stallion lowered his head to let her scratch his favorite place, just below the ear.

"I knew you had to have one in your life," MacCrea murmured, his voice coming from directly behind her. She hadn't realized he was so close, but a quick backward glance confirmed he stood mere inches away.

Her heart started pounding so loudly she couldn't hear anything else. Somehow she knew that all she had to do was turn around and face him, and she would once more feel his arms around her and know again the excitement of his kiss. That was all it would take — just one move on her part, one silent invitation. And some traitorous part of her soul wanted her to make it.

But Abbie wouldn't let herself be fooled into loving him again. Instead she stepped sideways, moving well away from him. "You were so interested in seeing my stallion, Mr. Wilder, go ahead and take a good look." She was surprised at how calm her voice sounded, considering the way she was shaking inside.

As MacCrea stepped up to the stall, Eden clambered atop the bales of straw next to him so she could see over the wooden partition. "Isn't he beautiful?" she declared. "I saw him the night he was born. There was an awful storm, and the wind blew and blew. That's how he got his name, Windstorm."

MacCrea frowned. "You must have been awfully small yourself."

"I was a little baby," she admitted. "But Mommy says I laughed and laughed when I saw him 'cause I was so happy about it." When the stallion affectionately nuzzled the top of her head, Eden grabbed his nose and pulled his head down, then lovingly rubbed a chiseled cheek. "Stop it, you silly boy," she scolded, then said to MacCrea, "See how you can see all his veins. That means he's dry. That's a good thing."

"You certainly know a lot about horses."

"I do," she agreed. "I have a pony of my very own. His name is JoJo. You'd like him, too."

Watching the two of them, with their heads so close together, Abbie wondered how MacCrea could fail to see the resemblance. To her, it was much too obvious: the dark, wavy hair, the full, thick eyebrows, the same chin and mouth. And the hands — Abbie caught the faint curling of Eden's little fingers as she fondled the stallion's head. She couldn't let him find out. She just couldn't.

"Eden, come down from there." She had to separate them, get Eden far away from MacCrea.

"But —"

"Don't argue with me. Just do as you're told. You've bent Mr. Wilder's ear long enough." As Eden reluctantly scrambled off the bales, Abbie caught hold of her hand and led her over to Ben. "Take her to the car and I'll meet you there in a few minutes."

"Good-bye, Mac — Mr. Wilder." Eden half turned to wave to him.

" 'Bye, Eden. I'll see you again sometime."

Something snapped inside her, releasing all the emotions she'd been holding so tightly in check. They swamped her as she swung around to face Mac-Crea. "No, you won't! You leave my daughter alone. Leave me alone."

She knew her voice had quavered badly, but she wasn't aware of the sudden rush of tears into her eyes until MacCrea cupped the side of her face in his hand and wiped away a tear with his thumb. "You're crying, Abbie. Why?" The gentleness of his voice, the concern in it, almost proved to be her undoing. She longed to lose herself in the touch of his hand.

But she couldn't. Neither could she answer him. Instead she pulled away from him and pivoted toward the stall, turning her back on him. She hadn't dreamed that after all this time — after all he'd done to her — she could still be so physically attracted to him. Why was her psyche so twisted that she kept loving men she couldn't trust?

"You haven't forgotten either, have you?" MacCrea asked.

"I never tried," she lied.

"Will you have dinner with me tonight . . . for old time's sake? You can bring your daughter and Ben along if it will make you feel safer," he mocked gently, confidently.

"The only 'old times' I'm interested in are the ones where you were gone. Why don't you arrange for that to happen again?"

"Hold it. You were the one who walked out," he reminded her tersely.

His anger gave her the control she needed to face him once more. "I was, wasn't I? I guess I just didn't like the way you used people."

"You accuse me of using people. What about you? Or don't you want to admit the real reason you married that farmer? You don't love him. You only married him to get your hands on land that originally belonged to your family."

"I don't have to ask who told you that. So why don't you go find Rachel? She's the one you came here to see anyway."

"I'm here to meet Lane."

"Then go find him. But stay away from me." She walked off briskly, her throat tight and a dull ache in her heart. It hurt more than she cared to admit that she hadn't guessed wrong. MacCrea was here to see Lane and Rachel.

34

WITH A NOD of his head, MacCrea absently acknowledged the hotel maid's greeting as he walked down the wide corridor to the double doors of the suite at the end. He knocked twice and waited, gnawed by the restlessness that had been eating at him since he'd left the showgrounds.

"Who is it?" The thick doors muffled the woman's voice, but he still recognized it as Rachel's.

"MacCrea Wilder." He still wasn't sure why he was there — why he hadn't headed straight for the airport and boarded the first plane out of Phoenix. Maybe he just didn't want Abbie to have the satisfaction of driving him out of town.

The security chain rattled a half-second before the left door swung open to admit him. Rachel moved away from it as he stepped inside. Her high heels made almost no sound on the thick carpet as she crossed to an oval mirror on the wall.

"The bar is fully stocked. Help yourself." She nodded in the direction of the paneled bar located in the corner of the suite's spacious sitting room.

"Thanks. I think I will." MacCrea tossed his hat on a rose-colored chair as he walked over to the bar and poured himself a glass of Chivas and water. "Where's Lane?"

"He's still in Houston." She removed an earring from the jewelry case on the side table in front of her and held it up to her ear.

MacCrea stopped with the glass halfway to his mouth. "He told me he was going to be here."

"I know. We were supposed to fly in together. But Alex has a bad case of the sniffles and Lane was afraid to leave him. You know how he dotes on his son."

Unconsciously MacCrea crooked an eyebrow at the hard, clipped edge of resentment in her voice, and the almost total lack of concern she expressed for her son. It was in such contrast to Abbie and her highly protective attitude toward her daughter.

"You don't sound worried about him." He sipped at his drink, studying her thoughtfully over the rim of the glass.

"Naturally I'm concerned when he's ill, but it isn't as if he's being left alone. Mrs. Weldon is a registered nurse. She is more than qualified to look after him. But Lane doesn't see it that way. Alex is his son."

"He's your son, too," MacCrea reminded her.

"Is he?" The words seemed to slip out. She attempted to cover them with a forced laugh. "Can you imagine a child of mine being terrified of horses? When he was two and three years old he used to scream his head off if one came within five feet of him. No, Alex is very much Daddy's boy."

"It won't always be that way."

"I wish I could believe that." She sighed heavily, suddenly no longer trying to mask her feelings. "You know that old saying, MacCrea, 'Two's company and three's a crowd'? I'm the one who makes it a crowd."

She looked so lonely and vulnerable that MacCrea couldn't help feeling a little sorry for her. "Lane does love you."

"Yes." Her mouth twisted in a smile that wasn't very pretty. "I'm the mother of his child. And that's a poor reason to love a woman, MacCrea." After trying on several earrings, she finally chose a pair of Harry Winston diamond-studded Burmese sapphires and clipped them onto her ears, then removed the matching diamond and sapphire necklace from the jewelry case.

"I suppose." But her comment made him wonder about other things — like the possibility that Abbie loved Dobie because he was the father of her child.

"When did you arrive?" She looped the necklace around her neck and fastened the clasp.

"About three or four hours ago. I figured I'd find you and Lane at the showgrounds, so I went there to look for you first. I ran into Abbie." He wasn't sure why he had told Rachel that. He hadn't intended to mention his meeting with her.

"I heard she was here." The icy-sharp bite to her voice left little room for doubt about her feelings toward Abbie. Not that MacCrea had expected her animosity toward her to have mellowed in any way over the years.

"Have you seen her stallion?"

"Oh, yes." She laughed shortly, with more bitterness than humor. "She's made sure I have."

"What do you mean?" He frowned at the curious statement.

"She makes a point of riding that stallion in the field right next to River Bend. I know she does it deliberately. She could ride that horse anywhere, but she has to do it right in my own backyard." Rachel swung away from the mirror and faced him, holding her head unnaturally high. "Believe me, she's never going to win the championship."

"You sound very confident of that."

"I am. The horse business is no different from any other business. Your success depends on the people you know and the amount of money you have available to promote your stallion. . . . Do you have any plans for this evening?" Rachel asked as she walked over to a chair and picked up the beaded evening bag lying on the seat.

"Nothing particular." He shrugged.

"Good. Then you can be my escort tonight since Lane isn't here." She picked up her mink jacket and handed it to him. "The Danberrys are having an aisle party. Ross Tibbs, the country singer, is supposed to be there."

"The one from Houston?" MacCrea set his drink glass down to help her on with the fur jacket.

"The same. He has a good-sized farm in Tennessee now where he raises Arabian horses. I've run into him a few times at some of the bigger shows." Pausing, she glanced at MacCrea over her shoulder. Just for an instant, the shadowed blue of her eyes reminded him of Abbie. "You will take me, won't you, MacCrea? I hate to go to these affairs alone."

"Sure." For some reason he was reluctant to try to get a flight out tonight.

And his other alternative — spending the night alone in a hotel room — appealed to him even less.

Rachel blinked as a flashbulb went off directly in front of her, momentarily blinding her. The stall area was jammed with people sipping champagne, munching on caviar, and wearing everything from Lauren to Levi, high fashion to no fashion. Everybody who was anybody in the Arabian horse business had come to the private party, making a curious gathering of celebrity entertainers, business giants, and the social elite hobnobbing with the top trainers, stud managers, and professionals in the business.

"I was told this champagne is for the lady with the bluest eyes. Where do you suppose I could find her?" The familiar voice came from behind her.

Rachel turned, her pulse hammering erratically. "Ross. How wonderful to see you again." She tried to inject the proper amount of pleasure into her voice as she accepted the wineglass from him. "Someone mentioned you might come to the party tonight. Did you just arrive?"

"No. I've probably been here about forty-five minutes."

"Really?" She pretended she hadn't known, even though she'd seen him arrive and made a special effort to ignore him. He didn't look or dress that much differently from when she'd first met him, but the trappings of success were visible. The bright blue shirt was silk, not polyester; the jacket was genuine suede, not an imitation; the jeans carried a designer label instead of J. C. Penney's; and the conchos on his hatband were solid silver, not silver-plated. More than that, everybody knew who Ross Tibbs was, and nearly all of them wanted to make sure Ross knew who they were.

"Where's your husband?" he inquired, his gaze never leaving her face, his intent study of her as unsettling as it had always been.

Rachel sipped at the bubbly wine, her palate sufficiently educated to recognize it was not one of the better champagnes, yet its effect on her was just as heady. "He's still in Houston. He plans to join me here in a few days."

She was tired of making excuses for Lane's absence from these affairs. If it wasn't business then it was little Alex that kept him away. Lane never seemed to have time for her anymore. His priorities were very clear to her: Alex was first; business, second; and she came in a poor third. Maybe it was wrong to feel jealous of her own son, but she had never anticipated that Lane would love him more than he loved her. Yet he did. There must be something wrong with her, some reason why people always loved someone else more than they did her. It wasn't fair.

"Tell me about this yearling filly of yours, Ross," she said, struggling to make conversation. "Everyone is talking about her."

"Have you seen her yet?"

"No."

Before she could react, the mink jacket that she had casually draped over her arm was in his hands. "Come on. We're going over to the barn so I can show her to you." He slung the fur loosely around her shoulders and kept his arm there to guide her toward the exit.

"Now? But . . ." Rachel protested half-heartedly, secretly wanting to be coerced into accompanying him and feeling vaguely guilty because she did.

"Wait until you see her." Ross propelled her through the crowd, talking over her faint objection. "She's a jewel. That's what I named her: Jewel of the Desert — in Arabic, of course, but I can't pronounce that."

Out of the corner of her eye, Rachel noticed MacCrea standing off to one side of the party crowd, talking to some man. She looked in his direction and saw that he was watching them. This was exactly the sort of situation with Ross she had wanted to avoid. That's why she had asked MacCrea to escort her to the party — to be her buffer, her shield. But now that it was happening, she didn't want it to stop. Yet she worried that MacCrea might tell Lane that she had gone off alone with Ross. She tried to convince herself that she had nothing to hide from Lane. After all, she was just going to see Ross's filly. It was perfectly innocent.

"Ross, please." She hung back, forcing him to pause as she glanced anxiously again in MacCrea's direction. "I really should let MacCrea know where I'm going. He brought me here. I just can't run off like this. What will he think?"

"Where is he?"

"Over there." Rachel pointed to him.

Changing course, he walked her over to MacCrea. "I'm taking Rachel to see my filly. Want to come along?" Rachel held her breath, partly afraid he'd accept and partly afraid he wouldn't.

MacCrea shook his head. "No, thanks. One horse looks the same as another to me."

"Tell you what, Wilder. There's no need for you hanging around here getting bored. I've got a car and driver right outside. I can make sure Rachel gets safely back to her hotel." Turning on a smile, Ross looked sideways at her. She was extremely conscious that his arm was still around her shoulders. "If that's okay with you, of course."

"I suppose it really doesn't matter how I get back," she began uncertainly, unable to tell by MacCrea's impassive expression what he actually thought. "I wouldn't want to inconvenience either of you."

"Whatever you want to do will be fine with me." MacCrea shrugged his indifference.

"Good. I'll take her back then." As they walked away, he tipped his head close to hers and murmured near her ear, "Didn't I tell you I'd handle it?"

"Yes." Maybe it was wrong to feel the way she did, but she was glad he had.

Any lingering misgivings fled the instant she saw the year-old Arabian. Totally enchanted by the bronze bay filly's exquisitely classic looks, she could talk of nothing else. She wanted to buy the horse on the spot. When Ross refused, insisting the filly wasn't for sale at any price, she begged him to breed the filly to her stallion, Sirocco, when she turned three, and Rachel made him promise that he'd sell her the foal.

Somehow she lost all track of time. She didn't even realize they never made it back to the party until she handed Ross the room key to her hotel suite. By then, it was too late to be concerned about any comments other guests might have made about the way she and Ross had disappeared without a word to their hosts.

"I think our arrangement calls for a drink, don't you?" Ross pushed open the door and followed her into the suite.

"I do, but you'd better make mine weak," Rachel declared, sighing blissfully as she tossed the mink jacket onto the sofa. "I already feel light-headed, and I'm not sure if I should blame the champagne or the prospect of a foal out of our two horses." She walked over to the small bar and leaned on the countertop to watch him prepare the drinks, barely able to contain the sense of excitement she felt. "Are you certain there's no way I can persuade you to sell that filly, Ross?"

"I can't think of anything I'd love more than to have you try. Lord knows, you're the only one who could tempt me into changing my mind." With the drinks in hand, he came out from behind the bar and walked around to her. Not more than a hand's width separated them when he stopped.

His nearness, the intimate look in his eyes, the feather-light brush of his fingers when she took the glass from him — all combined to stimulate the desire she'd tried to control from the outset. "You almost make me want to try," she admitted, catching the husky note of longing in her voice and knowing it shouldn't be there.

Reaching up, he lightly touched an earring with the tip of his finger. "Has anyone ever told you that your eyes are bluer than these sapphires?"

"Yes." Lane had, and Rachel wished Ross hadn't reminded her of that. All in one motion, she shoved the glass onto the counter and sidestepped Ross to walk over to the oval mirror.

As she stared at her reflection, she caught the diamond sparkle of the Harry Winston earrings and reached up to remove them slowly, one by one. Another gift, that's all they were. Gifts and empty words were the only things she received from Lane anymore, and all she had ever wanted was his love.

This was the way it had been with Dean, too, she realized, suddenly recognizing that she'd come full circle. Her reflected expression became grim as she considered the awful irony of the situation. She was as lonely now with Lane as she had been with Dean, forced to be satisfied with the scant remnants of his time and affection. All the expensive presents in the world couldn't make up for the love she'd been cheated out of again. What was wrong with her? Why couldn't anybody love her? She railed silently at the unfairness as she struggled to unfasten the safety clasp on her expensive necklace, a necklace she now hated.

"I'll do that for you." Ross's reflection joined hers in the mirror as he came up behind her.

When Rachel felt the warmth of his fingers on her neck, for an instant everything inside her became still. She stared at him in the mirror, absently studying his boyishly handsome features, remembering that reckless, happy-go-lucky smile that so often curved his mouth and that brashly flirtatious way he usually looked at her. She caught herself wanting to touch his curly brown hair, no longer hidden beneath his cowboy hat, and discover for herself if it was as soft and thick as it looked.

As she stood with her hand at her throat, holding the necklace in place, she considered the wedding ring Lane had placed on her finger. Once that ring had signified happiness and security to her. Now, when she looked at it, it meant nothing to her — just another pretty bauble Lane had given her to placate his conscience.

With its ends no longer fastened, the weight of the necklace sagged against her hand. She curled her fingers around the cold, hard stones and pulled them slowly away from her throat. A wonderful warmth replaced the inanimate feel of the necklace as Ross bent his head and pressed his lips against the side of her neck where a second ago the necklace had lain. Shuddering with the intense pleasure the kiss had evoked, she turned to face him, desperately needing to be loved by someone.

"Why did you do that?" She clutched the necklace tightly while his hands moved over the bare points of her shoulders, lightly rubbing and kneading her flesh with an odd reverence.

"Because I love you, Rachel. I've always loved you. You're the inspiration for every song about love, heartbreak, and loneliness I've ever written. I love you," he repeated, his voice so soft, yet so forceful. "And, right or wrong, I want to make love to you. If it's not what you want, tell me now. I don't know how much longer I can stand being this close to you without holding you and loving you."

"Ross, don't say you love me if you don't mean it. I couldn't endure that." She choked on a sob.

"I love you, my beautiful, beautiful blue eyes." He moved even closer, his mouth so near to hers that she could feel the warmth of his breath on her lips. "Let me show you how much I love you."

"Yes," she cried softly, and hungrily kissed him, going into his arms and clinging to him desperately, unable to get enough of the loving passion he showered on her. "I need you," she murmured against the smoothness of his shaven cheek. "You don't know how much I need you, Ross."

Lifting her off the floor, he cradled her body in his arms and carried her over to the bedroom door, kicking it open with his foot, kissing her all the while. It was like a romantic scene in a movie, only it was happening to her. She was the one being carried off by a man who loved her more than anything in the world.

Letting her down gently, he turned her to face him and took her in his arms, his lips caressing her brow and cheek with feather-soft kisses. She was trembling, frightened and excited by her own daring, as she felt his hand gliding up the back of her strapless gown, seeking and finding the zipper. The sound it made as he pulled it down reminded Rachel of a cat's soft purr. That's what she felt like —a purring cat rubbing herself against him and wanting to be stroked and petted.

As the loosened gown of velvet and satin began to slip, his hands helped it fall the rest of the way until the Blass original lay in a pile around her feet. A shiver rippled over her bared flesh in reaction to the sudden coolness. Needing his warmth, she pushed open his soft suede jacket and wound her arms tightly around his middle, pressing her body against him and feeling the heat of his body flowing through the thin silk of his shirt.

He cupped a hand under her chin and lifted it so he could once again kiss her lips. When his hat got in the way, he took it off and sent it sailing into a corner of the darkened bedroom, the silver conchos flashing in a whirling circle of reflected light, spinning off into the blackness.

As he shrugged out of his jacket, Rachel felt the play of the lean muscles in his back and closed her eyes, wanting to make sensations the reality. But his hands forced her to stand away from him, giving him room to pull apart the snaps holding the front of his shirt closed.

When she saw the curly dark hairs that covered his chest, she turned away and slowly began to remove her undergarments, her apprehension growing. She had gone too far to stop now, and truthfully she didn't want to stop, but she was afraid of standing naked before him — afraid he wouldn't want the plain Rachel he saw. Without the jewels and the designer gowns, that's all she was: the Rachel that nobody ever loved or wanted.

Yet she had to know. Slowly she turned to face him, grateful for the concealing shadows in the dimly lighted room. She heard him draw in his breath. Tentatively she looked up, but his arms were already going around her and his mouth coming down to cover her lips hotly, his tongue licking them open then plunging inside with a fervor and an urgency that caught her up in the force of his desire.

Then he lowered her onto the bed and joined her, his hands running all over her body as if they couldn't get enough of her — caressing the roundness of her breasts and rolling her hardened nipples between the calloused tips of his fingers, stroking her bottom and gliding between her legs, his fingers seeking the velvety moistness of her. Rachel shuddered uncontrollably at their entry, her hips arching instinctively to take them in.

He did not give her that pleasure for long, and she made a vague protest when he took his hand away. But already he was shifting to lie between her parted legs, his bone-hard shaft probing for the opening. Rachel tensed. She didn't mean to resist him, but she couldn't help herself. The reaction was automatic. As he entered her, Ross stretched out to lie on top of her. She tried to respond to the movement of his hips; she honestly tried, desperately wanting it to be different with him, desperately wanting to achieve climax with him inside her and enjoy more than the sensuous nibbling along her neck. For once in her life, she didn't want to fake it.

His hands slid down to cup her bottom, holding her cheeks to meet the grinding thrust of his hips and directing their movements. As the sweet pressure started to build, Rachel clutched at him, digging her fingers into his shoulders to hold him there, afraid he'd stop, afraid the wonderful rhythm would break. But it didn't. It didn't.

"Yes, yes, yes," she cried out without meaning to and felt the tempo of his thrusting hips change, driving deeper, lifting her higher, until the marvelous agony of it all exploded in a rush of pure rapture. Within seconds Ross shuddered against her, convulsed by his own throes of satisfaction.

As she lay in his arms, savoring that sensation of absolute fulfillment, she felt truly loved. Drenched in the scent of their lovemaking, she breathed it in, the musky odor headier than the most expensive Parisian perfume. She turned onto her side so she could see him, this man who had made her feel like a woman. She ran her hand over his chest, enjoying the sensation of his bare skin and silken hairs.

He caught hold if it and carried her fingertips to his lips. "I wish I were a poet, Rachel," he murmured. "I wish I knew the beautiful words to describe the satin smoothness of your body and the sweet perfection of your breasts. But the words that come to my mind sound so ridiculously corny —"

She covered his mouth with her hand. "Just love me, Ross," she whispered. "Love me." She said the last against his mouth as she took her hand away and replaced it with her lips.

35 ∿

PEOPLE SWARMED ABOUT the motel lobby, some arriving, some departing, and others entering or leaving the adjoining coffee shop. From her seat on a couch in the lobby, Abbie could see the elevators — when someone wasn't blocking her view, that is, which was nearly all the time. Impatiently she flipped through the morning edition of the Phoenix newspaper while she waited for Ben to come back. She couldn't understand what was keeping him. He'd only gone to get a jacket from his room. She had wanted to exercise Windstorm before the work arena became crowded with other horses and riders getting ready for their morning classes.

"Do you see Ben yet, Mommy?" Eden stood on the cushioned couch and leaned sideways against Abbie, trying to see around the people walking by.

"No, dear."

"Windstorm is gonna be wondering where we are, isn't he?"

"Yes. Now sit down. You know you're not supposed to stand on the furniture." Abbie absently turned another page of the newspaper and shook it flat.

"But I can't see, then," Eden reasoned, "and you told me to watch for Ben."

A grainy newspaper photograph practically leaped off the page at Abbie. She didn't hear Eden's reply or notice that she didn't sit down as she was told. She was too distracted by MacCrea's likeness staring back at her, exact in every detail, from the lazy gleam in his dark eyes to the complacent slant of his mustached mouth. He seemed to be mocking her, as if he knew she'd see this photograph of him . . . and the woman with him, none other than Rachel Canfield.

She told herself she didn't care, that he meant nothing to her anymore, that all she had to do was turn the page again. Instead she folded the paper open to the photograph and read the caption. "Rachel Canfield, wife of industrialist magnate Lane Canfield, escorted by millionaire wildcatter MacCrea Wilder to a party held last night at —"

"Look, Mommy!" Eden excitedly tapped her shoulder. "There's MacCrea!"

"I see him." She shifted her eyes back to the picture.

"MacCrea! Wait!" Eden bounced across the cushion in her scramble to get off the couch.

Startled, Abbie looked up as Eden darted toward a man crossing the lobby. MacCrea. "Eden, come back here!" She hurried after her, but it was too late. MacCrea had already seen Eden and stopped.

"Hello, short stuff." Smiling, he rumpled the top of her dark, wavy hair. "Don't tell me your mother's lost again." When he glanced up, he looked directly at her. Although his expression never changed, Abbie sensed shutters closing and a mask dropping into place.

"No." Eden laughed. "She's sitting right over there. We're waiting for Ben."

As Abbie caught her daughter by the shoulders and pulled her back out of MacCrea's reach, she realized she still had the folded newspaper in her hand. "There you are, Mommy. See, she's not lost."

"Come on, Eden." She took her firmly by the hand. "You're bothering Mr. Wilder."

Resisting Abbie's attempt to lead her away, Eden looked at him and frowned. "Was I bothering you?"

"No, of course not."

"Don't encourage her," Abbie warned, keeping her voice low to conceal her anger.

"How come you got that?" Eden pointed to the garment bag slung over his shoulder. "Are you going somewhere?"

"Yes, I'm leaving. I have a plane to catch," he replied, addressing his answer to Abbie.

"But aren't you going to stay and see Windstorm win?" Eden protested.

"I can't. I've finished all my business here and I have to get back to work."

"Business?" Abbie scoffed bitterly. "That's not what the morning paper called it. Here. You can read it for yourself." She shoved the newspaper at him. "Maybe you'd like to tell me again how little contact you have with her!" She had no intention of waiting around to see what kind of trumped-up explanation he would make. As she scooped Eden into her arms, she saw Ben coming into the lobby and headed directly for the front door to their car parked outside.

"Mommy, how come you don't like MacCrea?" Eden asked as Abbie lifted her onto the seat.

At almost the same instant, MacCrea walked out of the motel and signaled for a cab. Abbie watched him, with more pain than anger. "You wouldn't understand, Eden," she said regretfully and climbed into the car with her daughter.

36 ✒

MORNINGS, AFTERNOONS, and evenings, Rachel grasped every opportunity to be with Ross. The lavish parties and equally glamorous sales that were an integral part of the Scottsdale Show scene enabled her to meet him discreetly. Always arriving and leaving separately, they attended the elegant gala held at the Loews', an elaborate fete given at the Wrigley mansion, the staid brunch at the Biltmore, an intimate dinner party in a luxury condo, and countless casual aisle parties and formal receptions.

They arranged to sit at the same tables in the exclusive "gold card" sections and view the Arabian horses offered for sale in spectacularly staged productions against backdrops of larger-than-life reproductions of art masterpieces, a recreation of the Palace of Versailles, and sleek contemporary settings of chrome and crystal. They sipped champagne together and ate chocolate-dipped strawberries while celebrity entertainers performed for them and Arabians came floating onto the runways through mists of white fog.

They sat together in the show stands and offered each other moral support when their respective horses competed in elimination classes to qualify for the finals. But then there were the nights — the madly passionate nights when Ross made love to her so thoroughly and so completely that she found it impossible to doubt the depth of his love. It seemed that nothing could mar this happiness she'd found.

She slipped the satin nightgown over her head and felt the sensuous material slide down to cover her naked body. Absently she adjusted the narrow straps over her shoulders as she turned back to the king-size bed where Ross lay, watching her.

"You are supposed to be getting dressed," she chided softly.

"I was trying to decide if you're more beautiful with clothes or without."

"And?"

"I can't make up my mind." He raised himself up on an elbow and reached for her hand to draw her close to the bed. "Why don't you take that gown off so I can decide."

"No, you don't." She leaned away from him, slightly pulling from his hand without making any real effort to get free. "It's late, almost midnight. And I have to get up in the morning. Tomorrow's the big day." Sirocco was scheduled to compete in the finals of the halter class.

"So?"

"So, I need my sleep. And so do you."

"Why don't I sleep here tonight with you? I want to wake up in the morning and find you lying beside me."

"Ross, we can't." She wished he wouldn't ask. "Suppose you're seen leaving my suite in the morning. What are people going to think?"

"The same thing they think when they see me sneaking out of your room in the middle of the night." He pulled her down onto the bed and began kissing her arm. "You don't really think we're fooling anybody, do you? By now, everyone's seen the way I look at you with all the love in my heart shining in my eyes."

"I suppose." But she didn't want to consider that.

"I do love you, Rachel. And I don't care if the whole world knows it."

"Ross, I —" As she reached up to stroke his face, the telephone on the nightstand rang shrilly. Rachel jumped, startled by the harsh sound. For an instant, she could only stare at it as it rang a second time. She glanced hesitantly at Ross, noting his suddenly sober look, then picked up the receiver, cutting off the bell in the middle of its third ring. "Hello?"

"Rachel, darling, did I wake you?" Lane's voice came clearly over the line.

"Yes," she lied, clutching the phone a little closer and turning more of her back to Ross. "Is something wrong? Alex — is he all right?"

"Yes, he's fine," Lane assured her. "As a matter of fact, he didn't even run a fever today."

"Then . . ." If it wasn't an emergency — and from the sound of his voice, it wasn't — why was he calling her at this hour of the night?

"I tried to reach you several times today."

"You did? I . . . . I'm sorry. I've been on the run so much today that I never checked to see if I had any messages. I would have called but . . ." She hadn't wanted to talk to him. She didn't now, not with Ross lying here.

"I thought that was probably the case. And I'm sorry to call you so late and get you out of bed, but I wanted you to know that I'm flying out of Houston tomorrow. I'll have to stop and pick up MacCrea at our field in West Texas. I have some papers to go over with him. But we should be landing in Phoenix around noon."

"You will?" She didn't know what to think, what to say.

"I promised you I'd be there for the finals. Don't I always keep my word?" Lane chided affectionately.

"Yes, of course," she replied.

"You don't sound very happy about it."

"Oh, I am," she said in a rush. "It's just that . . . I'm only half-awake. Why don't I pick you up at the airport tomorrow?"

"I'd like that." He sounded satisfied with her explanation. "You go back to sleep, dear, and I'll see you tomorrow — correction, today."

"Yes. Good night."

"Good night, dear."

Rachel waited for the click on the other end of the line before she slowly replaced the receiver on its cradle. As she brought her hands back to her lap, she unconsciously touched the wedding ring on her finger.

"Your husband?" Ross guessed.

"Yes. He's flying in tomorrow."

The mattress dipped beneath her as Ross pushed himself into a sitting position behind her. He ran his hand up her arm in a caress that was no different from countless others she'd experienced, yet this time Rachel felt tense at his touch. That telephone call had complicated the situation. Not ten minutes ago it had all seemed so simple: Ross loved her; that Lane was her husband had seemed totally immaterial. But it wasn't.

"Are you going to tell him about us?" Ross asked, slipping aside the strap of her gown to nuzzle her shoulder.

The thought frightened her. What if she was wrong? What if Ross didn't really love her? This had all happened so quickly; how could she be sure? Agitated by his suggestion, Rachel pushed off the bed and took several steps away from it. "I don't see how I can, Ross. MacCrea will be with him," she reasoned with a forced calm.

"Rachel —"

"Please, Ross, I think it would be best if you'd get dressed and leave now." Nervously she twisted her hands together, unable to look at him.

"No." She heard the rustle of bedcovers being thrown aside and the squeak of the bedsprings, followed by the faint thud of his feet hitting the floor. "I'm not going anywhere until we get a few things straight." As she started to turn, he caught her arm and swung her the rest of the way around to face him. He wore a desperate look as he searched her face for some clue. "Just what are you telling me? 'It's been fun, but good-bye'? Because I'm not going to accept that. I can't just walk away and forget any of this happened. I love you. It isn't just a passing thing with me."

"Ross, I want to see you again, too. But, with Lane here, that will be impossible. And you have that television special to tape and all your other commitments to keep. It's not going to be as easy for us to meet after tonight."

"You could always leave Lane and come with me." He tried to draw her into his embrace, but Rachel flattened her hands against his chest to keep some distance between them.

"I want to be with you, Ross. I need you, more than you'll ever know. But, if you really love me, don't ask me to do that. I can't, not now anyway. It's too soon. There are too many other things to consider. I'm not even sure if I know this is right — for either of us."

"If I love you and you love me, it has to be right."

"You don't understand." She shook her head. "Once I thought I loved Lane, too. I want to be sure this time."

"Darling . . ." He started to argue, then paused and sighed heavily. "All right, I won't rush you, but it isn't going to be easy. Because I won't be happy until you're with me every day and every night. I know I'm not as rich as your husband is, but I'm not poor by any means, not anymore. I promise you you'll have everything you've ever wanted. Just name it and it's yours."

"I don't want anything." She didn't understand why every man thought he had to buy her love with expensive presents.

Another twenty minutes passed before Rachel was finally able to persuade Ross to get dressed and leave and she had time alone to think. As she lay awake, she almost wished she'd never gotten involved with him. True, she had been happy, but she'd been happy other times, too, and it had never lasted. Why hadn't she remembered that sooner?

ABBIE'S LEGS FELT as if they were made out of Eden's Silly Putty. And if the flutterings in her stomach were caused by butterflies, then Abbie was certain they were the biggest butterflies in the whole world. She'd been nervous before, but never like this.

She shivered, but it was from nerves, not the cool desert air. For at least the tenth time, Abbie brushed an imaginary speck of dirt off Windstorm's white satin coat and checked his polished black hooves while she waited for the stallion class to be called.

"This is it, Ben," she said grimly, wishing she felt as calm as he looked standing there holding Eden in his arms. "Windstorm has to win. He just has to. I couldn't stand it if Rachel walked away with the championship."

"He'll win, Mommy." Eden leaned over and petted the stallion's neck. "I just know he will. He's the most beautiful horse ever."

"Beauty alone does not make a stallion great, child," Ben lectured sternly. "If Windstorm should win this title, what would it prove? That he has courage, stamina, heart? No. It is the racetrack and only the racetrack that would show his true worth. This class is no more than a beauty contest."

"I'm not going to argue." Abbie knew she had about as much chance of changing Ben's mind on that as she did of convincing a bulldog to let go once he'd clamped his jaws on something. "But if he wins here and we race him this summer, we can have both."

"I'll bet he can run faster than any horse in the world," Eden declared.

Abbie started to correct her daughter, then changed her mind. She didn't feel like explaining why a Thoroughbred could run faster than an Arabian. Over the years, Thoroughbreds had been selectively bred for speed, even though the lineage of every one of those horses traced directly back to three Arabian stallions. Arabians, too, were born to run, but their physical differences gave them an astounding ability to carry weight and amazing endurance. But trying to make a five-year-old understand that would take too long.

"Hadn't you two better go get your seats?" Abbie suggested, wanting a few minutes alone to settle her nerves, if she could, before the class was called. "You be good and stay with Ben. Promise?"

"I promise." Eden wrapped her arms around Abbie's neck and gave her a big hug and a kiss on the cheek.

As she watched them leave, she realized that for the first time she was going head-to-head with Rachel, her stallion against Rachel's. She had to win. She couldn't lose to her again.

All around her, grooms feverishly brushed, combed, and polished their respective stallions whether they needed it or not, while the trainers jiggled lead ropes, swished their whips, or quieted a stallion already too fired up by the electric tension in the air. Alone, without a cadre of stable hands to assist her, Abbie smoothed the stallion's long forelock, arranging it to fall down the center of his forehead.

It felt as if her heart leaped into her throat when the call for the stallion class finally came. An eternity of seconds seemed to tick by before it was her turn to lead Windstorm into the arena. "Okay, fella," she whispered as she swung him in a tight circle to head for the in gate. "Show them who's the best."

"Heads up!" someone shouted as Abbie ran toward the arena gate, giving the stallion plenty of slack.

Windstorm bounded past her, a white flame of motion, neck tautly arched, mane and tail flying. As he charged into the arena ahead of her, Abbie knew their entrance looked to all the world as if he had bolted on her. But the lead never went taut as the stallion swung back to her and reared briefly on his hind legs.

When she heard the roar of appreciation from the crowd in the stands, Abbie smiled. "They're yours, Windstorm. Make 'em notice you." He trotted after her, floating over the arena floor as she moved to the outer perimeter of the oval ring. She knew they made an eye-catching pair — a sixteen-hand white stallion and a petite dark-haired woman. And she knew Windstorm loved the noise and attention of the crowd. The more they cheered, the more animated he became, firing up as only an Arabian could.

"Go get 'em, Abbie!" a man yelled to her as they passed his seat.

Abbie stopped Windstorm a short distance from the next stallion to wait for the rest of the qualifiers to enter the arena. Officially, the judging didn't begin until the two-minute gate closed. She glanced at the section of seats where Ben and Eden were supposed to be sitting. About ten rows up, a small arm waved wildly. Smiling, Abbie started to bring her attention back to Windstorm, but something — a movement or a sound from the seats to her right — distracted her.

With a sense of shock, she discovered MacCrea staring back at her. All the faces around him were a blur. His alone was distinct. What was he doing there? Why had he come back? Half turning in his seat, he looked in the general direction of Ben and Eden's seats. Abbie felt her heart knocking against her ribs.

At that instant, the man sitting beside MacCrea leaned over and claimed his attention. Abbie recognized that distinctive mane of white hair. Lane and Rachel were seated with him.

"The gate is closed," the announcer stated, his voice booming over the public-address system. "The judging of the stallion halter class will begin now. The judges ask that you space your horses along the rail and walk them, please."

On either side of her there was movement. Fighting the sudden attack of nerves, Abbie led an eager, dancing Windstorm in a snug circle, then walked him along the rail, letting him show off his leggy, smooth stride. The stallion was ready to get down to business, but she wasn't.

How many times had Ben told her not to look at the crowd? Don't pay any attention to them, he'd said. It's just you and your horse. Block everything else out. Don't worry about what the other horses are doing or how they're showing or whether the judges are watching you. Make him look his best at all times. Concentrate on the horse.

It began: the walking, the trotting, the posing with all four feet in picture-perfect position, tail up, ears pricked, neck stretched, first en masse, then singly. As always, the class seemed to go on forever, straining nerves and heightening tension.

At last the announcement came. "The judges have made their decisions. You may relax your horses while their scores are compiled."

Immediately Abbie stepped to the stallion's side and absently rubbed a white wither. Her legs were shaking and her stomach was all tied up in knots. Windstorm swung his head around to look at her as if to say, "Are you okay?" She wanted to bury her face against his neck and cry — with hope or relief, she wasn't sure which. Instead she stood there, trying to hide all the anxiety that came from not knowing the judges' result.

Almost unwillingly, she glanced down the line at Rachel's blood bay stallion. The Arabian surveyed the crowded stands with absolute arrogance. She couldn't help noticing how confident the stallion's trainer looked. She felt better when she saw him nervously moisten his lips. Her own were dry as paper.

The minutes dragged by with agonizing slowness as Abbie and everyone else waited for the judges' scores to be tallied. When the announcer declared he had the results, the crowd noise fell to a murmur. Before he announced the Reserve Champion and Champion Stallion, he began naming the Top Ten Stallions, first explaining that the stallions placing in the top ten were all regarded as equal in status regardless of the order in which they were named.

Seven stallions were called, then eight, each followed by cheers and whistles from the crowd. And after each, Abbie held her breath, wanting the championship too desperately to settle for the honor of Top Ten Stallion.

"Next, number four fifty-seven, Windstorm!" Abbie froze as her number was called, everything inside her screaming *no*, her heart sinking to the pit of her stomach. "Shown by owner and trainer, Abbie Hix."

In a blur of tears, she led Windstorm out of the line, deaf to the applause and a few boos of disappointment. They had lost. Engulfed by a terrible sense of defeat, she didn't even remember the ribbon presentation and picture-taking ceremony. She didn't hear the Reserve Champion Stallion named. Nothing registered until the Champion Stallion was called.

"This year's Champion Stallion is number three fifty-eight, Sirocco!"

As the announcement was made, Windstorm bounded into the air, nearly jerking the lead out of Abbie's loose grasp. Instinctively she checked his forward motion, forcing the stallion to swing in an arc in front of her. With a raking toss of his head, Windstorm came to a stop, then trumpeted a challenge at the bay stallion trotting proudly in the spotlight, as if disputing the decision.

Her stallion's reaction was almost more than Abbie's nerves could take. As quickly as possible, Abbie exited the arena, unable to acknowledge the congratulations offered her. For some, Top Ten Stallion might be better than nothing, but not to her . . . never to her. All her life, she had lost to Rachel. She hated the taste it left in her mouth.

Blessedly, Abbie had a few minutes alone in the stall with Windstorm to regain her composure before Ben and Eden arrived. No matter how bitter the disappointment was to swallow, she couldn't let her young daughter see how upset she was over Windstorm's placing.

The hardest thing Abbie ever had to do was to look at the tears in Eden's blue eyes and smile. More than anything she wanted to cry with her daughter. "It's about time you two got here. We've been waiting for you."

"I don't care what anybody says. Windstorm is the best horse ever in the whole wide world." Eden's lower lip quivered.

"He's *one* of the best," Abbie stressed carefully. "And he has a ribbon to prove it. Come on. Help me pin it on his stall so everyone who walks by can see it." As she started to lift Eden out of Ben's arms, she met his glance. For a split second she faltered, knowing that he saw through her charade.

"Remember what I said."

She nodded. "I know. It proves nothing."

"There can be no question of the winner of a horse race. It is the horse what crosses the finish line first. In Poland, it is a stallion's record on the track and his foals that prove his worth as a sire. That is the way it should be here."

"I know." Just as she knew that more and more Arabian horse breeders, including some of the big ones, were turning away from the horse-show arenas and to the racetracks to test the worth of their stock, as their counterparts in Europe and the Middle East had been doing for hundreds of years. Gathering Eden into her arms, she gave her the ribbon and helped her to hang it on the front of the stall. "What do you say we all go get something to eat?" she suggested, wiping the last traces of tears off Eden's cheeks.

"I'm not hungry," Eden said, still pouting.

"Not even for a hot-fudge sundae with whipped cream and cherries on top?" Abbie looked at her askance, doubting her daughter's sweet tooth could resist such a temptation.

"A whole one . . . just for me?"

"I think this celebration might call for a whole one."

"Didja hear that, Ben?" Eden turned excitedly to him. "I get to have one all to myself and I don't have to share it."

"It will take a very big girl to eat a whole sundae by herself."

"But I'm getting bigger every day."

"You certainly are," Abbie agreed and set Eden down. "And a big girl like you doesn't need to be carried."

As they left the barn to head for the parking lot, Eden skipped along beside Abbie, swinging her hand as if she didn't have a care in the world, the prospect of a treat banishing all sorrow. Abbie envied that ability to forget and put it all behind her. She'd been like that at Eden's age. Unfortunately she'd outgrown that too many years ago. A special treat couldn't make the hurt go away anymore.

With their path blocked by the crowd milling in front of the stallion barn, Abbie was forced to slow her pace. She paid little attention to the shrieks of joy and late congratulations being exchanged by those around her, intent only on keeping her small party together and not getting separated in the crowd. Suddenly she found herself face-to-face with Rachel.

After an initial look of surprise, Rachel's expression became serenely composed, mannequin-smooth and smug. "Are you leaving already?"

Abbie stiffened at the insinuation she was running off to lick her wounds, angered most of all because it was true. "Yes."

"We're holding a little celebration in the stallion barn. Would you care to join us?"

Abbie was tempted to accept the invitation just to aggravate Rachel, but she resisted the impulse, knowing that Rachel would love the chance to rub her nose in the defeat. "What are you celebrating? Winning a beauty contest?"

"My, but that sounds remarkably like sour grapes," Rachel taunted. "I wonder why I have the feeling you wouldn't call it that if your stallion had won."

Vaguely Abbie was aware of MacCrea looking on, as well as Lane Canfield and Ross Tibbs, but she was too intent on this confrontation with Rachel to take much notice of them. "You're wrong. I've always regarded the halter class as a beauty contest. It judges a horse's looks, not his athletic ability. Win or lose, I had every intention of racing Windstorm this year. And that's precisely what I'm going to do. But I'm curious what your plans for Sirocco are now."

"I'm taking him home, to River Bend" — she stressed that deliberately — "so he can rest before the National Finals this fall. That's all he has left to win."

"Except a race. It doesn't matter though. I think you've made the right decision." Abbie smiled complacently at the look of surprise that flashed across Rachel's face. "You and I both know your stallion couldn't stand up under the rigors of racing. If I were you, I'd be afraid of him breaking down, too."

"You don't know what you're talking about," she retorted stiffly.

"Don't I? My father had a breeding program very similar to yours. He believed in breeding beautiful horses." Abbie paused, smiling. "I believe in breeding Arabians. Like you, he never did understand the difference."

"That's a lie!" Her voice lifted angrily.

"My mommy doesn't lie," Eden protested.

"Be quiet," Rachel snapped at her.

"You have no right to talk to my daughter that way."

"Then why don't you teach her some manners?" she shouted.

"Don't you yell at my mommy!" Eden tore loose from Abbie's hand and flung herself at Rachel, her arms swinging like a windmill.

Before Abbie could grab her and pull her away, MacCrea lifted Eden into his arms. "That's enough." Shifting Eden onto his hip, he took Abbie by the elbow and propelled her ahead of him through the crowd.

"Let go of me!" Abbie struggled to pull free, but his fingers dug deeper, numbing the nerves in her arm and making it tingle painfully.

"Not until I'm damned good and ready," he growled, leaving her in no doubt that he meant exactly what he said. As long as he held Eden, Abbie realized, she didn't have any choice but to go wherever he was taking her. He didn't stop until they were nearly to the parking lot and well clear of the crowd.

The instant MacCrea released her, Abbie whirled around. "I want my daughter. Give her to me."

Staring at her, his eyes cold and angry, he continued to hold Eden. "You're two of a kind," he muttered. "I oughta drag both of you over my knee and give you the paddling you deserve."

"I wouldn't try it," Abbie warned.

"Why are you so mad at my mommy?" Eden looked confused and a little frightened.

MacCrea paused and briefly eyed Abbie, then glanced over his shoulder as Ben hurried toward them, puffing slightly. "We'll meet you at the motel, Ben. These two are riding back with me."

"I'm not going anywhere with you, MacCrea, until you give me my daughter," Abbie asserted.

He just smiled. "I'm no fool, Abbie. She's my guarantee that you come with me. I've got a few things to say to you and you're going to listen."

"That's kidnapping."

"Kidnapping, blackmail, call it any damned thing you like. But that's the way it's going to be." He started walking toward the parking lot. Abbie hesitated, then hurried after him.

"All right, you win," she said as she drew level with him.

"I never doubted that for a minute. The tan car in the second row is mine."

When they reached the car, MacCrea set Eden in the backseat. "Can't I sit up front with you and Mommy?"

"Nope. Little girls ride in the backseat." He started the engine.

"Where are we going, Mommy?"

"Back to the motel." At least, she hoped MacCrea would take them straight back. She didn't really trust him.

"What about my sundae? You said I could have one with hot fudge and cherries and everything."

"If you'll sit down and be quiet, short stuff, I'll buy you a giant-sized sundae with nuts on it, too," MacCrea promised.

"You shouldn't bribe her like that," Abbie said angrily as Eden quickly sat back in the seat.

"It can't be any worse than what you're doing." He followed the arrows to the parking-lot exit and accelerated onto the street.

"What's that supposed to mean?"

"Knowing you, you're probably damned proud of yourself." Anger thickened his low voice. Abbie glanced briefly at him, noticing the ridged muscles in his jaw. "You weren't content until you dragged your daughter into your stupid, jealous feud with Rachel, were you? Teach them to hate while they are young. Isn't that the way it's done?"

"I didn't start it. Rachel was the one who wouldn't leave Eden out of it."

"None of it would have happened if you hadn't been looking for a fight. And don't deny that you goaded Rachel deliberately. I was there."

"That's right. Defend poor little Rachel," Abbie retorted sarcastically, fighting to suppress the sobs of frustration that caught in her throat.

"I'm not defending her."

"What do you call it then?" But she didn't care to hear his explanation. "I don't even know why I'm talking to you. How I raise my daughter is none of your business."

"Maybe it isn't, but every time I look at her, Abbie, I see you — the way you must have been before you were warped by this jealousy and your heart got all twisted with hate. Do you honestly want your daughter to grow up with the bitterness and hatred you feel?"

"No!" She was stunned that he would even think that.

"Then you'd better wake up and look at what you're doing to her," he warned. "Your jealousy is going to destroy her the same way it destroyed us."

Abbie started to remind MacCrea that he had been the one who betrayed her, but what was the point? It was over. He hadn't understood then, and he certainly wouldn't understand now. If anything, the years in between had proved she couldn't trust him.

At the same time, she couldn't argue with him about Eden. Someday she would have to tell her daughter who Rachel was. If she didn't, Eden would hear the whole sordid story from someone else. But MacCrea was right; she shouldn't let her bitterness and hurt color it.

Eden leaned over the middle of the seat back. "Are you talking about that lady that yelled at you? I didn't like her. She wasn't very nice."

Abbie caught the I-told-you-so look MacCrea threw at her. "You shouldn't say things like that, Eden," she insisted tautly.

"Why? You didn't like her either, did you, Mommy?" She frowned.

"Get out of that one if you can, Abbie," MacCrea challenged. She couldn't — and he knew it.

"Look! There's our motel." Eden pointed at the sign ahead of them.

Abbie nearly sighed with relief as MacCrea slowed the car and turned into the driveway. No longer did she have to wonder whether he truly intended to bring them straight here. The instant he stopped the car, parking it in an empty space near the lobby entrance, Abbie climbed out of the front seat and opened the rear door to claim Eden. She resisted the urge to gather Eden into her arms and run away from him into the motel. Instead, she walked Eden to the sidewalk that ran alongside the building, holding her firmly by the hand. There, she paused to wait for MacCrea.

"Tell Mr. Wilder good night and thank him for the ride." She tried to act normal even though every nerve in her body was screaming for her to get Eden out of his sight.

"But what about my sundae?" It was all Abbie could do to keep from shaking her.

"That's right. I promised I'd buy you the biggest sundae in town if you were good, didn't I?" MacCrea said.

"I wouldn't worry about it. The coffee shop is still open. I can buy her one there. After all, you do have a party to attend, and we don't want to keep you from it."

"What gave you that idea?"

"You were with her. You know she expects you." Her voice vibrated with the anger she tried to contain.

"Maybe so, but believe me, I won't be missed," he replied, then smiled at Eden. "Besides, I'd much rather buy a little girl some ice cream than drink champagne toasts to some horse."

"And I'd rather you didn't."

"Anyone would get the impression you're trying to get rid of me."

"I am." She tightened her hold on Eden's hand.

"Do you want me to leave, Eden?"

"Don't bring her into this," she protested angrily.

"Why not? She's the one I invited."

"I don't care!"

Eden pulled on her hand, demanding Abbie's attention. "Mommy, why don't you like him?"

"Yes, 'Mommy,' tell her why you don't like me. I'd be interested to hear how you'd answer that," he said dryly.

Frustrated by his stubborn persistence, Abbie couldn't even begin to try. The reasons were all too tangled. "Why are you doing this? Why can't you just leave us alone?"

MacCrea paused, as if her question had suddenly made him examine his motives. "I don't know." He shrugged faintly. "Maybe because you want it so badly."

Was she too anxious? Had she aroused his suspicion? Did he wonder if it was something more on her part than just a desire not to have anything more to do with a former lover? She couldn't risk learning the answers.

"Join us if you want. But don't expect me to make you feel welcome." She pivoted sharply and started toward the motel door, dragging Eden with her.

"Look, Mommy. Here comes Ben." Eden waved gaily at the driver of the car pulling into the lot.

38

EXCEPT FOR TWO MEN sitting at a counter drinking coffee and four more people at a table on the other side of the room, they had the restaurant to themselves. Abbie sipped at her coffee and glanced toward the kitchen, wondering how long it could possibly take the waitress to bring Ben's banana cream pie and Eden's hot-fudge sundae . . . and how long it would take her daughter to eat it. It couldn't be soon enough to suit her. Maybe she should have ordered something to eat just to have something to do to make the time pass more quickly, but the way her stomach was churning, she doubted she could keep it down.

It was difficult enough sitting next to MacCrea, aware that he had maneuvered her into accepting this situation. Why hadn't she been smart enough to see it coming? Why had she allowed it to happen? Why hadn't she recognized that he was up to his old tricks? He knew that where Eden was concerned, she was vulnerable. As yet, he just didn't know why. And she couldn't let him find out.

"Are you staying at this motel, too?" Eden asked MacCrea, the two of them carrying on the only conversation at the table.

"I sure am."

"So are we. When are you going? We're leaving tomorrow. We've been gone a long time. Daddy is really going to be happy to see us when we get back. Isn't he, Mommy?"

"He certainly will." Unconsciously she twisted the wedding band on her ring finger. The instant she noticed MacCrea's glance shift to her hand, she realized what she was doing and reached again for her coffee cup. "And we'll be glad to see him, too, won't we?" She smiled at Eden, forcing an enthusiasm into her voice that she was far from feeling.

"You bet!"

When the waitress came out of the kitchen, balanced on her tray was a large goblet filled with vanilla ice cream covered by a layer of chocolate fudge and crowned with a tall swirl of whipped cream, sprinkled with nuts and topped by a red cherry.

"Look at the size of that sundae. Are you sure you can eat it all?" Abbie asked skeptically as she scooted Eden's chair closer to the table.

"Uh huh, I'm a big girl."

"It looks bigger than you," MacCrea remarked when the waitress set the sundae down on the table in front of her, but Eden corrected that problem by kneeling on her chair.

"Can I eat the cherry first, Mommy?" She picked up the long spoon, its length ungainly in her small hand.

"Yes. Just pay attention and don't get that sundae all over your good clothes," Abbie cautioned, knowing she was probably wasting her breath.

"I think I'll save it for later." She plucked the cherry from the whipped cream by its stem and laid it on the table, then proceeded to wipe her sticky fingers on her dress.

"Use your napkin." Abbie pushed it closer to the goblet, conscious of MacCrea's low chortle.

When Eden plunged her spoon into the sundae to dig out her first biteful, an avalanche of melted ice cream, thick chocolate, and whipped topping spilled over the rim of the goblet on the opposite side. Eden caught it with her fingers and pushed most of it back inside the glass, then licked the mixture off her fingers.

"Mmm, it's good."

"It looks good," MacCrea agreed.

"Want a bite?" Eden offered him the huge glob of ice cream and fudge on her spoon, then somehow managed to get it to her own mouth without dropping it when he politely refused.

Within minutes, Eden had almost as much of the sundae all over her face and hands and the table as she did in her stomach. Abbie desperately wished that her daughter was still young enough to be spoon-fed. Watching her eat by herself was an exercise in patience, and Abbie's was already sorely tested. She looked over at Ben, seeking a diversion.

"How was the pie?"

"It was good but not as good as your momma's."

"How is your mother?" MacCrea asked.

"She's fine." Abbie held out her cup as the waitress brought the coffeepot to the table.

"Do you know my grandma?" Eden spooned another partially melted mouthful of ice cream from the goblet, half of it dripping across the table as she tried to aim it at her mouth.

"Yes."

"I don't get to see her very much." Eden released a very adultlike sigh and absently stirred the melting remains of her sundae. As she scooped out another dripping spoonful, she glanced over at MacCrea and paused, with the spoon in midair. "Look, Mommy." Wonder was in her voice as she used the dripping spoon to point at him. "MacCrea has a crooked finger just like me."

For a split second Abbie was paralyzed by Eden's pronouncement as she stared at the little finger curling away from the handle of the coffee cup Mac-Crea was holding. Then she noticed the puzzled blankness in his expression and realized the significance of the comparison hadn't registered yet. There was still a chance it wouldn't if she acted fast.

"Eden, you're dripping ice cream all over the table." Quickly she grabbed the small hand holding the long spoon, covering the little finger so MacCrea couldn't see the way it arched, too. "Pay attention to what you're doing. Just look at the mess you've made."

"But, Mommy, did you see his finger?"

Abbie talked right over Eden's question, praying that MacCrea wouldn't hear it. "I think that's enough ice cream for you, little lady. You're just playing in it now." Out of the corner of her eye, she saw MacCrea set his coffee cup down, a frown deepening the lines in his forehead.

"What's she talking about?"

She ignored his question as she took the spoon from Eden's sticky fingers and put it back in the sundae dish, then reached for a paper napkin. "I bet you have more ice cream *on* you than *in* you. You've got chocolate from ear to ear. I wouldn't be surprised if you have it in your hair. And look, you've spilled some on your good dress. What am I going to do with you?"

Abbie went through the motion of wetting the napkin in her water glass and attempting to wipe the worst of the sticky residue from her daughter's face and hands. But Eden knew she had MacCrea's attention and centered all of hers on him. When she opened her mouth to say something to him, Abbie immediately smothered the attempt with the wet napkin, pretending to wipe the chocolate ring around her lips.

When the napkin had rapidly shredded into nothing, Abbie stood up and scooped Eden off the chair into her arms. "I think we'd better go to our room and get you cleaned up. It's past your bedtime anyway." Ignoring the objections Eden attempted to raise, she turned to MacCrea and met his narrowed gaze. Her heart was thumping so loudly she was certain he could hear it. "I'm sorry," she said without knowing why she was apologizing to him, of all people. "Thank Mr. Wilder for the sundae, Eden, and tell him good-bye. We'll be leaving early in the morning, so we won't be seeing him again." She hoped.

"But —"

"Eden." Abbie shot her a warning look, but an instant later she had trouble swallowing as MacCrea straightened from his chair and towered in front of them.

"Thank you for the hot-fudge sundae, Mr. Wilder," Eden mumbled dejectedly.

"It was my pleasure. Maybe next time your mother won't spirit you away before you get a chance to finish it."

"Yeah." But Eden didn't sound too hopeful.

"Good-bye, Eden." As MacCrea extended his hand to her daughter, Abbie felt her heart leap into her throat.

"No, you'd better not," Abbie intervened quickly. "You'll get all sticky." She darted a frantic look at Ben. "Are you coming?"

But MacCrea paid no attention to Ben. Instead he stared at the small hand on Abbie's shoulder. Abbie didn't have to look to know that, at rest, the first joint of Eden's little finger always jutted upward at a very noticeable angle. When his glance swung to her, he appeared puzzled and faintly stunned. Abbie held her breath, her mind racing, trying to think what she could do when he finally figured out the truth. Ben stepped in to distract him.

"I wish to thank you for the pie and coffee. It was good."

"You're welcome," he replied absently.

"Yes, good night, Mr. Wilder, and thank you for the coffee." Abbie moved away from him before she finished talking.

"Wait a minute." He started to come after her, but the waitress detained him.

"Your check, sir."

Once outside the coffee shop, Abbie broke into a running walk, hurrying down the long corridor to her motel room with Eden jouncing on her hip. She looked back once to make certain Ben was the only one behind her. But she knew she wouldn't feel safe until she and Eden were inside the room and the door was shut and locked.

Her hand shook when she tried to insert the room key in the lock. Impatiently she set Eden down so she could use both hands. She glanced up briefly when Ben joined her. Beyond him she saw MacCrea striding purposefully toward them.

"He knows," Ben said.

She knew he was right, and knowing it just made her all the more angry — angry at herself, Ben, MacCrea, Eden . . . everyone. Why did he have to find out? Why couldn't he have just stayed away? Finally she got the key to turn in the lock and pushed the door open, but she made no attempt to shove Eden inside. It was too late. MacCrea was there. Still she refused to look at him, refused to acknowledge him.

"I think you'd better take Eden with you, Ben, so Abbie and I can talk privately," MacCrea stated, his voice clipped and hard.

"We have nothing to discuss," Abbie snapped.

"We damned well do, and you know it." His voice rumbled at an ominously low pitch as if he were controlling his anger with difficulty. "If you want to have it out right here and now, that's fine with me."

Left with no alternative, Abbie gave Eden a little push in Ben's direction. "Go with Ben, honey. He'll help you wash up. I'll come by to get you in a few minutes." She waited until Ben had Eden securely by the hand, then she pivoted and entered her motel room, MacCrea following a step behind her.

As the door slammed shut with reverberating force, the blood ran strong and fast through her veins, pumping adrenaline through her system. She had hoped this confrontation with MacCrea would never be necessary, but now that it was here, she was ready for it — in an odd way, almost eager for it.

"She's my daughter, isn't she?" MacCrea accused.

Abbie whirled around to face him. "She's *my* daughter!"

"You know damned well what I mean." He was angry, impatient, his lips thin and tight, the muscles working along his jaw. "I'm her father."

"You're nothing to her. You're just some stranger who bought her a sundae. Dobie's the only father she knows. It's *his* name that's on her birth certificate."

"That's why you married him, isn't it? The poor sucker probably doesn't even know the way you've tricked him and used him, does he?"

Fighting a twinge of guilt, Abbie looked away and asserted forcefully, "My baby needed a father and a name."

"Dammit, she already had one! She had *me!* She had the right to *my* name!" Grabbing her by the shoulders, MacCrea forced her to look at him. "You damned little fool, you know I wanted to marry you. I loved you."

"But I didn't want you — or any more of your deceit and half-truths." It was odd how fresh the pain of his betrayal felt to her at that moment. The ache was as real as if it all had happened yesterday.

"But you wanted my baby."

"I wanted *my* baby."

He dug his fingers into her shoulders. "Deny it all you want, but the fact remains, I am her father. You can't change that."

"What difference does it make?" she argued. "Twenty minutes ago you had no idea you even had a daughter. Why is Eden suddenly so important to you now? You don't even know her."

"Whose fault is that? Or are you going to try to blame me for that, too?"

"She doesn't need you. There's nothing you can give her that she doesn't already have. She's happy and loved, well fed and clothed. She has a home and a family, people who care about her. You'd just hurt and confuse her. You'd never bring her anything but pain."

"You're talking about yourself, Abbie," MacCrea accused. "And I don't mean just our relationship, but the way things were with your father. It's that damned jealousy again."

"Maybe it is. Maybe I don't think any child needs a father, least of all men like you and my daddy."

"Hasn't it ever occurred to you that your father might have loved both you and Rachel? That, just maybe, he behaved the way he did because he was torn with guilt?"

"You don't know anything about it! How can you defend him?" She struggled briefly, trying to shake off the numbing grip of his hands, but he wouldn't let her go. He forced her to stand there and face him.

"I know how I felt walking down that corridor, for the first time realizing that I had a daughter and thinking that I should have been there when she was born; that I should have been there when she took her first step and said her first words; I should have been there when she cried. But I wasn't and I couldn't be. And I felt guilty even though it wasn't my fault. If I feel that way, imagine how your father must have felt over Rachel."

"That's not the way it was." She resented his attempt to defend a situation he knew nothing about, especially when she knew he was doing it to satisfy his own selfish desires. "He loved her, not me. All I ever got from him was a reflection of his love for her because I looked like her."

"He didn't love you both?"

"No," Abbie retorted sharply, too incensed by this entire conversation to think straight. "You can't love two people at the same time."

"You love Eden, don't you?"

"Yes."

"And your mother?"

"Of course." The instant the words were out of her mouth, Abbie saw the trap he was setting for her.

"And Ben?" he challenged. She glared at him, refusing to answer and damn herself with her own words. "Admit it, Abbie. You love him, too."

She couldn't deny it, and her continued silence seemed to be an act of betrayal against the one person who had always been there when she needed someone. She looked down at the gold buckle on MacCrea's belt and grudgingly replied, "In a way."

"In a way," MacCrea repeated her phrase with satisfaction. "That makes three people you love. How do you explain that?"

"It's not the same," she said defensively.

"No, it isn't. You love all three of them equally but differently, don't you?"

"Yes," Abbie said, quickly seizing on his explanation.

"Then isn't it possible your father loved you and Rachel equally but differently?"

"You always twist everything around." She felt strangled by the bitter anger that gripped her throat as she lifted her gaze to the ruthless lines in his face. "She was his favorite. He was always giving her things."

"Maybe he was trying to make up for the fact he wasn't there all the time. Maybe he was trying to cram all his affection into a few short hours."

"Look at the money he left her, while Momma and I ended up with practically nothing!" Tears burned her eyes until she could hardly see — hot tears caused by the pain of wounds that had never truly healed.

"For your information, he set up that trust fund for Rachel when she was born. That money was in place long before he got into financial trouble."

"How would you know?" Abbie jeered.

"I asked," MacCrea shot back.

"Then why didn't he do the same for me?"

"Probably because you were his legitimate heir and he figured you would end up with everything he had. Which, at the time, was probably considerably more than the money he placed in trust for Rachel. And maybe, just maybe, he did it because he knew what a spiteful little bitch you were going to turn out to be, and he knew that if he didn't make provisions for Rachel, you'd see to it she never got a cent — the same way you tried to keep me from finding out about my child."

"You're lying!" She struck out blindly with her fists, briefly landing blows on his arms and chest. Cursing under his breath, MacCrea hauled her roughly against him, using her own body to pin her arms against his chest. "Let me go!" Abbie continued to struggle, however ineffectually.

"I ought to . . ." But he didn't bother to finish the threat, instead using action to silence her.

Abbie made a vain attempt to elude the downward swoop of his head, but he grabbed a handful of hair and yanked it, arching her neck back as far as it would go. As he kissed her, his teeth ground against hers and his mustache scratched her skin. The brutal assault was a deliberate attempt to inflict pain. Abbie refused even to think of it as a kiss. She'd known too many of MacCrea's kisses to confuse this with one. The pain was in such contrast to the exquisite pleasure she had once known in his arms that Abbie couldn't help recalling the latter. He wanted to hurt her, but Abbie knew it was her heart that ached the most. She tried desperately to remember how much she hated him and forget the sensation of his heart thudding beneath her hands.

Breaking off the assault, he dragged his mouth across her cheek and down to her throat. "Damn you, Abbie," he muttered thickly against her skin. "Damn you to hell for doing this to me."

At first she didn't know what he was talking about as her bruised lips throbbed painfully. Then she felt the rubbing stroke of his hand on her spine — the beginnings of a caress. No! Abbie thought wildly. She couldn't, she wouldn't let herself be fooled by him again.

With a violent, wrenching twist of her body, she broke free of his arms, catching him by surprise. When he took a step toward her, she backed up two. "Stay away from me. I hate you. I can't stand the sight of you! Get out of here! Just get out!"

"You're good at that, aren't you? You've had plenty of practice at ordering people out of your life."

"Get out." She wanted to throw something at him, but instinctively she knew that would only provoke him.

"I'll leave." But he made no move toward the door. Unconsciously Abbie held her breath, not wanting to say anything that might change his mind. "But this isn't over."

"It was over more than six years ago."

"You're forgetting: there's still the matter of my daughter that needs to be resolved."

"Stay away from her." Abbie tried not to give in to the sense of panic she felt.

"You can shut me out of your life, Abbie, but I'm not going to let you shut me out of Eden's. You'd better get used to the idea."

"No." She knew how weak her protest sounded as he turned and walked the few steps to the door.

He opened it, then paused to look back at her. "You'll be seeing me again," he promised grimly.

No! Inside, the denial was an angry scream, but not a sound came out of her mouth as Abbie watched MacCrea walk out of the door. The door swung closed on its own. In a panic, Abbie ran after him, jerking the door open and rushing into the wide corridor. When she saw him striding away from her, she stopped.

"MacCrea, don't!" she called after him. "If you have any feelings for her at all, stay away. Don't hurt her just because you want to get back at me." She noticed the faint hesitation in his stride and knew he had heard her. But he kept walking. She didn't know whether she'd gotten through to him.

Turning, she glanced at the door to Ben's room, fear knotting her throat. She couldn't face Ben yet — or Eden either, for that matter. She needed some time alone to think this whole thing out.

The next morning, before first light, they checked out of the motel and drove to the showgrounds. By the time a red sun peeked over the eastern mountains to cast its eye on the city of Phoenix below, Windstorm was loaded in the horse trailer and they were on their way out of town.

For the first hour, Abbie kept one eye on the road and one on the side mirror, half-expecting to see the reflection of MacCrea's rented car coming after them. She didn't draw an easy breath until they crossed the state line. As she relaxed slightly, the tension easing from her neck muscles, a small foot pushed itself against her thigh. Smiling, Abbie glanced down at her sleeping daughter, curled up in the middle of the seat with her head pillowed on Ben's leg.

"She's so tired," Abbie said absently. "I knew she would be, getting up that early this morning. At least we won't have to hear her ask every five minutes, 'How much farther do we have to go?'"

"We did not leave so early because you wanted her to sleep," Ben stated. "You thought MacCrea would come back this morning."

"I wasn't sure. I couldn't take the chance." She paused. "He says he wants her."

"What did you expect?"

"I don't know," she admitted. "I never thought he'd find out."

"What will you do now?"

Abbie shrugged. "Maybe he'll change his mind. Why should he care anyway? He doesn't even know her. He can't possibly love her. Most men would be glad to let someone else take care of their child. They don't want the responsibility — financial or otherwise. Maybe after he has time to think about it, he'll feel that way, too, and forget all that stupid guilt."

"Guilt?" Ben frowned at her. "Over what?"

"He claimed he felt guilty because he wasn't there when she was born and a lot of other nonsense like that. I'd really rather not discuss it, Ben," she insisted impatiently, but the denial was no sooner out of her mouth than she remembered the other things MacCrea had said, specifically that whole argument they'd had over her father and Rachel. It had gnawed at her off and on all night long. "Ben . . . do you think Daddy loved both me and . . . Rachel?"

"Yes."

"But . . ." Abbie was thrown by his matter-of-fact response. "He gave her so much more than I ever got. How can you say that?"

"If you have a horse that is strong and one that is weak, to which one would you give more grain?"

"The weak horse, naturally."

"Correct."

Was he saying that Rachel was weak? Abbie wondered. She had started out with less and therefore received more? She realized that MacCrea had said almost the same thing, but in a different way. Was it possible she had been wrong to resent Rachel all this time?

39 ✑

As an airliner rumbled down the runway for takeoff, the thundering of its jet turbines shaking the air, a black limousine drove onto the concrete apron and stopped next to the private jet emblazoned with the logo of Canfield Industries. The driver stepped out and quickly opened the doors for his passengers.

Ross Tibbs climbed out first, then turned to help Rachel. When she placed her hand in his, his fingers closed warmly around it. He made no attempt to conceal the adoration in his look, and she felt a little tingle of excitement that he would show his feelings so openly with Lane standing only a few feet away. It was so reckless and daring of him that, even while it made her afraid, it also made her glad.

"What did I tell you, darling? Perfect flying weather," Lane declared, coming around from the other side of the long car to join her, followed by Mac-Crea. "Just look at that blue sky. And the pilot promised it's going to be like this all the way to Houston."

"I'm glad." But she almost wished it would cloud up and rain so she would have an excuse to stay behind — and steal a few more moments with Ross.

"Rachel is a white-knuckle flyer, I'm afraid," Lane said, smiling at her with an amused tolerance that she recognized too well. From the very beginning of their relationship, his attitude toward her had always been vaguely patronizing. Over the last few years, she'd grown tired of it.

"That's hardly true anymore, Lane." But she knew she was wasting her breath. He simply refused to recognize that she had matured into a sophisticated, worldly woman. He continued to play a fatherly role — that is, when he condescended to spend any of his precious time with her at all.

"I'm not the best of passengers either," Ross said, "so you're not alone in that, Rachel."

"I am not afraid of flying." If *he* started treating her like a child who needed her fears dispelled, Rachel swore she'd scream.

"In that case, if we ever fly anywhere together, you can hold my hand." As Ross gave her fingers a little squeeze, Rachel suddenly realized that he still held her hand. She darted a quick look at Lane to see if he had noticed, but it was MacCrea, standing slightly behind him, who appeared to be watching them with speculative interest. Rachel wondered how much he knew — or guessed.

Before Rachel could respond to Ross's comment, the pilot joined them. "All your luggage is aboard, Mr. Canfield. We can leave whenever you're ready."

"Thanks, Jim. We'll be right there," Lane said as the limousine driver closed the trunk and quietly took up his post by the door.

"I guess we have to leave. Ross, thank you for everything." Rachel pressed her other hand on the one still holding hers, then impulsively kissed him on the cheek. In a way, she didn't care whether Lane thought she was being too familiar or not. There was a little part of her that even hoped he'd be jealous.

"It was all my pleasure. You know that, Rachel." Reluctantly, Ross released her hand.

"You will stay in touch." Hearing the earnest plea in her voice, Rachel tried to cover it. "You know how interested I am in your filly."

"I'll keep you posted on her progress. I promise."

"Ross, let me add my thanks to Rachel's." Lane held out his hand to him. Ross hesitated a fraction of a second, then shook it. "We really appreciate the lift to the airport. I just hope it wasn't too much of an inconvenience for you."

"Not at all."

"If you're ever in the Houston area, give us a call. You know you're welcome at River Bend anytime."

"I just might take you up on that invitation," Ross declared, his glance skipping briefly to her. "It's been a long time since I visited my old stomping grounds."

After MacCrea had added his good-bye to the others, there was no more reason to linger. As she walked with Lane to the steps of the plane, Rachel felt torn. She waved to Ross one last time from the doorway of the private jet, then entered the plush cabin and took her usual seat. Once she had her belt fastened, she leaned back in the velour-covered seat and sighed wistfully.

"Something wrong, dear?" Lane inquired.

"No, nothing," she denied quickly, then saw he wasn't even looking at her. Already his briefcase was open on the tabletop in front of him and a sheaf of documents was in his hands. "I'm just tired, that's all. The party broke up so late last night . . ." She paused, suddenly noticing the way MacCrea was watching her. "I don't know whether I should even talk to you, MacCrea. You never did come back last night."

"I was detained."

"I don't suppose I need to ask by whom?" The mere recollection of that whole scene with Abbie last night made Rachel prickle with anger. God, how she hated, loathed, and despised that woman.

"No, you don't."

"What did you two talk about?"

"That, Rachel — to put it as politely as I know how — is none of your damned business." He wasn't in any mood to parry her questions about Abbie with nonanswers.

"MacCrea, you wouldn't be so foolish as to have gotten involved with her again? After the way she and that little brat of hers behaved last night, I don't —"

"Leave Eden out of it, Rachel," he warned.

She drew back slightly, her eyes widening at his threatening tone. "I never realized you were so sensitive about such things." Her curiosity was piqued.

Irritated with himself for arousing it, MacCrea pushed out of his seat. "Maybe I just don't like the way you and Abbie drag an innocent child into your petty feud. Excuse me. I think I'll sit in the back. I'm not exactly good company this morning." He moved to one of the rear seats in the cabin and strapped himself in.

Within minutes the private jet was airborne and streaking eastward. For a time, MacCrea stared out the window, watching the gray track of a highway below. Somewhere down there on one of those roads was Abbie . . . with his daughter. *His* daughter. He had a child. She was a part of him, his own flesh and blood.

He recalled the first time he saw her, a midget-sized blue-eyed beauty seeking help to find her lost mommy. At the time he'd wondered why she had picked him out of that whole crowd of people. But it was only right since he was her father. Instinctively she must have been drawn to him. Abbie could deny it all she wanted, but there was a bond between them.

But what was he going to do about it? What should he do? All night long he'd wrestled with the problem, but he was no closer to solving it than he had been twelve hours ago when he'd left Abbie's motel room.

"If you have any feelings for her at all, you'll stay away." That was the last thing Abbie had said to him. MacCrea wondered if she was right. If he tried to assert his paternal rights, what would that do to Eden? How much would that hurt her? She was a smart little kid, but there was only so much a five-year-old could understand.

But how could he walk away? He couldn't turn back the clock and forget last night had happened. He couldn't pretend Eden didn't exist. He lifted his gaze to the stretch of blue Texas sky above the horizon — a sky almost as blue as her eyes. He pictured her in his mind: the mischievous glint in her blue eyes, the rosy-cheeked innocence of her smile, and the bobbing swing of her dark ponytail. Damn, but she was a cute little mite, MacCrea thought. Almost immediately he could see Abbie's face next to Eden's, the same blue eyes, the same dark hair, but with a look of fearful wariness — the look of a mother willing to fight to keep her child from harm. He couldn't blame Abbie for wanting to protect Eden, but, dammit, what was he supposed to do? She was his daughter, too.

40

IN THE DISTANCE, a Caterpillar continued to growl over the former hayfield, its blade scraping away the thick stubble and taking the top layer of soil with it as the machine carved out the dimensions of the oval training track being built on the site. A quarter-mile away stood the Victorian mansion of River Bend, within easy sight of the track and vice versa.

When she had chosen the site, Abbie knew that Rachel would think she was building it there to antagonize her, but she had chosen that particular parcel of land because it was relatively level, well-drained, and far enough from the creek that it wouldn't flood in heavy rain. The track's proximity to River Bend was purely accidental, whether Rachel wanted to believe that or not.

As the compact car pulled out of the yard with the reporter for one of the major Arabian horse publications behind the wheel, Abbie sighed wearily. "I don't know about you, Ben, but I feel like I've put in a full day. Lord knows she has enough material to write several articles."

"Eden is home. There goes the school bus," Ben said.

"I think I'll go meet her." She started down the lane at a fast walk.

Ever since MacCrea had discovered that Eden was his daughter, Abbie had become overly protective and possessive of Eden, wanting to know where she was and whom she was with every minute. It had been almost ten days since MacCrea had found out about Eden. As yet, she hadn't seen or heard from him. She wanted desperately to believe it meant he was going to stay away.

Ahead of her, Abbie saw the reporter's car swing to the right-hand side of the lane to make room for an oncoming pickup truck. She didn't recognize the truck, but the pigtailed little girl waving gaily at her from its cab was definitely Eden. As Abbie waved back, she glanced at the driver. She suddenly felt icy-cold all over, as if a blue norther had swept in and chilled the air thirty degrees. She stared at MacCrea as he slowed the truck to a stop. The very thing she had feared the most had happened; MacCrea was here and he had Eden with him.

"Mommy!" Eden poked her head out the cab window. Abbie forced her legs to carry her over to the passenger side of the truck. "Look who came to visit us."

Her throat paralyzed by fear, she couldn't say a thing as she stared past Eden at MacCrea. "Hop in," he said.

With numb fingers, she opened the door and climbed into the cab. Eden scooted into the middle to make room for her and started chattering away like a magpie, but Abbie didn't hear a word she said. She thought she had prepared herself for this eventuality, but now that it was here, she wasn't sure what to do.

"Mommy, aren't you going to open the door?" Eden demanded impatiently. In a daze, Abbie realized the truck had stopped moving. They were parked in front of the house. As she stepped down from the cab, Eden was right on her heels. "Come on, Mommy. I promised MacCrea I'd show him my pony."

Abbie reacted instinctively. "First you have to change out of your school clothes, young lady." She pushed Eden in the direction of the house.

"Aw, Mom." She hung back, digging in her heels in protest.

"You know the rule, Eden." The crunch of gravel warned Abbie of Mac-Crea's approach as he came around the front of the truck.

"I know," Eden mumbled, then abruptly spun around to gaze earnestly at MacCrea. "It won't take long. I promise. You'll be here when I come back, won't you? You won't leave, will you?"

"No. I'll be here." His low-pitched voice came from a point only a few feet to her left. But Abbie wouldn't turn her head to look at him as Eden broke into a smile and ran for the house.

Abbie stood rigid, the banging of the back door reverberating through her heightened senses like a shock wave. She was afraid to move, afraid she might say or do something rash as she felt MacCrea's attention shift to her. She tried to ignore him, but just knowing he was looking at her made her aware of the wisps of hair that had worked loose from the sleek bun at the nape of her neck during the gallops on Windstorm for the photo session. The high collar of her blouse suddenly felt tight around her throat, the black jacket and gray riding pants too constraining.

The instant he turned away from her, she knew it, the sensation of his scrutiny lifting immediately. "You've made a lot of changes around here. I see the old stone barn is gone."

Turning, Abbie tried to look at the place through his eyes. "We tore it down to make room for the new broodmare barn."

All three of the new structures — the broodmare barn, the stables, and the stud barn — were painted the color of desert sand and trimmed in a dark umber brown. A coat of creosote darkened the wooden fencing around the paddocks, the arena, and the lunging pen. The whole place had a practical, efficient look to it. Abbie knew she had accomplished a great deal. She was proud of it — until she realized that MacCrea was bound to judge it by River Bend's ultra-modern facilities, and there was no way hers could compare to Rachel's.

"You're not interested in all this, MacCrea, so why don't you just tell me why you're here?" she demanded tightly, looking squarely at him for the first time. She was stunned by his haggard appearance, the gauntness in his cheeks and the hollows under his eyes.

"I tried to do it your way, Abbie," he said. "I've stayed away. But it's not going to work. I can't forget she's my daughter, too."

"No." It was no more than a whispered protest — a faint attempt to deny all that he was implying.

"I'm going to be part of her life."

"You can't!"

"Can't I?" His challenging gaze bored into her, then made a lightning skip to a point beyond her as a faint smile touched his mouth. "You just watch me."

Almost simultaneously, Abbie heard the slamming of the back door and the rapid clatter of booted feet on the sidewalk. She swung around, catching sight of Eden running toward them, her pigtails flying. One pantleg of her patched jeans was caught inside her boot top and the other was out.

"That was fast, wasn't it?" Eden declared as she reached MacCrea. Barely slowing down at all, she grabbed his hand and pulled him in the direction of the stable. "Come on. I want you to see Jojo. He's the nicest pony in the whole world. I'd let you ride him, but you're too big for him."

"That's all right. I'd rather watch you." MacCrea smiled.

Belatedly, Eden glanced over her shoulder. "You're coming, too, aren't you, Mommy?"

"Yes." She wasn't about to leave MacCrea alone with Eden.

But she deliberately held herself aloof from them, taking no part in their conversation. She was along strictly to chaperone them and help Eden saddle her thirteen-hands-high, Welsh-Arabian pony. Not by word or deed did she want to imply that this had her approval. And she certainly didn't want to make it a threesome.

Watching and listening to Eden, Abbie found it difficult to ignore how obviously taken her daughter was with MacCrea. She tried to convince herself that it didn't mean anything. Eden liked everybody; she always had. That's all there was to it. There was no special bond between them. Abbie repeatedly told herself to stop looking for something that wasn't there.

"She's quite the little horsewoman, isn't she?" MacCrea remarked, smiling as he watched Eden canter her pony around the arena.

Hearing the note of pride in his voice, Abbie wanted to cry in frustration. He was talking just like a father. "She is a very good rider for her age." To say less would be to deny the same pride she took in Eden's accomplishment.

As Eden circled the arena again, MacCrea shifted to stand closer to her and leaned his arms on the rail. "Just look at her, Abbie," he murmured. "That's a part of us out there — our flesh and blood."

Abbie stared at Eden and saw the dark hair that came from her and the waves in it that came from MacCrea, the blue eyes that were like hers and the crooked little fingers, like MacCrea's. She had refused to look at Eden in that way before. Now she saw that the evidence was irrefutable. Slowly she drew her gaze from Eden and turned to look at MacCrea. She found it difficult to meet the dark intensity of his eyes. At the same time, she couldn't make herself look away.

"We made her, you and I, Abbie." Something in the quality of his voice turned the words into a caress.

Suddenly it became frighteningly easy to imagine herself in his arms again. "Don't . . . say that." She took a step sideways, putting more distance between them. "Don't even think that way."

"You know it's true." He continued to lean against the rail, appearing oblivious to the tension that screamed through her.

She moved to the arena gate. "Eden! That's enough for today. Come say good-bye to Mr. Wilder. He has to leave now."

Kicking her pony into a gallop, Eden rode over to the gate. "Can't he stay just a little bit longer? I wanted you to set up some jumps so I could show him how high JoJo can jump."

"No. It's late." Abbie caught hold of the pony's bridle and led him out of the arena.

"But can't he stay for supper?"

"No." The last thing she needed was to have Dobie find out MacCrea was here. Out of the corner of her eye, she saw MacCrea push away from the fence and wander leisurely toward the gate. "I've already asked him. He can't." She glanced sharply at him, warning him not to dispute her claim.

"Maybe another time, Eden," he said.

"Then you will come see us again?" she asked eagerly.

"You can count on it."

"Mac—" Abbie didn't have a chance to say more.

"As I was about to explain to your mother, I'm moving back here to live." He said it so calmly that, for a split second, the full impact didn't register.

"You can't." Abbie stared at him, horror-struck by the thought.

MacCrea smiled lazily, but the look in his eyes was dead serious. "That's one of the advantages a wildcatter has. He can headquarter his company anywhere he wants. I've decided to move it here. It's time I settled down and found a place to live."

A thousand angry protests came to mind, but Abbie couldn't make a single one of them — not with Eden there. "Do you think that's wise?" she asked tersely.

"Wise for who?" he countered softly, then smiled with infuriating confidence. "I'll be in town for a couple of days looking around. Maybe we'll run into each other."

Abbie was so angry she couldn't even talk. He knew damned well she couldn't let his decision go unchallenged. She'd have to see him and try to talk him out of moving back. Somehow she had to convince him it would be a mistake.

MacCrea said something to Eden and moved away, heading across the yard to his pickup. Abbie watched him climb into the cab of his truck, relieved to see him go, but, at the same time, recognizing that she'd have to see him again.

"How come you didn't tell him good-bye, Mommy?"

"Mac, wait!" She suddenly realized she didn't know where he was staying. But it was too late. The roar of the truck's engine drowned out her call. He didn't hear her, and Abbie wasn't about to run after him.

"How come you called him Mac?" Eden looked at her curiously.

"I . . . don't know." Abbie hadn't realized she had. "I guess because that's his nickname." Yet she had rarely ever shortened his name — except when they were making love.

"I think that's what I'll call him, too," Eden stated decisively.

Abbie wanted to object, but how could she? Every time she turned around she seemed to have dug herself deeper into a hole. Somehow she had to find a way to get out of it.

"Unsaddle JoJo and put him back in his stall, honey. We still have the horses to feed and supper to fix before your daddy comes in from the fields."

The Truesdale building was a two-story brick structure built around the turn of the century. Once it had housed a bank, then later it had been remodeled into a retail shop with rental offices in the rear. When the retail shops had closed, the entire building had been converted into cheap office space. The last renter had moved out this past summer, but no one had bothered to scrape the name of the termite-and-pest-control company off the large plate-glass window in the front of the building.

But from the time Abbie was a child, she had been fascinated by the stately cornices that adorned the old building. Her eye was drawn to them again as she parked her car in the empty space in front of it. Stepping out of her car, she glanced around, looking for MacCrea's truck, but it was nowhere in sight, even though it was seven minutes after one. When she had finally reached him through his office that morning, he had agreed to meet her here at one. She walked up the steps to the main entrance and hesitantly tried the door. It swung open at the push of her hand.

She went inside and closed the door, then paused to listen. She could feel the damp chill in the stale air and doubted that anyone bothered to heat the empty old building. A loud clunk came from somewhere near the far end of the long, dark corridor before her.

"Hello? Is anybody here?" The echo of her own voice came bouncing back at her. It was like shouting into an empty oil drum. The bare rooms magnified the sound of the footsteps she heard, giving them a hollow thud. "MacCrea? Is that you?"

"Yeah. I'll be right there." The walls partially muffled his answer, but she was still able to recognize his voice. An instant later, he emerged from a shadowy alcove at the far end of the corridor and walked toward her, brushing at the sleeves of his jacket. "Sorry. I was checking out the plumbing. I didn't hear you come in. The realtor left me the key, so I thought I might as well look around a bit. What do you think of it?"

"I . . . I really don't know." She hadn't come here to discuss that.

"It's a stout old building. It wouldn't take much to whip the place into shape." MacCrea looked around, as if assessing the amount of work that needed to be done. "There's more space here than I need, but it will mean I'll have room to expand later on." Pausing, he turned back to her. "I've signed the papers to buy this building."

"No. You can't move here. I told you this morning that we had to talk. How could you do this?" All her well-thought-out arguments vanished with his announcement. "Why couldn't you have waited until we had a chance to discuss this?"

"There was nothing to discuss as far as I was concerned."

"Why can't you be reasonable? Don't you realize how impossible you're making things? Not just for me, but for Eden and everyone else involved. You can't just come waltzing back here and demand to see her," she raged helplessly.

"Why not? She's my daughter." He shrugged indifferently.

"I should have known that would be your reaction." Abbie swung away from him, outraged by his callous attitude. "You never did care about anybody's feelings except your own. You go around creating all these problems, then let others suffer for them."

Blindly she charged into a vacant room and threw her purse down on one of the wooden crates stacked against the wall. Hearing his footsteps behind her, Abbie stopped and turned to face him.

"I didn't create this problem, Abbie," he stated. "You did when you married Hix and passed our child off as his. I had no part in that decision. Now it's blowing up in your face. That's why you're so upset. You never should have married him."

He was right, and she hated him for it. "I suppose you think I should have married you," she retorted.

"If you had, you wouldn't be in this mess right now."

"No. I'd be in a worse one." She hugged her arms tightly around her middle, trying to hold in check all the violent churning tearing her up inside.

For a long moment, MacCrea said nothing. Then he wandered over to the wooden crates and stared at the lettering stenciled on the sides. "That last time we were together, after that Christmas party . . . that's when it happened, wasn't it? That's when you got pregnant."

"Yes." She was abrupt with him, impatient that he should even bother to talk about such a minor detail.

"I've thought a lot about that night lately." Turning, he half sat and half leaned against the stacked crates.

"Have you?"

"You're bound to remember it, too."

"I remember how it ended," she snapped defensively. Then a horrible thought occurred to her. "Who have you told about Eden? Does Rachel know?"

"I haven't told anyone." Reaching out, he caught hold of her hand and pulled her over to stand closer to him. "That's one thing I never have understood, Abbie. What the hell did Rachel ever have to do with us? What did she have to do with the way I felt about you — or the way you felt about me?"

"If you don't know by now, you'll never understand." She strained to twist her wrist free of his grip, but he merely increased the pressure.

"I want to know," he insisted. "Explain to me what she had to do with *us*."

"I can't!" All that didn't seem important to her anymore.

"Let me ask you a question. If she had a horse you wanted, would you buy it from her?"

"What difference does it make? She'd never sell it to me." Abbie didn't know why she was even letting herself get involved in this senseless discussion.

"For the sake of argument, assume she would. Would you buy the horse?"

"If I wanted it, yes."

"Even though you hate her and don't want anything to do with her?" MacCrea challenged.

"I don't hate her." The instant the words came out of her mouth, Abbie was surprised by them — surprised because she realized they were true. She didn't know when or how it happened, but she didn't hate Rachel anymore. "Besides, buying a horse from her, that's business. It has nothing to do with personal feelings."

"My dealings with her were — and still are — strictly business. How many times did I try to explain that to you? But you wouldn't listen to me. Why, Abbie? Why?"

"I don't know." She tried to give him an answer that made sense. "Maybe I couldn't then. Maybe I was too young — and too ready to believe the worst. So many things happened that year, I —" Realizing there was no way to pick up all the scattered pieces of the past, she pulled away from him. "What difference does it make now, MacCrea?" she said. "It's over."

He was on his feet and his hands were on her waist, turning her to face him before she was even aware he had moved. "It doesn't have to be, Abbie."

When she looked into his eyes, she could almost believe him. As she watched his mustached mouth descend, she made no attempt to avoid it. She let it settle onto her lips, its gentle pressure at once warm and evocative, stirring up feelings she thought she'd buried years ago. It had been too long since she'd known such tender passion, or felt the gentle strength of his caressing hands moving over her body, reminding her of the pleasures she'd once known in his arms. She pressed against him, aching with the need to love this man that had gone too long unfulfilled, and once she had loved him so very, very much.

"I want you, Abbie." He held her tightly, rubbing his mouth near her earlobe, his mustache catching loose strands of her hair. "I've never stopped wanting you, nor loving you, not once in all these years. And you still feel the same way about me. You can't deny it. Nothing's changed, Abbie. Not one damned thing."

But that wasn't true. "You're wrong." Abbie pushed back from him. "Things have changed, MacCrea. I'm not the same woman I was then, and you're not the same man. We've changed. I've grown up. I think differently and feel differently about things now. You don't know me. You don't know what I'm like now —what I want or what I need."

"No? I'll bet I could make some damned good guesses," he mocked. "Take your hair, for instance. Every time I've seen you lately, you've got it pulled back in this prim little bun. I'll bet you never wear it loose anymore, all soft against your neck." He trailed his fingers down the taut cord in her neck, stopping when he reached the high collar of her blouse. "And you wear a lot of turtle-necks and button your blouses all the way up to your throat. Your jackets are tailored like a man's. I bet if I looked in your closet I wouldn't find a single pretty dress that shows off your figure."

"You're wrong. I have several."

"New ones?"

"That's beside the point."

"Is it? You're a passionate woman, Abbie. But you've locked it all inside, beneath those high collars and that prim bun. You don't love that farmer husband of yours. You never have."

"What are you suggesting?" Abbie demanded. "That I leave him?" But she could tell by his expression that that was precisely what he meant. "And after that, what am I supposed to do? Come back to you?"

"Yes, dammit." He scowled impatiently, then tried to wipe it away. "Can't you see it would solve everything? The three of us would be together, you, me, and Eden, the way it should have been."

Abbie stared at him for several seconds, then pulled away from him and walked to the center of the empty room, unable to hold back the bitter laugh that rolled from her throat. "Why? Because you want your daughter?"

"Is it so damned impossible to believe that I might want you both?"

"No, it isn't impossible. Look, maybe you have the right to see your daughter and get to know her—"

"You're damned right I do."

"You also hold the power to force this whole situation out into the open. If I agree to let you see Eden, will you give me your word that you won't let on that she's your daughter—at least not for a while?"

"And if I gave you my word, would you believe me?" he asked, arching an eyebrow skeptically.

"I'd have to."

"That sounds remarkably like trust."

"You'd also have to let me choose the time and place to meet her." Unconsciously she held her breath as MacCrea studied her thoughtfully.

His answer was a long time coming. "Yes."

"Good." Abbie breathed easier, for the first time believing there was hope. "I'll be in touch. I promise."

"Abbie." He caught up with her in the corridor. "Before you go, there's one other thing. When I saw you in Phoenix that first time, long before I found out Eden was my daughter, it was you I wanted. Think about that. And think about this." He kissed her long and deep, not letting her go until she was kissing him back.

41 ~

As RACHEL PASSED the study, she noticed the door was ajar. She stepped back and pushed it the rest of the way open, but there was no one in the walnut-paneled room. Hearing the rustle of a starched uniform, she turned from the door just as one of the maids came around the corner of the back hallway.

"Maria, have you seen Mr. Tibbs?"

"Yes, ma'am. He's in the front parlor."

"Thank you." Quickening her steps, Rachel walked swiftly toward the high-ceilinged foyer. Intent on the double doors that led to the parlor, she almost walked right by the small boy standing by the front door, struggling with the zipper of his winter jacket. She stopped short of the double doors and swung back to face her son. "Where are you going, Alex?"

He darted an anxious glance at her, then lowered his chin, burying it in the collar of his jacket. "Outside," he mumbled, the mop of brown hair shielding his pale blue eyes from her sight.

"Did Mrs. Weldon say you could?" Rachel frowned, wishing he'd stop acting as if she were going to hit him. She'd never struck him in her life.

He bobbed his head up and down in an affirmative reply. "She said I could take the truck Uncle MacCrea gave me and play with it outside."

She glanced at the large toy pickup truck with oversized, "monster" wheels sitting on the floor near his feet. "You be careful and don't break it."

"Yes, ma'am."

"Can't you call me Mommy or Mother — something other than ma'am all the time?" Rachel insisted impatiently. "I know Mrs. Weldon is trying to teach you to be polite, but sometimes, Alex, you carry it too far."

"Yes, ma'am," he mumbled again.

Seeing it, Rachel felt absolutely helpless. She tried to be a good mother to her son, but she just couldn't seem to reach him. There were times when she wondered whether this timid, sensitive child belonged to her. It was so irritating to know that Lane could do no wrong in Alex's eyes, and she could do nothing right. Sometimes she even wondered why she tried. Neither of them cared about her — not really.

As Alex continued to fumble with the zipper, Rachel walked over to him. "Let me help you with that."

At first he pulled away, but Rachel persisted. She arranged his collar so it would lay smooth, then paused, with her hands on his shoulders.

"There you go." She smiled at him. When he smiled hesitantly back at her, she had the urge to give him a quick hug. As she started to pull him toward her, he hung back. Suddenly it all felt awkward and forced. Rachel straightened abruptly, unable to endure his rejection of her. "You can go outside and play with your truck now."

Still smarting from his rebuff, Rachel turned and walked stiffly to the double doors. As she entered the parlor, she forgot all about Ross being there. She gasped in surprise when her wrist was seized and she was spun halfway around.

"There's no escape, blue eyes," Ross declared, smiling as he locked his arms behind her back. "This time I've got you."

"Ross, you're —" But he silenced her protest in the most effective and demanding way, kissing her with an ardor that melted all her previous stiffness. Sighing contentedly, she relaxed against him and nestled her head on his shoulder. "I've missed you," she whispered.

At almost the same instant, she heard a faint noise near the doorway. Too late she remembered the door was still open. Maria, Mrs. Weldon — anybody could have seen her kissing Ross. Guiltily she pushed away from him and turned, half expecting to see one of the maids retreating from the doorway. Instead she saw her son, poised uncertainly on the threshold.

"Alex, I thought you were going outside. What are you doing here? What do you want?" she demanded sharply.

He backed up a step, his gaze falling under her glare. "I thought . . . maybe you'd want to come outside and watch me play with my new truck."

"No!" She knew she answered too angrily, but she couldn't help it. "Not now. I'm busy." Alex continued to stare at both of them as he backed up farther still.

"Maybe another time, sport," Ross inserted.

Rachel couldn't stand the way the child looked at her. Those pale blue eyes, the color of washed-out denim, seemed filled with hurt and condemnation. "Alex, please. Just go outside and play."

He took another step backward, then turned and ran for the front door. Rachel stood motionless, waiting until she heard the door shut and the clump of his boots on the porch outside; then, only then, did she hurry over and close the double doors to the parlor. She leaned weakly against them and half turned to look at Ross, a wild fluttering in her throat.

"You shouldn't have been so hard on the kid," Ross said gently.

"You don't understand. He doesn't like me. What if he tells Lane?" Agitated, she moved away from the doors, clasping her hands tightly together.

"What can he tell him?" Ross stopped her and loosened her clenched hands, holding them in his own.

"I can't help it." She sighed, feeling frustrated and confused. "You don't know how glad I am that you're here, but at the same time, I'm worried that Lane might find out about us."

He lifted her right hand to his mouth and pressed his lips into the center of her palm. "Would it be so terrible if he found out about us, Rachel? After all, I love you and you love me."

"I want to be with you, darling. You have to believe that. But it isn't as simple as you make it sound. If I walked out that door with you, I'd lose everything: my home, River Bend, Sirocco, and —" She had been about to say, "and all the rest of the horses."

But Ross broke in, "I know . . . your son."

"Yes, Alex, too." She felt guilty that she hadn't even considered him. But she'd always regarded him as Lane's son. River Bend, the horses — they were hers. But Lane would never let her have them; she was certain of that. "Darling, you know all you have to do is call and I'll meet you whenever and wherever I can. We love each other. Isn't that what counts?"

"I'm just greedy, I guess. I want you all the time."

"Silly, you have me all the time. I'm always thinking about you — except when I'm with Sirocco and my other horses," she teased.

Ross chuckled. "I never dreamed I'd have a stallion for a rival."

"Now you know." She laughed softly, relieved that Ross was slowly beginning to accept the idea that she could never divorce Lane. Naturally he didn't like it. She didn't either. But it was the only way things could be.

Looking back, she understood so well what Dean had gone through. This land, this home had been in his family for generations. How could he risk losing it in a divorce settlement? He had been deeply in love with her mother. Two people didn't have to be married to be happy. In time, Rachel was certain she could convince Ross that this arrangement was best. If he truly loved her, he'd accept it and not expect her to give up everything she'd ever dreamed of having.

"Do you have any idea how frustrating it is to sleep under the same roof with you and not in the same bed?" Ross drew her back into the circle of his arms and began nuzzling the little hollow behind her ear. "Let's go up to my room, lock the door, and make love the rest of the afternoon."

"You know we can't do that." Deftly she eluded his attempt to draw her into another embrace and stepped free of him. "Lane and MacCrea might come back anytime now."

"I've been here three days and all we've managed to do is steal a few kisses. Rachel —"

"I think we'd better talk about something else." She walked over to the front window and lifted the sheer curtain aside to gaze outside. There was no sign of Alex anywhere in the front lawn. A movement in her side vision drew her glance to the adjoining field west of the house. The dark ring of the oval track stood out sharply against the tan stubble of the former hayfield.

"Any suggestions?"

She ignored the faint edge to his voice. "Last night, when you were talking to MacCrea after dinner, did he give any reason why he suddenly decided to move back here?"

"No. Do you know?"

"I have the feeling he's gotten himself involved with Abbie again," Rachel said tightly, aware that he'd announced his decision shortly after he'd disappeared with Abbie that night Sirocco had won the championship. "He's a fool to get mixed up with her again."

"Speaking of Abbie, did you see the article on her in the March issue of the Arabian horse magazine?" With a wave of his hand, Ross indicated the magazine on the coffee table, the one with the color photo of Sirocco on its cover.

"This one?" Rachel picked it up, frowning in surprise. "I read the piece they wrote about Sirocco, but I haven't had time to look through the rest of it."

"I read it last night — while I was trying to fall asleep." His pointed remark indicated she was the cause of his insomnia as he took the magazine from her and flipped through the pages. After locating the article, he handed it back to her. "She's going to get a lot of mileage out of her decision to race her stallion. There are some great pictures of her training track under construction. 'Abbie's folly': isn't that what you call it?"

"Yes," she muttered absently as she quickly began skimming the article. Between the photos and the text, it was five pages long, a full page more than the cover story on Sirocco.

"You have to admit it's a good piece," Ross said when she'd finished it.

Rachel flipped back to the beginning and read it through again, her ire growing with each infuriating word. "They make that old Polack sound like some sort of a guru. And did you see this quote of hers?" Rachel read it aloud: "'Racing will have to play a major role in the Arabian horse scene in America the same as it does in Russia, Poland, and Egypt. It's part of Nature's selection process, the survival of the fittest. Races are won by the strong and the swift. Here, in the United States, we put too much emphasis on the beauty of the Arabian horse," claims Ms. Hix. "Too many of our recent national champions have had serious conformation faults — serious enough that they would automatically be eliminated as racing prospects by any knowledgeable horse trainer. Yet our judging system has proclaimed these stallions to be the best we have. If they are the best, then I'm afraid we're in serious trouble."' End of quote."

"She's only saying publicly what a lot of people in the business have been saying privately for years."

"Is that so?" Rachel angrily tossed the magazine onto the coffee table. "You are aware that she's referring to Sirocco in this article. She just doesn't have enough nerve to use his name. She can't stand it that her stallion lost to mine. Now she's doing everything she can to make Sirocco look inferior. I'd love to make her eat those words."

"Unfortunately, that's not likely to happen."

"Why isn't it?" she demanded, resenting his implication that Sirocco couldn't beat Abbie's stallion.

"Well, because . . . you're not going to be racing Sirocco. You've got the Nationals to get ready for. Besides, you don't risk injuring a valuable stallion like that on the racetrack."

"I suppose you think he'll break down, too."

"I didn't say anything of the kind." Ross raised his hands in a gesture of surrender. "Why are we arguing about this? You aren't going to race him, so —"

"Who says I'm not?" she retorted.

Totally bewildered, Ross sat down on the velvet cushions of the antique sofa. "I thought you did."

"Maybe I've changed my mind. If I put Sirocco in training, I'd get twice the publicity she would. Finding a trainer is no problem. I can hire the best in the country."

"You're not serious." He frowned.

"Why not? Sirocco's grandsires raced in Egypt . . . and won." The more she thought about it, the more determined she became. "She said something in the article about entering her stallion in the Liberty Classic at Delaware Park the Fourth of July, didn't she?" She reached for the magazine again.

"I think so."

"Sirocco's going to be in that race, too." She scanned the article again, then underlined the name, date, and place of the race.

"He's your horse, Rachel, but . . . are you sure you know what you're doing?"

"I know exactly what I'm doing. It's going to work out perfectly — in so many ways. Don't you see, Ross? Not only will I get tons of publicity out of this for Sirocco, but it will also give us a chance to meet somewhere away from here — away from all the people who know us. I'll have to send Sirocco somewhere to be trained. And he'll have to run in a couple races before the Liberty Classic. Lane won't think a thing about it if I fly there every other week or so. We can be together — alone — the way we were in Scottsdale."

"You don't have to say any more. I'm sold."

Rachel stared at the color photograph of Abbie. "I'd give anything to see the look on her face when she finds out." She laughed deep in her throat, relishing the thought.

A warm breeze, heavy with moisture from the Gulf, lifted Windstorm's silvery mane and sent it rippling back across Abbie's hands as she rode the stallion across the field, holding him to a trot. With the afternoon sun beating down out of a pastel sky, the heavy fisherman's sweater provided all the warmth she needed. It was one of those rare, fine days East Texas natives bragged about to their friends and relatives in the North, still shivering in March from the bitter chill of winter.

Slowing the stallion to a walk, Abbie started him around the training track, moving in a clockwise direction. Eden quickly joined her, the pony traveling at a jog-trot to keep pace with Windstorm's long strides. "If they had races for ponies, JoJo would win for sure, wouldn't he?"

Accustomed to her daughter's nonstop chatter and endless questions, Abbie let them wash over her, answering when it was necessary and nodding absently when it wasn't. The afternoon was too beautiful to let anything irritate her, least of all Eden's company.

As they rounded the first turn and started down the backstretch, Eden grew impatient with the slow pace Abbie set and cantered her pony ahead. Watching her, Abbie smiled. Eden always wanted to come with her when she exercised Windstorm, but invariably she grew tired of riding around the track and looked for something more challenging to do — like exploring the wooded creek bottom or stacking the leftover boards from the track rail in a pile for her pony to jump.

Somewhere a horse whinnied shrilly. Abbie glanced at the group of yearlings that crowded close to the white fence of the adjoining pasture at River Bend. The twin turrets of the Victorian-style mansion drew her attention, the peaks of their cone-shaped roofs poking into the pale blue sky.

"Hey!" Eden's sudden, sharp call snapped her attention back to the track. "What are you doing? Who said you could play here?"

Twenty yards ahead, Eden had stopped her pony and turned it crosswise on the track, blocking the trespasser from Abbie's view. Abbie dug a heel into Windstorm's side and the stallion bounded forward, quickly covering the short distance.

Before she reached her daughter, Abbie spied the young boy, Eden's age, with a toy truck clutched in his arms. The boy backed up quickly as if afraid she was going to run him down as she reined Windstorm to a halt beside Eden's pony. His eyes were saucer-round as he apprehensively glanced from Abbie to Eden and back, then darted a quick look over his shoulder as if gauging the distance to the track's outer rail and his chances of making it.

"What's he doing here, Mommy?" Eden demanded with proprietorial outrage.

"I . . ." The boy's mouth worked convulsively as he tried to get an answer out. "I was . . . just playing in the dirt with . . . my new truck. I didn't hurt anything."

Feeling sorry for him, Abbie smiled gently. "Of course you didn't. You just scared us. We didn't know you were here." But the boy didn't look altogether sure that they could possibly be as scared as he was. "What's your name?"

"Alex," he said reluctantly, backing up another step.

Abbie unconsciously lifted her head and glanced toward River Bend. Rachel's son was named Alex. Turning back, she studied him thoughtfully. Except for his light blue eyes, she could find little resemblance to Rachel. Yet he had to be her son.

"You live at River Bend, don't you?"

He bobbed his head in hesitant affirmation, then qualified his answer. "Sometimes."

Abbie vaguely recalled hearing that, even though Rachel spent a great deal of her time here, she sent her son to a private school in Houston during the week. "Does your mother know you came over here to play?"

"No." He stared at the ground. "She doesn't care. She doesn't care about anything I do." The mumbled answer carried with it a jumble of self-pity and resentment that caught Abbie by surprise.

"Oh, I'm sure she cares a lot," Abbie insisted, but Alex just shook his head in silent denial, forcing Abbie to consider how much more time Rachel spent at River Bend with her horses than she did in Houston with her son. "I'm glad to meet you, Alex. My name's Abbie and this is my daughter, Eden."

"How come that truck has such big wheels? It looks funny," Eden declared, frowning curiously at the truck he held.

"It's supposed to. That way it can go anywhere and run over anything. And it's fast, too. Faster than any horse," he retorted, eyeing her pony.

"That can't be faster than JoJo," Eden scoffed. "It's just a toy."

"Well, if it was real, it would be."

"Where'd you get it?"

"It was a present."

"Can I see it?" Kicking free of the stirrups, Eden jumped off her pony and walked over to look at his toy.

Abbie started to call her back, recognizing that Rachel would be upset if she knew Alex was here. Then she asked herself what harm it would do if Alex stayed a little while. Eden would certainly enjoy playing with someone her own age, and Alex probably would, too. Just because she and Rachel had had their differences in the past, there was no reason to drag the children into it.

When Abbie suggested that the two of them play in the track's infield, Eden blithely agreed and bossily shepherded Alex into it, leading the pony in tow. It never occurred to Eden that Alex might not want to play with her. Once again Abbie started the stallion around the track, this time at a rocking canter.

As Abbie cantered Windstorm past the first furlong pole, she noticed the white Mercedes driving slowly along the country road that ran past the field. She knew of only one car like it in the area, and it belonged to the Canfields.

Instinctively she checked Windstorm's stride and turned in the saddle to glance at the boy and girl playing in the infield, making mountains out of the clods of dirt for the toy truck to climb. She suddenly realized that she had no idea how long Alex had been playing here before she and Eden arrived. Someone might have discovered he was gone and come out to look for him. Why hadn't she obeyed that first impulse and sent him home? Rachel would be furious when she found him here.

As the Mercedes rolled to a stop, the trailing plume of dust ran over it, enveloping the vehicle in a hazy cloud. Abbie reined the stallion in and swung him back toward the infield. She started to yell to Alex to run for home, then she saw how flat and open the stretch of ground between the track and the white-fenced boundary or River Bend was. He'd never be able to cross it without being seen.

The settling cloud of dust partially obscured the man who climbed out of the passenger side of the car. Then, strangely, the Mercedes pulled away, leaving him behind. Abbie recognized that long, easy stride that had all the grace of a mountain lion. She felt a new tension race through her.

Unconsciously she tightened her grip on the reins and Windstorm side-stepped nervously beneath her, his ears flicking back and forth as his attention shifted from her to the man vaulting the fence and starting across the field toward them. As MacCrea approached the track, Abbie observed how rested he looked, compared to the last time she'd seen him. His handsome features now emanated strength instead of tiredness.

"Hello." He stopped on the opposite side of the track rail, his hands pushed negligently into the pockets of his leather jacket.

As she looked down at him from astride the stallion, she found the height advantage unsettling. She was too used to looking up at him. She swung out of the saddle and stepped onto the dirt track, gathering together the loose reins to avoid looking at him. "You were with Lane?"

"Yes, we had some business to finalize. You obviously meant it when you told Rachel you intended to race your horse." His glance made a cursory survey of the completed track.

"Yes."

MacCrea ducked under the rail and absently stroked the stallion's warm neck. "Looks like he's coming along all right."

"He is." She was conscious that his attention never really left her, not even when he seemed to direct it elsewhere.

"I got the picture of Eden you sent me."

Abbie was relieved that he'd finally mentioned Eden. She was tired of talking around the reason he was here. At the same time, she didn't want to be the one to introduce Eden into the conversation. "It's a school picture. I thought you might like to have one." She had hoped it might placate him a little and keep him from demanding to see Eden too often.

"Where is she?"

"Over there, playing." Abbie nodded her head in the direction of the infield.

A frown flickered across his face. "Who's the boy with her? That can't be Alex."

"I know I should have sent him home, but I didn't think it would hurt anything if they played together a little while." She turned as Alex hesitantly petted the pony's nose.

"I'll be damned," MacCrea swore softly. "Now I've seen everything."

Stung by the amused disbelief in his voice, Abbie reacted angrily, regarding it as another dig against her. "And just what does that mean?"

"Alex. He's always been afraid of horses. Now look at him."

"Alex is probably like a lot of boys," Abbie guessed. "He doesn't want to admit to a girl that he's scared. It would be too embarrassing."

"You're probably right."

Just then Eden saw MacCrea and let out a squeal of delight. "Mac!" She ran across the infield, pulling the pony along by its reins. Alex lagged behind, steering wide of the animal's hindquarters. Intent on the children, Abbie wasn't aware MacCrea had moved away from her until she saw him walking across the track to greet Eden. She led Windstorm over to them, reaching them as MacCrea swung Eden into the air and stood her on the top rail. "How did you get here?" Eden looked around for his company pickup.

"Magic." He winked.

Eden eyed him skeptically, then turned to Abbie. "Mommy, how'd he get here?"

"He walked."

"I knew it wasn't magic." She directed a sternly reproving look at MacCrea, then giggled. "You're silly."

"So are you." He tweaked her nose.

"No, I'm not." She jumped down from the rail and grabbed his hand. "I want you to meet my friend. He's got a truck and the wheels are bigger than it is. Wait until you see it." Turning, Eden waved at Alex, motioning for him to join them. "Come show him your truck."

But Alex hung back. "Alex knows I've already seen his truck," MacCrea said.

"When?" Eden demanded in surprise, then frowned. "Do you know Alex?"

"I sure do." He smiled.

"Do I have to go home now?" Alex raised his head, reluctance in every line of his face.

MacCrea glanced briefly at Abbie. She had the impression that he, too, was unwilling to break this up. "Your father's home. He will be wondering where you are. And your mother's probably missed you, too."

"No, she hasn't," Alex said, again with a bitter resentment that Abbie recognized too well. He added something else that sounded a lot like "She never misses me," but Abbie couldn't be sure.

"Just the same, we probably should leave," MacCrea said quietly, then cast a sidelong glance at Abbie. "You understand?"

"Of course." If they did start looking for Alex, she knew it was better that they didn't find him here.

"Does he have to go now? Can't he stay a little longer?" Eden pleaded in protest. "I wanted to take him to the slough by the creek. He doesn't think there's any alligators in it and I wanted to show him. Please."

"Maybe another time, Eden." He laid a hand on top of her head and gave it a little push down.

Eden grimaced at the refusal, then pursued the carrot MacCrea had offered. "Maybe you can come over tomorrow, Alex, and we can go then. We'll be here, won't we, Mommy?"

"Yes," Abbie admitted uneasily, realizing she was going to have to have a talk with her daughter. She dreaded trying to explain to Eden why Alex's parents might not want him playing with her. How could she make Eden understand, when she no longer understood it herself? Yet once she had hated Rachel with all the venom of a Texas rattler. Her hatred for Rachel was gone, but she feared their long-standing feud was about to start poisoning their children, and she didn't know how to stop it.

"Will you come, Alex?" Eden persisted.

"I don't know if I can." The boy shuffled his feet uncomfortably and stole a look at MacCrea.

"Please try," Eden wheedled. "We'll have lots of fun."

But Alex was obviously unwilling to commit himself as he chewed on his lower lip. MacCrea stepped into the void. "Come on, sport. We'd better go."

Stymied by Alex, Eden turned her persuasive efforts on MacCrea. "You'll come see us again, won't you?"

"Of course. Real soon," he promised, then glanced at Abbie, knowing it was up to her to set the time and place. "You know how to reach me."

She assumed it was through his Richmond office, but she simply nodded in affirmation rather than ask.

As they crossed the field, Alex walked with his head down and the truck tucked under his arm. The closer they got to the fence, the slower he walked, practically dragging his feet and forcing MacCrea to shorten his stride even more.

"You're very quiet," MacCrea remarked. It was something of an understatement. Alex hadn't said one word.

Beyond the dark trunks of the shade trees in the lawn, the large Victorian manor house glistened whitely in the sunlight. Alex eyed their destination with a look that was filled with misgivings. As his glance dropped away from the wide veranda with all its fancy gingerbread trim, he sighed heavily.

"Mother is gonna be mad at me 'cause I was over there." The corners of his mouth were turned down as far as they could go.

"What makes you say that?" MacCrea frowned sharply.

"'Cause I don't think she likes that lady."

"How do you know?"

"Sometimes when she sees her riding her white horse over there, her mouth gets all tight and her eyes look mean. And she . . . she says things about her."

MacCrea wondered how many more people besides himself were going to pay the price for Abbie and Rachel's bitter rivalry before it was over. For the time being at least, Abbie appeared to be unwilling to involve the children in it. But he knew her too well. All it would take was one push from Rachel and she'd shove back. Abbie wasn't the kind to turn the other cheek. She always struck back, and, dammit, he didn't want Eden getting caught in the crossfire.

"Are you going to tell her where I was?"

It was a full second before Alex's anxious voice registered. MacCrea paused a second longer, then smiled thinly. "Not if you don't want me to."

A smile of gratitude and relief broke across the sensitive planes of the boy's face. MacCrea wondered briefly whether he was right to encourage him, then decided it couldn't be any more wrong than what Rachel and Abbie were doing.

As they reached the fence, MacCrea heard Rachel calling for Alex. Then Lane's voice joined in. "Sounds like they're looking for you, sport." He picked up Alex under the arms and hoisted him over the fence. The search seemed to be concentrated in the backyard and over by the barns. "Better hurry. I think your father is in the back."

Alex broke into a run, darting between the young trees planted several years ago to replace the ones destroyed in the fire. As the boy angled for the rear of the house, MacCrea followed, taking a straighter route.

"Alex!" Lane called, his back turned to them.

"Here I am, Daddy!" Alex raced past the gazebo with its lacy white lattice-work, heading straight for his silver-haired father.

Turning, Lane saw him and called over his shoulder. "Rachel! I've found him. He's over here!" As he crouched down on one knee to greet Alex, Rachel hurried from the direction of the barns with Ross behind her. "We've been looking all over for you, Alex. Didn't you hear us calling?"

"I . . . I came as fast as I could." Breathless from running and uncertain of his reception, Alex moved hesitantly within reach of Lane's hands, then let himself be drawn closer when Rachel approached them.

"Alex! Lane, is he hurt? What happened?"

"He's fine," Lane assured her.

"How could you run off like that, Alex?" Rachel demanded, her anxiety turning to anger now that he was found. "Where have you been?"

Alex avoided her accusing look. "Playing . . . with my truck," he answered.

"Yes, but where? We've been looking everywhere for you," she stated impatiently. Alex darted a fearful glance at MacCrea, then clamped his mouth tightly shut. "You had us all so worried, Alex. I thought you were outside playing in the yard, but when your father came home and we couldn't find you

. . . I was afraid you were hurt or something—especially when you didn't come when we called."

"I'm sorry." He edged closer to Lane. MacCrea noticed the way Rachel's lips thinned. The door shut on the concern that had been in her expression. A coolness replaced it.

"Now that your father's home I'm sure you won't be running off to your secret place to play." She straightened and turned to Ross. "I think I'll go to the barn and talk to Mr. Woodall about my plans for Sirocco. Would you like to come along?"

"Sure."

As the pair set off together, Lane watched them, expressionless except for the pained look in his eyes. With difficulty he pushed to his feet, fighting the stiffness in his aging joints. "Come on, son." He took Alex by the hand. "Let's go in the house and get you cleaned up. It looks like you've been grubbing in the dirt."

MacCrea swung alongside as they headed for the house.

42

A ROAR CAME FROM the crowd in the racing stands, cheering on the horses running for the wire, as a groom led the gleaming white stallion past the stalls to the paddock area. Abbie walked alongside, the blue-on-blue jacquard silk of her dress and the silk scarf tied around the band of her wide-brimmed hat matching Windstorm's racing colors.

Her nerves were as tautly drawn as piano wire, and the palms of her hands were damp with perspiration. She was certain that she was more nervous than Alex had been last week when Eden had persuaded him to ride double with her on JoJo. Afterward Alex had said to her, "Maybe if I learned to ride, my mother would like me better." His comment had seemed an ironic echo of the past. Long ago, Abbie had turned to horses as well, in hopes of gaining her father's approval.

Alex had become a regular visitor, sneaking over to play with Eden whenever he could. Sometimes Abbie wondered whether she was right to let him come, but Eden needed a playmate her own age as much as Alex did, and his timidness balanced her boldness, each of them learning something from the other. But . . . there was Rachel to consider.

There was always Rachel, Abbie reminded herself, suddenly restless and agitated. Why was she letting thoughts about Rachel spoil a dazzling, beautiful June day? Windstorm was running in the next race. Why wasn't she enjoying the excitement instead of getting herself all worked up over Rachel?

But Abbie knew the answer to that one. This morning she'd learned from a fellow Arabian horse owner that Rachel's stallion, Sirocco, had won his race yesterday—by three lengths. In two and a half weeks, her stallion would be racing against Windstorm in the Liberty Classic, providing Windstorm finished well in this prep race today. He has to, Abbie thought, determined that he would not only win this race, but the Liberty Classic as well — the race that everyone was calling the Champion of Champions race. Windstorm was going to be that Champion. Abbie couldn't stand the thought of losing to Rachel again.

Eden tugged at her hand. "Mommy, do you think Mac's here?" A perplexed frown creased her child-smooth features as she scanned the small crowd that had gathered outside the paddock.

"I don't know." But Abbie knew he was supposed to be.

For the last three and a half months, she had arranged these "accidental" meetings so MacCrea could spend time with his daughter as she had promised, a task that had become increasingly difficult since Dobie had learned a month ago that MacCrea was back in the area. Twice Dobie had questioned her about him, wanting to know if she had seen or talked to him. Abbie admitted that she had, but she had tried to make it sound like that's all there was to it. She doubted that Dobie believed her. His unspoken suspicions and her own sense of guilt had added more strain to an already unstable marriage.

Abbie couldn't decide what to do about it. In the beginning, she had secretly hoped that MacCrea would get tired of playing father and go away, and things could be the way they were. But watching the bond between MacCrea and Eden grow, she knew now that wasn't going to happen. Sometimes she wondered who she was deceiving by maintaining this farce: Eden, Dobie, or herself.

"But Mac always comes to watch Windstorm race. Why isn't he here today?" Eden persisted, plainly troubled by his absence. More evidence of how much she looked forward to being with him.

"I don't know," Abbie repeated. "Maybe he was too busy."

When she had talked to him earlier in the week, MacCrea had told her that he planned to fly in from a drilling site in Wyoming and anticipated arriving around noon. Bad weather may have delayed him, since he was making the trip in the company plane instead of a commercial airliner. But if he'd run into a storm, why hadn't he called and left a message for her? Unless . . . Abbie remembered the photograph she'd seen in the morning paper of a private plane that had crashed during a storm. She suddenly felt cold — and a little frightened.

A large hand pressed itself against the back of her waist. Startled by the contact, Abbie turned into the curve of its arm and stared at MacCrea, alive and well, smiling that lazy smile that was so achingly familiar.

"MacCrea. You made it safely after all," she murmured, relief sweeping through her.

"Did you think I wouldn't?" His dark gaze centered on her with an intensity that gave Abbie the feeling that he could see right into her heart.

For a split second, everything was blocked out. She didn't even hear Eden clamoring to be noticed. "I . . . We . . . Eden wondered whether you were going to come today or not."

"Only Eden?" As the pressure of his hand on her back increased slightly, Abbie had the fleeting impression he was going to kiss her. Instead, he reached down and scooped up Eden.

"You really didn't think I wasn't going to be here today to cheer for Windstorm, did you?" MacCrea chided Eden. "You were the one who made me an official member of his rooting section."

"I know. But I looked and looked and didn't see you anywhere. And Mommy said maybe you were too busy to come."

"She said that, did she?" He hoisted Eden a little higher in his arms and partially turned to include Abbie in the range of his vision. "She was wrong. No matter what, I'll never be too busy to come. I can't stand up my favorite girl, now, can I?"

"You were awfully late," Eden reminded him. "It's almost time for the race. They've already taken Windstorm into the paddock so they can put the saddle on him."

"I know, and I'm sorry about that. I got caught in traffic on my way here from the airport. There was an accident and the road was blocked."

"Is that what kept you? I thought —" Abbie broke it off abruptly, not wanting to reveal the fear she'd had.

"Yes?" MacCrea prompted, casting a curious look in her direction.

"Never mind. Let's go into the paddock. I want to speak to the trainer before they give the call to saddle up." As she started toward the enclosure, she was forced to wait while a groom led another Arabian entrant through the opening.

"You're slipping, Abbie." MacCrea stood beside her, still carrying Eden in his arms. "You're going to have to watch yourself more closely."

"Why? What do you mean?" She frowned.

"The way you looked at me when I arrived, a person could get the idea you were glad to see me." His voice mocked her, but his gaze didn't.

Abbie didn't try to deny it. She couldn't. It was true. Just for an instant, she'd foolishly let her emotions rule. That was a mistake — a mistake she could easily make again with MacCrea. There were times when she wished she could just take Eden and run away — run from MacCrea and Dobie and this whole convoluted mess. But there were her mother, Ben, and the horses to consider. She wished MacCrea had never come back. Everything had been so simple before. She was trying desperately to hold on to that, but he was complicating her life in ways she didn't want.

In the paddock, Abbie conferred briefly with Windstorm's trainer, Joe Gibbs. She wasn't sure what she accomplished except to gain his reassurance that he considered the stallion fit and ready for the race — and to escape MacCrea's company. After weighing in, the jockey joined them, wearing blue-on-blue racing silks and carrying the light racing saddle and number cloth.

As the trainer personally saddled Windstorm, Abbie watched from the side, feeling totally superfluous. Still, she was reluctant to leave just yet. She glanced around the paddock at the half-dozen other Arabian horses entered in the race, all but two of them seasoned veterans of the track with respectable records. The favorite, a handsome chestnut with a slightly plain head, had lost only two races so far this season.

"You seem nervous," MacCrea remarked.

She glanced at him from under the brim of her hat, noticing that Eden was no longer with him. Ben was now the one being besieged by her endless questions. "Nervous, anxious, excited, worried," Abbie admitted, but she knew

MacCrea was responsible for part of her tension. "Windstorm has some stiff competition today."

"You don't sound very confident. Have you forgotten that he's won all three of his previous races?"

"No. But he's never raced a mile before either — or against horses of this caliber. I have cause to be concerned. I don't think you realize how important this race is. How well he does here will decide whether we run him in the Liberty Classic on the Fourth."

"I thought he was already entered."

"He is. But if he can't handle distance, we'll pull him. The Liberty is a mile and a quarter." She shifted her attention to the silver-white stallion, eagerly alert yet at the same time indifferent to the fussing of the trainer and groom. "He has to win. He just has to."

"You've heard then."

Abbie stiffened. She wanted to pretend that she didn't know what he meant, but she knew she could never fool MacCrea. "About Sirocco's victory? Yes."

Ben came over, firmly leading Eden by the hand. "We should go find our seats now. Soon it will be time for the race."

After wishing the jockey luck, they left the paddock area and made their way to their seats in the owners' boxes to await the parade to the post. Eden was too excited to sit down, leaving the seat between Abbie and MacCrea empty.

It was always a struggle for Abbie to pretend to ignore him, but today it seemed even more difficult for her. She tried to blame it on the rising tension she felt over the upcoming race, but she had the uncomfortable feeling that she had unwittingly admitted something during those few moments of fear earlier when she thought his plane might have crashed. For once she welcomed the distraction of Eden's nonstop chatter.

"Mommy, did you remember to bet the money Grandma gave you for the race?"

"Ben did earlier. He has the ticket."

"How much will she win?"

"Nothing if Windstorm doesn't, honey." Fully aware that that answer would never satisfy her daughter, Abbie glanced at the odds board. At the moment the number-four horse, Windstorm, was listed at seven to one. It was hardly reassuring to discover that the odds-makers obviously didn't regard her stallion as much of a threat. "She'll win somewhere around seventy dollars."

"Wow! Are you going to bet some money on Windstorm, too?"

"No."

"But you could win a lot of money," Eden protested.

"And I could lose it, too." But that wasn't the reason. Betting on her own horse just seemed to be inviting bad luck.

"Why? You know he's the fastest horse ever," Eden insisted. "He's going to win. I know it."

"A thousand things can go wrong in a race, Eden," Abbie tried to explain. "He could break badly from the gate or get caught in a pocket surrounded by other horses. A horse could run into him or one might fall in front of him. You just don't know."

"I do," she replied, unconcerned by such dire possibilities, and turned to MacCrea. "You're gonna bet on Windstorm, aren't you, Mac?"

"I already have." He pulled several tickets out of his shirt pocket and showed them to her.

"All of these! Can I hold them?"

"Sure." He gave them to her.

"How much money will you win?"

"A lot." MacCrea smiled.

"Boy, I wish I could have bet on Windstorm." Eden sighed longingly as she stared at all his tickets. "I wanted to take the money out of my piggy bank, but Mommy wouldn't let me bring it."

"I told you that you're too young," Abbie reminded her. "Children aren't allowed to bet money on horse races."

"Well, when I get big, I'm going to bet on Windstorm and win lots of money," Eden declared.

"Something tells me that there's a strong gambling streak in her," MacCrea said in an aside to Abbie.

"Obviously she inherited it from her father," she retorted, and instantly regretted the quick rejoinder and its reference to him.

"I agree," he replied, his gaze running intimately over her face.

As a warmth stole over her skin, Abbie looked away, concentrating her attention on the track. Just then, the first trumpeting notes of the Call to Post sounded, stirring the crowd to life once again. An Arabian horse carrying a rider festooned in a scarlet-and-gold native costume cantered onto the track to lead the procession of Arabian racehorses on their parade to the post. Their appearance drew a smattering of applause from the stands.

"Look, Mommy. There's Windstorm!" Eden cried excitedly, the first to spot the silvery-white stallion, officially listed as gray.

Snubbed close to his lead pony, Windstorm entered the track at a mincing trot, his neck arched in a tight curve, his long tail raised and flowing behind him like a white banner. One of the other horses shied at the noise from the crowd as the seven entries paraded past the stands on their way to the starting gate. But not Windstorm. He played to the crowd as if in a show ring instead of on a racetrack.

"Sometimes I wonder if we were wrong not to race him first," she said to Ben.

"Do not worry. He knows why he is here," Ben replied, studying all the horses through his binoculars.

Abbie thought she was nervous before, but she was twice as anxious now. When the horses reached the area behind the starting gate, cantering to loosen up, she shifted onto the edge of her seat. With only one other gray horse among the entrants and that one a dark gray, it was easy to distinguish Windstorm from the rest. But at this distance, Abbie could tell very little about him.

"How is he, Ben?"

"He is sweating a little. It is good."

"Let me see." She reached for the binoculars and trained them on Windstorm when Ben handed them to her. There was a telltale shadow on his neck, the sweat wetting his coat and letting the blackness of his skin show through. A little show of nervousness was good; it indicated alertness and an awareness of what was expected of him. But too much drained a horse's energy. Studying the white stallion, Abbie was forced to agree that Windstorm was by no means lathered. He looked ready. She hoped and prayed he was.

"Can I see, Mommy?" Eden tugged at her arm, jarring the focus.

"Not right now." Abbie briefly lowered the glasses to locate Windstorm again and noticed that the first horse was being loaded in the number-one post position. Quickly she raised the binoculars to observe Windstorm being led into the number-four slot without incident.

As the last horse went in, the track announcer's voice boomed through the stands. "They're at the gate, ready for the start of the fifth race." Her nerve ends picked up the expectancy in his voice, vibrating like a tuning fork.

An eternity seemed to pass as she kept the binoculars trained on the number-four position, watching the jockey's efforts to keep Windstorm alert and squared in the gate. The stallion's ears appeared to be on a swivel, constantly flicking back and forth, impatiently waiting for a signal from his rider. Finally he tossed his head, irritated with the delay.

Bells rang as the clanging gates sprang open and the horses burst out. "They're off!" A dull roar came from the surrounding crowd.

Abbie came to her feet, lowering the glasses. "How'd he break? I didn't see." By the third stride out of the gate, three horses had surged forward to vie for the lead. Windstorm wasn't one of them.

"He broke well." Ben stood up, adding softly, "Do not hurry him. Let him find his stride."

Abbie heard him as she concentrated on the loosely bunched horses thundering toward the stands, but a full second passed before she realized he was talking to the jockey riding Windstorm.

". . . Windstorm is fifth; Kaslan is sixth . . . ," the track announcer droned.

The white stallion was along the outside, five-and-a-half lengths back of the leader, but running easily, neither gaining nor losing ground as the horses approached the first turn. Abbie raised the glasses once more to follow him.

"I can't see, Mommy."

"Stand on the seat beside Ben." Abbie shifted to her right to make room for Eden. The horses entered the backstretch stringing out in a longer line. "He's in fourth now." Unconsciously she clutched at the sleeve of MacCrea's shirt, trying to contain her excitement as Windstorm began to close on the leaders. "I think he's making his move. I hope it's not too soon." But the stallion was still running with his ears pricked forward, a sure indication that he wasn't yet extending himself.

She lost sight of him as the horses went into the final turn. He was just a blur of white on the outside, obscured by the horses on the rail. She felt an unbearable tension in her throat.

The two leaders came out of the turn, neck and neck heading down the homestretch. But there, flying on the outside, was Windstorm, stretched out flat, each thrust of those powerful hindquarters driving him closer to the leaders, his large nostrils flared, drinking in the wind.

The cheers of the crowd were a distant roar in her ears, no match for the drumming hooves pounding over the dirt track. As Windstorm closed on the leaders, Abbie lowered the glasses, unconsciously using them to pump the air and urge him faster.

At the seven-eighth's pole, the white stallion caught the leaders and started pulling away. The other jockeys went to the whip, but Windstorm's jockey continued to hand-ride him, driving for the finish line. He was a half-length ahead . . . one length . . . two.

Abbie screamed as Windstorm crossed the line, still pulling away. "He did it! He won! He won!" She turned to MacCrea, her excited cry becoming a jubilant laugh.

"Didn't I tell you he'd win?"

Thrilled by his decisive victory, Abbie couldn't contain her elation. She had to express it, let some of it out. Impulsively she flung herself at MacCrea. He hooked his arm around her waist, lifting her off her feet.

The instant her lips touched his mouth, she realized what she was doing and started to pull back. His hand cupped the back of her head, checking the movement. There was a moment of stillness, broken only by the thudding of her heart, as the rugged planes of his face filled her vision.

"Oh, no, you don't, Abbie," he whispered.

He kissed her, his lips moving warmly, possessively, over hers, taking what she had been about to give him. Abbie couldn't deny that she enjoyed it. She returned the pressure, savoring the pleasure that flickered through her.

The whole embrace lasted no more than a few seconds, yet it seemed a lifetime had passed when MacCrea finally set her down and shifted to include a laughing, squealing Eden. Together they hugged and laughed and rejoiced in Windstorm's victory, drawing Ben into their celebration. But the sensation of MacCrea's kiss lingered on her lips. Abbie couldn't look at him without recalling it. But what was more unsettling, she saw the same reaction mirrored in his eyes, too, each time he looked at her.

Together they all trooped down to the winner's circle for the presentation ceremony. When it came time for pictures to be taken, Eden insisted that MacCrea be included, but he excused himself, convincing her that he had to cash his winning tickets in.

Abbie watched him disappear into the throng, knowing as well as he did that there was no way she could have explained to Dobie why MacCrea was in the photograph. MacCrea was right, for all their sakes, to stay out of it. Yet as the photographer positioned them next to the silver stallion, Abbie found herself wishing he was there.

After the ceremony was over, the groom led Windstorm away to have the mandatory check for drugs. The stallion moved off at a dancing walk, still looking fresh and eager to run.

As she left the winner's circle with Eden firmly in tow, Abbie thought about the coming mile-and-a-quarter race, now less than three weeks away. "There can be no doubt about Windstorm running in the Liberty now," she said to Ben, shortening her stride to keep pace with his slower steps. "It's going to be a treat to watch Windstorm kick dirt in Sirocco's face when they cross the finish line. Windstorm beat his time for the mile by a full second today."

"Not only that, he set a track record at the mile for Arabians," the trainer, Joe Gibbs, chimed in, bringing up the rear.

"He did?" Abbie turned to stare at the trainer, stunned by the news. "I knew his time was fast, but . . ." She started to laugh. She couldn't help it. "Can you believe it, Ben?" She wondered what Rachel would think when she found out.

A track record. She could hardly wait to tell MacCrea the news. She sobered slightly, remembering the kiss, and absently ran her fingertips over her lips as if expecting to find a physical impression to match the one he'd left on her mind . . . and, if she was honest, on her heart.

Automatically, Abbie glanced in the direction he would come. The stable row was quiet, an island of comfortable sounds, removed from the din of the grandstands. Horses stood with their heads hanging over the stalls, swishing their tails or stomping their feet at buzzing flies, munching on hay or banging their water buckets. Occasionally there was the clop of hooves as a groom walked by, cooling out a horse, or the soft voices of passersby as they paused at a stall to stroke a velvety muzzle. The yelling and cheering belonged in the stands.

As MacCrea came strolling leisurely past the row of stalls toward them, Abbie felt the quick knocking of her heart against her ribs. She stared at him, a fine tension running through her. But the feeling wasn't unpleasant; it was more like a sharpening of her senses than anything else.

"Eden," she called to her daughter chattering away at the groom, relating Windstorm's life story, from the sounds of it. "There's MacCrea."

"'Scuse me. I've got to go." She was off like a shot, running to meet him. "Did you collect your winnings?" she called before she even reached him.

"I sure did." He fanned the bills for her to see.

"Wow! Look at how much money Mac won, Mommy!"

"It's a lot, isn't it?" Abbie said as Eden skipped ahead of MacCrea to rejoin her. "Did you tell him our news?"

"What news?" Eden stared at her with a blank frown.

Bending down, she whispered in her ear. "Windstorm set a track record for Arabians."

"Oh, yes!" She turned to MacCrea, her eyes bright with excitement. "Windstorm set a record."

"He had the fastest time for an Arabian at the mile here at this track," Abbie explained, feeling again that little surge of pride over her stallion's accomplishment.

"That's great. Now we have three things to celebrate: Windstorm's time and my winnings."

"What's the third thing?" Eden frowned.

"I bought the Jeffords' property — house, acreage, and all." He looked at Abbie when he answered her. "Just about ten miles from the farm."

"I know the place," she said, even though she'd only seen it from the road.

"Maybe you can come by sometime and see it," MacCrea suggested, but Abbie wasn't about to commit herself to that. She didn't want to see where he ate or . . . where he slept. At her silence, MacCrea shifted his attention back to Eden. "How do you think we should go about this celebrating we have to do?"

"Well . . ." She pressed her lips together, considering the problem seriously. "We could all go get a bi-i-ig hot-fudge sundae and . . . maybe look at some toys. And we could go to a movie," she concluded proudly.

"Sounds good to me." MacCrea smiled faintly.

"Count me out. You two go ahead. Ben and I have to stay here and see to Windstorm." She always begged off so MacCrea could spend time alone with Eden.

"But I want you to come with us," Eden declared insistently. "It won't be the same if you don't."

"I'm sorry, but we can't go. Ben and I have to stay here." Abbie saw the tantrum coming on and braced herself for it.

"Then I'm not going to go either," Eden retorted, her expression defiant.

"Eden, you know you always have fun with Mac." She tried to reason with her.

"But I want all of us to have fun together like we did that time at the horse show."

"Don't be difficult, Eden." Abbie sighed, running out of patience with her recalcitrant daughter.

"If you won't come with us, we'll just stay here with you." She folded her arms in front of her, the gesture determined, and accompanied by a stubborn jutting of her chin.

"You're not spoiling anybody's fun but your own." But it was like talking to a mule. Abbie glanced helplessly at MacCrea, who seemed amused by their battle of wills. Just for an instant, she wondered if he had put Eden up to this.

"If you can't beat 'em, join 'em. Isn't that the way the old saying goes?" MacCrea said, his mouth crooking slightly beneath his mustache. "Come along with us. Windstorm gets along fine when you're not here. Why should this afternoon be any different?"

"I should have known you'd take her side in this," Abbie accused, but she couldn't summon any anger. She had the uneasy feeling that subconsciously she wanted to be talked into going. But to admit that, she'd also have to admit that she wanted to be with MacCrea.

"Please come with us, Mommy. They'll take good care of Windstorm. I know they will," Eden said, indicating the grooms with the stallion.

"Ben . . . ?" Abbie appealed to him for help.

"What is there to argue with?" He shrugged his square shoulders. "What she says is true."

"See. Even Ben agrees," Eden declared happily and took hold of Abbie's hand, then reached for Ben's. "You'll come with us won't you? We'll have lots of fun."

Eden was so obviously delighted at the prospect that Abbie felt it would be deliberately churlish to refuse. "You've talked me into it."

Together the four of them set off for the parking lot and the car MacCrea had rented, their destination a movie theater not too many miles from the track, one that MacCrea and Eden had discovered on a previous excursion in the area.

When they left the theater two hours later, dusk was spreading its mauve blanket over the sky, pushing aside the streaks of cerise. To Eden's dismay, Abbie insisted it was time they went back to their motel. She tried to convince Abbie she wasn't tired, but she fell asleep in the backseat within ten minutes.

MacCrea turned into the motel parking lot and drove past the lobby. "What room are you in?"

"One twenty-six. It's near that first side entrance." Abbie opened her purse to retrieve the room key. "Ben, would you wake up Eden?"

"Let her sleep," MacCrea said. "I'll carry her in."

Knowing how cranky and uncooperative Eden could be when she first woke up, Abbie didn't argue. "All right."

MacCrea parked the car near the side entrance and lifted Eden out of the backseat, then followed Abbie and Ben into the building.

Unlocking the door to room 126, Abbie walked in and stepped to the side to hold the door open for MacCrea, as Ben continued on to his own room. "You can put her down on the first bed," she said, indicating the double bed closest to the door.

When MacCrea started to lay her down, Eden made a protesting sound and clung to him. Gently he laid her down on the bed and untangled her arms from around his neck. Smiling absently, Abbie took off her hat and walked over to the suitcase lying open on the low dresser. Eden's nightgown, a long mock tee shirt, lay on top. As Abbie picked it up and started back to the bed with it, she noticed MacCrea sitting on the edge of the bed, pulling off Eden's socks and shoes.

"You don't have to bother with that. I'll get her ready for bed."

"I want to do it." The bedsprings creaked faintly as MacCrea shifted to glance at her, his angular features gentled by the underlying tenderness in his expression. "Is that her nightgown?"

"Yes." Abbie stared uncertainly at his outstretched hand.

"Putting Eden to bed is probably old hat to you," he pointed out, "but I've never had the opportunity to do this for my daughter before."

Abbie hesitated a second more, then handed him the nightgown and stood back to watch. Unwillingly, she was moved by the touching scene as MacCrea removed Eden's dress and slip, careful to disturb her as little as possible. He smiled at the frowning faces she made, his strong hands gentle in their handling of the sleeping child. Holding her, he pulled the nightgown over her head, slipped her arms through the sleeves, then laid her back down, sliding her legs between the sheets. Eden immediately snuggled into the pillow under her head. Bending, MacCrea lightly kissed her forehead, then straightened and pulled the bedcovers over her, tucking her in. He paused for an instant to watch Eden in sleep, then switched off the bedside lamp, leaving only the soft glow from the floorlamp between the two vinyl chairs to light the room. Moving with cat-soft silence, he came back to stand next to Abbie.

"Look at her," he murmured. "So small and innocent. A sleeping angel."

Admittedly that was the way she looked, the white pillowcase a halo around her dark head, her cheeks still baby-soft, her long-lashed eyes closed, all sweetness and innocence. But Abbie was well aware that Eden was no angel. Surely MacCrea didn't really think she was, but he had never seen her at her irritating worst. He'd only been exposed to her in small doses.

Surely he didn't think that today was an example of what it was like to be a parent. Certainly it had been fun and idyllic, but today was the exception rather than the rule. All he'd ever done was play at being a father. Living with Eden was something entirely different.

"Don't be fooled by her. She isn't always like this," Abbie warned. "You've never seen her when she's sick with the flu or a cold. She's whiny and demanding, always wanting this or that. Believe me, she's no fun at all then." Judging by his amused study of her, MacCrea wasn't at all convinced. Abbie hurried on, "Being a parent isn't all fun and games. That little temper tantrum you saw today — it was mild compared to some she's thrown when she didn't get her way. Just wait until she starts sassing and talking back. You won't think she's so cute and innocent then."

"Is that right?" The hint of a smile around the edges of his mouth seemed to mock her.

"Yes, it is," Abbie retorted, irritated that he might think she was making all this up. "And then there's the way she talks all the time. Look at the way she talked through the entire movie, asking why somebody did this or said that, wanting everything explained to her. Do you know that she even talks in her sleep? You've only had to put up with her endless chatter for a few hours at a time. Wait until you have to listen to her day in and day out."

"Talk, talk, talk," he said.

"Exactly. She just goes on and on . . ." Abbie forgot what she was going to say as he took her by the shoulders and squared her around to face him, all in one motion.

She stared at his mouth, surprised to find it so close, and watched his lips form the words, "Just like her mother."

Before she could react, he was kissing her, warmly, deeply. For an instant she forgot to resist, then she drew back, breaking the contact. "Mac, I think —"

"That's always been your trouble, Abbie." He didn't let her get away. Instead, he started nuzzling her neck and ear. "You think too much and you talk too much. For once, just shut up."

As he claimed her lips again, his advice suddenly seemed very wise. Why should she refuse herself something she wanted as much as he did, just because she didn't want to admit she wanted it? Denying it wouldn't change the longing she felt at this moment. As she allowed herself to enjoy his embrace, it was a little like coming home after a long absence. The joy, the warmth, the sense of reunion — they were all there . . . and something more that she was reluctant to identify.

He tunneled his fingers into her hair and began pulling out the pins that bound the chignon. As her hair tumbled loose about her shoulders, he drew back to look at her, his eyes heavy-lidded and dark. "I've wanted to do that for a long time."

Still holding her gaze, he scooped her off her feet and carried her to the nearest armchair and sat down, cradling her in his lap. No longer did she have to strain to reach him and span the difference in their heights. She was free to touch him, to run her fingers through his thick, wavy hair and feel the rope-lean muscles along his shoulders and back. His roaming hands stroked, caressed, and kneaded her body as he and she kissed and nibbled as if hungry for the taste of each other. Then his fingers went to work on the bow at her throat and the buttons of her shirtwaist dress, undoing them one by one. When his hand glided onto her bare skin, a rush of sensations raced through her body.

Caught up in the building passion between them, Abbie had no idea how long they had been in the chair, necking like a pair of teenagers just discovering all the preliminary delights that made making love the wonder it was. But when she heard Eden stir and mumble in her sleep, her maternal instincts reclaimed her. She couldn't tune out the sounds her daughter made, or ignore her presence in the room.

When she tried to inject a degree of restraint into their embrace, MacCrea protested. "Let me love you, Abbie. It's what we both want."

"Not here." She drew back, earnestly trying to make him understand. "We can't. Eden might wake up." A mixture of irritation, disappointment, and frustration darkened his expression when he glanced toward the bed. "We'd better stop before . . . one of us loses control," Abbie suggested, no more willing than he was to end this.

"Me, you mean." His mocking reply had a husky edge to it.

"I didn't say that."

He sighed heavily, giving her his answer as he sat her upright. She swung off his lap to stand on her own, feeling shaky and weak. She wanted nothing more than to turn and have MacCrea gather her back into his arms. Instead, she walked him to the door, holding the gaping front of her dress together. As he paused with his hand on the knob, she had the feeling that he didn't trust himself to kiss her again.

"This isn't over, you know," he said.

"Yes." She nodded, recognizing that she didn't want it to be over.

A slow smile spread across his face. "It took you long enough to admit it." Then he was gone — out the door before Abbie could say any more.

Automatically, she locked the door and slipped the safety chain in place, all the while thinking about his last statement. For the last four months, ever since she'd seen him that first time in Scottsdale, she had been telling herself it was over between them. Now she knew better. She wanted him so much it had become a physical ache.

She walked over to the open suitcase on the dresser. As she started to pick up her lace nightgown, she noticed her reflection in the mirror. Her long hair was all disheveled; her lips looked unusually full; her eyelids appeared to be faintly swollen; and the front of her dress gaped open all the way to her navel. She had the definite look of a woman who had just been thoroughly made love to . . . perhaps not thoroughly, she corrected, conscious of the lingering need.

As she gazed at her reflection in the mirror, Abbie found herself coming face to face with reality. A part of her had never stopped loving MacCrea — and the rest of her had learned to love him all over again.

She went through the motions of getting ready for bed — washing her face, brushing her teeth, and changing into her nightgown — but she didn't go near it. Instead she laid out clean clothes for herself and Eden and packed everything else into the suitcase except the toiletries they would need in the morning, postponing the moment when she'd have to climb into that bed alone.

At first, Abbie didn't pay any attention to the light rapping sound she heard, thinking that someone was knocking on a door somewhere along the corridor. Then it came again, slightly louder and more insistent, accompanied by the soft calling of her name. Frowning, Abbie started for the door. Halfway there, she realized that the rapping was coming from the door to the adjoining motel room. She stopped in front of it and waited until the sound came again.

"Yes?" she said hesitantly.

"It's me, MacCrea. Open the door."

She fumbled briefly with the lock, then pulled the door open. There he stood, leaning in the doorway to the next room and dangling a room key from his hand.

"I gave the desk clerk a hundred dollars and told him one twenty-eight was my lucky number. Is it?"

She stared at him, momentarily at a loss for even the simplest answer. Then she found it. "Yes." She was in his room — and in his arms — before she had time to consider the decision. But it didn't matter. It was where she belonged. Where she had always belonged.

43

MACCREA DRIFTED SOMEWHERE between wakefulness and sleep, a heady contentment claiming him. He was reluctant to waken and break the spell of whatever dream he'd had that made him feel this good. Yet something — or someone — stirred against him and coolness touched his bare leg where heat had been. Instinctively he reached out to draw that warm body close to him again. The instant he touched her, he knew. He opened his eyes to look and make sure he wasn't dreaming. It was Abbie he held, nestled in the curve of his body.

In sleep, she reminded him of a more sensual version of Eden: the same dark hair billowing about her face like a black cloud, the same long-lashed eyes and full lower lip. Now fully awake and aroused by the recollection of last night's passion, MacCrea couldn't resist the urge to lean over and kiss the ripe curve of her lips.

She stirred beneath him, drowsily kissing him back. He lifted his head to study her, watching as she arched her back, stretching her arms overhead like a cat waking from a nap, the action brushing her breasts against his chest. Then she snuggled back down, her eyes more than half-closed.

"Is it morning?" she asked, her voice thick and husky with sleep.

"Does it matter?" Supporting himself on one arm, he ran his hand over her body, pausing long enough to arouse a sleeping nipple, then traveling back down.

"Yes." But her body language was giving him an entirely different answer.

"This is the way it should be every morning, Abbie: you and me in the same bed and Eden sleeping in the next room."

"I'd better get up. I don't want her waking up alone in a strange room." Shifting position, she reached for his wristwatch on the nightstand and glanced at the dial. "It's eight o'clock already. I need to get Eden up, finish packing, and get out to the airport in time to catch our flight."

MacCrea checked the move she made to get out of bed. "Take a later plane. Stay here with me awhile longer."

For an instant she gazed at him longingly, then she shook her head. "I can't." She rolled away from him to the other side of the bed. "Dobie's meeting us at the airport."

Disturbed by something in her tone, he stared at her slim back, watching as she picked the short nightgown off the floor and slipped it on. He wanted to pull her back onto the bed and make her stay. With some women that might work, but he knew Abbie wasn't one of them. Stifling his frustration, he reached for the pair of slacks lying on the floor and stepped into them.

As he pulled them up around his hips, coins and keys jingling in the pockets, he turned to study her. "You are going to tell him about us, aren't you?" She hesitated ever so slightly, but didn't answer. As she moved toward the connecting door between the two rooms, MacCrea didn't like the implication of her silence one damned bit. "Don't leave yet, Abbie—not unless you want this conversation to take place in front of Eden."

She paused short of the door and turned back as he came around the bed. "Why? What is there to talk about?"

But he didn't buy her attempt to feign ignorance. "About us, of course. Or didn't last night mean anything to you?" He was certain it had. He'd stake everything he owned on it.

"Of course, it did." She avoided his gaze, the action telling him more than she realized.

Confident now of her answer, he could ask, "Abbie, do you love me?"

She sighed and nodded. "Yes."

"You know this changes everything, Abbie." He watched the play of warring emotions upon her face. "You can't stay married to him now. You have to tell him the truth. You know that."

"I don't know any such thing," she retorted tightly.

MacCrea gritted his teeth, wanting to shake her until her own rattled. "What are you, Abbie? Too stubborn or too proud to admit you made a mistake? Or are you planning to be just like your father and stay married to someone you don't love and make everyone's life as miserable as your own?"

"That's not true," she flashed, startled into anger by his accusation.

"Isn't it? Then tell me just how long you expect me to go on living with this lie of yours?"

"I don't know. I haven't had time to think. I—"

"You'd better find the time, and quickly," MacCrea warned. "I've played it your way long enough. I'm not going to live the rest of my life this way, sneaking off to meet you whenever you can get away."

"Don't threaten me, MacCrea Wilder." Tears glittered in her blue eyes, adding a hot brilliance to them.

"It isn't a threat." Sighing, he took her by the shoulders, feeling her stiffness. "We love each other, Abbie. And I'm not going to let you do this to us."

"It just isn't as easy as you think it is," she said, continuing to protest faintly.

"But it's got to be easier than living a lie the rest of our lives."

She leaned against him and hugged him around his middle, like a child seeking comfort and reassurance. "I do love you, Mac. It's just so hard anymore to figure out what's right or wrong. I always thought I knew."

He kissed her. He didn't know what else to say or do.

* * *

The farmhouse bedroom stared back at her, its silence somehow heavy. The old hardwood furniture of mixed styles was nicked and scarred from years of use, but still more than serviceable. Dobie didn't believe in replacing something just because it was old. He waited until it was practically falling apart. The pretty chintz bedspread and pale blue linen curtains at the windows were her choices. At the time, getting them had seemed a minor triumph, but now, Abbie didn't care at all about them.

With enough clothes packed to last several days, she closed the lid of the suitcase and swung it off the bed. As she set it on the floor behind the bedroom door, her glance fell on the gold wedding band she wore. She twisted it off her finger, hesitated, then slipped it into the pocket of her white cotton shirtdress.

Downstairs a door slammed. Frowning slightly, Abbie paused to listen. When she heard footsteps in the kitchen, she went to investigate. She found Dobie standing at the sink, filling a glass with tap water, his battered hat pushed to the back of his head and hay chafe clinging to his sweaty skin.

"What are you doing here?" She glanced at the wall clock. "It isn't even lunchtime yet. Did something break down?"

He shook his head briefly, then drank down the water in the glass and turned back to the sink to refill it. "I saw the car leave. I thought maybe you'd gone off somewhere again." Suspicion was heavy in his tone.

"Ben took Eden to her swimming lesson. Afterward, he's taking her out for a hamburger and french fries, so they won't be back for lunch." It had been her suggestion. She hadn't wanted Eden anywhere around this noon.

"You could have fixed some here just as easy. And it'd been a lot cheaper, too."

Irritated by his niggardly remark, Abbie nearly told him that Ben was paying for the treat, but she checked the impulse. She didn't want to get sidetracked into a meaningless argument with him over money.

"We need to talk, Dobie."

"About what?"

"Us. Our marriage. It isn't working out." It was ironic. She'd been through this before. She wondered why this moment wasn't any easier the second time.

"You seemed satisfied until Wilder showed up."

She didn't try to deny that. "Maybe I thought things would change — that we just needed more time. But it hasn't worked, not from the beginning. You have to admit, Dobie, that I haven't been the kind of wife you wanted . . . someone who stays home, who's waiting here when you come in from the fields every night."

"Have I complained? I let you have your horses, and go traipsing all over the country —"

"Dobie, stop." She wasn't going to let this turn into one of their typical arguments. "Please, all I want is a divorce. Believe me, it will be better for both of us."

"It's Wilder, isn't it?" Dobie accused, his jaw clenched tightly. "You've been sneaking around and meeting him behind my back, haven't you? You want a divorce so you can marry him. That's it, isn't it?"

In a way, everything he said was true. Only none of it was the way he thought. "I love him," she admitted simply, quietly.

For an instant, he just stared at her, his eyes wide, his expression raw with pain. Then he swung around abruptly, facing the sink and gripping the edge of it, his head bowed and his shoulders hunched forward. Seeing him like that, Abbie wanted to cry, but she determinedly blinked back the tears.

"Dammit, Abbie," he said, his voice low and half-strangled by his attempt to control it, "I love you too. Doesn't that count for something?"

"Of course, it does. Why do you think this is so hard for me? I never meant to hurt you, Dobie. You don't know how many times I wished there was some other way."

"Then why are you doing this?"

"Because . . . it's the right thing to do, the fair thing."

"Fair for who?" He turned back to look at her, his eyes reddened with tears. "For you? For Wilder? What about me and Edie?"

Abbie glanced away, unable to meet his gaze. "We need to talk about Eden. I know how much you love her—"

"What do you expect? She's my daughter."

Mutely she shook her head, finding it almost impossible to say the words. But no matter how much it hurt him, she couldn't hide the truth any longer. "No, Dobie, she isn't."

"What?"

With difficulty, Abbie forced herself to look at him. "Eden isn't your daughter. I was already pregnant with her when we made love that first time."

"You're lying."

"Not this time. I wanted my baby to have a father and I knew you would be a good one. And you have been. It was wrong of me to deceive you like that, I know, but—"

"If I'm not her father, then who is?" Dobie demanded, still doubting. "Not Wilder—"

"Yes."

"But you can't prove it. And you can't expect me just to take your word for it."

"Look at the way her little fingers curl—MacCrea has one like it. I've never seen such a thing before. It's a Wilder family trait."

"My God." He whitened. "All these years . . ."

"I'm sorry," Abbie said. "More than you'll ever know."

When Abbie tried to reach MacCrea at his office, she was told he was at River Bend, meeting with Lane Canfield. There was a moment when she almost decided not to call him at all, but she needed to talk to him. Tense and anxious, she dialed the number.

Rachel answered the phone. Abbie recognized her voice instantly and had to fight the urge to hang up. "I'd like to speak to MacCrea Wilder, please. I was told he was there."

"Who's calling?"

Abbie clutched the receiver a little tighter. "It's Abbie. I need to speak to him. It's important."

"I'm sorry. He's in a meeting."

"I know that," she inserted quickly, fearing that Rachel would hang up on her. "Just tell him I'm on the phone."

There was no response for several long seconds. Then there was a dull clunk, but the line didn't go dead. Abbie could hear faint noises in the background, then distantly MacCrea's voice saying, "Abbie? Of course, I'll take it." A second later, there was a click and he was on the line.

"I'm sorry I called you there, but . . . I had to talk to you."

"Don't worry about that. Just tell me what's wrong. I can tell something is."

"I told Dobie this morning that I wanted a divorce. He knew right away that you were involved."

"What about Eden?"

"I told him you were her father, not him."

"And?"

She took a deep breath, trying to steady her nerves. "And he walked out of the house. He hasn't come back. I don't know where he went."

"Where are you now?"

"At Ben's house. We're going to stay here."

"Eden's with you?"

"Yes. She's in the living room, playing checkers with Ben." She glanced at the two heads, one gray and one dark, huddled over the checkerboard on the coffee table.

"I'll be right there."

"Mac, no. You can't. It will only make things worse if Dobie finds you here when he comes back."

"Dammit, Abbie, you can't stay there."

"We have to . . . at least until we can find somewhere to take the mares and colts. I probably should have waited and talked to Dobie after we had found other facilities for the horses." When she thought of all the time and money she'd spent building her breeding farm there, she wished she had postponed her discussion with Dobie.

"I've got that handled. You can keep them at my place. I want you to throw some things in a suitcase, get Eden and Ben, and meet me over there in a half hour."

"But—"

"Abbie, don't argue with me. I don't want to take the chance that anything might happen to you . . . or Eden. If I can't come there, then you're going to come stay with me. Agreed?"

Abbie hesitated, then realized that if Dobie did cause a scene when he returned, it would be better if Eden didn't see it. She and Ben could always come back to take care of the horses. "Yes."

"Good. I'll see you there in half an hour. And, Abbie—"

"Yes?"

"I love you."

She felt the tears come. "I love you, too, Mac." And she loved him even more because he wasn't going to let her go through this alone. She continued to hold the phone to her ear after MacCrea had hung up, unwilling to let go of the closeness she had felt between them. She heard a second click, breaking the connection. Someone had been listening in. Abbie stared at the phone. That person had to have been Rachel.

* * *

After carefully replacing the telephone receiver in its cradle, Rachel turned to face the pocket doors to the library, and listened to the muffled voices of Lane and MacCrea coming from within. As the doors were slid apart, MacCrea stepped out and Rachel moved away from the telephone in the foyer.

"Leaving already, MacCrea?" she taunted, irritated at the way he was rushing to Abbie's side. Then she smiled sweetly at Lane, coming behind him. "I'll see him to the door, darling."

"Thank you. I do have some calls to make." Lane paused to shake hands with MacCrea. "I'll be getting back to you in the next week or so — after I've had a chance to review everything."

"I'll be waiting to hear from you. If you have any questions, just call." Then MacCrea turned, his glance briefly pausing on Rachel.

Smoothly, she slipped her arm into the crook of his and started walking him across the tiled foyer to the front door, waiting until she heard the retreat of Lane's footsteps before saying anything. "So. You've gotten yourself involved with Abbie again."

"That's my business, Rachel."

"You're a fool, MacCrea," she declared, releasing a sigh of disgust. "She only wants your money. Surely you can see that. You know as well as I do that she's determined to establish a stud farm that will rival River Bend. But that husband of hers won't give her the money to do it, so she's picked you."

"I'd be careful about pointing fingers if I were you, Rachel." MacCrea unhooked his arm from hers and reached for the solid brass doorknob. "Because every time you do, the other three fingers point back at yourself."

Stung by that complacent, knowing look in his dark eyes, Rachel drew back to glare at him. "I hope you remember that I tried to warn you." But he was already out the door, closing it in her face.

Abbie was waiting in the shade of the deck when MacCrea pulled into the driveway and parked his car next to hers. As she watched him come striding up the walk, indifferent to the broiling heat and stifling humidity of the East Texas summer afternoon, she felt some of her anxieties slipping away. He looked so strong and vital, so capable of handling any situation, that she finally really believed that everything was going to be all right. It was crazy when she thought about it. She had always prided herself on being independent, not needing anyone. Now she found herself wanting to lean on someone. Not just someone, she qualified that quickly in her mind. She wanted to lean on Mac-Crea.

As he reached her, he glanced around and frowned. "Where are Eden and Ben?"

"We saw the stables in back when we drove in. You know Ben. He had to check them out. Eden went along with him."

"How's she taking all this?"

"She doesn't know what's going on." Abbie shook her head, staring at the white buttons on his shirtfront and wishing he would take her in his arms and hold her. "I haven't told her yet."

"We'll do it later . . . together," MacCrea said, exactly as she had hoped he would.

"She's so young, I don't know how much of this she'll understand, especially about you."

"We'll take it slow . . . a step at a time." He gazed at her. "To tell you the truth, Abbie, I wasn't sure you'd break with him, at least not right away."

"If I'd thought it through, I probably would have waited. With the horses and a mare due to foal, and the race two weeks away, my timing isn't exactly the best." But the truth was, she didn't want to have to sleep in the same bed with Dobie anymore — not now, not after being with MacCrea. "But I had to."

"If you hadn't, Abbie, in another two days, I would have," he stated firmly, leaving her in no doubt that he would have done just that. "God, I've missed you," he said in the next breath and gathered her into his arms, kissing her hungrily, deeply. Just for an instant, Abbie let herself forget everything except the love that blazed between them — a fire that heated every inch of her body and lit every corner of her heart. When he pulled away, his breathing had grown ragged — as hers had. "It seems a helluva lot longer than three days since I held you like this."

"For me, too."

"How long do you think it will take Ben to look over the stable?"

"Not that long." She smiled.

MacCrea sighed as he released her, removing temptation to arm's length. "It's a damned shame there aren't more than six stalls down there."

"I didn't even know the property had a stable on it."

"That was one of my criteria when I had the realtor looking for a place. Horses were bound to be involved somewhere in the bargain, whether it was just Eden or it included you. I know it isn't River Bend —"

"There's only one River Bend." She wished he hadn't mentioned it . . . and she wished she hadn't said that. "I'm sorry." She couldn't look at him.

"I thought you'd gotten over losing it."

"It was my home. You never get over something like that. You just go on." She looked down at her hands, remembering the feel of River Bend dirt between her fingers. "You go on and hope that someday you'll find a place that will mean as much." Forcing a smile, she turned her face up to him. "You haven't shown me your house, yet, MacCrea."

He studied her thoughtfully, then turned. "Eden and Ben are coming. We might as well wait for them."

Eden came running up to show them one of the long seed pods from the catalpa trees that shaded the lawn. When Ben joined them, MacCrea led them into the sprawling adobe ranch house, built around a center courtyard.

White stucco and dark heavy beams dominated the interior design, with French doors in nearly every room opening onto the courtyard. Large skylights had been cut into the red-tiled roof, letting in the sun by day and the moon and stars by night, again incorporating the outdoors into the house. Throughout, floors of Tercate clay tiles gave way to sections of hardwood and Indian rugs.

As soon as Eden saw the huge stone fireplace in the living room, she immediately wanted MacCrea to start a fire in it, but Abbie managed to convince her that despite the air-conditioning, it was too warm for one. The room was done with antique English and American pieces and deep suede sofas.

When MacCrea showed her the child's suite, all done in light pink and mauve, Eden was enchanted by the canopied bed.

"We shouldn't have any trouble persuading her to go to sleep tonight," Abbie remarked as they left the room.

"I counted on that," MacCrea replied, his glance warmly suggestive of the plans he had for their time alone.

"Where's Mommy going to sleep?" Eden wanted to know.

"In here." He opened the door to the master suite.

A rounded fireplace of white adobe brick was nestled in one corner of the room, with a couple of easy chairs in front of it. Fur rugs flanked the king-sized bed that dominated the other side of the room. Two large closets were linked by a separate dressing room leading to an exquisite marble bath.

"Isn't it grand, Mommy?" Eden declared, sighing expressively. "Mac has the nicest home I've ever seen."

"I'm glad you like it, short stuff." MacCrea scooped her up to ride on his hip.

"I do, but, what about Ben?" She frowned at him. "You haven't shown us his room."

"I will not be staying here tonight, Eden," Ben inserted. "We have a sneaky mare who would pick such a time to have her baby."

MacCrea turned to him. "Can you handle everything all right, Ben?"

Abbie looked on as Ben let the question hang unanswered for several seconds while he quietly studied MacCrea with a critical eye. "I think there will be no trouble. One of the grooms will take part of the foal watch for me. You look after these two, and I will look after the horses."

Later that night, after they had tucked Eden into bed, Abbie lay curled on MacCrea's lap, her head nestled against his shoulder and her lips still warm from the kisses he'd given her when he'd pulled her into the chair with him. A heavy sigh broke from her, betraying her inner restlessness.

"What's wrong?" MacCrea asked, tipping his head to peer at her face.

"I feel a little guilty about Ben being at the farm, dealing with Dobie by himself and sitting up half the night with the mare. All this is my doing. I should be there taking the brunt of it, not Ben."

"Ben isn't going to have any problems with him."

"I hope you're right." She sighed again.

"I know I am."

She tilted her head back to study the quiet strength that was an innate part of his features — the sculpted cheekbone and slanted jawline. "Ben respects you. I was never sure how he felt about you until I saw the way he looked at you today."

"It's mutual."

"I saw that, too." She smiled.

He cupped her cheek in his hand and let his thumb trace the curved line of her mouth. His hands were no longer calloused, but Abbie found their smoothness equally stimulating. He bent down and rubbed his mouth across her lips, deliberately withholding the promised kiss to tease her. Reaching up, Abbie slid her fingers into his hair and forced his head down until she felt the satisfying pressure of his lips devouring hers, their tongues melding as they tasted each other.

Reluctantly MacCrea pulled back. "How much longer do you think it will be before that daughter of ours is sound asleep?" His hand slid under the long white skirt of her dress and caressed the back of her thigh.

"Not long." Abbie wanted to block everything else out of her mind except loving him, but she couldn't. She snuggled against him again and absently rubbed her cheek against his shoulder.

"What are you thinking?"

Abbie hesitated. "I was just wondering what . . . Dobie is going to do. I'd feel easier if I knew."

"Abbie." MacCrea lifted her chin, forcing her to look at him. "You're with me, and that's the way it's going to be from now on. There's nothing he can do that will change that. Not Dobie. Not Rachel. Not anyone."

"I know." She turned her face into his hand and kissed his palm, then rubbed her jaw and chin against it. "When I called you today, I think she listened in."

"I wouldn't be surprised." MacCrea paused, wanting more than anything to kiss her and kindle the passion he knew he could arouse. But he knew it wasn't what she wanted from him just now. "I was going to wait to tell you after the deal was finalized, but Lane agreed, in principle today, to sell me his interest in Wilder Oil. There's still a lot of details to work out, but in three or four weeks, it should be all signed and official."

"What?" She stared at him, her blue eyes wide with disbelief.

"I offered to buy him out shortly after I moved back. It's taken me this long to raise the necessary capital to make the deal. With the nosedive oil prices have taken lately, banks aren't exactly eager to loan money on something like this."

"Can you afford to buy him out?"

"To tell you the truth, I'm in hock up to my neck." MacCrea smiled. "I hope the Arabian horse business is good."

"But . . . why are you doing this?"

"Can't you guess?" he teased. "I lost you twice because of my business dealings with Lane and Rachel. I'm not about to let that be the reason I lose you a third time."

"You don't have to do this."

"That's a risk I'm not willing to take."

"You're crazy, MacCrea." But there was love in her eyes.

"You're damned right I am. All because of you." Seeing that look on her face, he couldn't keep a rein on his desire any longer.

Kissing and caressing her, he dispensed with the barrier of her clothes, turning her faint protests about Eden into low moans of need. When she was writhing against him, he carried her to the bed, stripped off his own clothes, and joined her there, immediately reaching out to gather her close and feel the heat of her flesh against his. He nibbled at her throat and breasts while his hands stroked the smooth skin of her thighs and hips, letting the tension build until the ache was mutual.

As he buried himself inside her, she arched her hips to take him all in. They rocked together, the tempo building, straining. For one brief instant, before the paroxysm of intense pleasure claimed him, MacCrea somehow knew that it would always be this way with them — thrust matching thrust, passion equaling passion, and love rivaling love. And he didn't want it any other way.

* * *

Three days later, Dobie's attorney contacted Abbie and informed her of Dobie's terms for an uncontested divorce. She was to agree to the immediate termination of her lease on his property, relinquish all financial claims to any permanent improvements she had made on his land, forfeit any rights to property acquired since their marriage, remove his name from Eden's birth certificate, and waive any claim for child support. In return, she was to keep all of her Arabian horses, the related tack and stable equipment, and the monies earned from them, plus any personal items that belonged to Abbie or her daughter, and allow him reasonable visitation privileges with Eden. Abbie agreed.

44 ⌐

LIKE A MONARCH SURVEYING his admiring subjects, the blood bay stallion gazed at the crowd gathered at the paddock rail. Magnificent and regal, he seemed totally indifferent to the saddle being placed on his back and the ministrations of the attendants — a king accustomed to being dressed by others.

"Isn't he just stunning, Lane?" she declared, unable to turn her gaze away from Sirocco to glance at her husband. "Have you ever seen him look so sleek and fit? He's going to win today. I know he is."

Hearing her voice, the stallion thrust his dark muzzle toward her, stretching out his long neck. Rachel moved to his head, rubbing him just behind the ear and studying up close the huge dark eyes and the network of veins on his face, so intent on her stallion that she didn't hear Lane's reply.

"We'll all be cheering for him."

"Who said beauty can't run?" she crooned softly. "We'll show her today, won't we?" She gave him a hug and a kiss. "Just for luck," she said and stepped back to stand next to Lane.

Out of the corner of her eye, Rachel caught a silver-white flash of movement and turned her head slightly to look at the white stallion, his head flung high, his nostrils widely distended as if trying to catch her scent. A little to the left stood Abbie with that old Polack guru of hers, Ben Jablonski. MacCrea was there, too, and the child. Rachel stared at the smiling and confident foursome, conscious of a faint bristling along her spine.

"May I give Sirocco a good luck pat, Mother? Will he let me?"

Distracted by the sight of her longtime rival, Rachel snapped an irritated, "Of course."

Then the unusualness of her son's request struck her and she turned to stare at Alex, dressed in short pants and a button-down white shirt, his brown hair neatly slicked in place. Warily, he approached the bay stallion and reached up to cautiously pet a muscled shoulder. "Good luck, Sirocco," he offered softly, then backed up quickly when the stallion dipped his head toward him. Alex stopped when he was safely between his father and Mrs. Weldon again.

"You have certainly gotten braver, Alex. I always thought you were afraid of horses," Rachel commented, wondering at the change in him.

He looked down, avoiding her gaze. "They're big, but they won't hurt you —not on purpose."

"I'm glad you finally realized that. Horses can be your dearest friends." She gazed at the stallion, this son of Simoon that meant so much to her, then glanced back at Alex in time to catch his small nod of agreement. "Has a horse become your friend, Alex?" Once she'd seen him duck under the fence to the broodmare pasture and disappear among the pecan trees. She knew how curious horses could be and wondered if one of them had come to investigate this small human who had entered their domain.

But her only response from Alex was a noncommittal shrug as he tucked his chin even closer to the collar of his white shirt. Frustrated, Rachel wondered why she even bothered to try to communicate with her son. He didn't want anything to do with her. He never did. Lane and his nanny, Mrs. Weldon, were the only two people Alex cared about.

Leaving the paddock area, they started making their way to their box seats in the grandstand. She knew that Ross would be waiting for them . . . as planned. Of course, she'd act surprised to see him and pretend that she didn't know he was in town—both of them ignoring the fact they'd been together last night.

It had been an absolutely wonderful evening, marred only by one small argument when Ross had attempted to give her the business card of a supposedly brilliant divorce lawyer. No matter how many times she tried to explain to him, Ross simply refused to accept the fact that she didn't want to get a divorce from Lane, not now and not later. Why should she? She had everything she could ever possibly want: her horses, her home, Lane, and Ross.

Rachel led the way as they approached the box. She spied Ross immediately, the cowboy hat on his head distinctly setting him apart from the crowd. He had on a pair of dark glasses, partly to shade his eyes from the bright July sunlight and partly to avoid being recognized by the large holiday crowd at the racetrack.

"Lane, look who's here." But she didn't wait for his reply, quickening her steps to hurry to Ross. "This is a surprise," she declared, briefly going into his arms and kissing the air near his cheek. "I thought you weren't going to be able to make it. You told me last week that you had a performance scheduled on the Fourth."

"I do," Ross said, speaking up for Lane's benefit. "I promised Willie I'd be on hand to sing at his annual picnic. If I leave right after the race, I can just make it. I told my pilot to have the plane fueled and the engines running so we could take off as soon as I got to the airport." As Lane joined them in the box, Rachel moved to the side to allow Ross to shake hands with him. "Hello, Lane. It's good to see you again. With your busy schedule, I wasn't sure you'd be here today either."

"There was no chance of that, Ross. I've always made it a point to be with Rachel at events that are important to her."

Startled by his statement, Rachel looked at him—startled because it was true. Even though Lane hadn't been at every single horse show or race, he had been present for the major ones despite his busy schedule. Until this very moment, she hadn't realized that.

Minutes later, the horses paraded onto the track, its condition officially listed as fast. Immediately she gave them her undivided attention, excluding every other thought from her mind.

As the horses were led into the starting gate, Rachel lifted the binoculars to watch the proceedings, using them as well to hide the mounting tension that stretched her nerves thin. Sirocco had to win this race. Right now, it was more important to her than winning the Nationals this fall.

When the gates sprang open to the loud clanging of bells, it felt as if her heart leaped into her throat and stayed there, a strangling ball of apprehension. The eleven horses appeared to explode as one out of the gates and ran stride for stride for several yards. Then she saw Sirocco surge forward to take the lead, a black-tipped flame racing in front of the field.

A chestnut came up to challenge on the outside. Rachel scanned the rest of the field, finally locating Abbie's horse, running in fifth or sixth position. Someone had told her that he usually came off the pace.

The other nine horses in the field didn't really mean anything to her. In her mind, this race was between Sirocco and Windstorm. As the horses rounded the first turn and headed down the backstretch with Sirocco still running in front, Rachel briefly lowered her glasses and stole a glance at Abbie, standing in a nearby owner's box. Even at a distance, she looked animated and excited, tense with emotion. Rachel felt like a statue by comparison, unable to let her feelings show. She wanted to yell and cheer, too, but she couldn't.

Instead she trained the binoculars on the blood bay stallion leading the field by three lengths. But that distance was quickly shortened as other horses made their move on him coming out of the turn for home. The silver-white horse along the rail charged closer with every stride. But Sirocco's jockey didn't see him. He was concentrating on the black bay charging up on the outside to challenge Sirocco.

Rachel wanted to yell a warning to the jockey, but she couldn't seem to open her mouth. The white stallion got a nose in front, but Sirocco came right back to race neck and neck with him, muscles bulging and straining, hooves pounding and digging the hard dirt.

An eighth of a mile from the finish line, Sirocco's jockey went to the whip. The bay stallion seemed to respond with a fresh burst of speed, but he couldn't shake off his challenger. The white stallion stayed right with him. Suddenly Sirocco appeared to stumble. The jockey tried to pull him up, but in the next stride, he fell, tumbling headfirst onto the track, directly in the path of the onrushing field.

"No!" Rachel screamed, trying to deny what her eyes were seeing as she struggled free from the pair of hands that gripped her. "Not Sirocco! No!"

Abbie never saw Windstorm cross the finish line in front. She felt numb with shock, her gaze riveted in horror on the fallen horse and rider, both lying motionless in the wake of the field. A hush had fallen over the crowd as several track personnel rushed to the downed victims.

"What happened, Mommy? Why isn't that horse getting up? Is he hurt?"

Hearing the fearful uncertainty in her voice, Abbie held Eden closer. "I'm afraid so, honey."

"Will he be all right?"

"I don't know." The jockey was attempting to get up despite the efforts of two men to make him lie still and wait for the ambulance speeding onto the track. But there was no discernible movement from the stallion. Abbie looked over at Rachel's box. Sirocco wasn't even her horse, but she could feel the pain, remembering her own terrible ordeal when River Breeze lay hurt.

Lane was at Rachel's side, an arm around her for support, as he cleared a path for them through the gawking crowd. Distantly Abbie could hear Rachel's hysterical, sobbing cries, "I've got to go to him. Please. I've got to go to him."

"Oh, God." Abbie turned away from the sight. She felt MacCrea's hand touch her shoulder.

"They'll want you down in the winner's circle for the cup presentation."

"I can't." She shook her head from side to side, protesting the need for her to be there. She'd won. At last she'd beaten Rachel. But she just felt sick inside.

"You have to. Windstorm won. The accident doesn't change that." Taking her by the elbow, MacCrea steered her out of the box toward the winner's circle below. Abbie knew he was right, but that didn't make it any easier.

Outside the winner's circle, she stopped, ignoring the attempts of a track steward to hustle her inside. The enclosure gave her a full view of the activity on the track. She could see the bay stallion lying in the dirt, the sunlight firing his red coat. The track veterinarian crouched beside the horse and several others stood around him. As two paramedics helped the jockey into the ambulance, Lane and Rachel walked onto the track.

"MacCrea, please. I have to know how serious it is. Will you go see?"

He regarded her solemnly for an instant. "Of course."

As MacCrea walked away, Abbie reluctantly allowed herself to be ushered into the winner's circle along with Ben and Eden. When Windstorm came prancing in, tugging at the groom's lead, lathered but still eager, she felt a rush of pride. She had bred and raised this stallion, a winner on the racetrack and in the show ring. Tearfully she hugged the Arabian stallion.

"We won, fair and square." The jockey was all smiles as he glanced down at her. "We were going past him before he went down."

"What happened? Do you know?" she asked.

He shook his head. "I heard a pop . . . like a bone snapping. He was a game horse, but we woulda won anyway. I asked Storm for more and he had it to give. The bay only had heart left."

"Like a bone snapping": the phrase echoed and reechoed in her mind. She tried to remind herself that a broken bone didn't necessarily mean the end of Sirocco. Look at River Breeze. "What about the jockey?"

"Joe, one of the stewards, said it looked like he broke his shoulder and maybe got a concussion out of it. Angel's tough. He'll be all right. I've seen worse spills."

A track official came over. "We're ready to make the presentation now, Mrs. Hix, if you'll just step over here."

As Abbie turned to follow him, the jockey repeated his earlier statement. "We woulda won anyway."

Numbly she accepted the congratulations from the race's sponsor, along with the silver trophy cup and the winner's share of the purse, and posed for the obligatory photograph, but she couldn't smile for the camera — not when, beyond it, she could see Rachel on the track, kneeling beside her stallion, mindless of the white linen suit she wore.

At last it was over. Abbie paused outside the winner's circle, watching as the jockey dismounted and pulled off the saddle to weigh in officially. A groom spread a blue blanket over Windstorm's lathered back and led him away.

"Aren't we going with Windstorm back to the barn, Mommy?" Eden frowned up at her, puzzled by this change in their routine and the strange undercurrents in the air.

"Not now. I want to wait for MacCrea." He was walking back across the track toward them now. She had to know what he'd found out.

"How come you look so sad, Mommy? Aren't you happy that Windstorm won?"

Sighing, Abbie tried to come up with an answer. "I am happy that he won, but I'm also sorry the other horse got hurt." But it wasn't just any horse. Sirocco was Rachel's stallion. Abbie didn't know how to explain to Eden why that was so significant. "Wait here with Ben while I go talk to MacCrea."

Ignoring Eden's protest that she wanted to come, too, Abbie walked forward to meet MacCrea. She searched his face for some clue as to the seriousness of Sirocco's injuries, but his expression showed her nothing. Unconsciously she tightened her hold on the silver trophy cradled in her arm as a truck pulled to a stop near the fallen horse, its bulk blocking the stallion from her sight.

"How bad is it?" she asked.

But MacCrea didn't answer until he was directly in front of her. When he gently gripped her shoulders, Abbie tried to brace herself mentally. "He's dead, Abbie. He broke his neck in the fall."

"No." It came out in one long, painful breath. "Oh, God, no." She sagged against him, moving her head from side to side, trying to deny it. "It can't be true. It can't."

"It is. I'm sorry."

"Why?" she cried, doubling her hand into a fist. "Why did it have to happen?"

But there were no answers to the questions she asked. Again, her gaze was drawn to the track as she pushed away from MacCrea. This time she understood the reason for the truck. It was there to haul away the dead stallion. Soon the horses in the next race would parade onto the track and everyone would be hurrying to place their bets, the tragedy of this race temporarily forgotten. But Abbie knew she would never forget that moment when Sirocco went down, or the tangle of legs as the onrushing horses struggled to jump the obstacle suddenly in their path, the stumbling, the near collisions, the wild swervings, and then, in the settling dust, Sirocco lying there, motionless.

Through a misting of tears, she saw Rachel, slowly walking her way, supported by Lane, her usually composed features wracked by grief. As she moved to intercept Rachel, MacCrea stopped her.

"Where are you going?"

"Rachel . . . I have to talk to her. I never wanted this to happen."

"Abbie, no. It's better if you don't."

But she wouldn't listen to him, pulling away to walk to them. Lane saw her first and paused, but Rachel stared at her without appearing to see her at all.

"Rachel, I . . . just wanted you to know that . . . I'm sorry." The words sounded so inadequate when she said them. "I'm truly sorry." But repeating them didn't seem to give them more weight.

Yet they must have penetrated, as Rachel looked at her with bitter loathing. "Why should you be sorry? Your horse won the race. That's what you wanted, isn't it?"

"I wanted him to win, yes, but . . . not this way." But the cup was there in her arms, evidence of Windstorm's victory.

"Why not?" Rachel challenged, her voice threatening to break. "Didn't you set out to prove that your stallion was better than mine? You've done it, so just go away and leave me alone. Sirocco's dead. Do you hear? He's dead. He's dead." She sobbed wildly and collapsed against Lane, hysterical now with grief.

This time when Abbie felt MacCrea's hand on her arm, she let him lead her away without a protest. "It's my fault," she said miserably.

"It was an accident, Abbie, an accident. It could have happened to any horse in the field, including Windstorm. I'm not going to let you blame yourself for it."

"But it was my fault. She would never have raced Sirocco if I hadn't goaded her into it. Remember that night right after Sirocco won at Scottsdale, when I told her that he'd won a beauty contest, that he didn't have the conformation to race? My God . . . I even told her he'd break down if she did race him. I forced her into this."

"She made her own decision. She knew the risk she was taking and raced him anyway. You can't hold yourself responsible for that."

But Abbie knew better.

45

THE MORNING BREEZE skipped across the swimming pool, then paused to riffle the pages of the purchase agreement on Lane's lap and scurried on. Automatically, Lane smoothed the pages flat as he continued to stare at the slight figure in the distance, huddled beside the freshly turned earth.

His half-lensed reading glasses sat on the umbrellaed poolside table next to him. He had yet to read the first page of the document on his lap. Not that he really needed to. He'd already gone over the agreement thoroughly the day before. He'd merely intended to look it over once more before MacCrea arrived this afternoon for the signing. But his concern for Rachel made it next to impossible to concentrate on business matters for any length of time.

"Watch me, Daddy!" Alex shouted.

With difficulty, he forced his attention away from Rachel and turned in time to see his son cannonball into the pool with a mighty splash that sprayed water far onto the deck. He waited until he saw Alex surface and dog-paddle vigorously toward the ladder.

"That's enough diving for today, Alex," he called to him. "You aren't that good a swimmer yet." If dog-paddling could be called swimming. "Get your inner tube and go play in the shallow end of the pool."

When Lane saw his young son trotting to the opposite side, he let his attention revert back to Rachel. She hadn't moved from her silent vigil by the grave.

"Excuse me, Mr. Canfield." Maria, the housemaid, approached his chair, the thick rubber soles of her white work shoes making almost no sound as she crossed the deck. "Mr. Tibbs is here." She partially turned to indicate the man following her dressed in new jeans and a pearl-snap western shirt.

"Thank you, Maria." Lane absently moved the papers off his lap and rose to greet his guest. "Hello, Ross. I wasn't aware you were expected." Briefly he shook hands with him, then motioned to the deck chair next to his. "Have a seat."

"Sorry, I can't stay." Ross removed his cowboy hat and briefly ran his fingers through his curly hair, then used both hands to turn the dark hat in a circle in front of him, inching it around by degrees. "I just stopped by to see how Rachel is. I know how upset she was over Sirocco. I only wish I could have stayed —"

"I understand." Lane found it strangely ironic to be standing here talking to Ross about Rachel. Although why not? They were two men who loved her. "She has taken the stallion's death very hard."

"Where is she?"

"Over there. By his grave," he said, pointing out the general location with a nod of his head. "She insisted on having him brought back for burial here at River Bend. At the time, I didn't see any harm in it. Now I'm not so sure it was a good idea."

"Do you mind if I go talk to her? I've brought something with me that might . . . well, make her feel a little better."

"Go ahead." At this point, Lane didn't care who brought Rachel out of her deep depression as long as someone did. He couldn't stand to see her this way.

With a self-conscious nod, Ross acknowledged the comment, then pushed the hat onto his head and walked away, cutting across the lawn toward the unmarked grave set off by itself near the fence line to the back pasture, halfway between the house and the barns. Lane watched him go, wondering if he would succeed, wondering if Rachel would wind up in his arms — this time for good. Yet she had turned to him, not Ross, when the accident occurred. Surely that action had to have been an instinctive one. At least, that's what he kept telling himself.

"Daddy. Daddy, did you see the big splash I made?" Alex came running around the pool to him, his wet, bare feet making slapping sounds on the concrete.

"I certainly did." Lane made a concerted effort to give Alex his whole attention. Too frequently in the last few days Alex had been shunted aside, Lane's concern for Rachel taking precedence over him. "You nearly got me wet."

"I know." Alex grinned with a trace of impish glee. "Would you like to swim with me for a while?"

"I'd like to, but I can't. I have some papers to go over, but I'll watch you."

Alex thought about that. "I think I'll just sit here with you for a while and rest. Swimming is pretty tiring."

"Yes, it is," Lane agreed, smiling faintly as Alex climbed onto the deck chair by the table.

Resuming his seat, Lane picked up the purchase agreement, but left his glasses on the table. Alex tapped his hand idly on the tubelike arm of the deck chair and gazed off in the direction of the grave. "What did Mr. Tibbs want?"

"He came to see your mother. He brought her something that he hopes will cheer her up a little."

"She's awfully sad, isn't she?"

"Yes. She loved Sirocco very much. She was there when he was born. You were just a tiny baby then. So she'd had him almost as long as she's had you. It hurts when you lose someone or something you care about a lot."

"I wish there was something I could do to make her feel better."

Lane caught the wistful note in Alex's voice and understood the need he felt to contribute something, however small. "Maybe there is."

"What?" Alex looked at him hopefully.

"A lot of times when you're very sad, little things mean more than anything else . . . thoughtful little things that say you care. For instance, you could pick your mother some wildflowers and give them to her so she can place them on Sirocco's grave. Or you could make her a card—"

"I could draw her a picture of Sirocco and color it for her. That way she'd always have a picture of him to remember what he looked like," Alex suggested excitedly. "She'd like that, wouldn't she? I can draw really, really good, Mrs. Weldon says. And I'd draw this extra good."

"I know you would. And I think your mother would like that very much." Lane smiled.

"I'm going to do it right now." Before the sentence was finished, Alex had scrambled out of the chair. He took off at a run for the house.

Watching him, Lane couldn't help thinking that it must be wonderful to be young and innocent enough to believe that you could find the answers for life's sorrows.

Rachel sat on the grass next to the long rectangular patch of freshly turned earth, something childlike in her pose: her legs curled up to one side, her head and shoulders bowed, one hand resting on the clods of dirt. A soft breeze ran over her dark hair, lifting tendrils and laying them back down like a mother lightly playing with a child's hair in an attempt to soothe and comfort.

As Ross walked up to her, she gave no sign that she was even aware of his presence. He paused, struck for a few seconds by the stark grief in her expression. There were no tears. He almost wished there were. He had the feeling they would have been easier to cope with than this intense sorrow that went so much deeper.

"Hello, Rachel."

At first he wasn't sure she'd heard him. Then she looked up. Her eyes were dull and blank, with almost no life in them at all. Even though she looked straight at him, Ross wasn't sure she saw him standing there. Then she seemed to rouse herself to some level of awareness.

"This is where Sirocco is buried. I'm having a marker made — a marble one, engraved with his name and the dates of his life, and a verse from a poem I once read. I've changed it a little to make it just for him." Almost dreamlike, she quoted the line, " 'If you have seen nothing but the beauty of his markings and limbs, his true beauty was hidden from you.' "

"It's beautiful."

"Feel the earth." She dug her fingers into the dirt. "It's warm . . . like his body was."

"It's the sun that makes it feel that way."

He started to worry about her, then she sighed dispiritedly and gazed up at him. This time the pain was visible in her expression. "I know," she said. "But sometimes I like to pretend it's from him."

"You can't do things like that, Rachel. It isn't good for you."

"I don't care. I want him to be here . . . with me," she declared insistently.

"Don't do this, Rachel. He's gone. You can't change that. I'm here with you. Please, come walk with me." Taking her by the shoulders, he gently forced her to stand up.

She offered no resistance, yet she continued to stare at the grave, reluctant to leave it as he turned her away. "He should be here, nickering to those mares in the pasture."

"I wish there was some way I could make you feel better — something I could say . . . or do. But I just don't know the right words." He felt helpless and frustrated, just like at the track. "You don't know how many times I wished that I hadn't left you that day, but I had to. There didn't seem to be anything I could do there. Lane was with you. I knew he'd look after you and see to everything."

"Lane's always there, every time," she murmured.

"I know." It bothered him that she had turned to Lane in those first shocked seconds after the accident occurred. She was supposed to be in love with him. "Look, I'm due back in Nashville tonight. My record company wants me to cut a new album and I have a meeting scheduled tomorrow with the producer. But if you want me to stay here with you, I'll cancel it."

"There's no need. It doesn't matter whether you're here or not. Nothing matters anymore."

She was so indifferent, so distant with him, as if he were a stranger, not the man who had held her in his arms and made love to her countless times in the past. They were walking side by side, his arm was around her, yet there was no sense of closeness. Somehow he had to change that.

"Come on. I have something to show you." He picked up their pace as they neared the palatial barn, but his statement sparked no interest from her. "Aren't you going to ask what it is?"

"What?" It was obvious she asked only because he prompted her.

"It's a surprise, but I can guarantee you're going to like it. Just wait and see if you don't."

But when Rachel spotted the truck and horse trailer parked outside the barn's imposing main entrance, she pulled back. "Somebody's here. I don't want to see them."

"It's okay. Honest. That's my rig."

"Yours? I don't understand." She frowned at him. For the first time, Ross had the feeling that he'd finally gotten through that wall of grief that insulated her.

"Remember I said I had a surprise for you." He motioned to the handler standing at the back of the trailer, gesturing for him to bring the filly out. "Well, here it is." Stopping, he turned to watch her face as the man walked the filly into her view. A puzzled look flickered across her face as she stared at the young Arabian, the morning sunlight flashing on her bronze coat. "It's Jewel," he said.

"Yes, but why did you bring her here?" She turned to him, her frown deepening.

"I want you to have her." As she drew back from him, still frowning, Ross went on. "I know how much you've always wanted her, and I meant it when I said she wasn't for sale. We're never going to have that foal out of her by Sirocco, so I'm giving her to you — as a present."

"No." She backed another step away from him, vaguely indignant and angry.

Puzzled by her reaction, Ross took the lead rope from the handler and offered it to her. "Please take her." But she shook her head and hid her hands behind her back. "I want you to have her, Rachel. I know she's not Sirocco, and . . . maybe I can't make it up to you for not staying with you after the accident, but let me try."

Something inside her seemed to snap. "Why does everybody always give me presents? Do you think you can buy me?" she cried in outrage. "Presents don't make up for all the hours I've been alone. I'm not a child that you can give a bauble to and think that will make the hurt go away. It won't work anymore!"

"I don't know what you're talking about," Ross said, confused and taken aback by her sudden outburst. "I'm not trying to buy you. I —"

"Then what do you call it? You feel guilty, so you want to give me your horse so you can ease your conscience. Well, I don't want your horse! And I don't want you! Just take your horse and get out of here. Don't ever come back! Do you hear? Not ever again!" Her hands were clenched into fists at her sides as she stood before him, trembling with anger, tears rolling down her cheeks.

"Rachel, you don't mean that. You're just upset." Stunned, Ross struggled to find an excuse for the abrupt change in her. "You don't know what you're saying."

"I know precisely what I'm saying," she retorted, her voice quivering with anger. "And if you don't have that horse loaded up and out of here within five minutes, I'm calling the sheriff and ordering him to escort you off this farm." She turned on her heel and headed for the barn, breaking into a run when she was halfway to the door.

"Rachel . . ." Ross took an uncertain step after her, unable to believe any of this was really happening.

"I think she means it," the handler said behind him.

Ross was forced to agree.

Sobbing in despair, Rachel ran straight to the section of the barn that housed the broodmares, not stopping until she reached the third one from the end. Hurrying frantically, she unhooked the webbed gate and went inside, pausing long enough to fasten it behind her, then throwing her arms around the neck of the dappled gray mare inside and burying her face in the charcoal-streaked mane.

"Simoon, Simoon," she cried brokenly. "Why do they always do this? Why? They keep trying to give me presents, when all I want is their love. Nobody really cares about me. Nobody." As she sobbed out her anguish and hurt, she felt the mare nudging her anxiously, accompanied by a soft whicker of concern. "No, that's not true, is it? You care, don't you, my beauty?" Rachel murmured, moving to face the mare and taking her head in both her hands, smiling faintly as the mare nuzzled at the tears on her cheeks, then, with a slurp of her big tongue, licked curiously at the salty wetness. "I love you, too, my Simoon. You've never let me down, have you?"

Straw rustled in the adjoining stall as the aging red gelding moved closer to the dividing partition and nickered for attention. Turning, Rachel scratched the underside of his grayed lip through the bars while she continued to rub the hollow behind the mare's ear.

"I know you care, too, Ahmar. I haven't forgotten you," she crooned, still intensely sad.

Overhead, circulating fans whirred, constantly moving the air and stirring up the strong smell of horse, hay, manure, and grain. Rachel turned back to the mare and rubbed her head against the mare's cheek, cuddling close to the Arabian, enjoying the slickness of her coat and the heat from her body, and breathing in her stimulating odor, finding a reassurance in the equine contact that she needed.

"Are you all right, Miz Canfield?"

Startled by the human intrusion, Rachel caught a quick glimpse of the groom standing at the stall entrance, then ducked back behind the mare, keeping her face hidden so he couldn't see her tears. She didn't want him or anybody else feeling sorry for her. She didn't need or want their pity.

"Yes, I am," she asserted. "I'd like to be alone. Please . . . go."

"Yes, ma'am."

Ahmar snorted as the groom passed his stall. When the gelding's attention swung back to her, Rachel knew they were alone.

"It always was the three of us, wasn't it?" she remembered, then reconsidered her statement. "Not always. For a while there were four. Now . . . Sirocco's gone. I miss him so much." She could feel the sobs coming again and hugged Simoon's neck. "Why did he have to die like that? It isn't fair. Your son's gone, Simoon. Do you understand that? Your son . . . and mine, too."

She began to cry softly, her tears wetting the dark gray hairs on the mare's neck. Here, she felt free to pour out her sorrows and her pain, free to grieve over the death of her beloved stallion and the betrayal by yet another man who hadn't truly loved her.

Simoon snorted and swung her head toward the stall opening, warning Rachel of someone's approach. Sniffling back her tears, she wiped frantically at her wet cheeks and eyes and struggled to summon a modicum of composure.

"Mommy?" Alex appeared, moving slowly down the wide aisle between the box stalls, cautiously looking to the right and left. "Are you here?"

She wanted to pretend she couldn't hear him, to slink into the far corner of the stall and hide from him — from everyone. But she knew she couldn't do that.

"Yes, Alex. What is it?" she demanded, her voice tight and choked from her recent cry.

At first he didn't know which stall her voice had come from, then he saw her. "There you are." He trotted eagerly to the webbed gate, trying to hide the sheet of paper in his hand behind his back. "I've been looking everywhere for you."

"If it's time for lunch, tell Maria I'm not hungry," she retorted sharply, impatient to be rid of him and be alone again. It was too difficult trying to hide all the hurt and pain she felt. She remembered the terrible agony of all his questions during the flight home: Why did Sirocco die? Why did he break his neck? Why did Mommy race him? Why was Mommy crying? Why did she love Sirocco? Why, why, why. She couldn't bear the thought of going through that ordeal all over again. Lane should be here to answer his questions the way he had on the plane.

"It isn't lunchtime yet. At least, I don't think it is. I brought you something." Stretching, he reached over the webbing, all smiles and eagerness, as he held out the paper he'd been hiding behind his back. "It's for you. I wanted to wrap it in pretty paper with a bow and everything, but Mrs. Weldon said we didn't have any."

Another present, Rachel thought bitterly. Why were they all trying to buy her? "I don't want it."

His smile faded abruptly. "But . . . Daddy thought —"

"Daddy was wrong! I don't want any presents! Not from you. Not from anyone. Do you understand?" She was too blinded by the angry tears that scalded her eyes to see the stricken look on his face. "Go. Go back to your daddy. I don't want you here!"

Whirling around, she sought the comfort of Simoon's warm body. Distantly, she heard the sound of his racing footsteps as Alex ran from the stall, the paper fluttering into the stall to land on the bedding of wood shavings.

She was alone with her horses again, and that was the way she wanted it. She didn't need anybody. And she spent the next hour trying to convince herself and them of that.

When she heard footsteps in the brick aisle approaching the stall again, she railed silently at the world for not leaving her alone. She saw Lane come into view, his leonine mane of silver hair distinctly identifying him as he glanced anxiously around.

"Alex?" he called.

Rachel nearly laughed out loud. She should have known he wasn't worried about her. He only cared about his son. She shrank back against the wall, trying to make herself small, hoping he wouldn't see her. But the movement seemed to draw his attention. He turned and looked directly at her.

"Rachel, have you seen Alex? Lunch is ready. But when Maria called him, he didn't answer."

"I don't know where he is," she replied flatly, her voice sounding as dull and dead as she felt inside.

Lane frowned and stepped closer to the stall. "But he must be around here somewhere. One of the grooms said he was positive he saw him come — What's that?" He stared at something on the stall floor. Reluctantly Rachel moved around to the other side of the mare to see what he meant. A paper, crumpled in the center by a hoof, lay among the shavings. Rachel saw it, but she made no attempt to retrieve it as Lane unhooked the gate and entered the stall. "Isn't that the picture of Sirocco that Alex drew for you?"

"I guess." She shrugged as he picked up the paper to look at it.

"Then he was here? He brought this to you?" He glanced at her questioningly, seeking confirmation.

"Yes." She stared at the paper Lane held, resenting all that it represented. "I told him I didn't want it. I thought he took it with him."

"You what?" Lane glared at her in cold, disbelieving anger. "How could you do that? He made this for you!"

"I don't care!" she hurled angrily. "Why should I? All my life people have given me presents, thinking that would make up for everything. Well, it doesn't! It never has."

"My God, Rachel, he's just a child. He wanted to do something that might make you feel better. Are you so wrapped up in your own self-pity that you can't see that we hurt because you hurt? This was more than a child's drawing. It was his way of letting you know he cared!"

Never in her life had Rachel ever seen Lane so angry. All his angry words hammered at her like blows to the head. For a second, she thought he was actually going to strike her. She shrank from him, cowering a little.

"I didn't know," she said faintly. "I thought —"

"You thought," he repeated harshly. "You thought only about yourself. I wonder if you ever think about anybody else." He left her standing there, still reeling from his angry condemnation.

As MacCrea drove past the massive white pillars that marked the entrance to River Bend, he glanced at the clock on the car's dashboard. He was five minutes late for his one-thirty meeting with Lane. As he sped up the wide driveway, he noticed two, no, three men, spread out in a line, walking through the pasture on his left. Initially it struck him as strange, then he dismissed it, deciding they were probably trying to catch one of the horses.

When he pulled into the yard, he saw Rachel come riding in astride the dappled gray mare she frequently rode. The horse's neck was dark with sweat. MacCrea frowned, wondering what Rachel was doing out riding in the heat of the day like this . . . and those men in the pasture . . . something was wrong. Quickly, he turned away from the house and headed for the barn, arriving just as Rachel dismounted and handed the reins to one of the grooms.

As he climbed out of his car, MacCrea caught the last part of the question she asked the groom: ". . . seen anything?" The groom responded with a negative shake of his head and led the horse away.

"What's going on?"

Rachel turned with a small start, a frantic look on her face. "MacCrea. I didn't know that was you."

"Where's Lane?"

"He's out with the others, looking for Alex. He's disappeared. Nobody's seen him since before lunch. We've called and called but" — she paused, drawing in a deep, shaky breath — "I'm worried that . . . something's happened to him. I'll never forgive myself if it has."

MacCrea started to tell her that he thought he might know where Alex was. After all, the boy didn't know Eden wasn't living at the neighboring farm anymore. But there was the chance he could be wrong. If he was, telling Rachel his suspicion would just stir up more trouble. It would be better to check it out himself.

"He'll turn up."

"I hope so," she replied fervently.

"If you see Lane, tell him I'll be back later."

"I will." She nodded.

But MacCrea doubted that she would remember, as he walked back to his car and climbed in.

Abbie carried the last box of their belongings out of the farmhouse and stowed it in the backseat of her car. Pausing, she wiped the beads of perspiration from her forehead and glanced at the rental van parked in front of the broodmare barn. Two of the grooms were systematically going through the barns and loading up all tools, tack, implements, and equipment they found. From the looks of it, they were almost done.

Dobie was out working the fields. With luck, she'd be packed and gone before he finished. She hadn't seen him and didn't want to. Telling him she was sorry again wouldn't undo the damage she'd done to all their lives.

Hearing the sound of a car's engine growing steadily louder, Abbie turned to glance down the driveway. When she recognized MacCrea's car, she frowned in surprise. What if Dobie saw him?

She tried to hide her concern as she walked over to him. "What are you doing here?"

"I was hoping to find Alex. You haven't seen him, have you?"

"Alex? No. Why?"

"I just came from River Bend. They're turning the place upside down looking for him. Nobody's seen him since late this morning. I thought . . . he might have come over here to play with Eden."

"We've been here nearly all day. Besides, after the heavy rains the other night, the creek between here and River Bend has been running bank full." The instant the words were out, Abbie felt a cold chill of fear. "Mac, you don't think he would have tried to cross it. I know he's only a little boy, but surely he would see that it's too dangerous."

Looking grim, MacCrea opened the car door. "I'd better go look."

"I'm coming with you." Abbie hurried around to the other side.

MacCrea drove out of the yard onto the rutted track that led to the lower pasture and the creek. When they reached the gate, Abbie hopped out to open it, then scrambled back inside after closing it behind them.

"There's a natural ford right along there where we usually cross." She pointed to a section of the tree-lined creek just ahead of them.

Short of the area she'd indicated, MacCrea stopped the car. "Let's get out and walk."

The blue sky, the bright, shining sun, and the rain-washed green of the trees gave a deceptive look of peace and quiet to the scene. But the stream was no longer a narrow rivulet of water trickling slowly over its bed of sand and gravel. The run-off from the recent heavy rain had turned it into an angry torrent. Its roar almost drowned out the sound of the two slamming car doors.

Linking up in front of the car, they paused to scan the shaded bank and the swollen creek, its dark waters tumbling violently down the narrow channel, hurling along branches, dead limbs — anything that got in their path.

"Where do you think he is?" Abbie was more worried than before. "He has to know they're looking for him by now."

" 'Let's hope he just doesn't want to be found."

"He wouldn't have tried to cross that," she insisted. "He's too timid." She couldn't find any consolation in that thought as she stared at a section of the bank on the opposite side that had caved in, undermined by the tremendous onslaught of water.

"We'd better split up and cover both sides." MacCrea headed for the creek's natural ford.

"Be careful," she urged.

Pausing, he smiled reassuringly at her, then waded into the rushing stream, picking his way carefully. At its deepest point, the water came up to his hips . . . well over a little boy's head. As she watched him fight to keep his balance in the strong current, she realized that Alex wouldn't have had a chance if he'd fallen in.

Safely on the other side, MacCrea waved to her, then looked around. Cupping his hands to his mouth, he shouted, "I found some tracks! He's been here!" He gestured downstream, indicating they should start their search in that direction.

Abbie was more worried than before, aware that MacCrea had chosen this direction thinking that if Alex had fallen in, the raging torrent would have carried his body downstream. His body. No, she refused to think like that. Anxiously she scanned the bank ahead of her, keeping well away from the edge as she moved slowly along, paralleling MacCrea's progress on the other side.

Thirty feet downstream, she spied something yellow caught in a tangle of debris by the opposite bank. "MacCrea, look!" She pointed to what looked like a piece of clothing and unwillingly recalled that Alex had a jacket that color. She held her breath, wanting to be wrong, as MacCrea worked his way to the spot and snared the yellow item from the trapped debris with a broken stick. It was a little boy's yellow jacket.

"Alex!" Abbie called frantically. "Alex, where are you?" She hurried along the bank, mindless of the thickening undergrowth that tried to slow her, now doubly anxious to find Alex. The roaring creek seemed to laugh at her as it rolled ahead of her, a churning, seething mass of water, silt, and debris.

She thought she heard a shout. She stopped to listen, then noticed that MacCrea wasn't anywhere in sight. Had she gotten ahead of him in her search? Hastily she backtracked.

"Abbie!" MacCrea waved to her from the opposite bank, holding a muddy boy astraddle his hip. "I found him!"

She started to cry with relief and pressed a hand to her mouth to cover the sob. Alex was all right. He was safe. Finding a place to ford the stream, MacCrea carried the boy across. Abbie waited tensely on the opposite side, not drawing an easy breath until they were beside her. "Where did you find him?" she asked as MacCrea set him down.

"He was hiding in some brush."

Abbie stooped down to look for herself and make sure he was all right. Up close, she could see the streaks on his grimy cheeks left by tears. "We've been looking for you, Alex. We thought . . ." But she didn't want to voice the fear that was still too fresh. Smiling, she lifted the brown hair off his forehead, damp with perspiration, and smoothed it back off his face. "We'd better take you home."

Abruptly he pulled back. "No. I don't want to go there."

"Why?" Abbie was taken aback by his vehemence. "Your mother and father will be worried about you. You don't want that."

"She won't care," he retorted, tears rolling down his cheeks again. "She doesn't want me. She told me to go away. I did and I'm never going back!"

"Alex, I'm sure she didn't mean it."

"Yes, she did," he asserted, then, as if it was all too much for him to bear alone, he threw himself at Abbie and wrapped his arms tightly around her neck to bury his face against her and cry. "I don't want to go back. I want to stay with you and Eden."

Moved by his wrenching plea, Abbie glanced helplessly at MacCrea. Mac-Crea crouched down beside them and laid a comforting hand on Alex's shoulders as they lifted spasmodically with his sniffling sobs.

"That's not really what you want, Alex," he said. "Think how much you'd miss your father."

"He works all the time."

"Not all the time."

"He could come see me when he doesn't," Alex declared tearfully, obviously having thought it all out.

"Oh, Alex," Abbie murmured and hugged him a little tighter, feeling his pain. "I'm sorry, but it just wouldn't work."

"But why?"

"Because . . . you belong with your mommy and daddy."

"Come on, son. I'll take you home." But as MacCrea tried to pull him away from Abbie, Alex wrapped his arms in a stranglehold around her neck.

"No!"

"I'll carry him," she told MacCrea. Alex clung to her, winding his legs tightly around her middle as she walked back to the car with MacCrea. She continued to hold him once they were inside, cuddling him in her arms like a baby.

"I'll drop you off at your car," MacCrea said.

"No. I'm coming with you." She'd made up her mind about that at the creek. "There are a few things I want to say to Rachel."

"Abbie." His tone was disapproving.

She didn't need to hear any more than that. "I'm going." Nothing and no one was going to stop her, not even MacCrea.

A half-dozen sweaty men, exhausted by their search for the missing boy in the full heat of the day, hunkered together in the shade of a surviving ancient oak, guzzling water from the jugs brought by the house staff and silently shaking their heads in answer to the questions put to them by both Lane and Rachel. Few even looked up when MacCrea drove in with Abbie and Alex.

Abbie struggled out of the passenger side, with Alex still in her arms. At first no one noticed her, their attention all on MacCrea, who was nearest them. As she came around the front of the car, Rachel saw the boy in her arms.

"Alex! You've found him!" Relief flooded her expression as she broke into a run. "Oh, Alex, where have you been? We've been so worried about you."

"He was over at the farm," Abbie answered as Alex tightened his arms around her.

At the sound of her voice, Rachel finally noticed Abbie. Immediately she stopped, wary and suspicious. "Why are you carrying him? Give me my son."

As she tried to take him from her, Alex cried out and hung on to Abbie more fiercely. "No! I want to stay with you."

"What have you done to him?" Rachel glared.

"It's not what I've done, but what you've done to him," Abbie answered as Lane joined them, his sunburned face still showing the mental and physical stress of the search, his shirt drenched with perspiration.

"Is he all right?" he asked worriedly.

"He isn't hurt, if that's what you mean," Abbie replied. Alex didn't resist when Lane reached to take him from her. Abbie willingly handed him over to Lane, but Alex continued to hide his face from Rachel. "You should know that he's been sneaking over to play with my daughter for several months. I probably should have tried to put a stop to it, but I didn't want our children to become involved in our personal conflict."

"You. You're the one who's turned my son against me," Rachel accused. "I should have known you'd do something like this. All my life, everyone's always loved you. Dean — everyone. You've always had everything. Now you're trying to steal my son. I never knew how much I hated you until right now. Get out of here before I have you thrown out!"

"I don't blame you for hating me. I probably deserve it. But I'm not leaving until I've said what I came here to say."

"I'm not interested in listening to anything you have to tell me." She started to turn away, but Abbie caught her arm, checking the movement.

"You have to listen . . . for Alex's sake," she insisted. "He thinks that you don't want him — that you don't love him. You can't let him go on believing that. I grew up thinking my father didn't really love me. So did you. Can't you remember how much that hurt? That's what Alex is feeling now."

"He's never cared about me," she replied stiffly. "It's always been Lane."

"And you resented that, didn't you? Don't you know that Alex picked up on that? Children are very sensitive. But they're still just children. You can't expect them to understand your hurt feelings, when they haven't even learned how to cope with their own. He wants you to love him, and he thinks there's something wrong with him because you don't."

Rachel tried to shut out the things Abbie was saying. Each was a barb, pricking and tearing at her. But none of them was true. They couldn't be. "You don't know what you're talking about," she protested.

"Don't I?" Abbie replied sadly. "Look at us, Rachel. Look at how bitterness and envy have twisted our lives. When I think of all the things I've said, the things I've done, the way I felt. And I blamed you for everything. We're sisters. What turned us into enemies? Why are we always competing against each other? It can't be for Daddy's love. He's gone. But if he could see us now . . . Rachel, you have to know that this isn't the way he wanted us to be."

"Stop it!" Rachel pressed her hands over her ears, but she succeeded in only partially muffling Abbie's voice.

"Maybe he did love us both. It's taken me a long time to realize that. You need to believe that, too. Maybe you and I will never be sisters in the true sense of the word, but can't we at least stop this fighting?"

"You'd like that, wouldn't you?"

Abbie looked at her silently for a long moment. "Just love your son, Rachel," she said finally, emotionally drained. "And let him know it, the way Daddy should have."

Rachel turned and ran, her vision blurred by tears. It was a lie — a trick. It had to be.

As Rachel disappeared from sight near the barn, Abbie felt MacCrea's hand on her shoulder. "You tried."

She glanced at Lane, and the boy in his arms. She hesitated. "I'm sorry for creating a scene."

"Don't be," Lane said gently. "A lot of it needed to be said."

Just then, a clatter of hooves came from the barn. A second later Rachel burst into view, riding her dark gray mare. For an instant, Abbie stared in shock. "She only has a halter and lead rope on that mare."

"Somebody, quick! Go after her!" Lane ordered.

Sobbing, blinded by tears, Rachel twined her fingers through Simoon's dark mane, holding on to it as well as the cotton lead rope. Digging her heels into the mare's sides, she urged her faster, needing to outrun the thoughts pounding in her head.

"It isn't true. She can't be right," she kept sobbing over and over.

But the drumming in her temples didn't stop as they raced headlong across the pasture, swerving around the towering pecans that loomed in their path and scattering the mares and colts that grazed among them. All the while she kept trying to convince herself that Abbie had said all those things just to confuse her. Dean couldn't have loved them both.

"Daddy." She buried her face in the whipping mane.

She didn't see the white board fence coming up, but she vaguely felt the bunching of the mare's hindquarters and the stiffening brace of the front legs as Simoon tried to get her hindlegs under her and slow down.

At the last second, the mare came to a jerking, sliding stop just short of the fence, unseating Rachel and pitching her forward onto the mare's neck. Simoon reared, twisting to turn away from the fence. Rachel felt herself falling and grasped at the one thing still in her hand: the lead rope. But the pull of her whole weight on it twisted the mare's head around, throwing her off balance. As Rachel hit the ground, the gray mare fell on top of her. Rachel felt first the jarring impact with the hard earth, then the crushing weight of the gray body pressing down on her, then pain . . . pain everywhere, intense and excruciating. She whimpered her father's name once, then let the blessed blackness consume her.

Severe internal injuries and bleeding was the diagnosis. They operated to stop the bleeding and make what repairs they could, but her prognosis was uncertain. Lane refused to leave the private suite in the hospital's intensive-care unit. Special accommodations were arranged to let him sleep in the same room. But Lane slept little during the three days Rachel lay unconscious. Most of the time he spent by her bed, staring at her deathly pale face, the tubes sticking out from her nose, arms, and body, and the wires running to the monitors, their beeps and blips constantly assuring him that she was still alive when his own eyes doubted it. He'd never been a praying man in the past, but he'd become one as he watched over her, willing her to come back to him.

Her eyelids fluttered. Lane wondered if he had imagined it. When it happened again, he held his breath and gazed at her intently. A moment later, she tried to open her eyes. After the second try, she succeeded. Lane immediately summoned the nurse on duty and leaned closer to the bed.

"Rachel. Can you hear me?"

She appeared to focus on him with difficulty. Her lips moved, but no sound came out. He clutched her hand in both of his and called to her again.

"Lane?" Her voice was softer than a whisper.

"Yes, darling. I'm here." He leaned closer, tears springing into his eyes.

"I . . . knew you . . . would be." The breathy words seemed to require great effort.

The nurse came in and he was forced to move aside. Several times that day, she'd drifted in and out of consciousness. Lane regarded it as a hopeful sign. The specialists he'd hired admitted that the next forty-eight hours were critical.

Abbie shortened her stride to match Ben's slower pace as they crossed the parking lot to the hospital entrance.

"She's got to be all right, Ben." She'd said that over and over the last three days, every time she came to the hospital to see Rachel. But she'd received no encouragement until Lane had phoned the house tonight. "If only I'd let Mac-Crea take Alex back alone," Abbie said ruefully.

"Do not play this 'if only' game in your head." Ben's lined and craggy face was grim with disapproval. "There is nowhere for it to stop. 'If only' you had not gone there must be followed by 'if only' Alex had not run away, then 'if only' you had not allowed him to play with Eden. Eventually it must become 'if only' Eden had not been born, 'if only' your father had not died. No one can say where the blame truly belongs."

"I know." She sighed heavily. "But I still feel responsible for what happened."

"I remember well the day you learned that River Bend would have to be sold. You also went galloping through the pasture like a madwoman. If you had fallen, if you had been injured, would you have blamed Mr. Canfield? He was the one who told you. Would you have blamed your father? Rachel?" He stopped to pull the glass entrance door open, then held it for her.

"That was different." Abbie halted to protest the comparison.

"The outcome was different, Abbie. You were not hurt on your wild ride." For all the sternness in his voice, his expression was filled with gentleness and understanding. "Abbie, you are not responsible."

"Ben." Her throat was tight with her welling emotions. " 'If only' Rachel had known someone like you when she was growing up."

"No more of that." He shook a finger at her, smiling warmly.

"Come on." Abbie hooked an arm around his waist. Walking together, they entered the hospital. The sterile atmosphere, the medicinal and antiseptic smells, and the muted bells, all combined to sober her. "I left word for MacCrea to meet us at the intensive-care nurse's station. I hope he got the message."

But he was waiting for them when they arrived. His dark glance swept over her in a quick inspection, a hint of relief in his expression. "I had visions of you racing through this traffic. If I had known Ben was with you, I wouldn't have worried so much."

"Have you seen Lane yet?"

"No. I just got here. Where's Eden and Alex?"

"Momma was at the house when Lane called. She's watching them." After learning the seriousness of Rachel's injuries, Abbie had persuaded Lane to let Alex stay with them rather than be looked after by servants, no matter how caring they were.

A nurse came to escort them to the private hospital suite. Lane emerged from the room as they walked up. Again, Abbie was struck by the change in him. Over the last three days, he seemed to have aged ten years, his face haggard and worn from the strain and lack of sleep. Even his hair looked whiter. The confidence, the strength that had been so much a part of him were no longer evident. Instead he looked vulnerable and frightened — and a little lost, like Alex had been.

"Abbie. Thank God, you're here," he said, grasping at her hand and clutching it tightly. "Rachel's been asking for you."

"How is she?"

But Lane just shook his head. Abbie didn't know how to interpret his answer, unsure whether he meant he didn't know or that Rachel's condition had changed. Hurriedly he ushered her into the suite, signaling to the guard outside that MacCrea and Ben were to be admitted as well.

He guided Abbie to the hospital bed, then reached down and took hold of Rachel's hand. "Rachel. It's Lane. Can you hear me?" There was a faint movement of her eyelids in response. " 'Abbie's here. Do you understand? Abbie."

As Rachel struggled to open her eyes, Lane shifted to let Abbie take his place at her side. Abbie stared at the pale image of herself in the hospital bed.

"Abbie . . . my almost-twin sister." Rachel's voice was so faint Abbie had to lean closer to catch the words.

"Yes. We are almost twins, aren't we?" She tried to smile at that, even as her eyes filled with tears. "You're going to make it, Rachel. I know you are."

"Abbie." There was a long pause as if Rachel was trying to gather her strength. "You . . . were right . . . the things you . . . said."

"I don't think you should try to talk any more." It hurt to see her like this and remember all the confrontations they'd had in the past, when they'd hissed and arched their backs like a cat startled by its reflection in a mirror.

Rachel smiled weakly. "Lane and Alex are . . . going to need you. And . . . let our children . . . grow up together . . . the way we should . . . have."

"I will." Tears spilled from her eyes. "But you shouldn't be talking this way, Rachel. You're going to be fine."

She closed her eyes briefly, almost displaying impatience with Abbie's protestation. "I love . . . my son. Make sure he . . . knows that."

"I will."

She glanced dully around. "Lane? Where is he?"

Blinking rapidly to control her tears, Abbie half turned to look at Lane. "She wants you." She stepped back to MacCrea, letting Lane take her place. She leaned against him, grateful for the comfort of the arm he wrapped around her . . . and for the fact that they loved each other.

"Darling." Lane stroked her cheek, his hand trembling. "I'm here. You rest now."

"I do love you," she whispered.

"I love you too." He started to cry, silently. "We're going to have a lot of time together. I promise you."

A faint smile curved her mouth — a smile of regret, then, strangely, peace. "I have to go now, darling," Rachel whispered, then added so faintly that Lane wasn't even sure he heard it. "Daddy's . . . waiting."

About the Author

Janet Dailey is one of America's best-selling female novelists, with more than 126 million copies of her books in print. Her most recent novels include *The Great Alone*, *The Glory Game*, and *Silver Wings, Santiago Blue*. She and her husband, Bill, live in the Ozark Mountain country of Branson, Missouri.